THE HENCHMEN CHRONICLES

SPECIAL EDITION

THE KING'S HENCHMEN

BOOK ONE

THE KING'S ASSASSIN

BOOK TWO

THE KING'S PRISONER

BOOK THREE

THE KING'S CONJURER

BOOK FOUR

THE KING'S ENEMIES

BOOK FIVE

CRAIG HALLORAN

The Henchmen Chronicles Collection

Books 1, 2, 3, 4, 5

By Craig Halloran

Copyright © 2019 by Craig Halloran

TWO-TEN BOOK PRESS

PO Box 4215, Charleston, WV 25364

eBook: 978-1-946218-99-5

Hardback:978-1-946218-64-3

Paperback: 978-1-088461-2-66

www.craighalloran.com

All rights reserved. No part of this publication may be reproduced, stored in a retrieval system, or transmitted in any form or by any means—electronic, mechanical, recorded, photocopied, or otherwise—without the prior permission of the copyright owner, except by a reviewer who may quote brief passages in a review.

Publisher's Note

This book is a work of fiction. Names, characters, places, and incidents either are the product of the author's imagination or are used fictitiously, and any resemblance to actual persons, living or dead, events, or locales is entirely coincidental.

Contact Information

*Check me out on Bookbub and follow: HalloranOnBookBub

*I'd love it if you would subscribe to my mailing list: www.craighalloran.com

*On Facebook, you can find me at The Darkslayer Report or Craig Halloran.

*Twitter, Twitter, Twitter. I am there, too: www.twitter.com/CraigHalloran

*And of course, you can always email me anytime at craig@thedarkslayer.com

Please, leave a review of Book 1, contact me, and I'll be happy to send you an eBook copy of Book 2, The King's Assassin.

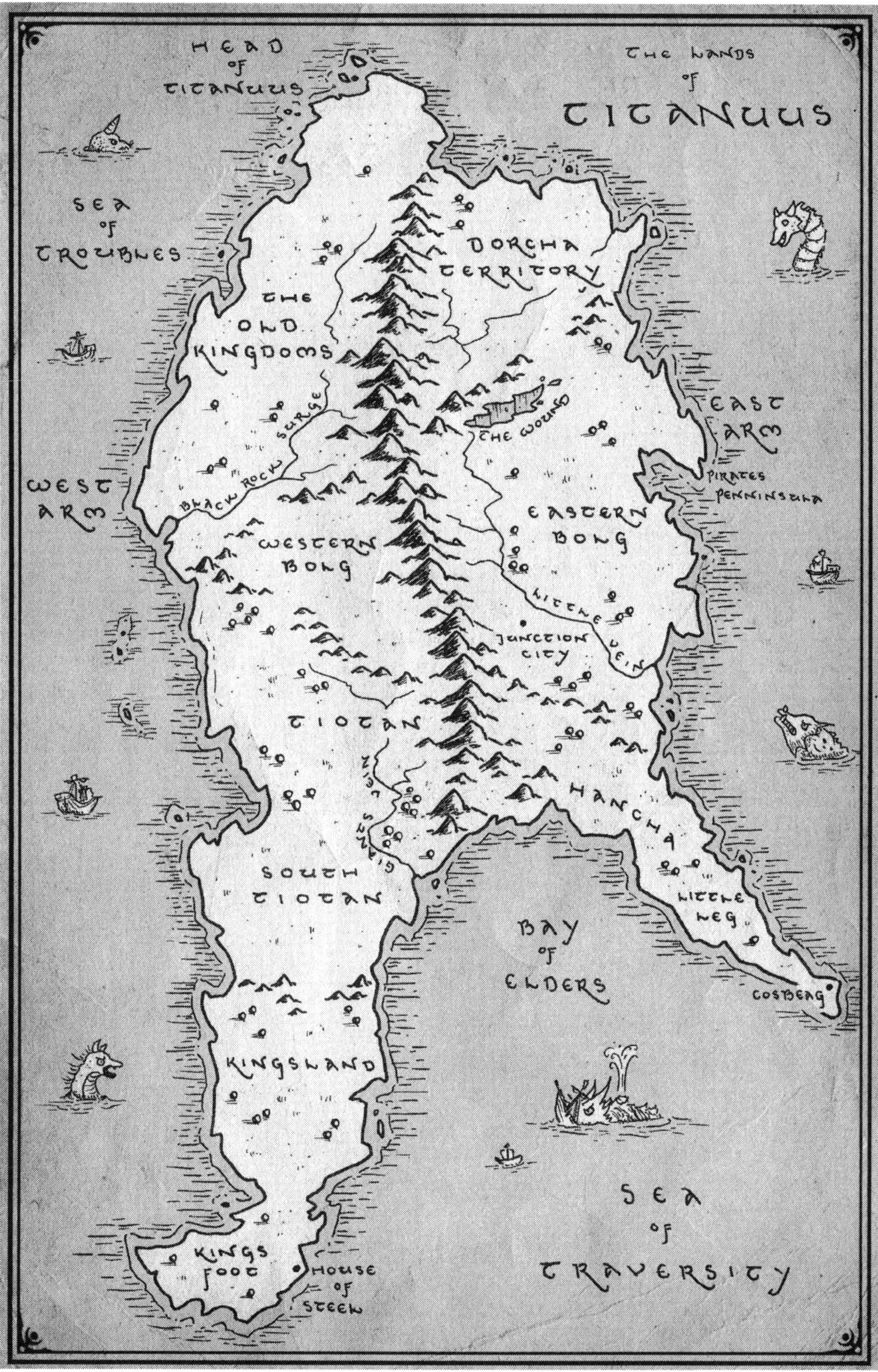

The Lands of
TITANUUS
Head of Titanuus
Sea of Troubles
The Old Kingdoms
Dorcha Territory
The Wound
Black Rock Surge
West Arm
East Arm
Pirates Penninsula
Western Bong
Eastern Bong
Little Vein
Junction City
Tiotan
Giants Vein
Hancha
South Tiotan
Little Leg
Bay of Elders
Costberg
Kingsland
Sea of Traversity
Kings Foot
House of Steel

TABLE OF CONTENTS

THE KING'S HENCHMEN 7

THE KING'S ASSASSIN 147

THE KING'S PRISONER 291

THE KING'S CONJURER 435

THE KING'S ENEMIES 581

BONUS BACKSTORY 761

FROM THE AUTHOR 789

OTHER BOOKS AND AUTHOR INFO 790

THE KING'S HENCHMEN

CRAIG HALLORAN

PROLOGUE

THE LANDS OF TITANUUS—NORTHERN TERRITORIES

"CAPTAIN." THE DEEP VOICE SPOKE softly. "Captain!"

Ruger opened his eyes. He lay on a bed of fur blankets inside a large canvas tent. The firm body of a woman lay beside him. She stirred as he sat up. The morning sun shone on the top of the tent, providing natural illumination. Drops of rain softly pelted the tent fabric. He pushed his fingers through his jet-black hair then breathed deeply into his nostrils and rubbed his eyes. He opened them. *Dirty donuts, I'm still here!*

On the other side of the tent's entrance flap, the person spoke more loudly and urgently. "Captain. Can you hear me?"

"Horace, I can hear you just fine! Hold your bloody horses!" Ruger said in a bitter voice. He shoved the leg of the woman wrapped up in the furs. "Sticks, get your scrawny arse out of my fox furs and go see what the lout wants."

"Did you say something, Captain?" Horace asked. "It's hard to hear through canvas."

"Give me a moment!" he yelled back.

Sticks rose to her feet. She wore a gray nightshirt that hung loose on her firm body. Her chestnut-colored hair was short and tied back in twin ponytails. The slightly fish-eyed woman with a tomboy demeanor bent over, picked up a bandolier of knives, and slung it over her shoulder. Barefoot, she headed toward the flap.

Ruger gave her a smack on the rear end. "Settle Horace down and come right back. No, bring me something to eat." He rubbed the hard ridges on his bare stomach. "I'm hungry."

Sticks gave him an expressionless nod. Quiet as a mouse, she vanished through the flap.

"Where's the Captain?" Horace asked.

"Will you tell me what it is?" Sticks replied in a stern manner. "He's dressing, and I need to fetch his breakfast. Out with it."

"Watch that brassy tone. My message is for his ears, not yours," Horace growled.

Ruger slipped on his trousers. He sat down on a cot, reached underneath for his boots, and stuffed his feet into them. *I hate these things. My feet will burn like fire before I'm half a day in.*

Horace's voice became louder. "You tell the Captain that my words are for his ears and not yours! It's urgent!"

"I don't care. You can tell me. I'm his eyes and ears," Sticks said matter-of-factly. "Spit it out."

"No!" Horace retorted.

Ruger's chin sank into his chest. Finally, he sighed and said, "For the love of money, Horace, just get your bloated belly in here!"

A strong arm with stubby fingers pushed the tent flap open, and Horace marched inside. The big husky warrior was as bald as an eagle but with a nest of beard down his chest. His eyes were as hard as diamonds. He wore a black leather tunic over an elbow-length suit of chain mail. A sword belt complete with long sword and dirk dressed his wide hips. He gave a firm nod. "Captain."

"Yes, I know. I'm the Captain. You don't have to call me that every time. Now, spit it out, *Horace*." Ruger reached behind himself, into the corner of the tent where his own sword belt was propped up. He lay it across his lap and ran his long fingers over the scabbard. "I really hope you didn't waste my precious moments of slumber." His eye slid up toward Sticks. "Not to mention other routines that I enjoy."

Eyeing Ruger's sword and scabbard, Horace swallowed and said, "Never, Captain—er... Never."

"So, what is it?"

"The frights. They escaped."

Ruger stiffened. He cocked his head to one side. His eyes narrowed. "What did you say?"

"The frights are gone," Horace replied. "Red Tunics are dead."

He stood up and buckled on his sword belt then glared down at Horace and sneered. "Show me."

Horace marched outside, followed by Ruger and Sticks. The morning light had come with heavy cloud cover and a steady rain. Surrounded by the tall trees of the forest, the campsite clearing was made up of small pup tents and stone rings around extinguished campfires. A man using a flint stone and hay struggled to light the fire in the rain. Horses nickered. Wagons were being loaded by workers in brick-colored tunics.

Hard-eyed men and women dressed in the same garb as Horace watched Ruger's every step from a distance. Horace led Ruger away from the camp to another clearing, where a nearby stream trickled a few dozen feet away. Three men in red tunics lay dead on the grass in drippings of their own blood. Branches with sharp ends had poked through their bodies with ghastly effect.

Ruger took a knee. He stared at the macabre scene and shook his head. *I hate this place.* "Who in Hades was on watch last night when this happened?"

"Vern had the last watch," Horace said. "These retainers were from his group."

"And where is Vern?"

"He came to me first, only minutes ago," Horace said as the rain came down harder, heavy drops splattering on his bald head. "He's trying to find the frights' tracks."

"A fat lot of good that is going to do in this rain!"

"We'll find them, Captain," Horace said. "We tracked the witches down once. We can do it again. They couldn't have gotten too far, and they don't move very fast. We have horses."

Ruger rose and kicked his black boots through the grasses. "We just spent the last forty days chasing them over one thousand miles! Now, we get to start all over again. I don't want to spend another hour on this. I want to return to Kingsland!"

"Captain, we'll pursue right away. Rain or no rain, we will find them soon," Horace promised.

"Get Bearclaw on it now. Find Vern and send him to me. He's the one that lost them, and I have no faith that he can find them."

Horace nodded and hustled away.

Ruger stormed over the grasses and stopped where a tree had fallen recently. Sticks shadowed him. He picked up one set of iron shackles with both hands. The frights were an odd group of gangly witches. They'd been tethered to the fallen tree.

"I can't believe this. They aren't supposed to be able to use their powers when iron is locked on them." He held the iron cuffs, bent outward, up to Sticks's face. "Look at this. Magic. Fetch Iris and have her take a look at this. Have the Red Tunics bring the shovels. Bury the dead. But not too deep. There's no time for that."

"The varmints will dig them out and feast on them," Sticks said.

"I don't care about your traditions. We don't have time to dig, dig, dig. We've dug enough on this journey." He shoved the heavy shackles into her chest. "Don't let Vern elude me either. I'll be in my tent."

Ruger paced inside his sixteen-by-sixteen-foot tent, wringing his hands behind his back. He ground his teeth and cursed and muttered, "It's bad enough that I'm trapped in another man's body. Now, I'm going to die in a body that is not my own. In a world that is not my home." He grabbed a cot and tossed it across the tent. "Dammit! I want out of this hellhole!"

Years ago, he'd been transported from America to the world that he now knew as Titanuus. He was changed from Professor Eugene Drisk into a warrior named Ruger Slade, in what he believed was an experiment all gone wrong. Now, he'd been thrust into the service of King Hector and charged with executing the king's business beyond the safety of Kingsland's borders.

Eugene Drisk had his moments as Ruger Slade, but for the most part, he was horrible at it—one mission failed after another. The king's grace was running out. His latest mission was to track down the frights and bring them back to Kingsland alive to be hanged on the gallows. It was a show of the king's strength in a crumbling kingdom, withering from the inside out.

The frights were a nefarious brood of witches who spread poison throughout Kingsland using venomous words and treacherous sorcery. They wrought evil wherever their crooked toes walked. In the city of Burgess, they'd burned down one of the king's cathedrals. Men, women, and children were burned alive within. The frights, five in all, were captured and imprisoned. A day before their execution, they escaped.

Ruger and the Henchmen were sent to hunt them down and bring them back alive. That was the last chance for this motley company of renegade knights and assorted prisoners to redeem themselves. It was their last chance because of all their past failures. The king's grace would end. The existence of Eugene Drisk might end as well if he didn't bring the frights back alive. Most of his Henchmen depended on him. If they failed, their sentences would be executed as well. The rest of the Henchmen would be disbanded or perhaps led by another.

He rubbed the lumpy brand of hardened skin shaped like a crown over his heart. "Cursed mark."

It was a mark of loyalty and faithfulness to the crown that meant "Glory to the king. Honor to the sword." It was given when the Henchmen gave their oath to the king. Breaking one's oath could be fatal. Henchmen who fled their duties were known to die—at the hands of their enemies, by being carted off by sky demons, or just because of sudden death. It was witchery that Eugene still didn't understand. Nor did he care.

"I'm marked like a prize horse. A horse with a time limit."

"Captain," someone with a gravelly voice said outside the tent. "It's Vern."

Ruger dropped his left hand to the pommel of his sword sheathed on his left hip. He faced the flap. "Enter."

Vern pushed the tent flap aside and entered. He was a well-built athlete with a pale complexion and short, kinky blond hair down to his neck. He had puffy lips and carried himself with aloofness. His eyes were sad and heavy. Like Horace, he wore a weathered black tunic over chain mail armor. A finely crafted longsword and dagger dressed his slender hips. "What is it?"

"Don't use that tone with me, Vern. And don't speak as if you don't know what this is all about.

I tire of your act." His fingers drummed on his pommel. "You were on last watch last night. Now, the frights are gone. Explain yourself."

With his head leaned over one shoulder and his thumbs tucked into the front of his sword belt, he shrugged. "I don't know."

"I am going to skewer you if you don't come cleaner than that. Now, tell me what happened."

"What difference does it make now? The frights are gone, and I should be out looking for them." Vern peered up then dropped his eyes back to Ruger. "And not staying dry in a tent like you."

Ruger's blood churned through his veins as his grip tightened on his sword. He stared Vern down. "I'm going to split your face in half if you keep up your obstinance. I have three dead Red Tunics. I can't help but wonder how they're dead and you're still alive."

Vern's eyes fell to Ruger's sword.

"What are you thinking, Vern? Do you think you can take me?"

"If you didn't have Black Bane, I have no doubt that I could. And I certainly wouldn't hide behind the retainers in battle, either. I'd use it."

"Oh, so you think that my sword makes me the better fighter, not the man. That's very interesting." He took his hand away from his hilt. "Have you been concocting these notions all on your own, or have the rest of the Henchmen been entertaining your musings?"

"No one used to concoct anything until you became cowardly and crazy. All you've done is lead us to our doom one mission after the other." Vern sneered at Ruger. "You've lost your edge—either that or your spine."

"Bold words coming from a man who nods off at his post." He patted the hilt of his dagger. "No swords. Just dirks."

"All right." Vern faced off against him. He crossed his left hand over his right hip, where his dagger was sheathed.

Ruger readied himself in a similar stance. "On your word, Vern."

Vern nodded. The moment Vern's lips parted, Ruger snaked out his dirk in a flash and pressed it against Vern's throat. The wide-eyed Henchman gulped. His hand was frozen on his dagger, still in his sheath.

As he pressed his dagger against Vern's neck, Ruger whispered in his ear. "Do you still think that I need Black Bane to kill you?"

With new sweat beading on his brow, Vern said, "No."

"No, what?"

"No, Captain."

Ruger cracked Vern upside the head with the handle of his dagger. The stunning blow knocked the warrior to the ground. He kicked Vern in the ribs. "Don't ever question me again, fool!"

He wanted to lay into Vern with all he had but held back. He needed every Henchman he had. And Vern was a good soldier, just difficult.

"You get your arse out there and find those frights. And you better hope by the Elders that you come through because if you don't, I'll make an example out of you!" He kicked him again. "Go!"

Groaning, Vern slowly crawled out of the tent.

Ruger huffed for breath. He jammed his dagger back in the sheath. Vern had made several pointed statements, and they were accurate.

He shook his head and said, "I didn't ask for this."

Another stern voice came from outside the tent. "Captain."

He rolled his eyes, took a deep breath, and stepped outside. Standing in front of him was a broad-faced bearish Henchman with a head of rain-soaked coal-black hair, a full beard, a hawk nose, and a dark complexion. He carried a twin-bladed Viking-style battle-axe.

"Bearclaw, why aren't you chasing down the frights?" Ruger asked.

"I can only chase one set of tracks at a time. There are five sets, going different directions. I need to split the company into small groups," Bearclaw said. "It will be a challenge to fetch them all, to say the least. We'll need all eyes on the trails. Including yours, Captain."

With a hard rain coming down, Ruger fought the urge to rip his hair out of his head and shouted, "I hate this place!"

Riding on horseback, Ruger led a pair of Red Tunics, who traveled on foot through the woodland. He was taking the path Bearclaw had pointed out to him. The rest of the Henchmen split up into small groups while a few Red Tunics remained back at camp. He rode with his keen eyes set for disturbances in the woodland. Even though the rain was coming down, the leaves slowed the hard rainfall on the ground. It took some time to get used to, but Ruger's body had great attributes and instincts. He picked up on things normal people wouldn't. He caught footprints in the soft ground and followed.

He looked behind him. The Red Tunics trudged along in the rear. They were a pair of grubby men, one heavier than the other, with mud-covered boots. They carried spears and had hand axes in their belts. Their tunics were dyed brick red, but they didn't wear chain mail underneath. They kept their eyes to the ground, heads scanning the area side to side.

"Sheesh," he said.

Normally, he'd have taken some of his better men with him, but in this case, he needed every skilled warrior out in the field. The frights had a jump of hours on them. With five of them gone, getting them all back might have been impossible. But he needed at least one—one alive. He was willing to risk all others, save for one. But even with the rain, their chances were good. The Henchmen were trackers, highly skilled woodsmen, and warriors. Some of them were knights, honed by the crown's finest training. They were ready for anything—what was left of them, that is.

He ducked underneath branches and weaved through the trees. They were heading north, above the Old Kingdoms, deeper into the head of Titanuus. The black horse he rode climbed the hilly terrain at a steady gait. Over the course of three hours, he only paused twice, to lock down the fright's trail again. The frights were women, witches to be exact, haggard crones with a stare that could turn a man's blood to ice. They were crafty survivors who had taken months to finally track down less than two days before. But now, the Henchmen had finally caught on to all their tricks.

The rain stopped, and the rustling branches fell silent. Water dripped from the leaves. Ruger tugged gently on the reins. His horse stopped and snorted. The air became still and quiet. Ahead, a steep slope of rocks and boulders made for a perfect den and hiding place. The muddy footprints came to an end. The last one he saw was deep and fresh. He grabbed the crossbow hanging from his saddle. He snatched a bolt from a quiver hanging on the other side and put it in his mouth. Using his strong fingers, he pulled back the crossbow string and locked it into place then loaded the bolt into the slide.

The Red Tunics crept up on his flank with big eyes sliding side to side. They held their spears at the ready.

Ruger didn't even know their names. He tipped his chin toward the rocks and said, "Go take a poke in those rocks."

The retainers exchanged a glance and started up the rocky hill at a slow pace.

"Today!"

The Red Tunics moved at a brisker pace. Up into the rocks they went, splitting up the higher they went. They cast their stares into the gaps in the rocks. They jammed their spears inside the gaps in the holes and hopped from boulder to boulder.

With his crossbow on his shoulder, he eased his horse forward. He only needed one good shot to cripple the fright. The retainers made for perfect bait. Eugene's approach had always been to lead from behind the lines and not in front, like a general commanding the field. Nothing was wrong with that. No doubt his men despised that about him, but he didn't care. It was simple strategy and a matter of survival.

The heavyset retainer traversing the rocks on the right froze in place. He stared down into a gap in the rocks, not moving. His body swayed side to side, and his spear dangled in his grip.

"Hey!" Ruger shouted.

The Red Tunic climbing on the left twisted in his companion's direction.

Without warning, a nest of red-backed and black-legged scorpions, each the size of a hand, scurried out of the gap by the dozens. They crawled up the rigid retainer's legs, over his torso, and over his neck. Scorpion stingers struck into the arms, legs, and neck of the man. His body quaked. Pumped with venom, his body puffed up.

"Get away from there!" Ruger said.

The retainer's face bulged and turned green. The scorpions had covered him up, their tails striking unendingly.

"What do we do?" the other retainer said, keeping his distance from the rocks by his comrade, which were a field of scorpions now. He looked about his feet and made a grim face as his comrade fell over. "He's dead. He's dead!"

"Yes, scorpions will do that to you. Just don't panic," Ruger said, his eyes wary. He didn't see any sign of the fright.

A shrill cackling of a woman carried down from the rocks and echoed all around.

"Show yourself, witch!"

A dozen feet higher in the crags, a gaunt woman in ragged clothing climbed out of a cleft. Kinky hair flowed back behind her head. Her eyes were pinkish red and demonic. The fingernails tipping her bony arms were black talons. She opened her mouth, full of sharp teeth, and said, "What is the matter? Don't you want to partake of my feast?" She held a scorpion in her hand, stuffed it in her mouth, and chewed. "Mmm… that's good."

Without a second thought, Ruger pulled the trigger on his crossbow. The bolt sailed true, impaling the fright through the chest.

Her legs wobbled. She straightened, tossed her head back, and cackled. The fright grabbed the bolt and pulled it out.

"Get up there and finish her!" Ruger ordered the Red Tunic.

The man crept up the rocks at an agonizing pace. The spear he carried shook in his hands.

Ruger fished out another bolt.

The fright leapt down from the rocks, covering over twenty feet in a single bound. She landed right in front of the stunned Red Tunic. With a swipe of her hand, she tore his throat out. He crumpled at her feet, clutching at his bleeding neck.

Ruger locked the bolt into place and aimed. He locked his eyes on the burning red eyes of the fright and fired. She vanished. The bolt clacked off the rocks and skipped out of sight.

"Sonuvabitch!"

The fright's wicked cajoling carried down the rocky slope.

He spurred his horse forward. This wasn't the first time he'd seen a fright's disappearing act. He led his horse up the rocks, away from the scorpions and past the dying Red Tunic, where he spotted new blood on the ground. The frights might not fall to wounds easily, but they still bled, though they used their magic to hold themselves together. A bad feeling crawled down his spine. This fright was probably the leader, the strongest of them all. He moved forward at a trot. He had her on the run and wounded. She'd be desperate and more dangerous. But so was he.

For a leathery witch who could have passed for a mummy, she covered ground as quickly as a rattlesnake. Her staggered trail climbed higher up the forest slope. Ruger fully expected a wild beast she'd summoned to burst out of the brush at any moment. That didn't happen. He climbed higher and higher, tracking her almost an hour. Clearing a tree line, he caught a glimpse of her less than fifty yards away. She looked back over her shoulder and hissed.

"Now I have you!" Ruger snapped the reins. "Eeyah!"

The fright fled on bony legs with the speed of a wildcat. Her eyes were fixed on a large cave mouth that opened up in the mountain.

"No!" Ruger roared.

He needed to cut her off. Inside the cave, he might lose her once and for all. He'd seen his share of caves filled with twisting caverns and jagged corridors. And he had no light to find the way.

"Go, horse, go!"

The horse thundered onward at a full gallop, making a straight line after the fright. She moved quickly on her sprinting legs, and with one last final cackle, she vanished into the dark mouth of the cave.

Ruger pulled his horse to a halt a dozen feet from the mouth of the cave and squinted. A strange sound caught his ears. A quavering light caught his eye. His heart raced. Bravery was not usually Eugene Drisk's cup of tea, but today it was.

"Fools rush in where angels fear to tread. Humph. What choice do I have? I'm going in."

CHAPTER 1
VIRGINIA, 2018

Abraham Jenkins took a yellow-and-black bandana out of the back pocket of his jeans. With the hot summer wind in his face, he mopped the sweat from his brow. It was the hottest time of the day, with the sun dropping above the Appalachian Mountains. The heat index was over one hundred five degrees. The back of his shirt was soaked with sweat. He'd just finished delivering several cases of beer at the Superfood Center in Wytheville, Virginia. He stuffed the damp bandana back into his pocket then loaded his dolly into the beer truck. He closed the side-panel slat doors. Clasping his hands on his hips, he arched his back and groaned.

He'd packed over thirty pounds onto his rangy frame over the past ten years. Sitting in the truck made his back as tight as a banjo string during a long ride. He was too young for that. Twisting at the hips side to side a few times, he moved around the truck, checking that all the rolling slat doors were closed. His coal-black truck shone in the sunlight. The old gold lettering, hand-painted, was like new.

The truck was a Chevy Kodiak crew-cab turbo diesel, the bed converted into a beverage hauler. It was a stout truck, unlike the others Abraham had worked with. This truck was his. It had three storage panels on each side. The middle panel had the beer-brand logo of a wooden keg with a steel helmet resting on the top and two battle-axes crossed over the front.

Abraham took his bandana back out and wiped off a smudge covering the helmet. "That's better."

From the passenger side, he made his way around the front of the truck, past the chrome headlamps, and climbed into the front seat. He slammed the door shut then turned the key in the ignition. As the air conditioning blasted out ice-cold air, he eased back in the seat. "That's way better."

The truck cabin, with a gray interior, had all the bells and whistles available for the 2009 model. That had been ten years before. It was relatively clean, with a small black wastebasket stuck in front of the passenger seat. It was full of crushed energy drink cans and fast food wrappers, some of which had spilled out on the seat. The only other thing in the passenger seat was a kid's Pittsburgh Pirates backpack. Abraham reached over and patted it. He shuttered a sigh.

He reached up and touched the truck's sun visor, feeling the edge of a photograph pinned to the visor. It was a family picture of him, his wife, and his son, the last photograph they'd taken together before they had died. He swallowed a lump in his throat, dropped his fingers from the visor, put the truck in gear, and headed for the interstate.

As soon as he hit the highway, he put on his sunglasses and ball cap. He turned on the radio, and the sad whine of a saxophone filled the truck cabin. "You've got to be kidding me," Abraham mumbled. "Nothing against you, Bob, but your timing couldn't have been more perfect. But lonesome highways aren't so bad. Just the people that ride them." He changed the radio channel.

He had one more stop left on his route before he could head back home. But he wasn't in any hurry, with no family to go back to. On the long open roads he tried to pull his life back together. Abraham had been driving the beer truck for two years. The eight years before that, he'd done next to nothing as he wallowed in sorrow over the loss of his wife and son. He'd been an ace pitcher for the Pirates and made a crap load of money, but after he lost his family, it wasn't long before he lost it all.

With nothing but endless green mountains to his left and right, he cruised north toward the Big Walker Tunnel. About two miles away, traffic backed up and slowed to a twenty-mile-an-hour crawl. Traffic was being merged into one lane.

"Ah, crap."

Abraham didn't mind being on the road, but he hated moving slowly. His beer truck wasn't a speedster, but at least he could get it to seventy-five miles per hour and keep with the flow. He reached back to the seats behind him and flipped open the white lid of a cherry-red Igloo cooler.

He grabbed a Mountain Dew out of the ice just as Metal Maiden came on the radio playing "Head to the Hills."

He cracked open the can's tab and said, "Maiden, I've already arrived. Now it's Zombie Dew time."

With gray clouds filling the sky, a spitting rain came down. Traffic in the southbound lanes was moving fine. Thirty minutes passed before he entered the mouth of the one-way tunnel. The eerie yellow glow of the tunnel shone on the pasty tiles making up the walls of the tunnel. Travelers were honking their horns. The tunnel was long. He and his son, Jake, used to try to hold their breaths from one side of the tunnel to the other. It was a fun game they played when they traveled south from Pittsburgh on vacation.

"I won't be able to hold my breath long enough this time, Jake."

A quarter of the way into the tunnel, he saw military vehicles lined up in the left-hand lane. Soldiers in camouflage gear, with flak vests, helmets, and M-16 assault rifles, were waving traffic through. Humvees with M-60 guns mounted in their turrets were there, as well as the big trucks called Deuces and several other armored vehicles that Abraham wasn't as familiar with. As he passed the first soldier, the young man with bright blue eyes and a friendly smile gave him a thumbs-up. The soldier's partner pushed his hand down.

Fighting the urge to slow down and ask them a nosy question, Abraham gave them a little salute when he passed. He got a thumbs-up from time to time in the beer truck. It was different and a hit at beer festivals. People liked to get their pictures with it.

About midway in the tunnel, a huge tarp was covering up the left side of the road, big enough to hide an eighteen-wheeler.

"Whew!" he said, pinching his nose.

He smelled something foul, like a car that had been set on fire and put out, but it wasn't that. It was something else, foreign and rank. Creeping by the odd military quarantine scene, he rolled down his window and stuck his head out like some of the other drivers. With his head out the window, he scanned the canopy's edges. Dark char marks were on the yellow-tiled walls. New cracks had started in the ceiling, and tiles had fallen onto the road.

A big soldier came right at him and stuck a meaty finger in Abraham's face. "Roll up that window, rubberneck! Certainly you've seen stranger things before!"

Abraham jerked his head inside, bumping his head as he did so. The gruff soldier looked as if he could chew lead and spit bullets. Abraham waved gently as he rolled up the window. Then all the overhead lights in the tunnel flickered and went black.

CHAPTER 2

Tire rubber squawked over the road. The cars in front of Abraham rocked forward and back, and the line of traffic came to a dead stop.

Abraham laid on the horn. "Come on, you idgits. Your headlights still work."

Even though the roof of the tunnel had become a strange canopy of blackness, the head- and taillights from most of the cars were giving off plenty of illumination. Suddenly, a beam of light struck Abraham's cabin, washing him in bright light. He shielded his eyes with his forearms.

"Gah!" He hit his horn again. "Turn that thing away!"

The white spotlight turned away from his cabin, toward the interior of military activity.

Abraham lifted his glasses off the bridge of his nose and rubbed his eyes. "Thanks for the new migraine, fellas. I was starting to miss the last one." He pulled the glasses down over his eyes and tried to blink away a few spots though they didn't go. "Jingle bells and shotgun shells. Misery loves company."

In 2009, Abraham had been in an accident that killed his wife Jenny and son Jake. Abraham didn't come out unscathed, either. He had a cracked skull and three brain surgeries that came with it, not to mention the other parts of his body that were busted up. As a result, he inherited the pain and discomfort that came with it. He inherited a drug addiction too: pain killers and antidepressants. It wasn't a lifestyle. It was survival that became a lifestyle.

With the help of energetic hardcase soldiers waving their black Maglites, traffic started moving again. A few minutes later, Abraham drove his truck out of the Big Walker Tunnel. For some reason, he let out an audible exhalation. The sky was cloud covered, and the rain was still spitting. The radio came back on, and some easy-riding classic rock came back on. Abraham was relieved by the cloud cover. Road glare from the sun might trigger his migraine, and he didn't want that. He just wanted to make his final stop, gas up, and go home.

Miles up the road, he took the interstate exit ramp into Rocky Gap. It was a very small town, and he wasn't even sure why it was on his route. The old man—his boss, Luther—had some connections there. He pulled underneath the gas canopy at Woody's Grill and Gas Up. He shut off the engine and got out. Then he opened the slat doors, fetched the dolly out, and loaded it up with cases of bottled beer. He pushed it toward the double glass doors leading into Woody's Grill. The grill had cedar wood siding, giving it a county-general-store look. Two soda machines were on the right side of the door and a sitting bench on the left side. He stopped.

Oh no.

Inside the doors, an attractive brunette woman was working behind the register. She wore a tight plum-colored V-neck T-shirt. Her name was Mandi. She'd been flirting with him ever since he started making deliveries to the store. Now, she was checking out an older man wearing a green John Deere ball cap. The older man made a toothless smile at her when she handed him his change. He ambled through the double doors. That was when she caught Abraham's eye, and a playful smile formed on her lips.

I was really hoping she wouldn't be working today.

The old man held the door open for Abraham and asked, "What are you waiting for, sonny? An invitation?" He waved his hand inside. "Get moving. Every minute is precious to an old goat like me."

Abraham pushed the dolly through the doors. "Thank you, sir."

The old man teetered off toward an old army-green Dodge pickup that had seen its best days thirty years before.

He walked up by the counter and said, "Hi, Mandi."

Twirling her finger in her ponytail, she popped a gum bubble and said, "Running a little late, Abraham?"

"I'm never late. I arrive at the exact time I'm supposed to be here."

She stood on tiptoe and leaned over the counter in a showy fashion. "Ha ha. Did you hear that one in a movie?"

"Sort of. I'll just put these back in the cooler." He patted the top case. "This is six."

"I can count just fine," she said as she popped another bubble. "And take your time. Now that you are here, we have some catching up to do."

He tipped his chin and headed away.

Woody's Grill was divided up into two sections. On the right was the convenience store. It was typical in fashion, mostly modern but with a decorative charm to it. On the left was the grill, which had a completely different look. The same checkered tiles were on the floor, but rose-red booths and shiny round bar stools were posted in front of the grill's service counter. The smell of hot delicious greasy American food lingered in the air. Several LCD screens were hanging high on the walls. A small mixed crowd of patrons watched sports while they chatted and ate. He slipped into the freezer section, pushed the cases off the dolly, and slid them back into the corner.

Then he turned around and froze.

Mandi was standing right in front of him with her hands stuffed into her back pockets. With a coy smile on her face, she slid her hands free of the denim, jumped into his arms, and kissed him.

CHAPTER 3

Mandi wasn't an ordinary kisser—she was an extraordinary one. Her soft lips drew Abraham deep into the moment. Standing a head taller than the shapely woman, he abruptly broke off the kiss and gently pushed her shoulders away. "What are you doing?"

"It's called kissing, Abraham. Did you forget what a kiss was?"

"No, it's just… inappropriate." He rubbed the back of his neck. "Awkward."

"Don't act like you haven't been kissed by a beautiful woman before. You might be kinda scruffy now, but you still have it." She took some lip balm out of her jeans and put it on. "I've been wanting to do that for over a year. I shouldn't have waited so long. You liked it, didn't you?"

"Look, I have work to do."

He tried to pass her, but like a playful teenager, she remained in his path. He liked Mandi. For a woman living out in the middle of nowhere, she had it all in the looks department. Abraham had gotten to know the family well. They owned most of the property in the area, from generations back. The grill was their business where they liked to play around and have some fun. "Besides, you're married."

She lifted her hand and wiggled the fingers. "Separated. So you can have me now," she said with frosty breath.

"I can see the tan line where your ring probably was a few minutes ago."

Mandi toyed with his beard and said, "I know you want to put those Johnny Bench hands on my tiny waist. Quick holding back, Abraham. I'm all yours. And just so you know, I am legally separated. You can ask Mom." She draped her arms around his neck. "Come on, stay with me over the weekend. You'll regret leaving on that long ride back home. You know it."

Abraham and Mandi had done this dance before. As reserved as he'd become, he still liked the attention. She was captivating. But there would be baggage, he was sure of that. She had a husband

and kids. He could never tell whether she was being fully forthcoming or not. He liked her, but not enough to take the risk. He'd had all the heartache he could stand in this world. Now, he was just passing through, waiting for a fresh start in another. He picked her up.

She let out a delightful squeal.

Then he set her down behind him, grabbed his dolly, and hustled out the freezer door, where he ran right into Mandi's mother, Martha. The matronly woman had her arms crossed over her chest as her foot tapped on the floor. Thirty years before, she could have been Mandi. Now, she was a pleasantly plump, gray-haired version of her daughter, with a warm sparkle in her eyes.

"Hello, ma'am."

"'Ma'am?' *Please* call me Martha, Abraham. You know better." She hooked his arm in his and said, "I came to rescue you… again. I'd apologize for Mandi, but I think we both know that it wouldn't change a thing. Once she sets her sights on something she wants, it's hard to pull her claws off of it."

"I know." He glanced back at the cooler.

With her eyes averted, Mandi started stocking the shelves.

"Is she really getting a divorce?"

"Who knows? I can't keep up with what she does. She does have a lawyer, though. It's a shame that Alex ended up being such a putz." Martha led them toward the restaurant section of the store. "Come on, now. I started them fixing you something to eat the moment you pulled up. And Herb is excited to see you."

"Just let me finish up my delivery, and I need to wash up."

"Oh, don't be silly. That can wait. Mandi will fetch the beer."

"But…"

Martha hustled him onto a bar stool. It was one of the round stainless-steel ones, like those in old soda shops, that spun around. She moved behind the counter and put on a black apron that said in white lettering, "God's in charge, but I'm the manager."

"I'm really not very hungry," Abraham said.

She gave him a warm smile and said, "I'll fetch Herb. He's so excited you are here." She scurried back into the kitchen.

Abraham set his ball cap down on the bar. He liked Woody's Grill but could never relax with Mandi prowling around. In his broken heart, he was still married to Jenny. They had been friends, boyfriend and girlfriend, on and off, since middle school. They married two years after he turned pro when he was twenty. Women had come before her, but none like Jenny. She was sweet and beautiful. She was his rock even when he thought the world revolved around him. He loved her but took her for granted. His wandering eye landed him in trouble more than once. The "all the babes love Abe" reputation didn't help much either. It made the road trips difficult.

Martha ushered Herb into the diner. If she was sixty, Herb was eighty and moved as if he was ninety. He had half a head of cotton-candy hair crumpled up on one side of his head that looked like it could blow away in a stiff breeze. His wore a long-sleeved knit shirt and checkered golf pants.

He pumped his shaky fist at Abraham and said, "If it isn't the Jenkins Jet."

"Stop saying that, Herb," Martha warned.

"Oh, he's fine," Herb said with youthful cheeriness. "No one around here knows him. Go fix him something to eat, will you, darling?"

She shook her head at Abraham. Herb was legally blind but refused to wear his glasses. On his own, Herb ambled around the bar and sat down by Abraham.

Herb grabbed his shoulder. "So, did you see any UFOs in Wytheville?"

CHAPTER 4

Old man Herb chuckled. His big ears wiggled a little as he did so, scratching his bushy sideburns. Then he said, "They think they are so important down in Wytheville… ever since they made up that bull-crap story about seeing a UFO and all of the national media came in."

"Herb, watch your language," Martha said.

"What? Crap isn't a curse word," Herb said.

"Yes it is." She set down a red plastic basket full of home-cut french fries covered in melted cheese and jalapeños. "There you go, Abraham. Eat up." She gave Herb a dirty look. "You watch your mouth."

"Ah," Herb said with disdain. "That's not a bad word. It's a little bad, but not that bad." He grabbed a napkin and rubbed an eye. "Anyway, they are full of bull crap down in Wytheville. I think they made it all up just so that they could get on television because no one wanted to stop in their crummy town."

Abraham tucked his napkin into the unbuttoned collar of his black polo shirt and started eating. He didn't understand what Herb's beef was with Wytheville, but Herb never failed to mention it. For some reason, the elder had a problem with that city. He was jealous, perhaps. Still, Abraham couldn't resist goading the man a little.

"I saw some signs in the Super Center down there about a UFO festival they were going to be having this year."

"What?" Herb flung his arms so hard he almost slipped out of his seat and would have if Abraham didn't catch him by an arm. Fastening both hands on the counter, Herb continued his tirade. "There ain't no such thing as UFOs in Wytheville! They say anything to draw attention to themselves. What's next? They gonna report a herd of unicorns prancing through their overrated city?"

"There was some military activity down in the tunnel. It seemed like something strange might be going on again."

"Pah!" Herb flapped his hands outward, and his lips twisted back and forth. "Ain't no such thing as UFOs. It's the biggest lie that was ever told." He looked at Abraham with his smoky bug eyes and made an impish smile. He gently punched Abraham in the shoulder. "At least in Wytheville!"

Abraham nodded as he pulled out a tangle of fries covered in cheese and jalapeños. The combination was a specialty at Woody's Grill. The secret was the home-cut fries with melted longhorn cheese and canned jalapeños out of Herb's garden. It was a local delicacy at $9.99 a basket. It was a little something Abraham got hooked on the first time he came through. A burning sensation started in his mouth, and he lifted a hand.

Herb cackled. "Sneaks up on you, don't it?"

Wringing her hands on a dish towel, Martha hustled over to Abraham. "Oh dear, I'm sorry. I didn't bring you anything to drink. What do you want?"

"Beer. It's always best with beer. Especially that ale he's hauling," Herb said. "That stuff keeps us in business. The locals love it."

After he swallowed his fries, he said, "Milk and an ice water." He tapped his chest. His eyes were watering. The first bit was always the strongest of the batch, and he needed the milk to break down the heat from the jalapeños caught in his throat.

Speaking with a spacey look that seemed to pass right through Abraham, Herb said, "The secret is chewing it up all together. You have to mix it. You didn't chew enough. So how's old man Luther? Is he still as cranky as ever?"

Martha set down tall glasses of ice water and milk filled to the brim. "Here you go, hon."

Abraham sucked down half the glass of milk. "Ah. Thanks, Martha. That hit the spot. I think I can handle it now."

"Well, your burger will be out in a few." She patted his arm. "Take your time, and chew at least twelve times before you swallow."

"Thanks." Abraham took a sip of water, turned his attention back to Herb, and said, "Luther's doing fine—a cranky curmudgeon twenty-four seven, waiting for the world to end. He sends his regards, as always."

"He's a good man. Rigid, but good. You'd think a man that ran a brewery would be more cheerful." Herb cackled. "Say, I could use one of those beers. We ran out two days ago, and people have been asking."

"They're in the cooler," Abraham said.

"Heck, it doesn't have to be cold. It's just as good warm, you know, like they serve in England."

As Abraham turned in his stool, his eyes drifted toward the diner window over an empty booth. Outside, Mandi was loading cases of beer onto the dolly. He could see the almost feline muscles in her arms as she stacked one box on top of the other. It was one of the sexiest things he'd ever seen. *Now that's a woman. Why don't I just give in?*

"She's something, isn't she?" Herb said.

"Huh?"

"Mandi really likes you. She wouldn't do that for anyone." Herb wasn't even looking outside. He was looking right at Abraham. "She wouldn't pour water on a burning man if she didn't like him. I think you'd make a good couple."

"I don't think I'm suited for marriage anymore."

"You just can't move on in this world, can you?"

"No, I think I'd be better off in another."

"That's a strange thing to say. Hey, maybe you could catch a UFO in Wytheville." Herb cackled loudly. "So, what's Luther into? Is he ever going to expand?"

"There are plenty of companies that want to buy him out. He won't budge." He started back in on his fries.

Martha reappeared and set down a huge hamburger that filled half the plate. Three pickle spears sat on the side.

"He says they'd just ruin it. As long as he lives, he'll keep it as is. He's content."

"Content is the best way to be," Martha commented. "Not wanting for anything. It brings a lot of peace. So many people running around like chickens with their heads chopped of, trying to find happiness… They need to find contentment in the surroundings they've been blessed with. People look too hard for happiness, not realizing it's on the inside."

"He doesn't need a sermon, Martha. Let the man eat," Herb said.

"You hush," she said. "Did you bless your meal, Abraham?"

"Uh, no, I just figured it was blessed since you made it."

Martha showed a serious look, letting him know that she wasn't buying it.

He closed his eyes and said the inward prayer he'd learned at the table when he was rehabbing in The Mission. The Mission had helped him crawl out of the well of despair and get him back on his feet again. He opened his eyes and said, "It's done."

"I always keep you in my prayers," Martha said.

"I appreciate it," he said.

Mandi pushed her way through the double doors. Hauling the cases of beer by the counter, she didn't even glance Abraham's way. He got the feeling that he'd hurt her, having brushed her off one too many times, perhaps. Perhaps today was the day that caught up with him.

"Hey, Mandi, bring me one of those beers," Herb hollered.

Outside, military vehicles pulled into the station, a Deuce and three Humvees. Their diesel engines rumbled loudly. Everyone in the diner stared out the window at them.

Scratching his nose, Herb said, "Humph. That's odd. We never get those convoys stopping here. They always stop in Wytheville."

CHAPTER 5

WITHIN SEVERAL MINUTES, THE ARMY men filtered into the grill. Uniform caps and helmets removed, they filled almost every table and bar stool in the diner. Martha hollered for Mandi. The daughter quickly made her way behind the bar, donned an apron, grabbed an order pad, and hustled over to the tables. With a welcoming smile on her face, she started taking orders from the uniformed men and women.

Martha's face was flushed when she said, "This is odd. We never get a rush like this. I'd better call in Maggie. Gonna need some help behind the counter and in the kitchen."

Facing Abraham to his left, Herb addressed a soldier on Abraham's left. "Hey, are there any UFOs in Wytheville?"

The soldier on the stool had the eagle rank insignia of a colonel embroidered on his camouflaged collar. In his thirties like Abraham, he had a high-and-tight haircut and a thick, neatly trimmed moustache. He smiled at Herb and said, "You know it."

Herb shook his head, harrumphed, and looked away.

Abraham chuckled. He nodded at the officer and started eating his burger. The officer gave a nod and peered deeply at his face. Abraham turned back toward Herb, who resumed their previous conversation.

"You know, I think Luther should sell out and make a pile of money off those big breweries." Herb licked his lips. "That's what I'd do. I'd just let them have it. Spread your brand all over the world. That's all it's about these days: the branding."

"I know," Abraham agreed.

He knew all about branding. He had been his own brand for a time, with T-shirts and hoagies named in his honor. The Jenkins Fastball. One Hundred Three Degrees Jenkins's Flame Thrower Hot Sauce, which was actually kinda mild. The Jenkins Jet Sandwich.

"But if the brand gets too big," he said, "they forget about little places like this. I think Luther likes it the way it is."

"Pfft. I can go buy it at the wholesale market. Plus, it'd probably be cheaper, too." Herb made a good, out-loud giggle. "I like to save a buck."

The diner became noisier as the new crowd settled in. Most of the soldiers had hard looks on their faces, but Mandi brought the smile out of all of them. She worked the room and must have sold everything on the menu. She giggled playfully at all the soldiers' flirtations and jokes. Never once did she glance back at Abraham as he sought her eyes out from time to time. He had been able to brush her off before, but this time, it was more difficult. That made him feel guilty too, as though he was cheating on Jenny and his son. His friends and family told him he needed to move on, but he kept telling himself he wasn't ready yet.

"So have you listened to any good books lately?" Herb asked. His heavy-lidded eyes followed Martha slipping back and forth behind the bar and kitchen as she took the orders and ran them straight back. "Hey, where's my beer?"

"Get your own beer. We are busy, hon," she said just before she vanished behind the kitchen's swinging door.

"I'll grab you one," Abraham said.

He moved out of his stool, slipped over to the store side and back into the freezer, and cracked open a case. He pulled out a dark bottle wrapped in the keg-barrel label. The logo read The Beer for What Ales You.

"That's a new one."

Luther alternated slogans back and forth. Some weren't bad, but others were just horrible. His favorite was Beer Happens. He made his way back to the diner.

Mandi was sitting in his stool, fully engaged in a friendly chat with the officer whom he'd been sitting next to. As she took his order, she would touch the man's shoulder and laugh at his comments. Abraham felt ashamed. At the moment, he looked like a slob compared to the neatly dressed man in uniform. He was out of shape and probably couldn't run a quarter mile to save his life. He remembered when he'd been fit as a fiddle and sharp as a tack in his dress. Now, he felt more out of place. He set the beer down hard on the counter.

"Oh, there it is," Herb said.

Mandi turned, gave Abraham an uninterested glance, and hopped out of his seat. As she continued her conversation with the officer, he eased back into his stool, huddled over his food, and slowly started eating.

Herb nudged him with his fist full of beer. "I need a little help. Will you do it?"

Absentmindedly, he said, "Huh? Oh."

He took the bottle in his hand. The beer bottle wasn't a twist-off. It required a bottle opener.

"Don't you have any paint-can openers? They work great, you know," Abraham said, thinking of the trick Luther had taught him.

The old man gave out cheap paint-can keys because they were perfect bottle openers and super cheap to buy in bulk.

"I got to see you do it," Herb said with a grin.

"Okay."

Abraham had hands like a gorilla's. They were strong as a vise, too—the one gift he had that he'd never had to work at. Using the power of his thumb, he pushed the cap right off the top of the bottle. The black cap, with its war-helm insignia, fell onto the bar.

Herb clapped his hands and cackled gleefully. He took the bottle from Abraham and took a long drink. "Ah, man, that's good. So tell me—have you listened to any good books lately?"

"Some." He had plenty of time to listen to lots of things in the truck. He tried to mix it up between audiobooks, radio, and satellite. But he preferred the quiet most of all. "You?"

"I like that *Game of Thrones*. I can't see it so well on the TV, but we listen on the road to Richmond. Man, that's good."

"It's awful," Martha said as she passed by with a coffee pot in hand. "They do the most horrible things to each other in those stories."

Herb grinned. "That's the fun part."

Martha rolled her eyes as she filled up a soldier's coffee.

"I still listen to a little bit of everything, that included," Abraham said. "I just have trouble sticking with the same story, so I jump around a lot. I like biographies about real people because you get a finished story. Some stories I don't like starting if there isn't a finish. But I figure I'll get around to finishing all of them one day. I've got nothing else going on."

"Huh. Well, what about sports? Do you listen to any games?"

"No."

CHAPTER 6

THIS WAS THE PART OF the conversation where Abraham would squirm. Herb tended to rehash the same topics, and baseball always came up. The elder wasn't preoccupied with the past. He was mostly only concerned about what he was interested in at the moment, which tended to be the same topics: money, beer, books, and sports.

Since the accident, Abraham had walked away from the game of baseball completely. Agents, managers, and reporters hounded him after the accident. He had a contract, a big one, that wouldn't be fulfilled. Maybe he could have played again, but he didn't care, and when the baseball business didn't leave him alone, he became bitter toward it. It amplified his sorrow. His life spiraled down further from there.

He was an ace pitcher, a strike-out king. When he was on the mound, he felt like a demigod. He'd struck out every batter he ever faced. He held that white leather ball in his hand like a lethal weapon. He humiliated batters time and time again. He would wind up that lanky arm of his and unleash the baseball off the tip of his finger as if it were shot out of a pistol. Batters went down, one after the other, pounding their bats on the ground to the roar of the crowd.

But the away teams hated him. They hated him with a passion. The signs in the stands read Jenkins the Jerk and Abraham Stinkin. He laughed at all of them. He didn't laugh after the accident. Plenty of flowers and fan mail came, even from the folks who despised him. But after that day, he realized life wasn't the mound, and some things in life, no matter how good you were, you just couldn't control.

He finished up his meal while Herb rambled on. He wiped his fingers on his napkin and pushed back the empty plate and the basket of fries. The sky outside was darkening.

"I need to get going. Let me go grab my delivery ticket and gas up."

"Sure, sure. I'll sign off on it. Looks like the girls are pretty busy," Herb said. "It's good seeing you."

Outside, under the gas station's canopy, he grabbed the gas-pump nozzle and fed it into the beer truck's tank. The digital meter converting gallons to dollars moved slowly. It was always slow at Woody's Grill but slower now as a few soldiers were also filling up their vehicles. His truck had a forty-gallon tank, so it would take a while.

Halfway through pumping, a man in a deep authoritative voice said, "Nice truck."

He turned to see the officer he'd sat beside in the grill. The man stood almost as tall as him.

"How are you doing, Colonel?"

The polished officer made an easy smile. "You know your insignias."

"I'm a military brat. My dad was an Air Force pilot in 'Nam. I wasn't born then, but he flew F-4 Phantoms during the war."

"I see. A napalm warrior, huh?"

"He used to say he set the world on fire. I was pretty young, and he was pretty old by the time I came around. I never knew what that meant until I saw *Platoon*."

The colonel chuckled. He brushed his finger across his moustache and said, "Look, I'm a big baseball fan. A big Buckos fan, as a matter of fact. I thought it was you back when I first locked eyes on you but wasn't sure until you peeled that cap off that beer bottle like it was the skin of a banana. Man, that was something."

"Oh."

"I don't mean to bother you, but I'm really a big fan. I don't want an autograph or anything. I just wanted to shake your hand and express my regards."

"Well sure, Colonel"—he looked at the man's name tag—"Dexter." He offered his hand. "And, I'd be happy to give an autograph, anything for you and your men."

"That's a mighty generous offer." The colonel shook with a strong grip. "It's Colonel Drew Dexter. But a handshake will do just fine."

"You mean you don't want a selfie with me?" he joked.

He dug in his pocket. "I'm not big on social media, but what the heck? How about one for me to show my family. My wife will get a kick out of it. Private Griffith, get your tail over here."

A young woman in uniform wearing a soft cap ran over to the colonel and saluted.

He returned the salute and handed her his phone. "Take a few good ones of me and my friend here."

"Yes, sir," she said.

The men stood shoulder to shoulder and smiled.

She silently snapped the photos. "It's done, Colonel."

"Thank you." Colonel Dexter took back his camera and said, "Dismissed, Private Griffith." He turned to Abraham. "Technology is something, isn't it? It's 2019, and our precious worlds live under our fingertips." He slid the phone into his shirt pocket. "I appreciate it."

"No problem. So are you part of that group that was working in the Big Walker Tunnel?"

"I can't say whether we are or aren't."

"No problem. I understand. I just hope the East River Mountain Tunnel is free of interruptions." Abraham checked the darkening sky. "Looks like it's going to be rain all the way either way."

"We came from the north. The East River Tunnel is smooth sailing. Anyway, my best to you, Mr. Jenkins. It's been a pleasure chatting with you."

"You too, Colonel. Say, would you like a couple of cases to share with your troops?"

The colonel's eyes got big. "We don't say no to beer." He patted the doors on the truck. "Especially this brew. You sure it's no trouble?"

"I get a few liberties on the job. Plus, the owner's a vet too. He'll understand." He unloaded two cases of the bottles and handed them over to the colonel. "Enjoy."

Taking the beer to his Humvee, the colonel said, "Will do."

The gas nozzle clicked. He racked the hose and finished paying with his gas card. The pump spat out a receipt. He took it and put it inside the truck. He made his rounds at the truck, checking the tires and making sure the slat doors were all closed except one left open for the dolly. He reached back in the truck, grabbed his clipboard, and headed inside.

Mandi was still working the tables. A skinny young man wearing a Woody's Grill T-shirt stood behind the register. He had jet-black hair that hung in his eyes. Abraham wondered if he was one of Mandi's kids.

He moved over to Herb, who was staring up at the television over the bar. "Time to hit the road. See you next week."

"You leaving already? It's gonna rain. A lot. I can feel it in my joints. The more rain, the more it hurts. I think it's the Indian in me," Herb said. "I'm one quarter Chippewa. One of a kind. Heh heh." With his tongue stuck out of his mouth, he signed the delivery receipt. "I can't read it, but I trust you."

Abraham gave Herb his copy then flagged down Martha, delivering orders behind the counter, and waved goodbye.

She caught his eye and waved. "See you next month. Be careful out there. Storm's coming."

He fetched his dolly, which Mandi had left in the cooler, and headed out. He glanced inside the diner. Mandi was on the far side of the room with her back to him, serving drinks to the soldiers. She never turned his way. *I guess I'll see her next month.*

Back at the beer truck, he loaded up his dolly and secured it inside the compartment. He closed the door and made one last walk around his vehicle. Coming around the front from the passenger side, he almost ran right into Mandi. Her arms were crossed over her chest. She tapped one foot, a storm brewing in her eyes.

"You're an idiot," she said.

"What did I do?"

"You could have at least walked up and said goodbye. Would that have killed you?"

"I think you were doing just fine entertaining the troops. Don't act like you were missing me." He tried to walk around her, but she stepped in his way.

She pointed in his face. "Ah ha! You do like me. I made you jealous, didn't I?"

Looking away from her penetrating stare, he said, "No."

"You're lying. You can't even look me in the eye. Just admit it—you like me. I know it because you never leave without two slices of Mom's homemade pecan pie."

He decided to flip the tables on her. "So you're an actress now. How can I trust someone that puts on a show like that? Look, I don't have time for games, Mandi. I've got to go. I've got work to do." He tried to move by her, but she shuffled in front of him. He rolled his eyes and sighed. "Will you get out of my way?"

"No. Not until you admit the truth. You like me."

"Don't make me do this."

"Do what, admit the truth? I know you are hurting, but let me help you unhurt," she said as she grabbed his waist and hooked her fingers in his belt loops. "I can help you move on."

"Mandi, you don't know me that well." He put his hands on her waist, lifted her up again, and set her aside.

"Hey!" she yelled, furious. Her cheeks turned as red as roses. Her stare filled with daggers that could kill him. Her fists balled up at her sides. She started to shake her head. Her hands opened up. Then the flames went out in her eyes, and tears started to form. "You know, Abraham, go ahead, let the road be your mistress." Her shoulders sagged as she walked away. "See you next month… or not. I don't care."

CHAPTER 7

Abraham hit the road feeling as empty as he'd felt in months. Mandi liked to dig her nails into him, and he would usually shrug it off, but this time, somehow, she got them in deep. He felt as though he didn't want to feel at all. As he was driving in the steady traffic north on I-77, he looked over at his son's backpack. It gave him comfort, as if his son were still sitting in the seat.

"I think I might have blown it this time."

Overhead, heavy clouds had built up, which came in from the ocean, to the east. The rain was barely spitting. No doubt a storm was coming. He didn't like driving in the rain. A single headlight in his sideview mirror caught his eye. Two seconds later, a babe on a jet bike zoomed by him, wearing only a red-white-and-blue helmet, cowboy boots, and a bikini. Her auburn hair was flowing out from underneath her helmet.

Abraham would have chuckled. He'd seen plenty of wild things on the road, but this view was a first. He figured she was leaving the lake and trying to beat the rain, not that it was any of his business. Three seconds later, another rider on a crotch rocket soared by. The man, with more muscle than motorcycle, must have been moving over one hundred miles per hour. The fool didn't even have a shirt on, just biker boots, jeans, and a black helmet.

"Idiot."

The last thing Abraham wanted was to have to pull over to scrape the two fools up off the road. It had happened before, and it was an ugly scene—wreckage and broken bodies all over the highway. It brought back memories that haunted him day in and day out. Now, his belly started to sour, and his head ached. The aggravation was probably activating his ulcer. With the combination of too many jalapeños and cheese and a juicy hamburger with almost as much grease as meat, things weren't gonna go well. His tummy gurgled in a loud, bad way.

"Oh no. Here we go."

His forehead broke out in a cold sweat. He fanned himself with his cap and turned the air conditioner up another level. The spitting rain came down harder on the windshield. He turned on the truck's wipers.

"I really need to cut back on the jalapeños."

For some reason, he reached up and pulled his sun visor down. While driving on a brief straight stretch of road, he took a long glance at the picture of his family, Jenny and Jake. Jenny was a tall athlete of a woman with pretty eyes and short sandy-blond hair that covered her ears. She always had a warm smile on her face. Jake, at eight years old, had more of his mother in him than his father. He was a handsome kid, lean as a string bean, but with big hands and feet like his dad. Both of them had ball caps on that day in the picture. It was the day he'd signed a huge contract with the Pirates. Not long after that, all their lives had turned inside out.

"I miss you, baby," he said as he kissed his two fingers and touched the picture. "Both of you, more than you'll ever know." His eyes watered. "I'm sorry."

His belly moaned. He reached over into Jake's backpack and fetched a bottle of Pepto-Bismol. He shook up the milky pink elixir, twisted off the cap, and drank. It was one of the few drugs he took, now that he'd cleaned himself up, and he felt guilty even for taking that. He'd lost faith in a lot of medicines that took hold of him. They were as bad as the depression itself. But with help from his friends at the mission, like Mike, Dave, and Luther, he was able to live with the pain and loss on his own. His heart ached because he missed his wife and son so much.

He put the bottle back in the backpack. "Thanks, son." He looked closely at the picture of his wife. "I love you, love. Sorry about Mandi. I hope you'll forgive me."

He knew in his heart that Jenny would understand. She had patience and a strong temperament and was as understanding as they came. But if he stepped too far from the line, she would let him know it. His head got swollen often, but she kept him grounded. She was the best thing that had ever happened to him: his best friend. No person could replace her.

A possum crept onto the highway and darted out from the berm on the right. Abraham jerked the wheel hard left. The truck wheels screeched and bumped over something.

"Geez! Stupid varmint!"

He pulled the truck back into the right lane and checked his mirrors. No other cars were around, coming or going. That was odd because this stretch of interstate stayed continuously busy, especially during vacation season.

With his belly gurgling like the crashing waters of a waterfall, now bloated and gassy, he unbuckled his belt. "Good Lord, this feels awful. No more jalapeños. I swear it. I swear that milk is curdling in my stomach. Go, Pepto, go. Work that magic."

He was about two miles away from the East River Mountain Tunnel. The storm clouds shaded the mountainous hills to black. Sheets of rain were coming down from the sky, and lightning streaked and flashed in the purple sky above the tunnel.

With almost two hours of driving left, Abraham said to himself, "Looks like it's going to be a long drive."

He rounded the last upward twist of the interstate that led him right to the tunnel. The subtle yellow glow of the tunnel mouth waited to swallow him whole. The rain came down harder, splattering loudly on his rooftop. A bolt of lightning that looked like it had been cast from heaven itself lit up the dark sky with white fire, striking the mountaintop. A thunderous boom followed, shaking the truck cabin.

"Whoa!" he cried out.

The beer truck engine sputtered. The dashboard lights flickered on and off. Still, the truck chugged along with the diesel turbo engine, renewing its laborious fury. With sheets of rain coming down, he plowed his way through into the tunnel, where he was alone—no head- or taillights in front of him or behind. It wasn't the oddest thing in the world to see, but normally, unless in the wee hours after midnight, plenty of company would be ripping through the tunnel. At 1,650 meters, the tunnel was just over a mile long, taking about one minute to pass through. The tires hummed through the tunnel, making a unique sound all their own. The lights inside the tunnel flickered on and off like the wink of fireflies.

"Not again."

Abraham liked the road, but tonight, he was ready to get back to the security of his cabin back home. Things just didn't feel right. The tips of his fingers tingled, his stomach ached, and his head pounded. Halfway into the tunnel, he saw a quavering light ahead. It made a sun ring inside the tunnel.

Squinting, he said, "What the heck?"

Suddenly, the eerie quavering pool of light shot right at him and his truck. It passed right through him, bathing his truck in strange light. An instant later, the truck started jumping up and down on its tires. The engine bucked and rattled. A sea of flying bats, in the hundreds, bounced off his windshield. He slammed on his brakes and screamed.

CHAPTER 8

Drenched in sweat, Abraham sat in the truck seat with his eyes wide open. The bats had cleared out. The truck lights shone on the dusty debris in the tunnel. It was a tunnel that wasn't the same one from moments ago. It was now nothing but black rock and clay.

"What on earth?"

He blinked hard several times as he caught his breath. His heart thundered inside his chest. Far ahead, at least over a quarter mile that he could tell, was an opening of daylight.

Rubbing his temples, he said, "No more jalapeño cheese fries for me."

The truck headlights and dashboard lights flickered. The diesel engine knocked hard and died. The cabin went black.

He smacked the wheel with the butt of his hand. "Ah, come on."

The tunnel was pitch black, but in his side-view mirror, he caught the quavering light hovering far behind him. "Lord, tell me this is just some episode, because things are getting creepy."

Abraham popped his door open a crack. It groaned as he pushed it wide-open. Slowly, he stepped outside. The ground beneath him was solid dirt. The tunnel walls around him were those of a cave just as big as the tunnel he'd been driving through. He peered at the quavering light. It was too blurry to see right through, where the rest of the real tunnel would be. All he could think of was his encounter in the Big Walker Tunnel. Perhaps this was a bizarre part of a military operation he'd gotten caught in.

He shouted, "Hello?" He did it again, but even louder. "Hello!"

He heard no response. The cave tunnel was as quiet as sleeping field mice. He looked in the direction the truck was facing. The daylight was natural, not alien like the strange pool of illumination behind him.

"I don't know what's going on, but I'm going to play right through it. I have to wake up sometime, dead or alive."

He got inside the truck's cab and cranked the key. The engine battery was stone cold. Shaking his head, he grabbed Jake's backpack. It had some of his son's personal items as well as a few of his own.

"Let's go on a little hike, son."

On foot, with an unsettled glance behind himself, he moved forward in the direction the truck was pointed. From Jake's pack, he grabbed a flashlight then flipped the switch. The light came on.

"Whew. At least something's working."

He lit up the field of dirt and rock at his feet with the welcome beam of illumination. It was as if nothing had ever passed through the cave before. It smelled like damp rocks and dirt, nothing out of the ordinary. He made it about fifty yards when the flashlight died. He slapped it on the side a few times. No light came.

"Great." He placed it back in his pack and shouldered it.

Trudging through the uncertain footing, he headed straight toward the tunnel's end light. He'd made it another hundred yards or so when he saw a figure darting into the tunnel.

"Hey," he said, waving his hands.

The figure sprinted toward him. Judging by her build, he guessed she was a bony woman. She moved quickly and looked desperate, taking glances over her shoulder as she ran. She had nothing on but a slip of ragged clothing. She didn't even look at Abraham the deeper she penetrated the cave. Twenty paces away, he got a closer look at her face as her demonic eyes locked on his.

Abraham's blood froze. "Sweet mother of mercy."

The pasty-skinned red-eyed woman looked like something spawned out of hell. She had a bushel of wiry brown hair that writhed like living wormlike snakes. Her eyes were red-pink angled slits, her leathery skin tight over her bony features. She showed a large mouthful of teeth as sharp as razors. She locked eyes on Abraham and changed direction, angling toward him.

Frightened out of his boots, he turned and ran away, yelling, "Lady, stay the hell away from me!"

He made three long strides before his toe clipped a hunk of sunken rock. He fell hard and sprawled onto the ground. He rolled onto his back just as the woman pounced on top of him. He screamed his own bloodcurdling scream.

CHAPTER 9

TERROR. IT SUDDENLY HAD A new meaning in Abraham's life. Now it took on the form of a bony witch who looked like an evil schoolteacher who had tormented him in second grade. Somehow, he fought the fierce little monster woman off as they rolled over the ground. She hissed awful sounds at him. Her teeth bit at his neck. He pushed her face away with his big hands. He set a boot in her gut and sent her flying.

She hit the ground hard, screeching like a wild banshee. Once she came to her feet, she eyed him and clacked her sharp teeth. Her talonlike fingernails clutched in and out at her sides.

Abraham sucked for his breath. His lungs burned, and his limbs were exhausted. The wiry witch woman had already taken the fight out of him. He was out of shape but managed to get back up on one knee. Before he made it to both feet, the witch of a woman was rushing him.

"No," he huffed. "No, get away!"

The whinny of a horse and clomp of horse hooves stopped the pink-eyed witch in her tracks. Her head lifted upward. Her slanted eyes turned big. The ugly scowl on her face turned to wroth anger. She shuffled side to side as if uncertain where to go.

With a concerted effort, Abraham made a backward glance. The last thing he wanted was for the wiry woman to pounce on his back. What he saw startled him. A man riding a black horse rode into the tunnel's entrance. He was some sort of medieval knight or warrior, just like he'd seen on television or heard about in stories. Abraham rubbed his eyes. *This can't be real.*

The horse trotted deeper into the tunnel. The rider's eyes were locked on the witch woman. His face was obscured in the darkness, and he held a crossbow in one hand.

The witch woman let out a screech, her gnarled hands and bony fingers massaging the air. The loose dirt on the ground shivered as her eyes rolled up in her head and turned black as pitch.

Abraham's heartbeat pounded in his ears. He couldn't catch his breath as the air turned icy and shimmered around him. The witch's breath turned frosty. Bugs and insects and worms popped up out of the ground. Centipedes crawled over his fingers.

He jerked away. "Gah!"

The witch spoke in strange words that twisted with arcane energy.

Clatch-zip!

A crossbow bolt struck the witch woman right between the eyes and stuck out from one end of the skull to the other. Her widened jaw hung open as her lanky, bare arms shook. She pointed a crooked finger at the rider and let out a deafening shriek.

Abraham couldn't believe his eyes as he plugged his ears with his fingers. The witch woman lived. She commanded bizarre power. Her crooked fingers needled the air. The icy wind in the caves howled, gaining strength and stirring his hair.

The rider and horse reared up. The warrior tossed his crossbow to the ground and slid a shimmering sword out of its scabbard. "Yah!" the man said. The horse lunged forward. The beast bore down on the screaming witch, who ran at the rider with fingers poised like daggers. The horse veered left. The shining sword sang. The witch's head leapt from her narrow shoulders, bounced off the ground, and rolled to a stop. Her black eyes turned pinkish red, flared once, and dimmed.

The tunnel fell silent. The crawling insects slipped back into the cave dirt. The icy chill in the air lifted away. Abraham clutched his chest, panting. He could feel his heart beating in his head. He swallowed the lump in his throat and slowly turned toward the man on horseback.

A few dozen feet away, the knight-like warrior sat coolly in the saddle. Eyeing the witch, he dismounted with casual ease. With long strides, he made his way through the cave toward the witch. Without giving Abraham a glance, he stood over the witch, pointed the sword at her chest, and stabbed her in the heart.

Abraham sat on the ground, sweating like a lumberjack and gasping. He knew what was happening wasn't real, but it felt real. *Wake up, Abraham, wake up! This isn't even entertaining.* He stared at the warrior. He was a tall athletic man, black haired with a neatly trimmed beard. His facial features were strong and angular, like many action heroes' he'd seen in the movies. The warrior wore a finely crafted metal breastplate that had seen action. He was dark, imposing and formidable.

Abraham lifted a hand and, not sure what to say, said, "Uh, hello?"

The warrior gave Abraham a sideways glance. His eyes hung on him long enough to soak him in. Then, the man's head snapped around and looked at the quavering body of light that hung deeper in the tunnel behind the truck. His glance slid over to the truck, and he shook his head. He did a double take between Abraham and the vehicle. He looked at Abraham and started talking in strong words.

Abraham couldn't understand what the man was saying. The warrior's words were a strange language, but he babbled on intently. He dropped his crossbow and drew his sword. It was a fine length of steel with a keen edge that shone in the dimness. He pointed the blade at the truck and started shouting.

Waving his hands in front of him, Abraham said, "I don't know what you are saying."

The man's dark eyes seemed to catch fire. His harsh words became stronger. The man's chest heaved, and his nostrils flared. He spoke in rough, broken-up English that Abraham began to understand. "What year is it?"

Finding his breath, Abraham managed to say, "Twenty eighteen."

"No!" The warrior hustled toward the truck and ran his hands over the hood. "I can't believe it. I thought I'd never see the day."

"What day?" Abraham asked.

"Your time has come. My time is done!" the warrior shouted at him. He stripped off his armor and slung aside his sword belt. Bare-chested, he was nothing but muscle and built like a linebacker. He looked at Abraham and in the same broken speech said, "Take off your clothing."

"What? No."

The warrior looked back into the tunnel. The quavering portal was shrinking. He turned on Abraham and, gripping his sword tightly, shook it at Abraham and said, "Do it now!"

"I'm not doing that! Who are you? Where am I?"

In two strides, the warrior crossed the distance between him, grabbed Abraham by the hair, and lifted him up to his toes. They were about the same size, but the man had the strength of a grizzly. The warrior then choked Abraham with his free hand while looking him right in the eye. "I am Eugene Drisk. This is Titanuus. It's a long story, and I don't have time to talk. Just give me your clothing!"

Abraham shook his head. "No."

The warrior looked back at the shrinking portal of light in the tunnel. Angrily, he shook his head then punched Abraham in his soft belly.

Abraham doubled over and let out a loud "oof" as he dropped to his knees.

The warrior ripped off Abraham's shirt and took his hat and glasses. He took his pants and shoes. He pulled Abraham's head back by the hair. He stuck the blade in Abraham's face and said, "Take my sword if you want to live."

"I don't want your sword."

"Take it!" The man tried to stuff the sword into Abraham's hand.

He clenched his fists and crawled away. "Leave me alone, you freak. I don't want your sword!"

The man pushed him to the ground. He pinned Abraham down with his foot on his chest. He lifted the sword high overhead. "Take the sword or die!" He stabbed downward.

Abraham flinched. He eyed the sword, stuck in the ground by his face. The witch's fresh blood ran down the blade.

The warrior kicked him in the ribs. "Take it. Take it, armor belt and all, or I'll kick the life out of you!" He drew back his foot again. "You must do as I say!"

"Fine!" Abraham fought his way up to a sitting position. "I'll take it! Just quick kicking me, you deranged Renaissance reenactor!" He reached for the pommel. "I'll take your bloody sword, seeing how none of this is really happening anyway! Then I'm going to beat you with it." He grabbed the sword and locked his fingers on it tightly. A charge of energy like a thunderbolt from heaven went right though him. He shook all over like a flag beating in the wind.

Energy exchanged between him and the warrior. An out-of-body experience occurred. Muscle and sinew popped. His entire body flexed and bulged, and he let out an agonizing scream. As quickly as the pain came, it was gone, and he was on his knees, chest heaving. The sword was clutched in his hand. The witch's blood ran back down over his fingers. He looked up and cast his eyes on a shabby-looking man holding a rock in one hand and his clothing in another. He was a balding, portly, scholarly-looking fellow, naked from the waist up. The man studied his own puffy fingers. He gave Abraham an incredulous stare and said, "Perhaps you'll be a better servant than me. But you're the king's fool now."

"Huh?" Abraham said. He took his eyes off the man for an instant.

The man walloped him upside the head with the rock.

By the time Abraham shook off the blow, the man was dashing away as quickly as his chubby legs would carry him toward the dying portal. He jumped through the ring of light just as it closed. The tunnel went black.

Abraham blinked his eyes. "What just happened?"

As he started to stand, the ground quaked, and debris rained down about him. The tunnel started to collapse.

CHAPTER 10

With hunks of dirt dropping down on his head, he yelled, "No! This isn't happening. No!" But it wasn't his voice that was speaking. It was the voice of the warrior who'd forced the sword upon him. With the weapon in hand and ground shaking beneath his feet, he started to run. On his way out of the tunnel, he snatched up his son's backpack and ran as if his feet were on fire. The tremendous sound of earth collapsing on itself followed after him. He dashed out of the tunnel into the shrubbery of the woodland. A blast of smoke and debris caught up with him, covering him in smoke and black soot.

Abraham coughed and stumbled around until he was free of the dusty smoke. Looking back at the tunnel entrance, he clutched his head and said, "No, no, no."

He sat in the daylight, staring at the collapsed cave. Huge hunks of rock had come down. He wandered back inside the entrance. Seeing only darkness, he came back out. He brushed the debris out of his hair, wondering what had just happened. *This doesn't make any sense.*

Abraham sat on the damp ground, staring at the cave listlessly for what could have been hours, trying to make sense of what had happened. His stomach's chronic gurgling finally came to a stop. He heard a horse nickering and followed the sound. Before long, he came upon the black horse the warrior had been riding. He'd never ridden a horse before but had been to races and knew this stallion was one of the big ones. It stood in a clearing, head down, chewing on the tall grasses.

Coughing a few more times, he said to the horse, "If this is a dream, then I want you to be a unicorn."

The horse's ears flapped.

Rubbing the back of his neck, he said, "Great."

He looked about. His surroundings weren't any different from the Appalachian Mountains he was used to driving through. The trees were tall and green. Pines, maples, birches, and oaks grew in any direction he looked. The odd thing was that it was daytime, not night, as it had been when he entered the tunnel.

He pinched a big hunk of skin on his forearm. "Ow!"

The effort didn't wake him.

"I suppose I'm going to have to ride this nightmare out." He rubbed his face. His thick brown beard had been replaced with one that was neatly trimmed. The hair on his arms was black. The muscles in his forearms twitched noticeably when he moved his fingers. Without being able to see himself, he surmised he was in the body of the man who had accosted him. A strange transformation had taken place. He looked at his hands. They weren't the same fleshy spades he had been born with, but big strong hands with hard calluses on his palms. "I guess it could have been worse. I could have been turned into that witch." He shivered and grimaced. "And my belly's no longer rumbling like an angry river." He made a slow pass through the clearing. "So where in the world am I?"

He took the horse by the reins. "I don't know how this is going to work out, but let's start moving."

He headed down the slope and walked aimlessly for miles. Riders on horseback crashed through the trees and into the clearing. It was a hard-eyed bunch of men and women, much like the warrior he'd crossed in the tunnel. Wary-eyed men and women brandished swords and spears. They all cast dangerous looks right at him as the group encircled Abraham.

He said, "I want to wake up now."

CHAPTER 11

Abraham didn't wake up where he hoped. Instead, he remained fully alert in his new surroundings. He could feel the heat of the sun, the breeze blowing through the branches, and the sweat running down his face. He scanned the company of coarse faces trapping him. A husky warrior spat brown juice on the ground. His head was bald, but his beard was full. He wiped his sleeve across his mouth.

The brooding men wore worn black tunics over shirts of chain mail. Two women were there, appearing just as rugged in their garb. They all looked Abraham up and down with their heavy eyes. That's when he realized that he was half naked, though he didn't feel as though he had anything to be ashamed about. He held his sword in a defensive manner. Making a slow turn, he eyed the rest of the group. Each of them seemed sullen eyed or carried a deadpan stare.

One woman spoke to him in foreign words. Her chestnut-brown hair was pulled back in twin ponytails. She had charm in a tomboyish sort of way. Her leather tunic was worn. She didn't carry a big sword, but a bandolier of knives crossed over one side of her chest. A sword belt carrying daggers rested on her curvy hips.

"What?" Abraham said.

The woman looked at the faces of the others in the company. A couple of men shrugged. The other warriors started looking concerned. The husky bald man in the saddle and carrying a spear started to speak. He was huge and heavy shouldered. He spoke to the woman. He pointed in the direction of the tunnel from where Abraham had come.

She nodded at the big warrior, and he, along with two others, rode for the tunnel and vanished out of sight. Then she dismounted. With her hands on the pommels of the daggers dressing her hips, she approached Abraham.

He stuck his sword out. She froze in place. With wary eyes, she lifted her hands up to shoulder height. Judging by the looks of the group he couldn't tell if they were some sort of fallen knights or misbegotten brigands he'd seen in fantasy movies.

Not knowing what else to say, he said what someone would typically say: "Who are you? What do you want?"

The half-decent-looking rogue warrior of a woman spoke at length. Years back, he'd had a friend that helped out with the baseball team. The man, Dougy, was deaf and always read lips. For some reason, Abraham picked up on it. He tilted his head and studied the woman's thin lips. Once she stopped, he shrugged.

He tapped himself on the chest and said, "Abraham. Abraham."

The rugged company exchanged concerned glances. Their hands and fingers toyed with their weapons.

He was making them nervous, but as far as he could tell, they knew him. He stuck his sword tip into the ground. "Abraham. Abraham Jenkins."

"Who is Abraham Jenkins?" the woman who had been speaking asked, clear as a bell.

Abraham gaped. He didn't think she was speaking in English, but he did think that it was a language that he could understand. The wheels in his new mind started to turn. A vague familiarity came over him. "Say that again?"

She looked at him and said slowly, "Who is Abraham Jenkins, Captain?"

"Captain?" He laughed. "You think I'm your captain? That's funny." He looked around. "So if I'm the Captain, then who are you? My first mate?"

The woman's eyes narrowed. Her slender hands deftly fell back to the weapons on her hips. "Sticks," she said.

A funny feeling came over him as the name did seem to ring a bell. He wondered whether she was an imaginary version of Mandi or someone else. In case he was the company's captain, in this imaginary world, he decided to play along. He rubbed the side of his head. Blood was caked on it where the strange man in the tunnel had clocked him upside the head with a rock. "The witch woman clubbed me."

"The witch woman?" Sticks said. "You mean the fright we are chasing down? She got to you, didn't she? Iris, get down here and check the Captain out." She scanned his body. "What happened to your belt and armor? Is the fright dead, or did she slip your fingers, Captain?"

"She's dead. Or it's dead, rather." He couldn't get the terrifying image of the fiendish-eyed witchy woman out of his head.

Looking at his blood-crusted sword, she asked, "Did you chop her head off with Black Bane?"

"Oh, the sword, eh? No, well, yes," he said, recalling the event in the tunnel. "I shot her then stabbed her." He looked at the sword and twisted it left to right. "With Black Bane."

The husky woman, Iris, ambled over in well-worn forest-green robes. Her auburn hair was tied up in a bun on her head. Unlike the others, she didn't carry armor or weapons but walked with a canelike cudgel. She had a leather satchel hanging on her shoulder. "Can I check that blow to your head, Captain? We want to make sure the hag didn't leave any lingering trouble."

"Sure," Abraham said in a language that he'd only moments ago somehow mastered. His memory was still in a fog.

Iris ran her soft, pudgy fingers over his face. She smelled like wildflowers, and cheap wine was on her breath. She moved all around him, brushing her curvy body against his. Her fingers probed the hard muscles of his body. She got in front of him and rose on tiptoe. She peeled his eyes open with her fingers and looked deep into them. "The Captain is fine. I think he might need some salve for his noggin for the swelling, but I can apply it back at camp. The bump on his head must have rattled his gray matter. It will come back with some rest."

"Thanks, Iris," Sticks said.

"Always an honor to care for the Captain."

Abraham wanted to ask, "Captain who?" but decided going along with it would be best. After all, he might not have more of a name than that. Whatever imaginary world he'd fallen into, maybe that was just who he was. *The Captain. Might as well stick with it. Perhaps I'll dream myself up a better name later. Though I wish I'd wake up first.*

The three warriors returned. The big bald rider had the breastplate armor, crossbow, and sword belt over his lap. Frowning, he looked down at Sticks.

"The Captain is coming around, Horace," she said.

"Aye." He dropped the gear down on the ground. "The cave collapsed in the middle, but the fright is dead." He frowned. "I thought you wanted her alive."

"Er... Why would I—" Abraham cut himself off, realizing the story clearly had more to it. "It didn't work out that way."

Horace grunted. "Are we returning to camp, Captain?"

Abraham felt all eyes on him. He was clearly in charge. All he could think to say was, "Aye."

CHAPTER 12

After a couple embarrassing attempts to get into his horse's saddle, Abraham finally got on top. He'd never ridden a horse before but told himself that since it wasn't real, he should just imagine he'd been doing it all his life. In moments, he had control of the black beauty and rode with ease in the saddle. Playing the role of the Captain while at the same time not having any idea where he was going, he ordered Horace to lead them back to camp. He rode back beside Sticks, stating that he still was under the weather. In truth, he felt better than he'd felt in years.

The horse ride was long. The dreary party traversed the forest without any incident. Two hours into the journey, his backside started to burn, but his new body was made for it. Instead, he took advantage of soaking up his new surroundings. His heart pounded in his ears. His mind raced to find a shred of reality he could relate to. The grim forest fed his despair. His face brushed against the branches of the pines.

No dream can be this real.

Abraham's mind backtracked through all the events that had happened over the last several hours. He was in his truck, feeling sick. Storms filled the skies. His head hurt as he drove into the tunnel. He saw a bright flash of light. That was when everything changed.

He ran through every possible scenario he could think of to explain the madness he was in. Perhaps the light was another vehicle that had hit him head-on. He recalled the floodlight in the Big Walker Tunnel, which the army had used. Maybe he'd had an aneurysm. Possibly, he'd had an allergic reaction to the food he was served at Woody's Grill and passed out from it.

For all I know, I probably crash-landed the beer truck in a creek bed and have been left for dead.

The longer the journey went on, the more real it became, beginning the moment a white mosquito the size of a slice of bread landed on his face.

He smashed it with his hand and wiped it on his legs. "Yecht."

The other odd thing was his backpack. He figured it would be a conversation piece, but no one had said a word to him about it. They didn't even look at it. One thing was for sure—he wasn't about to part with it. He was Abraham Jenkins, and it was keeping him attached to his world and not the fantasy one he'd somehow landed in.

Finally, at dusk, the company made it to a clearing down by a wide creek. At least a score of men wearing brick-red tunics were milling about the camp. Small pup tents were set up, a campfire burned, and meat cooked on a spit. Men carried sticks and chopped wood and branches. Others fished in the waters. They moved with a military purpose but, for the most part, were very haggard looking.

"Who are they?" he absentmindedly asked Sticks.

"What do you mean? The Red Tunics are our retainers. You handpicked them all, the same as us. Perhaps you need more time with Iris tonight."

He looked back at Iris, who rode in the middle of the ranks. The husky woman had a welcoming look in her eye. She lifted her eyebrows at him.

"Uh, I think I'll be fine after some rest."

"I was only jesting, Captain," Sticks said. "I hope you are feeling better tomorrow. You'll need your wits about you for the return journey."

Without having any idea where he was, he fought down the urge to ask, "What journey?" or "Journey where?" even though not doing so was killing him.

The company dismounted, and the Red Tunics took the horses away. As they did so, Abraham caught a glimpse of a group of two frights staring right at him.

"Holy sheetrock!" he said. "What are they doing here?"

Sticks looked at him as though he'd gone crazy. "They are our prisoners. We caught two but lost the other three, yours included. We are taking them back to the king to be executed. That's why we are here. To take these infidels to Kingsland and make an example of their troubles."

Eyeing the frights, Abraham arched a brow. The witches' hands and feet were bound with irons. That didn't stop them from hissing at him.

"How far is Kingsland?"

Sticks grabbed him by the elbow and pulled him away from the Henchmen working nearby giving him strange looks. She found seclusion near the creek, more than an earshot from all the others. "Captain, respectfully, please be mindful of what you are saying and who you say it in front of." She crouched back and winced slightly as though he was going to strike her. "You are not yourself. On a journey like this, they can't witness any weakness."

"Just refresh my memory. How long is this journey back to Kingsland?"

"Roughly a thousand miles."

He spoke so loudly the entire camp could hear. "On horseback?"

CHAPTER 13

One tent in the Henchmen encampment was bigger than the others. It wasn't huge by any means but was the size of a family camping tent, more or less, big enough for about four to six people. It was made of heavy tan canvas with a flap for a door. Inside were fox-fur blankets stretched over cots. A woven carpet covered most of the floor, giving it a cozy homelike effect. A small table had a top made of wooden slats. Oil lanterns sat on each corner of the table. Some other supplies and dried food were neatly stacked in the corners.

Abraham sat on the wooden folding chair with his elbows on the table. It seemed odd to him that the chair was collapsible, given his medieval-seeming situation. But he noticed the entire chair was intricately crafted with wooden parts, without metal pins or screws. He yawned. All that had happened in the past several hours had finally caught up with him. The rush was over.

Once I sleep, I'd better wake back up in my reality.

Sticks entered the room, still wearing her armor and weapons. Even though she was much smaller than Abraham, the bandolier of knives made her look as formidable as any man. The expressionless woman eased deeper inside with feline grace, sat down on one of the cots, undid her ponytails, and began stripping her gear off.

They hadn't spoken since Abraham's outburst over the length of the journey. Sticks managed to respectfully guide him into the tent, and he'd been waiting for her inside ever since. Now, he watched her with a drying throat.

The more Sticks took off, the more woman she became. She tugged her boots off and removed her bandolier and dagger belt. Gracefully, she wiggled out of her leather tunic and slid off her buckskin trousers. She was stripped down to a close-fitting white cotton jerkin that revealed she had a lot more to offer than her armor was hiding.

Abraham swallowed. Sticks's bare arms were taut with muscle. Her body was like a well-honed dancer's. Her dark eyes locked on his. She walked over to him and ran her gentle fingers through his hair. He looked up with his face at her chest level, and his blood churned through his body.

"We need to get you settled, Captain," she said.

"I, uh, what do you mean?"

She hauled him up to his feet, turned to grab the fox and mink blankets, and tossed them onto the ground. With ginger fingers, the inviting chestnut-haired woman started undressing him.

He stepped back.

She grabbed him by the waist of his pants and reeled him in. Sticks was all woman, a woman who wouldn't be denied. Thoughts about his wife, Jenny, and visions of Mandi raced through his mind. Absentmindedly, he shook his head.

Okay, Abraham, this has to be a dream. You know every time a dream starts like this, you wake up. So what the heck? Go with it. It's not real anyway.

Abraham grabbed her by the shoulders, pulled her up into his arms, and kissed her. Sticks didn't engage at first, but as their bodies came together, their lips caught fire. Moments later, they were on the ground, unleashed in the throes of passion, which went on deeper into the night.

Abraham was awoken by the sound of a wild rooster crowing. He rubbed his eyes and sat up on his elbows. Darkness surrounded him, so dark he could barely make out his surroundings. As his eyes focused, he began recollecting the intimate details of his dream. He rubbed his head. *I've never dreamed anything so vivid before.* He was ashamed to think it, but he thought it anyway: *That was awesome. Now that I'm awake, let's figure out where in the heck I am.*

A warm figure stirred beside him. A hand grazed his chest, and he felt a scar over the heart.

He jumped up with a shout. Backing up, he bumped into a cot and fell over. His eyes finally adjusted to the darkness, and he quickly realized he was in the same tent where he'd been. Sticks scurried to one of the corners. An oil lantern's flame created a soft glow inside the tent.

She peered at Abraham and said, "Settle yourself. You are among friends."

Pulling on his trousers, he said, "You're a friend, all right. Oh my, what have I done? What is going on?"

Wearing only her open-necked cotton shirt, she approached him. "Keep your voice down. The Henchmen don't want to hear weakness."

He tipped up the cot and sat down. Nodding his head vigorously, he said, "Oh, I'm sure they heard plenty of things last night. This is embarrassing."

"You are the Captain. Nothing embarrasses you." She kneeled before him and put a hand on his thigh. "You are the leader of the King's Henchmen, the boldest one of all."

He looked down her shirt. A king's crown was branded over her heart. He noticed it last night. He rubbed his fingers on his mark. *Why do we both have one of these?* He looked her dead in the eye and said, "Lady, I am not the Captain, I am Abraham Jenkins."

Sticks looked deep into his eyes. "I know that you are different, Captain. A woman knows these things. I… believe you."

Taken aback, he said, "How come?"

"Because… you've never kissed me before. Normally, you treat me like a tavern whore, but last night was… very different." She gripped his hand in hers. "You were… gentle, at times. Inexperienced at others."

"Inexperienced?" *Well, a long time has passed since I've been with anybody.* "Listen to me, Sticks. I am not from this world. The man, the Captain… Well, I took over his body."

She slapped her hand over his mouth. "Shush, you cannot say such things!" she said in a whisper. "You can be killed for it. If you want to live, you must be the Captain."

CHAPTER 14

THE COMPANY BROKE CAMP WITHOUT Abraham lifting a finger. The Red Tunics continued to move about their business in a very military fashion. None of the other Henchmen lifted a finger. Abraham, with Sticks's help, got all his gear on, including a new pair of trousers and a shirt under his breastplate armor. He looked like a warrior and felt like one too. Subtly following Sticks's lead, he got on his horse and followed after Horace, who led the company into the woodland.

Oddly enough, the terrain seemed familiar to him, as though he'd been there before. The woodland was much the same as it was surrounding his small farm tucked away in the West Virginia hills. He'd used it as a hideaway after the accident with his family. They'd died in a place like this. He started to wonder if he'd died again and didn't know it yet.

In the meantime, he tried to get familiar with what was going on. Sticks had really freaked out when he mentioned he was someone other than the Captain. Her eyes grew to the size of plates, making him think of the Salem witch hunts, where women were burned at the stake because of their abnormal behavior. He read similar stories in medieval history books when he was in high school. The priests and royalty of those days didn't tolerate the occult. He had a feeling he was in a place very much like that. The last thing he wanted was to wind up with his neck in a noose or exposed beneath a guillotine.

Just play along. It has to end sometime. I can't sleep forever.

He started sorting through what had been revealed to him. According to Sticks, he was the leader of the King's Henchmen. Very clearly, they served the king. In what capacity, he wasn't certain. The group was anything but a bunch of knights in shining armor. They were more or less a group of durable adventurers or a host of brigands if one judged by first appearances. But it was a large group, like a caravan, with the Red Tunics serving the others, making for a basic pecking order. Horace led the way on horseback, but two other Henchmen rode out ahead, scouting. All of them were well equipped.

Abraham peered about. *Let me see, I think I have this figured out. I have the Red Tunics, who don't have horses but drive the wagons. And the Henchmen all ride on horseback. I'm the Captain. The Red Tunics guard the frights. The Henchmen guard the group.* To him, they seemed like knights and squires but without all the cumbersome and gaudy armor. The arrangement seemed strange for "henchmen," which he normally would have considered to be a bunch of labor for hire. This group, however, was different. They were stalwart and stern looking, veteran soldiers who had seen a thing or two.

Shifting in his saddle, Abraham glanced backward at a pair of Henchmen riding behind himself and Sticks. One had jet-black tangled hair with coarse hairs on his forearms. He was broad faced and tan and had a dark scowl on his face. He carried a double-bladed battle-axe, fashioned in a Viking style with smaller axe heads, unlike the big, broad blades on his beer truck. "Bearclaw," he muttered.

Sticks leaned toward him and said, "What, Captain?"

"That's Bearclaw," he said.

"Yes," she said quietly.

Abraham didn't have any idea how he knew that, unless he'd picked up someone else saying it, but somehow he knew. He seemed to have gained not only a new body but also some of the knowledge that came with it. The other rider behind him was another man, thirtyish, tawny headed, with an aloofness about him.

"And that's Vern?"

"Yes."

An unsettling feeling turned his stomach. The last thing he wanted was to lose his own identity. *I am Abraham Jenkins.* He reached down and touched Jake's backpack, hanging from the saddle. *Don't forget it.*

As far as he could tell, the Henchmen were a mature bunch, war-torn and gritty. The Red Tunics were younger, hardworking, but not a smile among them. That was the group he was riding with now. They were soldiers, a team, on a mission for the king. The question was: who was the king? He didn't even know that man's name or his own, for that matter. *What the heck is my name? It can't be the Captain.* His back straightened.

Slade Ruger! That's my name. No, Captain Ruger Slade. At least I think it is.

Abraham didn't pick up any more bits and pieces that day. Instead, he rode, and the best he could tell, they were moving southwest. At least, based on the sun's position, that was the case. But he had no idea how that would actually work in another world. The times and the distances would change. Finally, the group broke out of the woodland into flatter prairies. Seagull-like birds were flying in the sky. A stiff, salty breeze rustled Abraham's hair. They rode on, over the rolling plains. A few hours later, they crested a hilltop. Abraham pulled his horse to a stop. Miles of shoreline stretched out along a seashore as far as the eye could see. The ocean, green and turbulent, crashed into rocky ledges. It wasn't possible for him to be in such a place so far from what he knew. It didn't make sense.

A flock of birds in a *V* pattern flew toward them. They were tiny at first but getting bigger. Every man in the group drew some sort of weapon. Even Sticks pulled her daggers. The closer the birds came, the bigger they grew. They weren't birds. Birds had beaks and feathers. These things had scales like lizards and were bigger than horses. They were dragons.

Abraham swallowed. His hand fell to his sword, and he said, "I'm not in Kansas anymore."

CHAPTER 15

ONE HUNDRED FEET ABOVE, THE dragons passed over the campaign without even giving the company a glance. The dragons had dark natural-colored scales and hard ridges on their bodies like desert lizards. They were ugly. Saliva dripped from slavering jaws in globs of rain that sizzled on the grasses. In seconds, the tight formation was gone out of sight.

The tension in the group deflated as they secured their weapons back inside their sheaths. Horace hefted his spear and said, "The dragons fear us. Ha ha!"

The Henchmen let out a cheer of relief.

"Either that, or fortune favors the foolish," Abraham said.

Sticks jammed her daggers into the sheaths on her hips. "It's about time we had some good fortune. We've lost enough men already."

"We have?" Abraham asked.

Taking a quick look about, she got close to him and said, "We've lost over a dozen men since we left the House of Steel. Fine men and women among them. I consider us lucky that we have this many left."

"It seems like a large group for such an adventure," he said.

"It was your decision."

Abraham didn't have any idea what she was talking about. And it seemed silly to send so many after the frights. The ugly crones were bound up and sitting in one of the wagons. They never said a word. He got the chills just looking at them. Goose bumps rose on his arms when—as one—their fiendish stares landed on him. He looked away.

He kicked his horse, and it lurched forward. They were heading downward toward the beach. "It just seems like a lot of trouble to round up a bunch of witches. If you don't mind, Sticks, would you fill me in?"

"Later, Captain. Everyone's ears are too big. We'll do it in privacy."

"If you say so."

"No, it's if you say so. I'll do it. You're the Captain." She rode farther away.

Abraham got the feeling she didn't want him to say too much. He needed to keep his mouth shut and start thinking. He'd just seen dragons. That wasn't a concept he was unfamiliar with. Plenty of dragons were in fantasy works he'd watched and read, but those he'd just seen were plain ugly. When he was younger, in middle school, before he blossomed, he played Dungeons & Dragons with his friends on the Air Force base. His dad used to tease him by saying he flew a real dragon, back in his days. Now, those imaginary fantasies had somehow become real.

I must have hit my head and engaged an overactive imagination. This isn't real. And I didn't have this big of an imagination to begin with!

The company hit the beach about two hours later. Of course, Abraham could only guess at the time, based on how quickly they moved. For all he knew, it could have been ten hours. But, to his relief, the sun was about to set in the west. It did appear bigger than what he was used to seeing. He couldn't glance at it long, but it had a purple glare around it. As they moved down the white sands of the beach, he couldn't help but think that would be a great spot to vacation. A big part of him wanted to jump in the foamy salt water. Instead, he drifted toward the back of the company.

No one said a word to him. They kept their eyes averted even when he looked right at them. The Red Tunics distanced themselves. One of them, carrying a pack as big as himself, waddled away in the other direction. That was when he decided to test the waters and ride up alongside Horace.

"Captain," Horace said with a stiff nod. The beefy man clawed at his beard.

"Are you sure you know where you're going?"

Horace's mouth clamped open and shut like a fish. "Er... Captain, the beach is the safest route until we get to the West Arm of Titanuus. From there, we'll take the land and navigate the mountain passes. There's no other way I know of, but if you have new orders, I'll follow them to the letter."

"No, Horace, that will do."

"Aye, Captain. Any other concerns?"

"It's a long way. At this rate, how long do you think it will take?"

"If we don't stop, twenty days, but I can only suspect as much trouble coming up as going down. With fortune on the king's side, I'd say thirty days but hope to make it in twenty-five."

"I see. Carry on, then."

He kept riding beside Horace. The man cast a nervous look at him from time to time. Behind him, Bearclaw and Vern were leaning forward in their saddles. Farther back, Iris eyeballed his back and looked away when he turned.

The company rode along the coastal waters until the sun dropped from the sky and the stars and moon hovered in the night. Standing far away from the others, Abraham studied the sky. The face of the moon was different. The constellations he knew were gone too.

This can't be possible. Tell me… please tell me I didn't drive through a portal to another universe. I might have wanted to leave home, but I didn't want to go this far.

CHAPTER 16

Abraham sat facing the ocean. Sticks joined him, her hair down. She carried a blanket.

"Your tent is ready," she said, "but it is probably safe for us to talk here. The breath from the Sea of Troubles will drown our conversation. Captain, speak freely now. My ears are yours."

Abraham had a thousand questions. Not sure where to start, he bluntly asked, "If I'm Ruger Slade, then why is it such a secret?"

Sticks spread out the blanket and sat down. He joined her. Together, they both stared out at the turbulent sea waters crashing in the distance.

Without looking at him, she said, "It's your order. Everyone calls you the Captain to keep your identity secret. That's what you say. Your name is renowned in Kingsland." She twisted her head left and right. "You are Ruger Slade, considered to be the greatest sword master in all of Titanuus. Now, you are secretly the sworn sword of the king."

"I have a sword, but I didn't think there was anything extraordinary about it." He rubbed his neck. "I mean, it's a nice sword, but I don't feel like a master of it."

He removed the sword from the sheath and thumbed the razor-sharp edge. The blade was a hard, dark steel with a dull shine in the metal. The broken runes carved above the cross guard were intricate.

He flipped it over with a twist of his wrist. "Have I killed many with my blade?"

She gave him a bewildered look. "You've killed every man or beast you've ever fought. Your skill is extraordinary. That's why you lead this group. They wouldn't follow just anyone. Well"—she shrugged her shoulders—"aside from the king that they've sworn their lives to. But leading this group… no easy task unless they respect or fear you. But many have been with you a long time. Don't you remember that?"

Abraham shrugged. He rubbed the hard calluses on his right hand with his left thumb. They were as thick as a bricklayer's. He had an uncle who did masonry work, Uncle Robert. He had big strong hands that were heavy and thick. A slap on your back from Uncle Robert's hands would knock the wind out of you. Abraham switched and started rubbing his left hand. The calluses were the same.

"I can use either hand, can't I?"

"You have no weakness. One is as good as the other."

He closed his eyes and tried to envision himself fighting with a sword. Bits and pieces of Ruger Slade's memories had come to him, but they were vague. At the same time, he couldn't imagine himself killing anything. He wasn't scared of doing so, but he'd never really hurt anyone with anything other than a fastball pitch. He knocked a baseball player out cold once. Now, to believe he was an incredible fencer seemed a stretch. No way could he be a master of something he'd never done before.

Well, at least I have a badass name. Maybe that will win some fights before a sword is even drawn.

He pulled his knees up to his chest and said, "You said we lost a lot of men coming up? North? How so? And give me the Cliff Notes version. Maybe it will jar my memory."

"What are Cliff Notes?"

"Never mind the Cliffs—just the short version," he said.

"There are the elements. Skirmishes with brigands and raiders. The battle with the hill folk in Bog was the worst. I think that is why Horace is wanting us to hug the coastline." The brisk sea winds stirred her ponytail from one shoulder to the other. "You bring plenty of Henchmen on every journey, but most of them don't make it back. The king's missions are dangerous, to say the least."

Abraham wished he knew the king's name, but he didn't want to ask her. For some reason, that seemed embarrassing, so he put his inquiry another way. "So we don't mention the king's name either, I take it?"

"No. We keep our mission very discreet. Only the ranking members of the Henchmen know what is going on. The Red Tunics don't. We pose as traders and well-armed merchants. If the others knew that we served"—she lowered her voice—"King Hector, the king's enemies would be upon us. We'll die before we reveal the purpose of our mission."

"But taking the frights to the, er..." he gave her a questioning look, "the House of Steel... Won't that expose us?"

"They are criminals, mostly. If anyone asks, we are swords for hire or slavers. Our business can easily be explained that we are dealing with someone else other than the king. In Kingsland, there are plenty that don't care for the king. And we, well, we aren't the type of group that fits in with the king's lofty standards."

"You make it sound like the king is not someone that you like. So why do you serve him?"

"No, we revere the king. It's an honor for miscreants to serve the crown. Whether for good or for bad, the king gave us purpose."

"Are there other kings or kingdoms?"

"Many. And they all want King Hector's head on a platter. That's where we come in."

CHAPTER 17

THE KING'S HENCHMEN RODE ALONG the shoreline the following day. Abraham stayed close to Sticks and Horace. The husky warrior said little but commented from time to time about the weather and expressed his concerns about the route they traveled. The man was clearly looking for approval. Abraham told him to stay the course. Sticks kept quiet and more or less shadowed him, riding at the back of his horse's right flank.

Abraham didn't want to say much either. He wasn't sure how Ruger Slade would have spoken. Who was the man at the tunnel, Eugene Drisk, who moved out of Ruger Slade's body? How did he act? Were they the same person, or were they two different personalities? He wanted to play the part. The last thing he needed was for someone to think he was possessed, like Sticks had warned him about, and to end up dead.

The two frights let out a unified bone-chilling shriek.

Many of the horses whinnied. Others stomped their hooves hard into the sand. Bearclaw turned his horse and led it toward the back, where the witches rode in the wagon. He untied a lash from his saddle and turned it loose on the wicked frights. With the sharp crack of leather on skin he beat the tar out of them. They grimaced and winced, but their leathery lips stayed clamped shut as they huddled over. Bearclaw handed the lash to one of the Red Tunics.

"Whip the wicked worse than I did if they do that again," the bearish warrior said. He shoved one of the frights in the back, knocking her to the floor. "Save your screaming for when you burn at the stake."

Abraham wasn't certain what to make of that. One thing was certain, though: the Henchmen were all business. But even after Bearclaw's theatrics, the frights kept their leathery scowls fixed on him. They flicked their tongues like a venomous snake. Their slitted pink-red eyes were narrowed as if they were creatures ready to strike at any moment.

"They were a lot of trouble to catch, weren't they?" he quietly asked Sticks.

"Tougher than a den of eight-legged wolverines," she replied.

He nodded. An eight-legged wolverine was something he could picture. In an odd way, that gave him some comfort.

Hours later, Horace slowed his horse until Abraham came along his side. "Captain, we are approaching Hamm's Inlet. It won't be so easy to slip along the coast without being noticed. The sea folk and pirates are territorial folk. They'll pry like a miner picking for gold."

Abraham narrowed his eyes at Horace. He slid his hand down onto the pommel of his blade. It was mostly an act, but something about it felt natural. "Don't you think I know that?"

Horace's eyebrows rose. "Aye, Captain. I'm just talking. No disrespect intentioned."

"Then don't state the obvious unless I ask for it."

New sweat trickled down Horace's bald head and ran past his ears. "Aye, sir, aye."

An emboldened part of Abraham wanted to laugh. In the real world, he'd never cross a man like Horace. The balding and bearded warrior was built like a defensive tackle or one of the massive overweight pro wrestlers who would squash men on the mat. Abraham wasn't any slouch for a pitcher, but he didn't have the look of a natural-born brawler either. Horace did. He looked like that kind of man who would run over kittens with a motorbike, and he'd just backed the man down.

"We should get some supplies in Hamm's Inlet," he said to Horace. "Some fresh food and drink is in order, too."

"Aye, Captain. Hamm's Inlet it is." Horace turned his back and trotted ahead.

Abraham straightened up in the saddle. He felt a degree of confidence that he knew what he was doing. He gave Sticks a sideways glance. She wasn't looking his way. He did have her to thank for much of his decision, though. In his tent the previous night, they'd looked at a map of Titanuus. She showed him the course they were taking and explained what lay ahead, like Hamm's Inlet, for instance. The coastline territory located above the West Arm of Titanuus was more or less hamlets and large villages filled with seafaring people. He didn't connect with the map at first, but the more he rode, the more familiar his surroundings became. At least he had some idea of where he was. He was in a world made just like other continents he'd seen.

He pulled his horse toward Sticks. "Why don't you make the rounds? Figure out what supplies we need. We'll take a small group into Hamm's Inlet, get what we need, and go. The rest can camp and keep moving. We'll catch up with them."

She nodded. "Aye, Captain. Is there anyone in particular you want to take?"

"You, Horace, Bearclaw, Vern, Iris, and two pack bearers. Just do the inventory and let me know if you think we need more."

Sticks's brow rose.

"Is there a problem?" he asked.

"No, Captain, it's a sound decision. I'll take care of it." She led her horse away.

Taking command felt good. He wasn't one hundred percent sure about his decision-making process, but he thought it might have something to do with the body he was in. His mind was still his own, but traces of memories of another consciousness seemed to be guiding him. Either that, or he was just doing what he did as a kid when they played Dungeons & Dragons. He just went where the adventure was. Perhaps that was the only way to find answers. If he was trapped in an imaginary world, he'd just have to play it out until it ended.

Horace led the small group of Henchmen, following the coastline to the top of Hamm's Inlet. They rode several miles before encountering the first city—out of dozens that ran along Hamm's Inlet—called Seaport. Wooden and stone buildings were built along the seashore, which ran from the water's edge into the gentle hills. Long docks stretched out to the sea, accompanied by fishermen's wharfs. The ships ranged from small skiffs and fishing rigs to mighty brigantines and galleons, without the portals for cannons.

They reminded Abraham of movies he'd seen about sailors or pirates from an early colonial period, or perhaps the Dark Ages. He didn't know which, but he did have some understanding of it. With the salty wind in his face, his thirst grew, and his stomach rumbled. He hadn't eaten much of anything recently, aside from dried strips of beef and some sort of hard fruit that tasted like chewy bark.

"Iris," he said to the husky woman, who had her hair in a bun and wore loose-fitting robes. "Take the reds and get our supplies. I think we'll eat. I'm starving. Once you've finished, join us." He sniffed in the smell of baking fish.

Iris gave him a pleasant smile and said, "As you wish, Captain." In a rugged voice, she said to the pair of Red Tunics, "Come on, boys, we have some dealing to do."

"Horace, find us a quiet spot to eat."

They stabled the horses in some barns just inside the edge of the fishing town. From the barns they followed stone walkways that led into the town. Many people were out along the dock, men wearing long-sleeved cotton shirts and the women just the same, but with skirts. Sailors were there too, walking arm in arm, with squarish caps on their heads and tassels on top. They swayed as they walked and sang while drinking from jugs of wine or rum hooked in their fingers.

Horace pushed his way through the double door of a whitewashed stone building with red clay tile roofing. The tavern was poorly lit by candlelight and small windows on the front of the building. The smell of fish and smoke was like a slap in the face. Not many people were inside, but the ones who were there shrank behind their tables with wary eyes. Horace found a table big enough to seat them all. He pulled out a chair at the head of the table.

Abraham took his seat at the head of the table. Sticks sat to his left and Horace to his right. Bearclaw and Vern followed suit. They sat like statues with tight expressions on their faces.

Abraham didn't care. He was starving. "Sit. Let's eat. Let's drink."

One of the other patrons with shifty eyes scurried through the tavern and out through the front door.

CHAPTER 18

The Henchmen quietly dug their spoons into the bowls of fish stew they'd been served. All of them huddled over their bowls like children who were being punished. Abraham wasn't certain what to make of it, but he was famished and ate. The fish stew, a gumbo-like mix, was loaded with savory hunks of seafood. He tasted lobster, crab, and scallops, along with some strong spices mixed in with broth and rice. It was good, far better than what he'd expected in a crappy run-down tavern where the floor creaked with every step. A spicy hunk of fish meat caught in his throat. He coughed and tapped his chest.

"Are you all right, Captain?" Sticks asked.

"Sometimes I forget to chew before I swallow." He grabbed a metal goblet. "Just have to wash the bait down." He drank. The strong spiced rum burned all the way down his throat. It did him little good, and he coughed more.

Out of the corner of his eye, the men at the other table gave him a funny look. He lifted his head, and they looked away.

Abraham would have killed for a glass of water. Asking for water instead of rum wasn't the best idea either. That would only make him a bigger fish out of water. So rum it was. He nursed it. The last thing he wanted to do was get drunk or even tipsy. After the accident, he'd used a lot of pills and alcohol to numb his pain, inside and out. He took years to regain control. He didn't want to lose that again, no matter what world he was in. He sipped more rum.

Looking at Vern, he asked, "How's your stew?"

"Er… fine, Captain." The aloof warrior pushed the wavy locks of blond hair out of his eyes. He drank from his goblet and resumed eating.

Those were the first words Abraham had spoken to the man. He wanted to see what sort of reaction he'd get. He hoped to trigger a memory, but the answer garnered him nothing. He sipped more rum. The liquid tasted sweeter after several sips.

Sitting straight up, Sticks said, "Iris should be along soon. If you like, I can check for her."

"I'm sure she'll find us."

Back in the corner opposite their table, two surly men were puffing on pipes. They would look at him and snigger. He could smell the bittersweet aroma of the burning leaves. It made him think of his father, who smoked cigars until the day he died.

"Did anyone bring any tobacco?"

Horace's eyebrows clenched.

"I guess not." He took another drink of rum. He finished his bowl of stew and ordered another one from the serving wench. She was attractive, wearing a loose blouse bound tight around her waist and very revealing. He gave her a big smile when she bent over to serve him a new bowl.

Sticks showed a Mona Lisa frown.

Abraham drank more rum and dug into his stew. Every spoonful tasted better and better. Halfway into the bowl, he stopped eating as every head at his table turned toward the front entrance. Loud and bawdy, a gang of greasy pirates entered the tavern, filling the tables and crowding the bar.

Abraham chuckled.

Pirates. Hah. I used to be a Pirate. No doubt this is a figment of my imagination. And if it's not real, then I might as well get drunk. He swallowed more rum.

Even though Abraham had pledged to himself not to indulge in the rum, its intoxicating effect blinded his reason. He sat in his chair, staring at the pirates. They were all Jack Sparrow types, a variety of shapes and sizes, but without the mascara. He burst out in loud laugher.

That drew the attention of every pirate in the room.

The tavern fell quiet, except for Abraham, who couldn't stop laughing.

Several feet away, sitting at the corner of the bar, a pirate slung a mug at him.

Without even thinking, Abraham plucked the speeding goblet out of the air.

Holy Big Trouble in Little China. *I have lightning-quick reflexes.*

"Did you see that?" he said to the Henchmen. He spun the mug on the tip of his finger. "Did you see that?"

"Aye, that was fast, Captain," Horace said.

A grizzly-sized pirate entered the tavern. The pirate stood tall and broad shouldered. He had a head full of red hair and a beard just the same. His overcoat was as red as blood with tarnished brass buttons running from top to bottom. His sword belt was black leather, and he carried a heavy cutlass on his hips. The pirates, one and all, stood at attention and saluted him.

One of them shouted, "Boyjas! Flamebeard! Boyjas!"

The excited cheers drowned out every sound in the room. Flamebeard lifted an oversized hand, and the pirates quieted. A parrot, which had escaped Abraham's notice, was perched on Flamebeard's shoulder. It let out a loud squawk.

Abraham erupted in uncontrollable laughter, and with his fist, he pounded the table. His wide-eyed Henchmen stiffened.

The pirates snaked out their blades and closed in.

CHAPTER 19

In a gravelly voice that carried through the tavern, Flamebeard looked at Abraham and asked, "Do we amuse you, stranger?"

Abraham took a breath and regained his composure. He studied the pirate, who had a countenance as fierce as any. He was a big man too, bigger than any other in the room. His red beard and hair came together around his face like a lion's mane. Abraham wagged a finger at the parrot, which, upon closer inspection, didn't have the feathers of a bird but leathery skin that resembled feathers. It made for a hideous bird, with solid yellow eyes and a thick black tongue that licked its beak.

Abraham cleared his throat. "Sorry, Flamebeard. But your ridiculous appearance and ghastly bird took me by surprise."

"Is that so?" Flamebeard's bushy eyebrows came together until they kissed. "I don't believe we've had a proper introduction. You are?"

"The Captain," Abraham said.

"That's it. The Captain." Flamebeard showed a sinister smile. "Certainly, you have a fuller name than that?"

"No, that's the name that I go by. I keep it simple for my friends and simpletons like you." Abraham's words flowed out with no thought behind them. To him, everything that was happening reminded him of a really well-done reenactment at a pirate restaurant, as a family might go to when vacationing at the beach. It was all make-believe. "Say, is that beard real, or is it a fake one like the mall Santas wear?"

Flamebeard stroked his bushy facial hair with his sausagelike fingers. "Keep up the insults, and you'll soon be the new anchor of my ship."

The pirates chuckled. One of them said, "Just kill him, Captain. He's earned a quick death."

Tilting onto the back legs of his chair, Abraham said, "I'm getting the feeling that this tavern is not big enough for two Captains. I tell you what. Walk out now, and you and all of your men will live to see another day at sea." He winked at Sticks, whose frozen look didn't change. "Fair enough, Flamebeard?"

"That's enough!" Flamebeard ripped his cutlass out of his belt. "Clear the floor, men. I'm going to teach the land hound a lesson that he'll never forget. On your feet, dust-eating coward. Let's see what you have to say with a belly full of dorcha steel."

The pirates pushed all the tables and chairs out of the way. They formed a ring around their captain, who unbuttoned his long red coat. The lizard-skinned parrot flew up into the rafters and let out a vicious squawk.

Every eye from Abraham's company was fixed on him. He put all four chair legs back on the floor. His chest tightened, and his nostrils flared. Back in his baseball-playing days, he'd talked a lot of smack. He'd let his emotions run high to pump him up for a game. Now, that spark of testosterone was running a new course through him. He couldn't turn it off. Without even thinking, he came out of his chair and crossed to the manmade arena.

The Henchmen rose from their benches and followed him.

Abraham was a well-built, long-armed athlete and one of the biggest men in the room, but the moment he stood across from Flamebeard, the wind went out of his sails.

Flamebeard stood taller and was built like a smokestack. The pirate had stripped down to his waist. He must have been a few inches short of seven feet. He didn't appear to be in the best shape, but plenty of muscle was packed underneath the thick skin of his chest and shoulders. He sliced his cutlass from side to side. The blade was curved, broad with a keen razor edge. He moved it like a part of his own arm.

He spat black juice on the floor. "Are you going to pull that steel or pee your pants, land dweller?"

Peeing his pants was the avenue Abraham was more likely to take. He had no idea what had compelled him to boldly stroll across the room to the center arena with iron in his limbs. He did it, though. That was certain. Something had possessed him. But standing before Flamebeard sobered him. His eyes slid over to his men. Horace, Bearclaw, and Vern stood nearby with their arms crossed over their chests and a wary look in their eyes. Sticks stood against the bar, leaning with one elbow resting on the edge.

Oh Lord, what am I doing? This pirate is going to butcher me.

"Quit stalling. Pull your steel, coward," Flamebeard said.

Abraham's right hand crossed over his body and fastened on the hilt of his long sword, Black Bane. Slowly, he drew the weapon out of the sheath. The blade scraped quietly out of the scabbard.

Its dark gray shone dully in the faint light of the tavern. He took a deep breath, hoping that would fill him with courage. It had no effect.

I'm going to die.

The corner of Flamebeard's mouth turned up in a knowing smile. "It's too late to surrender now." He brought his sword down and lunged with the speed of a fastball.

CHAPTER 20

Abraham swatted Flamebeard's sword thrust aside with a swipe from his own blade. The sharp ring of metal on metal filled his ears.

In a split second, his boots, which might as well have been fastened to the floor, were moving. That wasn't all that moved. The rest of his body did too, particularly his sword arm. It moved with a mind of its own. His sword crashed against the pirate's cutlass. It became a rigid metal snake on the attack.

Flamebeard backed away from the intense strikes. Using the range of his long arms, he slashed hard from side to side. Metal smacked against metal, parry after parry. The sting of the strikes raced from Abraham's hands up and through his shoulders. Somehow, he hung onto a sword that the larger man's blows should have ripped from his fingers. Thrusting and striking, he pushed the pirate back toward the corner.

How am I doing this?

Abraham wasn't trying not to do it, but he knew he wasn't doing it. His sword expertly moved in directions he never could have anticipated. His mind seemed to be trapped in a body not his own.

Flamebeard slid away from the dangerous range of Black Bane. He grabbed a chair by the leg and used it for a shield. Black Bane whittled down the chair stroke by stroke, hacking it into flying pieces. Flamebeard hurled the seat of the chair at Abraham. At the same time, the pirate lunged. "Die, land rat!"

Black Bane sang. *Slice!* Abraham cut Flamebeard's sword hand off at the forearm. Blood spat out of the stump.

Flamebeard let out a howl. "Impossible! No one douses the Flame!" The pirate took a knee and pulled a jewel-encrusted dagger from his belt. "No one!" He stabbed at Abraham.

Black Bane flashed before Flamebeard's eyes, and the pirate dropped the dagger. His head fell from his shoulders and rolled across the floor and into the bar with a *thud.* Flamebeard's big body fell over backward, blood pumping out of his neck.

A dead quiet fell over the raucous gang of pirates as they stared at their fallen leader.

"No one's ever defeated Flamebeard before. No one," one pirate said. He had a red cloth cap tied on his head in skullcap fashion. He wore a sleeveless jerkin and carried a short sword in his hand. "Only witchery could have done this. Flamebeard was the greatest sword of the seas."

Sticks made a callous statement: "You aren't at sea."

Abraham couldn't tear his eyes away from the man gushing blood on the floor. Flamebeard's body spasmed. Some fight was yet in him. Then his body went still. The blood no longer pumped out of his mutilated body. The leak turned into a drip. Abraham doubled over and vomited.

The pirates' hard eyes filled with fire. The one wearing the skullcap said, "There is more of us than them. Pirates don't lose to the land dwellers. Avenge our captain, Flamebeard." He lifted his sword high. "Kill them!"

Two pirates brandishing sabers chased Sticks into the back corner of the room. They were ugly men, built like rugged fishermen and missing many teeth. The one with a hawk nose with a ring pierced in the left nostril licked his lips and said, "Give yourself up, girlie. We'll all have at you one way or another. Make it easy on yourself by making it easy on us."

Sticks snaked two throwing knives out of her bandolier.

"Oh, those are very shiny toothpicks," said the other pirate, with a mane of hair past his ears. He shot her a grin. "Come and pick my teeth with them."

She flicked her pair of daggers upward. They stuck in a beam in the ceiling. The pirates' eyes locked on the knives, and they started laughing. The one with the nose ring dropped his eyes. Sticks jammed the daggers into his chest and the other's.

"You clever witch!" he spat just before he died.

Those pirates were dead, but the melee had begun. The clamor of battle reached a new crescendo inside the tavern. The pirates were hacking away at the rest of the Henchmen, who were brawling side by side for their lives.

Horace rammed his dagger hilt-deep in a pirate's belly.

Bearclaw swung his battle-axe into a man's chest. With a crunch of bone splintering a volcanic eruption of blood spewed from the pirate's busted chest.

Vern fought on his knees, with his long sword striking through pirates' legs and abdomens.

A pirate peeled away from the flock and flanked Horace, who was anchoring the right side of their defensive row. The bulky Horace—his arms locked up with another man's—didn't see the pirate coming. Sticks flicked a throwing knife from her hand. It hit the charging pirate right in the jugular. She searched out her Captain. He'd gotten separated from the group. A sea of men were coming at him from all directions. Fighting them all off would be impossible.

"Horace!" she shouted. "Get to the Captain!"

CHAPTER 21

In one moment, Abraham was puking his guts out, and in the next, he was fighting for his life. He hadn't even processed everything that just happened. As in a dream, he'd slain Flamebeard. He saw it but didn't feel it. It just didn't seem real. Adrenaline kicked in next. Suddenly, he felt everything as if it were his own body. He had the vomit to show for it.

That was when the pirates came. Sweaty, greasy, and angry, the dangerous gang of sailors attacked in a wave of destruction. At that point in time, all of it seemed very real. Abraham's own self-preservation kicked in. The fight became real. Either he died, or they died.

Abraham let out a wild howl. He thrust his sword through a pirate's clavicle. He ripped it out and chopped down another pirate. He spun away from a sword chop that would have split his head. He countered the pirate's swing by cutting his sword through the man's ribs. With the bottom of his boots mopping through the rising blood on the floor, he cut three more men down.

Abraham wasn't the only one swinging victory after victory. Horace, Bearclaw, and Vern, wearing their tunics over chain-mail armor, overmatched the unarmored pirates. The trio burst through the ranks with wroth force, piercing skin and chopping through bone. Over a minute later, the fight was over. Two surviving pirates dashed out the front door.

The blood-spattered Henchmen panted for breath as they looked over their fallen enemies. The dead pirates' wounds were ghastly. Abraham counted fifteen in all. Leaning with his arm braced against a wall, he threw up again.

"How do you fare, Captain?" Sticks asked. Specks of blood covered her face like freckles. Fresh blood stained her dagger-filled hands.

He gasped for breath and said, "There's no explanation for it."

The stench of new death wafted into his crinkling nose. He didn't dare another look at the slain. He'd seen more than he cared to see. It never looked so bad in the movies.

"I need some fresh air," he added.

Horace met Abraham at the doorway and pushed it open. He stepped aside and said, "Good fighting, Captain."

Abraham nodded at the bald warrior, whose beard was caked in blood. Once he got outside, he sucked in a lungful of air. He took several deep breaths and held out a hand. It was as steady as a rock. Inside his mind, he was shaking like a leaf. He couldn't believe his body wasn't trembling.

Iris and the two Red Tunics hustled over to the group. They all carried packs over their shoulders, and their arms were filled with sacks of goods.

Her soft eyes were as big as saucers. "What in the world happened?"

Bearclaw slung the blood from his axe onto the stones on the street. Blood dripped from a gash across his forehead. Another wound bled freely above the knee. "Seaweed-sucking pirates crossed the Captain. That's what happened. They paid for it."

"You need care, Bearclaw," Iris said. She put a handkerchief on his head. "Hold that."

The Red Tunics' packs were full to the brim with supplies, and they carried another between them. Their gaze jumped from bloody man to bloody man. One of them swallowed.

"Do we have everything that we need?" Abraham asked.

Iris nodded.

"Get the horses ready," Abraham said to the pack bearers. "We need to get out of here."

The waitress from the tavern came outside. Blood stained the bottom of her skirt. She was trembling like a leaf. Without looking at Abraham, she said, "Sire, my lord says that you did not pay for your meal. It's fourteen shards of silver. Forgive me for asking."

"Huh… oh." He looked at Sticks. "Pay her twenty."

Sticks's eyes lit up. "What? But their fish stew made you retch."

His eyes narrowed on Sticks. The fire in her eyes cooled. "Aye, sir." Emptying a purse full of small coins into her hand, she counted out twenty silver shards. The coins were the size of nickels and shaped like guitar picks with symbols stamped on them. "Here. Go. Tell your greedy lord that we might come for him next."

The bar maid curtseyed, turned, and vanished back inside the tavern.

"You're going to need to be stitched up, Bearclaw," Iris said to the bearish warrior.

"I'll heal just fine, but you can put those soft hands to work on me if you wish," Bearclaw replied to the pleasantly plump woman.

Iris smiled. "As you wish."

"Captain." Horace nodded down the street. A group of men had gathered several blocks down. They carried lanterns and were gesticulating in their direction. "The death of Flamebeard will travel fast. He has as many friends as he has enemies in the inlet, many of them prominent people."

It became clear that Horace, and most likely the others, had intimate knowledge of Flamebeard that Abraham had yet to recall. He had no doubt that the loud-mouthed pirate left terror in his wake, and Abraham had killed him.

"It was a fair fight," Sticks said. "None should have trouble with us. Flamebeard had it coming. He's a scourge of many."

Scowling, Vern said, "The sea folk won't take the word of strangers over the word of sailors. No doubt, the pirates' lies will catch fire and spread. They'll all come after us by the hundreds. We need to get to the horses and ride, before the *Captain* almost gets us killed again."

"Watch your tongue, Vern," Sticks warned.

"I can speak for myself," Abraham said. He stared Vern down. "Is there a problem?"

Vern shook his head. "No, Captain. I still breathe. It's good."

"Good. Keep it that way."

With the heat of battle still racing through his body, he didn't feel like taking any crap from anybody. He'd just killed half a dozen men or more. At least, he thought he had. One thing was sure—it all felt real. Leading the group, he headed down the road, following the steps that led into the city and back down toward the stables. The Red Tunics were leading the horses out of the stables when they arrived. Everyone mounted, Iris doubled up with Bearclaw. The pack bearers doubled up on her horse with one another.

Torch- and lantern-bearing sea folk had formed a blockade at the stable's exit.

Abraham turned his horse around. The citizens were blocking off the back entrance too. Scores of hard-eyed people were cramming the entrance. The Henchmen weren't going anywhere without another fight.

CHAPTER 22

Abraham stood with his hands on the rail of Flamebeard's galleon with the morning sun in his face. He'd never ridden on a ship that had sails, or on any large ship, for any matter. Now, he was the captain of a pirate ship. As it turned out, the citizens of Seaport were very grateful that Flamebeard had been slaughtered. The pirate and his gang of surly men were a menace. Since Abraham vanquished Flamebeard, he also had rights to his ship and his men. He swore several pirates into his service. The others, loyal to Flamebeard, were imprisoned. Apparently, the Henchmen, accompanied by the sailors, could handle the sailing of the ship.

Flamebeard's galleon was named the *Sea Talon*. It was every bit a pirate ship if there ever was one. Grand in design, the ship had three masts and white sails with flame colors woven into the fabric. The Red Tunics hustled over the decks. They climbed the ratlines and managed the sails. The decks were scrubbed with mops and brushes. Everything was done under the orders of the elder Henchmen.

Back at Seaport, he'd sold the horses and wagons. The Henchmen loaded up the frights and stuck them in the hold. That was Abraham's decision. No one questioned it, but no one gave him a pat on the back either. But in the past day, he'd slain a notorious criminal and a host of men, and now he had a galleon and all its treasures, plus Flamebeard's cutlass, to show for it. His fingers drummed on the railing.

Wait until the king sees this. For some strange reason, he felt good. *Whoever King Hector is.* He still couldn't picture the man's face.

Sticks brushed up against his arm. "Good morning, Captain."

"Good morning. I was beginning to think that all of you were avoiding me."

"Never. We've been busy manning the ship. It's no easy task to undertake, but it's all in good order now."

"I'll say. And we'll make it back to Kingsland much quicker. Tell me: why didn't we take a ship to begin with?"

"The frights didn't run on a ship. They fled on foot."

"Oh, I see. Sorry."

She showed him a puzzled look.

Abraham got the feeling that Ruger Slade wasn't a man who ever apologized for anything. He needed to bear that in mind.

The waters of the Sea of Troubles were choppy. Ahead of him was nothing but water. Behind him was the coast of Titanuus, a few miles away. He pointed west. "Do we have maps of what is out there?"

"Captain, there is nothing out there but the Elders. Only the boldest of fishermen travel beyond eyeshot of the coast."

"Why, will they fall off the edge?"

She tilted her head and gave him a perplexed look. Then that vanished, giving way to her normal, expressionless face. "No, the Elders will consume them."

He realized again that he should have known what she was talking about but didn't. But for some reason, he knew many other things that he hadn't before. He'd never sailed on a ship, but he knew what to call the three masts—the foremast, main mast, and mizzenmast—as well as the many decks—the main, forecastle, quarter, stern castle, charter, and poop. Belowdecks were the cargo hold, infirmary, brig, stores, and galley. He felt as though he'd been taken on a tour and was remembering everything.

He rested his elbow on the railing and said, "Let's go to my cabin to talk."

The captain's quarters was a twenty-by-twenty room with three windows in the back. A queen-sized bed was covered in linens and silks fit for a king. A small table for two was fastened to the floor for eating. A desk and chair sat against the wall. Two wardrobes and several wooden chests and strongboxes sat on the carpet-covered floor.

Sticks started undressing.

"No, I didn't bring you here for that," he said.

"Why else would you bring me here?"

"To talk."

She shrugged. "There isn't much else to do out at sea. You'll change your mind soon enough." She put her bandolier back over her shoulder then sat on the edge of the bed, crossed her legs, and put her hands on her knees. "I'm all yours."

Abraham knew what she meant. She was as frisky as he was and toying with him. In his new body, he found her hard to resist. Then he caught a glimpse of Jake's backpack on the bed among the pillows, and it brought him to his senses. He closed his eyes.

It's not real. It's not real. It's not real. For God's sake, it's not real!

Home. That was where he needed to be. He needed to be riding the lonely highways, living the life of a truck driver, and sorting his life out one day at a time. He took the position that whatever was going on wasn't real—it just felt like it. He decided to take the approach of a gamer. He was an avatar or a player. He'd have to ask questions to find answers about what he needed to do. Was it like the computer games he'd played as a kid? Ask questions that were simple and easy. Find out what you can. Move up to the next level. Complete the mission. Find your way home again. He opened his eyes.

Sticks hadn't moved an inch. Her pretty eyes remained on his. "Seasick?"

"No." He sat down beside her. "Tell me about the Elders. Tell me about Titanuus. Tell me about this world."

"Your questions are very strange. I know that you are not the same, but you still fight like Ruger Slade. If you hadn't slain Flamebeard, I'd have been worried. The men were starting to doubt. I was too." She shook her head and grinned. "You tore up Flamebeard. That was a sight to see. No one will doubt you—at least, not for a while." She touched his cheek. "And I like the new you. The old you was an ass. I hope this one stays." She leaned toward him.

The skin of his neck heated up. The rocking of the ship cutting through the waters further stirred the desire within him. He kissed her. She kissed him. It didn't stop.

CHAPTER 23

Abraham lay beside Sticks, who was leaning back against the pillows, the sheets pulled up over her chest. With his head on the pillows, he stared at the cabin ceiling. Their impulsive, lustful act left him feeling ashamed of himself, but this time wasn't as bad as the last time.

I'm sorry, Jenny. I couldn't control myself.

Sticks's tomboyish good looks and enchanting figure were more than enough to break any man. He knew. He was used to hearing stories of sexual triumphs and failures in testosterone-filled locker rooms. He didn't figure he knew any man, single or married, who could turn down a woman like Sticks. And with his body and hers, that made the tryst all the more compelling. He still wasn't sure whether he was performing his own actions or the actions of Ruger Slade.

"Do you still want me to tell you about the Elders and Titanuus?"

"Huh…? Oh, yeah." His fingers pinched the top of the sheets to cover his chest, like a frightened kid listening to a scary bedtime story. "Go on."

"Give me a moment." She crossed the room to a bar mounted against the wall. She took a bottle of port from the rack below it. "May I?"

"Sure. It's all ours now."

She filled a glass goblet with the chocolate-colored port and sniffed the bouquet. "Flamebeard must have had a refined palate. Would you like a glass?"

He held up his hand. "No thanks."

She sat back down beside him. "Titanuus is the name of a slain celestial giant whose body formed our world. He battled through the cosmos, against Antonugus, the Star Slayer." She took a long sip and cradled the glass to her chest. "Here, on the waters of this world, they stood toe-to-toe, fighting for the destiny of the universe. Antonugus carried a sword made from star fire. Titanuus was no match for its power. Antonugus gravely wounded Titanuus. He stabbed him right in the heart. He chopped Titanuus's arms off and one of his legs. Titanuus fell into the waters of the deep, watching Antonugus take to the stars, singing in victory. He pumped blood into the waters, giving it new life as he died. That's how the world was formed. That is how the Elders were born."

"That's a captivating story," he said, thinking of the map he'd seen. It did resemble the body of a man with arms and a leg cut off. The top of Titanuus even featured a large bump that could be taken for a head. "Wouldn't that make this giant a thousand miles tall? It seems preposterous."

She shrugged. "There is no way to truly measure the largest or the smallest of anything."

"So, what happened to the arms and leg that was chopped off? Did they float away? Wouldn't they make islands or something like that?"

"The Elders ate them," she said.

"And the Elders are giant people?"

She shook her head. "No, they are sea monsters. Gods to some. They live far out in the sea. They swallow ships like this whole. That's why the ships never sail out of sight of the shoreline. They never come back."

He raised a brow. "Has anyone ever seen one of these sea monsters?"

"Yes. But that was eons ago. I will tell you this: ships that sail too far into the Sea of Trouble do not come back."

He made a quiet applause. "Yay." He didn't mean to be rude, but the story, though intriguing, was little more than a fairy tale told to frighten children. It was little different from the Greek or Norse myths he'd read as a boy. But to Sticks's credit, the monsters did seem bigger. He scratched his ear. "Well, thanks for telling me. Now everything is making a lot more sense." He rolled his eyes.

"Captain, I can sense your sarcasm. I assure you that my story is true. Everyone knows it."

Abraham slid out of bed and started putting his clothing back on. "I'm sure they all do believe." Putting his shirt on, he turned toward her. "Do you think it's possible that, farther out in the sea, is another land like this?"

Her forehead wrinkled. "No."

"I see." He tucked his shirt into his trousers and slid his boots on. At least he had a better knowledge of the world he was in. Now, he had no doubt it wasn't real, no matter how real it seemed. For example, his cabin was stuffy and had a musty smell. The featherbed was comfortable but the sheets smelled. Thinking about sleeping in them gave him the willies. He lifted the sheets and asked, "Can I get these cleaned?"

Sticks gracefully slid out of the bed toward the wardrobe. She opened the wardrobe double doors. A red coat hung inside, along with other shirts and trousers and a stack of linens and towels.

"I'll have a retainer reset your room," she said.

By *retainer*, she meant a Red Tunic. That's what they called them. He'd recently caught on to that. Apparently, he called them Red Tunics. As far as Abraham could tell, they were part squire and part fraternity pledge, but without all the fun. He had a lot of friends who lived in frat houses when he'd played college baseball for two years, during and after high school. He made the rounds, and the pledges would serve the brothers, hand and foot, at least when it came to cleaning the frat houses and serving the drinks.

As for the senior Henchmen, like Sticks and Horace, the retainers called them what they were, Henchmen—that or "sir." The retainers strived to become Henchmen, but Abraham got the impression that they were expendable.

He snapped his fingers, making a loud pop. "Ah, I get it."

Sticks gave him a curious look. "Get what?"

He didn't say it, but he thought of the red-shirted security officers from *Star Trek*. Every time they showed up, they died. The man before him, Eugene Drisk, must have had a sinister sense of humor or been a Trekkie.

"Nothing." He pulled his shirt open, revealing the brand of the king's crown. "As long as we are going to be at sea for a few more days, you might as well tell me about this."

CHAPTER 24

STICKS PULLED HER SHIRT COLLAR down and over, showing her brand. As far as brands went, the skin was puffed up, but the detail, unlike most brands, was crisp. It didn't look like a burn or scar, much the way other brands did.

"All of the Henchmen wear the King's Brand. Not the tunics—they want to earn the brand. It's an honor. The adepts all have the brand. You really don't remember?"

"I can't say I do."

"You branded me. You branded all of us." She moved to the back side of the bed and stared out at the endless waters behind the window. "You seem to take pleasure in it. You were all smiles when you did me years ago."

"I'm not a nice man, am I?"

She started tying her hair into ponytails. "Are you going to let me speak freely? I don't want to be disrespectful and earn a whipping. Or be cast overboard like chum for the sharks."

"I've whipped you?"

Abraham prayed he wouldn't remember that. It seemed an unnecessary thing. The Henchmen were warriors, killers. They turned seasoned pirates into chop suey. No ordinary man would cross them after seeing that.

"I promise I won't whip you. I've never whipped anybody. Well, not in my world."

With her steady gaze on his, she said, "You are self-centered, arrogant, cruel, and malicious. You've killed your own men for speaking out against you. But they respect you even though our travels haven't been going so well. They are safer with you than without you. They don't have a choice, either way."

Abraham buckled on his sword belt. The boat rocked hard to the right. He danced a step back. Sticks grabbed hold of the headboard.

"Whoa! The floor's dancing." Spreading his legs out, he steadied himself.

They were definitely in a spot of choppy waters. Dark clouds now covered the sea as rain came down.

"If I branded all of you, then who branded me?"

"King Hector." Her shoulders swayed side to side with the jostling of the boat. "It's a great honor but not publicly known. You are marked for a reason. If you are captured, the enemy will see the mark. They will kill you or torture you. No, they will torture then kill you. That's why, at all costs, we avoid being captured. The mark is a death sentence even though it's a great honor to die in the service of the king. It's a better fate than what was already set aside for most of us."

"So the brand creates loyalty. That's interesting." He scratched the black whiskers on his chin. "We can't turn traitor because we'll be killed for it by the king or by the king's enemies. We are his property."

"Death before failure. We are all a living and breathing death sentence." She drank her wine. "The brand has powers too. It can stop a heart or summon a sky demon to anyone that deserts or is disloyal. It can bring luck, too."

"That's doesn't sound right," he said, rubbing his brand. "More stories to scare you. Besides, you said that the Henchmen were loyal to me."

"You, Horace, Vern, and Bearclaw have been together a very long time—before I met you, back when you were the old Ruger and not the new one that took over a few years ago." She finished off her port. "The king branded you, and you branded them. It's a longer story."

Even though thinking about it was grim, at least he had a clear understanding of what the brand was all about. He hoped it was another piece of the puzzle and that knowledge would lead him back to his world. He'd know who his troops were, too. The mark formed a brotherhood. All of them served the same king. They had the same mission. They were a team. He could relate to that. If there was one thing he understood, it was winning.

The King's Brand. It sounds like the name of a cigarette company. Maybe I'll be able to use it in the real world one day.

She finished braiding her ponytails and hung them over her shoulders. She approached him, touched his face, and asked, "Would you like a shave? You always liked it before. You'll want to look presentable for the king when the time comes."

"Do I shave me, or do you shave me?"

"Dominga shaves you. At least, that is your preference."

Of the ten Henchmen, he'd only gotten to know half of them. Seven were men. He knew Horace, Bearclaw, and Vern. The other four he hadn't become acquainted with. Three were women. He knew the faces of Sticks and Iris, but Dominga he didn't know. He remembered a few riders with their faces partly covered in cowls when he'd encountered them at first. He could see only their eyes. One was small, and he assumed it was a woman even though he could have been wrong.

"I'll wait," he said. "We still have a few days at sea, and I'm used to a fuller beard anyway."

"As you wish, Captain. Do you care if I move topside?"

"It's raining."

"I know, but I think you could use some time to yourself. I can send a retainer to set your bed."

He nodded. "No. Dismissed."

Without a word, Sticks departed.

Strangely, it felt natural to dismiss a woman he'd just slept with. The words came easy. Either he was getting used to becoming a captain, or the body he hosted was taking over. His fingertips tingled. He picked up Jake's backpack and hugged it tight and fell backward onto the bed.

Lord, please tell me I'm not losing my mind.

CHAPTER 25
THE PAST

On a hot and hazy day in Bradenton, Florida, in the spring of 2009, Abraham had recently signed a multimillion-dollar contract with the Pirates as their star pitcher. The Dominator, a name coined by his heated flock of fans, had come into his own. He pulled into the LECOM Field parking lot, driving a brand-new 2009 Chevy Kodiak truck with a smile as broad as the windshield.

Many of his teammates met him in the parking lot and checked out the new set of wheels. A lot of guys bought sports cars ranging from Ferraris to Porsches. Most of the bigger players could barely fit into the cramped cockpits of their European cars. Some of them were smart enough to buy a bigger Rolls-Royce or Mercedes. Abraham wanted to be different. He wanted big. He wanted roomy. He wanted American diesel. The Chevy Kodiak that Abraham rolled up in caught the attention of all of them.

The Kodiak was a vehicle true to its name. The midnight-black-edition turbodiesel king cab decked out in chrome made all the other cars look like kids' toys.

Buddy Parker, star outfielder for the Bucs, flicked up his black hand and whistled. "Woo-wee, now that's the perfect redneck vehicle. I'm going to get me one of them. I didn't even know they made 'em that big. No, I'm going to get two. Let me drive it."

"No, you have enough trouble keeping all four wheels of your cars on the road," Abraham said. "But when your Mercedes breaks down again, I'll be happy to tow you."

Buddy laughed.

He and Buddy had come into the league at the same time and hit it off pretty well. Buddy was from Alabama, a country boy raised on the farms, who knew more about running a farm than he did baseball. He talked about cows a lot but hated chickens. He had a five-hundred-acre ranch not far from his hometown. Once a year, he would have a massive team party and made the rookies milk the cows.

Jake hopped out the back door of the cab. The sandy-haired eight-year-old jumped up into Buddy's big hands. "Buddy! How many home runs are you going to hit this year?"

"One hundred," Buddy said. He always said that.

"That's impossible," Jake said. "Even Hank Aaron couldn't do that."

"No, but I'm going to try. You just watch and see. Buddy Parker and Abraham Jenkins are going to make some noise this season. This year, the P in *Pirates* stands for pennant!"

"Can I get a little help climbing out of here?"

Jenny asked. Abraham's wife climbed over from the passenger seat into the driver's. She wore a black Polo one-piece tennis dress that showed off her great tanned legs. Her light-brown hair was long, straight, and pulled behind her ears. A lot of people told her she looked like Diane Lane. Abraham told her she looked better.

Buddy set down Jake and hustled over to the truck door. "It would be my pleasure to help the most beautiful woman in Florida."

She let Buddy pick her up and set her down. She gave him a big hug and a kiss on the cheek. "Thanks, Buddy. My husband forgot to bring the fire-truck ladder."

Buddy tossed back his head and let out a gusty laugh that the entire parking lot could hear.

"It's not that high." Abraham pointed at the steps on the side. "You just have to step on these things, baby."

"I know dear, I just wanted Buddy to put his strong arms around me." She winked at Buddy.

Buddy kept on laughing and shaking his head. "Anytime. Anytime."

She walked over to Abraham, rose on tiptoe, and kissed him. "Just teasing."

"I know. But be careful. I'm not sure Buddy knows."

Jake grabbed Buddy's hands. "Come on. Take me to see the rest of the guys. I want to make fun of their errors and batting averages. Some of them really stunk last year. They need some motivation."

"You got it, kid." Buddy and Jake waved and walked away. "We ain't going to win no pennant if they are playing that way."

With her arms wrapped around Abraham's waist, Jenny asked, "So how am I supposed to park this thing at the shopping mall?"

"You aren't going to stay for practice?"

"Just teasing. I'm not going to spend all of *our* money yet. I'll wait until the end of the week."

"Just leave me enough to buy an airplane."

"I'll think about it."

He leaned down to kiss her perfect waiting lips.

Knock! Knock! Knock!

Knock! Knock! Knock!

Abraham's eyes snapped open. The dream from his past was gone. He found himself staring up at the wooden ceiling of the *Sea Talon*'s captain's quarters and cradling Jake's backpack.

"Oh no."

Sticks entered the room, accompanied by Horace. Both of them were drenched.

Horace closed the door on the storming rain. "Pardon us, Captain, but we have a problem."

The ship rocked hard to the left, half rolling Abraham out of the bed. He set his feet on the floor, set the backpack down, and rose. "Don't tell me we're taking on water. Or we're lost." He wiped the saliva from his mouth. The dream must have put him in a very deep sleep. He didn't even remember feeling tired. "How long have I been asleep?"

"Hours," Sticks said.

Beyond the windows of the cabin were nothing but stormy seas and sheets of black rain.

"Is it still daytime?" he asked.

"Yes."

The boat rocked side to side.

He faced them and nonchalantly said, "Okay, tell me what has happened. And it better not be one of those sea-monster stories. I've been in the belly of a tunnel, now of a ship, and I don't want to wind up in a fish belly like Jonah."

"Who is Jonah, sir?" Horace asked.

"Never mind. Just tell me what happened this time."

"It's the frights, Captain. They've escaped," Sticks said. "And two of your men are dead."

CHAPTER 26

Hard rain had soaked Abraham head to toe by the time he made it from his quarters belowdecks. The brig was located two levels below his cabin. It was an empty jail cell, made from iron bars that the rich sea-salt air had crusted over. Two Red Tunics lay outside the cell in pools of their own blood. Using a lantern for light, he bent over for a closer look. Their throats were torn open. They looked like an animal had attacked them.

The ship rocked.

Abraham caught one of the support beams, steadied himself, and stood up. "How could the frights have gotten out of there?"

The brig's door had a simple lock-and-key mechanism, and it wasn't damaged. He saw no sign of the key either.

"Who has the key?"

Horace pulled a key out of his pocket. "I have this one. Vern has the other. He's searching for the witches. These are the only keys that I'm aware of. And no one was in the brig when we boarded. The keys were inside the brig, Captain."

"Bring Vern down here, and find those witches," Abraham said. "There isn't any place to go on this ship. How hard could it be for them to hide? I want the ship searched from belly to mast."

"Aye, Captain." Horace hustled out of the room. His big feet pounded topside up the steps.

"This isn't what we needed. This stinks," he told Sticks, looking for some sort of affirmation. "Who in their right mind would have let the witches out?"

"The frights practice crafty ways of evil. They can beguile the mind if one is not careful. They should have been gagged," she said. "Women's words can be deadly."

"They can say all they want, but they can't make a key for the lock out of thin air." He stepped into the cell and looked for anything out of the ordinary. The hold was barren, free of any cots, chairs, or blankets. "Didn't they have shackles on?"

"Yes. But Vern took them off. He said if the ship sank, we didn't want to lose our prisoners to the sea. They'd need to swim."

"We aren't going to sink." The ship bucked up on a wave and crashed down again. Abraham corrected himself. "We probably won't sink." He made a disgusted look. The creepy frights on the loose opened up a nest of butterflies in his stomach. "If they were in shackles, we should be able to hear them from miles away. And this is a boat. I'm pretty sure chains on wood make a very noticeable sound."

"We'll find them, Captain."

"Will you quit calling me Captain when no one else is around!"

"Yes, Cap—" She closed her mouth.

Inspecting the lock, he asked, "How dangerous are these frights? I know a sword can take them, but they are strong as a wildcat. What do they do?"

"Evil magic," she said.

"Great." Abraham wasn't really sure what he was searching for in the cell. The danger was out of the cell, not in. But after having watched every episode of *CSI* twice, he felt as though a part of him knew what it was doing. *Who do I think I am?* CSI Titanuus. *What kind of trace am I looking for?*

Horace returned with Vern. Horace had the younger warrior by the nape of the neck. "Here he is, Captain."

"Where's your key, Vern?" he asked.

"It was stolen, Captain. I swear it." Vern spoke with desperation. The haughtiness he usually carried was gone. "The moment I heard the frights were out, I checked. It was gone. But I swear on my sword I didn't let them out." He looked down at the sword on Abraham's hip. "I swear it!"

Horace shook the man. "Quit whining like a dog. You're a Henchman!"

Vern clammed up.

It became perfectly clear by the tension in the quarters that the old captain would have killed Vern without a word.

Abraham dropped his hand to his hilt. "Vern, where is the key?"

"I swear I don't know. Captain." He blinked rapidly. "I'll help you find them."

Abraham squeezed his hilt. Part of him wanted to cut Vern down, but that part wasn't him. It was Ruger Slade, possibly taking control of him. He moved out of the cell. "Horace, lock him inside. And don't lose the key."

Horace closed Vern inside the brig. He twisted the key in the lock and tucked the key inside his tunic.

A pair of dark figures entered the tight quarters, Tark and Cudgel. They were a pair of well-built black men with light eyes that gave them a ghostly look. Tark had a beard, and Cudgel was bald. They wore tunics over the chain mail of the Henchmen. Stooped over, the lengthy Tark held out sets of shackles and irons. "We found these, Captain. Up on the poop deck. Didn't see the frights, but we'll find them. We always find them."

Tark and Cudgel were the company's scouts that rode out in front. Abraham didn't remember meeting them before, but he knew exactly who they were the moment they showed up. They were brothers but not twins. He wasn't sure, but Tark appeared to be the older, judging by the modest gray follicles in his hair and beard. They looked heavier in their wet armor but had sleek, wiry frames underneath. They carried long swords and daggers like the others.

Abraham cast a backward glance at Vern.

"I didn't even have the keys to the shackles. The retainers had them," Vern said.

Cudgel wiped the water from his face and asked, "What are your orders, Captain?"

Abraham had to think about it. Tracking down murdering witches was a new experience. Commanding a bunch of strangers who appeared to be a bunch of natural-born killers was a new adventure too. He thought of the only thing he could do. When the team had a problem, they would all gather in the locker room. "I want every Red Tunic and Henchman topside now!"

CHAPTER 27

THE COMPANY LINED UP IN the torrential sheets of rain. The only persons not in the lineup were Horace and Vern. He stood on deck, controlling the rudders from the ship's wheel. Every other man and woman stood on the main deck, hip to hip, at parade rest with their hands behind their back. The Henchmen formed the first row. The Red Tunics made up the second.

Bearclaw anchored the line of Henchmen. Sticks was next, followed by Iris, Tark, and Cudgel. Beside Cudgel was a smallish woman with her face wrapped up in a cowl. Abraham pulled the cowl down around the woman's neck and looked into the very pretty face of a petite black woman. Her kinky locks of hair rested on her shoulders. Her soothing light-blue eyes were captivating. That was Dominga, an out-of-place beauty, and he couldn't blame her for covering up.

With the hard rains drenching his face, he said, "I'm going to need a shave later."

Dominga nodded. He found it refreshing that she didn't call him *Captain*. He moved in front of the last two Henchmen and stood between them.

How old are these guys?

The last two men in the row were a pair of surly graybeards. He looked down at them. Neither man looked fit enough to wear the armor or swing a sword. Their unkempt beards enhanced their shabby appearance. They could have passed for Nick Nolte from *Down and Out in Beverly Hills* on his worst day.

Abraham eyeballed both of them. "Have you seen any witches?"

The two Henchmen spoke at the same time. "Nay, Captain."

Each man had a sword strapped to his back. Around their waists were assortments of pouches, purses, small daggers, and knives. The looked like homeless soldiers. Suddenly, Abraham recalled both of their names: Apollo and Prospero. The noble names fit the soggy, bearded faces like lipstick on a pig. He shook his head and walked to the back row.

A wave crashed over the starboard side of the craft, soaking every boot above the toes. The Red Tunics and pirates stood firm.

Abraham marched by each and every one of them. They were a motley group, tall and short, long haired, short haired, men and women. They wore swords and hatchets fit for a hero of a hermit's village. The best thing they had going on for themselves were the red tunics they wore like a badge of honor. He looked a young woman dead in the eye. Her unkempt hair hung over her pie-shaped freckled face. She had big dimples in her cheeks.

"Do you know why your tunic's red?" he shouted above the winds.

"Aye, Captain. To hide my blood from my enemies!" she brazenly shouted back.

"No." He touched her chest. "It's to make you easier to see than me!"

The row of Henchmen chuckled in the wind.

"Stop laughing," he ordered. "One of you… One of us, perhaps two, is a traitor. I aim to find out who it is and make an example of them." He studied the face of every man and woman in the ranks, hoping he'd pick up on something.

The hardened company didn't bat an eye. His efforts were looking like a waste of time. In front of the group, as time passed, he started to feel silly. He needed to make an impression on them. He needed to shake them up. He drew his sword. "I know who it is. With my sword, I'll kill who it is unless I get a confession."

Heads turned side to side. Some daring looks were cast toward Abraham.

He walked behind the retainers and, one by one, laid his sword on their shoulders. "Duck. Duck. Duck. Duck." At that moment in time, Abraham couldn't explain himself. He was caught up in it. Like a superhero whose identity transformed the moment he donned a costume or screamed "*Thundercats*" or "*Shazam*," he was in it. "Duck. Duck. Duck."

It's not real. It's a game. Or a figment of my imagination. Just kill one of them. See what happens. After all, you are a pirate.

He stood behind Apollo with his sword pressed against the man's back. "Tell me, Apollo, did you free the frights?"

"No, Captain," the man said fearlessly.

"Do you know who did?"

"No, Captain."

"You know what, Apollo? I think you are lying. And what's the penalty for lying?"

"Dying, Captain," Apollo replied.

With a dark glimmer in his eye, Abraham said, "That's right. Apollo never lies to the Captain."

"Gurk!"

Abraham twisted around. One of the Red Tunics standing behind him had the front end of a harpoon sticking out of his chest. A sinister shriek-cackle from the depths of hell erupted from behind the dying man.

The retainer crumpled onto the deck. Behind him, a thin-lipped, red-eyed witch had a wooden smile on her face. "Ship sail. Ship wreck. Ship burn above the deck," she said.

Abraham buried his sword hilt-deep in the witch's chest.

Her eyelids fluttered, and she repeated the same words again: "Ship sail. Ship wreck. Ship burn above the deck!" Her pink-red eyes locked on Abraham's. In a dying gesture, she reached for his face and said, "Kingsland is doomed, otherworlder. You cannot save it! The king is d—"

Crack! Bearclaw split the witch's head with his axe. Ripping it out of her skull, he said, "You can't let them talk so much." He pointed upward.

The rain stopped. The wind stopped blowing.

Abraham lifted his gaze. The top of the ship's center mast was burning like a torch.

CHAPTER 28

LIKE A GIANT'S MATCH, THE main mast burned. The flickering flames jumped onto the sails. The fire wasn't normal, as men would know it. The flames were a mix of blue, green, and red that crackled and hissed with a life of their own.

"There, Captain!" Bearclaw pointed at the mast.

Halfway up, the last of the frights clung to the wood. Vinelike tendrils jutted out of her body, making for additional appendages. Her hands and feet became sharp wooden claws. The flames in her eyes were the same as the burning mast's.

"Get the crossbows!" Bearclaw yelled.

"Red Tunics! Get the lifeboat in the water before this ship turns to a pillar of fire!" Abraham ordered.

The lifeboat sat in the middle of the main deck. The retainers scrambled into action.

"Where's my crossbow?" Abraham shouted.

"Coming!" Sticks said. She darted away and disappeared belowdecks.

Above, with a radiant pink glowing in her eyes, the fright chanted. The fires spread. The rain-soaked ship sails began to smoke. The flames ate the fabric.

Flatfooted, Abraham gaped at the bizarre occurrence. The bony witch had created a catastrophe.

Sticks reappeared and put his crossbow in his hands. He took aim at the hag on the center mast and fired.

The bolt zipped through the air right on target. The hag slipped around the mast like a scurrying insect, and the bolt buried itself in the large post.

"Bring her down! I want her alive!"

Bearclaw and Tark shot bolts from their crossbows. Both of them missed and started reloading.

"She is quick!" Bearclaw said.

The flames consumed everything they touched.

The Red Tunics started to lower the lifeboat into the water.

Abraham loaded another bolt into his crossbow. Eyeing the hag, he moved underneath her and aimed. He squeezed the trigger, and the bolt launched straight and true. The hag slipped around the post again, and the bolt hit the wood with another *thunk*.

"Stand still, you freaky cockroach!"

Bearclaw and Tark shot again and missed. They reloaded. So did Abraham.

Apollo and Prospero climbed up the ratlines toward the fright. Three retainers followed them up the ropes, making a line that trailed behind them. The passed spears up to the surly Henchmen. Prospero stabbed the witch in the leg, and she howled like a banshee.

"She bleeds! She'll die!" Prospero roared. Off-balance and clinging to the ropes, he poked at the hag, who nestled on the other side of the post. She had nowhere to go with the flames roaring several feet above her head and working their way down.

"Bearclaw! Tark! I'll shoot first, forcing her left or right. You have to nail her after that," Abraham said.

They nodded.

He locked his eyes on the hag latched to the center mast. She might dodge one bolt, but she couldn't avoid three of them. They created a half circle around the mast. Abraham stood in the middle, took aim, and fired. The fright scuttled left.

Bearclaw fired, and the bolt sailed true, hitting her right through the chest. She flung her arms outward. Tark slid around the pole and fired. His dead-on shot ripped through her skull, passing through one side and out of the other. She cackled maniacally. In a single bound, the witch woman leapt like a spider from the main mast back to the mizzenmast.

Abraham rushed toward the mizzen and bounded up the steps. By the time he got there, Sticks, Dominga, and Cudgel had climbed the mast using pairs of heavy gloves. They engaged the fright. The witch's tendrils coiled around their arms and legs. Sticks had a vinelike tendril around her neck. With one hand, the fierce woman clung to the witch's hair. With her other hand, she stabbed with a dagger.

With Sticks, Dominga, and Cudgel collapsing in on her, she could not withstand the brutal assault. The Henchmen, using small knives and daggers, chopped the hag away from the mast. The witch tumbled through the air and hit the planks, unmoving. The bold Henchmen climbed down with clawed animal skins on their hands, covering their fingers.

"Nice gloves," Abraham said.

The Henchmen huddled over the dead witch. The magic flames extinguished, but the damage was done. The tops of the masts were gone. All the sails on the main mast had been either chewed up by the flames or fully consumed.

Sticks cleaned her dagger off on the dead witch's clothing. She sheathed it and said, "The king won't like this. He wanted them alive."

"At least we have the bodies," Abraham said.

"They'll rot before we make it to Kingsland. No one will recognize what is left. The frights soil the earth from where they came," she replied.

"Toss them overboard, then," he said.

"We'll handle it, Captain," Cudgel said. He and Dominga hauled the body down the stairs and tossed it into the sea.

Abraham found himself alone on the sterncastle deck with Sticks. "Seeing you climb up that pole and taking it to the witch was incredible. This is one brave crew."

"Bravery won't do us any good now," she said. "Our mission has failed, and we drift further out to sea."

CHAPTER 29

THE *SEA TALON* DROPPED ANCHOR. At least for the time being, they weren't going anywhere. Abraham shouldn't have any sea monsters to worry about, either. He looked over the bow. The Red Tunics had the lifeboat in the water, ready to go. The shoreline was so far away he could barely see it. The sudden storm had taken them farther out than they were. He had decisions to make.

What in the heck do I know about sailing, anyway?

The center mast was toast. The sails on the other two masts were burned.

"What do you think, Horace?" he asked the meaty brute standing to his left.

Sticks stood to his right, watching the retainers climb back onto the main deck.

"The lifeboat will get us back to shore in a couple of trips. But the sails will function once we sew them up and catch wind again. It will be slower going, but it will do."

"Great. We're sitting ducks in the meantime."

"Pardon, sir?" Horace said.

"Nothing." Abraham changed course. "Is Vern still secured?"

"Aye, and whining like a hound. Permission to gag him."

"No. Whiny or not, I'm not so sure that he is to blame for all of this. But someone is, and they are still on this ship, aside from the Red Tunics that died. Take a head count. I want to make sure we aren't missing anyone else. Including me."

"Aye." Horace lumbered away.

With her elbows resting on the rails of the bow and her eyes cast toward the sea, Sticks asked, "Were you going to kill Apollo?"

"I don't know. I felt that was what my old self would have done. Am I right?"

"You've killed Henchmen and retainers before, so it was a good acting job. I was convinced you would go through with it."

"Well, don't expect mercy from me all of the time. I have a feeling I'll do things that are unpredictable."

"You're doing a fine job keeping the men on their toes. That's what matters most. Keep taking command. You have a knack for it."

That was easy for her to say. As for him, he didn't have a clue if what he was doing was right or wrong. He just made the best decision he could think of at the time. With no one else taking charge, he didn't have a choice. His fingers drummed on the ship's railing. He had a half smile on his face, remembering when he'd played Dungeons & Dragons. He and his friends confronted a hill giant. They all had different ideas on how to kill it. They emptied the toolbox, trying to bring the ten-foot brute down. Joe wanted to keep the giant alive so he could enslave it. Troy's goal was to decapitate it and mount the head on his war wagon. Tiffany ended up levitating the giant while Arley shot lightning bolts at it.

While all of that was going on, Alvin and Laid sneaked into the giant's lair and stole the treasure and hid it from the other party members. They were all so mad at one another that no one spoke or played again for months. In a way, what was going on now wasn't much different. Abraham made the best decisions he could, given the situation. He couldn't have cared less about treasure. He only wanted to wake up in his bed or truck cab again.

The black brothers, Tark and Cudgel, approached. With sweat dripping down his bald head, Cudgel said, "Captain, I think we have enough material to make sails. The boat might move at a crawl, but it will move."

"How long?" he asked.

"At least a day, maybe sooner."

"Make it so," he said. *Oh great, now who am I? Captain Picard?* His thoughts drifted to the other task at hand. *Who let the frights free? Who are the traitors among us?* All the Henchmen fought their guts out against the sea frights. They risked their necks to save the ship. He felt guilty for considering killing Apollo. Of course, the man couldn't be a real person anyway. It wasn't possible, so it didn't make any difference. But the old warrior had proved that his salt was as worthy as any. He fought without fear and with fire in his eyes.

Horace came back. "Ten Henchmen. One captain. Seventeen retainers. Twenty-eight. We started with thirty-one. Three retainers slain since we took the ship."

Abraham's past knowledge blossomed. He remembered traveling with a much larger group, as Sticks had suggested earlier in their travels. They'd had twenty Henchmen, forty retainers, and himself. Sixty was a large group. Now, they were less than half of that.

I can't believe we've lost so many. No wonder they don't care for me. I'm getting them all killed.

"That will be all, Horace. See to it that all our efforts are on the sails. I want to be sailing in the morning."

Horace departed.

For the rest of the day, the Henchmen and retainers went about their business as though they'd sailed a thousand times before. Abraham followed along with just about everything that everyone did. The sun set. A fog rolled in, and the sea vanished underneath the floating cloud.

He slept a lonely, restless sleep, tossing and turning between the dusk and the dawn. Sticks didn't stay with him. He wanted her there but didn't. Perhaps that was what made him so restless—either that or the horror he'd experienced the last few days: pirates, witches, and blood. The gruesome scenes appeared in his dreams, twisting them into nightmares. He wrestled internally with the events that he'd never seen or experienced before, things he'd done with the body that was not his own. Who was the man in Ruger Slade's body before him? He had a corrupted mind and dangerous intellect. That was one cruel, self-serving bastard. *I don't want to become that guy. I've got to be me.*

Abraham crawled out of bed and swung his feet to the floor. He rubbed his puffy eyes and yawned. He looked out the back window. The fog had lifted, and the sun shone on the sea. It shone on the sea and something else—ships full of stalwart, sullen-eyed, bare-chested men.

CHAPTER 30

Abraham jumped into his gear. He headed topside and met up with Horace, Bearclaw, and Sticks on the top deck. Two small galleys were there, with long oars in the water and no sails, at the fore and aft of the ship.

Buckling on his sword belt, he asked, "Who are they?"

"Buccaneers," Horace said.

"Well, if they are Tampa Bay Buccaneers, they shouldn't be a problem." He smiled.

No one else did. The rest of the company crowded the fore and aft of the ship from the lower decks.

"I take it that these buccaneers aren't here to help?"

"No, those oarsmen are the same as the vicious looters in Flamebeard's gang but worse," Horace said.

Abraham made his way to the back rail. The galley there had thirty strapping men sitting at the oars. Their skin was bronzed by long hours in the sun. They had red-and-white war paint all over their bodies and not a friendly face among them. At the fore of the ship, only one man stood. He had a long red-and-black braided ponytail that started on the top of his head and ran down the length of his back. The rest of his head was bald. He wasn't a big man but was built more like a middleweight boxer, and he carried a cutlass on his hip. No war paint was on him.

Abraham put his hands on the rail and asked, "Can I help you?"

"I am Totem, chosen leader of the Sea Savages," said the man with the ponytail. He gestured at the *Sea Talon* with his hand and spoke slowly, like an Indian from poorly done cowboy movies. "You sail a fine ship. It is a gift to us, from the Elders. We will take this gift. You will be our prisoners. You will be our feast." His smile showed a mouth full of teeth filed down to a point. He clapped his hands, and all the men behind the oars bared their teeth. "Give yourself up. We are hungry."

Abraham lifted a finger. "Uh, could you hold on a second, eh, Totem? Oh, and by the way, I am… Ruger. I'll be right back." He turned to his company. "Are they buccaneers or sea savages?"

"The same. We call them buccaneers, and they call themselves sea savages," Horace said. "They aren't very big. We can take them."

"No, but there are sixty of them, and I don't want to lose any more men," he said.

With a wary look, Bearclaw said, "That never stopped you before, Captain."

Whereas the Henchmen hadn't said much of anything at all before, now they'd become bolder—either that, or they loosened up.

Not sure which, Abraham said, "Sounds like that tongue of yours has a mind of its own. I'd hate to think that with your own mind, you questioned your captain."

Bearclaw's chin sank into his neck. "No, sir."

"Go to my quarters and fetch me one of Flamebeard's chests."

"Aye, Captain." Horace hustled away. He returned in a minute with a heavy wooden chest.

"Follow me," Abraham said. He moved to the back of the boat, looked down at the buccaneer, and said, "Totem, I think you have it all wrong. You see, I've spoken with the Elders, and they told me that you are supposed to pick up your gift." He looked at Horace. "Open the chest and show it to him."

"But Captain—"

Abraham gave him a hard look.

"Aye." Horace showed Totem the chest.

Totem shuffled backward. He stomped his boots on the deck, threw his head back, and let out a wild shriek. The sea savages jumped up on their benches with spears in hand and pounded the shafts on their seats.

"Huntah! Huntah! Huntah! Huntah!" they chanted. The same fully aroused cry went up from the other galley. "Huntah! Huntah! Huntah!"

Totem stopped screaming and lifted his sword in the air. "We accept the Elder gift!"

CHAPTER 31

After three more days of sailing, they made it to King's Bay without incident. King's Bay was the water north of King's Foot on the west shoreline. They docked the ship at one of the major port cities that ran along the leagues of coastland hugging the huge bay. They had no issues docking the *Sea Talon* though many eyes widened upon its arrival. Since they didn't bear the banners of the king's enemies in Tiotan and Bolg and paid the port fees, they had no issues with the king's port authority. Only those who didn't behave themselves in Kingsland had problems.

Abraham couldn't have been happier to be on land again. As a matter of fact, he got rooms for everyone at the seaside city called Swain. It was very much like the pictures he'd seen of Mediterranean cities that crowded the southern Greek and European shores. The buildings were made from big blocks of whitewashed stone. The rooftops were colorful. Seabirds squawked in the air and from lofty perches on the roofing, made from clay tiles.

The food and wine was good, and the people, who wore colorful, loose-fitting shirts, trousers, or robes, were friendly. He filled himself with sweet wine and food and retired alone in his room for the evening. It was a quaint room, ten feet by ten feet, with a bed, strongbox, and a long table against the wall with two candles on the tabletop beside an open window.

With a lot on his mind, he stared out his small cottage window overlooking the docks. Early evening had come, and the massive docks were a hive of activity. Sailors and soldiers were there in full armor. More big ships, galleons, brigandines, and galleys were there. Some were merchant ships, and the others were from the king's war fleet. Abraham didn't know how he understood all of that, but he did. All of it was vaguely familiar to him. The king's banners flapped from posts in the streets and on the top masts of the ships. One huge flag was mounted a hundred feet high on a small island of its own, like a memorial, between the docks. He couldn't take his eyes off the silky banner waving in the winds.

The king's banner was a flat golden lion head wearing a crown with six horns, with the white feathery wings of a bird for ears, on a royal-blue background. The crown on the lion's head brought back childhood memories. Abraham thought of the Cowardly Lion in *The Wizard of Oz* and King Moonracer from the Island of Misfit Toys.

This can't be real.

The seafaring citizens delighted themselves at the night festivals and ceremonies of lights going on. Colorful paper lanterns fueled by candlelight floated into the sky as in a Chinese festival. The people were a healthy mix of men and women, not so much different from home. It might as well have been a regatta at Three Rivers back in Pittsburgh but without the sternwheelers. Exhausted, he closed his shutters, took off his gear, and lay down in the bed. As soon as his head hit the down-filled pillow, he was fast asleep.

Knock. Knock. Knock.

Abraham opened his eyes. One eye was buried in his pillow. Bright daylight shone through the cracks of the shutters and onto his face. The bustling of commerce could be heard on the outside docks. The seabirds were squawking. The waves crashed against the shoreline and rattled the docks. That was the first night he'd slept through. No dreams. No disturbances. That would have been great, except for one thing. He was still in Titanuus. He rolled up and put his bare feet on the floor.

"Come in."

Sticks entered the room with a bundle of clothes. She closed the door behind herself. "You should have locked your door."

"I didn't realize it had a lock." He stretched his arms high and yawned. His body was alert and ready to go. "I slept like a baby. Must have been the wine."

"Swain is well-known for being a great place for rest despite the heavy activity. They say that the King's Bay is blessed. The sea wind caresses us all like babies."

"So I take it that you slept well too?"

She unfolded a cotton shirt, flapped it once in the air, and tossed it to him. "I don't sleep as well alone as I do with you."

"Sorry. I just needed a night to myself." He slid the shirt on then caught the clean trousers she threw at him. "We aren't engaged or anything, are we?"

She cocked her head. "Engaged? No. People like us don't get engaged. That's for royalty. We aren't royalty."

He stood up and slipped into his trousers. He grabbed his belt, which hung from the bedpost, and fastened it through the loops. He wondered when belt loops had been invented. He stuck his finger through the loops. "Do all pants have these?"

"No, you had a tailor sew them in. Your preference."

He rubbed his jaw. *Interesting.*

Knock. Knock. Knock.

Sticks opened the door. Dominga entered. The petite black woman with very pretty eyes carried in a bowl of water and set it on the table. She had a towel around her neck and a straight razor in her free hand. She smiled at him. "Are you ready for your shave, Captain?"

"I guess."

"You'll need to take that shirt off," she said.

"But I just put it on."

Dominga whispered in Sticks's ear. The expressionless Sticks lifted a brow.

"What?" he asked.

"We need to get you cleaned up." Sticks helped him out of his shirt.

"Why the sudden change?" he said.

She tossed the shirt onto the bed and said, "Because the King's Guardians have arrived."

CHAPTER 32

From his window, Abraham could see knights in shining armor riding on horseback in the streets. He counted twenty in all, in columns of two. Each of them wore a full suit of glistening full-plate armor. Their full helmets were fashioned like lion faces, each with a plume of lion hair at the top. The horses moved at a slow trot as they pranced down the stone road. They carried the banner of the king on a flagpole in the front and in the back.

Abraham swallowed. The King's Guardians were a formidable group who rode tall in the saddles and carried an air of superiority about them. The citizens that stood in the streets quickly hustled out of the oncoming horses' pathway. Some of them cheered the knights and applauded, but not all.

A group of miscreants dashed into the streets with their hands loaded up with rotting food and fish. The gangly group started hurling the waste at the knights. The filthy muck splattered on the King's Guardians' shiny armor.

The rabble-rousers chanted, "Death to the king! Death to the king!"

The horses came to a halt. The lead knights' helmets turned toward the rank assailants. The miscreants hurled more foul scraps and shouted curses. The knights in the front row spurred their white horses, and the gallant beasts charged forward.

The miscreants couldn't hide their shock-filled faces. A raw-boned man beat his chest and screamed at the charging knights. The rest of them scrambled away.

The first knight trampled the miscreant standing in his path. The second knight ran down another man. The merciless guardians chased down and trampled four more troublesome people though the streets and returned to their ranks. Not one citizen stood within fifty feet of the knights after that.

Crammed in the window beside Abraham, Dominga said, "That's what those dirty little lawbreakers get."

"The King's Guardians don't take any crap from anybody, do they?" Abraham said.

"No. An assault on his men is an assault on the crown itself," Sticks said.

The train of knights started riding out of town.

"Dominga, get him shaved. We don't want to keep the King's Guardians waiting."

Dominga gave Abraham a quick shave and quietly departed, leaving him in the room alone with Sticks.

With an arched brow, he said, "So I'm supposed to meet up with the King's Guardians, and they escort me to him."

"Yes, but with a great deal more discretion." She ran her fingers over his smooth face with a very soft touch. "The arrival of the King's Guardians is the way the king is letting you know that he knows you are here."

"How could he know that?"

"The king has eyes and ears everywhere. We are a part of that body. The moment we docked, I'm certain a rider or a pigeon delivered the message."

"I didn't think anyone knew who we were," he said.

"The king's allies do. I'd assume some of the king's enemies, too. Either way, the king is expecting you. May the king find favor with you, Ruger Slade." She gave him a goodbye kiss on the cheek and moved away.

He grabbed her hands. "Wait, aren't you coming?"

"There is a different path for the rest of us. If all works out, we'll meet you back at the Stronghold, the same as we always do. If not, it's been a pleasure serving the crown with you." She pulled free of his grip. "Goodbye."

Like a ghost, Sticks vanished on the other side of the door. Abraham sat quietly on his bed, scratching his head. *What in the world is going on now?* Sticks was the only person he could talk to. Now, she was gone. He jumped up and opened the door to see no sign of anyone in the hallway. He went back into the room, buckled on his sword, slung Jake's pack over his shoulders, and went down the steps to the main tavern floor. He expected to see the Henchmen and the Red Tunics having breakfast. Instead, the tavern was empty of any occupants—no serving girls at the tables and no bartender behind the bar. It was like an abandoned saloon in a ghost town but without all the dust.

Abraham made his way down the staircase. The boards groaned underneath his feet. He stopped at the bottom of the steps on the main floor. His nostrils flared. The smell of food cooking in the kitchen wafted through the room, but he still saw no sign of anyone. He wandered into the middle of the room.

Eyes narrowed, he said, "Hello?" The nape hairs on his neck rose. His hand fell to his pommel. He turned back toward the staircase.

Underneath the staircase was a small round table he had missed. A man was sitting in the chair behind the table with a long sword lying on top of it. He wore a traveling cloak with a silk collar. Black leather gloves covered his hands. He had the striking features of a nobleman, feathery black hair and a clean shave, but a white scar ran from his bottom lip to his chin. He had a scowl on his face.

"Feeling edgy, Ruger?" the man asked. He shoved the table back and stood. The man was lean, as tall as Abraham, and wearing a coat of blackened chain mail underneath his cloak. He picked up his long sword. The weapon was as well crafted as Black Bane. A lion head was fashioned on the pommel. He picked up his sword and walked toward Abraham, cutting the weapon's tip across the grime-stained planks of the floor. "I've been waiting for this a long time."

CHAPTER 33

"GO AHEAD, RUGER," THE MAN said. "Slide out that steel and see what happens. There's nothing I'd rather do than put your head on my father's platter."

Abraham's fingertips needled the handle of Black Bane. The contempt in the man's dark eyes clearly showed that they knew each other. He just needed a name. It was on the tip of his tongue, but he couldn't retrieve it.

He stalled. "I think we both know that if I drew, not only would I not be dead, but you would be dead."

"Puh," the man said. With a fine swordsman's grace, he slid his sword into his scabbard. "Father will have your head soon enough. Let's go."

Father. The man had said it twice. That implied he was King Hector's son. A lightbulb memory moment flashed in his mind. This man was King Hector's son, Lewis. Lewis had a long history with the Henchmen too. He hated them. He hated everyone who was not royalty. A new tide of information flowed though Abraham's brain. He closed his eyes and shook his head. He staggered to the bar as a migraine came on.

"What is the matter, goat lover? Are you having a spasm? That's what happens when you are in the presence of greatness," Lewis said.

With spots flashing in his eyes, he said, "I'm fine. But apparently, you aren't doing so well if the king sent you to greet me. What did you do this time, Lewis? Get caught screwing in the stables?"

Lewis sneered. "Watch your tongue, dog. Besides, I'd never be caught dead with some barefoot milkmaid like you."

"I wasn't talking about a milkmaid. What I was talking about has hooves, not toes."

Lewis slapped his hand hard on Abraham's shoulder. "Oh, Ruger," he said mirthfully, "the time will soon come when I'll see you gutted open or hanged. We'll see what clever words you have to say then. But in the meantime, you should watch your words, Henchman." He patted Ruger's face with his hand. "Come on, now. Let's get on the journey. I can't wait to hear all the details of your latest plunder."

Thanks to the new flood of memories, he was able to put more pieces of the strange world together. Lewis was one of King Hector's children. He was also the commander of the King's Guardians. He wouldn't be in that role if he wasn't worthy. Lewis was a knight with great expertise, as good as any.

Lewis also detested anyone not of royal blood. That was why no commoners were in the room. That was why the King's Guardians didn't hesitate to trample unruly peasants either. He had a very cavalier attitude, and so did his men. That was a big reason that he hated the Henchmen. It was a big reason that everyone who wasn't royal hated him. He was a grade-A spoiled jerk, but he could back it up.

Abraham stood up straight, looked him in the eyes, and said, "Lead the way, Guardian Commander."

Lewis snorted. He led them through the back, where two white stallions waited. The horses had the King's Brand on their left hindquarters. It was the type of crown that Abraham had. They climbed into the saddle and rode out of town. This was customarily what Ruger Slade did at the end of all his missions. At some point, he'd be escorted back to the king's castle, known as the House of Steel.

The show of the King's Guardians served as a distraction. The knights routinely made their rounds to the cities in Kingsland. No one knew when they were coming or going. Sometimes they escorted the Henchmen, and sometimes it was someone else. The king could send anyone he wanted—clerics, mages, spies, or merchants. One way or the other, once the Henchmen made it back to Kingsland, the King would know they were there. Only beyond his borders did he have no control.

In Kingsland, all roads led to the House of Steel. The road they were on had ankle-deep wagon ruts in some places. The sprawling countryside was rich in tall grasses and wildflowers that spanned as far as the eye could see. Rich farmland and cottages were spread throughout the territory. After an hour of riding out of town on a stifling day, they caught up with the King's Guardians and continued to ride behind them.

After a few more hours, Lewis—dabbing his forehead with a satin handkerchief—broke his silence. "Your mission was to return with several frights, and you didn't return with any." He huffed a laugh. "And now, my father's patience has run out. This latest failure will be catastrophic for you and your hapless men. Frankly, I'm glad to see it over with. I never understood why my father chose a rogue like you to begin with."

Abraham didn't reply.

"That's it. No clever remarks," Lewis added. "Did a cat catch your twisted tongue?"

Abraham thumbed the sweat from his brow and said, "I'll tell the king I did my best. If he doesn't like it, I guess I'll get what's coming to me."

"You'll get the guillotine. That's what you'll get. All of you!" Lewis tossed his head back in laughter. "Oh, how I hope to see it."

"If you think that you could do so much better, then why didn't the king send you to retrieve the frights?"

"You know full well that I have asked. My knights are more than qualified to handle these ridiculous missions." Lewis removed a glove and fanned himself. "What was the mission before last that became such a debacle?" His dark eyes brightened. "Ah, I remember. You were supposed to destroy a supply bridge in Tiotan, which you successfully did. But it was the wrong bridge, wasn't it?"

Abraham wasn't certain, but the words rang true.

Lewis went on. "And then there was a simple matter of retrieving the Ozam Tablets in the Dorcha territory. What happened there? Hmm? You brought them back in pieces and lost parts of them. Those were priceless artifacts. They contained historical information that was vital to the restoration of the crown. And what about the Shield of Puran? Consumed by a fire worm."

Abraham shifted in his saddle. The truth behind Lewis's sneering words stung. His mind started trying to put pieces of the memories together. He needed to talk to Sticks about what had happened on those missions. That was when he remembered something. His chest tightened. *Oh no.* Until he met with the king, all the Henchmen would be imprisoned.

CHAPTER 34

BARACHA WAS THE NAME OF the prison camp where the Henchmen were taken. It was a high-walled facility made from tremendous stones. Shaped like a hexagon, the Baracha wall stood fifty feet high and had only one entrance, a small iron portcullis. The only way out was either through that portcullis, or over the wall, which was heavily guarded. Baracha meant "place of misery" in the old language.

Sticks crinkled her nose as she fanned flies away from her face. The prisoners—sweaty and grimy—carried an unavoidable stink. The high walls of the Baracha kept the wind out, making it worse. The camp was one hundred yards from wall to wall. A lot of prisoners walked the yard. It was crowded, but the Henchmen clung together, keeping their backs to the wall. The men made a wall around the women, but the catcalls hadn't stopped since they entered.

The skies rumbled. The clouds were turning dark.

"A bad rain is coming," Cudgel said. He held out his hand and twisted it up and down. "In about an hour. Maybe it will wash some of the stink out of here."

"I doubt it," Sticks mumbled. She was squatting beside Dominga and Iris.

All of them covered up the best they could in their blankets. That was the only thing the prisoners were given when they entered. It kept prying eyes off them.

"It's only going to turn this dung hole into a mudhole. It always does."

The prison yard was packed dirt. No grass grew. With over one thousand people walking about, no vegetation would survive. No cells, dungeons, walls, bars, or chains existed. Each prisoner was on his own. They were treated like animals. Many newcomers didn't survive the first day because they were beaten to death and thrown into the pits below the Wall of Defecation. That was the southwest wall, converted into a massive latrine fifty feet long. A creek of sludge at the bottom washed excrement out to sea. It was the last place a woman wanted to be without an escort.

"I've got to go," Dominga said.

Sticks rolled her eyes. She'd been a Henchman a long time. This wasn't her first visit to Baracha either. She'd lived here briefly and in the king's dungeons. But this was Dominga's first time. She was a Red Tunic who'd only made her way up to Henchman on the last mission. She wasn't a former prisoner, either. She was a volunteer who started at the bottom, like the rest. Pretty but tough, she'd somehow made it.

"Come with us," Bearclaw said. Vern, Tark, and Cudgel joined him.

"I need to go too," one of the retainers said. She was the young pie-faced woman with a lot of freckles and dimples in her cheeks. Twila was her name, the only other woman left besides Sticks, Iris, and Dominga. She held her blanket tight around her body. Her hands trembled.

Tark waved the women over, and the men escorted Dominga and Twila away.

As soon as the group started walking away, the vulgarity came out from the surrounding prisoners.

Sticks shook her head. *Animals.* She did a head count of who was left: Horace, Bearclaw, Vern, Cudgel, Tark, Iris, Prospero, Apollo, and Dominga. Including her, that made ten of them, plus five Red Tunics. The rest of the Red Tunics and retainers had fled the moment they heard the word *Baracha*.

Aside from the Henchmen, plenty of rough characters were wandering the prison yard, hardened men and women, and others just pitiful. Most of them were waiting on their sentencing, but if they died, that made the entire process a lot simpler for the courts. Baracha made a fine crime deterrent, but too many troublemakers couldn't help themselves. If threatened, the Henchmen could hold their own. But some had died in Baracha. Sticks just hoped their wait wouldn't be too long.

Horace slid into Dominga's spot. Squatting by Sticks and Iris, he asked, "Do you think we are going to make it out of here this time?"

"I don't know. It seems like we've been getting by on borrowed time. After this last debacle, I think the king's grace will end for us," she said.

Rocking back and forth on her heels, Iris said, "Oh, don't say that. I'm facing life in prison for my mysticism. I only use it to help people."

Sticks scanned the crowd and saw the top of Bearclaw's head. Many lust-filled eyes were following the group. Baracha was the worst place for a woman to be. One had to be a very bad woman to get there. But they had their gangs in the yard too.

"It's death or the dungeons for us," Sticks said.

"At least we'll have our own room. Even though the grave is a very small one," Horace said.

"Yeah, if we have a body left to put in the grave," she said.

Iris plugged her ears. "Oh, don't say that either."

Horace chuckled. "So, what is your take on Ruger? He's not been the same since the tunnel."

"I don't know," Sticks said.

"Of course you know. You slept with him."

"So?"

"I'll sleep with him," Iris said. "I'll get a lot of information out of him."

Horace shook her head. "So you'll sleep with him and not with me?"

"You aren't Ruger, or even close," Iris said.

"What do you mean?" he objected. "I'm all man. I might not look like Ruger, but I've the same iron-made muscle under these puffy arms."

With a subtle neck roll, Iris turned her nose away and said, "It's not that."

"Well, what is it then?" he asked.

Sticks held a hand up. "Can the two of you do this some other time?"

Horace harrumphed and said, "I've been at this for over five years. Two good years, three bad ones. I probably know him better than any. Sticks, you know him second best. But I think something is wrong with him. Like before." Horace spoke quietly. "Do you think he's possessed?"

Sticks knew Horace knew him as well as she. Horace was a former Guardian like Ruger. They'd ridden together for years before the Henchmen. So had Bearclaw and Vern. The rest of them were convicts and hopeless misfits. They were an expendable resource given a new purpose to serve the king. The missions went well at first then started to slide backward a couple years ago. She told a white lie. "I think he got his courage back."

"I think it's too little, too late," Horace said. He looked about. "The king will be done with us."

"I hope not," Iris said.

"Hope isn't for people like us," Sticks replied.

Bearclaw, Vern, Tark, and Cudgel returned with Dominga and Twila. The women had deep frowns on their faces.

Horace moved aside and let the women take their place by the wall. "That was quick."

"That's because we didn't make it." Bearclaw turned toward a large unsavory group of men and women marching straight toward them. "They stopped us."

Horace looked at the ugly group of thugs. "What do they want?"

"They want to swap women."

CHAPTER 35

King Hector's castle, the House of Steel, was built on a bluff overlooking the Bay of Elders. The castle itself was nothing short of magnificent. It was one hundred thousand square feet of living space made of block stones, archways, and pillars of marble. The walls were blocks of white marble with golden and rusty flecks. The pillars and archways were black with swirls of gold and bronze in them. The hallways had carpets running the length of the floor. Great tapestries depicting stories of Kingsland's history adorned the walls. The stories they told were astonishing. Mighty fire-breathing beasts and heroes that looked as if they were hewn out of rock decorated the tapestries. The forces of light battled the invasion of darkness. Colossal beings with armor made of stars battled in the heavens. Abraham lost his breath looking at the detailed scenes, amazed that someone could sew something with such accuracy.

How in the world do they do this?

"Keep your unworthy eyes off of my father's tapestries," Lewis said. He shoved Ruger in the back. "Eyes on the floor, servant dog."

Abraham dropped his gaze to the floor and let Lewis lead him through the castle. The haughty prince marched on with his chin up in silent triumph. Lewis hated Ruger. It took a while for Abraham's mind to recollect exactly why, but when it came to him, he found it perfectly understandable. Lewis had crossed swords with Ruger once. The prince had the ugly scar on his lip and chin to show for it.

I'd hate me too.

With the King's Guardians posted all throughout the castle, he and Lewis traveled alone. They made their way to the parapets that made a pathway around the castle. From the top of the west wall, he could see the sprawling city of Burgess. A road of stone as wide as five wagons ran down from the castle to the grand capital city. The sprawling city stretched out for miles in a grid of well-built buildings and cottages. Beyond that city were farmlands. North and south of the castle were docks, beaches, and a harbor bustling with activity and commerce. From the castle's point of view, Burgess was perfect, but that was far from the truth.

The House of Steel's spires were another marvel of brilliant architecture. The six stone columns surrounding the castle rose a hundred feet high and were capped by twisting spearlike steel tips that shone in the sunlight. The House of Steel's gigantic flag hung outward from the top neck of the tower, flapping in the brisk ocean winds. But that wasn't why the king's castle was known as the House of Steel. Abraham's neck rose upward. It was called the House of Steel because of the gargantuan sword stuck downward tip first in the middle of it.

With the bottom end of the crusted-over sword standing fifty feet higher than the tips of the towers, it dwarfed everything else about the castle. The pommel had cross guards angled forty-five degrees downward. The blade sank into the top of the castle and vanished into the building. The gargantuan blade's steel showed a petrified look of gray stone covered in the gritty element carried by centuries of the salty sea winds. It was forbidden to touch the Sword of Stone. The Sword of Stone, according to the legends, was the weapon of Titanuus, buried in his leg after the celestial, Antonugus, defeated him. Seabirds nested in the hilt. Droppings and grit were all over the massive stone.

"Will you keep pace?" Lewis said. "You always gawk every time you see it. After you've seen it once, I don't see how you would ever forget. It's nothing but a poop stand now."

Abraham hustled up to Lewis. They rounded the southern wall toward the east side, where the king would be waiting. The east side was the safest place for the king, out of the view of his enemies. The backside of the castle was protected by two hundred feet of sheer cliffs, making it virtually impenetrable—not to mention the fleet of ships guarding the king's harbor and the soldiers who patrolled the entire castle. The King's Guardians in the castle numbered over one hundred. The king's personal soldiers numbered another thousand. He commanded an army over thirty-five thousand strong. They patrolled Kingsland cities, but the largest host of them were stationed at bases protecting the King's Foot and the border mountains between Kingsland and Southern Tiotan.

Two of the King's Guardians stepped aside, allowing entrance to the king's grand terrace, which overlooked the Bay of Elders. Lewis and Abraham approached a man wearing a garish blue-seafoamcolored robe with lion's fur around the shoulders. He had his back to them, his gaze fixed toward the sea. Abraham's heart started to race. Sweat gathered on his brow. He was in the presence of the king.

CHAPTER 36

STICKS SLID UP THE WALL. She had a small broken piece of stone in her hand. This wouldn't be the first prison scrap she'd been in, and it probably wouldn't be the last. Hanging back, she let Horace do the talking. He'd stepped to the front, facing the gang of goons who outnumbered them two to one. "Who is demanding a swap?" he asked.

A man pushed his way through the net of greasy bodies. He wore a cloak with a hood covering his eyes. A strange symbol was carved into his cheek. In a silky voice, the man said, "Why, that would be me, Horace. Baracha welcomes you back."

Horace stepped forward and glowered down at the man. "Save your pleasantries for some other fool stuffed inside these walls, Shade. Be on your way."

Shade lifted a finger. Unlike everyone else in the prison camp, his hands and clothing were clean. "Ah, ah, ah, I think that you would be wise to listen to me, you bearded egg. My offer is very generous. As you can see, I'm offering six of my finest maidens for only two of yours."

He stepped aside to show off the six ugly women he was talking about. Two of them were a pair of old crones, white eyes blinded by time, staring aimlessly and leaning on canes. The other four were flabby whores with hungry smiles that offered mouthfuls of missing teeth. They blew kisses at him with puffy lips.

"They will keep you warm when the winter comes."

Horace crossed his arms over his belly. "We won't be here for winter."

Shade rolled his neck. "Are you sure? As I understand it, you will be here for a long while. Take my offer. It's the best one that you will get from me. I offer protection. You don't want to be free game. Even men of your strength cannot overcome the sheer weight of superior numbers."

Horace looked down at Shade, who wasn't very tall but was fairly well built. He stepped on Shade's clean boots. "You're starting to piss me off, maggot. Begone."

Shade pulled his feet free. "You shouldn't have done that!" He didn't hide his irritation. "Be wise, and make a deal with me. If you don't, you won't be left alone. Not ever."

"It is not our decision to make," Horace said. He stepped aside. "I'll tell you what. If the women that accompany us are willing to make the swap, then who are we to stand in your way. Go ahead. Ask them yourself, worm."

Shade eased his way forward two steps past Horace. He cleared his throat. Addressing Dominga and Twila, he said, "Ladies, it would be in your best interest to accompany me to a more suitable arrangement in the camp. You will need my protection. Word has it that you won't be leaving, or you will at least be here for a long internment." He touched his chest and bowed. "I'll personally see to it that you are well taken care of."

"Does that include me?" Sticks said in her dry voice. She walked right toward Shade and stood eye to eye with him. "Well, does it, Shade?"

The swarthy man's Adam's apple rolled. "Why, Sticks. I didn't realize that was you. I thought you were just another one of the boys. But, yes, I would gladly extend my offer to include you, but I'd have to take two of my hags, er, maidens back."

Sticks grabbed him by the gonads and squeezed. "How about you stay on your side of the camp, and when we walk, you look the other way?"

The Henchmen chuckled with under-their-breath laughter.

Shade jumped away from her. "You will regret this misgiving, you plank-faced fool. I run this yard, not you!" He huddled inside the safety of his surly group and pointed his finger at all of them. "And don't you think for a moment that any of you are going to get out of here anytime soon. Not alive, that is. I have long ears. As long as any. The king is through with you." He started to turn around and turned back. "And make your own facilities. You are not welcome in mine!" Holding his crotch, he and his gang moved on.

Dominga stood beside Sticks and bumped wrists with her. "What's between you and him?"

"We have a history," Sticks said.

"It's pretty clear that he hates you."

"He hates all of us. He used to be a Henchman, but the Captain booted him out." That was only part of her story. Shade and Sticks had a deeper history than that, one she preferred to forget about. "He always gives us a hard time when we come back."

"Well, he's wrong, right? We won't be here that long, will we?" Dominga said.

"That I'm not so sure about. Shade might be a worm, but he doesn't make idle threats."

Near the middle of the courtyard, Shade had more prisoners gathering around him. He pointed in the Henchmen's direction. If he said something, he meant it. And he appeared to have taken control of one of the largest gangs in the prison. If he wanted them dead, he could probably get away with it. It would be a problem—a fatal one.

Heavy rain drops began to fall. Thunder rumbled in the sky.

Holding out his hand, Cudgel said, "The rain comes early. A bad sign."

A group of tall men with long ears and bulging trap muscles almost up to their ears broke away from Shade's pack. Not ordinary men, they were from a race of barbaric brutes called Gonds. They weren't good for much more than soldiering and farming. They were stupid but fought like their heads were on fire. Their impulsive urges got them in heaps of trouble. Now, eight of them were coming toward the Henchmen with their big fists swinging at their sides.

Horace cracked his knuckles. Vern clenched his jaws. Bearclaw cracked his neck side to side. Sticks rubbed her rock. In the background, Shade stood with his hands on his hips, smiling.

Horace breathed deeply in through his nostrils, and his broad chest expanded. "It looks like the dance is starting early."

CHAPTER 37

Lewis dropped to one knee. "Hail to the King." He bowed.

Abraham felt Lewis's hard stare on him and awkwardly sank down to one knee. He was about to repeat what Lewis had said but bit his tongue. He kept his eyes down, the same as Lewis, who sent an irritated sideward glance at him.

Nothing was said in a strange moment that felt like an eternity. The soft footfalls of King Hector approached. Abraham could see the hem of King Hector's robes dusting the tops of his shiny brown leather boots. The knot in Abraham's throat tightened. The king had an aura that stood his hairs on end. It was a foreign experience. He was dying to look up but dared not. He didn't know why, but Lewis wasn't looking up either, and he was the king's own son.

"Rise, son," King Hector said in the polished voice of an English gentleman.

Lewis slowly came to his feet, and the king embraced him.

In a warm and fatherly manner, the king said, "I take it that your journey to Swain was without incident."

"There was some rabble that attacked the King's Guardians. They were taken care of, Father."

"You killed them?" King Hector sighed. "I hate to hear it. But they must be made an example of. Just tell me that they weren't Kingsland citizens. That's hard to accept. Tell me they were more infidel invaders."

"I don't know. One enemy of the crown is the same as the other, citizen or not."

The king rubbed his hands together. "Sometimes I wonder if my stern tactics are the problem," Hector said. He walked back toward the patio wall as Lewis followed. "I have gallows in every quadrant of the city. Traitors are hung every day. Still, with a sickness, they assault the crown. I don't understand how that can be. Not so long ago, it didn't use to be this way."

Abraham lifted his eyes. He could see the back sides of King Hector and Lewis. The king was smaller in stature. He had a full head of wavy and curly gray-brown hair and leaned heavily on his left leg. Abraham dropped his eyes the moment the king turned back toward him.

"I could stand here and gripe about my problems incessantly for a week. Heaven knows that I've lost enough sleep." King Hector sighed again. "But let's get to the business at hand. Rise, Ruger. Rise and kiss the king's hand."

As if propelled by an unseen force, Abraham did as he was commanded. He looked at King Hector, and his knees wobbled. He fought to steady himself as the king's soft eyes drew him in. The king's strong aristocratic features had softened with time. The formerly prominent jawline sagged. His easy smile showed a few crooked teeth. It reminded him of an English gentleman from a movie that he couldn't readily recall. The king wore a small crown and had a sizeable teardrop-shaped emerald around his neck.

"Are you well, Ruger? Your back bends like a bow," the king said.

Abraham broke out in a cold sweat. New memories were flooding in. He and King Hector went back. Way back. Everything was jumbled together. "I'm sorry, Hector. I—*oof*!"

Lewis belted Abraham in the gut, doubling him over. "You mangy cur! You don't address the king by his first name!"

"Son, will you calm yourself," King Hector calmly said. "My servant doesn't look well. Perhaps it is the sickness from one too many failures. I don't see the need to quarter him over a slip of the tongue. At least not today. Besides, there is no one else around but us."

"Thank you for your mercy, King Hector," Abraham managed to blurt out.

Lewis had hit him like a heavyweight boxer. He could punch harder than he looked like he could, and the blow surprised him.

With a groan, he straightened his back. "I am sorry."

"I know you are, and you should be. After all, your last several missions have failed." The king clasped his hands behind his back. "Come, join me at the overlook."

"As you wish, King Hector," he said.

They stood at the patio wall together, gazing out over the sea. A sheer drop two hundred feet down led to where the waves crashed against the jagged rocks. Lewis stood behind Abraham's left shoulder, while the king stood at his right. He was certain Lewis would try to push him over.

"Look at all of those ships, Ruger," the king said.

At least one hundred warships were in the bay.

"The King's Fleet. The greatest fleet in all of Titanuus. At least it used to be. There was a time when the King's Fleet stretched all the way around the continent. Our territory was unlimited. But because of weak leadership, a spreading depravity, and faithless broods of people, Kingsland, once the capital of the entire world, has been pushed down to the bottom of the world like crap stuffed into a boot." He looked Abraham in the eye. "Dirty rotten scoundrels are taking over the world. My kingdom! We must stop them." He looked away and rubbed his temples. "Oh, my head hurts thinking about it. Lewis, will you get me something to drink?"

"Father, I will not leave you alone with this wretch," Lewis said. "I'll send a guardian."

"You'll do as I command! Go. I'm not a toddler that needs babysat. Go, son. Go."

Lewis gave Abraham a dangerous look and stormed off.

The king watched him go. "He's a good son. Loyal. More than I can say for the rest of them." He turned his attention to Ruger. "Now, tell me. Why is the best swordsman in the world failing me?"

CHAPTER 38

THERE WAS AN OLD SAYING about Gonds in Kingsland. *Never fight a Gond. Run like hell instead.* Aside from being as stupid as they were strong, the Gonds had animal-like endurance and a high tolerance for pain. Many of them pierced their bodies and had tattoos all over. That was what the Henchmen were up against now, a small host of rangy men who were more animal than man. The ashen-skinned men with cords of muscle from their toes to their chins thrust themselves into the Henchmen.

The rain poured down. Blood mixed with mud. Angry screams and howls of pain rose above the thunder. Big-fisted men swung their hearts out. Bone cracked against bone. Cartilage gave way. White teeth tore flesh away.

A blood-hungry crowd gathered around the brutal scene. Wagers were made.

Sticks slipped into the fray. A Gond had Horace pinned down in the mud with his hands locked on the man's neck. She cracked the ugly Gond in the temple with a stone. The brute shook his head and made an inhuman, horselike whinny. She hit him again and again, trying to crack his skull open like an egg.

"Get off, you beast!" she yelled.

The Gond punched his elbow back into her ribs.

She collapsed on the ground, clutching her sides, the wind knocked out of her. Her ribs felt busted.

Horace twisted free of the Gond's grip the moment the savage took his hand away. He locked up the Gond's wrist and applied pressure. Bone snapped. The Gond's jaw dropped open. Horace slammed his elbow into the man's chin, breaking the jaw and knocking the barbarian out. He crawled over the mud to Sticks.

"Get your scrawny arse away from here. They'll break you in half." He shoved her toward the frenzied crowd.

Another Gond jumped on his back and bearhugged him from behind. Horace hip tossed the man into the mud and kicked the man in the ribs.

Sticks rolled away from the danger. Horace was right. The Gond would break her in two. She was a great fighter with her daggers, but without them, well, hand-to-hand combat was not her strong point, especially against huge men who could squash her. But she wasn't going to sit around and watch, either. She scooped up a handful of mud and slung it in the eyes of Horace's attacker.

Horace got the Gond in a headlock and squeezed with all his might. "Well done, sister. Well done!" His jaw clenched. The barbarian picked up the beefy man and slammed him hard into the ground. "This one kicks like a wild mule! Smells like one too!"

Vern squared off with a Gond who fought with his mouth wide-open. The fit fighter jabbed punches into the Gond's face and ribs. The Gond smiled stupidly at him. Vern, not known for strength, hit him with everything he had. "I suppose you're too stupid to know when to fall down." He landed a right and left in the man's chin. Then he pulled back, shaking his hands. "What are you made out of, rock?"

Like a wild ape, the Gond lunged at Vern. His fingers tangled up in Vern's hair. The Gond headbutted the smaller man, and nose cartilage gave way. Blood dripped down into Vern's mouth. The Gond unleashed a relentless assault of hammer fists on him. Vern's legs turned to noodles, and he flopped face-first in the mud. The Gond kept whaling.

Bearclaw's kidney punch dropped a Gond to one knee. His fierce chop to the neck got the Gond clutching at his throat. He grabbed the man by the face and jammed his thumbs into the barbarian's eyes. The savage prisoner twisted away. Bearclaw let out a wild howl and chased after the savage, but his legs were tackled. He hit the ground hard as two Gonds jumped him then pounded him with hammerlike fists.

Five Gonds fought against Cudgel, Tark, Prospero, Apollo, and the other four Red Tunics. Prospero and a Gond were yanking at each other's beards as they headbutted each other. A Red Tunic jumped onto the Gond's back and bit his earlobe off.

Cudgel and Tark wrapped up the legs of a Gond and held on for dear life. The Gond whaled away at their backs. A Red Tunic latched himself onto the Gond's arms. The Gond slung him into the mud with a flick of his arm.

The other three retainers were getting manhandled by one lone Gond. The Gond busted two faces together. He picked another retainer up over his shoulders, slammed him hard into the ground, and stomped on him.

The ugly battle went back and forth, up and down, blow for blow, with feet sliding and faces eating mud for another minute. Then a bansheelike howl started, and the crowd fell silent. The Gonds broke off their attack.

The prisoner guards on the wall were swinging cowbell-shaped whistles that were attached to ropes over their heads and made the shrill sound of a siren.

Prison soldiers entered the prison yard, wearing plate-mail armor and open-faced helms. They carried spears and jabbed them into anyone who didn't clear their path.

One prisoner, a man well past his prime, ran into their path. He dropped to his knees with his fingers clenched together. They told him to get out of the way. He shook his head. They gored him. Order was restored.

Sticks counted forty Baracha soldiers. In addition to the spears, they had swords on their hips. They had the worst job a soldier could have in guarding a prison. They were ready to take a poke at anyone who crossed them and often did. She rubbed her ribs.

Horace wiped the mud from his face and huffed for breath. "Never thought I'd be glad to see them."

"Me either. What's wrong with all of you? I thought we were tough. You all got the crap kicked out of you," she said.

Prospero spat a tooth out of his mouth. He reached inside his mouth and pulled out another. Apollo did the same.

Cudgel was doubled over with his hands on his knees, sucking for air. "I hate barbarians." He huffed another couple of breaths. "There's no fear in them. Just stupid."

"Agreed," Tark said as he held a hand against his swollen face.

Two retainers dragged Vern by his boots over to the group. His nose was broken, his face bloody and swollen.

Sticks looked down at him and grimaced. "Did you even try to fight?"

Vern pointed a shaking finger at her and said, "Still prettier than you."

Bearclaw took a knee by Vern. "He won't be able to fight anytime soon. Shade is far from finished."

Sticks looked across the yard. Through the rain, Shade caught her eye and waved.

"Yeh, he's going to take us down one Henchman at a time." She looked at Vern. "At this rate, we won't last a week."

CHAPTER 39

"YOU'RE THE KING'S FOOL NOW!" Abraham saw those words in his mind as though they were written on a chalkboard. They were the last words Eugene Drisk had said at the tunnel, the mystery man who disappeared through the portal. Suddenly, the words came to mind and haunted him like the king's weary eyes.

"Where would you like me to start, uh, Your Majesty?" he asked.

King Hector tilted his head slightly over and looked deeper into Abraham's eyes. "Have you lost your edge, Ruger? And be honest. I don't have time for games. I have five kingdoms that want my head on a platter. A city of ungrateful citizens burgeoning to rise up. Tell me—do I need a new Henchman? Should the king's sword be somebody else?"

"Er… no." The pride of a ball player came out of Abraham. He would never sit down if he could pitch the winning game. "Absolutely not."

"What happened to those frights? They should have been an easy mark. Just put them in irons, and they are powerless," the king said.

"On the ship, they somehow escaped and wrought havoc. I can't explain it, but we killed them. Their bodies deteriorated. They were tossed into the sea." He held the king's stare. "But I defeated Flamebeard and brought the *Sea Talon* as a prize. I have his sword to show for the effort."

King Hector arched a brow. "Interesting. Flamebeard is renowned for his pillaging and swordsmanship. He's also worked for and against my crown." He stuck his bottom lip out and tilted his head side to side. "My crown is better off without his treachery. So you turned him into chum, did you?"

"He lost his head."

The king chuckled. "Despite that victory—and a new prize for my coffers—you still failed me, Ruger."

"I'm sorry. I did my best."

"Sorry. *Sorry* is for the weak. You are not weak. You can't be. And it sounds like you've lost control of your own men. Clearly, you have a traitor… or many. Have you executed any of them?"

"No. Until I prove otherwise, I assume they are innocent. I'm investigating."

The king shook his head. He walked down the parapet wall and sat on the edge. His shoulders sagged as if the weight of the world were collapsing on his shoulders. "In the streets, they call me the Ruthless King. Me. Ruthless. Yet they are the ones that are breaking the law. You can't have a country without laws. I enforce them. Without laws, there is no Kingsland. Without Kingsland, there is no law. There is only chaos. That's what thrives in Tiotan and Bolg. Hancha is no better. Their people are slaves, for all intents and purposes. My people are free, yet they complain."

Two seabirds landed on the wall near the king. He reached into a leather pouch and flicked bits of bread and seed at them. The birds pecked at the bits and flew away.

With his eyes fixed toward the Bay of Elders, the king said, "In the beginning, there was only one kingdom. Kingsland. It rested on the very heart of Titanuus. All of the races and creatures of the world were united. For centuries, we lived in peace, but over time, pride eroded even the best of us." He looked at Abraham. "My ancestors, in their efforts to please everyone, allowed this kingdom to be pushed aside, down to the bottom of Titanuus's foot. The people wanted new kingdoms and new leaders. They wanted to do it their own way. Before long, there wasn't one king to rule over the world but many." He waved his hands in an aggravated manner. "For the longest time, they fought each other, but now, they have all decided to fight against me. Somehow, Kingsland, the most orderly nation, is the problem."

Abraham started putting the pieces of the puzzle together. He'd heard the king's stories before, and he'd heard the stories from others. Ruger Slade had plenty of memories of them. Kingsland, the shiny star in Titanuus, was on the cusp of extinction. It was the last kingdom of the old world, where there had been order and peace. A dark poison had spread everywhere else, polluting the lands and devouring good people. All this had been done to insidious effect via a new cause of false righteousness spreading from generation to generation. The New Kingdom was what the movement was called. It promised glory for all but brought only strife.

King Hector had needed a long time to figure out what was going on. His ancestry had failed to protect the crown. They appeased their allies, not realizing they were enemies, and gave away their lands. They trusted the growing countries would do the right thing, as Kingsland always had, but that would not be the case. Each country fought to obtain more power. They used spies, espionage, sabotage, and marriage for their own personal gain. Alliances were made and broken. Skirmishes and battles raged.

As the situation got more out of hand, King Hector realized he had to do something. He had to fight fire with fire. He had to send spies into the other lands, so he created the Henchmen. They would be a nameless bunch of renegades who would spy and sabotage for the kingdom. For years, their missions were very successful, but lately, they'd hit a wall. And Abraham was their leader.

"There are so few that a king can trust," Hector said. "A man's oath is not as strong as it used to be. Men, women, pfft… They all lie for personal gain. They say practically anything. Ruger, I saw a light in you that others did not see. You proved me right, but lately, that light has been gone. I don't know what happened. You were my finest knight. The best sword. A renowned defender. And you deserted. Years of service, and you left. Why, Ruger? Why?"

Abraham wished he had the answer to that, but he didn't. It was another one of those fuzzy spots in his mind. If he had to guess, he would assume it had something to do with the body transformation. But one thing that did come to mind was that desertion by a King's Guardian meant certain death. Yet he lived. He was hated for it.

"I can't explain it, My King. I lost myself."

"Yes. Yes, you did."

More seabirds landed on the wall. The king tossed out more crumbs.

"You've had long enough to redeem yourself. But now, as much as I hate to do it, this experiment is over. I can no longer justify the risk. I'm disbanding the Henchmen." He stood, approached Abraham, fingered his emerald pendant with one hand, and put his hand on his shoulder with the other. "And I'm sad to inform you that your death sentence will be executed. Tomorrow. Guardians!" The knights who guarded the entrance to the terrace hustled over in their plate-mail armor. "Take him away."

CHAPTER 40

The king's condemnatory words took Abraham's breath away. Even though he was in the body of a fighting man, he had no will to strike. He stood dumbfounded. Everything around him turned into slow motion. The wings of the birds flying away from the wall flapped in a weird form of stop-motion. He could hear the metal-shod feet of the King's Guardians marching on the stone patio at a very slow rate. His head twisted toward the entrance to the terrace, leading back into the castle. A two-step stair led up to it. Three figures came through the billowing curtains of the archway's entrances. An older woman was being escorted by two men. One of the men was Lewis.

The Queen! Abraham dropped to a knee. It was Queen Clarann. She wore silk sleeping robes. Her hair was pulled up and braided. She wore a small diamond-studded tiara. Her pretty face appeared ashen and wrinkled. She shuffled when she walked with the men standing close by but not touching her.

Each of the King's Guardians dropped to a knee and bowed also.

The king rushed over to greet her. "My love, you should not be outside when you are so sick." He took her hands in his. "Please, stay in bed. You need your rest."

"Oh, I've been inside long enough." Queen Clarann let him kiss her on the cheek then brushed him off. "I want to see that sea one last time before I go."

"Don't say that," King Hector said. He fastened a hand around her waist and escorted her to the wall. "But if that is your wish, I will not deny it." He shot an aggravated look at the other man on the patio. "Viceroy Leodor, my queen is ravaged. When will you get this disease under control?"

"The Sect works at it day and night, Your Majesty. We come closer by the day," Viceroy Leodor said. He stood tall, wearing cream-colored robes trimmed with purple. He had a beak of a nose, bright, close-set eyes, and a sunken chin. He spoke in a respectful but forced manner. "But this disease is no ordinary disease. It is a curse. My healers and potion makers work endlessly to resolve the matter."

Queen Clarann sat down on the wall and groaned. She still had a spark in her eyes and strength in her voice. "Please, no more of those disgusting concoctions. I'd rather die now than swallow another." She stuck her tongue out. "Blecht."

"Don't say that, Clarann. I would not want to go on another day without you." King Hector spoke in a soft and soothing tone. "You are my wife. You are my life."

She touched his cheek with her trembling hand. "Hector, you have been good to me, but don't be so dramatic. It unsettles my stomach. You will always be more husband than king to me. That is more than any wife can ask for. But the citizens need more king than husband. I am holding you back. If my time comes, it comes."

"That is nonsense. You are far from full of years, unlike me. I will find a cure for you," Hector said.

"Don't be silly. Look at me. I look like I'm a thousand years old. I don't want to live my last days looking like a mummy." She brushed a withered hand across his check. "I'm sorry, Hector. I know this isn't fair to you. You never could have imagined this when you took such a younger bride. Now, I'm haggard and ugly."

"That is outrageous. You are as beautiful as ever."

She chuckled drily and rolled her eyes at him.

"Leodor!" Hector shouted. "This madness has gone on long enough. Certainly, you have some inkling that will end this disease. This is Kingsland. Anything is possible, or I am not the king!"

"Your Majesty," Viceroy Leodor said, "the only possibility is the egg of the fenix. Its yolk is said to cure anything. But as you well know, all of our expeditions to retrieve it have failed. And no one has sighted a fenix in decades. There are myths and legends, but that is all that we have."

The king stood. "No, they are not. My father saw one himself. They live if he says they lived." He clenched his fist. "If there is an egg to be fetched, we will have it."

"Father," Lewis said, "we have lost over five hundred men and women on these expeditions. The territories take them before they even arrive. It is a fruitless quest. Certainly, there is another way."

"What?" Queen Clarann asked. She started into a fit of coughing.

Hector, Leodor, and Lewis converged on her with outstretched hands.

"Oh, back away," she said, with steely resolve. "Hector, what news is this. You are sending men and women to their deaths, chasing after a silly legend for me." She grabbed Hector's hands in hers. "Hector, I know you love me, but I won't have you sacrificing lives of our loyal people on my account. That is foolishness."

King Hector stroked her cheek. "My dearest, you are the queen. The people are your humble servants. It is their duty. A kingdom must have a king and a queen. And selfishly, I need you."

"You'll have another queen. After all, there was one before me. I'm sure there will be one after. It's customary," she said.

"She didn't hold a candle to you. You know that." Hector kissed her hands.

Abraham noticed Lewis glowering at his father.

"Her sudden death was a tragic accident," Hector continued. "But I think it was destined to bring you and I together."

"Oh, don't say that, Hector. I feel so guilty. That's probably why I have this awful curse. It's payment to the Elders." She coughed. "Promise me you won't send any more to their deaths."

King Hector stiffened. "As you—"

"I'll do it!" Abraham blurted.

"Shut up, dog!" Lewis stormed over and kicked him in the gut.

CHAPTER 41

Abraham fell on all fours. With a groan, he fought his way back to his knees.

Lewis kicked him in the ribs. "Stay down, you walking, breathing, and sniveling wretch."

As tough as Abraham was, a kick in the ribs and gut still hurt like hell. On hands and knees, he spat out more words. "I can retrieve the egg. Please, one chance for redempt—*oof!*"

Lewis laid into him once more.

Squinting her eyes in Abraham's direction, the queen said, "Who is this man? And quit kicking him, Lewis."

"He is no one, my dear," the king said. "It's some finished business that I'd concluded when you arrived. Guardians, remove him immediately."

"Give me one chance, King Hector. Let me redeem myself. I beg you."

While listening to the conversation, Abraham had had a two-part inspiration. It was one part fear and one part *This has to be a part of a module or something.* If Titanuus was a fictional world wrapped up in his imagination, then maybe a scenario needed to be played out. Perhaps saving the Queen would lead him back home. He didn't know, but he knew that he had to act, or he would die in the king's gallows. The Guardians hooked their arms under his arms and began dragging him away.

"I can do it," he said. "I will do it. I swear it!"

The queen narrowed her eyes at Abraham. "Hector, don't I know this man?"

Hector opened his mouth.

She cut him off excitedly and said, "Ruger. Is that you?"

"Yes, Queen Clarann! Your devoted servant."

"Guardians, let him go," she said. "What is the meaning of this, Hector? I thought Ruger was dead." She eyed him. "Hector? Explain."

"I'd rather not, but I will," the King replied. "You know that Ruger deserted the Guardians and we lost sixty-five men. Several years ago, he resurfaced. I had him arrested." He eyed Abraham. "He deserved nothing less than execution, but I showed mercy. I gave him a choice: death or be branded as the King's Henchman."

Queen Clarann's mouth hung open. "Being a Henchman is a death sentence. Why didn't you tell me that a new sword had been branded?"

"There are more important matters. Besides, Ruger has failed his missions. I'm executing his death sentence tomorrow."

Lewis smiled. "An excellent decision, Father."

Queen Clarann stood up and teetered over to Ruger, her eyes shining like blue suns. She put a hand on his chin and lifted his head. She looked him over. "I was heartbroken when you deserted. But I am glad to see that you live. You were a true and faithful servant." She looked back at King Hector. "Is he still the best sword? If so, you'd have him killed?"

"Pfft, he's not the best sword, Mother," Lewis said. "I am."

"Oh, please. You are good, but your sister Clarice is better than you," she said.

Like a whiny snot, Lewis said, "She is not."

Queen Clarann held Abraham's face with both hands. With her thumbs underneath his eyes, she stared at him with eyes that looked as if they could see into his soul. "Give him one more chance. Grant him the expedition."

"Dearest, please, leave this business to us," Hector said. "There is much that you don't know. I will send out better men than him."

Lewis strutted forward, smiling with dignity. "Yes, Mother. I will go."

"No," she said. "You will send Ruger."

"One lone man will not be enough. It is an arduous journey. He will only desert us again," Viceroy Leodor said. He licked the sweat from his pale lips. "And men like him are not equipped for such an adventure. They are fighters. They need a group of skilled workers capable of finding the fenix and knowing how to handle it as well. I wouldn't venture it without the skills of priests and mages. It's a full-fledged campaign."

"I'll figure it out, Your Highness," Abraham said. "I have many Henchmen."

"Just do your best. Serve the kingdom, Ruger. Come home again."

She touched his cheek and looked right into his soul, and a spark that came straight from her fingertips went through Abraham's heart.

"Redeem yourself," she whispered softly in his ear. "Be brave, old friend."

The king rushed over to her side and took her from Abraham. "She's exhausted. Viceroy Leodor, take her back to her quarters." He kissed her cheek. "I'm coming along shortly, dear. Rest well."

"I'm tired of resting. I want to do something else besides sleep," she said.

Viceroy Leodor led her away. "I'll have the servants draw you a revitalizing bath."

Abraham wasn't certain where he stood. The queen might have a sharp mind, but she seemed so fragile. He feared that her words didn't have any weight. He waited as the king chewed his bottom lip while watching her go. He could tell by the worry in the man's voice and the look in his eyes that he truly loved her.

With a sigh, the King turned and faced him. "It looks like you have another chance—a futile one at best, but a chance."

"Father, this is outrageous," Lewis whined. "There is no fenix. It's a fool's quest. By tomorrow, Mother will forget about it. Put this traitor in the guillotine and get it over with."

"One day, when you have a wife that you love, you'll do anything for her. If she wants Ruger to seek out the egg, then so be it."

"Mother doesn't care about the egg, Father. She likes him like a loyal old hound"—Lewis sneered at Ruger—"and is granting him undeserved freedom. That is all. She is feeble and overly merciful. You know what Leodor says. He's done all that he can. There is no hope for her. She is strong. She understands that."

Shaking his fist, Hector said, "I need hope. This mission will give it to me. Ruger, if you pull off this miracle, your death sentence will be waived. And I will show you my gratitude."

Lewis stiffened. "Father, you can't trust him. He's a washed-up swordsman. His men are thugs. Let me and my men handle this. It might be lunacy, but for Mother, it would be an honor. We are the best hope that you have."

Hector shook his head. "You are not seasoned in the ways of the world beyond the border, son. I appreciate your offer, but no. You are the Captain of the King's Guardians. I need you here. Rise, Ruger."

Abraham did so.

"These are dire times. Bring that egg back to me. I know it exists."

"I am your Henchman. I'll do whatever it takes." He looked the king in the eye. "Death before failure."

Lewis laughed. "I'm certain that you'll soon experience both of them soon enough."

CHAPTER 42

Below the House of Steel were dungeons. Abraham was kept in a cell. He was the only one there. Made from blocks of stone and bars of steel, the drab place was clean aside from the cobwebs in the corners. Not even a guard was posted, or rats crawling along the floor. In his cell was a cot, a small pillow, and a bucket. He sat on the cot, lay down, and weighed his options. His situation was getting more uncomfortable and tenser. Since he'd arrived, he escaped one dire situation only to fall into another. The king meant business, but Abraham liked him. He liked the queen too. She was a salty woman, like his grandmother, who didn't let anything get by her. He wanted to help them. He didn't know whether he or Ruger wanted to help more. Something more seemed to exist between Ruger and the queen that he didn't comprehend. Her gentle touch jolted his heart. He wanted to go home, but he wanted to help them too. He'd gotten caught up in their lives. Now, he had to try.

In the meantime, he needed to figure out what was really going on in his mind. Everything he saw, tasted, or touched had been real. If he didn't know better, he'd swear that he had indeed been transported into another world and another body. But that was impossible. He'd seen movies like *Total Recall* and understood the basic concepts of virtual reality, but this was ridiculous.

Plucking at his lips, he said, "Am I Neo? Is this the Matrix?" He rolled onto his side as a multitude of new memories filtered through his mind. He felt as if a jump drive of information had been loaded into him. He recalled various sword-fighting styles: high guard, wrath guard, ox guard. People, places, and things crossed through his thoughts. Some of it was crystal clear, but the rest of it was fuzzy, as if he was sharing his mind with another person, or his had been transplanted into an android. "I just want to drive my beer truck again."

"What is a matrix?" an invading voice said.

Abraham sat up. Viceroy Leodor stood on the other side of the cell's bars with a curious look in his eyes and tapped his fingers on the bars. Abraham had a natural aversion to the bald and chinless man.

"It's a name for a puzzle," Abraham said.

"Life is a puzzle." Leodor looked at Abraham with a deep and spacey gaze. Then, he casually leaned against the bars. "Especially yours. Once again, you have escaped a certain death after failing another mission. I don't know if I should be more impressed or irritated."

"Why would you be irritated?"

"You're a Henchman. Less than a goat. You irritate me."

Abraham stood. "Ah, but I wasn't always a goat, now was I? I was the king's finest knight," Abraham said, probing Leodor. He knew who he was but thought he knew him better. "Was I not?"

Leodor's frown deepened. He stuck a key in the lock and twisted. "I want you to know that despite my love for the queen, I hope that *you* don't make it back. You have been nothing but a waste of time the last several years. I've supplied you with your needs. How many of your Henchmen and precious Red Tunics died this time? Forty."

"Thirty-eight." The amount jumped right off his tongue, and he felt guilty for saying it. "Why are you keeping tabs on me?"

Leodor rolled his eyes and stepped aside. "That's my charge, fool." He narrowed his eyes and looked deep into Abraham's own. "It seems that wound on your head rattled your gray matter." He let Abraham pass and led him out of the dungeons. "Based off my count, you've led over one hundred seventy-five people to their deaths."

"Hey, it comes with the territory. And like me, they volunteered for it. They took the King's Brand—nobody forced them. It's the same as any soldier." He didn't mean to say it in a callous manner, but it came out that way. He wasn't sure why. But he remembered his father telling him that the moment you sign up in the military, you sign your life away. "Maybe our odds would be better if you joined us?"

"Pfft. I'm in the business of saving our kingdom, not destroying it. Now, if you don't mind, keep your tongue bridled. Walk with me and listen. There is much that you need to know about the fenix egg if you are going to have a chance at finding it."

Abraham clammed up. But a voice inside himself wanted to shoot his mouth off. He wasn't sure whether it was himself or Ruger. After all, he had liked to talk a bunch of smack back in the day. It came out naturally. And if this was a fantasy or dreamworld, he saw no reason not to be whoever he wanted. He followed Leodor through a labyrinth of concealed corridors behind the castle's main walls and listened intently to the uppity man's words.

"The last two campaigns started at the same time. One campaign started at the top mountains north of Titanuus's spine, and the other campaign started at the bottom. The goal was to meet in the middle. The fenix or fenixes nest in those peaks. That's what the legend says. But it's thousands of square miles of treacherous terrain. Not to mention the other unexplored phenomena and creatures that indwell the Spine." Leodor stopped, spun on a heel, and faced Abraham. "Better men and women than you have boldly taken on this quest. None of them have come back. Of course, they may have fallen prey to our enemies, but more than likely, the Spine took them. I think that it will take you too."

"Thanks for the pep talk. It's no wonder the kingdom is doing so well."

Leodor shook his head and led Abraham up a long narrow flight of steps that twisted into one of the six outer towers. Halfway up, they entered a small enclosed room lit up by a pair of torches in brackets. The king stood inside with two Guardians and his son, Lewis. They were looking at a square table with Jake's backpack lying on top of it.

CHAPTER 43

Night fell upon the Baracha prison yard. On the inner ring halfway up the walls were huge torches in brackets. The guards on the top of the wall shimmied down ropes and lit the torch fires. They provided little illumination and created a darker spot in the middle. That was where Shade and his gang lurked. They waited in the shadows, like prowlers, waiting for the Henchmen to make a move.

The Henchmen huddled together against their section of wall. They were damp from the hard rain, which had finally stopped. The mud that they'd rolled in was caked and dried on their clothes.

Horace sat beside Sticks, clawing the mud out of his beard. Vern lay on his back, groaning from time to time. Bearclaw, Cudgel, Tark, Apollo, and Prospero stood guard, keeping their eyes peeled for another assault by the Gond. The Red Tunics, aside from Twila, stood with them.

"We can always attempt an escape if we have to," Horace said. "I'd rather die outside of these walls than inside here. I don't care if I only make it five feet." He looked at Sticks. "You're small enough to disappear. We can make the distraction."

Digging her rock into the ground, she said, "There is nowhere to go. Might as well stay here. I gave my word as a Henchman."

"We all did. But I'm not going to let Shade get the best of us." Horace cast his gaze outward. "He's a snake and a liar. Cost us two missions. He should have been dead, along with the others."

"I've got a shovel ready for him," Bearclaw said. He turned around. "When they come at us again, I say we all put our efforts on the biggest Gond. Take him down, and it will weaken the others."

Horace shrugged his heavy shoulders. "It will buy us time. It's sound enough. You, Cudgel, and Prospero do it. I don't think Vern will be able do anything. Maybe we can hurl him at them."

Vern groaned as he rolled onto his side and said, "Funny. Feed me to the dogs, why don't you?"

The heavyset black warrior Cudgel walked up on Vern and glared down on him. "You should be fed to the dogs. You let those witches out. You betrayed us, the same as Shade did. I ought to bust your melon open myself." He pointed a chubby finger at the incapacitated man. "Two of my brothers are dead because of you. There were four of us. Now, only Tark and I live!"

"I didn't do it!" Vern moaned and grimaced. "I swear it. By my brand and on the Elders, I didn't do that!"

Sticks kicked Vern in the backside. "Sure you didn't. Why would a liar lie about that?"

"I'm the best sword, after the Captain. You need me."

"Yeah, look at you. You're a real fine fighter, all curled up in the fetal position," Sticks said. All the Henchmen chuckled, aside from Cudgel. He turned his back toward the yard.

"I'm a swordsman, not a brawler. And I fought my guts out against the Gond." Vern winced. "Forgive me for not being born an animal."

"The rest of us fared well enough," Horace said.

"That's 'cause you're built like a chimney. Heavy as one too," Vern fired back. "And let me point something else out to you brilliant bunch of sages. Don't you find it funny that Shade, who was blamed for the prior calamities, wasn't around for this one? Maybe the Captain got it wrong. Maybe we all did, because the same stench of treachery lingers without him."

Sticks and Horace exchanged a glance. Vern was right. Shade had been the fall guy for the prior failures, but failures continued to happen. Now they were blaming Vern. If they were wrong about Shade, they could be wrong about Vern. When Shade had come on board, the well of success ran dry. Now, it was still happening without him.

"Vern's right. It could be any one of us," Sticks said.

"Yes, it's Vern," Horace said. "But Shade is still a snake. I never liked him before, and I don't like him now. He's come after us anyway."

"Well, forgive the man for holding a grudge. And it ain't me!" Vern said. He rolled over. Dominga was sitting with her back to the wall, looking at him. "See something you like, don't you?"

"No, I see a man with a face like a rotten tomato," Dominga said.

"You really know how to hurt a man when he's down." He turned away. "I guess I should have expected as much from one of the Captain's whores anyway. But you're missing out. My sword's just as big and shiny as his."

"Pig," Dominga said.

Vern shrugged. "I'm not a pig. I honestly and sincerely find you attractive. I couldn't say it before when the Captain was around. After all, he hoards all the girls, the same as everything else. But, seeing how we aren't going anywhere, I might as well spill my guts out. Dominga, I love you."

The pretty ebony-skinned woman had to fight back a smile.

Vern smiled through his busted lips. "I knew you liked me." He closed his eyes. "All women like me."

Sticks caught Dominga picking her lip and trying to hide a grin. *The little she-devil does like him. I'll be.* Vern wasn't bad. They'd been riding together a long time. He did his work. But he had brought up some illuminating points about Shade and Ruger. Ruger did hog everything, from the loot that they recovered to the women he bedded. He hadn't always been that way. He'd changed. Now, he'd changed again—for the better, she hoped. But they all still had the same problem—someone was betraying the group and making it look like an accident. *But who?*

"We've got company," Bearclaw said.

Shade approached with a larger group of goons. "Good evening, friends. I was strolling the yard, and I had a change of heart. I decided that I would give you one more offer: two of my finest ladies for just one of yours. I'll even let you pick which woman though I think Sticks is very much on the cusp between a man and a woman." He peeked at her. "I think it's the clenched brow that brings out the brooding man in her. But, like a prize sow, the woman of your choice will be well taken care of. You have my word."

Horace stood up and faced Shade. "Are you going to fight this time or talk?"

Shade spread his hands out. "I don't need to fight."

Horace threw a punch at Shade. The rogue slipped it, backed into his gang, and said, "Take them!"

CHAPTER 44

King Hector held up Jake's backpack and asked, "What sort of satchel is this, Ruger?"

It was a good question but hard to explain to someone who had not seen the likes of it before.

"A backpack," Abraham said. He rubbed the back of his neck. "For storage."

The king turned the backpack around in his head. He shook it. "Something rattles inside. Listen to me. This isn't the first foreign object that I've come across. I've seen other strange things not designed by anyone in my kingdom. Our enemies are developing new weapons to use against us. This might be one of them." He shook it again. "What is it? Where did you get it?"

"Your Majesty," Leodor said with his hungry eyes glued on the pack, "if you will allow me, I will be happy to use the Sect's resources to garner more information about it. The delicate services of the Zillons will unravel its mysteries." He reached for it.

King Hector pulled the backpack away like a child. "I don't want the Zillons to unravel the mysteries. I want Ruger to tell me." He narrowed his eyes at Ruger. The emerald pendant hanging on the king's neck sparkled. "That's an order from your king."

A strong force attacked Abraham's mind. The fighter inside him battled against it, but something was pulling information out of him. It dug for the truth. A new layer of perspiration broke out on his forehead. He wiped it away. With the king's intent stare haunting his soul, he reached for the pack. He decided not to fight it but to give in. He reached out and said, "All right, you want to know that truth."

"Yes." The king handed him the pack.

"Well… You can't handle the truth! But here goes." He pointed at the face of the badge stitched into the pack. "That's a Pittsburgh Pirate." He slung it over his shoulders, adjusted the straps, and buckled the fastener around his belly. "That's how this works." He took off the pack and unzipped it. "These little teeth make a zipper." He zipped it back and forth really fast. "It makes a very distinct sound."

King Hector, Leodor, and Lewis stood with their mouths agape.

"Now, wait until you see this." Abraham dumped the contents of the pack out onto the table.

The three other men made a noticeable *ahh* and crowded the table like flesh-eating vultures with eyes the size of saucers.

Abraham had stuck a few items into the pack over the years, but he never removed what was Jake's. He wasn't sure what all was in there, but his heart melted the moment he saw his picture on a baseball card. His throat tightened, and his jaws clenched.

The king's delicate hands rummaged through the foreign hoard. "What are these marvelous items?" He picked up a half-empty container of orange Tic Tacs and shook it. His eyes brightened. I know what this is." He put it to his ear and shook it. "It's a music box. I like it."

Abraham would have laughed if his heart wasn't swelling like a biscuit baking inside his chest. His picture and his boy's belongings got to him. He swallowed the lump in this throat and picked up a book. "This is a coloring book. Those robot things are called Transformers." He picked up a box of thirty Crayola crayons. "These are painting sticks." He opened the lid. "See all of the pretty colors." He tossed the box to Lewis.

Lewis swatted it away with an appalled look. "Father, these items are bewitched. I wouldn't touch them."

Abraham picked up the flashlight. It was yellow plastic with black ends. "This tube is a light, but it doesn't work." He started picking up and explaining one item after the other. "This is bubble gum. Long overdue homework. An unpaid electric bill. A bottle opener. An autographed baseball from Buddy Parker. A Zippo lighter and a pocket knife." He choked up. He and Jake had been planning a camping trip that never happened. He'd given those items to Jake. They were Jake's grandfather's.

Still filled with wide-eyed wonder, the King said, "How do you know the names of all of these things?" He picked up a multicolored cube. "What is this? It has so many teeny tiny gem-colored tiles." He hefted it in his hand. "And it's so light."

"It's a puzzle." He took a deep draw through his nose and took the cube. "Allow me." He started twisting the square. "It's a puzzle. You have to get all of the same colors matching on all six of the sides. It was created by the great wizard… uh… Rubik."

"What happens when you solve it?" Leodor said.

Abraham decided to have some fun. "Well, legend has it that whoever solves it will be granted a wish. But only the person that solves it."

When Leodor reached for the cube, King Hector snatched it away. "I will solve it." He started twisting the cube like a madman. "Hah! Look at that. I have three white ones in a row. This will be no problem."

"Your Majesty, it sounds dangerous. Perhaps you should let me work on it for you," Leodor pleaded.

"Nonsense. It's mine." King Hector held his audience's attention another ten minutes as he stuck his tongue out of his mouth. Finally, he hopped up and down and said, "This is impossible."

"Again, I will solve it for you, Your Majesty," Leodor said.

King Hector set the cube down on the table. He tapped it with his finger and said, "If anyone touches this cube that is not me, I will cut off both of his hands and feed them to the hounds." He poked his son in the chest. "That goes for you, too." He picked up Abraham's baseball picture. His head tilted. "What tiny people must have painted this strange portrait. Who is this man?"

Abraham looked the king dead in the eye and said, "That's me."

CHAPTER 45

THE KING HELD THE BASEBALL picture up to Abraham's face. "No, that is not you. And I don't understand why you said that, either. What are these strange symbols on the miniature painting?" He handed the picture to Leodor. "Can you interpret them?"

"No, but I will research it using the resources in the Sect's library the first chance that I get," Leodor said.

King Hector picked up a small black frisbee and flipped it with his fingers. "You have a great deal of explaining to do, Ruger. I don't understand how you came to knowledge of these objects. I need answers, clear and concise and not gibberish."

Abraham decided to spill his guts. "Your Majesty, I'm from another world. My name is Abraham Jenkins. That's my name on that card"—he pointed at it—"and my mind is inside the body of Ruger Slade. I don't know how else to explain it."

Lewis's sword whisked out of his sheath. He stepped in front of his father and held his long sword in the high guard position. "He is possessed, Father! He should hang!"

With an appalled look, Leodor said, "I agree. This devil should not be allowed to live within the walls of this castle. He must be executed."

"No," King Hector said calmly. "Son, put away your sword. I want to hear more about what this man—Abraham, is it?—has to say."

"But Father—" Lewis objected.

"Do as I say!"

Without taking his eyes off Abraham, Lewis sheathed his sword.

"Your Majesty, that would be quite foolish. He is a demon that can speak only lies," Leodor warned. "We must be rid of him."

Abraham swallowed.

"Perhaps," the king said as he tossed the frisbee up and down. "But at this point, what do we have to lose? The queen is dying. My enemies are chomping at the bit. We need something. An edge. Perhaps he can provide it."

"I agree with the viceroy, Father. Don't allow this," Lewis said.

The king pulled up a stool sitting underneath the table and sat down. He waved his hands over the objects on the table. "We have a vault that contains more objects like this. I collected some of it. The rest was inherited. Sometimes one shows up in the fairs, and my personal merchants bring it to me. But none of it makes sense. And when we come across these possessed people, what do we do? We kill them out of fear without acquiring any new understanding of what they are about. I think that it's time that we changed our tactic. Perhaps this is why our enemies have the edge. These otherworlders are on their side. It's time to change the tide."

Leodor's expression tightened as he stiffly shook his head. "Your Majesty, this is dangerous. As your chief advisor, I advise against it."

"That has been noted! If you object, then you may leave. Lewis and I can handle this… unless you want to leave too, son?"

Lewis jaw muscles flexed. "I'll stay. But if a demon climbs out of that body, I'll split him in half."

The king extended his open hand and said, "Go ahead, Abraham. Tell me about yourself. I'm eager to hear it."

What have I got to lose? This isn't real either way. Besides, maybe it's therapeutic.

Abraham opted for the truth and told the king everything that had happened after he drove into the East River Mountain Tunnel. By the time he finished, his limbs were weary. He was exhausted.

The king didn't say a word. He sat with his arms crossed, rubbing his emerald pendant between his thumb and finger. Finally, he said, "That's one whale of a story. It rings with truth. But I'm not sure what to make of it."

"Me either," Abraham said. "It's either true, or I'm dreaming. Or maybe we are all dreaming."

King Hector arched a brow. "Hmm… I see what you mean. The queen has many dreams. Wild ones. She tells me all the time. She won't let the scribes write them down because she doesn't want people to think that she was crazy. But maybe dreams are real. Who is to say? So the moment you took the sword, you changed. And another man appeared and disappeared through a mystical portal."

"Yes, sir."

"It's *sire*," Lewis said.

"A ring of light. Leodor, has the Sect reported anything about this?"

"I'll look into it."

"And this other man you saw. You said he was unfit," the king said as he took the baseball card from Leodor. "Not a well-knit man like this."

"No, King Hector. He wasn't fit at all. He was shabby looking. Older. Like Leodor but fatter and shorter."

Leodor looked as though he'd swallowed his chin.

The king chuckled and eyed the baseball card. "You have the look of a warrior though the clothing is very strange. Perhaps this other man was not fit for Ruger's body. That might have driven the failures. But with that said, Abraham, I have a question for you. You want to return to your own world, don't you?"

"Yes."

"I don't see how that fits into my service," the king said. "Your body is mine to command, but the mind is someone else's. I don't think that this can work out."

"King Hector, I gave you my word that I would try to find that egg. I'll keep it. If I return, I vow to continue to help you if you will continue to help me."

The king scratched behind his ear and said, "That sounds fair enough. I'll honor it."

"Thank you, Your Majesty!" He kissed the king's hand. "You won't regret it."

"Just bring back that egg." The king stood. "What about our men? What will you tell your men?"

"Nothing. The truth. I don't know."

The king laughed and tossed Abraham his backpack. "Let's hope this campaign doesn't end before it's started."

CHAPTER 46

Viceroy Leodor made his way to the House of Steel's archives. He was alone. His fingers twitched at his side as he moved quickly down the stairs, past a dozen wine cellars, and in through the wooden doors that led to the archives. It was a musty room with a vaulted ceiling and book shelving stacked twelve feet high. Large candles burned on the study tables spread out over the stone floor. Racks of scrolls sat against the walls as well. Inside were several scribes writing down the daily records with quill and ink. They wore blue robes with white collars.

"Get out," Leodor said firmly.

Five bookish men stuck their quills in their ink jars and hustled out. They closed the creaking doors behind them. The doors rattled shut.

Leodor made a quick pass through the premises. No one else was around. He headed to the back wall and passed underneath an archway, where a small door was blocking passage. He removed a key from underneath his robes and opened it. The room inside was pitch black. He muttered an arcane word. A soft yellow light illuminated the room with the quavering power of one hundred candles emanating from four globes that were attached to the top of a brass pole.

The room was a ten-by-twenty rectangle with a small rectangular table evenly centered in the middle. Wooden shelves full of books lined the eight-foot-high walls. Small cobwebs filled the empty corners of the cedar shelving. Tiny bugs and spiders crawled away from the light and disappeared into the cracks and crevices.

These were the oldest archives in the kingdom, eons old, but well-preserved in the cool dry climate. They contained records of the history of man near the beginning of time. They talked about life in Titanuus when only one kingdom existed. However, the language was ancient, forgotten, and very few could interpret it. The scribes would work on it slowly, but it was hardly a priority.

Leodor's hands rifled through a pile of scrolls stacked up neatly at the end of the farthest bookshelf. He'd studied in the archives for decades and knew them better than anyone. He controlled the scribes too, keeping their discoveries to himself. He kept his own enlightenment private as well. He slipped a small scroll out of the bottom of the pile. It was made of lamb's hide and bound by a leather cord. The scroll had a silky touch to it. He took it to the table and unrolled it.

It contained ancient script, but he could read it. It had been written during the era when all kingdoms were one, ages before. It told the story of King Ruoff and the Crown of Stones. It was the same crown worn by King Hector today. Six settings remained empty, made for six gems. The emerald in King Hector's pendant was one of those gems. King Hector's oldest ancestor on record was King Maceadon. He'd had five selfish children and one good. At their prompting, he agreed to bless each with a kingdom. He passed each of them a stone set in its own crown in his feebleness before he died. He gave his emerald stone, a crown, and Kingsland to his youngest and good son. The other five siblings were jealous and corrupt. King Maceadon's children and their children's children drifted further apart. King Maceadon's bloodline became so foul that only the good bloodline could be traced back to King Hector. Led by strife and greed, the new kingdoms continued to divide. Their true heritage was lost, along with their crowns and stones. In their anger, they all turned against the Kingsland, ruled by the youngest brother, and forced him from the main lands, south, to where the House of Steel resided.

Leodor traced his finger over the lettering. He mumbled the ancient text in his own language.

"Six stones. One kingdom. A crown with sturdy horns. Six stones unite all kingdoms. One land. One people. One king. One home. Six stones, the life of Titanuus. Six stones to rule the throne. Six stones to unite the world."

He knew the saying like the back of his hand, but more was there to be read. It told how the stones were meant to be together, working as one. But a devoted group of men and women hid the stones so that no one would ever find them again. Their location was kept secret for eons and their location finally lost. Only King Hector still had the one made from emerald. At least, that is what they all believed it was.

Leodor's fingers traced over the ancient lettering. He read aloud. "When the eyes of the other worlds open, the stones will reveal themselves." He rolled up the scroll and tapped it on his chin. "To tell the king or not to tell the king… That is the question."

CHAPTER 47

INSIDE BARACHA, THE HENCHMEN BATTLED the Gonds in the night. Cudgel and Tark latched onto a Gond's massive legs like ticks, while Bearclaw choked the man to death. The strategy proved futile. The superior numbers of Shade's gang overwhelmed them. Horace had both of his arms locked up by two men, while a third brute beat on him like a drum.

Prospero and Apollo were both facedown in the dirt, taking hard kicks to the ribs.

Bearclaw was the last to go down swinging before he succumbed to the thrashing.

Shade and his gang hemmed Sticks and the other three women against the wall. Vern crouched in front of them. He held his ribs with one hand and balled up a fist with the other. "Why don't we settle this between me and you, Shade?" Vern said. "Man to man!"

"Step aside, you fool. I'm not going to get my hands dirty on account of you." With his hands concealed in his cloak, Shade eased toward Vern.

Vern threw a hard punch.

Shade snaked his neck out of the way and drove a knee into Vern's ribs.

With a loud groan, Vern crumpled to the ground.

Sticks slipped into Shade's blind side, dropped low, and punched his ribs.

Shade fell onto both knees. Clutching his sides, he said, "Will one of you idiots contain her?"

Two Gonds pounced at her.

She kicked one that was missing his ears, in the crotch. The barbarian didn't wince. With a swipe of his heavy hand, he snatched her by the hair, yanked her up to her toes, and headbutted her. Painful stars exploded in her eyes, and her legs became noodles. She swayed but didn't fall on account of the Gond holding her up by her hair.

She looked up at the Gond and said, "I thought you mindless cow turds had standards."

"Uh huh," said the second Gond with tattoos all over his face just before he punched her in the gut.

The wind exploded out of her. As she gasped for breath, they let her fall to the ground.

Shade squatted down beside her and said, "Ah, looks like someone is bonding with her new lovers." He patted her on the head. "Good for you, Sticks. The Gond appreciate a humble woman. You'll make an excellent bride for the entire tribe."

The prison sirens whistled in the air. On the other side of the prison yard, the guards, spears in hand, charged toward the fight. They dug their spear butts into Shade's gang and the Henchmen with merciless force. The gang of Gonds dispersed.

Shade backed away from Sticks. As spears were pointed at his chest, he held his hands up high. "Heh, heh, heh." He grinned down at Sticks. "The guards won't care forever. Your time is almost up. Like them. Your numbers dwindle." He tipped his head at two dead Red Tunics who lay facedown in the mud. Their necks were twisted unnaturally toward their shoulders. "Bye… for now."

The pale-faced commander of the Baracha guards was the only one not wearing a helmet. He wore blackened plate mail, with the commander's eight chevrons stamped on the chest. Wolf fur was woven into the shoulders, and it made a short cape behind his back. He carried a studded mace with both of his hands. His face was ugly and pockmarked. His greasy brown hair was combed over. He spat tobacco juice on the ground and asked, "Which one of you goatherds is Horace?"

"I am," Horace said. He was on his knees with his hands sunk into the muddy ground. He pulled them out with a sucking sound. "Can I help you, Commander?"

"Yes, you can. You can round up your bastards and get your fat belly out of my prison." The commander spat juice on the ground. "Well, what are you waiting for? A wagon?"

With a groan, Horace came to his feet. "Aye, sir."

"Sergeant, see to it that they are properly processed." The commander looked down at the two dead retainers. "Are those your dead?"

Horace nodded.

"Drag them out unless you'd like me to have the Gond bury them for you."

"No, thank you. I'll take care of it." Horace picked a Red Tunic up in his arms. Bearclaw crawled out of the mud and hefted the other dead man over his shoulders. Escorted by the Baracha guards, Horace led the Henchmen toward the prison's portcullis exit.

Shade's gang beat their chests and jeered. Hundreds more prisoners joined in. Shade marched alongside the Henchmen, shouting at them with bitterness in his voice. "You'll be back! All of you! Tell Ruger I'll be waiting for him too! Tell him the Gonds will be waiting! Next time, all of you will pucker up and kiss my fanny!"

Sticks didn't look back. She held her stomach as she hobbled through the front gate with a growing headache.

Once outside of the prison yard, the Baracha guards returned all their gear to them. The commander pointed down the road and sent them on their way. Sticks trudged down the road with her chin dipped. Her headache was awful. Everything was sore. Everyone in the company moved at a sluggish gait, their shoulders sagging.

"Where to now?" Sticks asked Horace.

"I'm not sure. The Stronghold, I suppose," he replied. With the dead man in his arms, Horace took the lead.

They made it one hundred yards up the road when Horace came to a stop. At the top of the rise, a rider on a horse waited in the moonlight. The midnight rays glistened on the man's breastplate. It was Ruger Slade.

Slowly, the company slogged up to their captain and cast their weary eyes on him.

Sitting tall in the saddle, the strapping sword master asked, "What's the matter with you guys? You look like you just ate a mouthful of donkey dung."

The Henchmen exchanged glances with one another.

"Pardon, Captain," Horace said.

Ruger Slade's black horse nickered and stamped its hooves. It had a white patch of hair on the top of its snout and was geared up with a black leather harness and saddle.

"Easy, boy. Easy." He looked at the dead man in Horace's arms. "A sad thing seeing a Red Tunic becoming a dead tunic. Let's go make a hole and bury them."

The Henchmen followed Ruger Slade for miles, all the way to his stronghold south of Burgess. It was a small fortress built from natural stone, three stories tall, complete with battlements at the top, with its back against a steep hillside of rock. It was surrounded by acres of rich farmland and a small lake. A red barn with stables lay nearby. Livestock grazed. Hired hands slept in the surrounding storehouses. It was Ruger's home and the Henchmen's stronghold, a place that rivaled the lands of the local barons of Burgess.

They stopped at a graveyard overlooking the lake. Dozens of headstones were in the field. Horace and Bearclaw grabbed shovels and started digging. All the Henchmen took turns, even Ruger.

Sticks dug in disbelief. They hadn't buried a Red Tunic or Henchman in years. The old Ruger had stopped doing it. Now, the new Ruger dug and even said a few words.

"Ashes to ashes, dust to dust. May our brethren find a heaven where their steel does not rust."

CHAPTER 48

ABRAHAM WOKE IN TOTAL COMFORT. He lay in a down-filled bed, dressed in soft cotton. He was so comfortable he didn't want to move. He was sunk in, paralyzed in bliss. He didn't even remember having gone to sleep the night before. He didn't want to open his eyes.

Please let me wake up in the most comfortable hospital bed ever.

His nostrils flared. Somewhere, coffee brewed. The early birds chirped their morning songs. A breeze ran through the room, carrying the smell of baked bread to his nose.

Grandma?

When he was a boy, he would visit his grandmother in the country and stay a week at a time. Every morning at the table were flaky oversized biscuits stacked a mile high. That was decades before. He knew it couldn't be but wished it could.

A gentle hand caressed his chest. Soft, sweet breath touched his face. A nubile body brushed up against him. A sensual leg crossed over his.

Uh oh. Dare I look?

He thought at first that it was Sticks. But her touch wasn't so soft. He thought of his wife, Jenny. He wished it could be her but knew it couldn't be, for she was dead.

Perhaps I'm still dreaming.

He opened his eyes.

A gorgeous woman with piles of jet-black hair lay beside him with a smile in her gorgeous eyes. She ran her thighs up and down his. She said in a sensual voice, "Good morning, Captain." She kissed his shoulder with lips as soft as rose petals. "Did you sleep well?"

"Uh… I think so," he said, trying to recall her name.

From behind him, a second body wrapped him in a warm embrace. Lips kissed his back and neck. He thrust himself up into sitting position. Another woman lay on the other side of him. She was identical to the other one with the beautiful raven hair and dusky skin. They could have easily passed for the supervixen Hispanic and Italian movie stars he'd grown up watching.

"Wow."

"You fell asleep so quickly last night that we didn't get to have any fun," the one who woke him up said as she sat up beside him. She wore a short black nightgown that showed off her natural curves. Her hand worked its way down his chest. "Are you ready to have fun now?"

The other woman was dressed in pink. She looked underneath the furs and said, "I think he is."

With all his teenage fantasies suddenly coming to life, he needed every ounce of willpower to say, "No. Just, wait, uh, please, ladies." His heart raced like a galloping horse. He knew Ruger's body was about to take over, and he couldn't let that happen. "It's just a dream. Just a dream. Don't worry about it," he mumbled.

The door opened to his room. A third woman entered, carrying a serving tray. She wore a sexy white medieval teddy designed like the others. She was another identical twin.

Triplets! Now I know it's a dream.

The woman in white set down a platter of food on the end of the bed, with a mug of steaming coffee, a stack of what looked like crudely made pancakes, a pile of scrambled eggs, and cooked ham. "Captain, you must be very hungry from your journeys. You did not eat last night. Let me feed you, as I always do."

He was hungry, and not just for food. He gazed at her full breasts, swallowed, tore his eyes away and asked, "Sophia?"

"Yes," the woman in white said.

He pointed at the one in black. "Selma."

"Yes, Captain? What is your wish?" Selma replied.

He turned to the one in pink. "Bridget."

Bridget kissed his fingers. "You named me. You can rename me."

A new wave of memories came back to him. Viceroy Leodor mentioned setting the old Ruger up with property and servants years before. The triplets were a special gift. A lot of Ruger's history continued to pour back into his memories. The Stronghold was a fine piece of land that used to be the property of a retired Guardian. Leodor had the power to gift it to Ruger. Or perhaps, Ruger—or rather, Eugene—demanded it. He wasn't entirely sure. But based off the evidence, Eugene shamelessly took advantage of all the comforts that this fantasy life had to offer. He took a long look at the beautiful women surrounding him.

"Oh lord, I am Mudd."

"No, you are the Captain," the dreamy Selma said innocently.

Selma wore black, Sophia pink, and Bridget white. Eugene must have made them always dress in those colors so that he wouldn't mix them up even though each of them did have their own unique mannerisms.

At least he didn't name them Blossom, Bubbles, and Buttercup. That would have been really weird.

Abraham slid out of the bed and covered himself with a blanket. He was still grimy from his early adventures.

Bridget tugged at his blanket. "You need to bathe. The hot springs await, as always." She pulled her shoulders back and made a perky smile. "I will join you!"

He pulled away and headed for the window. The room took up the entire third floor of the Stronghold. It had wardrobes, chests of drawers, Persian-like carpets, and closets. The outer walls were solid stone, but the interior walls of the other rooms were wooden. The home had many modern aspects. He guessed it had five thousand square feet inside the rock. Outside were botanical gardens, hedges, a working farm, and at least a dozen hirelings that he could see breaking a sweat in the morning sunlight. With a great pond, its own hot springs, eye-catching gardens, and voluptuous women dwelling inside, it was nothing short of a medieval Playboy mansion.

This is ridiculous.

He crossed the room and stopped in front of a mirror angled so that he could see the women lounging enticingly on the bed. He took his first long look at himself.

Dang. Hugh Jackman, eat your heart out.

His sculpted frame wasn't layered in mounds of muscles. It was a finely honed physical specimen with well-defined, rippling muscles. He towered with broad shoulders and a narrow waist. He might as well have been cast from molten iron. With strong angular features and a steel-hard gaze, long limbed and big handed, he didn't look anything short of the deadliest swordsman who had ever been. He had the scars to show for it. No wonder men feared him. He feared himself.

He heard the rattle of a wagon rolling and saw it outside, hitched to a mule. Hay was loaded in the wagon, along with tools to work the fields. Far off in the distance, Bearclaw was manning a plow in the gardens. Sticks drove the wagon out of the barn. Cudgel, Tark, and two Red Tunics were sitting in the back. They were out of their armor and in work clothing. Sticks caught his eye and looked away.

Abraham started toward the steps.

What's this all about?

"Captain, where are you going?" Sophia said.

"Yes, we've missed you. Come back to bed," Bridget added.

Abraham left.

CHAPTER 49

"Whoa, whoa, whoa," Abraham said as he took the mule by the reins and brought the wagon to a stop. He looked at Sticks. "We need to talk."

"Certainly, Captain," Sticks remained in her seat and looked him dead in the eye.

"Let's walk, and don't call me Captain," he said. "Cudgel, Tark, don't go anywhere. We'll be right back."

Sticks hopped out of the wagon. She was still filthy dirty from the prison yard.

He followed the pathway that led out to the pond. No one else was nearby. Last night, he hadn't told the group anything new either. He just acted according to what he knew about Ruger. And burying the dead was the right thing to do, with a proper burial, when people gave their lives for you. He'd learned that from his veteran father.

"I'm still fuzzy on a lot of things," he said. "I know places and some people, but I'm not sure how it all works. So fill me in. When we come back to the Stronghold, all of you sleep in the barns? The house is plenty big."

"We used to stay in the house, but you removed us a few years ago. You said the hirelings work harder when we are out here." She shrugged. "We all work hard out here. It's what we do."

"But you only supervise, right?"

"It depends on the mood you are in. You say you want the Stronghold to be… tasteful. You are very proud of your wine cellar and gardens."

"I have a wine cellar?"

"Below the house, beside the dungeon."

He stiffened. "I have a dungeon too?"

"Yes," she said with a straight face. "But you don't use it for prisoners. You enjoy other things."

"Ah geez, I'm a pervert. Or I was a pervert. Listen, Eugene was the pervert, not me." Tapping his chest with his fingers and looking right at her, he said, "I'm not a pervert."

Sticks shrugged.

Ruger's eyes were like a scanner that would identify things and fill in the blanks as he saw them.

Ruger's mind would fill in some memory gaps, too. They walked out on a small dock at the pond. Ducks swam by. Facing outward, he said, "I was a real dickhead, wasn't I?"

"Dickhead?"

"A jerk."

She tilted her head. "You pull something hard? You are good at that."

By the blank look on her face, he knew she didn't understand. "No, let me see… Uh, I mean, oppressive, selfish."

Her creaseless forehead started to crinkle. She nodded. "Yes, very much so."

"Did I ever talk about my… inner self?"

She shook her head.

"Did I speak another name? Or call myself Eugene?"

"No."

Abraham couldn't blame Eugene for keeping it all to himself. Being trapped in a new body and in a different world was more than enough to drive a sane person crazy. He'd dreamed about such things as a teenager, but for it to actually happen was freakish. "Was the old me close to anyone in particular?"

Sticks took a knife out of her belt and spun it with a hand. "You preferred your privacy but indulged yourself in what you would call the flavor of the day."

"So I didn't have a favorite?"

She twisted her knife around, put it away, and shrugged. "You enjoyed new things. Pretty things."

"What about the me before the last me? What was he like?"

"You wouldn't be standing out here staring at ducks this time of morning. You'd be practicing with your swords. We'd all be practicing, and we wouldn't be gardening or farming, either." She kicked at the ducks that swam toward her. They quacked and swam away. "We all stayed in the Stronghold too, but not the retainers or hirelings. Plenty of room in the barns for them. They haven't earned the brand. Not all do."

Abraham scratched his cheek. He wanted to understand more about who Ruger Slade really was. *What happened to that man? Did he wind up in another body as well? Where is the real Ruger Slade?* "Tell me more, like, about my personality."

"Well, you were a knight once, the leader of the King's Guardians. So you were disciplined, stern, quiet. Those are the traits of a knight," Sticks said. "But, Horace, Vern, and Bearclaw know that old you better than I. They were Guardians too. Young and brave, they followed you after the first time you went crazy."

"Oh," he muttered.

She was talking about what King Hector had mentioned. Ruger Slade abandoned the Guardians, and many of them died. It sounded as though someone had jumped into Ruger even before Eugene Drisk did. Abraham wondered if that all had something to do with the sword, Black Bane.

Sticks continued. "There was always sadness. You didn't mix with the women like you do now and didn't engage in these casual conversations. You served the king, but it was all business. You conducted yourself with a heavy heart."

"So I wasn't much fun. But I didn't get as many killed then either, did I?" he asked.

"Many died, but no, not as many. You've never been afraid to put your Henchmen into battle for the cause. You would engage when what had to be done, had to be done. We've thwarted the plans of many of the king's enemies. We burned, we butchered any enemy of the king we came across. We've destroyed outposts, thwarted spy rings, purged the traitors from the sewers they hide in. You name it, we've done it. But we stopped getting our hands as dirty a few years ago."

"Dirty jobs, huh? I like that show." His stomach rumbled. "Have the Henchmen had breakfast?"

"A bowl of meal, as always."

Abraham didn't know any one of them very well, but he was disgusted by how they'd been treated. The Henchmen would have given their lives to him or the king. It was his crew now, and the time had come to make changes.

"Round the Henchmen up. It's time to break bread."

The first level of the Stronghold was a combination of kitchen, weapons training facility, and dining hall. During hard rains, they pulled the tables away and trained. They ate their meals there too, together, but that tradition had been abandoned years before. The second level of the building was a barracks made up of small beds and bunks, enough beds for one hundred soldiers to be quartered tightly together. At the top level was the Captain's quarters. It used to be divided into three sections, with two separate smaller quarters for the top sergeants. Now, it was only one room. Below the building was a dungeon, supply and weapons storage, and the wine cellar.

Abraham sat at the head of a long dark oak farm table, waiting for the Henchmen to join him. One by one, they came in the front door, with Bearclaw leading the way followed by Sticks, Vern, Cudgel, Tark, Dominga, Iris, Prospero, Apollo, and Horace bringing up the rear. Horace closed the door behind himself. Horace and Sticks sat at the head of the table, on either side of Abraham. The rest of the group took seats on the benches, spreading out but still filling only half of the huge table.

All the Henchmen were hard eyed, weary, and dirty. Prospero yawned and smacked his lips.

Horace broke the odd silence and said, "Good morning, Captain."

"Good morning," Abraham replied.

This was the first time he was able to take a really good look at all of them. Bearclaw had a fresh scab running down the length of his face. Vern's face looked like rotting pumpkin, and he wasn't a half bad-looking man to begin with, compared to the others. The rest were in better shape, all stripped down to muddy black tunics or shirts with long sleeves. Iris sent a warm smile his way. Cudgel and Tark looked at him intently with their smoky light-colored eyes.

Abraham scratched the side of an eye, unsure how to address them. He'd been a strong voice in his locker room, and words usually came easy, but at the moment, the uncertainty in their faces created doubt inside him.

He cleared his throat. "From now on, we all eat here. Together. Like we used to."

Bearclaw and Horace looked down the table at him. Prospero and Apollo pulled their elbows from the table. Dominga's tired eyes brightened.

"The hirelings are fixing breakfast. You can smell it, can't you?" he said.

Horace nodded. "Of course, Captain." He raked his fingers through his beard. "It all smells very good."

Abraham knew who these people were, but aside from Sticks, he didn't have a full grip on their personalities, aside from them being a fierce group of fighters. He felt as if he were in the locker room for the first time, meeting a new team. There was some awkwardness. He'd given thought to telling them who he was, as he had with Sticks and King Hector, but decided against it. He was just going to be who he wanted to be going forward, but he needed to break the ice with them. "From this point on, here in the Stronghold, let's all speak more freely with one another."

"But Captain, you told us if we didn't keep our tongues tied, you'd cut them out," Horace said.

"Well, after the latest lump on my head, I've changed my mind. So be yourself. That's an order."

A hireling woman appeared from inside the hidden kitchen galley. She was older, brown haired and bowlegged, with two metal coffee pots gripped in her leathery hands. She set the pots on the table as steam came from the spouts. Right behind her came another woman who could have passed for her daughter and had an innocent look about her. She carried a tray of clay mugs made with handles. The women set everyone up with a fresh cup of coffee, complete with cream and sugar that they made available. They vanished back into the galley.

The Henchmen stared blankly at their cups.

Abraham lifted his cup and said, "It's not Zombie Dew, but it will do. Drink up, everybody."

The hireling women brought out more platters of food: bacon, piles of ham and eggs, biscuits, ugly pancakes, and gravy.

The Henchmen heartily dug in.

Abraham was glad to see it. His grandmother had always told him that the best way to make friends was to serve them good food. Everyone liked good food. He enjoyed his own meal and the company. *The triplets' meal will have to wait.* Instead, his gaze was transfixed on the homeless-looking Prospero and Apollo, who were holding their plates up and licking them like hounds. *Clark Griswold, eat your heart out.*

Sticks carefully cut her food up with a knife and fork. Horace belched after every three mouthfuls. Vern chewed agonizingly slowly while Bearclaw stole food from his plate. He wasn't sure if they were a family, but they got along well enough with one another.

Abraham set down his utensils, deciding to take a crack at a little locker-room humor. "I'd like to share a joke that I heard long ago in a place far away."

Everyone stopped eating and looked his way.

Horace let out a final belch. "Sorry, Captain."

"It's fine," Abraham said. "So, a duck walks into a tavern and says, 'Hey barkeep, do you have any grapes?' And the barkeep says, 'No, I don't have any. Get out of here, you silly duck.' So the duck waddles away and leaves. The next day, the duck comes back and says to the barkeep, 'Hey, do you have any grapes?' Angrily, the barkeeper says, 'No. We only sell wine and ale here. Now, the next time you come into my tavern and ask me for grapes, I'm going to nail your bill to the bar.'" Abraham tapped the table hard with his finger. "'Now, get out of here, you stupid duck!' So the duck waddles out and leaves. On the third day, the duck comes back and says to the barkeep, 'Hey, do you have any nails?' The surprised bartender said, 'No.' Then the duck says, 'Well, do you have any grapes?'"

All the Henchmen looked at Abraham as though he were stupid, save for one.

Vern erupted in laughter.

CHAPTER 50

After the plates were cleaned, no one said much of anything. The environment remained as stale as bread. Drumming his fingers on the table, Abraham said, "I guess you're wondering what the king said to me or why my head is still attached."

"It's not our business. You're the Captain, and you give the orders," Horace said with a nod. "I think I speak for us all when I say that we are thankful for the meal. Shall we take the fields now?"

With a bewildered shake of his head, Abraham said, "No. This company has another mission. We'll be departing by tomorrow, if not today."

The group exchanged curious glances.

Cudgel leaned over, put his elbows on the table, clasped his fingers, and said, "Another mission? So soon?" When Horace glared at Cudgel, he glared right back. "He said we could speak freely."

"He didn't mean that freely," Horace fired back.

"Yes, I did," Abraham said.

Rolling his thumbs in front of his chest, Vern said, "Ha ha."

"Don't disrespect the Captain!" Horace roared. He pounded his fist on the table and pointed at Vern. "You giggling traitor!"

"Back off, Horace," Bearclaw said. "I've known Vern since we were young men. I don't think he's the traitor. Not now. For all we know, you are the traitor."

"What?" Horace's eyes twitched. "You hairy black snake! It makes perfect sense that you'd side with him. You're in on it, too!"

Sticks jumped in and said, "We don't know any of that! The frights might have found a way on their own. After all, they wield magic."

"And probably give birth to men like Vern!" Horace said.

Grimacing, Vern pushed himself up off the bench. "Listen, you bearded turd, you can call me a lot of things, but you aren't calling me a traitor. I say we settle this outside. Sword against sword. You might last five seconds since I'm wounded."

With a heavy shake of his bald head, Horace said, "I'll take that challenge. I'm going to put you down, and I'll put you down next, Bearclaw!"

Dominga jumped up on the table and said, "You two idiots shut your buttholes! No one's fighting anybody!"

Vern looked up at her and said, "Pretty thing, you aren't stopping anybody, but you're welcome to try."

"Vern, you couldn't whip me right now," she said. "I'd beat the hell out of you. Horace will stomp a mudhole out of you. You know that. Just sit down!"

"Your words cut deeper than any sword. I have pride." Vern sat down. "You know."

Horace made a triumphant harrumph.

"What are you guffing at, Horace?" she asked. "Sit your buttocks down."

Horace blanched. He started to sit, but Sticks stood up and said to Dominga, "You aren't anyone's leader. Horace. Sergeant. Me. Sergeant. You. Not sergeant!"

Dominga shrank under Sticks's hot gaze. Frowning, she did a back flip off the table and sat down at the bench. With the same fire in her voice she said, "The Captain said we could speak freely. What in Titanuus's tit do you think freely means?"

"I'm not sure what it means," Sticks said. She looked at Abraham.

Abraham smiled. "That's what I like to see out of my Henchmen. Some smack talk does the body good." He tapped the table with his fist. He'd been in the thick of his share of locker-room fights. "Real good. But I don't want anyone gutting anyone over a squabble." He showed his fists. "You can duke it out like brothers, but no weapons."

"But Captain, Vern betrayed us," Horace said.

"We've all ridden together a long time. Me, you, Bearclaw, and Vern were all the King's Guardians. You stuck with me when my failure happened. I don't think you'd betray us all now." Abraham shrugged. "Maybe things change. I don't know, but I'm not executing a man without proof or an admission of his crime. I don't know who freed the frights. It might have been one of us or one of them. Right now, we can't let it happen again. The slate is clean. We have to go forward. It's time for another mission. I can't make you get along. I can't make one believe the other. We're all going to have to trust that our actions speak for themselves. As for me, I haven't seen anyone here, or out there, do anything wrong. From this point on, the slate is clean."

The Henchmen exchanged uncomfortable looks. Some frowned, and others grumbled, expect for Prospero. His head was dipped onto his chest, drool running into his beard. He was snoring. Vern gave a stiff nod toward Abraham.

The bench groaned beneath Horace when he turned his body toward Abraham and said, "Fair enough. So what did King Hector say?"

"Well, he wasn't happy that we failed to return the frights. As a matter of fact, he was so unhappy that he decided to execute my death sentence," Abraham said.

Iris clutched her hands to her chest and moaned. "Oh no."

Horace stiffened. Several sets of eyes at the table grew big. If Ruger died, the Henchmen would be condemned. All of them would go back to prison, and the former knights would be hanged. The rest would be forgotten. Their fate depended on the company's success.

"So, the king's grace ended?" Horace asked.

"Yes, but fortunately, the queen's grace has not," he said. "If it weren't for her timely interruption, I believe I'd be swinging in the gallows this very morning. She is still fond of me, and sadly, she is sick."

"The queen is ill? What is wrong with her?" Iris asked in a sweet voice.

"I don't know. She's rigid, aging rapidly. Her vibrant beauty has faded." He took a swig of coffee. "It made my heart ache, but she still had fire in her eyes."

Resting his thick forearms on the table, Cudgel asked, "Certainly the viceroy can cure her? He's well-known for his methods and ability to heal."

"Pah!" Iris's cheery expression hardened. "The Sect is not as they say."

"I don't know, but Leodor has been doing everything that he can." Abraham finished his coffee and set it down. "He sent two expeditions to the peaks in Titanuus's Spine to find a cure. One north and one south. They never returned."

"Well, of course not. Not many that navigate the Spine ever live," Bearclaw said as he picked his teeth with his fork. "What were they looking for?"

"The egg of a fenix. He says its yolk can cure anything," he replied.

Everyone at the table started laughing so hard that Prospero was jolted from his slumber. He looked around and joined in with the cajoling. Even the stoic Sticks broke out in giggles.

Abraham sat in stunned silence, bewildered by their amusement. "Why is that so funny?"

Horace wiped his eyes and caught his breath. "Sorry, Captain. We all adore Queen Clarann, more so than the king, but sending a campaign into the Spine to search for a creature that does not exist… Well, that's plum foolishness." He hacked out a cough and tapped his chest. "You were jesting, weren't you?"

"No. The king and the viceroy were dead serious. King Hector claims that he's seen the fenix."

"No one sees the fenix and lives," Bearclaw said. "So that would be impossible. So say the legends. Are you sincere? They really did send out two campaigns into the Spine?"

"That's what they said."

"A campaign like that is over one hundred men each, and none of them returned?" Cudgel asked. "That is a shame for the queen. I've cast my eyes on her twice before. She was very beautiful. She had the strength of an eagle in her eyes. If the mythical fenix egg was her only hope, then her situation is fatal." He rubbed his chin. "I wonder who the next queen will be?"

"Ah, I'm sure the king will find a woman that is just as beautiful. After all, he is the king," Horace said. He put his hands down on his knees and rocked back and forth. "So, Captain, we are sorry for the news, but tell us, what is our next urgent mission?"

Abraham swallowed as he scanned the eyes of all the eager faces. His mind, merged with Ruger's, didn't recall anything about the Spine or fenixes. The Henchmen's reaction revealed that he'd bitten off more than he could chew. *Oh lord, what have I agreed to?* He sipped from his empty coffee mug. "Uh, well, King Hector wants to send one more campaign after the fenix egg."

With his hairy arms crossed over his chest, Bearclaw huffed and said, "Well, may the Elders favor them. What about us?"

Abraham intently looked at them all and replied, "We are the campaign."

CHAPTER 51

ROLLING HER NECK, DOMINGA SAID, "Well, somebody cut my jugular now."

"Yes, but shoot me with a crossbow first," Vern said. "Right in the heart, because without Dominga, I don't need it."

"Captain, tell me that this is not so," Horace said as he rocked back and forth on the bench. "We are soldiers. We use sabotage and espionage. We spy and gather information. Sure, we are expendable, but traversing the Spine to search for a fenix… That makes no sense. It's a suicide mission."

Everyone started to grumble and murmur. Prospero beat his head on the table. Apollo yawned. Sticks shook her head and chewed on her lip.

"Captain, we only have thirteen seasoned men left. Thirteen! Those expeditions had hundreds," Cudgel said. He wiped away the new sweat beading on his forehead with his forearm. "You've commandeered many more people, right?"

All eyes fell on Abraham.

"No," he said.

They let out a unified "Aaaaah!" and began shaking their heads and mumbling to themselves.

"It was either that or die. That would have been true for most of us," he said. "Henchmen, we are going after the fenix egg. That's an order."

"With only thirteen men?" Vern said. "The last mission we started with sixty. And now it's just us and a bunch of green tunics."

"Red Tunics," Dominga said.

"You know what I mean," Vern said.

"You bear the mark, Vern," Sticks said. "We all do. If he had to sail to the edge of the sea, we are bound to do it. No one forced any of us to take the King's Brand. It was voluntary."

"Yes, my brothers and I had such a great choice." Cudgel's nostrils flared. "Throw our lives away or rot in prison."

"At least you get fresh air," Bearclaw added.

"Not to mention that the king can release us from our pledge," Dominga said. "Can't he?"

"King Hector can do whatever he wants. It's just never been done before," Horace said. "Most of us die first."

"But you get a proper burial and your record wiped clean for fighting for the king," Sticks said.

"A fat lot of good that does our dead brothers," Cudgel said. He threw an arm over Tark. "We are the last ones. We'll never see my mother and father again."

Horace turned toward Cudgel and said, "Well, you shouldn't have been stealing from the king's livestock."

"We were starving. What else were we going to do? We were only children," the round-faced black man replied.

"Beg," Horace answered.

"Griping about the past isn't going to do us any good," Abraham said.

The hireling women slipped in from the galley, waddled over, refilled everyone's coffee, and disappeared back into the galley.

"Those campaigns were too big. A baker's dozen should work out better. Maybe we wouldn't have lost so many if we hadn't taken too many to begin with."

"It was your idea," Vern said with a stupefied look. "And what's a baker's dozen?"

"Thirteen. It means thirteen." He flipped his hand. "Listen, we are going to load up, take one small wagon, and head for the hills. There is no other choice that we have. Any questions?"

Cudgel lifted his hand. "We never go on a mission without at least one mystic. Who is going to care for our wounds and cast fire against our enemies?"

"You can let the dogs lick your wounds," Vern said.

"At least they'd like mine. They'd never touch yours," Cudgel fired back.

Vern rolled his swollen eyes.

"I can handle the wounds, mostly," Iris said.

Cudgel snorted.

"Who did we use before?" Abraham asked.

Sticks sat straight up.

Cudgel's eyes turned as white as the moon as he slammed both hands on the table. "Elgan did." He slapped his hands on the table again. He stepped over the bench as Tark did too. He stuck a finger at Abraham. "You might be the Captain, but there is something very wrong with you. I don't care if you slay me." The brothers stormed across the room, punched the double doors open, and exited with the door slamming behind them.

Abraham felt bad but remained poised. He wasn't going to remember everything. Mistakes would be made. He'd have to live or die with them. But this was what he had to do if he needed to find a way home. "Any other questions?"

No one said a word.

"Let's get ready then. Come on, Sticks."

CHAPTER 52

On separate horses, Abraham and Sticks rode to Burgess. The king's city was surrounded by miles of sprawling countryside and white cottages with light-blue roofs. Several stone-paved roads led into the city, miles away. On the way in, they passed plenty of travelers coming and going on foot, on horseback, or on wagons. The city itself was far vaster than his view from the House of Steel's high walls. Hundreds of buildings, made with stone and mortar, stood over fifty feet tall. He also saw great cathedrals with massive archway entrances and stadiums for entertainment and contests. The storefronts showed off colorful wreaths and decorations on their doors. Goods were enticingly displayed in the windows. Hard boots walked over the wooden porches. Old men and women were seated on benches outside. The city was laid out like a small fantasy version of Pittsburgh, with a constant sea breeze that stirred free-flowing hair.

Most of the people wore robes of different fashions and fine linens. Many men wore long shirts and trousers. Feet were shod with either boots or sandals. Barefoot children raced through the streets. Everything appeared orderly, well laid out, and splendid, except for the bloodstained gallows set up at the entrance to every quadrant.

One block ahead, crows and pigeons fought on the gallows deck, where criminals, treasonous men and women, were hanged. Two soldiers wearing steel cap helms and leather armor and carrying spears and swords on their hips guarded the gallows. The gallows had two nooses strung up and one guillotine stained black from dried blood. The nooses swung in the wind. The gruesome structure's posts and beams creaked against the ocean breeze.

Two men still hung in the nooses. They wore no hoods, tongues hanging from their mouths. Abraham and Sticks rode by, watching crows pick at the flesh. The rank-smelling sourness of rotting flesh filtered through the air. The soldiers were working their way up the steps. They lowered the dead bodies, loosened the nooses, and tossed them over the side into a wagon.

"That's probably going to be me if I don't bring that egg back," Abraham said.

He hadn't spoken since they'd left. Neither had Sticks.

Crinkling her nose, she asked, "Why are we here?"

"I don't know. I just wanted to get away from the others. I thought that coming here might refresh my memories."

"Is it?"

"Well, I know where I'm going, at least." He looked back at the gallows they'd just passed. "The people don't seem very fazed by the killings."

"Their hearts only harden against the king—not all, just most," she said.

A pair of long-faced women wearing black robes walked right out in front of their horses. The one on the right held up two fingers, wiggled them, and asked, "Death to the king, or life to the king?"

"Death to you if you don't get your wrinkled ass out of my way." Sticks reared up her horse.

The women dashed across the street and vanished into a small cathedral entrance.

"That was spooky," he said.

"They are probably members of the Sect. They control everything in Burgess but without saying so."

"Yes, so they work for Leodor?"

"Or Leodor works for them. No one knows. None of them ever admit to anything though they claim to support the king. I don't think a one of them would ever take the King's Brand, though."

They traveled from one side of Burgess to the other, where the road led out toward the sea. Levees, docks, wharfs, and boats of all kinds could be seen all the way up the shoreline. Some men fished from piers, while others hauled nets out of small boats. Abraham led them down to the beach, away from the crowds. The horses made their way down onto the wet sand. Surges of foaming green waves crashed over their hooves.

"What's on your mind?" Sticks asked.

"I needed to clear my head. Beaches are pretty popular for doing that where I come from." He breathed deeply through his nostrils and exhaled. "I think that's the first real deep breath I've had since I've been here. I did have a good sleep, though."

"I bet you did."

"Oh, the triplets. Well, nothing happened in there—this time, anyway." He laughed and made a sheepish smile. "Something must really be wrong with me to miss out on that kind of opportunity when this world is not real."

"You didn't tussle with them?"

"Did you hear any tusslings?"

"No. I wasn't listening, but usually, we can hear it. Hmm."

Staring out at the distant fishing boats, he said, "Okay, before I lead us into the jaws of death, I need to make sure I understand my men and women. I'm pretty hazy on all of our history."

"Me and Dominga worked our way up. Dominga's new and picked by, well, the other you. I came on because, well, I was on the run and had no place to go. You found me during recruiting Red Tunics. That was years ago. Horace—"

"No, don't tell me anymore. Horace, Bearclaw, and Vern were all knights like me." His eyes widened. "Ah crap, Prospero and Apollo are Guardians too, aren't they?"

"Yes."

"Oh man, when I lost my head, well, not me, but Ruger, they followed. They were to be punished the same as me. They weren't the only ones. So many others died." He leaned forward and patted his black horse's neck. "I recruited Cudgel and his brothers out of prison. They were young, barely men. Tark, Levi, and…" He squinted. "William were their names."

She nodded.

"And half of them died. Man, that hurts me. Do you know how many have died under my leadership?"

"One hundred and seventy-five Henchmen and retainers. Most of them retainers."

"You know this?"

"You used to keep a ledger. Now I keep it since you stopped doing it."

"And I've been doing this, how long, seven or eight years?"

"That's about right. I came on five years ago. I've been a Henchman for over three."

He shook his head. "Why would anyone volunteer to do this?"

She reached into her saddlebag, fished out two apples, and fed one to her horse. "It's a better life than farming or living in a prison. It's a chance for some nobody to serve the cause of the king. Not everyone can be one of the king's soldiers. Not everyone can find a place to work, either. It's a chance for status with promise of adventure, even treasure."

"I guess we are all a bunch of desperados in one way or another, I suppose." He opened his hands and caught the apple she tossed him. "It's no wonder we can't win if we are no more than a bunch of thieves and criminals."

"In the past, you brought the best out of all of us. We would fight hard for you, trust you before the change," she said. "They liked the old you. Besides, you used to say that everyone is a criminal in one way or another. Some get caught, and some don't."

He smiled. "I said that?"

"Years ago."

CHAPTER 53

ON THE SHORELINE, BELOW THE cliffs that rose up to the House of Steel, Abraham gathered the Henchmen. They were a formidable bunch, wearing black tunics over the chain-mail armor. All of them rode on horseback. The retainers, Twila and two young men, drove a two-team horse and wagon loaded with supplies. They also had three pack mules and five extra horses. The group looked as though they were ready for anything.

The King's Guardians, led by Lewis, approached from the south. Viceroy Leodor rode at his side. A dozen knights in full plate armor rode behind them. The sun shone on their lion-faced helmets. The lion's mane plumes billowed against the ocean breeze.

Abraham leaned over his saddle horn. Horace and Sticks were on either side of him. "You might want to make yourself scarce. You know how cavalier Lewis is."

"Aye, Captain," Horace said.

Lewis brought the Guardians to a halt with a raised fist. He and Leodor separated from the group and trotted up to Abraham. With the sun shining in his face, Lewis said, "It's a beautiful day to begin a dreadful expedition. What a shame I can't be joining you."

"Seeing how I'm trying to save the queen, you might want to give me your blessing," Abraham said.

Lewis reached over and pushed Leodor's shoulder. "That's what the viceroy is for. Go ahead, Leodor. Give him the fool's blessing."

Leodor frowned. From underneath his beige robes, he removed a scroll. "Ruger or, well, what do you want to be called?"

"Let's keep it simple and stick with Ruger," Abraham said.

"Yes, yes." Leodor licked his lips and handed Ruger a scroll. "That is the same information that I gave to the other expeditions. There is a history about the fenix and the names of peoples that have claimed to have seen it. Many people still worship the fenix but will guard its secret well. I cannot say if there is any truth to what is on that scroll or not. But there is a grain of truth in every lie and legend. Perhaps the elders will be with you. We will pray long life for the queen."

"Long live the queen," Ruger said. He tucked the scroll in his saddle and looked at Lewis. "Is there anything else? I'm ready to partake in this dreadful journey."

Lewis gazed behind him. "You don't boast very many. Is that because you led them all to their deaths?"

"No," Ruger said casually. "Some of them deserted."

Lewis laughed. "Those must have been the smart ones."

"So, what load of dragon dung did you put on that scroll?" Lewis asked Leodor. Both men remained on their horses, watching Ruger lead his company up the shore. "I hope you at least gave them a nibble."

"I gave them enough information to keep them busy," the clammy Leodor said. "And I'm certain that the result will be the same as the other two campaigns. Failure."

"It's a shame that you can't find a cure for Queen Clarann. She is a good woman. I like her."

"Sadly, some things cannot be cured. I fear that there is little hope for your stepmother. And I like her too." Leodor shifted in his saddle. "I really hate riding these things. They are so uncomfortable." He eyed the Henchmen. "I'm glad I'm not them. I'm not sure how they do it, how any of you do it. All of that armor must be very uncomfortable."

"You wouldn't say that if someone came at you with a sword. My chain and plate has saved me countless times." Lewis leaned over his saddle horn, his eyes intent on the campaign. "Is there any truth to the fenix and the powers of the yolk in the egg?"

"It is written. But proven… That's another thing."

"Tell me more about it."

"They histories say that the fenix is the spawn of the Elders, a truly magnificent and powerful creature. The images show part dragon and part monster, a great head and slavering jaws that can consume entire people. If one were to find it, we would not know. They would not survive the encounter. I think this will be Ruger's final journey."

"I don't know," Lewis said. "Sometimes I think the Elder of Luck is by his side. Even with eyes and ears on the inside, he keeps coming back. His last personality, well, that was manageable, but this one, this Abraham that speaks in his body now…" He shook his head. "He has an edge in his voice."

"I only heard desperation, my prince. He's still a far cry from the true Ruger that we know." Leodor jumped in his saddle as a seabird soared right over his head. "Bloody things. Why do they pester me so?" He composed himself, but his eyes searched the skies. "Besides, now that Ruger has lost his station and you have filled it, it becomes easier to fulfill the Underlord's demands. It's what you wanted, wasn't it?"

Lewis rubbed his hands together. "Yes. We should meet with the Underlord, shouldn't we?"

"Agreed. I will arrange it." Leodor cast a backward glance. "You'll have to separate yourself from the Guardians for a time."

"I know. That won't be a problem." The Henchmen faded into the shoreline. "I'll be curious what the Underlord has to say about this recent change in Ruger. The entire idea of different personalities taking over men's bodies is unsettling. Could such a thing happen to me?"

"I don't even think that the Underlord knows. But I sense change in the air. These possessed people are a sign of it." Leodor grabbed his reins in his soft hands. "And the portals that Ruger mentioned. That's another part in the puzzle. What unholy terror will come out of them next?"

"Humph." Lewis turned his horse around. "Holy or unholy, as long as it doesn't come after me, I don't care."

CHAPTER 54

THREE DAYS OF RIDING PASSED before the Henchmen arrived at what the locals called Titanuus's Crotch. They rode along the shoreline where they could and took the roads that snaked around the seashore cities of Southern Tiotan. At the moment, Southern Tiotan and Kingsland did not war with one another, but tensions were high. The Henchmen kept moving, camping outside the small towns that ran along the coast. Now they stood on the shores of Titanuus's Crotch, which was little more than a barren wasteland against the sea.

Abraham swayed side to side in his saddle. For the last several miles of riding, he'd kept his eyes fixed on the great mountain range called Titanuus's Spine. The mountains were leagues wide, and gargantuan hilltops rose beyond the height of the clouds.

Oh my.

This wasn't the first time he'd seen mountains like this. In West Virginia, hills were everywhere, but they weren't even above sea level. Titanuus's Spine was more like the Colorado Rockies, perhaps much bigger and longer. It reminded him of something else. When he was a teenager, his father had been stationed in Hawaii, and Abraham took a trip to Maui. He and his friends took a mountain-biking trip up to the top of a massive volcano called Haleakala. The mountain rose over seven thousand feet in height, where a great crater waited in the middle. They rode their bikes down mountains and back through the clouds that waited four thousand feet below. They didn't stop screaming down the road until it bottomed out at sea level. Acres of pineapple fields greeted them on the journey home.

Titanuus's Spine appeared to be very much like that except its peaks were jagged and dreadful.

Abraham snorted in a deep breath and slowly let it out. "This sucks."

Evening started to fall. The Henchmen's faces were already weary. No one had said a word in three days, hardly. Even the chatter by the campfire had been muted, as if all of them were on a long, quiet march to death row.

"Orders, Captain?" Horace said.

"Let's make camp."

"Aye."

Once that camp was set, Abraham rounded up the company by the campfire. "It's time for a little fellowship by the fireside," he said.

The Henchmen gathered. Some stood, while others sat. As always, Horace and Sticks remained to his right and left. "That includes you Red Tunics, too."

The Red Tunics, the pie- and dimple-faced Twila, along with the other two young gangly men, slunk over. None of them ever spoke to the Henchmen, aside from acknowledging orders.

He held up the scroll that Leodor had given him. "I'm going to keep it simple. We're going to try and retrace the steps of the other campaign. Certainly, that large of a group won't be that hard to follow. And according to this writing, we'll need to ask the people that reside along the base of the Spine if they know anything about the fenix." He opened the scroll and stared at it. "Uh, it appears that there are several tribes, or villages, that worship it. And I don't think they would worship something that they haven't seen." He thought about his own faith. "No, wait, I take that back. Anyway, that's the plan. But I'm open to suggestions."

No one said a word.

"Come on. I know that at least one of you has something to say." He rocked back and forth on his heels. He patted the pommel of Black Bane. "Someone say something."

"Er… well, Captain," Apollo said in a very gravelly voice. He scratched his scruffy beard. "Seeing how we are about to journey into the mountains and face a certain death, would it be possible to unwind one last time? You know, wet our tongues on some rum and ale."

"You want to go on a bender?"

"No, I want to get drunk and maybe cozy one last night with a trollop." Apollo scanned the women. "Seeing how all of these prudes are spoken for."

Iris lifted her hand. "I'm not spoken for, but I wouldn't sleep with you for a thousand shards of silver."

Twila perked up. "I would." She shrank back down under the stares of the Henchmen. "Sorry."

"Is this where the group stands?" Abraham asked. "You want a night of carousing? Huh." He used a serious tone. "Do you?"

"I do," Vern said after a brief silence. "And we haven't had a break since our last journey. We came back with our arses in hand and were tossed in Baracha." He touched his black-and-blue nose. "Then you show up all smiles. So, yes, I would like to go on a *bender*, as you say."

"We need to have our wits about us. We can't traverse the Spine hungover and drunk. We need to be sharp," Abraham said. "With our luck, we're bound to be in a fight before we know it."

"I fight better drunk," Apollo said.

"Aye, me too," Prospero agreed.

"Great, I have team Nick Nolte on my side. Anyone else?" he asked.

Tark lifted his hand. So did Cudgel, Vern, and Dominga.

"Oh, I see what the problem is," Abraham said sarcastically. "We've been failing all of these missions because we've been stone-cold sober." He looked at Horace. The beefy man shrugged. "We all know better than that. Besides, we're at the mountain's bottom. There's nowhere to go and get your freak on. Sorry, Apollo."

Vern took the toothpick out of his mouth and said, "We aren't far from Hackles, Captain."

"Hackles?"

Horace whispered in his ear. "It's one of the last stops at the base of the Spine. We've been there some time ago. Perhaps half a league up the shoreline. We'll still be on course before we enter the mountains."

Abraham took a long, hard look into the tired eyes of his command. Some held his gaze. The others looked away. He'd seen faces like that before in the locker room after a losing streak. Sometimes, a team played hard, but it wasn't working. Sometimes, people just tried too hard, and it wasn't happening. Everyone was stiff and rigid. They needed a break. They needed to loosen up. They needed one last night on the town.

"Well, what are you waiting for? Get this camp broken down. We're going to Hackles!"

The Henchmen, one and all, let out a roar.

CHAPTER 55

HACKLES WAS A SHABBY SEAPORT city where maybe ten thousand inhabitants thrived. According to local legends, it was the place where Titanuus had dumped his bowels when he died. The inky green seawaters were as foul as a dead sea. It was nothing compared to Swain in Kingsport. The rickety wooden buildings bowed and swayed against the wind. The floorboards on the porches creaked underfoot. Fishermen bandied about, singing songs about the sea, with jugs of wine hooked in their fingers. Others shuffled along, groaning about stiff backs and griping about the big fish they'd missed that day. The docks were small, and so were the vessels. The foamy seawater that beat against the rocks on the shore smelled strongly of salt and seaweed. Hackles was a rotten town.

The Henchmen loved it.

The tavern's regulars were a bunch of fishermen, mostly older, with thick beards and long-stemmed pipes. They grumbled and hunkered down over their drinks. Many eyes widened at the sight of the Henchmen, who came in with full armor and steel on their hips. Hackles wasn't much of a town. It was a place where many came for solitude, but it provided a little excitement from time to time when strangers passed through.

Within the hour, the Henchmen had nestled in. Apollo and Prospero practically dove into the first tavern they came across and vanished inside. The high-pitched squeals of women erupted from inside. Cudgel and Tark were the next to enter, followed by Bearclaw and Vern. By the time Abraham made it inside, all the men had giggling women sitting on their laps or hanging on their arms. The women's scant clothing revealed a lot of paint coating their nubile bodies. The body paint sparkled in the candlelight. The serving women brought tankards of ale and goblets made of steel. Apollo and Prospero opened their mouths wide, the women poured, and they guzzled it down.

Abraham took his seat at a corner table. Horace joined him.

Watching Apollo and Prospero, Abraham said, "And to think that they were Guardians once. Weren't they beholden to a higher standard?"

"We aren't Guardians anymore," Horace said as a curvy waitress set down two tankards of ale on the table. He gave her a nod and a wink and watched the sway of her generous hips when she walked away. "But even Knights celebrate victory, the same as others do. Including me. You remember that, don't you?"

"I think you've known for a long time that I'm not the same Ruger that you've always known," Abraham said.

Horace guzzled his beer. "Ah! What do you mean, Captain?"

"My strange behavior. Mannerisms. You know that I'm different."

Horace buried his chubby cheeks behind his mug and shrugged.

Ruger pressed the issue. "You think I'm crazy, don't you? And the men do too, don't they?"

"It doesn't matter what we think. You are the Captain." Horace set his goblet down and wiped his forearm across his mouth. "And I advise the Captain not to talk like this."

Abraham took a long drink of the warm and bitter ale. "This isn't very good. It tastes like boiled bark." He set it aside. "Horace, look at me. We have to talk this out. You and I were close once, right?"

Horace's neck rolled a little. "Aye, Captain. We all were, before the disgrace. We are loyal to you and the crown." He showed his intense eyes. "It doesn't matter who is in charge inside that body. We gave our word. We'll follow you to the depths of the ocean. Our word is honor. We don't need a brand to keep it."

Abraham rested his forearms on the table. "Even if I'm possessed?"

"Don't say that. I don't know what you are, but at least you have your spine back." He crossed his arms over his chest. "No pun intended, as you would say."

Ruger smiled. "I said that? When?"

"Not so long ago. Many times. You speak funny words time to time."

"Well, at least you are used to it."

Abraham thought he might talk more about who he really was but opted not to. The Henchmen were devoted men of their word. He was convinced that they would keep it.

"So that waitress gave you an approving look. Are you going to go for it?"

"Go for what?"

Abraham nudged the man. "Bed the woman. Copulate."

Horace's eyes were attached to Iris, who was sitting at the bar with Sticks and Dominga. They were all having a laugh. "No."

"You like Iris, don't you?"

Horace opened a hand and flung it outward. "What's not to like? She's a ravishing sight. I like the way the red in those auburn locks comes out in the sunlight. Her homely smile makes my heart sing."

"You should go talk to her."

Horace shook his head. "No. I've tried that. I've stopped that. She's a stubborn mule, that one."

"Have you ever tried to make her jealous?"

"What do you mean?"

Abraham reached out and grabbed a waitress passing by. She was the same one that had served them. He swung her around onto Horace's lap. He put a pair of silver shards in her hand. "Listen, gorgeous, you stay on his lap and make that woman jealous."

The curvy woman threw her arms over Horace's shoulders, hugged him tightly, and said, "My pleasure!"

"Captain! Captain!" Horace said. The waitress shushed him with a full kiss right on the lips.

Abraham grabbed his ale and giggled. If what was happening wasn't real, then he might as well have some fun with it. He drank. *I just wish the ale tasted better.* He left the table and crossed the floor. The tavern had two bars, one on the sea side and the other on the side of the Spine. Both bars offered large outdoor porches, making an excellent view of the Spine and the choppy waters in the Bay of Elders. He moved to the mountain side and took a seat on a stool, at the loneliest corner of the bar.

The Spine was nothing but black rock mountains jutting upward toward a dark-blue sky filled with faint, twinkling stars. He saw no sign of constellations like the Big Dipper, Draco, Orion, or even a North Star to go by. He sipped his brew. *This is not my world. Where in the heck am I?*

Sticks joined him. "Nice night."

He answered with his gaze fixed on the skies. "Yeah."

"So, will I be joining you tonight?" She put her hand on his arm. "It might be the last chance we have to enjoy ourselves, too."

He dropped his eyes to hers. Sticks had eyes as hard as stone, but a softer side of the woman waited deep inside. She was right. That night might have been his last time to have fun. He wondered if this was what it felt like before a soldier went to war, not knowing whether or not they would come back. He liked her. He didn't want to hurt her either. He took her hand and said, "Yeah."

She rose up on her toes and leaned in for a kiss.

A commotion of high-pitched voices came from the sea side of the tavern. The scuttle of boots rushed toward new screams.

Ruger and Sticks moved in behind a pack of angry fishermen, who started shouting obscenities. Another group climbed up over the porch railing. They were men and women, dripping wet from head to toe. Ruger got his first good look at the invaders. They were fish-like people with slanted black eyes, covered in skin like fish scales from head to toe.

"Myrmidons," Sticks said.

CHAPTER 56

THE MYRMIDONS CLIMBED OVER THE railing one by one. Water slipped down their sleek bodies, making puddles on the plank floor. They walked like men, with green-silver scales and black fins for ears on their sleek heads. Their eyes were black, with large white pupils in the middles. Not a strand of hair was on any of them. They were all scaled, bald, and sleek. They wore strands of seaweed for dress and carried no weapons but had very long black fingernails and sharp, spiny ridges on their backs. They spread out into the tavern, bumping into everyone they passed.

"Watch it, fish-face," Cudgel said right after an oily-scaled myrmidon jostled his table and knocked over his tankard.

Abraham dropped his hand to his sword. "What is it about these seaside taverns?" he asked Sticks. "Every time I enter one, trouble comes."

"The myrmidons are nothing but trouble." She hooked her arm in his. "They'll go away. Just ignore them before they do."

"Are you sure?"

"That's what you always told us."

Abraham rubbed his eyes. He—or rather, Ruger—had recollections about them. The myrmidons were an ancient race of seafaring people, small in number, who kept to themselves in the caves along the seashore and the smaller islands. They were great swimmers and fishermen and still mostly men despite their amphibian appearance.

"I guess so," he said. "I just hope our crew doesn't get all riled up over them."

Very quickly, the myrmidons made their presence known to everyone in the tavern. They dragged away chairs and tables, creating their own spots. They kicked back, swung their legs on the tabletops, and leaned backward on two chair legs. The waitresses were pawed at and victim to bubbly-voiced catcalls.

A myrmidon who stood seven feet tall lumbered through the tavern. His large hands had webbing between the fingers, and he wore many large gold chains over his neck like a gangster. His long arm was hooked over a female myrmidon. She was a beautiful and sensual thing with a necklace of violet pearls that dangled down between her plunging seaweed neckline. She winked at Abraham. The male stopped and looked at Ruger. The small black fins above his earholes bent downward.

In a bubbly voice, he said, "Keep your eyes from my lady if you want to keep them." He showed his hand, which could cover Ruger's entire face. The black claws on the tips of his fingers extended another foot.

Abraham sneered and said, "Go back to your lagoon, ya goon."

The spiny ridges on the myrmidon's back flexed up and down like dominoes and rattled like a snake's tail. He pointed a quill-like fingernail at Abraham's eyeball. He waved it back and forth. "No, no, no, no. Don't taunt Flexor. It will be your doom." He pulled his hand back, and the fingernail retracted. Flexor and his woman strode to the bar and sat down.

"Flexor. What the heck kind of name is that?" Abraham said. "Sounds like a rubber toy or something."

"If we leave them alone, they'll leave us alone," Sticks said. "Let's take a walk down on the shore since the night is so nice."

"All right," he said.

He scanned the room. Despite the myrmidons' loud voices and raucous mannerisms, the Henchmen seemed to be fitting in just fine.

"Just let me have a word with the men."

Bearclaw and Vern were playing cards at a table with two women between them. Vern rolled his toothpick from side to side. Bearclaw studied his cards and didn't bat an eye.

Abraham leaned over Bearclaw's shoulder and said, "We have bigger fish to fry. See to it that our men don't get into any trouble."

Bearclaw nodded. "If the fish men don't bother me, I won't bother them."

"Make sure they don't bother you." He looked at Vern. "Or you."

"Can I bother them?" a pleasant-looking waitress with flaxen curls asked. She scooted beside Vern with both hands under the table, massaging Vern's thigh. Her green eyes were smiling at Abraham. "We don't get many brawny men in these parts."

"Just keep them happy." Abraham moved over to Horace.

The waitress Abraham had put on Horace's lap was sitting in a chair beside the husky warrior with her elbows on the table and chin on her hands. Horace was frowning like a bearded bullfrog.

"He's not very playful," she said. "Can I use this silver for something else?"

He shooed her away. "Sure. What's the matter, Horace?"

He followed his stare. Across the room, a myrmidon appeared to be getting flirty with Iris. The big country-girl smile on her face suggested she was enjoying it.

"Ah. Listen, it will pass. For now, make sure the company stays out of trouble." He blocked his view of Iris. "Do you got it? I don't want any steel drawn."

Horace leaned to the right and looked around Abraham. "I got it."

He slid through the room and had to change course because a pair of myrmidons swung their legs across the gap between the tables and blocked his path. They made bubbly laughing when he went around them.

He caught up with Sticks and said, "They really are a bunch of annoying jerks, aren't they?"

"Jerks? You mean obnoxious by that, right? Like you used to be?"

"Right," he said.

They made their way down the wooden steps leading to the beach. The beach was covered in seaweed, and the foamy waters stank of strong salt and something like sulfur.

"Ew, this isn't exactly going to be the walk on the beach that I was hoping for," he said.

"Me either, but at least it's with you." She clasped his fingers in hers. "Even if it stinks."

Angry shouts erupted from the tavern. Abraham's head whipped around. A commotion had started in the rickety tavern. He and Sticks raced back up four flights of broken-up stairs. He cleared the final eight steps in an incredible leap and landed on the seaside porch. The Henchmen and myrmidons had collided in a wrathful tide of angry bodies.

CHAPTER 57

INSIDE THE TAVERN, ALL THE local fisherman had scattered. The quavering floor of the tavern became a battle royale, with the men with skin against the men with fins.

Horace had the myrmidon who had flirted with Iris hoisted over his head and pinned to the ceiling.

Tark punched a fish man in the face. Cudgel had a chair shattered on his back.

Bearclaw wrestled across the floor with two myrmidons at once.

Sticks ran down the length of the bar and kicked a myrmidon in the face.

A wine bottle sailed over Abraham's ducking head. "We need to break it up," he said as he prowled into the tavern. No weapons were drawn. It was skin and brawn locked up against muscles and scales. Fists collided with teeth. Sharp talons dug into flesh.

Horace let out an eardrum-shattering yelp. He dropped the myrmidon and backed into the wall. Black quills were stuck in his face, as if he'd been attacked by a porcupine. His sausage fingers started to pluck them out.

Iris rushed up to Horace and shouted, "Leave them alone!" She swung her metal goblet into an attacking myrmidon's chin. He hopped away from her.

Abraham battled into the fray with his fists flying. He landed an uppercut in a myrmidon's gut, which doubled the fish man over. From out of nowhere, a table crashed down on top of his back and drove him to his knees. He scurried out from underneath it and saw Flexor. The tallest myrmidon's talons had extended on all fingers, jutting out over a foot long. He clacked his sharp little piranha teeth together. Abraham started to draw.

"No blades, Captain!" Bearclaw said. He straddled a fish man and punched him in the face. "Let these little guppies fight with their fingernails if they want to." He grabbed the man by his seaweed collar, yanked him up, and headbutted him.

Abraham locked his sword back inside its sheath. He had no idea how good he was at hand-to-hand fighting, but he was about to find out. He rose and faced off against Flexor, lifting his fists. "All right, creature from the smelly lagoon, come on over, and I'll make clam chowder out of you."

Flexor spread his arms out and grinned. His arms looked impossibly long with the super-long fingernails. He slowly walked forward, saying, "I will peel you out of that armor and serve you to my sharks for dinner." He lunged in and swiped.

Abraham ducked, stepped into Flexor, wrapped the man in a bear hug, and slammed him down on the floor. The myrmidon tried to claw his way out of his grip. He rabbit punched the myrmidon in the back of the head.

The myrmidon thrashed on the floor and screamed with a high-pitched sound. "Reeeeeeeeeeee! Reeeeeeeeee! Reeeeeeeeeee!"

"Gah!" Abraham rolled off Flexor's back and stuck his fingers in his ears. "Geez, what is that?" He kicked Flexor.

The lanky myrmidon leader scrambled to his feet as the earsplitting screeching continued to gush from his lips. He waved his arm, and the myrmidons, one and all, slipped out of the tavern and over the porch rails and dashed down toward the sea. Flexor and his woman were the last to go. They vanished over the railing and disappeared. The screeching stopped.

The Henchmen slowly made their way back to their feet, shaking their heads.

"By the Elders, I didn't know that they could do that," Horace said. He was sitting on a barstool, letting Iris pluck the quills out of his face. "Dirty fighters. Cowardly. All of them."

Abraham and Sticks turned a table over and put it back on its legs. Then he pulled up a chair and rolled his jaw, trying to shake the ringing from his ears.

He sat down. "What happened?"

"Horace started it," Vern said. "He saw Iris getting cozy with that smooth-talking myrmidon and charged over there like a maddened bull."

"I did not!" Horace said.

"You did too," Iris said with a smile. She plucked a needle out from under his eye.

Horace's voice softened. "All I did was march over to have a word. That's when another one of those fish-eyed fools tripped me."

"Then Dominga slung her goblet at the fish-face hooked on Iris's arm," Vern added as he rubbed his swollen jaw. "Ol' Fish Eyes's scales turned red. That's when Horace drug his arse up off the floor and plowed into him."

"You didn't miss a beat, did you?" Abraham said to Vern.

Vern shrugged. "It was going to be a brawl. Everyone knew it the moment that they walked in, except you."

The Henchmen helped the waitresses set up the toppled chairs and tables. Prospero and Apollo lay on the floor, knocked out or passed out, snoring. Cudgel and Tark dragged them across the floor and leaned them in a corner. Within minutes, the deteriorating tavern was back under normal operation. The fishermen who had scattered returned. The place looked as if nothing had happened, aside from some scrapes, bruises, and the dark black heads that dotted Horace's puffy face.

Iris rubbed salve into Horace's meaty jaws. "You didn't have to go to such extremes for me."

"Well… I do."

She smiled warmly.

The Henchmen carried on for a couple more hours until Cudgel blurted out, "I've been pilfered!"

Cudgel's purse wasn't the only one missing. So was Bearclaw's, Vern's, Prospero's, Apollo's and Dominga's. Even Abraham's was missing.

"I think we've been duped," Sticks said.

The young Red Tunic, Twila, burst through the tavern doors. Drenched in sweat, her panicked stare searched the room until she found Ruger. "The horses! The wagon! They're gone!"

CHAPTER 58

On foot, the Henchmen took off after the thieves who had stolen their horses and wagons. It took coercion, but the tavern keeper and the waitresses had finally spilled their guts. As it turned out, they were in cahoots with the myrmidons, and not just them, either. They were part of a larger local network of brigands that operated on the shores of Titanuus's Crotch, called the Shell. The brawl was just a part of the bigger play. The Henchmen had been duped by thugs and thieves.

Abraham ground his teeth as they walked. Losing their gear was one thing. It was another to lose Jake's backpack. That was the only thing keeping him attached to home. Now, it was gone, and with that gone, he feared losing the lone connection that was a reminder of his greater purpose.

Vern walked up beside him and asked, "So, we can still speak freely?"

"Yes."

"Well done, Captain. We are off to the same lousy start as always." Vern shook his head and marched on.

According to the taverner, the Shell's hideout wasn't a secret. It was a small stone fort in the rocks that overlooked the sea line. It had been built centuries before, during the Coastal Wars, where Hancha and Tiotan fought for the territory. Seeing the land was barren and futile, both kingdoms abandoned the quest and left it to rot.

They walked all night, following the wagon-wheel tracks and hoofprints. They could do without the wagon, but the horses were another matter. They needed them, not to mention their rations. After a few hours of walking, Dominga and Tark, who'd been scouting ahead, returned.

Dominga shone with sweat in the moonlight. She said, "We've spotted the Shell."

The Shell was bigger than Ruger's stronghold, but not by much. It was nothing more than a rectangular fort with a three-story-high outer wall with battlements. A jetty of huge rocks made a natural dock that ran up to the portcullis entrance to the fort. Several small craft and barges were docked against the strand of land. No flags or banners flapped in the wind above the fort walls. The lonely-looking place was dim and quiet.

With the others, Abraham spied the fort from their position on the beach. The portcullis door was open. Several rogues sauntered in and out. Many of them stood along the dock and smoked.

"Huh," Gabe said.

"They don't appear to be worried about any pursuers," Sticks said. "Either the Shell has guts, or they are really stupid."

Horace grunted. "Look at their location. Tucked in those rocks, they could hold off an entire army for weeks if they needed to."

"Well, we aren't an army, and we don't have weeks," Abraham said. "But we have to get our gear back. The question is, how do we do that?"

"We kill 'em," Horace said.

"Yes, we kill them," Cudgel added.

"If they weren't smart enough to steal our blades, I agree, we kill them," Vern added.

"Aye, and they are thieves. They deserve death as punishment," Bearclaw stated.

"Well, we aren't here to start a war with the Shell," Abraham said.

"It's not uncommon for the rogues to sell goods back to the ones they were stolen from," Dominga offered.

All eyes turned to her.

"What? I know about these things. The same things happen in Kingsland. I used to be the eyes for a guild house before I got caught up doing this."

"Listen, darlin', we can't buy back something that was stolen from us with money we don't have," Vern said, "though I like the way you are thinking."

Abraham rubbed the scruff building on his face. "This sucks. But I think, talking to them, we'll fare better than fighting them. If Dominga's right and they have open doors for desperate customers, perhaps we can strike a deal with them."

"Let's just kill them," Apollo suggested. Prospero nodded and yawned. "Their ilk has it coming."

"We don't even know how many they have in there. And if we charge in there, they'll tuck their head back inside their shell." He stood. "I'm going in… alone."

"What about us, Captain?" Horace said.

"Just wait outside. If I don't come back out within a few hours, well, feel free to come looking for me. My guess is that in the worst case, I'll return with my tail tucked between my legs."

Iris looked at his behind. "But you don't have a tail. Does he have a tail, Sticks?"

"No, that's not what he means. It's an expression," Sticks said. "But he does have a tail on the front end."

Iris giggled.

"I would like to come with you," Sticks said. "You shouldn't go in there alone. I have some experience with people like this."

Abraham gave it some thought. "Fine. Just us. The rest of you, keep a hundred yards back. And keep your swords in place. I don't want to agitate them. Let's see what Flexor, or whoever is in charge, has to say. I mean it."

"We'll wait, but not forever, Captain," Horace said.

"Good." He looked at Sticks. "Come on."

Together, they made the trek to the Shell's fort. A handful of guards in plain clothing stood between the battlements, pointing crossbows at them. A handful of myrmidons and regular men met them outside the portcullis. Abraham was surprised to see Flexor's woman approach from the inside.

In her bubbling accent, the striking myrmidon looked him up and down and said, "Interesting. You may enter, but you must surrender your weapons."

Abraham unbuckled his sword belt and tossed it to the ground. "As you wish."

Sticks mimicked him.

"I am Kawnee," the lady myrmidon said. She picked up their weapons belts and slung them over her shoulder. "Follow me." She led them inside the fort.

The iron portcullis lowered, making loud squeaks and rattles. It came to a rest on the threshold, sealing them all inside.

CHAPTER 59

INSIDE THE FORT WAS A wooden building that ran from the front to the back. The bottom of the structure was an open-faced barn, with two levels of apartments above it. The apartments had a walkway and railing on the outside. Windows and doors were behind the railing, as on a motel. Surly men and women, in common garb, were spread out on the walkways, casting heavy stares at Ruger and Sticks. All of them were human.

The other side of the fort's courtyard was made up of storehouses residing beneath the parapets. Some had open bays, while others had closed doors. The air smelled of manure and hay. Kawnee led them straight down the middle. On the wall opposite the portcullis, another smaller portcullis waited. A pair of guards, holding spears, blocked the double-door entrance. They were brutes wearing leather armor, with heavy eyebrows, wide faces, and thick lips.

Kawnee waved her hand.

The lazy-eyed brutes stepped aside.

Ruger and Sticks followed Kawnee through the open gate into a smaller fort hidden behind the larger one. Unlike the outer fort, this fort was more of a grand hall with a pitched roof held up by stone archways. Six stone cauldrons of fire burned along the wall and corners. The smoke seeped up through small holes in the corner of the ceilings. The heavy doors closed behind them.

Six rogues, man and myrmidon, were posted on the right and left, armed with swords. At the end of the room were three empty wooden thronelike chairs sitting side by side, ascending from smallest to largest up a dais. Flexor sat tall in the chair in the middle, hands on his knees. But he barely caught Abraham's attention. Instead, the man sitting in the top chair caught his eyes. The man appeared to be in his forties, with short blond hair and a receding hairline. The round-faced man's penetrating eyes were as blue as the sky. He wore a black leather vest with a scarlet red long-sleeved shirt underneath. The buttons on the high-collared shirt were pearl white. The man leaned back with the bottom of one foot propped up in the seat of his chair. He didn't appear to be armed.

In a rich and welcoming voice, the blond man asked, "Who have you brought to me, Kawnee?"

Kawnee bowed her chin and said, "Lord Hawk, these travelers have made an inquiry about some of their belongings that they have lost."

"Interesting. What is that you carry, Kawnee?" Lord Hawk asked. He tilted his head. "Bring it to me."

Kawnee approached the wooden throne and laid Ruger's and Sticks's weapons at Lord Hawk's feet.

"Hand me that sword and take your seat," Lord Hawk said.

Ruger and Sticks exchanged a nervous glance. Lord Hawk slid Black Bane out of the sheath. The blackened steel glimmered in the dim light.

Lord Hawk's piercing eyes slowly ran over the blade from top to bottom. He twisted the blade over and again. His eyes slid over and met Abraham's. "This sword is unique. I like it. Who are you that brings me a gift like this?"

"Gift? Uh, no, my sword is not a gift. It's mine and mine alone," Abraham responded.

"Who are you?" Lord Hawk said in a more menacing tone.

"I am Ruger. This is Sticks."

"I didn't ask who she was. Nevertheless, it is good to meet the both of you. Now, tell me in your own words what brings you to the Shell?"

"Lord Hawk, your men stole a wagonload of our supplies, our purses, and over a dozen horses from us. I want them back."

Lord Hawk sat up suddenly in his chair. He turned to Flexor the myrmidon and asked, "Is this true? Did you rob these weary travelers of their goods?"

Flexor shrugged and said, "They lost them in a wager."

"That's a lie!" Sticks blurted out.

"Whoa, lady, you don't come into my fortress and make accusations," Lord Hawk said. He rested Black Bane on his shoulder. "That could be fatal. And before your tongues slip again, let me remind you that I am the judge and the jury around here." He narrowed his bright eyes at Sticks. "Now, let's back up a moment. You lost a bet with Flexor and his men. Perhaps you were drunk and careless. Believe me, I've lived in this part of the world a long time and met many that have made similar mistakes. It's nothing to be ashamed of. So you wish to buy back your gear? Right?"

Sticks's hands balled up into fists. Her mouth opened wide.

Abraham clamped his hands around her mouth, held her tight, and said, "Something like that, Lord Hawk."

"Ah. A man of reason. A very fit warrior of a man, at that." Lord Hawk sheathed the sword, tossed it onto the ground, and stood. "Tell me, Ruger, what did you have in mind?" he asked, patting a strange object on his right hip. "Make me a deal."

Abraham's eyes dropped. Lord Hawk carried a pistol on his hip.

CHAPTER 60

To say that Abraham was a little freaked out was an understatement. He lifted his eyes and found Lord Hawk's stare on his. He made a straight face and let go of Sticks. She stepped away from him.

Sonuvagun. Keep it together.

He'd gotten only a glimpse of the pistol and gun belt. It wasn't an ideal rig, but rather like one would see in the Old West. Lord Hawk wore a black leather belt, and the pistol, which appeared to be a six-shooter, was holstered in leather.

"Well, Ruger," Lord Hawk said as he stepped down from the dais, his hand remaining on the pistol's grip, "are you going to make an offer for your gear or not?"

"I think it would be a lot easier if you would tell me what you want, and we can negotiate from there."

Lord Hawk nodded. He looked back at Flexor and Kawnee and said, "You see, this is a good businessman. He doesn't come into the Shell and insult us. He wants to make a straight deal." He turned back to Ruger and Sticks. "I like that." He scratched the side of his clean-shaven face. "I'll sell you the wagon, horses, and all of the contents, for one thousand shards of gold."

"I don't have one thousand shards. Let me have your purse," he told Sticks.

With a deepening frown, she handed him her cloth purse.

He dumped the contents into his hand and counted. *It's not real. Have some fun.* "I can offer you five gold shards, fifteen silver, and thirteen copper. But I'll pay the rest back when we return from Alderaan."

"Where is Alderaan?" Lord Hawk said.

"Never mind. Do we have a deal, Lord Hawk?" Abraham said.

Lord Hawk leaned forward on one knee, and from several feet away, he said, "I think you are making light with me by offering a pittance." He rested his hand on the handle of his gun. "I made you a serious offer. You offer me a baron's tithe, and now, I'm insulted."

"I gave you the best offer that I'm able to offer. After all, you stole all of our gear. I think my offer is very generous, considering."

"Ruger, I'm going to counter your offer with another. Two thousand gold shards."

"I don't have that. You know it."

"Well, I guess we can't make a deal then. Goodbye, Ruger and Twigs." He moved back toward his chair.

Abraham moved to retrieve his weapon. The rogues, swords in hand, blocked his path.

"What do you think you are doing?" Lord Hawk said.

"Taking our weapons," he replied.

"No, those aren't your weapons. They are mine. It's the price that you pay for getting out of here alive." Lord Hawk sat down. He flicked his wrist at them. "Begone now."

He and Sticks turned away and walked toward the closed doors.

Under her breath, she said, "Great plan, Captain."

They stood before the doors waiting for them to be opened. It didn't happen. Abraham looked over his shoulder. Lord Hawk, Flexor, Kawnee, and the rest of the rogues all showed knowing smiles. Ruger smiled back. Out of the corner of his mouth he said to Sticks, "Why do I feel like we are about to be fed to the wolves?"

"Because you marched us right into their den," she replied.

"Is something wrong?" Lord Hawk said.

Rubbing the back of his neck, he said, "Uh, yes. The doors aren't opening."

"That's because you have to knock," Lord Hawk said in a suspiciously friendly manner. "Go ahead. Knock three times. Knock hard because my sentries are very hard of hearing."

Abraham rapped his knuckles against the thick wooden doors. Nothing happened. "This is getting worse and worse, isn't it?" he whispered.

Sticks nodded.

He turned around and shrugged. "It didn't work."

"Oh, that's because you forgot to say the magic words," Lord Hawk said. He smiled like a crocodile. "Open… Says… Me."

Abraham's eyes grew as big as saucers. "What?" Before he could move a muscle, the rogues in the corners flicked a handful of pellets at his feet.

The pellets burst open and spewed out a choking inky purple cloud.

Abraham and Sticks broke out in a fit of coughing. The strength in his iron-strong limbs faded, and he hit the ground headfirst.

CHAPTER 61
THE PAST

"Isn't this great?" Abraham asked Jenny and Jake.

They were flying inside a twin-engine Cessna. He was a big guy, and the cockpit was cramped, but a big smile covered his face. He loved to fly.

"What does the altimeter say, Jake?" he asked.

Jake sat in the copilot seat next to him. The light-haired kid wore an Optimus Prime T-shirt. He pointed at the plane's instrument panel and said, "Twenty-two thousand feet. Whoa, that's really high, isn't it?" He looked out his window. "Man, that's so cool. Those clouds look like a bed of cotton you could walk on."

The plane seated eight people, but the only other two on board were Abraham's wife, Jenny, and his best friend, Buddy Parker. They both sat in the next row of seats. Abraham popped a bubble-gum bubble. "Are you two doing all right back there? It's awfully quiet."

"It's just bumpy," Jenny said. The pretty woman wore a white sundress that showed off her tan figure. Her eyes were big. "But I'm getting used to it."

"You will," Abraham said. "And don't worry, this bird is as sound as they come. Hey, Buddy, say something."

"I'll say something. I can't believe that I'm dumb enough to ride in a plane that you are flying. That's what I'm saying." Buddy held his stomach. "How long is this flight going to be, anyway?"

"It's only two and a half hours. We'll land in Charleston before you know it. Just sit back and enjoy the flight. Besides, we have plenty of parachutes."

"Shut up." Buddy was hugging a small pillow. "I should have flown commercial."

"Ah, this is better. No hassles for you at the airport. Now, sit back and prepare for an inflight movie," he said.

"What movie?" Buddy asked.

Jake perked up. "We get to watch a movie?"

"That's right. We're gonna watch Buddy's favorite: *Major League*, starring Charlie Sheen."

Buddy grinned. "Will you shut up and just land this thing? Man, I can't believe I have to jet from Florida back to Pittsburgh for an autograph session."

"And my dad's birthday party."

"Yeah, that too."

"Where did you say it was?" Buddy asked.

"Hinton. Well, Dad's driving in from Hinton to meet us in Charleston. He doesn't know about this birthday present, so I can't wait to see his eyes when we show it to him." Abraham was thrilled to death to buy his dad a plane. His father, Captain Frank Jenkins, was a highly decorated war hero in Vietnam, who flew F-4 Phantoms. He became an instructor after he retired and taught Abraham to fly as soon as he was able. "Man, he's going to be thrilled."

"Let's just hope that he doesn't think that you overdid it, honey," Jenny said. "You know he doesn't like it when you spend money on him."

"That's why I'm going to tell him that it was your idea."

"Oh no, you won't!" She reached up and tickled Abraham.

He jumped in his seat. "Okay, okay, I won't. Just don't tickle me while I'm flying. I'll pee myself!"

Jake giggled. "You said *pee*."

"So, what's the plan, again?" Buddy asked. He leaned back in his chair and closed his eyes. "We land in Charleston, then what?"

"Well, we land, see Dad, give him his present, then I'm pretty sure that he'll want to fly his new toy. He takes us to Pittsburgh for the autograph session. We'll fly up, back, spend the night in Hinton for the party, and take a commercial flight back to Florida just in time to resume training camp."

"Man, being famous gets crazy," Buddy said.

"It's going to get crazier after we win the pennant. You can count on it," Abraham said.

"The Pirates are going to win the World Series," Jake said. "I can feel it!"

"That's just what I'll need. Abraham and Buddy with even bigger egos," Jenny said.

Abraham and Buddy chuckled. "You know it," Buddy said. "I'm gonna beat my best batting average and crack out over fifty home runs. It's going to be sweet."

"You know it," Abraham said. He looked over at his wiry, tawny-headed son. "So, do you think Grandpa Frank is going to like his present?"

"He'll love it! If he doesn't, I'll take it," Jake said.

"You know, I was about your age when Grandpa started taking me flying. He made sure that I got my pilot's license, too." He dropped his headphones down on his neck. "He used to say, 'You never know when you'll need to fly a plane.' So do you want to learn to fly?"

"You bet I do?" Jake said.

"Well, climb over here into the captain's seat."

"Really?"

"Hon, I don't think that's a very good idea," Jenny said.

"Oh, it will be all right."

"No, it won't be," Buddy objected. "You are the pilot, and you're going to get this metal bird on the ground. Sorry Jake, but ol' Buddy would rather play it safe."

"Aw, shucks." Jake slumped down in his seat.

Abraham hit him in the leg. "No pouting. Besides, those two buzzkills won't always be flying with us."

"Hey!" Jenny punched Abraham in the arm. "You better not."

"Ow, that's my pitching arm." He giggled. "Don't damage the moneymaker, baby."

"Yeah, damage the baby maker instead." Buddy tossed his head back and laughed. "Now that would be funny."

Jen cozied up to Abraham. Her soft lips kissed his cheek. She smelled great.

"What was that for?" he asked.

She took his free hand in both of her warm ones. She placed his hand on her belly and said, "Speaking of babies…"

CHAPTER 62

Abraham's head jerked up from the floor. He was in the same room. Lord Hawk, Flexor, and Kawnee were sitting in their chairs. He sat up and rubbed his eyes. He'd been dreaming about the past, the accident. It was a day he'd lived over and over again. It set his blood on fire.

Gathering his thoughts, he said, "Where's Sticks?"

Lord Hawk pointed to his left. Sticks was chained up to the wall between the burning cauldrons of fire. Her head was sunk against her chest. "She's resting. It takes some people longer than others to recover from the smoke of slumber. So how are you feeling, Ruger?"

"What do you want?" Abraham replied.

"Do you know what is more valuable than gold?"

A really good pizza. Ice-cold beer. It depends. "Good health."

"Ha! Well, I suppose there is some truth to that." Lord Hawk shifted in his seat. "Information. Yes, information is one of the most valuable assets that a man can acquire. Especially if it is information about a certain king."

Ruger stood up and swayed. The slumber smoke had dulled his senses. Blood flowed into his fingertips, which began to burn. "I suppose. What are you getting at?"

"Well, those horses that you gave to us… Some of them are branded with King Hector's mark. I find that very interesting."

Abraham shrugged. "So we bought some of the king's horses. It happens." He didn't have any idea whether it happened or not. But it could have.

"True." Lord Hawk got out of his chair and walked over to Sticks. He pulled her shirt down at the neck, revealing the King's Brand on her chest. "She is branded like a horse or like a Henchman."

Sticks's head rolled from one side to the other. Her eyelids started to open as she moaned.

Lord Hawk crossed the room and stopped in front of Abraham's sword belt. He lifted it up with his toe and pulled the sword free. He cast a sideways glance at Abraham and said, "Slade the Blade. I never imagined that I would meet you in person."

"I never thought I'd meet you either."

Lord Hawk eyeballed the sword and said, "This must be the infamous Black Bane. The craftsmanship is no doubt high quality, but as a whole, I find it unremarkable. I can say the same about you."

Flexor let out a bubbly chuckle. The rest of the rogues joined in.

"I have a weapon far greater at my disposal, which is more than a match for any sword." Lord Hawk pulled out his gun. The six-shooter had a blue finish and a walnut grip. He spun it on his finger. "This is a weapon greater than any sword ever forged." He tossed Black Bane onto the ground and holstered the gun after a spin on his finger. "But enough about weapons. You, Ruger Slade, are very popular outside of Kingsland. I believe there is a bounty on your head. At least two that I know of—one in Hancha and the other in East Bolg, I believe. It seems that your group gets around and does a lot of damage. I believe that King Elron in Hancha has offered ten thousand pieces of gold for your head and another five hundred per Henchman. That's quite a sum. He wasn't very happy about his aqueduct system that you destroyed."

Abraham didn't remember any such adventure and said, "It wasn't us. King Elron had plenty of other enemies."

"You know, you make a good point. But he blames Hector. Besides, it's not like people have a *picture* of you to go by or anything."

That's an interesting choice of words. Picture. When Lord Hawk spoke the "Open says me" phrase, it crossed up Abraham's thoughts. He couldn't help but wonder if Lord Hawk was someone like him. The way he talked and flipped the gun around like a cowboy couldn't have been learned in this world. *Or could it?*

"I don't recall ever being in Hancha," Abraham said. "I could have been mixed up with someone else."

"True. So, Ruger Slade, tell me what is going on and what you are doing. I know that you serve the king."

"Then you know that I can't tell you what I am doing. Not that I'm hiding anything."

"I was afraid that you would say that." Quick as a striking snake, Lord Hawk drew his gun, pointed it at Sticks, squeezed the trigger, and fired.

The bullet blasted into the stone wall right by Sticks's face. She flinched hard and let out a yelp. The loud *bang* echoed in the chamber. Smoke rolled out of the gun barrel.

"If I have to ask you what you are doing again, I'm going to send the next magic stone right through the center of her skull." That was the first time Lord Hawk said anything without even smiling. "Well?"

Abraham didn't doubt the man's intentions. He wasn't going to risk Sticks's life even though the Henchmen would rather die than reveal their service to the king. He eyed the gun. *I wonder how many bullets he has?* His father, Frank, was an avid hunter, and even though Abraham had never had a great love for it, he'd fired his share of guns. He even had a pistol that he kept inside his truck for his own protection. He wished he had it now.

"A campaign ventured into the Spine months ago," Abraham said. "It never came back. We're looking for survivors."

Sticks sighed.

"Fascinating. And what in the world would the king be sending his men into the Spine to find?" Lord Hawk asked.

Abraham's eyes slid over to Sticks. She gave him a subtle nod.

"If I tell you, will you let us go?" he asked.

"You aren't in a position to negotiate." He scratched an eyebrow with the tip of his gun. "But I'll consider it because I like you, Ruger. You're not the stiff neck I presumed. You're more… real."

"We are looking for the fenix."

Led by Lord Hawk, all the rogues in the room let out a gusty laugh.

Lord Hawk finally composed himself and said, "That's the stupidest thing I've ever heard."

"Nevertheless, it's true," Abraham replied.

Lord Hawk pointed his gun casually at Abraham and said, "I've got to tell you, this has been highly entertaining. You've really surprised me, Ruger. You really have. The insults just keep coming. Get back against the wall with your friend, Twigs."

"It's not a lie." He let out more of the truth. "The king's viceroy sent two campaigns into the Spine to find the fenix egg. The queen is sick. The egg is the only thing that can heal her."

"Oh, that is rich." Lord Hawk rolled his eyes. "And the leader of the Sect, Viceroy Leodor, I believe, told you that? My, Kingsland is in even greater flux than I anticipated. Why, it's no wonder that those campaigns failed. No manner of man can withstand the might of the spawn of the Elders. It's too bad for the queen, though. I heard she is very kind."

An awkward silence fell as all eyes in the room watched Lord Hawk pace, clearly mulling something over. Abraham noticed Sticks's nimble fingers working at her shackles.

Lord Hawk tapped his dimpled chin with his middle finger. In a hushed tone, he said, "The fastest sword in the world. Hmm… that makes me curious." He spun on a heel and faced Abraham. "I've heard that you can draw your sword faster than a man can bat an eye. I'll tell you what. I'm going to give you a chance to save yourself and your lady friend." He kicked the sword belt over to Abraham's feet. "Put it on."

Abraham complied, but his sword was still lying on the floor.

Lord Hawk picked it up and tossed it to him. "Sheathe it."

"Okay," he said and did.

Standing thirty feet apart, Lord Hawk holstered his gun. "I'm going to draw and shoot. You can try to block it with your sword. If you dodge, my bullet might not kill you, but it will kill your friend. What do you say?"

"You want me to stop a bullet with my sword? That's impossible."

"True, but it's the only chance that I'm giving you. If you block it, I'll set you free." Lord Hawk stood with his hand inches from his gun.

Abraham's fingers were inches away from his sword. He shielded Sticks with his body. There was no turning back now. He knew it.

Flexor and Kawnee sat on the edges of their seats. The rest of the rogues crept closer to the scene.

"We'll go on the count of three," Lord Hawk said. He fixed his eyes on Ruger. "Kawnee, count."

"One," the myrmidon woman said.

Abraham's hand moved closer to his handle. He kept his eyes fixed on Lord Hawk. He'd seen plenty of fastballs in his lifetime, but nothing like a speeding bullet. *Ruger, if you are in there, I'm going to need your help on this.* New sweat ran down his temple. His heart raced.

"Two."

Lord Hawk's expression never twitched.

"Three—"

Bang!

CHAPTER 63

The split-second moment moved like an out-of-body experience. Lord Hawk's hand grabbed the handle. He pulled his gun. At the same time, Abraham felt his sword sliding out of his sheath like a flicker of a snake's tongue.

Lord Hawk's aim straightened.

Abraham's sword twisted upward.

The bullet exploded out of the barrel.

He saw the bullet ripping through the air just as he brought the sword fully around.

Lead smacked into metal with a loud *crack-ting*.

I blocked it!

Lord Hawk's jaw dropped. His shoulders sagged. The barrel of his weapon dipped. In a long, drawn-out word, he said, "Impossible!"

Ruger had blocked the bullet. Black Bane quavered in his grip. The runes etched on the metal of the blade glowed the fiery orange of a furnace fire. An unanticipated surge of energy coursed right through him. He set his dark eyes on Lord Hawk. "You're going to pay."

With widening eyes, Lord Hawk pointed his weapon at Abraham and said, "Stop him! Stop him!" He squeezed the trigger.

Abraham positioned his sword blade right where Lord Hawk was aiming. The bullet skipped away from the loud steel with another loud *ting*. Then he blocked the next two shots. Lord Hawk kept squeezing the trigger. *Click. Click. Click.*

"You're empty, fool!" Abraham poised to strike.

Sticks twisted free of her shackles. She slipped two small thumb knives out of her sleeves and jammed the knives into the jugulars of the rogues standing guard beside her. A third rogue wearing a silver hoop in his nose chopped at her head. She ducked, dove for her bandolier, snatched it up, slipped it over her shoulder, and rolled flawlessly to one knee. She freed a dagger from her bandolier and stabbed the same attacker in the gut.

Kawnee jumped on her back. Sticks tossed the fish woman over her shoulder. Flexor appeared in the corner of her eye and slugged her in the side of the head. Her legs buckled. She saw stars and drew more blades. She squared off with Flexor. His black fingernails extended over a full foot in length.

She rolled her neck. "Let's do this, fish man."

Flexor chuckled.

A pair of rogues collapsed on Abraham just as Lord Hawk scuttled out of the way. Black Bane flashed in a right-handed strike. A mustached rogue's head fell from his shoulders. Abraham blocked a lethal strike, twisted Bane downward, and sank it into his attacker's heavy shoulder. The rogue let out a painful moan. Blood spat out of his mouth, and he collapsed on the floor.

Abraham didn't see Lord Hawk. "Where are you, coward?"

Sticks parried Flexor's fingernails with her daggers pumping through the air. Quick as a cat, the myrmidon stabbed with one hand and swiped at her with the other. His length was amazing. In between strikes, she flicked a dagger at his face, but he ducked the missile. She drew another.

Flexor showed his sharp little teeth to her. "Are you ready to die now?"

She wiped her sleeve across her mouth. Kawnee was back on her feet and circling her from behind. They not only had her in numbers, but also had a greater advantage in length. She flipped one dagger high into the air. Flexor's eyes drifted after it. Sticks lunged like a striking cobra. Flexor's quill-like claws slashed across her face, but the damage was done. She plunged her dagger deep into his heart.

"Gack!" Flexor gulped for air. "Gack!"

Kawnee rushed to his side. She caught him as he fell. "No, Flexor, no."

"Sticks!" Abraham said. He had Lord Hawk by the collar and was dragging him out from behind the wooden throne. Everyone else in the room was dead. "Are you all right?"

Her face was bleeding, but she said, "Yeh."

"Miscreants! You are not going to escape one way or the other. I have dozens of men outside that door," Lord Hawk shouted.

Abraham ripped the gun out of Lord Hawk's hand and cracked the man in the head with it. He eyed the gun. *Smith & Wesson. I'll be. An old police revolver, maybe. Thirty-eight special.* He tucked it into his belt.

"Ow!" Lord Hawk screeched as his head started to bleed.

Abraham didn't see any more bullets on the man. He patted the man down. "Do you have any more bullets?"

"No. Wait," Lord Hawk said. "How do you know about that?"

"I am Ruger Slade. I know things." He needed to feel out Lord Hawk. There was more to him than met the eye. "Is there another way out of here?"

"No. Brothers! Brothers! Enter!" Lord Hawk screamed. "You are finished now. Mystical sword or not, you won't overcome all of them."

The double doors burst open.

"Hahaha! You're doom—" Lord Hawk lost his voice. "You aren't my men. Who in Titanuus's Crotch are you?"

Horace, Bearclaw, Vern, Apollo, and Cudgel burst inside, coated in fresh blood from head to toe. Gore dripped from their weapons.

"Captain!" Horace said. "Are you well?"

"Well enough," Abraham said.

"My men, my men," Lord Hawk said as he craned his neck toward the door. His two brute guards lay in pools of their own blood. "What have you done?"

"We killed them all," Bearclaw said.

"All of them?" Lord Hawk said as the wind went out of his sails. "But there were dozens of them."

Vern slung the blood from his long sword and said, "*Were* dozens. Now, they are food for the scavengers."

Lord Hawk buried his face in his hands and sobbed. "They are all dead. All my men are dead."

"No, Lord Hawk, I still live," Kawnee said.

Lord Hawk lifted his face. "Yes, Kawnee, you know what to do."

Kawnee raised her arm and tossed pellets toward the floor.

"Get out!" Abraham said.

The chamber filled with inky black smoke. Abraham and the Henchmen blindly made their way out. When the smoke cleared, Lord Hawk and Kawnee were gone. So was the gun.

CHAPTER 64

Lord Hawk and Kawnee might have gotten away, but the Henchmen got their gear back. The Shell's fort looked more like a slaughterhouse than a battlefield. Dozens of rogues lay dead on the ground, on the parapet walk, and slumped over the railing of the apartments. None of them survived, that Abraham could see.

Near the middle of the courtyard, Iris was patching a wound in Prospero's thigh. A crossbow bolt protruded from it.

"This will hurt," she said.

"I know," the scruffy-bearded Prospero replied in his gravelly tone.

Iris ripped it out.

Prospero grimaced as his eyes watered.

Iris pinched the wound, and blood seeped through her fingers. She began dressing it with salve from a small jar and clean bandages. "You need to ride in the wagon for a while. My salve takes time to do its work."

"I think if you'd kiss it, it would make it much better." Prospero grinned.

"Close your eyes and keep dreaming," Iris said.

Abraham helped Prospero up to his feet. The older warrior hobbled over to the wagon, and with Abraham's help, he climbed in.

Abraham turned around to find Horace on his heels. He leaned back and asked, "Do we have everything?"

"All of the horses are accounted for, Captain. The company is still searching for Lord Hawk," Horace replied.

"Good. But let's not get preoccupied with it. After seeing this massacre, I don't think he'll show his face again anytime soon." He rummaged through the wagon and found Jake's backpack. His hand tightened on the straps. *Thank the Lord. If I lost this, I might lose myself.* He slung it over his shoulder. "Horace, let's walk."

"Aye."

Bearclaw, Vern, Apollo, Tark, and Cudgel were moving the dead inside the apartments. Vern had a sneer on his face when Abraham caught his eyes. The swordsman's flaxen waves of hair were mixed with blood. Abraham stared back until Vern looked away. Looking to the others, he said, "Tell me, how did you take so many? The rogues had the advantage."

"We tore through them like a wrecking machine. And we told you, we fight better drunk than sober. This wasn't the first time we've taken a fort like this," Horace said. He dug the bloody tip of his spear into the ground, coating it with dirt. "And it was a tactic that you created. Well, the old *old* you, that is."

"I hate to ask, but fill me in."

"Iris is our mystic. Better for healing than hurting, but she can make lightning in the sky so long as she is near water," Horace explained as they walked toward the storehouses below the parapets. "The eyes of the crossbowmen behind the parapets fastened on it. Tark and Dominga scaled the walls, gutted two of them, stole their crossbows, and shot the others. It was a well-executed assassination."

"I see."

Horace spat tobacco juice. "In the meantime, alone I approached the gate and started making a fuss. Hence, the two rogues guarding the portcullis were focused on me. They were laughing at me. Called me fat. That gave Tark and Dominga enough time to scout the fort's interior while the rest of the Henchmen started scaling the fort's wall. While they did that, Iris moved the lightning through the sky and above me. With all eyes on it, the Henchmen attacked.

"Tark and Dominga took the brutes down that guarded your entrance first. We didn't want whoever was inside to know that we were coming. The company worked their way down from top to bottom. Half of them were dead before they knew what hit them." Horace spat. "The rogues had steel but no armor. And not a one of them was a skilled swordsman. They didn't have a chance against the likes of us. We did as we always did—we butchered them. They're thieves. They had it coming."

Abraham entered the storehouse entrance. It consisted of a bunch of wooden shelves with barrels and bags of supplies. The storehouses were interconnected by one opening that led to each other.

"If you see anything we need, take it," he said absentmindedly.

He reflected on everything that had occurred. He'd underestimated the abilities of his own men. He should have known better by now. The Henchmen were seasoned fighters, one and all. He just wished he had more memories of their adventures. Then, there was the encounter with Lord Hawk. The man had a gun that looked like a beat cop's revolver that they didn't carry anymore. It turned his wheels, that and something else. He'd deflected bullets with his sword—a sword that glowed and sent an adrenaline rush right through him. *Holy crap, who am I?*

Sticks flagged them down from inside the walls of the last storage bay. "I found something." She led them inside the last storage room. A steel door, inches thick, was centered between huge stones that made up a separate wall. Dents had been made from the inside, bulging the door out.

"I think it's a dungeon," she said.

Horace fanned the air in front of his nose. "It stinks in here. Rotten."

"Did you hear anything?" Abraham asked as he ran his hand over the strange bumps on the door.

Sticks shook her head. She twirled a key ring on her finger and said, "No, but I found this."

"Open it."

CHAPTER 65

"DON'T YOU WANT TO KNOCK first?" Sticks said.

Abraham shrugged and rapped his knuckles on the door. It made a hollow echoing sound.

Horace awkwardly put his ear to the door. "I don't hear anything. But I'll be ready." He stepped back and lowered his spear. "If something jumps, I'll get it."

Sticks put the key inside the lock and twisted.

Abraham pulled his sword. A rung was on the door, so he grabbed it and started walking the door backward. He grimaced as he gave it a fierce tug. The door seal started to give. The metal door scraped along the metal frame.

"I don't think it's been used in a while," he said.

"Maybe there is treasure in it," Horace suggested. "It would be a good spot."

The door broke the threshold. A mighty stink came out.

"Eww!" Abraham covered his nose. His eyes watered.

"Close the door. Close the door. It smells like dead carcasses in there," Horace said with a souring face. "Ack! Ack!"

With a dagger in hand, Sticks peered inside. The cell was pitch black. The light from the lanterns hanging on the storeroom walls offered little illumination inside the cell. Sticking her head inside, she said, "I don't think the Shell stored anything valuable here. Something died. I don't care to find out what it is."

"Agreed," Abraham said. Flies buzzed out of the dungeon room. "Come on, let's close it. We need to move on. I don't want to disturb the dead's slumber in their tomb. Whatever dead they may be."

"Aye, Captain. Let's not bring any more bad fortune upon ourselves," Horace said.

Sticks stepped aside.

Abraham put his shoulder into the door and pushed it closed. The door groaned on the crust-covered hinges. The door stopped inches from being closed. He pushed against it. It wouldn't budge.

"Let me help you, Captain," Horace said. He leaned his spear against the wall and put his shoulder on the door. "Old doors often become askew on the frame if they haven't been opened in a long time." The burly man put his weight into it. "Hurk!"

The door didn't move.

"Wait!" Sticks said. "I just heard something move."

"What?" Abraham replied. His boots and Horace's boots slid over the ground. The door was opening by the power of some unknown force. He put his back into it. "Sticks, what do you see?"

Sticks walked backward, her eyes up and mouth agape.

Abraham and Horace jumped away from the door.

A towering shambling figure covered in long strands of gray hair stepped out from underneath the doorway. It looked like an old and malnourished bigfoot.

"Holy Harry and the Hendersons!" Abraham said.

Horace grabbed his spear and said, "It's a troglin!" He charged forward, thrusting his spear at the monster's side. The troglin snatched the head of the spear in its huge paw. It held the spear fast. It and Horace engaged in a tug of war.

Abraham closed in, carrying his sword in the wrath guard position. "Get back in your cage, beast!"

"Nooo," the troglin said in a very deep and weary voice. "I mean you no harm."

"Sure, he doesn't." Horace dug his heels into the ground and pulled his spear with all his might. "Turn your back, and he'll rip your head off and eat it like a melon." The troglin released the spear. Horace stumbled backward and crashed into the wall.

The troglin's head touched the eight-foot-high ceiling. It bent its neck over. It had large eyes and a long apelike face. Moaning, it dropped to a knee, took in a deep breath and said, "Ah, the air smells sweet again." Its eyes slid over to Abraham. "I can't stop you from slaying me. I'm too old and weak to fight. It took all I had in me to fight that bald big belly off. But, whoever you are, I give you my thanks for freeing me so I don't die in my own stink."

"Let's do it then, Captain. Brain him with Black Bane before he eats all of us," Horace said.

"I don't think he's going to eat us," Abraham said. *Oh my. A talking bigfoot. Now I know this world isn't real.* "Are you?"

"I am very hungry, and the fat one looks delicious, but no. I would not attack my liberator. I'm grateful," the troglin said.

"And smelly," Sticks said. She appeared smaller than a child beside the beast of a man.

"I'm sorry. I imagine I do reek, but I've become accustomed to it. Lord Hawk fed me then forgot about me." The weariness in his deep but pleasant voice strengthened. "If I find him, I'm going to squeeze his head until it pops between my fingers. The dirty little liar."

"Well, he's gone, and all of his men are dead."

Bearclaw, Vern, Tark, and Cudgel rushed into the room.

"We heard a scream," Cudgel said. He set his eyes on the troglin. "Gah!"

CHAPTER 66

After an hour of strong debating, Abraham got everyone settled down. By a large majority vote, the Henchmen wanted to kill the troglin. For the time being, they chained up the troglin and led him outside, under the stars, where he gazed with appreciative wonder.

With everyone gathered in the courtyard, Abraham said, "I've heard all your opinions, but this isn't a democracy. The troglin lives. Find some food and feed him."

"They eat people," Dominga said.

Sitting in the middle of the company, the troglin said, "That's not entirely true. Have we eaten people? Yes, but we thrive on all creatures in the animal kingdom. The same as you. We just don't cook it."

"If the Captain says feed him, then feed him," Horace said, looking at the two male Red Tunics. "Go!"

The Red Tunics scrambled into the stables underneath the apartments. The livestock had started to roam free. Pigs, chickens, and a pair of mules wandered aimlessly, and some came through the portcullis, now open.

With a torch in hand, Bearclaw said, "We are set to burn the fort from the inside out. All of the dead lie inside, prepared for a consuming burial."

"Just make sure all of the livestock is out," Abraham said.

The Red Tunics returned with a pair of chickens in their hands. The birds dangled lifelessly, their necks snapped. The troglin's tired eyes locked on the chickens, and he licked his lips. The Red Tunics shuffled toward and dropped the chickens at his feet. The troglin's chains rattled as he scooped one bird up and stuffed it all in his mouth.

"Ew, feathers and all," Dominga said.

As the troglin crunched down his dinner, Abraham turned to Bearclaw and said, "Torch it. Torch it all." He realized that he needed to exercise more faith in his men. All of them had proved capable, and they hadn't let him down yet. He hated to burn down a perfectly good building, but it was the right thing to do. The Shell was a bunch of petty thieves who preyed on the weak, extorted them, and hid inside their fort. This time, they'd crossed the wrong people and paid for it dearly.

The morning sun rose over the ocean. The new day had come. The burning wooden structures crackled and popped. Beams collapsed inside the flames. Black smoke billowed up and was carried out over the sea. On the other side of the portcullis, Prospero and Apollo covered all the ships in oil and burned them. If Lord Hawk returned, he'd have very little left to come back to.

Abraham looked out toward the jagged mountainous peaks of the Spine as Sticks stood with him. He yawned. "Say goodbye to a good night's sleep. I've got a feeling it's going to be a long journey. I hope everybody enjoyed unwinding last night! It sure beat the heck out of a good night's rest!"

Sticks rubbed his back. "Someone gets cranky when he doesn't get his sleep, doesn't he?"

"It's not the sleep. It's not knowing what's going to happen next. We haven't even kissed the toe of the mountain, and we're already weary. Now we have to navigate those hills." He shook his head. "At least we have our gear back."

The troglin gulped down the bones of his last chicken and said, "Pardon me, eh, Captain, is it?"

"Yes?"

Holding his hands out in a gentle manner, the sasquatchlike creature said, "First off, thank you for the chickens. They were a delicious appetizer." He licked his fingers and burped out a feather. "Excuse me. And, again, I'm grateful that you set me free. I'm happy to repay the debt, but not without a proper introduction. My name is Solomon. Solomon Paige."

"Uh, nice to meet you, Solomon," Abraham said. With inquisitive eyes he asked, "Do all troglins speak like you?"

"Troglins speak, but not like me," Solomon admitted. "I'm a bit of an outcast. Not because of my speech but some of my other mannerisms. It's a very lengthy story, and I'd probably die of old age before I managed to tell it all." He raked his fingers through his long gray hairs, which were thinning on the top. A few of his animal-like fingernails were missing. One shoulder stooped lower than the other. The muscles underneath his fur had probably bulged with the firmness of a young gorilla's at one time, but now, the hardened sinew sagged. He still must have been seven hundred pounds of man. He wet a thumb and smoothed over his bushy eyebrows. "Forgive me for eavesdropping, but I overheard that you are venturing into the Spine. Are you aware that my king dwells in crags and caves of those magnificent hills?"

"We know," Horace growled. "Everyone knows about the troglin that come down out of the mountains and raid villages. The women are carried off, the children eaten, and the men with arms ripped out of their sockets."

The Henchmen gathered around, their hard eyes locking on Solomon. Fingers tapped on their weapons.

Solomon scanned the group. "No doubt, there is truth to the stories that you have heard."

"Heard?" Horace tamped the butt of his spear on the ground. "I've seen it with my own eyes! Wild beastmen creeping down from the mountain and slaughtering everything in sight. I've seen the devastation with my own eyes! Captain, he was probably one of them! I say we kill him."

"I've made my decision," Abraham said.

He was fascinated with Solomon. The hairy old brute spoke better than he did. And something modern about his mannerisms perked his interests too.

"I'm not judging someone without proof."

"Of course not," Vern said. "You'd rather we lowered our guard first so it's easier to kill us."

"Shut up, Vern," Abraham said.

Solomon made a peaceful gesture with his hands and said, "I'm not debating the actions of my kindred. They are very territorial people. If you invade that territory, they will react. But they are content in the Spine's gaps. I'll tell you this, if you cross their path without some sort of guidance, you will have a fight on your hands." He looked up at Abraham. "May I ask what possesses you to traverse the Spine of Titanuus?"

Abraham threw him a softball question. "Ever hear of the fenix?"

Solomon's soft eyes grew. "Yes. I even know where it lives."

CHAPTER 67

LED BY A TROGLIN WEARING shackles and chains, the Henchmen traveled up into the Spine. No one talked to Abraham, not even Sticks. Horace, with the help of Vern, had them all convinced that the troglin would lead them straight into his den. Abraham didn't rule out the possibility, but they needed some sort of guide. Solomon would be as good as any. Plus, Abraham liked the troglin. He spoke more like the people he was used to being around.

I'm either stupid, crazy, or brilliant. Maybe all three. I don't know. But when I truly wake up, I'll have a lot to talk about. Maybe I'll write a book.

They rode all day, not stopping, through narrow paths without incident. That gave Abraham time to reflect on the dream he'd had when Lord Hawk knocked him out with the slumber smoke. If there was a blessing to be found in Titanuus, it would be that it kept his mind off the past. The loss of his wife and son made his heart ache every day. He could never stop thinking about the accident, could never escape from it. He relived the horror over and over. He didn't want to relive it again but felt ashamed for trying to forget it. He needed an escape.

The painkillers had given him a needed escape. They not only relieved the pain but also took the burden off his mind. He'd lived like a zombie for years, walking in numbness to the outside word, refusing to cope with his problem. But the time came when he had to pay his dues. That time came all too soon. The bills stacked up. The collectors came. He was miserable. He'd been on top of the world and crashed down out of the sky. And he hadn't even hit rock bottom yet.

I shouldn't like this world. But I kinda do. Forgive me, Jenny. Forgive me, Jake. I miss you.

The company came to a stop on a plateau halfway up the base of the mountain as they moved away from the sea. It was a patch of grass and shrubbery, with wild blue-purple berries in the branches.

Solomon pointed at the bushes and said, "The birds can eat them, but you can't." He sat down and hung his head. "By the Elders, my back hurts."

Abraham's dismounted his horse, which was lathered in sweat. He was too. "I thought it would get colder in the mountains."

"Why would it do that?" Solomon said. "You are closer to the sun."

"Yeh." The setting sun started to dip beneath the sea. "Huh, looks like the sun is going for a swim."

"They say the sun lights the waters from underneath," Solomon said. As the others started to make camp, he asked, "Abraham, I have a question I'd like to ask while the others are not around."

He eyed the troglin suspiciously and said, "All right. What is it?"

Solomon eyed his backpack that hung from the saddle. "How did you acquire that pack?"

His eyes narrowed. "I found it in a tunnel, the north end of the Old Kingdom. Why?"

"That design is very unique. Is that a pirate sewn into the pack?"

"I don't know, maybe. It sort of looks like a buccaneer or a pirate."

Abraham felt a tingle run up his spine. The two of them were having a mental chess match with one another. Or so it seemed. Whatever was going on, Solomon was very intelligent. Abraham could see it in his eyes.

"Have you ever seen a pirate before?" he asked.

"In a manner of speaking? Um…" Solomon rose up and looked over Abraham.

Abraham looked over his shoulder. The Henchmen were keeping their distance, setting up tents, including his own. "I don't think they are going to bother us. Were you getting at something?"

Solomon lowered his voice and said, "When I stepped out of the dungeon, you said, 'Holy Harry and the Hendersons.' What does that mean?"

Abraham's heart skipped, but he played it cool. "I don't know. It's just something I picked up. Why?"

"I'm going to say a few words. I'm curious if they might seem familiar. Television. Movies. Pittsburgh."

Goose bumps rose on Abraham's arms. "You're from Earth, aren't you?"

"Pittsburgh, to be exact."

"Holy moly. Tell me more." Abraham cast a backward glance. No one was looking. "So this is real? I'm not dreaming."

"Well, I don't know about that. Sometimes I think that I'm dreaming or trapped in a nightmare," Solomon said. "Back home, I was a vegetarian, and now, I'm trapped, or transformed, into this carnivorous body. I abhorred meat, and now"—he patted his stomach—"I can't get enough of it. I still appall myself, but when I'm hungry, I'm dangerously hungry."

"I can't believe this. So, you're from Pittsburgh?"

"Born and raised. I taught nutrition classes at Duquesne University. I was a well-educated hippie and driving a red VW bus. I thought I knew it all." Solomon shook his head and cast his stare toward the sky. "So, I'm driving down to West Virginia University for a series of nutrition seminars. I'm in my love bus, toking reefer, and jamming to the Beatles, when I cross through a sun ring of light in the Fort Pitt tunnel. I was pretty sure that I was tripping when my bus went from pavement onto dirt. The engine died, and I'm wandering aimlessly through a tunnel. That's when I crossed paths with, well"—he ran his hand over his body in a showy motion—"this horrid version of Chewbacca.

"At that point, I was pretty certain that I was tripping. Being a nutritionist, I had a thing for 'shrooming back then. Needless to say, I shouldn't have been behind the wheel because sometimes when I was, it felt like I was flying. Anyway, this old and shabby troglin body pounced." He held up two fingers and firmly said, "It wrestled me down and consumed me."

"It ate you?"

"I can't explain it, but it consumed me, entirely, in a very weird out-of-body experience. The next thing I know, I am it, and me is gone." He flapped an arm, shaking his hairy, dangling triceps. "Now I'm this. Is that what happened to you?"

"Something like that. So what year was it when you left?" Abraham asked.

"Nineteen ninety. You?"

"Two thousand and eighteen."

Solomon paled. "Oh my."

CHAPTER 68

THE HENCHMAN TRAVERSED THE RUGGED mountain terrain for two more days. Per Solomon's advice, they abandoned the wagon. It was sound advice, for the farther they traveled, the narrower the passages in the rocks became. The Spines' foreboding landscape was full of surprises. The wild mountain goats were bigger than horses, the dragonflies the size of crows. Pumas with blood-red coats lurked in the rocks. Strange valleys were nestled in the hills, which could contain entire civilizations. Hot breezes would come and go. The air was dry and stagnant at times, but in some spots, it became so humid that sweat soaked their clothing like rain. All in all, the treacherous trek was borderline miserable.

Abraham shifted in his saddle and used a cotton jerkin like a towel to wipe his face. He rode with Sticks at his side. She was the only one making conversation with him. Apparently, he'd gotten too cozy with Solomon. In privacy, he'd shared his history with Solomon. They seemed to hit it off—maybe too much. The others were grumbling, so they decided to keep their distance. Earning the trust of his men had been hard enough. Now, he was asking them to put their trust in a man-eating troglin.

"Everyone is giving me the cold shoulder, even you?" he asked Sticks. "Care to open up about what you are feeling?"

"You're the Captain," she said. Her two ponytails were down, and the ends of her brown hair were damp. "You decide. We follow."

"I might make the final decision, but I still like to entertain advice from my men. No one is saying a word." He looked back. Bearclaw and Vern rode five horse lengths behind them with sour looks on their faces. "Even Vern is keeping his mouth shut. Not even a jab."

"You're letting a monster lead. Not you. Besides, it's a fatal mission anyway. Everyone knows it. We won't be coming back."

Abraham gave her a stern look and said, "We aren't going to lose. I don't know how we are going to win, but we aren't going to phone it in."

"Phone it in?" she said.

"It's an expression from my world. It means give up before we've even started."

"I see. Well, at least I might get to see a fenix before I die. That should be something."

Abraham smiled. "See, that's a positive way of looking at it. Keep your little chin up."

Sticks made an odd expression and tipped her head back.

"That's better."

Tark and Dominga returned from the front. They'd been scouting ahead with Solomon. Their brows were knitted together.

"What's going on?" Abraham asked. "Where's Solomon?"

"He's waiting ahead at an impasse," Tark said. The lean, athletic bearded black fighter dripped with sweat. He wiped his brows with a forearm. "He said he'd wait for the others to catch up. It's treacherous."

"Let's go, then," Abraham said.

The Henchmen rode another mile until they caught up with the troglin. Solomon waited in front of a fiery chasm that had split a small forest of leafless, vine-covered trees. The chasm blocked the path with a stream of lava flowing through it. It was very wide, too wide for the horses to jump or cross.

"Crap," Abraham said.

Horace dismounted and marched over to the fiery gap. "Well done, troglin. I can only hope this is the river where the fenix lives."

Solomon shook his head. "No. This passage was free and clear before. Believe me, I've traveled these peaks for years. This is what happens as a result of the Spine contracting. It's always in travail. The fires below seep out when the rock cracks as Titanuus's body bows."

Abraham believed Solomon. The vegetarian turned troglin had spent years in the Spine, trying to find a portal back home. He'd first arrived in the Spine in his VW bus. It was here that the troglin consumed him.

He lifted his eyes. Thick corded vines hung in the surrounding trees' dead branches. Apparently, a thriving forest had been there at one time, but the vein of lava destroyed it.

"Solomon, is there another way around?"

The troglin lifted a long arm toward the rugged cliffs overlooking them. "It will be a dangerous climb, either up or down." He reached out and grabbed one of the vines that hung in the trees that dangled over the fiery gorge. "It's possible to use these vines."

The blackened trees were leaning over the gap from both sides. Some of them had fallen over and rested against each other.

Abraham waved the two male Red Tunics over. "Are you good climbers?"

Both the young men nodded.

"Take your hatchets, climb over using the vines, and chop down more of those surrounding trees. We'll do the same from this side and make a bridge for the ones that don't climb so well." He glanced at Horace.

"I can swing in the vines," Horace said, "carrying two people at the same time."

"Let's play it safe. And maybe we can get the horses across."

The two Red Tunics tucked their hatchets into their belts and hustled over to the chasm. The pair of wiry men, slight in build, jumped up and grabbed hold of the vines. The vines made for a natural ropelike bridge that dangled over the burning chasm. Using the gnarled knots in the vines like steps, they started crawling over the twenty-foot-wide chasm.

Abraham dabbed his face with his shirt and said, "This will work out."

A fiery wormlike creature burst up out of the molten lava. It had a head like a snake and little legs like a centipede. As it rose out of the lava, the Red Tunics screamed. One of them chopped at the monster with his hatchet. The fire worm opened its mouth, struck, and swallowed the fighting man whole. A second fire worm popped up out of the lava and closed quickly on the other trembling Red Tunic clinging to the vines. It gobbled the man up.

The fire worms plunged back into the liquid and vanished beneath the surface.

The Henchmen lined the edge of the chasm with their crossbows and spears pointed at the molten surface. They eyeballed the churning stream of death. The dark outlines of the fire worms could be seen swimming away below the surge. They were gone.

Abraham's heart raced. "That was fast." He glanced over at Twila, the last Red Tunic, who was shaking like a leaf. "Looks like you're the last."

CHAPTER 69

Using their hatchets, the Henchmen built a bridge and managed to safely cross the chasm of lava. No more fire worms appeared. The horses wouldn't cross with riders, but with effort, they finally traversed the bridge.

Loaded down with heavy packs, the horses climbed through the clouds hugging the mountain peaks. The lathered-up horses whinnied and nickered often on the trek. The company led the nervous horses up the winding mountain paths on foot.

"Your hairy friend knew about those fire worms," Horace said, leading his horse by the reins. He was huffing and puffing up the hillside, using his spear like a walking stick. "I wonder what he has in store for us next."

"He's not leading us to a trap, if that is what you are getting at," Abraham said. He and Horace were alone, as far as he could tell. He couldn't see twenty feet ahead or behind because of the fog. "We're going to go forward, not backward. Besides, we don't have anywhere else to go."

Horace's horse nickered and snorted.

"We should have left the beasts behind. This mountain spooks them," Horace said.

"You should have said something earlier."

"I hate leaving good horses behind." Horace's eyes slid up to where Solomon led at the front. "I bet if we left them, his kindred would eat them. They'd have a feast and laugh at us right now." Horace twisted his bull neck around and scanned the rocky ledges above. "I bet there are troglin all around us. Waiting to pounce on his signal."

"You've made it abundantly clear that you don't like him. I get it. But you need to move on, Horace, unless you have a better idea on how to find a fenix."

"Sorry, Captain. This is unfamiliar territory. It makes my stomach queasy." When Horace's horse nickered, he petted its head. "Easy, beast. Easy."

"We all feel the same."

Abraham moved along, carrying sixty pounds of gear on his shoulders for fear of the horses bolting away with it. They were jumpy, too jumpy to ride. His legs burned, and his lower back was on fire. They'd been walking for two days. The mountain was a hot and humid mess, like the dark recesses of a jungle. A breeze came but quickly went.

"Man, I'd do anything for a Dilly Bar right now."

"Pardon, Captain?" Horace said.

"It's a dessert in my world, an ice-cold cream coated in chocolate. You'd definitely like it."

"Sounds tasty."

"You have no idea."

The group walked until dark, taking turns on watch but staying close together. Solomon didn't sleep, that Abraham could tell. He still hadn't said another word to him. The next morning, the Henchmen geared up. The horses finally settled, so they loaded them up again and headed up the twisting paths, which ran along cliffs and into the clouded mountain peaks. Finally, hours into the long ride, they emerged from the clouds and came face-to-face with more mountains.

"Sweet Christmas, this place doesn't end," Abraham said.

The trek led them up another thousand feet until they could see the clouds like mist below them. They journeyed onward, climbing another peak until they all caught up with each other at the top of that hill.

Abraham and the company stood by Solomon and looked downward into the mouth of a crater that stretched as far as the eye could see. Parts of it were filled with black tar pits at the bottom. Birds' nests were nestled in the cliffs. Rocky formations like stalagmites seemed to grow out of the ground in both rounded and jagged formations. A sulfuric stink lingered in the stagnant air.

"This is the place that you seek," Solomon said as a chill north wind came down from the peaks, stirring gray hairs on his stooped frame. "The troglin call it the Elder's Birthing. They say the fenix is the guardian of the hive that spawned the Elders ages ago. All trespassers not born of Elder blood will surely die."

"It makes for a strange nest for a bird," Abraham commented.

"The fenix is not a bird. It's an abomination, they say," Solomon said.

Horace spat brown juice down into the crater. "Looks like a troglin dwelling to me."

"Agreed," Bearclaw said.

"Well, you can gawk at it all you want, but we're going in," Abraham stated. He scanned the eyes of everyone in the company. "Let's hear the Henchmen's creed."

"Death before failure," Horace muttered.

"What?" Abraham said loudly.

More of the company joined in and quietly muttered, "Death before failure."

He cupped his hand behind his ear. "I can't hear you, Henchmen!"

The Henchman's faces started to light up. On the signal of Horace's fist pumping in the air, united, all of them said, "Death before failure!"

Abraham gave an approving nod. His juices started to flow. "The hell with the odds. Let's go find that egg!"

THE HENCHMEN CHRONICLES

BOOK TWO

CRAIG HALLORAN

CHAPTER 1

THE GREAT CRATER CALLED ELDER's Birthing was as nasty a place as a person would want to be. The muggy and humid climate had Abraham drenched with sweat. Steam rose from the bubbling tarpits as he and the Henchmen rode past. A fine mist swirled over the ground made of clay and mud that clung to the horses' hooves and made sucking sounds. The air stank of sulfur.

Abraham sucked down half his water skin and wiped his elbow across his brow. "Ah, nothing more refreshing than a swig of hot water."

He scanned the faces of the somber-faced company. Sweat dripped down Horace's bald head like rain. Sticks's damp ponytails clung to her neck. Solomon, the bigfoot, walked along with sticky strands of long hair and mud up to his ankles. No one else looked any better.

Abraham tried to keep the mood light. "It's not so bad once you learn to ignore the smell, humidity, and heat. Right, Horace?"

With his bearded chin sunk into his barrel chest, Horace replied, "Aye, Captain." He spat out tobacco juice. "It's a fine place, better than the sands by the seas, if you were to ask me."

"No one asked," Vern said. His long flaxen locks were as wet as a mop. Sweat dripped off his chin onto his saddle.

The Henchmen had been following Solomon for hours through the crater, which seemed to have no end. They were surrounded by the oddly shaped columns of stone that stretched like stalagmites hundreds of feet in the air in some places. The rock formations were as smooth as river stone in some places and as jagged as broken rocks in others. Black-and-yellow moss grew on many of them. Trees and bushes grew with prickly leaves. Bugs the size of varmints flew and scurried over the ground. Some sort of cricket- or locust-like creatures were chirping constantly.

The insectoid chirping stopped. Some of the horses nickered. The group rode closer together, and not too far ahead, Solomon stopped. The aged eight-foot-tall sasquatch looked over his shoulder at Abraham.

"What is it?" Abraham whispered.

Solomon shrugged. "I don't have any idea."

Nothing seemed out of the ordinary. The terrain hadn't changed for miles. It had been one odd rock column, tar pit, and weird plant after the other. Every head in the group was slowly turning. Their eyes scanned the surrounding area, high and low. Swords and daggers scraped out of their sheaths.

Abraham's arm hair stood on end. He grabbed his crossbow and looked at Sticks, who was riding beside him. "Something's up," he said.

"That long-haired ape probably led us into a trap," Horace said as he slid his spear out of its saddle sleeve.

Dominga's horse reared up and let out a terrified neighing. The petite black woman clung to the saddle. Her horse went down. She leapt away and screamed.

Abraham turned his horse toward the commotion as the surrounding rocks and thatches came to life. A snapping turtle head the size of a man's burst out of a rocky shell and clamped down on Dominga's horse's leg. Similar attacks erupted all around.

"Holy crap!" Abraham yelled.

He fired his crossbow at a snapping turtle in a rock shell that scuttled toward his mount. The bolt skipped off the turtle-man's armored head. It snapped at his horse.

"Get the horses out of here!" he shouted.

Dominga dashed away from the turtle-men and jumped onto Vern's saddle. The strapping warrior unleashed his sword on a turtle-man running at him on two legs. The end of his sword split the hard shell-face right between the eyes.

The Henchmen turned their horses in every direction, only to face a swarm of attackers.

Abraham dropped his crossbow, which was tethered to his horse, and ripped his sword, Black Bane, from its sheath. The turtle-men's leathery skin was black, bright orange, and yellow. The irises of their eyes were large and bright. He hacked down at one that was biting at his horse with a fierce chop into its shell. A hunk of stone splintered off, but it kept coming.

"What in the seven hells are these things?" Abraham yelled.

"Terra-men, Captain! I've seen the likes on the shores of East Bolg," Horace bellowed. He jammed his spear into the rocky shell of his own attacker, but the spear skipped off the stony shell. "But they weren't so thick as this!" He gouged the terra-man again with his spear. "That shell is stone hard. Get away from my horse!" He gouged the terra-man in the eye with the tip of his spear.

The horse of the black-haired and broad-faced warrior, Bearclaw, went down to the ground. The well-built warrior landed on his feet. He chopped away at a yellow-eyed turtle-man with his two-headed Viking axe. Up on two legs, the terra-man came at Bearclaw with its powerful stubby arms and clawed fingers slashing. It ripped open Bearclaw's tunic, and its neck stretched out of its shell. It snapped at Bearclaw and caught the warrior on the forearm.

Bearclaw cried out in pain and, with the axe in his free hand, whaled away on the terra-man. "Unleash me!"

The terra-men had the Henchmen walled off at every turn. The creatures weren't fast, but they were deliberate. They'd clamped down on the legs of half of the horses and brought them to the ground. Abraham jumped off his horse and smacked its flank with the flat of his sword, shouting, "Eee-yah!"

The horse bolted away. Two terra-men snapped at the beast, just missing it before it vanished beyond the columns.

Sticks slipped beside Abraham, holding short swords in her hands. Her busy eyes followed the approaching terra-men. "How do we kill these things?"

He sliced the stubby clawed hand off one terra-man. Its head ducked into its shell. It came at them both. He stabbed it through the hard plates of its chest. The sword sank in halfway to the hilt. The terra-man's head popped out. Its neck twisted side to side, and the creature flopped over and died.

"Like that," he said. "Just use your length."

"Easy for you. You have Black Bane." Sticks slipped away from a clawed, two-legged attacker and cut her sword into its hand, slicing one of its claws off. "I guess I can do it bit by bit."

The terra-man crept steadily toward her.

She clipped it in the nose, cracking off a piece of shell from its beak. "This is going to take all day."

Abraham unleashed a sword swing from the wrath guard position. The sword tore clean through the terra-man's midsection, sending its sloppy gray innards flying. "No pizza for you!"

Like a mudslide, the torrent of terra-men kept coming.

Fearlessly, the Henchmen fought on.

CHAPTER 2

SOLOMON THE TROGLIN HOISTED A terra-man up over his head and hurled it into another. The monsters' shells hit hard with a loud clack. The flying terra-man bowled the other over. Both of the fallen terra-men struggled to rise, having landed flat on their backs. Their scaled limbs writhed outside their shells.

"They struggle as mightily as any turtle I know!" Solomon shouted in well-spoken English.

Apollo and Prospero rushed the fallen terra-men, baring their long swords and scraggly beards. They pounced high and stabbed their blades into the soft necks of the terra-men with wroth force.

Using his length, Abraham sliced downward into the rushing terra-men from the high guard position. Their hardened rock shells were no match for Black Bane's dully glimmering steel. Turtle skulls were cleanly cut open, exposed necks clipped like ribbons. Black Bane sang with kisses of steel that sent the terra-men into eternal slumber.

Cudgel, the burly bald black man, cried out as a terra-man bit down on his ankle. He bludgeoned it with tremendous overhanded swings of his flail that busted the grit off its shell. "Get this thing off of me!"

His brother, the lean, long-limbed, athletic Tark, dashed through hordes of terrapin attackers. With two hands, he thrust his sword into the shell of his brother's attacker. The blade sank into the shell and went hilt deep.

The terra-man's mouth gaped open, making a raspy sigh.

Cudgel popped the terra-man's face with a fierce swing from his spiked flail. "Eat spike!" He hopped on one foot as his other ankle bled freely. "Elders' blood, it hurts!"

Tark slipped a shoulder underneath his brother's arm. "Can you walk?"

"Not if it's broke," Cudgel said.

Abraham hacked down every terra-man who got too close to him or Sticks. They were no match for his speed. The shelled bodies were piling up, but they kept coming.

He stabbed. "Take that, Raphael!" He sliced. "Eat steel, Donatello!"

"How do you know their names?" Sticks ducked a clawed terrapin swing and punched her dagger into her attacker's throat.

"I don't!" he said as he butchered a terra-man's head like a sliced-open melon. "It's a thing in my world."

He fought on, uncertain whether his fighting prowess came from Ruger or the sword, Black Bane. He had an uncanny awareness of his surroundings. He sensed his men, where they were fighting, and where the enemy was coming from, like a sixth sense of some sort. He tried to back away from their attackers, but the terra-men had them surrounded in all directions.

"We have to find a way out of here!" he said.

The ground shook. An odd sound like thunder followed.

Thoooooooooom!

"What in the hell was that?" he asked.

The terra-men stopped attacking. Instead, they scurried together, making a wall with their bodies.

The ground quaked as if stomped by giant footsteps.

Thooom! Thooom! Thooom!

"Captain!" Horace cried out. He thrust his spear in the air. "Look!"

The terra-man of all terra-men stepped out from behind the strange columns. It stood twelve feet tall, with burning orange eyes. Natural yellow moss and knotty rock-like ridges grew on its shell. In one claw, it dragged a dead horse by a rear leg. Its great neck stretched out of its shell. Its eyes narrowed and scanned them all.

Dominga fired a crossbow bolt at the monster. The bolt skipped off its winking eyelid.

It opened its mouth and spoke in a great, hollow voice. "Who dares to slaughter my children?"

Abraham wasn't sure what was more surprising—a twelve-foot-high juggernaut turtle or the fact that it spoke. His fingertips tingled as Black Bane burned in his grip. *This is madness.* He swallowed the growing lump in his throat and spoke up. "Your children attacked us, Bowser! We did not attack them!"

The giant terra-man swung its head toward Abraham. "My children hunger. Your flesh and bones will feed them. You are meals from the Elders. All living are meals from the Elders and their children."

Abraham glanced at the others and said, "We aren't meals. We're men. Just passing through. And since when do turtles eat flesh? I thought they were all vegetarians."

"You speak strange for a man of Titanuus. No matter." The giant terra-man opened its great jaws wide and bit the horse's head off. Its mighty jaws crunched the skull with tremendous cracking sounds.

Holding her belly, Dominga said, "I think I'm going to be sick."

The great terra-man tossed the horse's corpse at the feet of his children. "Eat, my sons. Eat the wild flesh." It causally wiped its stocky scaled arm across its mouth. "We don't have such succulent food in the crater of birth. The Elders must be thanked. But my children that have fallen must be avenged. For they are so very, very precious to me."

Abraham wasn't very keen on fighting the enormous terra-man and all his children. From his point of view, the odds were stacked against them. Lowering his bloody sword, he said, "I am Ruger Slade. Can I ask what your name is?"

The terra-man tilted his head, and with unblinking eyes, he said, "I am Barath the Ancient." He managed to show the slightest smile. "Thank you for asking."

"Barath, feed your children the horses. But these men must come with me. They are food for… the Fenix."

Barath's eyes enlarged. "Whaaaaat?" He blinked. "Whaaaaat?"

Rubbing the back of his neck, Abraham casually said, "Er… well, if you are thanking the Elders for the horses, then you better make a tribute in return. These men will do. I'm sure the Elders will understand your mistake when you attacked the bearers of their soon-to-be sacrifices." He was throwing all the baloney he could at Barath. "The sooner we depart, the better."

"I'm not aware of any sacrifices to the Elder spawn, Fenix." Barath's clawed fingers opened and closed. "I think you are lying to me, flesh and bones. Children… feast on them."

CHAPTER 3

THE TERRA-MEN'S HEADS POPPED UP. Over twenty of them were still there, plus their father, Barath. The Henchmen backed into a defensive ring, brandishing their weapons.

His eyes fixed on Barath, Abraham asked, "Does anyone have any ideas?"

"We can take them, Captain," Horace said.

"Not without them taking some of us with them," he replied.

With Black Bane's handle hot in his grip, he felt more than confident to resume the fight. He wanted to fight, or at least Ruger did. But he didn't want to lose any men. Cudgel had a busted leg, and Bearclaw's arm might have been broken. He had to think of something.

He stepped forward and flashed his sword through the air. "Listen, Barath. You have our horses. Keep this up, and you'll have a fight on your hands that you don't want. I'll turn you and your boys into turtle stew. Or die trying."

Barath spread out his clawed hand, and his children halted. He eyes the sword. "That briar that you wield cannot hurt me. My shell is harder than steel… than iron of any kind." He thumbed his chest. "I'm indestructible."

"Maybe so, but your children aren't. How many more are you willing to lose? And do you really want to risk pissing off the Fenix?"

Barath rubbed his chin.

The Henchmen exchanged glances throughout the group. Every hard-eyed man and woman's knuckles were white from gripping their handles and pommels. They were ready to fight, every last one of them. Sticks twirled a dagger with one hand. Horace spat out brown juice. Vern's heavy stare was locked on the nearest terra-man to him.

"I adore my children. All are precious to me," Barath said. "You are bold, flesh and bones. I can honor that. Never let it be said that Barath cannot show compassion and mercy. My children will find your broken bodies soon enough in the crevices. Go on. Search for the Fenix. Greet death. We will dine on your bloody bones later."

"Grab what you can," Abraham said, as he picked up one of his packs that had fallen from the horses. "Thank you, Barath." He slung a heavy pack over his shoulder. "You wouldn't be able to point in the direction of the Fenix's lair, would you?"

Barath stretched out his arm and pointed a single finger. "You'll know it when you smell the breath of the Fenix. Keep walking as long and far as you can. Just put one foot in front of the other. In the end, it won't matter."

The Henchmen didn't waste any time distancing themselves from the terra-men. As soon as they were out of earshot, Horace sent Dominga and Tark out to search for surviving horses. They found three of them. Cudgel, with a broken right ankle, rode on one horse. The other two were loaded down with gear, which mostly consisted of water and rations. The rest of the Henchmen carried what they could, but that was it.

As for the head count, everyone was present and accounted for: Solomon, Sticks, Horace, Bearclaw, Vern, Iris the mystic, Prospero, Apollo, Cudgel, Tark, Dominga, and the last serving Red Tunic, the pie-faced Twila. Thirteen in all.

After making his head count again, Abraham muttered, "Long live the baker's dozen. Man, what I would do for a lox-and-cream-cheese bagel right now."

He had an aunt and uncle who used to own a bagel shop that he'd worked at one summer. It was hard work, baking in front of the bagel ovens, watching the rotisserie shelves roll over and over behind the glass shield of a five-hundred-degree oven. He'd thought that was hot, but it was nothing like the sweltering heat of Elder's Birthing. At the shop, he'd learned what a baker's dozen was. He'd learned bagels came in a voluminous variety of flavors, too. With sweat dripping in his eyes, he started naming them—anything to keep his mind off the madness. "Plain, onion, salt, poppy, sesame, everything, wheat, sourdough, cinnamon raisin, jalapeño cheese. Oh man, I loved those. Pumpernickel, blueberry, oh, and don't forget those bites with the cream-cheese frosting."

"What are you saying?" Sticks said. She had a small pack between her shoulders. Her brown hair was matted to her head. If she was as miserable as him, her expressionless face didn't show it.

"I'm thinking about the past. It was a lot friendlier than my present situation. I think I might have taken it for granted." Running his hand along the ledge of the path they walked, he noticed the corded muscles in his forearm. "Even though this body's much more fit than mine ever was. I almost feel like I can do anything in it."

Horace walked up from behind them and said, "You should have killed the turtle abomination with it, Captain."

"The answer to everything isn't always fighting. We all still live. We'll need every strong arm we have to face the Fenix, I figure," he said. "I can only imagine it's far worse than Barath."

"Aye," Horace brushed past him and Sticks. "If you say so."

CHAPTER 4

THE COMPANY TOOK SHELTER LATE in the evening underneath a large rocky overhang. A warm rain was coming down and splattering on the muddy ground. Abraham set his back against the rough stones, holding Jake's pack with his eyes closed. Sticks lay quietly with her head down by his legs.

Is all of this real or not?

He'd stayed so busy hauling through the crater with his nerves on edge that he'd only been thinking of finding the Fenix. So far, the king's quest turned out to be a mission in madness. The terra-men were an odd sort, as strong and violent as nature. Barath was an abomination that had bitten off a horse head with one bite. And the terra-men had talked, the same as any man.

He touched Sticks on the head. "Does everyone speak the same language?"

Without opening her eyes, she replied, "I don't understand."

"Well, everyone we've spoken to, man or monster, speaks the same."

"They all do, so far as I know. Perhaps there are other words that the secret societies and sects speak, but the kingdoms all share the same speech." She rolled her head toward him and asked, "Do you not speak one language in your world?"

"There are thousands."

"How do people get along?"

"It doesn't seem any different than this world. They still fight. And the more we understand each other, the worse it seems to get." Absentmindedly, he stroked her cheek. "I'm not sure if it's a good thing or not."

"That sounds confusing," she said.

"I think we made things too complicated where I'm from. As bad as this is, at least I feel like I know what to do and where I stand." He reached over, grabbed his waterskin, and drank. Out in the rain, Iris and Tark were filling up the waterskins. "Do you think I should have tried to kill Barath?"

"You've never lost a fight."

"He was huge. I'd have to stab him one hundred times before he went down. Besides, I don't think he is out to get us. It's his territory. We barged into it. But seeing turtles eat horsemeat like ravenous hounds… Well, that was creepy."

"How so?"

"In my world, turtles eat plants. Not meat or people, for that matter. They are smaller too."

"We have turtles but terra-men too." She laid her gentle fingers on his. "I think you did the right thing, not killing Barath. The old Ruger would have sent twenty Red Tunics to die before he would lend a hand."

"Yeah, well, with only one Red Tunic left, that just wasn't an option that I had." He eyed Twila, who had joined Iris and Tark in gathering the water. "Not that I would have used it."

Sticks didn't reply.

Abraham sorted through his thoughts. He wanted to get back home. In order to do that, he'd need help. He might have found help from King Hector, if he could retrieve a Fenix egg and cure Queen Clarann. If not, perhaps Solomon could help. At least with Solomon, he didn't feel alone in this world. The hippie-turned-troglin gave him a sense of normalcy. Without Solomon, he'd have gone completely crazy. *I'd be locked up in an institution somewhere in a twisted version of the movie* Dream Team.

Sticks began to snore softly.

Solomon ducked into the overhang and squatted in front him. His gray fur was dripping wet. Mud was caked on his legs up to his knees. "How are you holding up?"

"I'm not turtle food."

"I've seen my share of oddities in this world, but that Barath character might have been the tops." He looked from side to side then set his eyes on Abraham. "I had no idea. But I don't think your Henchmen will believe me."

"I can't control what they think. They are a stern lot. Let's just find the Fenix egg and get this over with."

He offered Solomon his waterskin, but he waved it away. Abraham was glad because he wasn't very comfortable drinking after the old troglin.

"You said the Fenix is an abomination?" Abraham said. "Worse than Barath?"

"I didn't say. I said the troglin said. I have no idea what it is. I just know that it is supposed to reside in this crater. A thorough exploration should reveal the location to us, even if Barath didn't point us in the right direction. We'll have to keep our eyes open. I imagine it won't be too hard to find."

"What about his warning you mentioned about not having Elder Blood?" Abraham asked. "Do you care to elaborate on that?"

"I'm only passing on what I heard. When I first arrived, I ran with a pack of troglin. We traversed the hills of the spine for years." Solomon scratched the hairy whiskers covering his chin. "There were children troglin that ran with the pack. The elder troglin would teach them. I would listen in." His protruding eyebrows wiggled. "It was a strenuous time, to say the least. Adapting to this body. Pooping outside in broad daylight and not using leaves to wipe because the others didn't. Anyway, I used my silence as a guise for knowledge. I learned things. But do you know what I learned most?"

"What?"

"That I really wish I had a big bag of weed. Because this place is crazy." He laughed quietly, and his nose crinkled. "But the troglin were adamant to stay out of the crater. And yet, here we are."

"So, you haven't talked to anyone else like us?"

Solomon shook his head. "There aren't many people that are friendly with the troglin. I hoped to find a portal in these hills and had all but abandoned hope until you came along. If there is one portal, there has to be another. Something must have caused them."

"I agree, but what?"

"If we can figure that out, then maybe we can find our way home."

Abraham nodded.

Horace crept up behind Solomon with his eyes so wide that the whites were showing. He pointed his thick finger out into the darkness and said, "Something lurks out there."

CHAPTER 5

"Let's get a fire going," Abraham suggested. "And get a head count too, Horace."

Sticks sat up and yawned. "What's happening?"

"We might have company." He came to his feet and walked the length of the overhang.

Cudgel was sleeping inside. Apollo and Prospero huddled nearby. Dominga and Vern were guarding the camp. On Horace's order, Iris and Tark started making a fire inside the overhang.

"What do you think is out there? The terra-men?" Abraham asked Solomon, who was shadowing him.

"This crater won't be void of its own critters. Lizards and big cats. Bugs as big as my feet. It's possible that your men might be jumpy."

"Jumpy? These guys? If they think something is wrong, then something is wrong. I trust them."

Solomon sniffed. "I have excellent senses, even for an old troglin. Let me wander." He stepped out into the rain and vanished into the night.

Horace returned a minute later. "They are all accounted for. Vern sent the word out. He's hunkered down thirty yards from Dominga. Something creeps through the brush, he says." He looked from side to side. "Where's the troglin?"

"Taking a look."

"It's probably his brood, waiting for our lids to get heavy so they can feast on our bones."

"I don't think he's something that we need to worry about. You have to trust me on this," Abraham said.

"You should trust your men. Once a troglin, always a troglin. They are hairy devils, I tell you." Horace moved to the group making the fire.

"I know," Abraham muttered.

He hoped he wasn't overlooking anything with Solomon. He was giving the man, allegedly from Pittsburgh, the benefit of the doubt. The Henchmen were a proven lot. They had instincts and had earned his trust. But until he saw something from Solomon that would change his mind, he wouldn't change course. He had a game plan and was going to stick to it.

After a few minutes of hard work, the fire, made from rotting limbs and gathered brush, crackled and glowed with orange light. The humid air was warm enough without the fire, but the glow offered security. Bearclaw stood over the flames. His right arm was bound in a sling Iris had made for him.

"You should rest," Iris said. Round-faced and well-built and curvy, she checked Bearclaw's sling and bandages. You're lucky that you didn't lose your arm."

"The king's ring mail saved me. It wouldn't be the first time it did," the broad-faced, flat-nosed Bearclaw said. "How long will the bone take to heal?"

"I don't know. Let the salve do its work. Everyone is different," she said.

With the new fire casting shadows into the overhang, the group spread out and stood out beyond the flames. The Henchmen's keen eyes searched the darkness, where night birds called out from time to time like squawking crows.

Abraham caught Prospero and Apollo yawning. The odd warriors said little if anything at all. They never seemed to have a care about anything. Apollo blew snot out of his nose. Prospero burped up something. They reminded him of a couple of guys he'd played baseball with. Cody and Roy Smith were brothers he'd played minor-league ball with. They were goofy and unkempt but could knock the cover off a ball whenever they got a hold of one. They never fit in. They never tried to, either. They just played ball with all they had in them.

Something approached from the darkness. It was Solomon, carrying a dead panther in his huge arms. He dropped it on the ground by the fire. The black cat had a silky black coat of white-splotched fur and must have weighed one hundred and fifty pounds. Its neck was broken.

"There's your invader. A black growler. I'm surprised you even heard it."

"And I'm surprised that you found it," Horace said. "We didn't hear so much as a scuffle out there. And we are supposed to believe that you caught this cat without a stir?"

"I got lucky." Solomon dropped to a knee. "It sprang at me. I grabbed that furball's neck and squeezed before it tore my heart from my chest."

Abraham took his eyes off the cat and looked at Solomon. Claws had raked his chest open. He bled freely.

"Solomon, you're wounded," he said.

"Only a flesh wound." The troglin teetered over and fell onto his side.

CHAPTER 6

Kneeling, Iris stitched up the deep claw marks in Solomon's chest. His fur was matted and bloody. Using a small knife, she cut the thread she carried and wound the remainder up on a spool. Solomon's chest gently rose and fell.

She patted his big face and said, "I guess he'll live. But those wounds were ghastly." She looked at her audience, composed of Horace, Sticks, Abraham, and Bearclaw. "I'd keep those claws of the black growler. They might come in handy."

Prospero and Apollo had begun skinning the beast. With the help of Tark, they cooked its flesh on a spit over the fire. The meat had a sweet savor to it, and Abraham's nostrils flared.

"That smells good," he said.

"Well, it should smell good," Horace said. "A black growler this big would fetch over one thousand shards of gold. The pelt alone is worth the most of that." He spat.

Iris frowned at him.

"What?"

Solomon's eye lids fluttered. He groaned and opened his eyes then sat upright, grimaced, and clutched his chest. "Oh! Grateful Dead, my skin feels like it's on fire." His long fingers caressed the matted hairs on his breast. "Oh man, that thing sliced me open like a sheet of paper, didn't it?" He looked at Abraham.

Abraham took a knee and said, "At least your guts are still in you. I have to admit I didn't expect you to fall like a tree over a little scratch from a cat."

Solomon managed a smile. "Me either. I don't think it was the wound so much as the hunger." His nostrils widened as he sniffed the air and started to slaver. "The black growler smells like quite a feast."

Abraham hollered to the men by the fire. "Apollo, prepare our big hairy friend here something to eat. As well as the rest of us. We should have our bellies full when we head out tomorrow. Maybe this cat meat is just what we need." He frowned at Solomon. "That didn't sound right, did it?"

Solomon shrugged. "Meat is meat to me."

The Henchmen divided up the growler meat and gave the largest portion to Solomon. He devoured the growler's two back legs raw and licked the blood from his fingers.

Abraham delighted in his portion. The cooked slab he had was savory and as tender as any venison he'd ever had. Almost everyone in the company devoured the meat and licked their fingers with juice dripping down their chins. It awakened his senses, and the weariness in his limbs began to fade. For the rest of the night, the group rested. The rain stopped. The dawn came. A headcount was taken, then they broke camp and resumed the quest.

About one hour into the walk, the Henchmen passed between two columns and by a bubbling tar pit the size of an Olympic-sized pool. A wretched stink drifted through the air like a slap in the face. Half of the company covered their noses. All three of the horses began to whinny.

Solomon approached from the front of the line, his great arms swinging by his sides. He passed Cudgel, still riding on the horse. They were eyeball to eyeball.

He stopped in front of Abraham and said, "I think we found it or something that might be it."

"Are you serious? We haven't been walking an hour," Abraham said.

"Come look," Solomon turned and walked back in the direction he'd come.

Abraham told Sticks and Horace, "If we were that close to our destination, I'll be amazed."

"I'll be relieved," Sticks stated.

"The troglin probably needed the night to set the trap for us," Horace replied.

"Let it go, Horace," Abraham said. "That's an order."

"Let what go, Captain?" Horace replied with a befuddled look.

"Never mind."

The stench of tar, sulfur, and rot came out of a tremendous cave partially hidden behind the rock columns. Like a straight mouth, the cave entrance was at least one hundred yards wide and less than half as high. Tar oozed out of the cave in hot, sticky streams that filled the pools below it. Stalactites hung down from the inside of the cave like great teeth. It was a breathtaking and ominous sight that could pass for the entrance to hell.

Abraham breathed in the foul air. "That must be the breath of the Fenix."

All the Henchmen stood in a row, looking up into the massive cave entrance. Iris, Dominga, Tark, and Twila pinched their nostrils.

"Ew, this will be new," Vern said as he cast his lazy gaze at Abraham. "If there's an abomination to be found, then it's to be found in there. Might as well say your prayers, Henchmen. The end is near."

Abraham would rather have done nothing more than turn around and depart. That was him speaking. But inside was another man, harder than iron, who didn't fear anything. Ruger Slade would move forward, inch by inch, foot by foot, no matter what. He gave Abraham courage that even the toughest of ordinary men wouldn't have. He scanned the faces of his crew. They'd all come together that far. He wasn't about to tell them they could back out now. He knew they wouldn't do it anyway. He took a drink of water and mentally prepared his speech.

"Listen up," he said.

All eyes of the party fixed on him.

"I can't say for certain that this is where the Fenix dwells. But judging by the looks of it, if it's the worst place to go, then that's probably where we need to be going." He pointed. "We aren't going inside that cave, looking for a fight. We're looking for an egg. It's an extraction mission." Abraham hadn't done anything like this before, but he made it sound as though he'd done it one hundred times. It came naturally to him. "Cudgel and Twila, you'll both stay back with the horses. And if anyone else wants to stay back, that's fine. Probably, the smaller the group, the better. Besides, if we don't make it back, someone will need to tell our tale of how the King's Henchmen battled the Fenix."

The comment drew many smiles, even from Vern.

Abraham nodded. "All right, then. Grab your balls and cover your nose. Let's take this stinkhole."

CHAPTER 7

The Henchmen climbed up the hill leading to the cave's entrance. They dipped torches in the stream of tar and lit them. The torches made black streamy smoke and cast a yellow-orange flame that crackled. Tark and Dominga scouted from the front, with Abraham, Horace, and Sticks not far behind them. They took their time entering the vastness of the cave. Abraham's eyes adjusted to the dim light. If the Fenix lived in the cave, he could only imagine it would be a massive birdlike thing.

"Everybody keep an eye on your neighbor. We don't need anyone getting lost," he said.

With a sour tone, Vern said, "This stink is almost blinding. It's worse than what comes out of Horace's butthole."

"Is not," Horace grumbled.

His comment brought forth a few dry laughs.

The cave sloped downward. They churned ahead slowly until the light from the cave mouth faded. The streams of tar that spilled out of the nostril-like orifices were gone. The cave ground was soft dirt with no signs of animals. No bats hung from the ceiling. Not a single cave bug crawled. The atmosphere was dead.

Holding a torch out in front of him, Tark said, "I can't see from one end to the other. It just goes."

Abraham expected the cave to narrow at some point, but it didn't. It stayed wide and continued long. "How deep are we in, Tark?"

"I'm over a thousand steps. That's pretty deep for a cave," Tark said. "I don't like it."

"Damn." Abraham had gone on a few hikes in his lifetime with his dad, Earl, who taught him how to count steps to keep track of his distance. It was all part of his father's pilot survival training, in case he was ever shot down in Vietnam. "A half a mile is pretty deep." He thought about the East River Mountain Tunnel, where he'd come through the portal. It was one mile long, but not nearly as deep and wide. He'd heard about caves that went on for miles and miles. This might well be another one of them. He looked down at his tracks in the ground. "Horace, make sure we don't lose our way out of here."

They moved on through the dark, murky stench, which continued as they walked downward. The rancid odor hung in the air like hot breath. The loose ground beneath their feet became slippery. Over one thousand steps into the trek, Abraham began to lose track of time as the pace ground on.

"Nothing could live down here," Vern muttered. "It's too foul for the living."

"They say the Elders can thrive anywhere," Iris said. She walked along with the hem of her robes pulled up. "But I have to admit I don't feel a thing. My own skills elude me, as if they've been sucked out of me."

"Don't anyone panic," Bearclaw said. "It's just a cave that smells like a bunghole."

"True, but something must be making that smell," Iris replied. "It's worse than rotting carcasses."

"Perhaps it's the bowels of Titanuus churning," Solomon suggested.

"Barath said that it was the breath of the Fenix that we smell," Sticks said. "Follow the breath—find the Fenix."

Horace clawed at his beard. "This is not a place for flesh and blood. That much I believe. But I agree. Follow the stink to the source."

Tark and Dominga shook their heads and carried on. Solomon followed behind them, drawing a curious look from Dominga. Solomon covered his nose.

Even Abraham had enough of the stench. His stomach turned, and he fought back the urge to wretch. The body of Ruger Slade seemed to have guts of iron, however. He had a steady hand that did not shake. As far as he could tell, the body that hosted him was unflappable.

"I see something," Solomon said. He stretched out his long hand and pointed his index finger. "Ruger, come and step beyond the torches."

Horace joined Abraham's advance. Far ahead, the slope took a steep incline into a wide channel cut in the rock, which had a green hue. "What is that?" Abraham said.

"An Elder's birth canal," Horace replied.

The group crept ahead. The stench worsened with every step. They made their way into the tunnel. The faint green glow came from tiny crystals in the channel's rock wall. The wide channel was still fifty feet wide but only twenty feet high. The light in the rock was very faint. The henchmen drew their weapons and walked through the channel of rock.

Sticks had her head down and was shaking it.

"What's wrong?" Abraham quietly asked her.

"I thought I could handle anything, but this place is turning my legs into noodles." Sticks swallowed. "All I want to do is vomit. This is awful."

"I don't think you're alone. Just stick together. No pun intended," he said.

Iris slipped in beside Sticks and took her by the hand. "I tremble within. Let's be strong together."

Sticks pulled away. "Let's just get it over with. If you want to hold hands, do it with Horace. This smells far worse than the tobacco on his breath."

Iris nodded. "You make a good point." She moved over to Horace. "Breathe on me."

"Er, certainly." He breathed in her face.

Iris smiled and held his hand. "As disgusting as I find your tobacco chewing, at the moment, I find it refreshing."

"Fresh enough to kiss?" Horace asked.

"Maybe, when we get out of here," Iris said with a playful smile.

Horace grinned from ear to ear.

Abraham's feet started to slide on the ground, and he fought to keep his footing. So did everyone else. The ground shifted beneath them like a living thing. One by one, with their arms flying outward, the Henchmen fell down. Abraham was the last to drop. He was sliding downward on a bed of black sand, and his hands desperately clawed through it. The slope suddenly steepened, and the slide increased in speed.

The Henchmen plunged deeper into the bowels of darkness.

CHAPTER 8

The heavy-shouldered Cudgel was sitting in the shade, sipping on his waterskin when his nape hairs stood up. He cupped an ear and turned toward the cave. "Did you hear something?"

Twila was feeding one of the horses a handful of oats. She turned and said, "No. What did you hear?"

"It sounded like a scream." Using a stick for a cane, he tried to stand.

Twila hurried over and stopped him. "Be still and rest your leg. There is nothing you can do for them now. Besides, the wind howls through that opening. I think that is what you are hearing."

"No, it was a scream," he said.

"I've been riding a long time with the Henchmen for some time, and I've never heard them scream, aside from crying out in pain. Even that doesn't happen much." She took a cloth out of her belt and dabbed the sweat on his bald head with it. "You worry about your brother, don't you?"

"I'm the oldest, and we are the last, so yes, I worry about him."

"I worry too. You are very handsome men. I love your eyes—so light and, well, what is the word for it?"

"Spooky?" he said.

"Well no, that doesn't sound complimentary. Maybe they are haunting, but in a good way," she showed a toothy smile and put her hand on his thigh. "They are pretty."

Cudgel couldn't help but smile. "I think your eyes are pretty too. They are very soft and kind."

She continued rubbing his thigh and asked, "So, how does your leg feel?"

"Whatever Iris wrapped around it makes it tingle all of the time. I think it's strengthening."

"That's good." She eyed the loaded crossbow lying at his side. "Can I ask you a favor?"

"Of course."

"Since we have some time on our hands, I'd like to be productive. Could you tell me how to use the crossbow?" She reached across him and let her fingers caress the weapon. Her full breasts brushed across his knees. "I think it is fascinating."

Cudgel picked up the crossbow as she sat back on her knees.

He eyed her and said, "The first rule of the crossbow is to never toy with it when it's loaded." He removed the bolt and pulled the trigger so that the string made a loud *snap*. "I shouldn't do that either, but for the sake of training, I don't think it will hurt it." Using two fingers like a claw, he pulled the string back and locked it in place with a grimace. "Not many can do that."

"You are so strong," she said, elated and clapping quietly. "I'll never be able to do that."

As if by magic, Cudgel produced a clawlike key, which had two metal fingers and a handle. "Take this. Put the bow down headfirst and secure it with your foot." He pulled the trigger again. *Snap!* "Use this to pull and lock the string back. You're a sturdy gal. If Sticks can do it, you can."

"Yes, she is very scrawny." She took the key and crossbow from Cudgel. She put the crossbow head on the ground and braced her foot against it. Using the key and both hands, she grunted and pulled the string back. Her arms trembled. "Ugh!" She locked the string in place. She panted. "Whoa, that was even more difficult than I imagined."

"It won't be so difficult when your life depends on it. You won't even think about it."

"I'd keep it loaded and ready just in case. I think I'd only be good for one shot if it was the last moment before melee." She aimed the crossbow at the columns. "So, can I load the bolt?"

He handed her the crossbow arrow and said, "Be my guest. Take a shot if you want. We have plenty."

She took the bolt and said, "I don't want to waste one."

Scratching behind an ear, he said, "I won't say anything, and I don't think anyone will notice."

She loaded the bolt into the crossbow slide and renewed her aim at the columns. "I wish I had something softer to shoot at so I could save the bolt."

"Again, don't worry about it. All you have to do is point and shoot. Hold in half a breath and aim the tip where you want it to go. Pull the trigger nice and easy." Cudgel pointed at a vine that had sprouted from the ground and grown around the rock column. "Try for that vine. It's pretty thick. You can do it."

She lowered the crossbow, looked at Cudgel, and said, "I want you to know that I appreciate this. Being a Red Tunic, I don't feel comfortable asking for help, seeing how I'm supposed to be the help."

"That's the military order of things. I started out as a Red Tunic too, and it wasn't easy, but I've made it this far. I figure after we get out of this fix, you'll probably be branded a Henchman too. Then the new Red Tunics can set up your tent for you. Heh heh."

"I'd be lying if I didn't admit that I daydreamed about it. But that's not all that I dream about." She looked him in the eyes and smiled. With her foot, she touched his leg. "I'd really like to be with you, and seeing how it's only the two of us, I think we can get away with it without anyone knowing."

Cudgel looked back into the cave and said, "You're right. But when I'm with a woman, I prefer to have her in a much more comfortable position."

"Listen, Cudgel, I'm a frisky woman, and right now, I'm feeling it for you." She started to set the crossbow down as she began unbuttoning her tunic with her other hand. "I don't care about the smell. I want you. Now, take those trousers off so I can take you."

"Heh. Why don't you take them off for me?"

She opened her tunic all the way, revealing her ample breasts clinging to a cotton jerkin. "As you wish," she said.

Cudgel made a smile as broad as a rainbow.

In a fluid cat-quick motion, Twila raised the crossbow, pulled the trigger, and shot him in the neck.

Making a gurgling sound, the wide-eyed Cudgel clutched at the bolt in his neck. His hot stare turned on her. He leapt at her legs, but she skipped away like a deer.

Laughing, she said, "Oh, Cudgel, what is the matter? You sound like you have something caught in your throat."

He limped at her and drew his sword. Through clenched and bloody teeth, he said, "Come here, you witch!"

Her warm and friendly voice had changed to a dark and deadly tone. "Now, why would I do that? You might try to hurt me."

Cudgel spat blood as he fought to catch his breath. He tripped and fell onto the ground then looked up into her face. He swung his sword at her feet, but she eased back out of range.

Twila squatted down. "I'll say this for the Henchmen. They all have a lot of fight in them. Too bad that just isn't enough." She pulled the sword free from his dying grip while he fought for his last breath. She leaned over and kissed him on the forehead. "If it's of any consequence, I really do find you very handsome. And if we ever had a moment, I'm sure we would have enjoyed it. Goodbye, Cudgel. Now the dirt will be your everlasting mistress. But her kisses will never be as sweet as mine."

Twila gathered the horses and rode away.

Cudgel sputtered his final breaths.

CHAPTER 9

THE PAST—2009

Beep. Beep. Beep. Beep. Beep.

Abraham woke with a sharp gasp. "Noooo," he moaned. A sharp pain lanced through his ribs. "Ugh." He blinked. His vision was blurry, and he thirsted.

Beep. Beep. Beep. Beep. Beep.

His heart pounded in his ears. He realized his body was immobilized. His legs had been lifted into the air and wrapped in casts. His arms were strapped down at his sides. He ached. His eyes drifted upward and to the side. He could see a heart monitor that he must have been hooked up to.

Beep. Beep. Beep. Beep. Beep.

"Jenny," he softly said, in a dry, cracking voice.

With a slight turn of his head, he realized he was alone in a hospital room. Faded green scrub-colored curtains hanging from the ceiling were half drawn around him. Flowers were everywhere in the room along with bright and colorful balloons that read Get Well Soon. Many of the flowers had begun to wilt in their faces. A few balloons hovered in the air, moving with the flow of the air conditioning. A dangling balloon string brushed across his chest. He tried to move his arms, but they wouldn't go.

He twisted his head left and right. "Jenny!"

Abraham's mind jumped back into the past. He was flying from Florida to meet his father, Earl, in West Virginia. The plane was a birthday gift for his dad, thanks to the big contract he'd just signed. From there, they were going back to Pittsburgh to sign autographs for the Pirates. It was him; his wife, Jenny; his young son, Jake; and his best friend and teammate slugger, Buddy Parker. Abraham was flying the plane. The flight was great. They started their descent above the mountain state. They'd dropped beneath the fluffy white clouds and cruised over the mighty hills of green when, from out of the rainless clouds, lightning struck the plane.

The instrument panel went crazy. A wing and the engine caught fire. Jenny and Jake were screaming. The plane descended quickly. Abraham did everything he could to keep the plane in the sky, but they were undoubtedly going to crash. The last thing he remembered yelling as he yanked on the plane's yoke was, "I love you, Jake! I love you, Jenny! I'm sorry, Buddy! Everyone hold on!"

Beep. Beep. Beep. Beep. Beep. Beep.

Tears streamed down Abraham's face. "Jake. Jenny." Fighting through the weakness, he managed to lift his voice. "Somebody help me!"

A black nurse peeked her head in the door. She was older, a little heavy, with kind eyes and wearing pink scrubs. She stared at him, and her eyes widened. "Oh my! You're awake!"

In a raspy voice, he asked, "Where's Jake? Where's Jenny?"

She hustled into the room, checked his vitals on the monitor, and said, "I'll be right back. Don't you go anywhere."

He caught her by the sleeve and said, "Where's my family?"

The nurse swallowed and gently pulled away. "I'll be right back, hon. Okay?" She vanished through the door.

Abraham's heart sank. He knew something was wrong. He'd seen it in the nurse's eyes. "Nooo."

His fingers found the remote connected to his hospital bed, and he blindly pressed the buttons. The bed lifted him until he rose far enough to see more of the room. A chair was in the corner, and Jake's Pirates backpack sat on it.

His lips trembled. "Please be alive. Please be alive. Nurse!"

The same nurse popped her head in the door and said, "Hon, it will be okay. The doctors are going to come to check on you. So be patient, please. I promise that we will do the best to take care of you."

"Can you tell me where my wife is?" he asked, but she'd already closed the door. "Please!"

CHAPTER 10

Abraham's Past

The doctor who had come into Abraham's room wouldn't comment on his family. All the tired-eyed man said was, "I just did the surgery, that's all I did. Things look good. That's all I did." He departed, leaving Abraham alone in his thoughts, swarming inside his head like a hive of bees.

Shortly after the doctor left, Abraham's father came into the room. Earl was a rugged-looking man with angular features, clean-shaven with a buzz haircut. He always carried the presence of a military officer wherever he went. He wore a denim jacket and had a sad look in his gray eyes.

"Dad," Abraham said, his throat swelling. "Tell me. What happened? Where's Jake and Jenny?"

Earl walked over and put his warm callused hand on Abraham's head. His eyes watered. "Son, they didn't make it."

Abraham's body shook. He sobbed uncontrollably. "No, Dad. No, that can't be true!"

"You're going to have to be strong, Son. They are in a better place now."

"No!" Pain coursed through his body. He hurt everywhere. "No!" He looked right at his dad. "What about Buddy?"

"He's gone, too."

Tears streamed down Abraham's cheeks. He felt hollow inside. His entire life had been wiped out.

"Dad, I didn't do anything wrong. We were just flying. Coming in for a landing. There were clouds in the sky, but they were clear. The lightning… It-it came out of nowhere. I tried to land safely. I tried." He broke out in tears.

His father leaned over and hugged him. He was crying too. He held Abraham tightly and said,

"I know, Son. I know. Nobody blames you. It was an accident. I'm just glad to have you back with us. You've been in a coma a long time."

Abraham stifled his tears. "What? A coma?" His lip quivered. "How long have I been in a coma?"

"Three months. You were all busted up when they drug you out of the plane. The doctors worked a day putting you back together. They got you stabilized, and the vitals were good, but you wouldn't wake up. Here." Earl grabbed a towel and wiped his son's face. "It's a miracle you made it, though. I'm glad you're alive."

"So, where are Jenny, Jake, and Buddy?"

"We waited as long as we could before we had the funeral services, hoping that you would wake, but when it didn't happen, we moved on." Earl rubbed his son's head. "No one blames you, Son. You have to know that. Jenny's parents understand. The investigation showed it was an accident. It's important that you understand this. It's going to be a tough rehabilitation for you."

"I don't want to rehab. I would rather I died with them. People are going to have to hate me. Buddy's family… They'd want to kill me. They loved him so much."

"Son, this might sound selfish of me to say, but I feel as selfish as you. You were bringing me a wonderful gift. Your intentions were good. I can't believe it turned into such a tragedy. Some things we just can't control in this world." Earl wiped his eyes on his denim jacket sleeve. "It's been hard on an old guy like me too."

Abraham had never seen his dad every cry before. Even when Earl accidentally cut the tip of his finger off with a skill saw, he didn't flinch. Seeing his dad cry made his heart tremble, and Abraham cried even more.

Earl patted him. "Let it out, Son. Let it out. Just let it all out."

Abraham had had everything he ever wanted: money, fame, and most importantly, a loving family. Now, all of it was gone. He had nothing left but guilt and emptiness. He cried continuously for minutes until his tear ducts went dry. "Poor Jake. He was so terrified when we were going down. I never saw anyone so scared before. Jenny was holding his hand, trying to keep him calm. She was so strong. So brave. I failed them. I shouldn't have been flying that thing."

"Son, you are a good pilot. I've flown with hundreds, and even the best have gone down because of bizarre circumstances and malfunctions. The important thing is that you don't blame yourself."

"They have to hate me, Dad. They have to. I was the pilot. They were my responsibility."

"It was a tragedy. It happens to the best of us. It happens to the worst of us."

He looked behind his father. "Hey, will you give me Jake's backpack?"

"Sure. Sure." Earl fetched the Pirates pack and set it on Abraham's chest. "One of the first responders fetched it out of the wreckage. It held up pretty well."

With pain running up his arms, he managed to lift his hands and grab the pack. He held onto it as if he was holding on for dear life. "Did you see them?" he asked. "Was it bad? Were they m-mangled?"

"I didn't see it for myself. The coroners told me. I wouldn't want to remember them any differently than the last time I saw them. The coroner said they died instantly, still strapped in their seats. It was a merciful way to go. They are with the Good Shepherd now, Son. You have to believe that."

He let out a shuddering sigh. "I know." Unlike his father, he didn't have the same final memory of his family's faces. What he saw was panic and fear. Jenny was strong, but the creases were deep in her face. Jake was a kid, scared to death. Buddy was bent over with his head between his knees, praying loudly.

But Jenny had said one thing he remembered. She said, "I love you, no matter what happens."

CHAPTER 11
THE PRESENT—TITANUUS

THE LAST THING ABRAHAM REMEMBERED was sliding down a slippery slope and into a void of darkness. He landed in a shallow puddle of tar that must have knocked him out. He was on top of someone and crawled off. His eyes adjusted to the tiny green lights illuminating the rocks. He was in yet another massive cavern. He hooked his arm around who he thought was Horace and dragged the man out of the tar and onto a sandy bank.

The Henchmen's fall had caused them to pile up on one another. Most of them were crawling out of the sludge. Abraham waded in knee deep and helped some of the others out. Most of them were coated in black, but it began to ooze off.

He found Sticks and pulled her to the bank. "Pretty sticky, huh?"

She looked up toward mouth of the tunnel they'd slid out of. "What happened? The ground just gave."

Iris was on her hands and knees, crawling out of the muck. She flipped her sticky hair from her eyes and said, "Something made it move. I felt it, like a living thing. I thought we were being swallowed."

Tark wiped his nose and sniffed the air. "It is foul like the innards of a belly. I think we were swallowed by the Fenix."

"That's preposterous," Horace said. "We're in a cave. Not that I know that much about caves, but we are in one. Not a stomach of some Elder beast."

"You don't know that," Tark said. He slung muck off his hands. "Titanuus still churns in his bowels. They say it's not dead yet. His heart beats beneath us. Who is to say that his spawn are not as tremendous as he is."

"She is," Dominga added.

Tark turned and looked at her and asked, "Are you saying that Titanuus is a woman?" He let out a gusty laugh. "Only a woman would believe that Titanuus is a woman."

"And only a man would believe that it is a man," Dominga replied.

"Because he is a man!" Vern said.

"If that is true, then how can a man give birth to the Elders," Dominga fired back.

Tark and Vern exchanged looks. Even Prospero scratched his head.

Bearclaw waded out of the sludge and said, "It doesn't matter because no one has ever seen an Elder. It's all legend."

"It's not legend," Iris stated. "And Titanuus is a man. That's how it's always been taught. Sorry, Dominga."

"You believe what you will. I'll believe what I will."

"We're here to find an egg, not identify Titanuus's gender. But judging by the smell, I'm pretty sure he's a man," Abraham said. "So, as long as we are here, let the search begin. Solomon, Tark, Dominga, lead the way. Keep following the smell."

"You heard the Captain," Horace said. "Let's find the egg."

Abraham wanted to get moving again. He didn't like the idle time. It made him think of his past, and looking back hurt too much. He'd thought he was over what had happened to Jenny and Jake, but when he dreamed about it when he was knocked out, it all came back. It was awful, worse than any stink he'd ever smelled. Anything was better than reliving his past.

The deeper inside the cavern they went, the worse the smell became. Tarlike pits were scattered like pools along the cavern floor. They bubbled, burbled, and popped. The Henchmen used the natural light emitted by the crystals in the caverns for direction. The cavern wasn't like a normal cave. It was different. The ground had a thin coat of slippery slime and wasn't hard as rock either. It was weird.

"I can't imagine anything thriving down here," Sticks said. "There is nothing to eat or drink. Not even the bugs have meat. It's barren."

"Something makes that foul odor," Horace commented. "Something must live down here."

"Yes, us," Vern said. "For now."

The company walked through the tunnels for a long time until they came to piles of petrified muck as tall as a man. Apollo scraped at one of the piles with his dagger. He sniffed the foul flakes on his blade and said, "It looks like excrement and smells like it, too." He wiped the blade off on his trousers. "Something lives down here, for certain."

"Captain, we still have some torches. Shall we light them and get a better view of our situation?" Horace asked.

"No. I don't want to alert whatever might be in here. Besides, that tar is oily. It might ignite if we aren't careful."

"Aye."

Ahead, Solomon drew deep breaths into his nostrils. His nose crinkled. "I think we are close to something." He lumbered forward with his long arms slowly swinging. He stopped in front of a moat of tar and oil that guarded a huge, long stone shelf. He pointed at it. "Look."

Sitting on the shelf of rock and partially hanging over the rim was a massive bird nest made of tree limbs, packed mud, and vines. It must have been over fifty feet wide.

Abraham couldn't believe his eyes. "I'll be. It is a nest."

Everyone stood at the ledge of the moat with their eyes fixed on the nest. The moat was ten feet across.

"I can jump it," Dominga said. She backed up twenty feet, set her feet, and sprinted ahead.

Vern stepped into her path and grabbed her.

"Let go of me, you idiot!"

"Oh, no you don't. Don't you remember what happened with those fire worms?" Vern warned. "We don't know what's in that moat."

"Good call," Abraham said. He picked up a branch that lay on the ground nearby. "Let's take a poke at it, shall we?"

He stuck the branch out over the waters. A globular tar man popped up out of the waters and snatched the branches from his fingers.

"Gah!"

Suddenly, the moat and the surrounding pools of tar began to gurgle angrily. Slimy, sloppy tar men emerged from them and came forward.

CHAPTER 12
LEWIS

DAYS HAD PASSED SINCE THE Henchmen departed. The handsome and well-knit leader of the King's Guardians, Prince Lewis, slipped out of the House of Steel in the wee hours of the morning, unescorted by his men. Cloaked head to toe, he snaked his way into Burgess, where the bald and chinless Viceroy Leodor waited for him in one of the smaller but oldest cathedrals. Alone in the grand stone building, Leodor secured the entrance doors and led Lewis into the stony vault below the cathedral's sanctuary. Ancient crypts lining that were stacked one on top of the other. Leodor knocked aside thick cobwebs with his torch.

"I take it that you weren't followed," the complacent Leodor said.

"I've been slipping out of the castle since I was five years old. No one caught me then, and no one will catch me now." Lewis ducked underneath an archway and tore off the cobwebs that stuck to his hood. He pulled the hood off. "If there was one Elder I wished were dead, it would be the Elder of Insects. I hate these things."

"Don't blaspheme. You are in the House of the Elders," Leodor warned.

"They aren't listening. And no one has ever seen an Elder, anyway. Just a bunch of fairy tales told to frighten children."

Leodor spun around, halting Lewis's advance. The placid viceroy looked him dead in the eye and said, "You don't believe in the Elders? Where do you think my powers are granted from?"

Lewis looked down at the viceroy and said, "I don't know, and I don't care. For all I know, they come out of your bung hole. Good for you. Now, let's get this over with so you can brag about your sorcerous powers to some big-eyed enchantress want-to-be later."

The viceroy snorted and led Lewis to the back end of the crypt. A large sarcophagus there had images of wild dogs carved into the stone lid. He stepped around it where a sheet of brown canvas covered something over ten feet tall. Together, they pulled the canvas down. An ornately designed bronze frame, ten feet tall and just as wide, was mounted to a blank stone wall. Demonic skulls with horns and fangs were woven into the frame, with shiny stones set in the eyes.

"Creepy." Lewis stretched his hand toward the frame.

Leodor smacked his hand away. "Don't touch it. It could kill you instantly."

"I have my gloves on."

"Your pretty little leather gloves won't save you from the Underlord's wrath. Now, step aside."

Leodor handed Lewis the torch and picked up the candlestands lying on the floor. Three of them were there, with three candles each. Each stand was as tall as a man, fashioned in twisted bronze the same as the frame mounted to the wall. The candle bases were small skull faces holding chubby black candles mounted in the skull. He made a triangle in front of the bronze frame and stood within the triangle of candlestands.

"Join me," Leodor said. After Lewis stepped inside the triangle, he said, "Light one candle and cast the torch aside."

"This isn't my first time. I know the routine."

Using the torch, he lit one of the small candles in the middle. A green flame burned. He tossed the torch outside the triangle. The flickering flames took the form of a tiny flaming demon. It hopped from candle to candle, lighting all of them one at a time before settling back into its burning place of origin. An icy chill went down Lewis's spine. The torch lying on the ground extinguished.

"Aren't you going to chant something?" Lewis asked.

"I will if you are silent. Be sure to stay—"

"I know—the protection of the triangle."

"Just be silent." Leodor closed his eyes, clasped his fingers together, and began to chant.

Lewis gripped his sword as icy arcane words spewed forth from Leodor's small mouth. The air left the room. The wall and frame before him warped and wobbled. A pinwheel of dark colors twisted inside the bronze frame. The spinning image slowed and took form. His heart thumped hard in his chest.

A man with blue eyes like burning crystals, wearing dark robes, his hands crossed over his chest, stood in the background. His head was bald and tattooed with black rings, the skin bluish, with a pewter pendant hanging from his neck with a demonic dog face on it. His iron-hard stare locked on Leodor. His words echoed loudly in the chamber. "What news do you bring forth, servants?"

"Oh worshipful Underlord, we humbly come to serve your needs," Leodor said with a bow. "It has come to our knowledge that Ruger Slade has changed personalities again. But in a more direct manner. He revealed himself fully, claiming that he was Abraham Jenkins, a man from another world."

The Underlord walked closer until the sunken leathery features of his stern face filled the frame. "And you killed him?"

"No. Not directly." Perspiration broke out on Leodor's forehead. "The king, well, put faith in the man. We sent them to the Spine on a suicide mission to fetch the Fenix egg and save the queen. We won't be seeing them again, ever. Ruger Slade, for all intents and purposes, is dead."

"Let's hope so, for your sake." The Underlord stepped back until he showed head to toe but still in a dominating size. He toyed with the pendant hanging from his neck. "The Elders have a way of meddling in my affairs. One never knows how or when they will show up. Be wary. The portals have unpredictable qualities, drawing in strange personalities and unique artifacts to this world. If they don't serve the Sect's intentions, continue to do away with the baubles that you find. We can't have King Hector gaining allies similar to our own. The portals are designed to give us an edge over him."

"None of that will matter once I am the King," Lewis said. "I'll rule the kingdom, and the rest of the lands will be yours, Master Underlord."

"Don't be overconfident, pampered Prince. Only a greedy coward would betray his own father, so I have little faith in you. But, to your fortune, your seed will be needed to feed the future, otherwise, I would do away with you." The Overlord moved away, and the image began to fade. "Keep me apprised." His picture in the mirror went blank.

"'Pampered Prince'?" Lewis scoffed. "Who does the Underlord think that he is? Wretched old fart. I'm way ahead of him."

CHAPTER 13

Abraham snaked Black Bane out of his sheath and cut a tar creature's neckless head from its shoulders. The swampy body of the monster sagged into the ground.

"They are coming from everywhere, Captain!" Horace roared. He stabbed his spear into another tar creature's chest, and it went through one side and out of the other. "I felt bones in it! Bone and sludge for blood!" Horace ripped his spear out as the creature kept advancing with its muddy tar arms outstretched. "It doesn't know it's dead!"

The Henchmen cut into the sludge men with unfettered vigor. Hard and heavy blades sliced through the tar-bodied monsters. The slow creatures fell under the cuts of steel. Others kept advancing.

Abraham swung his blade like a windmill and sawed away at them.

Bearclaw's double-bladed axe busted open face after face.

Apollo and Prospero swung their longswords with wroth force, splitting some of the creatures from the pits in half. Tar-coated limbs went flying. The battle turned into a bloodbath.

"There's too many!" Sticks said. Her short swords whittled away at her closest attacker as another slunk in from her flank. "Will our numbers ever find greater favor?"

"Just keep swinging!" Vern said. A tar creature drove its body into his legs. He went down to the ground. With his legs pinned, he chopped into it with two hands. "Get this thing off of me!"

The sludge monsters created a chain with their bodies, the last one standing inside the pit. Working as one, the sludge monsters dragged Vern toward it.

Seeing Vern scraping over the stone painted a horrific picture in Abraham's mind. Perhaps it was Ruger who told him what was happening. He didn't know, but his skin began to crawl. He noticed the bones of the dead at his feet emerging from some of the sludge men he'd slain. They were adventurers just like them, slain and turned into the living dead to serve as guardians of the Fenix and its egg.

"This sucks," Abraham said.

Vern was being dragged closer to the pit. "Somebody help me!"

Iris rushed to Vern's aid with her eyes glowing like stars. She chanted in a powerful voice. "Elders of Fire, bless these hands with flames that burn both the living and the dead!" Bright green-and-yellow flames engulfed her hands. She plunged them into the sludge monster holding onto Vern. The flames spread over the monster's body and spread to the others. They let out mind-jarring shrieks.

"Horace, get out those torches!" Abraham yelled as he chopped another monster down. "Iris, light them up!"

The spear-wielding bear of a warrior hustled away from the outstretched grip of his attackers and pulled the torches out of his pack. "Iris, set these torches aflame the same as you do my heart," Horace said.

"You have the worst timing when it comes to sharing your affection." Iris grabbed the torches by their heads and set them on fire. "But I like it. Maybe we'll share a kiss later if we make it."

"Ho ho ho!" Horace roared. He stuck his torches in the belly of his nearest attacker. "Merry kisses!"

The sludge man caught on fire. Horace tossed one of the torches to Dominga, who lit one sludge monster after the other.

The tar-dripping fiends retreated back toward their black pools.

"It's working," Abraham said. "Try lighting the pools."

Horace stuck his torch in the oily pit of tar, but the flame extinguished. Like a living thing, the oily tar tugged against Horace's iron grip. He braced his foot against the ledge.

"It's strong as a blacksmith," he said, grunting.

"Let it go," Abraham said, and Horace did. "We need to cross that moat. Use those flames to keep those things at bay. I have a feeling that fire won't keep them away forever." He approached the moat, looked at Iris and Dominga, and said, "Keep those flames above the waters. I don't think they'll come out if they sense the flame. We'll see." In a single bound, he jumped the moat and landed on the ledge of the other side. The moat didn't stir.

"Captain," Iris said, "my flames won't burn forever."

"I understand. Do your best."

Sticks jumped the moat next. She was followed by Bearclaw, Tark, Apollo, and Prospero.

Abraham started climbing the bed of rock that the great nest lay upon. Nearing the top, he grabbed hold of the nest's dangling vines. The nest was at least ten feet high. Like a squirrel, he slowly climbed it. *I can't believe how strong my hands are. I'm loaded down with armor and caked in tar, yet I can still climb this like a monkey.* He peeked over the rim of the nest, fully expecting to see a gargantuan bird ready to swallow him whole. Instead, he saw something else. Inside the nest was another swampy, gooey pit, with white foaming pus-like formations growing on top. It stank to high heaven.

The others climbed up by his side and beheld the foul sight within.

Sticks pointed toward the center of the Olympic-sized pool of goo. "I hope those aren't the eggs."

CHAPTER 14
LEWIS
THE HOUSE OF STEEL

On the morning after he had met with Viceroy Leodor and the Underlord, Prince Lewis was summoned to meet his father on the castle patio overlooking the Bay of Elders. He hadn't cared for the Underlord's undermining comments about him. He'd wrestled with them in his sleep most of the night. Yawning, he ran his fingers through his feathery locks of black hair. He was suited up in his suit of blackened chain-mail armor, covered by his emblematic maroon tunic, which showed the lion's face with wings coming out of it, the symbol of Kingsland. He marched down the grand halls of the castle, paying no mind to the subjects who bowed as he passed through.

I don't need Leodor or the Underlord. They are the ones that hesitate. When I'm king, I'll fix the both of them. Treating me like a pawn in some grand game… I am the game.

He met his father and Viceroy Leodor on the patio. King Hector stood by the wall, wearing a flattering suit of emerald and golden robes. The Crown of Stones hung over his brow. He was feeding the birds crumbs that he tossed into the air. Leodor stood near the king. The viceroy of the Sect had soft eyes with bags under them, looking as if he never slept at all. He didn't appear any different than he had hours before, when Lewis met him in the cathedral. Leodor was the one who had recruited him into the Sect as a young boy, and that was a secret they'd kept from his father ever since.

Lewis bowed. "Good morning, Father." He gave an irritated look to Leodor. "Viceroy."

King Hector gave his son a firm hug. "Good morning, Lewis. Have you had breakfast yet?"

"No. I'll pass through the kitchens later."

With the warm, goofy smile of a gentleman, the wavy-haired king said, "It's a sad thing when your mother is unable to force us to the tables. She always valued our time at breakfast. She would say it was the only time that she could round us all up before we all ran away from one another." He clucked and sighed. "We should keep with tradition."

"I agree. So, how is Lady Clarann? Her circumstance hasn't worsened, has it?"

"You would know if you would check on her once in a while."

"Father, forgive my detachment, but she's not my real mother though I am fond of her. She's been a good mate for you."

King Hector's brows buckled. "She has raised you like a mother since you were a boy. You bathed with her as a boy, for Elder's sake, and giggled all of the time. Shame on you and this twisted distance that you put between the two of you. Do you even remember your real mother?"

"Of course I do."

"Really, then what does she look like?"

"Beautiful. Curls of raven hair. A pointed nose and chin. She was a true aristocrat and not built with the broad face of a commoner."

"You disappoint me, Son. Clarann is not some commoner. Even your real mother would approve of her. She was a very understanding woman." Hector wagged his finger at his son. "She'd be disappointed with you if she saw how you were acting. It's neither princely nor knightly."

Lewis frowned and asked, "Did you summon me to lecture me on my estranged relationship with your wife, or am I called for a higher reason?"

"Funny that you should mention estranged relationships," Hector said. "I have a mission for you. Leodor informed me this morning that your half-sister, Clarice, has wandered from the castle. Apparently, she caught word that another expedition is underway to fetch the Fenix egg. If you'll recall, she tried to join the campaigns before, and we wouldn't allow it. Now your bull-headed sister has departed with her Guardian Maidens on her own personal quest. I need *you* to track her down and bring her back."

Lewis huffed. "Father," he whined. "That is a waste of my time. Send some of the Guardians after her. I'm certain they'll be able to track down that sawed-off little runt in no time. I have more important matters to attend too."

Hector poked him in the chest. "This is where you need a life lesson. There is nothing more important that family."

"She's not family. She's my half-sister."

"Listen to me, Lewis. She shares my blood the same as you do. That makes her whole blood. Do you understand me?"

Lewis looked down into his father's eyes and gave him a disappointed "Yes."

"Clarann doesn't know that Clarice slipped out. It would break her heart, so I want you to retrieve your sister and all of her maidens with all haste. We can't let anything happen to them. Do you understand?"

"I understand."

"Good. Now, you take twelve of your best Guardians and the fastest horses, catch up with her, and bring her back." Hector patted his stomach. "I need some milk. This news has my belly burning." He looked Lewis dead in the eye. "I'm counting on you to handle this, Lewis. Elder speed, Son. Elder speed." He headed back into the castle, leaving Lewis and Leodor all alone.

Lewis looked at Leodor and said, "Let me guess. You let the secret slip to Clarice, didn't you?"

Leodor replied, "It's possible my tongue might have slipped in front of one of the Guardian Maidens."

He smiled. "Good."

CHAPTER 15
THE SPINE – ELDERS BIRTHING

"What is it, Captain?" Horace shouted from below the nest. "Is there an egg? Yes?"

"There's something." Abraham had seen his share of eggs before. He used to eat them like candy when he was in training camp. He even tried drinking them raw like the boxer did in *Rocky*. But what he had his eyes fixed upon was different. Floating in the muck near the middle of the nest were three slimy green eggs the size of traveling trunks. "Man, that Fenix must be awfully big. I don't even think dinosaurs made eggs that big."

"What's a dinosaur?" Sticks asked.

"A giant lizard," he replied.

He scanned the nest and the surrounding area. On the other side of the nest was the cavern wall. He saw no sign of any creature or Fenix or any other monster that was living. Only the gooey bubbling waters remained. He looked down into the nest. The slimy waters filled up half the nest.

"That's still deep," he said.

Tark's smoky eyes were glued on the eggs. "Captain, how are we going to get one of those eggs out of there? They are huge."

"Probably heavy too," Apollo said.

"We'll figure it out." Abraham pointed around the nest's ring. "Bearclaw, you guys walk the perimeter. Make sure we don't run into any more surprises." He looked down at the others, who were standing on the other side of the moat. "Horace, do we have any rope?"

"We always have rope, Captain." Horace spat on the ground. His face clenched. "What do you need rope for?"

"These eggs are pretty big. We might have to tow them out if that can be done."

"I'll get the rope ready," Horace said.

Abraham sat down on the rim of the nest, facing inward. Sticks joined him. Bearclaw walked clockwise around the nest. Tark and Dominga walked the rim counterclockwise. Abraham kept his eyes on the eggs. They were lumpy things, coated in grit and grime, with little craters coating the shell. All of them were different sizes. The stinking waters bubbled around them.

"Any ideas?" he asked Sticks.

"Do we take one, or do we take them all?"

"A good question. I don't see us getting all of them out of here. Not to mention that it's going to be harder getting out than it was getting in. Unless there is another way out of here." He glanced up at the ceiling. "It would really suck to die down here. A pretty smelly place for a funeral."

Bearclaw, Tark, and Dominga made it to the other side of the nest.

"Do you see anything?" he asked them.

Tark shrugged. Bearclaw ran his hands over the back wall. Dominga stared down into the pool. Bearclaw's hands froze, and he muttered something. Tark and Dominga turned. Both of them kneeled beside Bearclaw, and they looked at the wall. Both of them jerked their hands back.

Abraham stood up. "What is it?"

"Not sure," Bearclaw said, "but it looks like this wall has eyes."

"Let me take a look."

Abraham and Sticks hustled over to the other side of the nest. He took a knee by Bearclaw. Sure enough, a reptilian eyeball bigger than his head stared right back at him. It was one of many. He waved his hand in front of it. It didn't blink.

Quietly he said, "Whatever it is, I think it sleeps."

"How do you know that?" Sticks asked.

"Did you ever see *Conan the Barbarian*? You know, when he drips sweat onto that giant snake's eye and its lens opens?" he asked.

They gave Abraham blank stares.

"Never mind. Wrong world. Wrong time. The point, if it's sleeping, don't jostle it."

"Do you think that it's the Fenix?" Tark asked.

"Probably."

"Maybe we should kill it," Bearclaw said.

"No, I don't think you want to wake a sleeping giant. Let's leave it alone and go. We're going to have a hard enough time getting the eggs out of here. Tark, you and Dominga keep an eye on, well, those eyes. We'll figure out how to get that egg out."

Sploosh! Sploosh!

Everyone's heads snapped around toward the center of the nest. Prospero and Apollo were wading chest deep through the pool of sticky slime.

"Are you guys crazy?" Abraham said in a hushed whisper.

The older Henchmen approached the eggs.

"They are crazy," Bearclaw said. "One should never be surprised by what they try and do. Better them than us."

"How's the water?" Abraham asked.

"Smelly and warm. A fine mud bath. No doubt that the swine would like it," Apollo said.

"I think the swine do like it," Dominga said with a smile.

Apollo and Prospero made their way to the eggs and pushed on them. "Captain, which one should we take?" Apollo asked.

"Let's start light. Try the smallest." He looked at the others behind him and shrugged. "Does anyone know anything about the incubation cycle of an Elder-spawn egg? If you do, speak up now or forever hold your peace."

Each one in the company gave him a stiff shake of the head.

"Is everything going well up there, Captain?" Horace shouted.

"Good Lord. Sticks, get over there and shut him up. Eventually, he's going to wake something up. Fetch the rope, too." He looked at Dominga and Tark, who were eyeing the eyes in the wall. "Did it blink?"

Dominga shook her head.

Apollo and Prospero pushed on the smallest egg. It wobbled in its floating perch. The bearded men huffed and puffed as they put their backs into it.

"Our feet are sliding. The egg clings to a perch of goo. Very stable." Apollo pulled out a dagger. "I'll try to saw it free."

On the other size of the nest, Sticks grabbed a rope. She started back around the nest. Abraham lifted a hand, and she stopped in her tracks.

"We'll try to reel it in from your side once Apollo frees the egg," Abraham said.

In the pool, Apollo—with his hands under the waters—sawed away with vigor.

"Any luck, Apollo?"

"My king's steel is sharp, but the effort is slow. I think it will come along eventually," Apollo replied.

"The sooner the better," he said.

"Captain," Dominga said with tightness in her voice.

"Yeah?"

"I think one of the eyes just blinked."

CHAPTER 16

As far as Abraham could see, the eyes hadn't moved at all. But the muggy atmosphere was becoming more prickly.

"Saw faster, Apollo!" he said.

"I am. Maybe that skinner you carry would fare better, seeing how it can cut anything," Apollo said.

Abraham's hand fell to the handle of Black Bane. He didn't know if there was any truth to Apollo's statement or not, but perhaps Black Bane's razor-sharp metal would do the trick. After all, as far as he knew, the sword was magic. He pulled the sword and climbed down into the pool. "Ew. I already regret this."

"Nice, isn't it?" Apollo said with a smile showing all beard and no teeth.

"Not unless you like living in a latrine. This is awful," he said of the warm, sticky sensation. He stuck his sword under the egg and started cutting. "This better work."

"It will. Black Bane cuts anything," Apollo said.

With one hand braced on the egg, he started sawing at the tendon-like objects below, which clung to the egg. "Sorry about this, Black Bane. Dominga, is anything winking up there?"

The petite Henchman squatted in front of the eye. She turned her head and said, "No."

"It winked," Tark blurted. He pointed his finger at one of the eyes. "That one. I saw it." He pulled a dagger. "It lives."

"Are you certain?" Abraham said.

"I saw it," Tark said.

"I don't know. I didn't see it," Dominga replied. "Just hurry up."

He sawed faster. The egg broke free of the cords that held it. The surrounding murky waters wobbled. The ground under the pool shifted. Apollo and Prospero's eyes grew big.

"Move!" Abraham yelled.

With the egg floating in the water, they pushed it toward Sticks.

She tossed one end of the rope into the pool. "You can't tie a rope around that egg?"

"No, we just need it to climb out," he said. "Bearclaw, get over here."

Bearclaw secured the rope over his shoulders. "Climb up."

The waters started to churn and bubble. Their gooey warmth was heating up.

Abraham took the rope and climbed out of the pool. "Hurry up!"

Prospero got on Apollo's shoulders. Apollo rolled the egg up the side of the nest. Prospero rolled it up the rest of the way to the nest's edge.

Abraham rolled it onto the rim. "Get up here!"

The old knights climbed the rope hand over hand and out of the pool. Both of them climbed down over the other side, in front of the moat.

"Drop it down to us, Captain," Apollo said.

Abraham picked up the egg. The massive thing filled his arms and must have weighed two hundred pounds. "I can't drop it over the ledge. It's too heavy."

"Is that the egg, Captain?" Horace said.

"It's either that or an awful-looking paperweight." The ground trembled. "Crapola!"

He could see where Iris had managed to make fires by the pools, which seemed to keep the sludge men at bay. Those fires appeared to be dimming.

"We need to move!" he yelled.

Prospero climbed back onto Apollo's shoulders.

Abraham rolled the burdensome egg down the side of the nest into Apollo's arms. Straining, Apollos lowered it to Prospero. The egg sank into Prospero's arms, and he lowered it with a grunt.

Tark and Dominga jumped off the nest to the ledge behind the moat. "All of that thing's eyes are moving," she said. "It's awake, Captain. The Fenix is awake!"

They still had ten feet of tar- and sludge-filled moat that they needed to cross with the egg. Jumping it would be impossible with the egg in tow.

"We need to toss it across," he said.

"I'll catch it!" Horace bellowed from the other side of the moat.

The ground shifted under their feet.

"Can you throw it that far?" Abraham asked Prospero and Apollo.

"Prospero is the strongest of us, and you are far stronger than me, Captain," Apollo said.

The egg was the size of one of the round stones in a World's Strongest Man contest. Even getting one's arms around it was a handful. Prospero waddled as he tried to walk with it. He grabbed one side of the egg as Prospero held the other. They started swinging it. It slipped in Prospero's grip and dropped to the ground. Everyone gasped.

"Whoops," Prospero said.

Apollo slapped his face and dragged his fingers down his beard.

The egg lay on the ground, unscathed. No crack showed on its exterior.

"Captain, you're the strongest. See if you can throw it over," Tark suggested.

"I am." He lifted his brow. "Of course I am."

Abraham had yet to test his limits on anything. He had no idea how strong he really was. From what he saw of his muscular self, he could have been as strong as a bull. But he certainly didn't feel herculean by any means. He squatted down and picked the egg up. He rolled it up onto his shoulder with a "Hurk!" Back in college, he'd participated in a hay-bale tossing contest. He had pretty good idea of what he was doing by launching it from his shoulder. Testing the weight, he twisted at the hips.

Put your legs and shoulders into it, he told himself. *Use all of your body.*

"You can do it, Captain. Toss it right to me!" Horace thumped his chest with his fist and opened his arms, waiting for the catch. "I could throw it, so I know you can throw it."

Abraham bent at the knees, said, "Here it comes!" and gave it a heave.

The egg sailed up two feet high in a gentle arc. It landed in Horace's awaiting arms and bowled him over. He pushed it up in the air, from the bench-press position. "I caught the egg!"

The Henchmen let out a rousing cheer. No one was more surprised than Abraham. *Dang, I am strong as a bear!*

The ground quaked. Something on the other side of the nest started moving.

CHAPTER 17

ABRAHAM, STICKS, DOMINGA, TARK, BEARCLAW, Prospero, and Apollo leapt over the moat, which was shielded by Iris's fire. Once they made it across, the lingering flames on her fingers extinguished.

"That took all I had left," she said.

"You did well," Abraham said. He was still marveling at his great strength. The minor herculean feat enthused him, but the awakening Fenix kept his senses level. "We need to find a way out of here. Horace, I need you and another strong back to carry the egg. I'll do it if I have to."

"Let me try to help," Solomon said. He stood over Horace, who was still on his back hoisting the egg up. Solomon plucked the egg out of Horace's hands and lifted it to his body like an egg carton. "I think I can handle it."

"Why didn't you do that before?" Abraham asked. "You could have probably jumped the moat with it."

"You didn't ask, and I really wasn't that sure myself."

Horace popped up from the ground. "Give me the egg. I'll carry it, you filthy troglin. You'll probably try to eat it."

"Be my guest." Solomon stuffed the egg in Horace's awaiting arms.

"Oof!" Horace said as the egg sank against his belly. He waddled as he walked away from Solomon. Puffing for breath, he said, "Don't worry, Captain. I have it. I'm the strongest bull in the valley."

Abraham wasn't sure about that. He knew Horace had the iron strength that matched his girth but figured he himself was a match for him. As for Solomon, the bigfoot man was part animal and eight feet tall. He might have been aging, but he was no doubt formidable.

"If you carry that egg, then Solomon will have to carry your spear," Abraham said.

Horace growled and gave the egg back to Solomon. "Fine, but he better not drop it or eat it."

"Ruger!" Sticks said. "We need to go!"

As a single unit, the Henchmen headed back in the direction they'd come from, leaving the nest and the sludge pools behind. They didn't stop until they arrived back where they'd started. Thirty feet above them, the tunnel they'd fallen through awaited.

"How do we get up and out of there without slipping?" he asked.

"We didn't have the rope ready the last time. I can climb up and secure it," Sticks said. She slung the coil of rope over her shoulder. The gritty woman started to scale the wall that led up to the opening.

"I'll go with her," Dominga said. When Vern tossed her a small pack, she snatched it and carried it on her shoulder. "Thanks."

A bone-chilling moaning carried throughout the massive cavern. It was part animal, part sub-human.

"It sounds angry," Iris said. The homely woman kept looking back over her shoulder. "I never imagined that I would have to face an Elder before. At least, not until I was dead."

"And you never would have had to until the new Ruger came along," Vern said. "Before, the Red Tunics handled the dirty work." He brushed the back of his hands over his grimy armor. "Now, we are the dirt. We didn't chase after monsters like this, either. It was men against men, not a bunch of adventuring monster hunters."

"Becoming a Henchman never promised any of us otherwise," Horace said. He spat out tobacco juice. "So, quit your belly aching, Vern."

"Can't help it. It's how I like to pass the time," the salty flaxen-haired warrior replied.

Abraham didn't pay him any mind. He'd been around his share of complainers. He watched Sticks and Dominga disappear into the tunnel.

The sound of rock cracking echoed throughout the cavern. Iris jumped and clung to Horace. He put his arm over her shoulder.

Skrreeeeeee. Skreeeeeee. Skreeeeee.

The weird animalistic sound was followed by a tight burst of huffing and snorting.

It was the weirdest, most mind-grating sound Abraham had ever heard. A power behind it filled up the cavern. Abraham had hoped that when they found the Fenix, it would be dormant or in some sort of deep hibernation. A reason must have existed that it had lain in silence for so long. No one had disturbed it. He could still see the huge, glaring eyes in his mind. No mortal saw the Fenix and lived. They were about to test that theory. He cupped his hands over his mouth and called up into the tunnel. "Uh... Sticks? How's that rope coming along?"

No one answered. The seconds went by like minutes.

"I'm sure she has it," he said in a reassuring fashion.

"Something comes," Tark said.

A loud hufflike bark started, followed by that mind-jarring *skreeee* sound. Iris and Vern plugged their ears with their fingers. Everyone that had a weapon had it drawn. Judging by the size of the Fenix's eyeballs, its head must have been the size of an elephant. Its body would fill half the cave. They would not be able to get around it.

"Sticks?" Abraham said. "Dominga?"

With his head twisting back and forth on his shoulders, Vern shouted, "Will you two dirty little whores hurry up?"

"I don't think your character assassination is going to spur their efforts," Solomon said.

"What do you know, ape?" Vern replied.

A long and loud sniffing sound began, following by a hungry sigh.

"The Fenix probably hasn't eaten in a very long time. I bet it's hungry," Horace commented.

Far back in the cave, a tremendous hulking body blacked out the twinkling green crystals that decorated the walls. It approached slowly and became bigger. The sniffing and screeching became louder.

"Start climbing," Abraham said. He shoved Horace and Iris forward.

The Fenix head appeared in the dim light. It was one of the most hideous things he'd ever seen.

"Go, everyone. Go, go, go!"

CHAPTER 18

A ROPE DROPPED OUT OF THE tunnel above. Sticks popped her head out from over the rim. "It's secured!" she said. She cast a daring look toward the commotion coming from the cavern, and her face turned ashen. Her little chin hung.

Iris, with the help of Horace, was the first person to climb from the cavern floor into the tunnel.

"Climb," Sticks told the mystic. "Climb!"

"I am," Iris said. She started to look back over her shoulder.

Sticks pushed her face away and said, "Climb."

Horace hustled into the tunnel after Iris. He clung to Sticks's side, and both of them assisted everyone else. Tark came up, followed by Apollo, Prospero, and Bearclaw. Solomon navigated the climb while carrying the egg with little difficulty. Vern and Abraham were still on the ground.

"Get up there." Abraham was holding Black Bane. "You'll only die if you stick around."

"You're the Captain. You should go first," Vern argued.

Abraham shoved him. "Get up there. That's an order!"

Vern sheathed his sword and hustled to the wall and started his climb.

Am I mad? Abraham thought. His feet were firmly on the ground. He held his sword out in front of him in the high point position. The battle would be like fighting a rhinoceros with a toothpick. The Fenix was huge. It was a hideous creature with a hammer-shaped head and four sets of enormous eyes. Its four nasal canals were hairy caverns. It had whiskers like a cat that probed the ground. The Fenix slunk forward on claws like a great bird. The monstrous wings folded alongside the spiny ridges on its back were leathery. Saliva dripped from huge fangs in its mouth and sizzled on the cavern floor. *Why am I still standing here?*

"Captain, run now while there is still time!" Horace shouted.

Abraham didn't understand what was happening. His feet were glued to the floor. He should have been the first one out of the tunnel and still running. Any normal man would have done that. Instead, he stood firm. He didn't want to fight the Fenix. Apparently, Ruger did. The flames of battle burned inside him. Ruger wanted this, not him.

"Captain! Get up here!" Horace shouted.

"Take the rope now!" Sticks added.

"Ruger," Abraham said to himself. "This is madness. Let me go. We can't fight this thing. It will swallow us whole!"

The Fenix crept forward. It was only one hundred feet away.

The tail end of the rope hit Abraham in the face. "Grab on!" Horace said.

Ruger's body gave in. Abraham entwined his free arm in the rope. "Pull me up! Pull me up!"

The Fenix came faster. Its great jaws opened wide as all its eyes locked on Abraham. It sped up as it scurried forward.

"Faster, dammit! Faster!" Abraham said.

Horace and Sticks reeled him in like a fish.

With its mouth spread wide, the Fenix lunged and snapped its jaws.

Abraham tucked his legs up to his chest.

The Fenix's teeth clacked loudly together. *Chomp!*

Aided by his companions, Abraham climbed inside the tunnel by the skin of his teeth. They started climbing up the slippery slope by using the rope hand over hand.

"Move it, Horace, move it!" Abraham said.

Led by Sticks, the trio traversed the tunnel. Horace's feet kept slipping on the slick ground.

Abraham put his shoulder into him. "We are almost there! Go!"

He stole a glance behind his shoulder. The Fenix had begun stuffing its head into the tunnel. Like a rat, it was squeezing its great body into the gap, which should have been too small for it. It was coming. Abraham could see that in its eyes. It would have them all dead in minutes.

"Go! Go! Go! Go!"

Finally, the last three Henchmen emerged out of the tunnel and onto the firmness of the cavern's ground. Every one of them was panting for breath. The rest of the Henchmen were waiting. Iris carried the lone torch.

"Is it trapped down there?" Tark asked.

"No, it's snaking its way up that wormhole," Horace said. "We must go."

"Agreed." Tark beckoned for the others to follow him. "I know the way."

"Hold on," Abraham said. "I'm staying."

Half the dumbfounded group said in unison, "What?"

"Listen. Get that egg out of here," he continued. "But that thing's coming, and our best chance of stopping it is fighting it once it climbs out of that hole. I don't know if we have the mettle to do it, but if we don't, well, I'm pretty sure we are all dead men… and women."

A savage growl came up out of the tunnel.

Iris covered her ears and cringed.

Horace tapped the butt of his spear on the ground. "It's a sound plan. I'm staying."

Bearclaw stepped forward. "No horse is going to be able to run that fast. We must fight it one way or the other." He spun his axe and kissed each blade. "I'm taking two eyes before I go."

"You do realize you are fighting the spawn of an Elder," Iris said. "Mortals don't kill them. They kill mortals."

"Perhaps the time for change has come," Solomon said. "For only the ridiculous achieve the impossible."

"Where'd you hear that?" Abraham said. "Woodstock?"

"No, I read it in a bathroom stall," the troglin replied.

"Just get that egg out of here. Tark, you, Iris, and Dominga get out of here. We'll buy you all of the time we can."

"Aren't you going to send me out?" Sticks said plainly.

"No, I thought you'd rather stick with me. No pun intended," he said.

"Actually, I'd rather go, but my knees are knocking so bad, I don't think I can move. You'll need me anyway," she said.

Tark and Solomon led the others away.

The Henchmen formed a semicircle in front of the tunnel entrance. Abraham stood in the middle of the pack. Horace stood on his right, with Apollo and Prospero. Sticks and Bearclaw were on his left, with Vern beside them. Horace spat. Shaking his sword, Vern cursed.

The Fenix squeezed up the tunnel. Its eyes glowed like blue ice. Its hot, rancid breath carried up the tunnel, coating them in stinky steam.

With a twist of his wrist, Abraham flipped Black Bane end over end. "This is it," he said. "Who wants to kill the spawn of an Elder today?"

As one, the Henchmen shouted at the top of their lungs, "Death before failure!"

CHAPTER 19

ABRAHAM LED HIS ROBUST GROUP of fighters into the mouth of the tunnel. The fearless knot of Henchmen charged through the hot, steamy breath of the Fenix as it squeezed its hulking body up through the tunnel.

"Die, beast!" Horace bellowed. He jammed the tip of his spear in the monster's nose.

Horace hacked at its eyes with his axe. Vern clipped at the Fenix's face with his sword while Apollo and Prospero chopped into the beast's skull with hard overhead chops.

"Taste the king's metal, foul, malodorous thing!" Apollo roared.

Steel sliced into the thick leathery hide and hard knotty ridges of the Fenix. Its great neck twisted from side to side. Steam continued to spew from its mouth, smelling like garbage. It let out an earsplitting *skreeeeeeeeeeee!*

Using Black Bane like a butcher's blade, Abraham turned the Fenix's nose into hamburger. It pushed forward, not slowing its sluggish charge. He hoped the sting of steel would push it back. If anything, it just made the monster mad. It was coming out of that hole.

"The spawn feels no pain!" Bearclaw said as he landed a two-handed chop into onto of the monster's eyes.

"Everything can die!" Sticks said. She tossed a dagger at its neck. The blade ricocheted into the ground. "Or not."

Its eyelid closed a split second in time, and Bearclaw's axe skipped off it. "Madness! Its eyelids are iron gates!"

"Keep at it!" Vern cried out. The swordsman was sticking his sword between the hard plates that covered the Fenix's skull in some places. "Everything has a weakness." He spun around and jabbed his sword at another of the monster's eyes. His blade bit home, plunging deep into its eyeball. "See, you need to aim better!"

The Fenix's eyelid closed down on the Vern's sword. With a shake of its thick neck, it ripped the sword out of Vern's grip.

"Ballocks!" Vern cried out. "That eyelid is as strong as a blacksmith's hand!" He kicked the monster with his boot. "Elder freak! Return my blade."

Bearclaw laughed while he was chopping. "It wouldn't be the first time that something dumber than you disarmed you."

Vern looked into the monster's eyes and replied, "I don't think it's dumb. I just need to start carrying more swords." He pulled his daggers, darted in, and started stabbing away.

Foot by foot, yard by yard, the abominable Fenix came forward, unslowed by the Henchmen's valiant efforts. It surged onward, its great jaws snapping at them. The Henchmen were in a slow retreat.

"Captain, this thing is not flesh and blood," Horace bellowed. He thrust his spear into the monster's cheek. "It does not bleed. Our strikes don't slow it. I'm putting everything I have into my blows. If it does not bleed, how can it die?"

"Something has to give!" Abraham rained down a two-handed chop on the bridge of the monster's snout. The steel hacked off a hunk of flesh, and blood spurted out. "It bleeds! It's hide's thick, but it bleeds. Put your backs into it, men!"

"Aye! Slay the spawn!" Horace roared.

The Henchmen's redoubled efforts were futile. The Fenix kept coming. They were backpedaling.

Abraham yawned. Out of the corner of his eye, he caught the others yawning too. *What is happening now?* He wasn't the only one yawning. Horace's jaws were wide open. Vern rubbed his eyes. Sticks rubbed her sleepy eyes. Prospero wandered away from the beast, found a spot along the wall, and lay down like a baby.

"Horace, do you feel sleepy?" Abraham shouted.

"My lids become heavy," Horace replied. "I'll keep fighting in my sleep, Captain. I promise."

"Crap!"

No wonder the Fenix wasn't trying to fight them. It had already sprayed them with its steamy breath, which must have been some sort of toxin. Abraham's limbs became heavy, his strikes slow and futile. He looked the monster in the eyes. A deep intelligence lurked in those massive orbs. It knew it had them. It knew it all along. It didn't have to fight because it had already won.

"Well played, monster."

Vern stumbled away from the Fenix and dropped to a knee. He started crawling away, out of the tunnel.

"Horace, we have to get out of here! Everyone, get out! Get out!" he said.

Apollo hustled to Prospero and started dragging him out of the tunnel. Bearclaw helped Vern and Horace stumble out of the mouth. All of them escaped the mouth of the cave with the Fenix right on their tail.

"What is this?" Horace said as he stumbled around in a circle, blinking his eyes and using his spear like a walking stick.

Vern sat down and fell backward with his arms spread out like wings.

Bearclaw swayed and dropped to his knees. He tried to prop himself up with his axe.

The Fenix's head popped out from the tunnel as it let out a victorious *skreeeeeeee!*

Abraham fought to keep his head up and his eyes open. He looked at the Fenix's widening, slavering jaws. He looked at his sword, Black Bane. The pommel burned in his hand. The sensation kept him awake. The arcane etchings on the blade above the crossguard started to glow like campfire coals.

He turned his head and gazed upon the Fenix and said, "Black Bane, this is it. I just need one strike to kill it. Whatever you have, whatever you are trying to tell me, just do it." He lifted his sword and cocked its burning steel back behind the shoulder and screamed, "Death before failure!"

The Fenix opened its mouth wide. Abraham rushed into the jaws of death.

The Fenix lashed out and swallowed him whole.

CHAPTER 20

Sticks, Solomon, Tark, Dominga, and Iris cleared the cave. All of them except for Solomon were puffing for breath. The troglin set the giant egg down. All of them looked back as the Fenix's screeching carried out of the cave.

"Ah, my poor Horace, I don't think he's going to make it," Iris said.

"I don't think any of them are," Dominga added.

"We need to keep moving. That's what Ruger wanted," Tark said.

"Let's go," Sticks said. She felt awful saying it, but she'd seen the Fenix. With or without Ruger Slade, she didn't figure they stood a chance against it. That would take a miracle. "There is nothing that we can do for them now. We need to keep moving."

Solomon picked the egg back up and cradled it in his lengthy arms. "May fortune favor the foolish."

"Where are the horses?" Tark asked, turning his head left and right. "Where's my brother? Where's Twila and the horses?" He cupped his hands to his mouth and meandered forward. "Cudgel! Where are you, brother? Cudgel!"

"Strange," Solomon said.

"Maybe the terra-men got them," Dominga said.

"Don't say that," Iris said.

"Well, either that or they had enough good sense to flee," the young black woman said.

"Don't say that! My brother is a Henchman. He wouldn't ever run, and certainly he'd never abandon me. Besides, his leg was brok—" Tark's eyes grew big as moons, fixed on a figure lying down on the ground at the shadowy rim of the cave. He scrambled over to the man, screaming, "Cudgel! Cudgel!"

Sticks rushed to Tark's side. He was on his knees, cradling Cudgel in his arms. Cudgel's eyes were wide open. He was dead, a crossbow bolt protruding from his neck. Tark rocked back and forth, tears flowing down his cheeks. "No! Nooo! This can't be. What has happened to you, Brother? Come back to me!"

Sticks stopped grinding her teeth and said, "Twila. She must have done this. I'm sorry, Tark." She laid a gentle hand on his shoulder.

"You really don't think that little woman would have done this, do you?" Iris said. "She seemed so sweet. So simple. I can't imagine."

"I always thought she was squirrely," Dominga said. "But she seemed harmless. It would make sense that she might have been the one causing all of the trouble. Nobody would know it."

"Regardless, we must go," Solomon said. "We'll have to sort this out later."

Skreeeeeeeeeeeeee!

"I'm not leaving without my brother." Tark wiped his eyes. "The rest of you go. He's all I have left. I don't care anymore."

"This isn't what Cudgel would want," Sticks said. "He'd want retribution. He'd do the same for you too."

"I don't care."

Thunder rumbled in the sky. Everyone but Tark looked up. A lone cloud started to build in the air in front of the columns. It hovered one hundred feet above them, a storm of energy brewing inside it.

Sticks's nose tingled.

Solomon set down the egg and stretched out his furry, grimy arms. The hair on his body was standing straight up all over. "It's like static electricity." He looked at the cloud. "Oh my." He dropped to the ground. "Get down!"

A huge bolt of lightning burst out of the cloud just as Sticks flattened on the ground. The bright stream of flickering light was thicker than a man's arm. It streaked into the cave in a crooked white-hot cord of fire. It lit up the cavern with scintillating light and kept going. She shook. The cave trembled. The bowels of Titanuus exploded.

Abraham charged. He didn't anticipate the Fenix moving so quickly. Its neck stretched out suddenly, and its jaws were wide enough to engulf him. He leapt into its great maw and stabbed Black Bane into the roof of its mouth. Grunting with tremendous effort, he pushed the blade in as far as he could, hoping to pierce its brain.

The Fenix's jaws started to close. Its tongue pushed Abraham back toward its throat.

He hung on to his sword as the suffocating blackness closed all around him. With slime oozing into his face, he twisted his blade one last time, saying, "Man, it can't end like this."

Suddenly, the inside of the Fenix's mouth lit up like the Fourth of July. A bolt of energy blasted out the Fenix's teeth and latched onto Black Bane. Wroth mystic power surged through Abraham's fingertips and coursed through the sword and into the skull of the Fenix. The body of the Elder spawn quaked. Its fleshy mouth dried up and sizzled. Out of its jaws came a mind-jarring screech.

Abraham didn't have any idea what was going on. But he liked it. He pushed the sword in deeper and yelled, "Eeeeeeeeeee-yaaargh!"

The Fenix sputtered and smoked. Its body crackled and popped. It bucked, twisted, and writhed.

The lightning faded.

The Fenix let out a foul, throaty sigh and died.

Abraham pulled the sword free of the roof of the monster's mouth. His limbs trembled as he walked out of the Fenix's gaping mouth. He looked back and saw the Elder spawn's eyes were burnt to a crisp in their sockets. Smoke streamed out of all its orifices. Hunks of burning flesh dripped off its body.

He scratched his head. He was alive. It was dead. That was nothing short of a miracle, and he had no idea how it had happened. He yawned. He was tired. He'd never felt so tired. All he wanted to do was sleep. In his shaking hand, the engravings on Black Bane had started to cool. Wispy fingers of smoke drifted from the tip of the steel.

All he could think to say was, "Thank you, Black Bane."

You're welcome.

"Huh," he said just before his eyes closed, as he fell down and fell asleep.

CHAPTER 21

Abraham woke. He was outside the Fenix's cavern. The sun had set behind the columns in the crater, covering him in partial darkness. Someone nearby snored loudly. He propped himself up on his elbows to see Horace, lying on Iris's lap. She was stroking the stalwart man's beard. Her eyes grew when she looked up and saw Abraham.

"You awaken?" Iris said with relief. "Finally. This one sleeps like a hibernating bear. I don't think he'll wake."

"Probably not, so long as he's lying on those comfy thighs of yours," Abraham said out of nowhere, not sure where it had come from. "Sorry."

Iris broke out in a smile. "No need to apologize."

The group was down and away from the mouth of the cave, below the ledge they'd climbed up earlier to enter. Sticks made her way over from a small campfire. Her creaseless face showed elation behind a rail-thin smile. She helped Abraham to his feet and said, "So glad that you could join us. How was your nap?"

"Fitting," he said, pinching the bridge of his nose. He had a migraine. "I just feel like both sides of my brain are on one side of my head." He scanned the area to see that all the Henchmen who had fought the Fenix were lying about on the ground. "I take it we all made it?"

"Not all," Sticks said.

She pointed at Tark. He'd set himself apart from the rest of the group and was leaning over Cudgel's body. He was on his knees, rocking back and forth and singing quietly.

"Cudgel is dead."

"Dead? What happened?"

"We think Twila killed him."

"What?" He pictured the young pie-faced woman with dimpled cheeks and freckles—she was a hard worker but seemed ordinary. "How?"

"She shot him in the neck with your crossbow," Sticks said.

"That doesn't sound right. Even with a broken leg, Cudgel wouldn't be caught off guard. Was he asleep?"

"No, it didn't look like it. There was a scuffle in the dirt. She got him. Pinned the bolt in his throat. He fought her with the bolt sticking out of his neck." She shrugged. "He bled out trying to crawl back into the cave."

Tark's shoulders were heaving.

Abraham's heart sank. Every one of them had been through hell. They were coated head to toe in gory, nasty grime. But none of them had lost a brother. Tark was the last one of them all. Abraham thought of his best friend, Buddy Parker. That loss felt as bad as losing his own brother. The grief in the faces of Buddy's family, when he finally faced them, had almost killed him. "I better go talk to him."

Sticks put her hand on his shoulder and pushed him back down. "I wouldn't." She glanced side to side. "The last time one of their brothers died, they were very emotional about it. Do you remember?"

He shook his head. "So, Twila took all of the horses and gear?"

"All of it."

"Damn. She's a little wolf in sheep's clothing, isn't she?"

"I guess."

Abraham suddenly realized that Jake's backpack was on those horses. It was his only connection to home. *No, I can't have this. I have to get it back. We have to get the egg back.* "Well, how far of a head start could she have?" He stood, and pain shot through his eyes. "We need to catch up. A handful of us can go."

"She's on horseback. It will be tough to catch up on foot," Sticks said. "And we need to be at full strength. There is no telling what other terrors we might face."

"She might have to face them too. She'll have to go through the terra-men."

"Only if she goes back that way." Sticks took out a dagger and spun it inside the palm of her hand. "Twila is clever. A saboteur, spy, or assassin. I don't know, but I'm pretty sure she's also a survivor." She spun her dagger one last time and slid it into her sheath. "But it's your call, Captain."

"I'm getting my gear, and we're taking the egg back to King Hector. I'm not staying in this hellhole any longer. Everybody get up!" he said. "Now!"

Iris patted Horace's face. "Wake up, ox. It's time to go."

Dominga shook Vern and Bearclaw from their slumber. Apollo and Prospero finally stirred. All of them were yawning and stretching, with Horace the last to come around.

"I dreamed I slept in a field of lilies, only to wake up in the field of my dreams," he said to Iris. "Do I live? What happened to the Fenix?"

"A lightning bolt blew it up," Abraham said. "Now get your ass up. Let's go."

"Oh," Horace said as he slowly came to his feet. "Where did the lightning come from, Captain?"

"I don't know," he said, unable to hide his irritation. Losing his backpack had shaken him. He felt that if he lost it, he would lose everything he knew. As for where the lightning bolt had come from, he'd have to sort that out later. And he thought that he'd heard his sword talk too—that lingered. "Let's get a move on. We have a mission to complete and a murderer to track down."

Solomon approached. "I don't think navigating this crater at night would be wise."

"Well, we can't catch up with Twila if we don't march day and night either. We have to do this, Solomon." He moved to Tark. "I'm sorry about Cudgel, my friend, but we have to go. He'd understand. Let's grab some rocks and give him a proper burial."

Tark stopped singing and began to shake his head. "Grab some rocks? And bury him out here like some wild coyote? We've abandoned enough of my brothers to the dirt. I'll not let it happen to another. I'll dig him a proper grave with the skin of my fingers. Go away, Ruger. Go away. The only thing you care about is your mission. So, go. Complete it! Kill me right here if you must. I don't want to be a Henchman!"

Vern hurried over to Abraham and Tark. "Cudgel is dead?"

"Twila did it," Dominga said.

"And you fools thought I was the trouble all along. I hope your heads are clear now! Sorry, Tark. Cudgel was a good man. All of you were." Vern's heavy stare landed on Abraham. "You aren't going to say a few words, Captain? Are we just going to leave him in a shallow grave and let the vultures pick him clean?"

"We have to track down Twila," Abraham said. "She can't get away." His guts were twisting inside. He needed Jake's pack. "Bearclaw, you and Dominga find the tracks. Start leading us out of here. Tark, you can stay, but at some point, you'll have to move on."

"I'll stay with you, Tark," Vern said.

Abraham grabbed Vern by the back of the neck and slung him down to the ground. "No, you'll go!"

Sitting on his backside, Vern said, "Sure, Captain, sure, but aren't you going to say a few words?"

Abraham found all eyes on him, even Tark's. All of them had been through hell, and they looked like it too. They were weary. Even Horace's chin was dipped. One and all of them had been fighting their guts out for him for days. They followed him like sheep. They deserved better than what he was giving them. He looked at Solomon, who stood behind the group, holding the egg in his hands. That might be the key to him getting home. He moved over to where he could get a better look at Cudgel. Cudgel had a caked-up hole in his neck. His dying must have been awful. He was betrayed by one of his own. Abraham sighed. Tark's distraught face changed his heart. *My backpack can wait.*

"I have a few words to say. Solomon, bring over that egg and plant it right here by Cudgel."

Solomon set the egg down where he was asked.

"We aren't going to kill ourselves over an egg that might not do anything. We're going to find out if it works first." He looked at Iris. "Can the dead be brought back to life?"

"The essence of the dead lingers in the body until it is buried or it's consumed by one element or another. It is well known that it can happen," Iris said. "Why?"

"Because I'm going to tap this egg and find out if it has any healing powers at all before any more of us get killed." He drew his sword, jammed it into the top of the egg, and twisted. A hole in the top cracked open.

"Captain, what are you doing? That is for the queen!" Horace said.

He withdrew his blade and pulled the goo-caked hunks of shell away. A sweet aroma drifted into his nostrils. After all the reeking smell they'd been through, nothing ever smelled better.

"I swear, that smells like vanilla ice cream and cherries," Abraham said.

"What are you going to do, Captain? Drink it?" Horace said.

"No." He picked up the egg and tilted it over Cudgel. "I'm going to give our brother a bath with it." He poured.

A syrupy white goo came out and splattered all over Cudgel's body. It filled the shallow grave the dead man lay in.

Tark's smoky eyes were glued to his brother. He looked up at Abraham. "You did that for me? For Cudgel? But the queen…" Tark said, his jaw hanging.

"Right now, Cudgel needed it more than her." Abraham nodded. "We all came to this dance together, and we're going to leave together if at all possible. I'm sorry, Tark, if it doesn't work. Cudgel is a good man. He deserved better."

"I just wish I could have told him goodbye. But thank you for trying," Tark said. "It brings me peace."

Iris knelt beside Tark. She dipped two fingers in the strange egg yolk and applied it to a deep laceration on Tark's arm. The wound quickly started to mend. "It might not bring back the dead, but it certainly regenerates the flesh. And quickly." She rubbed her fingers together. The egg yolk started flaking. "But I fear those properties won't last without remaining fresh in a seal. Captain, may I?"

Abraham nodded.

Iris started applying the yolk like a salve to everyone's wounds. While she did that, the yolk started caking around Cudgel.

Abraham put his hand on Tark's shoulder. "I really am sorry. I tried. Let's give him a burial that you like."

"What about Twila and the queen?" Tark said.

"We'll figure something out," Abraham said.

"Yes, we'll figure something out 'cause I'm going to find that pie-faced witch."

Abraham was looking at Tark, and his lips weren't moving. Tark was looking at him, and his lips weren't moving either. They both looked down. Cudgel's eyes were wide open. He was smiling.

CHAPTER 22

THANKS TO THE FENIX EGG yolk and Cudgel's revival, the Henchmen had a spring back in their step. They had a problem too. Without anything to seal the egg, the yolk quickly dried up, and its healing properties were ruined. They could all blame that on Twila, who'd stolen all their gear. In the meantime, Abraham was thankful they were all alive even though he was concerned he'd lose touch with all reality without his pack.

You know who you are. Don't forget it. You're Abraham Jenkins. A Pittsburgh Pirate turned beer-truck driver. Turned super swordsman. Ah man, this is nuts.

He led the group back into the cavern where the Fenix was lodged inside the tunnel. Using their weapons, they chopped the monster up. They had no other choice because they had to go back for another egg to return to Kingsland. It turned out to be a rigorous task, but at least no one complained about the stink.

They tied the ropes to the bones of the Fenix's carcass and shimmied back down into the cave. They took more fire with them and placed it by all the black pools to keep the sludge monsters at bay. With all things appearing to be in order, Abraham led Apollo, Prospero, Bearclaw, and Sticks across the moat. Solomon and Horace waited on the other side. Apollo and Prospero were the first to scurry up the nest and disappear over the rim with a *sploosh.*

Abraham looked over at Sticks and said, "Better them than me."

"Once odd, always odd," she said.

He climbed the nest with Sticks and Bearclaw bringing up the rear. Apollo and Prospero were wading chest deep through the pool of goo. "Are you coming, Captain?" Apollo asked. "The water is fine. Warm and reviving."

Abraham sighed through his clenched teeth. He'd just gotten out of the muck pit, and now he had to go in again. He considered passing his sword over to Apollo and letting them saw away. He shook his head and said, "I'm coming." He dropped into the pool, and his face drew up tight. "This is awful."

"Feels good, aye!" Apollo splashed the nasty waters at Prospero.

Prospero stiffened and splashed Apollo back. The exchange heated up. Both men started wrestling like pigs wallowing in mud.

Shaking his head, Abraham said, "Such fine company I keep."

"It looks like fun, Captain," Sticks said. She actually had a smile on her face.

"Yes, why don't you join me?"

"No, thank you," she replied.

Abraham took out Black Bane. "Sorry about this," he said to the sword, hoping it would reply, but it didn't. He reached underneath another egg and sawed at the strange cords that fastened the egg to its perch. He was working on the smaller of the two as the last one was much bigger. As he sawed away, he noticed a crack in the bigger egg. He stopped sawing. "Wait a minute."

Prospero dunked Apollo under the murk and let out a gusty laugh. Apollo's arms flailed above the waters.

Abraham made his way around to the other side of the bigger egg. A hole was in the egg. Hunks of the eggshell floated in the waters. He rose up on tiptoe. Nothing was in the egg. "Holy crap, this thing hatched."

Sticks called out to him. "What did you say?"

"This thing hatched!" he hollered as he scanned the water left and right. "Prospero, Apollo, cut it out!"

Prospero let Apollo out of the murk.

Apollo gasped for air and punched Prospero in the chest with both hands. "Don't do that again!" He pushed the hair out of his eyes. "Something wrong, Captain?"

"One of the eggs hatched. Be wary. Let's get this other egg out of here… fast." He hurried back to the egg that he was sawing on and started cutting again.

Apollo and Prospero put their hands on the egg and rocked it back and forth. With a snap, the roots underneath the egg finally came free.

"Let's go," said Abraham. "Go, go, go!"

They pushed the floating egg across the pool to where a rope waited to help them climb. Brandishing his sword, Abraham guarded their backsides. The only thing that moved in the waters was them. He saw no sign of a fledgling Fenix.

"Sticks, holler at Solomon," Abraham said. "We need to get this thing out of here fast."

Solomon climbed up on the nest. "Did you call?"

"Grab the egg."

Prospero climbed on Apollo's shoulders. Working in tandem, they rolled the egg up the inner wall of the nest, the same way they had before. With some heavy grunting, they pushed the egg up to the top, where Solomon was able to secure it with his big paws and roll it up on the rim.

Solomon picked up the egg. "Hmm, it's a tad heavier." He shook the egg, and something sloshed around inside. "A good fifty pounds, but my back can take it." He lifted it onto his shoulder and hopped up off the nest.

"All right, Tweedle-Dee and Tweedle-Dum, get out of there," he said to Apollo and Prospero.

The men grabbed the rope and climbed, leaving Abraham in the pool all alone.

Without looking up at Sticks, he asked, "You don't see anything, do you?"

"No. I'm certain that the little monster hides. Even if we encounter it, no doubt we can kill it. It's just a baby."

"Yeah, well, babies can grow up and become vengeful. One never knows." He reached back and grabbed the rope.

"Come on. I'm ready to get out of this place. I think I'm getting used to the smell," she said.

"Agreed," Bearclaw added. He climbed down off the nest. Sticks followed after him.

Abraham started to sheath his sword. The waters bubbled up behind him. He froze. The waters continued to bubble. Abraham jabbed his sword into the bubbles but hit nothing. He stabbed his sword in a few times. The pool bubbled in more than one spot. It appeared to be a natural occurrence.

He let out a breath and sheathed his sword. "Let's get out of here."

Abraham turned around and grabbed the rope with both hands. He felt eyes on him. His blood froze as he turned his head left and found himself almost nose to nose with the eight-eyed baby Fenix nestled in a cleft.

CHAPTER 23

Abraham's eyes were locked on the Fenix. The Fenix's eyes were locked on his. It was an ugly thing, like an eight-eyed hammer-head bat with a soft pelt of fur all over it. It was big, too, for a baby, possibly one hundred pounds and as big as a kid. Abraham slid his hand down to the dagger on his belt. He needed to kill it. One pair of eyes, the two rows at the top, stayed on him, and the other two sets followed his hand. He pulled the dagger free.

Sticks popped her head over the top of the nest and said, "Are you coming?"

"Quiet," he said. "I found the baby Fenix. It's right here, in the nest."

"Well, kill it."

"I'm getting there," he said, stealing a glance at her before dropping his eyes back on the Fenix, but it was gone. "What? Where did it go?" He jabbed his dagger into the spot where the Fenix had been nestled. "Sonuvagun, it's gone!"

"Are you sure that you saw it?"

"As sure as I can see you right now." He looked about with probing eyes. His keen senses could pick up anything most of the time, but the Fenix had vanished. "Damn. Let's just get the heck out of here." He put the dagger in his mouth and started to climb. Up and out of the nest he went and joined Sticks down by the moat.

"Maybe we should burn the nest," Sticks said.

Standing on the other side of the nest, Horace waved a torch back and forth. "Just say the word, Captain."

Abraham hopped over the moat, looked up at the nest, and said, "It's probably not going to survive very long without its mother or father or whatever. I think we've done enough damage. Let's just leave well enough alone. After all, we came after it. It didn't come after us."

"If you say so, Captain." Carrying the torch high, Horace led the way back out of the tunnel.

Finally, all the Henchmen were out of the caverns, and on foot, they resumed their trek out of Elder's Birthing.

Cudgel and Tark were all smiles that day. Both of them thanked Abraham at least one hundred times. Cudgel talked long about Twila. "She's a clever one, that one. She acted all innocent and stupid. She even offered to have a toss with me, and well, given the situation, I was tempted." He shook his head. "Mmm... mmm... mmm, that flowery voice of hers and sweet demeanor turned from one side of the hand to the other. She became cold and devilish. She shot that crossbow at me like she'd shot it one hundred times before. It hit, but I didn't feel it. I just wanted to kill her."

"We are going to get her, Brother," Tark promised. "You will be avenged."

Cudgel nodded. "That's kind of a funny notion now. How I can I be avenged when I'm still living?" He chuckled. "I'm just so happy to be alive, I could almost move on, but she betrayed the Henchmen, and she must pay."

Dominga walked close by with her hands on the hilts of the daggers. Her hips had a nice natural sway when she walked. "She'll pay, all right. For all that we know, she's the one that caused all of the misfortune that we'd run into. She caused the deaths of more of our brethren. I bet she let those frights loose that almost killed all of us. I knew we shouldn't trust her."

"Yes, well, the bigger question is, 'Why did she do it?'" Sticks asked.

"It sounds like someone is setting us up to fall," Abraham said. "There couldn't be a better explanation for it. The king has his enemies, and they can be within just as well as without. Someone doesn't want the king to win. They don't want the queen to survive. For all we know, they've poisoned her." He thought of Viceroy Leodor. The man was odd and very close to the king. It only made sense that a creepy man like that fit the bill. That was almost always the cause.

"Captain, we've never seen the king's servants. You would know better than anyone if that was the case," Vern suggested. "You bring in the new Red Tunics. You meet with Prince Lewis and Leodor. You make the decisions. You are as responsible for our calamities as any."

"What are you getting at, Vern?" Abraham said.

Vern stopped his march. Everyone stopped along with him. He walked up on Abraham. "I'll tell you what I'm getting at. Years ago, I was one of the King's Guardians. Most of us were. You were the captain, and we'd follow you to hell and back." He slid his eyes over Horace, Bearclaw, Apollo, and Prospero. "Then, you deserted. Many of us followed. Our lives have been chaos ever since. The man I followed, that we all followed, is gone. I don't what happened to the real Ruger, who stood with a spine filled with iron. But he's been gone a long time." He pointed a finger in Abraham's face. "You are possessed, and you need to hang!"

"You need to watch how you address the Captain, Vern," Horace warned. His voice was strong. "He has the right to cut you down if he likes. We gave an oath to follow Ruger Slade and serve the King. Possessed or not. It is what has been and what it will be."

"Horace, you are as blind as you are bearded," Vern said. "He could tell you to chop your own leg off, and you would."

"And you'd better, too, if he gave the order," Horace replied.

"He's crazy!" Vern shouted. "I know I'm not alone in my thinking. We've all had doubts. We've seen our brothers and sisters die. How much longer are we going to follow a man whose spirit changes with the wind? How many more of us have to die?"

"None of us have died," Sticks said. "We all still live. When's the last time we had a mission when someone didn't die?"

"Well, the mission ain't over yet," Vern replied.

Cudgel stepped forward, put a hand on Abraham's shoulder, and said, "I haven't been around long enough to understand all of the changes, but I'll tell you this. I like this man better than the last. His actions speak for themselves. I'll always follow him. Whatever changed, it's a good thing."

"I stand by Ruger and my brother as well," Tark said.

All the Henchmen surrounded Abraham, leaving Vern standing alone.

He shook his head and looked Abraham dead in the eye. "Who are you? Just tell me the truth."

Abraham couldn't help it when he replied, "You can't handle the truth."

CHAPTER 24

"You do a lot of talking these days," Vern said with a sneer. "I ought to knock your head off."

Several of the henchmen laughed.

"Vern, you're the worst brawler here. Iris could take you," Sticks said, stepping toward him. "But you can take a shot at me if you want."

"I'd like to see this," Tark said.

"Me too," added Cudgel. "My money is on Sticks."

"All right, that's enough," Abraham said. "Man, you guys want to scrap all of the time, don't you? Haven't we lost enough skin from our necks these past few days?"

No one said a word. Horace rubbed the back of his neck.

"As for my comment about Vern not being able to handle the truth, well, that was a joke from where I come from."

"I've never heard that expression before," Dominga said, "And I'm usually on top of things in Kingsland."

"It's from a movie," he said, fully anticipating the next question.

"What's a movie?" Iris asked.

"It's like a play or a puppet show. You have those sorts of things in the theaters, don't you?"

Many among the group nodded.

"Anyway, where I come from, the show is projected on a wall." He pinched the bridge of his nose. His migraine was still nagging at him. "Here is what I am trying to get at." He saw Solomon give him a concerned look. "Vern's suspicions are right, and I want to clear the air. I'm not Ruger as many of you had known him. I'm sure most have you have seen the changes. But you're faithful to your word, so you don't comment on it. All of you are good soldiers. As for me, well, I guess in order for you to understand it, we'll have to talk about possession. My spirit, or essence, is from another world, and somehow I wound up in Ruger's body. I can't explain how it happened any better than you could. But it happened. I came from another place and time. And now, I'm here, leading the Henchmen."

Abraham's words were met with stone cold silence. The company exchanged nervous glances with one another. Vern's hand went to his sword. Bearclaw's tight grip creaked on the leather bindings on his axe. Prospero and Apollo reached toward the swords crossed over their backs.

As Iris stepped behind Horace, he lifted his spear, pointed it at Abraham, and said, "You are saying that you are possessed?"

Horace didn't say *Captain.* That made Abraham's fingertips tingle. He'd tried to get Horace to stop saying it before, but he never did, until then.

Lifting his hands, palms up and outward, Abraham said, "I'm not possessed. Ruger Slade is possessed by me. But not by my choice."

"I told you," Vern said with haughty victory in his voice. "He is one of those otherworlders. The king and the Sect kill them. They are trouble. They are a curse upon all of Kingsland."

"King Hector knows," Abraham said.

"Lies!" Vern blurted. "If King Hector knew, he would have killed you."

Abraham reminded himself that none of this could be real. If it was a dream, he would have nothing to lose. If it wasn't, well, he had become one of the most incredible warriors who ever lived. He kind of liked it, but he didn't want to die either. "But he didn't. I'm a Henchman, on the same side as the rest of you, serving the kingdom. It's up to you whether or not you believe it. Personally, I have a hard time believing it myself, but I'm using the cards I was dealt." His stare grazed over the fingers fidgeting on the handles of their weapons. "So, what are all of you going to do, try to kill me?"

The Henchmen exchanged several looks amongst themselves. Finally, Horace spoke up and said, "Why no, Captain. We weren't going to kill you. We were going to kill Vern."

Vern's jaw dropped.

The company shared a jovial outburst of laughter. Even Abraham was nervously laughing.

Sticks slipped in beside him, and while the others were laughing, she said, "I think they like the new Ruger."

"Yeah, well, I'm glad. I started to think that they were going to run me through."

"Maybe Vern, but I think he's learned his lesson."

Vern walked away with a long face, his head down and shoulders slumped.

Abraham gave Sticks a pat on the rump. "I better go talk to him."

"Good luck with that," she said.

He caught up to Vern and said, "You don't have to like me, but we still need to work together and see this thing through. King Hector said that he may release us from our bonds of servitude. We've made it this far. Let's finish it together as one."

"I'm not very comfortable following a man with changing personalities. I need someone I can count on. You used to be rock solid, then you became a worm, and now, well, you're brazenly unpredictable." Vern took a deep breath and looked him in the eye. "You were my mentor. My trainer. A father or dear uncle I never had. Then you went away. Or Ruger went away. I don't understand it. I want Ruger back. Not something else. Not some impostor." He poked his finger into Abraham's chest. "Where is he?"

"I can't answer that. And I can't say for sure that Ruger is gone, either," he said. "Some of the things I do, I'm not doing—he's doing it. It's as if we are two personalities in one. I control the mind, but he still has the body." Abraham clutched his fingers in and out. "When I stood in front of the Fenix the first time, I wanted to run. Ruger wouldn't let me. He wanted to fight. He's fearless."

"You're damn right he is." Vern's hard expression softened. He studied Abraham's eyes and said, "Ruger, are you in there?"

Without thinking, Abraham placed his right hand on Vern's left shoulder and tapped Vern twice with his middle and index finger. Vern's eyes grew.

"I didn't do that," Abraham said.

"I know," Vern replied with astonishment. "He did."

CHAPTER 25
LEWIS

On horseback, Lewis led a train of his men up the coastline of Southern Tiotan. He was chasing after his half-sister, Clarice, and her Guardian Maidens. It was the last thing on earth that he wanted to do, but it had to be done. The sea breeze blew his feathered black hair into his eyes. He brushed it away. A flock of seagulls flew overhead. One of them pooped on his shoulder.

He took out a handkerchief, wiped the crap from his shoulder, and tossed the cloth away. "I hate birds. I hate the sea. I have much better things to do than this. We all do."

"Agreed," said the man riding beside him. His name was Pratt, Lewis's right-hand man. He was a big fellow, dark complected and heavy eyed, with very short brown hair, sideburns down to his ears, broad features, thick lips, and a lantern jaw. He was the biggest man in the group, by far. The King's Guardians no longer donned the customary full-plate armor and lion helmets. The group of twelve wore leather armor underneath traveling cloaks. Pratt had a gruff, ballsy way when he spoke. "We'll catch them soon. The Guardian Maidens know little about hard riding. They are birds that belong in the castle. We'll get them."

"Yes, well, we haven't caught up with them yet, have we?" Lewis said.

"No. But we will. I can feel it."

Pratt's eyes narrowed. Two riders were approaching, two more knights, dressed the same as the others. They'd been scouting ahead.

Pratt leaned over his saddle horn. "What have you found, Derik?"

All the guardians were well-knit men, and Derik was no exception. "Plenty of fishermen saw them pass no more than a day ago. By the sound of it, they are only half a day's ride, if that, and heading straight for the crotch of Titanuus. I'm not sure where they will enter the Spine, but it shouldn't be difficult to find out."

"Why do you say that?" Lewis asked.

Derik showed a pearly white smile and flipped Lewis a coin. It was a silver shard with Kingsland's marking. "Your sister is showing off her generosity. Apparently, the fishermen are doing a lousy job catching fish, and she gave them money for food. Oh, and she gave them a pack pony too. According to the fishermen, she said, and I quote, 'For you, your wives, your children. Let the king's grace be upon you.' She's so very kind. I admit I'm looking forward to seeing her again, as well as the maidens."

"She is an idiot." Lewis looked at the coin pinched between his thumb and finger. He flicked it away into the sand. "Only Clarice would prance up the shores of southern Tiotan and spew on about the king's grace. She'll have her throat cut if she parts her lips in front of the wrong people."

"We won't let that happen." Pratt took a slug of water out of his skin. "If anyone lays a hand on the princess, we'll butcher them."

Staring out to sea, Lewis absentmindedly replied, "Yes. Yes, of course."

He couldn't have cared less about Clarice, but he was in a tough spot. The King's Guardians were good men who would die trying to bring her back. None of them were aware of the game he played with Leodor and the Underlord. That was his secret that he kept to himself. Ultimately, the guardians served the crown, and they wouldn't go against the king, even on his own orders. That would be dishonor, and they would rather die first.

"We could catch up with them by nightfall, or at least Gravely and I could," Derik suggested. He slapped a shoulder of the rider beside him. "You don't have two faster riders than us. Right, Gravely?"

Gravely, stone faced and straight backed, nodded.

"Go on, then. We'll ride hard the rest of the day," Lewis said. He waved them on. "Go!"

"Off we go, then. See you tonight." Derik turned his horse and galloped off with Gravely.

"We'll have them by evening, then we can head back to Kingsland," Pratt said. "I have to admit I've enjoyed the trot along the shoreline. When my time is done, I'll live near the shore. It's peaceful."

"Pratt, I don't care." He dug his heels into his horse. "Let's get this over with."

"Just making conversation," Pratt added.

Pratt had a strong tendency to ramble on about mundane things. He wouldn't shut up unless Lewis ordered it. But Lewis respected the elder enough to let him ramble. Pratt had been a Guardian Knight for over twenty years. He'd ridden with Ruger Slade. He knew things.

"It will be a stone cottage set against the hillside, blending in with the rocks, one with natural light shining in from the morning sun. I'll keep goats and chickens and keep a shepherd on hand," Pratt said as he rode alongside Lewis. "It will be nice. I may even take a wife and have sons and daughters. They too could become Guardians, at least the boys."

Lewis blocked him out. He wanted to delay tracking down Clarice, but that wasn't happening. They were too close now. He'd hoped that misfortune would befall her. That would rid him of the pesky little menace. As much as he wanted to delay the quest, he couldn't any longer. He was just hoping she would make it into the mountains at least. That would increase her chances of encountering a fatality. But the last thing he needed was her being captured by the king's enemies. If that happened, he would be the one sent to rescue her. He couldn't let that happen either. He had to be the good son and play along.

Oh please, let her be dead by the time I catch her.

Lewis and the King's Guardians caught up with Derik and Gravely at the base of the Spine just before nightfall. Derik was on foot, checking horse tracks in the ground.

Squatting on one knee with his hand in the dirt, he said, "They were here, but they went up there." He pointed at the foreboding gargantuan mountains of the Spine.

"How long since they entered the Spine?" Lewis asked.

"A few hours at most. I can't imagine them traveling far at all at night," Derik said. "Are we going after them?" Thunder rumbled overhead. Dark clouds were rolling in from the sea. "I'm not going be able to track if that rain comes down. What do you say?"

Lewis studied the dreaded mountains and felt insignificant in their midst. This was the place he'd sent other expeditions to die. Now, he had to enter it himself. It started to sprinkle.

With a sigh, he said, "Ready the torches. We can't let them get too far. Let's go."

CHAPTER 26

Led by Derik and Gravely, the Guardians snaked their way up into the rigid mountains. The rough terrain was even more daunting to navigate at night, with strange trees and rocky outcroppings. Weird birds and critters made wild calls in the night that echoed through the channels. The sounds sent chills down Lewis's spine.

Pratt rode beside Lewis, carrying a torch and squinting.

"Perhaps you can settle down in the Spine," Lewis said.

"I'm curious to see what the Spine has to offer. I'm not beyond taking a journey through it. They say there are lost cities and civilizations unlike anything that lies beside the sea," Pratt commented. "I wish I could have been on those other campaigns."

"No, you don't. They didn't make it back."

"That doesn't mean they are dead just because we haven't seen them," Pratt said.

"You're annoying."

"I'm only being positive," Pratt replied.

He rolled his eyes.

Pratt stopped his horse and set his eyes on the rocky ledges above them. "Something moves above." He reached down and grabbed a light crossbow hanging from the saddle, and the other guardians followed suit.

Lewis squinted and followed Pratt's line of sight. One of the rocks had the look of a person on one knee. He couldn't tell whether it was real or not.

"Do you see a man or something else?" Lewis asked.

"I see a man," Pratt said under his breath.

Lewis started to slide his sword out of its scabbard. He saw no signs of Derik and Gravely, who were scouting ahead.

"You don't think—"

The distinctive sound of a bowstring snapping interrupted the silence.

Pratt rocked backward. "Argh!" A feathered shaft protruded out of his shoulder. "Bloody burdens, this is what I get for not wearing the king's armor!" He grabbed the shaft and ripped it out with a grunt. He eyeballed the arrow. "That's one of our feathers!"

The hidden archer fell out of their perch, and the person tumbled down the side of the hill and landed sprawled out on the path.

Lewis jumped off his horse and ran toward the archer, who was standing up. He tackled the archer and drove them hard to the ground. He pinned down the person's arms. It was a woman.

"Leah?"

"Prince Lewis?" she asked. She had beautiful round eyes and a long braided ponytail. She wore a bronze cuirass that enhanced her figure. She was one of the Guardian Maidens, one of Clarice's personal escorts. "What are you doing here?"

"Tracking down Clarice and you." He helped her to her feet. "Care to explain why you shot my Pratt?"

"I was only standing watch. Something startled me," she said.

Derik and Gravely climbed down from the spot where Leah was perched. "We slipped up on her, and just before I grabbed a hold of her, she fired," Derik said.

"You could have said something," Leah said. "I wouldn't have fired." She looked at Pratt. "Sorry. Is it bad?"

From his saddle, Pratt tossed the arrow at her. "It broke the skin. You'll have to pull the bowstring back farther if you want to do any real damage."

"I didn't have it fully drawn. Like I said, I was startled." She snatched the arrow from the ground. "I'm sure it would have killed you if it hit you in the throat."

The Guardians erupted in chuckles.

Lewis arched his brow and said, "Leah, I take it that Clarice isn't far away."

"No." She wiped her muddy hands on her britches. "You're going to take her home, aren't you?"

"Yes."

"Well, she won't like it."

He glowered at her. "Do I look like someone that cares what she likes?"

"No, Prince."

He took his horse by the reins. "Lead the way."

CHAPTER 27

"You are coming with me!" Lewis yelled. He'd been arguing openly with Clarice for over thirty minutes. They were at her camp, and she wouldn't budge. Her Maidens wouldn't either.

"I'm not going anywhere until I find that egg!" she shouted back. Clarice was a fifteen-year-old who thought she was thirty. She was short and shapely, with wide hips, a small waist, broad shoulders, long chestnut hair, and gorgeous fiery green eyes. She carried a rapier on her hip and two daggers. "Go home. Go home or join me because my quest has just begun." As pretty as Clarice was, she was stubborn as a bull.

Lewis shook his head. "You're leaving one way or the other." He grabbed her arm.

The Maidens slid their curved short swords out of their scabbards, all ten of them. Each was a tall athlete with pretty features, wearing a bronze cuirass that accented her sensual figures. Their braided ponytails were uniform, and the stern looks in their eyes meant business.

Clarice twisted out of Lewis's grip. "Don't you dare touch me again."

He looked at his open hand and said, "You're a strong little varmint, aren't you?"

She pulled her sword free. "I've warned you enough about calling me a varmint, critter, rodent—"

"Badger-face," he added.

She stabbed at him.

He jumped out of the way and pulled his sword free. "You better put that blade back where it belongs, or I'm going to teach you a very regrettable lesson."

"For you," she said. She sliced her rapier back and forth in quick flashes. "Let's have a go at it, Lewis the Lewd. Or are you afraid that I'll embarrass you?"

"I'm the best sword in Kingsland, child. Now, put your toy away before I throttle you." He poked his sword at her chest. He had superior reach and was glad to show it. "I mean it."

In a flash of steel, Clarice batted his sword aside with her blade, back spun her body into his, and put a dagger to his throat.

His eyebrows lifted. "Clever, little ferret."

"What did I tell you about comparing me to varmints?" she said.

"You might be fast, but you're far from fearsome." Quick as a cobra, he grabbed her wrist and bent it backward. She cried out and dropped to one knee. He applied more pressure, and the dagger fell free of her fingers. "If you're going to put an edge on someone's neck, then you better finish the job!" He pushed her down into the mud. "How's that for fast?"

Surrounded by the Guardians and the Maidens, with a steady rain coming down out of the night sky, Clarice said, "I'm still not coming with you. You'll have to fight all of us first. This cause is just. It is noble. It is for my mother, and I won't be turned away."

The rain came down harder.

Lewis looked into the sky. "Find shelter. We're going back home tomorrow. Pratt, make sure the Maidens don't scamper off in the middle of the night. If you need me, I'll be underneath that overhang."

"We'll leave in the morning. You can't stop us!" Clarice said.

"See you in the morning." He walked away.

Morning came. The rains stopped. The Guardians blocked Clarice and her Maidens from the slippery, muddy passage. Clarice's cheeks were rosy when she made her demands again. "Lewis, only a coward would prevent this noble expedition. Are you a coward? Or are you heartless?"

"Coward, no. Heartless, possibly." He yawned. "We can stand here all day, night, and day again, like monster bait, or we can go home, where you and I both belong."

"Why do you hate me and mother so?" she asked.

"You aren't from the proper lineage. Haven't you figured that out by now?"

"I share the same blood as you do," she said.

"No, your blood is tainted," he said. Clarice's frown deepened. Hurt showed in her pretty eyes. He combed his fingers through his hair and decided to try the nice-brother act. "Listen, it's not that I don't care about you or the queen. You're both, well, tolerable, but you need to understand that I miss my own mother. And I never found your mother to be a suitable replacement. Let me ask you: what if you were in my shoes? Would you just accept a new mother so willingly?"

"If she was my mother, yes. Mother is good and pure and strong. She abounds in love and grace. What child would not want a mother like that?"

Lewis caught Pratt looking at him with an arched brow. The hardened Guardian looked away.

Lewis sighed and said, "I'll make a deal with you. You come home with me, and I'll treat you and your mother much better."

"Our mother."

He shrugged his eyebrows and said, "All right, our mother."

Clarice's eyes brightened. She gave him a smug look, crossed her arms over her chest, and said, "I don't believe you. You've promised that before, remember? I'm not some stupid child that is going to believe you like I did the first time. I'm a woman now. Like my mother. I know better."

"You're a haughty little brat. That's what you are. If you march into those mountains, it will be to your doom. Just like the other expeditions that journeyed only to never return."

"I don't care. I have nothing to live for without mother."

"I wish I could let you go. I really do!" He threw his hands up. "Fine! You give me no choice. I'll disarm you and your Maidens and drag the lot of you home by your roots."

"You wouldn't dare!"

"You give me no choice. Pratt, take them!"

The Maidens drew their weapons and circled the princess. With their weapons drawn, the Guardians closed in. The knights, one and all, towered over the women even though some of the women were fairly tall. The Maidens were well-trained fighters and more than capable defenders. Not one woman batted an eye at the men who towered over them.

Pratt squared off with Leah and said, "No bloodshed. We use the cheeks of the steel only. Fair enough, Maiden?"

"Agreed," Leah said.

"You know," Pratt said in his slow rugged drawl, "I've never fought a beautiful woman before. It's awkward, but I won't insult you by going easy either."

"You're a true knight." Leah smiled. "En garde!"

Derik shouted from the top of the path, "Someone approaches!"

"A someone or something?" Lewis asked.

Derik rose on his toes and peeked around the bend. "A woman with horses. She's walking a trio of them."

Lewis lifted two fingers and said to Clarice, "This can wait, yes?"

"Lucky for you, it can."

"Well thanks to the Elder of Luck," he replied. Lewis immediately recognized the pie-faced woman in the red tunic. His throat tightened. He approached her and said, "Aren't you one of Ruger's retainers? Where do you come from?"

"Yes, I am Twila." She had scrapes all over her face, and the knees and elbows of her clothing were torn. "I came from a place called Elder's Birthing. A man named Solomon we met in a fisher town called Hackles led us there. He said that he would aid us in finding the Fenix's Egg. All that we found was our doom." She sagged to the ground.

"Get her some water," Lewis said.

Pratt put a water skin to Twila's lips and helped her drink.

Lewis kneeled beside her. "You said *us*. Where are the others?"

Twila guzzled the water, wiped her mouth, and said, "Thank you. I ran out of water over a day ago. As for Ruger and the Henchmen, they are all dead, and I want to get my arse off this mountain as fast as I can."

"Why?" Lewis asked.

"Because the terra-men and troglin are coming."

"How many?"

Twila shrugged. "The hills are filled with them. At least three for every man and woman."

"Saddle up," Lewis said. "We're going." He looked at Clarice. "Are you convinced?"

"I'll go, but at the bottom of the hill, I want the whole story. Maidens, let's ride."

CHAPTER 28

The Guardians and Maidens made camp a mile away from the bottom of the hills.

Fifteen-year-old Clarice grilled Twila with questions. "Tell me how they died, all of them."

"Go easy, girl, this retainer is traumatized," Lewis said.

Twila sat by the fire, shivering underneath a blanket. She nodded and said, "I can talk." She closed her eyes and took a breath. "We started with thirteen, and I'm the only one left. We didn't enter the Spine from this avenue. We started our trek above Hackles. We crossed a stream of lava and lost two Red Tunics. The guide took us to a massive crater called Elder's Birthing. He said it was the home of the Fenix. It's a wild place of tar pits and prickly vegetation. We encountered terra-men, fought through them, lost many horses, and fled to a cavern where our guide took us." Her nose crinkled. "The air was foul, rotting like refuse in a dung heap. I waited with the horses, with Cudgel. Led by Ruger, the Henchmen went into the cavern. There were screams. Weapons against bone clamored." She stared deep into the fire as she spoke. "I heard a sound so horrifying that my teeth clacked together. There was screaming. Yelling. All coming from the blackness. The screams fell silent.

"Deep in the cave, something massive dragged its great belly over the stones. Cudgel told me to run. I said no, but he forced me. When I looked back, I saw him standing like a tiny tooth in the mouth of the great cave. A creature with a head wide as three barns slithered out of the darkness and devoured him whole." Her fingers trembled. "In the daylight, I fled, praying that the creature would not dare the daylight, praying that it did not see me. I pray still now that it's not coming after me. For if that was the Fenix, then no one that sees it can live." She looked up at Lewis and Clarice as well. "I'm sorry. I was terrified. I failed the queen."

"This is not on your shoulders, Twila," he said, putting his hand on her shoulder. "We are grateful that you live. Now you can tell the tale of how the Henchmen valiantly battled the Fenix to their bitter ends. There is nothing but glory in that." He gazed at Clarice. "Don't you agree?"

Clarice nodded. "Don't fret, Twila. Your bravery may find you a place among my Maidens. Would you like that?"

"It would be an honor, of course. I just hope that I can stop shaking," Twila said.

"Get some rest," Clarice said. "We'll return to the House of Steel and inform my father. With this news, he can send a formidable force, defeat this beast, and take its egg."

"Are you mad?" Lewis said. "That might not have been the Fenix she saw. No one knows what it was."

"No, but it devours people whole. Horses whole. Father isn't going to send more men to their doom without knowing for certain where the egg is."

Lewis shook his hands. "You'll just have to have faith in the Elders that the Sect will come up with something."

Clarice shook her head. "We are going to find that egg. I know it's there. I'll be able to convince Father, and we will see this through. Whatever that beast is, Fenix or not, we will slay it."

"You're going to have to slay a lot," Twila said. She wiped the grime from her face with a damp rag. "Those jagged hills aren't meant for men."

"You made it out," Clarice said.

"Because the Elder of Luck was with me. That's the only way that I can explain it," Twila said. She rubbed her neck and grimaced. "Like the seers say, no matter the tragedy, like a scurrying rat, a remnant always survives."

Rolling her neck, Clarice said to Lewis, "Then that means that the other campaigns must have survivors, too. So, there is hope."

Lewis walked up to his half-sister, looked down at her, and said, "Just because they survived doesn't mean that they aren't imprisoned. Or worse."

CHAPTER 29

ABRAHAM WOKE FROM DREAMING ABOUT his past. He'd seen Mandi, from Woody's Grill. The gorgeous brunette who he'd shunned one too many times was holding hands with another man. A man in uniform. Colonel Drew Dexter. He had a thick moustache, like a young Sam Elliot. They had seemed happy. For some reason, it left him feeling empty, angry.

He yawned. He was underneath a rock bluff, lying on a bed of stone as something warm nuzzled against his backside. He was pretty sure that was Sticks. He peered outward. Dawn began to break. A fog lifted around the ugly, leafless trees. They'd been marching for two straight days, not stopping until they had to. All they wanted was out of that crater.

"Looks like another crappy day on Titanuus," he said to himself. "At least we have the egg." He yawned again and stretched his arms over his head. Then he reached down and jostled Sticks. "Come on. Early bird gets the worm. Let's get going." He ran his hands over her body. Her tunic felt soft and furry. He blinked and looked down at her. "What in the—*guh!*" He jumped up off the ground, grabbed his scabbard, and ripped his sword free.

The creature lying beside him popped up. It was an ugly eight-eyed bat-like creature, a small version of the Fenix about half the size of Abraham. It stood on little clawed feet. The small arms on the tips of its wings were spread out like Abraham's.

"Great googly-moogly!" he said. "Stay back!"

Abraham cocked his elbow back, preparing to thrust and end the thing. The baby Fenix mimicked his movement.

Horace, Bearclaw, Sticks, and more of the Henchmen rushed over. They had their weapons in hand and surrounded the Fenix.

"Let's gore the foul spawn of the beast," Horace said as he poked his spear at it.

The baby Fenix hissed at Horace and clacked its teeth at him.

"That's one ugly creature," Cudgel said. "It should not live. It should be burned."

"That's what we fought to save your brother," Tark added. "But it was one hundred times bigger."

"I don't know. It's sort of cute in an ugly way," Dominga said. "Look at that soft pelt. It gives the monster charm."

"Are you going to finish it, Captain?" Horace asked. He shuffled closed to the baby Fenix. "Say the word, and I'll end it."

The baby Fenix let out an earsplitting shriek that sounded like claws tearing across metal. The Henchmen winced and covered their ears.

"Back off!" Abraham shouted over the noise.

Horace backed up, and the shrieking ceased. The baby Fenix closed its mouth. Its wet nostrils flared, and it tilted his head from side to side like a bird.

"All right everyone, just calm down. Don't be so jumpy," Abraham said. "I'm going to try something." He slid his sword back into the scabbard. "I don't think this thing came to kill us. I do think it followed us. I saw it in the nest, back in the cavern."

He lifted both his arms. The baby Fenix did the same thing. He put his hands on top of his head. So did the baby Fenix. Abraham hopped on one leg, and the Fenix did too.

"It's dances!" Cudgel said with elation.

"The thing mocks you, Captain," Horace added. "I say we kill it."

Abraham stopped hopping on one foot. "It's not mocking me. It's imitating me. I think, when I saw it—"

"It imprinted on you!" Solomon said. "Ha! That is a wonder. A spawn of the Elders has become your hound."

Narrowing an eye at Solomon, Horace asked, "What is the troglin babbling about? It's not a hound, it's a–a bat or bird."

"A dragon," Iris said.

"It's not a dragon. It doesn't have scales," Sticks said. She sheathed her daggers. "Dragons have scales."

"Be still, everyone." Abraham stepped toward the creature. It stepped toward him. He stretched his hand out. It did the same. "It's like a baby duck. It bonds with the first person it sees. It thinks that I'm its mother. At least, I think that is what is going on." He was almost touching its creepy little hand. He spread his fingers out and locked fingers with it. The creature's grip was strong and warm as toast. "It's not a lizard. He's warm as baked bread."

Bearclaw flipped his axe up on his shoulder and asked, "How do you know it's a he?"

"I don't know. It just looks like a he to me." Abraham scratched the back of his head. "The question is now what do we do with him?"

Vern slipped alongside Bearclaw and said, "I'm with Horace—kill it. It's Elder Spawn. It will turn on us. Devour us." His lips twisted. "Look at it. We killed its mother. It will eat us. It might destroy all of Kingsland."

"Don't listen to him," Iris said, twisting her hair on a finger and staring at the baby Fenix. "Showing mercy to the Elder Spawn can garner Elder favor. And it was us that invaded its home. It was not the other way around. Are we pillagers that destroy families? And if this is the last of the Fenixes, a guardian of Elder's Birthing, what will replace it? All creatures have a purpose. So does this one." She walked up, stretched out her fingers and placed her hand on its head.

The baby Fenix's throat rumbled.

Iris made a big smile. "It purrs. Dominga, come, feel this."

Dominga eased up to the baby Fenix and started stroking its pelt. "My, it's warm. Ugly… but cute."

"Women don't make any sense," Horace said with a frown.

"Agreed," Vern replied.

Rubbing his chin with his great hand, Solomon said, "I think the Henchmen have a mascot." He chuckled. "I think you need to give it a name, Abraham."

"What do you call an ugly bat with eight eyes?" He shook his head. "Man, that sounds like a joke, doesn't it?"

Apollo perked up and said, "Horace's mother!"

Horace jabbed a finger at Apollo. "Don't you talk about my mother! Your mother's a… well… bearded lady!"

"How about Felix the Fenix?" Solomon suggested.

"That's not very imposing. Seeing how this thing is going to get very big," he said. "Man, he really does look like a hammerhead bat."

"You sound like someone that knows bats," Solomon said.

"I did a book report on them in grade school. It was one of the few projects that I enjoyed." Abraham unlocked his grip from the Fenix. "They mostly feed on insects. I hope that's the case with him." He patted its snout and cracked a smile as he remembered one of his favorite movies. "How about Simon?" He grinned. "Like Simon Phoenix."

"Short and sweet," Solomon said with a nod. "I take it there is a deeper meaning behind it?"

"You could say that." He scratched behind the Fenix's ears. "It's the name of a real bad dude from the movie *Demolition Man*. My dad and I loved it."

"Fitting. I'm sure it will come back to kill us one day." Solomon tilted his head and looked at the Fenix. "This should be interesting."

"What will be interesting?" he said. "Having two best buds named Solomon and Simon?"

Solomon chuckled. "Watching you teach it how to fly."

"Ha ha! I suppose it will be, but just so you know, I do know a little something about flying." Abraham's stomach knotted up as he thought about his dreams and the accident. He rubbed his aching forehead. "Henchmen, the king is waiting. Let's move out."

In a single column line, the company resumed their journey. The Fenix, Simon, walked behind Abraham like a man.

Sticks, walking right in front of him, looked back and said, "You attract interesting company."

"Yeah, don't remind me." He stepped over some stones, turned, and watched Simon climb over them. "I'm going to have a fine time teaching him how to ride a horse."

Sticks broke out in laughter. He'd never seen so much emotion from her.

"Somebody's feeling spry today."

"Perhaps," she said.

The column stopped. Word came from the front, where Tark and Dominga led, back to Horace, who turned to Ruger and said, "We have company ahead. Bad company."

"I wish," Abraham said.

He marched to the front. Down the hillside of the spine, dozens of terra-men had gathered.

"Great."

Barath the Ancient stood in the middle of the group. The giant snapping turtle stood like a man with his thick black-and-yellow scaled arms crossed over his shell chest. His bright orange eyes burned like suns. Towering at twelve feet tall, he glared at Abraham and said, "Children, take them."

CHAPTER 30

THE NEXT MORNING, LEWIS RODE along the coast in the back of the group, accompanying Twila. Both of them were on horseback, and she was leading the other two surviving horses of the Henchmen. One of the horses was Ruger's. The strange backpack hung from the saddle.

He cleared his throat and asked Twila, "Are you certain they are dead?"

"You doubt me?" she said.

"You spin a convincing tale, but you've left out many details. You might have sold Clarice, but you didn't sell me."

Twila cracked her neck from side to side. A cross look started on her round face that seemed unnatural. "You hired me to do a job. I've done it. I've sabotaged every mission they've undertaken since I joined the group. Dozens of men and women dead because of me. And now, you doubt me?"

"It might help if I'd seen the bodies."

"You didn't see any of the other bodies. Why do you need to see them now?" She glanced back at Ruger's pack. "That cherished item. Do you think that he would part with it? And if they lived, no doubt they would be coming after my head." She tilted her head to one side twice, like a nervous tic. "I can't wait to get out of this disguise. It's been too long. It's irritating."

"I admit I dearly miss your splendid figure. That one is a bit… lumpy."

"These lumps and curves made the job easier for me. No one would ever expect a rotund woman to be one of the king's assassins." She reached underneath her tunic to massage her bosom then straightened her back. "These things aren't your friend on a long ride, but they make for excellent distraction. I can't wait to get back into my natural form."

"Me either," he said quietly, "Raschel."

"I like the way you said that. I missed you too, Lewis." She reached over and patted his hand. "It's been too long, hasn't it?"

"Far too long," Lewis replied.

When Lewis came of age and was sworn into the King's Guardians, he took his place in the king's war room. King Hector proved to be willing to protect his kingdom by any means necessary. In addition to his vast army and fleet of ships, he hired mercenaries, spies, saboteurs and assassins, something like the Henchmen, to do his dirty work. The assorted lot of folk proved to be unreliable. However, because Lewis and Leodor held court with the kings, they were a part of the scheme that got their hands dirty. That was how he met Raschel. She was an assassin. The pair hit it off so well that they became as close as lovers. With the help of Leodor, they hatched up a scheme to put an end to the Henchmen, who—unlike the mercenaries and other ilk—would faithfully serve the king.

"What are you thinking?" she asked. "Your fingers are massaging the air."

He gave an absentminded look to his fingers. "Oh, well, I'm curious. Did you see what you said you saw?"

"No. But I'll tell you what I felt. I felt fear. And the smell was a muggy, putrid death. Nothing that ventured far into the cavern was coming out alive. It was the Fenix. And I believe the lore. No man who sees the Fenix will live to tell about it." She parted her lips and took a breath. "Out of all of my missions, nothing… nothing at all was scarier than that."

"But if you didn't see it, then how do you know it was the Fenix?"

She quickly shared the story about rescuing Solomon the troglin, the encounter with Barath the Ancient terra-man, and how Barath sent them to the Fenix's cavern. "My skin chills just thinking about it. I shouldn't be alive, but here I am. And lucky for you because if you ventured where we were, you'd all be dead too."

"No, we'd never be stupid enough to face the Fenix. The terra-men and troglin… Well, I'm certain we could hold our own if we had to battle. The King's Guardians are stalwart and formidable."

"Yes, but I'll tell you this, those Henchmen… They had true grit," she said. "I can't believe they had the guts to go into that cavern that smelled the way that it did. I wanted to puke, but somehow, they went in. I really don't understand how they did it. I couldn't have done it. Not with my knees knocking like they did."

Lewis gave her a curious look and said, "It's the brand."

"What?"

"The King's Brand. Leodor says that it has power. It gives the Henchmen inner strength. Fortitude. I never bought into it, but based off what you say, that is the only sense I can make out of it."

"Well, I agree that they have spines of steel, but why wouldn't such a thing be used on the Guardians?"

"The Guardians and the Maidens have other practices, and I know that my men are as brave as any."

"So, you think that you could march into the lair of the Fenix?" she said with a smirk.

"If I had to, I would." He arched a brow. "You don't believe me?"

"I think it's more than the brand. I think it's the man they follow. Ruger Slade, well, he changed up north when we encountered the frights. He's different now. The Henchmen like him. They follow him. He turned the tables."

"Yes, but he's dead now, right?"

"Of course. No one can look upon the spawn of an Elder and live. Trust me, he's dead, and all of the Henchmen with him. Nothing's ever come out of that lair alive except the Fenix."

Lewis shifted in his saddle and said, "I feel giddy and guilty."

"Why is that?"

"I'm finally rid of Ruger and the Henchmen." He smiled. "A thorn has been plucked from my side. But I feel bad for my father. He has no one he can turn to, and his wife is about to die."

CHAPTER 31

Lewis and Clarice returned to the House of Steel to deliver King Hector the news. The king met with them on the outside terrace that overlooked the Bay of Elders. Leodor and two of his personal Guardians were with him. He was flipping bread crumbs to the sea birds when Leodor announced Lewis and Clarice's arrival. When Hector's eyes fell on Clarice, he sighed with relief, rushed over to her, and gave her a hug.

In his gentle voice, he said, "My sweet little dove, I am so glad you have returned. My heart was twisting inside my chest." He squeezed her hard. "Promise me that you won't do something so foolish again."

"I'm sorry, Father," she said as she hugged him tightly. "I can't promise that. I want to go back and find the egg. We can beat the Fenix. I know it."

Hector pushed her an arm's length away and said, "You won't be leaving this castle, period."

"But Father!" she whined.

"You might have slipped me once, but you won't slip me again." His voice became strong as iron. "You'll remain in the House of Steel, where you belong, by your mother's side and mine. Do you understand?"

"We need to save her," Clarice said. "The cause is noble, and I'll give my life for hers. You must resume the quest, Father. I know the egg can be found."

"No," the king said. He looked at Lewis. "You've done well with your charge, Son. You and your men. And I am grateful. This family doesn't need to lose another one of our own. In times like this, we should stay together, be by your mother's side, to the very end."

Lewis nodded. "Has Clarann had a setback? I thought she was on the rebound before I departed."

"She has," Hector said with a frown. His gaze landed on Clarice. "And it has not helped that her one and only daughter is missing. Her heart broke the moment she learned that you left on her account."

"You told her?" Clarice said.

"I cannot lie to her. And what, did you not think that she would notice if you were missing? You abandoned her. You need to go to her now and apologize for what you put her through," Hector said.

Clarice's eyes watered, and her chin sagged. "I'm-I'm sorry, Father."

"Don't apologize to me." Hector squeezed her hands and kissed her on the forehead. "Apologize to your mother. And don't think she'll go easy on you, either."

"Yes, Father." Clarice gave a quick bow and hurried inside through the patio doors.

Hector let out a long sigh. "Lewis, I can't tell you how relieved I am that Clarice is back. You and your men deserve a feast." He glanced over his shoulder at Leodor. "Have the kitchen make arrangements."

The saggy-cheeked viceroy nodded and said, "Certainly, Your Majesty."

"You really don't need to prepare a feast. It wasn't so difficult a task," Lewis said. "But if it is your wish… And I'm sorry about Clarann. I wish that something could be done for her. Um… I fear I have more bad tidings to share as well."

"Oh," King Hector said. "Let's have a seat. I feel so exhausted." He moved to the chairs on the upper terrace as if his robes weighed a ton and sat down. "Ah… sit, Son, sit. Let's try to enjoy the shade. What other news do you have? Did you lose Guardians or Maidens?"

Lewis sat as Leodor stood behind them with his hands tucked inside the sleeves of his robes and frowning. Lewis eyeballed the pitcher of water sitting on the table then reached over and poured a glass. "No, all of the king's men and women are in good order." He drank deeply. "Ah."

"Well, tell me. What troubles you?" the king asked.

"It's Ruger… or Abraham. The King's Henchmen. All save one are dead." He gave his father a sad look. He pulled Ruger's backpack out of a sack he'd carried and gave it to the king. "I'm sorry."

Leodor's eyes widened.

The king held the backpack in his hands and deflated in his chair and said, "I knew that this attempt would be in vain, but I put hope in it." He looked Lewis in the eye. "How do you know this?"

Lewis thoroughly recounted his encounter and discussion with the Red Tunic, Twila. The king sat on the end of his chair, nodding, not missing a single word. Neither Hector nor Leodor asked a single question or tried to stop him. Sharing the entire tale took close to an hour. "Again, I'm sorry."

Aghast, Hector asked, "All of my Henchmen are gone now? I–I can't believe it."

"I would not fret, my king. Ruger was slated for execution," Leodor said. "At least he and his rabble died trying to fulfill a noble mission."

King Hector stroked the backpack. "I thought we might have turned a corner. That we might have an edge. Now, I have less than I had before."

"Sometimes, less is more." Lewis reached over and squeezed his father's knee. "They are one less burden to carry. Remember you have your armies and me. We'll do better. We can be more efficient."

Hector looked as though he'd lost his own son or a close family member, like a brother. He absentmindedly petted the backpack. "Ruger and I went so far back. I never thought it possible that he would die so soon. Then, these strange happenings. Possessions. Portals. Strange baubles." He gave Lewis a blank look. "What is happening to my world?"

Lewis gave Hector a polite smile and said, "It's changing."

CHAPTER 32

Raschel waited in her apartment for Lewis to arrive. The windowless apartment was located in the city of Burgess. It was a nicely decorated studio, small and quaint, with a double-sized bed against a wall, a sofa, a round table with two chairs, a cupboard, and a vanity. She sat in front of the vanity's mirror, looking at Twila's face. Twila was a cute but pudgy woman she'd met in the city's marketplace. Twila was a wholesome fruit vendor with a knack for selling customers more than they needed. Raschel had ordered several bushels of apples. Then she had Twila deliver them to her apartment and killed her.

"Oh Twila, you were such a nice person, too. I really hated to do this to you, but it served my purpose quite well," she said to herself. She twisted a ring on the ring finger of her right hand. It was quite ordinary to the naked eye, made out of onyx with diamond-shaped ivory teeth inlaid. She turned it on her finger until two small teeth, like a small snake's fangs, popped out. It was called the Ring of Tarsus. "Fascinating that it works so well."

After she'd lured Twila into her apartment, she struck quickly. Using the fangs in the ring, she grabbed Twila by the neck with the palm of her hand. The fangs sank into the innocent woman's neck and hooked on. The fangs drained Twila's blood and pumped it into Raschel's body. Magic and flesh worked as one. Second after second passed as Twila's dying eyes watched Raschel transform into herself. Drained to a husk, Twila felt her heartbeat fade. Her flesh and bone became brittle and turned to dust. Raschel turned into Twila. She spoke with Twila's voice and not her own.

With a smirk, she said to herself, "Bye-bye, Twila, and thanks for all of the good times." She took off the ring and the image in the mirror wobbled. Her face twisted and contorted. Twila's pie-faced features slimmed. A narrow chin formed. Her eyes turned dark and seductive. Once her pleasing lips formed, the rest of her body lengthened. She cried out and slapped her hands on the table with a painful shout. Arching her back, she opened her eyes wide and watched her sensuous hair lengthen. She shuddered. A film of sweat dressed her high cheekbones. Her full lips parted, and she let out a sigh. "Oh, I'm so glad that is over. I felt like a buffalo before."

She removed the clothing that was hanging from her body and checked herself in the mirror. Her stomach was flat, hips narrow, and breasts firm. She'd returned to her well-toned athletic form. "That's so much better, not that pleasantly plump was so awful. It had its advantages." She donned a black silk gown, stuffed the old clothing into a cloth sack, and tossed it into the corner by her door. She put the Ring of Tarsus back on and flopped back-first onto the bed. "That was miserable, but at least I'm going to be paid a lot of money for this."

Lying on a green satin pillow, she reminisced about all she'd done. In her travels with the Henchmen, she'd served as a spy for Lewis. Together, they doctored maps and plans and sent them on suicide missions. She turned Henchmen and Red Tunics against one another. She ruined food supplies and created faulty equipment. She made failures look like accidents. Men and women who battled back from the brink of death, she finished off. Raschel shook her head. "I can't believe I pulled all of that off. Ha. I'm even better than I realized. Lewis will owe me a fortune for all that I sacrificed. I'll be so rich I'll start my own kingdom." She yawned and took a nap.

Raschel had slept well the night before and spent the morning cleaning herself and disposing of all remnants of Twila's identity. That afternoon, a soft knocking came to her door. She opened it and found herself looking into Lewis's handsome face.

"What a nice surprise," she said. "I wasn't expecting you so soon."

She stepped aside, and he slipped in and closed the door behind him.

Lewis took her in his arms and kissed her passionately. He scooped her up and carried her to the bed. "I've missed you! You look ravishing!" He kissed her neck. "Don't ever change again. You can do your bidding without all of that changing."

She wiggled out of his grasp and from her knees held him at a distance with her hands. "Let's talk business first. I've been through sheer hell. Now, it's finished. I want paid."

"When you are my queen, you'll have all of the money you want, but"—he reached behind his back and produced a satin purse—"this is yours. Just as you requested."

She pulled the purse's drawstrings and spilled the contents into her hand. Large diamonds, rubies, and emeralds, fell out. The bright gems glinted in her eyes. "This is marvelous!" She hugged him. "This makes it all worth it. So, how did the king take the news?"

"He looks like a lost puppy. I almost feel sorry for him, but that's how one should feel about someone that is old and weak."

"Don't underestimate the elderly. They can surprise you," she said as she counted the gems in her hand. "I have to be honest. I'm not so sure that what I did was worth it, now that I have it. I almost died several times. I think I'll resort to straight-up assassination. Long missions like that… Never again."

Lewis pushed her down on the bed and said, "You don't need to kill anymore. You have plenty. There will be more."

"I enjoy the game. I'm young and not retiring. I'll only become weak without a challenge."

"Don't be crazy. There is nothing easy about being the queen. There are countless demanding duties." He pushed her down and straddled her and removed his jerkin. "The first one is pleasing your husband."

He bent down and kissed her all over. She kissed him and worked off his trousers. They made love on and off for hours.

Knock. Knock. Knock. Knock.

Lewis and Raschel's heads popped up. They exchanged a look. She grabbed a dagger hanging from a scabbard on her bedpost.

Quietly, he asked, "Are you expecting someone?"

"You are the only one that knows about this place. It might be a mistake," she said.

A parchment of paper was slipped underneath the door. They heard feet scampering away. Lewis swung his feet over the bed. Raschel picked the note up from the floor.

"It has your name on it," she said. "Shall I open it?"

He swiped at the note, but she deftly pulled it out of reach. "You'll have to be faster than that."

"There's no time for toying around. Hand it over."

Raschel gave him the note. It had a green wax seal with an elegant *L* stamped in it.

"It's Leodor. I should have known he'd know where I was. He doesn't miss anything." Lewis lifted a brow. "Unless he's been here?"

"No," she said. "Never."

He opened the triple-folded parchment and read. His jaw dropped to his chest, then he swallowed.

"What is it?" she asked.

Lewis's forehead creased. His nostrils flared as he held the note in front of her face and said, "It says, 'Ruger has arrived at the House of Steel. He brought the Fenix egg. Get your arse back here.'" He took the note and stuffed it in Raschel's mouth. "We'll talk about this later!"

CHAPTER 33
THE HOUSE OF STEEL

ABRAHAM SAT OUTSIDE ON THE King's terrace, which overlooked the Bay of Elders. He was behind a large table with a buffet of food, drinking the finest wine he ever tasted. Everything—the meats, cheeses, bread, fruits, and vegetables—was succulent and exquisite. He licked his fingers and wiped his mouth. At the moment, he was eating alone, waiting for the king to return. They'd already had a long conversation about everything that had happened. The only other people that were there were four of the King's Guardians. They were in full-plate armor and wearing their lion-faced helmets. He could feel their eyes on him. At one time, he must have known all of them, but he did not know them now.

He sipped his wine. "Ah."

King Hector hustled through the terrace patio doors and joined him at the table. The soft-eyed king had a hopeful smile on his face. He wore forest-green robes with golden trim. The golden Crown of Stone was cockeyed on his head. He put a napkin on his lap and raised a wine glass. "Leodor has informed me that the queen is bathing in the yolk of the Fenix." He fanned himself with his hand. "I feel giddy. I never imagined this would happen. In all truth, I thought the mission was futile. But nothing ventured, nothing gained, eh?"

"I couldn't agree more, Your Majesty," Abraham said. "Sometimes I feel as if I am dreaming."

Hector smiled and motioned for the Guardians to move away. The soldiers backed toward the terrace's outer walls. The dropping sun shone off the metal of their armor.

"Out of the sun. Into the shade," the king said. "Blend in, my Guardians."

The Guardians moved into the shadows cast by the sun setting west of the castle.

Abraham and King Hector were already in the shade that came at the end of the day. "I hope the ocean breeze is taking my foulness away from you, King Hector. When I came with the egg, I came with all haste."

King Hector, who sat at the head of the table but within one seat of him, leaned forward and said, "And you did the right thing. Now, please continue telling me about your second encounter with Barath the Ancient."

"Certainly." Abraham refilled his wine glass and offered to do so for the king.

The king shook his head, his light-green eyes intent on him. Abraham had already told the king about everything that had happened from their first encounter with Barath and the terra-men and how they slew the Fenix and retrieved the eggs. He even mentioned the baby Fenix that imprinted on him, and that led him up to that last encounter with Barath.

"So, we are trying to make our way back off of the Spine when we run smack into Barath. There he is, twelve feet tall and surrounded by what must have been fifty more terra-men that we could see. Barath says, 'Children, take them.'" Abraham leaned his chair back on two legs. "All of us drew our weapons, figuring to engage in the fight of all fights. Instead, Barath opens up his scaly paws, and he says, 'No, you misunderstand. My children will lead you off of the Spine with haste. They know a shorter way.'" He looked at the king, and said, "Naturally, I had to ask why."

"And what did he say," King Hector asked.

"Barath said that no one had ever faced the Fenix and lived. He said that was a sign. When he saw the baby Fenix, his eyes grew the size of boulders, and he knelt down. 'Just go. Go with all haste,' he said, 'and give King Hector my best.' Then he looked me dead in the eye and added, 'The tide turns. The Elders awaken. Tell that to the king.'"

King Hector leaned back in his chair, crossed his arms over his chest, and quietly restated, "The tide turns. The Elders awaken."

"I'm not sure what that means, but do you know?" Abraham asked.

"Long ago, the Elders walked among the world of men. Well, some of them, for there are so many. Most thrive in the seas. But perhaps the Elders will start to reappear." The king shrugged. "I don't know. But what I do know is that you killed the spawn of the Elders. You killed a Fenix. This is a godlike creature. It's quite possible that there might be repercussions, and what Barath said is a warning." He gave Abraham a curious look. "Where is the baby Fenix?"

"Before I came here, I had to stop by my stronghold and cage Simon. At the stronghold, we prepared the egg in a wagon loaded with hay and covered it up to keep prying eyes away."

Hector patted his knees and rubbed them. "Yes, yes. So, in all truth, the yolk of the egg brought a man back from the dead? Your Henchman, eh… What was his name?"

"Cudgel. And yes, he's bright eyed and bushy tailed."

"He has a tail? Like a squirrel?" the king asked.

"No, it's an expression from my world. It means 'ready to go.' Sorry."

"No Ruger, er, Abraham… I forget that we are dealing with an otherworldly personality. It's going to take some getting used to. But my hope for my dearest Clarann is growing. I feel that it is going to heal her fully." He slapped a knee and pointed at Abraham. "And if it does, you and your Henchmen will have your reputations reinstated."

Abraham arched an eyebrow. "And if it doesn't?"

Hector propped an elbow up on the table and said, "I like you, Abraham. I liked Ruger. I think in a way, you are one and the same, men with a strong sense of duty. But if the queen is not healed, I have no way of verifying your story. For all that I know, the entire tale is a well-fabricated lie. And given the daily climate that I face, I can't afford to take any chances. I'll have to execute your sentence."

CHAPTER 34

THE FRONT TWO LEGS OF Abraham's chair hit the terrace floor. "What? You're still going to kill me?"

"Easy, Abraham. We want to be hopeful in this situation. If all that you said is true, then you won't have anything to worry about," the king said. "But I can't put all of my faith in a man who rolls up to my castle door with a wagon and a boulder in the back of it. I saw the ugly rock, and though it is unique and I do have hope, only a fool would believe the entire tale that you've woven."

Abraham's jaw dropped. After all he'd been through, he couldn't believe Hector doubted him. And he'd been feeling pretty good about himself.

"Now," the king continued. "Lift your chin up from the floor and enjoy the fine meal that has been prepared for you. I'm sure Leodor will bring word to us soon."

Abraham clamped his mouth shut. Butterflies fluttered in his stomach. He'd never considered that the egg yolk might not work on the queen. That increased his worries. He didn't have much faith in Viceroy Leodor, either. The aloof mystic seemed like someone the king put too much trust in. *He could be with the queen, doing anything.* "Shouldn't you be there, to make sure that the yolk is properly applied? It dries up fast, like I said."

"No, I can trust Leodor. He heard what you said."

I don't know if he heard me, but he definitely saw me. When I showed up at the castle with the egg, he looked like he saw a ghost. Abraham swallowed more wine. It seemed as if, despite his efforts, the guillotine was descending slowly toward his neck again. *All of this time, I've been thinking I'm dreaming. The truth is it's a nightmare.* "It doesn't seem fair. I've… We've given all that we had."

"And all of you returned unscathed. That's miraculous," Hector said. "Ruger, I can see your disappointment. Put yourself on my throne. What would you do? The enemy closes in from all directions. The numbers dwindle. The expeditions fail. I have to be a king who is a king of his word. You were given a second chance, thanks to the queen. But if she dies, you die." He pointed at his Guardians. "I cannot lead men if I cannot enforce the law. A lawless society cannot survive. It will quickly die. The tall pines of the forest always start dying from the top. If my word fails, the kingdom falls. Do you understand?"

Abraham nodded. He had no desire to argue with King Hector. He had such a pleasant and likeable demeanor. Like a great oak, he wouldn't be shaken, either.

"I suppose," Abraham said. "But you are the king, and you could change the law."

"And bend eons of rules just to serve myself? Or you? If a law was truly unjust, I could understand it. But that isn't the case. You are a deserter. You abandoned your station. Many men died from it." King Hector took a goblet of wine in hand and drank. "You should be dead. However, I showed mercy and gave you the King's Brand. If you break your oath, you'll die from it. It was the best choice I had. We live and we die by our choices. Right or wrong, there are consequences. The law must enforce it."

"You know, you're a real hard-ass, but in a nice way." Abraham finished his wine. If it was possible that he was going to die soon, he might as well enjoy himself. "In my world, you'd make a fine president."

"Don't they have kings in your country?"

"Some countries do, but lately, they haven't worked out so well."

King Hector sniffed. "Interesting. So, the royal bloodlines aren't strong in your world?"

"Well, think about it. It isn't exactly a merit-based system when someone is born into it. And then the oldest male inherits the crown." He sniffed his wine's bouquet. "What happens if the oldest is wicked, pugnacious, spoiled, or depraved? He'll become a foul leader, his subjects enslaved or miserable. The country is not productive, and it is soon conquered by another."

"You are singing a familiar song. This is the dilemma the House of Steel has faced every day for centuries." The king grabbed a golden hunk of cheese and started to nibble at it. "What form of government does your country impose?"

"It's a republic, where the citizens elect their leaders by voting for them on a ballot."

King Hector spat out his cheese. "That's the most insane thing that I've ever heard. Let the people decide for themselves? It's preposterous!"

"And prosperous. You see—"

Prince Lewis burst through the doors onto the terrace. "Father, I came as soon as I heard the news." He eyeballed Abraham and clenched his jaws. "Ruger, it is surprising to see you again."

"I bet it is," Abraham replied. He was getting used to being called Ruger. He set down his goblet and drummed his fingers on the table. "So, Twila said that we were dead, did she? It's no wonder you look like you saw a ghost. Where is she?"

Lewis shrugged. His face was clammy, and his feathery hair dripped sweat down his cheeks. He dabbed it with a cloth napkin. "I haven't seen her since we departed the other day. I naturally assumed that she would return to the stronghold and bear the news to your hirelings."

Abraham shook his head. He'd already discussed with the king what Lewis had told him about Twila. "Oh, she wasn't anywhere to be found, but that wasn't any surprise to you."

"I beg your pardon?" Lewis said. "What are you saying?"

"Yes, what are you saying?" the king asked.

"I'll tell you what I am saying. I'm saying that Twila has been sabotaging our missions for quite some time. And someone that wanted us to fail planted her with the Henchmen. She made a fine job of it until I came around."

"Father, this man is insane." Lewis gave Abraham an appalled look. He poured a goblet of wine. "I don't know this Twila any better than a pig's elbow. And I don't pick his retainers, hirelings, or henchmen. He does."

"My son makes a valid point," Hector said. "You are allowed to pick your men. Not us. I've given you the freedom to do that."

"Why would I sabotage my own missions?" he said. "Twila killed Cudgel. She stole our horse and gear and abandoned us to the Fenix."

The king lifted a finger. "Ah, but we haven't been able to validate your story, have we? We only have your words, and we await Clarann's revival to verify it."

Lewis's eyes widened, and his tight expression eased. "Yes, you come telling tall tales, but you can't prove any of it."

The moment he saw Lewis's stiff expression ease, Abraham knew in his heart that the prince was in on it. Proving it would be another matter. He cleared his throat. "Your Majesty, I have a dozen men that can bear witness to my story. And don't forget: I have the Fenix."

"You have the Fenix?" Lewis said. "I don't understand. What sort of preposterous tale is this? Father, what sort of lies has he been feeding you?"

"Ruger says that he has a baby Fenix, in a cage, back inside his stronghold."

"Ha. I'll believe it when I see it," Lewis said. "I shall send my Guardians to fetch it. How does that sound to you, Ruger?"

Abraham got up from the table. "I'd be more than happy to show you the way."

"That won't be necessary," someone else said.

All the men turned toward the source of the voice. The king gasped. Queen Clarann was standing in the doorway.

CHAPTER 35

Queen Clarann was a fair-haired lioness with ice-blue eyes. Her wrinkly skin had been restored. Her lips were full and red. She wore a golden terry-cloth robe that caressed the firm curves of her body.

King Hector rose out of his seat, knocking his chair over. "My love!" he gasped. His hands trembled when he touched her face. "You've never looked so beautiful." He wrapped her in his arms, his body still shaking. "How do you feel?"

Clarann nestled her head in the king's shoulder and stroked his hair with his hand. "I've never felt better, Hector." She kissed his cheek and looked at Abraham. "Never better."

Abraham slid out of his chair and took a knee. His heart pounded inside his chest. He wasn't really sure what was happening. Clarann was a vision, but no more so than his wife, Jenny, or Mandi. But his body wanted hers. *Ruger! Oh no.* Something was going on. Apparently, a deeper connection existed between Ruger and the queen that he hadn't picked up on before. Perhaps it was Ruger's boldness that pushed them through to conquer the Fenix. *You old dog, what have you been up to?* He parted his lips and started to speak, but Prince Lewis beat him to the punch.

"Clarann, so glad to see that you are well." Lewis walked over to the queen and the king and gave them both a rigid hug. "It's cause for celebration."

"Indeed," Hector said. "We will have a great celebration, for Kingsland has its queen back."

Leodor walked out onto the terrace. His heavy eyes sought Lewis's. Abraham caught the uncomfortable glances between the two.

"You have done well, Leodor," Hector said. "I thank you!"

Clarann broke from Hector's embrace and said, "I don't think it is Leodor that deserves the credit. All he did was prepare a bath. Ruger is the one that brought the egg to us. Did he not?"

"Oh, well, of course, dearest. I'm sorry, but I'm simply giddy seeing you in your full glory. I only wanted to give credit where credit is due." Hector kissed her hands. "It was Leodor that made the suggestion. His idea bore great fruit." He turned his head toward Abraham. "Abraham, I doubted your word, but today you have proven yourself."

With a tilt of her head, Clarann asked, "Abraham? Who is Abraham?"

"Er, well…" Hector brushed a hand over his chest as if trying to wipe a mistake away. "Just a slip of the tongue."

"Hector, don't start fibbing to me now," she said. "Why did you call him Abraham?"

"Queen Clarann, I think that you should rest. Let me prepare a bed for you," Leodor suggested.

"Oh, shut up!" Clarann said with fire in her voice. "I've been bedridden for months. My restless slumbers were filled with the sound of wings from the crows that were coming. My dreams were filled with smoking steel dragons in foreign places. I might close my eyes to feel the caress of the sea winds on my face, but I'll be damned if I'm going back to sleep anytime soon. Leodor, why don't you go take a nap? You look like you haven't slept in a year."

Leodor's thinning brows rose and fell.

She turned on the king. "Now, tell me. Who is Abraham?"

"It's a long story and one that might trouble you," Hector said.

Clarann spread her arms out in a showy fashion and asked, "Do I look like anything is going to trouble me? After what I've been through, you no longer need to walk softly around your queen. I'm ready for anything. Please, do not mince words with me."

Hector nodded. "So be it, my love." He pointed at Abraham. "I'll let Ruger explain." He pulled out a chair. "I know that you aren't tired, but I want you to sit down for this."

With a surprised look she said, "As you wish." She sat down beside the king.

Leodor, Lewis, and Abraham joined them at the table.

She eyed Abraham. "Before you begin, first, I want to extend a thank you to your and your Henchmen. Thank you."

"You're welcome, Your Highness," Abraham said. He had to catch his breath for some reason. Finally, his racing heart slowed. "My name is Abraham Jenkins. I'm from another world called Earth. Man, it sounds weird saying that. Anyway, this is my story—this is my song."

He went on for an hour, explaining everything the best that he could. Everyone at the table hung on his every word. Clarann sat upright with her hands on her lap, chin up like a true queen. She hardly batted an eye as he spoke.

He finished up by saying, "And that's how I came to be in Titanuus."

Hector reached over and put his hand on hers and asked, "It's quite a story, isn't it? What are you thinking?"

The beautiful queen arched a brow and said, "It explains many things that we could not otherwise explain. If this… Abraham… truly is who he says that he is, and his essence resides in Ruger, then I wonder what happened to the essence of Ruger?" She seemed sad when she said it, as though truly worried. Her eyes searched Abraham's. "Where is he?"

"So far as I can tell, he's still a part of me, just not all of me. It's his body, my mind. Sometimes I feel it, and sometimes I don't. In his body, I do things that only he would have known to do." Abraham shrugged. "It's possible that his essence might be in the body of someone else."

Queen Clarann looked right at him and said, "Or in your body in your world."

CHAPTER 36

ABRAHAM HAD ENOUGH TO WORRY about regarding his own essence and didn't need to worry about Ruger's too. *Could Ruger be in my body? Back on Earth?* That didn't seem plausible. After all, when he made the transformation into Ruger, Eugene Drisk turned back into what appeared to be his original body and vanished through the portal in the tunnel. *None of this makes any sense. Every day feels more real than the last. But if I'm dreaming, I need to find out how to wake up. Otherwise, I'm in a world where anything can happen.*

"Your Highness," he said, "I sit on this side of the table with little more understanding than you do. It's as new to me as you. But we had a deal. I retrieve the egg, and you help me find a way back to my world. At the same time, I agree to help you with whatever you need."

Hector pulled his shoulders back and said, "I don't need you to remind to keep my word. My oaths will be kept."

Lewis jabbed a finger at Ruger and said, "You don't have to honor your word with this dog. He claims to be possessed. He has no credibility. He's a madman. You should finish him, Father. Be done with him!"

"No credibility," Hector said. "Son, are you blind? Look at your mother."

"She's not my mother." Lewis folded his hands across his chest. "And there's not so much of a difference that I can see."

Clarann let out a delighted chuckle. "Lewis, as always, your barbs tickle me. And so does your lunacy. You willfully blind yourself to Ruger's value and continue to disappoint."

"Leodor," Hector said. "Draw up papers for Ruger and all of his men that will clear their names under the authority of the king." He landed his gaze on Abraham. "I believe there are some Guardians among you that will be reinstated, if they like."

With an eager nod, Abraham said, "I'll let them know."

"Mother!" Clarice dashed onto the terrace and threw her arms around the queen. Cheek to cheek she hugged her mother tightly. "Oh, Mother, you look so well. So beautiful, like me!"

Clarann squeezed her daughter. "I'll never be so pretty as you."

Abraham rose from his seat and nodded at Clarice. She was a vibrant and beautiful teenager, dressed in a fanciful cotton jerkin and trousers.

Clarice's stare landed on him. "Ruger! So, you are alive!" She turned her glare on Lewis. "That woman Twila said they were dead. And you fell for it, Lewis. You fool. I knew we could not trust that woman."

"You didn't know diddly," Lewis said. "None of us did. The woman deceived all of us." He pointed at Abraham. "Including Ruger. She is his retainer."

"I didn't hire her. Er, well, maybe I did. I don't remember. Perhaps it was Eugene Drisk," Abraham said.

"Who is Eugene Drisk?" Hector asked.

"That was the man that possessed Ruger before me. The man I told you I encountered in the tunnel," he said.

Clarice's eyes moved from person to person. "What in Titanuus are all of you talking about?"

"It's a long story, dear," Clarann said, "I'll explain later."

Abraham's arrival had brought the Henchmen's losing streak to an end, but they still had a problem. Someone wanted their missions sabotaged. They must have planted Twila in the group. Or Eugene knew about it all along and was sabotaging their own missions. Perhaps he didn't share the same interests as the king. Perhaps he secretly served another. He pinched the bridge of his nose. Keeping track of everything made his head ache the more he thought about it.

"Are you well, Ruger?" Clarann asked.

"I have a lot on my mind. I realize that you have much to celebrate, but I need to get back to my men and share the good news. I need to figure out what happened to Twila. She'll have answers. We'll need them. I fear the king has spies in his midst. We have to find out who."

Hector held his emerald stone in his hand and rubbed a finger over the precious gem. "I trust everyone at this table with my life. Including you, Abraham. You've earned it. But if there is a fox in my henhouse, I will reveal them. Go to your men. Share the good news and give them our thanks. I'll summon you soon, and we'll talk in greater detail about your predicament, mine and the Crown of Stones."

Abraham nodded. "Thank you. I'll be at my stronghold, waiting for your call, and I'll probably be bathing the entire time. I apologize, ladies. I probably smell worse than manure. If I'd known you were coming, I'd have at least dunked myself in the ocean before I came."

Clarann made a pleasant smile. "Don't apologize. Every minute you've spared me from that withering husk means the world to me. Again, you have my thanks and gratitude."

Clarice hugged her mother. "Mine too. But thank you for clarifying what I was smelling. What is that, anyway?"

Abraham shrugged. "A little bit of the worst of everything."

Lewis rose from the table. "I'll escort you out."

With a final nod, Abraham departed with Lewis. The captain of the King's Guardians walked him all the way up to the stables of the House of Steel, near the wall of the main gate. Inside the stables, Lewis led him to the three horses that were taken. All the leftover gear lay on the hay in one of the stables, including his backpack.

Lewis shouted to a pair of stable hands. "Load up this man's beasts and take them to the front gate! He'll meet you there."

Abraham picked up the Pirates backpack and shouldered it, keeping his relief inside. *Ah. I'm not crazy.*

Once they were outside the portcullis, Lewis extended his hand.

With a cocked eye, Abraham shook his hand.

Lewis's iron grip locked on his. He said, "Don't think for a moment that you will be replacing me as captain of the King's Guardians."

"I have more important matters to attend to."

"Good. And tell your dogs that they aren't coming back either. I don't want them."

Abraham looked him dead in the eye and said, "Well, that's not up to you, now is it?" He squeezed Lewis's hand with a crushing grip until the prince paled. He pulled Lewis closer. "That's the king's decision."

Lewis ripped his grip free. "We'll see about that." He stormed away.

CHAPTER 37

His three-story stone Stronghold, with its rich farmlands, was a welcome sight. With the day's sun cooling behind the clouds, Abraham gathered all his henchmen inside the Stronghold on the first level. All of them sat at the large oak farm table except for Solomon. He sat on a milking stool beside the front door. The shaggy troglin still sat taller than the rest of them.

Abraham sat at the head of the empty table. Horace sat to his left, followed by Bearclaw, Vern, and Apollo. To his right, Sticks sat on her side with Dominga, Cudgel, and Prospero. Iris sat at the opposite end of the table. All of them had stripped down to normal clothing. The kitchen galley doors swung open. Two haggard-looking bowlegged women wearing off-white aprons teetered out, carrying trays of coffee urns and cups.

"Just leave the trays on the table, ladies."

The rough-looking sisters set down the trays, made unhappy mutterings, and waddled back into the galley out of sight.

"Help yourself," Abraham said.

No one at the table moved. All of them sat as stone-faced as ever. Sweat rolled down from Horace's temple. He had a serious look on his puffy face.

"Or not," Abraham continued. He poured himself a cup of coffee. "I guess I'll get on with it. As you can see, I returned with three horses, our lost gear, and my head. Which all of you should take as a good sign." He paused.

No one blinked.

"And it is. The yolk of the Fenix fully restored Queen Clarann."

Horace gave a short pump of his fist. "That is wonderful, Captain."

All the others at the table started to move. Their heads bobbed as they spoke cheerfully and quietly to one another.

Sticks even poured herself a cup of coffee and said, "So, we aren't going back to Baracha?"

"Nope," he said as he tilted his chair back on two legs. As a matter of fact, I don't know where any of you will go. King Hector is clearing all of our names. You no longer have to be one of his Henchmen."

The group fell silent. They all cast their eyes at Abraham, perplexed looks on their faces. Even Solomon.

Horace clawed at his beard then scratched the back of his head. "Pardon, Captain. We won't be Henchmen anymore?"

"No," Abraham said.

Long looks were exchanged among the company of hard-eyed men and women.

Vern, however, clapped his hands together and said, "That sounds great to me!" He got up from the table. "I'm out of here."

With big smoky eyes, Cudgel said, "So, we will receive the King's Papers? Tark and I are truly free men?"

Abraham shrugged. "The king is a man of his word. But listen, no one needs to run out of here. I have the Stronghold. All of you are always welcome to call this place home."

"Not me. I'm leaving." Vern headed for the door. "With the King's Papers, I assume I can take back my spot with the King's Guardians. You should too, Bearclaw."

"Go ahead," Dominga said. She crossed her arms, looked away from Vern, and frowned. "No one is going to miss you. Especially me."

Horace pulled his jerkin open, revealing the brand on his chest and, asked, "But Captain, what about the mark? We can't so simply be absolved of our duties. We gave our word to serve the king. We are branded for all eternity. To abandon our duty is to die."

"You are released from your duty," Abraham said.

"But how?" Horace asked. "We are still branded."

Vern had stopped by the front door and said, "Yeah, I've never seen a cattle brand go away. Once the king's cattle, always the king's cattle."

"Listen, I don't know all of the details other than what the king said. He's preparing papers. He's…" Abraham's voice trailed off.

The brand of the king's crown on Horace's chest started smoking. Audible gasps filled the room.

Tark jumped up from the table. His chest was smoking too. "I'm on fire!"

The chest of every Henchman in the room was smoking. It wasn't a burning-wood smoke but a misty, oily pink-red vapor. It drifted from their bodies up into the rafters.

"It burns again!" Vern yelled.

"We have betrayed our word!" Horace stammered. "Our treacherous hearts bring death!" He patted at his chest. "May the king forgive me!"

Sticks fanned her hand over the strange smoke coming out from above her breast. "It burns, but hardly like fire." She ran her fingers over the brand on her chest. The inky pink-red smoke dissipated. She pursed her lips and blew downward, and the smoke cleared from her body. The lumpy brand on her chest was gone. Her eyebrows rose. "It's gone."

Bearclaw had ripped his shirt off. The broad-faced warrior lifted his skinned-up hand from his chest and said, "Aye. Mine is gone, too."

One by one, the elated Henchmen looked one another over. All their brands were gone. Each and every one had vanished as if it had never even been there.

"I can't believe it, Captain," Horace said, his hand rubbing his chest. "The King's Brand is indeed powerful magic. Now, it's gone."

Abraham ran his hands over his chest. No smoke came from his body. "Yeah," he said, "everyone's is gone but mine."

CHAPTER 38

At the back end of the Stronghold lay an intimate cavern with pools of hot springs. Abraham sat chest deep in the churning mineral waters. Solomon sat across from him, only waist deep in the steaming waters. They weren't alone, either. Selma, Sophia, and Bridgett, three exotic women with dark hair and eyes, had joined them in the springs. They were lounging in medieval bikinis made from damp cotton that clung to their bodies. Selma wore black, Sophia pink, and Bridgett white. The colors were the only way Abraham could tell them apart. All of them were intoxicating.

Selma slipped over behind him and dipped her perfect legs into the water behind him. She started massaging his shoulders.

"You don't have to do that," he said as her strong fingers penetrated his muscles with a perfect touch. "Really, the water is doing the job."

"But Ruger, you are weary. I see it in your eyes. Let me tend to you," Selma said. She kissed his neck. "I have missed you."

"No more than I," Sophia said as she slipped into the pool.

Bridgett joined them. "None have missed you more than me, Captain."

Abraham didn't want Selma to stop. He didn't any of them to slow their advances. He lifted up his hands and said, "I'm sorry, but one at a time, girls."

Sophia and Bridgett stuck their bottom lips out.

Solomon lifted his massive hand out of the waters. "I don't have any objections to the extra attention." He winked at Sophia. "If they don't."

"Be my guest," Abraham said. He'd closed his eyes and laid his head back into Selma's lap. "Ah, that feels good. Too good. Help yourself."

"Sure thing," Solomon said.

Abraham opened his eyes. Bridgett and Sophia sat on both sides of the troglin. They ran their long painted fingernails over his hairy chest.

"This isn't right," Abraham said.

"It feels right to me," Solomon said. His smile filled the room, also revealing his canine fangs. "I think your predecessor did things right."

"I don't know about that. You should see the dungeon. That guy was a pervert."

"He clearly had a thing for Spanish and Italians." Solomon brushed the back of his chin over Bridgett's cheek. "What did he look like?"

"He was a flabby older white guy. The bookish type. You were one. You know what I mean," he said.

"I wasn't old, white, and flabby," Solomon said. "I was younger, fit. Well, not fit. I could run a hundred feet if I had to. Smoked too much hash and struggled lifting a bag of potatoes."

"Well you're old looking now."

"True, but stronger than ten hippies." He tossed his head back and laughed. Once he recovered, Solomon said, "Abraham, allow yourself to loosen up. Enjoy what this world offers. You've done well, by what I've seen. You've fared better than me."

"I don't know about that. All of the Henchmen left," he said.

A day after the company had met at the table and their brands dissipated, the King's Papers arrived. The Henchmen, one and all, left him, even Horace and Sticks. That really shocked him.

"I didn't think all of them would go," Abraham said.

"I didn't go."

"And I appreciate that. But it only makes sense because you and I have the same problem. We need to get back to our world."

Selma began massaging his head and asked, "What world are you talking about? The world beyond the sea?"

He turned his head, gave her a curious glance, and said, "No. What world are you talking about?"

"They say that another world lies beyond the Seas of Traversity and Troubles. But the Elders guard it," Selma said. "Is that the world you are from?"

Abraham and Solomon exchanged a look. Solomon shrugged.

Abraham told her, "I don't think so." He wondered if Titanuus might be a lost continent in some earthly place like the Bermuda Triangle or Atlantis. He turned his attention back to Solomon. "You've been here longer than me. Any ideas?"

"I fear that I've wasted valuable time desperately rummaging through the Spine. You're the best hope I've had since I arrived. You have the king's connection. Perhaps that will help."

"Yeah, well, I don't know about that." He rubbed his brand. "I still have to help him if he is going to help me. I'm not sure how I'm going to go about it without the others. I don't know my way around this world. I see things, and sometimes Ruger's memories will fill me in, but other than that, I'm lost."

"You'll just have to learn your way around, like I did. I'm going to help however I can. I have the same stake in our predicament as you do."

"I know. I just wish the others were around. I hate seeing a team break up." Abraham mostly missed Sticks. They'd formed a bond and had been intimate. He hadn't thought she would drop him like that. He even felt guilty being around the triplets. They were his to take, but that didn't seem right. He'd once had a wife and son. He even thought about Mandi. The triplets reminded him most of her. *I'm not sure what is going on, but I have to figure this out. If I'm in some sort of crazy coma, I have to wake up. But if I wake up, what do I wake up to?* "Solomon, do you really think that this is real?"

"A part of me hopes that it is."

"What part?"

"The strange peoples on Titanuus don't appear to judge others by appearances. They judge them by their actions." Solomon kissed Bridgett on the cheek. "That part I enjoy. But there are wicked hearts within—man, myrmidon, troglin, or zillons. The greedy heart of all the races is always the source of trouble. They can all be just as deceptive. I saw that with the troglin. They turned on me. I had to flee. Some are good, some malicious. It never ends, I think, no matter in what world we are."

"Oh, it will end one day," Abraham said. "If I don't believe that, then I might as well not believe anything."

"So, what are you going to do?"

"Await the king's orders and find some new Henchmen."

CHAPTER 39
LEWIS

In Kingsland's capital city, Burgess, the annual Sea Festival was in full swing. The evening sun had set, and the reveling on the cobblestone streets had begun hours before. Sailors back from long weeks at sea swayed arm in arm, singing in the colorful tongue of sailors. Women blushed as they covered the ears of their children when they walked by. The sailors winked and chuckled. One woman got goosed as she walked by.

Suddenly, scintillating explosions rocked the early night sky. Pyrotechnic after pyrotechnic was launched into the air. Umbrellas of fireworks rained down from the skyline. The children clapped and shouted with glee. Every eye in the streets was up. Hats were waving. Bonfires burned, and the great bells in the towers rang.

Lewis slipped into one of the haunting cathedrals adorned by insect-headed gargoyles with great pincers in their mouths. It was the worship place of the Elder of Insects. He closed the tall wooden door behind him and walked down the center aisle. The numerous bugs beneath his feet crunched underneath his boots. He sneered. The pews were half circles made from stone. At the end of the aisle, up the steps, on the stage was a twenty-foot-tall praying mantis made of jade.

He looked up at the creepy thing. "Stupid Elders."

"You might find greater favor in this life if you respected your Elders," Leodor said. He was sitting on a pew off to the left. He wore a heavy violet cloak with silver trim. His penetrating eyes were fixed on the mantis. "When is the last time you prayed?"

"Oh, that's easy. It was the last time after I saw an Elder. Never," Lewis said. He stomped more bugs underneath his feet. "There must have been at least one hundred better places that we could meet."

"No one comes here," Leodor said as he brushed some insects from his cloak.

"I can't imagine why. Does anyone even worship this Elder of Insects?"

"Certainly. The Sect controls all of the cathedrals. We have our clerics about this place, too. I cleared it out before you came."

"You cleared out everything but the bugs."

"We don't have control over them. They worship their master." Leodor nodded at the mantis statue. "Even they need a place to give thanks."

"Bugs? Really? Are you a complete fool?" Lewis spat on the floor. "You wonder why I don't worship. I'll tell you why. The Sect has made up an Elder for everything. The Elder of Insects. The Elder of Serpents. The Elder of the Sea. The Elder of Dogs. The Elder of Felines. The Elder of Weeds. The Elder of Gardens." He poked a finger at Leodor. "I have one for you. How about the Elder of Bung Holes?"

"Well, there actually is an Elder of Fools. I'd be happy to obtain a scroll of his prayers for you."

"So smug, aren't you, Leodor? You and the Sect have an Elder for everything and all of the people fooled, don't you? I think the Elder of Fools is fit for everybody."

Leodor hid his hands in the deep sleeves of his robes and replied, "You are the unbelieving fool, not me."

"I let you slide with your first jab, but I am the prince, and I won't let you talk to me like a child." He dropped his hand to his dagger. "I think you need a lesson in regards to your station, Viceroy." He tugged on the dagger, but it didn't come free. His hand was frozen to the weapon's hilt. A chill coursed through his body, like freezing blood in his veins. "What are you doing, snake?"

Leodor's eyes were aglow like silvery shimmering pools. His eyes, now spacey, locked on Lewis. He spoke with a deep hollowness that resonated in the small cathedral's chamber. "You are the one that needs to know his station, you spoiled, infantile child. I can turn your bones brittle as ice with a thought. I can boil your marrow." Through clenched teeth he said, "Respect is given when it is received."

Leodor let out a gasp as a shadowy figure appeared and held a blade against his throat. It was the assassin, Lewis's lover, Raschel.

"I always felt that the members of the Sect were overly chatty. Should I kill him, my love?" Raschel asked Lewis. "He'd make a fine sacrifice to the Elder of Insects. He could feed all of his little worshippers that scurry over the floors." She put her lips to Leodor's ears. "Wouldn't that be nice?"

"It would be," Leodor said in an unwavering tone. "But you would never get away with it."

"I've gotten away with plenty, and that doesn't include all of the dirty little things that you don't know about. The Sect has its people, and I have mine. Now, let me see the whites of your eyes before I nick you."

The silver pools in Leodor's eyes cleared.

Lewis freed his hand from the handle of his dagger and clutched his hand open and closed, frost on his fingernails. "I should behead you, Leodor."

"But you won't." Leodor lifted his chin. "Now, will you call your lady friend off?"

Lewis gave Raschel a nod. She lifted her blade away, spun it in her hand, and sheathed it. She stepped into full view, her eyes shaded by the hood of her cloak. She wore a tight-fitting leather jerkin with a cotton blouse underneath that revealed the womanly curves of her body. "The two of you need to get along better."

"That will be the day," Lewis said. "No more tricks, Leodor."

"Don't draw a weapon on me, Lewis." Leodor rubbed his hands on his knees and said, "Let's start with why we are gathered, shall we? I'll begin. I've reported to the Underlord—"

"What? You contacted the Underlord without me? How dare you?" Lewis said.

Leodor lifted his hands and said, "Don't get puffed up on me. You were tied up with our duties, and I had to report this immediately. If I didn't, my delay, *our delay*, would have drawn his ire. Believe me when I say that you don't want that. Needless to say, he seemed, er, concerned that Ruger completed the quest that should have destroyed him."

"It was your idea. I told you that we should have killed him outright. Instead, you sent him on a mission that not only gained my father's trust but restored the queen."

"Not to mention he killed one Fenix and captured another," Leodor said.

Lewis walked up on Leodor, looked down on him like a vulture, and said, "Are you proud of that notion? Sometimes I wonder whose side you are on."

"Need I remind you that it has been me all along that has been poisoning the queen?"

"Then poison her again," Lewis replied.

"No, that would be obvious. The queen is a strong woman, and she withstood the poison because of a fine constitution. It was a miracle that she hung on so long as she did. You underestimate her vitality."

"No, you underestimated it." Lewis propped his boot up on the bench beside Leodor and said, "So, what did our frightening Underlord say?"

Leodor looked up at Lewis and said, "You get your wish, Prince. He wants you to kill Ruger."

CHAPTER 40

Lewis and Raschel walked the streets of Burgess with their hoods over their heads. He couldn't help but smile. Finally, he could rid himself of Ruger and the Henchmen once and for all.

Raschel grabbed his hand, slowed his pace, and said, "Slow down. You're practically skipping."

"I can't help but feel glee. For years, my father has been tinkering around with the Henchmen, and slowly we've been picking them apart. But now"—he waggled his finger—"we can undo them in a straight-up slaughter."

"I don't think Leodor wants you to be brazen about it. You sound like you are going to fight him yourself," she said.

"Oh, I would love to finish the deed myself. If I could provoke him, perhaps, I could undo him."

"He wields Black Bane. Do you think you can overcome that?" she asked as they slipped into a narrower alley by passing underneath a stone archway that joined the buildings.

"Today, I feel that I can overcome anything."

"Do you believe what they say about Black Bane?" she asked.

"What do you mean? That ridiculous legend that it was forged by the Elders? Pfft. How can I believe that when I don't believe in the Elders?"

They entered Raschel's apartment building and walked up the stairs, two steps at a time, to the third floor, at the top. Using a small key, she opened the door then stepped aside, let Lewis in, and closed them inside. Both of them shed their cloaks and hung them on pegs by the door.

Raschel sat down in front of her vanity and began removing her small golden hoop earrings. "If you don't believe in the Elders, then how do you explain the Fenix?"

Lewis sat down on the bed to remove his boots. "The Fenix is a monster. We all know that there are all sorts of creatures that roam Titanuus. It is just one of them. For all we know, there are flocks of Fenixes elsewhere." He combed his fingers through his feathery black hair and began unbuttoning his shirt. "So, you spent a lot of time with Ruger. Do you know his weakness? After all, you are the one that is going to have to kill him. Thinking about it more thoroughly, I can't afford to get my hands dirty."

She dabbed perfume on her wrists from a glass jar and rubbed them together. "The last Ruger was a very simple animal to conquer. He used all of his physical advantages to his pleasure. He was a womanizer and a coward. He had the Red Tunics do all of the dirty work and shielded himself behind his Henchmen. But even so cowardly, he was naturally formidable and could fight like a lion. No one would cross him or Black Bane."

Lewis lay back on her pillows and said, "So, that straight-arrow became a womanizer. Interesting."

"What do you mean?"

"The Ruger I grew up with would not even look at a lady. He was the epitome of knighthood. Disciplined. Stern. Unwavering in the tenets of the Guardian Order. He trained. He overtrained. I hated him. I should have worshipped him, but I hated him." He turned his head her way. "So, Ruger was a womanizer. Did you have a few tosses with him?"

Raschel turned her head over her shoulder and said, "I wish."

Lewis chuckled. "Oh, you naughty little vixen. You are trying to fire my blood, aren't you?"

"I like seeing you worked up. I've always enjoyed the passion that your hatred brings."

"Nothing works me up more than you do. And when this is all over—and I am the king—we will marry."

"Is that a proposal?"

"Not officially. As for Ruger, you saw the change in him?"

"He told us that he was Abraham. A man from another world. He wanted to earn our trust, I believe. He's genuinely good-natured, unlike the other personality that must have been in him. I think he wants to do right. He's more of a leader." She removed her hairpins, and her brown hair fell down on her shoulders. "He rallied the Henchmen. There is something very different about him. He's… likeable."

"Well, don't go liking him too much. Or at all, for that matter."

She rose from the vanity chair. Tall, dark, and athletic, she stripped off everything but her cotton shirt. With the grace of a panther on the prowl, she crossed the room, climbed onto the bed, and straddled him. "So, how are we going to do this?"

"Did you want to tie me up again?"

"No, that's not what I meant. How do you want me to kill him?"

"Oh." He smiled. "That will make for some exciting pillow talk. Poison that makes him foam at the mouth would be nice. Perhaps an accident where an anvil falls and crushes his skull."

She put two fingers on his lips. "You really don't have a very good imagination when it comes to killing people. I'll handle it, but it's going to cost you because it can't be obvious."

"You are the best at that. You wiped out over half of his Henchmen."

"More like two-thirds. I'll handle this one. It will be interesting."

Lewis reached up, grabbed her locks with both hands, pulled her closer, and said, "Enough talk. Let's make this interesting instead."

CHAPTER 41
THE PAST
ABRAHAM'S PAST

ABRAHAM GOT OUT OF THE SUV he'd rented from the airport after the first flight he'd taken since the accident. He'd spent months in recovery and finally gotten himself into good enough shape to walk with a cane. It wasn't easy on his big frame. Now he was in Alabama, miles outside of Birmingham, in the driveway of Buddy Parker's family farm. It was a large ranch house surrounded by miles of split-rail fencing that went on and on. He headed up the walkway. The cane clicked with every step. With a grunt, he stepped out on the porch, faced the door with a brass horse-faced knocker in the middle, and sighed.

Rehabilitation had been hellish. The physical part of it was one thing. The mental and spiritual part was another. His spirit was broken. It was broken like the pieces of airplane he'd crashed all over the woodlands. Maybe worse. Jenny was gone. Jake was gone. Forever. That was only part of the pain. He never would have imagined the tidal wave of heart-twisting pain to come. He remembered when he'd picked up the newspaper in Pittsburgh. They'd thrown him under the bus. The paper said he was reckless and irresponsible. He found a headline on a national paper that read:

JENKINS THE JET KILLS FAMILY AND TEAMMATE
PIRATES' PENNANT HOPES CRASHED
HOTSHOT JENKINS FINAL FLIGHT FATAL

That was the beginning. The endless stream of reporters, questions, and accusations were more than enough to drive any man insane. They called him arrogant and inexperienced and said he had no business flying the plane. Abraham's father, Earl, tried to keep the press away. Like ravenous wolves, they came. The get-well flowers, balloons, and letters suddenly stopped coming. But the worst thing was the letter that never came. He never got word from Claude and Rose, the parents of Buddy Parker, his best friend and teammate. They were good people who had treated him like a son. But now, nothing. He had to see them. Today was the day he had the strength to face them. It couldn't wait any longer.

He felt a chronic, stabbing pain in his knees and shoulders. After reaching in a pocket and producing a prescription bottle, he fished out a pain pill with his finger, put it in his mouth, and swallowed. He used the knocker on the door.

Claude opened the door. He strongly resembled Buddy. He had dark black skin and graying hair with a matching moustache, and he wore a knit flannel shirt with jeans and a Pirates belt buckle. His eyes widened when he got a full look at Abraham. He closed the door behind himself and asked, "What are you doing here?"

Abraham swallowed. His tongue clove to the roof of his mouth. He could see the anger and pain building in Claude's warm, friendly eyes. With a growing ache in his heart, he said, "Mr. Parker, I came to say I'm sorry. I wanted you to know…" His voiced cracked. Tears started to flow. "It was an accident. I swear I wasn't careless like the papers say. I would never risk your family." He sobbed. "Or mine."

In a rigid tone, Claude said, "Do you think that is going to bring my son back? Do you? I don't care what the papers say or what you say. My son is gone, and he ain't coming back. That's on you!"

The front door opened. It was Rose, dressed in jeans and a nice black polo shirt. She was a pretty lady, but her eyes were tired and heavy. "Claude, do we have a visitor?" she asked in a sweet voice. She looked at Abraham. "Hello. I'm Rose." Rose was looking at Abraham as if she'd never seen him before in her life.

"Uh…" Abraham said. He glanced at Claude.

Claude hustled halfway inside the doorway, gently took his wife by the arm, and yelled, "Veronica! Veronica!"

A woman came running down the stairs. She was a younger white woman, dressed in brown scrubs that matched her short hair. She cradled Rose's elbows and said, "Come with me, Mrs. Parker. It's time for lunch and your medicine."

"But, we have company," Rose said. "Can we feed him too? He looks hungry. Where did you come from, young man?"

When Abraham started to speak, Claude cut him off. "We'll come and eat in a moment, dear. You go with Connie-Sue. Okay." He kissed her cheek. "I'll see you in a bit." He closed the women inside, stood in front of the door, and asked, "Did you see that? The moment Rose found out that Buddy was gone, she just checked out. Have you ever heard a broken-hearted woman wail for her lost son? Have you?" With clenched jaws, he shook his head angrily. "I lost my wife and my son the same day because of you. No apology is going to bring them back, either. This is your fault. It's on you!"

"Mister Parker, I-I swear, if there is anything I can do to make this right, I'll do it."

"Can you bring the dead back to life?" Claude stuck his chin out. "I didn't think so. The Lord might forgive you, Jenkins. But as of now, I can't. Get off of my porch and go." Claude opened the door and slammed it closed behind himself.

Abraham hobbled away with tears streaming down his face. He got in the SUV and drove all the way back to his home in Pittsburgh. His situation became worse after that. He tried to face the media, but the more he fought them, the harder they came. A few teammates and coaches reached out, but that wasn't enough. His downward spiral began, leading to an altercation in a grocery store with angry fans. He spent time in jail three times for fighting and public intoxication and urination. Finally, when he couldn't take it anymore, he moved to West Virginia with his father in Hinton.

Earl protected him as best he could. He kept him away from the articles and newspapers. They fished and went to church. Things seemed to get better, then Earl had a sudden heart attack and died. After that, Abraham wandered for years, deeper into the abyss, until he had next to nothing left. The elevator didn't go down any farther. His life was over.

CHAPTER 42
ABRAHAM'S PRESENT

ABRAHAM SAT IN THE CORNER of a small tavern located near the outskirts of Burgess. The local watering hole was filled with laborers from the city and farmers from the country. It smelled of sweat, dirt, and greasy food. He sipped his mug of ale, his second of the day. He wanted to forget the dreams he'd been having about his past. They all seemed very real—to the point that he feared he might not wake up again. *Weird.* He couldn't decide whether he wanted to wake up in Titanuus or wake up living his life over again.

In the meantime, he'd kept himself busy at the Stronghold. He got a feel for the work being done at the unique estate. The hirelings took care of the food and the fields. With the help of Solomon and himself, they fed the baby Fenix, Simon. Abraham wrestled with whether or not to dismiss the triplets, but Solomon talked him into keeping them around. They didn't seem to have anywhere to go, anyway. He tried to avoid them, but they didn't make it easy.

A scrawny young waitress wearing a blue skirt and white blouse with a matching hat that looked like a shower cap set a plate of food on the table. The portions of ham, bread, potatoes, and greens were generous, almost as generous as the gravy. He took up his three-pronged fork and started digging in.

Abraham missed the Henchmen. He missed Sticks. He couldn't believe they'd abandoned him. The company he'd kept with them was like that of a locker room. He really missed those fun days. They'd filled a void inside him. At the moment, he didn't mind eating alone. He needed the time to himself, and he'd gotten a feel for Burgess. It was a nice city and not very difficult to blend in, either. All sorts of people were coming and going. He even saw myrmidons and troglins, which he was a little bit leery of. The alien-looking zillons—with their big black eyes and white, almost translucent skin—were freaky.

He chewed up his food and took a swig of ale. It was a bitter brew but robust in flavor, which reminded him of a Great Lakes beer he'd once liked. He lifted his mug. "Here's to the *Edmund Fitzgerald*."

The waitress came back with a pitcher and topped his mug off. She gave him a wink. "Let me know if there is anything else that I can serve you."

"I will," he said, without hiding his smile. The waitress had flirted with him a little more and more every time he entered. He liked the tavern. The people were robust and hard working and didn't pay him any mind, and he was supposed to be famous. Slowly, he lowered his hand to his sword.

Two men were snaking their way through the crowd while continuing to cast looks at Abraham. They ordered beers and wove across the floor. They were young, but sword belts were strapped on their hips.

Abraham acted as though he didn't see them. Both men lingered near his table with their backs toward him. They were dressed like commoners, and one of them wore a cowl pulled over his neck. The meatier one with curly brown hair sipped and sipped his brew. The other young man stood loose as a goose, as if he was sleeping while standing. The bigger young man dared a look at Abraham then quickly turned away.

"What do you want?" Abraham growled.

Both men turned around. They both looked the same age but with different builds, and the broader man acted more serious and nervous.

"Excuse me, are you talking to me?" he asked.

"You've been eyeballing me ever since you stepped in this saloon," Abraham said. His grip tightened on his sword, the one he'd sworn had spoken to him once but never again since. "What do you want?"

"What's a saloon?" the other, sleepy-eyed man asked.

"A place where men die when they don't answer my question."

The bigger man elbowed the other man in the side. "Show respect, idgit. Apologies, but let me offer an introduction. I am Skitts, and this is Zann, my brother. Um, may we join you?"

"Sit."

Once the brothers were seated, Skitts continued in a low voice. "We know who you are, and we want to become Henchmen."

Abraham tugged on his ear. He'd spoken to his hirelings about discreetly spreading the word about finding new Red Tunics. That was days before. These men were the first two to show up. This was the main reason he hung around in the tavern. Without saying a word, he sized up the two men. Skitts had some brawn in his shoulders. He was a bit round-faced but a reasonable fit. He carried nervous energy. Zann, on the other hand, looked like he could sleep in the middle of a tornado, but he moved easily and was soft-footed. "Do you have shovels?"

Skitts leaned forward. "Pardon. Why would we need shovels?"

"To make a grave. You might have to make your brother's. He might have to dig yours. I might have to bury the both of you," Abraham said.

Zann's jaw hung low. He looked at Abraham as though he didn't understand what he'd said.

Skitts blinked repeatedly, his fingers fidgeting. "We have one shovel at home. Can we share it?"

Abraham drummed his fingers on the table. "I suppose. Now tell me about those swords you carry. Have you used them?"

"Well, er…" Skitts looked at this brother. "Not in a real battle. But we did our mandatory time in the king's army. We trained with the legions. We guarded the South Tiotan wall for two years. The entire length."

"I shot a Tiotan intruder," Zann mumbled, talking slowly. "Right in the back of the leg. He wailed like a hound and ran and fell and ran and fell."

"Yes, yes! We manned the ballistae and fired many times on the enemy. I'm certain I hit a couple, but the wounds were not fatal." Skitts kept nodding. "We are hard workers."

"You're telling me that your brother is a hard worker? He looked more like a hard sleeper."

"I don't sleep much," Zann said.

"That I believe. You have bags under your eyes like an Elder's grandmother." Abraham wiped his mouth with a cloth napkin. The men across the table eyed his food. Skitts silently smacked his lips. "Why do you want to be Henchmen?"

"We want to serve the king," Skitts said.

"But you did serve the king."

"Well, in a greater capacity. We want adventure. Treasure. See the world," Skitts said.

"Isn't that why you joined the King's Army? To be all that you can be," he said.

"No, I mean, we love our country, but we want more. We want glory. We want to be great swordsmen like you. We want to serve with a legend."

"Yes," Zann murmured in a slow, Southern-like drawl. "A legend."

Abraham leaned back and asked, "You two aren't deserters, are you?"

Skitts swallowed. "Not exactly."

CHAPTER 43

"OUT WITH IT," ABRAHAM SAID.

Scratching his head, Skitts said, "The colonel commander had it in for us."

"And why would the colonel commander have it in for you?" Abraham asked.

"Zann slept with his daughter," Skitts said.

"I wasn't the only one sleeping around. My genius brother was caught sleeping with the colonel's wife," Zann said. "Skitts takes a shine to the older women like a bear takes to honey."

"I don't have a thing for older women. She pursued me," Skitts said.

"Sure she did. And that's why you were caught slipping out of the colonel's tent." Zann's smiled showed his little teeth. "Heh heh."

"Anyway, Captain Ruger, we were both discharged without honor. We'd like to redeem ourselves." Skitts shrugged. "After all, men will be men, and women will be women." He worked up his best smile.

"Boys, you blow a lot of smoke. Everything you said might be a lie. I don't suppose you brought in references?"

The brothers exchanged a look.

"Where do you live?" Abraham asked.

Skitts blurted out directions.

Abraham shoved his plate across the table. "Take this food to another table. Eat and go. I'll think on it."

Skitts grabbed the plate, got up, and eagerly bowed. "Thank you. Thank you."

Zann nodded and slipped away with his brother.

Later in the evening, when the brothers were long gone, Abraham stepped outside to relieve himself by the creek. Once he finished, he sat down on a moss-covered boulder. A nice evening breeze was blowing, with a chill in the air. The clouds moved quickly across the moonless sky. "Plenty of stars, but I don't recognize a single one of them. No Orion, no Big Dipper, not a one of them. Lord, where in the heck am I? I miss my beer truck."

He snaked his sword out of its scabbard and held it up against the sky. Black Bane was a perfectly balanced longsword. He thumbed both of the keen edges. With two fingers, he traced over the runes engraved in the blade. An arcane source of power was within, and the sword had a voice, too. At least he thought it did. The lightning that had killed the Fenix came from somewhere.

"So, do you sing, Black Bane?"

The wind whistled through the trees.

Black Bane didn't say a word.

Abraham turned the blade side to side. It had an extra-long handle, making for a double-handed grip. He swallowed the grip up in his big hands. "Pitching ace to sword master. Incredible."

Back at the Stronghold, he'd come across hundreds of pages of parchment bound with twine. They had images of sword-fighting stances and directions complete with notes. He leafed through half of them in his free time, studying the material with eyes that had seen it before. His memory, or Ruger's, was refreshed. He even took time to practice for a few hours. All the moves came naturally to him.

His eyes studied Black Bane. "If you aren't going to talk, I'm putting you away." He waited a few seconds, slid it back into the scabbard, and headed back into the tavern.

A woman was sitting at his table with her back to him. Her dark hair touched the cloak on his shoulders. A quiver of arrows hung from her back, and a bow lay across her back. He eased around the corner of the table and slowly sat down. The woman was attractive and dark-eyed and reminded him of Mandi so much that his heart jumped. She filled out her shirt and leather jerkin well.

"Good evening," he said. "Uh, I don't mind the company, but this is my table. You are welcome to join me."

Sitting upright, she said in a soothing but slightly husky voice, "Thank you, but I believe you are the one I am looking for. You are Ruger Slade? Yes?"

"I am, but I don't want to make that public."

His eyes scanned the crowd. No one appeared to be listening. The loud talking carried over their voices. The bawdy drunks throwing darts on the opposite side of the tavern were the loudest ones of all.

"Let me guess. You want to be a Henchman?"

"I know I'm a woman, but I'm very skilled with a bow and my blades." She pulled back her cloak, revealing a pair of short swords strapped against her sides, otherwise well concealed. "I grew up a hunter, and for several years I've worked for the collectors as a bounty hunter. I'd make an excellent Henchman. I want to serve the king."

"There's more to becoming a Henchman than joining. You have to pay your dues as a Red Tunic."

She tilted her head. "A Red Tunic?"

"A retainer. You serve the Henchmen like a squire serves a knight. If you prove your worth, you become a Henchman."

"Oh." She sank down in her chair a little.

The woman's strong resemblance to Mandi got him caught up reflecting on his past. Mandi worked at Woody's Grill, and she had a thing with him. He brushed her off one final time. He wondered what would have happened if he had stayed. *Would I still be here, or would I be with her?* This woman was about his age, had a nice tanned complexion, the tiniest of freckles on the smooth cheeks of her face.

The woman leaned forward and asked, "Were you going to say something else?"

He blinked. "Sorry. I lost my train of thought." He lifted his mug. "Too much ale. Would you like one?"

"No, thank you. But I appreciate the offer. It's a nicer one than those men at the bar offered."

"They hit on you, huh?" he said.

"No, they didn't hit me. They offered to—"

"Never mind. It's just an expression. Do I need to have words with them?"

"Of course not. They are just a bunch of ornery farmers. I can handle myself. Trust me."

Abraham nodded. "Please don't think that woman can't be Henchmen. The ones in my group are as proven as the men. But I have to think about it. You know, I never even asked you what your name was."

"It's Raschel."

CHAPTER 44

LATER THAT NIGHT, ABRAHAM DEPARTED the country tavern and rode back toward the Stronghold. He swayed his shoulders as he sang an old Night Ranger song about rocking in America. Something about his meeting with Raschel got his juices flowing about Mandi. He missed the moderately spoiled woman's warm and friendly face. They both liked Night Ranger, too. It was old school for his age, but he liked it and most classic rock and country, which he'd listened to in his beer truck.

He changed his tune after he forgot the lyrics to the song he was singing and switched to another oldie: "Mandi, you're a fine girl. What a good—"

Out of the darkness, a bolt whistled through the air. Abraham's horse reared and tossed him to the ground. He scrambled back to his horse and hid behind it. The beast lay dead with an arrow in its neck.

"Sorry, fella," he muttered.

A group of men appeared from the surrounding trees and surrounded him. Ten in all were there, a rough-looking bunch in ragged clothing, carrying steel weapons in their hands. One man stood out among the others. He wore a leather overcoat and held a crossbow against one shoulder. His head was big, hair shaggy, and some of his teeth were missing.

He licked his mouth before he spoke and said, "Toss me your purse and your weapons."

"Am I being robbed?"

"No, this is the Burgess escort service," the leader of the highwaymen said. "Don't be stupid. Hand it over."

Abraham took a knee. His fingers loosened his purse away from his belt. "Why did you kill my horse? It was a fine steed, worth more than what I carry. That was stupid."

The highwayman pointed his loaded crossbow at Abraham. "We killed it so you couldn't run away to your mommy. Now, hand over the purse and the steel!"

He tossed his purse at the man's feet and said, "You shouldn't have killed my horse. That was a mistake."

The highwayman kicked the purse over to one of his men, who scooped it up. "Now your weapons," he said to Abraham.

Abraham scanned the crowd. They weren't the durable warriors he was accustomed to keeping with. They were armorless thieves who preyed on the weak.

"I don't think so," Abraham said. "If you want my sword, come and get it."

The highwaymen grunted. "Fool. I was going to slay you either way." He took aim at Abraham's chest. "Let's see if that quick tongue of yours can dodge this."

In that moment, Abraham realized he didn't have his armor on either. And he was too drunk to draw his sword quickly enough to block a crossbow bolt, as he had a bullet. He lifted a finger and asked, "Can I have a moment?"

"No." The highwaymen started to squeeze the trigger.

Out of the woods, an arrow whistled through the air and buried itself in the highwayman's side. The man let out a painful gasp and fired the crossbow at Abraham's head.

Abraham crouched, and the bolt whistled over his head. The money-hungry highwaymen came at him with weapons bared. He drew Black Bane as quickly as a man could bat an eyelash. He took his first attacker's head from his shoulders then sidestepped a downward sword thrust, snaked out his dagger, and pierced the attacker's chest. The man clutched at the bloody wound in his chest while silently screaming.

A second arrow whistled through the air, impaling a man's belly. A third arrow dotted the same man's forehead.

Black Bane rose and fell, hewing one man down after the other with the speed of a striking snake. Abraham lopped off another head and three more arms. The iron in his enemies' spines had turned to water. They fled. They bled. A volley of arrows and thrusts of steel dropped them all dead.

Abraham caught his breath and wiped blood from his eyes. He surveyed the fallen and let out a light chuckle. "I see dead people."

A woman carrying a loaded bow catwalked his way from the darkness. It was Raschel. "Are you harmed?" she asked as her intent eyes swept over the highwaymen.

"I'm fine, but my horse isn't," he said. He wiped his bloodstained sword over the grass and sheathed it. "Where did you come from?"

Raschel eased off her bowstring and dropped her arrow back in its quiver. "I have to apologize, but I was following you. I wanted to show off my skills by tracking you, and well, I needed to know where you lived, too."

"You didn't have to do that." He looked down at the leader of the highwaymen. He was dead with the arrow buried feather deep in his side. "You're a fine shot with that bow. Pretty impressive, given that it's dark outside and people were moving."

"I told you that I was good." She saw his purse on the ground and picked it up. "Is this yours?" She tossed it to him.

"Thanks. A man never goes anywhere without his purse." He took a knee by his horse. He stroked the star stripe on its head. "Sorry, fella."

He started removing the saddle, and Raschel knelt down and helped him. She had quick hands.

"Man, where do you think guys like that came from? Should we tell somebody?"

"Let the sheriff handle it. Men like these are low-end. I don't think he'll care that they are dead. But if he does, he'll probably find us." She smiled. "Well, you anyway. I'll disappear."

"You've come this far. You might as well come to the Stronghold. That's where you were heading, weren't you?"

"I'd like that."

"Consider this your initiation." He laid [illegible] her shoulder. "Welcome to the Red Tunics."

CHAPTER 45

"YOU TOLD HIM YOUR NAME?" Inside Raschel's apartment, Lewis wrung his hands behind his back and paced the floor. "What are you thinking? You joined the Henchmen again? Why didn't you kill him?"

"If you don't like my methods, then why don't you assassinate him yourself?" she said. She sat on the end of her bed, putting her pants on. "I'm glad I didn't tell you this before we slept together. It might have ruined the moment."

"The moment is ruined now!" He clenched his fists. "If you had a shot, you should have killed him, not the highwaymen. Poor saps. You put them in the crosshairs of a death trap."

Twirling her hair on a finger, she said, "Actually, they brought him down well. They just weren't wise enough to finish him. But it served my purpose. I gained his trust."

Lewis stood in front of her, put both his hands on her shoulders, and looked dead in her eyes. "Tell me. At that moment, could you have killed him?"

"I could have hit him. The question is 'Would that have killed him?' If it didn't, I would have been done in. He'd have killed me." She laid her warm hands on his. "Believe me when I say that I have seen him in action. He has instincts, a sixth sense. Ruger won't be so easy to kill. He has a way of slipping out of danger. No, let me do what I do. I'll set him up for a fall against a great horde of enemies. It will happen."

"Well, do it soon. My father is eager to send Ruger on a new campaign." Lewis started to pace again. "Thanks to my deranged stepmother, he thinks that Ruger is some sort of savior. Can you believe that?"

"What sort of campaign?"

"Leodor cooked up some quest about restoring the Crown of Stones to its full glory. It's nothing short of moronic. It's even a worse idea than fetching the Fenix egg. Those gems, if they even existed, could be anywhere in the world. It's madness."

"That will be difficult. Abraham's Henchmen abandoned him the moment the King's Brand cleared. He's somewhat depressed about it. The only one left around is the troglin. Hence, he continues to recruit."

"A troglin. That's three men in one."

"He's old and strange." She came to his side and gently put her arms around his neck. "Did you ever stop to think that if your father had the crown, then one day it will be yours to wear?"

"Of course I did. That's the only reason I am going along with it. But I don't think the Underlord will allow that to happen. According to Leodor, he wants the mission to fail before it's even begun." He took her wrists in her hands. "You need end your flirtations with Ruger and escort him to the grave. Just poison him and run. I'll hide you."

"Have faith in me, my love. I know what I'm doing. I've done this over a hundred times before." She kissed his cheek.

"I want him put in the ground. Next chance you get. Do it."

CHAPTER 46

Outside the Stronghold, Abraham worked with Skitts and Zann. The brothers were lathered in early-morning sweat. Abraham had been running sword-training drills for days. The brothers stood side by side with their longswords fully extended and pointed up. He kicked at their feet, and they adjusted their stances.

"Good," Abraham said. "Stand still and don't move before I say." He silently counted to thirty. Zann's arms started to shake. Forty-five seconds into it, Skitts's arms shook like leaves. "Fifty-seven… fifty-eight… fifty-nine… sixty. Sheathe your swords."

The brothers puffed for breath and slid their swords into their scabbards with clumsy effort. Skitts wiped his forehead with his sleeve. "I never trained this hard in the army. We just did regular drills."

"And that's why you are horrible swordsmen. Not to take a jab at the King's army, but their foot soldiers need more training." Abraham rubbed his jaw.

Skitts had already lost some of the boyish meat in his cheeks. Zann had come around and gained some thickness in his shoulders. He moved surprisingly well for a sleepy-eyed goon.

"Okay, high guard on one. One!"

The brothers drew their swords in the high guard and stood with alert eyes.

"Ox guard, two!" he said.

Skitts and Zann lifted their swords over their heads, tip first, blade parallel to the ground, and shifted their feet.

"Wrath guard, three!"

Again, the brothers shifted in their stances as they cocked the weapons back behind their shoulders.

Abraham repeated, "High guard, one! Ox guard, two! Wrath guard, three!"

The brothers stood unquavering.

"Let's go faster," he added. "Keep your feet or lose some meat! High! Ox! Wrath! High! Ox! Wrath! High! Ox! Wrath! High!"

Sweat dripped from Skitts's chin. Zann breathed deeply through his nose.

Abraham stepped between them and said, "I want to see a proper thrust from high guard. Shuffle step forward, plant the back foot, and put some weight down on the swing. You want to end a fight in one blow. Spit a man from skull to chin, the fight is over. It'll send the enemy running. Use your length. Your skill. I don't want to hear a ring of steel. I want to hear steel hitting bone. Thrust!"

The two men lunged forward and stabbed forward and pulled their swords back up.

Abraham backed up with them. "Thrust. Thrust. Thrust. Let's change it up. Switch from the thrust to the chop."

Skitts and Zann nodded.

"Chop! Chop! Chop! Chop! Chop!" Abraham marched them all over the yard, switching from position to position.

The brothers were exhausted.

On a break, Skitts drank from a water skin and asked, "When were you going to teach us any defense?"

"Killing first. That's the best defense," Abraham replied.

Solomon came out of the barn. His gray fur had fluffed up from where he'd cleaned the grime out of it. He wore a blacksmith's apron. "Your bird is becoming difficult."

"Why don't you two take a few laps around the lake," he said to the brothers. When they started to drop their swords, he added, "No, take those with you."

"Yes, Captain." Both of them took off running, shoving back and forth on one another on the way.

Solomon looked down at him and said, "I hate to sound impatient, but you appear to be more focused on the next campaign than getting us out of here. We've been waiting for word for days, and nothing has come."

"I can't really go anywhere with the brand without the king's permission. Besides, you seem to be enjoying your stay here." He passed Solomon on his way into the barn. "I just want to be ready. With only four Henchmen, I think I'm going to be doing much of the heavy lifting."

"If I'm here and you're here, certainly there are others like us. We need to seek them out. Burgess is a large town. Maybe you can look for more answers when you are recruiting."

"You should come with," Abraham said.

"Perhaps. But I'm beginning to feel that you are embracing this world too much. I'm not sure that I want to do that. Look at me. I'm a giant monkey."

"I'm not getting carried away. I promise. I can't help it if I like what I'm doing."

He stood in front of the stable where Simon stood inside. Steel bars went across the top, with wooden walls at the bottom keeping the Fenix inside. The creature walked over to Abraham on his tiny feet and looked right at him.

"Whoa, you're as tall as me. Man, birds grow fast."

"You think that thing is a bird? It's a bat-lizard thing. Perhaps an ugly dragon though the dragons I've seen are fairer."

"Either way, he needs to stretch those wings." Abraham opened the door. "Come on, Simon."

The Fenix followed Abraham out of the barn stride for stride. It swung its leathery winged arms like a man. Outside of the barn, Abraham started to slowly flap is arms like a bird.

Solomon slapped his face. "This is insanity. A man teaching a bird to fly."

"Listen, Winger, you have to jump and flap. Like this. Jump and flap." He did a pair of demonstrations. "Do it with me."

Simon cocked his head.

"I don't know." Abraham scratched his head.

Simon did the same.

"Do you think I can teach him to use a sword?"

"You couldn't do any worse than you are teaching it to fly." Solomon crinkled his nose. "It's a horrid thing. Malodorous. He spooks the horses. I'm sure they know one day he'll eat them. Be done with him. Kill it before it kills us."

"No, I'm not doing that. I don't know why I'm not doing that. Perhaps I should, but I just can't kill the thing in cold blood." He reached out and touched hands with Simon. "It's just a baby."

"True, but at the rate it's growing, it's going to be bigger than this barn before long. What will you do then?" Solomon said.

"I don't know. I'm trying to get it to fly away." Abraham started flapping his arms again. "Fly, Simon, fly."

Simon spread his wings out.

"Man, those things are big. What are they, twelve, fifteen feet?" Abraham started flapping again. "Come on, Simon. You can do it."

Simon batted his wings. His short knees bent. He launched himself into the sky.

"Whoa!" Abraham yelled. "Look at him go!"

Simon circled above them several times and let out a mighty screech. The hirelings who watched jumped out of their sandals. Others dashed into the cover of the barn. The Fenix let out one last squawk and turned north toward the Spine.

Abraham waved. He looked over at Solomon. "See, I'm an amazing teacher."

"Either that or you're really good at running your Henchmen away. I hope it doesn't come back."

"I don't think it is." Dropping his eyes, he saw someone coming toward the Stronghold on foot. At first, he thought it was Raschel, but it wasn't. "I'll be. It's Sticks."

The tomboyish and expressionless woman stopped in front of Abraham and said, "We have to talk."

CHAPTER 47

Inside the Stronghold, Abraham sat with Sticks at the farm table. They were alone. After they both sat down, he asked, "Where have you been?"

"Here and there," she said.

"I'm glad you're back, even it if is only for a little while. You're always welcome, of course."

Her brown eyes drifted toward the ceiling. "I figured you had all of the company that you needed."

"Huh? Oh, you meant the triplets. Listen, Sticks, Solomon is keeping them entertained. I know Ruger's last, er… personality was a freak, but I'm an old-fashioned kind of guy. I hope that makes some sense."

She shrugged.

"So, what did you want to talk about?"

"We've been trying to find Twila. Not much fortune with it. She seems to have disappeared."

"*We've*? We've who?"

"Well, Cudgel and Tark, for one. Did you think they were just going to let that go? Their eyes are filled with blood. Other than them, it's been me and Iris. But Horace checks in."

"What are you doing, forming your own band of Henchmen?"

"No," she said, "we are trying to avenge Cudgel. We can't have Twila running free." Her eyes narrowed. "She must pay."

"She could be anywhere by now. North, perhaps. She could have taken a boat and sailed away."

"We've checked all of the ports. No one has seen her. You do know that we've hunted down and found everything that we've tracked, right?"

"I'll take your word for it. So, what do you want from me? I'm all for finding Twila, but I have to find and ready more Henchmen for the king's quest. All of you left me." He tapped his knuckles on the table. "To be honest, it shocked me. I'm glad you are free, but honestly, I feel lost without the team."

"I don't think that it's you," she said. Her mouth twitched. "They want Twila. I want Twila. You should want Twila. Do you know how many deaths that woman is responsible for? Tark and Cudgel had two more brothers, not to mention the brothers you didn't know."

He knew the number was over one hundred. Whether it was directly or indirectly, he couldn't say. He felt that Eugene Drisk was as responsible as Twila was. "I want to help. You know I do. But isn't it possible that she could have disappeared?"

"What do you mean?"

"There are mages, wizards, you know, people that make portals, that brought people like me here. I think that anything is possible. You might be trying to pick up on a dead trail."

"Or a trail of the dead." Sticks got up from her bench. "That won't stop us. Only death will. Remember, someone put Twila in our midst for the reason. They are behind all of this. No doubt, whatever mission the king put you on, that will happen again. If we find Twila, then we find answers. I wanted to let you know what was going on. The others don't know that I came. They think that I'm beating the bushes."

"You're leaving?"

"I'm not even sure why I came."

Abraham rose. "I'm coming with you."

"No, you stay. Train your *new* Henchmen. Or Red Tunics. Don't let us impede you." She walked out the door.

He stood rubbing his head for a moment and walked outside after her.

Solomon was walking out of the barn with big bales of hay under his long arms. "Hello, Sticks," he said as she walked by.

She didn't reply and kept going until she passed over the slope and dipped and out of sight.

Standing beside Solomon, Abraham said, "Women. I don't even understand why she came."

"You must be daft. Even a troglin can see that," Solomon said.

"Oh, well, why don't you impart some of the divine troglin wisdom on me?"

"Simple. She wants you to chase her. You'd think a jock like you would know that."

Abraham tracked Sticks down to Burgess. She'd entered a tavern with a sign that hung above the door that read The Red Rooster. He walked up on the porch and through the open door. A handful of people were seated at the bar with their noses in their mugs of ale. The tables were empty save for one. Several familiar faces sat behind a medium-sized rectangle table. Horace filled his chair with his big frame. Iris, Cudgel and Tark, and Sticks made up the rest. All their eyes were on Abraham.

Sticks said, "I told you he would come."

He approached with a slight smile on his face and pulled back a chair. "I thought you said that no one knew you came to see me?"

"I lied," Sticks said.

Abraham extended his arm to Horace. They locked hands around each other's thick forearms. He did the same with Cudgel and Tark. "Good to see you. All of you."

"Same here, Captain," Horace said.

"Agreed," Tark and Cudgel replied in unison.

Iris looked at them with dreamy eyes, resting her chin on hands propped on her elbows. "You know I'm happy to see you."

He winked at her. "Ditto." Abraham rested an arm on the back of the chair. "All right, what's really going on? And where is everyone else?"

Horace clawed at his bushy beard and said, "Dominga is about. Haven't heard a word from Bearclaw, Vern, Prospero, or Apollo. They were heading to the House of Steel to be reinstated as the King's Guardians. We don't think that was such a good idea. That's why we hoped you'd come here."

"Why's that?" Abraham said.

Horace looked at Sticks. She gave him a nod.

"We think Prince Lewis is the problem," Horace said.

CHAPTER 48

"You know that I'm not going to jump on that wagon without some sort of proof," Abraham said.

A waitress set a mug of ale in front of him. She gave him a smile and walked away.

"I don't care for Lewis any more than you do, so I need to have some proof even though I have my suspicions."

Sticks tossed a skin of black fur and claws on the table. It was the same soft and shiny fur as the Black Growler they'd encountered at the Spine. "That's our physical proof. The rest comes from what I've seen with the naked eye."

He took the pelt in hand. "Where did you get this?"

"The dark markets. I inquired about it," Sticks said. "It was like pulling a tooth out of a live dragon's jaw. I knew that pelt was too valuable for Twila to part with. Only a fool would miss out on that opportunity. Anyway, she slipped."

"Wait a minute. I thought you said that you had no sign of her," Abraham said. As Sticks's mouth opened to speak, he said, "Never mind. You lied."

Sticks nodded. "I'm good at it. Anyway, we tracked the sale back to an apartment complex here in Burgess. There is no sign of Twila coming out, but Dominga stoops on it now. But, at night, we've seen Prince Lewis coming and going."

He leaned over the table. "You saw his face?"

"He was hooded. Same height and build. Same gait. It was him. I saw it myself," Sticks said.

"But—"

"And"—Sticks lifted a finger—"We followed three more similar figures into the Elder of Insects' cathedral. Again, they were cloaked, but we know it was Leodor. He moves like an old spirit. Lewis is more obvious with his natural strut. I didn't know who the woman was, but she wasn't built like Twila. It didn't stop me from following her, either."

Abraham lifted his chin. "And?"

"She went to the same apartments *and* to the Stronghold. It's your new woman."

"Raschel?" He leaned his chair back on two legs. "So, Lewis put a spy in the Henchmen?"

"Lewis and Leodor. That's the theory," Sticks said with a small smile.

"That sucks." Abraham liked Raschel. The thought of her being in cahoots with Lewis and Leodor was nothing short of disturbing. To make matters worse, both men must have been conspiring against King Hector. "His own son. I can't believe that Hector's boy would try to do him in."

"If he is truly behind this, then you need to warn the king," Cudgel said.

"Or we can kill him," Tark said. "A son turning on his own father is sickening."

Abraham dropped all four legs to the floor. "Am I supposed to tell the king? I don't think he'd believe me, an otherworlder, over them. How do I prove they did it?"

Horace leaned on his forearm and said, "You need to watch your back, Captain. This new Henchmen might be another pile of trouble that gets you killed."

"She does appear to be more formidable than Twila did. Maybe Lewis and Leodor want to have an inside source. Perhaps they don't trust us," he said.

"If it smells like a skunk, it's a skunk," Tark said.

Abraham had finally learned to put his faith in the Henchmen. He was better off taking their word for it. After all, they didn't have to be pursing Twila now that they were freed. They were doing it on their own out of honor and vengeance for the fallen.

"I agree," Abraham said. "So, what's the next move? Play along? Imprison Raschel and question her? I'm open to suggestions."

"I say we question her," Cudgel said. He had a bitter sound in his voice and a frown on his face. "I think she'll know what happened to Twila. We need answers. Clearly, they are protecting her."

Abraham sucked on his ale while he mulled it over. He was still the indentured servant of the king. That last thing he needed to do was make accusations and burn bridges. At this point, it was his word against Lewis and Leodor's. That would be a hard sell even if he had proof. He set down his mug. "At least I know there is a snake in the henhouse. For now, let's keep our eyes and ears peeled. Ordinary business. We'll see what reveals itself."

Horace gave a stiff nod, but his eyes were downcast. So were everyone else's.

"What is it?"

Horace spoke up. "Captain, you aren't in command of us now. We'll do what we want to do. You can't stop us. No disrespect, but what we do, we do for ourselves. And if we choose to pursue it"—he looked Abraham in the eyes—"we'll pursue it."

CHAPTER 49

Abraham parted his hands and asked, "Then why did you bring me here?"

"Out of respect," Horace said. "You've earned it. We thought you should know in case anything slides back on you." He touched his hand over his heart. "I admit I feel a hollowness within my breast now that the brand is gone. Something is missing. I liked being a Henchman. At least, recently."

Cudgel and Tark nodded. Iris tipped her chin.

Abraham could see some anguish in their faces. They really did want to stay at the Stronghold, but they had to find Twila first. They wouldn't follow him anymore without resolving that matter. He needed them, and he had a feeling that maybe they needed him too. They all gave each other purpose.

He lifted his hands and said, "Listen, I'm not going to get in your way. I appreciate you filling me in, but do what you have to do." He stood up. "If I can help, let me—"

The company's gaze moved past Abraham.

Dominga entered through the tavern's front door. With the grace of a cat, the sensual ebony woman made her way to the table. Her eyes rose when she saw Abraham. She gave him a quick smile and looked at the others.

"It's fine," Sticks said to Dominga. "We are all on board."

"Prince Lewis returned. He's back in the apartments." She grinned. "I finally know what rooms he's in. It's the top floor. I listened to his footsteps from the second."

"Well, who's watching to see if he leaves?" Horace asked.

"I have some reliable urchins keeping eyes on the exits." Dominga picked up Abraham's mug. "Do you mind?"

"Of course not," he said. "It's nice seeing you."

"I know." Dominga looked at Horace and Sticks. "So, what's the move?"

Horace glanced at Abraham and said, "We'll wait until the prince leaves. After that, we snatch this woman and question her. I'm pretty sure it would be a crime to interrogate the prince. That will only get us all back in prison. Was he alone?"

"Same as usual," Dominga said. "I found it odd that he came in the morning, for a change. Usually it's at night."

"I can answer that. Raschel was going to stay at the Stronghold beginning this evening. I was going to start her training tomorrow. Though she doesn't need any help with archery."

"No, she looks really good at handling arrows," Sticks said.

"Listen, maybe you aren't comfortable confronting Prince Lewis, but I am. I say we pay him a visit now. Perhaps we can catch him with his trousers down. Let's get answers. Let's get them today."

Horace nodded. "I support that."

Cudgel and Tark nodded. "Let's do it."

"No time like the present," Iris said.

Sticks shrugged and got up from the table. "So, who's in charge?"

Horace showed his teeth, slapped Abraham on the shoulder, and said, "The Captain is."

CHAPTER 50

On cat's feet, Abraham, Dominga, and Sticks crept down the hallway of the apartment building's third floor. The floors were hard wood, and the walls were made from solid stone. No balconies were on the outside, only windows. Dominga pointed out a door at the end of the hall. Sticks put her ear to the door and made a knowing smile.

Dominga mouthed the words "They are having sex" with affirmation.

Now the question was how to get in. Knocking was out of the question. Abraham moved toward the door. A board creaked loudly underneath his foot. He froze. The women looked at him.

He whispered, "So much for surprise. Let's roll." He lowered his shoulder and bashed right through the door.

Prince Lewis and Raschel were coming up out of the bed. Lewis was stripped down to his trousers. His well-built muscles tensed. Raschel had a silk robe on. She went for the dagger on her vanity. Sticks and Dominga cut her off with daggers pointed at her face.

"Ruger! What in blazes are you doing here?" Lewis reached for his sword belt, which hung on the end of the bed's footboard.

Abraham knocked his hand aside with the flat of Black Bane's blade.

Cringing and holding his hand, the prince said, "You dare!"

"I have a strict policy about my Red Tunics fraternizing with the crown. Especially you. Do you care to tell me what is going on?" Abraham said.

"I don't have to tell you anything. You are dead! You drew your weapon on royalty! Every one of you will hang in the gallows!" Lewis shouted.

Dominga pushed Raschel down on the bed. "Sit down. Relax, princess."

"Don't ever touch her again," Lewis said. "You'll regret it."

"Sit down and shut up, Lewis." Abraham held his sword blade on the cheek of the prince, and it drew blood. "I'm not playing around."

Lewis sat. "You are mad."

"You're damn right I am. And don't forget." He got nose to nose with Lewis. "I'm not from your world. I've got nothing to lose."

Lewis's Adam's apple rolled. "You're a dead man."

"Tell me about you and Raschel. Are you putting a spy in my company? Are you the one that put Twila there? Is this her replacement?"

"I don't know what you are talking about. I'm simply sowing my oats by bedding this whore. Who I sleep with is hardly any of your business, now is it?"

"We have an expression where I come from," Abraham said. "I wasn't born yesterday. Now, you tell me what is going on. Where's Twila? We know that she's been here, and you were the last one to see her, that I know of."

The floorboards outside the room creaked as someone big came down the hall. Horace filled the doorway with his frame. Cudgel and Tark stood behind him. "Do you need me, Captain?" Horace said.

"I might need you to sit on the prince until he cracks like an egg. He's not being very forthcoming."

With his finger, Lewis pushed Abraham's blade aside. "Seeing how you are a dead man, I'll humor you. I've hired Raschel to keep an eye on your mission. I need someone on the inside this time."

"So, you hired Twila."

"No. I don't know anything about that woman. What you are dealing with now is a coincidence. I'm sure many of your hirelings lived in these apartments at one time or another. There isn't anything so special about it."

"He's lying," Horace said.

"You fat oaf. You dare accuse a prince?" Lewis sneered. "I'll have you fed to the hogs."

"Lighten up, Lewis. You won't be feeding anybody to anything. I'm getting to the bottom of this one way or another," Abraham said. "I might not be able to prove you are behind it, but we know that Twila is. Give us her, and we'll part ways with you." He looked at Raschel. "But you're fired."

Raschel shrugged.

"You're a fool, Ruger. Abraham. Whoever you are. After today, you are finished. I don't know this Twila or where she is. You are barking up the wrong tree, and you'll pay dearly for it."

"Maybe not," Sticks said. She was holding something in her hand that she'd picked up from the vanity, a hair comb. "I know this. It was Twila's."

"You lying snake." Abraham locked his fingers around Lewis's throat. "Tell us where she is."

Prince Lewis's body turned ghostly. So did Raschel's. Lewis looked at his translucent hands and laughed. "Huh." As he faded out of Abraham's fingers, he parted with these final words: "I live, but you're a dead man now. You're all dead."

Abraham's hand passed through the vanishing man one last time. Lewis and Raschel were gone.

"What in the world just happened?" Abraham asked.

Sticks looked at him and said, "The snake slipped us. We're doomed, aren't we?"

"They were coming after us anyway. At least me, that is. He doesn't want our mission to succeed. Clearly, someone is helping him." He sniffed. "What is that smell? It's like lilac and spearmint."

Iris entered the room, and her nose crinkled. "They disappeared? Teleported. Whoa. That's thick. I can barely move a candle from one room to another. Someone moved two people. Only the most powerful members of the Sect can do that."

"Leodor. It has to be. We have to warn the king. Iris, how far can someone be teleported like that?"

"My guess, from one building to another. If it's Leodor, he's probably still in the city. In one of the cathedrals," Iris said.

"If that's true, then maybe we can get back to the king first," Abraham said. "Let's go."

"Captain," Horace said. He stood halfway in the doorway and was looking down the hall with Cudgel and Tark. "We might have a problem."

Tark and Cudgel drew their swords.

Abraham peeked around the doorway. Men in dark garb and birdlike black cowls covering their faces and carrying curved, wavy swords filled the hall from one end to the other. Over a score of heads were there.

"Yup," he said. "That is a problem."

CHAPTER 51

Lewis was on his hands and knees, spitting bile on the floor. The half-naked man's stomach was twisted in a knot. He was on a floor made of great stone tiles. He looked up and saw the grand support beams of a cathedral ceiling. Leodor stepped into full view.

"What did you do?" Lewis asked. "I feel the flu upon my bowels."

"I yanked you and your clever mistress out of the jaws of stupidity. That's what I did." Leodor hooked Lewis under an arm and helped him to his feet. "You had to take another dip in the pool, didn't you? Couldn't you have left Raschel alone to do her job?"

"What are you talking about now?" Lewis wiped his mouth. "Gack. And get me something to wash this yuck out." He looked side to side. "Where's Raschel?"

Leodor snapped his fingers. "Wine."

A young man wearing robes that were ringed like a racoon's tail appeared from behind the cathedral's stage. He carried a tray with a brass wine carafe and goblets. He poured a goblet full, left the tray on the pew, and vanished back behind the stage.

Lewis drank, swished, and spat.

"Do you mind? This is a sanctuary," Leodor said.

"No, I don't mind. Where is Raschel?"

"She solidified from the vanishing summons faster than you. Her stomach didn't sour like spoiled milk, either. She appears to have the fortitude that you lack. A good thing." Leodor dabbed the top of his sweaty lip with a rag. He sat down on one of the pews. "Now, she goes to finish what you started and finish Ruger Slade, once and for all."

"I don't suppose you brought my sword along? I can help with that." Lewis rubbed the blood on his chest from when Ruger had marked him. "He'll die for this."

"Yes, just like the time when you split your lip. You wanted to take his head then but didn't. Let me give you some advice. Let the assassin handle it."

"She should have done so by now. But she delayed." Lewis guzzled down a big drink. "I think she enjoys the long game too much." He pitched the goblet onto the floor.

"Now we don't have any choice in the matter. We can't let Ruger meet the king. He has Hector's ear. The last thing we need is for doubt and suspicion to be cast our way. We already dance too close to the flame as it is. He can't reach the House of Steel. You need to ride there and rally your men. Just in case. I'll come with. Let us make haste." Leodor rose with a groan. "The Elders really took it out of me when I cast that vanishing spell."

"How did you know where to find us?"

"The Sect has eyes everywhere. I keep eyes on you. They followed you to Raschel's complex. They caught Ruger and his men heading in and notified me. I had to act quickly, and it's a good thing I was in the area." He pointed at a stone pedestal that had two burnt marks on it.

Looking at the marks, Lewis said, "That smells like burnt hair."

"That's yours and Raschel's. It's the only way I could have snared the both of you. A good thing that I had it stored."

"How did you get my hair?"

"Oh, I've had it since you were a boy," he said with a gummy smile. "And I have plenty of it. Remember that."

"You don't think that Raschel can finish the job?" Lewis asked as they were walking out of the cathedral's back door into the alley.

"The man killed a Fenix. I won't believe he's dead until I see it. I would think the complex would be more than enough to handle him, though."

They moved into the alley, where a two-horse chariot waited.

Lewis stepped into the chariot and took the reins. "Complex? What do you mean?"

"Those apartments that you have been fornicating in? They are a front for one of the oldest assassin's guilds. It will be interesting to see how the fastest blade in Titanuus holds up against that."

CHAPTER 52

STARING DOWN THAT HALLWAY, WHICH was thick with ranks of assassins, Abraham said, "Sticks, find us another way out of here and fetch Horace Lewis's sword. He forgot his spear."

The assassins crept closer. They were only four doorways away.

Sticks tossed Lewis's sword belt to Horace then pulled her daggers from her hips. "This building doesn't have any windows. So, jumping or climbing down is out." She climbed onto the bed and poked the roof with her dagger. "We could try the ceiling."

"Better make it quick," he said. He looked at Tark, Cudgel, and Horace. "Gentlemen, we might have to punch a hole right through them. It's gonna be a tough fight in these close quarters. Make sure we don't hit one another."

"They only thing we're going to hit is them." Cudgel stepped beside Abraham. "We have the length. Let's use it."

Shoulder to shoulder, Abraham and Cudgel advanced on the assassins. "Let's go plow guard position." He lowered his sword and got into a fighting stance. The plow guard carried the sword handle down at the hip with the point pointed and angle upward.

Cudgel flashed a white smile. "Let's plow right through them!"

"Come on, dogs! Let's see what you got! Plow one!" Abraham ordered.

As one, he and Cudgel stepped forward and lunged. Two of the charging assassins were impaled by the blades. Their weapons fell free of their grips, and they died, clutching at the wound in their hearts.

"Plow two!" Abraham shouted.

Once again, he and Cudgel lunged forward and thrust with devastating effect.

"Plow three!"

The assassins had come prepared. They wielded shorter weapons, designed for close-quarters fighting, giving them the advantage. What they hadn't counted on was facing skilled swordsmen who had fought in every situation. They were losing.

Like a skilled advancing army, Abraham and Cudgel cut them down. They walked over the carpet of the dead. They plowed though the living. The bodies piled up. The armorless assassins kept coming.

"There is no end in sight of them," Cudgel said as he gored another assassin. "How many can there be?"

"I don't know. But their will should break at some point."

Abraham jammed Black Bane clean through a man's shoulder, just above the heart. The assassin twisted away with the sword still lodged in his body. He pulled against Abraham's grip, causing him to swing to one side. A third assassin slipped in between the two in the front and poked a dagger at Abraham's exposed belly. He jumped back just in time. The assassin's blade nicked his abdomen.

"Down with you!" Tark cried. He cut the assassin's arm off with a quick downward swing then advanced into Abraham's slot. "I'll take this!"

Abraham wrenched his sword free and fell back behind the brothers. He stood by Horace. "Getting bored yet?"

"If I had my spear, this fight would be over. I'd skewer an entire line of them." Horace fanned himself. "It's hot in here, and I'm not even fighting."

"I don't think the air conditioning is working," he said.

"The what?"

"Never mind."

Abraham scanned ahead. The apartment hallway was typical of many hotels he'd been in. Its hallway ran the length of the building with rooms on both sides of the hall. No exits were at the end, however. Instead, the exits were at the intersection in the middle. "We have to carve a path all the way to the middle. We'll make a break from the stairs from there."

In front, Tark and Cudgel continued to hew men down.

"What about Sticks and Dominga?" Horace asked.

Abraham yelled back down the hall. "Did you find a way out?"

Sticks popped her head outside the doorway. "No. Did you?"

"We're working on it!" He turned his attention to the pressing horde, but no end was in sight. "Man, I wish I had a machine gun."

The company had sliced their way within two doors of the intersection, which appeared crammed full of assassins of all shapes and sizes. Each and every one of them wore a black cowl that resembled a raven.

Cudgel and Tark were coated head to toe in splattered blood. Their boots were slick with fresh blood and ankle deep in the fallen dead.

Cudgel shouted the commands. "Plow one! Plow two!"

"There has to be a better way out of here." Abraham heard a click and turned as the doors they'd passed suddenly opened and more assassins poured out. "Horace, watch your back!"

CHAPTER 53

An assassin flung a black sack through the air. It appeared harmless, but when the sack struck Horace in the base of the skull, a tiny thunderclap followed. Horace wobbled on his legs and fell to the ground like a tranquilized moose.

"Hell's bells, what was that?" Abraham asked. His arm hairs prickled from the concussive force that came from the black sack. Another assassin tossed a black sack toward him. "Oh no, you don't." He didn't want it to hit Cudgel or Tark and batted it aside with his blade. Concussive energy exploded up his sword, through his arms and shoulders. The jarring impact knocked him into the wall.

The assassins pounced.

Abraham gored the first attacker in the neck with a quick stab of his sword. He pulled his dagger free from his belt and belly jabbed another. His body stung all over, but he fought the sensation off. The assassins were collapsing on them from both sides.

"Boys, we have a problem!" he yelled. "Girls, find a way out of here now!"

Dominga shouted back at him, "We're working on it! Keep your pants on!"

He eyed the assassins. "That's it. Ruger… Black Bane, show me what you can do!"

The assassins charged at him with swinging swords arcing downward at his head.

Ruger parried both swords. He punched holes in the hearts of both men with his dagger. As the assassins fell, he stepped between them. With dazzling speed, he unleashed Black Bane on the brood. He chopped, sliced, and thrust in blinding strokes. Black Bane turned the lesser men's bodies into chopped salad. The dark blade rose and fell, thrust and pierced. The assassins at the back fell dead.

Dominga stepped into the hall. "Ruger! We found a way out!"

"Brothers, we need to retreat," he said. He saw an unused black sack that had fallen to the floor. He picked it up and hurled it like a baseball between Tark and Cudgel. The sack struck an assassin in the face, and the concussion knocked two rows of the assassins backward.

"Now, that's what I call a fastball."

With a quick look over his shoulder, Cudgel asked, "What's the plan, Captain?"

"We're going backward." Abraham knelt down by Horace and picked the man up in a fireman's carry with a grunt. "Geez, this ox must be three hundred fifty pounds." He backed down the hallway. "Come on, fellas. Attack and retreat! Sticks, you better have a way out ready! We're coming!"

"Hurry up!" Dominga came outside. "Elder's Blood! How many are there?"

"I don't know," he said. "Do you see those black sacks on the dead belts? Grab those, toss them—"

"I know, I know," Dominga said as she hurried into the hallway and plucked out the black sacks. "I've dealt with the Brotherhood of Ravens' dirty tricks before." She flung two bags over Tark and Cudgel's heads. The concussive blast knocked a wave of assassins backward. "Let's go, boys. I can't bail you out all of the time."

Tark and Cudgel followed Abraham and Dominga into the room.

The bed was moved, revealing a trapdoor in the floor. Iris was in the room. She closed the busted door and circled one hand while chanting. The busted door mended back into place.

Sticks popped her head out of the trapdoor. "You can stare, or you can move. Your choice." She vanished back inside the hole.

Pounding started on the other side of the door. The hinges shook.

"I gave the door more strength with my spell," Iris said, "but it won't hold long."

"All of you go, ladies first," Abraham said as he helped Iris down the hole.

Dominga jumped down through the gap, followed by Tark and Cudgel. Abraham lowered Horace down to them. The big man slipped through the brothers' blood-slick fingers and hit the floor with a thump.

"Nice catch!"

The brothers shrugged at him.

Abraham jumped down through the hole. The room below was empty of furnishings and had a ladder that led down to the first level.

Sticks waved all of them over. "I've scouted this. It leads into the streets. Apparently, Raschel has a formidable station with her secret entrances."

Iris pointed one hand at the trapdoor and rolled the other in a circle. The door closed and sealed shut. Mystical green symbols covered the door all over. She looked at Abraham and shrugged. "Same as the other. It will slow them, but that's about it."

Stomping started on the trapdoor. Abraham shook Horace. The bearish man snored.

"Great." Abraham hefted him back onto his shoulders and started down the ladder. "It's like carrying lumpy keg barrels."

The ladder took them to another room with a secret door that slid open into an alley. On foot, they raced down the channel between the buildings. At the end of the alley, he puffed for breath, set down Horace, and said, "We need to split up. Meet back at the Stronghold. I'll lead them away."

Iris poked a glowing finger into Horace's ribs.

"Eeow!" The big man jumped up. "What? Who?"

"Just shut up and come with me." Iris took him by the hand, and they dashed into the streets.

"Are you sure you want to split up? That's not our way," Sticks said.

"I have a gut feeling they only want me dead. And there's no sense in them catching all of us. I'll be fine. Just meet me at the Stronghold."

Sticks nodded. She and Dominga went one way. Tark and Cudgel went another. The busy streets parted as they passed.

Abraham hung back in the alley and eyed the exit they'd come through. His heart raced. He wanted his friends safe. No sense in them dying on his account. As for him, he needed to lead the assassins off their trail. He needed to find a way to get word to the king. *This is madness. I don't know even know what I'm doing.*

Out of the secret exit, the assassins poured into the alley, their eyes set on him. With deadly weapons in hand, they charged. Abraham ran.

CHAPTER 54

THE SCREAMING IN THE STREETS didn't have anything to do with the battle-splattered warrior shoving through the civilians. It was the wave of black-cowled terror that had the women shrieking. They spilled out of the alley in twos, threes and fours. The Brotherhood of Ravens didn't hesitate to take a poke at anyone who stood in their paths. Word of the Brotherhood spread as quickly as the wind. The people scrambled. The streets cleared. Doors slammed shut, and shutters closed.

Abraham found himself running alone with the fleet feet of assassins hot on his tail.

Maybe this wasn't such a good idea.

He didn't know Burgess as well as he'd thought. He turned down an alley and found more raven-headed assassins barring his path. He jumped onto a storefront porch and tested the door lock of the first one he passed. It didn't budge. He continued down the western-styled porch fronts, jumping to the cobblestones and back onto the wood, pounding on doors that he passed.

"Go away!" someone yelled from inside.

The assassins were gaining ground. On fast feet, they sprinted behind like a silent wind of death. A long-limbed assassin closed the gap on Abraham and took a swipe at him with a wavy-bladed short sword.

Abraham sidestepped the swing, grabbed the man's wrist, and punched the man in the nose. The assassin's nose crunched beneath the power of his fist. He twisted the blade out of the assassin's hand and stabbed the man with it. It was a good move. *One assassin down, countless left to go. Where are all of them coming from?*

The short melee had shortened Abraham's lead. The plague of assassins were cutting off any avenue of escape from the city. Abraham leapt onto the next porch and jumped through the window, and the pane of glass shattered. The store was filled with clothing, dresses, shirts, and fanciful hats. The women in the store screamed.

"Pardon me," he said as he made his way toward the staircase leading up. He noticed a pretty lady in a purple gown and winked. "By the way, that looks great on you. Simply ravishing."

The woman in purple blushed.

He bounded up the steps and burst through the door that led to the balcony over the porch. Below, the Brotherhood of Ravens flocked toward the store. Assassins climbed over the balcony railing and hemmed him in between them. They hurled throwing stars at him.

Abraham ducked and dodged. "Hey! What is this, kung fu theater?" A throwing star lodged itself in his shoulder. He pulled it out and threw it down into the crowd of assassins, braining one assassin in the middle of the forehead. "That's what you get for staring." Black Bane in hand, he advanced with the hunger of a panther. He cut the first assassin down as he half drew his own blade.

Another throwing star whistled behind him and sank into his back. Abraham turned. "Now you're ticking me off!"

The assassin drew two short blades and darted toward Abraham, spinning his blades like a windmill.

Abraham saw a gaping hole in the man's offense and lunged. The tip of his longsword passed through the front side of the man and out the other. The assassin's arms dropped, and his blades clattered on the wood. Abraham shoved the man over the railing into the crowd below him. "How do you like those apples? Who's next?"

Dozens of assassins hurled throwing stars at him with flicks of their wrists. The spinning pinwheels of death whistled right toward him.

Abraham dove to the floor.

The stars thudded into the wooden walls behind him with a cascade of *thunk-thunk-thunk-thunk-thunk*.

"Smack-talking assassins. Maybe a bad idea." Aside from the star still lodged in his back, all the others had missed. He popped up from behind the railing. "Nyah! Nyah! You missed me!"

For the next several minutes, Abraham battled small groups of assassins from balconies, porches, and rooftops. He managed to keep control of the environment by moving. Assassin after assassin fell. They weren't any match for him. They dangled dead over the railings. They crawled in the streets, missing legs from chopped-through knees. Heads rolled down the planks and off the roof tiles, landing in troughs and flower boxes. Nicked up and bleeding, he killed them one after the other.

Facing two more attackers from another balcony, he said, "You guys are terrible." He'd surmised that the black hood didn't make the man. Most of them were novices with some training but far from advanced swordsmen. Compared to him, they seemed to have been dragged off the streets and given weapons. They were sheep for the slaughter. He killed two men in front of him with a single stroke.

He shouted down over the balcony rail at them. "Are you stupid? When you step into my zone, you step into the death zone. Do something else for a living!"

Three more climbed up on the balcony and approached. With sweat and blood dripping from his face, he said, "Great. Hard headed and hard of hearing. Just like I used to be." He motioned them forward with Black Bane. "Well, come on then, dog meat. I think the store owner wanted his walls painted red anyway."

A sharp flutelike whistle cut through the air, and the assassins froze in place. They turned their heads toward the sound of a wagon rumbling down the streets. Black chariots of men pulled by black horses were coming—men the likes of whom Abraham had never seen.

"Who in Sam Hill are they?"

CHAPTER 55

Four men stepped out of the four chariots. Their tall, well-knit bodies were dyed black as coal. White rings were painted around their bodies and appendages. Their heads were sleek, with eye sockets painted white. They strode down the streets like predators. All of them towered over the assassins. They must have stood seven feet tall. The assassins cleared away from the porch. The men in black ringed in white stood in front and looked up at Abraham.

"Nice costumes," Abraham said.

He noted the weapons they carried. Their right hands were missing. Weapons had been grafted onto the metal stumps that replaced their hands. From left to right, one carried a sword blade, the next a hook-nosed axe, followed by a spiked flail then a long chain with a hook on the end. They were wicked-looking devices, nasty, bloodstained, and dully shining.

"Do you have names?" he asked.

The one with the sword hand spoke well. "We are the Siblings of Slaughter. You are our prey." He waved his sword, beckoning him downward. "Come down, Ruger Slade. The time has come for our steel to meet. Let's us dance to the beat that metal reaves."

"That's very poetic, but I prefer the bird's eye view of things. Perhaps—"

"What is all the racket?"

A bitter voice spoke inside Abraham's head. It was the voice he'd heard from the sword when he battled the Fenix. "Black Bane?"

"No, I forget what my name is. All I know is that I'm trapped inside this steel cocoon and you woke me. Again. Keep it down out there, will you?"

The swordsman spoke again. "Are you coming, blade master? We will make it fair. If you find victory, you will no longer be pursued. But if you lose, you lose."

Abraham lifted a finger. "Give me a minute. I'm talking with my sword."

The swordsman continued in a polite accent, "I am Edge. These are my brothers, Axe, Spike, and Hook."

Abraham was about to address his sword when he leaned back over the rail and said, "Seriously, those are your names? You sound more like a garage band or a team of wrestlers." He stepped back and looked at his sword. "Do me a favor and blast these guys with a lightning bolt like you did the Fenix."

"Mmm, hold me where I can see them?"

He held Black Bane out over the railing.

"You can take them," the sword said.

"Can you even see them?"

"Of course I can."

"Then describe them to me."

"Er, well, the enemy is very dark, wiry with sharp little teeth. Is that close?"

"No, I think you just described a black cat." Abraham shook his head. "Who are you?"

"Ruger Slade, come down. The Siblings of Slaughter wait," Edge said.

"I said give me a minute!" Abraham's nostrils flared. "You have me surrounded. It's not as if I can go anywhere."

"I told you I don't remember who I am. The last thing I remember was a great battle. Light against darkness. I was spellcasting. Knocking spider things from grand columns. A world would be crushed beneath my power. I should have died, but I had a spell in my pocket buried in my mind. My essence transported from one body to another. Now I'm in this blade. It's peaceful, aside from the occasional banging of metal. We never stopped fighting where I came from. In this object, I can rest."

"Why don't you write a book about it? Are you going to help me or not?"

"No. Sometimes you have to do things for yourself. Tell me, what do the women look like in your world, are they ample?"

"That's it. I know this world isn't real!" He looked at his sword. "If you aren't going to help, stay out of my way." Abraham looked down at the Siblings of Slaughter. "Make a hole!" He jumped off the balcony into the street and landed in front of the brothers. All of them looked down at him with heavy stares. He walked to the middle of the street, where the Siblings of Slaughter formed a box around him. The Brotherhood of Ravens encircled the four warriors and walled them all in. "So are we going to do this one at a time or all at once?"

With his arms hanging down by his sides, Edge dipped his chin and said, "We are assassins. We don't reveal to the target how we are going to kill them. I will guarantee that it will be only us against you."

"Fair enough." Abraham cut Black Bane back and forth. "I'll be your huckleberry. If you will, give me a moment."

Edge shrugged, the sinewy muscles in his body flexing as he did. "Take all the time that you need. The Siblings of Slaughter have hunted all sorts. We've dethroned masters of all weapons and pierced the hearts of barons and kings. No man can stand against us. You, Ruger Slade, will only be practice. A rat fleeing the cat's claws. A dove that fights against a hawk. Fight with all of your heart and might. We'll appreciate what we learn from you. We'll use it."

"Yeah, yeah. I get it, you're a bunch of bad asses. Now, stop the monologue, and let's get this party started," Abraham said. *All right, Ruger, whatever you got, you better help me use it all now.*

"Are you talking to me?" the essence inside the sword asked.

"No, just shut up."

Abraham readied his sword in the high guard position. He turned slowly in a circle, studying the eyes of his opponents. They were seasoned warriors. Scars showed on their black-dyed skin. They'd been through a scrap or two. Each of them was tall and lengthy. They moved with a dancer's ease for big men, like something spawned from primordial jungles. At he turned, his head moved from side to side. "All right, then. Who wants to die first?"

The Sibling named Hook started swinging his chain over his head. The black links whistled through the air.

Abraham caught himself looking at the links. Behind him, the sibling called Spike bore down on him. The giant man swung his spiked mace in the direction for a collision course for Abraham's head. He chopped at the man. The man slipped to the side with the speed of a cat and rolled away from the sword strike. Links of chain wrapped around Abraham's ankle, and the hook locked into his calf. With a yank, Hook pulled Abraham off his feet. Down to the ground he went in a heap.

CHAPTER 56

THE BROTHERHOOD OF RAVENS—NORMALLY SILENT—LET out a gusty cheer the moment Abraham went down. Hook pulled on his chain with his free arm and dragged Abraham over the streets. Spike came right at him, swinging his spiked mace at his face. Abraham leaned away, and the mace bit into the stones. Abraham countered with a slice at Spike's feet. The assassin hopped away with a fraction of a second to spare.

"Geez, you freaks are fast!"

Hook towed Abraham over the road. The crowd went with him. Edge had a smirk on his face. Axe showed a white-toothed grin.

"I vaguely remember having a wife. She was built like a chimney stack and was a fine cook too. At night, she gave me the most amazing massages. I can almost feel it when I meditate upon it," the essence in the sword said. *"But for the life of me, I can't see her face or remember her name."*

"Will you shut up?" Abraham said. He hacked at Spike, trying to keep the assassin at bay, while Hook dragged him like a hunk of dead meat. "I don't need stories. I need help!"

"Fine. I'm going back to sleep. Try to keep it quiet out there, will you?"

Abraham managed to dodge another swing from Spike that would have busted into his hip. He used the length of his sword to keep the man at bay while at the same time keeping an eye on the other two Siblings. Their haunting stares soaked in every movement. *Ruger, we have to do something. Soon. Or there won't be anything left of either one of us.*

As Spike attacked with blow after blow, Edge and Axe walked alongside the battle.

Abraham twisted, scooted, parried, and butt hopped away from the heavy-handed blows Spike wrought. His imminent assassination was being put on display for all to see as the citizens of Burgess gathered on the balconies. Clearly, the Siblings of Slaughter wanted to create a moment to remember. He fell backward, feigning exhaustion, and let Hook drag him down the street.

Spike relented in his assault and laughed. Then he asked, "Do you tire so soon, little man?"

"Who, me? No, I'm not tired. I thought you were tired from all of that swinging and missing." He winked at Spike. "Nothing to be ashamed of. Some people just aren't very good at fighting."

Spike's brows knitted together. From a position behind Abraham's head, he brought his axe down with wroth force.

Abraham sat up as quickly as he could.

Spike's mace bit into the street.

In a fluid motion, Abraham leaned backward and thrust his sword back into Spike's neck. As the crowd gasped, Abraham turned his attention to Hook. He sat up fully and hacked into the chain binding him. Black Bane cut through the ebony links.

Hook lost his grip and stumbled.

Abraham bounded to his feet, cocked his sword behind his shoulder, and unleashed. Hook's head leapt from his shoulders and fell among the crowd.

In an instant, Edge and Axe attacked simultaneously. Edge swung his sword high, and Axe aimed low.

With a chain wrapped around his ankle and a hook in his calf, Abraham parried the axe swing and ducked underneath Edge's sword. The resounding blow of sword against axe jarred his arms.

The Siblings of Slaughter were as strong as they looked. He jumped back away from both of them and set his feet.

"Two down, and two to go," Abraham said. "The odds are getting better all of the time."

"You need to be more observant," Axe said.

Spike rose from his position on the ground. He had a hole in his neck, but he did not bleed. Hook's head was missing, but he still stood with balance. One of the assassins in a cowl picked up Hook's head and handed it to him. Hook cradled his head with one arm, like a football helmet. His eyes were wide open. He started swinging his severed chain overhead.

An icy caterpillar-like sensation crawled all over Abraham's body, a horrific sensation. His nerves of steel ebbed. "Nice trick. I didn't realize that you were already dead."

"We aren't dead by any means, as you can see. Another power courses through our veins that mortal men can't see." Edge eased toward Abraham. "You will soon know the sting of death, and the grave will hold you until the worms eat your flesh."

"We'll see. I was hoping to be cremated. You know, ashes to ashes, dust to dust. I've never had a fondness for burials." He spun his sword end over end. "Let's do this again."

"Siblings," Edge said, "no mercy."

CHAPTER 57

Once again, Abraham found himself surrounded by superior numbers. He was right back where he'd started, nicked up, sweat drenched, and his calf bleeding into the streets. He shuffled around in the plow guard stance, eyeing the moving enemy. His calf burned like fire. At times like this, he wished he'd worn his armor. *Breastplate. Don't leave home without it.*

Edge made the first strike. With his long half arm and half sword, he attacked with the blinding speed of a boxer's jab.

Abraham parried the strike. Suddenly, a funnel of sword-fighting techniques downloaded into his mind. His body immediately went to work. Black Bane came to life. The orange emberlike fire glowed.

The skilled Siblings of Slaughter converged on Abraham. They chopped, thrust, slashed, and jabbed. Hook's chain whistled high and cracked back down. Spike's mace whooshed by. Axe unleashed lethal blow after blow. Edge's sword twisted through air, clipping at Abraham's guts. He might as well have been stuck in a blender.

Body parts and the weapons attached to them started flying. Axe's weapon arm was the first to go. Black Bane chopped it off at the shoulder. Black Bane sliced Spike's arm at the elbow. His axe arm went flying midswing. The Siblings never saw it coming. A storm of blazing steel wrought havoc on their bodies. Hook lost his chain arm and fell to the ground from his leg being severed from the knee.

"Reap the whirlwind!" Abraham shouted with frenzied glee. He drove Edge back on his heels. The assassin's dark face paled as he parried desperately at the devastation being brought upon him. Abraham beat the man's weapon aside with ferocity. The blows would have disarmed the most extraordinary men. But Edge's sword was his arm.

With fire in his eyes, Abraham said, "Ah, screw it." He brought Black Bane down hard.

Edge parried. His blade snapped in two.

Abraham mutilated the weaponless warriors. He took limbs, starting with Spike and ending with Edge. With a single stroke, he removed Edge's head from the shoulders. He held the head up high for all to see. "This is what happens to assassins when they waltz into my world!"

The encircling Brotherhood of the Ravens backpedaled.

"Brotherhood! Cut down this hound!" Edge's head said.

Abraham looked at Edge. "You said I'd be free to go."

"I'm an assassin. I lied. You cannot kill us. You cannot win. We are the Siblings of—"

Abraham hurled the head into the crowd. "Yeah, yeah, I know." He held out Bane Blane. The blade's runes pulsated with angry life. "Who's next?"

A commotion of rumbling of wheels roared nearby. Horse-drawn chariots trampled through the knot of assassins. Three chariots and riders converged on Abraham, plowing through every one of the living.

"Get in, Ruger!" Vern said, his wavy locks waving in the wind.

He was driving a chariot of the Siblings of Slaughter. Bearclaw drove another one of the chariots into the crowd, followed by the third, driven by Apollo and Prospero. "What are you waiting for? I can't stop this thing. Jump in. We have to go!"

As Vern thundered by, Abraham dashed toward the cart and leapt into the back. "Where in Titanuus did you come from?"

"We were trying to have a drink when all the clamor started. Should have known that it was you."

The chariot bumped upward as it ran over two bodies.

"Woo hoo!" Vern said.

The three chariots driven by the Henchmen sent the assassins scattering through the streets. Abraham hung his sword out the window and took the lives of a few more dodging assassins.

"Can you take us to the Stronghold?" he asked.

"So long as the horses hold out, I'll get us there." Vern snapped the reins. "Yah!"

Behind them, Bearclaw, Apollo, and Prospero ran roughshod over the assailing masses. Bodies were crunched underneath horse hooves and hard wheels. Clearing a bloody path through the assassins, all three chariots thundered over the road like a black terror. The Brotherhood of Ravens gave chase, but the horses quickly outdistanced them.

Vern drove the horses through the city like bats out of hell. The chariot slung side to side as it skidded across the road and around the corners. He bellowed at the top of his lungs, "Yeehaw! I love driving these things."

To gasps and cries of alarm from bewildered onlookers, the train of horses broke free and made their way into the rolling countryside.

The runes of Black Bane cooled. Abraham slipped it into his sheath. His bloody hand trembled.

"Thanks for dragging me out of there," he said. "I was beginning to think the fighting wasn't going to end."

Vern showed a twisted smile. "I've seen you handle worse."

"You have?"

The chariot driver chuckled and said, "We better get some bandages. You're bleeding all over my new chariot."

The battle with the Brotherhood of Ravens and the Siblings of Slaughter hadn't come without its toll. He had lacerations and scrapes all over his arms, and that was only what he could see. He looked as though he'd run through a briar bush of razors. "I hope Iris and the others made it."

"What's going on?" Vern asked.

Abraham gave his best attempt at the Cliff Notes version. "Turns out that Twila was the assassin. I don't know if she is dead, gone, or someone else, but she was the saboteur of all our plans. We tracked it all back to Prince Lewis and Leodor. They are behind all of it."

"That explains the frosty reception that we received when we tried to rejoin the King's Guardians," Vern said as he snapped the reins. "That jerk wouldn't have any part of us."

"*Jerk*? Where'd you come up with that?"

"From you. Well, the other you. I can't keep track. Didn't I use it right?"

"No, you used it right. But *jerk* is an understatement."

He looked back at Bearclaw and the brothers, Prospero and Apollo. They raced through the cloud of road dust a few dozen yards behind them. He waved. Bearclaw saluted. Apollo waved, and Prospero appeared to be sleeping standing up. "At least we rooted out the enemy. The problem is how do we get the king to believe us?"

"I wouldn't have any idea." Vern drove mile after mile toward the Stronghold. Nearing the small plantation, he said, "Looks like we're going to have more visitors." He pointed eastward. "Look."

By the score, the King's Guardians were descending a hill less than a mile away. Armored in bright steel from head to toe, they rode on the backs of white horses. At the front, one man led, wearing a great coat. It was Lewis. His fist pumped in the air. A bugler sounded his horn. The flag bearer dropped the guard. In a cloud of thunder, down the hillside they came.

"Faster, Vern!" Abraham yelled. "We can't let them beat us to the Stronghold! We're dead men if they do!"

CHAPTER 58

THE HORSE-DRAWN CHARIOTS RACED DOWN the roadway leading to the Stronghold. Ahead, Solomon stood outside, towering over several others, looking to see what all the commotion was all about. Behind the chariots, the Guardians in armor led the charge down the slopes. They were a quarter of a mile away and closing fast.

Abraham shouted at the top of his lungs. "Get inside! Get everyone inside!"

Solomon waved his hands outward. The hirelings dropped what they were doing. With frightened faces, they hurried into the safety of the thick stone walls the Stronghold offered. The livestock scattered throughout the yard.

Twenty yards from the door, Vern brought the chariot to a rumbling halt. Bearclaw, Prospero, and Apollo followed suit. They took a look behind them and hurried inside.

Abraham met Solomon at the door. "Did Sticks and Horace make it? What about Iris?"

"They all are making preparations inside," the old troglin said. "You look like hell."

"You don't know the half of it. Let's get inside," he said.

Solomon shoved him through the door and said, "I'll be back. We need to turn the beasts free of the stables. Those butchers will slaughter them." He rushed toward the barn.

"There's not time, Solomon. Come back!" Abraham watched helplessly as Solomon vanished into the barn. A donkey and two horses bolted out of the barn after the alarming sound of a loud roar. "Hurry up!"

Led by Lewis, the Guardians galloped toward the Stronghold. They would arrive in the next few seconds.

"Solomon! Come on!" Abraham yelled. "Of all the stupid things to do."

Horace hooked Abraham by an arm. "Captain, you need to get inside. There is no time left."

He jerked his arm free. "Solomon! Solomon! Get your hairy butt back here!"

A few more horses bolted out of the barn, followed by cats, dogs, and a slow-moving cow. Solomon didn't emerge.

Lewis and his host of Guardians arrived. The Guardians dismounted in quick military fashion. They slipped their crossbows from hooks, loaded bolts, made a row in front of the horses, faced the Stronghold, and took aim.

Lewis looked right at Abraham and said, "Fire!"

Horace jerked Abraham inside. Bearclaw slammed the door shut. Crossbow bolts peppered the outside of the door with a *thak-thak-thak-thak-thak* sound. Bearclaw barred the door closed.

Abraham limped over to one of the small portals, the chain wrapped around his ankle clinking over the floor. Peering through the portal, he had a full view of the enemy. The King's Guardians were rows deep, showing at least sixty. The barn door was swung wide open, showing no sign of Solomon.

"Stupid hippie!"

Thak! A bolt splintered off the portal's rim. Abraham backed away. He couldn't do anything for Solomon now. All he could do was hope the big man escaped. He faced the crew. All of them were gathered around the room. Of the former Henchmen stood Horace, Sticks, Bearclaw, Vern, Dominga, Cudgel, Tark, Iris, Prospero, and Apollo. The two new Red Tunics, Skitts and Zann, were present, along with a group of hirelings.

"How long can we hold out?" Abraham asked.

"Weeks with food. With the springs in the back caverns, we can water ourselves for a lifetime," Horace said. "We might starve at some point, however."

"I don't think this battle is going to be a matter of weeks. Not even days. Lewis wants this done quick. The question is does he have the means to do it?"

Horace strode to the front and peeked out of one of the other portals without putting his head in it. "I see no wagon for siege. No doubt, they can fetch them. They could try to burn us out using pitch."

Iris stepped forward from the pack. "I can quench the flames to some degree." She studied Abraham with a worried expression. "We need to tend to those wounds."

Abraham peeked out of the wall portal, searching for Solomon. "I hope you headed for the hills."

From outside, Lewis called out. He had a red gash on his cheek where Abraham had marked him. "Ruger Slade! You and your men stand guilty of assaulting the crown! The penalty for that crime is death!" He rode his horse back and forth in front of his men. "However, granted that I am a merciful prince, I will entertain a second option. Ruger the fallen, surrender willfully, and I'll see to it that the sentence of all of your conspirators will be light. However, the penalty for you will be death!"

Ruger yelled out of the portal, "No deal, you lying sack of monkey dung! You are the one that betrays your father's crown, not me! It's you who should surrender to me!"

Lewis looked at his men and rolled his eyes. "A possessed lunatic."

Abraham moved away from the window. "Do we have any allies in the Guardians? Who's the big guy that breaks the horse underneath the saddle?"

"That's Pratt," Horace answered. "He won't bend against the prince. Not unless the king orders it. He never liked you much, either."

"Me? Why didn't he like me?"

"He was the commander of the Guardians until you came along. When you were gone, he took over briefly, but the king gave the command to the prince." Horace nodded his head. "It's called nepotism."

"I know. It's another name for monarchy. So, won't there be bitterness between Pratt and Lewis?"

"Actually, they've always gotten along just fine. Like brothers," Horace said cheerfully.

"You don't have to sound so happy about it."

"Yes, Captain." Horace frowned.

Abraham had hoped to create a seed of doubt and turn the King's Guardians to his side. Realizing that wouldn't happen didn't take him long. The Guardians were fiercely loyal. He knew that himself, or at least Ruger did. They could fight them and hope for the best, but it would be a bloodbath. The King's Guardians wore and wielded the finest steel. They were practically invincible in their armor against lesser-clad men. *Out of the frying pan and into the fire.*

Lewis started up again. "I'm not going to belabor my points, Ruger. Exit or suffer the consequences. I promise I won't leave a single one of you standing."

He shouted out of the portal. "Can I get a count of thirty? I need a little time to think." He ducked back as a crossbow bolt zinged through the portal. "I'll take that as a no. I've got to hand it to you, you're a lot smarter than Khan was when he dealt with Kirk."

"Who?" Lewis gave an irritated shake of his head. "Pratt. Start burning. Begin with the barn and make use of those chariots."

Within a minute, the Guardians had burning torches in hand and took them inside the barn. In seconds, the inside of the barn roared to life in flames.

"No!" Abraham said. "Solomon!"

The Guardians freed the horses from the chariots and rolled one of the chariots to the front door. With the other two they blocked the portals. Using their torches, they set all of them on fire.

"Chariots of fire," Abraham said in a deflating tone. "This isn't the way it is supposed to be." He caught Sticks staring at him, her eyes filled with worry. "Hello," he said.

Sticks rushed to his side and caught him as the floor seemed to bow beneath him.

"Abraham, can you stand? You wobble," Sticks said. "You are as clammy as a fish."

Outside, the flames licked through the portals, and the smoke came rolling in.

Abraham's head rolled from side to side. "Get me some water. I'm only a little dehydrated. And some aspirin too. I'm getting a bad headache." Abraham's knees gave way, and he fell over on Sticks.

CHAPTER 59
ABRAHAM'S PAST

Back in Hinton, West Virginia, Abraham walked the downtown streets. Years had passed since he'd lost Jenny, Jake, Buddy, and his father, Earl. Now, he strode down the sidewalks, wearing a flannel shirt, with his hands stuck in the pockets of his jeans. He hadn't shaved in months. His hair hung over his eyes. A light snow was falling.

He crossed the street and went into Lowman's Drugstore. A bell rang when he entered. It was an old-school store, complete with a small soda shop and ice-cream parlor. A gift shop and other general goods were there. He walked up two steps and stood behind the counter. A young lady caught his eye. Her eyes grew big when she saw him. Her name was Carly. She turned away, searching for the man working the drug-stocked shelves behind her.

"Mister Lowman, he's here," she said.

The pharmacist, Bill Lowman, was an older gentleman with dark, thinning hair and rectangular glasses on the bridge of his nose. He wore the standard white pharmacist smock with his name embroidered on it. He and the young girl spoke in lowered voices. They glanced at Abraham from time to time. Finally, Bill dabbed his forehead with a handkerchief and came around to the front counter. "Good morning, Abraham. How are you today?"

"I'm getting by. I'll be better if you have my pills ready," he said.

Bill had been a family friend for a long time. He was a soft-spoken fellow too. He ran a finger under his collar. "Uh, listen Abraham, I can't fill this script for five more days. I told you that yesterday."

"I just need a few to hold me over, Bill. Come on. I need them. My back's on fire. I can barely walk or sleep." Abraham arched backward and groaned. "Just give me the pills. No one is going to say anything."

"I-I can't. Abraham, you need to just go. You can't come in here every day, predicting a different outcome." Bill swallowed. "If you are having trouble, go to the emergency room."

Abraham banged his fist on the counter, shaking the countertop. "I've been there!"

Carly, a raspberry blonde with short hair, yanked the telephone off the wall and said, "Mr. Lowman, I'm calling the cops."

Bill lifted a hand and said, "No, no, I'll handle this, Carly. Just let me and Abraham talk this out. Put the phone down, please."

Carly hung the phone back up on the wall. Her blue eyes narrowed on Abraham. "Just say the word."

Carly wasn't the only other person inside the store. A young man, a high-school boy, was working the ice-cream bar. He held a broom across his chest like a weapon. Two other older ladies hurried out of the store.

Bill stepped out from behind the counter. He took Abraham by the arm and said, "Son, I know what you are going through. I know you are in anguish. You're alone."

Abraham opened his mouth to speak.

"But-but-but... hear me out. You think I can't understand. You think none of us can. But we do. Everyone's life is affected by tragedy in one way or another." He turned and faced Abraham. He held his arms at the elbow. "I'd been your father's friend a long time. I've known you since you were a boy. Abraham, you can beat this. I know you can. There are clinics. They can help you. Let them."

Abraham pushed the old man backward. Bill's grip broke from his sleeves. He stumbled over his feet and fell. His head cracked against the counter.

"Mr. Lowman!" Carly cried out. She rushed from behind the counter and came to his aid, kneeling beside Mister Lowman.

His head was bleeding, and he wasn't moving.

Carly laid him out on the floor. "He's not breathing! Joe, call an ambulance!"

The boy behind the counter dropped the broom and rushed to the phone.

Carly started giving Bill mouth-to-mouth resuscitation and giving him chest compressions.

Abraham went numb. Rushing blood filled his ears as he stammered, "It was an accident. I didn't mean to. He tripped and fell."

Carly kept trying to resuscitate the man. She didn't pay Abraham any mind.

Abraham's tongue clove to his mouth. He couldn't breathe. Everything looked and sounded as though it were inside a tunnel. He did the only thing that he could think to do. With a ring of the door's bell, he ran.

CHAPTER 60

Abraham spent the next six months in a state correctional facility. Bill Lowman spent weeks in a coma. Not long after Bill Lowman revived, he came to see Abraham. No one else in Bill's family did. Bill, now using a walker, forgave him, but he didn't drop the assault charges. Bill said, "I'm sorry, Abraham, but there are consequences for your actions. I'll pray that you survive this."

Prison wasn't a cake walk. It was miserable. It was worse than anything he'd imagined it to be. They shaved him down and called him "Superstar." There was mockery. There were fights. New wounds were opened. For the first time in his life, Abraham was surrounded by people more miserable than him. It served as a wake-up call, but the healing wasn't easy.

For the next six months, he did his best to be a model prisoner. That garnered his early release from a one-year sentence, but there were stipulations. He had probation. His new probation officer, Mike, was a good man, older and bald with a frosty moustache. He worked for the Mission, a church group that provided housing for young men going through rehabilitation. There were classes, Bible studies, hot meals, and hard work.

Abraham shrugged it all off at first. He still carried so much guilt. Forgiving himself was hard. He blamed himself for the loss of his family. But in truth, the only person he'd hurt was Bill Lowman. That time, he lost control. It was a fatal slip that stuck.

One night, after dinner, Abraham was talking with Mike and Dave, another counselor at the Mission. That was the first time he let it all out—the hurt, the tears, the pain. It kept coming. They counseled him. They prayed for him, and he prayed with them. They tried to teach him to forgive himself and set on a new course in life.

Finally, Abraham finished his course at the Mission. He had nowhere else to go and nothing at all to do. That was when Mike introduced him to one of his friends, Luther Vancross. The old man was seventy-five years old and as feisty as a flea. He owned a microbrewery.

Luther walked him through the brewery, introduced him to the small crew who worked there, and took him back into his office, which had dark wooden paneling, an ugly metal desk, and paperwork stacked everywhere.

"Have a seat," Luther said as he sat down in large green leather chair. Luther was shaved clean from the top of his head to the bottom of his chin. His round face had age spots all over it. He wore a black polo shirt with his brewery logo on it and khaki pants. He was very fit for such an old man.

Abraham sat down in a comfortable matching green leather chair. The leather groaned underneath him.

Luther looked at him with dark, piercing eyes and said, "I'll give you one chance. That's it. Do you want it?"

Abraham hadn't had a real job since he'd started playing baseball. At first, he wasn't sure what to say. After seconds of hesitation, he said, "I'll take it. And… thank you."

"Good." Luther slapped his hands on the desk. "Then let's get you started. There's some paperwork we need to do." He turned around in his chair and looked out the window, which had a view of the outside parking lot. "Say, that's a nice truck you have. Is that a Kodiak turbo diesel?"

"It is."

"You know, you can make some extra money if you want to use your own vehicle. It will save me the expense of buying a new truck."

"It will need some work. Paint and customization."

Luther flung a hand at him. "Ah, I've got a guy for that. He owes me plenty of favors." He turned back toward Abraham. "It's a strange marriage having a fella in rehab driving a beer truck. Do you think you can handle the temptation?"

"I never had an issue with drinking. It was the pills and some other stuff." Abraham shrugged. "I really don't think that will be an issue."

Luther leaned forward on his elbows. "And the other thing? You're truly clean?"

"I am. I don't see myself going down that road again even though my existence at the moment feels meaningless."

Luther leaned back in his chair and nodded. "Good work gives a man purpose and meaning. I think you'll like being a truck driver. I used to be one. It's what led me to all of this." He spread his arms out. "I like the time on the road. I did plenty of soul searching. Enjoyed the music and the news. But I think people talk too much anymore." He got up. "Let's get you started on the paperwork. I'll have Janice order you some shirts. Hmph. You're going to be a big one. What size, two X?"

"I wish." Abraham patted his stomach. "It's three X now."

CHAPTER 61

ABRAHAM TOOK ON THE MUNDANE task of beer-delivery man the best he could. The job had its merits. The local bars were always happy to see him. They liked his decked-out truck too. The Chevy Kodiak truck was spit polished black all over with gold lettering and lots of chrome. The job got him around people, but not too much. He had an excuse to skedaddle when the conversations started getting long.

The first couple of weeks kept him plenty busy. He ached all the time from the accident's injuries, but his time in prison had helped him handle it. The hard part was getting in good enough shape to carry the load. Bending over to pick up cases of beer tightened his back up like a drum. He'd be lying to himself if he said he didn't have an urge to take a pain pill, but he fought through it. He even put those round wooden beads on his truck seat. One stop at a time, he started getting better. He even got a call on the road from Mike at the Mission from time to time.

As he drove his route between southern West Virginia and North Carolina, he had plenty of time to think—too much time, perhaps. He became used to the isolation. He preferred the lonely existence—caffeinated drinks and truck-stop fast food for him.

With a picture of Jenny and Jake on his visor, along with Jake's backpack in his seat, he couldn't help but think about them all the time. If he didn't think about them, he felt guilty. Something, somewhere, hurt all the time. That was mostly his heart, however.

Day after day, he kept on trucking until he made a delivery at Woody's Grill and life started to change. He started to feel things.

Abraham pulled his truck underneath the canopy and beside the pumps. The fuel gauge was low. He exited the truck, made his way around to the pump, and unhitched the fuel nozzle. He opened his gas cap and started pumping. He reached into the cab and grabbed his clipboard and delivery docket. He pushed the brim of his ball cap up.

"Twenty-four cases, and I'm done." He tossed the clipboard onto the driver's seat.

He opened the back slat-panel door of the truck and grabbed the dolly from inside. Then he opened the next panel door to the left. Two cases at a time, he loaded the dolly until it was eight cases high. *Three trips to the walk-in. Easy-peasy.* He wheeled the dolly around toward the store and caught his breath.

A woman, about his age, blocked his path. She had straight dark ponytail hanging behind her shoulders. Her pretty face was sun bronzed with small freckles. She wore a hot-pink Woody's Grill T-shirt with black lettering, and her jean miniskirt showed off her great legs. She was tapping her foot and had her arms crossed over her chest. "What do you think you are doing?"

"Uh, making a beer delivery… ma'am," he said.

"Ma'am? That's strike two." She pointed at the truck. "You don't fill up during a delivery, newbie. You're blocking all of the pumps from other customers."

Woody twisted his head around. No other cars were in sight, aside from the ones passing by on the highway. "I didn't see anyone else around. And this isn't a typical delivery truck. It's not a commercial vehicle."

"It looks commercial to me," she said. "Why do you think they put all of that lettering on it? And that's strike three. If you want to drop that order, load it back up, pump your gas, take your truck over there"—she pointed toward an access parking area—"and then unload it."

Abraham's blood started to stir. His back had already tightened up like a banjo string. The last thing he wanted to do was load up his truck and unload it again. He'd already done over one hundred cases that day, not to mention the pony kegs. He rubbed his bearded mouth, looked down into the fiery woman's eyes, and said something other than what he planned to say. "Yes, ma'am."

Her eyes narrowed. "The name's Mandi." She walked back into the store.

Abraham started slinging the cases of bottled beer back into the truck. After his fuel pumped, he moved the truck and started the unloading process. He wheeled eight cases to the double glass-paned doors and waited. They didn't open automatically like the other stores he entered. Woody's Grill was an older business, off the interstate, beside what used to be the main highway back in the day. It was a quaint red-brick establishment, typical of what would be seen along country roads, but bigger. He turned his back and pushed through.

Mandi stood behind the cashier counter, leaning back and looking through the tabloids. "Figured that out all by yourself, did you?" she said with a smirk.

Abraham felt sweat begin to roll down his back. He was mad, too. "Where's the cooler, Mandi?"

"In the back of the store. You know, where almost every cooler in America is located."

He gritted his teeth, turned the dolly around, and gave her a smile. "Thank you, *ma'am*."

Mandi's cheeks reddened.

Abraham moved on. He loaded the beer cases and the walk-in cooler. On his way out, he smelled fresh pecan pie, hamburger grease, and french fries. His stomach rumbled. That was when he noticed the diner that made up the other side of the general store. It was complete with a checkered floor, red vinyl booths, and spinning bar stools. A venerable man watching one of the televisions that hung from the wall spun around in his stool. He squinted in Abraham's direction and waved him over.

He wheeled the empty dolly into the diner and asked, "Can I help you, sir?"

"Have you seen any UFOs in Wytheville?" the old man asked.

"Pardon?"

The old man cackled loudly. He grabbed a napkin from the bar and wiped the slobber from his mouth. He wore a Woody's Grill sweatshirt and checkered golf pants with white slippers. He hit Abraham on the arm. "I'm just joshing you. They make a big deal about that UFO sighting in Wytheville. You might not know about it." He leaned forward and looked at the brewery logo on Abraham's black shirt. "So, you're the new guy. Luther told me about you. Wow, I can't believe we have Jenkins the Jet in my store. I used to watch you play a lot."

"Luther told you about me?"

"We go way back. He said to keep an eye on you. My name's Herb, by the way. I own this place." He extended a trembling hand.

Abraham shook it. "Nice to meet you, sir."

"Is it true that you could throw a one-hundred-and-three-mile-an-hour fastball? I never believed what they said about that."

"I could throw faster."

Herb cackled. He turned his head toward the kitchen galley doors. "Hey, Martha! Martha! Come and meet the Jet!"

"I don't go by that anymore."

"Martha! Hurry up!" Herb shouted.

Abraham expected to see a venerable woman like Herb come teetering out from behind the double doors. His eyes widened the moment Martha came through. She was an older version of Mandi, pleasantly plump and far younger than Herb. She couldn't have been more than fifty. Abraham's jaw hung a little.

Wringing her hands in her apron, she met both men at the bar and said, "You must be Abraham?"

He swallowed. "Well, yeah, how did you know?"

"Herb's been rambling on about you since Luther mentioned you. And I overheard him say *the*

Jet." She shook his hand. "Nice to meet you. Say, I bet a big fella like you could use something to eat. How about I fix you something up?"

"I better be getting a move on," he said even though the food did smell mouthwateringly good.

"Nonsense. This is your last stop, isn't it?" Herb said.

"Yes."

"Well, sit down and eat." Herb hollered across the building. "Hey, Mandi! Get that fancy camera and take our picture. I want to put our picture on the wall."

"I'm not really famous," Abraham said as Martha disappeared into the kitchen.

Herb didn't pay Abraham's comment any mind. He started pointing all over the diner. "That's me and Johnny Cash. Over there is Charlie Daniels. Those are from years ago, some of them, before the interstate took our business away. Lots of famous people came rolling through. Glen Campbell. Hank Williams. Dolly was here twice! Man, you should have seen her. Hey Martha, who else used to come through?"

"Don't ask me," Martha hollered back. "Ask your late wife. I wasn't around back then."

Mandi strolled over with a sucker in her mouth. She held up her iPhone and said, "Say cheese."

Herb grinned so big that his dentures looked as though they'd pop out. Abraham made an uneasy smile.

"One for the ages," Mandi said as she walked way with a nice sway of her hips. She caught Abraham checking her out. "Don't you have some work to finish?"

CHAPTER 62
ABRAHAM'S PRESENT

Abraham woke up in fit of coughing. Iris had a hold of him and helped him sit up. The smoky air burned his eyes. They were outside, and people were scrambling over the rooftop. "What happened?"

Sticks stepped into view, her face marred with soot. Without any sign of emotion, she said, "You checked out again. Now we're on the roof, trying our best not to die. Lewis is determined to burn the entire countryside down. He's poured pitch all around the Stronghold."

He looked at Iris and said, "I thought you said you could control the flames."

"I was doing fine up until Leodor showed up. He spoiled my efforts. I can't match his powers," Iris said.

Horace approached and stood over Abraham. "Captain, we are out of options. I think they want to smoke us out. Surrender. But we wouldn't give, not without your awakening first. We'd die first. We're going to die anyway."

Abraham blinked his eyes. He felt as though he'd just relived a big part of his past in his sleep. Coming back to a new reality was jarring. "I'm Ruger Slade, aren't I?"

Sticks's eyelids lifted. She grabbed him by the collar. "Not this again. Are you Ruger or Abraham?"

"Both, I think."

She let out a sigh. "Good. I don't think I could handle a new personality now."

Iris put a flask to his lips. "Drink this elixir. It will help you recuperate on the inside. I've already mended your wounds on the outside." She grabbed his forearm and lifted it for him to see. She'd stitched it up. "See?"

He nodded as he drank. He guzzled the elixir as though it were water, but it was thick like a honey mead, and tasty. With a groan, he reached for Horace's meaty hands. Horace pulled him up to his feet.

The Henchmen were lined around the walls of the top of the Stronghold. They stood between the battlements, looking down.

Fanning the smoke from his face, he asked, "How long have I been out?"

"Since yesterday," Horace replied. "We survived the night only because the Guardians used the time to gather more fire-making supplies. They renewed the flames this morning. They've been piling wood at the bottom, trying to cook us. They keep jamming burning logs through the portal. We jammed that up with stones. We secured the door so they can't burst through. But it's still a smokehouse down there."

Abraham shook his head as though trying to wake from a dream. He had actually been enjoying the reality of getting to know Mandi again. Now, that was gone. He took a smoky breath and asked, "Is anyone hurt?"

"The Guardians have fired several volleys at us, but nothing is sticking," Horace said.

"Did we fire back?"

Horace gave him a funny look and said, "An assault on the King's Guardians is an assault on the king. You don't want us to do that, do you?"

"Right. I guess not." Abraham squeezed between the battlements where Dominga was keeping watch. The smoke obscured his vision, but he could see the barn was burned to the ground. So were the storehouses. Lewis was using the surrounding split-rail fencing for firewood. "Have you seen Solomon?"

With a sorrowful look, Dominga shook her head. "I'm glad you are up and about. Do you feel better?"

"No, I'd rather be sleeping."

Dominga offered a smile. "Me too. Won't be long before we get unlimited rest, it seems."

He laid a hand on her shoulder and said, "Don't give up hope yet." He stepped away from the wall and bumped into Horace, who stood right at his heels. "What's on your mind?"

"It's only a matter of time before the King's Guardians hoist the ladders." Horace walked his fingers through the air. "They'll climb them like metal spiders, and we'll have a full battle on our hands. I just wanted you to know. We spied them building the ladder this morning. And don't forget Leodor aids them as well. We won't be a match for a full regiment of the king's metal. I'd say only the Elders can save us now."

"Have we done anything to get word to the king about this madness?"

It was a hollow question. Convincing King Hector of Lewis and Leodor's treachery would be next to impossible.

"I tried to send some pigeons," Sticks said, tossing a dagger up and down. "Leodor blasted them out of the sky with his magic. We considered trying to slip out of here. At least, that is what myself, Tark, and Dominga wanted to do. We all agreed that we'd be slaughtered."

She looked at the steep hillside of rock behind the fortress. It was almost as sheer as a cliff. The hillside ran over one hundred feet high and peeled away from the fortress. The other side of the hill was a sheer cliff, making for a strange rock formation that created a massive wall. They called it the Shield.

"I could navigate the Shield at night," she said. "Perhaps I can get word to the king. I could at least notify him that a squadron of his men are assaulting the Stronghold. I bet he'd be curious about that."

"Without a horse, you'll be run down and butchered," Horace said. He tapped his spear butt on the stones. "We're going to have to fight against those soldiers. I never thought I'd see the day when something like this happened, the day I'd fight my own kin. We know those men."

Vern walked by with a sword in hand and said, "They should know better."

"That have to follow orders or lose their honor," Horace said. "But you never understood that, did you?"

"I served as well as any, Horace! So, don't you go barking at me. You are a deserter too," Vern flipped his sword around, sheathed it, and drew it again. "I just want to get it over with. I'm tired of standing around."

Cudgel called out from the battlements. "Captain! Horace!" He waved them over. "The assault begins."

The Guardians marched three massive ladders up to the walls and stopped short of the flames.

"What are they doing?" Abraham said. "They can't climb those ladders with all of those flames beneath them. They'll be burned to a crisp."

Down below, Leodor stepped to the forefront. The bookish older man lifted his hands to the sky. The air shimmered around him, causing his image to blur. He pushed his hands outward. The flaming wood built up along the wall scooted into separate piles, leaving massive gaps between them.

Leodor gave a shout.

The King's Guardians lifted their ladders up and set them against the Stronghold's walls between the gaps. All three of the ladders were wide. The lion-face-helmed warriors climbed up the rungs side by side, two men at a time. Like great metal beasts they came, cold and fearless.

Abraham's throat tightened. "Looks like it's on like Donkey Kong. Anybody got any barrels?" He pulled Black Bane free of the sheath. He looked at Sticks and said, "You better get some armor on. Horace, ready the Henchmen."

CHAPTER 63

Lewis stood beside Pratt, observing Leodor's work. The viceroy commanded powers that he didn't comprehend, nor did he care to. The Elders meant nothing to him. The only thing that mattered was the crown. He'd use Leodor and anyone else he could to get it. Pulling his black leather gloves tighter on his hands, he asked, "Pratt, how long do you think that this battle will take?"

Pratt had removed his helmet. He scratched behind his horselike neck and spoke poignantly, which was surprising for a brute of a man. "Under normal circumstances, I think this matter would be resolved within an hour. These aren't normal circumstances. Ruger Slade is on that roof, along with some of the finest Guardians from our ranks. This could well go into the night before we overtake them. But we will."

Lewis stiffly shook his head. "It should go a lot faster. I have eighty men. They don't even have twenty."

"They have position, but that will change." Pratt's heavy stare followed the Guardians climbing the ladders with ease and haste in full-plate armor. "They won't be a match for the king's armor. I just wish I had a bird's-eye view of it. Prince, I'll ascend the wall if you order me. It would be my pleasure to clash with Ruger."

"If anyone is going to have that pleasure, it will be me," Lewis said.

Leodor returned from the wall. His fingertips were smoking underneath the cuffs of his loose-fitting robes. He bowed. "The deed is done. Now, we watch."

"Isn't there more that you can do, Leodor?" Lewis asked with impatience and irritation. "Can't you summon lightning from the sky to shatter Ruger's troops? Won't the precious Elder of Light do that for you?"

"You speak as if you believe, O Prince. Have you had a sudden change of heart since I moved the flames and sticks?" Leodor asked with his usual forwardness.

"Don't poke at me, Leodor. Can you unleash something more assaulting or not? Summon a demon, perhaps. Maybe a giant insect."

"Summoning such a creature takes a long preparation. And the arrival of those beings is slow going. It takes planning. It's a shame that isn't one of your strong points," Leodor said.

"One of these days, Leodor… one of these days, I remove that tongue of yours."

Leodor rolled his eyes.

"I worship the Elder of Metal," Pratt stated. "He is strong. He builds well-knit men like me. No stone can crush him. The winds bust against his shield." He knocked on his chest plate. "He is good to those that are good to him."

"Good for you, Pratt. Be sure you don't let your Elder worship interfere with your duty to the king."

"Never, sire." Pratt cracked his neck side to side. "Ruger Slade. I never thought he would be so foolish to assault the crown. I never liked him, but he was loyal. It's almost a shame the madness has stricken him."

"Wild dogs must be put down," Lewis said.

"Agreed."

The first wave of Guardians climbed their way up to the battlements on top of the Stronghold. The clamor of battle begun. At the top of the ladders, the first Guardians forced their way between the battlements with shields. Below, their brethren were pushing at their backs. The Henchmen struck against the shield. Steel banged on steel like a small thunderstorm. Men yelled and cried out. They heaved against one another.

The Guardian at the top of the middle ladder successfully pushed his way between the battlements. Suddenly, his entire body catapulted backward. The Guardian plummeted to the ground with a crash. A bald and beefy warrior filled the gap between the battlements with a big grin on his face. He beat his chest.

"Who in Titanuus is that?" Lewis said.

"That's Horace. Four hundred pounds of horse manure in action. The only one as big as he is I," Pratt stated. "I can push through. Just say the word. I'll toss him off of that wall myself."

Lewis studied the bristling action building at the Stronghold's roof. He needed to get this over with before word got out to the king. "Pratt, you have my word. Finish this."

Pratt picked up his helmet and made a crooked smile and said, "My pleasure."

CHAPTER 64

Decked out in their chain mail and black leather tunics, the Henchmen fought valiantly against the forces surging between the battlements. Crossbow bolts whistled between the stones as cover fire came from the forces on the ground, making it impossible for the Henchmen to attack from the side.

Abraham and Bearclaw beat against the shields of a Guardian who'd begun powering his way through the gap. He jammed Black Bane clean through the shield. The man behind the lion-crested shield groaned as his body sagged. Abraham pulled his dark sword free. Fresh blood coated the blade. "Damnation!"

The vigorous Guardians behind their fallen brethren pushed their way between the five-foot-wide battlements standing almost as tall as them.

Bearclaw chopped his two-headed battle axe into their legs with devastating impact. He blasted between a Guardian's shin guard and tore out a knee cap. His second swing blasted into the Guardian's midriff. It dented the metal and sent the hobbled man teetering backward. "Death before failure!" He swung again and again.

A new Guardian climbed over the fallen and hacked away at Bearclaw's exposed head. Abraham stretched out his sword and parried the lethal strike away. Steel rang against steel. He batted the Guardian's weapon aside with a swing of his arms. He pulled back and stabbed the Guardian in the heart. The Guardian flung his arms outward and fell backward, yelling, "For the king!"

"This isn't right. It's twisted. We're supposed to be on the same side," Abraham said.

Bearclaw grunted. "The only thing that matters now is who remains above ground and who goes below."

A lion-face helmet popped up over the wall's rim. He struck it in the face. The helmet went askew, but the Guardian kept coming. Bearclaw chopped again. A second Guardian scaled the ladder and grabbed his arm. They wrestled over the weapon.

Abraham crammed his way onto the battlement. He and Bearclaw wrestled back to back against the Guardians. The King's Guardians fought like the lions that their helmets were fashioned after. The manelike plumes rustled in the wind. Fighting them was a shame, a tragedy to kill them. They were following orders with honor. He kicked one in the face. The man's head snapped backward. Bearclaw cut the man in the neck, and the Guardian stumbled from the ladder.

The last Guardian at the top plowed into Bearclaw. His clutching fingers grabbed a hold of Bearclaw's tunic and jerked him toward the ladder. Both men slid down the top steps. Abraham jumped on Bearclaw, grabbed him by the waist, and started hauling him in. "Get back up here!"

With a heave, Bearclaw pushed the Guardian away. The warrior tumbled down the ladder and took several more to the ground down with him. He pushed the empty ladder away from the wall, and it fell down on the Guardians who stood below, agape. The space between the battlement was cleared.

Abraham helped Bearclaw to his feet. They bumped forearms.

"That rocked!" Abraham said.

He'd bought some time on the left side of the Stronghold for the moment, but trouble was coming up the middle. The huge guardian, Pratt, started making his way up that ladder. It bowed and bent underneath his mighty frame. A train of Guardians fell in behind him.

"We better get over there."

Horace stood between the battlements, shaking his fist downward. "I see you, Pratt! You think you can get through me! Try me!" He thumbed his chest. "I'll flatten you!"

Abraham climbed into the battlement. "I'll lend you a hand."

With nostrils flaring, Horace gave him a hard look that could kill. "I don't need a hand. I want him to myself, Captain."

"We can't afford to let them breach the wall. It's a team effort."

Horace put his hand on Abraham's chest and said, "Don't deny me this, Captain. I want him. He's mine."

He looked over the wall, astonished at how quickly the Guardians moved up the ladder in full-plate armor, as though it was no more than chain mail. "I don't doubt you, Horace. You know that." He held out his hand. "I'll hold your spear."

Horace gave a stern nod and stuffed the spear into Abraham's hand. "Thank you, Captain. Death before failure."

"Aye," Abraham said as though he was one of them. "Death before failure."

Pratt's colossal head crested the wall. In his armor, he had the appearance of two men in one. Penetrating eyes burned behind the visor of the helm. The eyes slid over onto Ruger, narrowed, then found Horace. "Hello, fat man."

"Eat boot, Hog Head!" Horace kicked Pratt in the face.

The Guardian's head snapped back, but only a little. He laughed inside his helmet and forced himself from the ladder onto the battlement. Horace met him head on.

Abraham had never witnessed the likes of the battle he was witnessing. The two burly warriors were locked in a tangle of limbs between the battlements, thrashing back and forth. Pratt's metal glove clung to Horace's beard.

He said, "Smile," and punched Horace in the face.

Blood dripped out of Horace's nose. The burly fighter knocked Pratt's hand aside. He grabbed the Guardian's helmet by the mane, ripped it off, and flung it aside. He smiled with blood on his teeth and headbutted Pratt in the chin.

Pratt's shoulders sagged. His thick neck tilted. His pupils filled his irises.

Seizing the moment, Horace jumped Pratt and put him in a headlock. He ratcheted up the pressure. "I'm gonna pop that pumpkin head of yours like a pimple!"

Abraham exchanged a glance with Bearclaw. "I think he's got it under control."

"I never had a doubt," Bearclaw said.

He moved on to the parapets. The Guardians were still at least eighty men deep and still coming. The ladder they'd knocked over earlier was being lowered back against the wall. The Guardians resumed their ascent.

"Here we go again," Abraham said.

Suddenly, Horace let out an angry cry.

Abraham and Bearclaw turned in the direction of the voice. Pratt was standing between the battlements. He had Horace hoisted up over his head.

"Impossible," Bearclaw said with awe.

With fire in his eyes, Pratt glared at Ruger and said, "You're next." Then he hurled Horace over the side.

CHAPTER 65

"Nooo!" Abraham screamed. He raced to the wall and looked down where Horace had landed.

The bearish fighter lay face down in the ground. He didn't move. He didn't breathe. A small host of Guardians surrounded Horace. From all appearances, Horace was dead.

"Can he survive a fall like that?" Abraham muttered. He called out, "Horace! Horace!"

Bearclaw hooked his arm and spun him away from the wall. "It doesn't matter. We still have a fight on our hands."

The towering Pratt stood between the battlements. He waved his men through. "For the king, Guardians! Long live the king!"

The Guardians spilled through the gap. Vern, Prospero, and Apollo met them head on with steel banging against steel. The bright steel of swords flashed. Fighters grunted and cursed.

Pratt stepped off the wall and drew his sword out of its sheath, a long handsome blade with an extra-long pommel fit for his hands. He marched right toward Abraham. "It's over. Heh heh. Much easier than I thought it would be. How disappointing. But I don't want you to surrender. I want you to fight."

With his brows knitted together, Abraham said, "Trust me. You don't want that. I'll down you like a tree."

Pratt smirked, an unnatural fire behind his eyes. He bristled all over with new energy.

The hairs on the nape of Abraham's neck rose. Something was off, something uncanny. He took a peek over the battlements. Leodor was standing with his eyes closed, his thin lips moving like hummingbird wings. Lewis stood beside Leodor. He caught Ruger's eye and made the cut-throat gesture.

Abraham stepped away from the wall. "All right, Pratt. Let's do this."

Pratt's neck muscles flexed. Great veins rose underneath the skin of his neck. He bared his long sword and grinned. "I'm going to enjoy this."

"And I'm going to peel you open like a can of pineapple rings. When you're dying, remember I warned you." Abraham stood in the high point stance. "Show me what you got!"

Pratt cocked his sword back and swung. The metal blades collided with a long ringing effect.

Shockwaves went up Abraham's arms into his shoulders. He shuffled his feet over to the side, fighting to maintain full balance. He'd never been hit by anything so hard before. Pratt struck with the brute animal strength of a bull. His eyes became wild as fire.

Using his superior length, Pratt turned loose a series of one-handed windmill-like chops. The tip of his sword drew sparks from the stone floor he clipped.

Abraham backed away from the deadly windmill of power. He waited for an opening and darted in. He slashed Black Bane across Pratt's abdomen. The tip of his blade skipped off the hardened breast plate.

Pratt backhanded Abraham with a fist, catching Abraham across the cheek. The blow sent him spinning. Pratt followed up with an overhanded chop.

With stars in his eyes, Abraham moved with his momentum, spinning away from the strike and death blow.

"Stand still, you spineless weasel!" Pratt said with a roar. He spat saliva from his lips like a snorting animal. "It's only a matter of time before I finish you off! We'll finish you all off!"

Abraham's battle awareness kicked in. From the corners of his eyes, he could see the Henchmen were fading fast. They were crowded in a corner of the Stronghold's roof, fighting for their very lives, and it was all because of him. "You are a fool, Pratt. You are on the wrong side of right."

"And you are a deserter. I don't care what you say!"

The two warriors thrust and parried against one another with lightning speed. Pratt matched him strike for strike. The ring of steel sang like thunder. Abraham parried the bigger man's attacks and said, "Prince Lewis and Leodor allied against King Hector. If you're a good man, search your heart, and you'll know it's true. Look at you, trying to slaughter your former brethren."

Pratt sliced right over the top of Abraham's ducking head. "You speak the words of a man that is possessed. I don't believe the lies that you spew!"

Abraham stepped up his game. He sent Pratt backward with quick strokes that forced him to parry. He didn't want to kill the man. For the moment, all he wanted to do was talk. "Regardless of what you think, you shall know the truth, and the truth shall set you free."

The rugged-looking Pratt cocked an eye. "I tire of your funny talk. Look around you. All of you are doomed unless you surrender."

Back and forth they went. Sword against sword. Might against might. Skill against superior skill.

"Relent, Pratt, and listen to my words."

"Save them for the afterlife. You're finished, Ruger. The entire kingdom will know that I ended you!" Pratt locked both hands on his sword grip, put his hips into it, and swung.

The blow would have cut a horse in twain. Luckily, Abraham wasn't there to receive it. He leapt high in the air and cracked Pratt between the eyes with the butt of his sword.

Pratt dropped to his knees with a grunt. Blood trickled down into his blinking eyes. "Lucky shot."

Abraham popped him in the jaw. Pratt fell to the ground, his sword slipping free of his fingers.

Abraham kicked Pratt's sword away and said, "Really? I don't feel lucky."

"Ruger!" a woman shrieked.

He turned toward the sound of the voice. Iris was in a chokehold and being lifted off her feet. The Henchmen were outnumbered three to one. Vern lay bleeding on the ground. Bearclaw's shoulder hung low. Tark limped on a bloody leg. Dominga lay on the ground, not moving, and Sticks was cornered by two Guardians and parrying for her life.

He lifted his arms high and screamed, "I surrender! We surrender!"

CHAPTER 66

The fight was over. The battle was lost. Abraham and his henchmen were marched out of the Stronghold, where they kneeled in front of the gloating Prince Lewis and Viceroy Leodor. The only good thing to come out of it was that none of the Henchmen had died, including Horace. The big ox survived the fall. He wasn't moving but lay nearby, stretched out on the ground.

With his usual haughtiness, Prince Lewis said, "You just couldn't die in battle, could you. You had to survive. You had to surrender. Now, I have to do the dirty work."

"Perhaps if Pratt did a better job, you wouldn't have to get your hands even dirtier," Abraham said with a glance at Pratt.

The largest Guardian had blood drying on his face. The bruising over his eyes started to look like a mask.

Abraham looked at Leodor. "What are you smirking at? Even your magic wasn't enough to finish us."

Leodor sank his chin down into his chest. "I wasn't really trying."

Abraham shifted his attention to Lewis. The gloating look in the man's eyes told him that the end of the road was here. "Take me. Leave my men out of it."

Lewis drew his sword and said with an air of authority, "That time has passed. I gave you an opportunity to surrender. Instead, you burrowed. Now, the prince's grace has ended. Now, all of you have assaulted the King's Army. It's an affront to the king himself. The penalty for your reckless incursion is death. Bind him. All of them."

The Guardians bound the Henchmen's ankles together and tied their hands behind their backs. They even did so to the triplets, Selma, Sophia, and Bridgett. The hirelings and Red Tunics were bound up, too. Abraham caught Sticks's gaze, and she didn't have a crease of worry on her countenance.

He mouthed the word "Sorry."

She barely shrugged her brows.

Is this the end of a dream or the beginning of a nightmare? I guess it all has to end one way or the other. What a shame. I was beginning to like this place.

Pratt carried over a large block of wood and dropped it on the ground in front of Abraham.

"You're really good at lifting heavy objects, aren't you? Too bad you suck at swordplay," Abraham said.

"We'll see who sucks when your head hits the ground." Pratt walked away.

Two guardians bent Abraham over the crude chopping block. His head and neck were extended out over the rim. He glanced up at Lewis, who was resting his longsword on his shoulder.

"Don't worry, Ruger. They say the experience is painless," the prince said.

"Oh, I'm not worried about the pain. I'm worried that you'll miss and cut your foot off. You aren't so hot with that steel, either."

"You really know how to piss me off, don't you, Ruger." Lewis stuck his sword point-first in the ground. "How about some poetic justice? Pratt, bring me Black Bane."

CHAPTER 67

Lewis ran two fingers down the length of Black Bane's blade and smiled with satisfaction. "I must admit this weapon is quite possibly the finest craftmanship that I've ever seen. I hear that it can cut anything."

"Hand it over, and I'll be happy to show you," Abraham said.

Pratt punched him in the back.

Abraham groaned and said, "Thanks."

Flipping the sword end over end, Lewis said, "Leodor, it is said that the Elders made this sword. If that is true, then why does a man carry it?"

"The Elder's purposes are filled with many mysteries, left to us to figure out for ourselves," the viceroy said. "Then again, perhaps it is a sword made by ordinary men, forged by a craft that was lost ages ago."

Lewis smirked. "I like that answer better."

Abraham didn't care what Lewis thought. *Just keep this blowhard talking. Monologuing always ruins the bad guys. At least it does in my world.* He silently called out to Black Bane. *"Will you do something? Strike down Lewis with lightning. Do something."*

He looked toward the sky. No clouds or birds were there. The chirpings of nature were silent. As in so many fantasy books he'd read before, he hoped to see a dragon or wizard or even the baby Fenix, Simon, swoop down out of the sky and save the day. None of that happened. Not even a wind came. The humidity was stifling.

Abraham took a shot in the dark. "I have no doubt the Elders made it. Only a fool would believe otherwise. I hope you don't think that your feeble hand can wield it. It takes a special person to handle a superior weapon like Black Bane. Strike me down, and you'll only bring the Elders' wrath upon you."

"Your words might frighten the likes of Leodor, but as for me, well"—Lewis thumbed the sword's blade—"I don't believe in the Elders. Now, bite your tongue. It's time to execute your sentence." He lifted the sword over his head with both hands. "Any last words?"

Abraham's heart raced. Blood rushed behind his ears. He strained against his bonds. He tried to think of something riveting to say. Instead, the following words came out: "How much wood could a woodchuck chuck if a woodchuck could chuck wood."

Lewis snorted and said, "Goodbye, Ruger Slade."

"Goodbye, Captain!" Horace bellowed.

Abraham squeezed his eyes shut. With his heart beating in his throat, he managed to say, "Death before failure."

"Absolutely," Lewis said.

The sound of great horns filled the valley.

KAAAAAAH-COOOOOOOOOOO!

KAAAAAAH-COOOOOOOOOOO!

A rustling of armor spread throughout the Guardians' ranks.

"No," Lewis said in a hushed voice.

"The King's Horn!" Horace cried out. "That's the King's Horn!"

Abraham cracked an eye open. The King's Guardians were taking a knee. Lewis's face turned ashen. He stuck Black Bane in the ground, visibly shaken. He seemed to move under a compulsion that was not his own.

Abraham twisted his head around and caught Sticks's eyes. He mouthed the words "What is happening?"

Under her breath, Sticks said, "When the King's Horn sounds, all activity must stop. It's a crime to continue your labors."

Abraham let out a sigh of relief. "That's what I call being saved by the horn." He heard what must have been hundreds of horsemen galloping their way. It sounded like an army. He managed to get a glimpse of the oncoming legion. The soldiers were dressed in the same full-plate armor as the King's Guardians. The only difference was that their helmets were gold plated and the shining steel armor was trimmed in the same gold. They were the king's personal cavalry, known as the Golden Riders. A carriage drawn by a white horse rolled up between the ranks. The carriage was grand, made of polished black oak and painted in gold accents with the crest of the lion face with wings showing on the small flag posts decorating the corners.

Two Golden Riders moved down to the carriage. Someone on the inside pushed the door open, and King Hector poked his head out. He was wearing the small crown on his head. His face showed surprise and frustration, his gentlemanly manner erased from his face. Iron was in his eyes. His forest-green traveling cloak covered him down to his soft leather boots. Everything he wore was finely crafted. He stepped down to the ground and reached his hand into the carriage. Queen Clarann stepped out. The beautiful lioness of a woman wore travel garb similar to the king's. She held her chin high. Her light eyes took in her new surroundings. She looked back as Princess Clarice jumped out of the carriage.

"Oh great," Lewis said underneath his breath. "They even brought the brat with them."

Clarice stood beside her mother, short, young, and vibrant. She was dressed for action in a brown leather tunic. A single rapier hung on her round hips. Her eyes narrowed on Lewis.

King Hector marched right up to his son and looked him dead in the eye.

Lewis swallowed. "Father, what brings you from the House of Steel?"

"What brings me from the House of Steel? You have the gall to ask me that?" King Hector's strong tone carried the weight of a slap in the face. "Am I supposed to recount the running list of transgressions I so recently became aware of?"

Leodor interrupted and said, "Your Majesty, perhaps I can shed some light on the situation."

"You've done enough, Leodor," Hector said without looking at the man. He kept his eyes on Lewis. "You tell me, in your own words, what by the Elders is going on, Son."

Lewis pulled his shoulders back, took a long draw through his nose, cocked his head slightly and said, "It's quite simple. Ruger Slade assaulted me. An assault on the crown means death. I was willing to forgive him, but in his possessed state, well, he rejected my grace with insane and false accusations."

Hector looked down at Abraham and asked, "Is this true? Did you assault my son?"

"I did cut him, your majesty," Abraham said.

"I see many dead," Hector said as he looked at the gash on Lewis's neck. "My Guardians have been downed. Did you attack them as well?"

"We defended ourselves. We didn't want to fight, but we didn't have a choice. King Hector—"

"Silence!" Hector said. "An assault on the crown, its prince, its guards, is an assault on the king himself." He pulled Black Bane from the dirt. "What must be done, must be done."

Lewis's tight expression eased. He smirked at Ruger. "Well said, my king."

Abraham swallowed.

CHAPTER 68

"Son, you don't know the half of it," King Hector said. He used the tip of Black Bane and sawed through the cords that bound Abraham.

"Father, what are you doing?" Lewis whined.

"I'm getting to the bottom of this, once and for all." Hector helped Abraham to his feet. He pointed at the Stronghold's front door. "We'll convene in there. Lewis, Leodor, go inside. Clarann and Clarice, follow me. Pratt, you come, along with four of my Golden Riders. Ruger, choose one of your own to enter too."

"Yes, Your Majesty," Abraham said. He wasn't sure what to make of the sudden turn of events, but he felt something big was happening.

He'd never seen much of King Hector before. This time, however, a fire was in him. He stole a glance at Queen Clarann. She was looking right at him and quickly looked away.

He moved over to Sticks and undid the cords that bound her. "You're coming to the last dance with me."

"You're the Captain," Sticks said.

The inside of the Stronghold was mostly intact but smoky. It was stuffy and smelled of burning embers more than anything.

Queen Clarann coughed lightly. King pulled the chair out at the head of the table. "Seal those doors."

With the help of Pratt, two Golden Riders shoved a large slab of stone into the doorway.

"King Hector, shall we bar it?" Pratt asked.

"No, I'm only concerned with prying ears. I don't want the Guardians to see what is about to happen. What happens inside these rooms stays here." He tapped the table then rubbed the soot between his fingers.

Clarann and Clarice sat on his right. Lewis and Leodor took seats on the left. Abraham and Sticks hung at the other end of the table, sitting on the same bench as Lewis and Leodor.

King Hector reached for Clarann's hand and held it tight. He faced his son. "I want you to tell me the truth. What are you into? What is going on?"

"I told you. Ruger assaulted me. I wouldn't tolerate it any more than you would," Lewis replied.

Abraham wanted to object, but he kept his mouth shut.

"Father, you know that he lies," Clarice said. "He's always lied about one thing or another. Every path he takes is full of treachery."

Without taking his eyes off his son, Hector coolly said, "Be silent, Daughter. Lewis, am I supposed to believe that you and your cohort Leodor had nothing to do with the Brotherhood of Ravens overrunning the streets of Burgess? Am I to believe that they acted on their own volition because of him?" He pointed at Ruger. "It sounds preposterous."

Lewis sat with his arms crossed over his chest and said, "I do not keep track of the enemies that Ruger has made. I can imagine that he has many. Look at him. He has the look of a criminal, not to mention that he is a loon."

"So why didn't you notify me, eh?" the king asked. "You used my Guardians in an all-out assault. Now many of them are dead. In the midst of coming war, you treat my soldiers like chaff."

"I could not let this madman escape. He wounded me. He assaulted the crown. Ruger Slade is a wild dog that needs put down." Lewis took his gloves off and fanned himself. "I am the prince. I am trusted with many liberties that do not need your approval. Am I wrong, Father?"

"This is a special circumstance. You know that." King Hector looked down the table at Ruger. "Let's hear your end of it."

"Father, I insist, he's guilty. He's been judged. He is not worthy of your audience," Lewis said.

"This is the man that saved my queen. I will hear him out before I decide what is to be done. You be silent." The King looked at Sticks. "Who is this that you brought with you?"

"This is my second in command. Her name is Sticks," Abraham said.

"Ah, and she is your witness?" the King asked as his gaze gave her further study.

"She is."

"Out with it, then. And make it quick… Abraham," the King said.

Abraham ran through his theory of how Lewis and Leodor were sabotaging the Henchmen's missions. He explained how they'd caught Prince Lewis red-handed with the assassin, Raschel, who Twila either was or worked for. How that happened, he didn't bother to explain. It was still a theory. His story against Lewis and Leodor's. He finished the story by saying, "Prince Lewis and Leodor, I have no doubt, are behind many of your troubles. I don't know who they serve, but I don't believe it's you."

King Hector leaned back in his seat. His eyes looked upward and scanned the ceiling. He took a deep breath, dropped his eyes to Sticks, and asked, "And you verify this account?"

With her head down, Sticks said, "I do, Your Majesty."

"What do you make of this, Leodor? Is it true that my long-time servant is working against the crown?" the king asked.

"Your Majesty, I know that you cannot put your trust in an otherworlder. He is a demon that spews lies and tall tales. He's been desperate ever since he, well, changed." Leodor gave Ruger a sorrowful look. "You cannot trust a word that he says."

Clarice came out of her seat. "Father, they are lying through their rotten teeth!"

Clarann pulled her daughter back down. "Be silent, child."

Clarice grunted and glared at Lewis.

"As you should know, Abraham, it is your word versus the blood of the crown," the king said. "I have no choice but to take my son's word over yours."

Lewis gave Ruger a winning smile.

"However," the king said.

Lewis's head snapped around. His mouth gaped.

King Hector continued as he pulled out the emerald stone from the fold of his cloak. "I didn't bring all of us inside here to have a pissing contest. I brought us all here to find the truth, no matter how much it might hurt." He gripped the emerald pendant in his hand. Green fire illuminated between his fingers and knuckles. His eyes reflected the same mystic fire. "Golden Riders, see to it that Lewis and Leodor remain seated."

The soldiers walked up behind Lewis and Leodor and clamped their metal gauntlets down on their shoulders.

Leodor's jaw hung. His body trembled.

Lewis cried out like a spoiled child, "No, Father, nooo!"

CHAPTER 69

King Hector held his glowing fist in front of his son Lewis's face and said, "Tell me, are you using the Brotherhood or Ravens to thwart my plans?"

Lewis squirmed. His jaw opened and closed as he stared at the king's hand as if it was a snake about to strike. "Father, you must believe meee!" Sweat beaded his face. His skin became ashen and clammy.

"Answer me!" Hector demanded as he pushed the emerald stone up between his thumb and finger.

The gem floated into the air and hovered at eye level before Lewis. It shone like a brilliant star, lighting the room up with eerie illumination.

Abraham's own stomach twisted. The power of the stone gripped his heart. Something about it made all the darkness he'd buried want to come out. It was cleansing, and the king wasn't even targeting him, but the king had used it on him before. He glanced at Sticks. Her eyes were wide with fascination. She panted and held a hand over her heart. He reached over and held her other hand.

"Out with it, Son," the King said. "Did you hire the Brotherhood of Ravens to sabotage the Henchmen's efforts or not?"

Lewis growled in his throat as if a demon had been trapped inside him and wanted to get out. He rocked stiffly back and forth, but the Golden Riders held him fast. His facial features became a kaleidoscope of twisting emotion. The whites of his eyes cracked with red. With his fingernails digging into the table, he tossed his head back and shouted with unfettered rage, "Fine! I did it! Using the wings of the Ravens, I've sabotaged your stupid, ignorant, hopeless missions, Father!" He was sneering now. "You blind old fool, stuck in your old ways, refusing to budge when the world is changing. Yes, I did it!"

"Who else is behind this?" the King asked.

Lewis's eyebrows clenched together, and he looked at his father as though he was some kind of fool. He sneered and said with disdain, "Well, Leodor, of course. Who do you think made your whore of a queen so sick! Who do you think helped me plan the operations? Hmmm? Do you really think I could have done all of this alone? I had plenty of help."

King's Hector's nostrils flared. He breathed deeply, looked at Leodor and said, "So, Lewis's statement is accurate. You poisoned the queen. You conspire with him, and against the crown."

Leodor's sweaty lips wriggled underneath his nose. His tired eyes held the radiant shine of the stone. Finally, he licked his mouth and said, "I did not make the queen sick. She was diseased. I simply didn't aid her. Need I remind Your Majesty that, as a member of the Sect, I am a neutral party? I serve my order. I serve the Elders. I am washed clean of any crimes."

"Who else is in league with you? Are there more conspirators in my midst?" the king asked. "Tell me how all of this came to be?"

"The only other is Raschel," Lewis said as he tried to stare away from the stone. "She was my spy among the Henchmen. She used her power to steal the identity of a commoner named Twila. Aside from me and Leodor, she is the only one in the kingdom."

Abraham had the explanation he needed. He didn't understand it fully, but clearly, Raschel had become Twila. Given his own situation, anything was possible.

The king wasn't finished. "What drives this conspiracy, Lewis? Hmmm? Why would you turn your back against your own father, who has given you everything, you spoiled son?"

"Clarann. I hate her. She is not my mother. She's a commoner of the streets. No royal blood defines her. She is the scum that coats the bottom of my boots on my feet." Lewis managed to tear his eyes away from the stone to glare at Clarann and her daughter, Clarice. "They are cattle born."

The King grabbed his son's arm and said, "Clarann has been nothing but kind to you. You've had no reason to turn against your father or the crown. There is much more behind this. Perhaps your anger was used to turn your heart against me. Who is behind this attack? Hmmm?" His eyes slid between Lewis and Leodor. "Tell me."

"I'll tell you, Father. I'd be glad to. You don't even need your precious stone, now that the truth is out." Lewis looked his father dead in the eye. "I serve the Underlord. And soon, that crown on your head will be mine."

"No, that's not true, Son." King Hector held his open palm underneath the stone. Its fire went out, and the emerald dropped into his hand. He closed his fingers around it. "Both of you betrayed the crown. There is only death for you."

CHAPTER 70

"FATHER, YOU CAN'T BE SERIOUS," Lewis said with gaping astonishment. "You can't kill your own son. I'm your one and only heir. Your bloodline ends without me."

King Hector looked Lewis dead in the eyes and said, "Under eyewitness testimony, you've given me over a dozen reasons to have you hanged, quartered, guillotined. You've betrayed your king, queen, and country. Worst of all, you turned against your own family." The king let go of his son's forearm and shook his head sadly. "And I had such high hopes for you. No man is greater than his citizens or his country. You've been taught that a hundred times. It is a sad day indeed."

Abraham felt bad for King Hector. His only son had turned against him, for what seemed to be little or no reason at all. Lewis was an even bigger jerk than he'd imagined, a spoiled and pompous brat. He got the feeling that something else was brewing, something much bigger than the situation at hand. *Who in the world is the Underlord?*

King Hector stood up and pulled his dagger out of his belt. It had a razor-sharp edge and a jewel-encrusted handle. "Stand Lewis up, men."

"Wh-what are you doing?" Lewis asked. "You aren't going to kill me here, are you, in cold blood. I-I-I get a trial. I have to have a trial."

"I am the judge! I am the jury! I am the king!" Hector yelled. He pointed the dagger at Leodor. "Stand up that spineless jackal as well!"

As the Golden Riders jerked him up, the smarmy Leodor said, "An assault on me is an assault on the Sect, Your Majesty. You will lose all of their support in the coming wars."

"I reckon I lost it a long time ago," the king said. "Put them on their knees."

Abraham sat on the edge of his seat. *I can't believe the king's going to get blood on his hands.*

Leodor continued his rant. "I've always served you honorably, King Hector. I always will. I was only serving the interest of your son, which you asked me to do. Perhaps I became caught up in it. Spare me, O King. It is what is best for the kingdom. You can't win a war with the Sect against you. I can help."

"You can't be trusted. Neither of you can. As much as it grieves me, I have no other course but to take your lives for those that have been taken." He lifted the dagger before his face. "And I must do this by my own hand."

"Father, no!" Leodor whined. "You can't do this. I-I'll change. I'll make amends. I promise! Father, spare me, please spare me. You are the king. You can do it."

"No man is above the law. Not even me. Kingsland cannot survive on lawlessness. A kingdom without laws is not a kingdom at all." He looked from his son back to his dagger. "This is the Dagger of Death. Its strike is death. This will be the first time in decades I have used it." He looked at Golden Riders holding the two traitors fast. "Hold them still."

"No, no, no, no, no," Lewis pleaded.

Abraham knew the king was a man who would see justice meted out, but this was becoming disturbing. He didn't doubt that Lewis and Leodor had it coming. The number of crimes they had committed would have been countless, but to see the king undertake the execution was another matter. It didn't seem normal for King Hector to execute his own son. *Let Pratt do it or someone else.* He stole a look at Clarann and Clarice. Both of them sat rigid as a ramrod and holding hands with white knuckles. Mercy was in their eyes, in both ladies, but they dared not speak out in defiance of their king.

"It will be quick. It will be painless," the king said. "I'm sorry, Son, that I must do this. May the Elders forgive you." He slowly drew his hand back with the dagger poised to strike.

With his eyes locked on the dagger, Lewis gulped for air like a fish out of water.

Abraham couldn't take it any longer. "No, wait!"

The king froze and slowly turned his head toward Abraham. "Do you have something to say?"

"Brand them," Abraham blurted out. "They can't betray you if you brand them. They'll die if they do, right?"

King Hector lowered the dagger. His hard stare began to soften. "The branded must be a willing participant. I don't think these two are willing."

"I am, Father. I am!" Lewis seemed elated.

"I'd rather not, but I will," Leodor said with the energy of a defeated old man.

King Hector looked back at Queen Clarann and asked, "What do you think?"

"There is no other choice. It is the Brand, or it is death," Clarann said.

"Abraham, or Ruger, where is the Brand?" the king asked.

That was a good question. Abraham hadn't actually seen it before. All he knew was that Ruger's former host, Eugene Drisk, had branded many. Dominga was one of the more recent ones.

"I, uh..." Abraham said.

"I know where it is," Sticks said. "I shall fetch it with your permission. It's inside the Stronghold."

"Then fetch it, young lady," the king ordered. He looked at Lewis and Leodor. "Strip them down to the waist."

Sticks glided over to the right side of the room and stood before the fireplace, a large one made from stone. The hearth and mantle were made of granite. She got down on her knees and pushed the top of the hearth aside. She reached into the raised hearth and produced the Brand. It was a long rod of iron with a crown shape on the end. She walked it over to the king.

With a bow, she said, "Here it is, Your Majesty."

King Hector took the Brand and nodded. "Thank you. Pratt, start a fire. Let the King's Branding commence."

CHAPTER 71

Starting the fire didn't take Pratt long. The dried wood burned yellow-orange and started to pop and crackle. Abraham had seen enough fire for the day, but one more wouldn't hurt him. King Hector had given him the King's Brand. He wore a thick leather glove and held it in the flames. The brand wasn't an ordinary length of iron that one stuck to livestock. This one was different. Runes, much like the ones that decorated Black Bane's blade, twisted in rigid patterns all the way along the shaft. The brand itself was an open-faced crown with six horns. It glowed hot blue, not red. Wispy mystic smoke feathered up from the brand into the chimney. Bright bluish and green sparkles went with it.

"Come over here, Abraham. I believe the Brand is ready," King Hector said.

Abraham gave Sticks a long look as he turned away from the flames. Her eyes were fixed on the burning brand. He moved beside King Hector, who faced Lewis and Leodor, down on their knees. Leodor's body trembled as he wobbled in his stance.

King Hector took the brand from Abraham. "This is the King's Brand, created ages ago, as a seal of honor, to those who would faithfully serve the king. The king of Kingsland, that is. It is not an ordinary brand used for livestock or slaves. With this brand comes power. It grants life. It grants death. The Brand, this crown"—he pointed at the end of the Brand—"is placed over the heart. It will know your intentions. Serve the crown and be blessed. Betray the crown, be cursed and face death."

The well-knit Lewis looked up into his father's eyes and said, "Save the theatrics and get it over with. I don't want to hear some yarn about how Elders crapped it out, either. I'd rather—eee-argh!"

King Hector jammed the brand against Lewis's chest, just above the heart. The stench of frying skin filled the air. He pulled the brand back. It tore from the flesh it had charred. The burned image of the crown ebbed a deep blue. The color faded and reddened like blood.

"Titanuus's crotch, that hurt!" Lewis said.

Beside him, Leodor trembled like a leaf.

Panting, Lewis looked at the viceroy and added, "I can't wait to see how this turns out."

Leodor's sagging skin hung from his scrawny frame in a pathetic display of manliness. He didn't appear fit enough to push an empty wheelbarrow. His tired eyes blinked rapidly, and sweat ran down his temple. "Er, your majesty, this brand is a severe conflict of interest with my contract with the Sect. It cannot be."

King Hector jammed the brand over the frail man's heart.

Leodor flung his arms backward. His mouth dropped open, and black smoke came out.

The queen and princess gasped. The king stepped in front of them and said, "Elders of Light, what is that?"

The black smoke spilled out of Leodor's mouth like lava spewing out of a volcano. It took a humanoid shape and form, made like lumpy clouds. It floated around the room with two glimmering spots for its eyes, showing like bright diamonds. A haunting moaning sound came from its body.

"Begone, wicked spirit," King Hector said. He waved the brand at it.

The black spirit shifted away, floated quickly toward the fireplace, and went into the chimney. A gust of hot wind blasted through the room, and a shrieking moan followed. As quickly as the dark spirit had come, it was gone.

Leodor lay on the floor, hugging the Golden Riders like a baby. Chill bumps were all over his body.

"What happened, Leodor?" King Hector asked. "What was that thing?"

Leodor shook his head. He finally looked at the king and said, "That was the Spirit of the Sect. With it comes power of the order. Elders, no! I've been stripped of my majesty."

"At least you're not dead," Princess Clarice said.

"I might as well be," Leodor replied. He ran his shaking fingers over the burnt flesh on his scrawny chest. "I never saw this coming."

Sticks jumped in front of King Hector and took a knee. She removed her bandoliers of knives and her tunic and pulled her shirt down, exposing her chest. "King Hector, Your Majesty, will you brand me?"

Hector looked down on her and said, "No. I've done my bidding. I am king, not the leader of the Henchmen." He tossed the brand to Abraham. "He's the leader of the Henchmen, and under my authority, all that are branded must follow him, and he must follow me."

Holding the brand in his grip, Abraham looked down into Sticks's eyes and asked, "Are you sure you want this?"

"I never wanted it gone in the first place."

He branded her.

Sticks moaned, but not a tear was shed from her eyes.

Hector fanned his nose. "Good gravy, it's really beginning to stink in here. If we are done, then push away those stones. I want to get some fresh air." He faced Pratt. "You are the commander of the King's Guardians now." He glanced at his grimacing son. "Don't foul it up. There will be no mercy or brand for you."

The broken-nosed Pratt dropped to a knee and bowed. "I will not fail you, my king."

The Golden Riders moved toward the front and started moving the stones from the doorway that closed them in. King Hector started heading that way when Clarice dropped in front of him. "Father, stop. I have a request. You told me yesterday on my sixteenth year of life, that you would grant me anything I wished."

King Hector lifted a brow, gave Queen Clarann a curious look, and said, "Certainly I did, but now is not the proper time to settle the matter."

"But it is. I'm of proper age, an adult, ready for marriage, right?" she said.

"Oh, please don't tell me that you want to marry Ruger."

Clarice made a shocked expression and said, "Well, no. I'm not leaning that way at all. I would like him to train me."

"If that is your request, no doubt it can be arranged, but we have more important matters to attend to. Come, Clarice. Since you are an adult now, exercise the proper time and place to make your conversations. You need to work on that impulsiveness of yours."

From her knees, Clarice grabbed the king's hand. "You misunderstand. I don't want sword lessons as my gift. I want to be a Henchman. I want the King's Brand."

CHAPTER 72

"I must be a complete fool. It's no wonder my kingdom is in flux. Look at this place," King Hector said.

Late in the evening of the same day, Abraham discreetly escorted King Hector into the city of Burgess. They made their way into one of the Sect's larger cathedrals. Lewis and Leodor accompanied them along with half a dozen Guardians, led by Pratt, dressed in street clothes. Abraham walked quietly beside the king. That day had been a long one for the old man. He found out his own son and top confidant had betrayed him. To make matters worse, his coming-of-age daughter, Clarice, had been branded. Abraham felt for the man.

Gazing up at the rafters of the gaunt cathedral's ceiling, King Hector said, "This place is vile. There's no light, no hope, no soft burning candles. It was not like this when I was young. What sort of place has this become?"

"It gets worse," Lewis said. "I never cared for these false places of worship to begin with."

Leodor moved to the front of the cathedral as if his legs were made of stone. Since he'd been branded, he acted like a shell of the man he was before. He moved about like a wounded cripple. Leaving the Guardians behind, he led the rest of the group down to the vaults below, not stopping until they passed rows of sarcophagi and faced the great mirror in the back. His natural forwardness was gone, replaced by emptiness. "This is the place you seek."

"Get on with it, Leodor. I don't have time for your stalling," the king said.

The group stood in front of a brown canvas covering something hanging from a black wall. Leodor tugged on the fabric while Lewis lifted three candlestands made of bronze from the ground. Skulls were mounted on the tops of the stands. Candles were held firmly in the tops of the skulls. He made a triangle around the group. Leodor's efforts with the cover revealed a ten-foot-by-ten-foot mirror. The bronze frame was made of demonic images.

"What sort of practices have you embraced, Lewis? What perversion flipped your mind inside out?" the king asked.

Lewis looked away from his father with a deep frown on his face.

"So, this is where you speak to the Underlord," King Hector said.

"Yes, Your Majesty," Leodor replied.

Staring at the mirror, the king said, "Well, I didn't come here to look at myself. Summon this Underlord. I want to get a look at him for myself."

"I will warn Your Majesty that this is very dangerous. The Underlord wields great strength. It is imperative that you stay within the barrier." Leodor stepped inside the triangle.

He stuck his finger on the front candlestand's candle wick. A green flame ignited. A fat little demon like a jack-o'-lantern formed with a grin on his face. It jumped from candlestand to candlestand and merged into the last one with a giggling hiss. All the candles burned brightly. Leodor closed his eyelids and started chanting.

The candle flames quavered. Abraham's skin crawled. Dark, disturbing forces that unsettled his soul were at work. He put a hand on his sword as the air shimmered around him. The old Abraham would have bolted. The new one stood fast, strengthened by the steely resolves of Ruger's fearless body.

Their reflection in the great mirror pinwheeled into black, gray, and white. The tiny demonic eyes that dressed the mirror's edge burned like ruby-red beacons. A new image formed in the mirror as it became crystal clear, like a portal to another room. It was a throne room with black curtains outlining panes of glass filled with pale blue light that made for a dreary setting. A man sat on a king's throne made of ebony marble. His cruel expression was old, smooth, and wizened. With eyes like burning sapphires and skin as pale as stone, the man clad in black leather from wrist to ankle rose to his feet and came forward.

King Hector waited behind Lewis and Leodor. Abraham stood right behind him.

The Underlord came closer. From head to toe, he filled the mirror. "Leodor," he said in a strong voice that was as cold as ice. "What news do you bear? Who are these men that come with you?"'

As Lewis and Leodor shrank underneath the Underlord's iron gaze, King Hector pushed between them with his head held high. He spoke with a resounding authority that only the king could manifest. "I am no man. I am the king!"

The Underlord's dark, beady eyes widened as his head recoiled. "What treachery is this?"

"Am I to understand that you don't know treachery when you see it? That's disappointing to hear from a serpent as vile as you." King Hector pointed at the Underlord. "Wait a moment. You may have changed your image, but I know that face. You can't hide behind those veins of yours. Yes, yes, that build and frame, so womanly, but still a man. Arcayis! Ha, it is you, isn't it, you loathsome swine?"

"Mind your tongue, you spoiled brat," the Underlord said. "This switch I bring on you this time you'll never forget." His bright burning eyes darkened. "It will be fatal next time."

Abraham couldn't help himself and butted in. "You know this man?"

King Hector gave him a quick look and said, "Oh yes, I know this worm. This scum of the sewers. He was my father's right-hand mystic, much like Leodor." He glared at the forward mystic. "And betrayed him. I was a boy, very young, but I was around when this leech was banished. Hmmm." He rubbed his chin. "And now it seems that the crap has finally risen to the surface."

"You are the same fool that your father was, Hector. Except you are still the same naïve, pompous, useless brat." The Underlord spat after he spewed out the last words. "Your kingdom has unraveled beneath you." He spread his arms wide. "I control all of the armies north of you. I manipulate your cities. I am the shadows. I am the wind." He held out a stone the size of his finger. It was a dark-blue sapphire burning with the radiant fire of a star, much like the similar emerald the king held. He smiled like a crocodile. "I am Kingsland's end."

"You are a bag of wind!" Hector said with growing agitation.

"Good-bye, Hector. Enjoy your throne." Arcayis the Underlord walked backward. "And you can have those two stooges. I never really needed them anyway. For every one of them, I have many. And I have weapons the likes of which you've never seen before." With a wave of his hand, the image of the mirror faded.

Abraham stood staring at the reflection in the mirror. The king's eyes were heavy with worry.

Lewis and Leodor appeared uncertain. Abraham wanted to return home. Whoever Arcayis was, his reappearance shook the king visibly. Even though the king showed strength in the moment, he seemed to have aged.

"Are you okay?" Abraham asked.

King Hector gave Abraham a blank stare. Then his eyes hardened. He turned on Leodor and grabbed him by the neck. He pushed the former viceroy to his knees. "Leodor, what do you know about him? I want to know everything."

CHAPTER 73

EARLY IN THE NIGHT, ABRAHAM and Sticks separated from the king and made the long walk on the country roads back to the Stronghold. Some frightening things appeared to be going on in Kingsland. The once-peaceful land by the sea had become a place burdened by mistrust. He needed answers about his predicament. His gut told him that the Underlord might be someone that could help him. *If King Hector couldn't trust his own son, whom could he trust? Whom can I trust?*

Walking side by side with Sticks, he bumped shoulders with her. "How's your brand?"

"I'd be lying if I said it didn't hurt, but it will go away. I've been branded before," she said as she pulled her jerkin open, revealing the puffy pinkish-red wound. "Looks worse than it feels."

"Why did you do it? I mean, you could have started a new life."

"True, but I didn't have much of a life before I was branded, and I like being a Henchman." She gave him the eye. "There isn't anything wrong with that, is there? You almost sound disappointed."

He shook his head. "No, no, not at all. I mean, I don't have anyone else. I just wanted to make sure that you did it for yourself and not me." He gave her a sheepish look and said, "You didn't do it because you're in love with me, did you?"

"Ha ha," she said in a very dry manner. "Just because you're the last man I slept with doesn't mean you're going to be the last man that I sleep with. Don't get me wrong, I enjoy your company, but what I do, I do for me and the king. I like the purpose it gives me."

Sticks was as easy to read as a blank wall. Abraham was pretty sure she could keep her feelings to herself, and only she would know them. If she cared deeply, she wouldn't show it. If she hated him, she wouldn't show that either.

"It's not about me," Abraham said. "I figured it was possible that maybe you and Ruger had a deeper thing that I wouldn't be aware of."

"We didn't. With the last personality, it was only sexual."

Abraham couldn't help but smile. "If you say so, Lilith. That's good to know."

"Who's Lilith?"

"A frosty woman from a TV show. I'm not so sure you'd understand."

"Ah, from your world."

"Yes, a place where everybody knows my name."

They took the rest of the long walk in silence. The road to the Stronghold had become roughshod from all the king's horses and all the king's men. The smell of burning pitch and charred wood lingered heavy in the air. Smoke came out of the chimney's stack. Abraham scanned the area. The barn had burned to the ground, and heat was still rising from the ash. The split-rail fencing, aside from a few posts, was gone, burned with the rest of the wood piles used to smoke them out. It had been one helluva day. He wasn't sure how Ruger's body had held up under the grueling tasks he'd performed, but he felt fine. He stopped in front of the barn's ashes. It was the last place he'd seen Solomon.

"If his bones are in there, I don't want to know," he said.

Together, they went back inside the Stronghold. He expected to see some of the hirelings, but what he didn't expect to see was all the seats at table filled with the Henchmen. All of them turned and looked at him. Horace was in his usual seat, leaning heavily on his forearms. Dominga and Vern leaned against one another, battered from head to toe. Bearclaw had cuts on his arms and face. Cudgel and Tark stopped talking to look in Abraham's direction. Apollo and Prospero looked no different than they normally did, dirty and a little deranged. Iris got up from her seat, shuffled over to Abraham, and gave him a hug.

Slowly, Abraham walked into the room, eyeballing all of them, and said, "So, what's going on?"

"Captain, we've been conversing while we waited for your return," Horace said. He squeezed his eyes shut and grimaced before opening them wide again. "Did matters fare well with the king?"

"I don't think any of the king's business is going well." Feeling uncertain, Abraham pulled back his chair at the head of the table as Sticks took her seat across from Horace. "So, what was it that you were discussing?"

Horace looked down the rows of hardened men and women and said, "We want to be branded again. We want to stay Henchmen."

Abraham's eyebrows lifted. "All of you?" He looked at Vern when he said it.

The swordsman had taken more lumps than the rest of the group. His right eye was black, and he had a gash over the top of his head with a crude white bandage over it.

"Even me," Vern said through split lips.

"You don't want to be a part of the King's Guardians?" Abraham asked.

Bearclaw spoke up and said, "Lewis was such a jerkoff we decided against it. We'd made our minds up even before what happened today. And Pratt, well, horse-neck can have it. There is no sense in working with a man with a grudge against you."

"I don't think his grudge is against me but, rather, the old me." He waved his hands, tilted his head, and said, "Did you say *jerkoff*?"

"Is that not the proper use of it?" Bearclaw said.

"No, that's right, I didn't realize you'd picked that word up from me. It sounded strange coming from you, that's all." Abraham studied their eyes, which were looking right back at him.

The intent they wore on their faces was clear. They wanted to be Henchmen for some crazy reason. Inside his heart, he felt relief. If he was going to get out of this world, he would need help. He couldn't think of any better people than them. "Listen, I want to be clear about something." He touched his chest with his fingers. "I'm not from this world. I want to find my way home. I don't want to use you to do that. And what if Ruger changes again?"

Horace laid a heavy hand on his forearm. "No disrespect, Captain, but we've discussed that. We want to be Henchmen."

At a loss for words, Abraham blinked and managed to say, "None taken." He looked at the fireplace. The King's Brand was propped up against the hearth. The fire logs burned within. Abraham rose from his chair, picked up the brand, and put it in the fire. "I'm not going to mince words. Who's first?"

The branding started with Horace. The bearded and bald warrior stood on a shaky knee. The brand seared his hair and flesh, and he let out a joyous shout. After him went Bearclaw, Vern, Dominga, Tark, Cudgel, Iris, and Prospero. The scruffy-looking Apollo finished it off, holding his nose and shouting, "Shew! That's a stink you never forget!"

The great room was filled with painful grins as the Henchmen exchanged handshakes with one another. The hireling women brought in pitchers of wine and ale from the cellars and placed them on the table before waddling off again.

Abraham stood with the brand in the fire, scorching off any flecks of hair and flesh. The small chatter in the room quieted. A presence entered the room. He turned. Solomon stood inside of the front doorway.

"You're alive," Abraham said. "I thought you were burned alive. Where have you been?"

The troglin lifted up a long arm and wiggled his fingers. "I've been hiding. This race has a knack for hiding in the woodland." He walked over to Abraham and took a knee. "I've been waiting for your return. I wasn't sure how the others would receive me without you present." He glanced at Horace. "Brand me."

"What?" Abraham said. "Are you sure?"

"You heard me. It's not the hippy thing to do, but I need you, and you need me." He closed his eyes. "Get it over with. Brand me."

Abraham stuck the brand on Solomon's chest. The skin and hair sizzled.

Solomon let out a wild howl. Clutching his chest, he said, "Man, that was a stupid idea!"

"It will pass." Abraham slapped Solomon on the shoulder and extended a hand. "Welcome to the Henchmen."

CHAPTER 74

Abraham was summoned to the House of Steel, where he alone met with the king, queen, prince, princess, and ex-viceroy on the terrace that overlooked the Bay of Elders. Long looks were on the faces of everyone sitting at the long patio table. None was longer than King Hector's, who sat at the head. He was in a heated discussion with Clarice.

"Clarice, my daughter, my dearest, just because you have the King's Brand, it doesn't mean that you are required to go anywhere. You will stay at the castle, and that is final." King Hector rubbed his temples and sighed. "Why would you burden me with such a mad request?"

"Father, I am a woman, free to choose my own future. I don't want to be pampered and spoiled," Clarice said. She wore a black leather tunic, and her hair flowed back in a ponytail. "You see how that turned out with Lewis. This way, I can never betray you or the kingdom."

"Watch your mouth, you brattish hedgehog," Lewis said. "If you and your mother weren't in the picture, there wouldn't be an issue. You should have stayed in the streets where you belong. Instead, you've poisoned the bloodline."

"You are the one that poisoned the bloodline, Son, not Clarice," King Hector said. He noticed Abraham standing away from the table. "Oh, you're here. Good." He cast his glance behind Abraham to where Pratt, the new captain of the King's Guardians, stood. The knight seemed like a giant in his suit of full-plate armor. "Pratt, thank you for bringing him up. See to it that our privacy is maintained." King Hector got up, then reached down and squeezed the queen's hand. "Talk some sense into our daughter."

Queen Clarann gave the king a warm smile and said, "I will." When the king turned away, her beautiful light eyes fixed on Ruger and searched his for a moment.

Abraham nodded and followed after the king to the outer wall. The queen's deep look made the heart inside his body jump. *What was that all about?* Something had told him something more might have existed between Ruger and the Queen—he'd seen those looks before. *But what?* If something was there, only she knew. He looked back, but the queen was in a deep conversation with Lewis and Clarice.

He moved beside the king at the wall, hitched his thumbs inside his sword belt, and asked, "Did Leodor share anything revealing about the Underlord?"

"It appears that the fool is just a pawn. The same as my son was. Disgusting." From a pouch of bird seed and crumbs, he started feeding the sea birds flocking toward him. He flicked crumbs of bread at them. The gray-white birds would dive after what they didn't catch in the air. "I can't have a lineage to my heritage if I don't have a trustworthy son."

"Surely you have other sons and daughters?"

The king gave him a puzzled look and said, "I forget that you don't know things as you did. But Lewis is the one we have to dance with." He reached inside his green raiment and pulled out the colorful cube. "The Cube of Rubix. As you can see, I've completed one side," he said proudly. One side of the cube was green. "Tell me honestly—will it truly grant me a wish if I solve it?"

Abraham struggled between the truth or the lie but chose the truth. "No, I only told you that to save my own skin."

"That's too bad. I could really use a wish right now." King Hector twisted the blocks of the cube around. He looked as if he'd aged ten years in a day. "It is fun. Do me a favor. Don't tell Leodor that it lacks magical properties. It will be another carrot that I dangle before him if the need ever be."

"I won't, and I apologize."

"It is I that should be apologizing to you."

The way the king said that and looked at him made his hairs stand on end. "For what?"

"For using you, a stranger, in this strange world. After my lengthy discussions with Leodor and a thorough search of the library's annals, I've come to the conclusion that the only way to save this kingdom is to complete the Crown of Stones." He pointed at the crown on his head with six empty settings. "I have one stone. I believe that Arcayis has one other. I'm not sure what power it wields, but whoever has them all will have the power to reunite the kingdoms or dismantle them forever." He put the cube away. "You'll lead the Henchmen to find the remaining stones before Arcayis does. When that is complete, I'll see what I can do to help you find a way back to your world. Selfishly, I admit, I need you."

Abraham had hoped he would be given some time to sort through his own dilemma. Now he'd been placed in charge of a grand quest that he didn't want any part of. But he'd promised to help the king, and perhaps helping the king would help himself. Besides, if they found another portal back... *Who could stop me from going home?*

"I'll do my best, but I'm still a fish out of water in this world. Are you sure that you want to put your trust in me?"

"Regrettably, you're the only one proven to be trustworthy so far." The king set down the bag of bird meal and dusted off his hands. He stared down at the ships docked in the Bay of Elders. His eyes searched the skies where flocks of huge birds flew in the distance. "According to Leodor, you will have the better understanding of the artifacts that Arcayis claims to wield. I assume they are objects like the ones that you brought. It will give us an edge, I hope."

"Knowledge can be a dangerous thing. I hope what I have will best serve you." He followed the king's line of sight to the unusual flock of birds flying in wide circles far away. "I'll do my best, but can Leodor be trusted?"

"That's why I branded him. He can't call on the Sect. They'll kill him. And he believes that the Underlord is the head of them. It makes sense. I didn't know Arcayis deeply as a boy, but I know enough to know that he was a worm. How he manipulated my father so long I don't understand."

"Perhaps he turned. People change. It happens all of the time in my world."

Abraham's eyes widened as the great birds flew right toward the castle wall at a high rate of speed. Several of them were flying in a diamond formation. Riders rose up from the back of the birds, but the birds had scales. They weren't birds—they were dragons, with ruddy scales and hard spiny ridges on their bodies the size of horses.

"Your Majesty, those are dragons, aren't they?"

Clarice rushed over to the wall beside her father. "Zillon dragon riders!" she exclaimed. "I can't believe it!" She started waving.

The king lifted his chin, raised his eyebrows, and made a weak smile. "Long-standing allies," he said to Abraham. "From the Peaks of Little Leg. It seems they come to show support. A good sign from the Elders."

The zillon dragon riders formed a ring and circled about one hundred yards away from the wall. The zillons wore open-faced metal helmets with small purple plumes waving from the tops. They had skull faces and big black eyes, very much like aliens from movies, but they were built like men. They were shirtless and wore leather breeches. The dragons they rode were ugly lizards with wings and a little bigger than horses. They gave Abraham the creeps.

"Uh, are you sure that they are on your side?" he asked.

"They've never not been on the side of the crown," the king said as everyone now stood along the wall. "The zillons are renowned peacekeepers and fighters. That's how they keep the peace. Why?"

Abraham shrugged and said, "Because I feel like fire ants are crawling up my back." He leaned outward and narrowed his eyes. The lead zillon rider unshouldered what looked like a rifle. The zillon rider butted the weapon on his shoulder and pointed it at the king. A red dot brightened on the weapon. The same dot appeared on King Hector's chest.

King Hector looked at the laser dot on his chest and tried to brush it away. "What is this? A glow fly? I've never seen the likes of it before."

Abraham sprang into action. "Everybody, get down!"

He tackled the king just as a hail of gunfire began. The stone wall of the terrace spat chunks of rock as bullets blasted into it. The steady spray of bullets kept coming with a loud popping sound.

"Stay down! Everyone stay down!"

The king started yelling. "Archers! Archers! Pratt, summon the archers!"

A sharp whistle cut through the sound of the advanced weaponry being fired. Archers appeared on top of the castle, wearing acorn-shaped helmets. They drew their bows and fired from the castle roof in kneeling positions. Arrows sailed over the Bay of Elders to the snap of bowstrings.

Abraham dared a peek over the wall. Only one of the six zillons carried a rifle. The other five carried crossbows, and they returned their own volley toward the archers. They unleashed one last hail of crossbow bolts and gunfire. More stones were chipped away. The enemy turned the dragons away and flew back toward the coast of Little Leg.

"What in the Elders was that popping sound?" King Hector asked as he crouched behind the wall.

"That was an assault rifle. It makes a very distinct firing sound," Abraham said as the zillons distanced themselves. "It's a weapon soldiers use in my world. It's like a hundred bows in one." He scanned the group. "Is everyone okay?"

Clarann was covering Clarice with her body, but they seemed fine otherwise. Lewis and Leodor were wide-eyed but fine as well. On top of the castle roof, one of the archers lay over the rim, dangling lifelessly.

Pratt jogged over to the king. His head was bleeding, as though something had grazed his skull. "Sire, I'll send riders to destroy those assassins. Just say the word, Your Majesty."

"Keep your eyes on the skies, Pratt! It seems we have new enemies afoot. How disappointing." The king looked down on his robes and dusted his chest. "Where did that bright mark go?"

"It's gone. With them," Abraham said. "That was a laser pointer. They use it to aim at a target. I guess they were aiming at you."

The king gave Abraham a dumbfounded look and asked, "Did you say that weapon, eh, assault rifle, was like one hundred bows in one?"

"Sadly, I think that's a fair assessment. It's a good thing that they only had one." Abraham's heart beat in his ears. Something crazy was going on. He searched the skies. "And you better pray that they don't have more of them."

THE KING'S PRISONER

CRAIG HALLORAN

CHAPTER 1

ABRAHAM STOOD INSIDE THE CAPTAIN'S quarters of the pirate ship *Sea Talon*. He and the Henchmen had acquired it after he battled the terrifying Flamebeard, a notorious pirate of great repute. That was his first official sword fight—at least, for him. The same couldn't be said for the body that his mind currently occupied. Supposedly, Ruger Slade was one of the greatest swordsmen in the world called Titanuus. Now, Abraham was him.

Clasping his hands behind his back and rolling his thumbs over each other, he looked out his windows, which gave him a full view of the churning seas. The boat rocked and swayed, and the floorboards and walls groaned. The china on his small dining table rattled and bounced. Abraham's eyes were locked on another ship much like *Sea Talon*. The ship in pursuit had sails with black stripes crossing a field of maroon. It had given chase hours before, and two more ships sailed behind it. The Henchmen were in the enemy waters of Tiotan, headed north on a bold journey.

"I never figured myself for a navy guy," Abraham said.

His words were met with silence as he was the only person in the room. The captain's cabin was dim and wall to wall with dark polished wood. Most of the other hands were on deck, keeping a close eye on the closing enemy. The boat rocked, but Abraham's feet remained steady. His new body was no stranger to the seas. It didn't seem to be a stranger to anything. Ruger Slade's body was cold and as fearless as they came.

A hard knocking came at his cabin door.

"What?" he asked with irritation.

"Permission to enter, Captain?" a grizzly-voiced man said.

Abraham turned and faced the door. "Come in, Horace."

The door creaked open, and Horace entered. He was a bald-headed and thick-bearded bear of a man, wearing a sleeveless tunic that showed off his hairy, beefy arms that hid iron muscle underneath. The buttons of his leather tunic strained to keep his belly in one place. "Captain, Lewis and Leodor are having a tantrum on deck. They have everyone confused on who they should be listening to. He's tossing his heritage around."

Abraham's nostrils flared as he breathed in deeply. Lewis and Leodor were proving to be nothing but a royal pain in his backside. They were newly branded Henchmen, but the headstrong men had been nothing but obstinate since their sea quest began over a day before.

"Why don't you throw them overboard?" Abraham suggested.

Horace tilted his head toward Abraham and said, "Captain?"

"You know, have them walk the plank. Feed them to the sharks. Put chains on their legs and drop them to the bottom of the sea."

"Er… Aye, Captain." Horace turned around to exit the room.

"No, stop. I'll handle it." Abraham grabbed his sword belt, looped around the headboard post, and buckled it on. He ran his fingers over the leather grip of Black Bane like a gunslinger before an old western standoff.

Over one week before, zillon dragon riders from the territory of Hancha had flown across the Bay of Elders and tried to assassinate King Hector. They did it using a modern assault rifle that unleashed a dangerous hail of bullets. He managed to save the king's life. The old man was indebted, but he was determined to learn more about his enemies and their strange artifacts. He peppered Abraham with questions.

In a private group, he met with Queen Clarann, Pratt, Leodor, and Lewis. For two days, Abraham talked at length about his world. That seemed strange, but it brought him some comfort. With his help, they tried to get a handle on what they were up against. Arcayis the Underlord had made a bold move against King Hector. At least, that was where Hector laid the blame, and Abraham agreed with him. After all, Arcayis had made the threat. He followed up on it too.

King Hector vowed vengeance. He hatched a new plan: kill the Underlord. The froward viceroy, Leodor, let out a doubting laugh that drew the king's ire. King Hector busted the man across the jaw, and Leodor collapsed like a tent. Lewis laughed, but his chortling was quickly cut off by the king's glare. Abraham inwardly grinned at it all, but nothing delighted him more than the king's plan. The king wanted the head of the snake, and that line of thinking was right up Abraham's alley. It awakened the dominating spirit in him, lighting a fire under Jenkins the Jet.

Now, the original mission was askew. Originally, the king had wanted the stones from the crown found. He wanted the Crown of Stones restored. But now, he wanted his biggest threat dead: the Underlord. And the Henchmen had been sent to do it.

Abraham followed Horace up the stairs, which groaned under the weight of the hardy men. The ship pitched left, and Horace leaned into the wall of the shallow stairwell. Abraham didn't. At the top, the chill winds of the sea breeze bristled Horace's beard and Abraham's hair. Lewis and Leodor were waiting. So was Sticks, dressed the same as always, tight leather breeches, a loose white cotton jerkin, and a bandolier of knives across her shoulder. Her short dark hair and cute expressionless face made her fetching, in simple garb and gear.

Lewis faced Abraham. He was tapping his foot and still wore the same cap and the black leather armor under his clothing. The wind kept his hair in his eyes, though he kept sweeping it away. "What is your plan, Ruger? Those Tiotan warships are gaining on us. And in case you didn't notice, there are three of them and only one of us. You need to make a decision."

"And you need to shut up," Abraham said. "And you better stop ordering my men around. The only reason they are gaining is because we're losing wind 'cause your mouth is open."

Lewis's jaws clenched, and his eyes narrowed. His fingers drummed on the handle of his sword. "You should watch your tongue."

Abraham stepped toward Lewis. They were almost the same height, but Ruger was taller and thicker in frame.

"Are you going to draw that steel or stand there tickling the handle?" Abraham asked.

CHAPTER 2

LEWIS CAME NOSE TO NOSE with Abraham and said, "If it weren't for this ridiculous branding, I'd carve you up like a turkey."

"If it weren't for the brand, you'd be dead. Your own father would have hanged you," Abraham replied.

With a deepening frown, Lewis leaned back. He took his hand from the handle of his sword and said, "Someone had to take charge while you were stewing in your quarters."

"And that someone would be Horace."

Abraham brushed the hair from his eyes to take a head count of the Henchmen. The day at sea was sunny, and the scruffy fighters Apollo and Prospero were above in the crow's nest. At the front of the ship, on the foredeck, was the ebony sprite of a woman, Dominga, dressed in snug leathers. Vern was with her, geared up in his tunic and chain mail. The rest of the crew was dressed in a sailing outfit or some sort of pirate's garb.

The brothers, smoky-eyed Tark and Cudgel, searched the seas on the starboard side. The broad-faced and fierce-looking Bearclaw worked with the new Red Tunics, brothers, Skitts and Zann, who mopped the decks. Skitts was a well-built young man with a farmer's rugged frame. Zann was lean and moved slow, smooth, and easy. Also, a few holdover pirates from Flame Beard's crew had stayed with *Sea Talon*. All the men and women stayed busy. The sweet, pie-faced mystic, Iris, was prepping meals in the galley below.

Solomon Paige, the troglin, was on board but nowhere to be found. He hadn't come on deck since they'd departed.

Abraham moved up to the poop deck and gazed at the trailing ships. Horace, Sticks, Lewis, and Leodor climbed up the steps from behind him. He set his foot on the back rail and leaned forward.

In his strong voice, he spoke over the winds. "This is what we are going to do. We'll let them catch up with us."

"Are you insane?" the flummoxed Lewis asked. "If they don't butcher us, they'll enslave us! This is how you operate? With blatant stupidity?"

"No, that's how you operate," Abraham said as he turned. "There is a reason we stripped down this ship and put merchant's sails on it. All the markings of Flame Beard are gone. It's called preparation. We knew this would happen. That's why we disguised ourselves."

No one looked much different than they normally did, but nobody else would know that.

"This is what Henchmen do." Abraham looked at Lewis and Leodor. "You should know that. After all, you are the one that put a spy in our camp."

Leodor swallowed and pulled his billowing robes closer around his frail body.

Lewis shook his head. "You'll get us all killed before we even make it past the Left Arm. We should outrun them."

"And look guilty? It only makes sense that *you* would think that way. No, if anything, we should slow down a little."

"What if one of them recognizes me?" Lewis whined. "I'm the prince, a valuable prisoner."

"Ah, that's perfect. We can use you to barter for our release if need be." Abraham nodded with enthusiasm. "I never realized that advantage until now." He laid a hand on Lewis's shoulder. "Thanks for pointing that out."

Lewis slapped Abraham's hand aside. "I hate you." He departed with Leodor.

As Horace watched the two men go, he said, "I agree with your earlier sentiment. We should toss them overboard."

Sticks nodded. "I wonder if the brand will allow us to do that. Can one Henchman turn against another?"

Abraham shrugged. He didn't have time to worry about Lewis's hurt feelings or whatever troubles the man might cause. He had three warships to worry about. "Horace, go ahead and peel back on our speed, but not too much. We'll just have to wait and see what happens."

"Aye, Captain." Horace headed off the poop deck and barked new orders to the crew.

Sticks looked at Abraham with a straight face, as hard to read as ever.

"What's on your mind?" he asked.

"Nothing."

"It doesn't look like nothing… even though it's hard to tell. Do you disagree with my plan?"

"No," she said. "We've done similar things in the past. Sometimes it works, and sometimes it doesn't."

"Do you think this won't work?"

"I don't know, but we can't outrun them."

"Thanks for nothing."

She tilted her head. "You asked."

"Just make sure that everyone is ready. Tell them to stay calm. Me and Horace will do the talking."

Sticks turned and walked away. He couldn't help but notice her walk in those tight leather breeches. Sticks had something he'd always liked, though putting his finger on it was hard. As soon as she went down the steps, Iris came hurrying up. The curvy mystic's eyes were wide and her robes disheveled.

"What's wrong?" he asked.

Iris brushed away her wavy brown locks, which had blown into her face, and said, "We have stowaways!"

CHAPTER 3

"What sort of stowaways?" Abraham asked. The last things he wanted to see were the Frights. The strange albino, reddish-pink-eyed witches came to mind.

"I don't know. I was in the supply deck, gathering goods for cooking," Iris said as she led the way down the steps into the ship's hold. "I scooted aside some chests and barrels. That's when I saw a set of eyes looking right back at me." She stopped midway down the steps and grabbed Abraham's hand to place it right over her bosom. "Can you feel that? My heart jumps. It races." She smiled at him. "It's still racing."

"Yeah, I bet it is," he said as he pulled his hand away. "Are you sure you saw someone?"

"What I didn't see, I smelled. There are people in the hold. A bit fragrant at that, like perfume." She scuttered to the bottom of the steps and into the supply rooms, poorly lit by the ship's portals. She sniffed the air. "Do you smell that?"

Abraham's nostrils twitched, but it wasn't by any desire of his own. It was more of a reflex of Ruger's. He narrowed his eyes. The storeroom was loaded with crates and barrels. "Where?" he asked Iris.

Iris pointed toward the back of the storage room. A wall of barrels was stacked there, one upon another, and tied down with rope. Wooden crates sat waist-high on the floor.

She fastened her fingers in Abraham's pants and pressed her body behind his. "Protect me."

He couldn't tell whether she was fooling around or not. Perhaps this was a ploy to get him alone. She'd been close to Horace but always flirted with Abraham. With her tied to his rear end, he made his approach toward the back. The boat pitched hard, and some dry goods stored in the rafters fell from their perch in a storage net behind the barrels. A gasp escaped from behind the barrels.

Abraham pulled his sword. "All right. We know you are in there." He shook his head, realizing he'd used a line spoken in countless shows and movies. "Come on out. I'm serious." *I know that smell.*

No one said a word or moved. Iris's fingers started working their way across his abdomen and feeling his hard muscles. He ignored her.

"Listen, I heard your voice, and I can smell your perfume. If you won't come out, then I'll uncage the rats, the big ones that eat toes and fingers for breakfast."

A figure rose from behind the barrels. She had beautiful eyes and a rounded teardrop face. She wasn't very tall but was young and full-figured. It was Princess Clarice.

"What in the world are you doing here?" Abraham sheathed his sword.

"I'm a Henchman. I belong here." Clarice stepped out from behind the barrels, followed by two more women, taller than her, cloaked, and very pretty. "And now, I'm here."

"Are you out of your mind? Your father, King Hector, was very clear. You stay at the castle. He didn't want you going on this mission." Abraham wanted to grab the young woman and shake some sense into her. He had enough to deal with as things were. "And who are they?"

"These are my guardian maidens, Hazel and Swan." The women were attractive, in their thirties or possibly forties, stern looking with their hair pulled back tightly. They wore well-crafted, curve-enhancing breastplate armor with tight leather leggings

"Guardian maidens? Wow. They sound like a real big help." He rolled his eyes and pulled Iris's hands away from his waist. "There's your stowaways. I wish you never even found them, but you can have them. Your father must be having a fit trying to find you. Your timing couldn't be worse."

"No, I told my maidens to let them know what I did long after I'm gone. He'll have to understand. We only hid down here until you got far enough away that you couldn't turn around."

"Clever." He pointed in her face. "Don't think for one minute that I won't turn this boat around."

One of the guardian maidens sliced a dagger at his fingers, and he jerked his hand away in the nick of time. The two tall women formed a shield in front of Clarice, brandishing daggers.

"You insult the princess, dog," one of them said in a husky voice. Her hair was stone white, where the other's was pitch-black. "You must pay."

Quicker than the blink of an eye, Abraham yanked the daggers out of both of their hands and tossed them to the floor. "I'm in charge. You're trespassing."

The gaping women's hands went for their belts.

"Don't do it. I'm not in the mood."

The women dropped their hands to their sides.

"It's fine, Hazel and Swan," Clarice said as she stepped through the two guardian women. "Ruger is the Captain of the Henchmen. I'm under his orders, and you're under mine. Do whatever it is that he says. And Ruger, don't worry about my father or mother. My maidens will notify them of my whereabouts when the proper time comes."

"He'll come after you. All you are doing is putting Kingsland in jeopardy. What you did is a very selfish and stupid thing to do."

"It shouldn't surprise you, Ruger. The hierarchy rarely plays by its own rules," someone said in a chill but cocky voice that hadn't been a part of the original conversation.

Abraham found himself looking at a smallish man crammed casually on a storage shelf. The man had a strange mark on his cheek, like a star tattoo or brand. His body was wrapped up in a cloak, and a hood shielded his eyes. He bit into a small green apple, and juice squirted down the short tawny hairs on his chin.

"Who in the hell are you?" Abraham asked.

CHAPTER 4

"SHADES!" IRIS EXCLAIMED. SHE GRABBED a potato out of a barrel and threw it at him.

The man snatched the vegetable out of the air in a fluid motion. "It's good to see you too, Iris."

"You know this guy?" Abraham asked Iris.

Her eyes were hot as flames.

"Of course she does. The curious thing is that you don't, Ruger," Shades said as he started to exit his perch.

Abraham put the tip of his dagger on the man's throat. "Be still if you don't want to start leaking." He studied the man's face. It was familiar. A lot of things were, but he didn't recall the man. Ruger probably did. "Iris, refresh my memory."

"Shades was one of us. A Henchman. You banished him from the group. He was the one that we suspected caused all of the problems," Iris said with a frown.

"What's he doing here?" he asked.

Shades opened his mouth, only to shut it again as Abraham put more pressure on his neck.

"He's with us," Clarice interjected. "Shades snuck us on the ship. He's our guide of sorts."

Abraham put his dagger away and faced Clarice. "You're full of surprises, aren't you? Now I have four stowaways. How'd your paths cross, anyway? He doesn't look like the sort of fella that you would spend time with in the castle."

"My maidens hired him. I don't know him personally. If I'd known he was a Henchman, I'd not have done it," Clarice said unapologetically.

"He's not a Henchman," Iris stated. "And he was one of the king's prisoners in Baracha." She walked up to Shades and punched him in the thigh. "That's where he tried to have us killed. All of us!"

"When did this happen?" Abraham asked.

"After we docked at Seaport. We were held in Baracha while you met with the king." Iris's fingertips started glowing. "Shades tried to make us brides to those barbaric savages, the Gond."

"I can explain all of that," Shades said.

"Sure you can, rat dung!" Iris said.

Lewis and Leodor waltzed into the storage room. Lewis had his arms crossed over his chest and said, "I saw you rush off. I wanted to see what you were…" His voice trailed off as his widening eyes landed on his half sister. "You! What are you doing here? Ruger, what treachery is this?"

"Lighten up, Lewis," Abraham said. "Your sister is a stowaway. Apparently, she misses you."

"I do not!" Clarice said like a child.

"You little brat. You snuck onto this ship for what purpose?" Lewis asked. "To continue to be a thorn in my side. It's bad enough I had to rescue you once, but now I have to take you back again. Ruger, turn the ship around."

"I'm not turning anything around," Abraham said, realizing at that moment that he was beginning to respond more easily to the name *Ruger*. "In case you have forgotten, we have three warships that we have to deal with. We'll sort this out after that."

The long-faced Leodor stepped forward, his hands hidden in his sleeves. "Ruger, I would suggest that the princess be returned immediately. She and Lewis are valued by the enemy. They'll only use them for leverage against the crown."

With the butt of his palm bouncing on the pommel of Black Bane, he said, "This mission would have been a whole lot easier if neither one of them would have come."

"Ruger, my maidens want to become Henchmen, like me," Clarice said. "Can you brand them? That way, you'll know that we all have to be loyal to the king."

"It doesn't work like that," he said. "You're supposed to earn the brand. You have to prove yourself. You"—he pointed his finger at the princess—"and these two sandbags"—he pointed at Lewis and Leodor—"didn't earn it. The brand was used to save their necks. You were given it because you have a big heart, but you're hardheaded and spoiled. The three of you are nothing but baggage on this mission. We have to work as one. None of you seems to get it." He looked down at Clarice. "Let me make this clear, little sister. No one gets branded by me until they earn it."

"What if you had a brand and lost it?" Shades said.

"Iris, what is this clown talking about?"

The mystic reached up into Shades's hood, grabbed him by the ear, and pulled him off the shelf. He landed easily on his feet. He wasn't very tall for a man.

She reached into his clothing and felt his chest and said, "His brand is gone."

"Yes, my chest started smoking suddenly, and to be frank, it scared the skin right off of me. It took some investigating on my part, but I was able to put together what happened. Apparently, my freedom was granted, but no one stopped by Baracha to tell me."

"There would be a good reason for that." Iris tried to punch him in the crotch, but Shades turned his hips and blocked her effort. "I might not get you, but once the others find out you're here, they'll handle it for me."

"I can explain," Shades said.

"I don't care," the mystic replied.

"Who is the tiny man?" Lewis asked.

"That's your baby sister's guide," Abraham said.

"Don't call me that!" Clarice said.

"Yes, please don't call her my sister," Lewis requested. "Even though I do find *baby* to be perfectly fitting."

Horace's booming voice carried throughout the galley. "Captain! The warships are coming alongside. They are signaling for us to drop anchor. What do you want us to do?"

"Just wait. I'll be up."

Horace shouted back, "They don't look like they want to wait. They look like they want a fight."

CHAPTER 5

Before Abraham rushed topside like a chicken with its head cut off, he searched the lower holds for Solomon. The troglin had alluded to being very adept at hiding, and inside the bowels of a tightly quartered ship, that proved to be true.

"Solomon! Solomon! Where are you?"

"Never too far away. Never too near," the troglin said.

Abraham spun around. Solomon was squatting behind him with his neck bent over. The hairy old bigfoot, who normally stood eight feet tall, filled the narrow corridor between the storage areas.

"Are you all right?" Abraham asked.

"I have no idea. Would you be all right if you were a troglin?"

"Listen, I don't have time to discuss what you're going through. But I might need you topside. Tiotan warships are knocking at the door."

Solomon sighed as he used his long fingers to play with the long hairs underneath his chin. "I might look like a monster, but I'm not an apt fighter. Actually, I'm more or less a coward. You know how we hippies can be. We are peaceful. Abhor violence."

"I know, and you abstain from meat. Look, no disrespect, but you're a Henchman now. The sooner you learn to let those hairy knuckles of yours get bloody, the better. It's going to be a fight if we want to get back home."

"Anything is better than this," Solomon said as he gazed upon the naked palms of his hands. "Anything."

"The triplets didn't seem to mind your company, right?"

Solomon showed some teeth. "That's true." He scratched his head. "Huh."

"Now quit moping. Just make yourself available if I call." He put a hand on Solomon's big shoulder. "We'll get through this."

"If you say so. Just give me a shout," the troglin said.

Abraham tried to pass Solomon, which made for an awkward moment as he couldn't squeeze by. "We're gonna have to have this dance later. You need to back it up."

Solomon silently maneuvered his way backward and vanished into the blackness of one of the storage rooms.

Without a second glance, Abraham headed back up on deck. His brows rose. Two warships had flanked *Sea Talon*. They cut through the waves less than a stone's throw away. Soldiers were lined up along the railing, numbering in the dozens. They wore metal skullcaps with nose guards, and the spears they carried pointed toward the sky. Their leather armor was dyed a rich maroon and trimmed in black clothing underneath the supple gear.

Sticks slid alongside and said, "So glad you could join us. What are your orders? Perhaps we add more of them to your crew, along with the others." Her eyes were on Clarice and her maidens, standing by the mainmast.

There was no sign of Shades.

"One thing at a time," Abraham said. His crew was manning their stations, not a nervous look among them, except for Lewis and Leodor, who stood near the guardian maidens.

Abraham sought out Horace, standing at the helm, and shouted up to him, "Lower the sails and drop anchor!"

Lewis marched right up to him. "We'll be dead men if they attack us."

"No, you'll be a dead man. I'm confident the rest of the Henchmen can handle it."

Lewis turned his nose and walked away.

The crew of *Sea Talon* lowered the sails, and the ship slowed. The anchor was dropped. The Tiotan warships managed to close in within a few dozen feet. Their sailors tossed the grapples across the sea and hooked *Sea Talon*'s rails. Hand over hand, the sailors pulled the warships alongside *Sea Talon*. The boat rocked when they hit. The Tiotan soldiers stood almost eye to eye with Abraham's crew. None of the men or women blinked.

"Ahoy!" a man shouted from the helm of the warship's quarterdeck on the starboard side.

From the same deck on the other warship, on the port side of *Sea Talon*, another man shouted, "Ahoy!"

Abraham sized up the two ship captains. They wore grand maroon hats, like those of old eighteenth-century admirals. Their maroon uniform shirts had many large brass buttons. The decorative shirts had black shoulder pads with tassels. Their tall black leather boots shone. The men were rangy but deep chested, with angular features, and clean shaven. They carried curved sabers on their hips. As best as Abraham could tell, they were twins.

The Tiotan captain on the starboard side spoke with strong, confident, military authority. "Who is our ship's captain?"

Abraham took his place center stage on the main deck, where both of the brothers could clearly see him. "That would be me. I'm Captain, er, Slade."

"I am Captain Rafael Alphonso, of Tiotan, and those are my brothers, Captain Donello Alphonso on your port side, and Captain Sloven Alphonso in the ship behind your rear."

Abraham hadn't even paid attention to the third ship behind him. He couldn't see the other brother.

Captain Alphonso said, "Permission to come aboard? We need to execute an inspection. There are many smugglers and spies traversing the waters these days, and we make a quick account of them."

"Uh, yes, permission granted," Abraham said.

Captain Rafael Alphonso made his way down the steps and politely said, "Please have your ship's manifest ready as we cross. Tell your sailors to keep their distance. I'll have my soldiers gore them if they get too close."

"Yes, yes, absolutely," Abraham said. "Clear Captain Alphonso a path." He looked at the ship on his port side. The other brother was coming down his steps. "For both of them."

The *Sea Talon*'s crew made a path to Abraham wide enough to drive a wagon through. Captains Rafael and Donello Alphonso quickly made their way on board. They marched right up to Abraham. With their hats on, they stood a little taller than him.

Awkwardly, he said, "Welcome aboard."

"Spare me the pleasantries. I'm a quick judge of character, and your ship has stink all over it," Captain Rafael Alphonso said as he and his brother looked about, searching the faces of *Sea Talon*'s crew. The nostrils of his triangular nose widened. "Yes, stink all over it. Where is your manifest?"

CHAPTER 6

Sticks handed a rolled-up manifest to Abraham. Before they departed on their seafaring journey, they'd prepped plenty of documents that matched the supplies they carried. Captain Rafael Alphonso looked down his nose at Sticks. "Is this your first mate, Captain Slade?"

Abraham gave Sticks a sideways glance and said, "Yes."

"Interesting choice. A young boy instead of a seasoned man," Captain Rafael Alphonso said.

"I'm not a boy," Sticks retorted. "I'm a—"

Abraham shoved her away. "Give Captain Alphonso some space, will you? He's very busy."

"Unbridled tongues. No discipline," the other brother, Captain Donello Alphonso, said. "A sure sign of treachery. The boy should be whipped."

Sticks opened her mouth.

Abraham gave her the eye. "I'll see to it unless you'd be interested."

"Not our crew member, but outbursts like that are not tolerated in the ranks of Tiotan. I can assure you of that," Rafael said as he looked over the manifest. "Sugar, meal, grain, rolls of fine silk, pepper, spices, and potatoes. Hmm…" He kept reading the list and muttered, "Hmm… hmm… hmm. We need to verify all of it. This manifest might look authentic, but it smells of forgery. I know. I've destroyed my fair share of pirates posing as merchants. Have you ever heard of Flame Beard?"

"Er… yes," Abraham said.

"We are the reason that he doesn't traverse the Sea of Troubles anymore," Rafael said with pride. "We caught him and his crew smuggling from that wretch of a king, Hector. We slaughtered every last one of his crew." He patted his sword handle, which rattled in the sheath. "And him. My brother and I took Flame Beard down personally. Oh, he was formidable for a large man but no match for our speed."

Abraham wanted to say, "You lying sack of donkey dung. Punk." He held his tongue.

Horace, who stood behind the brother captains, stiffened as his meaty fingers clenched. Abraham didn't take it lightly either. That had been his kill. If anyone was going to boast about it, it should have been him.

"An impressive feat," Abraham said. "I crossed paths with Flame Beard once myself."

Rafael's eyes lifted.

"Let's just say, I'm glad to be here. So, he was smuggling for King Hector, you say?"

"Elders, yes," Donello piped in. He adjusted his large hat. "That's what pirates do. They play both sides, but they are only on their own side. But we caught him harboring the king's spies and killed them. King Hector. His very name makes me want to spit. What sort of man takes children for brides and slaughters innocent women that dare speak out against him?"

Lewis, who was leaning comfortably against the mainmast, shoved off with his shoulders. His handsome eyes narrowed, and the white scar on his lips tightened. Leodor's gentle hand pulled him back by the elbow.

Abraham didn't miss the entirety of the subtle event. Ruger's keen vision and senses never seemed to miss anything. *So, the young windbag still cares for the king. Maybe there is hope yet.* He decided to fan the flames. "From what I understand, ol' King Hector's days are numbered."

"You don't know the half of it," Rafael said as his gaze searched the manifest. "You and your crew better hope that you aren't on the wrong side of the storm that is coming. Kingsland, for all intents and purposes, is dead to the other five lands." He smirked as he rolled up the scroll. "Soon, it will be known as Southern Tiotan."

"Shall we begin the inspection?" Donello asked.

"Yes, brother, bring over the hatchet men." Rafael looked at Abraham. "Make sure that all of your men are on deck. If we cross any strangers, we'll kill them."

Donello waved a group of soldiers over from his ship. There were six of them. They carried hatchets. They saluted their captain and stood at attention.

"Go below. Open everything." Donello took the manifest from Rafael and handed it to the lead hatchet man. "Let us know if you find any surprises. We'll be waiting."

The hatchet men vanished down the steps leading into the bowels of the ship. Within seconds, the sound of wood being hacked into carried up on deck. Rafael and Donello had smug smiles on their faces. With their arms folded over their deep chests, they rocked on their heels.

Abraham fought the urge to bite his nails. Horace had given the order for all hands on deck, but Solomon had never appeared. Abraham popped his thumb knuckle with an index finger.

"Are you nervous, Captain Slade?" Rafael asked.

"No, but I don't like the sound of my cargo being busted open. I'm going to have to repackage all of that."

"If that is all that you have to do, consider yourself fortunate," Rafael said.

Abraham nodded. He scanned the faces of his crew. Horace's, Bearclaw's, and Vern's eyes were as hard as hammered iron. They looked like wildcats ready to spring from their cage. The rest of the crew that he could see were as still as stone, aside from the constant sea breeze stirring their hair. He was confident that the manifest and the cargo would match up, but something about the Captains Alphonso didn't seem right.

One of the hatchet-wielding soldiers hurried up the steps. His eyes were as big as moons. The captains turned to face the man.

Abraham's heartbeat spiked. *Holy baloney, here we go.*

"What is it, Corporal?" Donello asked.

"There is a troglin in the brig," the corporal said.

The brothers' bushy eyebrows almost jumped from their brows. "There's a troglin in the brig?" both men asked.

Rafael spun on the heel of one black leather boot and faced Abraham. "I didn't see any reference to a troglin on the manifest." He bared his teeth and drew his saber. "It's this sort of dishonesty that makes me have to kill people."

CHAPTER 7

Abraham lifted his hands palms out and quickly said, "The troglin is not cargo. He's a prisoner."

Rafael rested the edge of his saber on the top of Abraham's chest. The curved tip of the blade pointed at the soft flesh underneath Abraham's neck. "I don't care if the troglin is a prisoner or cargo—only a fool would not mention a troglin was on board. Captain Slade, I am disappointed. You appeared to be a man with good sense. Instead, you will die like a fool."

Donello lifted a hand and waved his soldiers over. Three dozen men carrying spears climbed from their respective ships onto the deck of *Sea Talon*. They held every crew member at the tip of a spear.

Abraham lifted his hands as his company did the same. "Captain Rafael, Donello, if you please, I can explain."

"Do we look like men that take matters lightly?" Rafael asked. "I didn't become a top commander in Tiotan's navy by bending my ear to every liar that pleaded. I show no mercy to smugglers and especially sympathizers to Kingsland." He leaned forward until the bill of his hat touched Ruger's forehead. "But don't worry, Captain Slade. I'll let some of your sailors live so they can swab the ship's deck with your blood. Then I'll sink it and them with it."

Without batting an eye, Abraham said, "Before you kill us, could you do me one favor?"

"What is your request?"

Abraham didn't know what to say. All he wanted to do was buy time. Then, he came up with something quick. "Make sure that the Sect in Dorcha gets the troglin. That's all I know."

Captain Rafael looked him dead in the eye, pressed the tip of his saber deeper into Abraham's neck without breaking the skin, and said, "No."

Abraham was a split second away from slapping Rafael's blade away when a pleading man's voice cried out from below, in the hold. "No, no, no… apologies! Please don't hurt my men!"

Captain Rafael lowered his sword, and along with his brother, he turned to face the man who scrambled up the stairs.

The man speaking with a thick drunken accent was Shades. He wore lavish robes too big for his body. His tawny hair was messed up underneath a soft cotton nightcap. He stood on the deck and swayed. "I-I… apologize, good captains of Tiotan." He said it with a gusty slur and waddled over to the captains, both of whom towered over him. He hiccupped and reeked of strong wine. "I am Slarten Manliest. A merchant. And this is my ship." He hiccupped again. "Forgive my captain. He means well but is not known for making sound decisions. Only executing orders." He put his arms around both men's waists. "My *henchmen* are rather stupid, but thank the Elders that I am finally awake."

Rafael and Donello looked down their noses at Shades, shoved him aside, and said, "If you would have awakened sooner, perhaps this coming tragedy could have been averted. But it's too late now, little merchant. Join the others."

"Oh, but wait, I think there has been a misunderstanding." Shades's deft hands vanished into his robes and reappeared with two hefty leather pouches that filled his hands. He tossed them lightly up and down, and the bags clinked with the rich sound of coins. "I believe this is what you were looking for." He tossed the sacks to each man.

The brothers caught the bags in their chests. They tested the weight of the coins with short tosses of their own.

"You better pray that these are golden shards," Donella said. "Insult us with silver, and I'll slit your throat first." He peeked in his sack and gave his brother an approving glance. "It's the right color but still light."

"The exchange is not complete. I hoped that your brother would be coming aboard." Shades hiccupped again. "Sorry, my heavy indulgence has made me sloppy." He produced another bag of coins. He handed it to Rafael. "*Hic*. I hope that will do."

Rafael and Donella looked at one another and nodded.

Then Rafael said, "It will. Slarten Manliest, I suggest that you search for a more apt captain when you port." He raised his voice. "Sailors of Tiotan, return to ship."

Without another word, the captains departed along with their crew. The Tiotan crew unhooked their grappling hooks and pushed away. Within minutes, their warships were breaking away from *Sea Talon*. Their grand sails filled with wind again.

Abraham couldn't help but feel dumbfounded at the sudden turn of events. He could have sworn that tense situation would have become a fight to the end, but somehow, Shades had twisted it away.

"So, that was a shakedown. Sweet donuts. I didn't see that coming."

Shades slipped his nightcap off his head and said, "I'll take that as a thanks. Once again, it seems that it's up to me to do all of the quick thinking. *Shakedown*. That's an interesting way of putting it."

The Henchmen encircled Shades. The rogue appeared like a child among the towering men.

"What is this conniving wretch doing here?" Sticks asked in a heated tone.

"As I stated, I'm saving—*ulp*."

Vern had whisked a dagger out of his belt and put it to Shades's throat. "I took one whale of a beating the last time we crossed in Baracha. Now, I can return the favor. Ruger, let me gut this fish."

"Ease off, Vern. I'm not disagreeing with you, but there's some sorting we need to do first," Abraham said. "The men of Tiotan are gone. We live without a scratch. There is something to be said for that."

"We could have killed them," Horace stated.

Abraham nodded. He didn't doubt his men anymore. "I know, but we need to get sailing. We have a mission to complete. Raise the sails. We'll talk later."

Vern jammed his dagger into his belt. His burning stare passed between Abraham and Shades. He looked the rogue dead in the eye and said, "I'll get you. No Gond to save you now."

Tark put a hand on Vern's shoulder and led him away. "You aren't alone, brother. We all want a piece of him. And we'll have it."

CHAPTER 8

IN ORDER TO SETTLE THE unease carrying through the ship, Shades was put in the brig. He was kept under guard too, by Solomon, which left Shades's eyes wide and mouth gaping. This gave Abraham time to sort matters out. He had four stowaways on board: Clarice, Hazel, Swan, and Shades. One was a Henchman and another a former Henchman. He trusted the ones he knew, but he had two more bags of trouble whom he didn't trust: Lewis and Leodor. So he called a meeting.

In order to keep the peace, he summoned Sticks, Horace, Bearclaw, Vern, and Iris to the private meeting in his quarters. He had Tark and Cudgel stand guard at the door. If they listened, he didn't care. He only wanted to keep the other prickly new Henchmen away. He poured everyone a goblet of rum.

"Time to chat," he said. "Tell me about Shades. And forgive me for not knowing better. Was he a Henchman, as we are?"

Rubbing his beard, Horace said, "One of the original. He started with us not long after we were formed. After we deserted the king and were branded. He's one of the survivors. He lasted, unlike over a hundred others that didn't."

"He's a weasel. A snake," Vern said as he sipped his rum and grimaced. "Mmm… that's good. Black rum from Dorcha. Ol' Flame Beard carried the best. I could set Shades on fire with this concoction. Be happy to do it, too."

"You'd waste good rum on him," the stark warrior Bearclaw said. "Use oil. He's not worth a dram of rum."

"It sounds like all parties present are against him. If he was a Henchman, why was he in Baracha and not with us?" Abraham asked then took a stiff drink. The black rum burned all the way down his throat to his stomach. "It does leave a mark in you, doesn't it?"

"You put him in Baracha, Captain," Horace said. "And all of us agreed. After one of our missions, while you met with the king, we waited there, but you didn't pick him to come out."

"And why was that?" he asked.

The Henchmen in the room exchanged looks.

"All of us were convinced that he was the saboteur of our missions," Horace said. "Especially you. You would have had him dead if you could have. And no one faulted you for it. We were losing men like sheep in a slaughterhouse."

"But we've since learned that Twila—or Raschel—Leodor, and Lewis were behind those failed missions." Abraham tapped a finger on the rim of his goblet. "Shades would have been cleared the same as the rest of us."

Iris raised her voice and said, "We don't know for certain that he wasn't in on it. He fits the part. Besides, he tried to put us under in Baracha. He nearly pulled it off too."

"I still have sore ribs from it. Those Gond got ahold of me and shook my bones loose," Vern said as he rubbed his ribs. "Just give me ten minutes with the little worm alone."

The company rattled off a few more points. They didn't want anything to do with Shades and made it clear that they didn't trust him. But if he'd been a Henchman at one time, then at one time, he must have been trustworthy. Or at least he should have been. "Sticks, you haven't said a word. What is your feeling about Shades?"

Without showing any emotions in her creaseless face, she said, "Aside from what happened in Baracha, I never saw Shades betray us."

"Ah, by the foul wind of the Elders, you got along with him worse than any of us," Vern said. "Now you side with him?"

"I'm not siding with him. I know what I know, the same as you, but even when Ruger tossed him, I had my doubts. I went along. It was better off not seeing him," she said as she wound her fingers in one of her ponytails.

"Tell me, if he was a Henchman in Baracha, how was he able to assault you?" Abraham asked. "Certainly, there would have been repercussions of it. A sky demon. Tragic accident. Some ill must have befallen him."

Iris drained her goblet and said, "As a mystic, I think that actions of a branded must be directly linked to the branded, as opposed to indirectly. Shades didn't attack us, but his legion of thugs did. I still think that it would bring forth ill will, but I cannot say for sure. The power of the brand seems to work uniquely depending on the person. I hate to say it, but Leodor might know more about it than me."

"For the time being, he's locked up," Abraham said. "So let's not worry about that. We can always leave him on the coast."

"Or strand him on an island," Bearclaw suggested. "Remember, he's not branded now. I say we do as you suggested. Get rid of him the first chance that we get. We'll be better off for it."

"Remember, this isn't a 'majority rules' situation. I have to make that decision. I think leaving him on the coast is the best decision. We'll move on after that. I don't want anyone among us that isn't a Henchman. It's bad enough that Leodor and Lewis have it but don't deserve it."

"They didn't want it," Horace said. "All of us wanted it. It's an honor, as dark as it might seem. I revel in the purpose that it gives me. I like serving the king. People like them… They only serve themselves."

"Hearts can change," Iris muttered.

"What do you mean by that?" Vern asked.

Iris let Horace refill her goblet and said, "Well, the first time I saw Shades in the ship's hold, I wanted him dead. But now that I think about it, we put him in Baracha in error. And he said he could explain his actions. He did bail us out above decks too. He didn't have to do that."

"We didn't need bailed out," Horace growled. "It was under control. We would have killed them."

Iris gripped Horace's hand and said, "I know, but we have a bigger crew. Sailors. They wouldn't have made it. Or the new Red Tunics. I'm all for getting out of a bind without bloodshed, and all of Tiotan's ships might have come for us after victory. And before, even when Shades was in question, well, he delivered as well as any one of us."

"Well, why don't you give him a big fat kiss and an apology?" Vern said. "I'm through talking about this." He made his way to the door and flung it open.

After he pushed by Tark and Cudgel, Bearclaw and Horace followed after him.

Tark and Cudgel, the smoky-eyed athletes, peered into the room, and Cudgel said, "I'll stand by what you say, Captain, but I feel the same as them. What Shades did in that prison was low. He needs punished." He closed the door again.

The ship rocked hard left then right.

"Choppy waters," Abraham muttered. "I don't like them. I can't have the company divided. Once we take to land, I think it will be best for all parties to cut Shades loose." He wished he had a better memory of Shades and what he was like, but it was a blank. He didn't even recognize the man, even vaguely, as he did the others. "I don't suppose anyone is going to object. Should be simple enough."

Sticks lifted two fingers and said, "There is one thing you should consider."

"Oh, what's that?"

"We need him."

CHAPTER 9

"How's it going?" Abraham asked. He was down inside the ship's hold, at the rear, where the brig was located.

Solomon sat outside the cell barred with steel, his elbows on his knees. Shades was inside the cell, sitting on a lone bench, his back to the wall. He still wore the garish oversized robes from earlier, when he'd posed as a merchant.

"He likes to talk," Solomon said. "Too much."

"Yes, he has always had a big mouth," Sticks said, hanging back behind Abraham.

Nobody else was with them.

Shades showed an easy smile that hid his teeth. He spoke again in his silky voice. "Oh yes, the unflappable Sticks. The princess of personality. How delightful it is that you should join me." He wagged his finger. "I must say, though, that those ponytails do little to make up for your boyish exterior. Perhaps if you let it all hang out, you would fare better as a woman."

Abraham slid his gaze between the two debaters and asked, "What's going on with the two of you?"

"Nothing," Sticks said. "He's all talk."

Shades stood up and grabbed the cell bars and said, "Now, Sticks, you know that there is much more to me than that. Much more."

"It doesn't look like it from where I'm standing," Abraham said. "But I'm used to runts with big mouths. It's how they protect themselves."

Shades lifted his eyes to Abraham and said, "You really aren't the same man as the last. You are someone different. Ha. Even I have to admit that this is fascinating, and very little fascinates me. Well, this troglin does too." He tapped a finger on the bars. "Tell me, what is your real name if it's not Ruger?"

"You're a smart fella. You tell me."

"Abraham. You can thank Clarice for filling me in. She's a young girl that likes to talk. But do not fret. I always figure everything out anyway." He licked his teeth. "So, you are the new otherworlder. I can only hope that you are better than the last one. He was quite the fool, trapped in Ruger's body."

Abraham exchanged a glance with Solomon.

Shades's light eyes brightened. "Ah! I'll be—the troglin is an otherworlder too. This gets better and better. Tell me, did you know one another from your world, or are you from different worlds completely? I say it's easy to pick up on because of the way that you talk. Your speech is very uncommon."

Abraham really wished he remembered more about Shades, who seemed to know more about Abraham than he knew about himself. He wasn't sure whether he liked him or not, but at least he had some personality. "So you're from Hancha?"

"I can't change where I was born. You should know that. But yes, I'll entertain your questions. I am from Hancha. It's a big part of my mysterious past. Why do you ask?" Shades sat back down. "Oh, wait. I know why. Princess Clarice blathered about everything. The zillon dragon riders attacked the king with a strange weapon that shot sling bullets. I assume it's another one of those crazy artifacts from your world or perhaps another. Who knows? Anyway, you need a guide through Hancha." He made a welcoming gesture with his hands. "And here I am, a man who has thoroughly leveraged himself to meet your needs. You can let me out now. Perhaps get me something to eat. Some of that Dorcha rum you've been drinking would be mighty fine."

"He's cocky," Solomon said. "I hate cocky."

"I'm an acquired taste. Just ask Sticks. She knows me more intimately than any," Shades said.

Abraham gave her a sideways look and said, "Tell me you're brother and sister or something."

She didn't say a word.

"Cousins?"

Shades popped up out of his seat and said, "I'll be happy to retell the story that you most certainly don't remember. It was years ago, when Sticks joined our ranks and quickly cozied up to me. She was so cute, trying to be so rugged and boyish, just to fit in, but it wasn't long before she proved to be all woman. Then there was some back and forth—awkwardness when you showed an interest. She seemed to be one that wanted to move up the ranks and stepped on me to get into the top tent."

The muscles in Sticks's jaw clenched. If her eyes could have shot poisoned arrows, she would have done so at Shades.

"Your gossip isn't very Henchmanlike," Abraham said. "It sounds more like the words of old chattering women. Sticks, do you really think that we need him to guide through Hancha?"

"I'm only saying that he knows it better than any of the rest of us. There were more Henchmen from Hancha, but they are all dead."

"Don't blame that on me," Shades said. "I wasn't responsible for any of what I was accused of."

"If that's the case, then why did you try to kill us in Baracha?" she asked, her voice cracking a little.

"Now that I have time to explain, I will explain." Shades poked his finger at Abraham and Sticks. "You abandoned me in Baracha. What was I supposed to do, lie down and die? In the past, we would wait as a group and be strong. But not this time. It was me. One on one." His jaw tightened. His small deft hands turned white knuckled on the bars. "So, I managed to join one of the gangs." He pulled up his sleeve, revealing white scars carved into his arm, making a crude image of a snake with fangs. "Over time, I proved my worth and overtook the gang called the Serpent's Tail. I recruited the Gond, which wasn't easy, and after that, we had the run of the prison yard. When you came, I had to prove who I was. It was only fighting. No one got killed. Sure, some broken bones and bloody noses, but the Henchmen can handle that."

"You came after the women. We know what they do with the women in Baracha," Sticks said in a tone that was almost a growl.

"Well, to be clear, all of the women except for you. Listen, it was for your protection. It might not sound that way, but there were other gangs bent on taking a fatal poke at the Henchmen," Shades said. "I know this because the Serpent's Tail was offered accommodation to bring about your demise. We were only one of the gangs involved, but I acted first." He pressed his face between the bars. "It… was… a… show."

Solomon clapped his hands together, making a loud pop. "I told you he was a talker. I tell you, if I could have woven my words like that back when I was young, I would have saved myself a heap of trouble."

"I agree," Abraham said.

"Sticks, you know better than any that I was never the trouble," Shades said. "I was a good Henchman. But I found out what was going on with Twila. But she got me first." He made an angry shake of his head. "Clever. So clever." He shook his head and frowned. "And I was onto the old Ruger too. He was letting her do that damage and put the blame on me. I should have acted quicker."

"Yeah, well, we have a long trip ahead. I'll decide tonight whether or not to cut you loose," Abraham said. "Solomon, do you want some relief?"

"No, I'll stay. I'm as comfortable here as anywhere."

"Good. Just holler if you change your mind. It's time to get back on track." Abraham pinched the bridge of his nose. A small headache was coming on. "I'll be in my quart—"

"Captain!" Horace called out from the main deck. "Trouble comes. All swords on deck! All swords on deck!"

CHAPTER 10

Taking the steps three at a time to the main deck, Abraham quickly found himself in a scene of chaos. At first, he imagined that the warships from Tiotan had returned. Instead, he gaped at something completing unimaginable, at least by Earth's standards. Flying men circled the skies above. They had great heads like pterodactyls' with lengthy gray beaks, the arms and legs of men, and talons for toes and fingers. Their skin was blackened scales like fishes', but thicker like a great lizard's. They had lean, wiry muscles, skinny arms, and bellies that appeared as hard as iron hide.

Horace, Bearclaw, and Vern stood on the main deck, aiming crossbows at the creatures. They fired volley after volley. The creatures twisted through the sky. Apollo and Prospero manned the crow's nest, brandishing their swords at flying fiends circling them.

Abraham had snaked out his own sword without even realizing it. Energy coursed through his hand. "Holy sheetrock! What are those things?"

"Windreavers," a pirate cried out. He was one of Flamebeard's old crew. "They are hellions of the skies." He ducked underneath a windreaver that dove at his head. As it took a swipe at the pirate with its claws, a hunk of flesh in his shoulder went with it. "Gargh!" the pirate cried out.

Horace shot a crossbow bolt into the windreaver's neck. It flopped on the deck like a fish and died.

Abraham climbed his way up to the poop deck of the ship, where Dominga and Vern were locked in battle with a small flock of windreavers that had landed. The windreavers' great snapping jaws, filled with rows of tiny sharp teeth, made loud clacks. Vern buried his sword in a creature's chest. Blood spurted from the wound as it twisted away and dove off the ship.

Dominga fought with sword and dagger. She stuck a windreaver in the arm. It lashed out with its winged arm with claws that cut her across the face. She dropped down and lunged her short sword into its belly with her full force. The blade went into one side of its abdomen and out the other. Its mouth opened wide, and a horrifying birdlike shriek came out.

Black Bane flashed across the shrieking bird-thing's neck and took its head from the shoulders.

"I had it under control," Dominga said as she jerked her sword out of the windreaver's belly.

Abraham didn't slow. Two more windreavers landed on the deck, and more were landing. They were long armed and quick, and their biting beaks struck out like serpents. The ferocity of Abraham, Vern, and Dominga sent the windreavers diving over the edge of the ship's stern. The fiendish flyers vanished underneath the surface of the choppy waters.

Abraham tore his stare away from the water to the commotion in the crow's nest above. He pointed his sword. "There!"

Apollo and Prospero were in the fight of their lives. Windreavers hung to the rim of the crow's nest, biting and lashing out with their talons. Prospero locked his arms around one of the windreavers' beaks and started punching the strange birdman in the face.

A windreaver clamped down on Apollo's arm, and the man let out a fierce scream. He turned wild-eyed and bit the windreaver on its arm. Then his sword cut clean through the membrane of its wing and sliced fully through it. With a quick punch of a dagger, he gored its heart. The windreaver fell away and tangled up in the ratlines, twitching.

The windreavers, dozens in all, circled above, screeching and squawking harrowing sounds. Without any warning, they dove into the waters and vanished underneath the ship.

The ship's company looked overboard.

"Does anyone see them?" Horace asked as he joined the other onlookers leaning over the ship's railing. He'd dropped his crossbow and rearmed with a spear. "They fly like birds and swim like fish."

"Keep this ship moving," Lewis ordered. "Those things probably had all of the taste of steel that they could handle." He had the drab red blood of a windreaver dripping from the edge of his sword. "They might look frightening, but they fight like stupid animals."

"Animals that fight in packs can be deadly," said Clarice's guardian maiden Swan in her husky voice. "Be wary."

Lewis spat off the railing. "The only one that should be wary is the fool that crosses me and the king's steel. It cut their scaly skins like butter. They won't be back," he said as he swept his dark hair from his eyes. "Like pigeons, they scatter."

Abraham counted six windreavers lying dead on the deck. One lay dead near the mainmast, its blood oozing from a gaping wound onto the wooden planks. The windreavers were ugly, with no charm about them at all. Their pterodactyl heads were oddly long and looked too heavy for their bodies. Like animals, they looked the same alive as they did dead. Their large eyes were like polished onyx, and they stood over six feet tall.

"Seems strange that they attack for no reason." He fanned his nose. "Whew, they smell like rotting sardines. What agitated them?"

The pirate who had called out the names of the windreavers earlier limped over to Abraham. He wore a vest and was hairy chested and lazy eyed. He said, "They are scavengers. They feed on men for meat. Anything. They like it fresh. I've only seen them twice before. Once when we crossed a sinking ship after a battle we came on. They snatched the dying from the waters and flew away. The other time, they flew away. A sky dragon was giving chase. 'Twas a scary thing with a tail like a stick of fire. Humph, the Sea Elders must be with us since they fled beneath. A good sign."

"Sea Elders. Yes, of course. They are looking out for us." Lewis sheathed his sword. "I wonder, was the same sea elder looking after them?"

With her flowing hair billowing in the wind, Clarice said to her half brother, "Vermin like them don't pray. Vermin like you don't either."

"Ha ha," Lewis said as he adjusted his leather gloves. "I've made it this far without the Elders." He twisted his head around. "Where is Leodor? Old sour face, are you hiding? It's safe now!"

Abraham walked away and looked over the rail down into the waters. The ship moved at a brisk pace, cutting through the choppy waters like a knife. He squinted. Several feet below the surface it looked like something swam like a dolphin by the ship's hull. "Guys, look closer. I think those windreavers are swimming alongside. Take a look for you—"

Like a salmon swimming upstream and jumping the breaks, a windreaver sailed up into the deck. They came all at once by the dozens from all directions. The windreavers let out fiendish earsplitting screeches as they launched themselves into the Henchmen and the crew.

Abraham split the nearest monster's face wide open with lethal blow of his sword. A woman screamed. It was Clarice. Two windreavers hooked her arms with their taloned fingertips. They launched themselves into the air and sped away in hasty flight. "Nooo!" Abraham yelled.

"Help meee!" Clarice screamed. "Help meee!"

CHAPTER 11

"Once again, the Sea of Troubles lives up to its name," Bearclaw said. The axe-wielding warrior's eyes were searching over the sea. In the distance, the windreavers were carrying off part of the ship's crew.

"Dirty donuts!" Abraham said as he helplessly watched Clarice, Sticks, Horace, and the Red Tunic Skitts being carried off by the strange creatures.

The reptilian birdmen sped toward the horizon and disappeared over the sea.

He pounded his fist on the railing. "Where are those things going? They can't be flying that far away…" He searched the eyes of his crew. "Can they?"

The pirate who'd spoken to him earlier stood beside Abraham and said, "Those windreavers reside on Crown Island. It's a place of horrors. No ships can dock there. At least, no ships such as this. The beaches are cliffs of stone. Even Flame Beard avoided it."

"Well aren't you a cluster of good news?" Abraham told the pirate. "What is your name, anyway?"

"Jander. I was Flamebeard's top deckhand, at least until you slaughtered him." He stuck his chest out and gave a crisp salute. "It's an honor to serve Captain Ruger Slade. Even this sea dog's ears heard about you."

Abraham pushed past the man and said, "Horace… ah crap, Horace is gone. Who can drive this ship to that island?"

Bearclaw arched a brow and said, "Drive, Captain?"

"I mean sail! Someone set sail to that island." He was trying to find the right lingo. All he could think of was *Star Trek* episodes. "Why are all of you looking at me like that? Helmsman, set a course for Crown Island."

No one moved. Horace had manned the wheel before, and Abraham wasn't sure who backed him up.

"Well done," Lewis said. "You have a ship and no one left to sail it."

Abraham gave Lewis a dangerous look and said, "Well look at you, all broken up about your sister."

"Half sister, and I'm all ripped apart inside," Lewis said with casual smugness. "She's gone now. I don't think there is anything that can be done to save her unless sailing in circles will somehow bring her back."

Abraham locked his fingers around Lewis's throat and said, "If you weren't a Henchman, I'd kill you." He pushed the man away.

Red-faced, Lewis rubbed his throat. "You'll pay for that."

Abraham ignored him. He needed to pull it together. Four members of his crew had been snatched, and he had to get them back. "Listen up. I know we can sail this ship. Who backed up Horace?"

Cudgel stepped forward and said, "Tark and I did. We can handle it."

"Good. Get us on course," Abraham said.

Jander spoke up and added, "I can sail the ship with a skeleton crew if need be. I've been on the waters all my life. None knows them better than me."

"Good. See to it that they don't get off course."

"All right, Henchmen, let's fill those sails with gusty wind and get this sea cutter moving!" Cudgel said in a booming voice. "It can't sail itself!"

The ship's crew scrambled into action.

Abraham moved back to the railing. Without Sticks and Horace, he felt more lost than ever, as if a part of him were missing. Everything that could have gone wrong was going wrong. *Man, I can't believe this is happening.*

"Tough break," someone said.

Abraham noticed Shades standing on his left. "How did you get out?"

"You should know me better than that, *Ruger*. There isn't a lock that can hold me. Besides, your furry friend went to see what the commotion was all about." Shades made a quick scan of the deck. "But perhaps he is still hiding. Anyway, quite a dilemma. Quite a—"

"Bearclaw, stick this rodent back in his cell. Bind him up if you have to. And tape his mouth shut."

"Pardon?" Bearclaw said.

"Never mind. Just get him out of here."

Bearclaw took Shades by the scruff of his neck, lifted the grimacing man up on tiptoe, and said, "Gladly."

"Ahem."

Abraham turned.

Leodor was standing behind him with his hands tucked in his rustling robes. "Abraham, may I have a word with you?"

"I'm kinda busy," he said.

"It will only take a moment. As much as I would like to support your efforts to save our comrades, I strongly caution against it," Leodor said.

"We don't leave Henchmen behind. Of course, you wouldn't understand that even though you are one," he said.

"If it was me, I would understand," Leodor calmly said. He rubbed his scrawny chest above his heart. "My life is the king's. I die in his honor. We serve the king and his glory. We don't serve ourselves, or rather, the Henchmen. We have a mission to complete. The quest is long. We need to move with haste in that direction."

Lewis popped up behind Leodor and said, "He's right. It might take weeks to find them. And then what? If we find their carcasses, we bury them? I know that I sound cold, but I speak truth, despite my lack of affection for my sister. We serve the king, not her."

Abraham rubbed his temples and said, "Good Lord, why couldn't have they just taken you two windbags? It would have made this a whole lot easier." He pinched the bridge of his nose and dropped his hands. "Even if the two of you were whisked away, I'd come. It's the right thing to do because we're a team, not a bunch of expendables even though, well, we are. But so long as I'm in charge, I'm going to keep the Henchmen together, hell or high water." He stepped up on Leodor, smashing the man between himself and Lewis and said, "Got it?"

Leodor nodded. Lewis shrugged, covered his mouth, and yawned.

"I respect your firm attitude about this," Leodor said as he squeezed out from between the two men. "But consider this. No one can serve the king if we all wind up dead."

"Yes, no one," Lewis scoffed.

Abraham's headache started to throb. He wanted to toss both men overboard. "Is that all? And before you say anything, know that I won't be changing my mind on this."

Leodor cleared his throat and added, "If you think your trek to the Spine was treacherous, I'll give you fair warning: based off of the histories I have studied deeply, for decades, I know that what lurks in Crown Island is infinitely more dangerous than what you've already seen."

CHAPTER 12

Dealing with problems was one thing. Dealing with problems with a headache was another. Abraham had a bad one, so bad that he took to his quarters and lay facedown on the bed. He put a Do Not Disturb sign in front of the door. It was Bearclaw.

The loss of Horace, Sticks, and Clarice wasn't something he needed now. *Just another debacle I have to fix. Sticks and Horace? Why them?* He also felt bad for the young fellow, Skitts, too. He hardly knew the young man. He rolled over on his back and stared at the ceiling. "This sucks."

Lewis and Leodor continued to prod him at length even after he ended the conversation a half dozen times. The problem was that they made sound points. The first point they made caused Abraham to have many regrets. As they'd mapped out their mission to invade Hancha, find the zillon dragon riders, and kill Arcayis the Underlord, he chose to take the long route, including what would have otherwise been a short trip across the Bay of Elders.

He wasn't alone in his reasoning. They could have sailed the southern seas below the Bay of Elders and found a place to dock at Little Leg in Hancha. This was Lewis and Leodor's suggestion. Abraham was naturally inclined to go against it. King Hector and Queen Clarann agreed with him. They opted to take their time, sailing north along the western coast of Titanuus and over his head, and settle down on the coastline south of Titanuus's East Arm. The logic was simple. Their enemies wouldn't be looking for them from there. The enemy would expect a southern approach.

As things turned out, perhaps Lewis and Leodor were right. If they had sailed south, perhaps they'd still have the crew intact. Sadly, the arrival of Clarice, though she was a Henchman, only complicated things.

Abraham pushed his face out of his pillow, sat up on the edge of his bed, rubbed the back of his head, and asked, "What is with that kid? She's as hardheaded as a bull. I just hope those windreavers haven't turned her into lunch meat."

Jake's Pirates backpack caught his eye. It was hanging on the headboard post. Abraham scooted over the sheets, leaned over, and grabbed it. As he held it in his hands and stared down at it, guilt swelled in his chest. The past several days had been so hectic that he hadn't even thought about Jake and his dead wife, Jenny.

He ran his thumbs over the straps. "Sorry, Son. Sorry, hon." His eyes watered. "What am I doing here? I don't even know if this place is real. I know my life with you was, though, wasn't it?" He flicked the zipper with his finger. He remembered the day he'd given Jake the backpack. It was a birthday present right before the accident, not too far removed from when he'd signed his big baseball contract. He swallowed the lump in his throat. "Ah, man. I hope you guys understand. I'm sorry." He hung the backpack up on the post. "I have to save them. But I'll never forget about you."

Outside, the moonlight shone through the glass panes of the window.

He walked over to the window and spread his hands out over the panes. Outside, the tips of the choppy waves twinkled with dazzling effect. For a moment, Titanuus seemed peaceful. He rubbed his head. He'd like to have a pain pill, ibuprofen or something to take the edge off. He hadn't had one of those in years. They brought only more sorrow and trouble. For the most part, Ruger's body handled everything extremely well, inhumanly well, aside from the occasional migraines.

"Come on, Ruger. I need to shake this. We have work to do." He stood. "Block it out. Just block it out, and it will subside."

At the moment, he had too much to think about. His problems were coming at him from all directions. Everything had started with the zillon dragon riders. The alienlike race with ghostly white skin and marble black eyes had tried to assassinate King Hector. It wasn't a customary assassination either, using poison or sharp weapons. The fiends used an assault rifle that looked like an M-16 or AK-47. That tossed Abraham for a loop and put King Hector in a panic. The enemy was using weapons the likes of which he'd never seen. At least Abraham had some idea what they were up against. But a fat lot of good it would do them if they had a lot more of them.

That led to planning the next step. King Hector didn't play games. If you took a shot at him, he took a shot at you, carefully and quietly. Abraham liked the mission. He was ready, but Lewis and Leodor created a problem. They weren't on board. Then, of all people, Princess Clarice showed up, and everything quickly started to unravel. Such was the luck of the Henchmen: turmoil, lots of it.

To make matters worse, that wasn't even Abraham's biggest problem. The fact that he was stuck in Titanuus had taken a backseat to the matters at hand. He, for all intents and purposes, seemed to be becoming someone else, which was madness. He hadn't even taken a sniff at trying to find one of those portals or doorways that would take him back home. The only things attaching him to that reality were his occasional dreams and Jake's backpack.

He rubbed his forehead. "I'd do anything for a Ziploc full of ice right now."

Knock. Knock. Knock.

The soft knocking came from the other side of his door. It was someone's knuckle being gentle on the wooden frame. Abraham opened the door.

Bearclaw stood outside. The warrior was all business behind his broad face and wild jet-black hair. In his direct manner, he said, "Crown Island is in sight."

"Perfect." Abraham grabbed his sword, buckled it on, and headed on deck. The entire crew, aside from Cudgel, who steered the ship, were gathered on the foredeck. Their wide eyes stared out over the foremast, which jutted out of the front of the ship, fixed on the haunting sight in the distance. He joined them.

"Ahoy," Jander said in a gravelly voice as he leaned out over the front, hanging onto sail lines that ran from the bowsprit to the forecastle mast. "Crown Island."

Located south of the West Arm of Titanuus, the stark sea-stranded landmass lived up to its namesake. A rim of jagged cliff faces peaked and dipped all the way around the island as far as the eye could see. The waves crashed angrily against the foreboding cliffs. Clouds, more like a fog, hung over the island, slowly moving in a ghostly fashion. The sea wind cutting through the choppy miles of rock whistled like a banshee gone mad. The rough waters appeared to be surrounded by reefs of coral and shallows of rock. No big ship could traverse it.

Lewis and Leodor approached Abraham. "It's not too late to make the right decision," Lewis said.

Abraham's jaws clenched. He looked them both dead in the eyes and said, "I've already made the right decision. Bearclaw, get the lifeboat in the water. Tonight, we're going in."

CHAPTER 13

LEWIS AND LEODOR PUT THEIR backs into the oars as they rowed feverishly against the sea. Leodor looked as if he was about to die, gasping with every effort he put in. He wasn't even doing much of the work. Swan sat beside him, and Hazel was beside Lewis, doubling up on the oars. The guardian maidens had insisted on coming.

From the bow of the craft, watching Leodor panting for breath, Abraham asked, "When's the last time you did any physical labor? You look like death warmed over."

"I've dedicated to my life acting from behind the scenes, not in them. It's a foolish thing to bring me. I'm of no use to you," Leodor said as he wheezed.

Luckily for Abraham, his headache had subsided. He said, "I agree with you, but you're a Henchman now. It's time to build some character. Now dig those oars into the water, grandpa."

The other Henchmen in the boat, aside from furrow-browed Lewis, let out some hearty laughter. Among the small ship's crew were Bearclaw, Vern, Dominga, Iris, Apollo, Prospero, and Skitts's brother, the Red Tunic Zann, who like the guardian maidens, had insisted on coming. The boat was plenty big enough to hold all of them and their gear. He'd left the others back on the ship, including Solomon. Something didn't seem right with the troglin.

The boat scraped over a reef, rocking the craft, and got hung up. Bearclaw grabbed an oar and pushed them free. They navigated through the reefs and shallows toward the rocky cliff faces, looking for a spot to dock the craft and enter the island. Crown Island had the foreboding presence of a prison, the kind where you went in and didn't come out.

"Does anyone see a good place to park?" Abraham said.

"Anywhere on these shallows will be fine. We go in any closer, and we're going to crash into those walls," Vern said. "And in this armor, all of us will sink like stones."

"I won't," Dominga reminded him with a smile. She wore only snug garb made of leather. "But if you sink, I'll try to fish you out."

"Brilliant idea, Ruger. Rowing in the middle of the night. A wise man would have waited until morning," Lewis said as he pulled at the oars.

"There's a method to my madness. Number one, the longer we wait, the more likely they are dead. Number two, I'm hoping those bird men, or whatever they are, don't fly at night."

"Is there a number three?" Lewis asked sarcastically.

"Yes—shut up and row."

"Ruger," Bearclaw said as he pointed a long, broad finger toward the island. "If we can get in behind that jetty, there might be a cover back there."

Abraham looked at the strapping women, Swan and Hazel. "Go for it."

With the help of Lewis and Leodor, the two of them guided the watercraft toward the jetty. Horace sat in the rear, while Abraham kept his spot on the bow. Suddenly, the waves picked up the rear end of the boat and sent it careening toward the rocky outcropping they were aiming for.

Abraham cried out, "Hold on! Everybody brace yourselves!"

The lifeboat moved with startling speed toward the jagged rocks. If the nose of the boat hit the rock, it would be shattered to pieces, and the company would be stranded if not sunk to a watery grave. He flung his arms out and braced his feet against the boat's bench. His fingers touched rock. His arms strained against the weight of the boat, which heaved its full weight behind him. With backbreaking effort, he pushed the nose of the ship away from the rocks, grunting with the strain.

The sharp rocks scraped against Abraham's cheeks and shoulder, but he managed to turn the nose of the boat. The side of the ship bumped hard against the rocks, bucking all the passengers.

Using his hands, and with the help of the others, he pushed the boat alongside the outcropping.

Abraham let out a sigh, looked at the wide-eyed crew, and kind of laughed. "That was a close call."

The back surge of waves heaved the boat upward.

A sharp pain lanced through Abraham's skull as he cracked his noggin on a rock sticking out from overhead. Warm blood ran down into his eyes. He touched it and looked at it on his fingertips. The world started to spin. His body swayed, and he faded into blackness.

CHAPTER 14
THE PRESENT

Beep. Beep. Beep. Beep. Beep.

Abraham woke up in a modern-day hospital bed. The lights were dim. The air was cool. Several blankets covered his body. He was warm, almost comfortable. He turned his head and looked at the blood-pressure monitor. He was at a perfect one-twenty over eighty. His heartbeat was steady at sixty-five beats per minute. His vital statistics were rarely ever that good.

Beep. Beep. Beep. Beep. Beep.

"Dirty donuts, that sound is annoying," he said and clawed a finger at the oxygen tube stuck inside his nose. "What is this thing? For a dream, this is a little too vivid."

Since he'd been on Titanuus, he'd had several dreams about his past. They were so real that he felt he was reliving it. Often, they came on after a headache. A deep sleep would follow. His past came back to haunt him. This dream was different. He was in a hospital room, but there weren't any balloons. It was like the one after his accident. The room was barren, and a flat-screen television hung from the wall.

"That's new."

The last thing he remembered was trying to save the lifeboat from crashing into the rocks. He cracked his head. Blood was on his fingers. He looked at them. His hands were clean. He rubbed his forehead. A bandage was on it. "Ah, no."

"Did you say something to me?" someone asked in a weak voice from the other side of a sea-green curtain drawn along one side of his bed.

With a grunt, Abraham rolled over on one side and pushed the curtain away. An old white man lay in his bed, hooked up to IVs and oxygen. With a bald face filled with age spots, he must have been at least ninety. He was scrawny, a withered man, but light was in his eyes when he tilted his gaze toward Abraham.

"Hi. Uh, no, I wasn't talking to you, just myself. Er… I'm Abraham."

"They call me Charles. Nice to meet you." Even though Charles had hardly a stick of hair on his head, he had frosty eyebrows so thick that he could comb them over. "I was wondering if you'd wake up before I died."

"Well, I guess you got your wish."

Abraham looked about. The room had that hospital smell of bedpans and cleaning agents. Charles didn't appear to have any belongings at all.

"Sorry, Charles, that probably sounded rude."

"Ah, no, not at all. It's good to hear a voice. Aside from brief interludes with the nurses, I haven't had many conversations." Charles closed his eyes. "Everyone is polite, though. They are always polite when they know that you're going to die. It's their job to make you comfortable, I guess."

Abraham grabbed his railing and pulled himself into a sitting position with a grunt. He managed to figure out how to push the support railing down and swung his legs over the edge of the bed. The first thing he noticed was his bulging belly. The rock-hard six-pack of muscles that Ruger boasted was gone. He placed both hands on his belly. "This is embarrassing."

"At least you have some fat on you. I'm little more than skin on bones," Charles said. "Heh heh."

"I can see that you are old, but you don't look like someone that is about to die," Abraham said absentmindedly. Like a slap in the face, it just hit him that Sticks, Horace, Clarice, and Skitts were in danger and needed rescue. "Ah, man. This can't be happening now."

"What, being old? I've been old a long time. But I get sick, come here—they move me floor to floor and bed to bed. Like I'm a purse or something. I don't know." Charles made a throat-clearing cough. "You know, you might find this hard to believe, but I used to be a big fella like you. Bigger. I was a bulldozer among my fellow infantry men. Now, I've shrunk down like a husk of mini corn. It sucks."

"You're a vet? Well, thanks for your service. My dad was one. A pilot." Abraham shook his head. "What am I doing? I know this isn't real. It's just another dream."

"Listen son, our lives are what we choose them to be." Charles pressed a button on the side of his bed rail, and the back end of his bed rose up. With a shaky hand, he reached over and grabbed a plastic hospital cup. "Say, do you think that you could fetch me some water? I'd buzz a nurse, but they take forever. Unless Lindsay is here. She stays on top of things, but she's always off on Sundays."

Abraham tilted his head toward Charles and asked, "Sunday? What is the date?"

"September something, I think. I'm good with days, but not so much the dates. The new memories fade like melting snow, but I really remember the old ones. My first wife—she was a house girl. I met her in the Philippines. Stark black hair and eyes that I'll never forget."

Abraham snatched the cup out of Charles's hand and asked, "What year is it?"

"Oh, that I know. It's 2018."

Abraham's knees buckled as his world came crashing down. Dreaming in the past was one thing, but dreaming in the present—that was a nightmare.

"No, no, no, this can't be!" He flung his room door open. "Nurse! Nurse!"

A nurses' station was nearby. The male and female nurses donning a variety of scrubs were drinking and talking, many eyeballing the screens of their smart phones. All of them stopped what they were doing, and their frozen stares hung on Abraham.

One nurse, a short husky lady with a braided ponytail, wore scrubs decorated with pictures of Hello Kitty. She set down a can of Red Bull and said, "Sir, let's get you back into bed. Larry, call the doctor. Tell him Mr. Jenkins is awake."

Abraham cast his eyes on the nurse. "Tell me, what is the date and year?"

"It's September 18, 2018," she calmly said.

Abraham lifted his chin, flung out his fists wide, and screamed, "Noooooooooo!"

CHAPTER 15

Getting Abraham settled down took some doing, but the nurse in the Hello Kitty scrubs didn't back down. Her name was Nancy, and when she told Abraham he was acting like a child, that got him. He might be torn between one world and another, but he wasn't going to get anywhere by having a fit. He climbed back in bed.

The doctors and nurses ordered a rigmarole of tests. Abraham played along. After all, if he was having a dream, then all he needed to do was wake up. The best way to do that was to get back to sleep. That would be the quickest way back to Titanuus. He requested something to help him sleep and told Charles and the nurse, Ann, "Good night. It was nice knowing you."

The sedatives worked. His lids became heavy, and he heard himself snore before he fell into a deep sleep.

He woke up in the same hospital room, well rested and bleary-eyed. His pulse picked up. "Dirty donuts, I'm still here."

A rustle of paper came from inside the room. Abraham peered that direction. A man sitting in a chair in the corner was folding up a newspaper. He was old and as bald as a cue ball and wore a navy suit, white shirt, and no tie.

"Luther?"

"Good morning, Abraham," Luther Vancross said as he stood up. He owned the brewery that Abraham drove a truck for. He had age spots all over but moved like a thirty-year-old in a seventy-five-year-old's body. "How are you feeling?"

"That's the last question that you want to ask. Believe me—the last question." He looked over to the right. The curtain was pulled back, and an empty bed was beside him. "What happened to Charles?"

Luther leaned forward and asked, "Who?"

"Charles, the man that looked like an even older you? He was here yesterday. He…" Abraham caught a knowing look in Luther's eye. "Did he die?"

"I believe so. It happened right before I arrived. They were straightening up the room. I didn't know that he was the Charles that you spoke of. Sorry, I guess you got to know him."

With emptiness filling him, he said, "I guess you could say that. Though it was brief. He said something about our lives being what we chose them to be. It was kind of cryptic. I hate that he's gone."

"At least you are alive," Luther said with a faint smile. "It sounds like this Charles was full of years. When the Lord takes you, he takes you. I'm glad that he didn't take you. I would have felt a great loss after your accident."

Aside from his original interview with Luther years before, Abraham didn't have much to do with the man. He did his job and went home, catching Luther every so often back at the brewery. Both men spoke little but did much. But Luther always was a straight shooter.

"What accident are you talking about?" Abraham asked.

"The one in the East River Mountain Tunnel. That is where they found you, battered up and knocked out," Luther said, not batting an eye. He'd always maintained a stern quality about himself. He tapped the folded-up newspaper on his hand. "I'll never forget that call. None of my drivers ever had a bad accident. We've always been fortunate. That's why I only hire good men and women. But that accident was freakish."

Abraham clenched his brow. He believed that Luther believed what he was saying, but he didn't believe it himself. He hadn't wrecked his truck. His truck was fine when he entered the tunnel, and he was alone inside it. He hadn't hit anything. "What was freakish?"

"Your accident. They said a hunk of the tunnel fell on top of you. Or the cab. It should have crushed you, they said."

"Who said that, the army? I want to tell you something, Luther, nothing fell on my truck. Believe me, something else that is strange has happened." Abraham looked the man in the eyes. "Have you seen my truck?"

"No. But if it's totaled, it's totaled. Don't worry about it. Insurance will cover it, and we'll get you a new one—that is, if you want to come back to work."

"No, seriously, Luther—have you seen my truck or the pictures? I want to see pictures!"

"I don't see the point, but I'll do what I can." Luther scratched at his sideburns. "Abraham, no one is blaming you. It was an accident. I'll see if I can get ahold of the West Virginia State Troopers. They should have the accident report. I'm assuming that they worked in coordination with the army, of course. I wasn't at the scene. I just got the phone call."

"From who?"

"Er… a Colonel Dexter. I could call him. I have his card back in my office."

The name rang a bell. Abraham remembered talking to a Colonel Dexter at the gas pumps at Woody's Grill. He'd taken a picture with the man. "Did he have a moustache?"

"I only spoke with him on the phone," Luther said. "I guess, to be fair, he sounded like he had a moustache. His voice was deep, very deep, like a Johnny Cash or Sam Elliot."

Abraham crushed the blankets with his hands. Something stank. It reeked. Bells and whistles sounded off like alarms inside him. "Why don't you get on the phone, call your office, and get that number. I want to talk to him."

"Will you please tell me what you are so worked up about? Look at your heart rate. It's rising." Luther put his hand on Abraham's shoulder. "You need to take it easy. Rest and don't worry about the bills. The brewery has all of that covered. If anything, I think that you have a case against the Department of Highways. I have a great lawyer. His name is—"

Knock. Knock. Knock.

"Mr. Jenkins, you have another visitor," Nancy the nurse said. She looked at Luther. "We try to limit to no more than one at a time if you aren't immediate family. But I'll give you a few minutes."

"Understood," Luther said with a gentleman's nod of the chin. "You're the boss."

Abraham couldn't imagine who else would be coming to see him. He didn't have anyone close left, and Luther was his emergency contact. A shapely woman entered the room. His heart skipped. It was Brandi.

CHAPTER 16

MANDI COULDN'T HAVE BEEN PRETTIER. The dark-eyed, deeply tanned brunette's hair touched the shoulders of a revealing, low-cut blouse. She wore a jean miniskirt that showed off her nice legs. She held a small vase filled with wild flowers. With a shy expression, she came inside. "Hi, handsome."

"Uh, hi, Mandi." Abraham cast a nervous look at Luther, whose stare hung on the very attractive thirtysomething woman. "This is Luther. I don't know if you've met."

Luther extended his hand and held hers and said, "It's a pleasure. We've met, back when you were a little girl. I used to run around with Herb a good bit. I was at his and Martha's wedding. How is your mother doing?"

"She's just fine but worried about Abraham. She's been sick since she heard about the accident." Mandi released her grip. "Nice to meet you, again, Luther. Um… thanks for letting us know about Abraham. We appreciate it."

"My pleasure." Luther stuffed his newspaper up underneath an arm and said, "I better skedaddle. I don't want to upset Nurse Nancy. I have a hunch she'd throw me out on my rear like a bundle of newspapers. I'll look into Colonel Dexter for you, Abraham. Now get some rest. You're alive. Be happy." He departed.

Mandi showed Abraham the flowers. "For you. I wasn't sure what sort of flowers you liked, so I picked these along the highway."

"Pretty," he said as he took the flowers in hand. "Uh… I've never gotten flowers before. This is a first." He politely sniffed them and set them down on the nearby food tray. "So, how have you been?"

"Worried," she said as she curled her silky locks around an index finger. "When I heard about the accident, I felt my heart jump. If something bad had happened… Well, I'd feel awful the way we left things."

"You shouldn't feel that way. I mean, I'm flattered. You look great, and you're a beautiful woman." He swallowed and averted his eyes. "I just… Well, I never thought it could work out, and I shouldn't have been so cold to you. I should be flattered." He reached out, took her hand, looked into her lovely eyes, and said, "I guess I'm trying to say that I'm sorry."

Mandi's eyes grew, and she leaned back. "Wow. I wasn't expecting that at all." Her cheeks flushed. She ran the fingers of her free hand through her hair. "That was so open and honest. I'm kinda overwhelmed."

"Well, a lot has changed since I've been gone."

She looked confused and said, "You haven't been anywhere but in this hospital. What happened? Did you have an out-of-body experience?" Her voice grew excited. "Did you see heaven?"

"No, I wish."

She squeezed his hand and said, "If it's hell, I don't want to know."

"No, it wasn't that either."

He sighed. The warmth of her hand was so real. Her full lips were perfect. He wanted to kiss her.

"It's a long story," he said. "You wouldn't believe me if I told you."

She sat down on the edge of the bed. "Do you mind?"

"No."

"So, what were you guys talking about Colonel Drew for? You seemed upset. He helped you out, didn't he?"

"You've talked to him? Drew Dexter. That's his name, right?"

"Yep. He's been stopping in the diner and checking on me. I pretty sure he is not as worried about you as he pretends to be. I think he, well…"

"Likes you? Ha, I'm sure he does. What man wouldn't like a woman with gorgeous legs like that?" He squeezed her thigh just above the knee.

Mandi let out a delightful squeal. "Abraham. What's gotten into you?"

"Nothing. I just know that I'm dreaming." He let out a mad laugh. "Oh, this is so crazy. You have to listen to me, Mandi, and if you will, just keep it between us. Something happened to me inside that tunnel. A big chunk of rock didn't fall on my truck. Or hit my head. And I'm only telling you this because, well, you're nice and have been nothing but good to me, so if I'm crazy, then you need to know it first so you don't get hurt."

She leaned over and caressed his bearded face with a gentle hand. "There is nothing you can say that can scare me. I live out in the middle of nowhere. All I do is watch too much Netflix and cable TV." She squinted. "You look a little different. Those soft eyes of yours have gotten harder. I don't know what it is, but it's sexier. Like there is more of you in there."

"Well, maybe that's because I have a split personality."

CHAPTER 17

Abraham fully expected Mandi to get up and leave the room. She didn't. She sat on the bed with a smile on her face that grew into a short burst of laughter.

"What?" he asked.

"First off, I've already seen two of your personalities. So you've already surprised me with the last one." She locked her fingers with his. "That was a pleasant surprise. I liked it. It was as if you were coming out of your shell."

"No, that's not what I'm talking about. This is serious. When I went into that tunnel, I ended up passing into another world, a medieval fantasy world. I'm talking knights with swords, monsters, and dragons. I've been fighting all of them. I killed a pirate named Flame Beard."

The smile on her face started to vanish. She said, "You've been listening to too many audiobooks. That's what I think." She shrugged. "But go ahead. Entertain me. I don't have anything better to do."

"You really shouldn't like me this much." He played with his beard. "Look at me. I look like Fozzie Bear or something."

She patted his belly. "Don't be so hard on yourself. I can whip you into shape."

"Ha ha, well, if you saw the other me, you wouldn't have to worry about that. He's in perfect shape."

Mandi tilted her head. "Oh, what do you mean? You aren't you in your *dream* world?"

"I'm a master swordsman named Ruger Slade. I look like the Wolverine guy but bigger and better."

"Ha, now I know you're dreaming. Okay, Ruger Blade—"

"Slade."

"Slade, isn't that an Australian band? You know, the 'Run Runaway' song. Maybe that can be your theme."

He remembered the band and rolled his eyes. "Oh man, don't ruin me." He shifted in his bed. "Do you want to hear this or not?"

"I want to hear it," someone with a scratchy old voice said.

Charles was in a wheelchair being pushed by Nurse Nancy.

"Charles!" Abraham hollered as if he'd just found a long-lost dog. "You're alive!"

The old man lifted his feeble arms and shook his little fists. "They gave me one more week to live. Whoopee!" He broke into a fit of coughing and wheezing.

"Stop getting yourself all worked up, Charles," Nancy said as she rubbed his back. "You don't want to shorten that week."

"The sooner you're off your shift, the more certain I'll be that I'll live longer. When's Lindsay coming back?" Charles caught his breath, twisted his neck around, and glared at Nurse Nancy. "Just get me in bed."

"My pleasure, you ancient goat," Nancy said. The brassy blonde loaded Charles into bed and wired him up to the oxygen and monitors. She made quick work of it then patted his forehead. "See you tomorrow."

"I hope not," Charles said as his wizened eyes watched her exit the room. "She's trying to kill me." He got his first good look at Mandi. "Oh my. She did kill me. I'm in heaven already."

Mandi giggled.

"Charles, where have you been?" Abraham asked.

"Who cares? The only thing that matters is that I'm here now. So, who is your radiant friend?"

"I'm Mandi. It's nice to meet you, Charles."

"The pleasure is all mine." Charles cleared his throat and adjusted the oxygen tube in his nose. "I hate this thing. Makes me look pitiful. But don't mind me. After that last battery of tests, I'm exhausted." He closed his eyes. "Nice to meet you, Mandi. I hope you stick around. You look like a woman that would be good for that guy."

"I will if he lets me," she said.

"Uh… well, Charles, I'm glad you're back. Next time, warn me before you leave," Abraham said.

"Who are you, my babysitter?" Charles waved his hand. "Good night."

Mandi shrugged her brows. "So, are you going to keep telling me your story, or do we need more privacy? We don't want Charles to think you are a nutcase. He might report you to Nurse Dr. Jackie."

"No, I won't," Charles quietly said. His voice trailed off. "I could use a good story."

"Whatever. I don't see the harm in it," Abraham said as Mandi brushed his hair away from his eyes. "Where was I?"

"You said that you were Ruger Slade. A sword fighter."

"A renowned sword fighter." He grabbed her hand. All of a sudden, the urgency to return to Titanuus came back. With awakening passion, he said, "And I was on a mission to save my friends. My Henchmen. They need me. Sticks, Horace, Clarice. They are in immediate danger. There are so many people counting on me. King Hector, Bearclaw, Vern, Iris, Dominga. And my sword even has a name. It's Black Bane."

"That's a pretty vivid dream when you know names for things. I studied psychology in college," she said. "I even thought that I might become a psychiatrist. At least I wanted to. But when I got married and had babies, all of that went by the wayside." She made a sweeping gesture with her hands. "Whoosh. The point is that you usually dream what you know but don't actually identify with new names."

"Wow, that's something I never knew about you."

"I'm a quick study of people. Some I like to study, but most I…" She stopped and looked at Charles.

The old man was sitting up on his bed. A new fire glimmered in his eyes as he stared hard at Abraham.

"Something wrong, Charles?" He glanced at Mandi. "Do I need to call a nurse?"

In a voice as strong as iron, Charles said, "You've been to Titanuus. So have I."

CHAPTER 18

Abraham cleared a catch in his throat and with wide-eyed wonder asked, "Excuse me? Did you just say that you've been to Titanuus?"

"Oh, yes," Charles said with a healthy luster in his eyes. "It is the home of Black Bane, and you wield it. That's fascinating."

"What is he talking about?" Mandi said. "What is Titanuus?"

Abraham peeled away from the woman and swung his legs over the rim of his bed. "Shh-shh-shh," he said softly.

"I'm not one to take kindly to being shushed," she said, rubbing her bare arms. "But since I have goose bumps popping up all over me, I'll allow it this time."

"Charles, what do you know about Titanuus?" Abraham said with desperate urgency. "I need to get back there now."

Charles's monitors began to beep loudly. His heartbeat and blood pressure spiked. His eyes became spacey and distant, and his mouth opened wide. He clutched his heart and moaned loudly.

"Gooseberries! He looks like he's having a heart attack," Mandi said. She repeatedly pressed the nurse call button located on Abraham's hospital bed. "Nurse! Nurse!"

With a wild-eyed look, Charles snatched Abraham's hands in his. His grip was as strong as a mason's. In a strong cryptic voice, he said, "Find the Big Apple, Ruger. You must find the Big Apple. The tide turns. The Elders awaken."

Nurse Nancy rushed into the room. "Let go of him!" She tried to peel Charles's grip away from Abraham's finger. "Geez, it's like there is Gorilla Glue on them." She stole a look at the monitors. "Charles, let go! You're having a heart attack."

Beep. Beep. Beep. Beep. Beep. Beee...

Finally, the old man's grip broke free, and he fell backward on the bed.

"Get the paddles in here, quick!" Nurse Nancy cried.

"Help him!" Abraham said.

"I'm trying!"

A pack of nurses rushed into the room, pushing a defibrillation machine.

Nurse Nancy removed Charles's gown then grabbed the paddles while a male nurse lubed them up. She rubbed them together. "Charge that thing."

The defibrillation machine made a distinct whine. The male nurse studying the machine gave Nurse Dr. Jackie the go-ahead nod. She lowered the paddles onto Charles's scrawny chest.

A tall and slender black man wearing black-rimmed glasses ran into the room. "Stop!" A physician's stethoscope bounced around his neck. He grabbed Nancy by the shoulders and pulled her away. "Do not resuscitate! Do not resuscitate! It's on his medical power of attorney!"

Nurse Nancy sank inside her Hello Kitty scrubs. "Ah, crap, oh no. I'm so sorry. I forgot."

"Why did you stop for?" Abraham asked. "Bring him back! Bring him back! Why isn't anybody doing anything?"

Dejected, Nurse Nancy said, "I can't. I'm sorry, but this is the way Charles wanted it."

When Abraham reached for the paddles, the doctor stepped in his way. In a firm voice, he said, "Mister Jenkins, you need to settle down. This isn't your responsibility. It's ours. Now, you seem awfully upset. Did you have some sort of relationship with Charles?"

Abraham sat down on his bed. "You could say that, but no, we weren't related."

The doctor nodded and turned away. He checked his watch. "Time of death, 2:10 p.m. Go ahead and take Mister Abney downstairs." He took off his glasses and wiped the lenses with a handkerchief. "Nurse Nancy... come and see me in my office."

Abraham dropped his face into his hands as his stomach twisted into knots. Charles knew about Titanuus. He had been there. Nothing but truth was in his eyes.

As soon as the doctors and nurses left the room, he quietly said to Mandi, "You heard what he said, didn't you? He named Titanuus. That's where I have been. For weeks."

"I heard it. That was intense." Mandi rubbed his arm. "It was intense even before, well"—she had a guilty look in her eye—"before Charles died. I've never seen anyone die before. Not in real life, that is."

If anything, Abraham's doubts about where he was and where he'd been had been eased. He wasn't crazy. He was traveling between two worlds somehow. He knew it in his gut. Everything was too real. The question was how. An explanation had to exist.

"Listen, I need you to do me a favor," he told Mandi. "I mean, I'll understand if you don't want to. But in case I go back out, will you look into a few things?"

She arched a brow and said, "Sure."

"I'll do it on my own, but man, my stomach is fluttering like butterfly wings, and a migraine is coming on again."

"Well, let me get you something for the pain."

"Oh no. Remember, I had a severe problem with that kind of medicine, and I don't want to go through that again." He pinched the bridge of his nose. "I need to maintain a clear head."

"So, what is it that you want me to do?"

"When I was in Titanuus, there were two men from this world that I met. The first one was named Eugene Drisk. He was a professor or something. The other one was another professor named Solomon Paige. He would have gone missing twenty years ago or more. He said he was a hippie nutritionist at Duquesne. Just see if you can find them. And try to find out what that Colonel Dexter is up to. Oh, and do me one more favor. Will you take some flowers to the cemetery? For Jenny and Jake. Just in case."

With a worried look in her eyes, Mandi said, "You're kinda scaring me, Abraham. I don't know what's going on, but I don't want you to leave me again. Abraham." She shook his arm. "Abraham!"

He heard her words, but he could not answer. He didn't want to leave her, but they needed him on Titanuus. Shocking pain splintered his mind. Bright, blinding spots flooded his mind, and he screamed.

CHAPTER 19

"He's coming around," someone said.

Abraham's eyes peeked open. The dark surroundings blocked out the skies. Nothing but walls of black rock could be seen. The roar of the waves carried to his ears, but he could smell the salt of the sea. Iris's face was looking right at him. Her round eyes and face had their usual warmness. Her soft hand was on his face. Her touch was warm and soothing, and he wanted to melt into it.

"How long have I been out?" he asked with a groan.

"Several hours. You took a nasty shot on your head. I had to mend the wound from all of the bleeding." Iris rubbed his face with a damp rag. "There was a lot of blood. I almost thought you were dead at first, but I knew better. It would take more than a bump on the head to kill Ruger Slade."

Realizing he was lying with his head on her lap with her bosoms in his face, he rolled over onto his side. His head pounded like a jackhammer. His skull felt as if it were split in half. "That rock about got the best of me."

He peered about. They were in some sort of cave with the top cut out. He could see a small part of the daylight sky. Ugly gnarled trees were growing above, and vines and roots were running down into the strange cave that he lay in.

"Where are we? Where is everybody else?"

"We are secluded while the others are scouting," she said as she reached over and rubbed his back. "Bearclaw carried you over. We are—I don't know—about a mile deep into the island. Crown Island is a strange place. Full of surprises." She flicked away a spider as big as her hand. It looked like a tarantula. "And bugs. Many, many bugs."

"Glad to see that you are among us again."

Squinting, Abraham noticed another person huddled in the corner of the cave. "Shades?"

"At your service, dear Captain." The man was hogtied. "I'd shake your hand, but as you can see, or barely see, I'm a bit indisposed."

"Where did you come from?" he asked.

Shades opened his mouth, but Iris slung a handful of dirt at him.

She said, "He stowed away on the lifeboat. The little bugger was crammed underneath the benches with our gear. I swear, I don't know how he does it. He's not that wee of a fellow. But it is a pain in the ballocks." She flung more dirt at him. "Bearclaw left him here until you woke up so you could decide what to do with him. If there was a vote, we'd vote to leave him here after we rescue the others."

Abraham sat all the way up. The last he'd checked, Shades was locked up in the brig. Somehow, he'd escaped and made the trip to Crown Island with them. He thought it strange that such a sudden change had occurred after he'd come back from his dream or other reality. He'd been in the real world for at least a day, and now he was back in Titanuus. One place was as real as the other. *What if I live in two realities? Is that possible?* Regardless, he had a mission to complete and was actually glad to be back in Titanuus—even if his head hurt.

"Ruger or Abraham, are you still with us?" Shades asked with curiosity. "There is a lost look in your eyes."

Iris got up and gave Shades a stiff kick in the gut. "Be quiet. Nobody needs any more of your agitation."

"It's fine." Abraham stood up. The cave walls were thirty feet up. A narrow passage led out. "Let's go after the others."

"They'll be back soon. Bearclaw said so," she said.

"Yes, Bearclaw said that several hours ago, and that's not soon," Shades said. With his hands and feet tied behind his back, he managed to wriggle his way up onto his knees. "Something is wrong. I've been trying to tell Iris that. I've been around this company a long time, and they should be back by now. Or at least one of them would have checked in. They are very military about that."

That made sense to Abraham. The Henchmen were thorough when executing their plans. They did what they said. And there was a big difference between soon, a few hours, and several hours.

"Iris," he said, "be honest. Do you think Shades might be right?"

"My hands are clammy. I know something is off. But I wasn't going to leave you." She had a guilty expression. "I don't trust that Lewis and Leodor. Those two windbags probably got them into trouble. I'm worried about Horace." She frowned. "Someone should have been back by morning. It's daybreak now."

The conversation about the missing Henchmen made Abraham's hairs stand on end. Something was indeed wrong. Ruger's body could sense it. His sword belt was lying on the ground, so he picked it up and buckled it on.

"Captain… Abraham… Ruger… uh, how should I address you?" Shades asked. "It must be very confusing. I only ask because I want to help. Why else would I come to this wretched island? I want to prove my worth to you. If you could only remember how it used to be. I was one of your best."

"Ha!" Iris said, strapping on a backpack. "He's double tongued. You can trust a hungry wolverine better than you could trust him."

Shades rolled his eyes. "It's not my fault that the ones with less intelligence don't understand me. I'm a complicated man."

Abraham drew a dagger and took a knee in front of Shades. "I'll let you go. I'm certainly not going to let you lie in here and be eaten by spiders or whatever."

Shades brightened. "Excellent. So what title shall I address you by? I don't want to sound disrespectful."

"Ruger will do." He reached to cut away Shades's bindings.

Shades slipped his hands and feet free of the cords with the ease of a magician, and he tossed the ropes at Iris's feet. He looked at Abraham's dagger and said, "No need for that. I could have escaped at any moment and even slipped out when Iris would doze off. She makes little chipmunk noises when she sleeps."

"Hey," she said.

"Whatever," Abraham said. There had been enough delays. He needed to save Sticks and the others. "Grab some gear. Let's go."

Outside, the sun was bright, but a haze hung over the island. The three of them marched to the top of the ridge that they'd been hidden in. With his back to the ocean, Abraham gazed toward the center valleys of the island. It was a jungle, thick with huge twisted trees and wild foliage. Skimming the skies, great birds flew from tree to tree. But something else strange stood out in the middle of the great trees like a thumb. A gargantuan mushroom towered over the tree line.

As the sea winds howled through the rocky seawall, Abraham's spine tingled. "Devil's donuts, they're going to be in there, aren't they?"

CHAPTER 20

The sweltering island jungle was alive with snakes and vermin. Dripping with sweat, Abraham pushed his way through the bush wherever they couldn't pass. With tiny biting bugs stinging his arms, he forced a path through the dense thickness. "Remind me to leave Crown Island off my list of vacation destinations."

"Will do," Shades said. "I think."

They managed to track the Henchmen's path a mile deep into the island. The company had left a trail. They numbered too many to pass subtly, and the guardian maidens and Lewis and Leodor were inexperienced at what they were doing, which didn't help. Normally, the group could pass unnoticed. But not this time. The effort was sloppy.

Trudging along behind Abraham, Iris pulled free of some colorful flowers covered with briars. "Are there any jungles that aren't miserable?"

"I don't know. I haven't been in that many," he said.

Shades picked his way through the brush and came up behind them. "I think staying on the boat would have been a better idea. It's no wonder that the windreavers fly. Who could live in this misery?"

"Us for now." Abraham noticed fresh blood on a fern's leaves at his feet. A bright-yellow mosquito was feeding on the blood. He flicked it away. "We have blood."

They moved into a clearing among the trees and prickly bushes. Bushes had been plowed through, and deep foot impressions were on the ground. Some were men's, others beasts'.

"A skirmish. A bad one," Shades said. He was on one knee with his hand on the ground, looking at some footprints in blood. "Whatever they fought won. Something carried off the dead. They are still heading the way we are going, toward that mushroom."

"Seems strange that the windreavers would fight on the ground," Abraham commented.

"It's possible that the windreavers serve something else. A higher power. An Elder," Iris said. She wore an onyx-shaped amulet with dull brass trim around black jade. "The primitive places make living sacrifices. It's possible that they prepare a feast to the Elder of the Sea or another."

"You guys sure have a lot of Elders," he said as he eyed the blood on the ground.

"I don't mean to pry, but don't you have Elders where you come from?" she asked.

Shades looked up at Abraham.

"Elders are the names of parents and older people. But you mean something different. You're talking about gods. People in my world worship many idols, much like your elders. Money is the most notorious one. I only believe in the one true God. No time to discuss that now. We've got Henchmen to save from the clutches of whatever is in that mushroom."

"Ah, the Elder of Coin," Shades said with brightening eyes. "I like that one."

The trio continued the agonizing trek through the rough terrain until some faint pathways cleared. Abraham led the way, sword in hand and ears perked. Birds' calling, insects' buzzing, and varmints' chittering carried over the sound of their feet on the path. Tracks were on the ground, pressed-down woodland and footprints. True to their discipline, if the Henchmen were overwhelmed, they would sometimes scatter. Signs of that were all along the path, as well as signs of something else, a beast, heavy like a horse, with hooves for feet.

An animal-like snort erupted from the jungle ahead.

Abraham and his companions froze. Slowly, on tiptoe, they advanced. They stopped behind bushes rich in cranberries the size of a knuckle. A blue-winged robin flew out of a nest within. The trio hunkered down at the sound of a great beast snorting again.

He mouthed the words to his companions, "What is that?"

Iris and Shades only shrugged.

With the smallish man and hearty woman by his shoulders, he split the bush with his hands and peeked through the gap. A weird pack beast stood on eight powerful legs. It looked like an ox, stoutly built, with a broad head and nose, but had the curled horns of a ram. It stood as tall as and twice as wide as a horse. It had a saddle built for two. One man sat in the saddle, carrying a long spear. His head was a bone-white skull without a stitch of hair or skin on it. The rest of his body was that of a man, strapping, with body carvings, tattoos, and a necklace of finger bones dangling around his neck. His skin was pasty white, and he wore only a belt of daggers and a hemp dress around his waist.

Iris pressed her body into Abraham's and spoke softly in his ear. "Ghouls. The henchmen of many Elders."

Super ghouls is more like it, Abraham thought. They weren't ghouls as he thought of them. He pictured ghouls as a bunch of twisted grave diggers that only came out at night. They preyed on rats, bugs, and birds. This group of ghouls was different. They were warriors, wild men of the jungle with skull faces—a perversion of the living and the dead.

Shades tapped on Abraham's shoulders. He was looking around the right side of the bush, and he pointed.

Abraham hunkered down beside him. Apollo and Prospero were sitting on the ground, back to back, corded in jungle vines. Their faces were bloody and swollen. A second ghoul lorded over the top of them. The ghoul cracked each man on the head with the shaft of his spear and shouted in a bizarre language.

"I can free them if you distract them," Shades whispered to Abraham. "I can free them if you don't distract them. Say the word. It's your call."

"Hold on," he said.

The ghoul screamed in Prospero's and Apollo's faces. Prospero spat on the ground. The ghoul grabbed Prospero by the hair and slammed his head into Apollo's then laughed, mocking them. Quickly, the ghoul tethered the strung-up Henchmen to the beast. The ghoul in the saddle kicked his heels hard into the beast's ribs. The beast lumbered forward, and the rope went taut. Prospero and Apollo were dragged down the jungle path with the second ghoul walking right behind them.

As Abraham watched with horror, he said to Shades, "Go cut that rope. I'll take care of the ghoul."

"What do you want me to do?" Iris said.

"Keep an eye out. There's bound to be more." He looked at Shades. "Keep it quiet."

"Quiet is my middle name," the rogue said.

"Let's go."

CHAPTER 21

Apollo and Prospero bounced down the path. Dragged at a brisk pace, both men fought their way to their feet, only to fall down again and again. Then they did manage to make it upright, but with vain effort, for the ghoul tripped them with his spear. Together, the scraggly Henchmen toppled and busted their knees on the jagged path.

Abraham gave Shades enough time to slip out ahead of him. After a mental count of sixty, he made his move. He dashed down the path with Black Bane in hand, as silent as a deer. The ghouls lumbered with an easy gait, oblivious of the death coming upon them. Ten steps away, Abraham's soft feet touched a dry twig, which made a loud snap.

The second ghoul spun around with casual coolness. Tiny fires like burning diamonds lingered evilly within its eye sockets. The ghoul made an uncharacteristic move, tossing its head back and letting out a deep, demonic cry.

Abraham unleashed a lethal swing that took the ghoul's head from its shoulders. The body collapsed, and the bone-white skull bounced on the ground. It was still screaming.

"Bloody meat pies, will you shut up!" He kicked the skull like a football, and it went shrieking into the jungle.

"So much for the element of surprise," Apollo called out.

He and Prospero had been cut away from their tether. The battered men stood beside Shades, who'd just cut them free.

"I hope you brought some extra steel with you," Apollo continued. "We're going to need it. Those ghouls don't fight in pairs. They fight by the dozens. The jungle's thick as soup with them."

"You're responsible for your own gear, Henchmen. Not me. My guess is that he has it." Abraham pointed at the ghoul riding the great beast, which had turned around.

The beast clawed its hoof across the ground and snorted. The ghoul lowered its long spear like a lance.

"Trouble's coming," Abraham said. "Step aside."

Iris came charging up the path. Her eyes were as big as saucers. "The jungle's alive. They come." She looked at Apollo and Prospero, who were both empty-handed. "Those aren't going to do you much good. Let's do this."

Apollo and Prospero stuck out their right hands.

Iris grabbed them and started muttering. The wind picked up her hair, and a soft pink glow emanated from her eyes when she started chanting. The men's hands that she held turned into sharp ends like machetes.

Apollo said, "That will do."

Prospero let out a pleased grunt.

As fascinating as Abraham found the moment of transformation, he didn't have time to linger. The ghoul on the beast started its charge down the path. Its great hooves thundered underneath its slavering snarl. It lowered its curled horns that same moment the ghoul lowered its spear.

Abraham felt his body come to life as adrenaline charged through him. He felt invincible. He let go and let Ruger take over. He lifted his sword, charged down the path, and screamed.

Ten feet from a colossal collision with the beast, he leapt high in the air. He cleared the beast's horns and the ghoul's stabbing spear. He hit the ghoul like a cannonball, and it tumbled from the saddle. Both men hit the ground and rolled, one over the other. The ghoul got the upper hand. His strong fingers locked around Abraham's neck and dug in deep.

With a swing of his fist, Abraham cracked the skull of the ghoul with the pommel of his sword. The ghoul's teeth clacked together in laughter. Abraham struck again and again. The blows glanced away from the skull, which was as hard as stone.

"Get off of me, Skeletor!" Abraham pulled a dagger and plunged it into the ghoul's side.

The ghoul let out a gasp as dark blood spurted out of its side.

Abraham bucked underneath the weakening ghoul. He flung the body aside and slipped a dagger into its heart. "I have the power!"

The ghoul died.

The clamor of battle rose.

Abraham popped back to his feet. A gang of ghouls were locked in battle with Apollo and Prospero. The pair of fighters fought with wild fury against the spear-wielding fiends. Apollo sank his hand, turned into a machete, into the body of a ghoul. Prospero butchered another with a swift downward chop that went through the meat of the shoulder. "Kazuna!" he roared.

Farther down the path, Iris ran from a brood of ghouls and vanished into the jungle.

Shades was nowhere to be found.

Abraham ran back down the path after Iris. As he passed the skirmish of Apollo and Prospero in his path, he sliced two ghouls down with one swing. Not breaking stride, he churned after Iris. He leapt a fallen tree and came upon the ghouls that had her trapped in front of a tree. Iris's eyes were aglow with pink fire. Her fingertips massaged the air.

Four ghouls rushed her at once with lowered spears. They would impale her in a moment.

Abraham couldn't get there in time. Iris was doomed.

Jungle vines dropped out of the branches like living snakes. The vines coiled around the ghouls and ripped them up off their feet.

Before Abraham could take a swing at them, the vines ripped the ghouls apart. Black guts spilled out of them.

Iris wiped an oily black smudge from her face and flashed a smile at Abraham. "They fell right into my trap."

"Impressive. If I'd known that, I would have stayed and helped Prospero and Apollo." He scanned the bodies. "They are dead, aren't they?"

"For now. Let's hope the jungle feeds on them." She ran after him as they hurried back toward the path.

They busted through the brush back onto the path. Prospero and Apollo were battling for their lives. Worse trouble was coming. The beast came with snorting fury to trample all of them.

Abraham yelled at the top of his lungs, "Get out of the way!"

If they heard it, they didn't give a sign. The wild bearded men kept fighting.

The ox beast didn't slow a step.

CHAPTER 22

Ten yards away from colliding with Apollo, Prospero, and a knot of ghouls, the beast veered left. The bearded warriors shoved away from the ghouls. The battling knot of skull faces stumbled right into the stampeding beast, which trampled the ghouls. Bones cracked, and guts splattered underneath the behemoth's hooves.

Suddenly, a head popped up atop the beast. It was Shades. He sat hunched over in the saddle, tugging hard at the reins. "Get out of the way! Get out of the way! I can barely control this thing!" He pulled the reins hard backward.

Ruger stood in the path in front of Iris with his sword ready to strike.

The ox beast skidded to a halt. Its wet nostrils snorted snot all over the ground.

Shades peeked out from over the top. "I think it's another dumb animal. Naturally, a smart man like me can learn to control—"

The beast bucked.

Shades sailed high in the air. He reached up and grabbed the branches overhead. His fingers locked in a cluster of leaves. Then his grip started slipping. Beneath him, the horned beast jumped upward. Its straight rows of teeth nipped at Shades's toes.

He curled up and yelled, "Slay it! Slay it!"

Abraham caught the horned beast coming down and stepped into a sword swing that cut its neck open. The beast hit the ground with a resounding thud. It bucked a few times and died.

Meanwhile, farther up the path, Apollo and Prospero were finishing off the ghouls with spears. Their hands that were once as sharp as machetes had turned back to normal. They were up to their elbows in blood and gore.

Shades dropped out of the tree and landed without a sound beside the beast. He propped his foot up on it and crossed his arms. "Remember this. I'd like a portrait of it."

"You didn't slay it," Iris said.

"True, but the person looking at the painting won't know that," Shades said.

Apollo and Prospero wandered over. They noticed their sword belts hanging from the saddle of the beast. They picked them up, and each strapped on his two long swords and crossed them behind his shoulders. "I thought more would be coming. We were fortunate. This must have been the last patrol," Apollo said.

"What happened to everyone else?" Abraham asked.

"Ambushed. Scores of them." Apollo spat a bloody tooth onto the ground. "Traveling with Lewis and Leodor was like dragging a wagon full of pottery. They wouldn't shut up. We should have left them with you, but they insisted. We scattered. Made the most of it, but the ghouls had the numbers. Bearclaw surrendered. We hung back and followed but got trapped."

"Trapped how?" he asked.

"Fell into a pit," Apollo said while Prospero clawed the grit out of his beard. "I'm not sure if everyone else is caught. I hate to say it, but I assume they were."

A rustle came from the branches. Someone pushed through the vegetated tangles. It was Zann. His face was all scratched up, and he had bug bites all over him. The Red Tunic held his hands up. "It's me," he said, in a murmuring southern drawl. "I heard the commotion and thought I'd take a look. Glad it's you."

"Is anyone else about?" Abraham asked.

"No. I followed all the rest up to where I could see that crazy mushroom. I heard the scuffle and came back. Walked right into a massive spider web and got bit a thousand times." Zann peeled some webbing off himself. "I used to hate bugs. Now, I hate jungles too."

Abraham nodded. "All right, then. This is it. Let's go."

CHAPTER 23

A GIANT MUSHROOM SAT IN A jungle grove and towered above the trees. The tremendous obelisk of oddity appeared to be at least half the size of a football field. Stout at the bottom and with an umbrella of a top, the gargantuan mushroom was petrified. Vines snaked up the mushroom's sides. Small colorful flowers budded between the countless grooves. The place was unlike anything Abraham had seen before.

"That's weird. A mushroom castle." He and the others were hidden in the jungle less than thirty yards away from the mushroom. They'd been observing the comings and goings around the mushroom for quite some time. A broad dirt road made a ring around the mushroom, where ghouls and their oxenlike beasts circled the castle. On top of the mushroom, the windreavers could be seen, darting through the skies and landing on top. They would vanish on the roof. For all intents and purposes, the mushroom castle was well guarded.

"Any ideas?" Abraham asked his crew.

Shades toyed with the fine hairs budding on his chin. Apollo and Prospero were silent. Iris and Zann shrugged.

"Excellent suggestions."

He got the feeling that it would be up to him to figure out what to do. After all, he was the Captain. At first thought, he figured they could enter in a disguise by posing as the ghouls. He thought that their skull faces might have been some sort of mask. He was wrong—their heads were living skulls. The creepiness sent spiders walking up his arms. They needed to find another way in.

Finally, Shades spoke up. "I can get in there and take a look. At least we'll know what we are up against."

"So can I," Zann said in his slow country-boy accent. "I need to get my brother out of there."

Shades rolled his eyes. "I think it's best that I travel alone. I don't need anyone to slow me down."

"I don't need anyone to slow me down either," the lazy-eyed Zann said.

"You're being serious?" Shades said with incredulity.

"Don't I look serious?" Zann said.

Shades eyed Zann up and down and said, "No, you look useless."

"Enough chatter," Abraham said. "It's broad daylight out, and we'll probably have to wait until nightfall. I don't think anyone will be able to waltz over there without being seen."

"Sure I can," Shades said. He slunk away toward the mushroom castle.

"Anything he can do, I can do," Zann said as he took off after Shades.

Abraham opened his mouth as he watched them go. The men were already beyond earshot. He was about to object but thought the better of it. He needed to trust his Henchmen.

"Are you really trusting Shades to go in there with that boy?" Iris said. The thirtysomething woman had a motherly tone in her voice. "You can't trust him."

"We've been about to trust him this far," Abraham said. He kept his eyes fixed on the road circling the mushroom castle. Teams of ghoul guards made a slow march around the mushroom, sometimes crossing paths with one another. Two teams of ghouls carrying their spears passed each other, and as the ghouls separated and meandered down their paths, Shades and Zann silently darted behind the ghouls' backs and huddled by the mushrooms. Abraham could barely see the men blending in with the vines. "Whoa. That was slick."

Two of the ghouls turned around. Their bright diamond eyes scanned the ground between them and the forest and the mushroom. They looked right at Shades and Zann.

Abraham's heart quickened as he gripped his sword handle. He said under his breath, "Get ready to bail them out."

The ghouls turned back around and continued their patrol. Shades and Zann began climbing the vines up the mushroom castle. The structure stood over one hundred feet tall. It had to have been massive inside. The pair of men scaled the walls like monkeys and vanished into the stem like rats scurrying into holes.

"They are in. We wait," Abraham said. In a kneeling position, he switched knees.

Iris sat down beside him and hooked her arm in his. "I hope Horace is well. I hope they all are, but mostly Horace. I like him much better since he gave up the tobacco. I liked him, but it always made his teeth so ugly. I couldn't stand that. Now, he's truly handsome. Not like you, but you know, for a bullish man like him. A different sort."

"We'll get him back," Abraham assured her. "All of him."

From inside the mushroom came a low moaning like a great brass horn. The birds in the surrounding trees scattered out of the branches by the thousands. The critters of the jungle scampered.

Iris covered her ears. The sound became louder. The ground trembled beneath them.

The jarring noise became so loud that Abraham couldn't hear himself speak, and he said in a loud voice, "Do you have any idea what that sound is?"

With her fingertips plugging her ears, Iris shouted back, "An Elder awakens! An Elder awakens!"

CHAPTER 24

ABRAHAM FOUGHT THE URGE TO cover his ears. He kept his eyes fixed on the mushroom castle. The vine leaves and wild flowers shook and bowed on the petrified construct. The ghoul patrol took to their knees and bowed. The cavernous sound softened, and a chanting came from within the macabre structure.

Abraham looked at Iris and asked, "What makes you think that an Elder awakens?"

"Only an Elder makes a sound like that. Their very breath can shake the earth. The scrolls of the Sect say so." She unplugged her ears. "Was it not like this when we encountered the Elder spawn? Sounds so horrifying that they turn your bones to jelly. If it awakens, then it will be hungry."

"Then we better get in there," he said.

"We are ready," Apollo said. He had both swords in hand.

So did Prospero. "It's time to fish our brethren out of there. That thing within sounds hungry. Let's feed it some steel."

Abraham caught a glimpse of Zann popping out of one of the mushroom's portals. The wiry man shimmied down the vines, checked both ways at the road, and darted back into the forest. He met up with Abraham and the others. His hands trembled as he fought for his breath.

Abraham put his hand on the young man's shoulder and said, "Take it slow. What did you see? Where is Shades?"

Zann caught his breath. "Everything was fine until that sound started. My heart felt like it headbutted my ribcage. So, we navigated through this canal toward the center. It's like the inside of a beehive inside the mushroom—all sorts of coves, different shapes and sizes. There was a ledge that overlooked the center of the mushroom. It reminds me of the arenas and coliseums in Kingsland, except it's all on the inside."

The chanting coming from the inside of the mushroom grew louder.

"What did you see? Where are the Henchmen?" Abraham asked, shaking Zann's shoulder. "Did you see them?"

Zann nodded. "Yeah, I saw them. There were loaded up in a wagon, like the ones we used to transport prisoners in the king's army. One of those beasts was pulling the wagon toward the center. Those bird people were looking upward in the dome of the mushroom, squawking like crazy. In the dome of the mushroom, something moved. It was a black glob, gelatinous, wet, and sticky, a churning bulging mass. Tentacles dripped out of its body and wiggled like snakes." He shivered. "That's when that thing spoke. I felt it from my toenails to my chin. Shades told me to go." He looked Abraham dead in the eye. "I didn't have any trouble running. My feet did it for me."

"We're going in," Abraham said. "Apollo, Prospero, make sure those ghouls don't get the jump on us. You have the back side. Iris, you can stay or go. Whatever powers you have, have them ready."

"I'm coming. I can't let you have all of the fun without me. Besides, Horace needs me," she said.

Abraham nodded. "Lead the way," he told Zann.

Zann nodded and took off in a straight line for the mushroom castle. He led the climb. Abraham followed, with Iris behind them. Down on the ground, Apollo and Prospero sneaked up on the kneeling ghouls and butchered them. Zann entered the portal, and the group wormed their way into the canal. A few dozen feet in, they could stand.

The corridors were a network of hollowed-out stone. Nooks and crannies of all shapes and sizes were everywhere, partially covered in moss and mold. They sped down the tunnels in the direction that the sound was loudest. They emerged on a ledge overlooking a natural arena. Windreavers were perched along the ledges by the score. The ghouls moseyed about by the hundreds on the ground floor. All the lost Henchmen, bound with ropes, were being led into the center, where they were tied up to individual posts fixed in the ground.

"This is bad. Really bad," Abraham said.

The Henchmen were outnumbered over twenty to one. He looked up into the mushroom's dome. The numbers were just as Zann said… but worse. The heavy glob half filled the cap. Cords of slimy tentacles dropped from its guts. A great circular mouth full of razor-sharp teeth opened and closed. It started a slow descent down the walls.

"That's disgusting. How are we going to kill that thing?"

"It's an Elder. It can't be killed," Iris said.

"It's an Elder of what, slime?" he asked.

She shrugged. "We need Leodor. He might have some idea on how to stop it."

"I don't think we're going to stop it. We need to get everyone out of here," he said with widening eyes as he watched the glob descend. "That big thing moves fast."

Apollo and Prospero filed in behind them and peeked over the rim. "I see it's going to be another one of those days," Apollo said. "What's the plan?"

"We need to cut loose our company and get them the heck out of here." Abraham scanned the ground. "That wagon pulled by the beast might do. We're going to have to load them up and drive them straight back through that tunnel. Those beasts pulling the wagon should make a path. What do you say?"

"Death before failure," Apollo said.

Abraham nodded. "Yeah, it's going to be a real tequila wine mixer."

A shrieking scream erupted from down below. The glob slunk to the ground. Its tentacles, dozens of feet long, lashed out and caught Sticks by the waist. The slimy tentacles pulled her off of her feet. The rope binding her wrists and tethering her to the pole snapped taut. With a pain-stricken face, she hung parallel over the ground, quavering like a strummed banjo string. She cried out, "Help!"

Abraham took off down the stairs, yelling, "Sticks! Sticks!"

CHAPTER 25

THE INSIDE OF THE MUSHROOM flared out like the inside of a football stadium. The levels tiered up ten feet at a time. Abraham jumped from one level to the other, catching the attention of the surrounding windreavers. The windreavers started to chirp and beat their wings. Abraham paid them no mind. Sticks was seconds away from having her arms pulled out of her sockets. Panic filled the devotedly expressionless woman's eyes.

A spear ripped right passed Abraham's ear from behind. The mushroom became a hive of anger. He didn't break stride.

"Hold on! Hold on!" he yelled.

Sticks screamed something back at him

Out of nowhere, a smallish man sped across the arena floor with a dagger in hand. He made it to Sticks ahead of Abraham by thirty feet. It was Shades. He cut through the rope with one quick swing. Sticks snapped forward, careening toward the black glob's opening and closing slavering mouth. She flopped on the ground no more than twenty feet away from those foul clenching jaws. The tentacle holding her by the waist dragged her limp form toward the mouth.

Abraham churned on. He stretched his stride and closed the distance between her and him. Tentacles whipped at his feet and body. He bounded over one, rolled under another, and sliced the third clean through. He arrived at Sticks only ten feet away from the monster's mouth. Small tentaclelike tongues shot out of the monster's mouth.

"No!" With a single downward chop, he sliced the tentacles away from Sticks's waist. A smelly, sticky, gooey puslike substance squirted out. "Run," he said. "Run!"

Sticks tried to crawl away to safety, but another tentacle snared her leg. Her fingers clawed at the ground as she started to be dragged back in and yelled, "You call this a rescue?"

Horace sawed the ropes binding his wrists against the sharp square edge of the post he was tied to. The twine rope coiled around his wrists started to fray. Even with great effort, getting free would take an hour. He would be dead by then. "Remain stalwart, Henchmen!"

The mushroom's arena broke out into absolute chaos. A handful of Henchmen erupted from the terraces, bringing a roaring shout of encouragement from the prisoners. At the same time, the black glob, some sort of ancient Elder, had come to life. Tentacles sprang from its mouth like snakes, and that fiend's slithering things came for them. That was only part of it—the other part were the windreavers and the ghouls. They were in a full-frenzied attack and had set their sights on the Captain.

"Be patient, big one. I'll be back for you," Shades said as he slipped by Horace and sawed at Dominga's cords where she was hung up on the next post over. "Ladies first."

"Take your time. I don't need you." Horace put his shoulder into his post. The six-inch-wide pole wobbled. Using his strong hands, he rocked the post back and forth. It broke free in the hard ground. With a loud grunt, Horace ripped the post out of the ground.

Bearclaw and Vern let out wild cries. "Wreak havoc, Horace!" Vern shouted.

With eight feet of hard wooden post in his hands, Horace took a swipe at three charging ghouls and knocked them over. "Kiss wood, abominations!"

Two tentacles coiled around his ankles and ripped him from his feet. A windreaver glided over him and dropped a hunk of stone.

The boulder landed square on Horace's belly. He let out a gusty "oof!" and the tentacles reeled him in toward the black glob's mouth.

Shades cut Dominga free, which had a domino effect. He gave her a blade, and she cut loose the guardian maidens while he freed Bearclaw and Vern. The bigger men burst into action, and along with the rigid guardian maidens, Hazel and Swan, the foursome unleashed an assault on the ghouls. Locking up in hand-to-hand combat, they took away the ghouls' swords and abused the fiends with them. Streams of black blood dripped onto the ground.

The last people Shades cut free were Lewis and Leodor.

While the old man rubbed his raw red wrists, Lewis glared at Shades and said, "Next time, free me first."

Shades made a quick bow and sarcastically said, "As you wish, son of the king."

Lewis turned away. Weaponless, he marched straight toward two ghouls coming at him with swords. Lewis darted between their simultaneous thrusts, twisted a sword from one ghoul's hand, and heel-kicked the second one in the gut. With a sword in hand, he disemboweled the one he'd disarmed with a lightning-quick stroke. Then he split open the white skull of the other. A rush of more were coming his way. "Leodor, do something! I'm not doing all of the work myself."

Leodor gave Shades a firm push. "Step aside, child of the star." He flicked his fingers. The bony appendages emanated a green fire. He spread out his fingers, pointed at the rushing knot of ghouls. Green darts shot from his fingertips, and the darts shot through their foreheads. They tumbled to the ground. "That's power."

Windreavers soared overhead, dropping rocks. Shades danced away from the shower. Leodor took a direct blow to his skull.

The hordes kept coming. The battle got worse.

CHAPTER 26

THE GUARDIAN MAIDENS CUT PRINCESS Clarice loose from the post by sawing the rope with a spear.

"Get me a weapon!" Clarice said.

A windreaver soared overhead and chucked a spear down at her. With catlike agility, Clarice jumped aside. The spear bit into the ground, inches from her toes.

The dark-headed guardian maiden, Swan, and the light-haired Hazel cocked their spears back over their shoulders. Taking aim with the skill of well-trained soldiers, they launched their spears.

The windreaver that attacked Clarice twisted away from Swan's spear, but Hazel's caught it right in the abdomen. The windreaver let out a squawk and spiraled downward. It crashed skull first into one of the hitching posts.

Two ghouls carrying swords rushed Clarice. The first ghoul moved with a notable limp, and the other's skull face had a busted socket. The swords they carried were corroded, but steel still shone from underneath the rust. The notched edges were keen in some spots.

Clarice ducked underneath a sideward swing from the limping ghoul. She hopped out of the way of the second ghoul's cut. The strapping fiends lifted their swords high and struck out at her at the same time. She hopped backward. The swords missed her chest by an inch. She tripped over the legs of the dead windreaver and fell to the ground. The ghouls pounced.

"Save the princess!" Hazel cried out. Without a weapon, the guardian maiden hurled herself in front of the ghouls. She absorbed the full brunt of their attack.

The ghouls' swords hacked deep into Hazel's body armor with vicious blows, and blood flew.

Clarice screamed, "No!"

Abraham chopped at the tentacles as quickly as he could. He freed Sticks more than once, but keeping up was hard as the tentacles kept coming out of the black glob. He severed one slimy cord after the other and shouted, "Sticks, get out of here! I can handle this!"

"I don't think so," she said as she made acrobatic leaps and rolls away from the tentacles. "There are too many of them." She kicked one tentacle away and jumped another.

"Get in that wagon, and get everyone out of here!" Abraham sliced through two tentacles at once. "This is a rescue mission. Be rescued!"

"Incoming!" Horace said in his bearish voice. He was being dragged by many tentacles coiled around his feet toward the great opening and closing mouth. He had the hitching post and was clobbering the tentacles, but they did not release. Eyeing Abraham as he was dragged helplessly toward the black glob, he said, "Death before failure, Captain!"

"Everybody is going the wrong way!" Abraham said. "Henchmen, all of you get out of here!"

Escaping was easier said than done. In addition to the black glob were the scores of ghouls and windreavers launching attack after attack. Everyone was engaged in a life-and-death struggle. Where there were blades, there was blood—lots of it.

A new wave of tentacles spat out of the black glob's mouth. Abraham sliced through half of them. The other half wrapped up his wrist and ankles. With a fierce yank from the tentacles, he hit the deck. The black glob drew him in toward its clenching jaws. He wasn't alone. Sticks and Horace were heading that way as well. Wrestling against the tentacles, he said, "Meatballs and spaghetti! This isn't good!"

The black glob reeled them in toward its hungry mouth.

"I can smell the foulness within! Like the sewers of Dorcha!" Horace bellowed. "There is nothing but rotting death in there!" He looked to Abraham. "I have an idea. I'll go first and buy you time. It's been a pleasure to serve, Captain *Abraham*."

"No, stop, Horace, what are you doing?" he asked. He was on the right, with Horace in the middle and Sticks to the left of Horace.

Horace managed to hop on his butt and inch ahead of Abraham. He came within a few feet of the black glob's mouth. Horace lifted up the post, and as soon as his boots touched the rim of the glob's chomping mouth, he shouted, "How about a toothpick?" With a well-timed effort, he shoved the post into the monster's mouth. The great jaws froze. The gelatinous black glob let out an angry moan.

Horace gave a big, bearded smile. "It's working!"

The black glob's mouth twisted left and right like a dial. Its massive gooey body trembled all over. Abraham found a sliver of hope in the futile moment. Horace had bought them time. It could go a long way.

The post inside the monster's mouth snapped in half with a loud pop. Its teeth clacked together. The tentacles that held them were severed. They were free.

Horace let out a throaty cheer and pumped his fist in the air. "Death before failure!"

A nest of slimy tentacles burst out of the slimy Elder's mouth, enveloping Horace. In one easy yank, Horace's big body was jerked off the ground, and he vanished inside the blackness of the monster's mouth.

CHAPTER 27

Abraham's fighting heart sank. The gutsy Horace was gone.

"No," he muttered.

As the dead tentacles fell away from his limbs, another surge of them came. He and Sticks jumped and twisted. The tentacles were too many, overwhelming them with slimy coils that bit into their limbs and bodies.

With vain effort, he tried to cut against the tentacles locking him up, with fierce motions of his wrist. He cut, but that wasn't enough. "Sorry, Sticks," he said.

As the tentacles slowly reeled her in toward the monster's mouth, she said, "It's not your mistake. We never should have been caught."

"I say, what is all of the commotion about?" Black Bane asked, speaking into Abraham's mind.

"Black Bane! Do something! We're about to be devoured by a glob. Stop it!" he said.

"Are you calling me Black Bane or someone else?" the sword asked.

"You! You never told me your name. You forgot it!"

Wriggling against her bonds, Sticks asked, "Who are you talking to?"

"The sword! It's a long story!"

"Hmm… I suppose Black Bane will do. It's a fine name for a sword, but I'm not so sure about for a person," the sword replied. *"Let me see what I can do. Drawing magic from different worlds can be tricky. What sort of spell are you needing? A shield. Perhaps flying. I liked flying, I think."*

With the black glob's mouth only a few feet away, Abraham yelled, "Fire! Lightning! Just do something!"

"No need to yell."

The engravings on Black Bane charged up with the hot glow of lava. The handle heated up quickly in his hand. "What am I supposed to do?"

"Point and shoot."

Abraham was more than familiar with the concept. He'd been to the firing range with his father dozens of times. Also, he was a pitcher. The problem was that the sword was pointed toward the ground. Tentacles pulled down his arms, making it impossible to aim.

He huffed and puffed. The hard muscles in his arms went to work, and Ruger's body responded. He grabbed the handle in a firm grip with both hands. With the muscles in his forearms bulging like roots, he lifted the sword and pointed it toward the glob. "Cut loose the chaos!"

A crooked stream of burning energy blasted out of the sword's blade as if fired from a cannon. The fiery bolt slammed into the glob's body. Shockwaves rolled through its gelatinous makeup. It let out a heavy moan that filled the arena. The black glob crept away from the wroth power. Its tentacles loosened their iron hold on Abraham and Sticks.

Abraham climbed to his feet and let the sword unleash its power on the monster. "Die, you pile of manure. Die!"

The black glob spat a huge black glob out onto the ground. It landed right before Abraham's feet.

He didn't change his efforts, keeping the stream of energy pointed at the monster. With alarming speed, it crawled back up the wall and into the cap of the mushroom, more than half filling the ceiling. The bolt of power sent out one final surge as the last blast of energy released from the sword. The black glob made an ear-jarring shriek. Its body heavy and bulged, and it exploded.

KA-POOOOOM!

The ceiling rained down big globs of goo, showering everyone in oily sludge.

The ghouls and windreavers scattered.

Covered in glistening ebony slime, Abraham said, "That was gooey. Ghostbuster gooey—like a burnt marshmallow." He smacked his sludge-covered lips. "But that ain't marshmallow. More like burnt dung."

"Tastes like life to me!" the small black blob at Abraham's feet said.

"Horace!" Abraham said.

Horace popped up. "Aye!" He pumped his fist in the air. "Henchmen! Henchmen! Henchmen!" All the others rallied around the men and joined in. "Henchmen! Henchmen! Henchmen!"—except for Lewis and Leodor.

Abraham walked over to Lewis, stood by his side, and put his hand on his shoulder. "What is wrong? Aren't you used to victory?" he asked the refined prince, who was now covered in muck. He wiped his finger over the man's cheek, revealing the white underneath. "Don't worry. You'll eventually get a taste for it."

CHAPTER 28

The Henchmen made it back to *Sea Talon* and continued the journey north through the Sea of Troubles. All of them were sticky with black glob goo and blood. The blood from their battle wounds washed off easily. The glob was a different matter. It was more like a tar. It clung and stank on all of them.

Only one of them had died on the trek into the detestable Crown Island. Hazel the guardian maiden was given a flaming burial at sea. The crew watched the pyre of floating smoke and flame from the rear decks of the ship. It sank with the dreariness of Crown Island in the background.

Horace said a few words. "She lived with loyalty and died like the guardian she was."

All the eyes of the hardened company were dry, save for Princess Clarice's. The sixteen-year-old fought hard to control her sobbing, but her chin quivered. She clung tightly to her other guardian maiden, Swan. Like a loving aunt or older sister, Swan stroked Clarice's tangled locks.

"Everyone," Abraham respectfully said as the funeral pyre was swallowed by the waters, "let's get back to work. Mend your wounds and fill your bellies. This journey has only started." As everyone got back into action and moseyed down the decks, he looked at Swan. "Let me have a word with Clarice."

The raven-haired woman with eyes as hard as stone deepened her frown.

"It's a polite request," he said.

Swan's nostrils flared. She kissed Clarice on the head and walked away.

Clarice wiped her eyes, which were fixed on the burial spot at sea. "What do you want?"

"I just wanted to say that I'm sorry about the loss of your friend."

"Hazel has been with me since I was born." She sat down on the railing and held on with shaky hands. "That should have been me that died. Not her. She gave her life for me. And just like that, it's gone. I didn't have the right to take that."

Abraham lifted a boot up onto the railing, leaned forward with his eyes on the shiny wavetops of the sea, and said, "It's a good thing that you care."

"What is that supposed to mean? Of course I care."

"Where I come from, there are a lot of entitled people, like you, that don't care. Life has little meaning to them."

"I'm not like Lewis. He's that way, not me."

He nodded. "I can see that. But her death is your fault."

She glared at him and said, "I know that."

"No, I don't think that you do. At the moment, yes, she gave a sacrifice for you, but it was you that put her in the dangerous situation," he said. "You see, you disobeyed your father. You stowed away on this ship. You didn't give any consideration to the consequences of your actions. And now, your friend is dead."

Clarice turned rigid. Her eyes had the poison of snakes. "How dare you? I'm the—"

"Princess! Yeah, I know that. But you're on my ship, and you're part of my Henchmen. From now on, you act like it. Keep your impulses to yourself. They get not only you into trouble, but others as well."

With her mouth hanging open, she stood up, shut her mouth, gave him a burning look, and stormed away from the deck.

Abraham didn't even watch her go. He'd said what needed to be said. Clarice, Lewis, and Leodor were proving to be nothing but trouble. They were dragging the Henchmen down. He couldn't have that.

Sticks slid into view. "Pretty tough on the girl," she said. Her clothing was sticky with black tar, and she had cuts and scrapes all over. Her hair was tied back in two twisted braids.

"You disagree?"

"No, you're the Captain. She needed it. I think what you said was spot-on." Sticks planted her rear end on the railing. "Let her go plant her face in a pillow."

"You don't cry, do you?"

"No. It's a waste of water."

He chuckled. He needed the laugh. The day had been a long one.

Sticks cocked an eye at him and said, "Your sword talks to you?"

"Huh, well, when it wants to." He locked his fingers on Black Bane's handle. "I was going to ask you or Horace about that. Did the other me ever talk to the sword?"

"Not out loud, that I recall."

"What about the power that I used? I mean, I cast lightning out of the tip."

"The old you used some strange powers. But he never attributed it to the sword." She licked her fingers and rubbed at a greasy spot of tar on her elbow. "This stuff is nasty. Yech. Anyway, the older you acted like he could do anything. Horace and I always suspected there was something with Black Bane. After all, the Elders made it. So *they* say."

"Who is *they*?"

"Isn't that always the question?" The straight-faced woman shrugged and spat over the deck. "I say, who cares? We live. We die. Don't dwell on it."

"You really know how to liven up a party, don't you. If for some reason you ever make it to my world, I'm taking you to a Catalina wine mixer."

"A what?"

"Nothing." He took his hand away from his sword and said, "Just keep this between us, but I think a wizard from another world lives in it. Like I live in Ruger's body, someone else lives in this sword. It's very weird. Like Excalibur with a personality."

"What's Excalibur?"

"A legendary sword from my world."

"So, your world is like this world?" she asked.

"It used to be, I suppose. I'm not so sure about the magic. But the supernatural was more prevalent in biblical times with wizards like Jannes and Jombres." He slapped a knee and smiled. "But what do I know? I didn't live back then, but I can't rule it out either." He pushed out his chest and said, "Frankly, I'm just rolling with it."

Sticks gave a concerned smile. "Are you well?"

"I can't say. For all I know, I've gone crazy, but let's keep that between ourselves. I'm going to go track Solomon down. I'll see you later."

"Your cabin?"

He lifted two fingers and started to think of Mandi. "Uh, possibly."

"I'll kill him!" someone shouted from the main deck. "I'll kill him!"

CHAPTER 29

It took some doing, but Abraham quickly brought the commotion of angry voices under control. Apparently, Shades had somehow fondled Swan inappropriately. He claimed it was a misunderstanding, and he claimed it from the safety of the crow's nest. Meanwhile, Swan had her sword out, eager to butcher the slightly built man. She tried to climb the ropes, but her clumsy effort only brought on chortling laughter from the crew. Swan apparently couldn't climb ropes to save her life.

The red-faced Swan put it all on Abraham and said, "Put that man in the brig! Cast him in the sea! No man touches me like that and lives!"

"Touch you how?" Abraham asked.

"I don't want to discuss it. Bring him down here, and let me cut him open. I'll have satisfaction!"

"I saw it, Captain," Tark said from the next-highest deck. "He squeezed her rump like a melon from the marketplace. He got both hands on the hind end. Both small hands, that is. I'm surprised she noticed it. She's got an ample rear end." He made a curved gesture with his hand. "Like an apple."

Swan waved her sword at Tark and said, "Keep your eyes off my hind end! I'll kill you too!"

Tark's light eyes grew big.

The Henchmen ruptured with chuckles.

Even Abraham couldn't help but laugh. As he regained his composure, he shouted up to Shades in the crow's nest. "Come down here, apologize, and let's be done with it."

"Do you think an apology will do?" Swan said to him with an angry white stare. "I will have satisfaction. I will have vengeance. That rodent is not worthy to touch the sanctity of a guardian maiden. He has soiled me."

"He squeezed your butt," Iris said. "You don't need to start a war over it even though you could probably fight one on it."

Swan paled. She was a tall, strapping woman, almost mannish in build, with a tailgate that seemed to bring with it a natural air of authority that she wasn't entitled to. "You gap-toothed trollop. How dare you speak to me like that. I'll kill you too!"

"At this rate, she is going to kill everyone," the puffy-lipped Vern remarked with a chuckle. "Everyone, keep your hands to yourself, or the princess's bodyguard is going to cut them off and shove them up your nose."

"Okay, that's enough!" Abraham threw his arms up. "We are all Henchmen, and we don't cut each other's throats. Sorry, Swan, but an apology from Shades will have to do."

Burly, bald, and bearded, Horace said, "Er… Captain, they are not Henchmen. They don't have to live by the same standards that we do."

Abraham remembered that neither Shades nor Swan was branded. Without the brand, he didn't have full control over them.

Lewis strolled into view. "Ah ha, yes, the guardian maidens live by their own rigid standards. And when I say rigid, I mean rigid. Certainly, you remember, don't you, Ruger? Or am I talking to the other man in the shell, Abraham?"

Abraham didn't know what the man was talking about. Swan had a seething look.

"Can't you let this go?" he asked.

"No," Swan said in her husky voice.

"Ruger, you know me, I can't always control my impulses when faced with a such a charming woman," Shades shouted down from above. "The moment I encountered her, I was… smitten."

"I won't be groped like a tavern trollop. I am a guardian maiden. This sullied man must pay. You should know that," Swan said to Ruger.

"Fine, Lewis, fill me in." Abraham hated to ask, but it was something that he should obviously know but didn't. "What am I missing?"

"The guardian maidens are virgins. Pure of heart. No man can touch them without permission," Lewis said happily. "Not me and certainly not that man in the roost."

With her arms crossed over his chest, Dominga said, "No wonder she is so uptight." She bumped forearms with Vern and Iris, who stood beside her smiling.

"So, let me get this straight. You want to fight Shades. To the death," Abraham said.

"It is our way," Swan said. She took off her sword belt but removed her poniard. "A dance of daggers will do. I aim to teach him a lesson, but I'll kill him if I want to. I have the right."

Abraham gave Sticks and Horace a lost look. They shrugged their brows at him. Apparently, this was a legitimate conflict, and he could do nothing about it.

"This is insane. Swan, you should set your pride aside and let me punish him. Cheese and crackers, all of this from a bump on the rump." He threw his hands up. "Shades, get down here. This lady wants to dance. Give her a dance."

Shades climbed out of the crow's nest and down the mast like a spider. "I love to dance. And with this fabulous vixen, it will be a pleasure."

Swan glared down on Shades and said, "Grab a dagger. You're going to need it."

CHAPTER 30

A CIRCLE OF PEOPLE FORMED AROUND the two combatants. The fight was on.

The belligerent Swan glared at Shades and said, "Arm yourself, little man!"

Shades showed his slender fingers and said, "There won't be any need for that. I'd never stab a woman. Especially a ravishing beauty like you."

"You are a fool," Swan said in a cold tone. "I will not show mercy on you."

"Ooh… you know how to say the things that I like," Shades said with a smile.

All Abraham could do was watch and hope that Swan didn't kill the mouthy man. As he stood with his hands crossed over his chest, Vern took wagers from the others. The Henchmen were whispering among themselves. Some of them, like Cudgel, were grinning. Apollo and Prospero were huddled together, gathering their own money.

Swan spun her poniard in her hand and cut it quickly back and forth. She'd proven to be a skilled fighter, slaying ghouls and windreavers alike. Shades, however, appeared to be a different sort of foe. He moved quietly and quickly in his cloak.

"Take off that cloak," she said. "I need to see that you don't have any tricks up your sleeve."

"Oh, I'd be happy to." Shades spun the cloak off his body in a showy display. He hung it over his arm as a butler would and made a quick bow. He was bare chested and little compared to the other men on the crew. His body had a thin layer of fat and some muscle showing. He was fit, but not as fit as most. White and red scars from battles and beatings covered his back and chest. He'd been through something—a lot of something. "Oh, sorry, I accidentally removed my jerkin. I hope you like what you see, dear guardian maiden." He flexed his meager arms.

Bearclaw chortled.

Swan, whose skin appeared unblemished, blanched as she eyed him top to bottom. She set her jaw again and said, "You talk too much. One last chance to take a weapon."

Dominga flicked a dagger at Shades's feet, where it stuck deeply into the planks. She said, "Don't be a fool. Take it."

Shades tossed his cloak aside, bent over, and grabbed the dagger with one hand. Straining with effort, he tried to pull the dagger free with a grunt. He dropped to both knees and pulled at it with both hands. The dagger didn't budge.

The Henchmen busted out with bellowing guffaws.

Abraham couldn't hold his laughter back. Even Sticks couldn't contain her smile.

Swan's face turned as red as a beet, and she cast a hot stare at all of them. "Foolish hyenas! I'll give you something to laugh at!" Cat quick, she lunged and stabbed at Shades.

Without the dagger, Shades rolled out of the way in one silent, smooth motion. He popped up to his feet and hopped away from a slice across his belly.

"Cut him open like a fish!" Iris shouted.

Shades shot her a look. He backpedaled, dodged, dived, and rolled away from Swan's lethal strikes with the grace of an acrobat. The more he moved, the angrier Swan appeared to become. She thrust hard and fast.

The Henchmen shouted cheers of encouragement.

The combatants worked the inner circle. Swan's nostrils flared. Shades shot a devilish smile at her. With a grunt, she rushed him and let loose an overhead cut. Shades spun underneath the strike and slipped behind her body. She overextended and lost sight of him. She spun around, but Shades moved more quickly than she. He stuck to her, back to back, without touching her. She turned around slowly, a lost look in her eyes. Even when she would spin more quickly, Shades remained smoothly behind her. He put his finger to his lips when she stopped.

The Henchmen couldn't contain their laughter.

Swan looked over her shoulder and kicked backward. As Shades leaned left, she drove her left elbow into his ribs. With a painful *oof*, he sagged to the ground. She pounced on top of the smaller man. Straddling him, she pinned him down by clamping one hand over his throat.

She poised the dagger above his eye. "What do you have to say for yourself now, worm?"

Shirking underneath her gaze, he said, "The flesh is weak."

"I'll show you how weak it is." She cocked back the poniard and started to thrust.

"Swan! No!" Princess Clarice shouted in a voice that all could hear. She had been down below earlier, but the commotion of battle must have caught her attention.

"This man violated me. He violated the guardian maidens," Swan said, out of breath and panting.

"I tried to apologize," Shade said, "but everyone knows that these hands can't be trusted. Not when beholding such rare and divine—"

"Shut your mouth hole!" Swan said.

The princess walked over to Swan and calmly said, "Set your weapon aside. That's an order."

"But…" Swan said, dejected. She stuck the dagger in the deck right beside Shades's face. When she stood up, she found Clarice looking up into her eyes, and she swallowed.

"Swan," Clarice said. "I hereby release you from your vow to me. You are no longer a guardian maiden. I am no longer princess. I am a Henchman. You choose to be what you choose to be."

A silence fell over the ship. Lewis stood nearby, leaning against the mainmast with an eyebrow lifted.

Swan's jaw dropped. "Princess Clarice… I know no other task."

"Neither do I. You'll just have to learn like me."

CHAPTER 31

As the ship sailed on, Abraham finally tracked Solomon down. Compared to a luxury cruise liner, *Sea Talon* was very small. However, finding Solomon wasn't so easy. The troglin had a knack for hiding. In this case, Solomon had hidden himself in plain sight. He'd locked himself in the brig. That was the last place Abraham looked.

"You really don't need to be inside there." Abraham stood outside the cell's bars, which were locked. "You aren't an animal. Care to tell me what is going on?"

Solomon sat on the floor with his head down. "I don't feel like troglin are meant to be sailors. The motion of this ship is torment to me. It puts me on edge, and that makes me hunger."

"You mean, you want to eat people?"

Solomon nodded. "It's a sick thing. I'm becoming a ravenous cannibal. I swear I did nothing to deserve this."

"We'll cast our nets and start fishing. Will fish fulfill you?"

"I don't know that that will sustain me. I could handle some sushi. About a ton of it." Solomon lifted his hairy face and managed a sharp-toothed grin. "But this isn't a fishing vessel."

"No matter. The Henchmen always surprise me. I'm sure they'll catch something. A shark, maybe."

"Jaws would be delicious about now."

Abraham slid down the wall and sat down. "I had another experience."

"Really, you mean, a dream? What happened on that island?"

"That's a long story, but you'll pick up on it." He rubbed the nasty bump and gash on his head. "We were rowing the lifeboat to Crown Island when the surf rode my head into the rocks."

"I can see that. Do tell more."

"I woke up in a hospital. There was an old man in the other bed. Uh…" His eyes searched the ceiling. "Charles. Charles Abney was his name. He was old but very lively. There was a whole lot of goings-on. But do you know what he said to me?"

Solomon's belly rumbled. "No."

He turned his head toward Solomon and said, "He said he'd been to Titanuus."

"But that was a dream?"

"It didn't feel like a dream. It felt as real as this, or as real as it ever was." He bumped his head gently against the wall. "My boss was there, Luther Vancross. And Mandi was there too. We had a very deep conversation."

Abraham spent the next hour going over the details, and Solomon hung on his every word.

"I'm telling you, Solomon—this place is real, and that place is real. I feel like we are part of a bizarre experiment. In my dream, I was back in my body too. Just like I had an accident, but in a way, I don't believe it."

"Maybe you are Ruger Slade, dreaming that you are in another world and in another body," the troglin offered.

"What? No, that can't be it. Anyway, if I go back again, maybe I'll get more answers. I told Mandi to look into a few things. I wanted her to find out what happened to you and look into that Eugene Drisk."

"That's very kind of you. I'd be very curious to know what happened to me too. I wonder if my gangly body has been running around grocery stores terrorizing butcher shops for the last twenty-plus years."

"What do you mean?" he asked. "You think that the troglin inhabits your body?"

"I don't know how it works. It just made sense to think of it that way. Anyhow, go on."

Abraham rubbed the back of his head and said, "I think I lost my train of thought." He snapped his fingers. "Oh, when I get a bad migraine, that seems to trigger it. I've always had them since the plane accident. It's what got me addicted to painkillers. So, you don't have dreams like I do?"

"No. I'm envious. I'd do anything to go back to our world, even for a day—drink beer, smoke pot, and eat pizza. That's what I'd do."

"You can't think of something more practical to do? Like see your family?"

"I just want to relax, man. My family is pretty intense, hence my early inclinations towards recreational drug use." Solomon chuckled.

"I think we could make pizza if we wanted to. We could introduce this world to a lot of things."

"Indoor plumbing would be delightful." Solomon scooted away from the back way to the front of the cell. "Abraham, I think you are enjoying this world more than the last. Would that be an accurate statement?"

"I hate to say it, but I think so. Back home, I didn't have anything but my beer truck. I felt guilty all the time. It was hard to overcome. Everything reminded me of them," he said. "I know that's not right. Is it?"

"Who is to say but you? But if you let this world take over, then you might not ever make it back to the other," Solomon said.

"The only thing back home is Mandi. But we haven't even been on a date. I feel guilty when I'm with her, but here, I don't feel as much guilt."

Solomon tilted his head back. "Ah, what happens in Titanuus stays in Titanuus."

Abraham chuckled. "That's messed up, but I guess so. We could probably make a killing if we opened up our own casino here."

"Assuming that no one else has thought of it. Perhaps."

"What do you mean by someone else?" Abraham asked.

"Well, dude, we can't assume that we are the only ones here, now can we? If we are seeing modern items, and I've met you, and you've met me, then it's safe to say that *we are not alone*."

"Holy baloney. I just remembered something. The old man, Charles—he told me to find the 'Big Apple.' Does that mean anything to you?"

"Aside from what I know of it back home, no. I've never heard the expression before. Not here, anyway."

"I guess we are going to have to start asking around, then." Abraham got up. "It might not hurt to ask around now. Hang tight. I'll see what I can do about getting you something to eat."

Solomon came to his feet. The hairy troglin had to bend sideways as his head hit the ceiling. He reached through the bars and grabbed Abraham by the arm. "Don't get caught up in this world. Remember, we don't belong here. I want to go back, and I'm counting on you."

"I know. I gave you my word. I'll keep it."

"You can't please everyone all the time," Solomon said. "At some point, it will have to be one or the other. We can never have it all."

Abraham pulled away and said, "We'll see."

CHAPTER 32

Sea Talon and its crew sailed for days without any more incidents on the turbulent waters. The pirate galleon made its way safely over the Head of Titanuus and was now making its way south, past the Pirates' Peninsula, located on the East Arm. Early in the day, the great sun shone over the sea. Tark and Cudgel were in the crow's nest, using spyglasses. They were far out at sea, where the land could not be seen. That left Abraham uneasy.

Sticks stood beside him, overlooking the port side of the ship and staring farther out to sea. She leaned against his body. He put an arm around her shoulder. The last few days had been quiet. In the evenings, they slept together in his quarters. She had been very affectionate, more so than before.

They didn't speak about it, but he had a feeling it had something to do with him saving her life. He was getting used to it and feeling less guilty.

"Feels like there is nothing out here but us, doesn't it?" he asked.

"I know I'm glad I'm not alone. I'd hate to be lost at sea. It's massive," she said.

"Have you ever wondered if there are other lands like Titanuus out there? In my world, there are many."

"I couldn't care less. So long as I'm on land, I'm happy, even though being on this boat with you has had, well, some advantages."

"Women find sailing romantic." He toyed with her braid that hung over her breast. "Do you?"

"I don't know about that, but it seems to make the sex better."

"Oh, so you're just using me."

"It's either you or any one of them," she said as she glanced at the working crew. "But you do have the larger bedroom."

One thing he liked about Sticks was her matter-of-factness. And she was certainly a lot more woman than she appeared to be. With her came mystery and excitement, which made the voyage more delightful.

"Let's hope we don't sail too far and run into one of the Elders. I'd hate for one of them to capsize our boat." Abraham looked toward Horace.

Manning the wheel of the ship, the warrior had his face to the wind, and Iris stood behind him with her arms wrapped around his belly. Her hands beat on it gently like a drum.

Abraham scanned the deck with a shade of a smile.

Vern and Dominga sat on the bow with their legs dangled over the rim. They held hands. He talked. She giggled.

Somehow, impossibly, Shades and Swan were speaking openly. They were both swabbing the deck. He constantly spoke with flattering words while she tried to fight back her smiles.

"It's becoming a regular Love Boat around here," he said. "At this rate, we'll be starting new families. Is there an Elder of Love or Romance?"

"The Elder of Passion, they call her. They say her essence is the same wind that kisses the seas. Perhaps she is kissing us now," she said with a playful smile. "Do you want to go back to your cabin?"

Without any guilt, Abraham tossed her up on his broad shoulder and said, "Sure. What happens on Titanuus stays on Titanuus." He slapped her on the rump. As he turned away from the ocean, he found himself face-to-face with Lewis and Leodor. "I don't want to hear it. We are going after the Underlord, just as King Hector wants. I'm not diverting on some other quest. It's Hancha or bust. Get over it."

"We've agreed to let you lead us down that treacherous path," Lewis said with a bored gaze. "And it wasn't I that wanted to interrupt your little tryst. It was Leodor. Now that he's come around, he has something to say."

"Something useful, I hope." Abraham set Sticks down and faced the viceroy.

Leodor had taken a rock to the skull back at Crown Island, and it showed. Half of his face was bruised. He looked like death warmed over, but the glimmering intelligence in his saggy eyes was still there. He'd been under the deck, getting treatment from Iris the last few days.

"Well, spit it out, Mister Magoo," Abraham said. "I can't wait to hear the next twist from your chicken lips."

With his hands tucked inside the sleeves of his tar-stained robes, Leodor said, "It was always my wish to expressly serve the king. Putting our differences aside, Lewis informed me that you had made an inquiry about the Big Apple. Is this true?"

Abraham arched a brow and said, "Yeah, that's true. What do you know about it?"

"Interesting that you should ask. I know this name, not intimately, but I know it well enough." He winced, took his hand out of his sleeve, and touched the lump on his head. "I know exactly what it feels like to be hit with a boulder. It hurts. I've gained perspective for the games of brawn that men like you play. As I was saying, the Big Apple is an odd name, but it does pass the lips of the Sect from time to time. He is a player in the grand scheme of things."

"He's a man?" Abraham asked.

"I can't say if it is a he or she. All I can say is that there is. Sorry, I didn't mean to mislead you." Leodor licked his pale lips. "Do you still have port on board?"

"Plenty," Abraham said. "Tell me more about the Big Apple. Who is he, and let's assume he is a he in the *grand scheme of things*."

"The Big Apple is a smuggler of goods and information. It's people like him that the Sect use for their benefit. That is how they have eyes and ears in all places. They take the donations to the Elders to finance it." Leodor took a gratifying snort of air into his nose. A wince followed.

Sticks touched Abraham's hand and spoke up. "Spit it out. Where is the Big Apple?"

"Don't speak like that to the viceroy, wench," Lewis said.

"You aren't on any different footing than me, oh mighty prince," she fired back.

"Why, because I'm not sleeping with the Captain?"

"No, because you don't have the big walls of a castle to protect you."

Lewis sneered. "I don't need a castle to protect me from the likes of any of you. I can handle myself quite well." His eyes shifted to Abraham. "Even without a magic sword."

"Is that so?" Abraham asked. "Care to find out?"

"Any time and any place," Lewis replied coolly.

CHAPTER 33

Leodor stepped between the two bristling men. "There has been enough fighting over the past few days. I don't think my head can stand the racket. Abraham, I'll make your task simple. After all, it is only information. This smuggler, the Big Apple, he resides on the Pirates' Peninsula on the East Arm. But that would dissuade you from your current mission. But"—he lifted a bony index finger—"perhaps the Big Apple can provide information that can serve us just as well. The trick is finding an audience with him."

"Why is that?" Sticks asked.

Leodor looked at her as though she were stupid and said, "Because nobody in Kingsland has ever seen him."

Abraham met privately in his quarters with Horace, Sticks, and Solomon. Horace kept his distance from and his eyes on Solomon. The guardian didn't care for the troglin at all. Abraham ran everything Leodor had said to him by them.

"What do you think?" Abraham asked.

"I think whatever you think, Captain. You lead. I follow," Horace said.

"You know that I'm all for it," Solomon said. The troglin looked crammed inside the cabin even though he was sitting down.

"And you?" he asked Sticks.

She was straddling a wooden chair that she'd turned backward. "I can't help but wonder if Leodor is pulling the wool over your eyes. He's a Henchman and shouldn't be deceiving you. It would be to his peril."

"That's what I was thinking. I was also hoping that I wouldn't be the lone voice in this line of reasoning." Abraham stretched his hands up to the ceiling as the boat rocked to the side. He looked at Horace. "And I expect the rest of you to have input, whether you think that I'll like it or not."

Horace clawed his fingers through his beard and said, "I trust that the brand will do its work if there is a betrayal. It has. It will. We've had deserters. They've never been seen again. Once, the blue demon plucked a man from the earth and took him away in the sky. I forgot his name, with so many, but it was before your time."

"I say, nothing ventured, nothing gained," Solomon added. "Perhaps this Big Apple is one of us. He might have the answers that we seek."

"Yeah, well, that's what I'm hoping for. In more ways than one. Horace, take the ship to Pirates' Peninsula. It's time to get docked."

"Who's going on land?" Sticks asked as she got out of her seat.

"We'll start with a small group. We better keep the others back with the ship in case they need to bail us out," he said. "Why, who did you have in mind?"

"We've let Shades linger because we needed him to guide us through Hancha," she said. "And he wants to be branded again. Have you come to a decision on that? Does he stay or go?"

"Go," Horace volunteered.

"He's been cleared of any wrongdoing that we accused him of," she said, "aside from the incident in the prison. I know it sounds strange coming from me, but I have to admit we need him. With the brand comes loyalty."

Horace frowned. "I'll support whatever the Captain decides. But I don't like the way he operates."

So far, Shades had proven to be nothing but loyal. He'd been a huge help on the ship and in the skirmish on Crown Island. "I'll bring him along. We'll see how it goes. If he fouls up, he fouls up, and we'll leave him."

CHAPTER 34

The Pirates' Peninsula resided in Eastern Bolg territory. Both Western Bolg and Eastern Bolg were enemies of King Hector. However, the Pirates' Peninsula and the East Arm were neutral territories run by an anarchist pirate government. The seafaring pirates, fishermen, merchants, and smugglers didn't answer to anybody. They served themselves and whoever paid the most. At least, that was what Leodor told Abraham.

Sea Talon docked at one of the large ports. Hundreds of vessels of all sizes were in the bay, including a smattering of warships from other territories. Hardy men and women in short clothing worked like ants on the piers, loading and unloading in the hottest part of the day. The sweat-drenched people were busy, eyes forward, and talking bitterly in the heat.

Abraham and a small company of Henchmen casually strolled down the docks toward the bustling activity of the seaside city often referred to as Pirate's Harbor. Pirate's Harbor started on the beaches and ran right up into the rolling hills. His company included Sticks, Shades, Iris, and also Leodor, Lewis, Clarice, as well as Swan, who insisted on coming. He wanted to keep the party small and not appear intimidating. Too much muscle might draw attention. But Solomon came too. He dressed in a stitched cotton vest and wore a skirt altered to fit him. Apparently, troglin were often hired as bodyguards in northern territories. Hence, typical of the Henchmen, they posed as merchants with a small squad of moderately heavy guards. From Abraham's point of view, they fit right in with the multitudes. Aside from that, he didn't have any idea where he was going. He let Sticks lead the way.

Pirate's Harbor was a large, expanding cluster of stone buildings with clay-tiled roofs and mud and stone roadways. The buildings had no porches. They were more or less tall, narrow buildings of stone side by side, which ran deep and away from the roads. The sound of seabirds and harsh voices haggling were commonplace. Men and women in fisherman coats walked the streets, smoking pipes. Vendors with carts loaded with fish shouted at them from the streets. The ocean breeze did nothing to carry away the pungent smell of fish and sweet tobacco.

Sticks led them up the network of streets past numerous windows of dolled-up women shamelessly flaunting their bodies and catcalling.

"One shard, one trick. Two shards, three tricks," called a rosy-cheeked strumpet who sat in a windowsill—all the windows of that building had red shutters on them.

Solomon waved at the women and grinned. "A red-shutter district. I guess it is fair to assume that every city in every world has one."

"It's the oldest profession in the world, they say," Abraham said.

Lewis sneered at the women and said, "This place is disgusting. Nothing but animals in houses. I hate commoners. They have the standards of a sow."

"Yes, we know how you feel," Iris said. "But you're worse than a commoner now. You're a Henchman, two steps lower than a shepherd."

"Never," Lewis muttered.

Sticks stopped in front of a tavern that had a wooden sign mounted above the door. The sign read The Greasy Pelican inside a drawing of an oversized beak of a bird. She opened the door. Smoke and loud voices and the twangy sound of stringed music rolled out of the doorway like a slap in the face.

"After you," she told Abraham.

He crossed the threshold of the stone-built building. The room was deeper than it was wide, and round tables, half empty, covered the floor. Surly men and hearty women in short clothing chattered all over the room. The laps of men of all sorts were filled with women in skimpy outfits. The smoky room was filled with a vibrant, exotic Arabian beat. At the far end of the room was the bar and a stone staircase that led up to three balconies overlooking the room. The Henchmen filed in. No one paid them any mind until Solomon, bringing up the rear, entered.

All the way in the back, the bartender pointed at the group. Looking dead at Solomon, in a loud and edgy voice, he said, "We don't serve his kind in here!"

CHAPTER 35

THE CONVERSATIONS INSIDE THE TAVERN came to an abrupt halt. The eyes of the patrons took long, hard looks at the Henchmen. Hands that were once wrapped around the handle of a tankard of ale found new homes on the pommels of weapons.

Abraham moved front and center.

The barkeep marched out from behind the bar and came right down the aisle. He was a burly, cigar-smoking older man with short, wavy jet-black hair and a pockmarked face. He wore a greasy white apron, and his sleeves were rolled up over his hairy, meaty forearms. He stopped a few feet short of Abraham and blew a ring of smoke in his face. "Get out. Don't make me tell you twice."

"Where I go, the troglin goes," Abraham said, "and I'd be happy to throw in a few extra shards to accommodate you."

Puffing smoke like a steam engine and with his arms crossed over his chest, the barkeep said, "It ain't the troglin I'm talking about. It's you. We serve plenty of troglin. They're our best customers. And troglin serve them." He shouted back over his shoulder. "Hey, Gertie! Get out here!"

The swinging kitchen door behind the bar flung open. A troglin in a pink apron bent down and stepped through. Wiping her huge hands on a towel, she said with irritation, "What is it, Sam? I'm busy, you know."

Abraham looked at Solomon, and Solomon was looking at him. Solomon shrugged. Gertie the troglin was a much younger version of Solomon, with a coat of rich brown fur. She wasn't built much differently from Solomon, though she was taller and had noticeable bosoms tucked behind her apron. Abraham scratched his head. "I don't understand the problem."

"You don't?" Sam the barkeep said. "The problem is you, cupcake. Trouble is written all over your face. I know that type. I've seen all sorts. You waltz into my bar, have a few drinks, and the next thing I know, I have broken furniture and blood on the floor. No challenges here. This is a well-run establishment."

Abraham scanned all the hard-eyed and disheveled people in the room. Surely, a handful of cutthroats were among them. Half of them could have fit in with his crew if they weren't so shabby.

"You're joking, right?" Abraham asked.

"Do I look like someone that jests?" Sam said.

Gertie strolled in behind Sam, towering over everyone. She tossed her dish towel over her shoulder and asked in a sweet and womanly voice, "Do you want me to escort these bums out?"

"Bums?" Lewis fired back. "Who does that walking flea catcher think it is?"

Gertie's massive hand shot out and grabbed Lewis by the collar of his coat. She lifted him up with one hand and said, "You have bad manners, little man."

Lewis's hand went to the handle of his dagger, but Abraham's hand stopped him from pulling it out.

"Stop. We'll go peacefully. Sorry for the trouble, Sam." He looked up at the female troglin, whose stormy blue eyes were locked on Lewis. "Will you please put my comrade down, Gertie?"

"Since you asked nicely." Gertie set down Lewis, who rubbed his throat and straightened his coat. She eyed Solomon and asked, "What are you looking at?"

"One hairy beauty," Solomon replied.

Gertie crossed her arms and said, "Dream on, old-timer."

The modern vernacular Sam and Gertie used left Abraham mentally scratching his head. He nodded at Sam and said, "We're going."

Shades piped up and said in an uncharacteristically whiny voice, "But we are supposed to meet with the Big Apple here."

"Shhh," Leodor said. "That's personal business."

Blowing smoke out of his nostrils, Sam said, "Bloody barnacles. Why didn't you say so in the first place? Have enough sense to keep your voice down when you talk about the Big Apple. Gertie, find them some tables. Give them some privacy too." He faced his patrons, lifted his arms, and said, "It's cool. Go back about your business."

The pirates and patrons carried on. The rattle of tankards and pouring of ale renewed. The stringed instruments were strummed again with the same Arabian beat. Gertie led them to the center of the tavern, where a curtain hid a short platform. She pulled back the curtain far enough for them to pass through. Three sets of tables sat on what looked to be a small stage. "Make yourself comfortable," she said. "I'll have a waitress bring you some pitchers of ale and wine. It's happy hour. Enjoy it, and try not to cause any more trouble." She walked away as everyone was seated. The platform boards creaked beneath their feet.

Clarice sat down in the chair that Swan pulled out for her and said, "We didn't cause any trouble. They did." Her nose crinkled. "What is that smell? It cuts through the body odor. I like it. Saucy."

Solomon and Abraham were sitting at the same table with Sticks. The troglin elbowed Abraham and tipped his chin toward the center of the tavern floor. A waitress in a floppy shirt and white blouse crossed the floor with a serving tray on her shoulder. She set the tray down in front of a pair of tattooed men with golden hoop earrings, licking their lips.

"That's pizza," Solomon said, elated.

"It sure looks like it," Abraham said with widening eyes. More pizzas were on tables throughout the room, loaded with all sorts of mouthwatering cheeses and toppings. "I wasn't expecting this. Were you?"

"I've spent most of my time on the Spine. If I knew about this, I would have been here long ago," Solomon said. His mouth watered as he watched a pirate pull away a slice that stretched with cheese. "Oh man, that looks good."

Abraham turned to Sticks and asked, "Did you know about this?"

"About what?"

"The pizza?"

She straightened her back and said, "I've seen it before—briefly, when we were on one of our missions that Twila sabotaged. Never tried it. It looked weird to me. Many weird things in the north."

"You can say that again. I get the feeling that this might have something to do with the Big Apple. Do you?" he asked Solomon.

"If it smells like a big apple, it must be a big apple. It explains the modern influence of their character." Solomon's belly rumbled. "I hope they have every meat topping imaginable on it."

Abraham caught Sam waving him over to the bar. "I'll be back."

"Order me at least ten of those pizzas. I'm really getting hungry," Solomon said.

"I will." He crossed the room to the bar that Sam stood behind.

Sam the barkeep was wiping out the inside of a mug. "I wanted to let you know that the Big Apple will prefer discretion." He eyed the curtains. "Didn't want you to get spooked when the girls closed them. The word is out on your arrival. The Big Apple will come soon."

"Really? That seems quick," Abraham said as he watched two leggy waitresses close the curtains.

Lewis and Leodor sat alone and were frowning. Clarice, Swan, and Shades were at another table, pouring the wine just served to them. Sticks sat with Iris and Solomon. They vanished behind the curtain. Abraham tilted his head. Shades had made up the meeting with the Big Apple. If that was the case, Abraham wondered how the barkeep knew the Big Apple was coming. He played along but felt a spider crawl up his spine. "Say, Sam, I'd prefer it if you kept the curtains open. I like to keep an eye on my company. You understand. Some of them can be trouble."

"Sure, I understand," Sam said. He put a tankard of beer down in front of Abraham and whistled to the girls who had closed the curtains. "Have a beer. It's on the house."

Abraham took a tankard and a sip. "Thanks." He watched the waitresses slowly open the curtains. Every seat at the tables was empty. The Henchmen were gone.

CHAPTER 36

At first, Abraham thought the Henchmen were playing a joke on him. The tingling nerves running through his extremities told him different. His hand went to his sword. He turned to Sam, grabbed him by the collar, and pulled him over the bar. "What sort of mischief is this? Where are they?" he demanded.

Red-faced, Sam said, "I don't have any idea. Magic isn't my area of expertise. Serving ale is."

Abraham had Sam laid out on the bar. He lifted him up by the collar and slammed him back down. "Don't play games with me!"

The surly patrons came to their feet. Some left. Others drew small, pointy weapons. Gertie lumbered through the swinging kitchen door, carrying a huge iron frying pan. "Do I need to get busy with this?" she asked.

"Don't even try me, lady." Abraham put more pressure on Sam's chest. The stout man puffed for breath. "Spit it out, Sam. I'm not the kind of man that plays games."

"I hate to insult you, partner, but you're the fool that waltzed into the Peninsula with a bounty on your head," Sam said. "People know you. You're Ruger Slade. I haven't seen anyone as brazen as you since, well, you."

Abraham's grip loosened.

Sam continued. "The Big Apple knew you were here the moment you stepped off your ship. You just happened to wander into my tavern. I didn't ask for it, but all of them would have been waiting on you. You probably would have been safe if you hadn't mentioned the Big Apple. But you did. Or at least, that runt did. I tried to warn you, but you gave me no choice."

Gertie came around the bar and crept up on Abraham.

"Back off, bigfoot," he said.

"Don't you know it's not polite to comment on a lady's feet?" she asked.

"Those aren't feet. Those are oars, and that's not what I meant. What is with this place and the vernacular?" In a way, Abraham liked it, but it was confusing at the same time. This tavern had a different vibe to it. He'd experienced some modernism in Stronghold that Eugene Drisk left behind, with pancakes and syrup and a touch of slang, but this was different. It seemed extreme, almost jarring. "Where do you go from here, Sam? Does the Big Apple want me dead?"

"Boy, you really don't remember much, do you? The Big Apple doesn't want you dead, but plenty of other people do. I can't read his mind, but I'd say he might be protecting you from them. His associates will be here soon. You should go with them or never see your friends again."

"I'm not going anywhere without my friends." He looked back at Gertie, who stood only a few feet behind him. "Where are they?"

"Only the Big Apple can answer that." Gertie flicked her long fingers at him. A stream of pink dust flew from her hand into his face.

Abraham couldn't dodge the dust, and it covered his face like flour. He tried not to breathe, but it was too late. He lost all feeling in his limbs. The sword he'd drawn slipped out of his grip. All he could think as he drifted off to deep sleep was, "Not again. Home, here I come."

CHAPTER 37

ABRAHAM WOKE WITH A JERK. Someone had splashed him down with a bucket of stagnant water. He spat the foulness from his mouth as sat up. He was inside a dungeon cell and stripped down to his waist. The only thing he had left were boots and trousers. On the other side of the cell bars was a beefy goon wearing a leather helmet that covered his eyes and nose. His chin jutted out.

He banged his bucket on the bars and asked in a gruff voice, "Are you awake?"

"No, I'm still asleep and having a nightmare, apparently." He rubbed his temples. He'd fully expected to wake back up at home. Not that he wanted that to happen. His mind was cloudy, however. Whatever Gertie had flicked at him was nasty stuff. Even Ruger Slade couldn't handle it.

"I'll be back," the goon said. He turned and walked away down a dim dungeon corridor and vanished around the corner.

Abraham climbed to his feet. The dingy cell had a wooden cot with the framework broken and the fabric torn. Rotting straw was spread out on the floor where he'd been lying. His arms and legs were shackled with tight chains. He checked the tautness of the chains. The links were thick, unbreakable.

"Dirty donuts."

He was in a lone cell at the end of a row. In the aisle ahead of him were more stone cells, guarded by steel bars.

He called out, "Hello?"

No reply came. A black rat the size of a squirrel squirted from one cell and vanished into a cell across the aisle.

He called out again. "Hello?"

Abraham wondered where his friends were. All of them had disappeared like an act from a

David Copperfield show. Either that had been an illusion, or some powerful magic was behind it, magic the likes of which he'd never faced before. He wondered where it had come from.

At first, he thought Leodor might have had something to do with it. After all, the viceroy had had the idea to venture after the Big Apple. Perhaps everything was a setup from the beginning. The only thing Abraham could hope for was that the brand kept Leodor in check. The mystic should be in the same danger as the others. He hoped they weren't dead.

The sound of soft footsteps caught his ear, more than one set. They became louder. The guard from earlier rounded the corner at the end of the aisle, followed by a much smaller man, about five feet tall, shirtless, and layered in balled-up muscle. He had two small horns like a goat's on his head, and his face was impish. He wore a collar with three bright-yellow gems in the middle. Another figure glided in behind both men, a tall, slender person with robes that covered the gaunt body like vapors. His or her hooded face could not be seen—only blackness.

The little muscle-bound man with horns marched out in front of the others. His eyes had a devious intent. He stood a couple of feet from the bars of Abraham's cell, put his fists on his hips, and said in an impish voice, "Ruger freaking Slade."

"Do I know you?" he said.

"Hmm-hmm, oh, you don't know me, but I know you. Doesn't everyone? Hmm-hmm." The horned man tilted his head to the left in a quick, birdlike fashion. "I see in your eyes that you are lost. Tell me—what are you looking for? Hmm-hmm."

Figuring that he didn't have anything to lose, he said, "The Big Apple."

"And you've found him," the little man said.

"You're the Big Apple?"

"In the flesh," the Big Apple said.

Big Apple, my butt. More like little apple. He's messing with me. He has to be. With his hands still glued to the bars, he said, "That's an interesting name. Can I ask how you came upon it?"

"I gave it to myself." Big Apple tapped his fingertips together. "Hmm-hmm. I can see something deeper in your eyes. Tell me. What are you thinking, Slade the Blade? I want to know what you are thinking."

"Reggie Jackson."

Big Apple's eyes brightened. A pleased smile formed on his lips. "Tell me more."

"Times Square. Manhattan Island. The Statue of Liberty."

Big Apple rocked up and down on tiptoe. "Interesting. Very interesting." He rubbed his fingers across his mouth. "You have made a connection." He turned and looked at the guard and the shadowy figure. "Give us some privacy."

The guard and the robed person moved back down the aisle and out of sight.

"Was that a thing or a person?" Abraham asked.

"That's my wraith. Fleece. I control it. My personal protection. Once a very powerful wizard and now my slave. Hmm-hmm." Big Apple lifted a finger. "Now that we are alone, it's time to swap stories. Who are you really? How did you learn about me?"

Opting to believe he was in a dream anyway, he let loose. "I'm Abraham Jenkins. I used to play for the Pittsburgh Pirates. I was told to seek you out by a man named Charles Abney, back in the real world. Sometimes, when I black out, I go back and forth."

"You learned about me through a dream? Humph." Big Apple nodded. "I don't know any

Charles, but I have met many people like us. However, most of them, as you know, are hunted down and killed." He circled a finger around his ear. "They think that we are madmen. Hmm-hmm."

"So, what's your story?" Abraham asked.

"I'm Edgar Gravely. From Queens. I was born with cerebral palsy. It was manageable for a long time, and I even had the exciting job of being a janitor at Yankee Stadium. But I had no life outside of that. A real loner. My parents were decent, but they died young. I think taking care of me killed them… or at least took a lot of years from them." Big Apple was as bright-eyed as ever. "But now I'm here, and even though I'm a horned halfling, I like it."

"A horned halfling? Aren't you big for a halfling?"

"I have to say I like it. And I'm not looking back. Do you understand me, Abraham Jenkins? I'm not looking back." Edgar thumped his chest. "This isn't *Lord of the Rings.* This is Titanuus, a real fantasy world, a world of second chances, and I'm thankful for mine. In this world, I have knowledge that others have." He poked a finger to his temple. "Like me, you should take advantage of that."

"I sort of feel like I already have."

Big Apple gave a big grin. "Of course you should. You're freaking Ruger Slade, the baddest swordsman that ever lived. I'd kill if I could have been you." Big Apple came closer to the bars. "You have no idea what you are, do you?"

He shrugged.

Big Apple let out a belly full of laughter and walked away, saying, "You are about to find out."

CHAPTER 38

HOURS LATER, A GROUP OF guards in leather helmets and worn tunics escorted Abraham out of the dungeon. They marched him, shackles and all, up a windowless stone staircase, level after level. He had no feel for the place and couldn't tell whether it was inside a building, like a castle, or in the belly of a mountain.

Finally, the stairwell came to an end, with a broad landing at the top and a wooden door with black iron fixtures. One of the guards with more belly than brawn pushed his shoulder into the heavy door and shoved it open. The door dragged over the ground, and a gust of salty air filled the stairwell. Moonlight spilled through the opening.

Rough hands shoved Abraham outside and closed the door behind him. He stood in the darkness of night alone.

Abraham wandered forward with the irons rubbing his ankles. The floor was solid stone. Sheer rock walls twenty feet high surrounded him. The area was square, about thirty yards wide, like a courtyard or arena. Great torches burning with flame lined the top walls from the inside of the arena. Shadowy figures sat behind the rim of the wall, their faces obscured from the light.

More doorways were there, similar to the one he'd walked through, one on each wall. They were closed.

A familiar voice spoke above the wind. It was Edgar, Big Apple. His voice was amplified and carried all over. "Welcome to the Rim, Ruger Slade. There is a bounty on your head. A sizeable one. But I have plans for you."

Abraham spun in a slow circle. His eyes adjusted to the darkness behind the rim of the wall. He could see the faces of many people, sitting in stands overlooking the arena. Men and women of all sorts were dressed in clothing, armor, and colorful garb. Finally, his eyes landed on Edgar. The horned halfling sat on a big wooden chair like a throne. Two comely women with painted bodies and skimpy exotic clothing clung to the small man's sides. More guards and the wraith, Fleece, stood nearby.

Abraham walked toward Edgar as though he were in a scene taking place in a much smaller Roman coliseum. "What's this all about, Edgar? I thought we were making some ground."

"No, no, no," Edgar said with a waggling finger. "I am the Big Apple. Always the Big Apple. Don't draw my temper. Hmm-hmm." He leaned forward, his hands gripping the ends of the arms of his chair. "You have enough problems to deal with."

"Well, aren't you the mighty little man." He looked about. "Let me guess, at any moment, those doors are going to open, and I'm going to have a fight on my hands." He wiggled his fingers. "Is this a fistfight?"

"No, it's a fight for your life, sword master. Do you see all of these people in the stands? They came to see you fight. They came to see you die."

"Fight or die, huh? It has a nice ring to it. The only problem is that I don't have a sword. I'm not much of a swordsman without a sword."

The Big Apple reached behind his chair. He lifted a sword and scabbard out into view and laid it across his armrest. Then he rested his muscular forearms on it and said, "The legendary Black Bane. It's worth as much as you. Today is a great day to be the king of the smugglers. This weapon, well, it stays here, with me. I want the fights to be fair, after all." He tipped his head toward one of the guards wearing a leather face helmet.

The guard tossed a sword into the arena. It was a short sword designed like a gladius.

Abraham picked it up. The edge was notched, the blade tarnished, and the pommel worn. He turned it side over side. "Nice toothpick. So, who am I supposed to fight with this?"

Big Apple stood up on his chair and pointed to the doorway on the far side of the arena. He looked at Abraham and snapped his fingers. The shackles that bound him fell to the ground.

In his enhanced voice, Big Apple said, "Let the chaos begin!"

The door opened. Six men wearing ragged clothing and carrying swords spilled out of the opening. Their eyes locked onto Abraham, and they lifted their weapons and charged. The crowd lurking behind the wall came to their feet with wild howls.

CHAPTER 39

Abraham sized up the would-be killers in a split second. The killers were the kind of men you'd hire to do dirty work, tough men who fought in gangs who grouped up and bludgeoned people. They ran hard, holding their long swords like loaves of bread. The fastest one drove in on Abraham with his sword lifted high.

Abraham thrust his gladius into the man's chest. *Glitch!*

The attacker's mouth dropped open. His sword fell from his fingers.

Smooth as silk, Abraham grabbed the long sword before it hit the ground. He spun around the dying man and hewed down another attacker with a fierce chop across the man's exposed temple. With his fist filled with sharp steel, he turned into a tornado of death. The attackers didn't have time to know what hit them.

Stab!

Chop!

Slice!

Glitch!

In a handful of seconds, Abraham left six men dying in pools of their own blood. He tossed the gladius aside and picked up another dead man's sword. He spun them both together in a twist of shining steel.

The blood-hungry crowd erupted in throaty cheers. They pumped their fists and flailed their arms in a wild frenzy. They began to chant.

"Slade the Blade! Slade the Blade! Slade the Blade!"

Edgar applauded in his chair. He jumped out of the chair and sat on the wall. He motioned Abraham over. "That was fantastic! I'm eager to see more. Hmm-hmm. Look around. You made many people happy and many sad. See, see the long faces. Many want you dead."

Abraham wished he knew exactly why they wanted him dead. He didn't know a single face in the crowd. He did, however, like them roaring for him. It reminded him of the days when tens of thousands of people had chanted for Jenkins the Jet. He loved that. Now, his hot blood churned again. Or at least Ruger's did. "What's this all about? Is there something in it for me? If I win, will my Henchmen be freed?"

The Big Apple tossed his head back and laughed. "You are making demands, and you haven't even started yet. You have much to prove before you have a say in anything."

"You're a real pal."

Big Apple smiled. "I know."

He stood back up on the rim and clapped his hands, and the door underneath him opened. A swordsman dressed in layers of fine golden clothing stepped through. Big Apple's voice amplified again, and he spread his arms out wide as the crowd of hundreds quieted. "Now a real challenge. A sword for hire, a legend of the shadows, the killer of all that cross his steel, Fonay Zar of the Barbican."

Whispers spread throughout the square arena. Abraham backed away. Fonay Zar wasn't some chump like the men whom Abraham had just slaughtered.

The swordsman had light-brown hair and striking features. The lean fighter moved into the area with the grace of a panther. His sword was finely crafted, a straight length of steel with a white bone handle. The edge appeared as keen as a razor. Fonay Zar held out one sword and said, "A blade for a blade unless you are a coward, Ruger Slade."

The swords in Abraham's hands were nothing close to a superior weapon like Fonay Zar carried. They might as well have been strips of steel with edges on them, by comparison.

Ruger tossed one blade aside. He saluted with the crude sword in his hand and said, "Let's see what you got."

Fonay Zar bowed. He then went into a showy display of swordplay. The shining blade flickered like lightning around his body. The blade's edge whistled and cut through the air like a living thing. His technique and form had no flaws. He was perfect.

Abraham ground his feet into a fighting stance, high guard position, and said, "Wow, that was amazing. But the wind still lives, and so do I. Bring it on, golden boy."

Fonay Zar crept forward with his sword cocked over his shoulder in the wrath guard position. The crowd applauded. A few steps from Abraham, he switched to the high guard position and attacked.

Sword tips kissed. *Clang!*

Abraham hopped backward. Fonay Zar moved with the speed of a striking snake. The man's light eyes were as cold as steel.

Fonay Zar pressed the attack. He lunged with one quick step and stab followed by another. Abraham backpedaled like a bull. The man he fought was as smooth as silk. Abraham parried one blinding stroke after the other. He countered with a sideward slash.

Fonay Zar slid away and smiled. He flexed his arms and said, "You are strong like a bull. Yes! So much I have heard about you. Fast as a cat too. You are all I ever hoped that you would be, Ruger Slade. And now, I get to kill you." He stepped back over one of the dead bodies. "Then I will be the greatest swordsman in the world."

"No, you're going to be another one of those dead guys." Abraham cracked his neck side to side. "I promise you that. Soon enough, you're going to have blood all over your pretty clothing."

Fonay Zar's smile vanished. "Your blood, yes, but my blood, never." Fonay Zar charged Abraham and brought his sword down in a flurry of precise strokes.

Abraham parried them aside. He felt every bit of the blows in his hands and arms. The cheap steel he wielded didn't absorb punishment like Black Bane did. The cheap length of steel shared it. He parried and countered, only to be countered again. The tip of Fonay Zar's sword flashed before his eyes.

The audience shouted with raucous elation. New chants began as the master swordsmen went back and forth.

"Slay the Blade!"

"Slay the Blade!"

"Slay the Blade!"

Fonay Zar shuffled backward and thrust forward as if shot out of a cannon. Abraham twisted left. He was too late. Fonay Zar's sword clipped him through the shoulder. Blood spat down his arm. He jumped away.

The audience broke out in a frenzied howl.

"Feeling tired, Ruger?" Fonay gloated. He cut his sword inches above the ground. "You look tired. I can't promise I'll make your death painless, but I'll try to make it quick. Even though I think that the audience would like to see you bleed to death."

"It ain't over until it's over," Abraham replied.

"A futile expression. Where did you hear that?"

"*Rocky* one and *Rocky* six."

"I've never heard of those places." Fonay Zar flipped his sword around and made a quick bow. "It's been a pleasure."

I need to finish this guy and finish him quick. Come on, Ruger. I feel like you're holding back. What gives? Abraham rifled through his memories filled with pages of sword technique. The memory that stuck was that when equally matched, often the fighter with the superior weapon won. It made sense. He didn't have Black Bane, which made him every bit of a hair quicker. That fraction of time made the difference between life and death. Any risk he might take would be fatal.

He squared off on his opponent once more and said, "The pleasure is all mine."

He pounced at Fonay Zar. Blades collided. His blade broke.

CHAPTER 40

Abraham twisted away from Fonay Zar's death stroke. His blade had snapped off at the hilt, leaving him all but empty-handed. He threw the handle at the swordsman. The handle flickered over Fonay's head.

The audience jumped onto their feet and screamed their lungs out.

"It will almost be a shame to see it end like this," Fonay Zar said. He crept toward Abraham. "You were every bit a worthy opponent."

Without taking his eyes off Fonay, Abraham backed toward the dead men. Plenty of swords were on the deck. All he needed to do was snatch one of them.

Fonay darted toward Abraham and sliced, herding Abraham away from the field of the dead. "No, no, no, you had your chance."

"I don't know about that," Abraham said. His shoulder burned like fire, the wound freely bleeding. "I should have had a choice of a better blade."

"From what I can see, you had six choices. You chose poorly."

With sweat dripping down his face, Abraham said, "I know this. I've never cut a man down in cold blood. That's the brand of a coward."

Breathing easy, Fonay circled the arena with him and said, "This is not an arena of honor, my friend. It is an arena of death."

"Oh well, I had to try." He continued to square off with Fonay, keeping his eyes fixed on the man. He had one chance—just one—depending on what Fonay Zar did. "Remember this. You might be good, but you'll never know for sure if you are better than me."

"I don't care. All they'll remember is that I slew you with my sword. In the end, that is all that matters." Fonay Zar poised himself in the high guard position and attacked.

The moment Fonay lifted his sword the slightest to initiate the downward chop, Abraham dove at the man's legs. The sword stroke came down in flash of silver and bit into the ground. Both men wrestled over the ground in a tangle of limbs. Fonay's wiry frame proved to be as fit as a wolverine's. Natural strength powered his lanky limbs. His grip on the sword handle was iron.

Abraham headbutted the man in the nose, and the bridge crunched. He pinned the younger fighter's sword arm down and chopped his hand into the wrist. The fingers opened, and the blade slipped free. Abraham grabbed the sword, rolled away, and sprang to his feet.

Fonay jumped back to his feet with a look of bewilderment. His light eyes darted to the swords on the ground. They lay behind Abraham.

"Looks like you have blood all over your pretty outfit. It gives it character." Abraham knelt down. He set down the good sword and picked up two of the bad ones then tossed one bad one at Fonay's feet. "Pick it up!"

Fonay glanced down at the inferior weapon.

The crowd chanted.

"Pick it up! Pick it up! Pick it up!"

Fonay Zan picked up the sword. He squared off with Abraham, who now carried a sword of the same poor craftsmanship as his.

Abraham looked the man dead in the eyes and said, "For once, you're going to fight like a man! And die like one!"

Abraham attacked. His sword slipped through Fonay's defense and cut the man clean through the neck. Fonay dropped to his knees, clutching his bleeding throat. He toppled backward and died.

The crowd went silent.

Big Apple had a grin all over his face. He applauded again. "Such honor. Such honor. Honor can be deadly."

Abraham took a knee beside Fonay Zar. He removed a light golden sash from the man's waist and wrapped up his shoulder, then he picked up Fonay Zar's sword. The weapon had great balance and was half the weight of the ones he'd been wielding.

He looked up at Edgar, the Big Apple. "Is that it?"

"No," the Big Apple said. "Not even close."

"Fine, but I'm keeping this."

"Good, because you're going to need it."

CHAPTER 41

ABRAHAM STOOD NEAR THE MIDDLE of the arena, panting. He swayed. Blood and gore coated him from the tip of his sword to his shoulder. All the rest of him was covered in blood. The dead of all sorts were piled up all around the square arena. Two dead lions and a giant white-haired ape were among them. Men were there, the Black Knights in blackened armor from the Old Kingdom, who fought with spiked chains, daggers, and axes. They were great, gruesome, and gaunt alive. Now, they lay in heaps of flesh and bone sliced asunder, dead.

A minotaur lay on the ground. Its head was chopped off. One horn was missing. Fifteen men in forest-green robes with eyes the color of silver had come at him with spears and throwing stars. They were from the peaks of the Dorcha territory and had been called the Monks of Mayhem. They soiled the hard ground now. More were there, many more—sword fighters by the dozens. He'd fought as if he had fire in his veins. Abraham killed them all. Or Ruger did. Abraham got his first real glimpse of who Ruger really was. He was a killing machine who fought as if fire were flowing through his veins. He was invincible.

The flies and mosquitos came to feed on the dead at dawn. Their buzzing numbers overwhelmed the crowd. The Big Apple's guests began to file out of the arena, their throats raw from the screaming. They had nothing left in them. Ruger Slade had escaped time after time after time. His enemies had no choice but to move on, with heads hanging in defeat.

Edgar the Big Apple sat on his wooden throne, bright-eyed and bushy-tailed. The girls who accompanied him were sleeping. Fleece, the wraith, hadn't moved since the battles started, but his robes rolled like smoky vapors around his tall body.

Abraham dragged his sword toward the main wall, where the smuggler sat. He lifted his chin and asked, "What's next? Dragons? Giant vorpal bunny rabbits? A pink unicorn that breathes fire? Let's make a deal and see what's behind door number three."

Edgar tugged at the collar on his neck, which had three yellow gems in the middle. His nostrils flared. He fanned the air in front of his face and said, "Whew! I should have dragged the carcasses off after you killed them. But I never thought that you would even make it this far. Not without Black Bane." He tapped on the sword scabbard lying across the arms of his chair. "What to do? What to do? Wow, I wish I could have been you, even though this body isn't so bad compared to my old one."

Only pockets of people were scattered about the rim of the arena. The morning sun shone on their sweaty foreheads. The crowd had cheered for and against Abraham. His titanic efforts against the odds swayed the crowd. The haters left. The hopeful stayed. He didn't recognize any of them. "Come on, Big Apple. Let me and my people go. After all of this, I think I've earned it."

"I decide what you have or have not earned. Hmm-hmm." Big Apple scratched his nose. He waved his hand in the air. "Let me consult with an old friend."

On the far side of the arena stands, two figures stood. Casually, they walked around the arena toward the Big Apple's chair. The sun shone in Abraham's eyes. The moment they rounded the first corner, they came into focus, a man and woman, both of whom he recognized. The man, tall and fit, light hair receding, wore a black vest over a maroon shirt. A gun was holstered on his hip. It was Lord Hawk, leader of the Shell. Ruger had tangled with him at the hideout where he found Solomon. He was handsome, with a strong chin and natural charm. Beside him was the gorgeous myrmidon woman, Kawnee. The woman was from the race of fishlike people who lived on land and in the sea. Her alluring eyes were solid black. The scales on her sensuous body shone in the sunlight, her leather garb accenting the natural curves of her body. Her arm was hooked in Lord Hawk's.

Lord Hawk clasped hands with Big Apple. "It's been quite a show. My kind of show, old friend. Thanks for the invite. Even though the results have been disappointing so far." He looked down at Abraham. "We meet again."

"The pleasure is all yours," Abraham said. "Big Apple, what does he have to do with this?"

The horned halfling smiled. "I am the Smuggler King. I have many associates. The Shell is part of that. Lord Hawk is another one with a bounty on your head… and the troglin's."

"The troglin. You want the troglin back?" Abraham said.

Lord Hawk put his foot up on the wall, leaned over, and said, "He was a special pet."

"You treated him like an animal."

"Well, he is a troglin. Smells like an animal, it's an animal." Lord Hawk spat over the side. His hand was on his gun, which hung at his side. He surveyed the dead. "Quite a mess. It makes me think of all of my men that you butchered."

"There is a price for stealing and kidnapping," Abraham replied. He looked past Lord Hawk, and his eyes caught Kawnee's for a moment as she winked at him. Moving on to Big Apple, he asked, "Is this a parlay?"

"No, it's a reunion." Big Apple stood up on his chair. "Lord Hawk, what are you in the mood for?"

"Well, it's early. We have the entire day ahead of us." Lord Hawk patted the grip of his gun. "I say, let them fight some more. A lot more". Lord Hawk looked dead at Ruger and smirked. "How about the Wild Men from the Wound?" He turned his head back toward Big Apple. "You still have some of them, don't you?"

"I have plenty. How many shall I set free?" Big Apple asked.

Lord Hawk opened up his hands casually and said, "All of them."

CHAPTER 42

None of the four doors leading into the rim's square arena opened. Abraham could hear scuffling behind them. The rattle of chains and harsh voices could be heard behind the iron hinges. In the stands, Big Apple and Lord Hawk and Kawnee had turned their backs. They were drinking from large goblets and talking in quiet voices.

Abraham licked his parched lips. He was as dry as a bone. All his sweat was gone. Blood had caked on his flesh. Ruger might have been tough, but even he was subject to dehydration. With a dry throat, he shouted up to the group and said, "Grant me a request and let me drink."

Everyone stopped and looked at him. Big Apple asked, "What is the matter? Is the master swordsman thirsty? Hmm… hmm. Flesh and bone cannot conquer him, but a lack of water will."

"You didn't bring me out here to die of thirst. You brought me out here to fight. I don't think a skin of water will hurt anything."

Big Apple and Lord Hawk shrugged at each other. Lord Hawk threw an arm over Kawnee's shoulder and said, "Look at this beauty. She's a myrmidon. Sea people. She doesn't complain of the sun or beg for a drink."

"She's hasn't been fighting her butt off for the last several hours, either," Abraham fired back.

Lord Hawk kissed the pretty myrmidon woman on the cheek and said, "I'll let her decide. Just remember, dear, he killed your love, Flexor."

Kawnee might not have been thirsty, but she blinked a lot. The gills on the neck of her pale-green skin opened and closed rapidly. She slipped away from Lord Hawk, bent over, and grabbed what looked like a skin of water from underneath the stadium benches. With the grace of a queen, she moved down the bench planks to the edge of the wall. She leaned over the wall and held the skin out. "Come, and I will give you a drink."

Abraham walked up underneath Kawnee's outstretched arms and swallowed. The damp water skin hung suspended twenty feet above his face. A drop of water dripped down onto his cheek.

Kawnee tipped the water skin over, and water poured from the spout. She flipped the tip back up.

The water splashed onto Abraham's face. He barely got a drop in his mouth. He could see the playfulness in her eyes, only between her and him. The others could not be seen.

He mouthed the words, "Thank you."

Kawnee lifted her eyebrows. She took the water skin, put it to her lips, and gulped it down. She drained the remaining water by squeezing the contents of the water skin. The cool liquid splashed all over her face and down her chest. She twisted the water skin in her hands. That last of the drops dripped onto her tongue. She flung the water skin down at Abraham's feet and walked away.

"Bravo!" Big Apple cried, elated.

Lord Hawk clucked with laughter along with the guards and the handful of people still left.

Abraham frowned at the discarded skin. He picked it up and squeezed out a few drops that landed in the dust. "You know, for a fish lady, you make one lousy water boy. I didn't want your lousy H2O anyway." He flung the skin up into the stands.

Lord Hawk swatted it down and said, "What is the matter? Don't you want a refill?" The audience started laughing again.

Abraham walked back into the buzzing flies and stink of the arena. He had bigger things to worry about than water. Survival came to mind. Lord Hawk had mentioned the Wild Men of the Wound. The name of the men didn't ring a bell with him, but the Wound did. He'd seen it on the maps of Titanuus. It was located in north Eastern Bolg. It was a great chasm, something like the Grand Canyon. According to Sticks, the Wound was said to be the fatal wound that the eternal being, Antonugus, had killed Titanuus with.

He began picking through the weapons of his enemies. He'd killed most of them with lethal precision—gouged hearts and slit-open bellies and necks. He couldn't afford to let them get a second swing. He had a sinking feeling inside his guts. The next wave that Big Apple sent was going to be bad—really bad, if that was possible.

The Black Knights of the Old Kingdom had been well equipped. Aside from their blackened armor, they had thick belts called girdes. Abraham suited himself up with a worn belt and loaded a few daggers he found into it. He still carried Fonay Zar's sword. The weapon wasn't Black Bane, but it was a difference maker. No other weapon could match it, but he needed one, a good one. He caught a shine of an axe head underneath one of the monks whose arm he'd cut off. The small wiry fighter had come at him with a pair of nunchakus.

He pushed the body aside with the heel of his foot and said, "You ain't no Bruce Lee." He picked up the axe, which had a wicked-looking singular head of steel, with a long beard and sharp chin. It was a true cleaver that one of the black knights had carried. He tossed it up and watched it flip end over end and caught it. "You'll do. You'll have to."

Big Apple and his small brood were all staring at Abraham. They had stopped talking and appeared to be waiting, the same as him.

A hard knocking came from the door below Big Apple's thronelike chair. One of the guards appeared on the upper deck. The brute hustled down the steps and whispered in Big Apple's ear.

"Good lord, your breath smells!" Big Apple shooed the man away. "Go, go bathe and brush with something besides manure. Man, these people have no hygiene. I got it." He tapped his fingertips together. He looked Abraham dead in the eye. "Hmm-hmm." He drew out the next two words, which had a familiar ring to them. "They're here."

Abraham spun around slowly.

The people who had left the Rim returned in a quick and orderly fashion. They had their hands full of bottles of wine, tankards of ale, and trays of food, much as one would see in a sports stadium. The hungry glazed look in their eyes returned.

They began to chant. "Wild Men! Wild Men! Wild Men! Wild Men!"

Big Apple raised his mighty little arms and clapped his hands.

All four of the arena doors opened at once. The Wild Men lumbered out of the great doors.

The crowd's chants turned to stone-cold silence.

Abraham's skin crawled into his toes.

CHAPTER 43

THE WILD MEN OF THE Wound weren't men in the customary sense of the word. Instead, they moved on all fours, knuckles on the ground, like white apes. Twenty appeared in all, five coming out of each door, grunting loudly when they entered.

The grimy men had shaggy manes of hair, bodies bulging and flexing with natural muscle with every movement they made. Like dogs, they moved deeper into the arena, snorting and sniffing the air. The half-naked men's large eyes grazed over Abraham before falling on the dead. Abraham stood still. The sight of the wild men jostled Ruger's senses. The hairs on his arms stood on end, which was a rare event. Nothing bowed the iron in Ruger Slade's limbs, but the Wild Men did.

They moved about the arena in small packs, their heads scanning side to side. They shoved, pushed, and rubbed up against one another. One of the Wild Men picked up the head of a Monk of Mayhem. He tossed it to another wild man, who caught it, stared at the decapitated face, and grunted. That Wild Man cocked the head back over his shoulder and slung it into the back of the head of another. That Wild Man rolled underneath the blow, popped up, and attacked the one that threw the head at him. They wrestled over the blood and the dead like fighting dogs.

While two of the Wild Men fought, the rest of the primordial pack milled through the slain. One Wild Man picked up a spiked flail. He swung it up and brought it down with great strength into a dead corpse. He kept swinging, turning the body into hamburger. Others were doing the same thing. They picked up weapons, toyed with them, and tested them out on the fallen.

One of the Wild Men sat back on his haunches. He held a sword in his hand and thumbed the edge. His eyes hung on Abraham. The others continued to pick through the weapons. Half of them armed themselves while the others seemed content to fight with their mallet-sized fists or thick fingernails that could tear open flesh.

"I should have put some armor on," Abraham muttered underneath his breath. "Times like this, a swordsman needs it." He eyed the pack of men. So far, they had shown very little interest in him as they sorted through the battlefield. Abraham tried to figure out who was the leader of the pack. If he took out the leader, that might scatter the others long enough to give him an advantage.

"What are you waiting for, Ruger?" Lord Hawk said from above. "Make some conversation with them. Say hello. The Wild Men love to chat."

"Oh, these are Wild Men," Abraham said. "I thought this was your family reunion."

"Ha ha!" Big Apple laughed, pointing at Lord Hawk. "He got you."

"You know, I'm really going to love watching them rip you apart, Ruger. And I know that the crowd is going to love it too!" Lord Hawk lifted up his fist and pumped it in the air. "Wild Men! Wild Men! Wild Men!"

Abraham took a deep breath.

The Wild Men clustered together, spread out, and encircled Ruger. The ones without weapons—ten in all—lurked on all fours, grunting and barking like hounds. The others stood tall and formidable with their backs bowed and metal weapons in hand. They cast deadly looks on Abraham from their dark eyes. The wide circle of the savage pack tightened.

The people in the stands chanted more loudly, "Kill the Blade! Kill the Blade! Kill the Blade!"

Abraham had slain over two dozen men in the past few hours. These men were different. They were a pack of wild-eyed animals hungry for blood and fearless of death. He could take down a few, but if they came all at once, their superior numbers would overwhelm him. *Come on, Ruger, what are we going to do?*

A Wild Man on all fours bolted out of his stance and charged.

Abraham brained the man with his axe.

The Wild Men growled and began to salivate. Two more barehanded Wild Men charged Abraham from opposite sides. They pounced like gorillas from several feet away.

With a flash of his sword, Abraham lopped the head off of one and cleaved the other Wild Man in the face. Both men dropped dead at his feet. Abraham jumped over the dead men and charged the biggest Wild Man of all, the one who carried a sword and had eyed him earlier. That Wild Man whistled under his breath just before the others attacked. He must have been the leader. Abraham drove a knee into the jaw of a Wild Man standing in front of the leader. He stabbed his sword at the leader's neck.

The Wild Men's leader slipped out of the way like a wild jungle cat. He made sharp whistles through his teeth. The throng of Wild Men came to life. All of them descended on Abraham in a frenzied wave.

Abraham sprinted after the leader.

The long-haired brute ran like a deer while screaming and holding his sword high. He spun around and backpedaled on bare feet away from Abraham.

Abraham closed the gap.

The Wild Man stopped on a dime and stuck his chin out.

Abraham lowered his sword and aimed for the heart. The Wild Man coiled his legs and leapt high into the air. Abraham passed beneath the Wild Man and cut the man's foot off. The leader let out a wild cry and fell into the knot of charging men. Abraham kept running.

With his attacker howling for his blood, he sprinted into the nearest corner and turned. "Come on, dogs!"

The Wild Men of the Wound converged on him as one.

Abraham hammered away at the rank knot of sweating bodies with his sword and axe. His sharp edges mangled bone and flesh. Blood sprinkled and splattered in the air. He chopped at the churning mass with everything he had in him. He moved like a human Cuisinart. His attackers became meat for a butcher shop. He ruined their sinewy flesh. *Slice! Hack! Chop!*

Strong limbs penetrated his defenses. Hands locked around his legs and arms. The Wild Men locked him up. They hit, punched, and bit. They brought Abraham down to his knees. They ripped his weapons from his grasp. Hard fists punched him senseless. He fought back. They beat him down, grabbed his legs, and dragged him across the ground, screaming like a pack of howling wolves.

CHAPTER 44

With the crowd cheering, the Wild Men dragged Abraham around the arena in triumph. They came to a stop near the middle and pinned him down by the arms and legs. Abraham wrestled against his captors. His own great strength could not match their numbers. One of the Wild Men kicked him in the ribs.

"Guh!"

A second Wild Man punched him in the face.

The leader of the Wild Men hopped into view. Blood dripped freely from the wound where Abraham had chopped the savage's foot. The leader used his sword as a cane for balance. He pointed at Abraham's foot with his free hand. He hopped closer to Abraham and hovered over his legs. Two savages pinned his jerking leg down.

"I guess it's nothing personal," Abraham said. "A foot for a foot. Just make it quick."

The Wild Men's leader lifted his sword.

A ball of blue fire soared across the arena, smote the leader in the chest, and knocked him from his feet. The Wild Men let out cries and scattered.

Abraham rolled up on one side. Iris and Leodor stood in one of the doorways. Balls of energy exploded out of their hands, smiting the Wild Men. The people in the stands stampeded out of the stadium.

Big Apple jumped up and down in his chair yelling, "No! No! No!"

In the stands and on the arena floor, the Henchmen came. Horace, Bearclaw, and Vern hustled through one of the doors and engaged the Wild Men. Horace gored two of the men at once on the end of his spear. Bearclaw savagely ended one Wild Man's life with a single stroke. Vern's long sword flickered in and out of body after body.

Clarice and Swan carved up one savage together.

Prince Lewis's lethal strokes were as smooth as silk.

By the time Abraham got to his feet and snatched up a weapon, all the Wild Men from the Wound were dead. Up in the stands, Solomon, Sticks, Shades, Dominga, Tark, and Cudgel had Big Apple and the wraith, Fleece, surrounded. The guards were dead, and Lord Hawk and Kawnee were nowhere to be seen.

Big Apple sank down in his throne and clapped his hands slowly. "Well done, Ruger Slade. That was extraordinary. Hmm-hmm." He scratched one of the little horns on his head. "Now, before you try anything stupid, such as kill me, I think we should talk first."

"If you want to talk, come down here, and we will talk," Abraham said. The Henchmen gathered around him. He wasn't sure how they'd escaped or come together, but the timing couldn't have been better. "Don't be shy."

"I like it up here," Big Apple said. "It's my comfort zone."

"Solomon, why don't you give him a hand?" he said. "And keep an eye out for Lord Hawk. He was here earlier."

Solomon's eyes grew big. "He was?" With a quick glance over his shoulder, he approached Big Apple. Fleece moved in front of him. "I don't think Mister Curtains is going to let me."

"Leodor, what is the deal with that thing?" Abraham asked.

"It's a wraith," Leodor said with a frown as he stuck his hands inside his sleeves. "Not to be taken lightly. Do not touch it. They are known to have very bizarre powers. In some cases, their breath can be lethal."

"I've experienced plenty of that already." Abraham wanted information from Edgar. Despite how much he wanted to kill the horned wretch, the time to play nice had come. He had to remember that this might be a game and none of it was real. "Edgar, how about the two of us have a nice little chat? Mano a mano. Capisce?"

Edgar stood up and said, "Very well. I always was a good listener. Give me your word that you won't kill me."

"I won't."

"Or your Henchmen?"

Abraham glanced at Horace. "They won't."

Cheerfully, Edgar said, "Then come on up."

"No, you come down."

Edgar rolled his eyes. He jumped down from his throne, walked the benches, and jumped off the wall. He made an acrobatic somersault in the air and landed on his feet. He strode up to Abraham and said, "Let's walk."

Abraham wasn't surprised by the horned halfling's bravado. He walked the walk and talked the talk of a five-foot-tall muscle man. They separated themselves from the others. "You might not want to go home, but I do. But first, I have to help King Hector."

"Ah, man, why do you want to help King Hector? The entire world hates him, even his people in Kingsland." Edgar shook his head. "You are on the wrong side of this. You should be on my side. We could rule this world together, you and me."

"I want to go home."

"Ha! No you don't. Hmm-hmm. I can see it in your eyes. You like this place, the same as I do. It's addictive. Listen to me. We have knowledge." Edgar put his finger to his forehead. "That is priceless. Hey, I heard that you had some pizza in the Greasy Pelican. Hmm-hmm. Where do you think that recipe came from? We can have so much fun in this place."

"I gave my word to the king."

"No, you gave your word to a dream."

CHAPTER 45

A *DREAM*. CERTAINLY, A STRONG CASE could have been made for that, especially with Abraham's last experience back in the real world. Charles Abney, the old patient, had mentioned the Big Apple. Now Abraham was standing face-to-face with a horned halfling from New York City. It was convenient, all too convenient. Covered in flesh wounds, he limped along and asked, "Should guys like us be helping each other?"

Edgar's face tightened, and he shook his head. "Hmm-hmm, I told you the last thing I want is to go back to the body I was in. I'm very content with this one." He flexed his biceps. "And the girls like it. And even though I am small, I'm strong as a bull. Horned halflings are special people."

"Will you tell me how you got here?"

"Nope."

"Fine, listen, I'll find out on my own one way or the other. But what I want now is to help the king. Zillon dragon riders tried to kill him using an assault rifle. I saw it myself." He looked down at Edgar. "Do you know anything about that?"

Edgar clasped his hands and smiled. "I know everything—you see, everything. It is the beautiful thing of being me." He lifted his fingers as he spoke. "One, I know that King Hector is seeking out Arcayis the Underlord. He believes that man is behind the attempt. Two, I also know that you are seeking to reassemble the Crown of Stones."

Abraham slowed.

"Ah, you are surprised that I know that, aren't you?" Big Apple said with a grin. "I told you that I know everything. You see, the Sect and I work close together. We use each other for information. Of course, they think they are using me more than I am them, but it's the other way around."

They finished one lap around the inside of the arena. Everyone else was standing around and watching.

"King Hector wants the Crown of Stones," Big Apple continued. "With it, he thinks that he can save the world and unite the kingdoms. I'm telling you, uh, Abraham, that will never happen."

"Why not?"

"For one"—Edgar stuck out a pudgy index finger—"more trouble from our world is coming every day. And number two—"

"Whoa, whoa, whoa, what do you mean more trouble every day?"

"You know, more stuff like guns and people. People with ideas like me. We aren't the only ones. There are many otherworlders in Titanuus. Be wary. I will tell you this. The Sect is snatching up them and their knowledge. They have been for quite some time. They are ten steps ahead of King Hector in this game where this world is quickly changing."

Abraham nodded, wanting to keep Edgar talking as long as he could. More information was more weaponry for his arsenal. *Keep yapping, you little goat.* "What is number two?"

"Those magical gemstones that you want to complete the crown—well, the Underlord has all of them save for one. Hmm-hmm."

"I don't believe it."

In a scratchy old voice, Edgar said, "That is why you failed."

Abraham tilted his head and said, "Funny. It's been a long time since I heard that line. Anyway, if he has most of the stones, wouldn't he have enough power to overrun Kingsland?"

"I don't know. I think he wants King Hector to punch himself out. But there is the matter of the King's Steel. It's the strongest metal in the world and only mined near the House of Steel. The Underlord respects its power. He wants it for himself too. But, metal or no metal, the way I see it, you and your Henchmen are the only hope that he has. I believe he is comfortable in destroying all of you one by one, the same as he did before with the assassin, Raschel. She was a good one, wasn't she?"

"You really do know too much. But since you are so smart, where is the Underlord?"

"Why would I tell you that?"

"Ah, so you do know?" Abraham asked.

They finished their third lap.

"Of course. I'll tell you this much. Why? Because I like a long shot. Being a smuggler, I'm a betting man, and I need friends on both sides when one wins and the other dies."

"All right, spit it out."

"The Underlord resides in Little Leg, near the zillon dragon-riders' peaks. It's a fortress or cathedral, something like that. I've never been. It's near Cauldron City. All I know is that he stays there all day, all night, running his operations. Oh, and those assault rifles that you were talking about, I'd expect more of them. Possibly worse. Arcayis the Underlord has been storing up artifacts from our world for quite some time. I'd be careful."

"I don't think I'd be any other way." Abraham stopped and faced Edgar. "Still think it's strange that you would offer anything useful."

"You fought with honor. I liked it. Besides, you don't stand a chance, but I'm willing to at least give you a fighting one. Perhaps I have a soft spot for a homeboy. May the Elders bless you. May they curse you too."

"Have you ever seen an Elder?" Abraham asked.

"Heck no. Hmm-hmm. These people worship everything. It's Elders this and Elders that." Edgar shrugged his arms and shoulders. "They are a bunch of pagans. They worship dog skulls, flowers, even funny-looking pastry dishes. Like pizza. Ah, when I made pizza, they started an all-new cult."

"What about the saying 'The tide shifts. The Elders awaken'?" Abraham asked.

"Pfft… these idiots say that all of the time. They don't know what that means."

"You sound like someone that has more faith in our world than this one."

Edgar lost his smile and said, "There is a world created by God and a world created by man. I made my choice."

"What does that mean?"

"I've told you enough. Hmm-hmm. Figure it out yourself."

CHAPTER 46

The Henchmen equipped themselves at Pirate City with horses, rations, and gear. They left *Sea Talon* in the hands of Jander, one of Flamebeard's former crew. Apollo and Prospero stayed back on the ship as well with a few other crewmen. No other volunteers stayed. Abraham led the company south, riding close to the shoreline toward Hancha.

Abraham rode out front with Sticks and Horace riding beside him. As usual, Dominga and Tark were scouting ahead on foot. Behind Abraham were Bearclaw and Vern, followed by Cudgel and Iris. Lewis, Leodor, Clarice, and Swan were in the rear, with Shades and Solomon—who was on foot—bringing up the very rear.

No one said so much as a word. Abraham gave the orders. They followed. The mission hadn't changed: kill the men that had tried to assassinate the king, the zillon dragon riders—not to mention the man who had most likely given the order, Arcayis the Underlord.

The beaten paths cutting through the forest hills weren't hard to follow. The roads were well traveled in the south.

Iris stitched Abraham up. His wounds still burned and were sore. He could still feel the hard claws of the wild men raking across his skin. Certain doom had fallen upon him, but he escaped, thanks to the loyalty and bravery of the Henchmen.

With the sun sinking behind the trees, Abraham, who had been mulling over the latest torrid series of events, broke his silence. "What happened on that stage at the Greasy Pelican? All of you vanished."

Sticks touched her stomach and said, "I don't know, but I puked my guts out after it happened.

We poofed from that stage into a dungeon. Ugh, my stomach twists like a vine from thinking of it. That thing, though—the wraith in the stands of the Rim. It was there when we arrived."

"We could have killed it," Horace said.

"How did you escape?" Abraham asked.

"Shades. He squeezed through the bars, killed the guards, and freed us." Sticks's horse trotted ahead of Abraham's. She tugged on the reins and waited for him to catch up. "The problem was we didn't know where you were or where we were. That took some time. We beat it out of the guards. Once we figured it out, Shades headed back to the ship. I led the rest of us in to find you at the Rim."

"You have my gratitude. I was seconds away from having my foot chopped off. And that was only the start of it," he said. "Your timing is impeccable."

"All in a day's work." Sticks's brown hair was tied behind her head in twin braids. Her single bandolier of daggers crossed her shoulders. She was missing a few of her blades. Blood stained her clothing. She had a mark on her upper left arm, which was swollen and bruising where one of the Wild Men had bitten her. She'd bitten the savage back with a dagger into the temple. "Care to tell us more about your conversation with the horned halfling?"

"Let me guess—inquiring minds want to know?"

"What?" she said.

"Never mind." Abraham sat slightly hunched over in the saddle and patted the side of his horse's neck. The horse was a chestnut brown with a black mane. He didn't have much experience with horses in his past, but he'd come to like them.

"Big Apple the Smuggler King says that he came from the same world as me," Abraham continued. "His real name is Edgar Gravely, and he likes it here. He doesn't want me to do anything that will screw it up for him."

"You can't trust horned halflings. They are nothing but trouble," Horace said. His sausage fingers combed through his beard. "I've crossed them before. They are as bad as the troglins."

"They eat people?" Abraham asked.

"No, they lie. They steal. They are trouble." Horace coughed, reached down, and grabbed a water skin. "Trouble."

"Well, he is a smuggler," Sticks said as she made a rail-thin smile at Abraham. "Horace doesn't care for the peoples beyond Kingsland, if you haven't figured that out. He thinks they are all trouble."

"They are all trouble," Horace fired back. "And that one has horns. Who would trust a wee man with horns? We should have killed him."

"We need information. We can't kill off the source of information. Besides, Edgar isn't really a horned halfling. He's an otherworlder like me." Abraham chuckled. "I just called myself an otherworlder. Interesting. Anyway, we'll track down these assassins in Cauldron City. That's our mission. Kill whatever zillons are associated with Arcayis and take the stones of power or whatever they are."

Horace bit off a crusty fingernail and spat it away. "The zillon dragon riders live in the high places."

"Your point is?" he said.

"They live in the high places, Captain. That's what I know, not because I have seen, but I have heard."

"That's a big help. Thanks, Horace."

Horace gave an affirmative nod.

Lewis and Leodor rode up alongside Abraham.

"Great, my favorite Henchmen," he said with a shake of his head. "Let me guess, you came to offer more advice."

"No… well, yes." Lewis said. His right arm was bandaged just below the shoulder. "Who wouldn't want the prince's advice?"

"Perhaps you mean Lewis the Lewd's advice," Sticks said.

With a sneer, Lewis said, "You better mind your tongue, you scrawny wench. Or I'll have it twisted out of your face."

"Lighten up, Lewis," Abraham said. "Try being nice to the ladies. It gets you a lot farther than being mean to them."

Lewis rolled his eyes.

Leodor cleared his throat and said, "I overheard you talking about Cauldron City. What is our business there?"

Abraham looked at Leodor as though he were stupid and said, "To find Arcayis. Big Apple says that he resides there."

Leodor shook his head and replied, "The only thing we will find in the Cauldron is certain death."

CHAPTER 47

Abraham rolled his eyes. "Listen, spooky old man, I don't know if you figured it out yet, but facing certain death is what we do." He looked dead at the older man. "Now, are you going to be part of the problem or part of the solution, Chinless One?"

Leodor blanched.

Horace laughed. "Har! Chinless One. I like it." He poked a finger Leodor's way. "It's because you don't have a chin. Aye!"

Leodor covered his small chin with his hand. "I have a chin."

"You have a baby chin," Abraham fired back.

Sticks trembled in her saddle, bent over with her own silent laughter.

He turned on Lewis. "And you have a chin like Waluigi."

Touching his chin, Lewis said with insecurity, "What is a Waluigi?"

Lewis had very handsome, chiseled features with a slightly prominent chin. Aside from the scar on his lip, he had no flaws at all. That was all the reason for Abraham to pick on him. "A Waluigi is a person with a giant chin that can poke an eye out in my world."

"I'm not a Waluigi," Lewis said. "I'm a prince. Don't call me that again."

Abraham looked away. The joke turned into something else as he remembered his son, Jake. The two of them had played a lot of *Mario Kart* together. Waluigi, dressed in purple overalls, was Jake's favorite character. Abraham and Jake used to joke about people with big chins. Jake would point and innocently say, "Waluigi." He reached down and touched Jake's Pirates backpack. He hadn't opened it in a while, but he always slept with it near his side.

"Joking aside, Leodor, do you care to fill us in on why Cauldron City can bring about our doom?"

"Cauldron City is not the problem. The Cauldron is. We don't want to venture into the Cauldron."

Abraham arched a brow. He didn't want to sound ignorant by asking, but he did anyway. "Are they different?"

"Cauldron City is not so different than any other city, but it resides in the shadow of the Cauldron," Leodor said. "The Cauldron is a fortress where many members of the Sect preside. They study. They train. They manipulate. The Underlord is now chief among them. No doubt, he will be expecting our arrival. And the zillon dragon riders, well, I think we can only assume that they are on his side as well. Their spiny pinnacles overlook the Cauldron. The Sect has eyes everywhere. I thought it pertinent that I pass this warning along."

"Have you been to the Cauldron?" he asked.

"Yes. My training as a mystic began there when I was young. It's the same with many chosen members of the Sect."

"Was Iris trained there?"

"No, she didn't come from a background of privilege," Leodor said with a glance behind his shoulder. "She uses a perverted form of Titanuus's powers. Her kind is not chosen to wield the stream, but some find it without proper training. Very reckless."

"You better watch how you speak about my lady, Chinless Man, or you might end up being a headless man as well," Horace said.

"Don't threaten me, big belly. I can turn your skin inside out," Leodor replied.

Horace grunted. "I'd like to see you try."

"The point is, as formidable as you might feel, even with Black Bane, you are storming a fortress with only a handful of men and women." Leodor moved his brows up and down. "You'll need a better plan than that. I'd focus on the zillons. They tried to kill the king. Perhaps the Underlord was not behind it. Of course, the zillons are another matter entirely. They have dragons. We don't."

"This is our mission," Abraham said. "There won't be any turning around. Aside from your chronic warnings, do you have anything positive to offer, Leodor?"

"No."

"I didn't think so. What about you, Lewis? What dreadful insights would you like to share?"

Leodor and Lewis turned their horses away and headed toward the rear of the company. With hard eyes, Bearclaw and Vern bumped horses with them as they passed.

Abraham hollered back at them, "Thanks for all of the help, guys! Real team players! You know, there is a saying back in my world: 'If you don't have anything good to say, don't say anything at all.'"

Horace nodded. "I like it, Captain."

"Yeah, well, I like it too." Abraham scowled. "But those two windbags are getting on my nerves."

CHAPTER 48

That night, Abraham warmed his hands over a small campfire. Solomon was with him.

The shaggy gray-haired troglin still wore his maroon vest. He was squatting near the fire and toying with the buttons. "If I'm not mistaken, I think these buttons are made of plastic. They feel like plastic."

"They aren't plastic. They are brass. I can see the shine still on them." Abraham pitched a stick onto the fire.

No one else was around. Several fires had been set up at the campsite in a clearing surrounded by great trees.

Abraham stared deeply into the fire. "But I guess anything is possible. They have guns. I have a backpack. Why not?"

Solomon scratched his neck and said, "I wish I would have got a crack at Lord Hawk."

"Yeah, I bet you did."

"He treated me like an animal. Tortured me. I'm not prone to violence, but I think I'd rip his arms off."

Abraham smirked. "No doubt you could, Chewie."

Solomon tilted his head. "Huh?"

"Nothing."

"Tell me more about Big Apple. Do you believe him?"

"I believe he's an otherworlder like us. I can't say whether or not his story checks out. He gave me the distinct impression that he had no interest in going back to our world. He said he had cerebral palsy." He flicked a twig into the fire. "I can't say I blame him."

"Sounds like this Edgar is sowing his oats for the first time. I don't think that I can blame him either." Solomon sat down cross-legged, stretched his arms upward, and yawned. "You know, I'm getting a lot less rest now that I'm a Henchman. But at least I'm off that boat. I tell you, Abraham, I don't think I'm going to sail back. I'd rather ride a horse back to Kingsland."

"No, you're coming with us. We stick together, one way or the other."

"I know." Solomon looked heavenward. "Just saying."

The night crickets chirped all around.

"I've gazed at the stars a thousand times since I've been back. I don't recognize a one of them. When I was a boy, my dad got me a telescope when I was ten—a birthday present."

"You like astronomy?"

"No, I couldn't have cared less. I liked girls. Those were the stars that I wanted to see." Solomon showed a smile of sharp teeth. "My first girlfriend was older. Not when I was ten, but in high school. I was a sophomore, and she was a senior. She taught me a lot about things. We'd even get together when she came back from college. She was a huge stoner and went on to become a law-school teacher. What a waste. I wonder what she's into now."

"She's probably a senator. What was her name? On second thought, I don't want to know."

"Heh, now that you mention it, her father was in politics. Congressman, I think. I didn't pay much attention. Anyway, her name was Alice. Kinda square, but she'd surprise you." Solomon lay down in the dirt. "I never paid the stars a lick of attention until I got here. What in the hell happened to us, Abe?"

"I don't know, but I have a feeling that the horned halfling does." He sat back and looked skyward. "He doesn't want us to find out either."

"We had the upper hand. We should've taken advantage of it. Maybe he does know the way home."

"I gave my word to take care of the king first. If I see that through, then he'll take care of me. At least, that's the plan."

Solomon sighed. "I think you like it here. Perhaps too much. If it were up to me, I think I'd take a crack at going back home. That's what I'd do."

"You aren't me, and I'm not you. Did you ever stop to think that you might be here for another reason?"

"Aside from some sort of punishment, no." Solomon rolled up onto one side. "Let me guess. You think that you are here to save the world, don't you?"

Abraham shrugged.

Solomon let out a hearty laugh.

"What?" Abraham said. "It's better than thinking that I'm here by accident."

"You jocks are all the same, aren't you?" Solomon's usual mild tone became bitter. "Every jock I ever knew had a hero complex."

"Hey, if the shoe fits…"

"Pah!" Solomon got up, dusted the dirt off his vest, and said, "I think I'll sleep elsewhere."

"Solomon? Come on, man."

The troglin vanished into the woodland as if he'd never even been there.

"Bigfoot, eat your heart out."

"Ahem."

Abraham turned his head. "Oh, hi, Shades. Have a seat. Solomon's spot is still warm."

Shades had his hood off. The smallish man brightened. "Don't mind if I do… Abraham? Is it all right that I call you that?"

"I'm good with both. What's on your mind?"

Shades sat in Solomon's spot and warmed his hands by the fire. "I was wondering if you had given any more thought to branding me a Henchman."

"From what I can see, you earned it. But I have to ask why. You don't seem like the type that would want to be a Henchman."

"I take offense," the silky-voiced man said. "Why would you discriminate between me and the others?"

"You come across as the self-serving type."

"Like Lewis and Leodor?"

"Ha, well, not like that. More like a thief or a rogue. You want to have something so that you can get something out of it." He pointed at Shades's face. "Besides, it appears that you have a brand."

Shades gently touched two fingers to the starlike scar on his cheek. "This little beauty mark. Ha, it's nothing."

"How'd you get that beauty mark?"

"Er, well, if I told you that I was born with it, would you be satisfied?"

"No."

"I don't want to lie about it either. It's my cross to bear. And, well"—Shades shrugged—"it's embarrassing."

"I don't think anyone in this group should have anything to hide. We have to trust one another."

With an easy smile, Sticks leaned back and said, "Oh, come now, do you really think this group doesn't hold secrets from one another? You are leading a bunch of criminals, for the Elders' sake. Look." He pointed toward Lewis and Leodor, huddled over their own fire. "Those two conspirators tried to kill the king." He made his rounds group by group. "Tark and Cudgel are common thieves. Dominga, a thief. Sticks, a former harlot and thief."

"Harlot?"

"Er, I mean Dominga. Not Sticks. No, Sticks has always been a thorn among the roses—er, I mean a rose among the thorns. And don't get me started on Iris." Shades leaned forward and said under his breath, "She's a mystic. Never trust a mystic. One like her practices the arts of the dark druids. Not a good thing, even by the Sect's standards."

"Well, aren't you a fountain of information?" Abraham would be lying to himself if he didn't admit that Sticks being a former harlot stung a little. Shades's words twisted in his heart. *Don't take it personal. Remember, this might not be real. And so what if she was?* He set his jaw and said, "You know, you have a fine way of deflecting attention away from the mark on your face." He touched the stitches Iris had sewn into his arm after the last battle. "Listen, bub, we are all a bunch of dirty rotten scoundrels. But with me, the slate is clean. It's all about what you do moving forward."

"If that is the case, why won't you brand me?" Shades said with an unusual tightness in his voice. "I haven't given you any trouble. I've been the best ally a friend can be."

"Sorry, Shades, but I have to trust my gut on this." Abraham lay down on his side and looked into the fire. "Say, you're from Hancha. What can you tell me about Cauldron City or the Cauldron?"

Shades stood up. "Sorry, Abraham. It will have to wait." He walked away.

Abraham made a big yawn. The battle, the ride, and the aching wounds had finally caught up with him. "Fine by me." With the crickets chirping and the small fire's embers popping, he fell asleep like a baby.

CHAPTER 49
BACK HOME

Abraham woke up inside a padded white room. He sat up. His arms were bound to his chest. He wiggled around and screamed, "Nooo!" He was in a straitjacket. He popped up to his bare feet. "No. No. No. No. No."

His heart fluttered—not the good kind of flutter but the bad kind. Helplessness assailed him. Wide-eyed, he walked the padded floor and bounced against the soft walls. The walls were dingy white. Everything had a stale smell. He looked about. A white camera shaped like a globe was anchored into the corner of the ten-foot-high ceiling. He looked dead at it.

"Hello? Can you hear me? What is going on?"

He paced, continuing to call out for help. The padded walls absorbed his pleas. Seeing the faint outline of a door, he threw his shoulders against it. He kept that up until he fell down in the center of the room, lathered in sweat and panting.

This can't be real. I'm not crazy. I belong in Titanuus. He squeezed his eyes shut. *Take me back to Titanuus!*

For the longest time, Abraham lay on his back with his eyes wide open. He had no idea where he was or what had happened. He had gotten used to bad headaches and blacking out and finding his way home again, but this was different. He'd fallen asleep by a campfire while talking to Shades. Now, he was in what he assumed to be the real world. He rolled over and looked at the camera. A tiny red dot glowed like a red eye underneath it.

"Why am I here?"

That was the bigger question. It made sense that he had wound up in a hospital before in a coma. He could believe that it was the result of an accident. But now he was in a loony bin of some sort. *Why?*

"Oh no," he said softly. The only thing he could think of was that he'd possibly spoken to the wrong people, and they had locked him up. He rolled over and scratched his itching nose against the floor. "This is crazy. Why would they have locked me up? I'm a nice guy, and I couldn't have said something that stupid. I wonder if that Nurse Nancy had something to do with it. She seemed to be kinda mean." He looked at the camera. *Oh great, I'm talking to myself. The first sign of crazy.* He sat cross-legged and faced the camera. "Could I please talk to someone? I'm Abraham Jenkins. The last thing I remember was being in a hospital after a truck accident." He tossed out more information about himself—where he was from, who he was, and even his driver's license number. "Please, someone talk to me."

Time passed. The only company he had was the chronic hum of the caged fluorescent lights above him. The bulbs were bright, but a few of them had gone dim and flickered. He lay on his back and stared at them for many long minutes. He closed his eyes and tried to sleep, but the straitjacket's constricting nature made getting comfortable impossible. His shoulders and arms itched, and he couldn't scratch them.

Abraham walked on his knees to the door and pressed his ear against it. The only thing he could hear was his heart thumping in his temple. He tapped his forehead against the door. He wanted to slam his skull into it but refrained. *Remember, they're watching.*

The question is, who is watching? How did I get here? Where is Mandi? Does she know about this? Did she put me in here? Perhaps Luther Vancross did. Maybe all of them think that I'm crazy.

Maybe he was.

He took in a deep breath of air from the stuffy room and shook with a shuddering sigh. He leaned back against the door and closed his eyes. He tapped his toes together. *I want to go to Titanuus. I want to go to Titanuus. I want to go to Titanuus.*

One of the flickering fluorescent bulbs went black.

Abraham huffed a depressed laugh. "I'm going to have to fall asleep eventually. Don't dwell on it, Abraham. Don't dwell on it."

He moved to one of the corners in the wall, the one below the camera. He closed his eyes and breathed deeply. His sore muscles began to ease. His breathing slowed. His eyes became heavy. *Yes, sweet sleep, take me away.* His chin dipped into his chest.

The door to his padded cell opened.

CHAPTER 50

Two men in the sea-green uniform scrubs of an orderly walked into the padded room. One of them carried a long metal stick with two prongs on the end. He was black, older, short haired, and built like a football lineman with his playing days long behind him. His nose was busted. The other was a white farm-boy type, young, about the same size as his counterpart. He had a black eye and a front tooth missing. Their wounds looked fresh. Both men wore frowns.

Their names were sewn into their shirts. The black man's read Otis, and the younger fellow's read Haymaker.

Abraham tried to make it light. "Good morning, fellas, or afternoon or evening... Uh, I hope it's time for my bathroom break because I really have to go."

The orderlies exchanged a glance.

The black man, Otis, stepped forward and stuck his prod into Abraham's ribs.

Abraham jumped from his seat. "Gah!" His nerves caught fire from head to toe. Cringing in the corner, he asked, "What did you do that for?"

"Because if you get squirrely, you are going to get more of that," Otis said in a deep voice. "Get up! And don't play games with me today, fool."

"Okay," Abraham said. Judging by the heavy stares in both men's eyes, he knew they meant business. And he certainly didn't want to get shocked again—it sent fire right through him. "Okay."

The orderlies got him up on his feet and led him out of the room. With their strong hands locked on his arms, they led him down the hall. The floor tiles were cold. Abraham's cold feet burned with every step. The floors felt as if they had tacks in them for some reason. The hallway was dim, the cinderblock walls were painted off-white, and the lights above showed off the dinginess. The place was definitely a hospital of some sort. They passed many closed doors. Some had portal windows, and others didn't. It was a dreary place.

At the end of the hallway was an elevator with metal doors so shiny Abraham could see his blurred reflection in them. *I look shaggy. Scary. No wonder I'm locked up. I look like I haven't combed my hair or trimmed my beard in weeks.* The big men were about the same size as him. Haymaker pressed the elevator button.

"So, is this the way to the bathroom? I really hate to sound like a baby, but I have to go."

Otis waved his metal stick in his face.

"I mean, I did have to go."

The elevator dinged, and the doors split open. The rough-handed orderlies guided Abraham inside. The doors closed. Haymaker hit the button. The elevator went up.

Abraham nodded. "Going up. A good sign."

He counted the floor buttons on the elevator panel—eleven floors. Haymaker hit the eleventh-floor button.

"The top. Even better."

Otis stuck his stick right underneath Abraham's chin and said, "Quiet."

The elevator stopped. The doors opened. The orderlies let him into the room. It was an office with a bunch of empty cubicles. The same fluorescent lights hung in the ceiling. Most of the bulbs were out.

The carpet didn't hurt as much on his feet as the cold tile floors in the hallway. The men led Abraham to the back of the offices into the corner. Otis knocked on an oak door.

"Come in," someone said in a sharp voice.

Otis pushed the door open by its nickel-plated handle. The office was very big, nicely decorated with warm wood-paneled walls and the heads of game. Deer, elk, and black bear heads were mounted on the wall. The overhead lights were off, but the cloudy sunlight of a hazy morning shone through the windows. Bookshelves, display cases, and sports memorabilia were there. A man sat behind an expensive cherry-wood desk in a high-backed burgundy leather chair with his legs propped up on the desktop. His face was hidden by an open newspaper, but Abraham could see curly locks of brown hair over the rim of the paper.

"Sit him down and gear him up," the man behind the desk said.

"Yes, sir," Otis and Haymaker replied. They took the straitjacket off Abraham. As they did so, they put two chrome-plated shackles on his wrists, with three small stripes of green light glowing on the cuffs. They shoved Abraham down into a green leather chair in front of the desk. "He's ready, Doctor."

"Good. Now leave us," the clean-shaven doctor said.

Both men exited without a word, closing the door quietly behind them. The man behind the desk dropped the paper from his face, folded it up, and placed it on the desk. He had a receding hairline, curly brown hair, and a round face and was in his late fifties, clean-shaven and dark eyed. He wore wire-rim glasses shaped like octagons. His expression was stern with a slight smile. He wore a camo hunting suit and clasped his rough hands on the desk. "Good morning. I am Dr. Jack Lassiter. Tell me who you are."

"Abraham Jenkins." He looked at the cuffs on his wrists.

"Don't worry about those," Dr. Lassiter said. "So long as you behave yourself and don't do anything stupid, like before, you'll be just fine."

Abraham lifted his chin and asked, "Before? What do these things do?"

Doctor Lassiter smiled. "Heh heh heh. It's a little therapeutic invention of my own. It will make that cattle prod that Otis carries feel like a tickle of a feather."

CHAPTER 51

Abraham rubbed his wrists. "Oh. I'll stay put. That cattle prod was enough. It almost shot the pee out of me, though." He looked over his shoulder at a door in the corner behind him. "And, well, I still really need to go."

"Keep the door open."

"Thanks, Dr. Lassiter." He got up, crossed the room, opened the door to a small, quaint bathroom, and turned the light on. Feeling as though he hadn't gone in days, he relieved himself, washed his hands, turned off the light, and exited. "Again, many thanks, Dr. Lassiter."

"No need to be so formal. Call me Dr. Jack. It's best we keep it simple, Abraham." Dr. Jack pointed at a little black button mounted on his desk. "That's the switch that will make you twitch. Remember that. I'm not the kind of man that jokes about a thing like that."

Abraham lifted his hands and sat down. "I believe you." He wouldn't learn anything about what was going on if he didn't cooperate. He stuck with the nice-guy act. Eyeing the trophy heads mounted on the wall, he said, "So, you're a hunter?"

"I've been sweeping the woods and skinning bucks since I was a boy. A fine sport, hunting." Dr. Jack rocked back in his seat and drummed his fingers on the end of his chair's arms. "What about you?"

"Never hunted much. I was more of a ball-sports guy."

"I know." Dr. Jack reached down into a drawer and pulled out a thick manila file with a red rubber band on it. He took off the rubber band and opened the papers. He licked his thumb and rummaged through the file. "You have had an eventful life. Some very unfortunate turns of events. Very sorry to hear about that."

Abraham leaned forward. "I have to say, you've lost me. Can you tell me why I'm here? I don't mean to be pushy, but I'm very confused."

"That's why I brought you here. Because you aren't the only one that is confused. I'm a bit confused myself." Dr. Jack picked up a remote from his desk. He pointed it toward a large flat-screen television that hung on the wall to his right, and the television came on. "Tell me, what is the last thing that you remember before coming here?"

I was lying by a campfire in Titanuus. That was the first thing that came to Abraham's mind, but he knew better than to say it. His turned in his chair toward the television. "I was in a hospital. I'd come out of a coma. I talked with my roommate, a very old guy, Charles Abner. A couple of friends stopped by—my boss, Luther Vancross, and a woman friend, Mandi." He buckled his brows and quickly lifted a finger. "Oh, and the nurse was Nancy."

Dr. Jack nodded several times. He took notes with a blue pen while Abraham spoke. He shook the pen. "Ah, crap. My pen's out of ink." He flicked it into a wastebasket beside his desk and grabbed another one out of a drawer. "If you are ever in the market for a good reliable ink pen, get the Bic Atlantis. It's my favorite. All of the other ones suck." He scribbled on a separate notepad. "Good. Good. So, you remember talking with your associates. Then what? Who did you talk to last?"

"Mandi. I think I fell asleep after that." He told a partial truth, not wanting to get into how Charles had jumped into the conversation too. "It was the last thing I remember before waking up here."

"Fascinating," Dr. Jack said with a shine in his brown eyes. "If I'm correct, what you are talking about lines up with what happened with the occurrence three days ago."

"Occurrence?" Abraham leaned back in his seat. "Did you say three days ago?"

"Abraham, you're a jock. You've seen your own kind of action, and you've been through a lot. I mean, have you ever been a striker, a brawler? You are a big fella. Rough looking, like a biker. One of those Hells Angels."

"Hey, I've never been into those types of things. I mean, there might have been some scuffles on the baseball fields, but I always tried to break them up." He broke out in a cold sweat. "I was cocky but mellow."

Dr. Jack picked up a piece of paper and said, "Says here that you punched a guy and knocked him out in college. Two teeth out."

Abraham sank in his chair. That had been an ugly day, one that he'd buried deep. He didn't even start the fight—he only went in swinging. The guy didn't see it coming. The young man's face caved in, and his body fell. "Look, that was more of an accident."

"Maybe. Look, all men have a violent nature. But that day, something uncorked in you. Right?" Dr. Jack said in a pushy voice.

"No." Abraham's neck reddened. "I was a talker."

"Did that provoke the fight?"

He bobbed his head side to side. "Probably. I don't know. It was long ago, and everyone was in on it. Wait, I remember, I hit a guy with a ball. In the hip. I didn't tip my hat. The bench cleared."

"Why didn't you tip your hat?"

"I guess I was being a jerk that day, but I learned my lesson. I swear I did."

Dr. Jack puffed up in his chair, flexing and gesticulating mildly with his arms. "You're a big rangy fella. That draws attention. I bet you liked that. Being a jock, you are probably used to getting your way. But when you don't, you get angry, don't you?"

"I, uh… no. No, I don't have a temper."

Dr. Jack made a devilish smile and picked up another piece of paper. "Sure you don't. And what about this man? The pharmacist you attacked. Bill Lowman. Did he provoke you?"

"No, no, I was hooked on pain pills. It was an accident."

"You've been in a lot of accidents. You know that? Accidents that hurt many and killed them." Dr. Jack leaned forward. "I know this is harsh, but trust me, it's therapeutic. Facing the truth. It's the best therapy." He looked Abraham dead in the eye. "Look at you. You're turning red all over. You want to hit me, don't you?"

Yes.

CHAPTER 52

"It's fine. Say what you are thinking," Dr. Jack said.

"What is up with the third degree? I've been through all of this. I want to put it behind me. How is it therapeutic to dredge it all up?" He flipped out his hands. "What man wouldn't want to hit someone treating him like this? Especially after all I have been through."

Dr. Jack pecked an index finger on the table. "It's a matter of trust. We need to establish that. You see, I think you believe that you have moved on, but you haven't. I'm going to show you why I believe that. It should shed a little light on my concerns." He turned toward the television. "After you fell into another coma, you had some violent convulsions. Your language was foreign. The local hospital didn't know what to do with you, so you were brought here—a special treatment center."

"Okay. Pardon, but I don't think there is anything wrong with me."

"Pain-pill addiction. Migraines." Dr. Jack shook his head. "There is something wrong with all of us. But most, we hope, can control it."

"There's nothing wrong with me. I'm normal," Abraham lied. *Abnormal is more like it.* His life had a new truth. He was the best swordsman in Titanuus. Many were dead to show for it. But that wasn't this world. It was another. He scratched an eyebrow and looked at the television. An image came up of a hospital nurses' station.

Dr. Jack glanced at him and said, "Here we go. I kinda wish we had some popcorn. Do you like popcorn, Abraham?"

He placed a hand on his belly. "I'd like about anything right now." He focused on the TV screen. A tall shaggy-haired man wearing a hospital gown approached the nurses' station. He dragged intravenous tubes behind him, along with the monitoring station. Two of the women looked up from their phones and jumped in their seats. One of them grabbed a phone. Nurse Nancy raced into the scene from out of nowhere. She wore a set of Hello Kitty scrubs, much like before. She put her hands into Abraham's belly. She was yelling at him.

Abraham broke out into a cold sweat. *Oh Lord, tell me I don't hurt her. Don't let me hurt her.* He watched himself pick up Nurse Nancy by the waist like a child and set her aside. He moved down the hallway. The camera view switched from the nurses' station to the hallway. In long strides, he made his way down the hallway, head twisting left and right like a trapped tiger's. He glanced upward for a moment in the direction of the camera. His eyes were wildfires. Abraham didn't recognize himself. The man was him but different.

A group of doctors and nurses, male and female, came rushing down the hallway. The men barred Abraham's path. He pushed through them. Two nurses, stout men but not as big, hooked his arms. Abraham slung them face-first into each other.

"Heh heh heh. I know I shouldn't laugh, but I love a good action movie. But this is better because it's real," Dr. Jack said. "Man, that hurt me to watch."

One of the doctors was screaming and waving his hands. He mouthed the words, "Call security! Call security!" The doctor backpedaled from Abraham, stumbled, and fell down. As he walked by, the doctor locked both arms around his leg. Abraham glared down upon the doctor. The doctor let go. Abraham moved down the hall. He poked his head into doors and walked into rooms and came back out. He ripped the intravenous needles out of his arms. He moved down the hall and disappeared from view.

The camera angle changed.

Abraham saw himself move into the lobby, where the elevators waited. He walked by one set of doors when they opened. Four security guards in blue uniforms came rushing out, carrying black billy clubs. A nurse pointed at Abraham and screamed. The guards converged on Abraham.

The first guard to approach Abraham clubbed him in the back of the head. Abraham spun around and backfisted the man in the jaw then snatched the man's club as he crumpled to the floor.

"This is where it really gets good," Dr. Jack said. He gesticulated with stiff open hands. "Wah tah!"

Abraham touched the back of his head and felt a knot on it.

The camera view caught the second elevator's doors opening. Six more guards, armed the same, came pouring out. Abraham, club in hand, squared off on the guards of all shapes, ages, and sizes. Two bum-rushed him with their clubs raised high. Abraham cracked them both in the tops of their skulls in the blink of an eye. The guards fell face-first to the floor.

One of the guards was barking orders to the others, a big black fellow. He waved his arms and was mouthing the words, "Pile on him! Pile on him! There's more of them than us."

The gang of guards bum-rushed Abraham. That was a mistake. He snatched another club from the ground, and fisting the two clubs, he beat the tar out of the inferior men. The black clubs busted out a man's teeth, smote temples, and dislodged an eyeball. Watching, Abraham winced.

Dr. Jack chuckled. "I've never seen a big man so out of shape move so fast. It's uncanny. Inhuman."

Abraham followed the fighter's perfected movements. Lightning-fast strokes. He knew them like the back of his hand. It wasn't inhuman. It was Ruger. A chill ran down his spine.

All the guards were sprawled out on the floor, groaning, bleeding, crawling, or all of the above. The men were wiped out, crying over busted elbows, broken noses, and arms. Three female guards remained. They had their taser guns out and pointed at Ruger.

Smart. They should have tried that first and saved the men from the macho act.

Two of the women guards trembled, but the third came forward, as steady as a rock. She was butch, with spiky black hair. She crept in on Ruger. Her lips were saying, "Give yourself up, big fella. I'll shoot."

Ruger took one step toward her.

She fired the taser. So did the other two.

Ruger's eyes lit up like a Christmas tree.

CHAPTER 53

Ruger's body shook inside his skin. His belly jiggled like Santa Claus's. Over a dozen strands of electricity latched onto his chest. The prods sunken into his flesh sent pulsating jolts of electricity through the strings. His hair stood on end, and his teeth clacked together. He swayed but did not fall.

The butch guard shouted to the other two. It looked as though she said, "Give him all the juice you got! Lay down, big fella." She continued to squeeze the trigger on her taser gun, as did the others. "Fall!"

The wild-eyed man swept two handfuls of taser strings into his big hands. With a fierce yank, he pulled them all out. The chest of his hospital-issued clothing showed small bloody marks on it. He dropped the wiry coils down on the floor.

The female guards' eyes widened. The butch one swallowed. She nervously looked at the others then faced him again. She took out her club and took a step forward.

Ruger gave her the no-no finger sign.

She rushed him, screaming. He snatched the club out of her hand and shoved her backward. The other two caught the meaty woman, and all three fell down.

Ruger turned his back and ran down the nearest hall.

"At least you play nice with the ladies," Dr. Jack said. "If not for that, I'd have figured you were completely out of your skull."

The camera angle changed. The view caught up with Ruger looking out a window. His head quickly turned side to side. He pounded his fist on the glass. He turned and saw an empty linen cart. The shiny metal frame sat on black heavy-duty casters. He hustled over to the cart and picked it up in his long, hairy arms. With a heave, he sent the cart crashing through the glass window. Moving with apish agility, he swung himself out behind the window's broken hunks of glass and vanished.

Abraham looked right at Dr. Jack. "Where did he go? I mean, where did I go?"

"Interesting that you put it that way." Dr. Jack held up the remote and waved it gently. He pressed the buttons. "Fortunately, we have plenty of cameras on the outside. Man, I must have watched this over a dozen times. Every time, I get the chills. But not so much as this next part."

A new picture showed up on the TV screen. It was outside and snowing. The camera showed the outside of a tall, impersonal, hospital-like building. Abraham guessed it was the building with the elevator he'd taken. It was surrounded by the tall trees of a forest. *What is this place?*

Dr. Jack leaned forward in his chair. He patted the remote in his hand and pointed at the screen. "Take a close look. This is a camera shot from the ground level. But up near the top, the eighth floor, well, tell me what you see."

Abraham squinted. A man was climbing the building like a spider. The winds tore at his hospital garb and beard.

Ruger's fingers and toes were lodged inside the cement grooves that ran vertically down the building. He descended slowly, foot by foot, level by level, without stopping.

Abraham's heart raced. It was him, but it wasn't. It could have only been Ruger. He didn't know Ruger for certain—they'd never met—but for some reason, he knew that was him. That was the only explanation he could comprehend. *How?*

"I've seen a lot of crazy things in my life. Crazy is what I do… but this?" Dr. Jack looked right at Abraham when he said it. "This is something straight up out of *The Terminator*. I kept waiting for your skin to come off. I'm thankful that didn't happen. I think."

Ruger made it down the building one level at a time. He didn't move like Spider-Man, but he moved.

"How is my body doing this?" he muttered.

Tapping the remote on his chin, Dr. Jack said, "I've been wondering the same thing myself. To the point that it is making me crazy. Every time I watch, I learn a little something else. Look at you, a big fella but out of shape. For your fingers to cling to those snowy walls, well, your grip would have to be stronger than steel. I understand smaller climbers doing feats like this, but you, a washed-up baseball pitcher turned junk-food-eating truck driver? Uh-uh, I can't buy it. There weren't any pentagrams tattooed on your body. So, I ruled out any demons, even though it's been recorded that demons that possess people give them super strength."

"I'm not a demon."

"No, but it would make a lot more sense if you were. I'd be sleeping better. I know that much." Jack smiled at him and looked back at the television. Marveling, he said, "You know, I must have watched this five times before I caught on to something."

"What's that?"

"Why didn't you take the stairs? Or try the elevator? Any normal person would have done that. But like some sort of alien, you went right through the window. Why? Why? Why?"

That was a good question. If it was Ruger, he wouldn't have been familiar with the layout of modern buildings. He might not have recognized the exit signs over the stairwells. And the red glow of the exits might have deterred him. *Man, if that's you, Ruger, then how are you suddenly in me?* "I don't know," Abraham said. "Look at me. I'm the kind of guy that prefers elevators."

"Uh-huh." Jack's stare was fixed on the television.

Ruger made his way down the wall and dropped from it the last fifteen feet.

"Look at that. You land like a cat. A fat cat, but a cat, nonetheless. You should have shattered your leg, but nothing in your body is broken."

Ruger prowled across the hospital grounds. The camera views changed several times as he raced across the campus grounds. A twenty-foot-high fence surrounded the building. Red warning lights were flashing on the tops of the metal fence posts. Ruger grabbed the fence then jerked his hands away.

"That fence is electric." Dr. Jack chuckled.

CHAPTER 54

RUGER SCALED THE ELECTRIC FENCE like a monkey. He pushed his body through the barbed wire at the top, shredding his hospital garb. After dropping to the other side of the fence, he didn't look back. He dashed through the snow and disappeared into the woodland.

The TV screen went black. Dr. Jack tossed the remote onto the table. "Tasers didn't stop you. The electric fence didn't either." He looked at the bracelets on Abraham's wrists. "Don't get any funny ideas. I promise you that those will stop you. Forever, possibly."

"I'm not going anywhere. I want the same answers that you want." He wiped the sweat from the side of his head. "So, where did you catch me? Or how?"

"Good question." Dr. Jack spun in his chair and faced the wall of mounted trophies. "I've been hunting since I was a kid. I love it, my dad did, my grandpa did, and so on. You see that buck up there." He pointed at the wall. "Twenty point. It took me years to get him. I knew he was there, and he knew that I was there. But one day, I got him. We left early, right after dawn. I camped in the same spot for three days. He appeared. One shot took him down."

Abraham played nice, even though massive confusion still raced through his head. "Impressive. He's very big. I take it that I was easier."

"You were a wild-eyed man in the woodland. Lost. Confused. Technically, you didn't hurt anyone… that bad. Aside from the fellow whose eyeball you dislodged." He spun back toward Abraham. "You left a trail of blood that the blind could see. The hounds gave chase. Cornered you in the cliffs. You know what we did?"

"I'm on pins and needles."

"Threw a net over you. My idea. There isn't much a man can do once he's all tangled up and you drag him away."

"Like in the *Planet of the Apes*. Nice."

Dr. Jack made a wicked chuckle. "Good one. A net and tranquilizers. The tranquilizers took a long time to wear you down. I didn't want you to hurt yourself or others, so it was the straitjacket and padded room for you." He leaned forward, clasped his hands, and put his elbows on the table. "So, Abraham Jenkins, can you tell me what in the hell is going on?" He looked him right in the eyes, searching for a sign or an answer. "Tell me what you are thinking. I can help."

Abraham had dealt with his fair share of intelligent people in this lifetime. Dr. Jack was one of them. He came across as the kind of man who was two steps ahead of everyone around him, the kind of man who knew more than he showed. Judging by the heads mounted on the wall, he was a dangerous man too.

"I think I might have been abducted by aliens. You know, we are close to Wytheville. Maybe they implanted something inside of me. It gave me superpowers." He smiled.

"You might want to cooperate."

He lifted his wrists. "I am. Look, I can't explain that. It's as impossible to me as it is to you.

Not to mention that I'm sore and burning like fire all over. Can I ask you a question? What kind of special treatment facility is this?"

"It's a WHS center. You've probably never heard of it, but we take care of privileged clients. Consider yourself lucky."

"Why am I special?" He frowned. "I don't get it."

"You are safe. That's all that matters. But we need to diagnose your problem. Your schizophrenia."

"I'm not schizo!" Abraham's knee started to bounce. He could live with the migraines and his past troubles, but he couldn't live with being called crazy. He wasn't crazy. Everything he did was real. There had to be an explanation for it. He was going to find out. He noticed Dr. Jack's finger hovering over the button. "I'm sorry, but no one has ever called me crazy before." He sighed.

"Just like most people that are incarcerated swear that they are innocent, well, people with mental disorders are pretty much the same. Don't take it hard. There is therapy for you. I can, and I will help." Dr. Jack leafed through the papers in the file, wetting his thumb as he did so. "You were roommates with Charles Abney in the hospital. Do you remember him?"

"I do. He died."

"Yes, he did. I shouldn't share this with you—it's privileged information—but seeing how he's gone and he doesn't have any family"—he made that smug chuckle—"well, who is going to know? Besides, if I get got, it's my word against yours. A crazy person."

"Isn't *crazy* a bit of an insensitive way of labeling people nowadays?"

"Do you take me as a man that gives a crap about political correctness? Sticks and stones, Abraham, sticks and stones." He fished out a piece of paper from one of his desk drawers and held it up—it was a map. "Charles drew this for me. Does it look familiar?"

Abraham swallowed. *Titanuus!*

CHAPTER 55

ABRAHAM TRIED TO PLAY IT cool. He tilted his head to one side and said, "It looks like a picture of West Virginia. I mean, if you flip it over." He shrugged. "I've looked at a lot of maps. I'm a local and a truck driver, you know."

Dr. Jack turned the picture around and flipped it over. He scratched his neck. "Huh. I never picked up on that. It actually does closely resemble the mountain state." He set the map down on the desk. "A funny thing. You know, one of my nurses—you met her, Nurse Nancy—overheard Charles talking to you about a something called Titanuus just before he died. She made it sound like the two of you might have had something in common."

With his fingers locked together, Abraham shrugged his thumbs and lied, "I didn't really make much sense of it."

Dr. Jack was playing a cat-and-mouse mind game with him. That wasn't Abraham's strongest suit, but he wasn't one to be played either.

He decided to flip the conversation. "It sounds like you might know more about this Titanuus than I do. Do you?"

Dr. Jack raised his brows. Stiffly, he said, "I hear a lot of things from my patients. Nothing they say surprises me. But one thing that I've become particularly good at is knowing when they are lying. Again, I want to emphasize that you and I need to establish a chain of trust. If we can do that, well, both of us will be better off. I'll be enlightened, and you'll be relieved of the burdens that you carry. You can hopefully return back to society, sooner than later."

"Return back to society?" Abraham rocked forward in his chair. "How long do you plan on keeping me?"

"I don't think you fully understand the severity of your situation. You assaulted several people. It's on video. I can keep you as long as I want. And be thankful—it's either this or prison."

Abraham paled and sat back in his seat. Dr. Jack Lassiter meant business. Abraham wasn't sure what sort of business the man was into or what he really wanted, but he'd made it clear that he was in control. Abraham's eyes swept the room as he searched for something to use against the man, something to remember. He needed to know more about who this man was. At the same time, he thought, *Prison might be the better option.* He cleared his throat. "Dr. Jack, I might think a lot better if I had something good to eat. After all, a lot has happened, and I'm starving."

"You'll eat. You'll eat sooner if you open up with me." Dr. Jack closed the file and tossed it in the drawer. "Do you have anything else that you'd like to add?"

"No."

"Then this session is over. Otis! Haymaker! Come on in."

The office door opened, and the burly orderlies strolled inside. Haymaker carried the straitjacket.

Abraham looked at the men from over his shoulder and said, "Is that really necessary?"

"You saw the video," Dr. Jack said. "You're very dangerous. You probably don't remember, but Otis and Haymaker caught a first-hand look at what you can do when you're unfettered." He glanced at Otis's shiner and Haymaker's busted nose. "Otis was an all-American lineman at Alabama. Would have been pro if not for a knee injury. You tossed him through a door like a sack of potatoes. Didn't he, Otis?"

With a scowl on his face, Otis made a quick nod.

Dr. Jack continued. "No, Abraham, a padded room is the safest place for you to be. Now, behave yourself. Me, I have some hunting to do." He gave the orderlies a nod.

The orderlies left the bracelets on and put him back in the straitjacket. They buckled the straps tightly and led him out of the room. Abraham took one last look back through the door at Dr. Jack. The man had turned in his chair and faced the snowy window. Haymaker closed the door. Down the elevator they went, and they gruffly shoved him back into the padded room.

"This is it? I'm back here, just like that. This is crazy! I'm not crazy!"

Otis looked at him with his heavy gaze and said, "Oh, believe me, you're crazy. And where I come from, we put crazy down. That's what I said that they should do to you."

"Come on, do you know who I am? You're an athlete, Otis. I'm Abraham Jenkins. The Jet. I've had rough times, but I've never hurt anyone. This is nuts. Come on, man. You have to help me out. Don't I get a phone call or something?"

"Nope," Otis said.

Haymaker stood behind Otis's shoulder with a syringe and a large vial. He poked the needle into the vial and drew a clear liquid into the syringe.

Abraham backpedaled into the corner. "What is that? What is he doing?"

"It's a sedative. A little something to help you rest and to keep you from hurting yourself. Not that I care," Otis said. "Dr. Jack's orders. Come on now—be still. Let's get this over with nice and easy."

Abraham violently shook his head. "I don't need to be sedated. I don't need it. Look at me! I'm behaving myself."

Otis waved Haymaker forward with a nod of his chin. He held his stun rod and smacked it gently into his hand. "Don't make me use this, Mr. Jenkins. Cooperate. Make it nice and easy."

Abraham cringed in the corner. Fear assailed him as his eyes locked on the man holding the needle. He wasn't sure what was driving his fear, but getting injected, well, it didn't sit well with him. Perhaps he feared a new addiction. "Don't, just don't." He looked up at the camera on the wall of his room and shouted. "I don't need it!"

"You're being difficult. I can't have that." Otis hit him with the stun rod.

Abraham wriggled in his skin and collapsed on the padded floor. Otis held him down. Haymaker stuck him in the neck. The taut muscles in his body eased. His eyelids became heavy. The images of the men towering over him blurred. He let go of his fear. The time had come to go back home. *Titanuus, here I come.*

CHAPTER 56

Abraham wiped the drool from his mouth. He was in the same padded white room he'd been in before. The red light on the globe-shaped camera stared down on him. He moaned, "Noooo." He rolled over to the wall and propped himself up in the corner. "How long have I been out?" He eyed the camera.

Stop talking to yourself.

The fluorescent lights flickered above him. The steady hum accompanied his nervous thoughts. He'd fully expected to wake up back in Titanuus. Instead, he was trapped in the real world, trapped back home in a world where he wasn't needed. In Titanuus, he was needed. His head sank into his chest.

I have to get back. I have to get back. I know it's real. It has to be real.

Abraham might have had some issues in his life, but being crazy wasn't one of them. Even when he was hooked on painkillers, he'd only committed one desperate act. He learned from it. He got better from it. What Dr. Lassiter was insinuating about him couldn't be more wrong. He wasn't a man prone to violence. Even when he'd lost Jenny, Jake, and Buddy, he didn't have a violent reaction. Instead, he sobbed and cried tremendously.

Be strong, Abraham. Be strong. There has to be an explanation for all of this.

He rehashed the video footage in his mind. His body had been doing the impossible. Even when he was in the best of shape, he could not have done what he witnessed. It was Ruger. He had no explanation, but he and that man had switched places, a bit, temporarily. There was no other way he could have controlled his body like that, not even after all the books he'd read and movies he'd watched. There was no way.

I am in Ruger, and Ruger is in me. That does sound crazy.

He gently bumped his head back against the padded wall.

Think. Think. Think. I can't live like this.

He eyed the camera. He couldn't tell whether it had a recording device or not. He assumed not, but maybe he was wrong. Dr. Jack might have been watching him right then. He had to be careful. He stood up and paced.

Ruger, Ruger, Ruger, if you are a part of this body, I need you to listen to me. He focused on the people in his life, people who could help. Mandi. Luther. *These are people that can help.* He didn't know what to make of Dr. Jack, but the confident psychiatrist might have actually been trying to help. *I don't know about him, but don't hurt anyone.* He envisioned the exits and the stairs out. He ran through the function of the elevator. He focused on anything that he could that might be useful in case Ruger came out again.

This is insane. What am I, Dr. Jekyll and Mr. Hyde?

He paced for minutes that became hours, thinking of everything useful to Ruger that he could. His belly groaned. His wounds ached. The muscles in his body burned as they did the first few days after training camp, but they felt three times as bad. Ruger had pushed him beyond his natural limits.

What is that guy made of, anyway? His will is as hard as iron. I just wish that my body was.

After circling the padded cell until he couldn't walk anymore, he went and stood before the camera. He tossed his arms out and said, "Fine, Dr. Jack. I'm ready to tell you about Titanuus."

He moved to the wall and sat back down. He waited. Another bulb flickered out and went dead. He waited.

His eyelids became heavy. He started to sleep. The door to his cell opened again. Otis and Haymaker came inside, each carrying a stun rod in his meaty grip. With a lazy roll of his neck, Abraham said, "I really hope it's dinner time."

Otis cracked him upside the head with his stun rod.

Abraham's hair curled. The room went black.

CHAPTER 57

THE SMELL OF FRIED CHICKEN and steamy mashed potatoes lingered in the air. Abraham's eyelids slowly rose. The surrounding light was dim. He hoped he was back in the woodlands of Titanuus.

That wasn't the case. The light came from a brass lamp with a green shade on Dr. Jack's desk. The psychiatrist sat at his desk behind a bucket of chicken. He was sucking his fingers and wearing the same camo suit from before.

Abraham sat up in the same chair he had been sitting in. His head throbbed from the stun rod Otis had stuck him with. "Dinner time?"

Dr. Jack pushed the bucket of chicken his way. "Eat up. Grab some rolls, potatoes, green beans, and fried corn." He waved a chicken leg at Abraham. "Extra crispy. The best. Oh, and sorry for the shock from Otis, but we had to make sure you wouldn't turn wild again."

He didn't have to tell Abraham twice. He reached into the bucket, grabbed a piece of meat, and filled his hands with three rolls. Abraham didn't eat like an animal, but it was close. If he could have, he would have consumed the bone. That was the best food he'd tasted in a long time.

"You might want to wash that down. I'd hate to see you choke yourself." Dr. Jack shoved a huge Styrofoam cup his way. "I hope you like Coca-Cola."

Abraham took the cup in hand and gulped it down to the bottom then let out a long "Aaaaaah!"

"Take it easy, Mean Joe Green."

"I forgot how much I missed that stuff. It feels like it's been forever." He continued eating.

After wiping his hands on a paper napkin, the doctor threw it in the waste bin by his desk and asked, "What do you mean by that?"

After swallowing his last bite, Abraham said, "Because I've been in Titanuus." He grabbed a Styrofoam plate from the desk and scooped out the potatoes and poured on the gravy. "I guess you've heard about it or else you wouldn't be asking me."

"You're prying about Charles Abney. Yes, he did talk about that place. He called it a medieval fantasy world. His descriptions were very vivid. I even had him take a lie detector test. He beat it, but I cured him."

"You cured him?" Abraham loaded in a spoonful of potatoes and spoke with his mouth full. "Was he dangerous?"

"No, not like you. I was young then. I wanted to prove myself. I really wasn't going to buy into *The Road to El Dorado* or this *Stargate* stuff." Dr. Jack grabbed a two-liter of cola and refilled his cup. "So, what do you drink in Titanuus? A lot of ale? Water? Milk?"

"There's nothing processed. It's like going back three hundred years in this world, maybe farther. We ride horses and fight monsters."

Dr. Jack lifted his chin and stroked his neck. He set a small recording device on the table. "I'd like to hear everything, and I want you to start from the beginning."

"Huh," Abraham said as a kind of laugh. "That's going to take a long time because an awful lot has happened."

"Start at the beginning."

"Fine. I hope you don't mind me eating while I talk, but the way my life has been going, I don't know when the next meal is my last one."

"Enjoy. You keep cooperating, and there will be more where that came from. But if you start feeling twitchy"—Dr. Jack held his finger over the button—"I'll be ready."

"Let's hope that doesn't happen." Abraham started at the beginning and recounted the time he'd driven through the sun ring inside the East River Mountain Tunnel and wound up in Titanuus. He talked nonstop for two hours. He ate every crumb of food. "They don't make those little parfait cups anymore, do they?"

"No."

"Man, those were good. I always liked the crumbled-up pie crust in the bottom."

Dr. Jack nodded. "Me too." The inflection in his voice was gone. He seemed listless. He clicked a button on his recorder and said, "Let's take a break."

"Okay. Did something that I said bother you? You seem disturbed."

"I am disturbed, only in a different way than you." Dr. Jack patted the files on his desk. "I've done my homework. Based off of my research, you and Charles Abney never met before, but both of you have described the same world. You have used the same names. Titanuus. Dorcha Territory. Kingsland. Eastern Bolg." He looked at Ruger. "The Spine. My first inclination is that maybe the both of you read the same fantasy books. But I"—he lifted his fingers and made air quotes—"'Googled' it. Nothing of the sort. And based off of my experiences, it's virtually impossible for two people to have the same memories without having been there themselves."

Abraham moved to the end of his chair. "So, you believe me?"

Dr. Jack laughed. "No, no, no, I wouldn't go that far. There is the crazy you know and the crazy you don't know. You usually learn that a few months after the wedding."

Abraham tilted his head.

"That was a joke."

"Oh." He patted his belly. "Sorry, but I haven't had much to laugh about lately. It's been one twisted adventure after the other. And they need me back there."

"You want to go back? In the thick of all of that danger?"

"Yup."

Dr. Jack leaned back in his chair, rubbed his hands together, and said, "I think that I know what is going on here. But please, continue again from where you left off. Try to shorten it, you know, the Cliff's Notes version. You remember Cliff's Notes, don't you?" He started his recorder.

"I do." Abraham refilled his Coke cup and fired out more of the story. He picked up where he'd left off, after he fought Redbeard and met Lewis and King Hector for the first time. He explained about the Henchmen, named them all, and talked about Stronghold. He did leave out quite a few details intentionally. He never mentioned Eugene Drisk or Solomon Paige by name, but he mentioned the talking troglin. After all, they were all people. He went on about the terra-men and the encounter with the Elder Spawn in the Spine. He went on about the mysterious deaths of the Henchmen that they pinned on Raschel, the assassin from the Brotherhood of the Ravens. He added in the Underlord, Arcayis the Arcane, Lord Hawk, the myrmidons… Abraham got some of the events out of order and had to backtrack from time to time because so much had happened. He could see Dr. Jack scribbling on a notepad. "How are we doing?"

"We can take a break." Dr. Jack looked at his watch. "Whew, that's a doozy of a tale." He lifted his glasses and rubbed his eyes. "You've told me many life-and-death experiences. I mean, one after the other, like an action movie. You know, Indiana Jones stuff."

"More like Conan the Barbarian, but I see your point."

"No, you haven't seen my point, but I'm about to make it." Dr. Jack dropped his glasses on the top of his notes and looked at his notepad. "Do you realize that every time that your life is in imminent danger, something or someone bails you out?"

Uncertainly, he said, "Yeah."

"Don't you get it? Let's see. For example, you are fighting against that Elder Spawn thing, a dragon or giant bat, but your magic sword—"

"Black Bane."

"Yes, Black Bane bails you out. Or your Henchmen—they show up at just the right moment. I mean, everything suddenly works out perfectly. Nothing in real life works out like that. You know that. But in this world you are caught up in, it does. I call it alter-escapism. It's a world that we build in our imagination, and everything turns out the way that we want." Dr. Jack leaned back over his desk. "Abraham, as much as you believe it, Titanuus is not real."

CHAPTER 58

Dr. Jack's words were like a punch in the gut. Abraham raised his brows and said, "But we were just talking about Charles Abney. You said it wasn't possible that two people could remember the same thing."

"No, I don't believe in the impossible, per se. Just because an event can't be explained at the moment doesn't mean that an explanation can't be found." Dr. Jack clasped his fingers together. "It's cases like this that make my job so interesting. It's fascinating." He took off his glasses and removed a handkerchief from his pocket. He huffed on his octagon-shaped spectacles and cleaned them. "You are in the right place. With my help, we'll see to it that you never go back to Titanuus again. I know that you like it there, but it's for the better."

"You don't have that right to determine what is best for me." Abraham's jaws clenched. "I can live however I choose."

"Not when you are hurting people. That makes you a danger to society. You need to be institutionalized for the time being." Dr. Jack put his glasses on. "You need to control that animal that is inside of you."

"I'm not an animal, and there isn't one inside of me." He raised his voice. "Do you really think that this is helping me? Is that how your practice works? By telling people that they are crazy?"

"Calm down and lower your voice."

Abraham looked beyond the doctor and at the windows. He wanted to toss Dr. Jack through them. One minute, the man was on his side, and in the next, he was the complete opposite. *Don't let him get to you. You've been through worse than this.* He took a breath. "I'm calm. But wouldn't you be edgy if you were in my situation? You like to point out that incident in the hospital, but I think the matter on your end could have been handled better. Don't you?"

Dr. Jack shrugged. "It was a unique event. But—"

"I don't think it was a unique event now that I think about it. Those guards, well, they were pretty well armed. And there was a lot of them. Have things like this happened before?"

Dr. Jack didn't bat an eye. "This is a secured facility. There are plenty of guards."

"Yes, but why is that? Are there more people like me here? Are there other people that claim to be from Titanuus?" He watched the doctor's eyes and expression widen the slightest bit. One thing was sure—Dr. Jack had a great poker face. If Abraham were to guess, the man lied. He lied a lot. That was his gut feeling. "Are there?"

"Of course not." Dr. Jack cleared the food containers and used napkins from his desk and tossed them in the trash can. "We've been at this a while. I believe it's time to take a break. We can reconvene in a few days."

"A few days? What? No! I'm not going back in that padded room for three more days. That's not right." Abraham got up from his chair. He poked a finger at Dr. Jack. "Quit screwing with my head. I know that is what you are doing."

Dr. Jack hollered, "Otis! Haymaker!" He held his finger above the button linked to the metal bracelets Abraham was wearing. In an easy voice, he said, "Abraham, settle yourself. What I am doing is for your own safety. This is only a precaution. In case the other person in you comes out."

Otis and Haymaker burst through the door with stun rods in their hands. They hustled over and flanked Abraham.

"Easy!" Dr. Jack lifted a hand. "I don't want to have another fight on my hands. Let's all take a breath." He looked at Abraham. "Are you going to cooperate?"

Abraham wanted to say no. The last thing he wanted was to go back into that cell. He would lose his mind in there. *It's no wonder people go crazy. I bet it gets worse after they arrive in places like this.* "I don't have a choice but to cooperate, but why don't you treat me like a man, and give me your word that we will meet tomorrow?"

Dr. Jack gave him an approving look and said, "No, Mister Jenkins, I'm not the kind of man that makes deals with patients. That's a very deadly road to drive down. It's three days, but I could make it four or five. I could use a little extra time in the woods."

"Don't you have any other patients?"

"I do, but right now, I'm losing mine." Dr. Jack gave Abraham a dangerous look. "Don't test me."

Abraham's efforts weren't getting him anywhere. He dropped his arms back by his side. He didn't have a choice. "Okay."

Dr. Jack gave the orderlies a nod.

Otis held the stun rod near Abraham's ribs while Haymaker picked up the straitjacket lying on the floor.

Abraham kept his heavy stare on Dr. Jack, whose index finger lingered beside the button. "You know, when I was playing ball, I used to play poker with the guys for kicks." He glanced at the button. "Most of them thought they were good bluffers, but they weren't."

"Interesting. You are a very observant man, and I agree. I've played my share of poker myself even though I'm more of a blackjack man." Dr. Jack tapped his finger on the desk. "Do you think this button is a placebo?"

"No," he said just as Haymaker started to slide his left arm into the straitjacket. "I think you are." He elbowed Otis in the jaw, lunged for the desk, and grabbed Dr. Jack's hand. He held the man in an iron grip.

Dr. Jack winced, but his eyes filled with fire. "You just made a big mistake," he said through clenched teeth.

"No, you did." Abraham slammed his hand down on the button. The entire room turned bright white as electricity coursed through his body. He screamed.

CHAPTER 59
TITANUUS

Abraham screamed and sat straight up. He was in the woods, surrounded by the clamor of battle. Hard voices were crying out in the darkness of the forest. Steel clashed against steel.

Sticks rushed over to him and dropped to her knees, her forehead dripping with sweat. "You're awake. It's about time. Can you fight?"

Abraham blinked his eyes. "I think so."

"Good." She stuffed his sword and scabbard into his gut and said, "Grab Black Bane. We need you!"

Abraham jumped onto his feet and ripped his sword out of the sheath. He didn't know what was going on, but he didn't care. "No more padded rooms for me."

"What?" Sticks asked as she led him through the forest. The overhanging tree leaves were so large that they blocked out the daylight, casting them in smothering dimness.

"I'll tell you later," he said. The farther they ran, the louder the clamor of battle became. "What is going on?"

"We were ambushed. At least, the scouts were." She ducked underneath some low-hanging branches and leapt a fallen log. "I've been staying back with you. The others are still fighting. It started moments ago. Dominga brought back the warning. Tark had fallen."

"Tark is fallen?" Abraham increased his stride. He passed Sticks, churning toward the sound of battle. In seconds, he arrived on the grisly scene. The Henchmen were down inside a narrow ravine, fighting uphill against a wave of strange attackers. *What are those things?*

Small people covered in long stringy hair rode in pairs on the backs of pony-sized beetles like rhinoceroses. The beetles sped down the hills on eight legs. The little men hurled javelins.

Horace gored a charging beetle through the head on the end of his spear. "Taste the tip of the King's Steel!" he bellowed.

Vern swatted a hurtling javelin aside with his sword and dove away from a charging beetle. It turned at the last second and rammed its strange horn right into him.

Abraham called out, "Vern!" and raced down the hill.

"It's the Captain," Horace roared. His thunderous voice carried down the ravine. "The Captain's awake! Now, put your backs into it, Henchmen! You're fighting like sheep!"

With a tremendous overhead swing, Abraham cleaved a beetle's head off. The hard black shell of its body cracked open like a nut. Green gooey guts spilled. The smallish fur-coated, sharp-toothed men with blood-red eyes jumped off their mounts and bared their sharp teeth. They carried crudely made javelins made from hard wood. They cocked them back over their shoulders.

Solomon emerged from underneath the dangling vines of a willow tree. He grabbed two men by the scruff of their necks and lifted them off their feet then smashed the little men's Cro-Magnon faces together. "Ugly little idiots!" He flung them aside. "Where have you been, Abe?"

"Long story. I'll fill you in later." Abraham jumped toward the next beetle that charged him. He cut through its mouth and horns. The beetles and little men were everywhere. They were a swarm. He turned Black Bane's wrath loose.

Slice! Chop! Slice! Slice! Slice!

With fresh gore coating him up to the neck, Abraham couldn't have been happier. Black Bane's blade burned red-hot. Its keen edge cut through their attackers like a hot knife through butter.

The ambushed Henchmen rallied. With fierce swings, their weapons sank home. Lewis and Clarice fought back-to-back, battling their hearts out. Leodor cast out shimmering shields of citrine energy that deflected the sting of the little men's javelins. Bearclaw wrought havoc with his double-bladed axe, busting open the husks of the beetles one after the other.

The little men swarmed from all directions. Ruger let Black Bane sing. He pressed the attack and shouted to Solomon, "Did you ever see *Land of the Lost*?"

"No," the troglin said as he swung one little man by the ankles into another. "Is that a movie?"

Abraham gored an attacker in the chest. "A Saturday-morning TV show. There were these cave men. One of them was called Chukka." He decapitated another. "He was nice, but he had two evil brothers. These guys remind me of them." He cut a beetle's horn off. "As for these rhino-beetles, well, they're new to me."

"It's all new." Solomon carried two of the little men in a head lock. He squeezed them in the nooks of his arms. Two sharp cracks of spines snapping followed. He let their dead bodies fall in the ferns of the ravine floor. "I really hated to do that, but these things are merciless."

Shades popped up in front of Abraham. His dagger-filled hands were stained with new blood. "They are woodlings. Tark and Dominga stumbled upon a nest of them. It's like kicking a hive of bees. They are people indigenous to Hancha." He ducked away and jumped on two woodlings riding a beetle. He knocked both to the ground and killed them. He popped up from the foliage. "Strong, but not the best of fighters."

A foursome of woodlings erupted from the brush and attacked Shades as one. They pushed him down the ravine then vanished among the ferns.

Abraham called out, "Shades!"

CHAPTER 60

Abraham launched himself down the hillside and found Shades tussling with the woodlings. They were about the same size as the small man. Their long fingernails tore at his clothing. Abraham clocked a woodling that had wrapped itself around Shades's legs with the butt of his sword. The woodling melted into the bush.

Shades's dagger flashed in the dimness of the ravine and poked a hole in another woodling's throat. It stumbled away, clutching at its throat. Shades squirted free of the last woodling. It gave chase. Abraham stuck it in the middle of the back.

A weird howling carried through the ravine. The woodlings disengaged from the attack. The ones on foot jumped on the backs of beetles. They sped away and disappeared into the woods.

The battered Henchmen gathered. Most of them were bloody from head to toe. Their armor had saved them.

Iris called out from the bowels of the ravine, "Help! I need help."

Abraham hustled down the hillside. Iris was holding Tark in her lap. The lightly bearded black man with light eyes had caught a javelin in the neck.

Cudgel knelt by his brother's side and clutched his hand. "Don't die on me, brother. Don't you die on me."

Tark tried to speak, but he only spat blood.

"I can't do anything for him," Iris said. "I don't have the power. The wound is too grave and delicate. Perhaps Leodor can help. I don't know. It's in the Elders' hands now."

Abraham looked about. "Where's Leodor?" He didn't see Leodor or Lewis among the Henchmen who had gathered. "Find him!"

The Henchmen scattered.

Taking a knee, Abraham put a hand on Tark's thigh and said, "You are going to make it."

Bearclaw erupted through the branches of the low-hanging trees. He had Leodor by the scruff of his neck and shoved the fragile man toward Abraham. "I found him. He was crawling up the hill with Lewis."

Abraham reached up, grabbed Leodor by his robes, pulled him down, and said, "Fix him."

Leodor's clammy face was pasted with sweat. He looked at Tark and said, "That wound is grave. I don't think there is anything I can do for it."

"You're going to try." He pushed Leodor to his knees over Tark. "Do it!"

"I'll need some water, to see the wound better," the mystic said.

Lewis marched down the hill and said, "You can't expect him to perform miracles. He needs to save his energy. What if more of those… er, what are they?"

"Woodlings," Sticks said. She cut away a water skin that was hanging from Lewis's chest. She tossed it to Abraham, looked at Lewis, and said, "Thanks, moron."

"Help me clean the wound," Leodor said to Iris.

Abraham handed Iris the water skin.

"Be strong, brother. Be strong," the bald Cudgel said to his brother. He gave Abraham a desperate look. "He's slipping. He no longer grips my hand."

"So much blood." Leodor's fingers massaged the air. "Very sticky. I hate sticky. I need leaves. Large green ones. Moist. Bring them quick."

Iris pointed into the branches, eyeballed Solomon, and said, "Those."

Solomon reached his great hands up into the branches and gently plucked out several spade-shaped leaves the size of his hands. He passed them down to Sticks, who took them to Iris. The lady mystic cleaned the leaves with water.

"Good, place them here." Leodor pointed at the gaping wound in Tark's neck, which pumped new blood out of it. "Quickly. His flow slows. The Elder of Death comes."

Cudgel gulped aloud. With sweat dripping from his chin, he said, "No, no, no, no…"

Leodor said, "Everyone, keep silent."

The Henchmen clammed up.

The wind stilled the moment Leodor parted his lips and muttered arcane words. He placed his hand and a few of the leaves over the wound. An orange fire emanated from his fingers. The lusty green color of the leaves browned and merged with the ebony warrior's skin.

Tark's eyes popped wide. With his body turning as rigid as a plank, he let out a painful gasp. Then he collapsed back onto the ground, limp and not breathing.

Cudgel bellowed at Leodor, "What did you do? What did you do? You killed him!" He shook the smaller man by the shoulders. "Murdering mystic!"

Iris wrapped her arms around Cudgel's back and said, "Calm yourself, friend. Your brother breathes. Look at the gentle rise and fall of his chest."

Cudgel released the aghast Leodor. He put his hands in his brother's, and Tark gripped his hand. "He squeezes!" Cudgel made a nervous smile. "He squeezes! Does this mean that he lives?"

"I don't know. I've done all I can." Leodor clutched at the neck of his robes. "Let the spell do its work and keep your paws off of me!" He stood up with an agonized sigh and looked at Abraham. "Happy?"

Abraham guided Leodor aside, threw his arm over the man's narrow shoulders, and said, "Now, that wasn't so bad, was it?"

Giving Abraham an appalled look, Leodor said, "What do you mean?"

"Helping someone. Doesn't that feel good?"

"I've helped plenty of people in my day. This moment is no different." Leodor glanced at Tark with sad eyes. "To be honest, I really don't think he'll make it. Will I get blamed for that?"

"All that matters is that you did your best. Did you?"

Leodor snorted. "My work is always the best." He pulled away from Abraham. "Lewis, will you help me up this hill? I can barely walk."

"What am I, your underling?" Lewis shook his head and walked away.

Solomon stepped in behind Leodor and said, "I'll help you." He showed Leodor an oversized smile.

"I-I-I'll manage," Leodor said while looking up with eyes the size of saucers.

Solomon scooped the man up in his arms and carried him up the hill, cradled like a baby. "You deserve a break today. I'll carry you."

The remaining cluster of Henchmen chuckled.

Abraham sought out Shades. Once he locked eyes on him, he asked, "Did you say we were in Hancha?"

CHAPTER 61

Using Shades for a guide, the Henchmen arrived at a small farm town called Earlin the next day. The farming community was rich with miles of plowed terrain and produce fields. Stone cottages with straw roofs were scattered in the hills and plains. Barns and storehouses were aplenty. The town itself was well equipped for visitors, complete with taverns and stables for travelers.

The majority of the Henchmen set up camp outside Earlin in a clearing near the riverbed. Abraham, Horace, Sticks, and Shades headed into town in the evening, just after the sun set.

With some pep in his step, Shades led the way. His hood was down, and his elbows were swinging. "I have to admit it's good to be back in my country. There is something about the salty air and smell of baking beast that does my essence good."

"Just find us a place to keep a low profile. Not the lowest—just low," Abraham said.

He'd had a lot to mull over the past day. Four days had passed since he'd fallen asleep by the campfire. The Henchmen put him on a stretcher and dragged him over hill and dale into Hancha. He woke in the middle of everyone fighting for their lives against the woodlings. Everyone survived, and Tark was awake. Being back in Titanuus was good. Anything was better than a straitjacket.

The hardworking people walking the streets wore long sleeves and trousers. They moved with hustle and carried cheerful expressions on their grubby faces. Small groups of men and women played music and danced on the street corners. Some men talked quietly on the porches, drinking ales, smoking pipes, and chewing tobacco. Many bellies bulged over their belts. Shades led them up a two-step staircase onto a porch leading into a wooden tavern. The steps and wood-plank porch groaned underneath their feet.

Abraham followed Shades inside the tavern. They took seats at a round table in the back corner of the building. The smell of roasting meat and vegetables lingered strongly in the air. The late dinner crowd had a few drinks in them. They talked with spirited voices. Men and women were there, but the oddest of all were the pale-skinned zillons. Seeing the alienlike people dressed like farmers in overalls and wearing straw hats was strange. A small group sat at a table playing cards. They had long, slender fingers that moved with the skill of a magician's. They quietly chortled with laughter from time to time.

Horace leaned over the table and rested on his elbows. "Strange country. Never been so deep in Hancha. My neck is itching."

"Don't act squirrely," Shades said as he lifted his hand and flagged down a waitress. "You always get edgy around new people. It shows even behind that beard on your face. Just keep quiet and eat something."

"They better not be serving that rat meat. I remember the last time you talked me into that," Horace said.

Sticks chuckled.

"I don't recall the incident. Should I?"

"You were there, but it was a time ago," Sticks said.

A zillon waitress walked up. Unlike the males, who were as bald as pickles, she had a long, flowing black ponytail sprouting from the top of her head. Her large black eyes were pretty, features sharp, with a tiny little nose and small nostrils. She had no ears but ear holes. She was bony but wore a blue blouse that showed off her bosoms. "Would you like to try our house ale? If not, we have several different varieties for your pleasure. Darks, ryes, stouts, fruits, ports, lights."

Horace slung his elbow over his chair and said, "What is a light?"

"An ale to keep husky fellows like you from becoming huskier." She reached down and patted his belly. "But I like a portly man. They make good eaters." She winked at Horace. Her tiny mouth expanded to show her tiny white teeth. "I think you will like the port. It's made by our own brew masters, Edmund and Fitzgerald."

Abraham waved his hand around the table and said, "How about a round of those ports? It sounds like a good start."

In a cheery voice, the zillon waitress winked at him and said, "I'll right back. I'll bring you some appetizers on the house too."

Abraham's jaw could have hit the table. "Did she say 'appetizers'? Is it customary that taverns serve appetizers? And serve light beer?"

"It's not a custom in Kingsland, but it's one of the charms that I like about Hancha. They offer variety," Shades said. A candle sat inside a glass globe in the middle of the table. He rubbed his thumb and finger together over the wick, and the candle started to burn. He made a charming smile. "One of my favorite tricks. I'll tell you what—why don't you let me order? My word that it won't be rat meat, either."

The zillon waitress returned with her ghostly pale fingers wrapped around four mugs of port. "I'll be back to take your order in a moment. But first, I have to help my cohorts honor a guest with a happy birth year song." She skipped away with her ponytail bouncing and hands clapping.

Abraham shook his head, buried his face in his mug, and drank.

CHAPTER 62

The zillon waitress brought small roasted hens for appetizers. Chopped salad, meat-and-cheese samplers, and several different pitchers of ale were brought out. Horace was determined to try all of them. Abraham didn't want his company to seem suspicious either. He let them enjoy the local fare, which also included sushi and egg rolls. The tavern served more than the local meat-and-potatoes fare. Their dishes were more sophisticated and just as hearty. The waitress, Anna, dutifully introduced them to the menus, as well as a wine, mixer, and beer list—and a dessert selection. Dishes had fanciful names, after local legends and stories from Hancha. The bustling inn had as many combinations of dishes as a Mexican-American chain restaurant.

Abraham settled for a bowl of Elders' Stew. It was a mishmash of meats from the fields and the sea, with bits of lobsters, red beans, and rice. The stew came in a Jethro-sized cereal bowl that could have served the entire table. Sticks ate a tossed salad with vegetables Abraham had never seen, loaded with crab meat and a sweet-and-sour-smelling celery dressing called the Plate of Ven. Shades drank many samplers of ale, pushing some aside with a "no" and smiling about the ones he liked with a "yes." Horace drank what the smaller man didn't drink but settled on a fine stout called Red Horse.

Anna, the cute and friendly waitress, advised him to "take it easy on the Red Horse." She winked at the big man. "It will sneak up on you and makes some men crazy."

The tavern became livelier as the evening went on. Excited customers came and went, mostly with warm smiles on their faces. Two large stone fireplaces roared with orange-yellow flames. A lone man sat on a stool in the corner, strumming an eight-stringed guitar and singing. The customers sang along to the dashing singer's campy music: "Sweeet Man-o-Waaahr, buh-buh-buh!"

Abraham dug his stew into a smaller bowl, ate steadily, and drank his ale. The tavern became a medieval version of a local Applebee's. Many twists existed in Titanuus, and this latest stop was a new one. In Pirate Town, they'd had pizza, and this Hancha farm hovel had menu lists as long as a roll of toilet paper. The waitress was an alien straight out of *Close Encounters of the Third Kind*, except she wore clothing and was fetching. He scanned the room. *Maybe I am crazy.*

Horace and Shades were turned in their chairs, engaged in conversations with the locals. Sticks gave Abraham a nudge in the ribs with her elbow and asked, "What is going on in that handsome melon of yours?"

"Nothing," he said dryly.

She gave him the "Do I look like I'm stupid?" look.

"Okay. Fine." He pushed his bowl of stew aside. "Something's bothering me."

"Why don't you tell me about it?" She gave him a pleasant smile, reached over, and held his hand. "You can tell me. I'm all yours."

"Yeh, I bet," he said, thinking of what Shades had told him about her being a prostitute.

"What is that supposed to mean?"

"Nothing."

She squeezed his hand. "Tell me, or I'll pin your hand to this table with one of my daggers."

"I didn't know you used to be a"—he looked at her and away and said—"a whore."

Sticks turned her stare on Shades where he sat beside her with his back turned. She rabbit-punched his ribs.

Shades melted in his chair and fell to the floor. The paling man gazed at her with widened eyes and asked, "What did you do that for?"

"You know what, weasel." She kicked Shades. On his back, he snaked away. She turned her attention back to Abraham. "You knew it from the beginning, though I was glad that *you* didn't know about me. To me, it was a fresh start."

"I guess everyone knew anyway. I really shouldn't judge," he said. "I wasn't braced for it."

"Look, I was young, but when I got my chance to escape with the Henchmen, I took it." She took his hand back in hers. "There isn't anything that you can say to me that will hurt me. You should know that by now. Words don't hurt me. Only steel and fire will."

"I have to admit you and the rest have thick skin. It's refreshing. A lot of people in my world have egos as fragile as snowflakes." He put his free hand over hers. "But I shouldn't have mentioned it. I did like watching you stick it to Shades, though."

"Aside from my whoredom, what really ails you? Is it the sleep?" she asked.

"Where to begin? But yeah, it was the sleep. I dreamed I was back in my world. Actually, I'd swear that I was there, the same as I'd swear on the brand that I am here. I was locked up in a place where they put crazy people."

"An asylum."

"Yes, an asylum. You have those here?"

"Yes," she said in her expressionless, matter-of-fact manner. "Nothing but horrors in those places. They say it's worse than the Baracha. They place people like you in there. Possessed. Otherworlders. Unless they kill you such as they do in Kingsland."

Abraham winced. "That's hard to hear. Sticks, I have to figure out what is going on. I know this world is as real as the other. It has to be. I can't explain how, but I know it is. So, you know that old Ruger"—he searched her eyes—"the real one… well?"

"Not as well as Horace, Bearclaw, and Vern. But yes. You've asked me this before, but why again?"

"Because I think that he is in my world, trapped in my body."

CHAPTER 63

While Shades made his rounds through the tavern, Abraham brought Horace into the conversation. He told them most of the pertinent parts in detail. But mostly, he wanted to get a better understanding about Ruger. He was in the man's body, and he felt as if they shared one mind as well, which was disturbing.

"Would Ruger hurt anyone, say, a defenseless person?" Abraham asked.

"No," Horace said in his bearish voice. "Ruger is a guardian's guardian. He'd never hurt anyone that wasn't trying to harm him. He lived by the highest of standards. That never changed even when he was a Henchman." He combed bread and cheese crumbs out of his beard. "I can't say the same for the rest of us."

"I see. I need to figure out a way to communicate with him. When I go back and forth." Abraham tugged at the scruff on his chin. "Our worlds don't speak the same language, but I understand them both. I need to try to find a way for him to understand what is going on."

Horace exchanged a quick look with Sticks. "Don't underestimate Ruger. He probably knows more than he shows. But maybe a symbol that you can write down will help."

"Like what?" she asked.

"The crown or the Kingsland Crest. He'd know that," Horace blurted out. "Draw him a picture of it."

Abraham envisioned the brand that was a crown with six horns, with a small round tip at the top. That wouldn't be a hard thing for him to draw. The crest of Kingsland, which the guardians wore, might have been a different matter. It was a crowned golden lion's face, with white wings for ears on a royal-blue sea background.

"I don't see why I can't pull that off. At least, without the details." Abraham sighed. "Man, I don't want to go back. Not like that. Shackled in a padded white room is no way to live."

"These are strange mutterings that you share. It awakens the moths in my belly." Horace quaffed a full tankard of ale. "Ale helps."

Abraham offered an uncertain smile. The ale wasn't doing much for him. If anything, it only made matters worse. He sat in a medieval microbrewery, feeling more nuts than ever, as if the world he knew was merging with another. He abhorred the dangerous thought.

"Do you dream?" he asked Sticks.

"Only about you," she said with a winsome smile.

"No, seriously."

"Of course I do," she said. "Not often, but I do dream."

"I dream," Horace added. "I'm hunting a man that I can't catch. He moves like a white stag in the woods. I never even get close. He springs away the moment I see him."

"So, you dream the same dream?"

Horace shrugged. "It's the only one that I remember. The others fade away."

Abraham understood. In the past when he'd had dreams, he didn't remember them shortly after he woke. But the last dreams he had, back home, were as real as the room that he was sitting in. "Keep an eye on me. If I act strange, let me know, in case I drift away."

His friends nodded.

The waitress, Anna, returned. Dipping her ample chest before Abraham's eyes, she asked, "How is your food?"

"Fulfilling," he said. He noticed more of the barmaids, including zillons, sitting in the laps of the hearty patrons. "This is a very nice tavern. Very lively."

"It isn't usually so busy, but this is the date of the Alefest, and many of Hancha's finest soldiers are arriving tomorrow."

He arched a brow and asked, "For the festival?"

"No, silly man." Anna tousled his hair. "The soldiers come to rally the town and raise money for Hancha's noble forces. They raise money to overthrow the evil tyrant King Hector. His wicked treatment of his enslaved citizens must be undone." She gave Abraham a funny look. "Surely you have heard about this? Where are you from, if you don't mind me asking?"

"Tiotan," Abraham said.

"Dorcha," Horace blurted out at the same time.

Sticks jumped into the conversation and coolly said, "We hail from Tiotan but just finished our travels for business in Dorcha. Our guide, well, he's showing us around on our visit to Little Leg. He's a Hanchan, but the area is unfamiliar to us."

"Ah." Anna started picking plates and dishes and loading him on her tray. "I can tell that you are new to the area. Please pardon my intrusion, but I am enjoying getting to know the people." She brushed by Horace as she made her way around the table. "I enjoy a lot of different things."

Horace glanced at the cute zillon and swallowed. "I think I'll get a breath of fresh air."

Anna giggled. "Let me know if any of you need anything." She winked and departed.

Abraham leaned back and watched Anna go. "I wonder if all zillons are so forward."

"You call that forward?" Sticks slipped out of her chair into Abraham's and straddled him. She dropped her hands around his neck. "How is this for *forward*?"

"I'd be lying if I said that I didn't like it." He noticed the passion in her eyes. The strong ale fueled their emotions. He placed his hands on the small of her back and pulled her chest-to-chest with him.

Sticks kissed him.

He crushed her in his arms and kissed her back.

Kissing him fiercely on and off, she said, "I missed you."

Between kisses, he said, "I think it's time we checked into our room."

She nodded and nibbled on his neck.

He picked her up and found Anna looking at him with a lipless frown. He fished out several shards and set them on the table. "I'll need a room for the night as well."

Anna scooped up the coins and grinned. "You will have the best. Take the steps. I'll see you at the top."

With Sticks nuzzling his body, he picked his way through the crowd and made his way to the stairs leading up. Shades appeared in front of the steps, his eyebrows creased. Abraham stopped in his tracks. Shades pointed toward the front door.

Well-armed soldiers entered the tavern. The people and the songs fell silent.

CHAPTER 64

THE HANCHAN SOLDIERS WORE OPEN-FACED metal helmets with burgundy tunics crested with a black ankh embroidered upside down on the front. Underneath the fine tunics was chain-mail armor. The four sturdy soldiers escorted a towering man who wore a bastard sword strapped to his back. He wore the same gear as the soldiers, but a black riding cloak covered his shoulders. The man's hair was short, and he had gray eyes as hard as stone. A lantern jaw hung half open over his bull neck. His gaze swept the room.

Abraham held Sticks in his arms and leaned against the banister. He averted his gaze from the soldiers scanning the quiet room. Horace stooped down and took a seat in the chair.

Shades melted into the steps behind Abraham. He whispered in Abraham's ear, "Over one hundred Hanchan soldiers rode into town. They've spread out and were asking questions. I got wind of it the moment my toes hit the porch."

"Are they looking for us?" Abraham asked.

"A large company of well-armed travelers," Shades replied as he put his hood up over his head. "A good thing we entered in a small pack."

Across the room, chair legs scraped over the wooden floor. Every head turned and looked. A rickety-limbed farmer with more beard than face lifted up a tankard of ale. He glanced at the soldiers and said, "Long live Hancha. May I buy its finest solders a round?"

The leader of the soldiers stared down on the farmer from across the room, with broad hawkish features. In a rugged voice, he said, "Of course you may." He lifted a fist the size of a mallet and added, "We drink to the conquest of Kingsland! Death to the tyranny of King Hector! Death to his supporters one and all!"

The patrons let out a chorus of wild cries. They stomped their feet and waved their hats. The excited people pounded fists on the tables. The barkeep served the soldiers tankards of ale. The soldiers eagerly took the ale and drank to a chorus of cheers.

The raucous crowd finally quieted. The music started again. The farmer approached the soldiers. He shook the men's hands.

"We need to move on," Abraham said.

"Hold on, Captain." Shades had his eyes on the farmer and the soldiers. "Let me see what they say."

"Are you reading lips?" he asked.

"Shh-shh-shh," Shades said. "Oh, that's interesting."

"What's interesting?"

"The farmer is asking the man with hair as short as my finger what his name is. Oh, that's not good."

Abraham gave Shades an aggravated look.

"Not good at all," Shades continued.

"Will you spit it out?"

"That soldier in the black cloak is Commander Cutter, leader of the king's Black Squadron."

Horace stiffened.

Shades continued, "They are the elite soldiers of Cauldron City. Hancha's finest. Much like the King's Guardians. It's no wonder that crowd froze at their tables when they waltzed in. Their symbol, the black ankh, means death."

"I thought that you were taking us to a place to lay low," Sticks said. "Instead, you brought us right into a viper pit. Idiot!"

The soldiers sauntered into the bar. Commander Cutter remained at the bar, talking with the locals. The farmer moved away and started sharing the name of Commander Cutter to the other patrons. New and excited whispers spread throughout the room.

"Shades, what's going on now?" Abraham asked.

"Commander Cutter is well-known. The leader of the Black Squadron is famous and infamous. He's the best sword in Hancha, with over two hundred kills to his name," Shades said.

As the word spread about the identity of Commander Cutter, the barmaids cozied up to the well-hewn warrior. They posed with him while a local artisan sketched out their picture on parchment.

"You've got to be kidding me," Abraham said. "A medieval selfie? Listen, you two keep our table. Slip out later. Meet us at the camp in the wee hours. Sticks and I will take our room and slip out later. Avoid Captain Cutter and his squad at all costs. We've got a mission to complete."

"Aye, Captain," Horace replied. "We know the drill."

Abraham carried Sticks up the stairs. He took a backward glance. Commander Cutter's penetrating eyes locked on his. He turned away.

"That man looks mean," Sticks said, a slight slur in her speech. "Do you think you can take him?"

"I don't want to find out." He headed down the hallway of the second level.

Anna waited in front of the door at the end of the hall. She opened it. "The best room available. Soft bedding and a fine window view." She stepped aside.

Abraham entered. It was a cozy room with plush quilts, many pillows, and a storage chest at the end of the bed. A small table sat by the window.

"I can bring up breakfast in the morning, and you can watch the sunrise. It's very nice," Anna said. "And if you need anything else at all, let me know. It would be my pleasure." She winked at him and closed the door behind her.

Abraham tossed Sticks on the bed and said, "Hooters, eat your heart out."

Sticks giggled. She took off her bandolier, stripped off her tunic, and tossed the gear to the floor. She nuzzled the pillows between her arms and thighs and said, "What are you waiting for?"

"I don't know if now is the time." He pulled the curtains back and peeked out the window.

Dozens of members of the Black Squadron were patrolling the streets.

"Really not a good time."

Sticks slid onto the floor, glided to the curtains, and closed them. All she wore was a cotton shirt that clung to her fetching figure. She unbuckled his sword belt and dropped it on the floor and said, "I don't take no for an answer."

CHAPTER 65

ABRAHAM AND STICKS LEFT THEIR passions unfettered. The surrounding element of danger heightened the moment. More than once, they exhausted themselves in one another's arms. After each time, Abraham would check the window. The Black Squadron remained in the streets, posted like watchdogs. Sticks reeled him back into the bed again and again.

With Sticks lying on his chest, he said, "We have to get out of here before dawn breaks. We should have met back at camp hours ago."

Sticks yawned. "I know. But once more. We never know when we'll get this chance again."

"I'm surprised that you, well, let your hair down. Was it the ale or me?"

She kissed his chest. "A healthy mix of both." She ran her hand down beneath the quilt that covered him. "But mostly you."

This is great and weird, being me in another man's body. I don't think I've ever had a night like this. Sticks pressed her face into his neck. Her lips were thin, but her kisses were as soft as rose petals.

He sniffed. "Do you smell smoke?"

She inhaled through her small nose. "I smell smoke." She sat up. "Do you hear that?"

Heavy footsteps ran up and down the halls. Harsh voices called out, "Fire! Fire! Fire!"

Abraham and Sticks jumped out of bed, put on their clothing, and gathered their gear. He opened the door, and smoke poured into the room.

"Holy sheetrock, we have to go!"

They merged with a panicked knot of people crammed into the hallway. The wave of fear-filled faces thundered down the steps. The tavern floor was filled with smoke. Orange flames burned inside the kitchen.

"Fire! Fire! Fire!" several folks called out.

Through the haze, Abraham headed toward the front entrance.

Sticks hooked his arm and pulled him another way. "No, this way." She led him to a window in the back of the room. She picked up a chair and tossed it through. "Let's go!"

They jumped through the window together into a back alley. They raced from it to the barn where the horses were stabled, and Abraham found his horse. Horace's and Shades's were gone. Already saddled, his horse stamped its hooves and whinnied. Slowly, he led the horse out of the barn. He opened the stable gate and led the horse out, and they mounted together.

Down the street, people and soldiers scrambled with buckets of water toward the burning building. They made a chain of buckets scores of people long.

Abraham checked the streets in all directions. The coast was clear. He gently spurred the horse. It trotted down the streets and into the darkness of the night. With the voices fading, he spurred the horse to a gallop and headed back to camp.

"You burned down the tavern? Why would you do that?" Abraham yelled at Shades.

They were back at the camp set up by the river. The Henchmen had broken camp and were on horseback and ready to go.

Perched in his saddle, Shades shrugged and said, "There wasn't much of a choice. The Black Squadron had eyes everywhere. We needed a distraction, and we needed a big one."

Still on horseback, Abraham walked his horse over to Shades, leaned over, and said, "You could have killed innocent people."

"They are Hanchans—far from innocent and enemies of Kingsland. You heard them roaring on about King Hector. If they died, they died."

Abraham punched Shades so hard in the chest that he knocked the man out of the saddle. "We don't do that!"

"Actually, we do," Sticks said in his ear. She'd remained in the saddle with him. "To speak ill against the king means death."

Clutching his chest, Shades climbed back into the saddle and said, "If it's any consolation, I don't think anyone died. Maybe a few, but doubtful."

Abraham searched the faces of his Henchmen. The solemn group averted their eyes except for Vern, Lewis, and Leodor. They held his stare, testing him.

"We don't butcher and burn people." Abraham thought of the waitress, Anna, and wondered if she was safe. "We find a better way."

Sitting proudly in his saddle, Prince Lewis said, "We are at war. No one is innocent in war. We will have casualties, and they will have casualties. The important thing is that they have more of them than we do."

Abraham turned his horse aside, let it walk away, and said, "Shut up, Lewis. Shades, Horace, get us back on the trail."

The Henchmen rode in the darkness of the night. Abraham couldn't help but think about how cavalier the company might have been when led by Ruger. Perhaps they did do devastating things behind enemy lines. Maybe countless innocents were killed. He could have asked but didn't. He'd never been to war before. That wasn't something he fully understood, but at the moment, he was in the middle of a war. So were his men. He had to make sure that he could lead them.

"I don't think what Shades did was bad," Sticks said to him. "Actually, I expected it."

"You did?" he asked, while taking note that the others weren't around.

They were keeping their distance.

"This wouldn't be the first time that we had to create a diversion. I'd thought the same thing myself. I was surprised that you didn't," she said.

"So, Ruger would have done the same thing?"

"Death before failure. Their deaths or ours," she said.

"But those people. They were only enjoying themselves. They were farmers and laymen. I don't want their deaths on my conscience. I have enough on my mind as is."

"Think about it, Abraham. Everywhere we've been outside of Kingsland, haven't people been calling for our heads?"

He nodded, then his back straightened. "But wait, what about the sea captains from Tiotan? We averted them."

"True, and I hate to say it, but that was because of Shades, or else they would have killed us."

She nuzzled her chin in his back. "Those soldiers, Commander Cutter and the Black Squadron, do you think they were fools, or do you think they were onto us?"

Abraham saw Commander Cutter's face as clear as crystal. A warrior knew a warrior. The battle-bred crow's-feet in their eyes gave it away.

"You're right. He knew I was trouble the moment he saw me."

"And a man like that won't forget you either," she said. "He's coming. They'll all be coming."

CHAPTER 66

The Henchmen kept their heads down, rode hard leagues away from the east coast, stopped late, and rose early. Two days later, they were on the coastal plains in the Little Leg of Hancha, viewing Cauldron City.

"That's it," Shades said. The man hadn't approached Ruger since they'd last spoken. "The great dogwoods with black bark and white leaves are only found in these valleys."

The petals of the gnarled dogwood trees drifted through the air like snow before landing gently on the ground. They were all over the valley that led to Cauldron City. The plains surrounding the city weren't the same lush green fields of Kingsland. The tall wind-swept grasses were brown and almost gray, giving it a barren look. In the distance, Cauldron City's buildings, made from black stone, could be seen in the morning light. Only the glass-paned windows shone. The city was large, like Burgess, possibly bigger. Travelers and workers moved along the stone-paved streets.

Abraham craned his neck and asked, "If that's Cauldron City, then where is the Cauldron?"

Shades pointed above the city. A ridge of mountains in the south was covered in mist. "There, in the bluffs. A one-way road leads up to it."

Lewis and Leodor approached. Lewis yawned and said, "What is that grand plan? Are you going to duck into Cauldron City and burn it down like the last one? I myself wouldn't mind a hot meal and a glass of red wine."

"We aren't going into the city. We're going straight into the Cauldron," Abraham said.

"Now? In broad daylight? How stupid is that?" Lewis said.

Princess Clarice rode up to the group and asked, "What is going on? Are we going into the city?" Her eyes were big and bright. "I've always wanted to visit Hancha. I'm told that they have fabulous wares, festivals, and delicacies."

"Yeah, they probably have a shopping mall and petting zoo too, but this isn't a shopping trip. But," Abraham said, "with a show of hands, who would like to take a tour of the city?"

Lewis, Leodor, Swan, Sticks—back on her own horse—Iris, Shades, Solomon, Clarice, Dominga, and the ailing Tark all raised their hands. Only the grim-faced Horace, Bearclaw, Vern, and Cudgel kept their hands down.

Abraham smiled. "It looks like we have a majority, but this isn't a democracy. I vote no. That means we all vote no. Let's go."

The Henchmen stayed on the outskirts of the city's countryside, using the paths along the hillsides. They continued toward the high hills in the south, where the Cauldron resided. Those black hills bottomed out miles away from the city that the Cauldron overlooked. A light fog lingered at the base.

Abraham gazed upward. The hills were high, the same as the ones that bordered the interstates in the Mountain State. The trees were dark pines, maples, and oaks. A road made of black gravel-like pebbles snaked a pathway up a steep incline and disappeared into the hillside.

He looked at Leodor and asked, "That way?"

"The fog lifts at night, but yes," the older mystic said. "We can't ride up there. Not like this," he said.

"Sure we can. We'll ride up, knock on the gate—there is a gate, isn't there?" He smirked. "And we will ask to see the Underlord. After all, you and Lewis are friends with him."

Leodor scoffed. "That's preposterous."

"Why?" he asked.

"Those hills have eyes. They will know that we are coming," Leodor fired back. "We don't look like members of the Sect. Only members of the Sect may enter."

Gazing up the stark hillside, Abraham said, "Interesting. So, what does a member of the Sect look like? Do they wear special robes, perhaps?"

"Of course they do. In Hancha, they were the burgundy with gold trim," Leodor said. "The leading priests are trimmed in white. They are devoted worshippers of the grand dogwoods."

"Imagine that. So, all we need are some robes. I bet there are a lot of them to be found in the cathedrals inside Cauldron City, right Leodor?"

The froward viceroy said, "That would be a smart place to look."

"Sticks. Shades."

"Way ahead of you, Captain," Sticks said. She rode with Shades back toward Cauldron City.

"Where are they going?" Lewis asked.

"To fetch our robes." Abraham led his horse and the others away from the road leading up to the Cauldron. He eyed Leodor and Lewis. "Come on, you two windbags. We need to chat more about what you know about this place."

The Henchmen found a spot at the base of the hills where the tall treetops and branches concealed them.

Abraham dismounted, looped his reins on a branch, and said to Leodor, "You said the hills have eyes. What did you mean by that?"

Leodor licked his thin lips, looked up into the hills, and said, "The zillon dragon riders. They live in the pinnacles behind the Cauldron. Like hawks, the dragons watch the Cauldron like a nest."

CHAPTER 67

"SO, ARE YOU GOING TO tell me more about where you've been?" Solomon asked Abraham as they were sitting apart from the others, who were on the lookout. "We haven't talked since your *return*."

Nearby, Iris was checking Tark's wounds, but the rangy black fighter had said, "I can ride, so I can fight. We go up, I'm going."

Abraham chewed on a small hunk of dried meat, washed it down with water, and said, "What makes you think that I went anywhere?"

"Come on, I know you dreamed. I'm not stupid."

"I hate to mention it. But if you insist, I woke up in a loony bin. There were more twists and turns too." He watched Solomon's eyes widen. "For example, I think that Ruger's essence is inhabiting my body back home. Does that make any sense to you?"

Solomon scratched the thick hairs on the back of his neck and said, "Unlike you, I'm stuck here, but it's an interesting concept. You aren't pulling my hairy leg, are you?"

"I wish I was, but no. I don't want to go back there. I know that sounds strange, but I'm a nutcase there as opposed to here."

"Actually, you are a nutcase here. Remember how they treat the possessed? They kill them. Man, beast, or troglin."

Solomon dropped a hand to the ground and opened the fingers of his huge paw. He whistled softly. A chipmunk with black-and-brown fur slunk out of some dark-purple ferns right into the palm of his hand. The chipmunk's little nose twitched. It crawled up Solomon's arm and over his shoulders.

"Tell me more," Solomon continued.

With time to burn, Abraham filled in his friend from the home world. "This dream state is really messing with my mind, I have to admit. You said that you came through a portal, didn't you? Or am I remembering that wrong?"

"No, I burst right through a halo of energy, and I've been trying to find that selfsame portal for years." Solomon sighed and glanced up the hill. "Maybe there will be some answers up there."

"Maybe. But I don't think answers are very easy to come by." Abraham finished up his jerky, washed it down with water, and said, "No portals so far. Something isn't right. I know everything is a mess and our lives are upside down, but I believe in my heart that these are two separate worlds and that they are connected. But man, that Dr. Jack really got into my head, telling me it's a dream. No dream can be this real. It can't be."

The chipmunk popped up on top of Solomon's head and started eating an acorn of some sort.

Iris giggled.

Tark managed a smile.

Abraham gave them both an easy look and asked, "So, what's it like for you two to follow a madman?"

"It's fine by me so long as it's a good madman." Tark groaned as he sat up from lying down. With Iris's help, he came back to his feet. "You're doing fine so far, but if I can give you some advice, Captain, don't think about it too much. Let things come to you. And trust your gut. We trust it. So should you."

Iris nodded. With her hand around Tark's side, she led him away.

"Thanks," Abraham said under his breath.

Solomon twisted his head side to side and lifted his eyes upward. "Is he still up there?"

Abraham lay down, propped himself casually on an elbow, and asked, "How do you know it's a he?"

"Ha ha."

The chipmunk scurried right down Solomon's face, jumped away, and dashed into the wood.

"Hey!"

"Looks like you're stuck with me, hippie."

Solomon rubbed his chest where the brand was. "My choice. You know, Abraham, if we are trying to get back to our world, then don't you think that Ruger, for example, is trying to get back to this world?"

Abraham's neck hairs rose. "I hadn't thought about that. I'm not sure that I like that idea either. Is that selfish?"

"Considerably." Solomon arched his back. "I don't think he wanted to leave here, just like I don't think that the people we inhabited wanted to go there. At least you know who you were. Me? I don't know much about the old troglin I became. The troglins don't care much for their elderly. Like lions, they are led by the strongest in the pack."

"Oh man," Abraham said.

"What?"

"I just had a dark thought." He clenched his jaws. The tapping of his heart sped up in his ears. "What if the same thing that is happening to us is happening back home?"

"You mean, our otherworlders are being hunted and killed?"

"Yeah, but maybe locked up. Maybe that was what was going on in that hospital I was in. Perhaps there were more like you and me."

Solomon sat with his fingers locked and rolling his thumbs. "Bizarre. I'm not fond of the idea. It's like coming off of a bad acid trip." He winced. "Oh man, this brain session is giving me a headache."

"Don't say that. I don't want any more headaches."

"Sorry." Solomon lay flat on his back and closed his eyes. "You might want to get some rest."

Abraham sat up. "At this juncture, I think I'll pass."

CHAPTER 68

LEAVING THE HORSE OUTSIDE THE city, Sticks and Shades slipped into Cauldron City and quickly blended in with the assorted crowd. With night falling, chill winds came down from the high hills, and the citizens were bundled in woolen garb and winter cloaks. Cackling women and carousing men could be heard from open tavern and apartment windows. Eerie music and songs winded through the city blocks' channels. The people, men and women, including a lot of zillons, carried themselves with purpose from building to building, winding down from a day's work. Cauldron City was festive in a dark sort of way.

The black-and-gray stones that made up the buildings and cobblestone streets gave the city a drab atmosphere. The roofs were covered in dark-red clay tiles. Lanterns hung from posts in the streets with the candles shielded by green glass that made for eerier illumination.

Talking quietly, Sticks said to Shades, "You still can't bridle that tongue of yours, can you?"

"Whatever do you mean?"

"You know what I mean. Telling Abraham that I was a whore."

"Ah, so you do have a soft spot for the otherworlder. I knew that you did. I wanted to hear you say it."

Sticks pushed Shades into an alley and shoved him into a wall. She put a dagger against his throat.

"Well, well, well," he said, "I see you are still kinky."

"Shut your mouth hole, or else I'll give you another one. Tell me what game you are playing. I want to know."

"Whatever do you mean? I only want to serve the king."

"Don't feed me that manure. I know better than that. I know you better than anyone."

"I know you do." Shades slipped a hand on her rump and squeezed. "And I know you the same."

She pressed the blade harder on his neck. "Remove your hand."

"You wouldn't kill a man over a little squeeze on the tush, would you?"

"I've killed men for less," she said.

"You won't kill me. But I reluctantly remove my hand from the most delightful part of your body." His Adam's apple rolled against the edge of the blade when he swallowed. "I hope that didn't leave a nick. As for my purposes, I swear they are sincere. And my name's cleared, is it not? I just want to be a Henchman again."

She searched his eyes. Years before, she and Shades had had a strong and passionate relationship. She was naïve and needed a man to lean on. As she grew, she grew away from him. True to his name, Shades was shady. She could never put her finger on it, but he was.

She took her dagger away from his neck, spun it in her hand, and sheathed it back in her bandolier. "I'll figure it out."

Shades rubbed his neck and said, "There's nothing to figure out. Now, if you don't mind, let's go find those cloaks. There are plenty of cathedrals and temples around here. The Hanchans are very fond of their elders." He grabbed her hand. "Come on, dearie."

She jerked her hand away and shoved him forward. "Quit playing games."

With a cheerful step, Shades took the lead. He hopped up on a stone porch front and strutted underneath the tavern and store decks. He weaved his way through the people, nodding politely and offering a greeting from time to time.

Sticks kept on his heels. Whenever she was with him, she felt as though he was a moment away from bolting off. He made her feel like a nervous mother watching over an overactive child. She glanced into some of the windows they passed. Painted strumpets, clad in dark sheer silks, danced shamelessly for the patrons. She didn't miss those days. From what she could see, the assorted life in Hancha was worse. Inky smoke spilled out of the door and windows. The lusty smell of strong perfumes and incense wafted into her nose. She fanned it away.

She caught up with Shades, who'd stretched his lead. "It figures that you are from this place."

He let out a low chuckle and darted across the street into a section of town where the streets were almost barren, aside from the beggars huddled underneath stone benches. He stood in front of a thirty-foot-high portico leading into another section of town.

Sticks stood beside him and looked up at the portico, with three giants within its archway. Every creature and race she'd ever seen or imagined was carved into the stone.

"What is in there?" she asked.

"This is what locals call Elders Alley," he said. "Not really an alley, per se, but a place where the multitudes worship their favored Elders. Come on." He tried to take her by the hand.

She peeled away and headed into the archway on the right. "I'll take it from here."

Sticks didn't have much else to figure out, she realized once she crossed to the other side. Temples and cathedrals of all sorts were everywhere. Finding her way out wouldn't be a problem either.

Just inside the threshold of the giant portico, she said, "That's a lot of temples."

Shades pointed at the biggest one. It had open iron gates leading into a courtyard. "That looks like a place filled with ample contributions."

She led the way. They weren't the only ones wandering through the area. Acolytes aplenty were wandering the streets, murmuring and praying. They were clad in dark robes, some of which were made of the finest materials and others as moth-ridden as paupers'. Shades moved into the courtyard right up the steps of the cathedral. Stealing into the temples wasn't anything new. She and the Henchmen had done it dozens of times. The temples were some of the safest places, considered hallowed ground. She walked right through the great doors, which led directly into the pews facing a stage and altar. Some sort of ceremony was going on. Men and women were gathered on the stage, dancing and singing among the smoke with a glowing paint on their eyes and bodies.

"Can you make out what they are saying?" she asked Shades.

"I never understood their strange tongues," he replied. "I always figured that they made it up. But this appears to be a very popular place. Most seats are filled. I'd imagine they are about to make a sacrifice to the Black Kraken."

Sticks shivered. "I can't stand slimy things. Come on, let's find the cloak room and get out of here."

"You know, the penalty for stealing from a temple carries a death sentence. That's why they are safe havens," he said with a smile.

"Has that ever stopped us before?"

He shook his head with a grin on his face.

Sticks stole through the darkness of the side aisles. The storerooms weren't hard to find, nestled away behind the side entrances of the stage in the basement. The temple had many lavish decorations set aside for ceremonies. Bronze candlestands, pewter goblets, silver trays, and bowls loaded with chunks of incense were there. The walls were lined with cloak hooks. Sticks grabbed a dark-gray cloak trimmed with purple satin. Many of them were there.

"These will do. Find a sack or something to put them in," she said as he slipped the cloak on over her body.

Shades had a cotton sack in hand. "Way ahead of you." He stuffed more cloaks into the sack. "The Black Kraken will have our heads for this."

"For what, stealing?" she said. "Who says we are stealing? We are only borrowing them." She rummaged through the variety of sizes of cloaks on the pegs. "Who says that we aren't borrowing them? Besides, we are going right into the heart of the Sect. Right? I have a feeling that we'll be leaving them there."

"I miss your dry wit. It made for grand pillow talk back in the day."

"Keep dreaming." She finished filling her sack and slung it over her shoulder. She tilted her head and looked toward the stairs as the chanting and singing grew louder. "Our timing couldn't be better."

"Agreed." Shades stepped aside. "Lead the way."

She hustled up the steps and stole her way back into the aisle from which they'd come. The petitioners were shaking their hands and arms and singing in a wild frenzy. Something was happening on stage, a living sacrifice perhaps. She dared not look. She didn't want to know. She kept her head down and moved forward. Breaking free of the temple doors, she hurried down the steps and caught her breath.

Sticks, wearing the same robes as she, stood beside her, looked back, and said, "Vile. Simply vile. One of the reasons that I left, and it's only getting worse."

A sharp scream erupted from within the temple.

"I've heard enough." Sticks took off toward the three arches in the portico. Her heart was racing by the time she got through them. She didn't stop as she cut into the alleys. She stopped and caught her breath.

"Is something wrong?" Shades asked as he looked back over his shoulder. "I think we are in the clear."

"Those places. I hate those places." She took a deep breath. "Hate them."

"That's what is coming to Kingsland. An invasion of darkness. Unless we stop them." He shifted his sack from one shoulder to the other. "Lawlessness shall abound. I might be a rogue, but even I see the need for order. Come. I know a shorter way. You tucked us deep in the alleys."

"Go, then," she said as she followed after him.

They avoided the lively crowds building in the streets. Once they broke free of the city's main structures, they took a small road that led back to the horses. A large group of riders came their way. They were well-armed soldiers wearing metal helmets that glimmered dully in the starlight. Sticks and Shades moved aside and kept their hooded heads down. The sound of the approaching horses grew, along with the rattle of armor and gear.

"You, priests," someone called out in a gruff voice.

Sticks knew the voice immediately. It was the harsh tone of Commander Cutter. "Yes, my lord," she replied.

"Tell me, priest, why do you travel away from the city? Is something amiss?"

"No, my lord. We are meeting with our brethren in the woodland to draw strength from the Elder of the Moon," she said. "It is imperative that we work away from the distractions of the festivities."

Commander Cutter's horse snorted near her face.

The commander said, "The Elder of the Moon, aye. Offer him a prayer from Commander Cutter and his men. Tell him we need light shed on the men that we track."

"Certainly," she said, holding out her hand. She stole a glance at Commander Cutter, seeing that the short-haired and iron-jawed man carried himself with a great presence. "I will see to it that your request is heard."

Commander Cutter fished into his purse and dropped two silver shards into her palm. "Make sure that it sticks."

Shades let out a soft giggle and followed it up with gentle coughing.

Sticks slapped him on the back. "Apologies. My fellow layman needs prayers as well. Are there any other services that I can provide, my lord? Anything more specific to pray for?"

"And cost me another round of drinks?" Commander Cutter laughed. "Ha ha. I can't afford the payment. The sack you carried is probably filled with shards as is." He kicked her bag. "What burdens do you carry?"

"Blankets. It will be a chill night, and we've got to set the camp for the ceremony," she said.

"I see. Make sure that you don't forget my prayer, priest. I always follow up with the viceroy of your Sect," Commander Cutter said. "Let's move out, Black Squadron." He waved his hand in a forward motion and marched down the road.

Once the soldiers passed, Sticks and Shades quickly ambled down the road. She glanced back in time to see the last of the soldiers disappear around the bend. "Sounds like Commander Cutter is on our tail for certain."

"He could be looking for someone else," Shades suggested.

Sticks shook her head. "I don't think so. He's onto us. I know it."

"I agree. Back at the tavern, he was sniffing around but being very subtle about it." Shades took a path into the woodland, where the horses waited. "He wasn't going to let us leave without asking a few questions. He's a clever tracker for certain."

"How do you think he came to be on our trail so quick?" she asked as she mounted up.

"Big Apple. Lord Hawk. Those men might have spread the word. Either that, or the dubious Commander Cutter is looking into the slaughter of the woodlings that we encountered. After all, they are citizens of Hancha. He could be investigating that."

Sticks led her horse back onto the road. "I doubt it." She galloped back to camp.

CHAPTER 69

Abraham held up a Black Kraken robe. It showed the head, face, and eyes of the great sea monster subtly woven throughout the entire body of the dark robes. "This is nice." He slipped the robes over his armor. "Leodor, what's the protocol? Are we walking or riding?"

"We must go on foot if we don't want to arouse any suspicion," Leodor said as he draped the new set of robes over his frail body. "The walk is long, winding, and steep. I dread it."

"We'll get you there." Abraham donned his hood as the others did the same. "Is everyone ready?"

"Ready, Captain," Horace replied. He was twisting off the tip of his spear that he'd tooled to stay on with a small pin. He put the spear head away and used the shaft like a walking stick.

"If we aren't back in a couple of days, well, come looking for us if you want," he said to Solomon.

The troglin was remaining back with Tark, Shades, and Dominga as lookouts. Sticks had already brought Abraham up to speed in regard to their run-in with Commander Cutter.

"I don't expect you to be a hero," Abraham said. "Lay low. Get word back to the king."

Solomon shook his head and said, "Death before failure. You fail, we will go in, so do me a favor and don't blow it."

"Let's go." Abraham led the Henchmen up the black gravel roadway into the dark and dreary fog. He could only see several feet in front of himself. For all he knew, snakes and dragons could be nestled in the rocks all around them, waiting to strike. Keeping those thoughts in mind, Leodor reassured him that barring an army marching up the path, a small group like this wouldn't draw any suspicion. Any attempt to attack the Cauldron would be suicidal.

The Henchmen trudged up the hill behind him. The fog began to thin. Daylight crept into their eyes.

Abraham shielded his eyes from the bright sun rising over the jagged hills. The road opened into a full view of the Cauldron. It was a great castle carved out of the great hillside, complete with a barbican, a drawbridge, and battlements on the top. It was every bit as long as half a football field and thirty feet of black stone tall. High on its perch, the Cauldron was perfectly fortified like the House of Steel.

"Whoa," Princess Clarice said. "Are those dragons or statues?"

"I'm hoping they are statues," Vern replied with an uneasy gaze.

Stationed along the parapet walls were small towers on the corners and one in the middle that broke the main wall into two sections. On top of those towers were three dragons, similar to the horse-sized ones the zillons had used to attack the king at the House of Steel. The dragons had the rough, bumpy hides of horned toad lizards and burning yellow eyes narrowed into slits. Forked tongues flickered from their mouths.

"Do they breathe fire?" Abraham asked.

Lewis scoffed. "A dragon breathing fire… Who ever heard of such a thing?"

Abraham resumed his march. "All right, everyone, stop gawking. Let's look like we belong. Leodor, get up here."

Panting for breath, Leodor shuffled his way up to Abraham.

"Do the zillons live here as well?" he asked the mystic.

"No, they are in the pinnacles. Look beyond the walls. You will see them."

Beyond the dragons and the wall were pillars of stone stretching toward the sky like great gnarled fingers. Dozens of them towered at least a hundred feet in height above the hills themselves.

"The dragon riders live there?" he asked.

"They are the Keepers of the Dragons that kept eyes on the Cauldron for centuries. It seems we can confirm that they are the Sect's allies now," Leodor said with a glance drifting up. "I've never seen dragons here before."

"Just remember, there is a zillon out there with an assault rifle. And there might be more of them. I know you don't know much about what that is, but if those guards marching behind the battlements had them, they'd be about to pick us off with ease." Abraham increased his stride. "Do they have horses?"

"Much like the House of Steel, the Cauldron is equipped with everything, including a personal army posted throughout the structure." Leodor kept up with Abraham. "I'll do the talking. And please, no one else say anything."

Abraham looked back at the company and said, "You know that plan. Stick to it." He rubbed his chin and kept his eyes ahead.

They had two objectives. Kill Arcayis, and secure the zillons' assault weapon. One would have been a lot easier to do with the other. He crossed the drawbridge, which was lowered over a twenty-yard-long crevice in the hillside. A mist wavered in the depths. "Is this bridge always open?"

"So far as I know," Leodor said.

On the other side of the bridge stood a host of soldiers carrying spears and wearing short swords on their hips, bronze helmets with nose guards and flared spikes on top, and brown leather tunics. They stood at attention and nodded when the company passed by and went into the inner courtyard sanctum of the castle.

The Cauldron's courtyard was rich in gardens and planters with beautiful flowers rich in deep, velvety colors. The dogwoods growing along the walks were small but plenty. Their white petals drifted through the air. All sorts of robed priests and mystics were about, walking with their hands tucked inside their robes. Wearing the Sect robes of all sorts and colors, they strolled down the brick walkways, sat on wrought-iron benches, and gathered in small groups. Scores of men and women were there from all walks of life, whose idle chattering gave life to what otherwise might have been a dreary and depressing place.

In the center of the castle courtyard stood a stone keep, twenty yards tall, with a split-iron fence wrapping around it. At the top of the stark cylindrical structure were the bone-white leaves of a dogwood tree, capped in the middle. A dozen guards were stationed around it.

The Henchmen moseyed through the courtyard, where many of the priests gardened while others prayed, ate, and drank from slender glasses of wine.

"Tell me about that keep," Abraham told Leodor.

"The Tree of the Elders thrives within that stony case. The priests minister to the soil. It grows without the sun or the rain. It is also the location of the Sect leaders' high offices," Leodor said as he looked at the entrance door.

Two men walked out from the dark-red split doors that led into the keep. The burning blue eyes, dark robes, and bald head of one of them were unmistakable. It was Arcayis the Underlord.

CHAPTER 70

A ZILLON SOLDIER WITH AN ASSAULT rifle hanging from his shoulder walked beside the Underlord.

Leodor gasped.

The Underlord's gaze started to drift their direction.

Abraham's fingertips tingled with fire. Ruger's body charged with energy. He pulled his sword out from underneath his robes and charged. "That's them!"

Arcayis's eyes widened. He darted back into the keep, yelling, "Guards! Guards! Stop them!"

The zillon soldier swung the assault rifle around and onto his shoulder. He took aim at Abraham and fired. Muzzle fire flashed.

Bullets ricocheted off Abraham's breast-plate. His stride didn't slow. His swing didn't either. He cut the zillon down with a sword strike that cleaved the zillon's skull.

"For the king!" he yelled. Without breaking stride, he rushed toward the keep's quickly closing door. He jammed his sword through the narrowing slit and put his shoulder against it. The door didn't budge. "Get me some help over here! Sticks, grab that dead zillon's rifle! And his belt!"

Alarm horns sounded in the courtyard. The priests and mystics scrambled to life. Hands holding concealed knives burst out from underneath their sleeves. The soldiers carrying spears charged. Dragons took flight from their perches on the wall.

Horace bulled his way down the path and lowered his shoulder into the door. The red door gave way.

Abraham slipped inside. A dozen men and women in loose-fitting robes scrambled away from the tree that grew in the center. They vanished into the alcoves that lined the keep's inner rim. He caught a glimpse of Arcayis running up a flight of stairs to the second level. Outside the keep's front door, the clamor of battle raged.

"Get everyone inside!" Abraham yelled.

Horace stood inside the doorway, waving his arm in a huge circle and shouting, "Inside, Henchmen! Inside!"

One by one, starting with Leodor, the Henchmen poured into the keep. Bearclaw and Cudgel, led by Sticks, dragged inside the dead zillon carrying the assault rifle.

"I couldn't get the belt off," she said to Abraham.

Horace and Vern shut the door and dropped the locking bar into place.

"Make sure it doesn't open," Abraham said to Iris.

"I will," Iris said. A rosy glow emanated from her fingertips the moment she touched the door. The red-pinkish hue spread over the door.

Abraham knelt down by the dead zillon. A black web belt like the ones the military used was latched around the zillon's waist. He pinched the locked plastic mechanism right before Sticks's eyes and pulled the belt, which included an ammo pouch, free from the body. He gave it to Sticks. "Don't lose this or the rifle."

"How do you use it?" Sticks asked.

"Aim and squeeze the trigger." He clenched his index finger. "I'll show you later." He pointed toward the top balconies overlooking the keep's inner courtyard. "The Underlord went up there, Leodor. What's up there?"

"The Sect's special chambers."

A foursome of robe-wearing, dagger-wielding priests burst out of the alcoves, screaming shrilly at the top of their lungs.

Prince Clarice and Swan dashed into their paths and cut them down in four quick thrusts. Clarice wiped her rapier off on the dead's robes and winked at her brother.

Lewis shook his head. "If you were good, you would have taken all four of them."

A fierce pounding started on the door. Yelling and coarse shouts started from outside.

With all the Henchmen assembled, Abraham headed for the stairs leading to the upper chambers. "Let's go." He took the steps four at a time to the second level.

A ring of arched doorway entrances went all the way around the inner circle. All the Henchmen were gathered on the balconies except for Horace, Iris, and Cudgel, who guarded the door below.

"Leodor, you've been here before," Abraham said. "Any ideas where his special chamber might be?"

"I can't say. They are mostly places for mediation and study," Leodor said. "I've only been in one once before, decades ago. Things can change."

"Spread out," Abraham said. "If anyone sees a creepy bald wizard with blue diamonds for eyes, holler!" He tested the first door handle that he came to—the mechanism was locked. "Dirty donuts."

Sticks knelt down beside him to pick the lock. She gave him a look and nodded.

Abraham shoved the door open. A powerful clawed hand grabbed his arm and yanked him off his feet, pulling him inside. The door slammed shut behind him.

CHAPTER 71

Abraham slammed into a wall. A muscle-bound man with a boar's face had him pinned to the wall by the neck. His toes dangled above the floor. He was in a study of some sort, complete with chairs, small tables, and bookshelves. A chandelier of candles illuminated the room. He kicked at the creature that held him fast. The boar-faced man had the jutting bottom fangs of a hog. It sank its nails into Abraham's neck with an iron grip. The inhuman man headbutted Abraham in the face and slung him aside. Black Bane slipped from Abraham's fingers.

"He will be a tasty one, brother!" said another boar man standing by the door. The gruff-voiced boar man dropped an iron bar over it, sealing the three of them inside. "Just as the Underlord said. Today, we dine on the flesh of heroes!"

Abraham rolled up and put his back against the wall. Bright spots filled his eyes. He shook his head. The boar men were bare chested, with bulging muscles popping up underneath the coarse black hair covering their bodies. He saw his sword lying on the floor and dove for it.

The ugly boar man that had grabbed him kicked the sword away with a hoofed foot. "No, no, no," the man said. "That is not how we fight." He balled up his fists.

His brother came and stood behind him, punching a meaty fist into his hand. One of his fangs was broken off. He was shorter, but both of them stood taller than Abraham. "This one wears a shell. Let us crack that shell and dine."

Abraham climbed to his feet. "You two don't look like you've missed any meals. Are you sure that you want to eat me?"

The boar-faced brothers exchanged a look and let out gusty snorts and laughs. "This one jests," the taller one said. "He won't joke soon enough." He raised his fists. "Time to have some fun with the dinner meat first."

"Oh, so you want to box," Abraham said, balling up his fists. "Fair enough." He moved forward and punched the boar man in the face with a right cross. He finished the combo with a punch in the belly. The boar man's hide felt as hard as stone. He unloaded a quick combination of punches to the ribs.

The boar man balled up, winced, and said, "You hit hard for a man. My hide can take it." He started punching back.

Abraham ducked the hard and heavy swings. He blocked a punch and countered with a jab in the ribs.

"Brother, this one fights well," the taller one said. "Help me finish him quickly. I hunger."

"Of course," the shorter one said. He slipped in behind Abraham and unloaded a flurry of punches. "Smash him. Beat him. Eat him!"

Abraham backed into a corner. He forearm blocked their attacks, which rained down on him like sledgehammers. They hit him like heavyweight boxers working him on the ropes. He slipped his head away and blocked. Their hard punches plowed into his breastplate and glanced off his head. He kicked the short one in the gut, and the boar man doubled over. Abraham rammed his knee into its nose. He squirted free of the other and went for his sword.

One foot away from scooping the sword up, he was tackled by the taller boar man. They rolled across the floor in a tangle of limbs. The boar man had the animal strength of a bear. He pinned Abraham down by the neck with his hands. Abraham chopped at his arms.

"You fight well," the boar man said. "When we roast you, we will honor your flesh with a sweet, succulent sauce from the Old Kingdom."

The boar man's fingers dug deeper into his throat. The steel-hardened thews layering his neck saved his throat from collapsing. The boar man squeezed.

"I'm softening him up for you, brother." The shorter one egged him on and kicked at Abraham's ribs, saying, "There's nothing sweeter than the taste of succulent pulverized meat."

The breastplate saved Abraham's ribs from shattering, but painful shockwaves carried through his body. He locked his hands on the bigger boar man's wrist, wrenched, and twisted.

"Ho ho, you will not break my grip. Nothing can. You will die under it."

Abraham's sword lay within reach. He stretched his fingers toward it.

"No, no, no." The brother kicking Abraham hopped to the sword, picked it up, and said, "I have the power. Ha ha ha. Not a fan of the steel, but this would make a fine spit to cook his flesh on. Won't that be fitting? Cooking on your own sword." He tossed it away.

Abraham punched at the ribs of the boar man straddling him. The slavering boar man didn't budge. A thought struck Abraham as he started to lose air and his vision came to blacken. *Use your dagger, idiot.* He'd been so used to using Black Bane he'd completely forgotten about the daggers tucked underneath his cloak. *Bloody Mary, always carry an extra knife.* He squirmed his fingers down by his side, found the hilt of a dagger pressed along his side, and ripped it free. He stabbed the boar man clean through the ribs, piercing the thick hide and hitting the pumping heart.

The boar man arched his back. His pig jaws opened wide. The life in his eyes faded.

Abraham pushed the boar man away and sprang to his feet. He squared off against the other brother, still standing. "You should have searched me, stupid pig."

"Nooo!" The boar man clutched his head and shook it like a bull. "Nooo!" With rage burning in his eyes, he shouted, "You killed my brother! I will kill you!" He scraped his hoof across the floor, snorted loudly, and charged.

In a lightning-quick downward stroke, Abraham stuck the boar man through skull and brain. The boar man died instantly, falling to the carpet underneath their feet.

Abraham retrieved his sword. A loud commotion of battle sounded from the other side of the door. He lifted the bar away and flung the door open.

The Tree of the Elders was burning. The dragons were inside.

CHAPTER 72

DRAGONS ROARED INSIDE THE KEEP. One dragon lay on the floor of the keep by the burning tree, dead. The entire keep was filled with smoky vapors. Crackling flames licked at the bark trunk of the dogwood tree. Skirmishes raged all around.

Abraham cried out across the balcony, "Sticks!" She was on the other side, with Lewis and Leodor, battling two dragons that hemmed them in on the ledge of the balcony. He ran toward them, racing around the outer ring of the keep.

A dragon streaked through the air, crashed through the railing, and blocked his path. Head low, it crept toward him with a hungry growl in its throat. It came at Abraham on the quick, scurrying legs of a lizard.

Black Bane flashed right between the dragon's eyes. The blade sank deep in the dragon's snout.

The dragon recoiled and let out a pain-filled roar. Its breath reeked of rotten flesh and sulfur.

Abraham pressed the attack. He brought the blade up and down on the horse-sized dragon's snout. Hunks of lizard flesh were hacked away. Teeth were chopped out of its mouth.

It charged.

Abraham braced his feet, lunged forward, and stabbed.

The hulk of the dragon barreled into him, and the balcony railing broke. Man and dragon plummeted to the ground.

Abraham twisted in the air, distancing himself from the dragon. He hit the ground flat on his back, and the wind burst out of his lungs. The dragon landed beside him with Black Bane embedded in its eye socket. It twitched as its tail flapped back and forth, scraping over the ground. Fighting for breath, Abraham crawled over the tail where the dying dragon spasmed. He grabbed the sword hilt, put some weight on it, and jammed it deeper.

The dragon stiffened and lay still.

He pulled his sword free just in time to confront two soldiers rushing him with lowered spears. He knocked one spear aside and spun back into the Cauldron soldier's body and smote the man with an elbow in the face. The man staggered backward. Abraham cut the arms off the second soldier. That soldier lifted up his bleeding stumps for hands and fell over dead. Abraham made quick work of the first soldier he'd attacked. A stab in the heart did the trick. Then he was on the move again.

Horace, Cudgel, and Iris were battling at the keep's front door, slaying new attackers and keeping them at bay. Iris sent fiery rose-pink hornets from her fingertips spraying into the enemy. Cudgel dislodged a soldier's jaw with a fierce hit from his spiked mace. Horace gored man after man on the end of his thick spear. Bodies piled up in bloody heaps around them.

"Horace, do you need help?" Abraham asked as he raced past.

Horace ran two enemy soldiers through at once and said, "No, Captain. Don't spoil our fun. Kill those dragons!"

The rest of the Henchmen were locked up in mortal battle with the dragons on the balcony. Swan and Lewis hacked away at the beasts, keeping them at bay. Through the smoke, Abraham didn't see any more of the dragons as he bounded back up the steps. He raced around the curve of the balcony. Running up on the backside of the dragon attacking Swan, he lopped its tail off with a lethal swing.

The dragon spun around on Abraham.

Swan sliced open the dragon's neck the moment it twisted away from her. "Taste my steel, beast!"

Together, Abraham and Swan carved up the dragon. Its scaly hide was no match for Black Bane and the King's Steel wielded by the guardian maiden. Hunks of flesh flew from the dragon. It thrashed on the balcony with blood spurting from the deep gashes in its body. Its serpentine movement began to slow, and it spread its wings.

"Never!" Swan leapt onto the dragon's back and sliced through both of its wings.

It jumped through the railing, flapping furiously as it nose-dived toward the ground.

"Princess!" Swan called out. She hung from the railing by one hand. Her feet dangled over the edge.

Clarice arrived at the same time Abraham did. The princess wrapped her fingers around Swan's hand. "Hold on!"

Abraham grabbed Swan by the back of the pants and hauled her up. "Next time, let go of your sword in case no one is around."

"Never," Swan replied.

The last dragon lay dead at Lewis's feet. The prince had lizard guts and blood all over him. On the back end of the dragon were Bearclaw and Vern. Their weapons were also drenched with blood.

Abraham surveyed the surroundings. The soldiers were dead, and the tree still burned. Branches were falling from the tree's trunk. He waved at Horace. The bearded warrior waved back. Dozens of soldiers were dead on the balconies and the ground. If any others survived, they were hiding.

"Leodor, are there any other ways out of here?" Abraham asked.

"Only through the roof and through that door. It's a keep. There is only one way in and one way out." Leodor rolled his eyes. "They are designed that way, you know."

"Yeah, thanks, Leodor." Abraham eyed the hole in the roof, which had no access, aside from the tree that burned. "We have to search this place room by room. The Underlord has to be here, somewhere."

"I find that unlikely," Leodor said. "I see no reason why he wouldn't be able to remove himself from the keep with a transportation spell. I'd do the same."

Sticks spun her short swords in her hands and asked, "Wouldn't you need to have one prepared?"

"One can only assume that the Underlord is prepared for everything," Leodor replied.

"I say that we get out of here," Lewis suggested with his eyes locked on the hole in the roof of the keep. "Before more dragons flood through that gap."

"Captain!" Horace shouted from below. "This door won't hold much longer! Magic or no. The wood begins to splinter."

"We're trapped in here. The only way out is against the Cauldron army. No, we're too close. Maybe we caught the Underlord with his pants down." Abraham headed to the next door. "Let's turn this place upside down before time runs out." He knocked on the door. "Room service. It's time to clean your room."

"ARE YOU LOOKING FOR ME?"

Everyone turned. Arcayis the Underlord stood on the other side of the balcony, twelve feet tall with one hand filled with blazing blue bolts of lightning.

CHAPTER 73

The towering figure of Arcayis loomed on the balcony like a great shadow in his black robes. A necklace of bright stones hung around his neck. The stone in the middle burned with blue fire, while the others were white, yellow, orange, and red. His voice filled the room and shook the branches burning on the trees. "I applaud your boldness, Ruger Slade. Ha ha. I didn't expect to see you so soon or at all." He craned his neck. "Ah, I see that you brought my former servants, Lewis and Leodor. Are you ready to come back to the winning side?"

"We didn't come to chat. We came to kill you," Abraham said. He moved down the balcony, where he had a better look at Arcayis. He moved to the right, while Bearclaw and Vern moved left. "You could make it easier on yourself and surrender."

Toying with the necklace draped over his chest, Arcayis asked, "Now, why would I do that? I'm all but invincible. Can't you see that I've already acquired five of the six stones that you seek?"

Abraham shot a look back at Leodor, who shrank inside his robes. "Tell me that you didn't know about this."

"I didn't. I'm as shocked as any," Leodor said. "We are finished."

"Yes, listen to Leodor, Ruger. You are finished. Your quest ends here with me." Arcayis eyed the burning tree. "You really do need to pay for setting fire to the Tree of the Elders. The Sect will frown heavily over that. Someone, most likely you, will suffer eons for it."

"It's just a tree, man," Abraham said. He crept forward and made it one quarter of the balcony ring away from Arcayis. He tingled from the bottom of his spine to the top. "How about we talk about this?"

Arcayis gave him a scornful look and said, "I don't think so. Prepare to watch your Henchmen die."

He flung a bolt of energy at Bearclaw and Vern, who dove as the bolt exploded into the balcony, collapsing it beneath them. The warriors fell to the ground, and the Underlord let out a triumphant laugh.

Abraham charged.

With a flick of his fingers, Arcayis blew away the balcony, leaving a chasm between them. "No, no, no. I want you to stand and watch this."

He hurled bolt after bolt across the deck. The lightning blasted Swan's and Clarice's bodies. The barrage of energy collapsed more of the balcony beneath them. All of them fell to the ground.

"Perfect. It's always easier to kill from a dragon's point of view."

Abraham banged his sword on the railing. "Wake up, Black Bane. I need help."

Arcayis pitched away, flinging bolt after bolt at the bombarded Henchmen.

Bearclaw ran for cover and took a bolt square in the back. His arms flung wide as he sailed into a support column below the crumbling balcony.

Leodor and Lewis hid behind an orange shield of energy. A bolt of energy shattered it.

"You have made my task easy by coming here, Ruger!" Arcayis threw bolt after bolt like a mad god of thunder. "No more elaborate schemes. Instead, a straight-up fight. Once you perish, King Hector will follow. You are the last hope that he has." He laughed like a madman. "Ah ha ha ha ha!"

"Black Bane, wake up!"

The sword was the only thing he could think of that could match the same wroth power that Arcayis wielded. The runes engraved in the blade, which glowed red-hot during moments like this, grew cold.

"Fine! I'm not going to stand here and watch my men get slaughtered." Abraham backed up, sheathed his sword, faced the gap in the balcony, ran, and jumped. He landed with his arms on the rim of the broken ledge.

Arcayis peered down at him with blazing eyes and said, "That was a very stupid thing to do. You are defenseless. Oh well. I'll end this early." He lifted a lightning bolt over his shoulder and drove it down into Abraham's head.

Every nerve ending in Abraham's body exploded with vibrant pain. His sight washed over in blue. He saw himself falling away from Arcayis's leering face. The picture jostled. He was on the ground with his ears ringing and scorched hair stinking. His mouth tasted like the tip of a nine-volt battery. Everything hurt. It all hurt badly.

Above, Arcayis slung his lightning bolt into the fire and smoke. The floor quaked. The keep shook.

Move, Abraham. You have to move! If Abraham was moving, he couldn't tell. *Ruger, get your ass off of the floor and do something!* A body sailed over his eyes. It was Cudgel. His robes were on fire. *No!*

Arcayis continued his barrage of fire with fathomless energy. Bolts appeared in his hands one after the other. Like a hawk's, his eyes locked on a target, then he cocked back and threw.

Rushing blood roared through Abraham's ears. He turned his head. Horace lay on his chest, face down, with the Robes of the Black Kraken on fire and smoldering. As Iris frantically tried to pat out the flames, a blue bolt exploded at her feet. The smoke cleared. She was gone.

CHAPTER 74

Sticks popped into Abraham's view. Her face was skinned up and bloody. She grabbed him by the boots and dragged him underneath the balcony. Her lips were moving, but he couldn't make out a word she said. The explosions and sharp ringing in his ears drowned her voice out. He managed to lift a shaking arm.

He waved her away saying, "Go, go, go!"

"Such a delight!" Arcayis's great voice thundered from above. "The King's Henchmen are sheep for the slaughter! Die, Henchmen, die!"

Searing blue bolts of light soared through the keep.

Kra-koom! Kra-koom! Kra-koom!

Sticks held out the assault rifle and waved it in front of Abraham in a frantic motion. Her hands were on the trigger housing. She looked at him and spoke.

Abraham tried to read her lips. He wasn't sure but thought she was asking, "What do I do?" Without full control of his body, all he could manage to do was say, "Pull the trigger." He squeezed his own trigger finger. "Pull the trigger." He couldn't hear or understand his own words.

Sticks tilted her head. Her eyes ran the length of the weapon. Using both hands, she held out the assault rifle. She didn't brace the stock of the weapon against her shoulder but held it straight out in an awkward position. Backpedaling, Sticks slowly walked out from underneath the balcony with the weapon pointed toward the ceiling.

With agonizing pain shooting through his head, Abraham twisted his head around. She didn't know what she was doing. Arcayis would blow her away. He let out another garbled warning, "Nooo!"

Blue lightning lit up the room.

Chunks of debris went flying.

Flaming branches fell from the tree.

The muzzle of the assault weapon flashed.

Arcayis dropped from above and landed hard on his back. A bullet had blown out the back of his head.

Abraham's eyes popped. "Huh?"

Sticks held the assault rifle up, nodded, and smiled. She said something inaudible.

The inner walls of the keep quieted. Only the cracking sound of the burning tree remained.

Abraham managed to fight his way up to his hands and knees. His limbs shook with effort. *How am I not dead? I just took a lightning bolt to the cranium.* He caught Sticks looking at him and said, "Good shot."

Arcayis's giant body shrank back down to normal size.

Sticks slung the rifle over her shoulder. She took the necklace off Arcayis's neck. The burning blue stone had gone cold. She walked over to Abraham and put the necklace around his neck. "Let's go home."

Bearclaw and Vern helped Abraham to his feet.

A limping Lewis used his sword for a cane.

Leodor's robes were in tatters. He swayed with every step.

Swan and Clarice were marred with soot and caked black from head to toe.

Cudgel moved slowly toward the group with a nasty gash on his bald head.

Horace cradled Iris's limp body in his arms. Tears filled his eyes. "She's dead," he sobbed. "He killed her. That fiend killed her!"

Abraham's heart sank.

Everyone's chins dipped.

Horace sobbed loudly. "Curse the Elders and their games!"

Iris placed her hand over Horace's mouth and said, "I'm not dead. Can't you feel that I'm still breathing? I can barely move. The king's armor saved me," she said, glancing at the others with a wobbling neck. "I'd say it saved us all."

"She's alive!" Horace elated. "She's alive!"

The keep's door shook on the hinges. Axes chopped into the wood. Something rammed it from the other side.

Abraham slipped out of the arms of Bearclaw and Vern. His vibrant strength returned to his limbs. He wasn't sure how he'd survived, but based on what Iris had said, he thought the king's breastplate he was wearing had something to do with it. The king's steel, he started to believe, was special. "All right, listen up, there's going to be more soldiers and dragons out there." He glanced up, imagining scores of dragons pouring through the opening of the keep and devouring them whole. "If anyone has any bright ideas, now is the time to share them."

"If I may," Leodor said. His eyes were locked on the bright gemstones dangling from Abraham's neck. "I could harness the necklace's powers and possibly put an end to all of this."

Iris shook her head. "Those are for the king only."

"You know nothing about it," Leodor told her with a cross look.

"I know that you don't deserve it. You might kill us all with it," Iris fired back.

The soldiers outside the keep chopped a large hunk out of the door. Angry stares peered through the gap.

"I'm a Henchman," Leodor said. "I can't use it against the king's will, or I will die."

"Yes, let Leodor have the necklace," Lewis said. "He is the only one that possesses the knowledge to use it," He moved toward Abraham and held out his hand. "My father would approve it. And I am the prince who endorses it. Are Leodor and I not proven?"

"You've pulled your weight," Abraham said, surrounded by doubting eyes. He felt Lewis and Leodor still had a long way to go, despite having gained some favor. As dire as his situation was, he wasn't desperate enough to turn over the necklace. He flicked his fingers. Invisible needles burned all through his body, especially from the elbow up. He clenched his hand. "But not that much weight."

"Don't be a fool!" Lewis pointed at the door. "They'll swarm us the moment they burst through there!"

"We can kill them," Horace said.

The enemy whittled the door down more, bigger chunks at a time.

Bearclaw, Vern, Cudgel, Swan, and Clarice, bearing their weapons, made a fighting line between Abraham and the door.

"This is madness!" Lewis said.

"Indeed," Leodor agreed.

"There's an old saying in my world," Abraham replied. "Sometimes you have to know when to hold them, when to fold them, when to walk away, or run. Now is one of those times."

"What in Titanuus's Crotch does that mean?" Lewis asked.

Abraham smiled. "Horace, I'm going to need your spear. It's time to go Frazetta on them."

"And what, pray tell, is Frazetta?" Lewis asked with a snide look.

Abraham smirked. "You'll see."

CHAPTER 75

Abraham decapitated Arcayis with Black Bane and mounted the Underlord's head on the tip of Horace's spear. Horace hoisted the head up.

"That's Frazetta," Abraham said.

He marched in front of the keep's door with Horace standing on one side and Sticks on the other. Horace held the spear and head upright. Sticks had the assault rifle across her chest. The rest of the Henchmen stood behind them. He watched as the Cauldron soldiers finally burst through the door.

Over a dozen soldiers poured through the busted opening, bearing swords and spears. They came to an abrupt halt. Their battle-hungry gazes hung on the image of the Underlord's decapitated head skewered on a spear.

"Now that I have your attention," Abraham said in a strong authoritative voice, "let me make what is about to happen crystal clear for you. Number one, as you can see, the Underlord is dead. So is everyone else in here, including the dragons. Number two"—he bandied the necklace jewels before their eyes—"I have the Underlord's power. Number three, we are going to walk out of here without any trouble from you at all. Capisce?"

The soldiers deflated inside their armor, and their hard-eyed stares softened.

Abraham stepped forward as the soldiers cowered back. He marched them back out of the keep. Scores of soldiers and priests were gathered in the courtyard. Several zillon dragon riders were perched on the outer wall. Dozens of the Cauldron's throng gasped at the sight of Arcayis's head.

"Listen up!" Abraham shouted in a harsher tone. "Attack us, and I wipe you out of existence." He shook the necklace at them. "I wipe you out, your wives, your husbands, your children, and baby dragons! I'll kill every last one of them. Do you hear me?"

The crowed murmured in agreement and cleared him a path to the gate.

"I want horses! And I better not see one single cross look!" He looked at a soldier who quickly looked away. He spotted a priest with a lazy eye and poofy hair. "Or any cross-eyed looks!"

The lazy-eyed priest gulped and wormed his way into the crowd.

Abraham continued, "I'll find your cousins, your kin, your house, your fields, and I'll burn it all!"

"Hear, hear," Horace said out of the corner of his mouth.

"Laying it on a little thick, aren't you?" Sticks quietly asked.

"It's my *Unforgiven* moment," he said from the corner of his mouth. "Roll with it."

The Cauldron's enclave made a clear path to the portcullis gate. They brought horses for everyone. Outside the gate, the Henchmen mounted up.

Abraham stared up at the Zillon dragon riders. They showed no expression at all. Saliva dripped from the dragons' fangs. "King Hector lives. All who oppose him die. Pray you don't ever see any of us again. We show mercy once, not twice." He turned his horse toward the fog. "Yah! Yah!"

The Henchmen thundered down the road and vanished into the fog.

At the bottom of the massive hill, the Henchmen met up with Solomon, Tark, Dominga, and Shades.

"All of you look like hell, but I see that you brought us a souvenir," Solomon said.

"Nice head," Dominga added.

Shades sniggered. "And to think that you pulled it off without me."

"I wouldn't be overconfident," Leodor said. "They let us escape. They must have."

Abraham shook his head and said, "It's a bluff, old man." He reached across the saddle and grabbed Leodor's narrow shoulders. "You see, sometimes you don't have to fight when you're a man, and it doesn't mean you're weak if you turn that other cheek."

Leodor turned up his nose, slipped from Abraham's grasp, and led his horse away.

With his head turned toward the hills, Solomon said, "What happened up there? I didn't expect you back so soon."

"I guess the element of surprise was on our side." Abraham couldn't help but smile. He'd dodged death again, and all the Henchmen returned intact. "I'll tell you on the ride back. A very interesting story, but we got what we needed and more." He pulled out the necklace from underneath his cloak.

"Are those all of the stones?" Solomon asked with the jewels shining in his eyes.

"All five. Apparently, the Underlord had them. I thought he was going to wipe us out, but Sticks shot him."

"Shot him?" Solomon looked at Sticks. "An assault rifle?"

"And ammo. We ran smack-dab into the zillon that shot at King Hector and Arcayis himself." He chuckled. "They didn't see it coming."

"If you don't mind me saying, you seem a little punch drunk," the old troglin added.

"That's probably because the Underlord jammed a lightning bolt straight through me." He tapped his armor. "This sheet metal kept me together." He lifted an arm. "Horace, Shades, lead us back to the *Sea Talon* with haste." He winked at Solomon. "Don't tell Leodor or Lewis, but I agree—my bluff might not hold, and I don't know how to use this necklace."

"But the dragons… Were there dragons?" Solomon asked.

"More dragons than I have toes and fingers, that I could see. The farther away from them, the better. They are the things to fear most. I'm shocked that the zillons fell for my bluff at all."

"We would have killed them," Horace said as he rode by. "Move out, Henchmen!"

The company moved at a trot and stayed on the back roads. They put the Cauldron's clouded hills far behind them and broke away from the city. Over a mile from the city was a stone bridge over a deep trickling creek.

Horace lifted a fist and stopped at the beginning of the bridge. "Whoa."

Abraham rode alongside Horace and asked, "What's going on?"

Horace pointed at a small army of men gathered on the other side of the bridge. Their burgundy tunics with upside-down black ankhs were a dead giveaway. It was the Black Squadron.

CHAPTER 76

"I'll handle this," Abraham said. He led his horse out onto the bridge.

Sticks and Horace followed but kept their distance behind him. The horses' hooves clomped on the wooden bridge. The wind picked up, and the horses nickered.

On the other side of the bridge, three riders approached. The biggest man rode in the middle, the man they'd identified as Commander Cutter in the small-town tavern Shades set on fire. Commander Cutter had a short military-style haircut. The hawkish man had a broad face with strong angular features, great shoulders, and grizzle on his face. A white scar split his chin. He wore a pitch-black cloak over his burgundy tunic. The handle of a bastard sword stuck out behind his back.

He narrowed his eyes at Abraham and spat over the bridge. "I am Commander Cutter. This is the Black Squadron."

"You are in our way, Commander Cutter," Abraham said.

Cutter's hardened stare shifted to the head that Horace carried on his spear. "I'm curious. Where is the body that goes with that head?"

"What business is that of yours?"

"Everything that happens in Hancha is my business," Cutter replied. He dropped his focus back on Abraham. "I'm an important man around here. I don't find favor with people riding the country with heads mounted on spears. But I get the feeling that you and your company aren't from around here, are you?"

"Just passing through. We are taking the head home as a souvenir."

Cutter spat on the bridge. "Let's quit playing games. You were in the tavern the other night, weren't you? The one that burned. I saw you, the big belly and the woman, plus that little fella back there."

"That was us," Abraham replied.

"And you're Ruger Slade, aren't you?"

"Yes and no, but that's a long story."

Cutter rested his corded forearms on the saddle horn. "And the rest of you are King Hector's Henchmen."

Abraham shrugged. "Is there something that I can help you with? You see, we are in a bit of a hurry."

"I imagine that you are. I'd be in a hurry too if I was in enemy territory." Cutter sniggered. "Slade the Blade. The moment I heard about your exploits in Pirate City, I knew I had to find you face-to-face. They say you are the best with a blade. Perhaps the best ever." He spat. "I don't believe it."

"If you were there, you would have." Abraham pushed his fingers back through his hair. "Listen, as you can see, we've had a few tough days, Commander. And yes, I know you're a fine swordsman yourself, and you probably want a piece of me. But before you do something stupid and draw your blade, let me fill you in." He pointed at the decapitated head. "That's the Underlord. The head of the Sect. The prince of the Cauldron. He's dead. Very dead." He gave Sticks a sideways glance. "She shot him with that weapon of mass destruction in her hands. It blew out the back end of his head."

Sticks aimed the weapon at Commander Cutter's face.

Abraham continued. "Not to mention the zillon dragon riders that fell." He dangled the necklace before Cutter. "And I have the Underlord's most precious source of power. Now, I'm going to tell you what I told the others that were smart enough to get out of our way and not die. We'll show mercy once. After that, you die." He tugged his earlobe. "I'll extend the king's same grace to you." He buckled his brows, darkened his tone, and said, "Get out of our way or die."

Commander Cutter's stare swept across the three of them before stopping back on Abraham. "I want sword against sword. Me against you."

"It will have to wait. I'm not in the mood. Step aside, all of you, or my little friend will do the same to you that she did to the Underlord," he replied.

"You are a coward." Cutter spat on the ground and backed his horse away. The other two soldiers did the same. With a wave of his arm, the Black Squadron cleared the road.

Abraham led the Henchmen over the bridge. As he passed Commander Cutter, he said, "I'm not a coward. And you aren't as stupid as you look." He put his heels into the ribs of his horse and galloped away. The Henchmen rode after him, leaving the onlooking Black Squadron eating their dust.

They rode the countryside for miles without stopping. Then Abraham slowed to a walk, allowing the horses to rest.

Horace caught up to him and said, "Captain, I'm not one to question you, but I have to ask, why didn't you fight him?"

"Because," Abraham said, tightening his tingling grip on the reins, "not only can I barely feel my hands, I can hardly lift my arms." The corner of his mouth turned up. "Then again, maybe I have the strength after all. Drop. Your. Sword."

Horace gave him a curious look. "Pardon, Captain?"

Abraham chuckled. "Nothing."

Horace grunted. "Just so you know, we could have killed them."

"I know." He could still smell his singed hair. Painful shards ran up and down his spine. The lightning bolt to the head had some severe lingering effects, and a migraine had come on. "But I had to make sure that we all made it out alive."

CHAPTER 77

The Henchmen reunited with the ship crew at Pirate City. They sailed on *Sea Talon* all the way back to Kingsland without incident. Night had fallen when they ported. A season-changing wintery chill swept through the air. Abraham, Leodor, Lewis, Princess Clarice, and Swan headed straight to the House of Steel that evening. Abraham ordered the rest of the Henchmen back to the Stronghold.

King Hector and Queen Clarann welcomed Princess Clarice with warm hugs and tears in their eyes. Clarice apologized all over herself and shared the demise of the Guardian Maiden Hazel. They had reunited on the king's terrace overlooking the Bay of Elders. Pratt, the commander of the King's Guardians, along with two other Guardians, stood guard on the terrace. The king and queen were quickly brought up to speed on their journey by Clarice.

With a smile of relief, King Hector strolled over to Abraham with his arms swinging by his sides. He practically walked on tiptoe, his eyes glued to the necklace hanging on Abraham's neck. "Surely, those can't be the jewels from the Crown of Stones."

As Abraham opened his mouth, Leodor stepped forward and said with a bow, "Your Majesty, I cannot vouch for the authenticity of the stones myself. Abraham refused to part with them."

"Yes, well, he is the Captain," Hector said, "and wise to keep them in hand." His fingers kneaded the air between them. "So, the Underlord is dead?"

"Dead as stone," Abraham replied. "We killed the would-be assassin too." He reached behind his back, where the assault rifle hung from a strap on his shoulder. He showed it to the king. "This is an assault rifle. An M-16 is what it is called, to be exact. Sticks shot Arcayis in the head with it. It turned his head inside out." He glanced at a round wicker basket sitting in front of Lewis's feet. "It's gruesome, but we brought his head in a fish basket if you want to look."

King Hector looked at his son and nodded.

Lewis squatted down and flipped open the basket's lid.

Queen Clarann walked over at that moment. She and Hector bent their necks over the basket together. She pinched her nose and, with watering eyes, looked away.

Hector's nose twitched, and he said, "Ghastly. And to think that could have been me." His gaze hung on the head. "The entire back of his head is missing, but I know it's him. Those eyes… I'll never forget them." He flipped his hand.

Lewis closed the basket and asked, "What would you have me do with it, Father?"

With his lips pointed toward the sea, he said, "Pitch it over the wall. Let the sea birds dine on it. If memory serves, Arcayis hated birds. It will be a fitting funeral for him."

Without a word, Lewis walked over to the terrace wall and dumped the head out. He tossed the basket after it.

King Hector eyed Abraham, the rifle, and the necklace. He shook his head and, with disbelief in his voice, said, "I am without words, otherworlder. And you have my entire gratitude. To think that I was going to hang you." He dropped a firm hand on Abraham's shoulder. "You have earned the king's gratitude."

"Just me?" he asked.

"All of the Henchmen, but most especially you, Abraham." Hector glanced at Clarann, who was nothing short of a lovely vision. "Not only did you save the love of my life, but my daughter, possibly my kingdom, not to mention my son." He turned his attention to Lewis. "I hope you learned something from this man, Son. Did you?"

"I learned there is nothing that he did that I could not have done," Lewis replied with a heavy crease in his brow. "Besides, it was a united effort. I'm not sure that any of them would have survived without myself and Leodor to pull them through."

"You smug, snotty little liar!" Clarice yelled. Her fists were balled up at her side, and her hot stare could have killed her half brother. "Father, the only thing those two sandbags did was drag us down. The Henchmen are better off without them."

King Hector rubbed his chin, which sagged with age, and asked Abraham, "Is that so?"

His gaze drifted toward Lewis and Leodor. "I think everyone pulled their weight. I can fill you in at length."

The king nodded. "No, I accept your statement. I mean, look at Leodor. He looks like a pauper's dish towel. He must have done something. I can see dirt underneath his fingernails and an ugly bump on his head. We can hash out the details later." He dropped his eyes on the necklace. "May I?"

"Certainly."

King Hector waved at Pratt. "Bring the crown over."

Pratt lumbered over to the patio table where the crown sat with bright moonlight twinkling on its metal horns. The big man, who appeared exceptionally huge in his armor, picked the crown up as though holding a baby. He marched over to King Hector and took a knee before him. "Your Majesty," the man said.

King Hector took the crown and said, "Thank you, Pratt. That will be all."

Pratt gave Abraham a heavy look and moved back to his post.

"I guess I won't be needing this anymore." King Hector reached into his pocket and produced the colorful cube. "Your Cube of Rubik. I never solved it." The orange side of the cube had been solved. The other five sides and colors were a jumbled mess. He placed it in Abraham's palm.

"At least you finished one side. That's far better than most that try to solve it." Abraham noticed Leodor staring at them. He turned his broad back to the man, shielding the viceroy's view from the cube. Under his breath, he said to the king, "Hang onto it. Let Leodor still think it's magic."

King Hector took the cube, looked past Abraham at Leodor, and said, "Good idea." He tucked the cube away. Then he handed the crown to Clarann, reached inside his robes, and withdrew his necklace with the emerald jewel set in it. He popped it out of the casing, looked at Clarann, and said, "The moment of truth."

Abraham's throat turned dry. His fingers clutched at his side. With the king and the crown's help, he might be able to go right back home. The problem was, he wasn't so sure that he wanted to. As bad as Titanuus was, he liked it—the people too. The only thing tying him back home was Mandi. He swallowed. *What if this crown opens a portal and sends me back, and I don't want to go? I don't think I'm ready to leave yet. Am I?*

The king set the emerald stone in the front horn's facet. The tiny pronglike claws in the facet locked onto the jewel, which fit inside perfectly. Five more facets were left to fill, two on each side and one in the back. He popped the jewels out of the necklace's golden casing. He began with the blue stone. It clamped perfectly into the facet of the crown's horn in the back. "Marvelous," he said with a warming smile.

The blue stone shone dully in the moonlight.

Leodor moved closer to the king. "It's magnificent, Your Majesty. Gems worthy of a true king."

"I hope you aren't groveling," King Hector said. "I hate groveling." He tried the orange stone next. It didn't twinkle the same as the emerald. The stone wouldn't fit in any of the facets even though it looked as though it would. He turned it upside down. It still wouldn't go.

"Strange," King Hector said.

"Perhaps I can make it fit," Leodor offered.

The king pulled the crown away. He next took the ruby jewel, shaped like a giant teardrop, the same as the others. It wouldn't fit either.

"What is wrong?" Queen Clarann asked.

The entire group formed a circle around the king. All of them watched with bated breath.

King Hector swallowed. He tried the yellow stone next. "I don't know. The crown rejects them." He held the yellow stone up in the moonlight. The shining light reflected dully on the stone. "Clarann, lift the crown into the light."

Clarann's graceful arms pushed the crown into the light. The emerald and blue sapphire stones shone with the glimmer and twinkle of a colorful star. She gasped quietly.

Hector dropped the yellow stone onto the stone patio, where it clacked off the pavement. He lifted his foot and crushed the yellow jewel under his boot heel. A crunch of glass crackled on the rocks as the jewel smashed into several broken chunks of glass.

"What sort of ruse is this?" he asked, anger filling his voice. He smashed all four of the other stones—orange, red, and ice white—the same way. He lifted his voice in anger. "Leodor, explain!"

Stammering, Leodor said, "I am at a loss, Your Majesty. If I only had a moment to inspect them, I would have seen them more clearly." His tired gaze drifted to Abraham. "You could have avoided this embarrassment. I thought that the Underlord fell too easily. This explains very much. Perhaps Arcayis wasn't the Underlord that we seek."

Abraham ground his teeth.

Clarice jumped at Leodor, jabbed her finger in his chest and said, "You saw the Underlord. We all did. He hurled bolts of lightning like javelins. And he stood like a giant. He tried to kill us all. This is not Ruger's fault! Shame on you for implying so!"

Lewis covered his mouth and chuckled underneath his breath.

Leodor shrugged his scrawny shoulders. "With or without the stones, Arcayis would still be one of the world's most formidable mystics. He didn't need all the stones to unleash the potent wrath of his craft. One stone alone would enhance such power."

"At least you have one more stone, Father," Lewis said as he looked at the crown. "Pretty."

"What, then, in the name of the Elders, happened?" King Hector asked.

The sea winds died down, and the group fell silent.

Abraham's heart deflated. At first, he hadn't wanted to go back home. The moment he realized the stones didn't work and he couldn't make it back, he wanted to go. Now, that had changed. Victory had been snatched out of his grip. *How?* He clenched his jaws. An impish face appeared in his mind, and it all came together. They had been set up. He turned and kicked the patio wall and said, "I know what happened."

All eyes fell on him.

"The Big Apple." He turned and faced them all. "That dirty little horned halfling betrayed us."

"But why?" King Hector asked.

"Because he doesn't want to accidentally be sent home, that's why." Abraham smashed his fist into his palm. "But we'll see about that." He walked away from the others and stopped at the farthest end of the patio. He wanted to be alone, but he could hear the anger and disappointment in everyone's voices. They would have to start all over again, and Lewis and Leodor were the unhappiest about all of it.

"Abraham," someone said in a soft voice. It was Clarann, a golden-haired lioness of striking beauty walking in the moonlight. "Can I have a word with you?"

"Sure you can. I deserve it."

"Not about that. I feel you did well. All that you could." She stood shoulder to shoulder beside him with her hip touching his. "Clarice wouldn't boast of your efforts if it wasn't true. She is a very straightforward young woman and full of fire."

"Yes, I can see that. She made mistakes, but she handled herself quite well."

"She gets it honestly from her father."

Abraham nodded and said, "I would have guessed that she gets it from her mother."

Clarann turned and looked at him with eyes searching for something that was lost and said, "No, it comes from her father, the man in my eyes, Ruger Slade."

THE KING'S CONJURER

THE HENCHMEN CHRONICLES

BOOK FOUR

CRAIG HALLORAN

CHAPTER 1

At midday, the sun was shining behind the clouds on a brisk day that kept the leaves rustling in the wind. He stood on the mound and dug his toe into the dirt. Ninety feet away, the smoky-eyed Tark stood over a flat piece of limestone that represented home plate. All the bases were made from slabs of limestone that formed an imperfect baseball diamond. He held the autographed baseball of Buddy Parker—his former teammate, now perished—behind his back. He ran his fingers over the red laces. He looked out from underneath the bill of his baseball cap.

"You aren't going to hit this," he said to Tark.

Tark held a club whittled down into a crude baseball bat. He wiggled it in the air, took a couple of test swings, and said, "We'll see about that. As you say, 'Bring the heat.'"

"Bring something," Horace said in a grumpy voice. The bearded big belly squatted behind home plate. He wore a full helmet and leather chest-plate armor. His beard spilled out from underneath his helmet and over his chest. He had a catcher's mitt too. His voice rang hollowly inside the helmet when he spoke. "I'm getting hungry. We've been at this silly game long enough."

Narrowing his eyes, the strapping athlete Tark said, "I like it."

Six more Henchmen were on the field. Vern, Bearclaw, and Dominga were in the outfield. Sticks stood on first base, Apollo manned second base, and Prospero stood over third. Shades played shortstop, between second and third base. All of them wore thick leather gloves, for Abraham had shown the picture of himself on a baseball card to a leather worker who in turn made the gloves.

"Now remember," he said, "three strikes, and you're out. Someone else will bat after that. We'll rotate you in the field."

"So all I have to do is hit that little white ball? And run around those bases. And I win?" Tark asked. He showed a big white smile. "This will be easy."

"One thing is for sure. It will be interesting," Solomon said. The towering troglin stood behind Horace in the umpire position. He looked at Abraham and said, "You better not hit me with a wild pitch."

"I won't. Besides, how bad could it hurt? You're a troglin."

"An old troglin." Solomon flipped up his thumbs and said, "Play ball!"

Abraham took a breath. His haphazard Field of Dreams was far from perfect, but it kept his mind off other things.

Standing in the fields at a distance were the rest of the Henchmen and his retainers. Iris the mystic was there, along with the young brothers, Skitts and Zann. The three dusky-skinned beauties, Sophia dressed in black, Selma wearing red, and Bridget draped in white, were present. They stood out like gorgeous flowers among the weeds.

Lewis, Leodor, and Clarice were not present. They'd been retained at the House of Steel by the order of King Hector. Abraham couldn't have been more relieved after the bombshell Queen Clarann had dropped on him: that Ruger was Clarice's father. He and the queen had talked briefly, but he made himself scarce after that. She hadn't called on him since.

"Are you going to throw that thing or not?" Horace shouted. "My knees are aching."

"All right. All right. Here it comes." Abraham wound up the pitch and let the ball fly.

The baseball slipped right underneath Tark's powerful swing. *Swish.* He spun around, off balance.

Solomon made the call, showing the strike signal. "Strike!"

Horace threw the ball back to Abraham.

He caught the ball in his homemade mitt and smiled. "You know, Solomon, I didn't take a hippie for a baseball fan."

"Hippies like baseball too. Heck, I played in Little League for years. The old man wanted me to even though I hated it—of course, every boy did it back then—not because I didn't like it. I just sucked at it. I was more fit for watching it on television." Solomon shrugged. "But I was pretty good at ping-pong."

Tark took his place back over the plate. "Let's try that again."

"My pleasure." Abraham looked over at Sticks, who was hovering over first base with her usual straight face. He couldn't tell whether she was bored or not. He winked at her and said, "Having fun?"

Sticks shrugged.

"I must say, this is far from stimulating," Shades said as he tossed his glove up and down in the air. "And I don't see the need for this leather gauntlet. It's a clumsy device."

"You'll understand soon enough." Abraham ground his feet into the mound. Ruger's body was the makeup of a perfect athlete. Generally speaking, the man could do it all. He could pitch too, but not like the real Abraham Jenkins. Abraham had a gift. It was how his shoulder, arm, hand, and fingers were made. Whenever he would wind up and throw, the ball would whistle out of his hand. Only God could make an arm better. But at least Ruger was accurate.

He eyeballed Tark. *I'll take some heat off so he can get a good crack at it.* He wound up and threw the moderately fast pitch straight down the line.

Tark unleashed a mighty swing.

Crack!

The ball skipped across the dirt field right between first and second.

"Run!" Solomon yelled at Tark.

Tark sprinted toward first base.

"Drop the bat!" Solomon hollered.

Tark arrived at first base as fast as a jackrabbit with the baseball bat in hand. He handed it to Sticks. She chucked it aside.

"Keep running!" Solomon hollered.

"Will somebody get the ball?" Abraham yelled as the ball skipped toward right field, where Vern was standing. "Vern, get the ball!"

"You get it!" Vern said.

Tark rounded second base and sprinted toward third.

Cudgel ran over from center field and snatched up the ball, which came to a stop at a knee-high outfield wall made from large stones.

"Throw it home!" Abraham yelled. "Throw it home!"

"Where's home?" Cudgel shrugged.

"To Horace! Throw it to Hor—"

Cudgel chucked the baseball three hundred feet toward Horace, hovering over home plate.

Tark sped past third base toward home plate. Solomon kept waving him in.

Abraham watched the ball sail over his head. *Nice throw.*

The baseball dropped right into Horace's mitt.

"Tag him! You have to tag him!" Abraham shouted at Horace.

Horace tossed down his glove, and the ball rolled out of his mitt and across the dirt. He stepped in front of home plate and braced himself for Tark's charge. Horace tackled Tark and pinned him to the ground.

"I did it, Captain. I tackled him!" He nodded with excitement as he sat on Tark's back. "I like this game."

Tark stretched out his fingertips and touched home plate.

Solomon loomed over home plate, stretched out his arms, and swiped them through the air. "Safe!"

Abraham slapped his forehead and ran his fingers down his face. "Good grief."

CHAPTER 2

SINCE THE HENCHMEN HAD RETURNED to Kingsland in triumph from their invasion of Hancha, where they'd killed Arcayis, life had become somewhat normal. By King Hector's order, they weren't allowed to travel away from Kingsland but otherwise were given full liberty. For all intents and purposes, life had been normal for Abraham. Aside from creating a baseball field, he and the Henchmen managed the Stronghold and its fields and conducted training.

Several weeks passed without interruption from the House of Steel. Lewis and Leodor never showed up. Ruger's alleged daughter, Clarice, didn't show up either. He tried not to think about her or Queen Clarann. Whatever had happened between Ruger and the queen was their business. The last thing he wanted now was to be drawn into any sordid affairs.

Outside of the Stronghold, Ruger labored in the heat of the day, rebuilding the barn that had burned down, courtesy of Leodor. He was on the top pitch of the roof, hammering in shingles, with Prospero and Apollo helping him. Prospero hummed a cheery tune that carried an Irish-sounding jingle while Apollo sang the words:

"Her name was Sherry, and she said we should marry.
And I said, 'I'll have to ask my horse first.'
She said to let me know what the horse says,
And good luck finding her after that.
'I need a fit man that is smart as a beast
And not a man that can't think for himself.'
I chuckled and giggled, and I tickled her rump
And said with delight, 'I'd rather marry a horse
Than a stubborn old goat.'"

Abraham mopped his sweat from his brow with a navy-blue handkerchief as he laughed. "That's not half bad, Apollo. Has anyone ever told you that you have a voice like Tom Petty?"

"No." Apollo clawed at his scraggly beard. He and Prospero, no matter what time of day, always maintained their haggard and older appearance. "Who is Tom Petty?"

"A famous bard back in my world. I think you'd like his music."

Apollo lined a nail over a shingle he put in place, and Prospero drove it halfway in with a single hammer strike. He pulled his fingers away and readied another shingle and nail. "Was this Petty man a knight in your world?"

"No, nothing of the sort. Just an entertainer."

"They make a big deal about entertainers in your world." Apollo tacked on another shingle.

Across the courtyard, Sophia and Selma were sitting within the top window of his bedroom in the Stronghold, eyeballing him. They used their slender hands to fan the sweat glistening on their necks. Abraham swallowed.

Prospero hit Apollo on the hand with his hammer.

"Ow!" Apollo rubbed his hand and said, "Pay attention to what you are doing and stop gawking. Those are the Captain's concubines. You should know better."

Prospero grunted.

"Actually, they aren't my concubines. They are holdovers from the, well, last guy that was in charge." Abraham watched as the gorgeous women waved at him. He waved back. He still hadn't worked up the nerve to sleep with them, though he badly wanted to.

They were all a man could hope for. He'd ended up sleeping in a separate room with Sticks even though she made it perfectly clear she was all right with him sleeping with the trio of beauties.

"You know, you can talk to them," Abraham said. "They might be waving at you, not me. Those ladies aren't spoken for."

Apollo and Prospero exchanged a look. Apollo looked at him and said, "We can't do that, Captain. We are married."

Abraham tilted his head and gave them a funny look. "What do you mean, *married*?"

Apollo set his hammer down and asked, "Don't you have wives in your world? Like the king and the queen. We are married. Married to our women."

"What women?"

"Our wives?" Apollo shook his head and said, "You were at the wedding. A double wedding. We married twins, but Prospero and I are cousins. Many think we are brothers, but there is a distinction in our family line that carries."

"Well, why are you here?" he asked with incredulity. "You should be with your family. Your children. Do you have children?"

"Aye, we both do," Apollo said as Prospero nodded. "But they are grown now. They live in the foot of Kingsland. They are fine."

"I think you should go see them."

"No. They understand. When we go back, if we make it back, we'll be staying." Apollo clenched his leathery hand, which showed thick calluses on the palm. "The king comes first. It's our sworn duty."

"You are good men—faithful to the king and your wives. I appreciate it."

"It's an honor to serve whether it's good or bad."

Apollo and Prospero got back to work. Shingles were laid down, and the hammer drove in more nails.

Abraham resumed his work. He had never been much of a handyman back home, but Ruger seemed to take to it with vigor. Once they finished up the rooftop, he let the hirelings cover it with an inky tarlike coating that waterproofed the roof. He watched from below while he sucked on a flask of water. By the end of the day, the barn would be finished.

Sticks walked out of the Stronghold's open door. She had a small basket of rolls in her hands. "Why don't you eat something? I helped out with these."

"Sure." He grabbed a roll and ate. "Mmm… that's good. And you stuffed the sausage and cheese in them. You girls are getting there."

Sticks looked up at the women perched in the master bedroom's window. Their shapely legs dangled over the sill. Sophia and Selma looked at Sticks, whispered to one another, and giggled.

"Don't you think it's time to cut them loose?" Sticks asked. "They don't cook, and you aren't sleeping with them, so why keep them around? They don't do anything."

"I thought I'd make them Henchmen," he said. "They only need a little work. Perhaps you can train them."

Sticks made a dry "ha ha" and headed back toward the front door. "Enjoy your sausage roll."

"I am," he said with a smile. Then a sharp pain split him between the eyes. He hadn't had a migraine in weeks. This one hit him like a freight train, and he dropped to a knee. "Uh, Sticks."

Sophia and Selma screamed his name.

The ground began to twist. A sun ring burst in front of his eyes. A portal opened before him. Two men approached from the darkness of the portal's tunnel.

Sticks appeared in front of him. Her warm hands cupped his face. "Ruger! Ruger! Stay with me!" Her eyes widened. "Ruger, stay awake! Stay awake…" Her voice trailed off.

Abraham descended into darkness.

CHAPTER 3
BACK HOME

Abraham woke with a nagging headache. He cracked his eyelids open. A small fire was burning inside a stone fireplace. Nothing was between him and the low-burning fire except a wooden coffee table with deer antlers for table legs. He blinked and rubbed his temples. A heavy quilt covered his body.

Where am I now?

He shifted inside the sofa. His body sank deeper into the foam cushions. A musty smell mingled in the air with the burning wood. Aside from the fire, the room was dim. He was inside a log cabin with an open ceiling. Cobwebs were spun in the corners. The building groaned against the wind whistling outside.

Abraham sat up and took a closer look around the room. The dreary log cabin couldn't be any bigger than a thousand square feet. It appeared to have been abandoned years before. Closed curtains hung in windows. A wrought-iron chandelier hung over a small dining table. A midsize bed stood with a chest of drawers and a few other modern furnishings. The cabin had *woodsman* written all over it. The deer heads mounted on the walls were testament to that.

"Oh no," he said quietly. The hairs on his neck stood on end.

Clearly, he was back home. Or somewhere like that. He envisioned Dr. Jack Lassiter, the psychiatrist he'd encountered before. The curly-haired man reminded him a lot of Gene Hackman. The doctor was a devoted hunter, and this cabin looked like something Dr. Jack would thrive in.

Abraham sat up. "Whoa." His arms and legs were free. No straitjacket or shackles bound him either. He rubbed the back of his head. "Ruger, did you get this place all to yourself? Did you escape that hospital? Good for you."

Outside the front door, wooden boards groaned underneath the sound of footsteps.

Abraham moved to the fireplace and grabbed the metal poker leaning against the mantel. The front door swung open with a groan. The chill night air swept through the room. A shapely woman backed her way into the cabin. Her brunette hair was braided into a single tail. She wore a heavy cotton sweater, tight jeans, and work boots. Her arms were loaded with snow-covered logs. She shut the door with her toe and turned. Her jaw dropped. The wood she carried fell on the floor with a clatter. "Ruger. You're awake."

"Mandi?" Abraham said. His heart swelled. "What are you doing here? What is going on?"

A smile broke out over Mandi's face. She hopped over the logs and rushed into his arms. "Abraham! It's you, isn't it? I knew you would come back. I had faith."

He wrapped his bearish arms around her and said, "Of course it's me. Who else would I…? Wait a minute." He pushed her back gently and looked into her pretty eyes. "You called me Ruger. Why'd you do that?"

"I'll explain in a minute." She rose up on her tiptoes and kissed him fully on the lips. She wouldn't be denied. Her long fingers pulled his long hair. She walked him backward toward the bed and pushed herself down on top of him. She sank her face and soft lips into his neck.

He pulled away.

She straddled him and pulled off her sweater. Her full breasts jiggled inside her black bra as she tore at the buttons on his flannel shirt. Her athletic thighs clenched his own.

With his heart racing, the captivated man mumbled, "Resistance is futile." He turned himself over to her, and she turned herself over to him. They made love until the logs in the fireplace dimmed.

They lay underneath the covers. Mandi lay against his side with her gentle fingers touching his chest.

"Uh, I hate to spoil the wonderful moment," he said, "but what is going on?"

She kissed his neck, sat up in the bed, and said, "I don't even know where to start." She shivered. "We need to keep the fire burning. It's going to get cold if we don't. Not that I can't keep you warm all night."

"I believe that." He pulled her back as she tried to get out of bed. "I'll take care of it. You talk."

"So much for pillow talk, huh?" she replied with a playful smile.

He slipped on his boxers, grabbed the wood logs near the front door, and placed a couple of them in the fire. "Hope this wood is dry."

"It is. There's a shed filled with it." She started dressing. "I'm sorry, Abraham."

"For what?"

"You know. Jumping your bones."

He looked at her with a big smile and said, "Apology accepted."

"Well, aren't you the spry and cheerful one. I like it."

He dusted the grit of the snow and wood from his hands and said, "I've been through a lot. Let's just say it changed me." He replaced the screen in front of the fireplace. "It loosened me up, in a way."

She stood up in her bra and panties, arched her back, and stretched. "Listen to me, apologizing for having sex with a man. Me."

"I see your point. So why are you making an apology?"

"I just told myself that if I ever got you back again, I wouldn't hold back." She pulled her sweater down over her shoulders. "I believe you, Abraham, and I wanted you to know that. I am here for you."

He crossed the room and clasped her hands in his. "It means a lot. I swear, this Titanuus place is the real thing."

"Oh, I don't have any doubt about that. I did before, but given all that has happened, I'm more than convinced. Ruger took care of that."

"Ruger?" He gave her a serious look. "That's right. You called me that when you came in. He didn't hurt you, did he?"

"No, no, he's a perfect gentleman. Perhaps too perfect." She made a sheepish look.

"Did you and he, you know...?"

"No, but it wasn't from a lack of me trying." She pulled him over to the couch. "You better sit down."

CHAPTER 4

She set a protein shake in a carton on the coffee table. "I'd make coffee, but I don't have the means. This place doesn't run electric. It's off the grid, so to speak. It's our family cabin, dating back a few generations." She sat down.

"So where are we?"

"Down by the Greenbrier River in Summers County."

"Back in West Virginia, huh?"

"Yeah." She leaned forward with her elbows on her knees and stared into the warm fire. "Where to start? Where to start?"

"How about from the last time you saw me? Back in the hospital. With Nurse Nancy."

"Oh yeah. That seems like it was ages ago even though it's only been several weeks. Anyway, I did what you said. I tried to look up Eugene Drisk. I'll tell you more about that later. But he exists. Saw his name in an article in a Pittsburgh paper." She rubbed her hands on her thighs. "So, you went into a coma. I came to visit a few days after. Then, *poof*, you were gone. That nasty Nurse Nancy in the Hello Kitty scrubs treated me like a red-haired stepchild."

"Really, I can't imagine," he quipped. "That little Billy Goat Gruff."

"You can say that again. I almost put a fist through her pudgy face. But I wasn't direct family, and Luther Vancross wasn't either. Given the Health Information Portability and Accountability Act, we had as much of a chance in finding out where you were as breaking into Fort Knox. It's asinine."

He patted her knee. "What did you do?"

"What any gorgeous and sexy woman like me would do." She crossed her legs and put her warm hand on his. "I used my powers of seduction. Do you remember Colonel Drew Dexter?"

Abraham looked up in the corner of his eye socket and said, "Oh, you mean Mr. Moustache."

"Yeah, him. If you remember, he took a shine to me and had been calling on me. Pretty regular. When I mentioned you and what was going on in the hospital, he would change the subject." She looked into Abraham's eyes. "But I saw that shift. That flicker in those hazel eyes. I knew that he knew something. Believe me, I know. That douchebag I married has been cheating on me for years. He never fooled me. My attorney got it out of him on paper."

"Sorry to hear about that," he said.

"Don't be. I was a faithful and dutiful wife. I don't have anything to be ashamed of. It's the kids that I worry about. But they are mostly grown, and given the screwed-up nature of this world, they understand."

Abraham studied her face, not a wrinkle of worry on it. She was like Sticks in that manner, but far prettier. But her eyes were tired. Puffiness and a slight red rim showed before her eyelids.

"Keep going," he said.

"Just so you know, I didn't sleep with Colonel Drew. He kept coming around. I continued to warm up to him. I'd get close and pull away. We kissed, but that was all. But I finally knew that I broke him when he said, 'I know things. But I can't say because of my top-secret clearance. I'll see what I can find out.'"

His belly moaned. He reached for the protein shake. "And?"

"And that's when it really got weird." She moved away and grabbed a red Playmate cooler sitting on the floor near the dining table. "I have some snacks."

"Snacks?" He arched a brow, and his mouth started to water. "I could go for some snacks. Titanuus is severely lacking in the snack department. Tell me, you have some Dilly Bars?"

"No." She set the cooler down on the coffee table. "Sorry, didn't make it by Dairy Queen when we fled. But"—she opened the cooler—"I have plenty of protein bars and Little Debbie snack cakes."

He snatched the box of Oatmeal Creme Pies out of her hands. "I love these things!" He tore the box open and ripped away the clear plastic wrappers. He stuffed three in his mouth at once and chewed with joy.

"I guess I can say goodbye to those washboard abs," she replied.

"Huh?" He lifted up his shirt. His belly was long gone and replaced by a rock-hard stomach. "Oh. Well, that's what happens when they starve you, I guess."

"I don't think you've gotten a good look at yourself. You are you but built like a chimney stack."

He flexed his big forearm. It was knotted with muscle as in his playing days. He swallowed. "Man, those are delicious. The food in Titanuus—it's good, but it's not this good."

"Clearly. Can I continue, or do you want to finish the box first."

He grabbed two more Oatmeal Creme Pies. "I'm good. Go on."

She unwrapped a protein bar. "I really put a spell on Drew. He was smitten by me. After staying clammed up, he showed up at Woody's Grill late in the evening. I was closing, along with Herb and my mom, Martha. As usual, Mom had to try to feed him, but he was in a hurry. He didn't even crack a smile when Herb joked about the UFOs. He whispered to me that he knew where you were. It was top secret, but he managed to use his connections and get me clearance."

Abraham stopped chewing and asked, "What happened then?"

She shivered and said, "He took me there."

"Where?"

"Facility 117."

CHAPTER 5

Abraham squinted. He could see in the recesses of his mind a bronze nameplate on a building marked Facility 117. "It's a cement building with grooves running vertical from top to bottom. About ten stories tall. A high chain-link fence all around it."

"That's it." She rubbed her arms. She got up and put another log on the fire. "Sorry, but the place gave me the chills." She rubbed her hands in front of the flames. "Drew drove me up there in a black Humvee. That was the first thing I thought was odd because there weren't any markings of the Army on it, but there was some special gear inside. He took me up a gravel road that winded through the hills near the East River Mountain Tunnel. I never would have imagined that a huge building was up there in the middle of nowhere."

"Yeah, me either."

"Drew said it was an old military hospital that was built after World War II. I didn't think much of it. We checked in at security and went inside." She took her spot back on the couch. "There weren't a lot of people around that I could see. There were the four guards at the front gate and two waiting behind the security desk. All of them wore the same security uniform. They weren't military. I gave them a big smile. They didn't crack a grin, but they went all TSA on me when they searched me."

Mandi started taking the braid out of her hair. "Once I passed through the scanner, I had chill bumps all over. I felt like I might be going in but not coming back. There was this weird humming, like a generator running, but more natural."

Abraham felt a sinking feeling in his stomach. "You shouldn't have gone there. Not over me, anyway."

"Well, it's too late for that. Besides, I'm nosy. All of the women in my family are. I have a cousin, Tori, up in West Virginia. You'd be amazed at what her big nose got her into several years ago." She reached over and locked her fingers with his. "Anyway, I was worried about you and needed to see that you were all right. Up the elevator we went to the fifth floor. We met Dr. Jack Lassiter."

"Yeah, I know him."

"You do?"

"Another long story, but keep going," he said as he gave her hand a firm squeeze. "I'm listening."

"Thanks, Dr. Crane." She giggled. "Dr. Jack, as he preferred to be called, was very polite. He explained your condition by using a bunch of medical terminology that lost my attention. Sorry, but I really hated biology and other complicated college courses like that. So I dropped them. Finally, after some flirting and pleading, they took me to your hospital room. It was a quiet place with only one nurse on call. You were shackled to the bed but sleeping as sound as a baby. You had cuts and bruises all over you. That made me mad, and I let them have it.

"Dr. Jack went on to explain that you were only being protected from yourself. He talked more about the delirium and schizophrenia that you were dealing with. As truthful as he sounded, I didn't believe a word of it. Dr. Jack was likeable but more of a wolf in sheep's clothing. While you were sleeping, Drew and Jack started talking. I don't know why, but I whispered in your ear who I was and who you were. I even mentioned Titanuus and said the name Ruger Slade." She looked up and shook her head. "It was all a bunch of senseless babble. The kind of babble that Drew and Jack didn't like."

"'Let's not irritate him,' Jack had said. 'He's prone to violence when he wakes. But he is doing fine. You can see the IVs and monitors. I promise, he's getting the best care he can get.' Well, I insisted on giving you a kiss before he hauled me a way. When I did, I placed that picture you gave him in his hand. You know, the crest of the lion's head with the wings." Her eyes searched Abraham's. "You swallowed the note up in that big palm. They didn't see a thing. I knew something was brewing."

"Wow," he said in a low voice.

"After that, I didn't overdo it. I said what any naïve woman would say. 'Let me know if he wakes up. Keep me posted.' You know." She shrugged. "Jack said he'd have me over again. He hoped that my presence might be helpful and perhaps, if you woke up and behaved, I could visit again. But he was very specific when he said, 'Don't tell anyone about this place.' I agreed, and Drew and I left. I was careful to thank him all over."

Abraham scratched the scruffy hairs on his chin. "I don't know what to say, Mandi. I can't believe that you did all of that for me. I don't understand why."

"A man should never ask why a woman loves him. He should only accept it."

He nodded, reached into the cooler, and grabbed a canister of cashews. "Mmm, Planters. The best. No peanuts in Titanuus either."

"You really speak like you are fond of that place. Is it better than here?"

"Sort of," he said. He stuffed in a handful of salty cashews. "Then what happened?"

She leaned back into the sofa and said, "Everything pretty much went back to normal. I tried to not overthink it and checked in with Drew from time to time. We went to the movies… twice."

"I see, and…?"

"He only got to second base."

"No, not that part."

"Oh, well then. Per the routine, me, Mom, and Herb were closing the Grill. You showed up, drenched by rain, wearing hospital garb. Except it wasn't you—it was Ruger. I knew it when he said, 'Take me home to Titanuus.' We've been on the run ever since."

CHAPTER 6

Abraham combed his fingers through his hair. "Man, that's a whale of a story."

"What do you mean? It's no bigger than yours."

"I know that. It's just…" He gave her a blank stare. "I'm not crazy, am I? All of this? Me… you?"

"Don't start riding the crazy train now," she said with a huff. She got up and paced around the sofa, making the boards creak underneath her feet. "Because if you're crazy, then I'm crazy too."

"So, you really do believe this?"

"Well, the Titanuus story is a tough sell, but Ruger did a fair job convincing me of that."

"You talked with him? He can speak?"

"Turns out he's a pretty sharp fella. He picked up our lingo while he was in the facility. It seems that Dr. Jack spent a lot of time with him. He learned enough about how everything works and managed his escape." She stopped in front of the fire. "He called it playing possum."

Of course Ruger would be able to figure out the language the same way that Abraham had quickly picked up the words of Titanuus. *Man, this all better not be a part of my imagination. I can't be crazy.* "Tell me more about being on the run."

"I don't know how Ruger slipped from the facility, but I knew that they'd be looking for him and eventually come to me. I decided to skedaddle. Ruger was reluctant. All he wanted to do was get back to Titanuus. I didn't know the way, but I let him know that you were working on it on your end. He's working on it on his end. So we headed down the road. I told Herb and Martha not to say a word about it, that I'd be back to keep up appearances. But we've been staying here for the past few days."

Abraham dusted the salt off his hands and said, "Tell me more about Ruger. What is he like?"

"Determined. There is a restlessness in his eyes," she said, "but he's confident and in complete control." She sat back down beside Abraham. Her fireplace-warmed thigh rubbed against his. "I can see who is who by the eyes. And tell by your mannerisms. That's how I knew it was you. The funny thing is that I feel as safe with you as I do him."

"He made you feel safe?"

"Yeah. It was like being with the perfect gentleman but one that could really kick ass if need be. He can do things, or at least he can do things with that body that I never imagined."

"I thought you said you didn't sleep with him?"

She pushed his shoulder. "That's not what I mean. Something tells me that he wouldn't have me anyway. Like I said, he's a straight shooter."

"Well, I think I can understand why he would resist. In his world, he was the Guardian Commander. They were knights who lived by the highest standards. A code." He rubbed her thigh. "Don't feel bad. He's already committed."

"He has a wife? Have you been sleeping with his wife?" She looked appalled.

"Well, you have to keep up appearances."

She playfully shoved him. "You pig."

"I'm only kidding. He's not married, but it's still complicated. As it turns out, he has an illegitimate daughter with Queen Clarann." Abraham gave a quick account of the who's who and what's what, bringing Mandi up to speed on the Henchmen and King Hector's family. "Needless to say, that puts me in a fine predicament as well. It's one more complicated thing after the other."

Mandi buried her pretty face in her hands and moaned. "This is better than anything that I could have imagined." She looked at him. "So what are you going to do? What are we going to do?"

"Somebody has to know something, and my guess is that it's Eugene Drisk. You said that you saw something about him? What did you see?"

"I did what you asked, including taking flowers to Jan and Jake at the cemetery. It's a very pretty place and well taken care of. There were some fresh flowers still there."

Abraham's throat tightened. He hadn't given them a thought since he'd arrived back home. He'd been too wrapped up in himself. He wiped his eyes. "Thanks."

"It's okay." She squeezed his hand. "They would understand what you are going through. I'm sure of it."

"I feel guilty for not feeling guilty. I'm so used to carrying all of that guilt. Now, I carry other problems. My own."

"You can't feel guilty. That plane accident wasn't your fault. They are in Heaven, right? They are better off."

He nodded. "I know." Then he sobbed.

Mandi wrapped him up in a hug and stroked his hair. "It's okay, Abraham. You're allowed to let go."

He took a breath and broke off the embrace. "Not yet. I'm not ready. Tell me more about Eugene Drisk."

"I found microfiche of the old newspapers that talked about his appearance. He vanished without a trace. Anyway, I have another cousin in Washington, DC, named Sid. She used to be in the FBI. I asked her to look into it. She's really cool and has a bounty-hunter business. Anyway, she set me up with a man that writes a magazine called *Nightfall DC*. I think his name is Russ. Believe it or not, he had an article mentioning Eugene Drisk. The lost man suddenly reappeared, along with a few other sightings, only to disappear again."

"Do you have a copy of it?" he asked.

"No, it was on the web when I looked. I'd try now, but I don't want to use my phone. I've been keeping it off. For protection."

"Good thinking. But I'm not so sure that keeping your phone off will eliminate any tracking. Did you bring it with you?"

"Well, yeah. In case of emergencies. But I've been careful. And if they would have found us, they would have done so by now." She winked at him. "See, I'm careful. Besides, I don't think you can get a signal down in this river valley."

"I hope you're right." He sank into the couch and stared into the fire. "Would it be bad if I told you that I'd rather live in Titanuus?"

"No." Mandi snuggled her cheek against his shoulder. "Not as long as I can go."

"Mandi, you're something."

"I know."

Abraham's ears caught the sound of tires rolling over a gravel road. He sat up straight.

"What is it?" she asked.

"Someone is coming." He moved to the front-window curtains and peeked through.

Bright halogen headlights shined at the dingy windows.

"Devil's donuts. I think they found us."

CHAPTER 7

MANDI LOOKED THROUGH THE OTHER side of the window and said, "That's Drew. He's got a ball cap on, but it's him."

A man with rugged good looks, a black ball cap, and a caterpillar moustache exited a black Humvee.

Colonel Dexter was dressed in blue jeans and an army-green hoodie. A semiautomatic pistol was strapped on his hip. He walked slowly toward the cabin with an air of confidence in his stride.

"Come here," Abraham said as he walked back to the fire. He wrapped his arms around Mandi and kissed her head. "You've been great, but I'm not going to let you endanger yourself over me. But I want you to listen."

With her face buried in his chest, she nodded.

Quickly, he told her everything pertinent that he could remember about Titanuus. He explained about the Crown of Stones and their quest to obtain all the gems. He mentioned the death of Arcayis the Underlord. "Look into a man named Edgar Gravely from Queens. He had palsy, but now in Titanuus, he's a horned halfling that calls himself Big Apple. He doesn't want to leave, and I think he wants to stop us. I've got to track him down next."

"Why are you telling me this?"

"In case I flash back to Titanuus, you need to fill Ruger in if you can. Every bit helps, but most of all, I think Eugene Drisk is the key."

"I'll keep looking," she said.

Drew Dexter knocked on the door and said in his deep voice, "Mandi, I know you are in there. I tracked your phone."

Whispering to Abraham, she said, "I would've sworn they couldn't do that. I'm sorry."

"It's okay. Just ask him what he wants."

She nodded. "What do you want, Drew? Why are you stalking me?"

"I'm not stalking you. I'm worried. So are Herb and Martha. You are running around with a schizophrenic, you know."

"What I do in my personal time is my business, not yours," she halfway yelled. "Just go away, or I'll have *you* charged with stalking."

Abraham heard the porch boards groan when Drew moved toward the window. The hairs on his neck stood on end, and the tips of his fingers tingled. *He's not alone. I can feel it in my bones.* He rolled his hand, motioning for her to keep talking.

With her hands jammed in her back pockets, she said, "Uh, why don't you go away, Drew! I need some time to think."

"Is Abraham in there with you? I need to know that you are all right. How do I know that you are safe?"

"Don't I sound safe?" she fired back and shrugged at Abraham.

He whispered in her ear. "If anything happens, let them think I'm Ruger and not Abraham. Okay?"

Mandi nodded. "Just so you know, after this, I'm not going on any more dates with you. And I don't like your moustache either! It's creepy!"

Abraham peeked through the window curtains in the back of the cabin. The wind swayed the trees, and snow swirled off the roof. He crept back over to the front door. The floorboards groaned.

Drew called out from the other side of the door. "Mandi! Are you okay? Is he armed?"

"No! He's sleeping."

Abraham shrugged at her.

She shrugged back.

He tiptoed back to the couch and lay down.

"Don't lie to me," Drew said. "This is a potentially dangerous situation, and we can't afford to play any games."

"I'm not playing games. Fine! I'll let you in, but don't do anything stupid. And you better be alone," she said.

"I'm alone," Drew replied.

"You better be," she said.

Abraham heard her footsteps walking over to the door. The door opened. A heavier person walked inside, bringing cold air with him. The door closed.

"Will you put that gun away?" Mandi said. "He's asleep or catatonic. I don't know. He went blank yesterday and hasn't moved sense."

Abraham let his body relax, but he could hear everything around him. Colonel Drew's footsteps were a dead giveaway to his location. The man bumped into the coffee table as well, and the legs scraped over the floor.

"I said put the gun away," she repeated.

"No can do," Drew said. "This old fox caught the guards in the facility with their pants down more than once using this act. He's not going to fool me." Drew spoke louder. "And just so you know… Try anything clever, Mr. Jenkins, I have over two dozen men outside, waiting on you."

"You liar," Mandi said.

"Ah, come on, you knew that I was lying. Here, take these flexicuffs and bind his wrists and ankles together."

"What?" she said. "I'm not doing that. Look, he hasn't broken any laws. The only thing he is guilty of is being in a coma."

"No, he's guilty of being crazy. He's a danger to society. There are a whole bunch of people running around with these delusional fantasies. Dr. Jack is trying to cure them." Drew cleared his throat. "Trust the process."

"You trust the process. I'm not binding up my friend."

"Listen, Mandi, you are already looking at criminal charges: aiding and abetting a fugitive as well as a psychopath. This is the moment where you need to earn our trust and help out."

"Well, I'm not doing it."

"Fine, I'll just shoot him," Drew said.

"Nooo," she pleaded.

"Relax. It's a tranquilizer gun. But it has enough juice to take down an elephant… or two. This Abraham is really something, I've seen the video. Really something."

Something buzzed.

"Hold on," Drew said. "I need to take this."

"How'd you get a signal?" she asked.

"I'm Army. We always get a signal," Drew said. "Colonel Dexter here. Yes, we have him in custody. Uh-huh. He's catatonic again. Uh-huh. The area is all secure. Uh-huh. Got it."

Abraham could visualize Drew sliding the phone into his jeans pocket.

"What did he say?" Mandi asked.

"He said don't take any chances. Trank him and bind him with all that I got." Colonel Dexter charged the slide on his gun. "Sweet dreams, Abraham Jenkins, or whoever the hell you are."

CHAPTER 8

Abraham kicked where he heard the weapon being charged. He opened his eyes in time to see the gun sailing out of Drew's hand.

Drew threw a punch at Abraham.

Abraham slid his head aside and sank his fist deep into the colonel's stomach.

Colonel Drew let out a *woof* and sagged to the floor, holding his belly.

"Cuff him," he said to Mandi.

"Gladly." She secured Drew's wrists and ankles with the flexicuffs in a matter of seconds.

"You're pretty quick with those things," Abraham said as he hauled the man up onto the couch. "Why do I get the feeling that you've used those things before?"

"I'm a sorority girl. I'm sworn to secrecy, so I'll only kiss but never tell." She winked at him and picked up the gun. "What do you want me to do with this?"

"You mean you don't already know?" he said sarcastically.

"Oh, okay."

She pointed it at Drew, whose eyes turned as big as saucers. She shot him in the chest. Drew's eyes bugged out, rolled up, and showed their whites. He wilted on the sofa like a leaf.

"Nooo!" Abraham grabbed the gun out of her hand. "Are you crazy? I was joking around. You know, the sorority thing?"

"I wasn't joking about that! And you shouldn't have joked about shooting him with the gun."

"I didn't say shoot him with a trank gun. Man, who are you? Mad Mandi?"

"Thanks—not very nice."

"Sorry." He opened Drew's eyelids, and only the whites showed. "I hope his heart can take it, because he's going to be out for a while." He plucked the dart out of Drew's chest and held it out for Mandi. "Care for a souvenir to show your sisters, or would you rather scalp him?"

"Ha ha," she said dryly. "I don't see what the big deal is. He had it coming."

"True, but I wanted to question him. He knows stuff. I need those answers." He went over to peek out the windows. He didn't see anyone else. "We need to move. They'll be expecting us to come out soon."

"How are we going to pull that off?"

Abraham started taking off his shirt. "He's about my size. We'll switch clothes."

"Uh, a little hard to do since I cuffed him," she replied. She searched Drew's belt. "Never mind—he's got a knife and, it appears, plenty of cuffs. Army man is well prepared." She started stripping him down.

Abraham slipped into the man's hoodie and placed the black ball cap on his head. "I've got everything but the moustache."

"Yeah, let's leave that in the seventies, where Ron Burgundy left it," she replied as he fitted Drew into Abraham's clothing and cuffed him up. She clasped the man's face in her hands and stared at his sagging face. "Stay classy."

Abraham picked the man up and slung him like a carpet over his shoulder. "Grab his phone. And the cooler. We can't leave Little Debbie behind."

"Of course not."

Abraham kept his head down, opened the door, and headed outside while holding the gun on Mandi. The icy wind stirred up flecks of snow and chilled his face. With frosty breath, they crossed the headlights, and she got into the passenger side of the Humvee. He loaded Drew through the back doors and hopped into the driver's seat. He closed the door and turned over the engine. The Humvee rumbled to life.

"I haven't driven in a while. You might want to buckle up."

She clicked her seat belt in place and said, "Just don't go catatonic on me again. Please."

"We'll switch the first chance that we get. You might want to pray in the meantime."

"So where are we going?"

"Back toward the facility. At least, that's what I want them to think."

He put the car in drive and backed up. He turned the wheel and headed back up the gravel road. As he sped his way up the hairpin turns that led out of the river valley, they zoomed by several Jeeps pulled alongside the narrow road. He didn't slow or look at any over them.

"I want to see if they follow," he said.

"You're the boss."

"No, I'm the leader of the Henchmen."

They hit the main roads several minutes later. A train of black Jeeps followed them as far as the interstate ramps and then started to splinter off. One Jeep sped past them. Abraham flashed his lights at them, and the Jeep moved on.

He checked the rearview mirror. "It doesn't look like we are taking a full escort back to Facility 117. It's just us."

Mandi leaned her chair back and closed her eyes. "I hope so."

He glanced at her. She was as pretty as an angel, with her hair cascading onto the shoulders of her creamy white sweater. With her full lips barely pursed, she couldn't have been more beautiful.

A few more minutes into the drive, she began to whistle softly through her nose. Abraham turned on the radio. The sad whine of a saxophone played.

"Really? The first song I've heard in months, and they're playing Seger again."

Directions to Facility 117 were already locked into the Humvee's navigation system. He drove down the interstate exit ramp that was a few miles away from the road leading to the facility. He woke up Mandi. Her head was propped up against the window.

Stretching her arms, she asked, "Where are we?"

"Near the facility," he said.

"Now what?"

"We need to ditch the phones and find another car. There's a mini-mart up the road. We can make the swap there."

She yawned. "Okay, but I'm not very keen on ditching my phone."

"It's either that or I ditch you." He shrugged. "Sorry."

"No one ditches me. Besides, we can get a burner phone in the store. I have cash." From her back jeans pocket, she took her phone, in a sparkling pink jewel case. "Let me check and see if I have any messages."

Abraham drove down the road.

"Oh!" she said, excited.

"What?"

"It's from my cousin, Sid. She said they found Eugene Drisk!"

"No way."

Mandi held the phone in front of his face, showing a picture of Eugene Drisk sitting at a bar. "Is that him?"

Abraham nodded. "Way."

CHAPTER 9

ABRAHAM WAS RIDING IN THE back seat of a shiny sea-green Cadillac Coupe DeVille. An older couple sat in the front. Abraham and Mandi had met the couple in the Mini-Mart Gas and Go. The old man driving had recognized Abraham. He was from Pittsburgh, and they were returning there from a trip in Florida.

Miles and Carla were the names of the old couple. They played gospel music, sang along, and hummed as the Cadillac floated over the highway ten miles an hour under the speed limit. The trip with the older couple made for an ideal cover. No one stopped them along the way.

"You know, I never believed a word about you being at fault in that plane accident," Miles said. He had a full head of hair, neatly cut and swept over to one side. He'd look in the rearview mirror when he talked. "You were one of the good guys. Real good. I can't wait to tell my pals that Jenkins the Jet rode in my car."

In the passenger seat, Carla was knitting. "The papers say the most awful things about people." Her cotton top had a blue sheen that seemed to reflect the ocean-blue dashboard and upholstery. "You can't believe hardly any of it. We hardly read it anymore." Her glasses on the rim of her nose, she asked, "So, tell me, how long have the two of you been a couple? Are you engaged?"

"No, we just started a new relationship," Mandi said. She was cozied up to Abraham with her head on his shoulder. "But it's looking more promising by the day."

"That's nice to hear. You know, Abraham," Carla said. "This is a nice place to pop the question. This is where Miles asked me, some twenty-five years ago."

"You mean you haven't been married longer?" Abraham said.

"We were both widowers," Miles fired back. "We met at my wife's funeral. But it's not weird. They were distant cousins, second cousins, I believe. I never thought I'd fall in love again, especially at my wife's funeral. Heh heh. But it happened. The Lord works in mysterious ways." He leaned over and tried to kiss her.

Carla shoved him back. "Will you watch the road, you silly goose? You're gonna wreck us."

Mandi leaned forward. "We can't thank you enough for giving us a lift. When the ol' Hummer broke down, I thought we were screwed."

Carla stopped knitting.

Mandi continued. "Sorry. But we really needed to make the trip, because the wedding is tomorrow and I'm running kind of late. I was supposed to be there yesterday, but we lost our luggage at the airport check-in, and well, it's been a mess ever since."

"I see," Carla said.

Mandi gave a frozen grin and shrugged. Abraham tipped his chin. They were lying about everything, but what else were they supposed to do? They needed to find answers. The hard part had been abandoning Colonel Drew Dexter in the Humvee. Mandi assured Abraham that it wouldn't be long before his people found him. Abraham agreed. He had enough to worry about, let alone one of the bad guys.

"Only thirty miles to the Fort Pitt Tunnel," Miles said cheerfully. "You know, when I was young, I'd sit in the back seat of my parents' car with my girlfriend, and we'd kiss the entire way through. We called it the Love Tunnel." He looked in the mirror and shrugged his brows and winked.

"You never told me that," Carla said.

"Well, you never asked," Miles replied.

"A fine time to bring it up in front of company. You could have prepared me for it," Carla said in a bickering tone. "That's embarrassing."

"Embarrassing. This coming from a woman that made out with me at my wife's funeral."

Carla gasped and stuck him with a needle.

"Ow!" he said. "Take it easy. I'm driving."

As Miles and Carla bickered, Mandi gently took Abraham by the chin and said, "Are you okay? You looked like you saw a ghost."

"No, but my friend, Solomon Paige, the one that looks like Bigfoot, well, he transformed when he passed through the Fort Pitt Tunnel." He shifted in his seat. "Needless to say, it's in the wee hours of the morning, and hardly a car is on the road. Pretty weird that we have old folks driving us too."

"We are night birds," Miles said. He tapped his ear, where a hearing aid sat. "Less traffic on the road. Great for travel, and we sleep a lot in the day. I hate traffic. Carla hates it more."

Abraham and Mandi exchanged a surprised glance.

"Shame on you for eavesdropping, Miles," Carla said as she gave him another poke with her needle. "That's rude. It's rude to them, and worse, it's rude to me 'cause you weren't listening again."

"Sorry, folks. But these hearing aids are great. They take the ringing out of my ears, and I can hear all the sounds of music. All thanks to the VA." Miles grinned in the rearview mirror. "Your time will come. You need them. So, Abraham, do tunnels make you nervous? I only heard part of it."

"I guess you could say that."

"Well, do what I would do if I had a pretty lady in the back seat like that. Make out from start to finish."

"I'm going to throttle you when we get home," Carla said to Miles. Her needles resumed their clicking.

"Thanks for the advice," Abraham said. He pinched his nose as he saw the sign for the Fort Pitt Tunnel, which was only five miles away. His head started splitting.

"Oh no," he muttered.

"What is it?" Mandi asked.

"I'm feeling it again."

"Don't look at it. Just lay down in my lap."

He did so.

"Say, that's a nice move," Miles said. "Ow! Stop doing that."

Mandi ran her fingers through his hair. She gave him a warm smile. "It's going to be all right. You're with me."

He held her hand in his sweaty grip. "I hope you are right."

"I'm a woman. I'm always right." She kissed him full on the lips just as the Fort Pitt Tunnel swallowed them whole.

CHAPTER 10

Abraham and Mandi walked through the busy streets of Pittsburgh, trying to find a hotel. They parted pleasantly with Miles and Carla, both of whom gave them a long and loving embrace.

"The two of you should get married next," Carla said with a tear in her eye. "I have a good feeling about you. Enjoy the wedding."

Mandi secured a room with the help of her cousin Sid. With Sid's direction, she'd acquired paid credit cards and a burner phone with the cash she had. Now, they were secure in a nice hotel room that had a nice view of the three rivers.

Abraham took a shower and cleaned himself up while Mandi went out and purchased new clothing. Inside the steamy bathroom, he wiped the mirror with a towel. Bruises, cuts, and scrapes decorated his body, but otherwise, he was in pretty good shape.

He nodded. "Not bad. I might not be Ruger, but I still have something going on."

He threw a terry cloth robe on and sat down on the bed. Dirt was still underneath his fingernails. The television was on, and a group of men and an attractive woman were talking about Pirates baseball.

He found the remote on the nightstand and turned it off. "I don't even want to know."

Abraham flopped back on the lone king-size bed and stared at the ceiling. "How long is this going to last?"

A chill went through his bones. The last few times, his encounters back home hadn't lasted very long. This one was going on two days. He expected to be zapped back to Titanuus at any moment. However, no pain was brewing inside his skull. This was, for the first time in as long as he could remember, normal.

He continued talking to himself. "Don't get caught up in it, Abraham. This might be real for now, but it won't stay real." He sat up and looked out the window at a perfect view of PNC Park. "Ah man, I must be dreaming. This is all so twisted."

Seeing the ballpark left an emptiness inside him, a void that could not be filled. He thought of Buddy Parker. His close friend and teammate had never gotten to see the field again. The airplane crash took that all away from the man. It had taken everything away from Abraham too.

"I don't belong here," he mumbled as he shut the curtains. "Why did I even come here?"

He knew why. They needed to find Eugene Drisk. The professor would have answers. He had to know the truth.

The hotel room door opened. Mandi entered, carrying a couple of shopping bags. She'd changed into a new pair of blue jeans and wore a Steelers jersey fit for a woman with the number fifty-eight.

"I don't think Jack Lambert ever looked that good in his jersey," he said.

"Who?" She looked down at her chest. "Oh, this. I just bought it because it was on sale."

"A Lambert jersey on sale, here?" He shook his head. "It must be a knockoff."

"Maybe." She shrugged and tossed the bags on the bed. "So how are you doing?" She caressed his face with her hand, rose up on tiptoe, and kissed his cheek. "You look good, all cleaned up."

He combed his fingers through his beard. "I was gonna shave but thought I might be recognized. So I didn't bother."

"Well, it's pretty scraggly. A trim wouldn't hurt. I can do that if you like."

He shrugged.

"I'll take that as a yes. Have a seat on the bed." She headed to the bathroom. "Are you okay?"

"I don't feel right being back here. You know, lots of memories. I upset a lot of people."

"I think they'd be over it by now." She had a small pair of scissors in her hand. She dragged over a chair from the small desk, placed it in front of him, and sat down. "People will get over it."

"Not in Pittsburgh. They don't forget, trust me. There were some pretty angry people out there."

Mandi started trimming his beard. "I'm sorry for how you feel. It's not fair."

"What's the plan? Any word from your cousin?"

"Yeah. Her contact got a hold of me. Russ. He said that Eugene hangs out at a place called the Yard." She flicked Abraham's hairs into a wastebasket.

"Wait, we're tracking him down at a bar? Don't we have a home address?"

"Yes, I have that too. But it's a high-rise. Decent security. I don't think we could barge in there if we wanted to." She cut off another section of beard. "You're looking even better. I like it."

"Don't take off too much. I don't want to be recognized."

"Do you really think they'll remember?"

"Trust me—they remember. I've signed thousands of autographs in this town."

"True, but there are millions of people."

"Yeah, millions of people with television."

She straddled one of his legs and started cutting some more. Her perfume smelled great.

"We can play this however you want to," she said. "I'm here to help. I thought it would be best to catch him, you know, by surprise."

Abraham had been on plenty of dangerous missions on Titanuus, and he thought this one should be a piece of cake. He didn't want to lose any time either. There was always a chance that he'd zip back to Titanuus. He couldn't let that happen without more answers about how to stay back home. This time, he'd be sure that Eugene Drisk didn't slip through his fingers.

"What are you going to do if I turn back into Ruger?" he asked. "You know it will happen."

"Maybe it won't. But he seems to understand what to do. I guess I'll hope for the best," she said with a no-look smile.

His current situation seemed to be working out too perfectly. Perhaps Dr. Jack had been right. Things worked out the way he wanted because he imagined them. Abraham was living in a fantasy world he had created. It was either that or reality. He worried that he couldn't tell which was which.

"This is crazy," he said.

Mandi lifted his chin and met his eyes with hers. "Hey, now is not the time to doubt. I believe in you. You have to believe in yourself."

He nodded. "Death before failure."

"Huh?"

"It's something that we say. You know, the Henchmen."

"Interesting. Sounds like a really fun place to be." She brushed fingers over his beard. "Think that will do it." She put all her weight on his knee. "Don't you run away yet. Let me ask you something."

"Sure."

She looked deep into his eyes. "Would you rather be stuck here or there?"

Abraham started to say "here," but that would have been a lie. He liked Titanuus and who he'd become. A fresh start might have been just what he needed, and he got off on it.

"Honestly, I think I like it there better."

Mandi frowned as she rose up from his knee. "I guess it's true what they say."

"What's that?"

"The truth hurts." She walked away and shut herself in the bathroom.

CHAPTER 11

ABRAHAM AND MANDI WERE SITTING at a booth in a large microbrewery restaurant called the Yard. The large sports bar offered plenty of seating and had a very long L-shaped bar front with scores of tall stools. Flat-screen televisions could be clearly seen from any angle. Sporting events filled all the screens. The time was after five o'clock, and the robust restaurant, which smelled like beer and buffalo wings, was filling up fast.

"Come on, Mandi. You can't be mad at me for being honest. Besides, you said you would want to come to Titanuus," Abraham said.

She was giving him the cold shoulder since they'd talked in the hotel. Her words with him were short but not sweet.

"Would you rather that I lied?"

"Yes, Honest Abe. I would have." She sipped on her mug of an amber-colored beer. "Will you drop it? I'll get over it. I always do."

A waitress wearing a zebra-striped apron set down a mixer of appetizers on the table. "Can I get you anything else?" she asked in a perky voice as her stare hung on his eyes.

He lowered the bill on his Steelers cap and said, "No, this will do."

"I'll bring you both your free round in a bit. Just raise your little Pirate flag on the table up if you need me." The waitress vanished into the tables.

He reached over and covered Mandi's palm with his hand. "Do you know that feeling you get when you get back home after a long vacation? You make it back from a long trip, and you are so relieved to be back home and in your bed."

Mandi barely looked at him and nodded.

"Well, when I come back home, I don't get that at all. My bed in Titanuus is more comfortable than my bed here. I know that sounds strange, but it's true. And I'm sorry."

"Just stop apologizing. I understand. I can't help it if I want you to myself. I think if you gave it a chance, we could have a good life here together."

"I'm not in any kind of position to commit to anything now. You know that."

She pulled her hand out from underneath his and said, "Sure."

"Well, what do you want to do? Go to Vegas and get married?"

She shrugged her eyebrows.

"Wow." He slumped back in the booth.

His problems in both worlds continued to mount. Mandi was beginning to complicate things. *Maybe I need to cut her loose. Keep her out of danger. It's the best thing to do in the long run. Especially if I'm nuts.* He glanced over her inviting features. *Besides, she's too hot to be this helpful.*

Mandi kicked his shin.

He sat up straight. "That's fine. Let it out."

"No, you dope. Look. That dude taking a seat at the bar." She had her eyes locked on a man wearing an oversized beige overcoat. "Isn't that Eugene?"

Abraham recognized the shabby man from his encounter in the East River Mountain Tunnel from what must have been months before. Eugene had thinning hair on his balding head. The remaining locks were stringy. He had a pronounced nose for a small man. He hunched over the bar and raised his hand, and the bartender brought him a mug of dark beer.

"That's him," Abraham said.

Mandi started up out of her seat and said, "I'll feel him out."

"No, stay put. I made it this close, so I'm not going to miss out on the opportunity." He got up and beat another man to the stool beside Eugene.

Eugene's big eyes were glued to the television screen. He stuck his lips out and sucked on his beer. His hand trembled when he drank.

"Do you have any money on the game?" Abraham asked politely.

Without looking at him, Eugene said in a condescending tone, "No. Betting is for fools."

With the crowds whistling and cheering at the television screens, he said, "It looks like you are in the company of fools."

"Yes, well, it's been that way all of my life." Eugene turned his back farther toward Abraham. "It seems this moment is no different."

"You know, I'm a betting man, and I'd be curious to get your take on this game. Just for kicks, who do you like? The Penguins or the Brewers?"

"There are hundreds of people in the room. Why don't you ask them?" Eugene swallowed a couple more gulps of beer. "What are you, one of those vagrants looking a free drink? I say hit the road. They don't take kindly to your ilk here."

"Sorry, old dude, I was just making conversation."

Eugene shuddered inside his overcoat. He clenched a fist, took a deep breath, and sighed. "Mister, will you please leave me be? I'm not bothering you, so don't you bother me."

"I'm not from around here. I only wanted to make conversation. I just thought an elder like you would be more hospitable," Abraham said.

"Oh lord, you're one of those obnoxious Canadians, aren't you? Coming down here to gloat over some ancient Stanley Cup string of victories."

"I'm not Canadian, but you have some respectable knowledge of the sport." He glanced at his booth and found Mandi was gone. He scanned the room but didn't see her anywhere. *Crap.* "Look more like the academic type. Perhaps, back in your day, you played the very dangerous sport of ice hockey."

"Hockey, dangerous? Pah. If you think hockey is dangerous, then you don't know what danger is. Trust me."

"I guess you're right. But hey, I got you to make some conversation, didn't I?" He chuckled and gave Eugene a hearty slap on the back, knocking the older man toward the bar. "Where I come from, we are people's people."

Eugene shrugged in his coat. "Fine! If you are dying for me to ask, I'll ask. Where are you from?"

"Titanuus."

Eugene set his beer down, turned, and faced Abraham. His eyes filled with recognition. He leaned toward Abraham. "I'll be. It's you. Or is it?"

CHAPTER 12

"No, it's me, Abraham Jenkins," he answered. "The real one." He laid a heavy hand on Eugene's shoulder and squeezed. "I've come a long way. We need to talk."

"Talk about what? You're back, right? Consider yourself lucky. I was stuck in the hellish place for years." Eugene made a bitter face. "It was one insane mission after the other. More treachery afoot than a pirate's ship. No, you consider yourself lucky that you found a portal. Even in ol' Ruger's body, eventually the place would become insufferable." He hoisted his glass. "Here's to you!"

Abraham gave Eugene a doubting look as he clicked mugs with him. The older scholar hadn't reacted the way he'd expected.

"You really thought Titanuus was that bad?"

"All of the fighting and killing? Me? As you can see, I was never built for that. I'm an academic." Eugene's eyes brightened. "But being so youthful and vibrant wasn't without its benefits." A goofy smile crossed his wizened face. He licked his lips. "So tell me, how are my triplets?"

"They are living like queens in the Stronghold."

Eugene poked him in the chest. "So, I imagine that you've taken full advantage of their erotic abilities."

"No."

Leaning away, Eugene lifted an eyebrow and said, "What happened? Did Ruger become impotent?"

"No, he's fine in that department."

Rubbing his saggy chin, Eugene said, "Oh, I see. You courted with another one of the Henchmen. Sticks, aye?" He tapped on Abraham's ribs with his fist. "Yes, I can see in your eyes that you did. She's a raw gal, isn't she, with a smile like a fish."

"I'd rather not talk about it." Abraham set down his mug. "Look, we need to talk about more serious business."

Mandi cozied up to his side and hooked his arm. "Am I interrupting anything?"

Eugene seized her hand in his and said, "No, not at all, you lovely vision." He winked at Abraham. "It didn't take you long to get back on track, did it?" He gave her hand an awkward smooch. "Well done, young man."

Mandi pulled her hand away and wiped it off with a napkin.

"Eugene, this is Mandi."

The older man nodded and asked, "Does she know?"

"Yes."

Eugene searched her eyes with a penetrating stare. "And you believe your friend, about Titanuus?"

She gave a little shrug and said, "I wouldn't be here if I didn't."

"Fascinating. You found yourself a keeper." Eugene took out a handkerchief and blew his nose. "So, what is the problem? Why did you seek me out? Better yet, how did you find me?" He rose up in his chair and scanned the crowd. "I'm very discreet."

The crowd let out a roar. The Penguins had scored a goal.

"I need to understand what is going on." Abraham leaned toward Eugene and spoke over the riled-up people. "You see, I keep going back and forth between worlds."

"You mean through a portal? You've seen more than one?"

"No, not a portal. I fall asleep or get a bad headache, and I bounce between one world and another. I need to find a way back. And there are others like us back there."

Eugene tucked his handkerchief away and said, "This is very interesting. You really didn't see a portal?"

"He said he didn't," Mandi said.

"No need to be snippy, my raven-haired goddess." Eugene rubbed his jaw and stared at the ceiling. "You know, you really caught me off guard. I thought I was finished with the entire matter. Your appearance is quite distressing."

"Why don't we start at the beginning? These portals—are they some sort of experiment? Were you a part of it?" Abraham asked.

Eugene's head dipped down to his chest, and he sighed. "Well, I guess it won't hurt to tell you who I am. I'm a scientist. I was a tenured one at Carnegie Mellon. A very prestigious position. I was part of a team that did research and experimentation aimed at discovering other dimensions. Purely fantasy, and I thought it was a joke when I was assigned to it, but the work proved to be fascinating. The theory, so to speak, grew on me."

"So you opened a portal? Titanuus *is* real?" he asked.

"Oh yes, it's as real as this place or any other," Eugene admitted. "But the problem is that once the portal opened, we didn't have any control of it. And like those ancient *Stargate* theories that we studied, this portal was different. It moved but seemed to like tunnels."

Abraham leaned back against the bar. Eugene had given him an answer that he needed. He felt a tiny bit of relief. His concerns about being crazy faded.

A waitress walked up to Mandi and handed her a strawberry daiquiri.

Mandi looked puzzled and said, "I didn't order this."

"No, that group of guys in the corner booth did," the waitress said. "Here is one of their numbers."

A bunch of young men with preppy haircuts, wearing Pittsburgh sports regalia, waved at Mandi. One of them winked at her.

"What a bunch of douchebags." She handed the drink back to the waitress and said, "Take it away." She held up the napkin with the number on it so that the young men could see then ripped it up.

"It's mating season in here sometimes, but I can't blame them for showing you attention," Eugene said as he slid out of his chair. "I need to excuse myself. This old bladder doesn't hold up for days like the one in Titanuus did. More like minutes, and the first beer runs through me." He patted Abraham on the shoulder. "Now, don't go anywhere. I'll be right back." He teetered away.

"What do you think?" Mandi said as she watched Eugene head toward the bathrooms.

"Pretty surprising. I thought he'd be a real jerk. I guess he's glad he's back."

"Yeah well, you should be too."

"Come on, you know this won't last," he said as he reached for her.

Mandi backed away and bumped into one of the young men who had sent her a drink. The rest of the group was standing behind him.

With an irritated stare, she said, "Pardon me."

"It's okay, gorgeous. I just wanted to come over here and give you another chance to get to know me. You see, I'm a real nice guy." The young man talking was tall, handsome, and built like a quarterback.

His friends sniggered behind him.

"I'm Colt."

"Listen, junior, I'm with someone. Go find someone else your own age." She turned her back.

Colt hooked her elbow and pulled her back. "I don't think you understand. I'm Colt. Don't you know who Colt is?"

Abraham came to his feet and stepped toe to toe with Colt. They were about the same height. The other young men with Colt were just as big and bigger.

"Back off, Colt," he said. "You're being rude."

Colt flipped Abraham's ballcap off. "Sit down, old man."

"Hey!" someone in the crowd said. "That's Abraham Jenkins!"

CHAPTER 13

The bar immediately filled with a chorus of boos and jeers, and the patrons shouted a bunch of rude comments.

"Killer!"

"Murderer!"

The list went on and on.

"It looks like you aren't a very popular guy around here," Colt said to Abraham. "What are you, some old sports jock?"

"No, that's Jenkins the Jet," said a black young man standing behind Colt. He was built like a chimney stack. "He's the one that killed Buddy Parker and his family in that crazy plane wreck. I know the Parkers."

Abraham grabbed Mandi by the arm and said, "Let's get out of here."

"What about Eugene?" she asked.

"I'll get him. Maybe there's a back door." He started to move away from Colt and his crew.

Colt stepped in his way. "Hey, we aren't finished talking yet. I still don't have the lady's name and number."

"I don't have time for this." Abraham balled up his fist.

Mandi took him by the wrist and said, "Don't you dare. You get Eugene. I can handle this." She stepped between him and Colt. "Okay, big fella. You win. Let's talk."

With trepidation stirring inside him, Abraham picked up his hat and took off to the bathroom. The crowd wasn't kind to him at all. The men, with their fists loaded with bottles of beer, wouldn't budge as he tried to push his way through them. He escaped into the bathroom hallway. A line was at the women's door, and he pushed the door into the men's.

A large stainless-steel trough for a urinal was crowded with men lined up in front of it. Three bathroom stalls were there also.

He peeked underneath the stalls and saw three different pairs of shoes. He had no idea what Eugene was wearing, but the man had said he had to pee. He knocked on each door saying, "Eugene? Eugene?"

"Wait your turn, idiot!" a man shouted from the middle stall.

"Did anyone see an old man in a beige overcoat, about yea high?" Abraham asked. "Devil's donuts, he's not in here?" He hustled out of the bathroom.

Eugene had given him the slip. *I knew he was being too nice.* He hurried down the hallway. Two college-aged goons blocked his way. They were beefier versions of Colt and built like linemen.

He stopped. "Guys, I don't have time for this. It's an emergency."

"Yeah, well, Colt and your lady aren't done talking yet. When he's done, you can go," said the black man who had spoken earlier.

"Are you guys on scholarship?"

"Yeah."

"Interesting. I'm close friends with the athletic director. I could make a call and change that scholarship situation," Abraham said.

The young men exchanged a look and stepped aside.

Abraham squirted between them and hustled over to the bar where Mandi was seated with Colt. "He slipped us."

"What?" She started out of her seat.

Colt hooked her arm. "Hey, where are you going, baby? Huh? We aren't finished talking yet."

"How about a shower, Biff?" She poured Abraham's beer over Colt's head.

Colt gawped.

Together, Abraham and Mandi raced through the spirited crowd and out the front doors.

"What are you idiots looking at?" Colt screamed. "Go get them!"

Outside, Abraham caught a glimpse of Eugene on the other side of the street. He started crossing the adjacent street. "Eugene, stop!"

Eugene looked at him, turned, and broke out into a run.

"Hey, he's moving pretty fast," Mandi said.

"You can say that again."

They ran through the slow city traffic and picked their way to the other side of the road. Small-business buildings made up block after block of the area. They chased after Eugene.

Behind them, Colt hollered after them, "You can run, but you can't hide, Rose!"

"Rose? You told him your name was Rose," Abraham said to Mandi.

"He's stupid. He bought it," she said, racing alongside Abraham with her hair trailing behind her.

Half a block away, Eugene ducked into an alley.

"There he goes," she said. "Man, we didn't even catch up with him?"

They turned into the alley and saw green dumpsters and bags of trash. A few fire escapes were anchored to the buildings on both sides. The alley dead-ended half a block up. Abraham saw no sign of Eugene.

"Oh where, oh where did that tricky fish go?" Abraham muttered.

Several back entrances to business buildings were there, but after business hours, all of them were closed.

"He could have gone into any of these doors," she said.

Security cameras were posted over the doors, and two sedans were parked in the alley.

Abraham got down on his hands and knees and looked underneath the cars. "Not here," he said as he stood up and dusted off his hands.

"Abraham, we have company," she said.

Colt and his crew entered the alley. Six of them were marching behind the young man's lead. Colt stopped twenty feet away and pointed at Abraham. Some of the others smashed their fists into their hands. All their eyes had a starry glow.

Colt said, "Now you're going to get what's coming to you, Ruger Slade."

CHAPTER 14

With chills running up his spine, Abraham asked, "What did you call me?"

"We know who you are and where you are from. Titanuus," Colt said with a darkening expression. "We are from Titanuus as well. Now trapped in this abominable world." He came closer and leered at Mandi. "But it has its perks."

Abraham stepped in front of the brood of men with his thoughts racing. "Who are you? Where are you from?"

"That's not what you need to be concerned with. Right now, your situation is, well, a lot more terminal, Blade Weaver," Colt said. "But we are otherworlders like you too."

Mandi clung to Abraham's arm and said, "I'm scared."

"It's okay," he said, backing them both up. "I'll protect you." Abraham's head was spinning at this darker twist of fate, and his heart pumped like a piston. "You guys, whatever you are, need to leave us alone. We just want Eugene."

"Yes, well, your mistake was finding him." Colt nodded his chin to one side.

His men fanned out in an arc, walling off the escape route behind them. Three of them had lengths of pipe in their hands.

"You should have behaved, Ruger. That would be best for everyone. Get him."

The thugs closed in.

Abraham stepped in front of Mandi, who started texting. He knew how to fight, but he hadn't done much fighting in his own body. Ruger had fought and made mincemeat out of some other people. Now, the time had come for Abraham to see what he could do.

"You better be glad that I don't have a sword," he said.

"It wouldn't make a difference if you did."

Abraham lifted his arms and scanned his opponents. Each and every one was as stout as a telephone pole. *I hope they can't fight as well as they look.*

The black man he'd spoken with at the bathrooms came at him first. He swung hard and heavy punches.

Abraham slipped out of reach.

"Stand still, you big chicken," the burly man said. "Redge is going to bust you up!"

Abraham punched Redge in the throat. Redge floundered backward, clutching at his throat.

The other five men came at Abraham in a rush. He dropped one man with a shot in the ribs, ducked underneath a haymaker, and dislodged the attacker's jaw with an uppercut.

A meaty fist caught him hard in the belly.

Abraham grunted and countered with a leg sweep. Three men were down on the ground. The last two on their feet plowed into him with throaty growls. He tumbled hard onto the street. They wrestled over the pavement, kicking, clawing, and throwing elbows.

He twisted a man's wrist and snapped it. The man let out a painful howl and kicked away.

A rabbit punch to the ribs crumpled another man on the pavement.

"I don't know who you guys are, but you fight like a bunch of daisies."

Abraham tore into them. His big fists broke noses and ribs. Whoever they were, they weren't like Ruger Slade or him. They were cowards trapped in the big bodies, making them ideal bullies. He beat the crap out of them and watched them limp and crawl away. Blood dripped from his swelling knuckles.

"Abraham," Mandi said desperately.

Colt had a long arm around her waist and was pointing a gun to her head.

"Help me."

"Shut up," Colt said. "Listen up. This fun is over. It's time to give yourself up. You don't want this pretty lady to get hurt, do you?"

"No." Abraham lifted his arms.

The back door of one of the cars parked in the alley popped open, and Eugene came out. "I can't believe you missed me. Interesting."

"What is going on here, Eugene? What is this all about? Who are these guys?" he asked.

"Some of my old friends from Titanuus that have proven themselves useful to our cause," Eugene replied. He walked over to Abraham with a very easy stride. "I see you are surprised that I'm not so, well, shabby as I appear. Well, when I came back, I too carried over some of the attributes of Ruger. You see, the experience has done us both very well."

Struggling in Colt's arms, Mandi said, "What kind of snake are you?"

"Why, I'm a snake that can shed his skin and grow it back again. It's something that you wouldn't understand, honey." Eugene looked at Mandi. "I really hate it when innocent people get caught up in our affairs. You made a very big mistake, young lady. You have become collateral damage. And all for what? A truck driver."

"You leave her out of this, Eugene!" he yelled.

"Sorry, but the matter is out of my hands." He looked at Redge as the big man was rubbing his throat. "Get a stun rod and some cuffs. It's high time that we fully restrained this pest."

"If you hurt her, I swear I'll tear all of you apart," he warned.

"Don't make threats that you can't back up, my good man." Eugene took out a handkerchief and blew his nose. "That will prove fatal."

"You won't kill me. I know you need me, don't you?"

"Huh..." Eugene reached over and grabbed the stun rod from Redge. He twirled it in his hand. "Yes, they do need you. Dr. Jack and the others. Yes, they need you. But I don't agree. Tell you what—I'll see to it that Mandi won't be harmed if you behave. Deal?"

"Like I can take your word for it?"

"True, but you don't have a choice," Eugene said.

"I'll be fine," Mandi said. "Don't get yourself hurt."

Redge walked behind Abraham with flexicuffs in his hands.

"What is with you guys and flex cuffs?"

Redge cuffed his wrists and ankles.

"Good." Eugene walked up to Abraham. "Now, say your goodbyes."

"I'm going to get you out of this," he said to Mandi.

Colt scoffed a laugh. "Yeah, right."

"I believe in you," she said back to Abraham.

"Smooch, smooch, smooch—isn't that nice?" Colt said, making kissy lips. "Don't worry. She'll be just fine with me. She'll come around. They always do."

Eugene hit Abraham in the gut with the stun rod.

Fire shot through Abraham's veins, and he dropped to his knees.

"You are still strong. Very strong. Let me try that again, Abraham." Eugene hit him again… and again.

Mandi screamed, "Stop it! You're killing him!"

He fell to the ground with a dark veil falling over his eyes. His heavy lids started to close. All he could see was Mandi kicking and screaming. He read Eugene's lips as well.

"Dispose of her."

Noooooooooooo!

CHAPTER 15
TITANUUS

ABRAHAM WOKE WITH A SPLITTING headache. His eyes felt as if they had sandbags on them. He scratched away the crust and opened them with his fingers. The bright sun shone into his eyes. He was lying on a bed of blankets. The sound of a rolling wagon rattled underneath him. He grabbed a hold of the side and sat up.

"Look who is awake," Vern said. The warrior was riding a horse behind the wagon. His wavy blond hair bounced on his shoulders as his puffy lips maintained a permanent sneer.

Bearclaw rode beside Vern. The broad-faced warrior with wild black hair and a thick beard eyed Abraham like a hawk.

Both men wore their black leather tunics over chain mail. Their sword belts bounced at their sides.

"Captain! You are awake!" Horace said. The beefy warrior was driving the wagon.

Sticks rode on the bench beside Horace. Her hair was tied in twin ponytails. One bandolier of knives was strapped over a shoulder. Her sword belt was full of more sharp weapons. Wearing a tight sleeveless leather jerkin over a long-sleeved cotton shirt, the expressionless woman climbed into the wagon with Abraham. "Welcome back," she said. "Did you sleep well?"

"I wouldn't say that." He rubbed his temples with his fingers. "Oh man, Mandi is in trouble. I have to get back home. Where are we? What's going on?"

"We are in Kingsland on the road to the House of Steel," she said as she handed him a water skin. "You've been catatonic for over a week. But the king just summoned us. We didn't know what to do, so we put you in the wagon."

He gulped down the water and wetted his parched lips. His stomach growled like a wolf. "I've been out that long?"

"Yes."

"Has anything else happened?"

"The barn is finished, Captain," Horace said with a look over his shoulder. "The Henchmen and Red Tunics labor in the fields. The weather has been good. The lilies bloom. The songbirds sing. I think it's the calm before the storm."

Staring out at the rolling hills and lush valleys leading toward the city of Burgess, he asked, "Why would you say that?"

"Because we are going to see the king," Horace replied.

Abraham clutched his head. He couldn't stop thinking about Mandi. She was in danger, all because of him. He had to find a way back. Looking at the supplies in the wagon, he told Sticks, "Hand me that shovel."

With a blank look, she reached over, grabbed the shovel, and dragged it scraping over the wagon bed. She put the shovel handle in his hands. "What are you going to do with a shovel?"

He wrapped his hands around the neck of the shovel and looked into the spade as he would a mirror.

Sticks tilted her head to one side and looked at the spot where he was looking.

"I need to go back home," he said. His heart started to race. All he could think about was Mandi being hauled away by Eugene and his goons. He bashed himself in the forehead with the shovel. "I need to go back home!" He did it again, popping himself hard, square in the noggin. "Now!"

Sticks jumped on the shovel and bear-hugged it. "Have you lost your mind? Who hits themselves with a shovel?"

"I do," Horace offered. "Good show, Captain."

"He's insane," Vern said. He'd moved his horse to the left side of the wagon as Bearclaw trotted up to the right. "Possessed. I told you all he's a madman."

"Give me the shovel back!" Abraham said. A trickle of blood ran down his forehead and over the bridge of his nose. "I have to get back home!"

"What is going on back home?" Sticks tried to stop the blood dripping from his forehead with the sleeve of her shirt. "You really made a fine mess of yourself. Horace, did we pack any bandages?"

"Why would we need bandages?" He looked back over his shoulder at Abraham. "Oh, that is bad. Usually Iris brings those. I told you that we should have brought her."

"Yeah, everywhere we go with him, someone ends up bleeding," Vern said. "Or dying."

Sticks glared at Vern. She whisked a dagger out of her bandolier and cut part of the sleeve off her shirt. She put the crude bandage on Abraham's head. She took his hand and slapped it over the bandage. "Keep it there. Now, explain yourself."

"I was back in my old body. Back home. Needless to say, a friend of mine is in big trouble." He studied the concerned faces of the group. "You know the person that used to host this body? Well, the other personality?"

All of them nodded.

"His name is Eugene Drisk. We tracked him down. I tried to get answers, but the weasel flipped on us." He rolled his neck. "Poor Mandi. She's not equipped for this. I have to get there now."

"Perhaps the king will have answers, Captain," Horace said. "Look ahead. The House of Steel awaits."

Abraham climbed out of the wagon bed and into the front of the wagon. He sat on the bench beside Horace, who was driving a team of two horses. Their destination was only a mile away. The House of Steel was a magnificent castle made from alabaster stone. Huge colorful flags made a ring around a humongous sword driven into the earth ages before. Legend said it was the sword of Antonugus, which slew the celestial warrior, Titanuus, the universal being that had formed the world.

"It's a beautiful thing," Horace said as he snapped the reins.

"Yes, it's quite a castle," Abraham replied.

"I'm not talking about the castle. I'm talking about that sword. I marvel."

Abraham checked the blood on his rag. He'd made quite a mess of himself. He sighed. *No more playing around. I have to get back home. And King Hector is going to help.* Another thought crossed his mind. "Ah crap."

"What's the matter, Captain?"

He put the rag back on his head. "Nothing." *Except Queen Clarann is going to be there.*

CHAPTER 16

Abraham left his accompanying Henchmen outside the castle's front gate. The King's Guardians, led by their commander, Pratt, escorted Abraham onto the castle grounds.

"What happened to your face?" the horse-necked Pratt asked. He stood half a head taller than Abraham and had shoulders as wide as a deer's rack.

"I hit it with a shovel," Abraham said dryly. He shielded his eyes from the sun, which shone off the shoulder of Pratt's full-plate armor.

"Hmm," Pratt replied. "It looks like you did a fine job if that was your intent. But you shouldn't appear marred up in the king's presence."

"Yes, well, I'll try to be better put together the next time." Abraham wasn't in the mood to chat. He had another mission. He scanned the outlying walls and windows decorating the beautiful castle and saw no sign of the queen. *I hope she isn't there. I don't want to talk about Ruger's illegitimate daughter. Oh man, what if this is what it's all about? King Hector would behead me!*

One of the other two Guardians opened a wrought-iron gate. The pathway entered a walled channel paved with decorative stones. Stairs led upward toward a terrace. The group was met at the top landing by two more Guardians standing on the other side of another iron gate. They saluted Pratt with hand chops to their temples and opened the gate.

Pratt led the way out onto the king's terrace, overlooking the Bay of Elders. They were alone. "Wait here. I'll announce you." In one stride, he took all three steps leading up onto an elevated patio and entered through the curtains there.

Abraham checked his self-inflicted head wound with his fingertips. Blood had dried on his fingers, but the bleeding was staunched. He gazed down into the bay. Flocks of birds floated in the winds over the choppy waters. He counted dozens of warships docked and out in the sea. He'd never seen so many before.

He rubbed his chin. *Something's brewing. I smell war.*

Abraham leaned his back against the terrace wall and waited for the first person to come through. *Please don't be Clarann.* He wanted to get down to business. No doubt King Hector wanted them to continue their missions, and most likely, this was what it was all about, but he had a mission too: save Mandi and put an end to this mess.

Pratt came through the curtains and pulled them to one side.

Oh Lord, who is behind curtain number one, Monty?

Queen Clarann stepped out onto the patio. Pratt let the curtains go behind her.

Son of a biscuit!

CHAPTER 17

Queen Clarann was a fair-haired lioness with ice-blue eyes. She wore a long silk gown that showed off all her natural curves. The beautiful woman dismissed Pratt, who abandoned the terrace.

Abraham took a knee. As his heart thundered in his chest, his palms began to sweat.

She gracefully walked over to him and said, "Please stand, Abraham. It's good to see you."

As lovely as she was, she had a don't-beat-around-the-bush air about her. He rose and faced her.

"By the Elders, what happened to your head? That wound is fresh."

He looked over at the terrace gate where the Guardians were posted and said, "Pratt did it."

"What?" She twisted her head around and glared at Pratt, standing more than an earshot away.

Pratt's eyes grew big, and he stiffened.

"I'm only kidding," he said. He wasn't in a joking mood, but he couldn't help taking a shot at Pratt. "I had a small accident on the way over."

"You don't have accidents," she said matter-of-factly.

"I'm not Ruger, remember. Maybe he didn't, but I do." He looked away from her penetrating gaze. "Is the king coming… soon?"

"I've made you uncomfortable, haven't I?" she asked.

He shrugged.

"I have felt horrible for unloading my burden on you. That wasn't right for me to do." She sat on the terrace wall. "I hoped that maybe, well, that might bring Ruger back. I guess I wanted him to know." She shook her head. "I feel like a whore."

"Huh," Abraham said with amazement. "Why would you say that?"

She hugged her arms, looked out over the sea, and said, "Because I am. I'm the cause of all of this. I don't deserve to be a queen, and King Hector is a fool for falling for me."

With a sheepish look, he asked, "Does the king know?"

Her eyes started to water. Teardrops ran down her cheeks.

CHAPTER 18

I'M A DEAD MAN.

"I'm going to the gallows, aren't I?"

"What? No." She grabbed his hands. "Of course not. Hector doesn't know. I would hate to hurt him like that. He's a true king, and he deserves much better than me. I'm a commoner, not meant for royalty. I should have died."

He patted her back and said, "Don't be so hard on yourself." He wanted to walk away, but being close to her stirred him.

She wore an intoxicating perfume with a lavender scent. Her wine-colored lips looked soft, and her enticing figure, accented in her silky dress, was to die for. The platinum blonde could bring any man to his knees.

"And you don't look like a commoner. You look like a queen."

She choked out a sob and said, "Thank you, even though I know you are feeding me false sympathy."

"No, that's not true, and you know it."

Seabirds landed on the terrace wall. He shooed them away.

"You know, I didn't stick around for the entire story," he said. "Can you tell me what really happened between you and Ruger? It might help."

Queen Clarann wiped her tears away and said, "It's an awful love story. Ruger and I met through my family's connections with the House of Steel. They are merchants that deal in fine tapestries. That's how I met Ruger, and we fell in love. But the Captain of the King's Guardians is forbidden to marry. His focus must be on the king."

"I thought Pratt was married," he said.

"No, Pratt is a talker who enjoys speaking about his imaginary family." She toyed with the sapphire necklace hanging over her breasts. "He makes it sound real. I overhear them talking sometimes. A family serves as a distraction. That's why most of the older knights marry younger women at a much older age."

"It's not such a bad plan," he grinned.

She laughed. "It's not as if they abstain from all relations either. The Guardians are, well, as you know, private. So an unexpected twist of fate occurred when King Hector fell for me. His wife had died, and I managed to catch his eye. Don't mistake me. I love Hector, truly, but the marriage was, well, arranged."

"Let me guess. You and Ruger had an affair?"

"Not at all. Ruger would die first. There was no greater Guardian than him, but before I married Hector, well…" Clarann's chin started to quiver. She took a deep breath through her nose and said, "I seduced him. That wasn't easy either, but my tugging on his heart wore him down. He gave in to me just days before the wedding. I fear I broke him."

"Broke? That's a strange thing to say."

"It wasn't so long after that when all of the crazy things started to happen. Ruger abandoned the Guardians. More possessed people walked the kingdom. The brewing rumors of war grew teeth. I swear I've tainted Kingsland. My wicked heart wanted what it wanted, and now we all suffer for it. Worst of all, Ruger is lost. All I wanted to do was tell him that I was sorry. He needed to know about his daughter too. He never knew."

"You never told him?"

"How could I? It would ruin him."

Abraham scratched his neck and said, "I think he might be glad to know it. It's possible that he might know already."

She looked deep into his eyes and asked, "Is Ruger still in there?"

"No, but he's back home in my world, trying to find a way back here."

"How do you know this?" she said.

"It's a long story, but trust me when I say he's not lost. He's in the wrong body. He's in my old body."

She threw her arms around Abraham and gave him a warm embrace.

Abraham felt himself melt in her arms. The chemistry between them was the kind that should be forbidden.

King Hector's authoritative voice interrupted the moment. "What is the meaning of this?"

Queen Clarann and Abraham separated. She bowed. Abraham took a knee.

"Rise, Abraham!" King Hector said.

He wore the Crown of Stones, which showed the shiny emerald in the front horn. He wore kingly robes, deep red and trimmed with silver fur. Lewis and Leodor walked behind the king, along with another man, who wore juice-purple hooded robes.

The king extended his hand toward Ruger. "A happy queen makes a happy king! I can see the joy on her face. What good news do you bear?" He looked at Abraham's forehead and winced. "What happened to you?"

"I hit myself with a shovel. It's a long story."

"You did a fine job," Lewis said. He was dressed in his cape with new clothing and armor underneath. "I'm certain I could do better."

"Stop it, Lewis, or I'll make a bridle for your tongue," King Hector said. He turned his attention to Clarann. "Well, what are you glowing about?"

"I never gave him a proper thank you, Hector," Clarann said quickly. "He saved our daughter and my life. I finally had a moment to express my sincere gratitude." She dipped her chin. "I'm sorry if I broke the crown's etiquette, but I was suddenly overwhelmed."

"It certainly looks like it," Lewis said.

King Hector ignored his son and said, "Of course you didn't break any formal protocols. You are the queen. You can express your gratitude however you see fit." He put his hand on Abraham's shoulder. "I trust this man. He's more than proven himself."

Abraham nodded. So did the queen. Their eyes met briefly.

Abraham said, "It's an honor, Your Majesty."

"Excellent. Shall we get down to business?" the king said. He turned toward the table on the terrace's upper deck.

The shine of the blue gem on the back horn of the king's crown caught Abraham's eyes. Life sparkled within it. He took a seat at the table with the others. The king sat at the head, the queen to his left, and his son to the right. Abraham sat by the queen with Leodor across from him. The man in purple robes sat beside the viceroy with his face covered by a hood.

"Where is Clarice?" the king asked.

Clarice stepped through the curtains a moment later. The beautiful girl with flowing chestnut hair and gorgeous eyes sat down beside Abraham. "Sorry, Father." She glared at Lewis. "I believe that I was delayed receiving the word."

Lewis smirked. "Of course you were."

King Hector rolled his eyes.

CHAPTER 19

"Abraham"—King Hector opened his hand toward the man seated beside Leodor—"I wanted to introduce you to Melris."

His eyes hidden in his hood, Melris slowly dipped his clean-shaven chin.

"Nice to meet you," Abraham said. He felt Clarice staring at him and gave her a quick look. As her big eyes soaked him in, he looked away. "Let me guess, you're another one of Leodor's cronies from the Sect."

"Hardly," Leodor scoffed. The old mystic's snobbish expression was as froward as ever. He spoke as though he had a bad taste in his mouth. "Melris comes from the outer sect."

"We are the Elders' chosen," Melris said in a soft voice. He had a pleasant yet cryptic manner about him. "We don't pervert the arcane."

"Pah!" Leodor rolled his eyes. "King Hector, I don't understand why you wish to consort with this lunatic. His ilk are an assorted lot of conjurers and enchanters spawned from drunken gypsies. They are tremendous weavers of words, but that is all. Don't let his forked tongue spellbind you."

"I didn't," King Hector said as he drummed his fingers on the table and rested his chin on his palm. "I used the stone of truth on him. Melris answered my questions without fault. He is an Elderling."

"Pfft!" Leodor sank back in his chair and stuffed his hands in his sleeves. "We'll see."

Abraham lifted a finger and asked, "What is an Elderling?"

Leodor flung his hands out of his robes and said, "Oh please, Your Majesty, let me handle this?"

"Be respectful, Leodor. All of my guests in the House of Steel are worthy of the king's respect," Hector replied.

"Certainly, Your Majesty," Leodor droned. "You see, Abraham, Melris claims to be a direct servant of the Elders. Though he cannot speak of them. Or describe them. He has, however, been in direct contact with him. According to the Elderlings, they are born with magic ability and do not require any tutelage or training. They claim that it comes naturally."

Melris held a hand out over the table. His fingernails were perfectly manicured, with a pale mulberry shade. His hands were unblemished and soft. He turned his palm upward, and a beautiful violet flower made of energy appeared.

The women at the table gasped.

"How beautiful," Clarann said with awe.

With a gentle flip of his hand, Melris cast the burning magic flower into the air. It floated higher and higher and then transformed.

"Look, it's a bird," Clarice said.

The bird flapped its wings and streaked into the sky and disappeared.

Hector, Clarann, and Clarice applauded.

"Magnificent," the king said, elated.

Leodor's chinless face tightened. "It's an illusion."

"Illusion or not, I still don't follow what is going on here," Abraham said.

Lewis gave Abraham a haughty look and said, "My father wants Melris to become a Henchman."

"I can't become a Henchman," Melris said as he blew the magic's vapors from his fingers. "I am an Elderling, but they sent me to help."

"And why would they do that?" Lewis asked. "They've never helped before." He shook his head. "There aren't such things as Elders."

"Don't be a fool, son. Of course there are." Hector cleared his throat. "Abraham, Melris is going to assist you on your quest to recover the four remaining stones. He offers knowledge given of the Elders that we can use. His recent arrival couldn't have come at a better time."

"Your Majesty, how can I trust a man that does not wear the King's Brand?" he said.

"Not all in your company wear the brand. They earn it, don't they? Hmm?" Hector replied. "You take Red Tunics and Hirelings, don't you?"

"I suppose that is correct, but we can handle them if they step out of line. I'm not so sure about this guy." He eyed Melris. "No offense."

"None taken," Melris replied.

"As I recall, you didn't handle the assassin Raschel all that well," King Hector replied.

"Yeah, but that's because those two sandbags"—he pointed at Lewis and Leodor—"were behind it all. They hired her. At least they are branded now. But this guy… Well, honestly, King Hector, I have enough personnel to deal with."

"One more won't hurt. Besides, Melris is more than capable of handling himself. He's assured me of that." King Hector stood up and put his index fingers down on the table. A fiery edge built up in his voice. "Melris will accompany you, but Abraham, you are in charge. Melris also has intimate knowledge on the location of the stones. He will guide you on the journey. The two of you can begin sorting out the details on our way out." He adjusted his crown. "Any questions?"

"King Hector, I'm not sure what path we are taking, but we should be going after the horned halfling, Big Apple. That little bald-headed ball of muscle has the answers that we need. That I need." Abraham stood up and planted his knuckles on the table. "Your Majesty, I have problems back home. I need to return as soon as possible."

The friendly demeanor of an Englishman vanished from Hector's face when his eyebrows knitted together and he said, "Sit down!"

Abraham's legs turned to jelly, and he dropped into his chair. *What in Titanuus's Crotch was that all about?*

CHAPTER 20

Abraham left the House of Steel like a dog with its tail between its legs. King Hector's orders were clear. They were to find the gems to the Crown of Stones at all costs.

"This sucks. This sucks. This sucks," he muttered to himself. He was in his bedroom inside the Stronghold, packing his gear for the long journey.

The triplets, Sophia, Selma, and Bridget, were in the room with him. Each of them was a vixen with piles of dark hair, a rich caramel tan, and seductive *I Dream of Jeannie* eyes. They folded his clothes and helped him pack.

"You seem angry, Master," Selma said. She looked ravishing in her pink tunic dress trimmed in black fox fur. She was sitting on the edge of the bed with her legs crossed and stuffing his clothing into his sack. "Must you go so soon? It's pouring, the rain."

"And it storms," said Sophia, who was dressed in the same outfit but in all black. "You could get hit by lightning."

"Huh huh," he laughed, recalling his battle with Arcayis the Underlord. The powerful mystic had rammed a bolt of blue lightning into his skull. "Let's hope not." He picked up his son's backpack with the Pirates logo on it. Staring at the logo, he could see his boy's face. The lightning storm had cost him everything. A lightning strike had caused his plane to crash.

Bridget, dressed in white, rubbed his shoulders. "Stay with us, Master. Enjoy yourself by the fire. Let us care for you, for once."

"I've got the king's business to do," he said as he ground his teeth.

King Hector really hacked him off. The man had changed. Abraham couldn't put his finger on it, but adding that blue gemstone to the crown appeared to have enhanced his power and confidence.

"Thanks for the offer."

The upstairs bedroom fireplace crackling nearby set the perfect scene. The triplets converged on him. Their hands and fingers massaged his muscles. They pushed him back into the bed and sat him down.

"Hey, whoa!" he said.

Selma was on her knees, behind his back, rubbing his shoulders. Sophia sat beside him, rubbing his forearms. Bridget was on her knees, rubbing his calves. All three of them smelled great. Their perfume filled his nose with intoxicating effect. His heart started to race.

"Master, it's been so long since you spent time with us. We miss your intimacy. You saved us from treachery," Selma said.

"That wasn't me. That was, well, the other me," he said as he closed his eyes and let Selma rub his temples. "Oh, and by the way, he misses you."

"Really?" Sophia said brightly. All three of them started to glow.

"He's a very bad man, you know. He took my girlfriend back home hostage."

One passion was replaced by another as he thought of Mandi. She was in danger, and he had to get back home. He politely tore his way out of the sensual touches of the three women. He saw Sticks leaning against the door frame.

"Hey… Sticks. We were packing."

"I can see that." Sticks pushed off of the door frame and said, "The Henchmen are gathered downstairs, per your request."

"I'll be right down."

Sticks vanished down the hallway. The triplets giggled as they watched her leave. She wasn't the ravishing beauty that the triplets were, but she wasn't a dog either.

"You guys are harsh," Abraham said and headed downstairs.

Downstairs, all the Henchmen were seated at the great table. The head seat was empty. Sticks sat on the left row beside Prospero, Apollo, Dominga, Tark, and Cudgel. On the right were Horace, Bearclaw, Vern, Iris, and Shades. All of them were in full gear. They were a hard-eyed bunch, to say the least. Last of all was Solomon. His oversized body sat in the chair on the opposite end of Abraham's seat. His matted fur had been combed out. The bigfoot-like troglin had a gentler look about him. He still wore the vest and trousers he'd acquired in Pirate City.

The table was loaded with a feast of roast beast, meats, rolls, and cheese. The two older hirelings, sisters Elga and Eileen, teetered out of the kitchen with bent backs, half hobbling, carrying serving trays. The salty women filled all the goblets with wine and the mugs with hot coffee. They grumbled, hacked, and coughed as they worked.

Abraham sat down and dismissed the hirelings with a wave of his hand and said, "That will be all."

The stringy-haired Elga mumbled in a mocking fashion, "That will be all," and teetered away with her sister.

The galley door to the kitchen slammed behind them.

"Grumpy old women," he said to himself.

He looked down the table. Despite the pouring rain and thunder, the great room had a warm and cozy feel. The huge strong fireplace burned with several roasting logs. Curtains and animal pelts on the walls softened the room's interior. He'd let the triplets handle the decoration. They'd given the Stronghold more of a lodgelike feel.

He lifted his wine goblet. "Let's have a toast."

With befuddled looks, the group lifted their glasses.

"To the Henchmen. Death before failure," he said.

"Hear! Hear!" Horace added.

They drank with unease.

Abraham looked over at Sticks and said, "Let's eat. Pass the potatoes." In a sullen mood, he loaded his plate as they all passed the food around.

Eating utensils scraped against bowls as the food was scooped out in heaps. No one was saying a word. All of them loaded their plates and ate quietly.

Abraham picked away at his food. He sawed up hunks of beef with his knife and fork. He chewed slowly and washed it down with sour purple wine. He couldn't stop thinking about Mandi. He was eating, and back home, she was suffering. He didn't know what to do, and King Hector had sidetracked him.

Vern dropped his utensils on his plate with a clatter and asked, "Captain, what in the Elders is going on? Have you become possessed by someone else again?"

CHAPTER 21

"MAINTAIN RESPECT, VERN!" HORACE BELTED out. "You don't question the Captain!"

"Hey, I thought we'd become all chummy now," Vern replied.

"It's not your words—it's your tone," Sticks said.

Everyone at the table broke out in an argument… except for Prospero, who gobbled up his plate of food. Half of the table defended Vern, while the other half attacked him.

Abraham raised his voice. "That's enough!"

The company quieted.

"I'm the same Abraham Jenkins. I have a problem back home. A friend of mine is in danger."

Vern tossed his cloth napkin on his plate and said, "Great. Here we go again, out on another mission while he's worried about another world and not this one."

"Shut up, Vern," Iris said. The mystic, dressed in green robes decked out in subtle arcane symbols, had a frown on her comely pie face. "You took the Brand again, so don't complain about it now."

"Yes, do be quiet. I don't even have a Brand, though I've asked for it." Shades had a mark on one cheek and a scar on the other. He wore no armor underneath his loose-fitting garb. He eyed the fireplace, where the King's Brand was propped up against the mantel. "Now would be a fine time before the mission begins."

"Oh, don't start this again," Iris said.

"Agreed," the attractive black woman, Dominga, added.

"Haven't I proven myself?" Shades said.

Half of the people at the table responded together. "No!"

Shades ran his fingers back through his tawny locks of short hair. "I don't know why you people don't like me."

"It's because of what you did at Baracha, you fool!" Iris said.

Shades rolled his eyes. "You need to let it go. I've saved all of you several times since."

"You imagine things!" Horace fired back.

"Yes, you delusional little creep!" Dominga said.

The bickering resumed.

Abraham opened his mouth to shut them down again.

Then Shades flipped a spoonful of mashed potatoes into Iris's face.

Aghast, she cried out, "You little devil piglet!" She picked up her plate and flung the entire meal at Shades.

Horace jumped out of his seat and said, "Iris! Show some decorum! Shades, I'm going to break you in—ulp!"

A heap of potatoes smote him in the nose. A turkey leg sailed at Shades. He plucked it out of the air and took a bite out of it.

"Thank you, Dominga," he said with a wink.

In the next instant, hands were filled with food. Hunks of meat and bowls of vegetables were being flung from all directions. Rolls and biscuits and bowls of stew went everywhere.

A huge smile broke out on Solomon's face as he filled his hands with hunks of beef and said, "Food fight!"

Abraham sat at the end of the table, watching the meal go to waste.

Sticks crawled underneath the table.

Solomon cowered behind his forearms and hands and moved away from the table, saying, "Don't get food in my fur!"

Hot rolls were chucked like snowballs. The goblets of wine were spilled.

An errant throw sent a bowl of green-pea soup splashing off Abraham's chest.

The Henchmen froze. All of them were covered in farm table grit of one sort or another.

Abraham rubbed his eyes and face. Pea soup dripped into his lap. He clenched his teeth and felt his ears turning red.

All the Henchmen slowly sat back down in their seats.

Solomon took his place at the end of the table. With noodles dangling from his fur, he said, "Sorry, Abraham. I don't know what got into me."

Abraham set the empty bowl of pea soup that had landed on his lap back on the table. "It's all right. Everyone is entitled to a Belushi moment. Now, where was I?"

Sticks crawled back into her seat from underneath the table. "I thought that you were going to tell us about the mission. You hadn't said a word about it since we left the House of Steel. All you said was start packing."

"No, that wasn't it," he said. "Vern questioned me." He gave Vern a hard look. "Just so you know, as well as the rest of you, the real Ruger, it appears, resides in my body back home. I can't explain it. But he lives, somehow. But I don't want to talk about that." He saw Solomon raise an eyebrow. "That's all you need to know."

"In the meantime," Abraham continued, "we are heading north to recover the rest of the stones. And we'll have a new Henchman, so to speak, among us."

The company exchanged confused glances.

Horace said, "What do you mean, Captain? Do you brand another Henchman? Did the king?"

"No. His name is Melris. He should be arriving with those other sandbags, Lewis and Leodor."

"What about Swan and the princess?" Shades asked. He and the Guardian Maiden Swan had connected on their last trip.

Abraham shrugged. "I suppose they'll all be coming along too."

"Captain," Horace said, "the more of us, the harder to navigate in discretion. Are we taking the ship?"

"I don't know."

"It doesn't sound like you are in charge anymore," Vern said in a snide manner.

Bearclaw popped Vern with an elbow.

"The king insists that we let Melris guide us. Not lead." Abraham's jaw muscles clenched. He couldn't stop thinking about Mandi. "Don't have any confusion. I'm in charge."

Iris spoke with the polite airiness of an Englishwoman and said, "What does this Melris do?"

"According to Leodor, he's a mystic from the outer sect. The old chinless wonder doesn't care for him." Abraham smirked. "But apparently, the king summoned him. And Melris calls himself—"

A loud thunderclap filled the room, followed by a quick flash of lightning.

A newcomer spoke a moment later and said in a clear but soft tone, "An Elderling."

Every head at the table twisted toward the front door.

Decked out in the wine-purple garb of a wizard stood Melris. Despite the rain outdoors, his raiment was as dry as a bone.

CHAPTER 22

Abraham rested his elbows on the table and asked, "Where are the others, Melris?"

"They won't be coming," replied the taller-than-average and slender Melris.

Using a metal rod like a cane, he approached the table. The rod was made out of black iron. It had three feet, like prongs, on the bottom. It didn't clack when it touched the stone floor. Melris's steps didn't make a sound either. "I sensed your distress in working with them. I suggested to the king that they remain behind."

Horace smacked a meaty palm on the table. "I like this Melris."

"I'd like him better if I could see his face," Dominga said as she strained her eyes to look underneath the stranger's hood. "He has skin like a baby."

With his hands, covered in black gloves, Melris lowered his hood. He had short strawberry-blond locks of wavy hair and boyish good looks. Like a rose among thorns, he had not a blemish on him. His lavender eyes had an omniscient spark to them.

"How old are you?" the moony-eyed Iris asked. "You look like a child."

"I'm an Elderling. We don't keep track of our ages, but it would be reasonable to say that I exceed all of the ages of you put together."

Horace pumped his fist in the air. "Hear! Hear! I'm not the oldest one anymore!"

Tark scratched the back of his skull and asked, "Captain, what is an Elderling?"

Abraham was about to speak, but Iris cut him off. "They are supposed to be the direct servants of the Elders. But I've never seen one before, nor any of the other mystics that I've trained with. They are as rare as the Elders. Not that anyone has seen any of them either."

"I believe you are mistaken. You have seen two," Melris said as he made his way around the table. He carefully stepped away from the piles of food. "There is the Fenix, the Elder Spawn. That is an Elder of sorts. Also, you killed the Elder of Slime at Crown Island. The Elders took note of that. That experience will serve you well."

"We've killed Elders?" Bearclaw thumped his chest. "Well, well."

"There are minor Elders and major Elders," Melris replied.

"Which kind were they?" Horace asked.

Melris stood by the fire and picked up the Brand. "It's not my place to say." He studied the crown-like design and set it back down. "Abraham, are you and your Henchmen ready to go now?"

"Er… yes, we are always ready, but it would help if we knew where we were going."

"Yes, it would. We are going to the Wound. Are you familiar with it?"

Abraham teetered on the back two legs of his chair and tried to search Ruger's memory banks. He knew where the Wound was on the map. The canyon could be easily found, located in the northern hemisphere of Eastern Bolg. That was all he recalled. He eyed Horace. "Am I familiar with it?"

"No, Captain. None of us are."

"I see." Melris passed his hand over the log fire, extinguishing the flames. "Shall we go, then?"

Abraham dropped his front chair legs to the floor, got up, and walked to the front door. He felt every eye in the room on his back but Melris's. He opened the door. Sheets of rain were coming down outside. Mud puddles had formed all over the courtyard.

He cupped his hands over his mouth and hollered toward the barn, "Skittles and Zanax!"

A few moments later, two figures crept out of the barn and into the drenching gloom. The Red Tunics Skitts and Zann, brothers, splashed through the mud and made a beeline for Abraham. He called them Skittles and Zanax—one after the candy and the other after the drug Xanax back home—because the names seemed to fit their temperaments. Plus, they were catchy.

The brothers stood before him, soaked to the bone. "Yes, Captain?"

"Get the horses and wagon ready. We are moving out now."

"A nice day to travel," Zann said in a slow and scratchy Southern drawl. "Can't wait to ride in it."

Shielding his eyes from the blowing rain, Skitts asked, "Are we going?"

"You don't think I'm going to pitch my tent, do you?"

"No, sir," Skitts replied. He shoved his brother, and they hustled back to the barn.

Abraham moved back inside, looked at his group, and asked, "What are you waiting for? The sun to start shining? Sunshine or rain, we've got a kingdom to save."

CHAPTER 23

The Henchmen headed back up the Kingsland coastland toward Titanuus's Crotch. That was still the safest route of travel. Southern Tiotan and Kingsland were in full alert along the border between the two great territories. Not even commerce moved back and forth between the two countries anymore.

Abraham and company had gathered plenty of intelligence while they were waiting on King Hector's direction. They had contacts in the King's Army that kept them informed. There were spies too—spies on both sides. Abraham couldn't help but wonder if Melris might be one of them.

He led the way up the stormy coastline where the Bay of Elders' angry waters crashed. The company moved in the same double-column formation. The Red Tunics towed behind the wagon in the rear. Dominga and Tark scouted ahead. Even the daytime was as dark as night.

Abraham didn't really care. This was the first time since he'd lived in Titanuus that he was mentally detached. He couldn't stop thinking about Mandi and the danger she must have been in. He had no way of protecting her, and his heart ached. She'd been good to him without him giving her any sort of reason.

Solomon caught up to Abraham with his long-drenched arms swinging. He was traveling on foot but had little trouble keeping up with the horse, with his giant stride. "A word?"

"Of course." Abraham peeled his horse away from Sticks and Horace, who were always fixtures in front of him. He led his horse toward the sandy beaches and the crashing waves. "What's on your mind?"

"We haven't spoken since your last episode. At the dinner table, you mentioned an encounter with the real Ruger Slade. That threw me." Solomon slung the water from his hands. "Stinking fur. It adds another hundred pounds when it's wet. You know, I think we could make a killing selling umbrellas."

Abraham's horse nickered and shook its neck.

"A great idea. A fortune for the taking," Abraham said glumly.

"You're all eaten up. More so than before. We all sense it. So fill me in."

"It's a long story."

"We have a long journey."

Abraham told Solomon everything that had happened when he was back home. If he left out any detail, it wasn't intentional.

Toying with the wet hair underneath his chin as though it were a goatee, Solomon said, "Interesting. I sympathize with your distress, but at least you are back on board with getting out of this place. I was beginning to feel like a lone wolf."

"Yeah, well, the both of us might be a pair of lone wolves. I don't feel like the king still has my back either. He's more interested in the gems." He shifted in his saddle. "And Mandi is all alone."

"It sounded to me like she has Ruger to help her. Maybe it won't be that bad. It's best to assume that she's safe."

Abraham frowned and cast a look behind, to where Melris rode on the wagon Iris was driving. "What's your take on that guy?"

Solomon wiggled his protruding eyebrows and said, "Weird but smooth. I can't really make much of a judgment on him."

"Yeah, me either. I haven't even bothered to talk to him."

"Compared to Leodor and Lewis, he's a breath of fresh air."

"Agreed. But at least I knew what to expect from them."

"You can't have it all," Solomon replied. "So, what is the plan?"

"Junction City is on the way up to the Wound. I'm hoping to stop there and pick up the trail of Big Apple."

Solomon nodded. "Yeah, if that guy thinks we are a threat, he's going to keep tabs on us." He cast a glance back at Melris. "Tell you what. How about I try to feel the strange fellow out? You seem too tense right now. I'll take a crack at it."

"Go ahead. I don't feel like talking—not much, anyway."

Solomon drifted back into the ranks, and Abraham took his spot in the front.

"Trouble, Captain?" Horace asked.

"No, we otherworlders were only touching base," he told both of them. "Keep your lips sealed, but we'll go to Junction City and see if we can sniff out the horned halfling there. Just don't let the newbie in on it."

"Aye, Captain."

Sticks nodded at him and said, "My lips are sealed."

CHAPTER 24

The Henchmen were riding along the bottoms of the eastern hills of the Spine, a few days from their destination in Junction City. Abraham, as well as the others, would scan the stark mountain range as strange sounds and calls would echo down from its jagged ravines and valleys. Abraham had no desire to navigate the treacherous mountain terrain again. The mere thought of such a trek in the odd, barren, and humid climate gave him the willies. The company traveled at a brisk pace through the grassy plains.

Domingo, who had been scouting from the front with Tark, galloped back to the main party. A worried look crossed her pretty teardrop-shaped face.

Halting his horse and the rest of the company, Abraham asked, "What is it?"

"I can't say," she said with a quick look over her shoulder. She pointed behind herself. "That stretch of wheat grass that we are about to cross through has a stink about it."

"A stink?" Horace sat with a mirthful look. "Perhaps that's Tark?"

Dominga made a gentle eyeroll and said, "No, it's not an odor so much as a feeling. There is a silence. The grasses do not even rustle."

"The wind is not blowing," Sticks said.

"Come on, I'll show you what I'm talking about." Dominga led them another half mile through the fields.

They found Tark standing behind a long rise. His horse grazed a few yards behind him.

She followed the path of pressed-down grass right toward him. "Did you see anything?"

Tark kept his smoky eyes on the expansive field of tall brown and fertile green grasses. "Nothing. It's alive but stagnant. But these goose bumps on my arms haven't departed either."

Abraham rode up on top of the rise. The fields were like a desert that went on endlessly in all directions. It would be a perfect place for hunting varmints and deer.

"I don't *feel* anything." Ruger's body had a strong sense when it came to danger. "Not that I think you are mistaken."

"I've been at this a long time," Tark said, rubbing his forearm. "When my hairs stand on end, I'm usually right."

"True," Dominga agreed.

"We can go around the field, but that might take an extra day," he said. "I hate to do that when we can make a straight path for those mountains. We'll be home free then. Besides, we can't risk the open roads and crossing Hanchan soldiers. It wouldn't surprise me a bit if Commander Cutter and his men were keeping an eye out for us. That guy's a bad penny. He'll show up again, I figure."

"It's your call as always, Captain," Tark said.

Abraham eyed the horizon. Leagues away was a bordering set of mountains, much smaller than the Spine. Those ranges made up the borders that separated Hancha from Eastern Bolg. The goal was to cross the open range, navigate the mountains, and make their way to Junction City. With the sun setting behind them, the Spine cast a shadow over the range. A pit started to form in his stomach. He eyed Sticks. She had the assault rifle slung over her shoulder.

"Ready that weapon," he said. "Horace, tell the troops to have the crossbows ready. I'll lead."

Horace turned his big horse around and hefted his spear. He circled the spear tip and thrust it in the air.

Immediately, Bearclaw and Vern loaded their crossbows. Behind them, Apollo and Prospero did the same, and so on with all the well-equipped Henchmen.

Abraham gave Tark and Dominga a nod. With crossbows in hand and resting on their laps, they resumed their scouting position at the forefront. Flanked by Sticks and Horace, he followed their lead. The entire company ventured two hundred yards deep in the eerie silence. The sound of his heart pumped in his ears.

"Why are we moving so slow?" Vern asked. "It's just a bloody field. At this rate, we'll never make it to the mountains until tomorrow morning. Let's ride."

"If you want to ride out ahead, feel free," Abraham said. "As a matter of fact, maybe it would be best to put you on permanent scout duty."

Vern replied, "Look, I'm just saying we could move quicker. It's not like we are going to get attacked by a bunch of varmints."

"Tark warned us," Sticks said.

Vern rested his crossbow against a shoulder and said, "He gets spooked all of the time."

"Did you see that?" Sticks asked. She pointed the barrel of her assault rifle toward a small rise in the grasses to her left. "I saw the grasses move."

"So did I, Captain," Horace said.

Up ahead about thirty yards, Tark and Dominga came to a stop. They pointed their crossbows at the grasses.

A chill raced up and down Abraham's spine. The tall grasses rose up in a circle that surrounded them. Aboriginal men stood up in the field, wearing the grasses like hats. They were lean, tall, and muscular. Their brown bodies were painted with white patterns, with swirls, streaks, and dots on their bare faces and chests. Some of them had long throwing spears hoisted up on their shoulders. Others had primitive bows and arrows.

Horace spat black juice onto the ground. "Pitters."

The name didn't ring a bell. "We've fought them before?" Abraham asked.

"Aye, years ago," Horace replied. "They live in the low ridges of the Spine and hunt in the fields. We waltzed into one of their hunting grounds once before. They didn't like it."

"What happened?"

Horace lowered his spear. "Three of us died that day."

CHAPTER 25

Abraham counted at least fifty Pitters whom he could see. Hundreds more could have been hiding in the tall grasses.

"Will they negotiate?" he asked Horace.

"No. We tried that last time where we encountered them on the other side of the Spine. They don't speak."

"We can run for it or circle the wagon. They aren't faster than horses, are they?"

"They are fast," Horace replied. "We'll have to bust through their front ranks, but Captain, they won't stop until they catch us."

"Maybe, but we can at least fight with the mountains at our back. With our weapons and armor, we can whittle down their wooden weapons."

"Agreed, we can kill them," Horace replied.

Abraham lifted his hand. "Everybody, get ready to run to the hills. Run for your lives," he quipped. He dropped his hand and kicked his horse in the ribs. "Eee-yah!"

The Henchmen's horses, led by Tark and Dominga, bolted into a full gallop. The wagon, drawn by a team of two beasts, rattled to life. Iris drove the wagon, with Melris clinging to his seat. As one, the company thundered through the grasses.

The Pitters called out in a cacophony of wild hooting. They snaked through the grasses, keeping pace with the horses. As their bowstrings were plucked, a barrage of arrows whistled through the air. Smooth as silk, they drew arrows from their animal-skin quivers and fired again.

An arrow pierced Sticks in her thigh, and she let out a sharp gasp. A Pitter closed in on her from a forward angle with his spear held high. She shot the wild man in the face with the rifle, and blood sprayed out of the dying man's back. He stumbled and vanished into the tall grasses.

The Pitters chasing them started to fade behind. The ones ahead came at them at an angle. With hollering hoots, they closed in on the fleeing gang of hardened fighters. One lanky Pitter crashed spear first into Horace's beast. The spear snapped on impact. Horace rode the beast over the man and gored another charging Pitter with his spear.

Bearclaw and Vern fired into the frenzied throng. They slowed and lined up their horses beside the racing wagon then threw their crossbows into the back. Bearclaw waved his arm at Skitts and Zann, and the Red Tunic brothers sped up to the wagon.

"Get into the wagon, load those crossbows, and keep firing." Bearclaw readied his twin-bladed Viking-style battle-ax and peeled away. The Henchmen formed a battle ring around the wagon and horses.

Vern whisked out his sword and followed Bearclaw back to the front of the wagon. They swung the King's Steel into their rushing enemies. Steel and bone clashed. Hot blood sprayed the fields. The Pitters fell but kept coming in gnashing swarms.

Solomon snatched up one Pitter and threw him into two other pursuers.

Skitts and Zann jumped from their horses into the wagon. Zann loaded the crossbows, and Skitts aimed and fired. They worked in perfect tandem. Pitter after Pitter fell, gurgling in their own blood.

Abraham pulled Black Bane free of its sheath. The darkened steel of the broad blade shone with its own inner light. He leaned over his saddle and swung at an attacker. The savage's head leapt from his shoulders.

"Eat dung, Pitter!"

The horse-riding Henchmen stormed ahead at full speed toward the mountains. Spears and arrows whistled by. An arrow skipped off Horace's armor. Their armor saved most of them. The fine metal, crafted from the King's Steel, offered the ultimate protection. No finer metal existed in all the land.

Black Bane sank into the neck and clavicle of another Pitter. The savage dropped like a stone.

Two Pitters zeroed in on Sticks and her horse. One of the wild men grabbed onto the horse's reins and tugged while the other latched onto the back of her saddle. Sticks slung her weapon over her shoulder and pulled free a long dagger. She cut one Pitter across the forearm, but he hung on, with his feet dragging across the ground.

"Give off my horse!" she yelled.

Abraham dug his heels into his horse and chased after Sticks. "I'm coming!"

Sticks gave him a quick look and rolled her eyes. She leaned backward and lunged at the savage clinging to her saddle. She stabbed the wild man in the neck, and he fell away. She pulled herself forward and flicked the same dagger into the second Pitter's chest. The man held on. She whisked out her short sword and chopped his arm off at the forearm.

The Pitter let out a wild cry and slipped into the grass. Sticks's horse trampled over him.

Abraham gave her a thumbs-up. She shook her head with a disappointed look.

He caught up to her and spoke over the wind and the pounding hooves of the horses. "Forgive me! I need to remind myself that you can handle yourself! You are a fine marksman with those daggers."

"I could have shot them, but you said to save the bullets. But I needed the practice," she said, with her twin ponytails bouncing on top of her head.

"You're a natural! You don't need practice. You have a gift. In my world, you are what we'd call a crack shot!"

"Crack shot?" Sticks gave him a funny look.

The Henchmen pulled away from the front waves of the Pitters. The savages in grass hats fell behind them but didn't slow their chase. Nothing lay between the company and the mountains. They had broken free.

Abraham twisted his head around and made a head count. Solomon, Cudgel, Apollo, and Prospero were bringing up the rear. Bearclaw and Apollo were riding on either side of the wagon. Skitts and Zann were in the wagon, loading crossbows. Iris was driving the wagon, and Melris was sitting beside her. Sticks and Horace were riding beside Abraham, and Tark and Dominga were keeping the lead out front.

"It looks like we are in the clear," Abraham said.

"Aye, Captain!" Horace bellowed. "But we could kill them!"

Abraham made a light-hearted chuckle. He caught Dominga looking back at him. She smiled and waved.

A huge pantherlike creature as big as a horse launched itself out of a concealed spot in the grasses. It took Dominga and her horse down.

Tark screamed, "Nooo!"

CHAPTER 26

A SECOND PANTHER BEAST POUNCED ONTO Tark and his horse. He tumbled from his saddle into the tall grasses.

"Yah! Yah!" Abraham yelled.

He and Horace raced neck and neck to the aid of Dominga and Tark. They arrived a few seconds later.

"What are those things?" Abraham asked.

"Wild panthers!" Horace said.

Each giant cat had the light coat of a lion and a tuft of thick brown fur on top of its neck.

Horace lowered his spear and charged the panther that had sunk its sharp fangs into Tark's horse's neck. "I'll kill them!" He bore down on the panther before it sprang away at the last second. "Missed!"

"Horace, watch out!" A third panther sprang out of the grasses and knocked Horace from his saddle. More huge cats appeared and converged on the Henchmen. They attacked the horses and brought them down by biting their legs. Abraham pulled back on his reins and wheeled his horse around. The Pitters and their panthers encircled the stalled company. "Bloody meat pies!"

"What do we do?" Sticks said.

"Circle the wagon!" He waved his hand around in the air. "Henchmen, circle the wagon! Let loose the horses! These cats will eat them alive!" He jumped off his horse and swatted its rear flank with his sword. "Yah!"

The horse bolted.

"Aaayeeee!" Dominga screamed.

Abraham's head snapped around. The silky black woman was riding on the back of a panther. Her fingers were lodged in its thick patch of neck hair. It twisted around, bucked, and bit and clawed at her. With a kick of its hips, the panther bucked her into the air.

Dominga flipped into the air and landed on her feet. She pulled short swords free from her scabbards and got into a fighting stance.

The wild panther charged her. She split its nose and went down in a flurry of slashing claws.

Abraham sprinted toward the panther. He caught up just as it bowled Dominga over. He swung Black Bane hard into the beast's hips. The blade cut clean through the skin, taking bone and sinew with it.

The panther kicked with its back claws, knocking Abraham off his feet. It turned around, saliva dripping from its slavering jaws. Its piercing green eyes lapped him up with hungry intent. It pounced.

Abraham lifted his sword and held it fast.

The panther impaled itself on the blade. Its claws tore at Abraham in wild death throes. Warm blood oozed from its wound over Abraham's hands. It died and sank down on top of the man.

With a grunt, Abraham pushed himself out from underneath the massive beast. Dominga grabbed his arm and tugged. Her upper arm had huge gashes in it. The wounds were nasty.

"I hope you aren't allergic," he said.

Grimacing, Dominga asked, "What's that mean?"

"I'll explain later."

The Henchmen were embroiled in a heated battle around the pair of horses and wagon.

Solomon had a wild panther by the neck and was punching it in the face.

Dominga fired mystic hornets of energy from her fingertips. The humming swarm bore into the Pitters. The savages hopped and jumped and slapped at the glowing insects.

Iris's attacks served the Henchmen well. Cudgel pummeled the ill-equipped savages with bone-jarring swings of his spiked mace. Teeth clacked together and shattered. Skulls were crushed.

Apollo and Prospero swung their long swords with devastating effect. Apollo disemboweled two charging Pitters at the same time. Prospero hacked the arm off of one and sliced out the knee of another.

Horace lumbered out of the grasses, holding his gory spear. Blood was on his face and beard. The wild hooting increased all around them. "We can kill them, Captain!"

Abraham joined his men. "Death before failure!" He turned Black Bane loose on the enemy.

Slice! Chop!

Hack! Glitch!

The dead fell in heaps. The army of Pitters didn't dwindle. More came at them from all directions.

"How many of them are there?" Sticks said.

"Who cares! More food for the Elders!" Bearclaw said.

"None can withstand the might of the King's Steel!" Vern shouted as he ran his blade through a Pitter's skull. "We are invincible!"

A stone tomahawk tumbled through the air and clocked Vern in the skull. He collapsed like a tent.

"Vern!" Dominga cried. She ran to the man and stood over his body with her swords in hand.

Solomon moved alongside her at the back corner of the wagon.

Skitts and Zann kept firing the crossbows into the horde.

Abraham swung Black Bane through a savage's chest as a wild panther charged him. "Oh no, another bad ol' puddy tat." He split its nose in twain before Horace gored it with his spear. "Thanks."

Horace charged back into the fray.

There was no end to the sea of Pitters. They continued to crop up by the dozens.

"Black Bane, if you are listening, we could use a hand," he said.

The only things keeping the Henchmen in one piece were their superior skills, weaponry, and armor, but that wouldn't hold forever. The Henchmen, after all, were only human. He banged the tip of his sword on the wagon's wheel. "Black Bane, wake up!"

The sword quavered. The runes in the blade glowed like embers and went dim. Abraham cut down another attacker and shook his head. Perhaps his predecessor, Eugene Drisk, had it right.

"Dirty donuts! I should've brought more Henchmen."

CHAPTER 27

THE BATTLE RAGED. THE SECONDS felt like a minute. The Henchmen were pressed, their backs to the wagon, fighting for their lives.

Vern was down.

Tark was nowhere to be seen.

Solomon's fur looked like a pincushion of arrows.

Sitting in the wagon seat, Melris yawned. The Elderling stood up and spread his arms wide. His wine-colored robes hung from his arms like a sheet, and his long fingertips needled the air.

While fighting, Abraham watched the young mystic out of the corner of his eyes. Arrows shot by the enemy veered away from the strange man. Melris's robes rustled with a life of their own. *What is he doing?*

Melris pushed back his billowy sleeves. He flipped up his hands.

Dozens of Pitters in close-quarters battle near the wagon were lifted from their feet, along with their big cats. The savage horde levitated in the air, higher and higher. The confused throng of sweaty painted bodies swam and twisted in the air. They hooted and panted with wide-eyed astonishment.

The clamor of battle fell silent.

The rest of the Pitters looked up in the air with the whites of their eyes locked on their clan. They watched as the cluster of suspended men and wild animals were gathered together in the air.

With Sticks and Horace at his side, Abraham and the other Henchmen watched the marvel take place in the sky above. The knot of hooting Pitters and their wild panthers were bunched together. The distraught cats let out angry growls and lashed out at their masters.

"You don't see that every day," Solomon said.

The Pitters stranded on the ground gathered underneath their brethren with their necks bent toward the sky.

Abraham glanced at Melris. Facing away from the living tangle in the sky, the Elderling turned up the corner of his mouth. He dropped his hands. From over a hundred feet above, the Pitters and wild panthers went into a hooting and mewing freefall.

The Pitters on the ground let out a feverish gasp. Many scattered. The rest were crushed underneath their brethren. It became a pile of dead men, their limbs broken and twisted. The living survivors writhed underneath the pile as they tried to claw their way free.

A ball of purple flame started in the palm of Melris's hand. The size of a tomato, the ball grew to the size of a pumpkin. With a swipe of his hand, he lobbed it toward the pile of Pitters and big cats. It sailed through the sky and landed square in the middle of them. The flames exploded. They consumed every man, living and dead. Their flesh turned to ash. The pile became a bonfire of burning bones and awful stink.

The dozens of surviving Pitters fled.

Horace wiped his bloody spear tip in the grass and said, "I don't think Leodor could have done that."

Iris covered her nose and said, "I agree."

CHAPTER 28
LEWIS

BACK AT THE HOUSE OF Steel, Lewis and Leodor were sitting in a small living room, drinking wine. A board game with chess-like pieces sat on a small round table between them. Leodor's wizened face and knitted eyebrows were focused on the board.

Lewis stared into the fire nearby, flipping a dagger up and down in one hand and drinking from the other. "Come on, Leodor, make a move."

"I will when I'm ready," Leodor replied in his snobbish manner. He started to move one of the game pieces but moved it back. "When I'm ready."

"You act like the very heavens will fall if you make the wrong move," Lewis said.

"One never knows for certain the weight of their decisions. So the Elders say."

Lewis rolled his eyes. He stood up, walked over to the fire, set down his wine, and sheathed his dagger. He spread his fingers in front of the flame. "Don't try to segue into another speech about your precious Elders. I'll believe them when I see them."

"You've seen one."

"That *thing* on Crown Island? It was merely a monster, worshipped, well fed by foolish men. What sort of person feeds a monster? That is stupid."

"It's still an Elder." Leodor placed his piece on another position of the checkered board. "Gratius Victorious."

Lewis stiffened. He picked up his wine goblet and swallowed the remains. He walked over to the gameboard and looked down. "Hmm… It seems that you have erred, my friend." He moved one of his white ivory pieces, shaped like a knight in armor. He smirked. "Gratius Victorious."

Leodor stiffened in his chair. His fingertips clawed at the thinning hair on his head. "How do you do that? I don't understand it."

"I'm brilliant." Lewis refilled his goblet. "And I play better when I'm tipsy." He bumped into the table and knocked several game pieces over.

"More like drunk." Leodor started resetting the board. "Play again?"

Lewis yawned. "I don't know. Believe it or not, I'm getting tired of beating you. I'm getting tired of everything."

"Is that so?" Leodor said with an arched eyebrow. "And could it be that you miss adventuring with the Henchmen?"

"Pfft. Hardly. Perhaps I miss leading the King's Guardians, but the Henchmen, no. I'm glad Father saved us from another doomed mission. Aren't you?"

Leodor shrugged.

Surprised, Lewis plopped down in his seat across from the older man and said, "Really? This is a startling admission coming from you. What is going on in that age-spotted forehead of yours?"

"I can't say. But my chest nags me."

"Well, my horrid brand itches too. Maybe it's because they all died."

"They are the kingdom's hope. Your father places his faith in them." Leodor finished setting up the board. He moved a piece. "Your move."

Lewis frowned. "I don't want to play again. I want to drink. A night on the town wouldn't be so bad."

"But we are restricted. Besides, I can't leave. The Sect would find me and peel the skin off of my back. No thank you. I'm safest here or among the Henchmen."

Lewis moved a piece. "It's ludicrous that you think that way. Ah, I know what it is. It's that Elderling, Melris, isn't it?"

Leodor shrugged in his robes. "No. I could care less about that imposter." He moved a piece.

"Do I sense a note of jealousy rolling off of your slithering tongue?"

"Don't be silly. I care nothing about some enchanter off of the streets."

"An enchanter that conveniently appeared in the king's chambers undetected. That is no easy feat, my friend."

"Why are you calling me 'friend' all of a sudden?"

He paused in thought and said, "I have no idea. Perhaps it's because, at the moment, I don't have any." He moved a piece on the board. "Pathetic. I prefer your company compared to drinking alone."

"Even worse, I prefer your company without drinking at all. Oh well, I suppose we should consider our confinement a blessing from the Elders." Leodor moved an onyx game piece.

"Don't start with the Elder talk. Save your breath for some other fool that is dumb enough to worship the very dung-covered ground they walk on." He slid a piece diagonally from one checkered square to another. "Gratius Victorious."

The tired-eyed Leodor made a sound as though he were choking. "Three moves. You bested me in three moves!" He backhanded all the pieces off the table, sank back in his chair, and stuffed his hands in his robes.

"I told you I get better when I'm drinking." He sloshed his wine in his goblet. "It's a gift."

"A shame that you can't use it toward something more beneficial."

"I can. I'm a genius in military organization. For five years, I kept the Guardians organized and crushed any uprisings. I'm quite suited for the field, if I don't mind saying so myself. My gift is anticipation followed by focused action."

"Well, you are the king's son. And he's no fool."

"If it's any concession, I've never beaten my father."

Leodor straightened up in his chair. "Interesting."

Lewis guzzled down more wine. "How's that?"

"Because I have beat him several times."

"Hmm, I can see your frustration. Perhaps you are getting too old."

"With age comes wisdom."

"More importantly, power. You know, we were so close to having the kingdom to ourselves." Leodor rubbed his chest. "Do you really think that we will die if we work against the Brand?"

"Something terrible will happen. I'm certain of that. The Blue Demon will come, they say."

"Another myth, I say."

"Are you willing to risk it? To be honest, I find it refreshing knowing where I must stand. I am tired of all the scheming."

Lewis set down his goblet. "My, you are getting old."

As the door to the living room burst open, Princess Clarice entered. "There you are. I've searched all over for you."

"Why is that?"

"You know why. We can't just sit here. It's time to escape."

CHAPTER 29

LEWIS MOVED TO A PLUSH sofa near the fireplace, stretched out, and sank into the cushions. "This castle isn't big enough, apparently. Over five hundred rooms, and she still found us." He stuffed a pillow over his face and in a muffled voice said, "Go away."

Clarice shut herself inside the room, took a seat on Lewis's sofa, tugged on his trouser leg, and said, "Hear me out."

With the pillow still over his face, he replied, "I'll do no such thing. Talk to Leodor. He might take you up on it, but not I."

"Listen to me!" she urged. "We are Henchmen. Part of a group. It's not natural for us to be so far apart. I can feel it. I sleep with demons in my dreams."

"Does your brand itch and burn?" Leodor asked.

"It nags me like buzzing flies that won't go away," she replied earnestly.

Lewis lifted the pillow off his face. "Speaking of buzzing flies that won't go away…" He threw the pillow at his half sister. She slapped it aside.

"I know you feel it too, Lewis. We aren't supposed to be here. We are supposed to be out there. It's driving me crazy."

"Not me—I'm fine. If it bothers you so much, then have a drink. Either that or find a suitor. You're about at childbearing age. Go make some babies. You'll soon forget about all of this."

She punched him in the leg.

"Ow! Do that again, and I'll toss you into that fire." He sat up and rubbed his eyes. "So, where is that hound of yours, Swan? Let me guess, she's snapping chicken necks."

"She'll snap your neck," she replied. "I gave her the slip. Seriously, Lewis, Father is wrong to keep us here. We don't belong at the castle. We are Henchmen."

"He's only saving face. The real reason we are here is because of you. You are the one being protected. He couldn't have cared less about us." Lewis got up and prepared another goblet of wine. "If you want to run away again, I won't stop you. It will be our little secret."

"The king will only send us after her again," Leodor replied.

"I assure you that won't be happening," a woman said. She stood in the doorway.

"Leah," Lewis said with delight. "What a pleasure it is to see you."

Leah was the head of the Guardian Maidens. She was a striking beauty, all warrior, all woman, wearing a bronze cuirass that matched her coppery locks. He strolled across the room and kissed her hand. "I've missed you."

"Yes, so much that you ran into the arms of an assassin, I heard," Leah said. Her big beautiful eyes probed his.

"I was seduced. Bewitched. But as I recall, you rejected my advances, time and again."

She wiggled his prominent chin with her fingertips and said, "That's because your reputation precedes you, Lewis the Lewd."

Clarice and Leodor let out a giggle.

With his hand still clasping Leah's, he said, "You cut to the heart."

Leah gave him a rueful smile and said, "That's why I'm the captain of the Guardian Maidens." She slipped from his fingers and ventured deeper into the room. She stared down at Clarice. "Planning a little excursion?"

"No, I was only visiting with my brother," Clarice replied nonchalantly.

"Half brother," Lewis fired back.

"Please, Clarice. You've been trying to duck the Maidens ever since the Henchmen left. But I promise you this—you'll never slip me. Not like you did the others that failed me recently. Hazel is dead, thanks to your foolishness." Leah sat down on the sofa beside Clarice. "You'd do well to forget about it."

Clarice huffed, folded her arms across her chest, and said, "You don't understand. You aren't a Henchman."

"No, I'm a Guardian Maiden. We are bonded and have a special brand of our own."

"I'd like to see that brand," Lewis said with a dashing smile. He moved to the wine hutch and pulled out a new bottle. "How about I pour you a glass? It's from the Old Kingdom. Centuries old. The best."

"You know that the Guardians don't drink on duty, and I don't drink off duty either." She gave him a friendly nod. "But I appreciate your offer."

Lewis sat down between the women and said, "I'm with you one hundred percent, Leah. I've been telling the little princess that her efforts are nothing but foolishness. It might be best to lock her up in the dungeons."

"If only I could," Leah said.

"Hey, no one is locking me up anywhere." Clarice jumped out of her seat and pointed at the other three persons in the room one at a time. "You're a coward! You're a coward! And you're a coward!"

"You dare!" Lewis said. He jumped up to his feet and pulled his sword. "You might call me many things but never a coward!"

Leah rose from the sofa and said, "Agreed."

"I don't mind it so much. Cowards are survivors," Leodor added.

"You sit here on your arses, hiding behind the castle walls, while the kingdom is in flux!" Clarice pulled her rapier. "Our brothers and sisters, Henchmen, need us! I challenge you"—she pointed the tip of her blade at Lewis—"and you"—she did the same to Leah—"to a duel of swords. I win, then you have to follow me after the Henchmen. I lose, I'll leave you alone."

"You are a delusional little gal," Lewis said with incredulity. "First, you can't defeat either one of us. Second, we would make it a hundred yards from the castle. The King's Guardians, not to mention scores of other soldiers, would see us."

Clarice smacked his blade with her blade. "Coward!"

Lewis's high-boned cheeks reddened. "I'm losing patience." His grip tightened on his hilt.

"There is no point in this foolishness," Leah said. "Lewis is right. There is no way out."

"Leodor can get us free of the castle's walls and far from the soldiers' sight," Clarice said.

Leodor picked up the game pieces he'd knocked from the table. He placed them in the appropriate positions back on the board. "It's true. I can."

"Leodor!" Lewis whined. He'd been a part of Leodor's portal incantations before. "Why would you say that? She's only guessing."

"It's true. I can. But just because I can doesn't mean that I will."

"So, if I outduel Lewis and Leah, then you will teleport us out of here?" Clarice said.

Leodor shrugged. "I don't see why not."

Lewis and Leah gave Leodor incredulous looks.

Lewis shook his head and said, "No matter. It wouldn't go that far." He pointed his sword at Leah. "We'll finish this in the proving grounds."

CHAPTER 30

Iris stitched up a nasty gash in Horace's forearm where a wild panther's claw had torn it open. "You should be more careful," she said. "Get a suit of the king's chain mail that will cover all of your arms."

"My forearms are too beefy," Horace said. He was chewing a wad of tobacco in his jaw and spat.

Iris glared at him. "I told you I don't like that stuff."

"I know, but it takes my mind off the pain. I'll spit it out later." He winced. "Ow, woman. Are you stitching from the inside out or outside in?"

"Spit it out," Iris said.

"Ah..." Horace took the wad of tobacco out of his mouth and tossed it into the campfire. "There. Happy?"

Abraham managed a smile. He sat near the campfire, warming his hands over it. The company had made camp at the base of the mountains. The stark jagged hills were a natural border between Hancha and Eastern Bolg.

Sticks, Solomon, and Tark helped Iris bandage the wounded.

Not one Henchman had escaped without new scars. The battle with the Pitters had been nasty.

Dominga and Cudgel were cooking over another campfire.

The Red Tunics, Skitts and Zann, pitched Abraham's tent.

Abraham stood up and made his rounds, making sure that no one was going to die.

"How are you guys doing?" he asked Vern and Bearclaw.

Vern was holding a bandage on his head that Iris had made for him. That stone tomahawk had clocked him good. "My head pounds like a drum, and my ears are ringing. Sadly, I still breathe."

"I know the feeling. You?" he asked Bearclaw.

Bearclaw was scraping a stone over the blades of his axe. "I sewed up my thigh. But my wounds were minor. The king's armor kept my bowels intact."

"Good. Get something to eat. Sticks is making Pitter panther stew," he said. "Good stuff. Can't you smell it?"

"Aye," Bearclaw replied.

"Yeah, we could eat for months after slaying all of those Pitter panthers." He scanned the camp.

Melris stood on the edge of the camp in the shadows, staring at the mountains. The gentle winds stirred his robes. Abraham hadn't said a word to him after the battle, for too many had wounds to attend to.

Abraham walked to the Elderling. "I think it's time that we had a chat."

"Certainly." Melris kept his eyes fixed on the rocks. His hood still covered his head. "What do you wish to talk about?"

"First, take that hood down. I feel like I'm talking to a ghost."

Melris complied. He wasn't nearly as haunting with the hood down. He had a boyish quality in his face that made him more approachable. Like Sticks, he wasn't one for showing expression. "Is this suitable?"

"I like to see your eyes when I'm talking." He locked eyes with the man. Melris's eyes had a twinkle like purple stars. "Uh, I suppose I should thank you for that trick you pulled out in the fields."

"Trick?"

"You know, levitating the enemy and doing a watermelon drop with them. That was amazing, but the timing could have been better."

"That wasn't a trick. I learned it from Trinos," Melris replied. "So, should I have executed it sooner or later?"

Incredulous, Abraham said, "Sooner. And who is Trinos? Never mind."

"I merely sped up the process of elimination. Your company would have prevailed with minimal losses by my estimation."

Abraham's voice became harsh. "Listen, Commander Data, it's not my company, it's *our* company. You are a part of it. We fight—you fight. You don't sit in the wagon and watch the birds fly by."

"I see," Melris said. "Is there anything else?"

"Look"—he thumbed back toward the camp—"I know these people. They are Henchmen. But I don't know you. You aren't a Henchman. You are an Elderling, whatever that is."

"We are direct servants of the Elders, born with the land's magic coursing in our veins." He leaned to one side, past Abraham. "And you are mistaken. Shades, Skitts, and Zann are not Henchmen. They don't have the Brand, but you trust them."

"They earned it. They proved themselves."

"I took the lives of sixty-eight enemies singlehandedly. Have I not *proven* myself?"

Abraham nodded. He had to admit Melris had the right answers. He pushed his fingers through his hair and said, "Let's run through a few things. I need to know that we are on the same page. First, who is in charge?"

"You are in charge. I am merely a guide. I hope that you don't feel threatened by me."

"No." Abraham absentmindedly put his hand on Black Bane's handle. "It's good we are clear about that. As for the Henchmen, we all perform like a military unit. I know what to expect from them, but I don't know what to expect from you." He glanced down at the iron rod Melris carried. "What does that do?"

Melris flipped the rod around like a sword. "This is a rod of devastation. That should speak for itself."

"I see," he said, taking his eyes off the thing. "Listen, Melris, if we fight, you fight. We fight for the king. We fight for one another. 'Death before failure' is our credo."

"I admire your spirit." Melris turned his back and faced the mountain. "I shall do my best to fit in. In the meantime, I am solely focused on recovering the stones from the Wound. If you'll pardon me, I must meditate."

Abraham shook his head. His thoughts wandered back home. He was worried about Mandi. "I don't need this." He started to walk away. "I need to get back home."

Melris turned. "You desire to find a portal?"

Abraham stopped in his tracks. "Yes."

"I know something about that."

CHAPTER 31

"Speak to me." Abraham draped his hand over the mage's shoulder. "Let's talk by the campfire. I'm getting hungry. Let me ask, do you eat?"

"Some," Melris said with an uncomfortable look.

Abraham locked his strong fingers on the Elderling's shoulders. Melris was a slender six-footer. The man's velvety robes felt thicker than him. Abraham wasn't about to let him go now. He wanted information.

He led the man to Horace's campfire. "Sit. Speak."

Melris quietly sat down in front of the flames.

Abraham waved at Sticks and Solomon. "Bring some food. You'll want to hear this. At least, Solomon will."

Solomon lumbered over and squatted down beside Melris. "Fellowship by the fireside?"

"More than that," Abraham stated. "Ol' Melris is going to shed some light on the portals."

Solomon's brows rose.

Sticks brought over two bowls of Pitter panther stew. She handed one bowl to Abraham. "Hopefully, this will be better than the story you told about that man running from the giant rock and losing the golden idol."

Nodding his head, Horace said, "Yes, that was a bad one. Why would the treasure hunter throw a hireling the prize? That was a foolish thing to do. I'd die before imparting my treasure to a hireling."

Abraham spread his hands out and said, "The hireling died."

"Yes, but you said that he never got the idol back either," Sticks said as she dug her spoon into her bowl. "The treasure hunter lost the small idol and the golden coffin."

"That was the Ark of the Covenant. Not a coffin. It's the place where Moses kept the Ten Commandments," Abraham said. "I don't want to explain this again. It's not about the treasure."

"It's always about the treasure," Horace said as Iris walked over with a bowl of stew and handed it to him. "That's what treasure hunters do."

"Never mind."

Abraham started eating. As much as he wanted to hear about the portals, he had to eat or pass out. He considered passing out, as that might get him back to Mandi, but Ruger's body wouldn't allow it. The salty broth with chewy panther meat hit the spot.

"All right, Melris," he said. "What do you know about the portals?"

"King Hector is on the right path. His cause is just even though not all Elders agree. The portals are created by another world, a world of invaders." He refused a bowl of stew that Iris tried to hand him. "I assume that would be your world, Abraham Jenkins."

"Mine too," Solomon said. "But we didn't have anything to do with it."

"No, of course not. You are only fish that were caught in the net," Melris said.

Shades slipped into view and leaned against the wagon. Using a knife, he cleaned his nails.

Melris continued, "The king was wise to eliminate the otherworlders such as you. But the numbers have grown to many."

"You are saying we should be killed?" Abraham said.

"At first, that was the best course of action, but the Elders reconsidered since you wield Black Bane," Melris replied.

"What does that have to do with it?"

"The sword was crafted by the Elders. It can't be wielded by just anyone. It is bestowed on the one that can protect Titanuus."

Abraham rubbed a palm on the blade's handle. "Huh. I didn't know that."

"I can't explain all of it entirely, but the sword possesses special qualities," Melris added.

"You can say that again," Abraham said.

"The metal is from the blade of Titanuus. The sword shattered in his battle with Antonugus ages ago. Black Bane is but a sliver. The rest lies in the ocean deep." Melris held his gloved hands over the flames. His hands began to glow, and he flicked his fingertips.

The embers of the fire drifted into the air above them and formed tiny bright-orange stars above the group's heads.

Melris massaged the air. Flames snaked out of the fire and formed the outline of two flaming sword-wielding warriors. They were covered in full-plate armor and battle helms made of brilliant lights. They battled among the stars.

"Titanuus and Antonugus battled in the heavens for centuries. Finally, Titanuus fell."

One warrior gutted the chest of the other.

"Titanuus suffered a mortal wound and fell from the heavens and into the waters of an empty world."

The orange embers cooled and disappeared.

"Titanuus was formed. His blood gave us birth. But now, the very life of Titanuus is under a darker threat, an invasion from another world." Melris sighed. "This is a bigger threat than Antonugus."

Abraham rubbed his head. Another headache was coming on. "So what are we supposed to do? And how many people like me are out there?"

"It is hard to say. Even the Elders don't know, but anyone could be an otherworlder like you."

The Henchmen grouped at the fire exchanged glances.

"The Elders call it soul swapping. Their essence is moving out of one body and into another. Through the portals. How it happens we can't explain. But I am here to investigate," Melris said. "The portal has been opened in another world by means we don't understand. Only the Crown of Stones, we hope, can counter it."

"Can't it be closed from the other side?" Abraham said.

"Possibly. But sometimes, when a gate is opened, it is impossible to close. But the Crown of Stones, we hope, will suffice."

"This is crazy." Abraham set down his bowl. "The only thing that makes sense is that I'm crazy and none of this is real. If we close the gate, everyone will be stranded here, like me and Solomon."

"That, I can't say for sure," Melris said. "Even the Elders don't know. But the Crown of Stones should be able to control both opening and closing. But the other world is opening them on their own."

"Well, isn't that just great." Abraham kicked at the dirt with a heel. He suspected the Big Apple would have more answers. He had to find him again and figure out what his motivation was. He pinched the bridge of his nose. "I've heard enough. I'm going to sleep."

"Captain!" Horace said.

Two winged shadows appeared in the sky. They dropped down on Shades, hooked their talons into his arms, and flew him away. They were gone by the time Abraham pulled his sword free.

All he could hear was Shades yelling, "They found me! They found me! Help meeeee!"

CHAPTER 32

Lewis, Leodor, Leah, and Clarice gathered in a small training ground inside the House of Steel designed for the Guardians. The proving ground was located in the sublevels of the castle, having the appearance of a modified dungeon. Cells were there with no bars. The limestone walls were slick with moisture in some places. Racks of weapons and armor filled the stony cavities.

Clarice stood on a square platform of risen stone, fifteen by fifteen feet wide. She buckled on a suit of padded armor. She tied her flowing brown hair back in a ponytail.

Leah warmed up her bare arms with two wooden practice swords. She spun them in her grip with fluid expertise.

"Seriously," Lewis quipped. He carried a jug of wine in his hand. He took a long sip. "You are challenging me with children's toys? I thought this was going to be a real fight." He set the jug down, walked over to a weapons rack, and snatched up a wooden sword, which was little more than a polished stick knotted up with a leather binding around it to make a handle. "How dangerous."

Leodor took a seat on the edge of the platform and yawned. "Can we get this over with? I'm ready to retire for the evening. I had to be up when the roosters crow. I'm not myself without proper sleep."

"Says the man that always looked tired." Lewis propped a foot up on the steps of a small set of bleachers facing the arena. He set his jug down to stretch. "Don't fret. This won't last long."

"No, it won't," Clarice said. She spun two swords in her hands. "Who goes first?"

Lewis gestured toward Leah and said, "Ladies first. And do me a favor. Teach her a lesson so I don't have to."

"You'll have to do your own dirty work." Leah hopped up onto the platform and squared off on Clarice. "Are we using two swords or one?"

Clarice said with a shrug, "Since I made the challenge, I'll let you choose."

"We can keep it interesting." Leah flipped her swords with her wrists. "Two swords it is."

Lewis rolled his eyes. "Is this going to be a fight or a show? Two swords. Pah."

"Just keep score." Leah eyed Clarice. "How many strikes to the victor?"

"Best of five," the princess replied.

"Five? You seek to delay the inevitable." Lewis crossed his arms while still holding his sword in hand. "Take your mark."

The women faced off. They each held two wooden swords and took a battle stance. Their eyes locked.

"The rules. The rules." Leodor sauntered over to the bleachers and sat down. "Be clear about them."

"Yes, yes. We'll adhere to the standard. No strikes above the neck or below the knee. A point, if earned, will be deducted. Agreed?"

Both women nodded. Clarice's forehead started to bead with sweat.

"Someone is nervous. Let the battle begin." Lewis pulled his shoulders back and smirked. Leah was taller and longer, giving her a key advantage in reach. "Engage!"

Leah lunged forward, stabbing at Clarice's chest.

Clarice parried the attack by batting the swords to either side. She countered with a twin downward thrust and struck both of Leah's shoulders.

"Hit!" Lewis said. He gave Leah an incredulous look and said, "I hope you are awake now."

Leah's nostrils flared. She rolled her neck from side to side and fixed her stare on Clarice.

Clarice had a stone-cold look in her eyes.

"One strike, Clarice. Take your positions," Lewis said firmly.

The women resumed their battle stances.

"Engage!"

Clarice thrust. Leah parried. The wooden swords clacked off one another like the sound of popping wood. Violent thrusts and parries were exchanged. Leah pressed the attack. *Thrust. Thrust. Chop. Thrust. Thrust. Chop.*

With astonishing agility, Clarice glided away from the attacks. She twisted her swords between Leah's attacks and smote her hard in the belly.

"Hit!" Lewis shouted. "Two strikes, Clarice. No strikes," he said with disappointment, "Leah. Try hitting her back this time. You are captain of the Guardian Maidens, aren't you?"

Sweat glistened on the skin above Leah's breasts, which heaved underneath her figure-enhancing bronze cuirass. A snarl formed on her face. "At least I'm still a captain." She resumed her battle stance and faced off with Clarice. "You've been practicing."

Clarice stared Leah down like a panther hunting its prey. "I'm a Henchman. Fighting for your life is practicing," she replied coldly. "Death before failure."

Lewis chuckled. "She's a volatile little chipmunk, isn't she. Engage!"

The two women fought. Swords impacted one another with wooden fury.

Leah pressed the attack. Her thrusts were parried, spun away from, or countered.

Clarice snaked her body away from the flurry of skilled attacks. She shuffled away, ducked, and countered. The women battled back and forth, using every square inch of the arena platform.

The sword-on-sword strikes echoed hollowly in the proving chamber.

Leodor sat on the edge of his seat, tired eyes wide, fists clenching.

Lewis yawned. He followed the yawn with a belch.

Leah overextended herself on a thrust.

Clarice whacked her opponent in the ribs.

"Hit!" Lewis shouted. The women disengaged and faced one another in the middle of the platform. "Three strikes, Clarice. The victor," he said with noticeable disbelief.

"Good fight," Leah said to Clarice. "You've grown much, and I underestimated you. I let you get in my head. It won't happen again." Panting for breath, she gave Clarice a hug. "I'm proud of you."

"Thanks," Clarice said. She broke off the hug and faced her brother. With a confident smile, she said, "You're next."

CHAPTER 33

"WHAT JUST HAPPENED? WHAT WERE those things?" Abraham shouted.

Shades had vanished into the midnight sky. Strange hulking winged creatures had swooped down and snatched the rogue away in a blink of an eye.

"I've never seen the likes of them before," Horace said as he poked his spear toward the sky. "He's gone now. Could be anywhere."

Abraham spun around on his heel. "Does anyone know what in the hell those things were?"

All the Henchmen were on their feet with weapons ready. All eyes were searching the sky and the surrounding scenery. Prospero and Apollo shrugged, sheathed their swords, sat down, and resumed eating.

"He's gone now," Iris said. The rose-colored fire in her hands went out. "I don't suppose there is much we can do about it."

Sticks slipped her daggers back into her bandolier and said, "'They found me.' You heard him say that, didn't you?"

"Yes." Abraham gave her a probing look. "What did he mean? Who found him?"

"I know Shades as well as any," she said, "and he's been edgy. I got the feeling that he was worried about someone coming after him. I even caught him checking the skies from time to time. I found it weird."

"I noticed that too," he said, still searching the skylines. "He seemed very desperate to get the Brand. Do you think that might have something to do with it?"

Horace stuck his spear into the ground. "No telling now. He's gone. Better get some rest, Captain."

"What? We just lost a man. I'm not going to sleep on that. We have to get him back."

"If you say so, Captain," Horace replied. "But he's not a Henchman, so I wouldn't fret."

"Skittles and Zanax aren't either, but I'm not going to abandon them either."

He scanned the faces of his hardened crew. They all clearly held a grudge against Shades. Despite the rogue's loyal efforts, he still hadn't won them over.

A pit grew in Abraham's stomach. He hadn't put his faith in Shades either. He'd refused to brand him. He clasped his hands behind his head and surveyed the stars. "Blue blazes."

"Your friend bears the mark of the Targon," offered Melris, who hadn't budged from his spot in front of the fire.

Abraham dropped his hands and gave Sticks a curious glance. She shrugged. So did Horace. The word *Targon* didn't jostle anything in Ruger's memory banks either. He stood over Melris and asked, "What is a Targon?"

With his eyes fixed on the fire, Melris said, "The Targon are slavers from the Old Kingdom. They serve the High King of the Mountains. They prepare the finest specimens for the king's service."

"By specimens, you mean people, right?" Abraham asked.

"I'm sure they mark beasts for service as well. The slaves to the Targon are like cattle. Hence the mark. Like the King's Brand."

"Well, aren't you a fountain of information? Why didn't you try to stop them, Melris?"

"I was as surprised as you," the Elderling replied.

Abraham paced around the campfire. The Old Kingdom was in the northeast territory, days away. He didn't owe Shades anything, but the rogue was part of his team. Abraham couldn't abandon him.

"Do you have any idea what will happen to him?" he asked.

"I cannot say. Perhaps he will be made an example of. I'd assume the worst. The Targon are ruthless people." Melris stood up and faced Abraham. "Sorry."

"What are we going to do?" Sticks asked. "Even with horses, we can't track something that is flying."

"I'm tired of my crew getting snatched away." Abraham clenched his jaws.

Sticks was right. They had no way to catch the Targon and no way to tell if Shades would still be alive either. He watched the clouds passing in the sky. He had a mission to complete. He needed to get back to Mandi. *Lord, what am I going to do? I need some help on this one.*

"Clearly, Shades has a past that pre-existed his time with the Henchmen. It's no surprise for such a sneaky fella," Iris said as she began gathering the empty bowls of stew. "I don't think it was meant to be. They don't call him Shades for nothing. It's probably not his real name."

"Since I've been here, Shades has done no wrong."

"You weren't in the prison," Iris said.

"Love"—Horace put his hand on Iris's shoulder—"careful how you speak to the Captain."

Iris moved out from underneath Horace's meaty hand and said, "I follow, but that doesn't always mean that I have to agree." She hustled away.

Melris tilted his head toward the sky. The bottom end of his rod started to glow a faint purple.

Abraham's neck hairs stood on end. High above, something circled in the air. He gripped the handle of Black Bane. "Is that them? Are they coming back?"

"No," Melris said in his soft voice. "That is something far more dangerous."

The great creature in the sky dove toward the camp.

"The sky lives," Horace said.

Abraham pulled his sword and said, "Henchmen, to the ready!"

CHAPTER 34

Lewis stepped up onto the training platform with the wooden sword resting on his shoulder. He hiccupped. "A shame to let all of that good wine go to waste on this meaningless exercise."

"It's far from meaningless," Clarice said. "If I win, we are all leaving."

"Don't count on it," Lewis said.

"You gave your word!" she fired back.

"I'm talking about you winning. It's not going to happen."

Leah dabbed her sweaty face with a towel and asked, "What will it be? One sword or two?"

"As you can see, I only brought one, but I'm perfectly fine letting this little rodent fight with two," he said, a noticeable slur in his words.

With an incredulous expression, Leah asked, "Are you certain? She's as quick as a cat."

"Yes, I saw the little kitten whip you like an old dog." He leaned into Leah's pretty face. "I think you and I should spend time together. I could teach you my excellent swordplay."

Leah patted his cheek and said, "Let's see how you do against your little sister first."

"Half sister."

"Prince," Leodor said, "your timing is going to be way off, on account of your inebriation. I'm employing the Rictarn Tactic. It should spare you from immediate humiliation."

"Are you instructing me on the usages of steel? Or wood, rather. A mystic. Now I've heard it all."

"I spent some time in the army when I was younger. All servants of the crown required training back then."

With a side look, Lewis replied, "Obviously, you were horrible at it."

Leodor lifted his scrawny shoulders. "True. My body aches just thinking about it."

Leah stepped off the platform and said, "Shall we get on with it?"

Lewis and Clarice faced off in their battle stances. He kept his sword on his shoulder. She had both blades out in front of her.

"I'm going to enjoy throttling you," Clarice said.

"The first competitor to score three hits wins," Leah reminded them. "Engage!"

With the quickness of a springing cat, Clarice stabbed at Lewis with both blades.

Lewis brought his sword down like a flicker of a snake's tongue. *Whack.* He hit Clarice hard on the top of her skull.

Clarice jumped back, grimacing. "What in Titanuus was that?"

"It would have been your funeral if this sword were real," Lewis quipped.

Tossing her towel over her shoulder, Leah said, "That's a point for Clarice."

"I thought I lost a point," Lewis said, "and I don't have any to lose."

"No, these are Gin-gin rules," Leah said. "If you don't have a point to give, your opponent gets your point." She smirked at him.

"So be it," he said.

Clarice rubbed her head on her forearm. Her eyes were watering.

"Did you feel that through your pelt, little badger?"

"I'm going to pelt you," Clarice replied.

"Resume your places," Leah said.

The fighters stood a few paces apart, Lewis towering over his sister like a cat over a mouse.

"Engage!"

Clarice parried Lewis's downward strike with both of her swords. *Clack!*

Lewis chopped harder into her swords. The strength of his long sword arm knocked her parries aside. Stretching and striking, he swatted her behind.

Clarice let out a yelp and skipped away.

"Hit!" Leah said. "One strike, Clarice. One strike, Lewis. We are tied."

"Bravo," Leodor said from his seat.

"Take your positions."

Clarice's nostrils flared. Her eyes narrowed with growing hatred.

Lewis turned up the corner of his mouth.

"Engage!"

Clarice's swords struck out in a blinding whirlwind of fury.

Clack. Clok. Clack. Clack. Clok.

Lewis caught every blow on the length of his sword. With one hand behind his back, he danced backward around the ring, blocking every strike she made. "You are fast. Your skill is average." He ducked one sword strike and sidestepped another. "Your footwork could use much work as well," he added as he glided around the ring.

Clarice broke off her assault. Panting, she backed away and lowered her swords.

"Are you quitting?" Lewis asked.

"I want to see you fight and not dance."

"Oh, if that is your wish, let me grant it." He gripped the sword with both hands and charged.

Clarice's eyes grew. She parried the fierce blows that Lewis rained down on her with wroth force. He knocked her swords down. She brought them up again and absorbed more punishment. She backed toward the rim of the stage, cornered, and one foot slipped off.

"Hit!"

"What?" Clarice exclaimed.

"You came off of the platform. That's a hit," Leah explained. She gave Lewis an approving look. "One strike, Clarice. Two strikes, Lewis. Take your positions."

Clarice moved to her spot with her shoulders hanging. Eyebrows knitted together, she shook her head and resumed her battle stance.

Lewis moved into his spot and said, "One more strike, and I can go to bed. I know what you are thinking, ratling. You seek to dupe me and catch me off guard. But I can see the fire burning in your eyes. I won't be fooled." He moved into his stance and put both hands on his sword. "But you can try me."

"Engage!"

Clarice came at him.

Lewis knocked both swords out of her hands with one mighty swing. He put the sword on her neck.

"Hit!" Leah said.

Leodor clapped. "Bravo. Bravo. I'm not a fan of you, Lewis, but that swordplay was exquisite." He smoothed his thinning hair back. "And I really didn't feel like casting a dimension spell. They are very dangerous."

Clarice kicked both swords off the stage and stormed out of the room.

Lewis dropped his sword on the deck. He stepped off the platform, put his arm around Leah, and reeled her in. "Well played, my dear."

"Indeed," she replied.

As Leodor's tired eyes awakened, Lewis kissed her full on the lips.

CHAPTER 35

A WINGED BEHEMOTH NESTLED IN THE mountain's rocky ledges. It sat perched over a hundred yards high on the hill. Its beastly shape contoured with the hill.

Sword in hand, Abraham moved toward the base of the mountain with his eyes glued on the creature. Sticks and Horace flanked him.

"It's a big thing, whatever it is," Sticks said.

"We can kill it," Horace added.

Abraham's arm hairs stood on end. His earlobes burned. Fear didn't course through Ruger's veins. Excitement did. The thought of battle aroused him. He tried to quell Ruger's natural enthusiasm. "That thing is bigger than an elephant. And it flies as well."

"What's an elephant?" Sticks asked.

"Melris, you seem to have some inner knowledge. Can you tell us what that thing is? Is it another one of those Targons?"

"No, I sense the beast is of a different complexity. I will shed more light on it." He shot a pale purple beam of light—like a flashlight—out of his hand.

Iris gasped.

"The Fenix," Abraham said as he stared in horror at the hideous beast.

The ugly creature had eight eyes, four on each side of the head. The eyes burned with citrine fire. A long, broad snout was that of a hammer-headed bat. Its fur was ruddy and brown. Saliva dripped from the fangs protruding underneath its thin black lips like a bulldog's. Great black wings were folded behind its back.

The Henchmen loaded crossbows.

"Take aim, Henchmen," Horace said.

Fingers started to squeeze the triggers.

"No, wait," Abraham said. "I think that is Simon."

"How can you be sure?" Solomon asked from his position behind the wagon.

"Because we killed all of the others," he replied.

"No doubt, this creature, if it is the same, it comes to kill us," Solomon added. He stretched his long arm out and pushed forward Skitts and Zann, who sat in the wagon with crossbows ready. "Go ahead. Shoot that thing."

"No, don't shoot it. Everyone, stay calm." Abraham motioned downward with a hand.

"Abraham, that thing is ten times bigger than the last. It couldn't be the same one. Even if it was, you killed its father or mother or whatever," Solomon added.

Speaking in a slow Southern-like drawl, Zann said, "Well, I'm not taking any chances." He squeezed the trigger.

Clatch-zip!

The bolt sailed true and struck the Fenix in the nose. It let out a moan like a wounded lion. Fog spilled from its great mouth. The inky white mist spilled down the mountainside like an avalanche of snow.

"You idiot!" Abraham said. "Everyone back away. Everyone back away!"

The Fenix launched itself into the sky.

Zann stood up in the wagon and shouted, "Woohoo! See, I scared it away."

Backing away, Melris kept his light on the creature and followed it through the sky. "The breath of the Elder Spawn is subtle." The light from his hand went out.

Abraham lost sight of the Elder Spawn. "Everyone, get out of here before that breath freezes your limbs."

"And the Fenix makes a snack out of us." Solomon bolted toward the fields.

The Henchmen hurried after the troglin. With a screech, the Fenix dove down from the sky. Swooping over the camp, it unleashed its vaporous breath. Its vapors splashed out like falling rain. A sticky substance coated the fleeing Henchmen and their camp.

Horace fell first, and his big belly squashed the campfire.

Iris fell next, followed by Sticks, Vern, and Bearclaw.

Abraham's limbs moved like molasses. He watched more Henchmen fall one by one. His lids grew heavy, and his flight came to a stop. He fell to his knees with his sword locked in his grip. Melris moved in front of him. Bolts of fire flew skyward from his fingertips. The Fenix dropped out of the sky and landed on the Elderling.

Abraham screamed, "Nooo!"

Shards of pain sliced through his head. He fell on his back. The Fenix loomed over him. Hot saliva dripped from the monster's mouth and onto his armor. Its rancid breath could have woken the dead.

"Man, you really need a Tic-Tac," he said.

Abraham's new world went black.

CHAPTER 36

Abraham woke to the sound of the wind ripping through his hair. Giant talons were latched around his body. The world waited to greet him hundreds of feet below.

He squirmed inside the viselike grip. "No. Nooo!"

In the fleeting moment when he'd blacked out, he hoped he would return to Mandi's side. Instead, he flew through the sky like a rodent being taken to a hawk's nest. He pulled his arms up. Somehow, impossibly, Black Bane remained in his grip.

The Fenix had a furry coat over its belly. Its legs dangled low, making it too far for Abraham to take a stab at it.

He decided to take another stab at it, a different kind of stab. "Simon! Simon Fenix! I know it's you! Take me down!"

He'd named the elder spawn after the movie character Simon Phoenix, from the movie *Demolition Man*. Before the great dragon-bat thing departed, he'd called it that at least one hundred times when they bonded.

"Simon! It's me. Abraham. Take me down!"

"What is all of the shouting about?"

Black Bane, the sword, was speaking in Abraham's mind.

"Well, look who decided to join us," Abraham said with his mouth to the wind. "I can only imagine that you have nothing to offer."

"I wouldn't say that. I always have something to offer. Mostly advice… about women. Er… what is your name again?"

"Abraham Jenkins." He looked down at the treetops they were flying over. "I don't guess that you ever remembered yours?"

"I can't say I do. Perhaps it changed one too many times. So tell me, Abraham, how are things going for you? It sounds quiet. No banging around. That's a good thing."

"Not really. I'm captured by a giant dragonlike creature. I think it's taking me back to its nest. The funny thing is you helped me kill its mother before. Now, I think it's about to kill me."

"Hmm… it sounds dangerous. Can't you hit it?"

"Sure, but I might fall a thousand feet."

"In my past, there was a dragon, with shining black scales the size of small shields. It had a great belly, for a dragon, that dragged over the grasses. I used to run. It would fetch me but never kill me."

Straining his neck as he searched for some possible way to escape, he asked, "So what happened to it?"

"I believe it married a druid. A fetching woman, not a sample I prefer, but very ghostly and exotic. Rose-petal lips. Skin as soft as—"

"Not helping!" Abraham squirmed in the Fenix's clutches. "Listen, Black Bane, I need to get down on the ground before this thing takes me back to its nest. Or wherever. Can you help?"

"Did you call me Black Bane?"

"Yes!"

"Interesting. I have the worst trouble with names, though I do recall being referred to as that before. You see, the other personalities would call me that from time to time. But I keep forgetting. Thanks for reminding me. Now, where were we?"

"I need to get out of this creature's grip and back onto the ground."

"And you said that it is a dragon?"

"Yes!"

A jolt of energy coursed through the sword and into Abraham's body.

"Gah!"

The Fenix's claws opened wide.

Abraham plummeted toward the earth. "Black Bane! This isn't what I had in mind. I'm falling!"

"You are free of the beast, aren't you?"

"I'm going to die any second now!" Holding the sword in two hands, he screamed at it. "Help me!"

"I thought that I did. Let me see what I can do. The magic resources in this world are tricky. If I only had my spell book... Yes, I recall having a spell book."

Abraham twisted his head around just in time to see the green treetops rushing to greet him. All he could think to do was scream, "Nooo!"

The Fenix swooped underneath him, and he grabbed onto a handful of fur. Hanging on for dear life, he pulled himself up into a sitting position.

"Simon! It's you, isn't it!"

Over the sound of the wind, he heard a rattle of acknowledgment coming from the Fenix's throat. A catlike purr rumbled beneath him. The ugly beast craned its neck and locked four eyes on Abraham's own.

"It is you!"

He started floating upward. His fingers grasped the thick patch of fur on Simon's back while his feet started to rise into the air. An unseen force was pulling him upward.

"Hey, what is going on?"

"Is my spell working, er, what was your name again?"

"Ruger! I mean Abraham! Your spell is a little late. I'd be looking like roadkill only seconds ago. Turn it off!"

"Turn it off? That is an odd phrase. So, your present condition is safe?"

Abraham kept trying to pull his body down, but it kept floating up. "I'm riding on the back of the dragon. I think I'm safe. It would be better if I could get him to land."

"I see. Hold on, Ruger."

"The thought had occurred to me," he replied as he recalled a line from an old spy movie. His body suddenly dropped onto the creature's back. He found himself sailing through the starlit skies. With the wind kissing his face he said, "James Bond, eat your heart out."

As he sailed the skies on the back of the great living beast, a feeling of exhilaration swept through Abraham. He'd flown planes and felt the special freedom that it gave, but that was nothing like riding on the back of the Fenix. Its body churned with warm life. Its outstretched wings beat the winds with power. Abraham let out a triumphant cry at the top of his lungs.

"Interesting."

"Huh." Abraham came to his senses. "What's that, Black Bane?"

"I can hear the thoughts of the Fenix. It is talking, but it's more of a childlike gibberish."

Abraham stroked the pelt on the Fenix's back. "That makes sense. It's only a few months old."

"Maybe so, but it's a strong-willed thing with a deep intelligence of its own. So, you want him to land?"

"Tell him to take me back to the camp. No, wait. Tell him to follow after the Targons."

"Targons?"

"They snatched away one of my Henchmen. Shades. Only a few minutes before Simon appeared. If he can find the scent, maybe he can catch them. They would have been heading toward the old kingdom."

"I'll ask."

For a moment, all of Abraham's concerns faded away. He felt no guilt. No pain. No crosses to bear. Now, only he and the open sky remained.

Simon the Fenix veered away from his eastward path and turned north.

"Whoa," Abraham said. Black Bane's grip was warm in his hand. The runes in the blade had a soft glow. "What's going on?"

"I communicated your desires to the beast. I believe he understands. Apparently, he has a nose like a dwarven setter."

"What is a dwarven setter?"

"Funny that you should ask. A big dog, I think. It's fascinating that I can recall the breed but little to nothing else. But I can still picture many comely women clearly in my mind. How are the women in this world? Are they fetching?"

"Some of them are as fine as wine and sweet as honey."

"It sounds like a fine place to be. What I wouldn't do to sample some cuisine. I don't hunger, but I admit, this metal coffin leaves me quite bored."

"Perhaps when I find a way back to my world, it will send you back to your world too."

"Eh… I'd rather be here. Where I come from is a hellish place—hot, dry, and overrun by evil."

"What about the women?"

"I'll take my chances elsewhere."

Simon's wings beat faster, and they gained speed.

The wind tore through Abraham's hair. "Man, he's moving. He must have picked up on something." With the warm winds caressing his face, he felt like a kid on a roller coaster.

Black Bane didn't reply.

Simon let out a rumble in his throat and dived. His wings stretched to their limits, over thirty feet wide. In a spiral, he glided downward.

Abraham felt the warm handle of the sword grow cold. The fiery glow in the sword's blade went cold.

"Black Bane?"

No response came.

"Asleep again. Well, thanks."

In the fields below, a train of people was moving at a brisk pace. A caged wagon pulled by a horse was among them. Abraham squinted. A man huddled in the cage, but in the night, at that great distance, he was hard to see.

He patted Simon's neck. "Take me closer."

The great batlike dragon swooped lower. He flattened out one hundred feet above the party, like a silent shadow sailing over their ranks.

Abraham caught a better look at that rolling cage. Shades was on his knees with his fingers locked around the bars, looking up at him. The rogue was being led by large men in heavy cloaks with bulges in their backs. He waved at Shades.

Shades made a subtle wave back.

There was no sign of the tigerish creatures that had snatched up Shades earlier, which Abraham had figured to be some sort of wraith or demon. Only the big people in hooded robes were there, moving at a brisk pace. At least twenty of them were there.

Simon circled around.

"Let's make another pass," Abraham said into one of the Fenix's earholes. He had no idea whether the Elder Spawn understood him or not, but he seemed to feel a connection. "A little closer this time."

Simon dipped closer to the ground. The Fenix practically skimmed the ground at fifty feet in height.

The slavers, or whatever they were, didn't tilt a head.

Shades waved his arms wildly.

Abraham tilted his head toward the man and said, "What?"

Shades pointed into the air.

Abraham whipped his head around. A tiger-faced man with the wings of a bird, holding a spear, flew right at him. Abraham knocked the spear aside. The big-bodied attacker's momentum knocked him off Simon's back. Abraham tumbled toward the ground.

CHAPTER 37

Abraham landed flat on his back, and the fall audibly knocked the wind out of him. Fighting for his breath, he rolled over onto his side, sucking for air. He fought his way to his hands and knees, still gripping Black Bane in his hand.

The Targon formed a ring around him. They had the faces of great cats and bodies like Olympian wrestlers. Muscles bulged underneath their robes. They lowered their spears at Abraham. Their hands had fur on them. The fingers' nails were sharp and black.

Abraham sucked for air and finally managed to say, "Hello, kitty."

A Targon with a face like a leopard's rushed over and kicked him in the ribs with the toe of his boot. It sprang away with its green eyes narrowed and whiskers twitching.

"That's the King's Armor I wear. It takes a licking but keeps on ticking." Abraham rose to his feet. He counted eight of the Targon.

A loud screech erupted in the skies above them. Simon the Fenix was locked in battle with four flying Targon. The winged lionlike men cut through the air with the agility of small birds. One jabbed its spear into Simon's hide.

Simon's tail snapped through the air. The barbs growing on the end of his tail struck a Targon in the chest. *Thump!* Blood sprayed from thc wound.

The Targon died in midair. His wings collapsed, and he plummeted from the sky.

The battle above was enough to catch the Targons' attention, allowing Abraham to catch his breath. He couldn't be sure, but some of the Targon appeared to have wings, while the others didn't.

He brandished his sword with a few twists in the air and said, "Listen up, Thundercats. We can do this the easy way or the hard way. And to be clear, the hard way will be fatal."

Two Targon charged him with spears lowered.

Abraham chopped the tip off one spear and sidestepped the other. One Targon impaled the other on the end of his spear.

The battle above kept raging.

Abraham fought for his life below. With roars like lions', the cat-men charged. He split a panther-face's skull. The other five attackers wrestled him to the ground. Teeth bit into Abraham's thigh. A clawed hand slashed his face. He fought through the wild sounds of angry mewing.

He punched.

Kicked.

He slid a dagger out of his belt and stabbed an exposed belly.

The Targon were fierce fighters, cat-quick and nasty. They were light on their feet, perhaps too light…

Abraham rolled on top of a Targon and thrust his weight down. Ribs cracked underneath his power. The cat-man hissed. A claw swiped his face. Abraham gored its chest with the dagger.

"Bad kitty."

Ruger's endless endurance and superior strength slowly overtook the litter. The Targon were big but not strong. Unlike men, they weren't heavy boned either. They were light on their feet. Perhaps that was why they were able to fly.

A Targon sprang onto Abraham from high above. He stepped underneath it and cut clear through its abdomen.

A spear whistled through the air. Abraham slipped his neck aside, though he hadn't seen it coming. Ruger must have had something like a sixth sense. The Targon regrouped. Five of them were left. They jumped Abraham like a bag of kitty litter. Two came at him, spears lowered. Two more flanked to one side and hurled their spears at him.

Abraham jumped forward, avoiding the hurled spears. With sword in one hand and dagger in the other, he hacked down the two charging felines.

Wet blood dripped from his blades. He took the fight to the other attackers. Cloth, fur, and flesh ran red. Black Bane slaughtered. The Targon died with their bright cat eyes fixed on the sky.

Abraham stood in the blood-slicked grasses, searching for more enemies. None came.

He lifted his sword in both hands over his head and said, "Thunder! Thunder! Thundercats! Hoooo—oof!"

A flying Targon flew into his backside, and they tumbled over the grasses. Abraham's grip failed him. He was in a fight for his life against a Targon that was bigger, stronger, and faster than the others.

Abraham punched its face.

The Targon locked its fingers around Abraham's neck and squeezed. The black nails bit into skin.

Abraham latched his fingers around the Targon's neck and squeezed with all his might.

Holy sheetrock, this thing is strong!

The flying Targon had the face of a leopard and carried a superior air about it. It showed no fear in its eyes—only victory. With raw strength, more like an animal's than a man's, it growled in its throat and squeezed hard. The Targon's nails dug into Abraham's thick neck muscles, which did not give.

Abraham wedged his fingers into the thick muscles of the Targon's neck. The cat-man glared into his eyes, its face turning red and purple like Abraham's. His facial fur didn't stand on end. Victory lurked in its eyes, fueled by vengeance.

With a grunt, Abraham squeezed with all his might. "Urk!" The veins in his forearms sprouted like worms. Ruger's engine turned on. Losing air, his engine started to fade. The cat-man's raw power was suffocating him.

What is this thing made of?

The steel-strong limbs in Ruger's body started to give way. Triumph showed in the cat-man's eyes. It had Abraham. He could do nothing.

Farewell, Titanuus.

CHAPTER 38

GLITCH.

The Targon's eyes widened. It let out a ragged mew and slumped over to one side of Abraham's body.

Gasping, Abraham kicked away from his dead attacker. Shades held Abraham's dagger in his hand. The tip dripped blood.

Rubbing his throat, Abraham said, "Good timing. How'd you get out of that cage?"

"No cage can hold me," Shades said. The light-in-stature man extended a hand. "And it is I that should be thanking you, Captain." He flipped the dagger and offered it pommel first to Abraham. "The Targon would have made an example out of me."

Abraham wiped his blade in the grass and sheathed it. All the Targon were dead. The ones that had flown in the sky lay dead on the ground.

Abraham saw no sign of Simon. "Where did the Fenix go?"

"To dinner. He had a Targon in his talons and flew that way." Shades pointed toward the Spine. He made a gritty look. "Your head looks like it's been ripped off and stuck back on again."

"Yeah, well, it feels like it too." He spotted his sword lying in the grass and picked it up. "Man, I thought I was a goner. Those Targon weren't so bad, but the winged ones are tougher than nails."

"The Targon possess natural skill that they rely on more than routine training. Their weakness is their refusal to wear armor." Shades patted down the robes of a dead cat-man. "Like the great cats of the wild, they have incredible instincts, making them excellent trackers. The winged ones are felines supreme, the strongest of the lot. They lead the hunts. If it weren't for that bat thing, I fear you would not have made it. Or would have been enslaved the same as me." He winked at Abraham. "You have interesting friends. But this brood is a bunch of slavers." He moved to another body, rummaged the robes, and fished out a small leather purse. "And slavers have money."

"What is your tie to them?"

Shades shrugged and said, "Well, the Targon seek talent to serve the King of the Mountains."

"In the Old Kingdom."

Shades arched a brow and said, "Yes. You know that."

"Melris had knowledge of the Targons' history."

"I see. Well, the Targon are a very secluded race, as is the King of the Mountain. They have a strange relationship, eons old."

Abraham studied the dead. "These Targon are striking. They don't come across as something that is wicked."

"If you think these men catch your eye, you should see the women. But they aren't any different than the rest of the races. There is good and evil in all of them. This group survived on money." He spilled out the contents of a purse into his hand. Silver shards shaped like guitar picks gleamed dully in his palm. "A decent score."

"So, how did you wind up at the King of the Mountain?"

"Easy. My parents sold me straight out of my homeland in Hancha. That's right. My own flesh and blood sold me for a few rotten songs." He started juggling four shards then added the fifth, sixth, and seventh. "I made money on the streets as an entertainer of sorts." His hands and fingers moved in a blur. "I was good at it. Actually, the thieves' guilds had their eye on me at first, but the Targon came and snatched me away.

"For the king, I worked as a jester and sleight-of-hand magician. I can perform acrobatics, act, and be an expert marksman. In truth, it hadn't been a very bad life. If you took care of the king, he took care of you. At least, so long as your skills remained worthy. He had an assortment of great talent, but the older ones, when they lost a step, would disappear."

"So you escaped?"

Shades touched the star tattoo underneath his right eye. "Escape is not so easy. Like the King's Brand, the Targon slavers have a brand of their own. It allows them to track you no matter where you go." He caught all seven coins in the palm of his hand and lifted a finger. "It's magic, but I learned its secret when I worked as a scribe for one of the king's sages. That's when I learned that another mystic brand can cover the slave brand's detection. I planned my escape and sought to become one of the king's legendary Henchmen." He ran a finger down the scar under his left eye. "That's when I acquired this."

"So that's why you want the brand?" Abraham sheathed his sword. "It figures." He started limping away.

Shades hustled over to him. "I earned the Brand. The same as the rest. I delight in the company of the Henchmen. I'm a faithful follower. And need I remind you, I just saved your life and risked my own." He moved in front of Abraham. "Captain. I need this. The Targon will be back. They'll publicly flay the skin from my bones. I'm not one to beg, but please."

Abraham moved past him. "I'll think about it."

CHAPTER 39

Two mornings later, the Henchmen reunited at the base of the mountains on the side of the Eastern Bolg territories. Abraham and Shades were waiting on them at the bottom of a key mountain pass. Tark and Dominga were the first to track them down.

All the Henchmen had survived the encounter with Simon the Fenix, as his paralyzing breath wore off.

The Henchmen gave Shades a half-hearted welcome back.

Abraham got slaps on the back and hearty handshakes. He brought them all up to speed.

Iris rode in the back of the wagon, tending to Melris. The Elderling had been crushed underneath Simon the Fenix, which was bigger than two elephants. He lay in the wagon, underneath a blanket, with his eyes closed and breathing gently.

"How is he doing?" Abraham asked. He was back on his horse, riding by the wagon.

Sticks was doubled up behind him. They had lost many horses battling the Pitters and the wild panthers.

Iris was stirring ointment in a small bowl with a mixing spoon. She applied the bluish salve to Melris's lips. "He's not dead, and so far as I can tell, he's fully alive. When that beast landed on him, he was crushed into a dip in the ground. His ribs are bruised, but nothing else appears to be broken. Methinks his bones might be soft, like a baby's. Perhaps the Elder of Fortune is his mentor."

"You can't wake him up?" he said.

"I've tried using strong-smelling scents. Nothing stirs the man's sense. I do the best I can to keep water in him." Iris stroked Melris's face. "He's pretty for a young man. I've never felt skin so soft." She tugged on his cheek. "Yet firm as leather."

Abraham nodded. "Let me know when he wakes."

"I will."

They were only two days' ride from Junction City. Abraham's wheels were turning. With Melris down, he could start his hunt for Big Apple. The Elderling had been very persistent about moving straight to the Wound, but his present condition presented the perfect opportunity for Abraham.

"What are you waiting for?" Sticks asked. She gave him a little squeeze from behind.

"What do you mean?"

"I know you're heading straight to Junction City. Now's the perfect time. I'm ready. Let's do it."

Abraham glanced over his shoulder. Vern and Bearclaw were walking alongside Solomon. He waved at the troglin.

Solomon lengthened his stride and caught up with Abraham and Sticks in no time. "Any revelations?"

"No. I wanted to let you know that we are going to ride ahead to Junction City. We want to keep a low profile," he said.

Solomon wiggled his eyebrows and said, "I see. Because I'm giant and hairy, you don't want me around. Ha. I'll get over it. So, you are going after Big Apple, huh?"

"I've got to take a crack at it. That little dingleberry threw us completely off track. He knows more than he lets on. I'm certain the rest of the Sect knows more too." He twisted his head around and looked at the wagon. "And Melris, he's not sharing his entire story either, I'm sure."

"I'll keep an eye on things." Solomon covered more than half of Sticks's back with his paw of a giant hand. "I assume you are taking this butterfly with you, but who else?"

"Shades will come."

"Are you certain?" Sticks said. "He brings danger."

"We had a long talk the past two days. I'm certain."

"Are you going to make him a Henchman?" she asked.

"I'm thinking about it."

"If you want my opinion, I like Shades," Solomon said. "He brings some flavor to an otherwise drab party."

Abraham nodded.

"What does *drab* mean?" Sticks asked.

"Dreary," Solomon replied.

"I'm not drab," she said.

"No, you aren't drab… or happy or sad or angry. I don't know what you are." Solomon chuckled. "It's sexy, and it's not." He eyed Abraham and discreetly asked, "Does she show any kind of emotion? You know…"

Abraham managed a smile and said, "A gentleman never tells."

"You can if you want," Sticks said.

"Oooh, spicy. Now, I like that." Solomon grinned widely. "And she didn't even bat an eye. I like the mystery that comes with this woman." He punched Abraham in the arm, which jostled Abraham in the saddle. "You lucky dog."

"You could have stayed back with the triplets, you know," Abraham said.

"And miss out on all of the fun of being a Henchman?" Solomon tossed his head back. "Ha! I'm seeing this through. Unlike you, I want to get back home."

Abraham instantly thought of Mandi. "Yeah, me too." He felt Sticks's grip tighten around his waist. He'd become a man torn between two worlds and desirable women aplenty. The question was which world was more important—back home or Titanuus. Telling the difference between the two had become impossible. *The only thing I can do is move forward and hope I do right.*

Abraham turned his horse around and brought it to a stop. The Henchmen gathered in front of him.

"Red Tunics, start a fire," he said as he dismounted. He found Shades quietly standing among the group, his hands clasped as he rolled his thumbs over one another. "Horace, fetch the King's Brand."

Several of the Henchmen rolled their eyes, and others sighed.

"Shades, come forward."

CHAPTER 40

"How are you feeling?" Abraham said to Shades.

Shades was slumped over in his saddle, clutching his chest. "I don't recall the last brand hurting so much. I feel like my chest is on fire."

"Consider it payback for what you did to us in Baracha," Sticks said. "If it were up to me, I'd have stuck the hot iron all over you." She was still doubled up in the saddle with Abraham. Only the three of them were traveling.

"I bet you didn't crack when it burned you either," Shades said.

"Never."

The trio was on a roadway leading to Junction City. They rode through light rain along a muddy road with deep wagon-wheel ruts. Their wet cloaks did little to keep their clothing from becoming damp.

Abraham had left Horace in charge of the Henchmen—as long as Melris remained asleep. They were to wait three days on the north side of Junction City for Abraham to return. If they didn't return, Horace could come after them. Shades had been to a tavern called the Broken Wing. Their hunt for Big Apple would start there.

Sticks sniffed the air. "What is that burning smell?"

"We are downwind of Junction City. Those are the smokestacks you smell," Shades said. He pointed ahead. "Once we clear that next rise in the plains, we'll be able to see the city."

Abraham kicked his horse into a trot. Even though he had a mission to complete, he wouldn't mind a hot meal and soft bed. Having Sticks riding behind him got his juices flowing too. She leaned on him from time to time, pressing her breasts into his back.

I'm a dog. Sticks in one world and Mandi in the other. Cheesy time-traveler romances, here I come.

Over the rise, he got his first glimpse of Junction City. "Whoa."

The horse came to a stop, though that wasn't his intent.

Junction City resembled Burgess in layout: stone buildings and stone-paved streets. Huge smokestacks made of cut rock were spread throughout the city, towering over everything else. They were at least one hundred feet high and half as wide as they were tall. Giant plumes of smoke billowed out of the tops of the stacks. The smoke colors varied among a putrid yellow, filmy moss, and dingy white.

A river ran behind the city and snaked through the valley.

Travelers entered and exited the city from all directions, on a variety of roads. The town bustled with activity on all corners.

"A thriving place, eh?" Shades said.

Abraham crinkled his nose and asked, "What are they burning?"

"Refuse. Wood. Coal. People." Shades bobbed his hand. "It keeps the people warm at night."

"Coal? That's interesting. Do the stacks always burn?"

"I haven't spent much time here, but I'd suppose so. Maybe not. I traveled here when I was a boy. Made another pass after I escaped. With hundreds of thousands of people, it's a good place to get lost in." Shades leaned over his saddle horn. "And it appears to be growing."

"Do they have an army? Does the King of Eastern Bolg live in there? I don't see a castle."

"The king lives on the other side of the Little Vein River. Junction City has its own garrison though it's a trading city, open to all territories. Aside from Kingsland, of course. You won't see any blue banners with lion's heads and white wings here. I'm certain of that. Shall I lead?"

"Take us to the Broken Wing. I don't want to waste any time."

"Aye, aye, Captain." Shades gave his horse a kick and led them toward the city.

One hundred yards out, a group of four riders wearing leather armor dyed gray and skull-cap helmets rode right toward them.

"Who are they?" Abraham asked.

"Representatives of Junction City's garrison. They are called the Gray Guard. They aren't the friendliest bunch either." Shades lined his horse between Abraham and the oncoming men. "It's best that you let me do the talking."

Abraham recalled Shades's work on the *Sea Talon* when they'd been boarded by the trio of brothers called Captain Alphonso. They were from Tiotan, and Shades had bribed them.

He gave the rogue a nod and said, "Go for it."

The soldiers closed in at a full gallop.

"They aren't slowing," Sticks said. "Shouldn't they be slowing?"

"I would think so." Shades stopped his horse.

Abraham did the same. He dropped his hand to his sword. "I don't think that's a welcome wagon. They look like they want to kill somebody."

His heartbeat pumped in his ears. Something was up. Big Apple must have known they were coming.

Sticks's hands slid away from his body as she pulled his dagger from his belt. "I need to borrow this."

CHAPTER 41

The Gray Guard thundered past the visiting trio at full speed. They didn't even give the small company a glance. They rode fast and hard and disappeared over the rise.

"See? I told you that I would handle it," Shades said. "Did you even notice that they didn't have weapons drawn?"

"Weapons that we could see," Abraham said. "I wonder where they are going? There isn't much of anything between us and the others."

"There isn't much traffic coming from the south either," Sticks added. "But the Henchmen can handle themselves."

Abraham flipped out a hand. "Lead the way."

Their horses' hooves hit the cobblestone streets several minutes later. Junction City was a nice city, by medieval standards. The people were just in an array of robes and fine linens. Merchant carts and merchant wagons rattled over the streets.

Abraham's forehead started to bead. He watched a wagon full of coal roll by. The churning fires in the smokestacks created an extra layer of warmth in the city. They created a stuffiness too. A mild odor lingered in the street. The wind shifted direction, bringing forth the smell of burning wood.

They stabled the horses and walked the streets. Men and women shouted back and forth from their windows. Children raced through the streets, pushing a metal ring with a stick.

A group of gawkers gathered around a salesman who stood on a small platform and had a curtain stage behind him. His thumbs were in his suspenders. He had a tall hat and handlebar moustache. Behind him was a contraption that looked very much like a bicycle.

"Oh no," Abraham muttered as an icy shiver raced down his spine. He saw men and women pulling carts like rickshaws.

Women shielded themselves from the sun with medieval umbrellas.

A lanky fellow with hair down to his waist carried a wooden sign that said Showgirls. He twisted it around his body in a showy fashion.

People from all walks of life were strolling through Junction City as well: scale-covered Myrmidons, bruising barbarians, pale-faced zillons and troglins appearing here and there, cat-faced Targon gliding through the crowds.

He gave Shades a worried look.

"Let's hope they aren't slavers," Shades said coolly.

Sticks nudged Abraham's ribs with an elbow. She pointed her eyes toward the top of a smokestack. A dragon like the ones the zillons flew basked in the warmth of the stack's smoke.

"It seems they take all kinds in this town. Shades, how many taverns do you think this city holds?"

"Dozens. Is that where you want to start looking?"

They walked by a haunting garden protected by a wrought-iron gate. A Sect temple loomed in the background.

"We could always start there. They know where the trouble is," Sticks said. "They'll be distracted since we killed Arcayis."

"True, but someone must have stepped up. No doubt they will have named a new Underlord," Shades added.

"Yeah, I think the Big Apple would have answers to that too. That mission had his stink all over it," he said.

A trio of jugglers waltzed by, tossing fruit and knives between their hands.

Shades walked right between the juggling act, plucked two knives out of the volley, and tossed them each into separate fruits. The move left the jugglers gaping.

"We are keeping a low profile," Abraham warned.

"Sorry, I couldn't help myself," Shades quipped. "Ah, here it is." He moved toward a tavern painted a dull red.

A heavy-set woman sat in an Adirondack-style chair, fanning herself. Beside her was a pretty young woman in skimpy clothing with the dark eyes and straight hair of an Asian. She stood behind a booth, selling wooden tokens.

"You, sir. Big strong man. For only five silver shards, you can drink all you want from our chain of taverns." The young woman slipped from behind the stand, grabbed his hand, and rubbed her nubile body against him. "Your choice of ale, grog, and fruity mixers." She glanced at Sticks. "We have many prettier girls too."

Abraham tried to pull his hand away, but the little woman wouldn't let go.

Sticks belted her in the stomach.

"Hey! Don't you hit my ladies!" The big woman sitting in the chair started to rise. Her face was turning as pink as her robes. She had a scratchy, husky voice. "I'll have the bruisers skin you alive!"

Shades slipped some silver shards into the fat of the woman's palm. "We'll take three tokens. And there is a little something extra for you. You'll have to forgive my little brother. He doesn't get out much."

"She's a he?" the fat woman asked.

"In most territories." Shades gave Sticks an ornery look while the woman counted the coins in her hand.

She bit down on one shard with her bad teeth and nodded her saggy chin. "That's good coin. Targon. I'll take it." She kicked the young girl in the ribs. "Will you get moving and give these fine customers their tokens?"

The girl fished the coins out of a box in her booth and gave them to the older woman. She bowed and moved away.

The big woman in the chair stuffed the tokens into Shades's hand. "Have yourself a good time, you handsome little fella. The Broken Wing welcomes you! Ha ha!" She swatted Shades on the behind as he entered. She did the same to Abraham and Sticks. "You two fellas have a good time as well."

The Broken Wing was another decrepit tavern filled with broken tables and chairs that had been mended back together time and time again. Oily-skinned men and women drank, ate, smoked, and cursed at the tables. The bar on one side of the tavern and the granite-block fireplace on the other side of the bar were the main fixtures.

The food smelled fried and greasy. The smell of baked hot rolls tickled Abraham's nose. A scent of spiced pumpkin lingered in the sweltering air.

That was the first thing Abraham noticed. The second was the strands of eye-popping bikinilike clothing worn by the fetching women. They walked the floors with hips swaying and eyelashes batting. Trays of drinks were balanced delicately in their hands. The strumpets were a mixed lot of women, Myrmidons, zillons, and cat-faced feline women who had to have been Targon.

Abraham swallowed the lump in his throat.

A woman slipped behind him and purred in his ear. She had white fur with tiger stripes, pink eyes of a rose, a wisp of black clothing, and a human body to die for. "Hello, handsome," she said. "Let me find you a seat. I'm Lila."

"It's no surprise that you picked a dwelling full of trollops," Sticks said to Shades.

"And it's no surprise that others easily mistake you for a man."

Sticks punched the man in his arm.

Mesmerized, Abraham let the gorgeous tigerish woman seat him at the table. He wet his lips and said, "Thank you."

The Targon waitress caressed his face, gently scratching it with her clawed fingertips. With a sexy purr in her voice, she said, "Just whistle if you need me." She strolled away.

That was when Abraham noticed the third pertinent thing. He turned to scan his surroundings with a smile all over his face. As he swiveled around in his chair, he found himself looking at the broad side of a huge man's back.

Their elbows bumped.

The man turned.

It was Commander Cutter from Hancha.

CHAPTER 42

Abraham was a second from ramming his elbow into Commander Cutter's broad face when Sticks jumped into Abraham's lap and kissed him.

Commander Cutter shoved his elbow into Abraham's shoulder. The blow knocked him and Sticks onto the floor.

"Watch what you're doing, whore," Cutter said in a grizzly voice. Without even looking at them, he picked up his pint of ale and guzzled it. He wiped his forearm across the white scar on his chin. The man was a mass of muscle, with a short haircut and strong angular features. He wore a black cloak and grabbed his bastard sword, propped up against the wall. "Let's go, Black Squadron. This whore hole is getting too crowded for a big fella like me."

Abraham and Sticks continued to kiss. She started to get into it, and his heart raced—not because of her but more because of the presence of the Black Squadron. They were a company of Hancha's elite soldiers. They wore burgundy tunics with upside-down black ankhs over suits of chain mail. The Henchmen had encountered them before in a small town in Hancha. Commander

Cutter had hunted them from Pirate's Harbor. Shades had burned that tavern down as a distraction. They crossed them again after their victory in Cauldron City. Commander Cutter challenged Ruger Slade, but Slade the Blade had refused.

Commander Cutter and his small company of four departed the Broken Wing to the disappointed flattering and musings of the serving girls.

Abraham sat up. Sticks broke off her kiss but still straddled him. He scanned the room. No more members of the Black Squadron remained to be seen.

Shades stepped into view and offered his hand. "I see our mighty friend is back."

Abraham took Shades's hand and stood up with Sticks's legs still locked around his waist. He gave her the big eye and asked, "What's gotten into you?"

"Perhaps it's the competition. I saw that hungry look that you gave the Targon."

"My my, Sticks has a jealous bone. I never thought I'd see the day," Shades said cheerfully. "She's human after all."

"We have bigger things to worry about." He set down Sticks even though he was so riled up that he didn't want to. "Shades, get us a room with a view of the street. A balcony would be great." He cast his glance all over the bar. "I've got a feeling that if Cutter is here, so is Big Apple. It's no coincidence. Keep an eye out for Lord Hawk too. Probably a bunch of members of the Shell about. We better lie low."

Shades scored a room on the second level of the tavern. Using a key, he let them inside. "It's all yours. I'll send up some food."

"Where are you staying?" Abraham asked.

Shades winked at him and said, "With all of these ladies strolling about, I won't need a room. They'll offer me one of theirs." He closed the door.

The room was large, with a queen-size bed covered in a purple quilt and pillows. Two storage chests sat along the wall, along with a desk and mirror and a table for two by the window. A single door opened to the outside balcony.

Abraham opened the door and said, "I bet I could be rich if I invented the sliding door for this country."

Sticks sat down on the edge of the bed and started taking her cloak off.

"Uh, what are you doing?"

She took the long braids out of her hair and combed them out with her fingers. She flipped her head down and tousled her hair and flipped it back. Her dark-auburn locks hung on her shoulders. Her tomboyish good looks started to stand out. She removed her bandolier and unbuckled her tunic.

Abraham swallowed. "Uh, Sticks, Shades will be back with food at any moment."

She raised a brow, made a quirky smile, and said, "No, he won't."

"We need to find the Big Apple and see what Cutter is up to. I know they are here. We have a mission."

Sticks pulled off her trousers. All she wore was a cotton shirt that hung down past her waist. She walked over to him, took him by the hand, and led him to the bed. She pushed him down onto the bed, tugged his trousers off, and straddled him. "I have a mission too. I want you, and I want you now."

CHAPTER 43

Abraham and Sticks hit the festive streets of Junction City. Some sort of celebration was going on. People marched over the paved roadways, playing instruments, wearing costumes, and carrying a variety of flags and banners. He got a vibe like what he'd gotten before when he visited Mardi Gras on Bourbon Street in New Orleans.

Sticks held Abraham's hand and walked with her, arms swinging.

What is going on with her?

The expressionless woman showed little emotion in her face or otherwise. But when she wanted something, she didn't hesitate to take it. She might not say much, but she carried a passionate intensity in her eyes. Those eyes said it all, and she had taken Abraham.

Still, the hand holding and arm swinging seemed awkward. She led the way.

"Come over here," she said in a chipper tone.

Along the streets were small booths where women painted the faces of men and women celebrating in the parade. He overheard people talking about a contest of costumes going on. The more he looked about, the more odd characters he saw. People were dressed like dragons, birds, rodents, cats, and even clowns of a sort. Some disheveled drunken men even mimicked the Gray Guard soldiers while they sang at the top of their lungs, swinging arm in arm.

The array of custom clothing was bright and colorful in some cases, dreary and dark in others. The women strutted about shamelessly in tight silken bodysuits that left very little to the imagination. They rubbed up against Abraham when they walked by with smiles and flirtatious giggles.

What is this, Comic-Con?

"Come on, Abraham, sit down," Sticks said. She patted a stool.

"What are we doing?" he asked as he pulled his head away from a cute teenage girl with roses in her hair, who tried to apply makeup to him. "Hey, I'm not into that!"

"Shush, we can't look like ourselves and risk being seen." She planted her rear end on a stool beside him. "Now, what sort of creature would you like to look like?"

"I don't know. Back home, we had a holiday called Halloween. We'd dress up in something scary. I liked doing scary." He saw some men strolling by with ugly masks on. "Can't I do that?"

"No." She sat with her back straight and her cheeks sucked in as the girl attending her put on a base layer of makeup. "A mask will distort your senses."

"What are you going to be?"

"A cat," she said.

"Really, a cat? That's not very original."

She eyeballed him and replied, "Back in the Broken Wing, you seemed to like them."

He'd seen more women dressed up as cats at Halloween parties than anything else he could recall. In some cases, it might have been sexy, but it wasn't very original.

"It's fine," he said.

Sticks frowned. "Fine? Is there something else that you'd rather I be?"

"No, I'm good with the whiskers. Go for it." He looked at the girl powdering him up. "Give me a white face with two blazing silver stars over my eyes."

The girl shrugged and quickly got to work. A few minutes later, the makeup job was over.

"How do I look?" Sticks asked.

She had her face painted white and was given black whiskers and a red button nose. The makeup artist accented her eyes with black and gold, giving her a very desirable feline look.

"Pretty hot. I take back what I said about the cat thing."

"What are you supposed to be? I don't recognize that image. Is it something from your world?"

"Yeah, I'm Ace Frehley. Do you like it?"

She lifted her shoulders as she paid the young woman. "I think a cat would have been better."

"Nah, Space Ace is the way to go." He played the air guitar. "Lead the way, cat lady."

Sticks led them through the raucous crowd. Bars and taverns ran from one end of the road to the other. The bars associated with the Broken Wing each had a blue front door.

They crossed the street, and as they did so, Abraham caught four dudes in Kiss makeup marching by. They flashed him the Kiss sign. He gingerly flashed them back.

Oh man, this isn't good. This is crazy. I'm crazy.

They spent the next few hours moving from bar to bar, trying to locate Commander Cutter and his men. The tavern floors were sticky. The sweaty people coming in and out started to smell. Smoke in the barrooms became a thick fog.

Abraham sipped on his beer. His eyes burned. Sticks would sit hip to hip beside him. He felt lost, but in a good way. People would look right through him. He bobbed his head to the thumping beat of the music. *I could get used to this.*

They made it through four bars and spent a little time in each before moving on to the next.

Commander Cutter was nowhere to be found. They hit three more blue-door taverns. Sticks made her rounds and asked a few questions. Abraham sat quietly and observed. The townsfolk of Junction City lined up shots of liquor and played drinking games. Hearty men bounced shards into glass tumblers and drank.

The party atmosphere was like ones he'd seen at college. It reminded him of his time with the team after baseball games. It was close to home—too close. A headache started to build between his eyes. He set down his beer and wetted his lips. He needed water.

Sticks came back and joined him at the table. "Are you well?"

"I don't know."

A woman in a long red coat with a matching wide-brimmed hat came in. Men with leather boots, moustaches, and cowboy vests strolled in after her.

"Did you find out anything?" He gripped the table with the end of his fingers. "Big Apple is here. I know it." His chair started to turn underneath him. "Sticks, is the room moving?"

"No," she said.

She sounded as though she were on the other side of the bar. "I need to get out of here. I need fresh air." He stood on wobbly knees.

A man shoved him down into his chair and said, "You aren't going anywhere."

CHAPTER 44

ABRAHAM GRABBED THE MAN BY the chest and reeled him in. The man wore a mask with the face of a chimpanzee. A hooded cloak covered his head and shoulders.

"Who are you?" Abraham asked.

"Easy, easy," the man behind the monkey mask said. He lifted the mask.

"Shades." Abraham shoved the man back. His own head started to spin a little.

Sticks tucked away her daggers. "What are you doing, fool?"

Shades made a meow sound and said, "I like the makeup, kitten. Quite the improvement. Is there any chance that it's permanent?"

"Shut up," she replied.

Abraham shook the fog from his head and asked, "Where have you been?" He looked the man up and down. "And why are you taller?"

Shades plopped down in a chair, bent over, and lifted his cloak. One-foot-high wooden stilts were fastened to his boots. "It's all part of my disguise, Captain." He stared hard into Abraham's face. "No fancy makeup required. Uh, what are you supposed to be?"

"Ace Frehley. A famous bard back home."

"Ah, I see. It's quite fetching." Shades rolled his eyes. "So, have you had any luck tracking down Commander Cutter?"

"No." Abraham fanned himself. "I need some water. What about you?"

"As a matter of fact, I came from his very spot."

Abraham sat up.

Sticks leaned forward. "Well?"

"Two blocks over is a tavern called the Showboat. There are many pretty dancing girls." He shrugged his pale eyebrows. "They have Commander Cutter and his brood captivated. Shall we press on?"

Abraham rose to his feet and headed to the door. He stumbled out into the street and gulped for fresh air.

Shades and Sticks followed behind, with Shades asking, "What's wrong with him? Did the Captain have one too many?"

Sticks hooked a hand around Abraham's waist and said, "No, I don't think so. What's wrong, Abraham? You aren't going to black out, are you?"

He took a deep, long breath through his nostrils, and his head started to clear. He straightened back up. "No, I'll be fine. Whew, I don't know what came over me." He wiped the cold sweat from his brow on a sleeve. "The bar was suffocating. I don't know what it was."

"I'll lead the way," Shades said with an uneasy glance. He pulled his monkey mask down. With his stilts on, he stood only a few inches shorter than Ruger. "I like being taller. I can get a better view of people, and it's not as smelly. Trust me when I say there is nothing worse than standing underneath a dirty man's armpit."

The word Showboat was painted on a wooden sign hanging over the tavern's blue door. A burly bouncer type in common garb stood outside the door, with arms crossed and a wary look in his eyes. The bruiser had a mohawk and goatee. The bouncer grabbed Shades by the collar and said, "You again? I don't like you."

Shades flashed the token. "I have this."

"I don't care. I don't like your face!" The bouncer spat as he talked.

"It's only a mask," Shades said as he wiped the spit from his mask. "I can take it off."

"No." The bouncer shoved him away. "Get out of here before I break your legs."

Abraham and Sticks were the next in line.

The bouncer eyed them both, took a long, hard look at Abraham and said, "You're a big one. Bigger than me." He nodded and eyeballed Sticks. "Lucky for you, I like cats. I have a couple myself in my flat. Lilly and Tiger." He stepped aside. "Enjoy, but don't make trouble, or I'll bust you up."

Abraham nodded, took a deep breath, and shuffled inside.

Incense burned in the tavern like a bad perfume. The bar sweltered. Big bodies were crammed behind small tables. The tavern dwellers faced a stage full of dancing girls on the opposite end.

Sticks zeroed in on two stools open behind the bar. She dropped on one before another man and woman could take them. She hitched her thumb and said, "Find another spot."

The man started to say something back to Sticks but had second thoughts when he looked up at Ruger. The couple left.

Abraham took a seat. "Man, these places smell."

The bartender was an Asian-looking woman who wore a white shirt underneath a black vest. She set down a pair of steaming towels on a plate before them.

He and Sticks exchanged a glance.

"It's for your sweat!" the bartender said in a smart-alecky Chinese-like accent.

"We have makeup on," Sticks fired back.

"So!" The bartender gave them both a disappointed look. "You got coin or just hogging stools?"

Abraham and Sticks flashed their tokens.

The bartender filled two shot glasses with a wine-red liquid. "Cherry brandy. Drink up. It's good for the sweats. Go ahead, drink it."

Abraham didn't want to drink, but he tapped his glass against Sticks's and said, "Bottoms up." After they both drank, his face soured. "Ugh, that tastes like cough syrup."

"No syrup. Cherry brandy. Do you want ale? Devil's fire? A prairie fire. I'm busy. Tell me what you want," the bartender said.

Sticks lifted two fingers and said, "Ale." She turned her back to the bar and faced the stage. "Looks like Shades was right. There's Cutter."

Cutter sat behind a small table, like a man among boys, hunched over. His bastard sword was propped up against the wall nearby. A group of his Black Squadron were with him. They were all armed, but judging by the women on their laps, they were having a good time—except Cutter. No woman accompanied him. His eyes were on the stage.

The exotic dancers moved their nubile bodies to the thumping beat of bongos, chimes, and the sound of a flute. They were short ladies, representing many of the races, and they would weave their way through the crowd in an enticing manner.

Cutter shrugged off their advances. He'd look them up and down and push them aside.

"It looks like he's a picky one," Sticks said.

"He's probably waiting on someone and doesn't want to be distracted," he said.

"I bet I can distract him," Sticks said.

"What do you mean?"

She departed for the stage, saying, "Watch and see."

CHAPTER 45

Sticks vanished into the crowd, leaving Abraham scratching his head. He turned his attention back to Cutter's table. Cutter's men pawed the women and pulled them into their laps. Some of the dancers squirmed away, and others didn't.

Cutter slugged down his ale and scratched his ear. The man had a high-and-tight military cut and was built and looked like a bulldog.

Abraham eyed the man's bastard sword. *I wonder how good he really is.*

Ruger Slade was rumored to be the best swordsman in the world. The competitive spirit of Abraham embraced that, and he had a feeling that the body of Ruger did too. The raucous atmosphere stirred something inside him. He touched the pommel of his sword, wanting to test his mettle.

The thumping beat of the music shifted to a sultry melody. The rowdy men in the room fell silent for a moment. They craned their necks as the light on the stage dimmed.

A woman appeared on the stage who stood out among the other dancers. Her hands carried flames. She swayed to the beat and moved the flames from one hand to another.

Abraham narrowed his eyes. The woman's face was painted like a cat. A skimpy two-piece outfit hugged her sensual curves. It was Sticks.

With a body that was the envy of all the other dancers, Sticks made her way off stage and into the crowd. She moved with the sexy prowess of a feline. Sweat glistened on her flat belly. Her hips swayed with every step, leaving men's tongues hanging out of their mouths.

Sticks's captivating movements had his heart beating in his throat.

"I really like this cat version of her better," Shades said in his smooth Australian-style accent. "She's a real dog otherwise."

Abraham twisted his head around and said, "I didn't think you were allowed in here."

"Pfft, do you think that sack of meat could keep me from slipping into a tavern?" Shades took off his mask. "They have a back door, you know. The cook let me in. She was a cutie."

The bartender set down a steaming cloth, a mug of ale, and a shot of cherry brandy in front of Shades. "You need anything else?"

"How about some mix?" Shades said.

Abraham turned his attention back to Sticks. She was making her way through the crowd and moving the flames from hand to hand. She would blow out the candles on the tables in an enticing fashion and light them again with her own flame.

Shades nudged Abraham. "Have some mix? It's good stuff."

Abraham found himself looking at a bowl of peanuts. His jaw hung.

Shades cracked open a shell, ate the nut, and tossed the shell on the floor. "Have you had some? I bet they don't have a treat like this in your world."

As alarming as the sight of peanuts was, it didn't hold a candle to the performance Sticks was giving on the floor. Lust filled the eyes of men. They hooted and hollered for more.

Shades crunched down on his bowl of mix and said, "She has a fine rear end, doesn't she? It's her best asset, if you ask me."

"What is she doing?"

"She's working on the big fella, Cutter. You know, she's going to seduce him." Shades grinned. "You know, squeeze him for information."

Abraham didn't hide his shock.

"Don't worry, I'm sure she'll hate every bit of being with a large fella like that," Shades added. "But a Henchman has to do what a Henchman has to do."

"She's going to sleep with him?"

"We are spies. We do what we do."

"Great," Abraham said with a disappointing shake of his head. "I'm dating Jane Bond."

"Don't worry, there are more Sticks in the sea."

"Don't you mean *fish*?" Abraham asked.

"Sure. You do remember that Sticks and I had a thing for a good while," Shades added. He tossed more shells on the floor. "It's best not to get so attached. But we are a tight group. Hard to avoid those love triangles that surface."

Abraham swatted the bowl of peanuts out of Shades's hands. The mix scattered, and the bowl shattered.

"You pay for that!" the bartender said. "That was my number-one bowl. It will cost you extra."

Abraham turned his back on the bartender with his nostrils flaring. He focused on Sticks. He'd just slept with her, and now she was seducing a room full of men. It shouldn't have bothered him, but it did.

"Don't let your skull boil," Shades said as he slipped the bartender some shards. "It's the king's business. Make the most of it." He handed Abraham a mug of ale. "Have a drink. You're too rigid to blend in."

"Ooh, I see the problem. Big man with star face has a slutty woman," the bartender said. "I would like to hire her." She started wiggling her shoulders. "She make my customers very happy."

Abraham took a deep breath. *Don't let it eat you up. None of this might be real anyway.*

Sticks made her way toward Cutter. The warrior's gaze swallowed her body as he rubbed his chin. The expressionless woman went right at him. Her eyes locked with his and burned with sultry intensity. She held her hands in front of Cutter's face, flames dancing in her palms. Cutter blew them out and grinned. She hopped into his lap. He picked her up with a smile on his face and walked by Abraham and straight out of the bar.

CHAPTER 46

"WHAT WAS THAT ALL ABOUT? I thought he was waiting on somebody," Abraham mused.

"He was," Shades replied. "Her."

The four remaining soldiers of the Black Squadron started to depart. The hard-eyed soldiers, who had a Henchmen-type quality, escorted dancers out of the bar.

The soldiers walked by with drunken grins on their faces.

Shades tripped the one third from the back. The man tumbled into the backside of the man in front of him. The first soldier went down as well.

"Say! I saw you do that!" the soldier in the back said.

"I did too," said one of the pretty dancers. She pointed at Shades. "It was this little weasel."

"I reckon this little hound needs to be taught a lesson," said the soldier in the back.

Abraham punched the talking man in the face. The man fell like a stone.

Shades kicked the soldier he'd tripped in the side of the face. He said to Abraham, "Take care of this mess. I'll catch up with you." He bolted for the front door.

"Wait!" Abraham said. He started after Shades. One of the soldiers on the floor tackled his legs and drove him back into the bar. He punched the man in the ribs. The soldier was well padded up with a tunic over chain mail.

He hit the man harder.

The man let out a groan.

"Stop fighting! Stop fighting!" the bartender said. She cracked Abraham over the head with a ceramic jug, and ale spilled all over him.

The dancing girls screamed and scattered.

The soldiers in front came to their feet and rushed Abraham.

Abraham wrestled against two men. They whaled on one another.

"You want a fight? We'll fight! No one attacks the Black Squadron and lives!" the first soldier said.

A burly patron smashed a chair over the talking soldier's back.

Abraham twisted away from the man he'd been punching and shoved the man into the crowd.

A bar brawl broke out.

The bartender jumped up on the bar and screamed, "See what you did?" She thrust a finger at Abraham. "You are paying for this!"

Abraham dropped some silver shards on the table and bolted out of the front door.

The wee hours of the night had come, but the streets were still bustling with celebration. He saw no sign of Shades or Sticks.

"Great!" Abraham rushed through the streets, trying to find his friends.

A parade of costumed people marched by, blowing horns and tossing confetti.

All four Black Squadron members spilled out of the Showboat. They spotted Abraham from across the street. One of them pointed at Abraham and shouted, "There!" They pulled their swords and ran after him.

Abraham jumped in with the parade.

The Black Squadron, drunk or not, weren't fooled. They plowed into the paraders and shoved them aside. They hacked at Abraham with their swords.

A sword tip came within a whisker of Abraham's nose. *That was too close.* He bolted away from his pursuers and ducked into a dead-end alley. With his back to the wall, he pulled his sword just as the Black Squadron closed him in.

"You're dead now, painted fool," said the tallest man in the front. "No one crosses the Black Squadron and lives."

"Wouldn't the Gray Guard take issue with you killing one of their citizens?" Abraham fired back. "Murder is a crime."

"Not when it's self-defense, plus"—he glanced at his men—"I have three witnesses, and you have none." He advanced with his sword ready to parry.

Two street urchins bolted out of the alley. Three cats bounded after them.

"I'm really good with this sword," Abraham warned. "You might want to reconsider and walk away."

"Just because you're big doesn't mean you're good with a blade. I've cut down much bigger, you painted-face oaf." The soldier waded in and lunged. It was a good jab from the ox guard position.

Abraham slid to the side, swung, and cut the man's head clean off.

The dead soldier fell to the ground with blood spurting from his neck.

The remaining three soldiers gaped. Their astonished eyes were blinking.

Abraham twisted his blade in the air and said, "A lucky stroke. Who is next?"

Two Black Squadron soldiers crept in as one. With their eyes narrowed, they came in at high guard position.

They were skilled and seasoned soldiers. Abraham could tell even though their drunkenness made their movements sloppy. On a sober night, they might have proven a better fight.

As one, the soldiers advanced and thrust downward.

Abraham blocked both swords. He shoved them backward, turned his hip, and slashed Black Bane through their guts.

The disemboweled men dropped to their knees.

"That was fast," the last soldier said. His sword hand trembled. "Who are you? You're as good as Cutter."

"I'm Ace Frehley. Rock star." Abraham held Black Bane like a guitar and started to air jam. "Black Squadron, I hear you calling. What's it going to be? I tell you what. I'll even close my eyes."

With a sneer, the soldier gripped his sword with two hands, tilted his head, narrowed his eyes, and said, "Say, I recognize you. We tracked you in Hancha. You're Ruger Slade."

The sweat and spilt ale must have washed away part of Abraham's makeup. "No, I'm Space Ace."

The soldier tipped his chin. "Sure. If you say so." He took a step closer. "Go ahead. Close those eyes, Ace."

Abraham shut his eyelids. The sound of running boot steps caught his ears. The heavy steps weren't closing in. They were going away.

The Black Squadron soldier was running away like the six-fingered man in *The Princess Bride*. He raced toward the end of the alley.

"Crap!" Abraham sprinted after the man. The last thing he wanted was for the soldier to warn Cutter. "Coward! A member of the Black Squadron shouldn't run."

The soldier disappeared around the corner at the end of the alley.

Abraham barreled into the street and headed in the direction where the man had run away.

The soldier was gone.

Abraham wiped his sword off on his cloak and sheathed it. "What a cluster."

CHAPTER 47

Abraham jogged the streets and sidewalks, ducking into alley after alley but finding no sign of the soldier, Shades, or Sticks. His search went on for minutes as he drifted anxiously through the city. Standing inside an alley, he kicked a crate.

"Bloody meatballs!"

He didn't have any doubt that the soldier had run off to warn Cutter. He could only hope that Sticks wouldn't blow her own cover. Cutter had gotten a good look at her before.

Abraham turned over a barrel and sat down in the shadows of the alley. He watched the thinning parade of people strolling by. He took a deep breath, leaned his head against the wall, and closed his eyes. Another headache was coming on. He thought about Sticks. Mandi. The thought of both women being in danger tore his heart in two.

He beat his head against the wall.

"What are you doing?"

Abraham's eyes snapped open to see Shades in front of him with his monkey mask on. "I could ask you the same."

"I'm not kissing stone with the back of my head. What's the problem?"

"One of the Black Squadron recognized me. I killed the others, but he ran. I lost him." He sighed. "I'm certain that he'll tell Cutter that we are here. Sticks could be in more danger."

Shades looked out on the street and back at him. "I found the dwelling where Cutter is. I managed to catch up with him. Would you like to see it?"

Abraham jumped up. "Why didn't you mention that in the first place?"

"I didn't want to interrupt your sulking. Besides, she can take care of—"

Abraham shoved him out of the alley. "Lead the way."

Shades picked up the pace and led him to a ratty tavern on the river side of the city. It had a double-door front entrance with one door closed. Two drunken women staggered outside. A stairwell leading to the top room's balcony started at the bottom of the tavern's alley. He pointed at the balcony, which wrapped around the rickety tavern. "They went up there. Headed to the back."

Just inside the alley at the bottom of the stairs, a Black Squadron soldier was leaning against the wall.

"I think he's good." Shades waltzed right at the man.

Abraham tried to hook the rogue's arm, but he slipped out of reach.

The man didn't move when Shades approached.

Creeping forward, Abraham said, "Is he sleeping?"

"You could say that." Shades tapped the man on the chest. "Are you asleep?"

"What are you doing?"

Shades lifted the man's head back, showing his cut throat. "I caught up with the rat at the bottom of the stairs. He didn't see me coming. They never do."

Abraham recognized the soldier that had fled in the alley. "I guess my secret is safe with him."

Some familiar gusty laughter could be heard from inside the rundown tavern. Abraham put his ear to the wall. More hearty laughter belted out again on the other side.

"That's him."

"Him?" Shades asked.

Abraham pulled the mask off Shades's face. He put it on and said, "Watch my back."

He staggered into the tavern doorway and leaned heavily on the door frame. The eyelets in the monkey mask were small, but the visibility was decent. Hunched over, he teetered in the bar area. The tables were half full of dwellers in sordid clothing, with bloodshot eyes. The smoke was as thick as pea soup.

In the back of the bar, by a cold fireplace, Big Apple sat on a barstool. A woman's muddy blouse was stretched between the stubby horns on his head. He puffed on a thick cigar. The bare-chested, musclebound halfling tossed his head back, chortling. Women were wrestling in a mud pit. His eyes were lit like fire.

"I'll be," Abraham muttered. He pushed some talents onto the bar and sank into a stool.

Big Apple was surrounded by a bunch of goons who looked like executioners from a medieval dungeon. They wore black hoods, and chains crossed over their backs. Each of them carried a mace.

The bartender, an ugly guy with a pitted face, slid a tankard of beer his way. He looked just like Sam from Pirate Harbor and gave Abraham a wary eye.

Abraham managed a loud belch underneath his mask.

The bartender moved away.

He moved down to the end of the bar, where he could get a better eye at the festivities. Three women were in the ring of mud, slugging it out with a fat man in white. *It can't be.*

A man walked behind Abraham and rubbed shoulders against his. He and his escort took a seat near Big Apple. Abraham immediately recognized Lord Hawk. The leader of the Shell wore his signature black vest over a maroon shirt. The gorgeous Myrmidon woman, Kawnee, escorted Lord Hawk. They glanced at Ruger, but he looked away from both of them, focusing on the action in the ring.

It looks like the gang is all here. His fingertips tingled. *Now what?*

Big Apple clucked away as though he'd never laughed before. The obnoxious horned halfling shouted over every blurry-eyed patron in the room. "Fight, fat man! Fight!"

Abraham dared a glance at Big Apple's table.

Lord Hawk was whispering in Big Apple's ear. He subtly pointed at Abraham.

Oh no, they recognized me. He scooted away from the scene from one stool to another.

Big Apple huffed smoke out of his nose, pointed his stubby cigar hand at Abraham, and said, "I want you! Don't move a muscle."

CHAPTER 48

Abraham pointed at his own chest in a "who, me?" gesture.

"Yes, you, monkey face!" Big Apple said boldly. "I want you to get in the mud ring with my girls. I've never seen them wrestle a monkey before." He stiffly clapped his hands. "Get in there."

Abraham shook his head.

Big Apple tilted his head to the side and asked, "Are you telling me no?" He looked at Lord Hawk. "Is he telling me no?"

Lord Hawk leaned back in his chair, hooked his arm over the back of his chair, and said, "I believe that he is. He's a large man too. Like one of those mountain gorillas. You know, I bet he thinks he can handle the likes of me and you."

Big Apple grabbed a mug of ale from his table and slung it into the fireplace. He jumped up and stood on top of his stool. "Me! You think that you can handle me 'cause I'm little?" He flexed his arms and chest. The horned halfling's muscles bulged like a little Hercules. "Come and see if you can take me."

Abraham waved his hands in front of him. He noticed Lord Hawk toying with the handle of the revolver on his hip. Kawnee sat beside him with a playful smile on her fish face. He slid off his stool and backed away. His body, on the other hand, had other ideas. Ruger's body wanted to fight. He wanted to fight all of them—kill them all. They reeked of evil.

I'd probably be better off if I killed them. But I need answers.

"Hey, monkey face," Big Apple said. "Why don't you take that mask off?" He looked him up and down. "And stand up straight. I want a better look at you. You can't fool me by hunching over."

This is going bad.

He backed toward the door. The air surrounding him turned ice cold. He twisted his head over his shoulder and looked up.

In black robes, the towering wraith, Fleece, stood behind Abraham. No face could be seen inside the hood, only pitch-black darkness. The tatters of Fleece's robes moved with a ghostly life of their own.

Frost came out with Abraham's breath. His skin crawled. Arcane power emanated from the wraith. It had power, true power. Abraham started backing the other way. His hand found the pommel of his sword as he moved out of the radius of cold.

"What is the matter, monkey man?" Big Apple asked. "Don't you want to dance with my servant, Fleece?"

Abraham glanced back at Big Apple.

The horned halfling tugged at the jewel-studded collar on his neck. His eyes narrowed on Abraham. "Are you going to get in the ring now, or are you going to wind up like one of them?" He pointed into a corner.

Two men were leaning in a corner, shriveled to husks. Their eyes and mouths were wide open, as if gasping in torment and horror.

He swallowed. *They know it's me.*

Fleece drifted toward him. The cold air came back. Chills ran down Abraham's spine.

He cleared his throat and, through the muffled mask, said, "If you insist, I'll wrestle."

Big Apple's eyes brightened. He clapped his hands together with a loud smack. "That's the spirit!" He made an impish laugh. "Huh-huh-huh-huh-huh. You made the right decision, monkey man. Now, go show those girls what you can do."

Lord Hawk put a boot to Abraham's rump and shoved him forward.

He feigned tripping on his robes and sprawled out on the ground, hitting it with a loud thump. His sword belt clattered against the floor.

"Whoa!" Lord Hawk came to his feet. "This fellow is loaded down like a soldier."

From his hands and knees, Abraham said, "I'm a Gray Guard. Out having a good time. I don't want to get reported to my commander. They frown on this sort of behavior. I hope you understand."

"Gray Guard?" Big Apple asked. "Did you say Gray Guard?"

Without looking back, Abraham said, "Yes." *Oh man, this is going to be bad. I should have said anything else. Mercenary. Black Squadron.* He started crawling toward the mud pit. "Does that matter?"

"We aren't very fond of the Gray Guard. Look where you are, man," Lord Hawk said. "This is a hive for criminals. The Gray Guard likes to keep an eye on guys like us. You know what, Big Apple, it's all coming together."

"What is that?" Big Apple said.

"This man is a spy."

You got it half right. He kept moving toward the mud pit. "I'm not a spy. I only want to have a good time. I swear I won't say anything."

Two of Big Apple's goons blocked Abraham's path. One of them stepped on his fingers. He let out an exaggerated scream. "Gah! Please don't hurt me! I said I would wrestle."

"He doesn't sound very brave for a Gray Guard. The Gray Guards I know would die before they humiliated themselves," Lord Hawk said.

"We'll take him on anyway!" one of the sultry women in the mud ring said. Mud dripped over her voluptuous body. She slung her hair back, revealing a few missing teeth. "We aren't particular." She slapped the belly of the fat man, who was tied up by the arms of the other two women. "Just look at this ox!"

"Shaddup, you stupid wench," Big Apple said. "I see what you are saying, Hawk. This fella is very… wimpy."

"Cowardly," Kawnee added. "I don't even think he is worthy of the mud ring."

Something stirred inside Abraham's gut. It was Ruger. No one was going to call him a coward and get away with it. The acting job was over. *Enough is enough. Screw it!* He grabbed one of the goons by the ankle and jerked the man to the floor.

CHAPTER 49

BEFORE THE SECOND GOON TOWERING over him could act, Abraham reached up and punched the man in the crotch.

The goon doubled over with a loud "Oof!"

Abraham socked the man in the jaw, stood up, and with his chest heaving, said, "Nobody calls the monkey man a coward!"

Lord Hawk pointed his revolver right at his chest and said, "Don't do anything stupid."

Abraham played dumb. "What does that do?"

"It blows your head open like a rotting melon."

Big Apple chuckled. "I like the monkey man. Let's see him wrestle."

Abraham had a plan. Covered in mud, his face wouldn't be seen. He took off his cloak and wrapped his sword belt in it. After setting that aside, he stood in front of them, wearing breastplate and trousers. He couldn't let them see his brand. "I'm ready."

Big Apple, Lord Hawk, and Kawnee lifted their eyebrows.

One of the women in the ring said, “Ooh yeah, bring him on in. I want the monkey man.”

“I saw him first,” said another one of the muddy ladies.

Suddenly, Big Apple’s goons on the floor tacked Abraham. One of them grabbed his hair and pulled. The other one hit him in the gut.

The three men wrestled over the floor in a knot of angry flying limbs.

Abraham bent one goon’s wrist backward and snapped it.

The man let out a howl of pain.

He cracked the last goon in the jaw. The blow knocked the man out cold.

“Fighting dirty, huh?” he said. “I can take it.”

He looked at Big Apple and Lord Hawk. Their eyes were bigger than saucers.

“What?” he asked.

Something wasn’t right. He glanced down. The monkey mask lay at his feet.

He looked back at them and smiled. “Did you miss me?”

“Ruger Slade!” Lord Hawk pointed the gun at him and squeezed the trigger.

Abraham jumped high.

The bullet blasted out of the barrel and ricocheted off Abraham’s breastplate. He landed on Lord Hawk and drove the man to the ground. He punched Lord Hawk in the throat and wrenched the gun from his hand. He jumped up and turned the gun on Big Apple. He thumbed the gun hammer back. “Don’t move!”

Big Apple lifted his hands and said, “Don’t shoot!” As his remaining goons started to flank Abraham, he said, “Back off! I don’t want him shooting me on account of you idiots. You got me, so what do you want?”

“Answers. Sit down.”

Big Apple plopped down on his stool and puffed on his cigar. “I might not have the answers that you want.”

“You have them. I know you have them. You wouldn’t have sent us on a wild-goose chase to Cauldron City if you didn’t.”

Big Apple chuckled. “I was hoping that you would have been killed. It seemed unlikely that even you and your Henchmen would be about to kill Arcayis. That was impressive.”

Lord Hawk got up, rubbing his jaw. “It would have been more if the Black Squadron would have had the stones to finish you off. That’s why I sent them. You scared the crap out of them. That’s for certain. Kill Arcayis. Didn’t see that coming.” He shot a look at Big Apple. “I thought he was strong.”

“Maybe he would have been stronger if he was the Underlord,” Abraham suggested.

Big Apple’s eyes lit up. “You don’t think Arcayis is the Underlord? That’s an interesting theory. Why is that?”

“Leodor didn’t buy into it. That’s good enough for me. The Underlord is still out there, alive and well.” He eyed Big Apple. “Perhaps it’s you.”

“I assure you that I am not the Underlord.” Big Apple blew a smoke ring. “I’m not your enemy. I just don’t want to go home. I don’t want to be Edgar the invalid again. That’s why I don’t want you finding the king’s stones.” He spread his arms out. “Be content with who you are. You are Ruger Slade, the best swordsman in the world. Enjoy it. Join me.”

“He can’t join. He’s branded,” Lord Hawk said in a condescending way. “He must follow the king's orders. That's how I understand it. This man has no choice but to bring us down. After all, we are the king's enemies."

"Kingsland is dying. Eventually, it will fall," Big Apple said. "A new world is coming to take over. You can do what you want with us, but you can't stop it."

"Tell me who is behind it. It's the Underlord, isn't it?" Abraham looked between both men. "Or is it someone from *back home*?"

"Perhaps they are one and the same," Big Apple said. "You might as well put the gun down. You aren't the sort of man to shoot me in cold blood. You're just another pawn like me, trying to find his place in this world. Well, your place is with a dying kingdom. My place is with a rising one."

Abraham knew that both men had more information than they'd ever let on. He'd have to torture them to get it out of them. That wasn't his style, but the Henchmen weren't above it. He studied Big Apple's impish face. He was cocky but careless.

"Humor me," Abraham said. "Is there a portal? You know, a permanent one." He wiggled the gun. "This didn't magically appear, did it?"

"I don't know." Big Apple stared at the gun. "But I do know there are more of those out there. Do you really think King Hector stands a chance against that? Swarming men loaded with modern-day artillery? The time will come. It will be a slaughter."

"You know, *Edgar*." He watched Big Apple's eyes narrow—now was the time to get all the information he could out of them. He might not get another chance. "You are wearing on my patience." He lowered the gun barrel and shot the stool between Big Apple's legs.

Big Apple jumped over to the fireplace hearth. "Hey! Hey! Hey! What are you doing?"

"Stand still!" Abraham fired again. The bullets blasted away chips of the fireplace's heart. "Where's the portal?" he yelled. "Who's the Underlord?"

The women in the mud pit stuck their fingers in their ears and raced out of the bar, screaming.

"Quit wasting my bullets!" Lord Hawk said.

Big Apple cowered inside the fireplace. "I don't know!"

Abraham fired into the fireplace again.

Blam!

"Tell me what I want to know!" Abraham's frustration boiled over. "Tell me now!"

Blam!

Big Apple yelled at him. "Nooo!"

Abraham pointed the gun at Big Apple's leg. "Now I'm going to hurt you!" He squeezed the trigger.

Click.

"You're empty, fool!" Lord Hawk said.

Big Apple grinned and touched the gemstones on his collar. "Fleece, get him!"

Abraham threw the gun at Big Apple's head. The weapon bounced off the man's hard head and horns. He dove toward his cloak and sword.

Fleece swooped in above him. His shifting mass of swirling robes enveloped Abraham's body.

He crawled on, fighting the icy numbness and pain coursing through his extremities. The wraith was draining the life out of him. He clawed his way toward Black Bane. He could see the pommel sticking out from underneath his cloak. He groaned and cried out as the might in his arms was sapped away.

Abraham flattened on the floor. He rolled over on his back. His fingers clutched in the air as he writhed.

The wraith loomed over him, a huge, haunting apparition. In the darkness beneath its hood, two eyes like bright stars appeared.

Abraham's blood froze. He couldn't move.

Big Apple and Lord Hawk looked down on him. The horned halfling was smoking and grinning. Lord Hawk kicked Abraham in the ribs.

"You wanted to know who the Underlord is," Big Apple said. "Like I said, it wasn't me." He pointed his cigar at the wraith. "It's him." He ran his stubby finger over the collar on his neck. "And you'll never guess who controls him. Me. Ha ha ha. Now I have you, Abraham. Don't I? Don't we all?" He waved his meaty palm. "Bye bye, Abraham Jenkins. Bye bye, Ruger Slade."

Screaming at the building intense pain, Abraham lost his sight and descended into darkness.

CHAPTER 50
BACK HOME

Darkness. Pain. Abraham could hear himself breathing. Slow. Easy. Quiet. He didn't open his eyes. He was seated. Soft-rock radio was playing. The familiar sound of rolling down a highway caught his ears.

I'm in a car!

He kept his eyes closed. Something was restraining him. It must have been a seat belt. He wiggled his fingers. His wrists were bound in front of him.

Blazing saddles! More flex cuffs!

He didn't move. The last thing he wanted to do was alert his captors to his condition. He'd need to take them by surprise. He needed to listen and learn about Mandi. His nostrils flared. The faint smell of sweet perfume, good stuff, lingered in the air. It didn't smell like something Eugene Drisk would wear—or his goons, like Colt.

Mandi?

Abraham couldn't be certain. Mandi always smelled good. All he could do was hope this was her.

The car he rode in accelerated and pushed him back in its seat. The car had a throaty roar in the engine.

"That's it. Open it up, babe," a man said in a casual and quiet manner. "It's a long drive. Might as well have some fun."

Someone was tapping on the steering wheel to the rhythm of the song's beat. She was humming the words of a Rupert Holmes song. "Shh," she said. "I'm listening."

The woman who spoke clearly wasn't Mandi. She had a firm voice and carried authority. Abraham didn't recall having seen any women in Eugene's group either.

Who are these guys? What have they done with Mandi?

"I don't know about this yacht-rock radio. It's not a good fit for the Hellcat," the man quipped.

"Of course it is. It's the perfect cruiser," the woman said quietly.

"If you say so," the man replied. "You're always right."

Sounds like I've been abducted by a pair of newlyweds. Oh man, how much time has passed? I've been days in Titanuus.

Abraham took a peek. Moonlight shone through the car's glass. Through his narrow eyelids, he could see a nice-looking brunette with medium-length hair driving the car. Both her hands were on the wheel, fingers tapping. He slid his eyes over to the passenger side. The man in the seat sat with his head higher than the headrest. His shoulders were almost too wide for the racing seat.

Another big goon. I can handle him. I think.

He closed his eyes.

He'd have to wait it out and see where they took him. In the meantime, he'd listen. He would make a move the first chance he had. The only problem was the flex cuffs. His ankles were free, and he could still run. Even with his hands bound, he could fight if he had to.

I'll play possum. Knock them out and steal the car.

The car motored down the road mile after mile.

As glad as Abraham wanted to be, he wasn't. He was back home, but at what cost? Ruger Slade's body was back in Titanuus. Big Apple had him. And the Underlord had been revealed. Sticks, Shades, and all the Henchmen would be in danger now. Plus, his enemies would have Black Bane. Everything was a mess.

What am I doing?

Perhaps he was better off back home than in Titanuus. Or was it vice versa? He had a hard time telling.

One step at a time. Keep it simple. Find Mandi. Save Mandi.

Another song started playing on the radio.

"Ah, I love this song," the man said. "It's good but twisted by today's standards. There's an interesting bit on Wiki about it."

"I didn't think you liked yacht rock," she said playfully.

"Not me. The car."

"Ah, I always take pleasure learning new things about you. Benny Mardones. 'Into the Night.' Check," she replied.

Benny Mardones? Seriously?

Abraham dared another peek. The woman driving was staring dead at him in her rearview mirror. He snapped his eyes shut. *Devil's donuts! I know she saw me. Just act like you're still asleep.* He shifted in a slumbering fashion and rolled his head over to one side. *Please buy it.*

The voice of Benny Mardones died.

"What did you do that for?" the man on the passenger side asked.

"Because Sleeping Beauty has awakened."

CHAPTER 51

"Should I shoot him with the juice?" the man said.

The car seat's leather groaned as the man twisted around in his seat.

"No. Hey, Mandi," the woman said. "Wake up."

Someone stirred beside Abraham.

"What is it?" Mandi asked.

"Your boyfriend's awake, but he's playing possum," the woman driving said.

Mandi unclicked her seat belt and scooted toward Abraham.

"I've got your back," the man said. "Any sudden moves, and I'll zap him."

Abraham kept his eyes closed. He felt Mandi's warm hands on his face.

"Ruger. Ruger." She gently slapped his cheeks. "Are you back?"

He opened his eyes. "I'm not Ruger. I'm Abraham."

Mandi threw her arms around him and hugged him tightly. "I'm so glad you are back! I didn't think I'd see you again."

"I didn't think I'd see you either. I was worried." He got a good look at her face when she pulled back and saw her cheeks were bruised and swollen. "What happened?" He kicked the man's seat in front of him. "Did they do this?"

"Heavens, no. That's my cousin, Sid, and her husband, John. Remember I told you about them," Mandi said.

"Hi," Sid said.

John turned farther in his seat and extended his hand, which was as big as Abraham's. He was a nice-looking guy, clean shaven with angular features and wearing dark sunglasses. "Call me Smoke."

Abraham took the man's strong grip and asked, "Got a knife, Smoke?"

"Sorry about that," Mandi said as she whisked a knife out of her boot. She cut off the flex cuffs. "You twitch a lot. And when you wake up as Ruger, you're very intense. You still aren't used to this place."

Abraham rubbed his wrists, looked at Mandi, and said, "Thanks, warrior princess. Care to catch me up to speed? What happened to Eugene and those goons?"

"Man, this is eerie," Smoke said. He looked dead into Abraham's eyes. "You are completely a different person. I can see it and hear it. Him and Ruger aren't the same. Maybe it's strong hypnosis."

"Or he's a shifter," Sid chimed in.

"No, he's in the same body." Smoke's nostrils flared. "He doesn't reek of evil either. But those other dudes did."

Abraham looked at Mandi and said, "So, your cousin's husband can smell evil? How convenient."

"It's not so much a smell as it is a feeling," Smoke replied coolly. "It comes on primarily when dealing with the supernatural elements. I want to hear more about this fantasy world. Titanuus?"

"John, don't push it," Sid warned.

"Come on, hon, if there is a portal to a fantasy world, then we have to go," Smoke said. "It can be a second honeymoon."

"What about the kids?" Sid said. "Can they go on the honeymoon too?"

"No, that would be a vacation. But I don't see why not. I'm sure Keith and Sally could use the break," Smoke replied.

"We aren't going to another fantasy world," Sid replied. "We don't even know if this one is real."

"Are you talking about my fantasy world or this world?" Abraham asked.

"Take your pick," Sid said dryly.

"Titanuus is real," Abraham stated.

Smoke tapped Abraham's knee with the back of his hand. "I believe you, dude. We'll find that yellow brick road and take you back there."

"I don't want to go back. I mean, I do, but I don't. Mandi, what is going on? Bring me up to speed."

Mandi held his hand and said, "It's a bit of a story, and I'm not the best at it, but I'll try." She glanced up. "Let's see. We were in the alley in Pittsburgh. Eugene and his otherworlder goons got the drop on us. They had a gun to my head. Eugene gut-punched you with a stun rod."

"Yeah, that's the last thing I remember."

"You went down, and I was scared. Colt and those guys, they were possessed with a strange darkness in their eyes." She shivered. "I tried to fight them off, but I'm not that strong. The only thing I did was send Sid a text before all of that happened. I jammed my phone in my pocket." She swallowed. Her voice trembled. "I wanted them to at least find my body if they killed me."

He squeezed her hand. "I'm so sorry, Mandi. This is all my fault." He touched her bruised cheek. "You need to stay out of this."

"She won't be able to stay out of this until it's over," Smoke added.

Sid elbowed him.

Smoke shrugged. "Sorry, but it's true. It's like Rocky said: 'It ain't over till it's over.'"

"I agree. I'm in this to the end," Mandi said. Her beautiful eyes were intense. "Don't try to talk me out of it. Besides, when you went down, Ruger came back."

"He did?" Abraham asked.

"Yeah," Mandi said. "Eugene's goons were carting us both to the cars that pulled into the alley. More men in black SUVs came."

"I hate black SUVs," Sid said.

Mandi continued, "Just as they were about to load you into the car, you came to life like a wild tiger. I'm not sure how you got out of the flex cuffs, but you did."

Smoke interrupted. "I can show you."

"Mandi, ignore him," Sid said.

Mandi cleared her throat. "Man, could you move. I mean, you could move before, but when Ruger takes over, it's different. He's merciless."

"You can't treat evil any other way," Smoke said. "You have to bash their face in with a shovel. Strike first. Strike hard. No mercy."

"Take it easy, Karate Kid," Sid replied with a chuckle.

Smoke shook his head. "No, that's Cobra Kai I'm quoting."

"Weren't they the bad guys?" Abraham asked.

Smoke twisted around in his seat again and said, "Now there is a new series on YouTube that spins the story around from Johnny Lawrence's side of things."

Sid punched Smoke in the leg again. "Let her finish the story, please." She looked in the rearview mirror at Abraham. "Sorry, but my husband hasn't gotten a lot of guy time lately, since the kids are still little."

"It's okay," Abraham said. He wet his lips. "But you'd get plenty of that in Titanuus with the Henchmen."

The leather groaned in Smoke's seat when he started to turn.

"No," Sid warned.

Smoke looked mysterious but had some playfulness about him. The more he talked, the more Abraham liked him.

Abraham took a water bottle that Mandi offered him and twisted the cap off and drank. "Ah, that's better. You were saying?"

CHAPTER 52

MANDI'S FACE LIT UP AS she told the story. "You turned those thugs into broken pottery. I've never seen a big man like you move so fast."

Smoke cleared his throat.

"Every punch you threw broke something," she said with excitement rising in her voice. "I heard ribs snap. A man's jaw broke. Three men were knocked out cold with one blow. I didn't see all of it, but those dudes were going down like the Hindenburg. Colt had a gun on me and told you to back off. I don't know what overcame me. I guess I got Ruger syndrome, because I drove my elbow in his belly.

"That's when you, or Ruger, pounced. A gunshot went off, but you had him on the ground and were beating the hell out of him." Mandi took back the bottle and drank. "Whew, Sid, turn the air conditioner up. Anyway, Eugene was screaming at his men. That's when you locked eyes on Eugene." She tensed. "There was murder in your eyes. Not like when you fought those men—that was focused. Intent. But once you looked at Eugene, it was nothing but deep hatred. My toes tingled. Eugene shrank under your gaze, dove into the car, and locked it. You punched out the windshield."

"Cobra Kai," Smoke said subtly.

Sid shook her head.

"Anyway," Mandi continued, "Eugene stomped on the gas and peeled out of the alley. We grabbed another car and chased him through the city. That was my first car chase, but I think I did pretty good. Then you grabbed the wheel and almost turned the car over. I swatted you back and said, 'Let the woman do the driving.' You actually listened, but your arms were bleeding all over the car. You started to bandage it."

Abraham checked his forearm and saw some scarring, but the wounds were mended.

"We took care of that," Sid said. "It's a special healing foam that we use. It's more effective than stitches."

Abraham lifted a brow and said, "I see. So, what happened in the chase?"

"I caught Eugene's bumper on a corner. He rolled over, and we rolled over in the middle of the street." Mandi rubbed her cheek. "That's how I got this bruise. We squeezed out of the SUV, and you rounded up Eugene. He was squirming his way out of the car's window. You knocked him out cold. I don't think you meant to.

"By this time, the cops were coming. I told you that we needed to run. You tossed Eugene over your shoulder and started running. I'm pretty sure that you didn't know where you were going, but you ran like a deer and almost lost me more than once. Somehow, we beat the cops and ducked into a parking garage and hid. You laid Eugene down in the stairwell. Your eyes could have bored holes through him. Ruger hates that guy."

Abraham could understand why. Eugene had used Ruger's body for his own selfish and immoral purposes. Somehow, Ruger had a sense of what was going on with a body he hosted or through the eyes and actions of another. They were all connected.

"As we huddled in the stairwell, things went south. You blacked out again," Mandi said. "Stone-cold comatose."

"What have I been doing all of this time? Sleeping?"

Mandi shrugged. "Lucky for me, I had texted Sid, and they picked us up a few hours later. We've been on the run ever since."

"Super Uber," Smoke muttered.

Sid drove the car off the highway while Abraham sorted out his thoughts. They pulled into a shopping plaza. A Pizza Hut and a Baskin Robbins were there. Smoke got out of the car and hustled inside.

"We're stopping for pizza?" Abraham asked Sid. His belly growled.

Sid turned in her seat. She was fetching, like Mandi, but taller and more athletic. She carried a dangerous air about her, and a gun was holstered on her hip. "Smoke has a very strict dietary regimen that he must adhere to."

Abraham watched Smoke walk out of the Pizza Hut with four pizza boxes. He moved into the Baskin Robbins. "Pizza and ice cream?"

"Milkshakes," Sid said.

"Huh." Abraham peered through the window. "Where are we?"

"Morgantown, West Virginia," Mandi said.

"What are we doing here?" he asked.

"Smoke wanted to catch a Mountaineer basketball game. We are hiding out too, lying low until the channel's clear," Sid said. "Our people will let us know when we can move. In the meantime, we'll keep trying to fish more info out of Drisk."

"You sound like someone with a law-enforcement background, but Mandi said you were bounty hunters?"

"I used to be FBI. Circumstances changed the day I met him." Sid pointed her gaze toward the window.

Smoke was coming back. He had four pizza boxes and four milkshakes in one arm. He opened the car and slid in like a big cat.

"Did you get milkshakes for the rest of us?" Sid asked him.

"No. I got you guys a pizza. Pepperoni," Smoke said as he filled all the available cupholders with the milkshakes. He handed one pizza back to Mandi and eyed her and Abraham. "Do you want a milkshake? I'll go back."

"I'm fine," Mandi said.

Abraham almost answered the question then instantly asked, "Where in Titanuus's Crotch is Eugene Drisk? You didn't leave him alone, did you?"

CHAPTER 53

SID DROVE THEM DOWN A long stretch of country road. They stopped at an old white two-story farmhouse with a wraparound porch. The house was pitch black inside. The large gravel driveway had a few abandoned vehicles. A red storage barn stood nearby, and one of the doors was open. A red Massey Fergusson tractor was stowed inside.

Everyone got out of the car. The winter air was cool, crisp, and breezy. Snowflakes lingered in the air.

Abraham's legs were cramping. The back seat of the Dodge Hellcat hadn't been made for a big man like him. He felt as though he'd run a marathon, and his body ached all over. Ruger had pushed him to the limits again.

He closed the door to the phantom-black Hellcat and said, "Nice car."

"Thanks," Sid said.

He eyed the porch. The farmhouse looked abandoned. He expected to see someone on the porch, but nobody was there. "You didn't leave Drisk alone, did you? There's a guard here, right?"

"No, no guards," Smoke said. He tossed the pizza boxes in a small dumpster then moved to the trunk. "Mr. Drisk isn't going anywhere."

"You can't trust that guy. He's like me. He'll squirm out of wherever you put him!"

"No, he won't." Smoke studied Abraham's eyes. "Are you taller than me?"

Smoke stood a half inch taller if Abraham had to guess. He was about six-foot five himself.

"No."

"Good," Smoke replied. He eyed Sid.

The trunk popped open.

Eugene Drisk lay inside the trunk. His eyes were closed. His mouth, wrists, and ankles were bound with flex cuffs.

Smoke lifted the man out of the trunk as if he were stuffed with feathers. He dropped Eugene on the ground.

Abraham took a long look inside the trunk, seeing a few shotguns, assault rifles, and metal briefcases—an arsenal. "Are you sure you're just bounty hunters? That's some serious artillery."

"The Challengers have great trunk space, don't they?" Smoke closed the lid. "The things we hunt, let's just say, are full of surprises." Smoke picked up Eugene by the back of the pants like a piece of luggage. "Let's go inside and start a fire."

Abraham headed toward the house.

Smoke pushed him toward the barn. "That way."

The inside of the barn was in good shape. No straw or livestock was there. The floors were solid planks of wood. Some of the stalls had been converted into camping rooms. A kitchenette and a coal-burning stove were there.

Mandi closed the barn door.

"I'll start the fire," Sid said as she walked by Abraham. She was only a few inches shorter than he. She briskly made her way to the Buck stove sitting in a corner of the barn. Some blankets and mattresses lay on the ground. It made for a livable indoor camping environment.

"You guys have been staying here?" he asked.

"The last few days," Mandi said.

"I've been out that long? Geez. The time is a mess. An hour in one world might be a day in the other." He scratched his face. "I guess we need to make the most of it."

Smoke propped Eugene up in a chair and tied him up to a support beam. He lightly smacked the man's face. He pushed open his eyelid. "He's still out."

"I told you that serum was too strong for an old man," Sid said with a shiver. When they got a fire going in the stove, she rubbed her hands in front of it. "Get warm, you guys. We'll probably be here a while. Smoke overdosed him again."

"Better safe than sorry," Smoke said. He walked over to Sid and gave her a kiss. "I'll let you give him the shot next time."

Mandi hooked Abraham's arm and said, "Come over by the fire. Let's warm up. I'm cold."

He didn't move. "No. Eugene ain't no fool. He might be playing possum. I'd rather watch him." He eyed Smoke. "Did you pat him down?"

"The only thing he has is his clothing." He opened an old ice chest and grabbed a can of Coke. "No phones or wires. We scanned him for tracking devices too, even the ones that go in the skull. He's cold." He raised the Coke can. "Want one?"

"No."

"Cheese popcorn?"

"Later. The pizza held. I could do for some snack cakes later."

Smoke pointed a gun finger at him and said, "I'll make it so." He headed outside and made some trips back and forth, carrying in the metal briefcases and a few weapons.

Abraham stood in front of Eugene and studied him. The older man's skin was sagging, but he had a firm jaw. He was definitely more fit than the shapeless man he'd encountered in the tunnel cave months before. Abraham rubbed his own jaw as if he were Indiana Jones staring at the golden idol. "You said that you talked to him before? He was awake?"

Sid walked over to him and said, "Yes. He's a real smart aleck too. We didn't push hard because we weren't sure what to ask. We thought we'd wait it out for you."

"Can we wake him?" he asked.

"Of course, but I don't recommend it. For ethical reasons," Sid said. "It's basically torture. He might have a heart attack."

"He might be old, but he can take it. And my time is limited. I might drift off at any moment. I need to interrogate him now."

"Have you ever interrogated someone?" Sid asked.

"No."

Sid glanced at Smoke. "Then you might want to let us handle it. Does he have any fears that you know of?"

Abraham shrugged. Ruger didn't fear anything, but Eugene was a different story. "Spiders, maybe?"

CHAPTER 54

SID HELD A SYRINGE IN her hand and asked, "Are you sure that you want to do this?" She squirted a little juice out of the tip. "Mal warned me that it might be fatal."

"Mal who?" Abraham asked.

"Mal Carlson. A friend of ours. He's a scientist," she replied.

"Do you think that he could help out with my situation?"

"We'll keep him apprised. He's definitely interested. But he and his wife, Asia, are on vacation right now." She approached Eugene, who had been secured to a barn support post, and rolled up his sleeves. "Be glad she's not around. She's bossy."

Abraham gave her a smile. Sid carried herself with a businesslike approach. She obviously had a law-enforcement or military background. Smoke, however, was harder to judge. He stood nearby, eating an apple and wearing a Starslayer T-shirt. Both of them were as fit as a fiddle. They complemented each other well.

"The moment of truth," Sid said.

Abraham nodded.

Sid stuck the needle an inch deep in Eugene's forearm and pressed the plunger.

Eugene's eyes popped open. He convulsed.

"Shoot, we should have put a bit in his mouth," Sid said and caught a towel that Smoke tossed her. She shoved it into Eugene's gaping jaws. "Don't bite your tongue off, old man."

Eugene spasmed for about a minute then finally went limp. His forehead was beaded in sweat as he looked at Sid.

She took the gag out.

Eugene spat, eyed the syringe, and asked, "What did you shoot me with? *Gasoline*?"

"I told you it was harsh." Sid stuck the needle in the post. She moved back and stood by Smoke.

Eugene's eyes slid up toward Abraham. His lips twisted. In a ragged voice, he said, "Oh, it's you." He leaned his head to the side. "The weak one. I can see that Ruger isn't back. Good for me."

Abraham dragged a stool over and sat down in front of Eugene. "It's time that we had a talk. I want to know what's going on, and you aren't going anywhere until I do."

Eugene leered at Mandi and Sid and licked his lips. "Pretty women. Very pretty. Ruger always did keep fine company. I must admit, I miss that body of his. The stamina."

Abraham pushed Eugene's head back into the pole. It made a *thunk*. "Nobody cares about your sex life."

Wincing, Eugene said, "I do." He coughed. "I can't talk so well if my mouth is dry. Can I get a drink of something?"

"No," Abraham said. "If you want a drink, you'll have to talk first."

"And if I don't get a drink, I can't talk."

Abraham shoved the man's head back into the pole again. Eugene might appear older and weaker, but he knew better. He'd been Ruger Slade for years. The old man still carried that dangerous edge with him. "Cooperate."

"Ha. You aren't the sort to torture me. I know who you are—a washed-up baseball player. A child of privilege. A drug addict. No, you don't have the stones to get anything out of me." Eugene glanced over at Smoke and Sid. "That's why you have them. Isn't it?"

"No. They are my Uber drivers." He leaned into Eugene's face. "Don't underestimate me. I'm a desperate man. Since I've been Ruger Slade, I've killed hundreds," he exaggerated. "I've even slain two Elders. Do you really think I won't hesitate to put the hurt on you? Your mind might be able to take it, but your body can't." He locked his hands around Eugene's throat and squeezed. "So far as I am concerned, this is the king's business."

Eugene's face started to turn red.

The Henchmen weren't above torture when it came to the king's business. They wouldn't show mercy when it came to completing a task. They were spies, secret agents in a medieval fantasy time.

Abraham normally didn't have the stomach for it, but the enemy had put him through enough. Now he needed answers. He let go.

Eugene gasped for air. He coughed and said, "Now I'm really thirsty."

"Tell me what is going on, Eugene. There are portals. Someone controls them. Our world is invading their world. Why?"

Eugene gave him a knowing look and asked, "What makes you think there is an invasion?"

"That's what the other side tells me. I've come across a few other people like us. I dealt with the Shell and the Sect. Someone on that side is working with someone on this side. I want to know who it is and why."

"Hmm..." Eugene said. "You are further along than I could have imagined. Interesting. Can I have a drink?"

"Tell me something first."

"Okay." Eugene sniffed. "There is an invasion. This world into theirs."

Abraham nodded at Mandi.

She fetched a bottle of water out of the old ice chest and slowly walked it over. She twisted the cap off, tilted up his chin, and let Eugene drink. Water dribbled onto his shirt. She wiped it away with her gentle fingers. "Let me wipe that off."

"Feeding me like a child. So pathetic." He couldn't take his eyes off her. "Why don't we take the cuffs off, and we can have a nice chat. I'll tell you what you want," Eugene said to Abraham while looking at her.

"Why the sudden change of heart?"

"I'll tell you why," Eugene said as he took another drink. "No matter what you know and no matter what you do, it won't make a difference. That's why. Pandora's Box has been opened. It can't be closed again."

"Anything that can be done can be undone," Smoke said.

"Is that so? You can undo the damage when a dam's wall breaks? I don't think so. It wipes out all in its wake." Eugene managed another drink. "That is the problem with heroes. They think they can fix anything, but they can't."

CHAPTER 55

"KEEP TALKING," ABRAHAM SAID. CLEARLY Mandi's presence was having an effect on the man. He liked women. He liked them a lot. "I'm listening."

"I'm listening too," Mandi said in a sweet voice.

"You remind me of the triplets back in Titanuus," Eugene said, with hungry eyes that could devour Mandi whole. "I miss them. They were the perfect mates."

Mandi looked at Abraham and asked, "Do you know these triplets?"

"Oh, he knows them," Eugene said. "There is no way of not knowing them once you are in the same room with them. They are Ruger Slade's servants. Wholehearted ones, I might add."

"I don't know them like *that*," he reassured Mandi.

"Oh yes, he does." Eugene giggled. "Unless he's made of stone, but even Ruger is flesh and blood." He turned his gaze back on Mandi. "My, you are a vision. Will you feed me?"

"I have some leftover pizza and Ring Dings," Smoke offered.

"I'll take anything she touches," Eugene added.

Mandi raised her eyebrows at Abraham, making it clear she would roll with it. Much like Sticks, she would apparently go to great lengths to complete a mission.

Smoke handed her a box of Ring Dings. With her chest lowered in front of Eugene's face, she slowly fed the pastry to him.

"Mmm. Mmm. Thank you," he said.

Abraham moved back to Smoke and Sid and said under his breath, "Man, this guy is a real perv. I'm not like that. It's no wonder Ruger hates him so."

"Roll with it," Sid said. "Every man has a weakness. You got lucky and found it early."

After Mandi finished feeding Eugene, she sat down beside him and placed a hand on his leg.

Eugene's eyes were filled with glee. "The flesh is weak. Especially mine." He swallowed. "Hey, I'm a sucker for a cheap thrill. So, Abraham, I'm going to try to tell you what is happening in layman's terms. Again, it won't make any difference, the way I see it. And all of you will wind up dead soon enough. They'll find us. Trust me."

"Who?" he asked.

Eugene sighed and said, "That's the harder question to answer. The military. The government. Venture capitalists. I'm a scientist, a researcher at Carnegie Mellon. We had a research grant to study the existence of other dimensions. I can't say who the grant came from. It was top secret but had the stink of government all over it. We call it the Corporation. With the harnessing of nuclear power, we began studies that would affect time and space. The splitting of atoms has a multifaceted destructive purpose.

"The scientific community was abuzz about the ancient star gates scattered all over the world. We created a gate of our own, using nuclear power. In theory, it would create a rift in space. And remember, we didn't come up with this preposterous notion either. We were hired to create it. Needless to say, without any scientific basis to rely on, I had major scientific doubts. Still, we built what we called the Time Tunnel. It's a ten-foot-high doorway framed out of titanium and tungsten. The name is horrible. Professor Maurice coined it, and despite my objections about a doorway that opens another dimension, such as the Dimension Tunnel, Time Tunnel stuck.

"I'm playing nice. Can we remove the bonds?" Eugene asked.

"No." Abraham said.

Mandi patted Eugene's head.

"Fine. You're lucky she is here."

"And to think that you were going to *dispose* of me," Mandi said.

"I was only putting on for the troops. I'd never allow anything bad to happen to you now that I know you. Anyway," Eugene continued, "we turned the Time Tunnel on. It worked. I'm talking, my hair was standing on the top of my head. The raw power… It was, well, amazing. The doorway was black like a sheet of ice. We came out from behind the barrier and looked at the wondrous vision. It began to change. The blackness turned to color. A painting of endless fields formed. All of us saw a new frontier unlike anything we'd seen before. It was a new world.

"The frame of the Time Tunnel started to bow. My team fled. I stuck my hand in the doorway. I felt the warmth of the new world. So real. The frame collapsed as I pulled my hand away. The portal hovered with a life of its own. I looked back at my colleagues, waved, and jumped toward it, but I bounced off the shimmering image. The portal vanished.

"After that, we created one door after the other. The frame could never hold the portal for long. We learned that flesh and blood could not pass through, but inanimate objects could. Our team put everything we had into it. Our donors gave us unlimited resources. But the same result came time and again. The Time Tunnel frame would collapse. The portal would vanish. Then we came to learn about the mysterious disappearance in our highway-system tunnels. The portals we opened were on the loose. People were disappearing. Along with their vehicles.

"I came up with an idea. I volunteered to drive into the tunnel using a vehicle, figuring if I was inside the casing, I could cross. Using a small car, I drove right into the Time Tunnel. That's when I became Ruger Slade. I was in his body, but my body remained here, I came to find out recently. I was comatose the entire time. I hosted a new body."

"It's called a soul swap," Abraham said.

He rose from his chair and paced. Eugene's story sounded believable, but he had to assume lies were twisted in with the truth. He looked at Smoke and Sid. She was whispering in Smoke's ear.

"Eh, you called it a soul swap?" Eugene said. "Where did you come up that? It's profoundly accurate."

"And Elderling named Melris told me," he said.

"An Elderling. Interesting." Eugene shifted in his chair. "Will you please take these off of me? I'm exhausted. And to be honest, I find sharing refreshing. And I have more information, believe me, much more. The Corporation is investing more funding into the Titanuus project. You see, they have been able to pick my brain and more—others that have been through this, as you coin it, soul swap."

Smoke looked at his watch.

"What is it?" Sid asked.

"We have company." Smoke took off out of the barn.

CHAPTER 56

NOT A MOMENT AFTER SMOKE exited the barn, the *wuppa wuppa* of an oncoming helicopter could be heard overhead.

"I told you that they would find us," Eugene said. "And I'm not bragging. They find everyone."

Sid put on a black web belt and holstered two automatic Glock pistols. She put on her jacket. "Looks like the interview is over."

Smoke appeared inside the room as the sound of a helicopter soared overhead. "I don't know how they found us."

"Probably the GPS in your vehicle," Eugene suggested. "That gets a lot of people."

"No, I disabled it. Our phones can't be tracked either." Smoke eyed Mandi.

"This is a burner." Mandi held out her phone. "Did that do it?"

"I don't think so." Sid moved over to Eugene and ran her hands over his face and neck. "He must have some other sort of tag on him that we missed."

"Oh, that feels wonderful. Your hands are very warm," Eugene said as he nuzzled her hand with his face. "Don't stop, gorgeous."

"Ew, you really need therapy." Sid patted him down all over. Her hands stopped on his dress shoes. She yanked them off and twisted the heel off one. "Smoke? Did you check his feet?"

"Of course I did," he said.

Sid turned the heel over, and a flat round battery like the one used in a watch fell out. She gave Smoke a disappointed look. "We're compromised."

Smoke shrugged and said, "Bish happens."

Eugene looked at the battery and with a smile said, "I told you."

"Everybody, get to the Hellcat!" Sid ordered. "We can lose 'em in the hills."

"What about Eugene?" Abraham asked.

"He's dead weight. We have to go." Sid grabbed the metal suitcases.

Smoke snatched up more weapons. "Grab and go," he said.

"Bye bye," Eugene said with a devilish grin. "I hope to see you ladies again."

The party broke free of the barn's front door.

A streak of fire raced through the sky with a roar. The fire collided with the Hellcat.

KA-BOOOOOM!

The car turned into an inferno of explosions.

"My Hellcat!" Sid screamed with anguish in her soul.

"My LAW rockets!" Smoke added.

With fire in her voice, Sid said, "Everyone back inside!"

Abraham closed them inside the barn.

"Morning glory!" Sid cursed.

"Looks like we have a fight on our hands," Smoke quipped.

"Ah, you missed me," Eugene said, delighted. "So glad that you are back. I missed you too. I have a feeling that we are all going to become very close. At least those of us that are still living."

"What are we going to do?" Mandi said in a loud, worried voice. The whirling propellers of a military-grade transport chopper roared overhead.

Abraham put his arm around her waist. "I'll protect you."

"That's a very sweet thing to say," Eugene said, "but it won't do you any good. Those are soldiers out there. If there is one helicopter, I bet two more are near. Probably a score of well-armed men at least. It looks like you have firepower, but it's not as if you have Black Bane." He tensed in his bonds. "It's times like this I wish I was back in Ruger's body. Talk about exhilarating."

Sid took a knee and opened both of the metal briefcases. "I didn't think it would come to this." She pulled out a sleek bodysuit and tossed one each to Abraham and Mandi. "Take off your clothes and put those on."

Abraham held the suit up before his eyes and asked, "Are we going scuba diving?"

"No. It's called a sweetheart suit. Bulletproof." Sid stripped down to her black bra and panties. For a taller woman, she had great natural curves. The muscles in her arms flexed when she pulled her own suit on.

"Hubba hubba," Eugene said. "Teacher, take me back to school."

"Will you shut up?" Sid said.

Mandi stripped down to her bra and panties. Her body left Eugene's tongue hanging out of his mouth. Her curves jiggled when she pulled the tight suit on.

Smoke was nothing but sculpted muscles with scars all over. He was built a lot like Ruger but sleeker.

Abraham, by comparison, had plenty of meat packed over hard, unseen muscle. His belly, though much slimmer, still hung down. He fought to pull the sweetheart suit on. Mandi helped him by tugging fiercely on his sleeves. They zipped each other up.

Sid and Smoke put on their old clothing and boots.

A spring of new energy coursed through Abraham's body. He couldn't help but smile. Mandi gave him a frisky look.

"It's nice, isn't it?" Smoke said.

"I feel like I could run a hundred miles." Abraham's gut still bulged, but not as badly. "Slimming too."

"One of these fools does not belong here," Eugene sang in a familiar *Sesame Street* tune. "One of these fools is not the same. One of these fools is too fat for his suit."

Smoke walked over to Eugene and said, "My wife told you to shut up."

"I'm sorry, I didn't hear her. I was too busy drooling," Eugene fired back.

Smoke pinched the man's neck.

Eugene's eyes closed, and he slumped over.

"What's the plan?" Smoke said.

Sid loaded more extended ammo clips into her gun as Smoke did the same—some of the clips had blue, green, and red tape on them. "Those bastards took my car. We'll take their helicopter." She tossed Abraham and Mandi each a gun. "You know how to shoot, don't you?"

"Right now, I feel like I can do anything," Mandi said. "Can I keep this suit?"

"We'll see, cuz," Sid replied. She opened a small metal bottle and spilled four emerald-green pills into her hand. "Everyone take one."

"They look like vitamin D pills," Mandi said. "What does it do?"

Smoke grinned. "We call them super vitamins. They give you a real boost. They'll heighten your senses and enhance your strength. Keep one handy in case of emergency."

Mandi took a pill in hand.

Abraham backed away. "I don't mix well with pills. I'd rather not."

"We're going to have to scrap," Smoke said. "Can you fight and shoot if you have to?"

"I can handle it."

Smoke nodded. He bent over and grabbed some goggles with round blue lenses from the metal case and tossed them to Abraham. "Good. Then you come with me."

CHAPTER 57

Abraham and the others followed Smoke out through some loose wall panels in the back. They headed away from the landed chopper and into the woods.

"We'll split up," Sid said. "I'll keep Mandi safe. You and Smoke take care of them." She kissed Smoke. "Be careful."

Mandi gave Abraham a quick kiss. "You too."

The women moved deeper into the woods and vanished in the trees.

Smoke crouched down and eyed the barn. He was like a big cat waiting to pounce.

The goggles Abraham wore did wonders for his night sight. The house and barn looked as though they were sitting illuminated by a blue daytime sun.

"These things are incredible," he mumbled.

The helicopter had landed behind the farmhouse. Its blades were still whirring loudly. Another helicopter flew overhead, slowly hovering over a hundred feet high. Soldiers appeared on the lawn, over a dozen of them snaking through the yard. They surrounded the house and barn. The red lasers from their automatic pistols were on.

"There's a lot of them," Smoke said. He spun his pistols on his fingers. "It's going to be a party. Can you use that weapon?"

Abraham looked at the gun in his hand and said, "Yeah, but I'm a lot better with a sword."

Smoke took a long black-handled hunting knife out of his belt and said, "Take this, Highlander."

Abraham spun it in his free hand. "That'll do. So, are you going to kill these guys?"

"I hate to kill 'em. But those folks are black ops. Off the record. They know what they are in for. My guess is that they are on a capture mission. But if they blast away, take them out before they take you."

"Got it." Abraham eyed his gun. It had a long blue clip in it. "What is the difference in these clips?"

"The blue pierce armor. The red are explosive. The green, well, take them out as a last resort." Smoke nodded at him. "Stay close. Follow my lead. Let's go."

The soldiers entered the house and the barn in small teams while other soldiers stood guard. They used flashlights and turned the beams over the fields. Above, the helicopter activated a spotlight. The huge light scoured the area.

Abraham and Smoke crouched behind a well while the helicopter beam passed over them. They peeked over around opposite sides of the rim. Some men with flashlights were walking the grounds, while others slunk toward the forest. Two soldiers came out of the back of the barn where Abraham's group had come out earlier. The soldiers pointed into the woods, away from the well.

"It's time to find out if they are here to kill us or not," Smoke said. "Wait here."

"What are you going to do?"

"Be ready," Smoke said. He took off at a dead sprint back toward the woods.

The soldiers shouted out. "There's one!"

The helicopter light shined down on Smoke. Smoke stood in the beam with his arms raised and guns waving.

He's crazy!

"Take him out!" one of the commanding soldiers said.

The farmland exploded in a hail of gunfire.

Smoke sprang toward the woods like a deer.

Holy sheetrock! They are trying to kill us!

Abraham had fully expected that the soldiers were trying to capture them. They'd fooled him. They were shooting. He huddled behind the well.

Smoke vanished into the woodland's edge. A squad of four soldiers quickly worked their way up the slope, going after him. They passed the well no more than thirty yards away.

Abraham aimed at the soldiers. His hand was shaking. *I can't shoot those men in the back… can I?*

Smoke raced out of the woods with his guns blazing and the helicopter spotlight right on him. Two soldiers fell. Two more fired back.

More soldiers converged on Smoke.

Abraham started pulling his trigger. The muzzle of the Glock flashed. Men were falling. Others were coming running at him and firing. Before he knew what happened, his clip was empty. *Blazing Saddles!* He discharged the weapon's clip and fumbled to reload another magazine. His ear caught the sound of footsteps crunching over the stiff grasses. He turned around as he stuffed in his clip. A soldier had him dead to rights with a pistol pointed at his chest. The soldier wore a black ball cap. He cracked a wicked smile and opened fire. *Blam. Blam. Blam.*

CHAPTER 58

ABRAHAM GROANED AS HIS CHEST caught fire. The full force of every bullet sent shards of pain exploding through him.

"Say, you ain't bleeding, and you're still breathing," the thuggish soldier said.

Gasping for air, Abraham managed to say, "No. Sorry to disappoint you." As much as his chest hurt, he might as well have been dead.

The soldier shrugged. "I guess it needs to be a head shot then."

Abraham kicked the man in the shin as the gun went off. A bullet whizzed by his ear. He jumped on the soldier and drove his knife into the man's gut. The soldier let out a ragged sigh and died.

With blood on his knuckles, he pulled the blade out and crawled back behind the well. He charged the slide on his weapon and fired at another wave of soldiers coming right at him.

Smoke jumped behind the well and asked, "How's it going?"

"I've been shot three times, but I'm still breathing," Abraham said. "You?"

"I took a couple of rounds. Hurts, don't it?"

"That's putting it mildly."

"You'll get used to it."

"Believe me, I am, but I'd rather not."

The helicopter spotlight shone on both of them.

Hails of gunfire blasted into the water well's stones.

"We need to move!" Abraham said.

"Follow my lead." Smoke rolled across the grass and fired into the soldiers. Two more soldiers dropped. He came to his feet and sprinted right at them. "Eee-yah!"

Abraham took off after the ranging man. He fired at everything moving that wasn't Smoke. One of his shots ripped through one man's chest and knocked down another. *Man, these bullets are nasty.*

They skirmished with the soldiers all over the yard. They battled behind the barn and the house. Soldiers came at them in twos and fours.

The sting of a bullet punched into Abraham's shoulder. He shrugged it off. Even in his old body, his blood was running battle hot.

The helicopter chased them over the yard. Automatic gunfire blasted out from the chopper. The grass spat up behind their fleeing feet.

Smoke dashed up the steps onto the front porch as Abraham followed behind him. Smoke crashed through the front door. Abraham dove through a glass window.

A man tackled Abraham, and a knife cut his cheek. They wrestled over the floor, knocking over light stands and bumping into a china cabinet. The soldier was a large man, strong as an ox. He wrestled like an angry bear.

"I will break you like egg," the soldier said in a thick Russian accent. He busted Abraham in the nose with his forehead.

Abraham's nose caved in, and his eyes watered. Warm blood ran down his chin. He punched his knife at the man and fired a shot.

The soldier grabbed both of his wrists in a viselike grip. He wrenched both weapons free. In a sudden movement, he hip tossed Abraham to the floor. He pinned Abraham down and locked his fingers on his throat.

Abraham whaled away at the man's ribs. The soldier's body armor absorbed the blows. *Who is this freak?*

The soldier put his weight on Abraham's neck. He was bigger than Abraham and built like a defensive lineman. The soldier's crushing grip started to collapse the muscles in his neck.

Nooo!

Abraham grabbed the man's wrists and tried to pry them apart. The soldier applied more force. In Titanuus, Ruger would have made mincemeat out of this guy. Back home, it was different. He was only Abraham Jenkins, an out-of-shape truck driver fighting for his breath.

No! I'm Ruger Slade. I've fought far worse than this!

He let out a loud grunt. He squirmed and thrashed. His body shifted underneath the hulk trying to kill him. He grabbed one of the soldier's ring fingers and peeled it back. He gave it a yank, and the finger bone snapped out of place.

The soldier let out a yelp and punched Abraham in the face.

Abraham twisted out from underneath the man. He sprang back to his feet, gasping for breath.

The soldier charged and rammed Abraham back into the fireplace. Both men went back and forth, whaling on one another.

He hit the soldier in the face as hard as he could. The fighter spat out a tooth, snapped his finger back into place, and kept coming, huffing for breath.

"You haven't been in a long fight in a while, have you?" Abraham asked, his own lungs burning.

The bearish soldier pulled a knife from somewhere behind his back and started slicing at Abraham.

Abraham blocked the deadly cuts with his forearm. The soldier sneaked one slice across his chest. His clothing was slashed, but the sweetheart suit kept his bowels intact. Back and forth, the men battled through the farmhouse's living room. They fell over a couch in a tangle of limbs. Neither man gave. The fight was still on.

Somehow, Abraham found deep reserves that kept him from being pummeled to death. His will and Ruger's will started to become one. He fought like a demon. He liked it.

"I will break you," the soldier said.

"Keep dreaming, Drago."

The soldier feinted in with the knife and slipped a hard punch across Abraham's jaw.

Abraham fell to one knee. His body wobbled as he became woozy. The soldier's punch had been dead on.

The soldier lifted the knife.

Abraham couldn't lift his arms to block. His strength fled him. He was stunned.

The helicopters light shone into the living room, and a loud whirring came from outside.

"Get down, Abraham!" Smoke cried out.

Abraham fell over.

Bullets ripped through the house. Glass shattered. Wood splintered.

The big soldier gaped as bullets cut the man in two. The top of his body fell from the bottom.

Smoke crawled over to Abraham, blood all over his face. "I told you it was going to be a party."

Abraham spotted his gun and grabbed it. He pulled a red clip from his belt and reloaded. As the house was being cut in half, he asked, "Are they firing what I think they are?"

"A Vulcan Gatling gun. You got it." Smoke pulled a big piece of glass out of his hand. "They must think we are predators."

Abraham rose and fired at the chopper. The bullets ripped out of the gun barrel like red tracer rounds. They zipped through the busted windows and into the chopper.

BOOM!

The chopper turned into a ball of flame and peeled away. It crashed hard and loud into the driveway. A pyre of burning metal ensued.

Both men stood.

"Good shot," Smoke said. "I was wondering if you'd remember about the red bullets. Cool, aren't they?"

"Yep," Abraham said. "Man, I'm thirsty."

"It's the suit. It will dehydrate you."

The house groaned and swayed.

"Uh oh," Smoke said.

The second floor of the house collapsed on top of them.

CHAPTER 60

BLACKNESS. SUFFOCATING AIR. ABRAHAM TOOK a short breath, and something bit into his lungs. "Ugh."

Half of a house had just fallen on top of him. He could still hear muffled gunshots, but he couldn't see a thing. Abraham pushed out from underneath of what felt like a chandelier. His leg was pinned somewhere. "Smoke," he called out dryly.

"I'm here," the voice muttered in the darkness. "Stuck at the moment, but I'm working on it."

"You're not chewing your arm off or something like that, are you?"

"Too early for that."

Wood and paneling popped and cracked.

Old plaster drywall dust was everywhere.

Abraham spat and said, "We sure know how to bring down the house, don't we?"

"You can say that again." Smoke grunted. Something heavy scraped over the floor. "I think I can see light. Can you?"

With one armed pinned against his chest, Abraham wiped dust out of his eyes and blinked. "It's as black as a coal mine. Man, I hope Mandi is okay. I've got to get out of here." He clawed at the roof that had fallen on him, old plaster and wood framing. He didn't have much wiggle room at all but fought against the weight of it. "Guh!"

"Don't blow a gasket over there," Smoke said. "We'll manage."

The sound of footsteps could be heard outside. The gunfire had stopped. People were walking through the collapsed house. They moved on cats' feet, but the stiff boards groaned underneath them.

"They sound light," Smoke said in a hushed voice. "Women?"

Abraham nodded in the darkness.

"Sid!" Smoke said.

"Smoke," a woman responded in a muffled voice. "Where are you?"

The men tapped on their ceiling, calling out.

Above, the women busted away the roof and subflooring.

Abraham pushed his free arm against the ceiling.

Someone was ripping away his prison. He made out the faint outline of fingers.

"Abraham," Mandi said. She was nothing more than a silhouette. She grabbed his shoulders and started to pull him.

"Gah!" he said. "Sorry, but my leg is pinned under the subfloor."

"Where?" Mandi asked. She ran her hands down his body and followed it down to his leg. "Oh, I'm standing on the section that's pinning your leg down. Hold on." She punched through the flooring. "I just need to get a good grip on this beam. I'll lift, and you slide out."

"You're going to lift the house off of me?"

"Yep," Mandi said. "I took one of those pills. I've got pregnant-woman strength right now. Like Octomom or something. Let's go for it."

Mandi huddled over the beam and put her back into it with a grunt. The joists pinning his legs rose. He slipped out from under them and punched his way up to his feet.

Mandi lowered the joists, jumped over to him, and gave him a bear hug that might have broken a lesser man's back.

"Ow! I don't need any more cracked ribs."

"Sorry." She pulled him down by the hair and kissed him fiercely. "You have to try these vitamins. I feel like some kind of superwoman."

"Come on, lovebirds, let's go," Sid said.

The gang of four barreled their way through the upstairs window and climbed down the wraparound porch. The helicopter and Hellcat were burning side by side in the driveway. Dead soldiers were scattered all over the grounds.

"I killed those dudes," Mandi said with fire in her eyes. "I mean, I could see them moving, like they were in slow motion. It was point and shoot. Like I was playing *Duck Hunt* or something." She wrapped her arms around Abraham's. "I've never killed anyone."

"Sorry." Abraham didn't know what else to say as they followed Sid and Smoke to the other helicopter. "At least you're alive."

"Oh, I don't regret it. It was them or me. Better off them. Evil men. I could see it in their eyes. They had it coming."

The helicopter started to take off.

"Wait! What is happening?" Sid asked and ran toward it in a long-legged sprint. She was fast, but Smoke was faster. They both jumped onto the skids of the helicopter as it took off.

"Are they crazy?" Abraham yelled. As the helicopter rose higher, he could make out the face of Eugene Drisk staring out of the copilot's window. The professor was waving.

As it took off, another helicopter dropped out of the sky. Its spotlights illuminated Abraham and Mandi.

Abraham shielded his eyes.

The Vulcan machine gun on the helicopter fired. Red-hot blasts of gunfire erupted out of the chopper.

Mandi pushed Abraham out of the way. "I'll handle this." The wild-eyed woman stood in the path of bullets that chewed up the grass on their way toward her. She squeezed off bullets in rapid succession.

"Get out of the way, Mandi!" He climbed back to his feet. "Run, Mandi! Run!"

The Vulcan bullets made a path right through Mandi.

Abraham screamed, "Nooo!"

CHAPTER 61

THE HELICOPTER PITCHED LEFT, AND the hail of bullets went with it. It crashed into the trees, blew up, and caught fire.

Abraham rushed over to Mandi, who lay on the ground. The bullets had made massive divots all around her. He picked her up in his arms and cradled her. "Mandi," he said softly as he shook her. "Mandi. Don't die on me."

Mandi's chest rose and fell as she breathed. Not a scratch was on her.

"They missed!" he said with elation. He shook her, but she didn't wake. "What's wrong?"

The last helicopter in the sky flew in an erratic pattern above him. One person fell out of the chopper, and another person fell after the first. They plummeted through the roof of the barn.

Abraham's heart jumped in his throat.

The helicopter lowered, its lights on Abraham.

He stared it down.

The spotlight dimmed.

Sid jumped out of the helicopter and asked, "What are you waiting for? Let's go. Get in!"

She didn't have to tell him twice. With Mandi in his arms, he rushed over to the chopper. Crouched low, he slipped underneath that chopper's blades and climbed inside. "She's out cold."

The helicopter rose upward.

Smoke was sitting in the pilot's seat with a headset on.

Eugene Drisk was slumped over in the copilot's chair.

Sid checked Mandi's pulse. "She's fine." She spoke loudly, the wind in her hair. "Dehydrated. The super vitamins drained her. Sorry about that, but it was the only way that she could keep up with me. And I didn't have to twist her arm to take it."

"Are they addictive?"

"No. But they give you a hangover." Sid tugged off Mandi's bodysuit. "These suits will burn you up if you aren't used to it. Find her a blanket."

Abraham nodded. He rummaged through the military gear and found a green blanket. He wrapped it around Mandi. "We need some water," he said in a loud voice.

"I'll look." Sid took a turn making her way around the cabin.

"Where will we go now?" he asked.

"What?"

"Where are we going?" he repeated more loudly.

Sid shrugged. "I'll get a headset. There's no telling where Smoke will take us. After a night like this, he'll probably land at the nearest diner to get some milkshakes and pancakes." She found some canteens in the cooler and tilted her head. "Are you all right? You don't look so well."

"What's wrong?" he said, "I feel fine."

"You're as pale as Mandi. Peaked." Sid touched his face. "Oh man, you're dehydrated. You need some serious H2O." She handed him a canteen. "Drink."

He nodded, gave her a faint smile, felt the helicopter start to spin, and passed out.

CHAPTER 62

Suffocating smoke burned Abraham's lungs. He woke in a fit of coughing. Every inch of his body felt as if thousands of needles were trying to poke out of it. His eyes burned, and he couldn't see a thing. The only moving in his body came from his hoarse coughing.

The helicopter must have crashed. Where's Mandi?

Flames were all around him. He couldn't see a thing. The wroth heat of the fires started to cook him.

He coughed and hacked as the flames took his breath away. He rolled onto his belly and started to crawl slowly away from the heat, but he didn't have the strength.

I'm going to burn alive!

Wooziness assailed him, and he felt faint again. With his head down, he summoned his reserves and pushed forward. He inched ahead. The flames were so hot that they burnt his toes.

Someone grabbed him by the arms and began pulling him away from the fire. He couldn't make the person out, for he couldn't lift his head to see. The person didn't seem particularly strong.

Mandi? Sid? Get me out of this hot mess!

The flames roared. The fire crackled and popped. Someone let out a bloodcurdling scream. A loud explosion jolted his body.

Whoever was pulling him from the fire was moving slowly and coughing too.

"Hurry up," Abraham groaned in a dry, cracking voice. He kicked with his feet. "Hurry."

The heat felt as if he were lying just inside a fireplace. He was roasted all over. The smell of his singed hair carried into his nose as if his flesh were cooking.

Please don't be hell. I don't want to go to hell. I believe. Lord, I believe!

Abraham's body bounced down over something hard. His eyes were so watery that he couldn't see. The person pulling him grunted and coughed. He went into another fit of coughing as well.

Someone else latched onto his other arm and helped the other drag him farther. The hot flames enveloping his surroundings started to cool. He coughed and sucked in a lungful of breathable air. He gasped in more air as he was dragged farther from the flames.

Thank heavens!

He opened his eyes and wiped the tears away. "Thanks, guys," he managed to croak. "What happened? Did the chopper crash? Where's Mandi?"

"Who's Mandi?" Horace asked. The beefy man helped Abraham into a sitting position. He slapped Abraham on the back and said, "Cough out that smoke. You need to clear it."

"What?" Abraham's head snapped around. A tavern was burning in the streets of Junction City. It was the one he'd been in with Big Apple, Lord Hawk, Kawnee, and the wraith, Fleece. He clutched his head. "Nooo! Black Bane!"

"Be happy that I pulled you out when I did," Shades said. "It was getting hot in there. A few more seconds, and we might not have made it." He slapped Abraham's shoulder. "No need to thank me. As for the sword, well, I figure it had a good run."

CHAPTER 63

Black smoke spilled into the streets. Men and women raced from the river with buckets of water, making a chain of people who tossed water onto the burning building.

"You set the tavern on fire, didn't you?" Abraham asked Shades as the flames consumed the tavern like a giant box of matches. "Didn't I tell you not to do that?"

"I don't recall those exact words. I believe that you were speaking generally," Shades said. "Such as, don't burn a building down because you don't like the service. Or the people that are in it. But, in case of a dangerous situation, set the building on fire."

Abraham was only half listening as his mind tried to sort things out. Minutes before, he had been back home, but now, he was in Titanuus. Smoke and Sid were gone. So was Mandi. She was unconscious, but at least she was safe with her cousin. He hoped.

The upper level of the tavern collapsed on the bottom. A new plume of flames and smoke went up. The old dry wood popped and cracked loudly. In a few minutes, nothing would be left.

His back straightened. "Where's Sticks?" He reached up and grabbed Shades by the collar and pulled the small man down. "You didn't kill her, did you?"

"Of course not," Shades replied. "I'd never harm a lady."

Abraham looked around. A crowd had gathered around the tavern. Most of them were cheering and partying. Abraham saw no sign of Sticks, Big Apple, Lord Hawk, Kawnee, or Fleece. He recalled his last moments with Big Apple. The horned halfling had stated that he controlled Fleece, who turned out to be the Underlord. If that were the case, then Big Apple controlled a lot more than he'd let on. By the looks of it, the horned halfling controlled the Sect and quite possibly Lord Hawk's guild, the Shell. The question was how… and why. Abraham stood up and asked, "Then where is she? Where are the rest of them?"

Shades lifted a finger, paused, and said, "That's a long story."

He pointed toward a group of soldiers gathering around the fire. They were the Gray Guard. The stalwart group of soldiers grabbed the folks nearest the fire and started asking questions. People were pointing in Abraham's direction.

"I think we should move on," Shades said.

"I'm not leaving Black Bane in that pillar of flame. I have to get it!" Abraham said.

"I'll fetch it, Captain." Horace tapped the butt of his spear on the ground. "I'll deal with the Gray Guard too, one soldier to another. I can speak the language."

Abraham gave Horace and the fire a long look and walked away. He followed Shades into the back alleys and took a seat on a box crate with his head down. He coughed and said, "Spit it out, you little pyromaniac."

"Pyromaniac?" Shades glanced upward and rubbed his chin. "That's a term from your world, isn't it? I think I like it."

Abraham slumped against the wall, grimacing. He could barely move. His bones ached, and his muscles were as tight as bowstrings. He accidentally took a deep breath of the alley's stink and said, "Whew! And make it quick. I don't want to sit in this cat box all night. And where the heck did Horace come from?"

Shades casually leaned his head from one shoulder to the other and said, "Let me start at the beginning. You went in the tavern. I went up the stairs and listened at the doors. I had no trouble tracking down Sticks. Commander Cutter is a loud one, if you know what I mean." He winked. "Once I secured her whereabouts, I decided to slip into the tavern. I made my move from the back alley and into the kitchen. Well, I got there soon enough to overhear your conversation with Big Apple. You had him pinned inside the fireplace, pointing that gun at him. It is called a gun, right?"

Abraham gave a weak nod. He could hardly lift his chin. The spell that Fleece had hit him with sucked the vitality right out of him.

Shades pulled back his sleeves, revealing his bare forearms, and squatted down in front of Abraham. "That thing got its bony fingers on you, and my hair stood on my arms. I froze in my tracks, but your scream got me going again. That wraith is an omnipotent sort. Otherworldly. I was sure you would be undone, because I've never heard a man wail so loudly."

"It wasn't that loud." Abraham didn't remember screaming, but he didn't doubt that he had. Fleece's touch felt as if his soul were being ripped out.

"Oh, it was. I can still hear it ringing in my ears." He pushed down his sleeves. "That's when I did the only thing that I knew to do."

"Start a fire?"

Shades shrugged his eyebrows. "Create a distraction that happened to be a fire. I had to do something that would stop all of the screaming." He covered his ears. "Other than this. I managed to clear the kitchen quick because the cook was drunk and outside smoking. I locked him outside. It didn't take long to get the coals and the chicken grease burning. I flung it on the curtains outside of the kitchen near the seats. No one was paying attention to me—just you and the harrowing sound of sheer torment.

"The smoke began to carry, and one of the girls from the mud hole was the first to notice the flames and shout, 'Fire!' Just when the goons scrambled to put the flames out, you'll never guess who entered through the front door."

"Sticks?"

"No." Shades backhanded Abraham's shoulder. "Melris."

Abraham made a surprised look and said, "He was comatose."

"*Was* being the key word. The purple man's eyes lit up like the stars the moment he set his eyes on the shade's back. The room brightened in a wash of purple as his hands caught fire. The rod he carried came to life like a burning torch. He slammed it into the floor." Shades flicked his fingers out. "Boooom."

CHAPTER 64

"EVERYONE IN THE ROOM FLATTENED as if they were hit by a sudden gale," Shades said with awe. "They were tossed like a bull had bucked them. The floor underneath my feet heaved. The bar bowed. The glasses and pottery jangled, fell, and broke. I was on my knees, and very little takes me from my feet. By the time I climbed back to my feet, I found myself sitting in the midst of a storm with flashes of purple and black.

"The purple man and the black shade had locked horns. Like sheets in the wind, without a toe touching the floor, they battled through the tavern. Their bodies blasted through the bars. The flames of the fire spread faster. The purple man, well, he had some sort of aura around his body. The wraith couldn't get a grip on him. Purple smote the wraith with his rod. It made the sound of timbers breaking."

Abraham hung on the rogue's every word. He nodded as he visualized the scene.

Shades paced the alley, gesticulating as he continued the story. "They punched through one wall and reentered through another. Spinning like a dust devil of arcane energy, they trashed the tavern floor. Tables and chairs were lifted from the floor and sent crashing into the walls. The wraith let out an angry shriek. His hands filled with black flames. He tried to choke the purple man to death.

"The purple man slipped his clutches. He swung his rod like a club. The two of them whaled on one another with flaming fists. Their robes came alive like a writhing nest of snakes. They tangled, tugged, and I swear by the Elders, they screamed screams of their own. By the time I gathered my bowels, the two of them blasted through the ceiling and carried on through the roof." He punched his hand in the air. "Pow! They were gone.

"I jumped through the wreckage and headed outside. There they were, standing in the streets, hurling bolts of light at each other. The town lit up with a new daylight. The sounds of a storm rolled through the streets. Cries arose from the rooftops. The little ball of muscle charged at the wraith. He was thrusting his finger at it and yelling at the top of his lungs. He said, 'Take us away. Take us away. Now!'" Shades flicked his fingers out. "Poof. They were gone. The wraith and the halfling. Lord Hawk and the fish lady. Even the goons. Vanished into thin air. Melris took off down the street. His burning eyes were searching the sky. I have no idea where he went."

"What about Sticks?"

Shades shrugged. "I think she and Cutter disappeared with them. I rushed back into the fire to save you. Don't worry, she can take care of herself."

Abraham stood up and kicked the crate. "We don't know that." His head started to ache. He wanted to rest, to take a breath, but he couldn't. "What about the other Henchmen? Are they here?"

"I've only seen Horace. Well, him and the purple man." Shades moved to the end of the alley and peeked into the city. "Horace is out there talking to the Gray Guard. It looks like a bunch of drunks have cleared out. They've already rounded up a heap of them. Got them face down in the road, spread-eagle."

Abraham rubbed his neck. He needed a break. Traveling between two worlds was beginning to catch up to him. He trudged over to Shades and saw Horace making small talk with the Gray Guard. "Fetch him."

"Consider it done." Shades departed.

"This is getting old. I'm getting old."

He didn't have any idea how old Ruger was, but he guessed the man was in his mid-thirties. Most of the Henchmen were, if he were to guess. After the shock he'd taken from Fleece, he felt more like seventy.

The tavern was burning, but the flames were dying down. The hungry flames quickly turned the ancient dry wood to ash.

"Black Bane," he muttered. He had enough problems. The last thing he needed was to lose his sword. He needed something he could get a grip on. The heft of Black Bane in his grip gave him a sense of security. Now, it was underneath piles of burning ash. "Better to have some bad luck than have no luck at all. Gloom, despair, and agony on me."

Horace and Shades approached. Horace gave him a stiff nod. "The Gray Guard cooled. They aren't so bad to chat with. They recognize a soldier's soldier. I told them I saw wild mages battling in the sky. Plenty of other folk support the situation." He clawed at his beard. "What now, Captain?"

"Where did Melris come from? He was out. Simon sat on him," he asked.

"He popped up several hours after you departed. I told him where you went and tried to stop him. He insisted on getting you. There wasn't no telling him no." Horace wiped the beading sweat on his forehead. "Why is this place so hot? It's the cool season."

"The others are coming?" Abraham asked.

"Aye, I told them we'd meet at the river. That was Melris's idea. He said the Little Vein is the fast way to the Wound." Horace cleared his throat. "Any fool knows that. We've seen the maps."

"Did you see Sticks?"

"No. As soon as we entered town, Melris moved like a hound dog right toward the blaze. He's got some sort of intuition. I didn't even see the fire," Horace said. "He lost me in the streets. The man can run like a deer. I can say that much for him."

Abraham wandered into the street with his brow furrowed. "All right. Get some men and some gear. We need to dig my sword out of that burning heap the first chance we get." His palms itched. Losing Sticks terrified him for some reason. "Shades, get with Dominga and Tark. You need to find Sticks."

"Will do." Shades slapped Abraham on the shoulder as he walked by. "You have to believe she can handle herself."

His jaws clenched. "I'll believe it when I see it. Now go!"

CHAPTER 65

Posing as volunteer medieval firefighters, a group of Henchmen went to work at the burn site. The fire was extinguished. The sun rose. Nothing was left of the tavern except piles of charred wood and ash.

Horace and Bearclaw were covered in soot as they shoveled piles of roasted wreckage away. Vern clawed the fallen coals away with a rake. The Red Tunics lent a hand. Skitts and Zann were on their hands and knees, digging through the rubble.

Solomon hauled away half-burnt beams and tossed them into a pile.

Abraham stood over the spot where he thought his sword might have been. Iris knelt beside him, her eyes closed. She held her palms downward and mumbled strange chants.

"Anything?" he asked.

Iris didn't reply.

Cudgel wandered over to him, his face beaded with sweat. His clothing was marred with black soot. "Anything, Captain?"

Abraham shrugged. "No. Keep on digging."

Cudgel flipped his shovel over his hand and said, "I wish we had more Red Tunics to do the digging. I'd like to get some breakfast. And look at me now. I'm all messy."

"You'll live," Abraham said absentmindedly.

He couldn't stop thinking about Sticks. She was in the clutches of Cutter. The thought of her being with Cutter soured his mood.

As Cudgel wiped his bald head with a rag, his eyes popped, and he said, "Look, it's Melris."

Abraham turned. Melris was casually walking down the street as if nothing had happened at all. He cradled his rod of devastation in his arms.

"Where have you been?" Abraham asked angrily.

In his quiet voice, Melris said, "I've been trying to locate the wraith."

"Well, did you find him?"

Melris shook his head. "No. I have no sense of them at all. The wraith is endowed with significant powers."

"The wraith is the Underlord. The halfling controls him," Abraham said. "Did you learn anything about him from your fight?"

Melris hefted his rod onto his shoulder and asked, "Like what?"

"I don't know. Who is the Underlord? What are they doing? Or want?"

"The Underlord is a wraith. He is the living, now undead. His mastery of magic is far-reaching. He sold his mortal life for the power of magic. That is how he acquired abilities. That is why he leads the Sect. He completed their trials and is blessed by the Dark Elders." Melris dusted some wooden splinters from his robes. "I sought him out the moment I had a sense of him. I should have killed him, but he is strong, stronger than I imagined."

With his head rolling, Cudgel asked, "Well, how strong are you, Elderling?"

"I'm trained by the Elders. We are equipped to handle anything in the common world," Melris replied.

Cudgel rolled his eyes.

"What does that even mean?" Abraham asked.

"Yeah, apparently you didn't handle the wraith so well," Cudgel said.

"It means that I am more than flesh and blood. I have Elder magic coursing through my veins."

"Well, I'd like to have some biscuits and gravy running through mine." Cudgel huffed, moved away, and started digging.

Abraham gave Melris a curious glance and said, "What did you mean by the Dark Elders?"

"There are good Elders and bad. The Elders are supposed to keep harmony in the world. They protect the races, but they use them too. Normally, they are inactive. Elderlings like me care for them. When there is a shift in Titanuus, they become restless and active."

"The tide turns. The Elders awaken," Abraham said, quoting a phrase he had heard repeated several times. "Is that what is happening? Is that why you are here?"

"The balance of nature is unbalanced. Titanuus is shaken. We must stop it. We must stop the invasion. That is why I am here."

Abraham wondered who Melris meant by the Elders. *Are they a race of omnipotent beings, like the Greek and Norse gods of mythos? Or am I just crazy?* "I want to find Sticks. Can you help us with that? Or help me find my sword?"

"We need to depart," Melris said. "You should have stayed the course to begin with, but you chose to take a different path. We must follow the king's command and retrieve the stones."

"I'm not going anywhere without Sticks. She's a Henchman. We find her first." He looked down at Melris. "Besides, finding Big Apple and the Underlord is a good thing. We know that one controls the others. We know they stand between us and the truth. If we stop them, the king won't need the stones."

Melris narrowed his eyes and said, "Otherworlder, the king needs the stones now more than ever. Kingsland, the last bastion of hope, will be destroyed without them. The enemy grows stronger every day. The very Spine of Titanuus tremors."

"If the stones are so important, then why aren't Big Apple and the Underlord going after them?"

"Because they have chosen to side with the invaders. Their faith is in the artifacts that they bring. To them, the magic of Titanuus is part of an antiquated past. They embrace a new future."

"Great, free pizza delivery and thirty-one thousand flavors of ice cream, here we come." Abraham sighed aloud. "Is nothing sacred?"

"Ice cream?" Melris said.

The floorboards beneath Cudgel collapsed, and he let out a surprised shout.

Everyone rushed over to the hole in the floor. A basement lay beneath the tavern. Cudgel was flat on his back.

"Are you well?" Iris said.

"Well enough." Cudgel wormed around. "Nothing is broken. Well, look at what I have here." He lifted up a charred scabbard with a sword in it. The pommel of Black Bane shone.

"Toss it up," Abraham said.

Showing a mouthful of white teeth, Cudgel said, "Finders keepers."

"Get him out of there," Abraham ordered.

Solomon bent over the gap, stretched his long hairy arms down, and grabbed Cudgel, who reached up. The troglin reeled the stout man up as easily as lifting a baby.

"Thanks," Cudgel said. He gave Solomon a pat on the back and handed Abraham the sword. "Here, Captain."

Black Bane's scabbard was crusted over with char and soot. The leather encasing it appeared dry and cracked. Small flecks of charred leather fell off the sheath. Somehow, the flames hadn't entirely consumed it and eaten it away. The sword's grip and pommel were intact but blackened with ashes and char.

Abraham pulled the sword halfway out of the scabbard. The blade shone in the sunlight.

"It's good, eh, Captain?" Horace said.

He nodded. Out of the corner of his eye, Shades, Dominga, and Tark approached. They were accompanied by three men wearing the burgundy tunics over the chain mail of the Black Squadron.

"What's this all about?" Abraham asked as he stared down the Black Squadron members, all of whom had short hair on the top and were shaved on the sides. He looked at Shades. "Well?"

Shades opened his mouth, but a Black Squadron soldier with a full brown beard cut him off. "You are Ruger Slade?"

"Yes," Abraham said.

"Commander Cutter sends a message. He has the woman. Follow me if you want her back. Only you and one witness," the soldier said.

"A witness for what?"

"The duel."

CHAPTER 66

Abraham raised an eyebrow and asked, "What sort of duel?"

The brown-bearded soldier looked at his men and chuckled. He spat on the ground and said, "If you don't know what a duel is, then you are dead already."

The other two Black Squadron members chuckled and spat. They eyed the members of the Henchmen who began to gather.

Vern strolled forward with his hand on his sword belt and said, "I'd be happy to duel with any of you Hanchans. You are the worst swords in the world. I'll prove it."

One of the soldiers wandered in Vern's direction. His leader pulled him back by the collar.

"You'll get your chance," the leader said. "Once Cutter finishes off Ruger, we'll dispose of the rest of them. They are wanted men, after all." He fixed his hardened stare on Abraham and spat again. "You and one witness from your Elder-forsaken group. You have Commander Cutter's word that no harm will come to you once it's over. He wants all of your men to hear it for themselves from the lips of your own vermin."

"Commander Cutter sounds very confident in his abilities. But tell me, eh, what is your name?"

"Tomas. Second in command."

"Tomas, second in command, I don't think that you thought this through. What happens when he dies?"

"Well, er, the woman will be returned to you," Tomas said.

"You can't take the word of a Hanchan," Horace warned. "They are all liars."

"And lousy fighters," Vern added.

"It's a trap, Captain," Horace said.

"Time is pressing. If I don't return with you soon, the woman will be killed," Tomas said. "You should come with me immediately. You and one man. Command your company to stay behind. All of them. If so much as a one of them shows, the woman's throat will be cut."

Abraham turned and faced his command and said, "Everyone stay put except for Horace. He'll come with me." He saw the disappointed expressions on their faces and winked even though he felt like crap. "I'll make it quick. Come on, Horace."

Tomas and his men led them back into the city, leaving the Henchmen behind. Horace strutted with his chest out and spear in hand. "You should let me fight him, Captain. I can take Cutter. I'll kill him."

There was nothing Abraham would rather do than take Horace up on the offer. He was empty. His bones ached, and his muscles throbbed. Fleece had really done a number on him, and he hadn't recovered. He was drained. Normally, Ruger's body was up for any fight. At the moment, his body could barely walk, but he didn't show it.

The road led them to the exterior of one of the giant stacks. The top of its chimney, hundreds of feet in the air, spewed out clouds of gray smoke. A suffocating warmth emanated from the great pillar. An open doorway led inside the stack.

Tomas led the way. Abraham and Horace walked between them and the other two men. A stone stairwell led in a tight downward spiral with burning torches hung on the wall. After a thirty-foot descent, they entered a grand circular chamber underneath the stack. Torches lined the walls. Ash piles were everywhere. The suffocating warmth increased. The great stones above them pulsated with an orange heartbeat glow of their own.

"Welcome to the Waste," Tomas said. He navigated through the piles of ash on the dusty floor toward the other side of the chamber. "Commander Cutter awaits."

On the other side of the room, Cutter stood with his men, over a score of them. Cutter, the biggest of them all, sat on a large wooden chair built into a wooden podium like a throne. His bastard sword lay across his lap. He rubbed a finger underneath his lip as he eyed Abraham.

"Where is the woman?" Abraham asked.

Cutter took a deep breath through his nose. Without looking, he hitched his thumb toward his men in the back. Two men came forward with Sticks locked in their arms. One of them was wearing her bandolier of knives.

Abraham's blood ran hot the moment his eyes found hers.

CHAPTER 67

Sticks's right eye was swollen shut. Her cat makeup had smeared on her face, and she had a split lip. A rope was tied around her neck, raw with burn marks. She sagged in the soldiers' arms. She lifted her chin and glanced at Abraham through her one good eye.

"What did you do to her?" Abraham shouted.

"I didn't do anything," Cutter said. "She tried to escape. We had to subdue her. She fights like a wildcat, that one. Took one of my men out. That's grounds for killing her." He tapped his fingers on the blade of his sword. "Be thankful that she is still alive."

Abraham wanted nothing more than to split the man in half. The problem was he wasn't sure he could do it. Even speaking took effort. He decided to delay. *Keep him talking.* "I'm here. Let her go. There is nowhere for me to go, and I never run from a fight."

"Never? Ha! When we crossed paths in Hancha, you avoided it then," Cutter said.

"No, you backed down. I was being merciful to you and your men. We killed Arcayis the Underlord that day. We'll kill the rest of your brood too. Big Apple, Fleece, Lord Hawk… all of them are going down."

"The only one going down today is you. As for them, they have their visions, and I have mine." Cutter rose from his chair and stepped down off his podium. "Mine is to be known as the greatest swordsman in the world. I'll settle for that."

"More like the greatest lackey. Big Apple has you twisted around his finger. He is only using you for his gain."

"Says King Hector's fool, who wears the King's Brand. You are the one that is a slave, not I." Cutter rested his sword on his shoulder. He gripped the hilt of his sword in two hands. "Enough chatter. It's time to duel. I've been waiting a lifetime for this."

"Your lifetime is over," Horace stated.

Cutter eyed Horace and said, "We'll see, spear chucker." Sweat ran down from the corner of his eyebrow. "Let's discuss the terms of the duel. Death. Mercy. Yield."

"Why not make it to the death?" Abraham asked as he pulled his sword free from its deteriorating scabbard.

"I want you to beg for mercy. I want you to yield from fear," Cutter said as he narrowed his eyes on Abraham. "I want all of my men to see it. Your men to see it. For death is the easy way out. Even though, most likely, I will kill you."

"And when I kill you, your men will stand down? Sticks, Horace, and I go free."

Cutter raised one hand and said, "You have my word as the Commander of the Black Squadron. Tomas will see it through."

Tomas nodded.

Cutter moved by Abraham and Horace. He made his way past the head-high ash piles toward the center of the chamber, where no piles sat. A thirty-foot-wide ring of black stone lay in the floor, partially covered in ash. He stepped to the middle.

Abraham moved inside the ring.

The Black Squadron members stepped onto the black line, enclosing the swordsmen in the middle. Horace stood among those men, arms crossed with the butt of his spear on the floor.

On the opposite side of the ring from Horace stood Sticks, her knees wobbling and her chin sagging into her chest.

Abraham faced off with Cutter, ten feet between them. He rested Black Bane on his shoulder. "I want more than our freedom after I win."

"Oh, and what might that be?" Cutter said.

"I want to know what Big Apple and Lord Hawk are planning. I want to know where they went to."

"We are not their handmaidens. We are soldiers of Hancha. That is who we serve."

"I know better than that."

Cutter shrugged his mountainous shoulders. He was a huge man, much like the current Guardian Commander, Pratt. He waved a hand. "Fine, I'll agree, but only because it won't come to that. Are you finished delaying, Slade the Blade? I'm ready to fight. I've been planning this day for all of my life."

Abraham nodded and sized Cutter up as he did so. Cutter tended to put his weight on his left foot. His arms were long, and his bastard sword had a couple more inches than Black Bane. No doubt the swordsman would use his length as his strength. The question was how quick he was with his steel.

Abraham had yet to see the man fight. But he reminded Abraham of the large pirate, Flamebeard, who was a reputed swordsman and whom Abraham had cut down with a few strokes. The problem was Abraham didn't feel anything. He was flat. Seeing Sticks gave him fire, but he soon cooled. His body ached. He remembered having to pitch a game when he had the flu. That was how he felt now. Sick. Tired. Drained.

He glanced at Sticks. She gave him a dull stare. He turned to Horace, who gave him a nod.

Cutter spread his feet out and got into a sword-fighting stance. He held his sword in two hands, low, and in the plow guard position. He set his gaze on Abraham. His nostrils started to flare. "Are you ready for your final duel, Ruger Slade?"

Abraham got into the same ox guard position and faced the bigger and longer man. The leather on Black Bane's handle squeezed in his gripping hands. He locked eyes on Cutter, gave him a nod, and said, "Death before failure."

CHAPTER 68

Cutter lunged.

Ruger parried.

Steel kissed steel with a clang.

The Black Squadron let out a wild cry.

"Kill him, Commander!" they chanted. "Spill his bowels on the deck!"

Abraham backpedaled and parried. Cutter's hard flashing strikes jolted his arms and up into his shoulders. He was in a fight—a fight for his life. Cutter was good. Very good.

"You're an excellent defender!" Cutter said as he lunged forward, his sword licking at Abraham's eyes. "But do you know how to fight?"

Abraham kept his lips sealed and breathed through the nose. He had to focus. One miscalculation might cost him his life. He circled away from Cutter's strikes and parried with the tip of his sword.

"Ha! You are weak, Ruger Slade. I always knew it!" Cutter put more shoulder into his swings. His bastard sword crashed into Black Bane with resounding effect. "Swing, man! Swing!"

Cutter's men let out raucous cries and jeers. Their leader was wearing down the greatest swordsman in the world.

Abraham parried with taxed limbs. He backpedaled from the fierce strikes. Fending off the expert swordsman took everything he had. His arms burned. He could see the moves coming before they happened, but his body could barely react to them. Fleece had really drained him. It was worse than he'd thought. *Come on, Ruger. You have to do this!* He jumped to the side, out of Cutter's reach.

"Stand still long enough to die!" Cutter said as he poked his sword forward like a striking snake. "It's time to put an end to you. You are an embarrassment. I expected a much better fight than this."

"And I expected better conversation," Abraham fired back. He countered a strike with a swing of his own. Metal crashed together.

Cutter blocked then unleashed a fatal swing at Abraham's neck.

Abraham crouched underneath the decapitating swing.

Cutter kicked him in the chest.

He fell on his backside. The soldiers let out victorious cries as Abraham scrambled away.

Cutter's sword bit into the stone, making sparks and just missing Abraham by inches.

Abraham swatted wildly at the bastard sword. He fought from his backside. He turned loose a desperate chop that forced Cutter backward. Abraham popped up to his feet. He braced his feet for Cutter's next charge. It didn't happen.

With his eyes fastened on Abraham, Cutter paced. He wiped a forearm across his mouth. "One swing. A weak one at that. I must tell you I am disappointed. Unless you are playing games with me. Is that the case? Hmm… a bit of possum."

With his head hung low, Abraham said, "No. You are far better than I expected."

"Kill him, Captain!" Horace said. "Quit toying with the bastard wielder!"

Abraham thought for certain that Ruger's vitality would have kicked in by then, but it hadn't happened. His chest heaved. Cutter was barely breathing heavily. Abraham licked his lips. He felt like a cat fighting against a wolf. He didn't have it.

He lifted his sword. "Let's finish this."

"Good! I want to hear you beg for mercy." Cutter came at him with his sword cocked back in the wrath guard position. He turned loose a swing with wroth force.

Abraham brought his sword up to block.

Clang!

Black Bane almost tore free from his grip. He staggered sideways.

Cutter pressed. He kept swinging, trying to chop Ruger Slade down like a tree.

It took everything Abraham had to bring his sword back up in time. He was losing. In seconds, it would be over with.

"Abraham! Fight!" Sticks shouted.

Something about the woman's words tapped the recesses of his mind. Abraham reached down deep and summoned his reserves, praying the tank wasn't empty. He braced himself for another blow. He took the full force of Cutter's swing on the edge of his sword. Steel scraped against steel. They locked up their crossguards.

Chest to chest, the men glared at one another. Cutter leaned down on him with eyes full of fury.

Abraham pushed back and said, "You ain't so tough. Is that all that you got?"

"No!" Cutter said. He gave a mighty shove that pushed Abraham into backpedaling. He flipped his sword around his body. "This is!" He charged.

The wild cries of the Black Guard renewed. Their loud voices echoed throughout the chamber.

Fight. Sticks's words echoed in his mind. *Fight!* His blood churned. He stared down Cutter and said, "You might be good, but you aren't no Conan."

"Who?" Cutter asked. He shrugged with a scowl and attacked. "Who cares!"

Abraham waited for Cutter to make his move. The bigger man rushed him with his sword in the high point position and lunged. Abraham turned his hip into his parry and batted the man aside. The fighters battled back and forth. Their swords clashed with the sharp ring of steel. Putting everything he had into his swings, Abraham attacked.

Within moments, both men were frothing at the mouth. Like two heavyweight fighters, they pounded at each other blow for blow. The swords rattled in their hilts. They struck like snakes. Neither man gave ground as they shuffled back and forth.

Ruger's body came to life. Abraham felt hot blood flowing through him again. Black Bane warmed in his hands. He got it going. He anticipated Cutter's moves. His body responded in kind. He pressed the attack.

Cutter parried and backpedaled.

Abraham came at the man in a storm of steel. Clutching his sword in both hands, he started beating down Cutter's sword. "What's the matter? Are you tired of fighting?"

"Never!" Cutter bull-rushed Abraham sword first.

Their blades collided together and locked up.

"I'll beat you!" Cutter shouted.

Abraham looked up into the man's face and said, "No, you won't!" He shoved the larger man backward.

Cutter stumbled in the midst of backpedaling.

Abraham rushed the man and swung low. He took Cutter's right leg off at the knee.

Cutter screamed as he toppled to the ground like a tree. "Nooo!"

Abraham stood over Cutter, sword in hand, and said, "It's over. Tell me what I want."

Cutter's eyebrows knitted together, and he said, "Never. Black Squadron, kill them! Kill them all!"

CHAPTER 69

Horace gored two soldiers at once with his spear. It happened the instant the enemies whisked their swords out of their scabbards.

Abraham caught the action out of the corner of his eyes as he moved toward Sticks. Two soldiers pulled out daggers to plunge into her gut. They weren't quick enough. Sticks appeared to be magically free. Small knives were in both of her hands. She stabbed both men in the neck. She snatched up her bandolier from the dying man's body and dropped it over her shoulders. She took the rope from her neck and slung it aside. She winked her one good eye at Abraham and said, "You're too late to come to my rescue."

Two attackers wielding short swords flanked Sticks. She ducked underneath a swing and stabbed the man in the belly. Her second attacker had the drop on her. His sword was raised and was coming down on her head.

Abraham closed the distance in two giant strides and took the man's head from his shoulders with one swipe of his sword. Blood gushed from the neck as the dead man fell over. His head rolled over to Cutter.

Cutter picked the head up and threw it at Abraham. "May the Elders curse you!"

Horace rushed into a pile of ash and stirred it up with his spear.

"Good idea!" Abraham knew they were outnumbered ten to one, and taking them all on at once would be risky. "Dust it up, Sticks! Split up!"

Sticks dashed through a pile of ash, which exploded into a cloud of smoke. The soldiers chasing her slowed.

Abraham did the same thing. He jumped into the ashes and started kicking and swinging. In moments, he lost sight of his enemies, and they lost sight of him. They fumbled and muttered angrily in the dusty murk. Focusing on the creaking of leather rubbing against skin, Abraham found his mark. He thrust into the chest of a coughing man.

The dead man's final last word sputtered out. "Gah!"

More alarmed shouts followed.

Men groaned and cried out.

The Henchmen struck like thieves in the night. The Black Squadron were seasoned soldiers, but they were taken off guard by this attack. Their warped cries and death throes filled the room.

"Shut your holes, you fools! Shut up and think!" Commander Cutter shouted. "Be silent! Use your ears and listen! That is what they are doing to you! Idiots!"

More bodies fell in one notable thud after the other.

Abraham moved like a ghost. He sank Black Bane deep into at least ten men.

Blood mixed with ash. The floor became sticky with dust and gore. The battle raged on until the final enemy soldier fell silent.

The Black Squadron were no match for the Henchmen.

The dust settled.

Abraham, Horace, and Sticks surrounded Commander Cutter. All of them were splattered with blood and covered in ash. They looked as though they'd climbed out of an incinerator.

Cutter had made a tourniquet by using his belt on his right thigh above the knee. Seated on the floor, he gripped his sword in both hands. "Come on, I'm still a fighting man!"

With a hard swipe of his sword, Abraham knocked Cutter's sword right out of his fingers. He gazed at the man's bloody stump. The dismembered leg lay nearby. "Yes, and you should keep on fighting. After all, it's only a minor flesh wound." He stuck the tip of his sword underneath Cutter's chin. "Don't make this difficult. Tell me where Big Apple is and what his plans are."

Cutter looked him dead in the eye and said, "No."

"You gave your word."

"To who? You? I gave my word to my men." Cutter scanned the room. "You killed all of them! Even Tomas! My finest man!"

"As I recall, you told them to kill us. What choice did we have?"

"You could have died," Cutter said with a shamed face. He spat. "You should have died. I was beating you. Only your sword makes you better. I should have made you trade the blade and made it an even fight."

"That didn't work in the tournament of swords, and it wouldn't have worked here." Abraham smacked the man's cheek with the flat of his blood-and-dust-caked sword. "Tell me, where are they?"

"What's the difference? You're going to kill me anyway," Cutter let out a ragged sigh. "Kill me. Without this leg, I have nothing to live for."

"Tell me where Big Apple is and what he is doing, and we'll stitch you up. We have a mystic," he offered.

"Can you put back the rest of them too?" Cutter surveyed the dead. "By the Elders, you slaughtered them. My men were better trained than that. I know it."

"Your men stink, and so do you," Horace said. "Let the dog die, Captain. He doesn't deserve any better. He's an enemy soldier that assaults the king. Our king! He deserves what is coming to him."

Abraham could see the desperation in Cutter's defeated eyes. "Sticks, notify the others. Bring Iris and Melris to me."

Sticks departed.

"Start talking, Cutter. Don't let this battle that you lost be the end of you. I can see that you don't want this to end. Isn't being able to fight again worth it?"

Cutter made a painful grimace. "Heh. You put my leg on, and you promise to fight me again with neutral swords."

Abraham glanced over his shoulder at Horace's disapproving frown, shrugged, and said, "Fair enough. Spill it."

"Spill what?" Cutter said.

"Tell me what you know about Big Apple. What are his plans? Where does he hide? All that you know."

"I will tell you this. Big Apple is not worried about you or the stones that you seek because he says you will never find them all. It is a waste of time. The Elders have them." Cutter spat again. "He only cares about controlling the otherworlders and what they can bring. He wants those strange weapons. King Hector cannot stand against them. He wants the King's Steel. The people on the other side want it."

"People on the other side of what?"

"The portal. I've seen them once. Fleece can open them. Sometimes, those artifacts fall out. Most of it is worthless junk, Big Apple says." Cutter turned green, and he yakked on the floor. "Ugh… losing your leg makes you feel awful."

Abraham's eyes brightened. If Big Apple could control the portals through Fleece, then the horned halfling could possibly figure out a way home. "But where is he?"

"Big Apple likes to travel, but he is not so far to find. He will hide among the Shell and the Sect. They have posts in every city on Titanuus. Someone always knows something." He poked his finger at Abraham. "That is where he is trying to build a permanent tunnel to the other world. They have a lair in the Spine. He sends workers to build there. They have been doing it for years. He says it will make gateways that will take them everywhere."

Abraham wasn't convinced that Cutter knew what he was talking about. Sweat beaded the man's clammy face, and he'd lost a lot of blood. He doubted Iris could put his leg back on, but they could stop the loss of blood, and the man could keep on living.

Cutter's eyelids fluttered.

Abraham tapped his face. "Where is Big Apple now? Tell me."

"He's says he's going back to the lair…" Cutter passed out.

He shook the man, asking, "Where is it? Where is it?"

Cutter was out cold.

CHAPTER 70

Abraham and the Henchmen traveled by boat up the Little Vein river toward the Wound. Melris insisted that they get back on course. Abraham didn't put up much of an argument. They were under the king's orders, and he wasn't about to dare a side journey into the Spine searching for Big Apple. He was exhausted. He might have gotten enough fire back to beat Cutter, but he still wasn't himself. His body was drained.

The wind filled the white sails of the galleon the company rode on. All of them were on the main deck of the big river boat. The sun shone in the sky. Making it to the Wound would take at least a few days.

Horace and Iris had a group gathered around them. They were clucking on about the battle with the Black Squadron. Iris wasn't there, but she, with the help of Melris, had put Commander Cutter's leg back on. They just put it on backward.

Abraham called Horace out on the cruel gesture.

In his defense, Horace said, "You only said to put it on, not how to put it on, Captain. He didn't deserve better either. We should have killed him. That snake will only strike again. He's a Hanchan. Let me be an example of what happens when you cross the King's Henchmen."

"That's my call, not yours," Abraham said. "Perhaps I'll leave someone else in charge next time."

He had left Horace in disgust. Tormenting people wasn't his way, but perhaps Horace was right. Cutter should have died. He was evil and wouldn't bat an eye over killing somebody. He'd broken his word too. Payback had come, an eye for an eye and a tooth for a tooth.

He sat on the railing, watching the tree line as they sailed past. The winds rustled his matted hair. As refreshing as it had been, he still felt like crap. A shadow fell over his shoulder. Solomon joined him.

"Do you feel like talking?" asked the former hippie turned troglin.

"Do I look like I feel like talking?" he asked.

"You look like you'd rather be dead."

"Heh, you got that right." Abraham looked back at his company. "Let's head to the bow and have some privacy. We have a lot to talk about."

Solomon raised his eyebrows, started walking, and said, "I hope it's good news."

"Yeah, well, I've been to Pittsburgh." Abraham settled himself on the ship's bow and filled Solomon in on all the details of meeting up with Mandi, his encounter with Eugene Drisk, and Sid and John Smoke.

Solomon was all ears and hung on every word. "That's quite a story. More like a modern-day fairy tale." He rubbed his face with one big paw of a hand. "I envy you. I'd do anything to see home again. I wonder who I swapped souls with?"

"My guess is that we will find those answers in that secret Facility 117. I think they are there. At least, that is what Eugene Drisk alluded too." With his hand on the lines, he said, "I really think we are getting closer to figuring this out. The parties are working at it on both ends. They are bound to figure it out."

Solomon closed his eyes, shook his head, and said, "I really need to wrap my head around this. It sounds like an acid trip. Go back to the part about people wanting to come to this world. I don't understand that. Why would anyone want to come here?" He raised his voice. "They don't even have air conditioning!"

Abraham let out a weak chuckle. With the wind in his face, he said, "I know, this is as good as it gets. I think there are a lot of miserable souls in our world that think they would be better off in this world. They are using the portals to move their souls from one body to another. I believe that they believe that they can create a new paradise."

"What are they trying to do, create a permanent Woodstock? I was there, you know, and I had my fun, but man, I can't do that every day. Troglin or not." Solomon toyed with the end of a coil of rope lying by his side. He swung the short end like a lasso. "Do you really think we are getting closer to figuring all of this out? You don't still think it's a dream, do you?"

"Nah. I know that all of this is out of the norm, but anything can happen once we put our minds to it. That's the scary thing about us. But unlike you, I don't think that Titanuus is so bad. I kinda like it."

"Well, you aren't a troglin. Perhaps I'd like it better if I was only me." Solomon curled the rope over his neck and shoulders. "But I enjoy the modern-day pleasantries."

"Back home has changed a lot since you were there. We have portable phones the size of an index card that you can do all kinds of things on."

"It sounds like something from *Star Trek*."

"It's more advanced in some ways, but we haven't conquered space travel."

"We haven't colonized the moon?"

"No, we haven't even been back. A lot of people don't even believe that we were there to begin with. They think the government lied to us. There's a bunch of videos on YouTube about it."

"YouTube?"

Abraham cracked a smile. "It's another thing from the internet. Ah man, when we get you back, you might freak out. I tell you, I got tired of all of the commotion back home. I think that's why I like the simplicity of this world." He cast his gaze toward the mountains on the distant horizon. "It's quiet. It's peaceful. Natural. Back home is a mess."

"Even so, I'd like to see it. I have family that I miss." Looking sad, Solomon turned his head away. "They probably have me locked up like some sort of animal back home. I'm probably foaming at the mouth right now."

Abraham felt strongly that Facility 117 might be the place where otherworlders like Solomon or the troglin whom he now hosted might be kept. The building had a cold creepiness that had seeped into his bones when he was there. He thought about Dr. Jack Lassiter. *That man seemed to be behind it all. I need to get my hands wrapped around that man's throat and squeeze the truth out of him.*

"Keep your chin up, Solomon," he said. "You have to have hope. I can't say for sure, but my gut tells me there is a reason why I am here."

Solomon turned his head slightly and said, "Really, and what might that be?"

"I think I'm supposed to close the portals. I think that is why I go back from this body to that one. I have to work both sides. I don't know why it's me, but so far, I'm the only one that can do it. Does that sound like a crazy theory?"

"No. I've never had faith in a lot of things, but I have faith in you, Abraham. I hope that you can lead me back to my promised land."

As he rubbed the back of his head, Abraham said, "Oh man, that's deep."

Solomon lay down and rested his big troglin head on the coil of rope. He closed his eyes and said, "I've spent enough time in this wilderness. Take me home."

CHAPTER 71

Days later, the Henchmen disembarked from the riverboat. They sold their horses and wagon in Junction City and traveled on foot. Melris led the way through the harsh terrain, rocky and full of sparse shrubbery. Nothing creeped or crawled over the bitter land leading toward the Wound. The farther they traveled, the more barren it became in the rugged outback climate.

Per usual, Dominga and Tark scouted ahead.

Abraham walked with Horace, Sticks, and Melris.

Bearclaw and Vern trailed behind them, followed by Iris, Shades, and Cudgel, then Solomon and the Red Tunics, Skitts and Zann, with Apollo and Prospero bringing up the rear. All of them carried heavy packs on their shoulders, along with quivers of bolts and crossbows.

Sticks switched her assault rifle from one shoulder to another. The swelling in her face was down, and her bruised eye was half open.

All of them were sweating like pigs in the intense heat of day, except for Melris. His soft skin appeared as cool as a cucumber.

Step by step, the company moved up one rocky rise after another. The ground shifted underfoot. Broken bits of black shale were everywhere. They walked from morning until night and set up camp underneath a crag that shadowed them from the moonlight.

No tents were set, but campfires were made. Strips of dried beef and bread called sun cakes were quietly consumed.

Horace scheduled the watch. Everyone else rolled out their bedrolls and hunkered down for the night.

Abraham stared into the fire. Sticks, Horace, and Melris were with him.

He wet his thirst with a long drink of water, handed it over to Sticks, and said, "Melris, we haven't talked much about the Wound. What should we be expecting?"

"You should expect that not all of us will make it," Melris replied coolly. His spacey eyes were fixed on the flames. "It is a place of death. It rots with decay. It leads into the very bowels of Titanuus. Vermin still feast on his innards to this day."

Abraham picked up a handful of dirt, let it cascade through his fingers, and said, "Are you telling me that there is flesh and bones beneath this rock?"

"Absolutely. Much of it is petrified, but there is still succulent marrow deep inside his bones." Melris gave Abraham a long look. "It would be very beneficial if you could summon your dragon. We will need the assistance."

Abraham leaned forward and said, "My dragon? You mean Simon, who almost killed you?"

"Yes."

"I can't summon him. He just came. And you attacked him."

"That was a misunderstanding on my part," Melris replied. "I didn't realize that you had acquired such a powerful ally. We will need it, for the dangers are great inside the Wound."

"And how do you know that the stones are even in there?"

"I don't."

Abraham's jaw hung open.

Horace made a throaty gasp.

Sticks scraped her knife over a round stone.

"Are you telling me that I'm going to risk my Henchmen pursuing a bunch of magic stones that might not even be there?" He dusted off his hands. "I don't think so."

"You don't have a choice. It is the king's orders," Melris said in his strangely youthful, cryptic manner. "The fate of the entire world lies in the hands of a few men. You should feel honored."

"I'll tell you how I feel. I feel stupid." He kicked the dirt, shook his head, and said, "I'm going to bed." He pinched the bridge of his nose and squinted his eyes. "Where's the Tylenol?" He stormed off.

CHAPTER 72

ABRAHAM HAD HAD A RESTLESS sleep on the hard ground. Sleeping in a breastplate only made it worse. Typically, he had his tent set up and enjoyed the soft pleasures within. One of those pleasures was Sticks. She would curl up in his arms, and he would sleep like a baby. He'd slept alone the past night even though she'd slept nearby. She was up and gone now. He trailed behind the others, yawning.

On a good note, his headache was gone. He trudged along in the back with the Red Tunics, Apollo and Prospero. They didn't say much, and he didn't feel like talking. He'd hoped when he went to sleep the previous night that he would wake up back home. He wanted to be with Mandi and make sure she was okay. He also didn't like the fact that Melris had said some of his Henchmen would die.

"Summon my dragon," he muttered. "He's not even a dragon. What am I supposed to do, whistle?"

Apollo gave him a funny look. Prospero strutted on, eyes forward, arms swinging. Both of the older, durable men wore their crossed swords over their backs. They must have been the oldest in the group. They had tufts of gray in their ginger-brown hair.

Skitts cast a sheepish look over his shoulder at Abraham. The stalwart young man carried a pack fit for three men on his shoulders. His brother Zann carried the same.

Both brothers were likeable in their own ways. *I don't want to see them die. I don't want any one of them to die.*

According to Prince Lewis, over one hundred Henchmen had died over the past several years. Most of that was thanks to Raschel, the assassin. Eugene Drisk had played a hand in that too, as did Lewis and Leodor. Eugene had treated the Henchmen like sacrificial lambs to save himself, a cowardly thing to do.

That's what soldiers do. They die for their country and what they believe in. It's the same with our veterans back home. All gave some—some gave all.

"Pardon me asking, Captain," Apollo said in his scratchy voice, "but why are you lingering with us? You should be in the front, leading. Are you squabbling with Sticks? I can see that, the dry tart that she is."

"No. There comes a point when you start dreading the mission. Facing the unknown. Don't you get tired of it?" he asked.

"I don't have a choice." Apollo winked at Abraham. "You don't either. I don't think about it. I move forward. It's the only way to end whatever it is that we are ending. I'll see it through until they run me through."

"Tell me more about the old me, the real Ruger. You knew him a long time?" he asked.

Apollo nodded. "I'd been a Guardian for a long time before Ruger came. I wasn't cut out for leadership. I was good for following orders, though. I'm a natural with a sword too, though not as quick as I used to be. A hair slower but"—he tapped his noggin—"quicker up here. Ruger is a natural leader. The best. Fearless. Determined. He's a rock. You fill his boots well. You'd fit them better if you didn't doubt. He never doubted. He just did."

The older warrior's scratchy words lit a fire underneath Abraham. He pulled his shoulders back and said, "Thanks for the chat."

"Any time. If it's any consolation, you're a lot more fun than the old Ruger. He's all business. You're fun."

Abraham nodded. He caught up to Skitts and Zann, who walked with shovels in hand, and said, "Good morning, men. Are you ready to face death today?"

"Feels like my back has tasted death already," Zann groaned. The pack he carried was half as big as him. "It's burning like it's in the netherworld."

Abraham slapped Zann's oversized pack. "Good. Feeling means you're breathing. Shout if you need a break."

The broadly built Skitts said, "I can walk with my pack all day." He shot a glare at his brother. "We won't need a break. Death before failure."

"Yeah, my death is going to be your failure. Because you're going to be carrying my pack." Zann spat. "You can't carry the both of them."

Abraham chuckled and moved on. Something about Apollo's words had gotten a light shining in him. He made his way toward the front of the ranks. He made light conversation with Iris, Cudgel, Bearclaw, Vern, and Solomon. He even cracked a few locker-room jokes that drew forth some chortling laughter. He kept the routine up for hours.

Finally, he made his way back up to Sticks, Horace, and Melris. They all gave him concerned looks.

Horace said, "Do you fare well, Captain?"

Abraham patted his sword grip and said, "I never felt better. Why?"

"Because you are acting crazy," Sticks said flatly.

"Maybe? There's no maybe about it." He looked at her with wild eyes. "I am crazy."

CHAPTER 73

THE SUN SET IN THE west, behind the great mountains of the Spine. The Spine's shadows swallowed the valley's. North of the Henchmen's position, miles away, were pinnacles of rock, mashed together in a leagues-long wall. Tiny flocks of birds swooped in and out of the rocky crevices and nestled in the high nooks and shelving. The wall was a foreboding monument weathered and tested by time.

"Welcome to the Wound," Melris said.

The Henchmen stood on a rocky hill, gazing side by side at the great wonder of the wall around the Wound. It stood over seventy feet high and was nothing short of captivating. The wall was steep at the base, angling up at a sheer but climbable pitch. Tower pillars of rock merged together around the top. At the base of the walls were clay huts with straw roofs that appeared tiny from the distance.

Abraham wet his parched lips with a drink from his water skin and asked, "Why does it have a wall around it? I thought it would be a gaping hole, like a canyon."

"Those are the scars and scabs of the wound. It is crusted over by time. There is a canyon on the other side of the wall. A deep one." Melris started forward. "Come. The journey begins."

Abraham caught Melris by a shoulder and asked, "What about the people in those huts? Aren't they the Wild Men from the Wound? They are quite vicious." Abraham recollected his encounter with the savage men, who prowled like a wild pack of dogs. He'd battled them in the Tournament of Swords at Pirate's Harbor, and they'd nearly killed him. "I don't think they will allow us to waltz through their… well, territory."

"True," Melris replied quietly. "We will have to do our best to avoid them."

"And if we don't?" Abraham asked.

"We will have to fight them and kill them."

Abraham scanned the small village outside the wall. Hundreds of huts were scattered along the wall's threshold. A pit formed in his stomach.

Horace practically stood on Abraham's toes and said, "I'd wager those savages stuff a family of ten to twenty in those huts." He laid a heavy hand on Abraham's shoulder. "We can kill them."

"No, we aren't going to kill anybody if we don't have to. Melris, it's time that you earned your salt on this mission. If there is a way of avoiding them, then you do that."

Melris shrugged his thin, pale eyebrows and said, "I can manage a diversion, but it is best that I save my magic. Have you summoned your dragon?"

"He's not a dragon. He's a Fenix."

"I think he's a dragon," Shades chimed in.

"He's dragon spawn. He might not look like a dragon, but he is still a dragon." Melris started walking east and held a finger up. "We are downwind. That should help. Summon your dragon."

Dominga and Tark approached and gave Abraham impatient looks. Dominga was drumming her fingers on her hips. Tark's smoky eyes were wide.

Abraham nodded.

Dominga and Tark took off down the slope, running like a pair of deer. They ran silently through the dry bush and vanished over the next rise.

"Don't worry about it. I can help if he can't," Iris said. The mystic was twitching her fingers, the nails glowing with rosy light. "I'll be able to conceal our location if need be, but we need to stay close together." She gave him a funny look. "We've done this before, you know."

"Of course we have," he said as he followed after Melris, who was on the move.

The Henchmen ran missions that took them in and out of many dangerous places. They were used to it. They were prepared. He should have known better.

He looked back at the company and said, "Transformers… Let's roll."

Dusk settled as the company started their miles-long trek toward the Wound. Tark and Dominga led the tight-knit group into a very steep and wide dry gulch that snaked its way toward the wall. The gulch was thirty feet deep and over twenty feet wide. Dry bushes and old branches and logs filled the lengthy washout. A tiny stream of water, only a few inches wide, trickled through the winding channel.

Dominga raised a fist and stopped. Tark moved along the top of the gulch, keeping his eyes toward the villages on the west side. He came to a stop as well. His eyes were big as he pointed down and ahead.

Abraham couldn't see past the next bend. On cat's feet, he caught up with Dominga, who was peeking around a mud-covered boulder. She pointed also.

A large group of Wild Men were hunched over a pool of water. Using their big hands like cups, they drank, washed, and splashed one another.

Blazing Saddles!

Abraham eyeballed a score of the wiry men, built like gorillas and moving about like dogs. They had bestial faces, flat noses, huge nostrils, and pale skin covered in a thin layer of hair. They grunted and barked at one another. He motioned toward Iris.

Iris crept forward with a sheepish look on her face and followed Abraham's stare. Her eyes grew. Without actually saying a word aloud, she said, "I have an idea. It will take a few minutes."

"What?" he mouthed back.

She flicked her fingers out and said, "Don't worry." She nodded at Horace and tiptoed toward him to whisper in the bearded man's ear.

Horace motioned to Cudgel, Bearclaw, and Vern. The three men huddled around Iris. She vanished among their big bodies.

Abraham perked his ears. He could barely make out the sound of her arcane mutterings, which were muffled by the men. He sought out the faces of the rest of the group and held out a hand so they would hold.

Solomon, Apollo, Prospero, and the Red Tunics froze in their positions.

Abraham locked eyes with Tark at the top of the gulch. The ebony warrior glistened with sweat. His athletic body hunkered down in the rocks.

Tark nodded at Abraham.

Abraham nodded back.

The loose rocks underneath Tark's foot gave way. Small stones tumbled down into the gulch.

The heads of the Wild Men of the Wound popped up. They sniffed and snorted loudly. Their big eyes peered about. Two of them scurried up the gulch and made a beeline for Tark.

Abraham lost sight of the Wild Men scrambling silently up the hill.

A crossbow fired. *Clatch-zip!*

A Wild Man howled.

Holy sheetrock!

CHAPTER 74

A LOUD BARKING SOUND AROSE FROM the savages. "Haroot! Haroot! Haroot! Haroot!"

"Captain, here!" Iris tossed something to Abraham.

He snatched it out of the air. It looked like a potato that had been dug out of the ground. Abraham gave Iris a blank look and shrugged. "What do I do with it?"

"Throw it at those mongrels and hold your nose," she said. "It's a stench bomb."

He stepped around the bend in the gulch. The Wild Men were beating their chests and howling. They started to climb up the gulch after Tark.

"Hey, dog face!" Abraham shouted.

The dog-faced savages froze. Their ears bent behind their heads. They turned their beady hound eyes on Abraham. He took aim and lofted a perfect throw into the center of the pack.

"Fetch!"

The Wild Men watched the potatolike projectile land in their midst and explode in a cloud of inky steam. The stench cloud enveloped all the apish men and continued to fill the gulch. The Wild Men's eyes puffed up like balloons. They coughed, hacked, and yelped. On all fours, the whimpering savages scrambled up the wall of the gulch and out.

"A stench bomb?" Abraham said.

Just as he finished, Tark raced down the side of the gulch. He had a crossbow in one hand and his sword in another. Wet blood dripped from his blade.

"How many did you get?" Abraham asked.

"Three," Tark said. "The good news is spreading fast. Listen."

A strange barking carried across the plains. "Haroot! Haroot! Haroot!" Some of the voices were distant. The others were farther away. The Wild Men were communicating.

"So much for going into the Wound unannounced," Abraham said. He watched the heads of the Wild Men peeking over the top of the gulch and down at them. "We need to get to the wall… now."

"Into the stench! They won't come near it. That's why I cast it." Iris pinched her nose and took him by the hand. "Where we go, the stink goes."

Abraham drifted into the stinking cloud while still holding hands with Iris. He immediately started to retch but somehow held it back. The sour skunk stink burned his nostrils and gagged his throat. His eyes watered.

This is horrid. Sewer gas isn't this bad. He had a vision of Cousin Randy emptying his mobile home in the movie *Christmas Vacation*. He gagged. *I can't do this.*

The Henchmen churned ahead, racing down the gulch and holding their breath. Wherever Iris went, the cloud went.

Abraham released her hand and increased his stride. He had to get clear of the foulness. He'd rather fight one hundred Wild Men than spend another second in the putrid, stomach-turning smell. He lengthened his stride and moved ahead of the company. With the wind whistling by his ears, he moved out of the midst and gasped for fresh air.

Sticks burst free behind him, followed by Dominga and Tark.

Pinching her nose, Dominga said, "Worst plan ever!"

Tark pointed ahead. "The wall!"

Just over one hundred yards away loomed the naturally formed wall. A wide set of rough-hewn steps carved out of the rock zigzagged upward. Hulking forms of men bulging with muscles were nested on their stairs. They howled and beat their chests wildly.

Abraham pulled his sword free of its scabbard. "I don't care. I'm killing them."

The Henchmen and the stench cloud gathered at the bottom of the steps. The Wild Men pelted them with rocks.

Solomon burst ahead, climbing the rock wall like a monkey. "I can't take the stink any longer! Gangway!" His big paws and feet raced up the wall. A rock hit him full in the chest. He shrugged it off, bore down on a Wild Man, grabbed his head of hair, and flung him off the wall.

One by one, the Henchmen emerged from the stinking cloud. They coughed and hacked their way up the stairs as the cloud hovered beneath them.

Standing on the rim of the gulch, the Wild Men continued to hurl fist-sized rocks at them. A few of them flung crude spears. One such spear zinged toward Shades's head. He snatched it out of the air, flipped it around, and flung it back. It impaled a Wild Man in the chest.

"Bull's-eyes!" he yelled.

"It's *bull's-eye*!" Bearclaw said. The wild-haired man snatched up a hunk of stone and hurled it back. He missed the attacker he was aiming for, who ducked underneath the rock. The rock hit the Wild Man behind him in the crotch. "That's a bull's-eye!"

Abraham led the charge up the steps. The Wild Men hidden in the rocks came at him from both sides and above. He ducked flying rocks, caught one in the chest, and sliced off clutching hands and fingers.

Horace forced himself up to Abraham's position and gored a jumping Wild Man in the heart with his spear. He used the attacker's momentum to fling him farther down the hillside. "Kill them all, Captain! Kill them all!"

Step by step, the Henchmen slowly battled their way up the zigzagging steps. Above them, the Wild Men's ranks were thinning. Below them, the group let out throaty howls. They slavered, hurled, and hooted. Fewer than a score of them were left. The stink cloud kept them at bay, but it was dissipating.

From the highest position, Solomon bashed a Wild Man's head into the rocks and pushed the attacker aside. With a gaze outward, he said, "Abraham!" and pointed east toward the villages. "Someone's going to crash our party!"

Abraham chopped off a man's head and whipped his head around. Scores of Wild Men were running on two feet and others on all fours, racing toward the gulch. They left a trail of galloping dust behind them. For men, they moved at alarming speed. They would arrive within the minute.

"Let's get a move on!" Abraham yelled.

Without warning, the cluster of Wild Men gathered at the rim of the gulch burst through the fading stench cloud. They bounded up the twisting stairs like a wild pack of dogs.

Skitts and Zann fired their crossbows into the oncoming swarm then backed behind Apollo and Prospero to reload. Apollo and Prospero's swords glinted in the day's fading light and came down in lightning-quick chops. The brutes' thick skulls were no match for the razor-sharp steel, which split their heads open like melons.

Cudgel bounded down the steps. He swung his mighty mace into the ribs of a blood-hungry attacker. A loud crack of ribs busting was followed by the elated battle cry of the smoky-eyed warrior. "Taste my thunder!"

The Henchmen skirmished in heated battle along the stairwell. The Wild Men kept coming, fearless and savage. They fought with their huge fists, sharp fingernails, and rocks.

Vern caught a fist in the face a split second before he cut a man's belly open. His second weapon hand, filled with a dagger, gouged out a neck.

Bearclaw's double-bladed axe rose and fell, gore dripping from both sides.

The Wild Men of the Wound were falling, but they weren't falling fast enough.

"Faster!" Abrahams said. "Fight faster!"

"You heard the Captain. Kill them faster!" Horace bellowed.

The Wild Man horde closed the gap. Like the last sands of an hourglass, the void was filled with muscular bodies, heaving and howling, running with ferocious hunger. With blood in their eyes, the attackers surged across the gulch and up the stairs.

Abraham took a final quick glance above. At the top of the wall, fifty feet away, was a gap that could be defended. He needed to get his men there now. Waving his sword, he said, "Take the high ground! Take the high ground now!"

Twenty feet below him, the Henchmen at the bottom of the ranks were fighting their guts out. The new swarm of Wild Men came up the rocky precipice like an angry tidal wave. The knot of surging bodies consumed them. The Henchmen started to fall.

Sticks was near Abraham when she gasped.

Horace started charging down the stairs.

Iris flung hornets of fire from her fingertips.

Melris stood quietly among the chaos, observing. He made his way toward the top and passed Abraham.

Abraham grabbed him by the robes and yelled, "What are you doing? Get down there and fight those things!"

"I need to save my energy. I'll meet you at the top." Melris slipped Abraham's grasp as if he were a ghost. "You can handle it."

Momentarily slack-jawed, Abraham said to Sticks and Shades, "Go with him!"

"What are you going to do?" Sticks asked. "We can't beat all of them."

Abraham looked upon the tide of hulks overrunning his men. His heart pounded like a mallet in his chest. His blood rushed in his ears. He set his volcanic gaze on the enemy and shouted at the top of his lungs, "Henchmen!" He jumped onto the side of the steep mountain wall, ran down the slant, and dove sword first into the churning fray. "Cut loose the chaos!"

CHAPTER 75

ABRAHAM PLUNGED INTO THE FRAY. Carnage. The Wild Men flung themselves fearlessly at the Henchmen. The Henchmen hewed them down with precision.

The Wild Men weren't the skilled fighters that the Henchmen were. They lost limbs but kept coming.

"Wall them off! Wall them off!" Abraham shouted. Black Bane became a living weapon in his hand. Stab. Thrust. *Glitch.*

The Henchmen in shirts of chain-mail armor formed a shell around the lesser-armed men. Iris was in the middle of the knot, flinging wild fiery hornets into the sky. Dominga helped the Red Tunics load crossbows and fired from close range.

The bodies started to pile up. The Henchmen rose valiantly on the bodies of the slain.

Abraham whisked out a dagger and launched a two-handed attack. He twisted his dagger in a hound-hulk's belly. Black Bane split open the face of another.

The relentless Wild Men collapsed on them. They hurled their big bodies into the Henchmen's rigid ranks. The sheer weight of numbers began to overwhelm them.

A Wild Man caught hold of Skitts by the hair and yanked him out of the ranks.

Vern chopped the Wild Man's arm off at the elbow, freeing Skitts.

With a crossbow bolt, Dominga shot a Wild Man in the face, who was about to clobber Vern in the head with a rock.

"Thanks, gorgeous," Vern said with a wink.

Horace started half chanting and half singing, "Kill them. Kill them all. Kill them. Kill them all." He sang it in rhythm as he thrust his sword into one hard body after the other. "Kill them. Kill them all!"

The sea of the enemy continued to rise. Abraham couldn't see an end to it. The harder they fought, the more Wild Men kept coming. He whittled down two more men to bloody stumps when a wave of savages tackled him.

The Wild Men had him on the ground. One bit his leg, and the other locked his fingers around his neck and started beating his head into the ground.

Abraham wriggled against their fierce clutches. The enemy had him pinned down, beating, biting, and choking him. *Must! Get! Free!* A hard kick slammed into his face from a third attacker that jumped into the melee.

A red dot appeared on the kicking attacker's head. Suddenly, the back of his skull blew open. As the dead body stumbled backward and fell, another bullet turned the head of the man choking

Abraham into a canoe. He sat up instantly and rammed his dagger into the earhole of the Wild Man biting his legs. He rolled to his feet and glanced up the stairs.

Sticks was nestled in the rocks, aiming her assault rifle at the battle raging below. The glow of a laser dot gleamed on the black rifle. The muzzle of the weapon flashed. Bullets tore through the enemies' skulls. One Wild Man fell right after the other.

The Henchmen surged and hacked back the attackers.

A loud barking could be heard over the clamor of battle.

"Haaaroooot! Haaaroooot!"

The Wild Men scurried back out of striking distance.

Sticks stopped firing.

The Wild Men started up in a chorus of their chant barks. "Haroot! Haroot! Haroot! Haroot!"

Down in the gulch, a giant imposing figure made his way through the winding channel. He was a Wild Man, walking on his feet and knuckles, standing eight feet tall at the shoulder. He had a beastly face, bulging biceps, and corded neck muscles. A furry loincloth dressed his hips. He came up through the ranks with his massive head tilted and moving with a primordial gait.

"Haroot! Haroot! Haroot! Haroot! Haroot!" the smaller Wild Men chanted.

A red dot appeared on the giant's head.

Sticks locked her sights on the huge man.

Abraham looked up at her and said, "Do it!"

A crack of gunfire echoed over the valley.

The giant Wild Man's head snapped slightly back.

The chanting stopped.

Blood trickled down the giant Wild Man's forehead and over the bridge of his nose. He wiped the fresh blood on his lengthy fingers. He tasted the blood. Shrugging his hairy black unibrow, the monstrous man said in a throaty voice, "My blood tastes good, but your blood is much sweeter."

Sticks put the laser dot on the giant's eyeball.

The giant blocked the beam with his hand. "Don't be foolish. I am Haroot. Your powerful sling bullet cannot harm me. My skin is steel, my bones granite." He lowered his hand and stared right at the laser. "Try me."

A bullet blasted into Haroot's eyeball. Juice spat out. The white of his eye cracked with red.

Haroot tossed his head back and laughed. He rose to his full ten feet in height. He scanned the Henchmen, who were huddled together on the steps. "Which one of you wants to fight me?" He pointed at Solomon. "How about you, hairy one? I have not eaten a troglin in a long time."

Solomon crouched behind an outcropping of rock and said, "I'll wait and see how you fare against the others."

"I'll fight you!" Horace stormed forward. "I've killed giants before, and I'll kill them again, you big-eared fool!"

"Ah, a fat rodent. I like it." Haroot rubbed his jutting chin. He opened his mouth, revealing rows of slavering canine teeth. "Come, fight me, beat me, and you'll be free to pass into the Wound."

"Hold off, Horace." Abraham made his way down the steps and stood alongside the beefy man. "You won't fight him. You'll fight me. I win, you leave, but I'll give you a choice. You can let us pass now, or you will very well die. I've never lost a fight."

"Ho ho. You are a flea. I am a god. We are the guardians of the pass. No one has entered in my lifetime, and no one shall enter now." He wiped the saliva dripping from his jaws. "I assure you. I am Haroot. I am never wrong. My skin cannot be destroyed." The blood on his head started to dry.

The skin over the bullet wound healed to a small bump. His red eye cleared. "But your skin…" He leaned forward. "I will peel it like a grape."

Abraham flipped his sword around. "We'll see about that." He lifted his sword over his head into the high guard stance. "Let's have at it, then."

Haroot nodded. "Good. I hunger." He turned his shoulders away and instantly unleashed a backhanded swing.

Abraham jumped backward and chopped off the knuckles of Haroot's fist.

The snarling giant lowered his brawny shoulders and charged like a dog.

Standing his ground, Abraham delivered a deep chop into the meat of Haroot's neck and shoulder. Haroot let out an ear-busting howl as he trampled over Abraham.

The two men rolled through the dust in a tangle of muscular limbs.

"You hurt Haroot!" the giant said. "You will pay!" He snapped at Abraham's ear. "I will eat your head."

Abraham twisted out from underneath the much larger man and sprinted back to his feet.

Haroot chased him down and slammed him into the gulch's winding wall. The men locked up.

With a dagger in his hand, he started punching holes between Haroot's ribs. The giant's efforts to crush Abraham didn't slow.

"You might hurt me, but you cannot kill me!" Haroot continued to slam Abraham into the wall.

Fighting to keep his grip on his sword and dagger, he headbutted Haroot in the nose. Bright spots exploded in his eyes.

Haroot coughed a wicked laugh.

Horace called out, "Good fighting, Captain."

The giant put Abraham in a headlock with one arm and started beating him in the chest with his other fist. "Now you die! Soon I eat!"

Haroot's powerful punches rattled Abraham's bones. His jaws clacked together. Only the King's Armor saved his bones from being broken into a dozen pieces. The recesses of his mind were calling out to him. Ruger's body mixed with his mind, shouting, "Fight, Abraham! Fight!" He reached down into his reserves and summoned Ruger's great natural strength. In a desperate lunge, he wedged his dagger inside Haroot's mouth.

Haroot's mouth clenched. His eyes crossed. He released Abraham from his crushing grip and staggered back. He reached inside his mouth, pulled the dagger out, and flicked it away. He spat blood. "You fight dirty."

With his eyebrows knitting together, Abraham gripped Black Bane in both hands and said, "You haven't seen nothing yet." He instantly visualized what he needed to do to the giant fearsome warrior. He'd found his second wind. Blood coursed through his veins like fire. "Let's dance, hairy pants."

Haroot charged.

Abraham sidestepped and chopped an outstretched hand off at the wrist. He dashed behind Haroot and cut the tendons behind his knees.

The giant dropped.

Abraham twisted his hips into the final swing. Black Bane sliced Haroot's head clean from his shoulders. Warm blood spat. The massive man toppled over.

The chanting of the Wild Men fell silent.

Abraham picked up Haroot's head by the hair and held it high for all to see. "Haroot this!" He spiked the head in the dirt with all his might. "Yaaah!"

The Wild Men from the Wound cleared out on all fours, whimpering like wounded wolves all the way home.

CHAPTER 76

Catching his breath as he headed up the stairs, Abraham said, "Get a head count."

"Good fight, Captain," Horace said as he wiped off the gore on the tip on his spear, on one of the dead. "What do you call the move you did?"

"When I cut his head off?"

"No, when you bounced his skull off the rocks."

"Ah, that's called a 'spike.' Something from my world," he said, scanning the piles of the dead.

Heaps of Wild Men with rent flesh lay scattered everywhere. Abraham marveled that they had fought off so many muscular men at once. But the Henchmen were good, very good—the best who endured. Still, he searched for the Red Tunics. They had been the first to fall underneath the wave of bruising bodies. He didn't see them or Apollo and Prospero. His spine tingled.

Vern and Cudgel were lifting bodies out of the way and slinging them aside.

"I found some!" Cudgel shouted brightly.

Skitts and Zann climbed out of the bloody pile. Caked in blood, they both sucked for breath, cuts and scrapes all over them.

Zann spat a finger out of his mouth. "That's nasty."

Abraham put a hand on Skitts's shoulder. "Are you well?"

"Never better." Skitts's eyes were wide. His crossbow trembled in his hand. "Sorry I fell, Captain. It won't happen again."

"Yes, it will. Just make sure that you get back up again."

Skitts nodded.

"Ruger, up here!" someone yelled.

Tark and Bearclaw were lifting Apollo out of a pile of dead Wild Men. Hunks of flesh hung from his armor. A nasty gash was still bleeding on his forehead.

The woozy Apollo asked, "Where's Prospero?"

All the Henchmen were accounted for except for Prospero. The company rummaged through dozens of the dead. Above, flocks of buzzards with black wings and white bellies began to circle.

Abraham's hand needled his palm. He couldn't bear the thought of losing anybody. It made him sick. It made him think of Buddy Parker, his wife Jenny, and his son, Jake. He'd been so busy he'd hardly given them a thought.

Solomon waded through the aboveground graveyard. He plucked bodies up in his mighty hands and tossed them aside. "Shush!" he said.

The company quieted but brought weapons to bear.

Abraham crept toward Solomon and bent an ear. A muffled snoring sound was coming from underneath the heap. He gave Solomon a curious look.

The troglin dropped his long arms down into the pile and started lifting away bodies. Inside a dugout of the dead, a battered and bloody Prospero snored loudly. He had a peaceful look on his face as if he were dreaming.

Solomon shook his head and said, "We found Prospero. It appears he had a better time than the rest of us."

The Henchmen roared with throaty laughter.

Abraham led the way up to the top of the stairs, where he met Sticks and Shades at the top. "Good shooting," he told her. He glanced at the magazine clips fastened to her web belt. "You didn't use them all, did you?"

"No."

He glanced at Shades. "Where's Melris?"

"Inside the gap, waiting on you… or us, rather," Shades said.

Two stone pillars created a doorway that led into the black space. The pillars were carved out of the natural rock and showed an assortment of monstrous faces. Abraham stepped up to the gap. A chill wind of stagnant air hit him like a slap in the face. He gave the Henchmen a nod and entered.

Melris was standing on a wide shelf of dirt, cradling his rod of devastation in his arms. His violet eyes had a soft glow, fixed on the black abyss looming below them.

Abraham moved out toward the ledge by the Elderling. The Wound was a humongous oval-shaped crater. Its depths were fathomless and as black as coal. A chill wind like an icy breath from an unknown source tore briskly at Melris's robes. Abraham could make out a narrow pathway that led down into the depths.

He looked at Melris. "Do you still think the stones are down there?"

"Yes," the Elderling said softly. "I can sense it."

Abraham lifted his brows, turned, and faced his party. "This is it. Everybody get patched up and eat something." He looked over the rim. "I don't think we're going to find any fast food down there." He sheathed his sword, moved up to Sticks, and grabbed the water skin she offered. "Thanks."

She nodded. "How do you feel?"

"Like I just killed a hairy hound giant. Why?"

"Your pupils are big."

"That's because it's pretty dark in…" Abraham's legs buckled. His view of Horace and Sticks swayed, and he collapsed into darkness.

CHAPTER 77

Lightning coursed through Abraham's veins. He jumped out of his skin. His eyes popped open. Bright lights hanging above him shone in his eyes. His arms and legs were strapped to a medical table. He squinted. The surrounding room was black. A man wearing an all-white set of scrubs approached.

"You!" Abraham said.

The hard-eyed, curly-haired psychiatrist, Jack Lassiter, smoked a cigar. The two beefy orderlies, Otis, an older black man, and Haymaker, a big dumb-looking older man, walked behind Dr. Jack.

"You!"

"Well, look who's back." Dr. Jack leaned over Abraham's table and blew smoke into his face. "Is that you, Mr. Jenkins? Tell me, whatcha been dreaming?"

THE HENCHMEN CHRONICLES

BOOK FIVE

CRAIG HALLORAN

CHAPTER 1

Smoke drifted into Abraham's nostrils. He coughed. Lights burned his eyes. The surrounding room was dark. Dr. Jack Lassiter paced around his table, puffing on a thick cigar. The orderlies, Otis and Haymaker, stood nearby with their stun rods in their big mitts.

Abraham wet his lips and asked, "Don't hospitals have a strict no-smoking policy, you jerk?"

Jack leaned his head back and chuckled, continuing to pace. His eyes were hard as coal, and he spoke with a strong, penetrating voice. "Glad you are back, Abraham." He stopped at the end of the table, where Abraham's toes were covered by a hospital blanket. Jack looked him dead in the eye and scratched the short, curly brown hairs on his head. "I could see it in your face the moment that you woke. Your eyes, they aren't like the other man's. There is a softness to them. The other's are like burning daggers. The jaw isn't as tight either." He huffed out a stream of smoke. "Very telling."

"If only I could applaud your brilliance," Abraham said as he wiggled his fingers. "A true master of psychiatry. I mean, you aren't Freud, Niles, or Frasier Crane, but you have some savvy."

Jack chuckled heavily. He poked a finger at Abraham and said, "You know, it's good that you have maintained a sense of humor about all of this. It's quite remarkable. The others don't fare so well, making you… unique."

"Momma always told me that I was special." He eyeballed Otis and Haymaker. "And not ugly." Talking smack came easy to him. He used it as a tactic while he tried to gather his senses. The last time he had been back home, Mandi was with him. They were with her cousin, Sidney, and Sidney's mysterious husband, John Smoke. They were in a helicopter when he passed out and wound up back on Titanuus. His nose itched. "Uh, I've got a bad itch that I can't scratch, right on the tip of my nose." He eyed Otis, who was built like a tackling dummy and had a swollen jaw. "How about you help a brother out?"

Otis rapped his stun rod in his hand and said, "I've got a cure for that itch."

Abraham clucked with laughter. He tugged against his bonds as he did so, testing the firm leather straps binding his wrists and ankles. Short of transforming into the Hulk or some other super-strong beast, he wasn't going anywhere. *Where are Mandi, Smoke, and Sid? What the heck happened?* Continuing to delay, he directed his voice toward Otis and said, "You remind me of Luke Cage. Do you know who that is?"

Otis gave him a funny look.

"Mister Jenkins, you can stop with the charades. I already know that your brash attempts at humor are a coping mechanism when you are uncomfortable," Dr. Jack said. He was dressed in camo hunting gear complete with a beige vest, and he had a sidearm on his hip. "I've read your file many times."

Abraham eyed Jack up and down and asked, "So you've been hunting again?" He said this as his thoughts raced back to Titanuus. He'd been with the Henchmen, and they'd just entered the mouth of the Wound. Melris the Elderling was going to lead them into the dark bowels of the chasm to find two more gems of power for the Crown of Stones. "It's been a long time since I've had some venison. I could go for a nice cut of deer steak with a side of scrambled eggs. And some butter biscuits. Like the ones my grandma used to make."

"Otis," Dr. Jack said, "Why don't you come over here and scratch his nose?"

"Oh, it's fine now," Abraham said.

Otis strolled over to the table with a lazy stride. He scratched Abraham's nose and stuck the stun rod in his side. Abraham cried out as his body arched and spasmed on the table.

Otis stuck him again and again, and Abraham's body jumped on the table.

"That's enough," Dr. Jack said.

Otis shocked Abraham again.

"That's enough!" Dr. Jack replied.

With a nod of triumph, Otis pulled his stun rod away and resumed his place by Haymaker with a grin on his face.

Abraham groaned. Painful tingles coursed through his body. The spot where Otis stuck him ached and burned. With sweat beading down his face, he panted and asked, "What's with the *One Flew over the Cuckoo's Nest* treatment? I haven't done anything." He glared at Dr. Jack. "What is your deal?"

Dr. Jack's eyes narrowed. His voice rose. "Haven't done anything? Haven't done anything? You are the one fouling this entire operation up!" He sucked hard on the cigar, making the ashes burn bright red. "I don't know what you are doing in Titanuus, mister, but you need to stop doing it now! Do you understand me?"

Abraham's eyes widened. He'd never seen Dr. Jack lose his cool. The man had become incensed. *The dude is having a meltdown. Good.* "Hey, I didn't ask for this to happen to me. It happened not because of something I did but because of something that you did."

Dr. Jack approached from the right side of the table and said, "You are the only one, the only one, that is giving this operation fits. Why can't you be like the others and butt out?"

"I don't even know what you are talking about?"

"Don't play games with me. You know what you are doing. You are fighting for the king. King Hector." Dr. Jack hit the edge of the table. "You side with him!"

Abraham had no idea what to make of that illuminating statement. His fingers danced at his sides. He looked deep into Dr. Jack's stone-cold eyes, unsure if that was the same person he'd met before or not. For some reason, he was getting a strong vibe that Dr. Jack might have been to Titanuus—either that, or he'd talked to someone that had. Someone like Eugene Drisk. He wouldn't be the only one either.

"If I'm such a problem, why don't you kill me?" He regretted saying it the moment the words came out. The last thing he needed was to suggest his own death.

Dr. Jack blew another blast of smoke in his face and said, "Because, just like you said, you are special."

"But you tried to kill me already."

"Not you. Just the fools that have been helping you."

I've got to find out what happened to Mandi. How did I get captured? What happened to her? "You seem to have a good grasp of what is going on in Titanuus, but what do you want from me?"

"I want to know how you move from body to body. As you've figured out, there are others, otherworlders, like you, that come, but they cannot come and go. Only you." Dr. Jack started to pace around the table again. "Out of all of them, only you have this special talent. We need to harness it. You are the gateway from here to Titanuus." He stopped, turned, and poked Abraham on the head. "Perhaps I can drill it out."

The heat of the cigar burned just over Abraham's eye. His watery eye sent a tear down his cheek. The truth was, he probably could work with Jack Lassiter. It might get him everything he ever wanted. The problem was that he didn't want to. He wouldn't, either. After all, he served the king. *Right is right, and wrong is wrong.* But that didn't mean he couldn't play along. "Look, Dr. Jack, I didn't ask for this, but maybe we can work something out."

Dr. Jack held the cigar over Abraham's eye. "Oh, you want to bargain now. Interesting. The other man inside you, Ruger Slade—he was hard as a stone. He wouldn't mutter a word. Nothing I tried would break him." He pulled the cigar away. "A fascinating case, actually. But he is the bigger problem, it seems. Bigger than you, a washed-up, entitled athlete turned into a worthless trucker."

"Hey, don't knock truckers. They are the lifeblood of this country. Who do you think hauls your twenty-dollar cigars to your humidor and fills your fridge with imported beer?"

Dr. Jack grinned and said, "My wife. And by the way, it's a one-hundred-dollar cigar."

"Good for you." Abraham sighed. "Look, man, I'm tired of all of this. I want to stay home. What do you want to know?"

CHAPTER 2

"GOOD. YOU ARE WILLING TO play along," Dr. Jack said with a puff on his cigar. "That might make all of the difference. You see, I'm not a man known for endless patience. I demand results."

"This might go better if I was in a more comfortable position." Abraham flexed his hands. "I'd be lying if I didn't say that I missed your office. Being strapped to a table—well, it's weird. Even talking from behind steel bars would be better. Besides, I have to pee."

"Go ahead. My orderlies will clean you up," Dr. Jack said. "They just love that stuff, dontcha, boys?"

Otis and Haymaker didn't utter a word. They glared at Abraham with their usual dull, heavy stares.

"I think I can hold it a bit longer," he said.

"Tell me, Mr. Jenkins, what happens right before your essence moves from one world to another?" Dr. Jack asked.

He didn't see the harm in answering and said, "Usually, I start to get a headache, you know, like a migraine, right between the eyes. I see those rings too." That was the truth but only part of the truth. The last time it happened, back at the Wound, he hadn't felt anything at all. He was talking with Sticks, and the world became a black swirl. "A big part of me still has trouble believing that this is real. For all I know, I might be strapped to a table elsewhere, in a coma."

"Does anything trigger these migraines?" Dr. Jack asked.

Abraham managed a shrug and said, "Stress. Normally, I'm in a lot of danger when it happens."

"What sort of danger?"

"You know, the usual fantasy fare. I'm killing monsters with my magic sword, and they are trying to kill me. Just before I arrived here, I finished butchering a ten-foot-tall monster that looked like a man and walked like a dog. They are called Wild Men. The carnage I left would fill this room from one side to the other." He noticed Otis and Haymaker exchange a glance. "It wasn't long after that I fell back here."

"Wild Men, huh? And a magic sword. Interesting. What does this magic sword do? Can you fly with it? Heh heh."

"No. It has strange properties." Abraham figured he might as well lay it on thick while playing a little dumb at the same time. "It's razor sharp, can talk in my head, and sometimes it will shoot a bolt of lightning."

"A sword that shoots fire." Dr. Jack smiled at his orderlies. "Man, this world has it all. Are there flying rugs too?"

"I think you mean carpets, and no, at least, not that I've seen. There are dragons." He swallowed. "Look, my throat is dry, and I'd like a drink, and I'd like to not pee all over myself either. How long have I been laying here? I feel like I haven't gone in days."

"That's about right," Dr. Jack said. "At the moment, you are in a very secure location. No doubt, your friends will try to rescue you. You've picked up some very interesting allies, it seems. It surprised even me."

"Mandi is okay?" he asked sheepishly.

"Since you are attempting to be forthcoming, I'll lend you that branch. Your girlfriend, or whatever she is to you, is on the loose with her peculiar cousin and her husband."

"How'd you get me?"

"Huh, funny that you don't remember." Dr. Jack puffed out a smoke ring. "You took off in that helicopter you stole. You landed in a field behind a truck stop in the dead of night. Believe it or not, we got kind of lucky. As it turns out, someone called the cops because four strange people walked out of the woods without a car or truck. They ordered a table full of pancakes and milkshakes. Not that that was the oddest thing for a trucker, but the descriptions paid off. We picked up on it right away. The government has eyes and ears everywhere."

Abraham's belly gurgled. "Those pancakes and milkshakes sure sound good about now." He rolled his head toward the orderlies. "Do you think you fellas could whip us something up while we are talking? I like my milkshakes cold and my syrup warm." He turned his attention back to Dr. Jack. "Not a fan of cold syrup. You?"

"I'm an oatmeal-for-breakfast kind of guy." Dr. Jack took another draw on his cigar and said, "It didn't take long for us to close in on you. We managed to be discreet. It seemed that you and your cohorts were planning to roll out with a friendly trucker. It might have worked too if we didn't sniff you out. Lucky for us, Dirty Lyle made that call. No one was going anywhere. We blocked the truck stop and closed in. Colonel Dexter led the charge. He was hungry to get you."

Me or Mandi. "So, did the trucker rally behind us? Did they crash your gates doing ninety-eight? Man, I would have loved to have seen them drop the hammer down."

"Sorry, Rubber Duck, but you gave yourself up."

If Abraham could have sat up straight in an instant, he would have. "Are you serious?" It was a fair question. For all he knew, Dr. Jack was lying to him. It was best to assume that.

Dr. Jack nodded. "In terms for your surrender, we let your cohorts go. But we're keeping an eye on them. You wish you could scratch your head, don't you?"

Abraham nodded. *What in Titanuus's Crotch is Ruger up to?*

CHAPTER 3

At first, Abraham wondered if the person hosting his body was Ruger. It might have been another otherworlder from Titanuus. Ruger had been becoming more active, however. Before, Abraham would have lain comatose. Now, Ruger was alive and well. Even Dr. Jack seemed to believe it. He parted his lips to speak, but Dr. Jack spoke first.

"Colonel Dexter agreed to your terms or, rather, Ruger's terms. He came quietly, and when he got here, well, he clammed up." Dr. Jack's jaw tightened, a thin film of sweat building on his brow. "Needless to say, I'm not so happy about that. He agreed to cooperate. He lied."

"It's not as if you are running this secret organization on honesty. And your methods"—he glanced at his bindings—"are far from humane. You've tortured me."

"All for the greater good."

"For some, perhaps, but I seriously doubt for all. Jumping from one world to another—let me tell you, it ain't no picnic. And I don't think you are going to be able to control it."

"We can make anything we imagine happen." Dr. Jack held his pinched fingers about an inch apart. "We are this close. In some areas, we've already succeeded. It's the soul swapping that we haven't mastered. That's what we need you to help us with. We need to learn how to control it."

"Maybe there is an antenna in my brain. Perhaps aliens put it there."

Dr. Jack chuckled. So did his stone-faced goons.

Abraham felt the hair rise on his arms. "Whoa, are you suggesting that aliens are in on this?" His mind started racing. He could hear old man Herb from Woody's Grill joking about the alien sighting in Wytheville, Virginia. Those words came back to haunt him now. He broke out in a cold sweat, and a well of doubt started to swell inside him. *This must be a dream. But it can't be!*

Visions of the zillon dragon riders crossed his mind. He remembered the zillon waitress in Hancha, Anna. She was sweet and pretty in her own unique way. He couldn't help but think that she was a distorted figment of his imagination.

"What's the matter, Abraham? You look pale," Dr. Jack said.

"You realize that this entire ordeal is hard enough to buy into, and now you are tossing in the existence of aliens."

"Is it really so hard to believe now, after all that you have seen? I've heard plenty of wondrous stories about Titanuus, the kind of stories that make my kinky hair straighten and my toes curl. I can't wait to see it. A new frontier ripe for the picking."

"Sure, if you want to take yourself back to the Dark Ages." Abraham played along, wanting to get more answers out of Dr. Jack, who was being very forthcoming. "Listen, there are monsters, literal physical monsters, that aren't going to give their world up without a fight. You can do what you want to do, but you better be careful what you wish for—what you wish for and your associates. It looks like people like you have enough already."

Dr. Jack raised his brow and said, "Well said, from one elite to another. Did you have enough, Abraham, when you bought your father that fancy plane? Or did you want more? A pennant? A World Series championship? A bigger contract perhaps, for Jenkins the Jet?"

"I was grateful for all of it and never wanted for anything more. I just happened to be a great baseball pitcher back then. But one thing I realized while I was trucking down the road was this: none of those privileges made me happy. The only thing that mattered was what I missed, my family. My world was empty without them."

"Well, not all people feel the same as you. They want their own world to rule. A fresh start. One without all of the red tape." Dr. Jack tapped the ashes off his cigar.

Abraham fought off the urge to roll his eyes. He understood men like Dr. Jack and Eugene Drisk. People like them would become power mad. They thought they knew what was best for everyone else. He'd had teammates, coaches, and owners like that. He'd heard their slants in their boorish meetings. They were the "me" in the "team" that they prattled on about all the time. It was all about their hidden agendas. He said to Otis and Haymaker, "So, what's in it for you guys, a little castle and some pretty wenches? I have a Stronghold. Maybe I'll let you guys see it. You can come over and have a beer."

"I don't drink," Otis said.

"Or blink. Good for you. I'm not so much of a drinker either. I used to have a problem." He lifted his head up. "Jack, I really need some relief and sustenance. I'm cooperating. Do you think you could make that happen? It would go a long way with me."

Dr. Jack rubbed an eyebrow and said, "You think this is a big joke, don't you?" He came closer. "But there is a lot more to this than meets the eye. A whole lot more. You've talked at length with Eugene Drisk, haven't you?"

He nodded.

"We've come a long way since we began what he started. He's just now learned what he helped give birth to." Dr. Jack stoked the fire on the end of his cigar with a few stiff puffs. "We're moving more and more through the working portal that we have. But it can serve a greater purpose. What if I were to tell you that I could send you back in time before you had your plane accident?"

"I'd say those curls in your hair are a little too tight."

Dr. Jack nodded at Otis. "Let our guest in, gentlemen."

The orderlies vanished into the exterior darkness of the room. A heavy door opened and closed, then the heavy footsteps of the bulky orderlies approached. They resumed their spot to the side. No one was with them.

Abraham looked at Dr. Jack, and not having seen anyone, he asked, "Am I missing something?"

"No, not at all." Dr. Jack looked past Abraham.

Abraham twisted his head around and looked upward. His heart jumped in his chest. He was face-to-face with a zillon.

CHAPTER 4
TITANUUS

"He's coming to," Sticks said. She held Abraham's head in her lap. She petted the short grizzly beard building up on his face. "A good sign."

The Henchmen stood inside the interior wall surrounding the Wound. A chill, gusty wind came up from the black mouth of the great canyon. Iris and the Red Tunics were mending the wounded with spells and stitches. Dominga and Vern had built a small fire.

Horace took a knee beside Sticks. His beard was caked in both the dried blood of the Wild Men from the Wound and his own. His arms were covered in bloody bandages. He stuffed some tobacco chaw in his mouth and pinched it between his teeth and gum. He sucked his teeth and said, "I hope he's back. I hate it when he goes into the deep sleep. We have a mission."

"Horace!" Iris's voice carried with agitation. "Are you sucking on that chaw again? You know I don't like it. Spit it out."

Horace's bald, bearded, and beefy face soured. "There won't be any time for romance on this mission. I'd appreciate some slack."

"There won't be any romance after, either, if you don't spit that foul foliage out." Iris gave him a demanding glare. "I mean it."

Horace grumbled, took the juicy wad of tobacco out of his mouth, and flung it against the wall. "If it was my dying wish, you wouldn't let me have it either, would you, woman?"

"No, I wouldn't!" Iris said.

Horace sucked his teeth. He winked at Sticks and said, "I always leave a little bit to suck on. She'll never know the better."

Abraham's eyelids snapped open, and he sat straight up. His eyes were alert, like a wary panther's.

"Abraham, take it easy. You'll get a head rush," Sticks warned. The plain-faced woman touched his neck and rubbed it. "You might have a knot on the back of your head from where you fell."

The swordsman quickly stood up, leaving Sticks and Horace gawking at him. The pair exchanged a glance.

"Captain," Horace said, "it's good to see you up and about. Can I get you anything? Food, perhaps. According to Melris, there won't be any food to plunder down there." He cast a look toward the dark belly of the cavern. "Just death, he says."

The rest of the Henchmen were going about their business, tending to the fire and their wounds. Prospero and Apollo were leaning against the wall, eating strips of dried beef. Dominga and Shades joined them.

Sticks took Abraham by the hand. He pulled his strong fingers away. He cast a long glance between her and Horace. A shiver ran down her spine the moment they locked eyes. A fiery intensity grew on Abraham's face. His eyebrows were knitted together, and his shoulders were pulled back. Even though he was looking with his eyes downward, his chin was still up.

She swallowed. "Let me fetch you a skin of water."

Abraham looked as if he hadn't ever seen her before in his life. He reached down and cradled her by the chin with his hand. He lifted her to her feet. His eyes looked over her bandolier of knives. His stare hardened.

The strength of his hand kept Sticks frozen in place. Immediately, she thought of the man that had possessed Ruger Slade before. He was a womanizing maniac who sent his men out like sheep for the slaughter. Her jaws clenched as she battled against the urge to tear her gaze away. This man was not Abraham, but she wasn't sure exactly who it was either.

"Perhaps the two of you need a moment alone," Horace suggested. "I'll have the Red Tunics pitch you a tent and give you some privacy. The heat of battle brings out the lust in all of us in one way or the other."

Slowly, Abraham turned his downward gaze on Horace. In a voice filled with tempered elation, he said, "This flower in my hand I do not know, but I certainly know you!" He released Sticks and caught up Horace in a bear hug. He lifted Horace up off his feet. "Handsome Horace, my, have you grown!"

The moment Horace's toes touched the ground, he took two steps backward. With wide eyes he said, "I haven't been called that in years. Captain?"

Bearclaw, Vern, Apollo, and Prospero approached with cautious looks in their eyes. All the rest of the party stopped what they were doing, including Shades, who slid in behind the four warriors.

The wild raven locks of Bearclaw shook with a nod of his chin. "Do my ears deceive me? Has my old friend returned? Is that you, Ruger?"

"It is," Ruger Slade said as he held his fingers out before him and clutched them open and closed. "For a spell, anyway."

Vern stepped forward and said, "I don't believe it. It's a deception. It has to be."

Sticks watched the men face off with one another. She wasn't sure what to think. She'd never met the real Ruger, but this man certainly wasn't Abraham. It wasn't the demented soul named Eugene either. Her gaze slid over to the baffled Horace. "How can you know that it is him?"

"It's him," Horace said. "I can feel it in my belly. I see it with my very own eyes as well. I would know."

Sticks's heart sank. The thought of Abraham being gone created a cold void inside her. She cared for the man more deeply than she would admit.

Vern swiped his wavy blond locks out of his eyes and said, "Don't get all gooey eyed, Horace. We've been deceived how many times before?" His hand fell on the handle of his sword. "This man might be as possessed as the others." He pulled his longsword. "There's only one swordsman better than me in this group, and that is supposed to be you." He flipped his blade around. "Let's see what you can do, Ruger."

CHAPTER 5

STICKS PICKED UP THE TATTERED scabbard containing Black Bane, leaning against the wall. She walked toward Ruger.

"No, no, no, no," Vern objected. "The real Ruger won't need his precious magic sword. Get him another blade. Something on par with mine."

Ruger gave Vern a dangerous look and said, "You're always up for a challenge, aren't you, Verner? It brings me joy to see there is fire in your guts." He eyed Black Bane's scabbard. "Who is the fool that is mishandling my equipment? Never mind." He pulled free a short sword from Sticks's hip. He patted her on the side. "May I borrow this?"

"You're the captain," Sticks said coolly. Ruger's direct mannerisms caught her off guard. He wasn't pushy but polished, direct but polite. He carried a natural charm that was captivating. Her heart sped up. She made an unlikely comment. "Be careful."

Ruger spun the sword by the handle inside the palm of his hand. He flipped the blade side to side and studied its sharp edge. "It's notched. Looks like you've been neglecting to put the stone to it. Has everyone forgotten how to care for their weapons?" He eyed Vern. "Let's hope you haven't forgotten how to fight."

"I don't know where you've been, Captain," Vern said. He got into his sword-fighting stance. "But I've been fighting plenty. What have you been doing with yourself the last few years?"

"A good question. If I could only answer it in its entirety." The company surrounded the combatants. "My, it's good to have hard steel in my hand once again. Come on, Vern. Have a go at it. Make a move."

"Whoever you are, you're going to regret taking a shorter blade. I'll carve you in two." Vern locked his eyes on Ruger, dropped his sword into the ox guard position, and lunged.

Steel rattled against steel as Ruger snaked to the left and batted the longer sword aside with jarring effect.

Vern stumbled sideward, fought for his footing, and faced off again. He licked his puffy lips.

"You dropped your shoulder too soon," Ruger said with a disappointed shake of his head. "Once again, you telegraphed your move. Whoever you have been fighting must not have been very good."

Bearclaw and Horace chuckled.

Vern set his jaw and came at Ruger again. He turned his hips into a powerful swing.

Ruger jumped several feet backward as the edge of Vern's sword tip scraped across the metal covering his chest. "That's the spirit!"

Ruger and Vern exchanged sword-on-sword strikes with blazing fury.

Bang! Clash! Ting! Slice! Whisk! Clang! Clang! Bang!

Vern poured it on.

Ruger parried with grace and power, dropping in tutorial tidbits as he did so. "Your elbows are extended. You flap like a chicken." *Bang!* "I've seen bears with better footwork than you. Are your boots tied together?" *Ching! Slice!* "Oh my, this is worse than I thought. Your skill has deteriorated."

Lathered up in sweat and chest heaving, Vern shouted, "It has not!" He locked both hands on his handle and redoubled his efforts. He unleashed all hell with his steel. He stabbed from the high guard, ox guard, and plow guard. He turned loose a final lethal wrath-guard swing.

Ruger knocked every strike aside in a blink of an eye. Without attacking, he batted aside Vern's snakelike strokes with raw power. Sticks caught her breath. She'd seen Ruger fight before, but it wasn't anything like the display he was putting on now. His form was perfect from head to toe. He was a true sword master.

In a blur of movement and with a flip of the wrist, Ruger knocked the longsword out of Vern's grip and held his short blade on the panting man's throat. "Do you still take me for an imposter?"

Vern's Adam's apple rolled against the edge of the blade. "You are my brother in arms, my captain, Ruger Slade. Of this I have no doubt."

Ruger's eyes narrowed. Tension hung in the air. Every breath was stifled. "You were insubordinate, Vern. You should never question the captain, no matter who is in his skin. I could cut your head off... but I won't. This time." He flipped the short sword back to Sticks. She snatched it out of the air and sheathed it. He grabbed Vern and wrapped him up tight. "'Tis grand to see you, brother!"

"You too!" Vern hugged him back. "You too!"

The often-quiet Prospero threw up a fist stained with Wild Men blood and said, "Slade the Blade returns! The captain of captains is back!"

Ruger embraced all his men with hugs and fierce armlocks. Sticks had never seen a group of men so tight. It was a brotherhood with roots that ran deep.

"I see many new faces, but many are gone as well. Dare I ask?" Ruger said.

"I couldn't keep them all alive without your help," Shades said as he stepped into Ruger's view.

"Ho! If it isn't the Night Possum!" Ruger swallowed Shades up in his long arms and crushed him like a child. "I should have known that you would squirt away from any disaster." He let Shades free of his powerful embrace. He addressed them all. "You'll have to forgive my elation. My rigid demeanor that you're accustomed to escapes me at the moment. I've come from a strange land ruled by greed and despair, polluted by chronic noise that would jangle a troglin's bones… Hello…" His voice trailed off as his eyes landed for the first time on Solomon. "What do we have here?"

Horace put a meaty hand on his shoulder and said, "Captain, there is much to talk about."

"I can see that."

CHAPTER 6

By torchlight, the Henchmen ventured on to the narrow ledges and into the icy chill of the Wound. Aided also by a soft glow from Melris's and Iris's hands, the surefooted group navigated deeper into the black terrain.

Ruger led in the front with Horace by his side and Melris a half step behind and between them. Sticks was bringing up the rear, with Solomon and the Red Tunics, Skitts, and Zann. She rubbed her hands together. Frost came from her breath. She brushed against Solomon's furry body and said, "What do you make of our new leader?"

The aged troglin shrugged and said, "I hope Abraham comes back."

Lifting an eyebrow, the normally unflappable Sticks asked, "Why do you say that?"

"I put my trust in Abraham to take me home. I'm not so sure about this man. His purpose might not be the same. To make matters worse, if Abraham does not come back, then that only means that I am stuck here as well." Solomon frowned. "Perhaps it serves me right for getting my hopes up of seeing my home again."

Sticks nodded. She felt for the troglin and could see the lost look in his big brown eyes. "This Ruger is better than the other one. At least we have that. The old guardians have truly embraced him. I don't have much of a problem with it myself, but I miss Abraham."

"Funny, but I still feel compelled to follow this man." Solomon rubbed his chest on the spot where he'd been branded. "It's the magic in the Brand, I guess. I was hoping to talk with him, but Horace wouldn't stop blathering. This Captain Ruger, he really jumped feet first into the king's mission. It was as if he hadn't missed a beat."

Ahead, the group slowed. The shelf that made a path down into the great canyon's interior narrowed to a ledge twenty feet long and just barely big enough for one man. Ruger crossed first with his back against the stone. He tossed a length of rope back to Horace. "Take no chances. One by one. We don't want to risk this shelf cracking."

One by one, the others crossed, holding the rope in hand. Debris on the outer edge broke off and chipped. The small rocks bounced down the rock wall, echoing at first then falling silent.

All the Henchmen moved across the ledge without hardly a one touching the rope. Sticks crossed in a few quick steps. She was followed by the Red Tunics, both of which were carrying heavy packs full of gear. Skitts used the rope, but Zann didn't.

"A bold pair of rabbits, I see," Ruger commented as they crossed. "You should grab the rope. Your packs will leave you off balance, and I don't want to lose any gear."

Skitts locked his hands around the rope. He was facing the wall and sidestepping along the twenty-foot gap. The back of his heels barely hung off the ledge as he moved slowly.

"Will you hurry up?" Zann suggested in his Southern drawl. "Or are you waiting for the ledge to break underneath of you?"

"I'm moving fast enough. You hush," Skitts said with a shaky voice.

"Keep it moving, young fellow. Only a few steps left to go." Ruger slid a look at Sticks. "This place would benefit from one of those elevators from that other world." He extended his arm and grabbed Skitts's pack the moment the Red Tunic came close enough. He assisted him all the way across. "Your heart won't shoot out of your throat so much the next time. You'll get used to it."

"Thank you, Captain," Skitts said as he moved on.

With an impish grin, Zann navigated the foreboding ledge with ease, leaving Solomon and Horace on the other side.

"Go ahead, Horace," Solomon said. "I'll hold the rope."

Horace handed him the rope and started to cross. The portly warrior walked on tiptoe with his free hand grazing the wall of rock. He crossed the gap in seconds.

Solomon tossed the slack in the rope over. He signaled to the others with a casual flip of his hand. "Scoot back. My feet are far too big to walk this dainty ledge."

Ruger coiled the rope over his head and moved back the onlookers bunched up on the ledge. "Let's give him some room. Have at it, troglin."

"Call me Solomon," the old troglin replied. In a single leap, Solomon jumped across the twenty-foot chasm. He landed gingerly on the full ledge. "Easy peasy."

"Well done, Henchman," Ruger remarked. "Though I'm not surprised. I've seen your ilk leap thirty feet like great cats. I was only concerned because you appear old."

"Yeah, well, don't let appearance fool you," Solomon replied with a quick look at Sticks.

"I assure you I don't." Ruger turned.

The shelf that Solomon was standing on broke underneath him. The troglin slipped into the chasm with his claws raking down the chasm wall.

Ruger dove belly first onto the ledge. His strong fingers clutched over the rim. "Horace, anchor my legs—I have him!"

Horace dropped down on his butt and hooked his meaty arms around Ruger's ankles.

Sticks burst into action, grabbing the rope and tossing it over the rim. She flipped the excess rope to the Red Tunics. "Anchor it!"

The Red Tunics fed the rope back to the others. A strong chain of rope and men was set.

"Where is he?" Horace asked.

"I don't know. I thought I had him. It appears I have not," Ruger replied.

Sticks gazed over the ledge. There was no sign of Solomon, only blackness.

CHAPTER 7

"Is he gone?" Horace said. He took a peek over the ledge as he did so.

"Shhh," Ruger said softly.

Sticks turned an ear. Small chunks of rock were bouncing down the wall. Something scraped against stone. The Henchmen lowered their torches into the black gap.

Suddenly, Solomon appeared, climbing up the wall like a squirrel. A broad grin crossed his face as he shouted, "Waaahooo!" He clucked with thunderous laughter as he climbed up onto the smaller ledge. He fastened himself to the wall with two black fingernails. "Have you forgotten that troglins are the greatest mountaineers in this world? Climbing through this chasm is easy peasy."

"Why don't you climb back down and find the bottom of this abyss?" Horace said as he hauled Ruger back in.

"I'm following orders," Solomon replied.

"As you should," Ruger said as he climbed back to his feet. "Next time, I'll have a better recollection of your skills in mind." He turned and face the group. "Enough gawking. Onward, Henchmen. We have the king's stones to find."

"'Tis a sad day to serve a king that has no stones," Shades remarked.

Many of the Henchmen chuckled.

"Not those stones," Ruger replied as he passed Sticks and shoulder bumped Shades. "Don't quip about the king. It can bring misfortune."

Sticks watched Solomon make his way back to the ledge. He still had a smile on his face. "Did I have you worried?" he asked.

"I never worry," she replied. Her ears perked. "Did you hear that?"

"What?" Solomon said.

She stepped to the ledge and looked downward as a moist sucking sound caught her ear. The fine hairs on the nape of her neck rose. "You didn't see anything down there, did you?"

"It's pitch-black. I can't even see my paw in front of my face." Solomon started forward. "It's probably the blood rushing through your ears."

Sticks gripped her handle of her sheathed sword. "You're probably right. Let's go." She glanced at Solomon just as a moist and fleshy tentacle wrapped around his waist. She pulled her sword and screamed, "Solomon!"

Solomon was ripped from the ledge by the powerful tentacle. The slimy thing had thousands of clutching suckers all over it.

"Gah! Get this thing off of me!" Solomon shouted. He was suspended by the massive tentacle, which plucked him off the wall like a bug. He thrashed against his bonds with his face in horrified agony. "Help! Help!"

Sticks chopped at the octopod tendril but was far from the mark.

The Henchmen, led by Ruger, rushed to their aid.

More tentacles crawled up the ledge and swiped at Sticks's feet. One tentacle had a bulging eye on the end of it. It lunged at Sticks. With a swing of her sword, she cut the eyeball off. She danced between the tentacles, cutting fiercely at everything that moved.

"Gaaah!" Solomon screamed. "Somebody do something!"

"There!" Ruger stabbed his sword downward at a hulking blob churning up the canyon wall. "Death to the slime dweller, Henchmen!"

Skitts and Zann fired a volley of crossbow bolts into the massive blob. A mouth opened and closed that could swallow a horse whole. The bolts sank into its flesh and disappeared. More tentacles exploded from it and snaked their way up onto the rim.

The Henchmen burst into action.

Horace stabbed his great spear into the tendrils.

Vern and Bearclaw slashed away.

Prospero hurled a burning torch into the monster's mouth.

The monster shrieked as it began to burn from the inside out. Its tentacles clenched and recoiled. The creeping slime began a rapid descent down the wall. It's bulging froglike body glowed with burning fire from within.

"Help me!" Solomon cried out. "Help me!" The troglin was being pulled down into the inky depths. His long, hairy fingers clutched at the air.

Ruger grabbed the rope and hurled it at the troglin, shouting, "Grab hold!"

Solomon grasped the rope with the tips of his fingers then coiled it around his hands.

"Henchmen! Take the rope!" Ruger commanded.

Every able hand in the company grabbed hold of the rope and pulled. Sticks stood behind Ruger, digging her heels into the ledge. Ruger's forearms knotted with muscle. He threw his head back and heaved. Behind her, Horace panted heavily and said, "This thing is heavier than me!"

The creeper wasn't going down without a meal. It pulled against them with unearthly force.

The boots of the Henchmen began to slide across the ledge.

Solomon cried out, "I can't hold much longer. Save yourself!"

"Put your backs into it!" Ruger shouted as he set his feet on the ledge and squatted down. "Death before failure. Hurk!"

Inch by inch, the Henchmen pulled the rope back. Every person holding the line groaned. Sticks's teeth ground, and her jaws clenched. Her back and thighs burned with fire. Out of the corner of her eye, she caught hornets made of rosy-purple fire shooting down into the abyss.

The monster let out a moan that would have turned a softer man's bones to jelly. It pulled down the wall with the strength of an elephant.

The rope burned through Sticks's hand. Horace bumped up against her.

Ruger gave his final order as he teetered over the edge. "No one lets go of this rope but me. That's an order!" He snatched up his sword and dove point first toward the monster.

"Captain, no!" Horace yelled.

Ruger vanished.

The rope juddered on the other side of the ledge. The great weight at the other end broke free a few moments later. The company backpedaled with the sudden change in weight and slammed into the wall. Not one single Henchmen lost grip.

Solomon climbed up over the ledge. His long, hairy arms were shaking like leaves. Sticks and Horace crawled over and hauled him all the way up.

"Thank you," Solomon said with a trembling voice. He looked over into the black expanse. "He dove right in. He dove right into its very jaws." He swallowed. "And like a wind blowing out a flame," he cast a sad look at Sticks, "he was gone."

CHAPTER 8

STICKS RUBBED THE RAW PALMS of her hands. Hours had passed since they battled the monster Ruger had called a creeper. Her hands burned like fire. That would pass. The loss of Ruger wouldn't. Nor would the loss of Abraham. If Ruger was dead, she had no chance of ever seeing Abraham again.

"Are you sure you don't want me to have a look at that?" Iris said in her naturally cheery voice. "After all, I've patched up all of the others requiring aid."

"It's only a burn," she said flatly.

The Henchmen had reached what appeared to be the bottom of the canyon. Above was a skylight the size of a fingernail, which showed the night sky. The canyon floor must have been a mile down, perhaps deeper. Sticks wasn't the best judge of such things.

"I'll live."

"Suit yourself. Holler if you need me." Iris moved back toward the rest of the group.

The men were gathered around, grumbling back and forth. Horace's, Bearclaw's, and Vern's heads were down. Vern was cursing. Fingers were being poked at one another. Without the captain, no one was there to control them.

Shades squirted away from the pack and squatted down by Sticks and Solomon. "This is going to be ugly with the captain dead."

"Don't say that," Solomon said. "We don't know that."

"Ruger might have been the greatest sword, but even he can't kill a thousand-foot free fall," Shades said with his usual rugged playfulness. "I imagine that only makes your predicament worse. Sorry, hairy fella."

Solomon shoved Shades onto his backside. "That man saved my life. Show some respect."

Shades climbed back to his feet and said, "You are right. Ruger deserves that. It was good to see him one last time and watch him save our backsides again. Believe me when I say when I grieve, I grieve as much as you."

Sticks sat with her legs crossed and the assault rifle across her lap. Her fingers toyed with the weapon's carrying strap. "I should have shot the thing. Like Abraham taught me. I didn't even think of it."

"Everyone is blaming each other. At least you aren't. I'll let you take full responsibility if you like." Shades grinned. "For a change, no one is blaming me, which is refreshing."

Horace's and Vern's voices started to rise. The loud talking became loud shouting.

"You are not going to lead this expedition. If anyone is going to lead, it is me!" Horace bellowed at Melris. "You are not even a Henchman! We are going to search for the captain!"

"No," Melris replied in his smooth voice that could penetrate a wall. "All of us are under the same order from King Hector. We are to make haste to recover the stones. Ruger Slade would have understood that. The mission comes first. We've been sidetracked once. I cannot allow it to happen again."

Vern jabbed a finger at the Elderling and said, "You listen to me, you little worm, we are in charge, not you!"

With a flick of his finger, Melris hurled Vern off his feet and sent him skidding over the ground. The Henchmen's weapons whisked out of their sheaths. They walled in Melris with shining steel bared.

Horace held his spear tip in Melris's face. "Henchmen don't turn against other Henchmen."

"I'm not a Henchman," Melris replied. His iron rod glowed in his hand. "And you err, Horace. I am in the right. You are in the wrong. The king placed me in charge of the expedition. Captain Slade understood that. Now he is gone, leaving me in charge. Though you can choose a leader among yourselves, you still have to follow me."

Sticks quietly approached the arguing men and said, "He's right, Horace. You know it. We don't have a choice."

"Then you can follow him," Horace said. He yanked his spear away from Melris's face. "I'm going to find the captain. Who is with me?"

Rising back to his feet, Vern said, "I am."

"As am I," agreed Bearclaw.

"We aren't going anywhere without the captain, dead or alive," Cudgel said.

His brother, Tark, nodded.

Apollo and Prospero stood gathered behind Horace. So did Dominga.

"I don't know, Horace," Iris said with her fingers fidgeting by her side. "It's bad luck to split up and even worse to go against the king's orders. I have to stand by Melris. Methinks any other move will piss the Elders off. We need them."

Horace stuffed his fingers into his pouch and said, "Then I'm chewing my tobacco!"

Shades and Solomon joined Iris behind Melris.

"Well, what in the Crotch are we supposed to do? We just take orders. Who do we take them from now?" Zann asked.

Horace pointed at Skitts and said, "You come with us. Zann, you can go with them." He gave Melris a final hard look. "Henchmen don't abandon Henchmen."

"Henchmen are expendable. That's why they are Henchmen," Melris said. "I'll warn you your chances of survival greatly diminish with your numbers divided. All of you would be wise to follow me. Believe me when I say that I know what I am talking about."

Horace spat on the ground. He eyed Sticks and Iris and said, "I'm disappointed in you." He turned his back and led his group into the darkness of the canyon.

Skitts carried a torch. He gave Sticks and her group one last long look before they disappeared around a bend in the rock and vanished into the darkness.

"I have a bad feeling about this." Zann sucked his teeth. "I'm not used to being separated from my brother. It makes me feel like a dove is flapping inside my chest."

CHAPTER 9

Aided by the illumination from Melris's and Iris's hands, the small company moved across the bottom of the Wound's canyon floor. Sticks could make out the rolling dark clouds high above, through a shrinking eye-shaped window. She felt small, tiny, like an ant in a strange but new world that lurked in the ground below. She tucked her hands against her sides and churned on.

Melris was in the front, Iris in the rear. Sticks, Solomon, Dominga, Shades, and Zann walked between them.

"Say, mage," Shades said to Melris. "Do you have a sense of where we are going? All of this place looks the same to me."

"I can feel it," Melris said. "The stones are in this place, deep in the bones of Titanuus."

"What does he mean by that?" Zann said with a frosty breath. "And wouldn't it be wise to make a torch or something? It might keep us a little warmer."

"Strange that it feels so cold down here," Solomon commented. "And where does the wind come from?"

"I don't know," Dominga said as she cozied up to Solomon, grabbed his arm, and draped it over her shoulder. She snuggled into him. "I hope you don't mind, but I hate being cold."

"Not at all," Solomon said.

"I can keep you warmer than him," Shades commented.

"I seriously doubt that," Dominga said.

"Well, I bet I can do a better job than Vern," Shades said.

"We'll never know." Dominga clung to Solomon more tightly, looked up, and gave him a smile.

Solomon smiled back.

Melris cradled his Rod of Devastation in his arms like a man holding a baby. He moved at a brisk pace on ghostly-soft footsteps.

They walked for hours. Sticks's teeth chattered though she tried to control it.

Finally, Melris moved over a rise on the hard rock floor and stopped.

A pale-pink light emanated from a hole in the ground. A slope inside the hole led downward.

Zann stretched his fingers over the twelve-foot-wide gap and said, "It's warm."

"We are going into the bones," Melris said. Without another word, he walked down the slope.

The remainder of the Henchmen stood outside the gap, exchanging glances with one another.

"I don't know about this place," Iris said with her fingers strumming the air. "Something very alive is down there. My very bones tingle."

"I'd rather die warm than be left out in the cold." Sticks hopped into the tunnel.

"Aye, I'm with her," Shade said.

"You don't have to tell me twice," Dominga added.

Solomon and Zann were still standing outside when Sticks looked back over her shoulder. Solomon was shaking his head. Zann was mumbling and nodding.

"Are you coming?" she asked.

"Perhaps we should wait for the others," Solomon said. "Something doesn't smell right."

Sticks sniffed. "I don't smell anything odd."

"Yeah, that's what bothers me," the troglin replied.

"We need to stay together. What's left of us, at least," she said.

"Yup," Zann croaked, "someone needs to protect the rest of them. I guess that's us." He waltzed into the tunnel. "Come on, hairy fella. They need us. And I don't have fur like you. I hate the cold too."

Solomon ventured in, casting his eyes all around. The tunnel was twenty feet high, and the walls were the color of red brick and perforated with holes. He scratched his fingers over the crusty coating of the walls, which were bone white underneath.

"Interesting," he said. "If I were to guess, I'd say that these walls were made of bone."

"Bone?" Zann asked.

Solomon looked at the dried dirt underneath his fingernail then at the strange flooring beneath his feet. The floor was no different from the walls.

"And this is blood or the dried marrow."

That's very observant, Solomon," Melris said. "We are inside the very bones of Titanuus. Feel them." He touched the perforated surface of the wall. "There is still life inside the celestial titan. And where there is life, there is more life."

"Now it's getting creepy," Solomon said.

"Shall we proceed?" Melris turned his back and continued walking down into the tunnel.

The walls were twenty feet high and just as wide. The passage led straight forward.

The small company moved at a brisk pace through the odd corridor. Sticks wondered if what Melris had said was really true about the titans that formed the world. *Are we actually inside the bones of a celestial titan that died eons ago? Is Titanuus still alive?* She rubbed the goose bumps popping up on her arms. *Creepy.* That wasn't something she would have ever dwelled on, but now, the odd circumstances told as stories to excited children before bedtime had become very real. She was on a bigger stage than she had ever been. *I miss Abraham.*

The longer they walked, the more she thought about him. Ruger Slade had come back, but then he died. That meant Abraham was gone, which wasn't something she was prepared to deal with. Her feelings for him ran deep. She didn't want to accept that he was dead. *I hope he still lives on his world.*

Iris drifted back and said to her, "You've got a long face for a girl who shows no expression at all. I figured you'd be feeling better now that we are all nice and toasty." She fanned her glistening face. "Perhaps too toasty."

"I think you know by now that I'm not the chatty type."

"Oh, well, we don't have much else to do, seeing how this walk might go on for days," Iris said.

Plenty of distance remained between everyone. Melris and Shades were in the front, while Dominga, Solomon, and Zann were in the back.

"Come on, have a go at it with me. I know it's your man that's missing."

Without batting an eye, Sticks looked at the pie-faced mystic and said, "I don't want to talk about it."

"Fine, then I'll do the talking. Abraham had you feeling all rosy inside, didn't he? And now, you don't know if you'll ever feel that way again. Well, let me tell you, you probably won't. Those kinds of feelings are fleeting in this world, but consider yourself lucky that you felt them because most don't."

"It won't ever come back," Sticks said.

"I had a fellow once. I felt like I was on a cloud when I was with him. Sometimes, the timing isn't right. Life gets in the way. People move on. It's a very sad thing." Iris offered a warm smile. "I think about him a lot still. I always will."

Sticks nodded. "I only wish I could have said good-bye."

CHAPTER 10
BACK HOME

ABRAHAM BLINKED. THE ZILLON STANDING beside his table didn't disappear. The alien-like person, unlike in the movies, had a black ponytail hanging from the back of her head. His oval eyes were large and black. A small nub of a nose was set in the middle of his face. She had a mouthful of many straight teeth. The zillon was no different from the ones he'd seen on Titanuus. The only difference was this zillon was here.

"Welcome to Earth," Abraham said.

Dr. Jack Lassiter chuckled. "You're a real funny guy, Abraham. No, this isn't an alien from another world. This is a zillon from Titanuus. Pretty interesting, wouldn't you say?"

In a voice as normal as any human woman, the zillon woman said, "I am Ottum from Hancha. A dragon rider. Do you know the dragon riders?"

Abraham looked the shapely zillon up and down. Ottum was wearing a set of black-and-gray camouflage clothing.

"Yeah. I know 'em. Killed them too. How'd you get here?"

Ottum kneaded her fingertips together and replied, "I came through a portal." Her spacey eyes did not blink. "It was long ago."

Dr. Jack intervened and said, "It's still a mystery how she got here, but we are unlocking more secrets about the portals every day. It's only a matter of time until we have it under complete control."

"Are there more zillons out there?" Abraham asked.

"It's a big world," Dr. Jack said. "We only see what the bigshots want us to see, so it's safe to say that yes, there are plenty of strange beings walking this world."

If Abraham could have sat up, he would have as he thought of Solomon and said, "Like Bigfoot!"

Dr. Jack shrugged. "So, Abraham, what do you think? How would you like to go back and start all over again? With your cooperation, we can make that happen."

"I don't believe that we can travel back through time. That's crazy."

"And you didn't believe that you could travel from one world to another, now did you?" Dr. Jack asked. He eyed the zillon. "But now, you have proof."

A big part of Abraham wanted nothing more than to go back to the time just before the plane crash. If he could do it all over again, he'd never get on that plane. He'd never fly either. He could be with Jenny and Jake again. He would hold them both in his arms and never let go. Life would be perfect. *This is madness. I can't go back in time. Of course, I can't live in two worlds at once either. God help me.*

"You should work with Dr. Jack," Ottum the zillon suggested. "Like you, I too want to return home."

"Well, back in your world, your people are trying to destroy the king of Kingsland. The dragon riders tried to assassinate him with modern weapons." He glared at Dr. Jack. "I bet you knew all about that, didn't you?"

"Come on, Abraham, don't be naive," Dr. Jack said as he puffed out a stream of smoke. "No kingdom lasts forever."

"Except the Kingdom of Heaven."

"Yeah, if you believe that sort of thing. You know your history. Every nation has been conquered at one time or another. Now is our time to be a part of a new world, a world where we can do things right. After all, this world is collapsing. We need a place to escape. There is no telling where this might lead."

"I don't know."

"Think about it," Dr. Jack said. "You saw the movie *Back to the Future*, didn't you? With the DeLorean that went back and forth through time. They set the wrongs right. You can have your life back."

"You make it sound like you have this mastered. If that's the case, why me?"

"I guess it's because you're special. You are the only one that bounces back between both worlds. The others can't do it. They come, they stay, they can't commute. For some reason—I don't know what it is—you can do both. It's causing problems. Work with me, and you can have your life back, and we can get back to our work."

Abraham imagined going back eight years in time. It didn't seem possible. Something inside his gut twisted. His father, Earl, had often said, "Life happens. It's not always good. It's not always bad. But you have to move forward." He wanted more than anything to hold Jenny and Jake one last time. In truth, he hadn't been able to move forward in life without them. He never moved on—at least, not until this maddening twist of fate, where he found himself traveling from one world to another. It had to end. But he had to end it correctly.

"What's on your mind?" Ottum asked. She stroked Abraham's face with a feather-light touch of her long, slender fingers. "Tell me. I want to help you, and you can help me. I understand. You can trust me. I've lost loved ones as well."

"I bet you have."

He tried not to have a grudge against her. Not all zillons were bad—he'd met many. But the zillons had attacked King Hector.

"Listen, I don't think I can handle much more of this," he said. "I'll deal with you, but I want to use the bathroom and have something to eat first."

Dr. Jack gave him a nod and said, "Deal."

CHAPTER 11

After Abraham was fed under the watchful eyes of Otis and Haymaker, he was strapped to another gurney and loaded into a green military ambulance and hauled away. Otis and Haymaker sat inside the ambulance cabin with their stun rods in their hands. Neither man took his eyes off him. The ambulance bounced over potholes and swayed on the hard bends in the road.

Abraham had no idea where he was. He opted for small talk. "So, how much does a good orderly make these days? Fifteen, twenty dollars an hour?"

"Shut up," Otis said. He stuck his stun rod on Abraham's nose. "Don't make me shock you."

"I'm not so sure that you want to do that. You might bring Dr. Jekyll out." He eyeballed Otis's swollen cheek. "You have a tough time with him, don't you."

"I'll say," Haymaker said in a cheery country-boy manner. "You tossed us around like bales of hay the last time you switched. But we'll be ready for you next time. We can handle it."

"Yeah, with me strapped up like this, you might." He strained against his cuffs. "Pretty strong, but I think Ruger Slade is stronger. In the other world, I have superpowers. I can snap these bonds like twigs." He shrugged his eyebrows. "Like twigs."

"Yeah, well, if Dr. Jack was smart, he'd let us kill you. You're the source of all the trouble. I don't know why, seeing how you are one man, but they are obsessed with you." Otis sniffed. "They'd be better off without you."

Abraham had no idea why he was more special than the other otherworlders that had soul swapped. He understood that he traveled between both worlds, but why it was him but not the others, he didn't know. *Why me?* For the life of him, he couldn't recall anything special having happened in his life, aside from the plane wreck, when the plane was struck by lightning and he somehow survived.

The ambulance rumbled down the road. It bumped and jostled over rugged terrain. With no windows inside the cabin, Abraham had no idea if it was day or night. Suddenly, the rough road became smooth. The ride went on for a few more minutes, then the ambulance's brakes squealed to a halt.

The double doors on the back of the ambulance popped open. Two soldiers in black-gray camouflage, wearing machine guns strapped over their backs and mesh baseball caps, stepped aside while Otis and Haymaker pushed the gurney out of the back.

The gurney's legs dropped open underneath Abraham. The orderlies pushed him along on the casters. They were inside an old tunnel, the walls made of old cinder blocks. The ceiling was at least twenty feet high. The tunnel was lit by military tree lights. Gas generators made a steady hum. On the walls of the tunnel were more heavy equipment and generators. A Jeep and a Humvee were there. Long black power cords ran along the floor.

"Nice place. Let me guess, Batman lives here," Abraham said.

"No, that's another cave," Dr. Jack said.

Abraham heard the man's voice but didn't see him. He craned his neck around. Aside from Otis and Haymaker, he saw only the two other soldiers. "You aren't really going to keep me strapped to this thing forever, are you? I said I'd help."

"Stand him up," Dr. Jack said.

Otis and Haymaker adjusted the custom-made gurney with a tilt that stood Abraham almost straight up.

He was facing the entrance of the tunnel, where he could see the ambulance, other vehicles, generators, and the other equipment. The bigger, rectangular generators were loud. A fuel tanker truck was pulled into the tunnel as well.

"What is this, one of those underground bunkers like that place in Colorado called NORAD? Or is this NORAD?"

Dr. Jack stepped into view and said, "No, it's not NORAD." He wasn't smoking.

"What's the matter, did you run out of cigars?"

"We don't smoke in this facility." Dr. Jack gave Otis and Haymaker a look and said, "Go ahead, turn him around."

With one arm, Otis spun Abraham around one hundred eighty degrees. Teams of men in white lab coats were strolling through large ground-level computer stations. At least a dozen soldiers were standing guard back against the tunnel's walls. He could make out a few familiar faces. Eugene Drisk, older and frumpy, was talking to Colonel Drew Dexter and Ottum the zillon. Colonel Dexter held an iPad and dotted it with a pen. His moustache twitched when he glanced at Abraham.

Well, if it isn't a couple of my favorite persons. Evil scientist and power-mad military man. "Ah, I see more of my favorite people," Abraham said. "Is this the secret lair of evil geniuses?" He nodded his head. "It's very sinister."

Dr. Jack moved deeper into the tunnel. "You're a funny man."

The orderlies shoved Abraham forward. He noticed some odd lettering on the generators that they passed. In large letters painted white, it read, Drakeland Corp. The letters were configured like a logo, and they ran through a rising sun. *Interesting. This isn't military equipment. It's private industry. I bet Sid and Smoke would want to know about this.*

Dr. Jack shook hands with Colonel Dexter.

Eugene Drisk almost jumped out of his lab coat when he saw Abraham. Shielding himself with his iPad, he said, "That's not…?"

"No, that's not Ruger. It's Abraham. Good ol' washed-up Abraham," Dr. Jack said. "And he wouldn't be here unless he'd agreed to cooperate. He's game for our big plan… Aren't you, Abraham?"

"I just want to get this over with one way or the other," he said.

"Good." Dr. Jack grabbed Ottum's hand in his and said, "Well, what are we waiting for. Let's turn the Time Tunnel on."

CHAPTER 12

EUGENE DRISK MOVED OVER TO one of the large computer stations and started punching keys. The five main computer stations were fanned out in front of an intricately crafted metal ring that made a thick hoop inside the tunnel. A new hum carried throughout the tunnel. Small twinkling LEDs in a variety of colors came on inside the loop. Like the stars in the sky, thousands of them appeared.

Abraham saw Haymaker's arm hairs stand on end. His own hairs stood as though they were filled with static electricity. Great power was coursing through the tunnel. The steady hum of the gas-powered generators chugged and suddenly heaved.

Dr. Jack stood with a triumphant smile on his face. "Watch this," he said.

Eugene gave a single finger signal to the other scientists wearing lab coats, standing along the tunnel wall. On both sides, each manned a large electrical switch with a long black handle. At the same time, they pushed the levers upward. The tunnel beyond the hoop filled with light, and the droning hum of lights became louder.

Abraham squinted. He couldn't shield his eyes, but he wanted to.

"It's not on!" Dr. Jack said in a loud voice. The curly hairs on his head were standing taller, as if he'd just walked through a wind tunnel. "It's only warming up!"

The tunnel walls behind the hoop were made up of large tiles of shiny steel. The glimmering tiles stretched back another fifty feet, where a bright ring of yellow light burned at the end.

"Very nice," Abraham said, "but I don't see a passing lane. And shouldn't there be a toll booth? You know, make sure you use one of the EZ Pass services. It makes a trucker's life a lot easier."

"Huh huh," Colonel Trotter laughed. "I might have liked you if you hadn't killed so many of my soldiers."

"What's a trucker supposed to do, let them kill me?" He was referring to the battle near Morgantown, when the choppers came. "It was us or them."

"They wouldn't have fired if you'd given yourself up," Colonel Dexter said. "The rest of it was miscommunication. I wasn't there. With that said, I hope this next trip of yours is a one-way journey. And don't worry about Mandi. I'll take care of her."

"I'm pretty sure you've burned that bridge." Abraham would have knocked the moustache off Colonel Dexter's face if he could have. His heart burned for Mandi. She'd stuck with him through thick and thin, and he hardly knew her. Now, he was thinking about his family, about going back to them, but he didn't believe that was possible. *What about the Henchmen—Sticks, Horace, and my friends? Will I ever see them again?* "So, what's the story, Jack? How does this thing work?"

"I'll let Eugene and his allies handle that. The question is, are you willing to go back and quit this nonsense with the king of Kingsland? You need to tell them to surrender. Tell them that we will give them whatever they want. Just cooperate."

Ottum approached Abraham, put her cool hand on his face, and said, "King Hector is not a good man. He rules with an iron fist. You cannot trust him. The gems in the Crown of Stones were taken from his family for good reason. They are power mad. It runs in his blood. That bloodline must be destroyed."

The inflection in Ottum's voice suggested she believed what she said. Abraham liked the king. He'd been fair. However, the last time he saw him, the king had changed. He had the green and blue Stones of Power, and the air about him had changed. *I hope I haven't been fighting on the wrong side of this the entire time. No, that couldn't be.* He eyed the men surrounding him. *These dudes are a bunch of tools.*

"Abraham, we aren't out to kill King Hector. We aren't out to kill anyone. What we want is the King's Steel. That's how we can keep the portal open." Dr. Jack pointed into the portal. "You notice that some of the plates shine more than the others. That's the King's Steel we've acquired. We need more of it. It keeps the tunnel and the gate intact. There is no metal on Earth like it."

"I don't think I'm going to be able to talk Hector into surrendering. He'll kill me. That would be treason. I'm no good to you dead."

"You're going to have to convince him. But we can help with that." Dr. Jack nodded at Colonel Dexter.

The colonel gave a hand signal to a group of soldiers. In the middle of the tunnel was a set of railroad tracks that led in and out of the tunnel. Behind them, way far in the back, something heavy started to roll over the tracks.

"Otis, do me a favor and turn me around," Abraham said.

"No," Otis answered.

"It's okay—do as he asks," Dr. Jack replied.

"As the gurney turns," Abraham said as he was wheeled around.

A train flatcar rolled down the tracks. It was loaded with a tank, racks of assault rifles, and crates that were marked Ammunition. He paled.

Eugene Drisk snaked his way over to the group and chuckled wickedly. "They've made more progress than I even dreamed of. What I told you back in Pittsburgh was misleading. Progress in this world moves faster each day. It's… uncanny."

Abraham was turned as the flatcar passed by. It stopped right before the mouth of the loop. The army-green tank might as well have been a harbinger of doom. Titanuus was being invaded. They wouldn't be ready for it.

"I know it's only one tank and a few hundred assault rifles," Dr. Jack said. "But it should be more than enough to send a message."

CHAPTER 13

"Fire up the Time Tunnel, Colonel Dexter. Let's show Mr. Jenkins what we can do," Dr. Jack said. He looked at Abraham and said, "This part makes me giddy."

Each computer station had several large LCD screens. Most of the images on the screens were of the Time Tunnel shown at various angles. The other screen showed the insides of tunnels from other places. Some of them had traffic passing through them like the Big Walker and East Mountain Tunnel. The other tunnels were abandoned.

"I thought the portals opened at random places and you couldn't control them," Abraham said.

Eugene Drisk overheard him talking to Dr. Jack, walked over, and said, "Your memory serves you well. I can't help but be amazed that this traveling back and forth doesn't jar your memories more."

"Did it jar your memories?"

"No, but I haven't been back and forth so many times as you," Eugene said. He stroked the scraggly whiskers on his chin. "I would think that would make a man crazy. As for the portals, when we turn the tunnel on, sometimes the other portals become active. They are most effective inside tunnels and possibly caves. I believe it has something to do with the contour and the darkness. So far, they are mostly active in the Fort Pitt, Big Walker, and East River Mountain Tunnels, plus some of the smaller railroad tunnels between here and there. That's why we practice this at night, when the roads are not so busy. The portals only open for a few seconds before they close again. We do our best to avoid casualties."

"Is that how I was pulled into all of this? You fired this tunnel up, and I happened to drive through it?"

"It's a theory. But"—Eugene lifted a finger—"we believe these portals have been around a very long time. Anomalies in time and space. We just happened to be the ones that discovered them."

"Good for you," Abraham said.

A black camping trailer over thirty feet long was parked on the left side of the tunnel. A rectangular row of windows ran from one end to the other. Men and women were standing behind the glass, wearing white lab coats.

Abraham tried to dig for every bit of information that he could get. Ruger Slade hadn't surrendered himself for just any reason. He must have wanted to get closer to the operation. Perhaps he had some faith that Abraham would do the right thing too. Abraham knew how clever Ruger could be as well. The sword fighter had an indomitable will, but he was more than that. He was a tactician, which made him dangerous.

"So," he said with a nod of his chin toward the trailer, "who are they? More otherworlders, I bet."

"No, that's the A-Team," Eugene said. "They are the geniuses that kept this project alive when I was gone."

Dr. Jack moved away and started talking to Colonel Dexter.

"Listen, Abraham, I don't know when you are going to speak to King Hector again, but I'll tell you this, it's very unlikely the old man will budge. Kingsland will die with him. As for you, well, you should do what is best for you. Just like I did what is best for me. Believe me, I was trapped inside Ruger Slade for years. It gets old. It can make you crazy, and I tried to make the most of it. The world is inhospitable. But we will make it so much better."

"Wouldn't you rather be here instead of there?"

"These people think that they will make Titanuus a vacation resort for the rich. That's only a ploy for money. There is more at play here, more than what wealth and riches could ever offer. It's a chance at immortality, by moving from one body to another, or rather, controlling time itself."

"We'll see."

"Yes, we will, because you are going to be the first pilot that we send through space and time." Eugene sniffed. "You'll be like the first space pilots that landed on the moon."

"Except many believe that never happened."

"Poppycock. People believe what we tell them."

Red lights mounted on the tunnel's interior walls started to flicker. An annoying buzzer went off.

"It's showtime," Eugene said.

The lab assistants started handing out rubber goggles with dark lenses. Otis jammed a pair over Abraham's eyes and snapped them shut tight.

"Thanks, big fella. Say, are these 3-D?"

"Shut up," Otis replied.

A digital female voice sounded overhead: "Countdown begins mark thirty. Twenty-nine. Twenty-eight."

The gas generators chugged more loudly. Their power cords ran across the ground, along the tracks, and were hooked into two five-foot-high-and-wide metal boxes fixed to the ground in front of the tunnel. Each box had a yellow nuclear-power warning sign. Heavy black power cords, each a foot thick, ran from the nuclear boxes to the Time Tunnel ring. A purple glow emanated from the tops of the boxes.

"Twenty-one. Twenty. Nineteen. Eighteen."

In that instant, Abraham understood what he needed to do. He had to destroy the Time Tunnel on Earth, and the portal gates on the other side of Titanuus had to be sealed as well. Forever. All he could do was hope that the Crown of Stones could do that.

"Twelve. Eleven. Ten. Nine."

The onlookers moved back from the Time Tunnel. They stood behind the computer stations, where Abraham was. Everyone had their goggles on, standing with bated breath.

Abraham's chest tightened. He was about to witness history. He didn't want to see it.

"Five. Four. Three. Two. One."

The LED lights inside the time tunnel switched from multiple colors to a bright purple. The plates inside the tunnel started to glow white hot and spin, slowly at first, then faster and faster.

Cold air blasted out of the tunnel in a hair-stirring *whoosh*.

A bright sun ring formed inside the tunnel. The bristling-cold air started to warm.

An image started to form inside the tunnel. Walls of a cave appeared that had not been there before. Great torches were hanging from the walls. Figures of men and women stood in a background cast in shadows.

Colonel Dexter started barking orders. "Send in the flatcar. Send it now!"

The flatcar loaded with the tank and modern weaponry was pushed into the tunnel.

The people on the other side of the tunnel waved swords in the air and cheered. They were rugged men, barbaric brutes with neck muscles up to their ears. Black tattoos decorated their bodies like snakes.

Abraham's blood chilled. They were Gond. That wasn't all he recognized, either. Standing in the wild crowd was the wraith, Fleece. Right beside him was the horned halfling, Big Apple. Big Apple waved his stubby little fingers. He pointed at the tank and grinned impishly.

The portal closed.

CHAPTER 14

"DID YOU GET A LOOK at those guys?" Dr. Jack asked with a shiver of his shoulders. "They were huge. It gave me a chill."

The scientists and soldiers were shaking hands, high fiving, and talking with elation about a job well done.

The light inside the Time Tunnel had cooled. The flatcar was gone. The loud humming in the background went quiet.

Abraham had chill bumps all over. "Do me a favor and take these goggles off, will you?"

Otis complied. With a rough yank, he pulled the goggles from Abraham's face.

"Gee, thanks. So, did you guys see some of your cousins over there? Those Gond are your kind of people."

"Shut up," Otis replied.

"Mr. Drisk," said one of the scientists monitoring the computer station closest to Abraham, "we had activity inside the Fort Pitt Tunnel."

Eugene hurried over to the man. Dr. Jack and Colonel Dexter joined him.

The scientist pointed at one of the overhead monitors. A van decked out in Pittsburgh Steelers logos passed through a bright sun ring that suddenly appeared in the tunnel. The van vanished. A young woman and her small daughter, decked out in Steelers jerseys, sat stranded on the stretch of road. Their eyes were big as saucers. They dashed across the road, away from the fast-moving traffic.

Colonel Dexter got on his phone and said in his deep voice, "We've got two live ones in the Fort Pitt Tunnel. A woman and her girl. Decked out in Steelers gear. Hard to miss. I'll upload more data." He stuffed his phone into his pocket. "Got to go. Let me know if you discover any more of them." He gave Abraham a quick disapproving look and hustled away.

Abraham mulled over his plans for the next hour or so while everyone else scuttled about like a hive of bees, congratulating themselves. He didn't have any doubt that what they did might have been one of the greatest achievements of mankind. *If men like this keep such secrets, then what other secrets do they keep?* "Otis, will you pinch me? I'm having a hard time believing this is real."

"Shut up."

"How about you, Haymaker? You don't look too busy."

"It's real," Haymaker replied. "As real as the hair on my head. I can't wait to get to Titanuus. I'm going to be a baron. Acres of land and many wives."

"You know the women are really hideous over there, don't you?" Abraham said.

Haymaker's bright expression dulled. "What?"

"I mean, if you like the husky, cornfed type, let me say they are aplenty. But don't expect them to have all of their teeth. They don't have toothbrushes, you know. Or running water or television."

Haymaker scratched his head. "I never really thought about that."

"He's pulling your leg," Otis said. "I told you to shut up, Abraham." He waved the stun rod over his face. "You don't want to make me use this."

"I think we both know that *you* are much safer with me than the other guy, aren't you?"

Otis paled. "Shut up."

Dr. Jack and Ottum strolled over. Eugene came with them. "Did you enjoy the show?" Jack said.

Feigning awe, Abraham replied, "So that is what happened to me? I drove through a sun ring, and that's how I became like this. A schizophrenic."

"You aren't a schizophrenic. You are an experiment," Eugene smugly said. "A lab rat."

"A lab rat, huh? I want to be clear about something, and I'm not one to use profane words, but I think all of you are bunch of first-rate arseholes." He eyed Ottum. "Including you."

"*Arseholes*—now that really is a harsh word," Dr. Jack said. "Where'd you come up with that one? Your friends in Titanuus?"

"No, it's from one of my favorite books. It's where guys like you wind up with an axe run through them, but in this case, it will probably be a sword."

"Black Bane," Eugene said.

"Anything can happen."

"What's Black Bane?" Dr. Jack asked.

"It's a sword in Titanuus with magical properties. An artifact of sorts. There is no blade sharper than it in all of the world." A hunger grew in Eugene's eyes. "It cuts bone and flesh like butter. Steel too."

"Hmm… sounds like something I'd like to add to my collection. I don't see why we couldn't acquire it. It's sounds like something that I would love to see." Dr. Jack eyeballed Abraham. "That's another little thing that I'd like to add to the list. Have King Hector stand down, and bring me that sword. Do this, and we can send you back to your wife and kid."

"Not to mention that you'll get back your friend Buddy Parker too. You might even earn a few pennants," Eugene added.

"You know, I've seen you transport people and things from one world to another, but I don't believe that you can send me back in time. Even though I want to."

"Yeah, well, watch this," Eugene said with a cocky smile. "Wheel him over to station one."

Otis pushed Abraham over to the computer station.

Eugene typed on the keyboard, and a new image came up on the overhead screen. It was daytime at an airfield. Jenny and Jake were standing outside Abraham's father's birthday-present plane with smiles on their faces.

Abraham's blood ran cold. The image was clear as a bell, real as could be. "How… how are you doing this?"

Dr. Jack looked right at him and said, "With our imagination combined with magic and technology, anything is possible. All you have to do is believe."

CHAPTER 15

Abraham's heart pounded. Jenny and Jake looked real enough to touch. All he wanted to do was reach out and hug them. Buddy Parker entered the picture on the screen. He hugged Jenny, and she gave Buddy a kiss on the cheek. He picked up a loaf of bread and swung the boy up into the air.

A tear ran down Abraham's cheek. "Stop it. Just stop it."

"What's the matter?" Dr. Jack asked. "Is this a little too close to home?" He nodded at Eugene. "Go ahead. Turn it off."

"If you can travel through time, why don't you just bring them to me?" Abraham said. "That would make it easier for all of us, wouldn't it?"

"We can only work with what we know," Eugene said. "Our Time Tunnel technology allows us to look into the past but not the future. What you just saw is an image created by data we knew of from that very day. Since 2010, modern-day technology has been very accurate. And because you can travel from one world to another without ill effect, we think that you can travel back into time."

Abraham scratched his chin on his chest. He was sweating profusely. Somehow, they were using magic and technology, based on the sound of it, but he didn't know where the magic was coming from. He didn't have time to get it all sorted out, but at least he was getting closer.

"So, if I am to go back to Titanuus," he said, "you want me to talk King Hector into surrender and bring you the sword, Black Bane. And then you'll send me back in time to my family."

"That's the plan," Dr. Jack said.

He chewed his lips and asked, "How are we supposed to know that I'm keeping my end of the bargain and that you are keeping yours?"

"Oh, well, we'll be sending more weaponry over with very specific instructions. We have plenty of agents that are working with us now in Titanuus. They are doing very well with communicating our agenda. That fella, Big Apple, Edward Gravely… It turns out that he's been a really fine help. We made a deal with him. A pretty incredible story for a man that was once an invalid. Turns out he had great ambition."

"Yes, I've met him. So, there only seems to be one problem left," he said. "I'm still here. I can't really control when I go back. It just happens."

"No, no, I think we've got that one figured out," Dr. Jack said with a wave of his finger. "Just remember—a deal is a deal. And our eyes, even in Titanuus, are everywhere."

"You're talking about the Sect and the Shell, aren't you?"

"Bingo. We made a deal with them some time ago. They all stand to profit every bit as much as us in the bold trek into a new frontier. It's going to be glorious." Dr. Jack pulled a cigar out of his pocket and put it in his mouth. "I can't wait to light up the moment I'm out of here. I'm going to have some bourbon too. Do they have good bourbon in Titanuus?"

"I don't know. I don't drink too much. Not here or there that much. I think you know my history."

"That I do. Try to find out for me on this next go-around."

"Again, I don't think I can click my heels together and go back. But most of the time, there's a headache involved."

Dr. Jack chuckled and said, "Yeah, I know." He nodded at Otis and Haymaker. "Let him have it, boys."

Without a moment's hesitation, the brutish orderlies drove their stun rods into Abraham's ribs with hungry glee all over their faces.

Abraham's toes and fingers curled. He thrashed violently in his bonds and let out an earsplitting scream.

Dr. Jack and Ottum plugged their ears with their fingertips.

Abraham's blood ran hot with lightning like fire. He glared at Dr. Jack's sneering smile. Another moment passed. Fire ran through his heart. His world turned black.

Thump-thump. Thump-thump. Thump-thump.

He felt as if someone was driving a nail into his skull. The loud, painful thumping started to slow. Abraham stirred. His burning limbs swam in a warm pile of goo. He fought for his breath. Something squishy suffocated him, covering his mouth and nostrils.

What is this?

Abraham started to swim. He kicked and punched. He spat out something gooey. More rancid goo poured into his mouth.

Nooo!

Something hard was in his grip. His arms and legs were free. He wasn't strapped to a gurney anymore, but he was dying.

Black Bane, help me!

The fiery runes etched in the great longsword glowed. Abraham found himself in something like the body of a jellyfish. He grabbed the pommel of his sword with both hands and started hacking through the blubbery flesh with broad strokes. He carved up the alien body from the inside out. He sliced open a gap and felt fresh air hitting his face.

Freedom, oh sweet freedom!

He shoved his head out of the body. Huge octopod tentacles were all over. He couldn't tell if he was facing up or down. He was attached inside the strange thing.

What is this place? I feel like I am being born again!

Black Bane's light helped, but above and below him was only blackness.

"What kind of monster is this? Did I get eaten?" He squirmed farther from his captor, inching his body out one limb at a time, until he squirted out and fell into the black depths below. "Nooo…!"

CHAPTER 16

ABRAHAM HIT THE GROUND A split second later.

Thud!

He lay flat on his back, sword in hand, looking upward at a bulging hulk made of tentacles with eyeballs. It reminded him of the monster Elder they'd fought at Crown Island. It was a huge creeper but much smaller. It started rapidly sliding down the rock wall.

"Holy sheetrock!" He scrambled on all fours away from the descending sludge pile.

It hit the ground with a squish.

Abraham gasped. His legs were pinned underneath the bulging hulk. He pushed away from the slimy creature and, with a fierce grunt, finally freed his feet. Panting, he stood up on noodle legs and swayed. He used Black Bane as a crutch.

"Where am I?"

A tentacle with an eyeball coiled around his calf.

"Gah!" He chopped right through the tendril and jogged away. "Blazing saddles! It's still alive!"

With a shiver, Abraham limped farther away from the creeper. In seconds, the monster was gone from sight. He was on a cavern floor. A thousand feet above him was an eye of wide-open sky. *Looks like I'm in the Wound. I wonder what happened to everyone else.* He shivered. "Frosty the Snowman, why's it so cold?"

Step after step, he stumbled over the rises of the black canyon. He didn't hear another soul. The land was cold and barren. Slowly, his natural strength started to return. He moved at an easier gait and tried to remain quiet. He let Ruger's senses do the work.

I can't believe I'm back. Just like that. I wonder how Ruger is doing. He contemplated everything that had gone on in the last several hours. Dr. Jack and Eugene Drisk had revealed a lot. They had a way to get his family back… *Or do they?* He shook his head. *So far on this misbegotten adventure, anything seems possible. I have to end this. It's getting too crazy.*

He wandered—step after step, hour after hour. He had to be able to find the Henchmen. Certainly, they would be near. They had to be.

"Did you say something?"

"Huh," Abraham muttered aloud, noticing that the engravings in the sword's blade brightened when it spoke. "Is that you, Black Bane?"

"I don't think that is my name."

"No, that is the sword's name. You go by another name, but we don't know what that is yet."

"Hmm… did we kill that monster?"

"Yes, I think."

"Interesting. Who are you? You sound different than the other man I was speaking to. Ruger. I like him. You're that other fella. Softer, but serviceable."

"I'm Abraham, and I'm not soft. Are you freely talking with Ruger but not me?"

"We go further back. It's a well-established relationship. But I have some good news."

Abraham held the sword before his eyes, looked at the gently pulsating orange runes, and said, "I can't wait it hear it."

"You sound like someone that doesn't want to know."

"No, I want to know. I'm confused, though. So, you've been talking to Ruger recently?"

"I don't have the same concept of time that you do, but I've spoken with him thoroughly since the last time I talked with you."

"And?"

"I like Ruger Slade. He has the grit of old friends I can't remember, but I can see them like ghosts from the past. He said that I should help you."

"Wow, it sounds like a real game changer," he said sarcastically, recalling that the essence within Black Bane had been extremely unreliable. "So you weren't willing to help me before?"

"I admit, I had my suspicions. Now, if you were an ample woman, there would be no doubt about it. But some strange fellow that holds me by the handle, eh, I'm not warming to that."

"What difference does it make? You can't see."

"Who says I can't see? I can see. I just didn't tell you that I could. But of course I can. I have a strong intuition about things."

Abraham spun the sword in his palm and said, "In that case, can you help me find my friends?"

"Perhaps. Are there any ample women among them?"

Abraham started to say no but switched his thoughts and said, "Of course there are. Some of them are plump, others athletic, but all of them bosomy."

The engravings inside the sword blade flared the bright orange of a fire. *"Tell me more!"*

"Show me the way, and I'll tell you about the triplets."

"Did you say triplets?"

"Yup, and I hope you like piles of silky black hair cascading over heaving mounds of cleavage."

Black Bane moved under its own power, pulling Abraham briskly through the caverns.

"Whoa," Abraham said as he was practically jerked out of his boots. He tugged back on the sword and said, "Slow down. What are you, a dog in heat?"

"No—more like an old dog in heat. Come on, young fellow. We have vixens to fetch. Tell me more."

Restraining himself by giving more modest visual pictures, he accurately described Sophia, Selma, and Bridgett.

"Those are pretty names. I like them all. I can see them in my mind. Black. Red. White. The perfect trio. And you didn't marry any of them?"

"No, I've been married, but now I'm a widower. I had a son too."

"Hmm… I seem to think that I had a son. I'm not sure though. I sense your friends are near. Very near." The sword pulled Abraham at a quick pace then forced him to break into a jog. Finally, it stopped in place. *"Is this them?"*

Abraham moved toward a cluster of standing men. In the dim light given by the blade, he squinted and said, "Horace?"

It was Horace. He was standing like a statue, his body unmoving. He was with Bearclaw, Vern, Prospero, Skitts, Apollo, Tark, and Cudgel. Their limbs were frozen stiff, as if they had been marching in place and suddenly came to a stop. Abraham touched Horace on a cheek. It was frosted with ice and cold.

"No, no, don't be dead. You can't be dead. Not all of you."

CHAPTER 17

Abraham wiped the ice from Horace's eyes. The big man's eyeball twitched.

"Horace? Horace, are you alive?"

Horace's eye didn't move again.

Abraham placed his hand on the man's chest. He checked Horace's pulse on the wrist. He swore he felt a beat, but it was very slow. "What in the world could have done this?"

"I don't know. Are the women all right?"

"There aren't any women with this group." Abraham walked through the group, inspecting them all. Not a single one of them had a horrified or shocked expression. It was as if they'd been frozen in time. He waved his hand in front of Vern but got no reaction. "Can't you see them? I thought that you could see them."

"I can't see anything. I'm a sword. I don't have eyes."

"You said you could see."

"I can sense things as well as sight. I suppose it's another gift. Hmm."

"Hmm, what?" Abraham tried to take the extinguished torch out of Skitts's hand, but the Red Tunic's fingers were locked around it like a vise. "Do you sense any other people? There should be at least seven more from the group."

"I sense something."

As fate would have it, Skitts was carrying Abraham's backpack. He reached inside the pack and fished out a Zippo lighter. He popped the lid open and flicked the flint wheel. He got small sparks. "Come on." He shook the lighter and flicked it again.

A flame started. He lit the torch, which slowly caught fire. The flame grew, casting soft light over the rigid company.

"That's better. You said you sensed a presence. What sort of presence?"

The engravings in Black Bane cooled.

"Oh great. You're sleeping again just when I need you most. And not like the love song 'I Needed You Most' either. In more of a macho way."

Abraham scanned the area. Nothing was there but pitch-black beyond the torchlight's thirty-foot radius. The chill winds rustled his hair. He moved over to Horace and said, "Hey, big guy, can you hear me?"

"Of course he can… for now."

Abraham spun around, brandishing Black Bane. He peered into the blackness toward the sound of the voice. It was a woman's voice, low, wicked, and gravelly, like an old witch's.

"Show yourself," he demanded.

"What is your name?" the voice in the darkness said. It came from a different location, on the other side of the Henchmen.

He spun around and said, "Show yourself, and I'll tell you."

No reply came. He didn't hear a word.

He envisioned the Frights that he'd first encountered when he came to Titanuus. They were bony pink-eyed women with strands of wiry hair. "Did you do this to my friends, witch?"

"Don't insult me. I am no witch!" The voice darkened. "I am much, much more. What is your name, human?"

"Show yourself, and I will tell you. I think that is fair."

"You invade my territory and now give me orders? You fool of flesh and blood. I will end you…" Her voice was followed by a hiss and a soft rattle. "But I will honor your final request and show my face."

Abraham turned. The woman's voice had moved behind him. Something told him he should run. His knees should have been knocking, but they weren't. Ruger's body held fast. The sword warrior didn't fear anything.

With his heart pounding in his throat, he said, "I'm waiting."

Twenty feet ahead, a light shone on a face in the darkness. It was a woman, fair and beautiful. Her skin appeared radiant and lit up from within. He saw no body, only her beautiful face with haunting good looks.

In a seductive voice, she asked, "Do you like what you see?"

With icy breath and jaw hanging, he said, "Absolutely."

"Good." Her words wrapped around him like a warm blanket. "Now, tell me what your name is."

"Ruger, er… Abraham. Abraham Jenkins."

The face hovered in the darkness, moving gently side to side but coming no closer. "That is a strange name, Abraham Jenkins. But we like it."

"We?"

Another face appeared, just as pretty as the other. Both of them had long, flowing, illuminated white hair that moved as if it was floating in the inky depths of the ocean. "Yes, me and my sister."

They spoke as one but changed who was speaking between words and sentences. "Do you find us divine?"

He licked his lips and said, "Certainly. Can I see the rest of you?"

He lowered his guard, and his knees bowed. A cool, fragrant mist drifted through the air and coated his body like dew. His taut muscles started to relax.

"I can't wait to see you."

"Yes, I can't wait for you to see us either. We are called Duplii. We don't receive visitors like you very often." Duplii's heads came closer together. Like Siamese twins, they almost touched cheek to cheek. "Please, relax and let us welcome you to our home."

"That sounds like a good idea," Abraham replied. He'd completely forgotten about the Henchmen and everything else. He felt as though he was entering a spa of some sort. Swaying a bit, he said, "This is nice, but it's getting chilly. Do you have any blankets?"

"Of course we do." Duplii's exotic faces drifted apart, farther and farther.

Abraham's eyes danced between both of them. The mist coating him started to crystallize on his body. He felt as though he'd fallen into a blanket of snow.

"Are you ready to see us fully?" Duplii said.

"Y-yes," he muttered as a fiery warning started pricking in the dulled recesses of his brain.

Duplii's heads came back together and forward. His heavy eyes widened. Duplii's heads grew bigger the closer they came. They were twice as big as his. He didn't see the sensuous bodies that he expected either. Instead, he saw something else as he watched the heads rise.

"Oh no."

Duplii's heads were attached to the ends of fleshy strands. Those strands were attached to a monstrous hulk that towered twenty feet high. Its jaws were wide open and filled with rows of thousands of sharp teeth. An inky mist came out of its mouth, still covering Abraham like soft rain.

It was the most hideous thing Abraham had ever seen.

"Do you still think we are beautiful?" Duplii said.

"Absolutely not," Abraham muttered as he watched the great mouth full of slavering teeth descend upon him.

CHAPTER 18

Abraham's grip tightened on his sword, but he could not move. Duplii came closer. Each head was on either side of him. Their icy breath was on his cheeks.

"Relax," Duplii said as one, "this won't hurt a bit, Abraham. Soon, you will be one with us."

Ruger's hot blood started flowing. Abraham couldn't move a muscle. He could barely think. The nagging in the back of his head grew stronger. It had to be Ruger. *I'm trying. I'm trying. I can't think of anything. So tired. So comfortable.* His eyes slid over to the beautiful faces of the alien women. "You're so pretty," he mumbled, "but so mean."

"We are Duplii. Aren't we beautiful?" They kissed his cheeks with soft lips as cold as ice. "You are warm. Warm is delicious."

Abraham fought to keep his mind alert. His eyelids felt heavy as rainclouds. Suddenly, a thought struck him as he stared at the beautiful women.

Black Bane! Wake up! There are two voluptuous women out here! You are missing it!

Black Bane's engravings turned bright fireplace orange.

"Did you say voluptuous?"

With Black Bane's handle hot in his hand, Abraham's sword arm filled with new strength. He lashed out at Duplii's face on the right side of him. He cut the head off, clean through the tendril.

Duplii's monster jaws crashed down.

Abraham dove out of the way.

"No!" Duplii screeched. "You killed my sister! Nooo!"

"Where are these voluptuous women? I don't see any. I only see a monster."

Abraham crawled to his feet and took a swipe at the beast. It didn't have legs like a dragon. It moved on thousands of small black ciliary feet underneath its body. Black Bane took a hunk of flesh out of it. "So you can see! You said you would help me. Help me kill that thing?"

"I want to see the women."

Abraham backpedaled away from the charging monster.

"I swear it! I swear it, you will!"

"All right, you don't have to sound so strained about it. I'm only making a modest request. Let me see what I can do. Give me a moment."

Running backward, he said, "I don't have a moment."

Duplii might have been huge, but the titanic beast moved quickly. "You will die!" the woman's head said as it stretched out toward him. She spat black needles out of her mouth. "Die, Abraham, die!"

A ball of white-hot lightning appeared above them, lighting the canyon floor up for one hundred yards.

Duplii fixed her gorgeous eyes on the ball and asked, "What is that?"

"It ain't a snowball."

The great beast turned from Abraham and looked upward. It roared with its mouth wide open. A freezing mist spewed out.

The bowling-ball-sized globe of energy dropped inside the monster's mouth.

Duplii made a gulping sound and exploded from the inside out with a notable *kah-poom!*

Fleshy guts sprayed all over Abraham. He was covered in gory grit from head to toe.

"Did that work?"

"Like magic."

"Good. I'm going to sleep now. Don't you dare wake me up again without the company of ample women. I swear I won't help you."

Abraham wiped the slimy flesh away from his face and hair and said, "You got it." He flicked the slime onto the ground. "Yuck."

The torch burned in the distance.

He walked toward it. The Henchmen were slowly moving.

He broke into a jog. "Horace!"

The bearish man gave him a dumb look, lifted an eyebrow, and said, "Captain?"

"The one and only. What happened?" he said.

"We were searching for you. That mist fell over us. We didn't even take notice. The next thing I know, we were frozen." Horace rolled his jaw and clenched his fingers. "I see you are back."

"What do you mean?"

Vern walked over, stretching his arms and yawning. He said, "He means you aren't the same captain that we were hoping for. It's a dead giveaway in how you talk."

"Don't start, Vern," Horace warned.

"No, that's all right. So you're telling me that the old Ruger was back in this body?"

Horace nodded.

"You better believe it. He lifted our spirits out of the throes of doom," Vern said.

"We're on the same side, you know." Abraham eyeballed the group. "How is everyone else?"

"Limber again," Bearclaw commented as he swung his axe from side to side. "What happened to us?"

"I'll show you."

He led the way to the fallen hulk called Duplii. The beautiful faces had turned as hard as stone. The body was a ton of mush scattered like mashed potatoes on the cavern floor.

"That's what happened." He noticed everyone seemed downcast. "Look, we're getting closer to getting everything back to normal. I haven't failed you yet. I won't fail you now. Ruger won't either. Now, where are Sticks and the others?"

"We split up hours ago," Horace said.

"Well, wipe those frowns off of your faces, and let's go get them."

CHAPTER 19

The Henchmen were the best trackers in the land. Picking up the trail of Melris, Solomon, Sticks, and the others didn't take them long. Their prints showed well on the canyon floor. That led them inside the strange wormhole that was filled with natural light and warm and humid instead of cold.

Abraham and Horace led the way, but Cudgel and Tark scouted out front. The flooring inside the strange twenty-foot-high tunnel didn't leave any prints, but it went one way.

"So, what was it like to have the old Ruger back?" Abraham asked.

"No disrespect, Captain. I'd follow you into the Sea of Troubles if need be, but it was a good thing to have him back, even if for only a short time." Horace scratched his eyebrow. "I'm glad he still lives, however that be."

"Yeah, he's living, all right. Listen, there is a lot that we need to talk about, between us and when Ruger comes back." It had become natural to talk about Ruger as if he was a different person who hosted the same body. "And I'm assuming he will. Things are coming to a head. The people in my world are invading Titanuus. We have to stop it." He brought Horace up to speed on everything. Horace wasn't slow by any measure, but he always felt more comfortable telling it to Sticks. "No matter what happens to me, you have to warn King Hector. The sooner we get back to Kingsland, the better."

"You know I won't let you down. We won't let you down, you or Ruger." Horace grinned. "It's kind of exciting."

"What do you mean?"

"We'd been cast aside so long that we'd become insignificant. Now, well, the fate of the very world might rest on our shoulders. We can take it."

Vern caught up with them and said, "It all sounds like madness to me."

Horace gave Vern a disappointed look and opened his mouth to speak.

"But"—Vern lifted a hand—"I'm in sword deep. Ruger was here. He filled me in. I have a better grasp of the situation. We've got to win this." He put his hand on Abraham's arm and said, "If you ever doubted my sword before, doubt it no more. It's yours. For the king. For the Henchmen."

"You can be my wingman anytime?" Abraham said.

"What does that mean?" Vern said. "I don't have wings."

"It's a thing in my world. I'll explain later."

When they caught up with Cudgel, he was standing at a tunnel intersection that split off in at least twelve different sections. "I have no idea which one they took. There isn't a sign or anything. We always leave a sign. There is not one."

"Where's Tark?" Abraham asked.

"He's running along these ribs, looking for a sign." Cudgel cradled his club in his hands. His eyes scanned the ceiling. "This is a strange place. I don't like it. Watch this." He pressed his hand into the crud caked up on the tunnel wall, leaving an impression. A few seconds later, the impression was gone. "See. You can scrape it with a knife too. I see bone underneath. I think we are inside a living thing."

Tark came hustling back. His smoky eyes were wide, and he was holding a flat knife in his hand. "I found this. It belongs to Sticks. I'm sure of it." He flipped it up and caught it. "You know she never loses a knife."

"Show me," Abraham said.

Tark led them to the fifth tunnel and stepped inside. The tunnels were half as wide as the one they'd been walking in. "It was stuck in the way." He jabbed the knife in. "Like this."

The tunnel gently quavered underneath their feet.

"I hope that's a coincidence." Abraham stuck his sword in the ground, and the tunnel didn't shake. "Good. I'd hate to think I've been eaten again." He looked ahead. "That way."

"Captain, do you want to split up?" Horace suggested.

"No, splitting up the last time is what got us into this mess. You should have stayed with Melris." He eyed the company of men. "We'll talk about that later."

"A punishment is coming, eh?" Horace asked.

"One thing is for sure—no soup for you." He nodded at Tark. "Lead the way."

The farther they traveled, the more the walls dripped with humidity. Sweat dripped from their chins and splashed on the ground. They walked for an hour on a straight path without the slightest bend in the tunnel. They heard no other sounds among their quiet footsteps.

"Captain." Tark had stopped ahead in the tunnel and was holding another small knife in his hand. "Another one."

"At least we are on the right path." Abraham lifted his shoulders. "Keep rolling."

"Sticks doesn't leave her knives unless she's in some kind of trouble," Horace commented. "Methinks that something is wrong—very wrong."

"I know, but how is this any different than any other day. Tark, pick up the pace. The sooner we find the trouble, the sooner we can put an end to it." *I hope.*

The company moved on hour after hour, or so it seemed. Abraham couldn't tell. He had much on his mind during the droning march. He had been asked to betray the king and promised that he could go back to his family. All this madness could come to an end, and he could make that happen.

He looked at his men. Their faces were hard, filled with deep cracks, scars, and lines. Their hands were hard with calluses and as thick as leather. The Henchmen were something, the ultimate teammates. They did what they were told to do without question.

But there was another question. *Are we on the side of right or the side of wrong? After all, what kind of king would brand a man with a hot iron?* The zillon, Ottum, had gotten him thinking. Abraham gave all his men a careful study. Not one of them wouldn't pass for a hardened criminal.

What if—just what if—the king fooled me?

CHAPTER 20

TARK HURRIED BACK TO THE company, showing a smile of white teeth. "We found something." He cupped his ear. "Can you hear that?"

Abraham bent his ear toward the tunnel ceiling and asked, "Is that water?"

"Yes, there is a large stream that runs in the bowels of the world. But that is not all. You have to see this. Hurry." The warrior took off in long, graceful strides and raced up the tunnel.

"Really, we are running now?" Vern said. "I seriously doubt that the stream is going anywhere."

"A little run never hurt anyone. Henchmen, let's go." Abraham took the lead. He couldn't imagine what could have gotten Tark so excited, but it had his blood pumping too. The journey through the sweltering tunnel had been long enough. The time had come for a change.

Skitts raced up beside him. He sniffed the air. "I can smell them now."

"You can?" Abraham asked.

"I can smell like a bloodhound," Skitts added. "It was hard to smell inside this tunnel. These walls seem to absorb the stenches. It's weird."

"Well, follow your nose," Abraham said. "It always knows 'the flavor of fruit.'"

"What?" Skitts said.

"Nothing. I just had a hankering for a bowl of Froot Loops." He and the Henchmen caught up with Cudgel and Tark.

The black brothers stood on an overlook where the tunnel ended. A steep drop over one hundred feet down led into a forest.

"Whoa," Vern said as he leaned over the ledge. "Are you jesting? There is a giant forest in the middle of the dirt."

For as far as Abraham could see were miles of treetops, shrubs, and other greenery. The cavern went on for miles, possibly leagues. The ceiling of the cavern was speckled with crystalline rocks that glowed like stars. The gargantuan cavern was still dim, but the rocks cast light similar to moonlight. The loud rush of water caught his ears. A smaller river was snaking its way through the underground forest away from them.

"Huh, looks like we are going down. Watch out for dinosaurs and underlings."

The Henchmen climbed down the steep incline with boots slipping and sliding over the wet rocks. Within a few minutes, they made it to the bottom of the forest floor.

A mix of oak and maple, the trees stood thirty to fifty feet high. Many of them had white bark, like dogwood. Their leaves were mostly green, with some maroon and yellow. Small forest critters jumped through the trees' branches. Tiny black birds flew in small flocks from one tree to another.

Abraham squatted beside an orange mushroom as tall as his knee. "That's worth some money." He turned his head and found Tark. Tark and Cudgel were on their hands and knees, running their fingers through the dirt. "Any sign of our friends?"

Tark nodded. "We have prints a blind man could follow." He pointed up the river. "That way."

"What about you, Skittles?" he asked. "Do you smell any trouble?"

"Solomon's scent lingers the strongest. I could find him a mile away. I am smelling plants and the dirt. It's heavy. But I don't smell any other people. I'd have to be in contact with them before I smelled them."

Abraham looked down at the tracks Cudgel had pointed out. "I don't see any other tracks. Just theirs." He looked up and down that path. "Do you?"

"No signs of duress," Tark said. "They move—they move quick."

"What are you thinking, Captain?" Horace asked.

"I'd think there would be trouble down here. It doesn't seem right that we can waltz right down here without any trouble."

Vern cleared his throat and said, "If people live down here, I don't think they'd get many visitors. Who else would come down here if you didn't have to?"

"Good point, but don't take any chances." Abraham drew his sword. "From here on out, we stay close. Let's move."

The deeper the company went, the more Abraham worried about getting out. He'd been spelunking before, when he was younger, and didn't like it. The mere thought of being hundreds of feet below ground and getting trapped left a sinking feeling in his stomach.

Tark and Cudgel led them alongside the stream. The banks were sandy, and the stream appeared shallow. Fish with glowing scales swam quickly underneath the waters. In groups, the fish would follow the company upstream, stop and face them, then move after them.

"Perhaps we should refill our canteens, Captain," Horace suggested. "After that walk in those tunnels, my whistler has become dry as a tomb bone."

The group had walked for hours without taking a drink. Abraham realized he was parched the moment Horace mentioned it. He stepped out to the edge of the water and filled his nostrils with the freshwater air. Then he scooped his hand into the cool waters and sipped. "It's no wonder trees grow down here. Their roots are sucking up this refreshing water." He swallowed some more. "Everyone fill up."

Apollo and Prospero kneeled down and scooped handfuls of water into their mouths. Bearclaw refilled two water skins. Horace and Vern drank straight from the stream.

The fish floated in the stream, facing the men in separate schools.

Abraham eyed them. "Either they don't like us drinking their water, or they are the nosiest fish I ever saw."

"They look delicious to me. Perhaps we need to do some fishing. I wouldn't mind a bite," Skitts said. He rinsed his face off in the surging waters. "I'm hungry."

Horace waded deeper into the waters, eyeing a small school of glowing fish. He held his spear over the waters. "There's nothing like fresh fish meat. These look particularly delicious."

Schools of hundreds of fish surrounded Horace. Abraham's eyes widened as a tingle ran through his bones. "Horace," he muttered.

Horace stabbed into the stream. An unseen force pulled him under.

Abraham shouted, "Horace!"

CHAPTER 21

Abraham dove into the spot where Horace had submerged. The fish swarmed him and latched onto his body with sucking mouths. In seconds, he was covered by dozens of them. He fought through the fish, searching for Horace. The fish had latched onto the warrior and dragged him toward a deep cave. Abraham swam after the man.

Horace thrashed underneath the deep waters, jabbing his spear wildly through the murk. He let the spear go and ripped the fish away from his body.

The fish latched onto Abraham's arms and legs guided him deeper into the water's black hole. *Madness! They are pushing me into the cave!*

Horace hit the bottom of the black pit. Bones of men and armor were resting on the stream's deep floor. Bubbles burst out of his mouth. He grabbed a fish and bit its head off.

Abraham reached out and hooked Horace underneath the arms. He tried to swim upward, but the fish forced him down. Bigger fish that did not glow swam out of dark holes. They were bigger than a man's head and had black scales and rings of blue stripes. They had mouths and teeth like piranhas' but were far bigger. He punched one away.

Horace shoved up from the ground. The glowing fish pushed him back down again.

Abraham held his breath, which burned in his chest. Above him, the glowfish formed a blanket in the waters. When he swam up, they pulled him down.

Horace ripped off a piranha that had latched onto his flesh. He choked on water and spasmed.

Warm blood flowed in the inky stream. Horace's eyes rolled into his head.

Abraham's mind screamed, *Nooo!* He locked onto Horace and pushed upward. The fish swam him back down. He was trapped. *This can't be. It can't be!* He gawked at the umbrella ceiling of glowing fish. They'd sealed them inside a watery grave and prepared for the feast.

Skitts burst through the barrier of fish with his arms stretched out. Covered in the glowfish, he plunged deep and grabbed hold of Abraham. Suddenly, like an anchor being pulled out of the waters, he, Horace, and Skitts were being pulled free of the fish trap.

Abraham held onto the beefy Horace for dear life. They burst through the ceiling of scales and were lifted through the waters. Underneath the waters, Bearclaw was latched onto Skitts's ankles, Vern had Bearclaw, and so on. They pulled Abraham and Horace into the shallow waters on the bank. Abraham gasped for air.

The fish jumped up and down in the waters like salmon during the spawning season.

Abraham rolled Horace onto his back. The spearman had turned blue. Abraham started chest compressions. "Don't you die on me, Horace. Don't you die! What kind of man dies at the hands of a little fish?"

"More like a thousand cuts," Vern said. He lifted Horace's limp arm. Jagged bite marks covered Horace's hands. "What did you run into down there, a wolverine?"

"Wolverines don't swim." Abraham kept pumping Horace's chest. "It was some sort of piranha. I have no idea what you would call them in this world."

"A fish that eats flesh—I've never heard such a thing." Cudgel leaned over Horace. "He is dead, isn't he?"

Horace spat a mouthful of water into Cudgel's face and started coughing.

Cudgel wiped his face and grinned. "I knew that would wake him up. He hates being called dead. Horace is a stubborn man."

Blinking his eyes, Horace said, "Captain, those are some tricky fish. I will kill them all. Where is my spear?"

Tark walked up with Horace's big spear in his hands. "It's all secure." One fish flapped its tail on the end of the spear. "It comes with dinner."

Horace chuckled.

Abraham slapped Horace on the back and helped his friend up to his feet. "I guess those fish were fishing for us."

Blood dripped from his arms into the waters. Minnow-sized fish darted into the shallows and sucked up the blood.

"Let's get moving."

For another hour, they walked in a single column farther away from the stream, where the grass stood ankle high. The trail of Sticks, Melris, and the others was still fresh. It appeared that they hadn't been dumb enough to venture into the waters.

The stream dropped off a cliff, creating a waterfall that crashed down onto rocks another fifty feet below. It formed an underground lake over a mile in diameter. Deer with white skins and black horns drank from the cool waters.

Tark led the climb down the rocks toward the lake.

The deer sprang away.

"I don't understand how life can live without sunlight. How can there be beasts such as this in the belly of Titanuus?" Horace said. "Bats and bugs, maybe, but living creatures?"

Abraham descended to the bottom, keeping his toes away from the lake waters. The rest of the Henchmen climbed down alongside the cascading falls.

Tall reeds and cattails surrounded the lake. The surrounding grasses stood the height of wheat. Abraham could see a new path where the grasses were pushed down.

He caught up to Tark. "Still them, huh?"

"Yes, but this path is well worn. I think it's a path used to fetch water and fish. Look." He pointed at the lake. "There are other footprints, not like deer but a two-toed man."

Abraham took a close look at the impressions in the mud. Each was a large footprint with two big toes and one smaller, like a thumb.

Cudgel put his hand in the print. "I've never seen tracks like this. Whatever it is is very heavy." He eyed more footprints. "They are very heavy, like a bull."

The beating of tom-tom drums carried over the strange valley.

Toom-tah-tah. Toom-tah-tah. Toom-tah-tah. Toom-tah-tah.

Pungent black smoke drifted into Abraham's nose. Somewhere, flesh was burning.

Skitts sniffed and said, "I can't say for sure, but that's either animal or people."

A shrill cry carried over the tall trees.

"That's my brother! That's Zann!"

CHAPTER 22

Skitts raced down the path toward the wailing sound of pain. The stalking man moved as if his head was on fire. Up one rise he went and down the next.

Abraham and the Henchmen gave chase. If Zann was in trouble, the others would be too. Abraham thought about Sticks. She'd been imprisoned and tortured enough before. He couldn't bear to see it. *Not again!*

The path led them downward to a clearing where several bonfires were spread out over the grounds. Stout men squatted around the flames. They had bald heads, large protruding ears, and big eyes. Their squat heads rested right on the neckless men's shoulders. Barrel-chested and thick thewed, they fanned the flames with big, long, thick fleshy fingers, their thumbs matching their feet.

Other strange men faced a great stone statue standing over forty feet high. Some of the men pounded the drums in a steady beat.

Toom-tah-tah. Toom-tah-tah. Toom-tah-tah. Toom-tah-tah.

The statue appeared to have been cut from limestone, like something one would see in the Aztec pyramids. A large ugly face made the head. One eye burned bright red and the other bright orange inside their sockets. A wheel made up of stone hands slowly spun in the middle of its stone body. Inside those hands were Sticks, Solomon, Iris, Dominga, and Zann. All their arms were pinned to their sides. The pinwheel of arms was slow-roasting them over a huge wooden bonfire.

Zann passed over the flames with his tail end smoking. Sticks was the next in line to pass over the flaming pyre.

"Yaaah!" Skitts screamed with his sword raised over his head.

The Henchmen descended on the corded men like a crashing wave.

Skitts brained the first neckless hulk with his sword.

The neckless brood came to life. They snatched up flaming logs in their great hands and attacked from all directions.

"Tark! Get that wheel stopped!" Abraham ordered. "Henchmen, clear a path! Mow these suckers down!"

He uncorked Black Bane with a lethal swing. The blade sank into the side of one creature's chest. It made the sound of an axe chopping wood. No blood spurted out. An inky smoke oozed out as it clutched at Abraham. He split its face open, and it fell away.

"Keep hacking."

Horace gored a monster on the end of his spear and flung it into the fire.

Vern sliced off their groping hands.

Bearclaw brutalized them with his double-bladed battle-axe. With thunderous overhead chops, he turned the creatures into firewood.

"What in Titanuus's Crotch are these things?" Cudgel cried. He popped a black bully in the head, sending hard chips of its skin flying. Then he stuck his boot in its chest, shoved it away, and hit another. "They are made of rock and wood."

"Slay the granite men!" Horace roared. He rammed his spear through two of the men at once, and smoke bled out of their bodies. He charged into them, pushing them backward one step at a time. With a final heave, he shoved them into a flaming pyre. "Burn the granite men!"

Abraham fought his way toward the wheel over the flames. Tark and Skitts plowed into a knot of the granite men. Their swords rose and fell on the chunky bodies, splintering away the fleshlike bark. The swords chopping into wooden bodies did less damage than the hollow sounds seemed to indicate. The King's Steel started to stick in the odd flesh. The granite men piled onto the Henchmen.

Sticks shouted out from above, "Get this wheel stopped! With every turn, we hold over the flames longer!"

"Henchmen! To the wheel! To the wheel!" Abraham shouted and barreled into the cluster of granite men battling Tark and Skitts. He busted Tark out of the swarm and said, "Stop that thing!"

"Aye, Captain!" Tark squirted out of the pack and began his climb up the statue.

Abraham landed one flashing stroke after another. Skitts slid in behind him. The rest of the Henchmen converged on the wheel. They formed a semicircle in front of the bonfire at the bottom of the wheel.

"How do you turn this thing off?" Skitts shouted to his brother.

"I don't know. Put the bloody fire out!" Zann yelled back.

"With what?" Skitts asked.

"Find a bucket or something!" Zann said.

"Ruger, hurry up!" Solomon said. "Sticks is going to die! She was first on the turn. This next one will be the longest!"

The flames licked upward at Sticks's clothing as she descended closer to the flames, gradually moving down from the five o'clock position to six. Her lips drew back, and she turned her red-hot face but didn't scream.

"Burn my biscuits," Abraham muttered. Only one thing could stop the flames from cooking her alive. "Horace, I'm going in!"

"In where?" Horace replied.

"The woodpile! It's the only way to knock those flames down!" Abraham turned and faced the flames. "Blazing saddles, away I go!" He jumped toward the flames.

Horace caught Abraham by the collar and hauled him back. "No, I'm bigger than you." Like a bull in a china shop, he plowed into the flames. He busted into the piles of wood logs and hot coals and ash. He made it halfway to the middle when the flames suddenly dropped. Horace stopped as well. The suffocating flames started to consume him.

Abraham shouted, "Death before failure!" and rushed into the inferno.

CHAPTER 23

ABRAHAM PUSHED DEEP INTO THE searing inferno and plowed into Horace. The white-hot flames scorched the hairs on his body. He thrust forward, shoving Horace toward the other side of the pyre. Suddenly, a great weight plunged into his back.

Over the roaring flames, he could hear men screaming, "Death before failure!"

The Henchmen rammed their bodies through the logs and shoved Abraham and Horace through one side and out the other.

The burning heap collapsed.

Bearclaw and Vern jumped on Horace and patted out the flames.

Abraham coughed as he caught his breath. He smelled like a stick of burning hair. The rest of him seemed okay. He wasn't sure why that was, but he had bigger problems. The granite men continued to swarm on the other side of the flames. They started chucking logs at the Henchmen.

Vern and Bearclaw doused Horace with the water from their skins. The beefy man's beard was smoking, and his forearms were red with blisters.

Sticks dangled from the stone hand that held her fast. Her body hung limp. Sweat dripped from her chin onto the ground. Panting, she locked eyes with Abraham and said, "Thank you."

Apollo, Prospero, and Cudgel kept the hordes at bay. Both Apollo and Prospero battled with a longsword in each hand. They blocked the granite men's flanking advances with the wall of flame between them.

Cudgel defended the other side of the collapsed bonfire. With tremendous overhead swings, he bashed one skull after another.

"Are you going to get up," Vern asked Horace, "or lie there while your chestnuts roast?"

"I can fight!" Horace stood with the help of Bearclaw and Vern. He glanced up. "Hello, everyone. Where is my Iris?"

"I'm here, you big fool! Quit doing stupid things and burning yourself alive," Iris said.

"Why do you say that? I always thought you like your buns toasted," Horace replied.

Tark flagged Abraham down from the stone statue. "I locked the wheel!"

"Find out how to get them out of those stone mitts!" he shouted back.

Skitts had climbed onto the wheel. He hung on the same arm that held his brother Zann. His hands rummaged over the stone hand. "How do you unlock this?"

"You don't unlock it. This thing is real," Zann said. "These fingers move with life of their own."

"Solomon, where is Melris?" Abraham said.

"He left us!" Solomon yelled back. "We haven't seen him since we were captured by those things."

The ground trembled. *Thoooom!*

"What was that?" Abraham asked, peering toward the direction of the sound. Over the flames, he saw a gargantuan granite man walking their way. It stood over thirty feet tall. "Oh, it looks like Daddy is coming home for dinner."

Thoooom! The heavy footsteps came down like thunder. *Thoooom! Thoooom!*

The smaller granite men backed off. They formed a semicircle on the ground, facing the giant granite man, and bowed down. On their hands and knees, they rose up and down and made worshipful moans.

"Look, it's Melris!" Vern said.

Melris was riding on the shoulder of the giant granite man. One hand held on to an ear, and the other hand held his Rod of Devastation.

The giant stopped in front of its group of worshippers and scanned the dead on the ground. In a cavernous voice, he said, "They killed my children! Why did they kill my children?"

From his perch, Melris looked down at Abraham and asked, "Yes, why did you attack Osgard's children? We were in the middle of negotiations."

"Really?" Abraham said. "You were in the middle of negotiations while our people were roasting like marshmallows."

"I was almost finished. Osgard *the Elder* and I struck a deal." Melris gave Abraham a nod that seemed to signify that he really needed to be paying attention to this. "A very favorable deal."

"No deal!" Osgard the Elder said.

"What?" Melris replied. "Osgard, don't let this misunderstanding disrupt our negotiations. The very fate of the world is on the line."

"No one is going to come down here. I don't care. No deal," Osgard said with heavy breath. "You've invaded my home. Slain my children. Now, you must make the sacrifice." He held out two monstrous fingers and thumb. "Crush them, my totem. Crush them all!"

Twila and Zann let out pained cries. Solomon let out a grunt.

Dominga cried out, "This thing is squeezing us to death!"

"Make it stop, Melris! Make it stop now!" Abraham ordered.

"I'm sorry, but it appears that Osgard has made his mind up. There won't be any changing it now until blood is shed," Melris replied. "Osgard, will those people be a suitable sacrifice? Can we have the stones after that?"

"No," Osgard said.

"Sorry," Melris replied.

"You snake!" Twila yelled. "Ugh… my bloody bones are cracking!"

Skitts tried to pry back the fingers locked around his brother. Zann screamed with anguish.

Abraham started to climb up the stone statue. He found a landing and started chopping at the wrist of the hand crushing Sticks. "Hang on! Melris! Do something now, or I swear, I'll cut your head off!"

The purple-clad Melris nodded. "Yes, yes." He stuck his iron rod inside Osgard's head like a Q-tip and said, "Osgard, are you sure that you won't change your mind?"

With his dark eyes intent on the men and women being crushed, the Elder said, "Nooo."

"I see," Melris replied. "You give me no choice." His purple robes billowed out from an unseen wind. His hand and eyes glowed with raspberry fire. A blast of angry flames shot through one side of Osgard's head and out the other.

Osgard's minions cried out. The Elder swayed. His head smoked out of both ears, and his eyes rolled up in his head. He spoke with black smoke pumping like a chimney stack out of his mouth, saying, "Elderling, you will pay for this."

Melris feather walked down the Elder's falling body to the ground.

Osgard fell flat on his back. His minions died at his feet.

CHAPTER 24

The Henchmen pried their own kind free from the stone statue's grip. Sticks rubbed her ribs as she was lowered back to the ground. "Abraham?" she asked as he assisted her.

"Yeah, I'm back," he said.

Sticks put her arms around him and gave him a warm hug. "I'm glad. I thought that you might have been gone forever."

"Well, look at you, getting all weepy on me."

"Just because you've rubbed off on me doesn't mean that my heart will break without you." She jabbed him in the ribs. "I'm a survivor. I think you know that."

"Yeah, I love you too."

Solomon dropped his big paws onto Abraham's shoulders and reeled him in for a bear hug. "I thought that was it. I couldn't help but wonder if I was ever going to see a Dairy Queen again. Glad you're back."

"Whew," Abraham said. "Me too, sort of. Man, your fur stinks."

"I got toasted, but my fur is very resistant to fire. Remember the barn?" Solomon said. "Troglins can be cooked, but it ain't easy."

"Yeah, well, I think that goes for all of us." He glanced at Horace. Even though the big man wasn't in the flames long, he still should have been roasted.

Melris approached with his iron rod cradled in his hand. "You bear the brand. Did you not know that it makes you resistant to fire?"

Sticks lunged at Melris and punched him in the face.

Melris fell flat on his butt. His eyes widened when he found a dagger pressed against his neck.

"I wonder: do you bleed purple, Elderling?" Sticks said.

"There is one way to find out," Melris replied.

"You've got some explaining to do," Abraham said. "You left our men in the lurch."

"No harm had been done until your arrival. Besides, I knew you could handle the fires. I'm really surprised that you didn't know that," Melris added.

"I'd like to find out how fireproof you are," Twila said. The pie-faced mystic kicked Melris in the back. "'Cause those flames sure felt real to me!" She tried to kick him again, but Horace pulled her back.

"We need to secure the stones instead of bickering," Melris said, "The sooner we leave, the more likely we all get out of the Wound alive. You don't think we are going to be able to walk right out of here, do you? Osgard isn't the only Elder in the canyon. There are more."

"Then get your magic wand ready, and be prepared to blow more wax out of their earholes. But I'll tell you this, I've had my fill of Elders for the day. Including Elderlings." Abraham looked at Tark, who was standing on top of the statue. "Get those stones out of the eyeholes and toss them down here."

With a nod, Tark climbed down the giant golem's face and peered inside the eye socket emanating red light. "I don't mean to disregard an order, but is this burning stone safe to touch?"

Melris nodded and told Abraham, "He will be fine. It takes a mystic's touch or royal blood to activate the magic within."

Abraham opened his hands. "Toss it down. According to the purple wizard, you should be just fine. Let's get a look at those Easter eggs."

Tark reached inside the eye socket and pulled out the gem. He held the burning red stone between his thumb and index finger. "This little stone makes a big light." The fire went out. "Or it did make a big light."

Some sort of big bird flew overhead.

Abraham and the others looked up. Something was flying above them. It wasn't alone, either.

"Let's speed it along, Tark," Abraham said.

The other socket that glowed orange cooled. Tark reached inside and grabbed the gem. He held it out for all to see.

"Catch," he said and tossed the stones down.

A black hawk dove from above toward the falling stones.

A crossbow bolt fired. *Clatch-zip.*

The bolt ripped through the big bird's chest. It crashed into the statue just as Abraham caught the stones in midair.

More flapping and fluttering stirred the air above them in the darkness. Echoing squawking began.

"Let's move out, Henchmen," he ordered. "Unless you want to stick around and find out what else wants to eat us."

The Henchmen grabbed their gear, formed two single columns, and followed Tark and Dominga as they always did. With the great birds *ka-caw*ing and squawking and diving at their heads, they ran faster.

Up one rise and down another, they made it to the waterfall and scaled the rocks. Abraham made sure every man made it up. Apollo and Prospero brought up the rear.

The company raced by the stream, covering their heads from the diving hawks. Solomon swatted several of them out of the air. Finally, they made it back into the sweltering tunnels that appeared to be made out of bone. The black hawks did not follow them in, so they slowed to a trot.

A few hours later, they crawled out of the tunnels and back into the icy air of the canyon floor. Melris urged Abraham to stop.

"What?" Abraham asked.

"Now would be a good time to summon your dragon," the Elderling said.

"Why?"

He pointed up at the open sky of the canyon, where daylight showed one thousand feet above. "The Elders will let us pass in the presence of the Elder Spawn. Otherwise, they will try to kill us. For none that enter the Wound have ever lived to escape."

With the chill winds rustling his charred head of hair, Abraham said, "I'm starting to think that your precious Elders aren't gods—they are monsters. Besides, I've already killed one on the way down, some two-headed chick that called herself Duplii."

Melris's eyes grew. "Duplii is dead?"

"Deader than the last guy we killed." He patted his sword on his hip. "You can thank Black Bane for that. He's cooperating now. Oh, that reminds me." He took off his sword belt. "Iris, come here."

Iris hustled over. "Yes."

"I need you to hold my sword," he said to the amply built woman. "Cradle him like a baby."

Iris gave him a funny look and said, "Yes, if you say so."

"Captain," Horace said, "We best hustle out of here while we have light in the sky."

Abraham smiled. "No, we're gonna stroll out of here, 'cause we own this place."

CHAPTER 25
THE HOUSE OF STEEL

After several long days of travel, the Henchmen arrived back in Kingsland. Abraham and Melris were immediately escorted to the House of Steel by the King's Guardians within an hour of crossing the border.

As usual, they were led through the shining gates of the grand castle that overlooked the Bay of Elders.

The Guardian Commander, Pratt, greeted both of them inside the gate. The oversized man appeared like a giant in his full-plate armor, towering above both men. "You are too unsightly to stand in the presence of the king. Couldn't you have washed up first?"

Abraham looked at his bare arms. The fish bites were scabbed over. Blisters were covered in caked blood and dirt. He eyed Pratt and said, "If you'd like to draw me a bath and bathe me, then have at it."

Pratt snorted. "Come along. Be sure to stay downwind of the king and queen. You reek." He led them up to the large terrace located on the back of the castle, which overlooked the Bay of Elders, the same place where Abraham had first met the king. "Wait here."

"We will, but if you could, will you check with the dry cleaners and see if my tuxedo is ready?"

Pratt sneered at him as he moved up to the upper patio and disappeared through the double door leading inside.

Abraham sat on the edge of the wall overlooking the sea. Hundreds of ships were in the bay, many more than before. He soaked up the sea wind while letting the sun shine on his face. It wasn't home, but being back at King Hector's castle felt good for some reason.

Melris dropped his hood. The ocean winds rustled his fair head of hair. "Four down and only two left to pursue. Impressive."

"Yeah, well, we still have to figure out where the other two are." Abraham fished the stones out of his pocket. The ruby and blazing orange gemstones sparkled in the sunlight. "What sort of special fire do these jewels have? Or do you know?"

"Not all their properties are fully known, but they do reveal themselves to the bearer. They do have names, however. The emerald is the Stone of Truth. The blue sapphire is the Stone of Lightning. The ruby you hold is the Stone of Blood, the orange the Stone of Power. That leaves the yellow amber as the Stone of Piety and the white diamond the Stone of Cleansing. All as one, though, can make chaos or harmony. When the king has them all, he'll be the most powerful person in Titanuus."

"Even greater than the Elders?"

"They aren't persons, but one could make a strong case for that." Melris gazed toward the horizon beyond the sea. "I only hope that King Hector can control this great power. After all, there was a reason why they were split up before."

Abraham thought about the zillon Ottum's warning about King Hector. *I hope I'm not creating another monster.*

Pratt returned, escorting Queen Clarann and Princess Clarice. The women hustled Abraham's way. Queen Clarann looked gorgeous in a short yellow dress the color of sunflowers. Princess Clarice wore the cuirass of a Guardian Maiden. Her long hair was pulled back in a ponytail, and her beautiful eyes were as bright as ever. Both women covered their noses.

"I know—I reek," Abraham said as he dumped the stones back in their pouch. He bowed and moved downwind. "It's wonderful to lay eyes on the both of you again. You both look beautiful."

"Tell me what you fought!" Clarice said as she bounced on her toes. "I want to know everything. I should have been there."

Abraham touched the young woman's chin and said, "I'll tell you everything. Perhaps we can go back to Stronghold. No doubt your fellow Henchmen would love to fill you in."

"You look like a burning behemoth spat you out," Queen Clarann said.

"I feel like it too."

"Are you well? You look grave," the queen said.

"Nothing some soap and suds won't cure." He clasped the queen's hand and gave her a knowing look. "All is well."

The queen lifted her eyebrows.

Prince Lewis and Leodor stepped out onto the patio. King Hector came behind them. The dark-headed prince's black cape rustled in the winds. The wizened Leodor's hands were hidden in the large sleeves of his robes. King Hector stood tall. The bend in his back was gone. Some red had returned to his white beard. He wore a stately suit of black robes trimmed in gold. The Crown of Stones rested tightly on his brow, pinching the skin as if it were grafted to his head.

The king's black garb sent a chill through Abraham.

King Hector threw up an arm and said, "Please, come sit! All of us." He gestured toward a table that held pitchers of wine and glass goblets. Diced fruit, cheeses, and crackers were spread out on platters on the table. "I can't wait to hear about all your adventures in the Wound."

After the queen and princess seated themselves on the right side of the king, Prince Lewis sat on the left. Abraham took a seat at the end of the table, leaving only Melris and Leodor between them.

"Why so far away, Abraham Jenkins?"

"I'm afraid my smell might make you retch."

King Hector let out a hearty laugh. He slapped Lewis on the back and said, "Now, that is a champion if there ever was one." His light tone became more serious. He lifted an eyebrow and shot Abraham a lustful look. "The stones. Do you have them?"

CHAPTER 26

ABRAHAM PASSED THE TWO STONES to Melris, who passed them to Leodor, who gave them to Lewis, who handed them to the king.

King Hector's eyes filled with the color of the sparkling stones. He licked his moustache and removed his crown. Two of the six horns were filled with gems. The blue stone was in the back and the green stone in the front. The king rolled the new stones in his hands, one in each. "I feel the life in them. They are excited. It's as if they are a family being reunited."

"The annals tell of the stones having their own unique essences," Leodor stated. The chinless man continued, "Essences that can be quite persuasive."

Abraham noticed a look of concern growing on Queen Clarann's face. She swallowed, reached down, and held her daughter's hand. Her eyes slid over to Abraham, but she quickly looked away.

King Hector clicked the new stones into the open clawlike prongs in the front of the crown. Left to right, the stones were red, green, and orange, with the blue one in the back. Each precious gem caught the sunlight and twinkled.

"It's magnificent, Father," Lewis said with a nod. "There is nothing that compares to it."

"And to think that it isn't even complete. Imagine how radiant it will be when all of the stones are put back in place," King Hector said. He lifted the crown and placed it back on his head.

A sudden wind whooshed over the terrace. The winds rustled King Hector's beard, enhancing a momentary wild look of power in his eyes.

Abraham shielded his face with his hand until the high wind died down. He grabbed a goblet of wine, filled it up from a carafe, and drank. *I got a bad feeling about this.*

As the windy stirrings at the table settled, King Hector eyeballed Abraham and said, "An excellent idea, my otherworldly friend. A toast! Everyone, grab a goblet. We've much to celebrate." He clenched a fist. "Victory is within *my* grasp!"

"Hear! Hear!" Lewis said.

Leodor echoed the sentiment.

Even Melris took up a goblet and sipped.

Abraham found Melris's actions odd because he'd never seen the Elderling eat anything. He felt eyes on him. Queen Clarann's wary eyes were on him again. He needed to talk to her about Ruger Slade, but for now, that would have to wait.

King Hector guzzled down a goblet and refilled another. "I feel so spry. Like the days of my youth when I hunted the great elk with nothing but a knife and a spear. I yearn to fill my hands with steel again and take it to my enemies." He hefted up the goblet. Red wine sloshed over the rim. "Another toast, to Abraham and Melris. Your aid came in the nick of time."

Neither Lewis nor Leodor spoke this time. Instead, the queen and princess offered their own "Hear! Hear!"

Abraham looked at Lewis and Leodor, the most discontent of all Henchmen. *I see someone still has a bug up their butt.*

"Tell me all that I need to know and more if need be," the king said as he looked between Abraham and Melris.

Melris opened his mouth.

Abraham cut him off. "Your Highness, we cut a bloody path from here to the Wound and back. We journeyed into the belly of the deep. Elders rose up, and now they are dead. All the Henchmen survived. Two stones were recovered. That's the CliffsNotes version. But there are more important matters at hand that need to be attended to."

King Hector nodded. "Yes, of course, we need to find the other stones. Leodor has been neck deep in the libraries, searching for their location. Certainly, it's not a priority."

"No, that's not it." Abraham took a breath. This was the part where he had to decide to tell the truth or not about his being able to go back in time and see his family. All he had to do was convince King Hector to stand down. "It's about the invaders. They are going to come hard and fast. But they have an offer."

King Hector sat up in his chair, put his hands on the table, and leaned over. "I beg your pardon? Have you been consorting with the enemy?"

Lewis jumped up out of his chair, jabbed a finger at Abraham, and said, "I told you that he was a traitor. We should have killed him long ago."

"Melris, do you know anything about this?" the king asked.

"This is news to me," Melris said quietly. "But in Abraham's defense, I do not recall him consorting with any of the king's enemies. Any enemy we crossed, he killed, or we killed, rather."

With a wave of his hand, the king said, "Sit down, Lewis."

Lewis plopped into his chair.

King Hector rolled his hand and said, "Out with it."

"As you know, my essence has been switching between this world and my world on occasion. It is in my world that the enemy created a rift, or dimension door, between my home and yours. They are making great strides controlling a portal or, as they call it, a Time Tunnel. I have seen it with my own eyes, and they are sending powerful artillery the likes that you and your armies have never seen.

"I'm sure you recall the weapon that the zillon dragon riders used to try and assassinate you with. It's called an assault rifle. They shipped hundreds of them, perhaps thousands of them, and are giving them to the Gond and whoever else. There is a weapon called a tank. It's a chariot made out of solid metal and bigger than elephants. It has a nose that fires a missile that would blow a hole clear through any side of this castle. That's just the beginning. There will be more—much, much more. They can't be stopped."

Everyone at the table paled except the king. He rubbed a finger over his chin and said, "We'll see about that."

CHAPTER 27

"THEY WANT ME TO MAKE a deal with you," Abraham said.

"A deal?" King Hector huffed a laugh. "Who wants to make a deal?"

"The men on the other side. My world. Dr. Jack Lassiter. Colonel Drew Dexter. Eugene Drisk. He's the man that used to inhabit this body before me. You see, the military in my world created the rift, and now, well, they want to take up full occupancy here."

"Why do they want to come here? Is your world so bad?" Queen Clarann asked.

Abraham scratched the scruff on the side of his jaw and said, "Something like that. My world has a lot of pleasures and conveniences that this world doesn't offer. That's not enough for some. They think they can do better. They want a new frontier to conquer, so to speak."

The king straightened up in his chair and said, "You tell them the next time you see them that this king will never surrender. I say we find this tunnel and we take their world by force." He slammed his fist on the table. "I'll invade them!"

"They don't have the process mastered. They can send weapons and other vehicles over, but they can't send people. It's this essence swap that they need control of." Abraham poked his finger on the table. "There is still time to put a stop to it. We only need to find out where their lair is, and we know that it is in the Spine, but that is all."

"This is outrageous." Lewis gestured toward Abraham. "This fool barters with our enemies, who we haven't even seen, and now he is negotiating on their behalf. He's making up stories, Father."

"No, he's not," the king said. "This otherworlder has done nothing but serve with honor. And he bears the brand. You cannot betray the crown without consequences." He nodded. "There he sits, a true Guardian of Kingsland."

Lewis shook his head.

"I only want what is best for both worlds," Abraham continued. "Even if that means that I don't make it back home. I do think there are more problems than the oncoming invasion that you need to be warned about."

"It gets worse?"

"Apparently, there are more otherworlders like me. They are already working with the people on the other side. Part of that is the Sect. The Underlord, a wraith called Fleece, is controlled by a horned halfling named Big Apple. Big Apple's real name is Edgar, and he's from my world. Somehow, I don't know how, he controls Fleece, who controls the Sect. He also leads the thieves' guild called the Shell. All of those people are under his thumb from here to the Old Kingdom. He has spies everywhere, some from this world and others not. King Hector, you can't trust anyone, except maybe your Henchmen."

Pratt cleared his throat.

King Hector grabbed Clarann by the hand and said, "I can certainly trust my queen."

"That goes without saying," he said though he was thinking about the queen's secret relationship with Ruger Slade and their daughter, Clarice. "You have to be careful who you trust from here on out. Very careful."

"Anything else?" the king said with a bemoaning sigh.

"They want the King's Steel."

King Hector raised an eyebrow and asked, "Why?"

"The metal is precious, unlike any other metal. It contains qualities that they need to manage their Time Tunnel. The more steel they have, the longer they can keep the portal open. It's the key ingredient they are missing." Abraham drank the rest of his wine. "Wherever it is, I'd triple the guard on it."

King's Hector's face sagged. "Oh."

Abraham leaned forward. "Oh, what?"

"Nothing that concerns you." King Hector clenched his fists. "These people in your world—if I find them, I'll put a noose around their necks." He wagged a finger at Abraham and said, "The next time you are in your world, you kill them. That's an order."

"Your Highness, I can't just murder someone in my world. There are laws against that, the same as the laws you have here."

Prince Lewis jumped up. "You will do as the king says! Are you defying his order?"

"No, I mean"—Abraham lifted his hands—"I can't kill in cold blood."

"This isn't cold blood. This is war!" King Hector stood up. "I want the enemy dead!" The gems in his crown burned with new fire. His eyes glazed over. "I will have their heads. And you will bring them to me."

The queen and princess pushed back in their seats.

"Hector, control yourself," Queen Clarann said.

King Hector glared at the queen. "You dare speak to me in that tone? I am the king." He hit the table. "I am the king!"

The table burst into cinders, and a force of energy knocked everyone back in their seats. The queen and the princess lay on the ground, holding onto one another, shaking. Shards of wood were sticking out of their faces.

Abraham rolled over on one side and plucked a splinter from his noggin. Everyone at the table was on the ground with splinters in their faces and specks of blood behind them, except for Melris. The Elderling sat in his chair, dusting the splinters off his robe and shaking them out of his hair.

King Hector's fierce expression softened the moment he saw Clarann and Clarice lying on the ground bleeding. He dropped to his knees and reached toward the queen. "My love, I'm sorry!"

Queen Clarann slapped the king's outstretched hands away.

CHAPTER 28

Abraham returned to Stronghold alone. King Hector and Queen Clarann's spat became an ongoing argument. King Hector had quickly dismissed him, but Melris and the others stayed. As soon as he entered Stronghold's threshold, he greeted all the Henchmen that he saw. The triplets, Sofia, Selma, and Bridgett, gave him welcoming hugs and kisses.

"Master, you stink," said Selma, who wore a short strapless dress. She escorted him downstairs to the dungeon level. "You need washed. Very much."

The dungeon was a basement with stone walls, where one part had hot springs turned into a grotto. Steam made for a warm fog that filled one of the rooms.

The triplets stripped Abraham down. Bridgett, wearing a skimpy white cotton dress, fought to tug his boots off. His bare feet slapped on the wet stone floor. Several large pools of churning water waited for him to enter.

Through the steam, he noticed several figures moving out of the waters. "Horace? Iris?" he said.

"Sorry, Captain, we'll give you some privacy," Horace said.

"No, get back in the tub. Geez, it's not just for me. It's for all of us." Abraham let the triplets lead him into the waters. He noticed Sticks in one of the other hot springs with Solomon. Shades was in the same one that Abraham got into.

Shades waved a hand and said, "Hello, Captain."

Abraham soaked in the tub. The triplets sat on the edge of the pool and began rubbing him down.

"Uh, that's not really needed, girls. Not that I don't appreciate it, but I really just want to sit here and soak." He nodded at Shades. "That fella there might need a rubdown. The others too."

Shades grinned. "That would be lovely."

"As you wish," Sophia said.

"I'll rub down my own man, thank you," Iris warned.

The triplets split up. Sophia joined Shades, while Bridget and Selma moved in on Sticks and Solomon. Sticks shooed the attractive women away, so they both went to work on Solomon's shoulders.

Abraham lay his head back against the damp towel Selma had laid on the rock ledge. He closed his eyes and breathed deeply. The hot bubbling pool of water was just what his aching body needed. His nostrils flared. The minty steam began to soften his hard muscles. The aches and pains that throbbed all over began to fade away.

This is better. Much better.

Ruger Slade's body was more or less a restless device. The slightest abnormal aberration in the environment would fire up his instincts. He was as alert as a prowling panther, always ready to strike at any moment.

Abraham managed winks of rest. He dozed off while the others talked, but every so often, his nerves would fire, waking him up and putting him on edge. Abraham tried to get the body to let go, to relax. They were safe inside Stronghold.

Relax, Ruger, relax.

Normally, Abraham slept well when he slept, though lightly. Ruger's body could make do on a few hours. Right then, that rest, despite all the creature comforts, wasn't happening. For some reason, Ruger's body wasn't settling down. He cracked an eye open.

Sticks lay with her head back, eyes closed, her creaseless face as expressionless as ever.

Solomon had Bridgett in his lap while Selma sat behind him, rubbing his hairy shoulders. Bridgett's fingers were playing with the troglin's gums and teeth, and Solomon would chuckle.

Horace and Iris sloshed around in their own pool, giggling quietly.

Sophia's legs were draped over Shades's shoulders while she gave him a temple massage. The man looked as if he was in heaven.

The room was filled with happy people, yet Ruger's instincts were still firing. Abraham had been in Ruger's body long enough to know to trust it. *Something's wrong.*

Abraham caught Sticks looking at him. She quickly looked away. He lifted an arm out of the water and waved her over. Quietly, she came. His eyes popped when she came out of the water not wearing a stitch of clothing.

"Why are you looking at me like that?" Sticks asked as she sank back down into the water beside him. She slid a look at the triplets. "Is it because I don't look like them?"

"Uh, no, it's not that. You look great. I guess I was expecting to see you in a bikini."

"A *bikini*?"

"It's something that the women wear when they are in the water back home."

She nodded. "I see. So, you wanted something?"

"I just wanted to see how you were doing."

"I'm fine." She sat so close their thighs were touching. She touched his leg. "You?"

"Feeling better, but it's hard to unwind after a trek like that. We still have a big situation to deal with. The king sent me away, so I don't know where things are going."

Shades jumped into the conversation and said, "So, what did the king say?" He scooted toward Abraham.

All of a sudden, Horace and Iris climbed over from their small pool into Abraham's bigger one. Solomon stretched out from his pool and leaned over its rim, which poured into the bigger pool as well.

"Huh, when King Hector speaks, people listen." Abraham cleared his throat. "I laid it all out for him. I told him about my world and the corporation behind the portals. We gave him the red and orange stones. I think they changed him. Let me ask all of you this: have you ever wondered how you know for certain that you are on the right side of things?"

Horace gave him an appalled look and said, "We always know we are on the right side of things because we serve the king."

"Yes, but there are other kings in Titanuus."

"No, there is only one true king." Horace's brows knitted together. "Captain, I find your words unsettling." He grabbed Iris by the hand. "We have to go."

"Horace, wait," Abraham said. "It's only a hypothetical question."

Horace and Iris vanished into the mist.

Abraham's shoulder sagged. "Crap."

CHAPTER 29

"WELL, THAT WAS REALLY SMOOTH," Solomon said to Abraham. He squinted an eye and said, "A little lower, Selma."

She grimaced as she dug her tiny mitts into the troglin's back.

"Ah, that's the spot," he said. "I swear, for little women, you have magic fingers. Strong fingers, at that."

"The better to please you with," Bridget said.

"Abraham, I understand where you are coming from," Shades said as he squirted water out of his hands. "There are many kings, and every one of them had their own ideas about what is right and what is wrong. I come from Hancha. The rules in that country are oily. I'll say this for King Hector: the people might not like him, but you know where he stands."

"What brought this on, anyway?" Sticks asked.

"Ah, I've been fine with it until my last trip back home. There is a woman there, a zillon named Ottum. She warned me about the king."

Solomon gaped. "A real live zillon? How is that possible? I didn't think that our bodies could travel from one world to another."

"I don't know, and the good thing is that they don't know either. That's a good thing. They plan on moving people back and forth by soul swapping." He sat up and brushed his damp hair away from his face. "Man, the possibilities."

"Was the zillon a prisoner, like you?" Sticks asked.

"No, she was one of them. At least, I think she was."

"If it's any consolation, Abraham, I've never known a man with greater honor than Ruger Slade," Shades said. "If our king did something wrong, he wouldn't stand for it. Believe me, I've seen him do much. With Ruger, the standard is the standard. He is the standard."

"I guess me opening my big mouth did him a lot of injustice."

Sticks hugged his arm. "You have to be you. He has to be him. I know you are a decent man. We all do."

He rubbed the back of his neck and said, "Yeah, I just have a heck of a standard to live up to."

"Horace will stop pouting soon enough. Just remember, a lot of those old soldiers practically worshipped Ruger. That's why they left with him when he fled… even though it wasn't him," Shades said.

Abraham scratched the brand on his chest. The raised crown was thick and tough. He wasn't so sure that King Hector was the bad guy. He'd seemed fair, but power could change people. One thing he was sure about was that Eugene Drisk, Dr. Jack Lassiter, and Colonel Dexter were bad. So was the corporation they worked for.

It's time to suck it up, buttercup, 'cause one way or the other, this thing is coming to the end. Maybe that's why my guts are turning.

"So, what do we do now? Wait?" Solomon asked. "Not that I mind waiting at the moment. I could get used to this."

"I'm sure that we will hear from the king soon enough. We still have two more stones to recover. My guess is that Melris and Leodor are trying to figure out where that is." He rinsed off his face. "Let's enjoy the moment. I'm driving myself crazy thinking about this all of the time."

"It sounds like a fine idea to me," Shades said. "I can let me plums shrivel in this water all day. It would be nice to have some beverages to partake in."

"I'll take care of it." Sophia rubbed Shades's shoulder and took off with her damp pink clothing clinging to the curves of her body. "Any requests?"

"Bring the best that you have," Abraham said. "Heck, we've been successful. Why not celebrate?" He nodded. "And that goes for all of us. Tell Elga and Eileen to bust open the wine cellar. Let's have ourselves a Catalina Wine Mixer!"

The Henchmen built a huge bonfire outside, in front of the Stronghold. The men and women—Henchmen, Red Tunics, and hirelings—were dancing arm in arm and hand in hand.

Skitts and Zann had a talent for playing five-stringed lutes like guitars, and they weren't half bad singers. They sang countrylike tunes about adventures in the fields of farm country.

Solomon carried around a full-sized keg of ale. He poured it straight from the tap into the open jaws of Vern, Bearclaw, and Prospero. Bridgett sat on top of the troglin's monstrous shoulders, tossing her hair from side to side and playing a tambourine.

Abraham strolled the courtyard area, smiling, dancing, and patting his men on the back. He started to drink but thought better of it. If Ruger was the standard, he would be wise to be so as well. Plus, his history with too much drink in the past had proven dangerous, and he had yet to shake a heavy wariness that made him feel that something close was amiss. He made his way over to Horace and Iris, who were standing in front of the new barn they'd recently built. Horace had his arm wrapped around the mystic's waist.

"Iris, do you mind?" Abraham asked.

"Certainly not, Captain. I've been dying to go and dance, but I couldn't get out of this bear's grip." She pranced off with her robes hiked up and joined in a dance with Dominga and two of the triplets, circling and skipping together like children.

He looked at Horace and asked, "Do we have a problem?"

"No," Horace said, his eyes fixed on the cavorting.

Abraham bristled. "No, what?"

Horace growled in his throat and said, "No, Captain."

"Was it hard to say?"

Horace gave a stiff chin nod.

Abraham stood beside Horace and watched the celebration with his arms crossed. Neither man said a word for the longest time.

Finally, Horace broke the silence. "I've heard worse from your lips."

"Pardon?"

"The last one, Eugene. He mouthed off about the king all the time. I wanted to kill him. When you said what you said, it hurt coming from you. How can you believe that King Hector is in the wrong? He is the only king that boldly declares what is right. He doesn't mince words and dance in the middle. Ruger did not either."

"I let that zillon push doubt into my brain."

"What zillon?"

Abraham brought Horace up to speed about the discussion at the Time Tunnel.

"Zillons can't be trusted unless they wear the brand. Did you see a brand?"

"Of course not. She wasn't naked."

Horace harrumphed. "Captain, your actions have shown me your heart. I should know well enough to give your comments a pass." He extended his hand. "Death before failure."

Abraham shook Horace's mighty grip with his own. "Death before failure."

"Abraham!" Tark was standing on top of their war wagon, waving a red handkerchief. He pointed down the dirt road. "Look!"

A white carriage was approaching, escorted by riders, Guardian Maidens.

"More women for the party!" He lifted up a flagon of ale. "Woo-tah-woooo!"

Abraham recognized one of the Guardian Maidens. She was the tall one with raven hair, named Swan. She dismounted and opened the door to the carriage.

Princess Clarice stepped out. She was followed by the queen.

All the Henchmen stopped reveling, bowed their heads, and took a knee.

Abraham's knees locked, and as he saw the distraught face turn toward him, he muttered, "This can't be good."

CHAPTER 30

Queen Clarann and Princess Clarice met with Abraham inside the Stronghold, away from the others. They were on the main floor, beside the farm table facing the fireplace.

The queen paced. "Hector is losing himself. Those stones—I fear they make him mad with power."

"Did he hurt you?" he asked.

"No, at least not since he turned the table to splinters." Queen Clarann wrung her hands. "I think that taught him a lesson, for now. Still, he did other things."

"Other things?"

Clarice toyed with her ponytail and said, "He knows."

Abraham's heart skipped. "You mean he knows that you are not his child?"

"Yes, he knows. He used that gem on Mother. Now, he's mad. Very mad. I've never seen him so distraught before. I don't think he likes you anymore."

"Me? I'm not your father. I mean, Ruger is, but not me. I'm innocent."

Clarann's pale-yellow summer dress dragged over the hearth stones and snagged on the corner. She ripped it away, tearing the fabric. "It's that crown. My Hector would understand this, but now, he's hot as fire. He threatened to kill you. Well, Ruger." She sat down on the end of the hearth and clutched her heart. "I'm the one that should swing from a rope, not you."

Clarice clicked her sword in and out of her scabbard. "You should have seen Lewis and Leodor clucking. They think that they are so right and righteous. Lewis moves to turn my father against his queen and me. At least I have the pleasure of knowing that he's not my *real* brother."

"Holy sheetrock, this is bad. So, Hector let you leave?" he asked.

Clarann shrugged. "I don't think he cares what happens to me. Hector has been such a good husband. I know that he only feels betrayed, and it's true. I betrayed him, and I am his queen." She sobbed.

Abraham grabbed a cotton napkin from the table and walked it over to the queen.

She took it and blew her nose. "Thank you, Abraham."

He rubbed her back. "I hate to ask, but do you know what his intentions are? Is he bringing a rope for me?"

"No, when I left, he'd taken up counsel with Lewis, Leodor, and Melris. He is very obsessed with recovering the other two stones. I think he thinks that he can control all of Titanuus with them."

He sat beside her while Clarice pulled her sword and practiced several strokes. "I can kill Lewis now, can't I? I'm going to slice him like an apple."

"You can't attack another Henchman," he reminded her.

Clarice slid her sword into the scabbard and said, "Oh, but I can. My father—er, well… King Hector—removed their brands shortly before we left. Those dogs don't have a leash on them any longer."

Abraham jumped up. "What? He lifted the brand on them and left it on us? But they tried to kill him!"

Clarann grabbed his hand in hers and said, "Hector does not think he has much to worry about. He thinks he's become invincible. I fear that he is blinded by the stones."

Abraham tried to pull free of her grip, but she held him fast and looked into his eyes. "This is not your fault. You are doing the right thing. No one could have foreseen this—not me and not Hector and least of all you. You have been nothing but a good and faithful servant."

Her words didn't make Abraham feel a whole lot better. He had a bigger problem. If Hector was not on his side, then he might not ever get home. He could be trapped in Titanuus forever, with a sea of enemies at his back. He could survive, but he didn't know if he could survive without the protection of the king. He would be on the run all his life.

"No sense in crying over spoiled milk." He found the queen's eyes and said, "There is something I need to tell you. Both of you. I left out this detail before."

"Yes," Clarann said.

Clarice sat down beside him. Both women were joined at his hips.

"It's about Ruger. He and I have been switching places, it seems."

"What do you mean?"

"Did you ever see *Freaky Friday*?"

"Freaky?" the queen asked.

"Friday?" the princess added.

"Bad example." He continued, "In the Wound, my essence went back home to my world. Ruger's essence came back to his body." He pocked his chest. "This body."

Clarann and Clarice threw their arms around him and squeezed him tightly.

CHAPTER 31

Abraham woke up the next morning, lying on the farm table. He'd offered his room upstairs to the queen and princess. He sat up, rubbing his stiff back. He smelled bacon and eggs cooking. A few bright coals were still burning in the fireplace.

Prospero was passed out on the right side of the fireplace. His nose twitched. In his sleep, he sniffed. His eyelids started to open. He knocked an empty goblet onto the floor.

Other stirrings started in the room. Vern and Dominga were cuddled up together in the corner. She started to yawn. Cudgel was passed out halfway between the kitchen galley and the farm table.

Elga came out with two canisters with steam coming out the top. The haggard-looking elderly woman stepped on Cudgel as she crossed over to the table and set the pot down. "Fresh coffee, Captain." Turning back, she kicked Cudgel in the gut. "Coffee's on!"

Abraham slid off the table and stretched his arms. He'd talked into the wee hours of the morning with Clarann and Clarice. Clarice was excited to meet her father, once and for all. Abraham felt tired. Once again, his sleep had been restless. He dreamed of being back home, facing danger and an uncertain fate. King Hector entered his dreams. The king was angry, disappointed. He'd sent fiery hounds of hell after Ruger.

Eileen teetered in, stepping on Cudgel as she did so. The rickety-limbed woman set down a tray of earthenware cups. She poured a cup of hot coffee with a steady hand. "This will wake you, sire. As you know, my brew can wake the dead. The meal will be served shortly."

Abraham took the coffee, and the cup warmed his hands. "Thanks." He walked outside.

The morning sun had begun to rise over the lake. The birds sang their morning songs. The Stronghold's estate couldn't have been more perfect. Shades stood by the bonfire, bright eyed and bushy tailed. The guardian maiden, Swan, was with him. The two had hit it off not too long before. The braids in her long black hair were down. She was still hard eyed but, in her own Amazonian way, beautiful too.

"Good morning, Captain!" Shades said brightly.

Abraham approached. He could still feel the warmth from the hot ashes in the fire. "Morning." He took a sip of coffee. "Let me guess. You two have been up all night."

In a mannish voice for a woman, Swan said, "The Guardian Maidens require little sleep if not no sleep at all if the queen demands it."

"Yeah, what a bunch of beautiful bloodguard." He rubbed his face. It started to bother him that he wasn't bright eyed and bushy tailed also. Normally, Ruger's body remained vital as a busy beaver, but he felt drained. *Is it me, or was it Fleece? I just can't get my jump back.*

The rest of the Guardian Maidens were standing on guard in front of Stronghold. Every one of them appeared as formidable as the next, in their bronze breastplates and tight leggings. Each carried a spear, with a rapier hanging on her hip.

"So, how did last night go?" Shades asked with a smile. "Are you and the queen, you know, planning another princess?"

Swan backhanded Shades in the shoulder. "I told you not to mention that. Respect the queen's privacy."

"I already knew. I've always known. Good lord, look at the girl. A blind man can see the resemblance." Shades chuckled. "How the king missed it, I'll never know. Of course, maybe the beard threw him off."

"Yeah, well, the king knows now, and I'm not so sure where we will stand after this." He squatted down, picked up a piece of kindling, and tossed it into the fire. "I think we made our leader mad."

"Which kind of mad?" Shades asked.

"Huh—good question."

Horace and Iris walked out of the barn. Chickens and chicks marched by their feet.

"Well, it looks like someone had a roll in the hay," Shade said. "Lucky you."

Iris smiled as she hugged Horace's side. "It was more than a roll."

Horace slapped her behind. "You can say that again. We're making a family." He sniffed. "And they are hungry!"

"Has anyone seen Solomon?" Abraham asked.

"He was down at the lake last night. We saw him when we took a stroll," Shades said as he grabbed Swan's hand though she jerked it away. "He was with the one in white, and the one in pink, Sophia, I think."

"All right, I'll go find him. The rest of you go and grab some McVittles. I'll be back." He headed toward the large pond. He wasn't halfway there when Solomon appeared on the horizon.

The troglin was walking arm in arm with two of the triplets at his sides. He had a content look on his face. He lifted his arm and waved. "Good morning."

Selma and Bridget gave Solomon a squeeze, smiled at Ruger, and hurried back inside.

"Not as good as yours, apparently," he said.

"Probably not. So, you and the queen didn't…?"

"Lord, no. I'm in enough trouble with the king as it is. Needless to say, that puts our little situation in a bind."

Solomon clawed his fingers through the long hairs under his chin and said, "Yeah, you know, I've been thinking about that."

Some squealing pigs ran by their feet.

"About what?"

"Well, I was thinking, if I go back, I'll be about forty years older, won't I?"

Abraham shrugged.

"That would put me in my seventies, at least, I think. And heck, what sort of shape would my body be in?"

"You're an old troglin now. What's the difference?"

"Troglins live a longer time then men, I think. And I'd be lost, possibly." Solomon shook his head. "Heck, I don't know. Perhaps I enjoyed myself too much last night. This world's kind of funky."

"Yeah, and you be the funky monkey. Look, I don't know what's going to happen, but I do know it's going to happen. I can feel it in my bones. Once we find those other stones, well, either we stay here or go home. And if we stay here, the king might not be so kind to—"

Riders galloping toward the Stronghold appeared, kicking up dust and scattering grazing livestock. They were King's Guardians, riding tall in the saddle, with their full lion-face helmets on. They were led by Prince Lewis.

CHAPTER 32

THE GUARDIAN MAIDENS BRISTLED. THEIR ranks were outnumbered two to one. Swan lifted an arm, and the anxious women stood still.

Prince Lewis dismounted. His black cape stirred in the morning breeze. He had a smug look of satisfaction on his face. Abraham followed him over to the smoldering bonfire.

Prince Lewis held his gloved hands over the coals. "Nothing like a dying fire during the morning chill, eh Abraham?"

"If you say so."

He looked back at the mounted King's Guardians. Pratt had taken his helmet off. The big man no longer wore the badge on his armor that signified him as the Guardian Commander. That badge, birds' claws holding golden maple leaves, was sewn into Lewis's leather armor.

"I see you got a promotion."

"Yes, I have my station back, now that I am no longer tarnished by the brand of the Henchmen."

"Are you going to try to kill your father again?"

"Heavens, no. My father and I have mended our fences. I realized that I have erred in my judgment. But I was youthful and, well, poisoned by the Sect and Raschel." Lewis looked Abraham dead in the eye. "I hate to admit it, but I believe I have your intervention to thank for that."

Abraham's skin crawled as Lewis spoke with a serpent's tongue, with words full of guile. "What brings you here? You aren't going to try and burn it down again, are you?"

"Pfft… of course not. As I've said, I'm a changed man."

The queen and the princess came out of Stronghold's front door. Shock and distrust were on their frowning faces.

"Hello, Clarice," Prince Lewis said to his former sister. He tipped his chin at Clarann. "My queen. Father sends word. He would like you to return to the House of Steel immediately."

Clarann had a blanket drawn over her shoulders and said, "I'll return when I am ready."

Prince Lewis rocked his head from side to side. "That wouldn't be wise. Not that it matters to me. You can live here for all that I care. I've always thought that you were more fit for farming and the outdoor life rather than the majestic setting of a royal courtyard. However, for your own safety and for the sake of the crown, it's best that you come home."

"All of a sudden, my husband cares," the queen said.

"Only the Elders know why, but yes." He reached underneath his cloak and pulled out a white handkerchief. Wildflowers were sewn into the fabric. "He offers this. I imagine it has some sentimental value."

Queen Clarann stepped forward and took the handkerchief. Her eyes watered. She glanced at Abraham then back to Lewis and said, "I made this for him."

"Good. Perhaps you can make him another. You should have plenty of time to practice your embroidery inside the walls of the House of Steel." Lewis smirked. "It's time to return, either of your own free will or by force. Please don't make it by force. My men and I have a long journey ahead. We'd rather not scuffle with your personal guard." He glanced at Swan. "They are vastly outnumbered."

"Did you come here to start a fight," Abraham asked, "or is there another purpose?"

"As a matter of fact, there is." Lewis produced a scroll that had the burgundy wax seal with the king's mark. "I have your orders. And he also told me to give you this." He handed Abraham the Rubik's Cube. It had been solved. "He said that he was disappointed."

Abraham blankly looked at the cube in his hand. It was his son Jake's. His neck tightened. He'd given so little thought to his wife and son. He hadn't even been sleeping with the backpack at his side. An awful feeling sank in: guilt and something else. The thought that King Hector had solved it unveiled a new intelligence.

"Are you going to play with your little puzzle, or are you going to read your orders?" Lewis asked.

Abraham broke open the seal and read the scroll. The written words were as clear as English to him. He read in silence, but his lips moved. He looked up at Lewis and said, "We are going to the Wall? To the border of South Tiotan. To engage the enemy."

Lewis smugly replied, "Yes. After all, you are the most qualified person to carry on the fight. It appears that those iron chariots have appeared outside of our walls. Envoys from South Tiotan's officials, along with the prestigious elite of Hancha, demand our surrender. They are quite emboldened by their new foreign allies. My father wants you to take those iron chariots out or die trying."

Abraham swallowed. His fingertips turned numb. "What about the last stones? We should set out on a mission to retrieve them."

Lewis rubbed his hands together and said, "Viceroy Leodor and Melris are working on that. King Hector has put his trust in them rather than the man that impregnated his wife and deceived him for over a decade."

"But the king gave his word!" Abraham said as his plans crumbled. "We need the stones to control the portal. The king gave his word!"

"I witnessed it, and so did you, Lewis," Clarann stated. "The king would never go back on his word." She snatched the letter out of Abraham's hand. Her eyes scanned the parchment. "It is his signature."

"Of course it is," Lewis said. "His contract with this man was broken the moment he learned the truth of his bastard daughter. It's nice to be right. It gives me such a warm and fuzzy feeling. And if you read the letter in its entirety, he also mentions that if you travel between this world and the other, tell them he won't surrender. Ever."

CHAPTER 33

THE WALL STOOD THIRTY FEET high and ten feet wide. It was constructed of huge blocks of quarry stone. It ran for leagues between the mountains that created a natural barrier between South Tiotan and Kingsland.

There was passage through the Wall, the Shield of Steel. The gate was twenty feet wide and had a grand set of thirty-foot-high solid-steel doors that opened outward and another set of doors that opened inward toward Kingsland. Between both sets was a portcullis made of heavy woven strips of steel.

On the backside of the Wall were tremendous ramps leading to the top of it. Forts that were interlinked on the Wall made up a small city. Thousands of Kingsland's soldiers guarded the wall, from one end to the other. They moved like ants today. Armed with swords, spears, and crossbows, they marched up the ramps to the Wall's battlements and manned the ballistae, small catapults, and vats filled with boiling pitch.

Abraham stood on top of the Wall near the gates with the sun on his face, marveling. He'd never been to the Great Wall of China, but he'd seen plenty of pictures, and the Wall looked very much like it. He and the Henchmen gazed over the battlements. Lewis and the Guardians were nearby.

The lands of South Tiotan were miles of rich green grasses as far as the eye could see. Now, those fields were littered with enemy camps. Soldiers from Tiotan and South Tiotan were lined up by the thousands out of bowshot distance. South Tiotan's banners, with angled black stripes over a field of yellow, were on one side. Tiotan's flags, with black stripes angled a different way on a field of maroon, were on the other side. Those weren't the only enemy flags posted in the ranks. Flags from Hancha, Dorcha, and East and West Bolg were there. The enemies' numbers had grown to over ten thousand or more.

"The Shield of Steel can never be penetrated," Lewis said proudly. "It is the greatest fortification in the world. The army that stands behind it is invincible. My ancestor built it."

Unlike Ruger, Abraham wasn't a master at military combat strategy, but even he tended to agree with Lewis. Even with all the enemy's armies gathered outside the Wall, outnumbering their troops ten to one, he still felt secure.

"There is a wall just like this in my world. It ran for three thousand miles. It did its job… for a while," Abraham said. He leaned between the battlements and eyeballed the tanks in the field. He counted ten green army tanks. He didn't know one tank from another, but to him, they looked like big ones. "But time and technology caught up. Now, the enemies can fly over it."

Lewis scanned the skies and said, "I don't see any zillon dragon riders. I think we won't have to worry about that." He stroked the furs on the collar of his cape. "Those iron chariots haven't made any noise, and they look quite small from here. What do they do?"

"Blow walls like this to smithereens," Abraham said. He ground his teeth. *If the Drakeland Corporation had sent ten tanks through already, how many more could they send?*

"Well, we can't let that happen, or rather, you can't let that happen." Lewis took off his gloves one finger at a time. "Though, those iron chariots aren't so frightening, like you described. They appear quite minuscule compared to the Wall. Besides, the gate won't fall. The portcullis is made out of the King's Steel. It can handle anything."

"Those iron chariots are called tanks—get it right, *Lewis*." Abraham moved from one battlement to another and looked over the ledge at the Shield of Steel. "That's a lot of steel. Have the tanks fired a shot?"

"A shot of what?" Lewis asked.

He rolled his eyes. "You don't want to know."

Well over a week had passed since he'd departed in essence from back home. He was supposed to negotiate with King Hector and be the back-and-forth between them and the Corporation. But he hadn't gone back and hadn't been able to get word back to them either. That was a problem. If they didn't hear back from him, they would no doubt attack.

A group of riders approached the Shield of Steel on horseback carrying a white banner.

"What's that?" he asked.

"They carry the banner of truce. They want to talk," Lewis said.

"Well, let's see what they have to say," Abraham said.

Passing through smaller doors built into the large gates, Abraham, Lewis, and a host of Guardians rode out to meet the enemy. Abraham's eyes widened when he noticed Lord Hawk among the generals of Tiotan. The savvy-looking leader of the Shell was leaning over his saddle horn with a cocky grin on his face. "I've been waiting for days for you to show your face," Lord Hawk said.

"What's this about?" Lewis asked as he steadied his horse. "Who is this man?"

"This is Lord Hawk, the leader of the Shell. We've crossed paths a few times." Abraham scanned the faces of the generals. "Where's your little friend, Big Apple?"

"One never knows when he might pop up," Lord Hawk said. The rogue with receding blond hair looked between Lewis and Abraham. "I take it you've had time to counsel with King Hector and have disclosed to him our offer?"

Prince Lewis bumped Lord Hawk's horse with his horse. "Listen to me, you thieving rodent. Listen, all of you. Titanuus will freeze over before King Hector surrenders. You best pack up your armies and return home. The Wall will never fall."

Lord Hawk chuckled. "Is that your final answer?"

"What is this, *Who Wants to Be a Millionaire*? Of course it is," Abraham fired back.

"I can speak for myself!" Lewis stated. He glared at Lord Hawk. "This negotiation is over."

Lord Hawk lifted a finger and said, "Before we part, I was ordered to show you an example of what you are up against." He raised a hand high.

The tank closest to the roadway leading to the Shield of Steel churned forward with its metal wheels grinding inside its tracks. It stopped fifty-five yards away from the Wall. The top hatch of the tank opened.

Big Apple popped out. The horned halfling wore a flak vest, smoked a cigar, and flexed his muscular arms. He took the cigar from his mouth and flicked the ashes. He had a grin on his face from ear to ear. He placed some goggles over his eyes and stuck his fingers in his ears.

The hairs on Abraham's neck rose. "Holy sheetrock! Get down!"

The tank fired.

Kaboom!

Every soldier and horse jumped.

A huge chunk of the Wall exploded.

CHAPTER 34

Abraham and Lewis retreated back behind the Wall. The prince had paled after that initial cannon shot, and his back quickly straightened. He had given Lord Hawk a hot stare and said with a shaking voice, "We will not surrender! You want a war, then you will have one!"

For the next hour, every ten minutes, all ten of the tanks fired. The missiles blasted in the Wall. Running soldiers stumbled. Cries of alarm went up.

The Henchmen stood on the Wall, watching in awe. The barricade was slowly getting chewed up, one ton of rock at a time. A steady breeze blew stone dust into their eyes. Battlements and the manned ballistae on top were being blown away.

"They are very noisy contraptions," Horace said as he wiped stone dust from his eyes. "How do you kill them?"

"Easy, with an antitank missile," Abraham replied, "but the problem is, we don't have any."

The ten tanks, twenty yards apart, formed a line in front of the Shield of Steel seventy-five yards away. Ballista bolts and arrows shot from Kingsland soldiers bows plinked off the tanks' iron hides.

Prince Lewis's cheeks were flushed red. The white stone dust covered his black cape like falling snow. He pointed a finger in Abraham's face and said, "You will stop those tanks! That is the king's mission!"

"You can't be serious. You can't expect us to ride out there and fight those things. Our weapons are useless against them!" he yelled back.

"I don't care! You are the Henchmen. That is what you do! Now gather your men, and do what you are ordered to do, or I'll hang all of you by the noose!" Prince Lewis signaled to his second in command, Pratt. "Gather the Guardians. We depart to the House of Steel immediately. We must warn the king."

"You mean you aren't going to stick around to watch us die?" Abraham said to Lewis. "Imagine you, tucking tail and running. I'm shocked."

"I don't need to watch. I'll have Pratt stay behind." Lewis nodded at his second in command. "Once they die, you ride."

"And if we don't die," Abraham said, "what does Mr. Pratt do then?"

His words fell on deaf ears as Lewis had already snaked his way down the ramps and was out of sight.

"Wow, he's going to make a fine king someday. Not!"

Pratt and Horace stood side by side, overlooking the battlement together. Both men were shaking their heads.

Pratt turned. "Ruger, or whoever, I've never cared for you much, but I'll tell you this. This is the battle I've been waiting for. Those metal dragons and smoking snouts, hah! Let me ride at them with my own thunder underneath my hips!"

"You are ready to ride with the Henchmen?"

Pratt bent his thick neck back and laughed. "Elders no. Only as a last resort. I'd rather wait and see what becomes of you first. So go on, get at it before this bloody wall falls down."

"It's not going to fall down, at least, not anytime soon," Abraham said.

The Wall was ten feet thick and would hold up against the barrage for days, if not weeks, possibly.

"They are firing every hour. Perhaps they don't have enough missiles in their quivers, and they are hoping to scare us. Let's wait it out a bit and see what happens."

Every hour, the tank guns fired. Every blast chewed up the wall, and the Shield of Steel rattled like a giant saber.

Night fell. The torches of the enemies could be seen for miles.

The tank guns' muzzle fire flashed bright orange and red.

Horace, Sticks, and Solomon stood by Abraham, watching the enemy.

"You know, I protested the Vietnam War," Solomon said. "It seemed like the cool thing to do at thc time, and I was trying to impress this girl. I never imagined I'd ever be on the front lines of a real battle. This is crazy. Every time those guns fire, my bones rattle. Never understood how a soldier might feel. I feel bad now."

"Yeah, war is hell," Abraham replied. "My dad told me that more than once. Heck, if I wasn't in Ruger's body, I'd probably be crying like a baby. I really don't have any idea how to stop them."

"You'll think of something," Sticks said.

"What makes you think that?"

"Because you have to."

The tanks were one problem, but Abraham sensed there was another. Something else was eating at him. His enemies were right in front of him, but something was missing. He couldn't put his finger on it. He scratched an eyelid and asked, "Horace, did you see any Gond?"

"No, Captain. The Gond would never fight alongside an organized army. Why?" Horace asked.

Abraham recalled seeing the Gond being armed with machine guns at the Time Tunnel. He'd expected they would appear with the army. *If they aren't here, where are they? Guarding the lair, perhaps?*

Another hour passed.

Ten tanks fired as one, rocking the Wall.

The pit in Abraham's stomach sank even further.

CHAPTER 35

THE ARMIES BEHIND THE TANKS would let out a rousing cry every time the tanks fired.

"Those cheers are beginning to annoy me," Horace said.

Dawn broke. Blurry-eyed soldiers of Kingsland patrolled the Wall and kept at their daily preparation duties.

Abraham leaned against the battlement wall with the rest of the Henchmen. They'd been ordered to stop the tanks, but a restless night didn't blossom any new ideas.

Pratt marched up to Abraham, kicked him in the boot, and said, "What are you waiting for?"

"An A-10 tank killer? You haven't seen one flying around here, have you?" he replied.

"Don't jest with me. You need to take action immediately. By sitting here, you accomplish nothing," Pratt said. "The longer you wait, the sooner you will be charged with treason. You are under orders of the king."

"I know that!" Abraham stood up. "And what are you going to do, Pratt? Huh? I'm gone, and all of a sudden, you're going to figure out how to stop ten tanks?"

Pratt blanched.

"I didn't think so," he said.

We have to act, Captain," Horace said while leaning on his spear. "I'll ride out there and stick it with my spear. We can kill them."

Bearclaw came to his feet. "I'm with Horace. We must fight. It's what we do. The longer we wait, the less fortune will favor us."

"I'm not going to stage a charge if we don't have some sort of edge," Abraham said. "We have to be patient."

"The Wall crumbles," Pratt said as he cast his hand outward. "Have you not looked for yourself? Those dragon snouts are chewing holes through the exterior."

"Captain," Shades said. He was sitting between the battlements. "You might want to have a look. The iron chariots' heads are swiveling."

The tanks' turrets started to turn. All the tanks' gun barrels pointed directly at the Shield of Steel.

"Sticks, how long has it been since the tank guns last fired?" he asked.

"It's coming up on that time. Any second now," Sticks said.

All as one, the tank guns blasted out their thunder.

Metal smote metal like a great gong falling to the earth.

BRRRWWWRRROOOONNNGGG!

The Shield of Steel rang like a gargantuan tower bell.

Soldiers fell to their knees, clutching their ears.

Abraham covered his ears with his hands. The ear-shattering sound was deafening.

The tank guns fired again and again.

The armies of Kingsland trembled underneath the blast of that limb-shaking sound.

With his hands pressed tight over his ears, Pratt yelled at Abraham. "You will end this now! Do you hear me? End it now!"

The tank gunfire stopped.

With his ears ringing with a thousand buzzing bells, Abraham leaned over the Wall. The Shield of Steel stood intact. The huge outer doors had huge divots and scorch marks all over, but they remained fully intact.

"That's the King's Steel for you! No power can tear down this wall!" Horace shook his spear in the air. He let out a roar.

Horace's bellowing created a chain reaction and caught on. The King's Army came to life. They belted out wild yells from one end of the Wall to the other. They jabbed their weapons toward the sky.

The tank guns turned. The noses of the barrels started to rise. The tanks fired one right after the other. A steady *ka-poom ka-poom ka-poom ka-poom* followed.

The tanks' missiles ripped through the battlement and tore men from the seats of the giant ballistae.

The King's Army dropped on their bellies, covering their heads and faces.

Pratt stormed down the walk. "Get up! Get up! Grin in the face of death, you hounds!"

The soldiers climbed back again and started shouting back over the Wall.

"That's more like it! The Shield of Steel is invincible!" Pratt yelled.

The tank turrets turned again. The barrels lowered toward the same spot on the Wall, to the left of the gate below where Abraham stood.

Like a woodchuck, Big Apple popped his head out of his tank's hatch. He still had an impish grin on his face.

"Let loose the arrows on that little hedgehog!" Pratt ordered.

The king's archers stretched their bowstrings. Crossbows and ballistae were pointed at the horned halfling.

"Fire!" Pratt shouted.

A volley of arrows and bolts whistled through the sky.

Big Apple waved just before he slammed the tank lid over his head.

Arrows and bolts ricocheted off the tank's metal.

The tank guns came to life and fired.

One missile blast after another blasted away at the outer wall. The tank shells pounded the same spot over and over.

"They're turning the Wall into a tunnel!" Abraham shouted. Ten feet of stone or not, those tanks would be able to drive right through the Wall in less than an hour.

The Wall shook underneath his feet. He watched in horror as bigger sections of the Wall started to crumble.

Pratt grabbed him by the shoulder and said, "Get out there and fight those things, you coward!"

Abraham knocked Pratt's hand aside. "The next time you do that, I'll take your hand from your wrist, and that won't be all." He pushed by the bigger Pratt. "Come on, Henchmen. Our time has come!"

Without a word of complaint or the slightest grumble, the Henchmen, one and all, followed Abraham Jenkins down the ramp to the bottom of the Wall. They stood as one and watched the Wall shake until one missile finally burst through. The barrage didn't stop until the Wall crumbled, leaving a tunnel large enough to drive a tank through.

Abraham pulled his sword. "Death before failure."

CHAPTER 36

After the shelling of the Wall stopped and the dust settled, Abraham headed into the tunnel. With Sticks and Horace in tow, he sloshed his way ankle deep through pulverized rubble. Out on the field of battle, five of the ten tanks turned and started rattling their way.

"Does anybody have any big ideas?" he said.

Horace's face was as blank as Sticks's. No one in Titanuus had ever seen a tank before, let alone fought one. Abraham had seen them but never fought one either. However, he had seen movies and read his fair share of *G.I. Combat* and *Sgt. Rock* comic books. Those childhood images sparked some ideas.

"Listen up!" Abraham shouted out of the tunnel. "We are going to let the first tank through. Tark, Cudgel, Prospero, and Apollo, as soon as that tank rolls through, start covering it in pitch. We'll set that thing on fire and smoke the men out."

"What about the others? How are we going to stop them from barreling through?" Horace asked.

Abraham flipped his sword around. "Leave that to me and Black Bane."

The first tank thundered down the road, pointed toward the tunnel. The other tanks blasted cover fire at the Wall. The tank rolled into the tunnel at twenty miles an hour.

"Now!" Abraham yelled to Tark and Cudgel, who were waiting above.

Tark and Cudgel poured two vats of hot pitch over the Wall and down onto the tank. The hot black goo spattered everywhere. Then Apollo and Prospero hefted bags of pitch and slung them onto the tank.

Small slit doors on the tank opened. The rat-a-tat of machine-gun fire blasted away from within.

Apollo and Prospero dropped to the ground.

Ranks of the king's foot soldiers were mowed down.

The tank gun turned and fired on the largest mass of soldiers gathered near the Wall. A loud booming blast sent men and their dismembered body parts flying.

"Burn that thing! Burn it now!" Horace bellowed.

Shades and Sticks rushed the tank with torches in hand and flung them onto the tank. Flames covered the tank. It rolled on, crushing, shooting, and killing everything in its path.

Gripping his sword in hand, Abraham said out loud, "It's showtime, Black Bane. I need you now."

The second tank entered the tunnel with its tank gun lowered.

"Black Bane?" He shook the sword. "Black Bane! I need lightning! I need it now! Oh man, this is a bad idea. Will you wake up?"

The tank started to pass out of the tunnel.

Abraham pointed the sword at the tank and yelled, "Lightning now!"

There was a momentary pause followed by a calm, *"All right, then."*

A globe of white-hot light dropped out of the sky and plowed into the tank, knocking it back into the tunnel. A jarring explosion knocked Abraham back off his feet. Tendrils of energy created a sparkling net all over the tank. Inside the tank's metal belly were the sounds of men screaming. As the mystic fires died out, the men's dying screams died out as well. The second tank was stuck in the tunnel.

A cry of victory went up from the soldiers on the top of the Wall.

"The tanks retreat!" Cudgel yelled from above. "The tanks retreat!"

The first tank rolled on like a flaming juggernaut. The Henchmen continued to throw on more pitch. The flames and black smoke grew higher. Suddenly, a man popped up out of the tank's turret coughing his lungs out and firing a machine gun.

Skitts and Zann shot the man in the face with their crossbows.

Another enemy soldier squirted out of the tank. The hot flames of pitch seared his hands and face. He dove off the tank. Before he could get up, the king's soldiers cut him down.

The tank rolled on, aimlessly, took a sudden turn back toward the Wall, barreled through a storage building, and crashed to a stop at the Wall.

Abraham breathed a sigh of relief and said, "Thanks, Black Bane."

"You're welcome."

"Now let's go and take those other tanks out."

"I beg your pardon? I'm might be powerful, but I'm not a miracle worker. I can only store up so much energy." Black Bane made a yawning sound. *"I'm spent after that. Good luck with your little skirmish."*

"Wait, how long does it take for you to store up enough energy to do that again?"

"Days. Weeks. It can vary. Say, where is that woman, Iris, that you matched me with earlier? She was some warm and cozy. I'd like to—"

Abraham sheathed the sword and said, "Good night."

He made the climb up the ramps to the top of the Wall. Cudgel was spot on—the tanks were retreating to their initial positions. The king's soldiers cheered in victory.

Pratt spat over the Wall and said, "There are still eight more of them out there. What are you and your magic sword waiting for?"

More ideas started to come to mind. He wasn't sure if they were his or Ruger's. He answered Pratt by saying, "Nighttime."

All day long, the tanks continued their hourly shellacking of the Shield of Steel. For the time being, they backed off from blowing another hole in the Wall. They seemed intent on doing something else. They blasted away at that Shield of Steel's weak spot, the stones around the hinges.

Abraham paced. "Blazing saddles!"

One of the front doors of the Wall stood in place, but it had fallen askew. The tanks continued to hammer away every hour on the hour. The enemy took their time about it. The inevitable began to sink in. The doors would fall, leaving an opening big enough to drive four tanks through. There would be no stopping them.

"So, what's the plan?" Solomon asked. The hippie troglin had a few more creases of worry in his brow. "Why do we wait for the night?"

"Because we have to be sneaky."

"Night is a good time for that. What are you going to do?"

"Something crazy. Did you ever see the movie *Beverly Hills Cop*?"

Solomon gave him a funny look and said, "Another movie reference? Seriously? Well, what's the plan?"

He looked at the tanks and said, "It's banana-in-the-tailpipe time."

CHAPTER 37

That night, Abraham asked Sticks, "Are you sure that you want to do this?"

"Of course I do. This is what I like to do," she replied.

"Me too," Shades said. He held a tank shell in his hand. "It's exciting playing with an explosive egg. You must come from a fascinating world."

"You have no idea," Abraham replied. He'd removed several shells from the tanks that had invaded them. The shells looked like giant bullets, more or less. With all the Henchmen gathered around him at ground level, he ran his finger over the tip. "Put them nose first inside the barrel. When they fire the tank guns again, they'll kiss. And then *boom*. No more tank."

"No more tank," Dominga said with a nod. She carefully loaded two tank shells into a leather satchel. "I like it."

Tark loaded two shells into his own satchel. "I like this idea too. I can't wait to see those iron devils go boom."

The Henchmen chuckled.

"We are going to beat those demons, aren't we, Captain?" Horace said.

Yeah, we're going to get them. But we are going to need one heck of a distraction." He addressed Sticks, Shades, Tark, and Dominga. Each of them had two shells. "You listen to me. If they sniff you out, tuck tail and get out of there. We'll find another way. Do you understand?"

The squad of four nodded.

"Come on." Abraham moved toward the tunnel the tanks had created with the Henchmen clustered behind him. The eight tanks remained stationed on the battlefield with their guns still pointed at the Shield of Steel. "Any time now. Iris!"

Iris pushed her way past the others to the front. "Yes."

"Do what you have to do to give them some cover."

"Of course." Iris grabbed Dominga by the hand. "Come with me." She led them to the other side of the tank.

"Horace, bring the horses up. We need to be ready to go," Abraham said. His heart pounded, and he was lathered in sweat. "Man, this is a bad idea."

Solomon wandered into the tunnel and peeked at the sky. "It's a good night for the attempt. Lots of clouds. No moon. Pitch-black. It might work."

"I'm still waiting to hear some better ideas."

"Well, you're asking the wrong person." Solomon patted Abraham on the head. "How's your gut feel?"

"Huh, never better."

The tank guns fired more shells into the Shield of Steel, and the great wall shook. New dust stirred.

Abraham flexed his hands, looked back down the tunnel, and said, "It's showtime."

Horace led two horses to the front. Bearclaw, Vern, Cudgel, Prospero, Apollo, Skitts, and Zann towed their own horses behind them.

Abraham took a horse outside by its leather reins and climbed into the saddle. The horse jumped, stamping its hooves.

"Easy, boy, easy." He led everyone outside.

Iris caught up to Abraham and said, "They are ready."

He looked down over his shoulder. The armor and clothing of Sticks, Shades, Dominga, and Tark had sprouted tall grasses all over. He moved toward Sticks.

"Don't say it again. We are all in this together," she said.

"I know. Just remember my orders. If they sniff you out, tuck tail and run." He scanned the row of tanks. Seventy-five yards of open field lay in front of them and another hundred yards behind them. The enemy army continued to keep its distance from Kingsland's ranged weapon defenses. "Otherwise, you know what to do." He stretched out his fist.

Sticks bumped his fist with hers. "We got this."

Abraham led the horsemen along the base of the Wall toward the Shield of Steel. Up top, the torches that lit the night had been extinguished, leaving them in the shadows that were black as night. They crossed over from one side of the gate to the other. In the rear, Zann carried a burning torch.

The tanks in the field remained stone-cold quiet. Only the rustle of the tall grasses could be heard.

"Send up the flame." Abraham grabbed the torch tucked into his saddle.

Zann lit Skitts's torch, and Skitts lit Prospero's. From the back to the front, one torch was lit after the other.

Abraham moved forward for all to see. "Follow my lead. All of you remember the chant, don't you?"

The grim-faced men nodded.

"After that, we'll scream our heads off like a wild bunch of Indians. 'Cause if we are going to go out, we are going to go out in style." Abraham used to watch a lot of westerns with his father and grandfather when he was a boy. There would be scenes where the Indians would charge out in a showy fashion, posturing in front of settlers and armies in a show of intimidation. He was fool enough to try the same thing today. "Time to ride out, Henchmen."

They formed a row and meandered on horseback toward the line of tanks with their torches held high in their hands.

Abraham cast a sideways glance. He could barely make out Sticks and the others, forty yards away, low crawling over the grasses. Ahead, the tank turrets didn't move. The wind whistled over the tanks' gun barrels. He stopped the horse line twenty yards away from the front end of the tanks.

The torch flames flapped in the wind.

Abraham fished a stone out of a saddlebag. He hurled it at the tank where he'd seen Big Apple last. "Listen up, you little billy goat! I'm going to give you to the count of ten to surrender, and if you don't, I'm going to do worse to these tanks than I did to the others. One! Two! Three! Four!"

The turret of the tank in the center turned and pointed its barrel right at Abraham.

CHAPTER 38

"Ah, it looks like I have your attention." He moved his horse out of the tank gun's aim. "Listen up, Big Apple. This isn't going to end well for you. I have a secret weapon. A really, really, big one."

"We have a secret weapon?" Horace said as he cast his glance all over. "Where? I don't see it."

"Shhh. I'm bluffing," he said under his breath. He resumed his count. "Five! Six! Seven! Eight!"

The hatch door of the center tank opened. Big Apple's horned head popped out. He pointed at his ear and said, "I can hear everything that you are saying, you fool. You don't have a secret weapon."

Abraham patted his sword handle. "Of course I do. Would you like to see it?"

"Huh huh. If that were a true threat, you would have used it by now. Besides, you can take out all the tanks that you want, but more will be coming." He pointed his stubby fingers at the Shield of Steel. "And once we have those doors down, we'll have enough steel to keep the Time Tunnel forever. It's over, Abraham Jenkins." He took out a new cigar and lit it with a fancy three-flame butane lighter. He puffed up a hot ring of smoke. "All of this fighting now is nothing more than window dressing."

"Don't get cocky, buckling."

Big Apple blew out a smoke ring and said, "Yeah, whatever. Do you have anything else that you wish to say before I destroy you?"

"Yeah, I do." Abraham tossed his head back, opened up his full voice and shouted. "How many Yankees?"

"Ten thousand!" the Henchmen cheered back.

"How many corn-fed, Southern-bred, never-dead re-e-ebels?" he bellowed at the top of his voice.

"Three!"

"What the hell you gonna do?" he finished.

The Henchmen yelled back with throaty voices, "Charge!"

Abraham kicked his horse into a full gallop, and the Henchmen followed. The group of riders raced around the tanks in a wide circle, waving their torches and screaming wildly.

On the Wall, the Kingsland soldiers gaped and exchanged dumbfounded looks with one another.

Solomon leaned against the Wall with his arms crossed, chuckling.

Abraham chanted loud chants of "Yip! Yip! Yip!"

The Henchmen did the same or worse.

Big Apple followed their every move, turning inside the hatch and glaring.

Abraham knew he looked like a fool. He hammed it up like a bad remake of *The Three Amigos*. He yelled out to his men, "Sew, Henchmen! Sew like the wind! Eee-yah!"

They rode long enough for Sticks and the others to snake through the grass and load the shells into the front of the tank barrels. The daring group finished the job and slunk back off.

If Big Apple caught on to what they were doing, he didn't show it. He continued to laugh and chuckle. He yelled at Abraham as he passed. "Hey, idiot, I've seen *Gunsmoke* before. Are you seriously trying to scare us?"

Abraham gave him a wild-eyed look and squalled, "You may take our gates, but you will never take our *freeedom*!"

Big Apple rolled his eyes. He knocked on the tank and shouted down the hatch, "Ready the machine guns. It's time to waste them." He saluted Abraham, dropped into the tank, and slapped the hatch lid over top of him.

The Henchmen were riding down the grasses, making a clear track in an oval circle. The rat-a-tat of machine guns started from the outmost tanks. Horace, Prospero, and Zann were shot out of their saddles. All three of them tumbled into the grass, and their horses crashed into the ground.

Abraham pulled back the reins of his horse. He charged through the field of machine-gun fire. He grabbed Horace's outstretched hands.

Apollo picked up Prospero, and Skitts snatched up Zann. They thundered back toward the tunnel with a hail of bullets ripping up the ground behind them.

"Yah! Yah!" Abraham galloped his horse into the tunnel.

All the rest of the Henchmen made the Wall's interior safety. The roar of machine-gun fire died down.

"Horace, are you okay?"

"What in Titanuus's Crotch did I get hit with?" The bearded bald man slid off the saddle and back onto the ground. He fell down, holding his thigh. "It burns like fire. Put it out!"

Iris rushed over to her man and said, "Be still, and let me have a look at it."

Horace had a bloody wound showing through his trousers. "What is it? It feels like an entire spear is inside my leg."

"It's a bullet. A big one," Abraham said. "Everyone get out of the tunnel. Treat the wounded." He couldn't see everyone with the tank wedged inside the tunnel. "Sticks!"

"Over here," she called back from the interior side of the Wall. She'd gathered with Shades, Dominga and Tark. "We did as you said. All of the shells were loaded into the noses of the iron beasts."

"It was a good plan," Shades said. He plucked grass out of his clothing. "I don't think that even ol' Ruger could have come up with a better one. But his plans always worked. Let's see if yours does."

A man cried out.

Zann lay on the ground, writhing and spitting blood out of his mouth. The young man's face was ghostly white. His brother fought to hold him still.

"It hurts!" Zann said as he spat more blood. "It bloody hurts!"

"Where?" Skitts asked.

Zann pointed to the side of his red tunic. A bullet had ripped through him from one side to the other. He collapsed on the ground, clutching the wound. "I'm dying, brother. My time has come. I go to kiss the Elders."

"Nooo!" Skitts said. Tears streamed down his face. "Twila, Twila, help him!"

"I'm coming. I'm coming." Twila hustled over with her robes hiked up over her ankles.

Abraham kneeled down beside Zann and grabbed his hand. "Zanex, hang on. Hang on. Don't let that little bullet get the best of you."

Zann stared blankly into the sky. "I can't see nothin'. It's been an honor, Captain. Finish them bastards." He stretched out his bloody fingers and touched Skitts's face. "I'll miss you, brother." He died in his brother's arms.

"Nooo!" Skitts yelled. "Save him, Twila! Nooo!"

CHAPTER 39

ABRAHAM STOOD ON TOP OF the Wall with his head down. The Red Tunic Zann was dead. Zann's brother, Skitts, sobbed behind the battlements. "He shouldn't have gone. He didn't have the King's Armor on. He died because of me. He's just a kid."

"No, he was a man," the iron-jawed Bearclaw said. "A soldier. Soldiers die so others don't have to. He gave his life the same as all of us. There is no shame in it." He cast his dark stare at Skitts. "They are brothers. There is no shame in his weeping. It will pass."

Vern had his boot up on the Wall with his eyes on the tanks. "We should all be dead by now. Every day is a miracle, if you ask me. Sooner or later, the rest of us will have it coming. It used to be that way before you came. You've spoiled us by surviving." He spat over the Wall. "Take heart, and move on."

"I wish it was that easy." If Abraham could've stopped his heart from clenching in his chest, he would have. But he couldn't stop it. He wasn't a general that led thousands of troops into battle to see many if not all slaughtered. Death bugged him. He'd rather no one die at all. He didn't use to be that way either. He was more callous in terms of war, with so many veterans in his family that had done soldiering. But when Jenny, Jake, and Buddy died, that changed his perspective on life. He realized he cared for people. He cared deeply. Abraham cleared his dry throat.

Vern passed him a skin of water. "Drink the wine, and pray you live to drink again."

"Huh." Abraham drank deeply and wiped his mouth. "You know, back in my world, there were wars where millions of men fought at land and sea. One of the most famous soldiers was a man named General George Patton. My coach used to play his speeches to the troops in the locker room before the games we played." He took another long sip.

Vern and Bearclaw shared a mutual high-eyebrow glance.

"Do you know what he said?" Abraham could feel the eyes of the lingering Henchmen on him. "He said, 'The object of war is not to die for your country but to make the other bastard die for his.'"

Horace was sitting on the back side of the Wall with his leg bandaged. He said, "I like this General Patton. Tell us more."

"Yes," Vern and Bearclaw agreed.

Abraham took another pull from the wineskin and said, "Okay, let me see what I remember." The slightest guilty smile broke out on his face. "My father, Earl, used to quote him all the time too. Hmm… this is kind of therapeutic. Let's see." He started the list.

"May God have mercy upon my enemies, because I won't."

"A good plan violently executed right now is far better than a perfect plan executed next week."

"Wars may be fought with weapons, but they are won by men."

Abraham passed the wine around for the others to share. Skitts tried his wine. Abraham's back straightened, and the strength in his voice slowly returned.

"A pint of sweat saves a gallon of blood."

"Nobody ever defended anything successfully. There is only attack and attack and attack some more."

Pratt was standing away from the company, but he lifted up his voice and said, "Hear! Hear!"

Abraham added a few more.

"Courage is fear holding on a minute longer."

"Americans love to fight. All real Americans love the sting of battle."

"When you put your hand into a bunch of goo that, a moment before, was your best friend's face… you'll know what to do."

Skitts sniffed.

Abraham finished with "It is foolish and wrong to mourn the men who died. Rather, we should thank God that such men lived." He walked over to Skitts and hugged him tightly.

"Hear. Hear," Skitts said as he returned the firm embrace. "Hear. Hear."

"Sorry to spoil the moment." Sticks was sitting between the battlements. "Shouldn't the iron chariots have fired by now? It's been an hour."

"Has it?" Abraham said. He moved to the spot where Solomon was standing. "I lost track of time. What do you think?"

"Let me check my watch." Solomon looked at his wrist. "Oh, sorry, I left my watch in the Fort Pitt tunnel. Do they still use watches back home?"

"Yeah, sort of."

The tanks hadn't moved, and no one had popped out of the hatches either. The field remained dark and overcast.

"I haven't seen anything budge," Sticks added, her assault rifle laid across her lap. She rolled a bullet between her fingers. "Maybe they ran out of those shells."

"No," Abraham muttered. "Big Apple isn't stupid. Maybe he's on to us." He hated to think that Zann had given his life for nothing. "Let's give them a few minutes. Perhaps we spooked them."

The minutes became an hour.

An hour became two.

The wee hours of the night dragged on.

The morning sunlight peeked over the tall hillsides.

Pratt strode over to Abraham and said, "Your plan bears no fruit. What is the second option?"

"They aren't attacking. That ought to count for something." Abraham rubbed his temples as a nagging headache was coming on. "Be patient."

"What about your General Patton? He was an attacker. You should attack," the horse-necked guardian said.

"Sure, I'll attack, but only if you are going to let me lead all of your men. How does that sound?"

Pratt rubbed his lantern jaw and said, "No."

"Abraham, the iron chariots move," Sticks said.

The Henchmen leaned over the Wall.

The tank turrets turned away from the Wall. Their rattling treads backed away.

Abraham slammed his fist on the Wall. "Devil's donuts!"

CHAPTER 40

"PRATT, TURN YOUR ARCHERS LOOSE on those tanks!" Abraham ordered.

"I don't take any orders from you. This is my wall and my charge. I won't waste arrows and bolts on an enemy that is retreating." Pratt bumped chests with Abraham. "And if you ever talk to me again, I might toss you over the Wall."

"Really?" In a blur of movement, Abraham grabbed Pratt by the neck and waist of his breastplate and heaved him up over his head. The huge man in full armor must have weighed over four hundred pounds of dead weight. Abraham had forgotten Ruger's great strength. His angry effort surprised even himself. "Is this what you had in mind, Pratt?"

Pratt blanched. He stammered when he spoke. "I don't like heights. Put me down. An assault on me is an assault on the king."

"The king isn't here! It's us against them. Are you going to be an anchor, or are you going to act like a Guardian?" Abraham asked. He shook the man over his head. "The standard is the standard. What is your standard, Pratt?"

The big-eyed Pratt let out an angry grunt. "I'll cooperate, but we will settle this. You and I."

Abraham put him down. "You need to quit acting like Lewis and get off of your high horse. Now, rally your men. Tell them the enemy is retreating. Unleash havoc on those metal beasts!"

Pratt marched away and flagged down his generals, shouting, "Archers! Archers! The enemy retreats! To arms!"

In a matter of seconds, bows, crossbows, and ballistae fired volley after volley. The missiles sailed up and streaked down, hitting the enemy soldiers' foremost ranks. The ballista bolts landed even deeper, impaling bodies over two hundred yards away.

Kingsland soldiers shouted over the Wall in a clamor of victorious cries. They beat their swords on their shields.

The tanks stopped in their tracks. The tank guns turned, and the green machines advanced back to their original position facing the Shield of Steel.

Abraham pumped a fist at his side. "It's working. It's working."

Kingsland's missile weapons rained down by the hundreds and rattled off the tanks.

"Keep firing! Keep firing!" Abraham said as he moved between the battlements. "That's it, make them mad!"

The eight tank guns took aim at the gate and the archers on the Wall.

Abraham's breath caught in his throat.

Every Henchmen hung over the Wall with eyes as big as mirrors.

"Come on, come on, come on," Abraham muttered.

Big ballista bolts rocketed into the tanks. A few of them stuck in the metal.

The enemy tank guns fired.

Boom-boom! Boom-boom! Boom-boom!

Red-hot flashes exploded from the barrels.

Boom-boom! Boom-boom!

The barrels peeled back like banana peels.

Boom-boom-boom-boom!

The entire field lit up like the Fourth of July. The explosions inside the barrels created a chain reaction. The turrets blasted off the tanks and into the sky. Two tanks flipped over.

Boom-boom-boom-boom-boom-boom!

Strips of metal, barrels, and tank treads flew through the air into hundreds of pieces.

Boom-boom!

The tanks caught fire. Oil and gas burned. Dying men screamed, their charred bodies torn asunder.

An eerie silence fell over the masses on the Wall. Jaws hung open. Once the explosions were over, the King's Army let out a loud chorus of triumphant cheers.

The Henchmen were all smiles. They slapped Abraham on the back.

Abraham couldn't help but grin all over himself. But his eyes were still searching the fiery mess of metal. One tank remained unscathed. It retreated from the rest. It was Big Apple's.

"Will you look at that? The little billy goat is getting away."

Horace limped over to him and said, "I don't suppose they will fall for that one again, will they?"

"Probably not. We got away with one. It will buy us some time."

The rest of the day, the King's Army resumed preparations for the assault. Everyone knew that more trouble would be coming, but for the moment, the invasion of Kingsland had been halted.

South of the Wall, in a meadow where the spring flowers bloomed, the Henchmen had a funeral service for Zann. Skitts dug the grave himself with the shovel Abraham had told him to bring. He offered some comforting words and helped fill the grave.

"He was a good brother in his own way," Skitts said with a long look on his face. "I always figured he could squeeze out of anything. I thought I'd go first, being much slower and all." He wiped his eyes on his sleeve. "I'm going to miss him. I've never lived a day without him."

Abraham swallowed the lump in his throat. He knew exactly how Skitts felt. His bowels twisted into knots. "I know it hurts. I know."

The Henchmen made camp away from the army. They needed rest. They hadn't stopped since having departed for the Wall. Black rings were underneath all their eyes. A campfire burned, and a few of the company set up their tents. Most of them drank and celebrated the same as the soldiers did.

Abraham lay down on his bedroll by the fire, staring up into the sky. His head throbbed. He closed his eyes, but the nagging pain didn't go away.

Sticks took a spot beside him, and so did Solomon. They were both sitting up with their arms wrapped around their knees and the flickering flames shining on their faces.

"Old Blood and Guts," Solomon said.

Abraham shut his eyelids and said, "Yeah, it all came back to me. Like a boomerang. I don't guess a hippie like you was a fan of his."

"Well, I don't know. His brutal philosophy makes more sense to me now than it did back when.

Boy, the things you forget about. It gave me a warm and fuzzy feeling, hearing it again." The troglin stretched his long hairy arms to the sky and yawned. "It makes me wonder if I've gone crazy."

"Don't fret it—you have," Abraham said. "Now, get some shut-eye. I figure we'll have another big problem to solve tomorrow."

A galloping horse could be heard thundering up the southern road leading to the Wall.

Abraham rolled over onto his side. A King's Guardian riding a large white horse whipped the beast's flanks. A man was draped over the front of his saddle. That man wore a black cape.

Abraham sat up. "That's Prince Lewis."

CHAPTER 41

Prince Lewis sat on top of a barrel inside an infirmary tent. He'd been shot in the leg, shoulder, and side. Lucky for him, the gut shot wasn't critical. He still breathed. He should have been dead.

Iris wound cotton straps around Lewis's muscular frame. "Those things, those bullets, are nasty. They tear holes out of the back end of you." She grimaced. "Never seen the likes."

"Yeah, they tumble," Abraham said. "They are designed that way. Nasty stuff."

"You come from a very vicious place," Lewis said. His face was beaded with sweat. "I feel like my entire backside has been ripped out." He had a bullet in his hand, one that they had removed from the tanks. "How can a little thing do so much damage?"

"It's called gunpowder. At least, that's a more primitive word for it."

The only other persons in the room were Pratt and the Guardian that had carried Prince Lewis back to the Wall. That rider had short brown hair and long sideburns. He was young and unscathed.

Lewis pointed a finger at the young Guardian. "Alshon, I owe you a great debt, dragging me out of the jaws of death."

"What happened, Prince?" Pratt was standing in the corner of the tent with his arms in front of his chest. "You looked like death warmed over when you arrived."

"Well, if that's how death feels, then I don't want to die." Prince Lewis took off his bloody gloves and tossed them away. "We were only a few miles north of the House of Steel's front gate, trotting through the passage between the high hills. Without warning, the bushes erupted with the bright glow of fireflies. The horses jumped and bucked. That maddening popping sound sent the beasts kicking into a frenzy.

"The barbarians charged out of the brush with those weapons firing. I've never seen men so big. They almost make Pratt look normal. Tattoos. Piercings." Lewis grimaced sharply and eyed Twila. "They screamed maddening bloodcurdling chants. One group fired those strange weapons, and the other group came upon us with axes." He dipped his chin and said, "None of us saw it coming.

"Horses went down. Guardians tumbled after them. I had enough wits to tell them to ride for the castle. To stay and fight would have been a slaughter. I spurred my horse in the same direction. One of these bullets, or more, took it down. I went down with it. I came to my feet, sword in hand. I made quick work of two Gonds trying to brain me with axes, but I was cut off from the others.

"I was about to chop off the head one of those long-eared Gond when those nasty metal hornets tore through me." Lewis rolled the bullet through his fingers. "I've felt pain but never pain like that.

I thought it was over. That moment was my last duel." He paused and looked at the others in the tent. "I swore off the King's Armor. But I'm swearing it back on again. It's the only thing that saved us from being cut to ribbons. Hmph. Then I was cut off from the others. The barbarians continued to swarm. Somehow, Alshon pulled me out of the flames of Sheol. I don't remember much until we made it back here. It is fortune that we had a horse between us and they didn't."

"How many?" Pratt asked.

"The ones carrying the rifles"—Lewis shrugged—"dozens, at least, but I fear there are many more. I fear the barbarians are invading the House of Steel. We need troops. We need to get back. Even the Guardians' finest will be outmatched by those…" He clenched a fist. "Weapons!"

"Will the king be able to hold out very long?" Abraham asked.

"The House of Steel has the strongest fortifications in all of the world," Pratt argued. "They can hold out forever."

"Don't be a fool, Pratt," Lewis said. "Where there is one Gond, there are ten more. There might be thousands that we missed. You know that. The castle has two hundred Guardians and fifty Golden Riders. The bulk of our armies are here, at the Wall." He eyeballed Abraham. "Speaking of which, how have you fared against the iron chariots?"

"Nine down, one to go," he said.

Lewis gave Pratt a doubting look. "Is this true?"

Pratt nodded. "I saw it with my own eyes. But the Shield of Steel is severely damaged."

"There will be more tanks," Abraham said. "It's only a matter of time. I won't be able to stop the next round. Do you want me to stay here, or do you want me to go to the House of Steel and help fight?"

"Certainly, you don't think that you and your Henchmen can stop hundreds of Gond?" Lewis asked with a smirk.

"Maybe. Maybe not. But I'm willing to try."

"Try. Ha. It will take more than blind effort," Lewis said.

"Of course." He rubbed his throbbing temples. "But I have an idea."

CHAPTER 42

"WHAT DO YOU THINK?" ABRAHAM asked Solomon.

The troglin was standing beside the tank that had crashed into the Wall a day earlier. Aside from the blackened scorch marks from the pitch, the tank was still in serviceable condition.

"Can we drive it?" Abraham asked.

Solomon held a large tank-operation manual, which looked like a pocket paperback book in his huge hands. He thumbed through the pages and squinted. His long finger ran over the lines. "I don't think it's so complicated. There appears to be a sequence to start the ignition, but the driving will be… kinda easy, I guess." He scratched behind an ear. "Things have really changed since I've been gone. All of the buttons, lights, and gauges are so tiny."

"So, do you think that you can squeeze in there and drive it?"

"Me? I can't jam myself inside there. It's going to have to be you or someone else that we can train." Solomon tucked the book underneath his arm. "If they were able to train those other people, then I don't see why we can't do the same. We might have to do it on the way to the castle, though, seeing how time is pressing."

"Agreed. And it won't be all about the tank either. We have more rifles. That should do us some good."

Sticks and Shades had gathered up four more assault rifles from the soldiers inside the tanks. Canisters of ammunition had been inside the tanks too. They had set up a pile of munitions by the campfire.

Abraham patted the tank's hull. "I find it interesting that these electrical systems operate in this world. My beer truck died moments after I drove through the tunnel. Heck, I can't remember if I even tried to start it again."

"These are diesel-fired engines. No reason it would work an entire electrical system," Solomon said.

"Yeah, that's true. But I doubt the GPS system will work."

"The what?"

"I'll explain later. Come on." He led Solomon back to the Henchmen's camp and stood in front of the fire. "Everyone gather around."

The tight group formed a semicircle around him.

"I want to make sure that we are on the same page. We'll ride with the King's Guardians and soldiers back to the House of Steel. And when I say ride, I mean on horseback and inside the iron chariot. Do I have any volunteers to drive it?"

The Henchmen exchanged many uncertain glances.

Shades and Skitts stepped forward.

"Good," Abraham said.

Four assault rifles were standing up butt down like a teepee, and he picked up one of them out of the pile.

"We are going to be doing some on-the-job training on the trip down south. I want all of you to learn how to shoot these weapons. Four of you will be assigned to take care of these weapons. Now I can pick, or you can volun—"

Dominga jumped forward. "I want one!"

"Me too," Tark said, lifting his hand.

"Anyone else?" Abraham asked.

Vern spat into the fire. "I'll stick with my sword. It's like Ruger taught us—it's the best weapon in the world."

"Aye," Bearclaw agreed. "I'll be having at them with my axe."

"Regardless, every man and woman here is going to learn how to use them."

"Sorry," Solomon said, "but I don't think my finger will fit inside the trigger guard."

Abraham nodded. "We won't get a whole lot of practice in because we need to save ammo, but all of you are plenty apt. You'll figure it out. Once we near Kingsland's border, we'll begin recon. Prince Lewis's troops will stay behind, waiting on our report. As I understand it, the Gond are tribal, so they don't know each other so much outside of the tribe. When we roll in, we are going to look like them."

"Some of us are a little small to be taken for barbarians," Shades said.

"Yeah, well, I think some of us can fit the bill. We're going to slap on black paint and ride to the castle on the tank."

Shades flicked a fly out of the air and said, "The Gond might be as brawny as they are stupid, but they can have a good nose for things. I'd be very wary of that plan. But I'd say that you have a fifty-fifty chance to fool them."

"We are going to get a close look at their forces, get a head count, and report back to Lewis."

"If they have hundreds of those guns," Shades asked, "how do we expect to beat them?"

"We have a tank, guns, and wits, and the King's Steel on our side. We'll figure it out when we get there."

"We can kill them," Horace said. He tapped his spear butt on the ground. "The Henchmen will kill them all."

"Well said." Abraham set down the rifle. "Any questions?" He scanned their hard-eyed faces. "Good. Let's roll out."

To everyone surprise, Solomon, Shades, and Skitts fired up the tank and got it moving. Shades and Skitts could be heard giggling like children inside.

Abraham led the group on the southern road back to the House of Steel. Horace and Sticks resumed their places beside him in the front. All of them rode horses. Dominga and Tark scouted ahead. They moved day and night, stopping only for a few hours of shut-eye before moving again. With the slow-moving tank, they needed to cover as much ground as possible when they could.

The bridges on the roads wouldn't hold the tank at a few junctions, but the rivers and streams were shallow enough for the tank to plow straight through. Abraham watched the surge of water rising over the tank treads as he waited for it to cross the river.

"It's a mighty beast," Horace said.

"Indeed it is."

They were only one day away from the House of Steel. Abraham shared all his thoughts with his Henchmen and even Prince Lewis too. He wasn't certain, but he got the feeling that Prince Lewis might be coming around. He seemed to show gratitude, and the smart-aleck remarks to Abraham had subsided.

"If I depart, make sure to tell Ruger everything I've told you. Don't leave a single detail out," Abraham said.

"We won't," Sticks said in a voice that seemed more sad than neutral. She seemed to have a hard time looking at Abraham.

"Horace, why don't you fall back a moment," he said.

"Aye, Captain." Horse slowed his horse.

Abraham moved closer to Sticks. Their thighs bumped as they moved forward. "What's on your mind?"

She kept her eyes forward on the green hills in the distance and said, "Nothing."

"I know you well enough by now to know that isn't true. It's Ruger, isn't it? You don't like him?"

"I don't want to talk about it," she said.

"So, something *is* bothering you? Just let it out. We never know when we might get this chance again." He wanted to be fair and address this strange love triangle. He had Mandi back home, whom he felt deeply for. Sticks had more than grown on him, but he'd never seen her laugh. Then there were Queen Clarann and Princess Clarice. The queen was Ruger's lover, and Clarice was his daughter. It all would have made for a great time-travel romance series. But with Sticks, he didn't see any point in putting the matter delicately. "Listen, Sticks, if I go, I'm really going to miss you. And if I stay, I'd like to stay with you."

"How easy for you to say." She spurred her horse into a trot with her hips bouncing on the saddle.

The haggard-looking Prospero wandered alongside Abraham, smacking his lips and sucking his teeth. With his eyes on Sticks, the man who never said anything said, "I bet that saddle's happy." He led his horse away.

Abraham let out a silly laugh. A bright sun ring with black spots formed in his line of sight. Then he shielded his eyes and fell out of the saddle.

CHAPTER 43
BACK HOME

"Wrong! Conan!" said someone with a fierce voice and an Asian accent. "What is best in life?"

"Crush your enemies. See them driven before you and hear the lamentation of the women."

Abraham rubbed his eyes. He was sitting on a sofa facing a large flat-screen TV. The movie *Conan the Barbarian* was playing on the screen. A bowl of popcorn, which was sitting on his lap, fell onto the floor. He was in a strange apartment that looked as if it had been made out of an old gas station. The ceilings were high, and a huge garage door had a phantom-black Dodge Hellcat parked behind it.

"Oh no."

He looked to his left. Smoke was leaning back in a fully extended leather recliner. He wore a black dragon T-shirt, blue jeans, and sunglasses with large lenses. His corded forearms rested on the chair's armrests. He held the remote control in his fingers and was snoring softly.

Abraham twisted his head around to see a kitchenette and full-sized kitchen table. Closed doors led to other rooms. It was nighttime outside. *Where am I? Where's Mandi and Sidney?* He reached down and picked up the bowl. His fingertips were coated with cheese dust. *What have I been doing?*

"You just *Quantum Leap*ed, didn't you?" Smoke asked in his mysterious tone.

"Huh?" He blinked his eyes.

Smoke hadn't moved.

"You just said that, didn't you?"

"Yup." Smoke collapsed the recliner and turned the TV volume down. He looked at the TV screen and said, "You have been glued to that movie nonstop since I caught it channel surfing. Well, Ruger has. He is really disappointed in the sword-fighting techniques, but he still likes it. Welcome back, Abraham."

"How did you know it was me?" He set the popcorn bowl on the coffee table, which had a small stack of car magazines on the corner and automatic pistols too.

"I can tell. Your eyes. Mannerisms. You weren't moving as sure of yourself." Smoke swiped his thick black hair out of his eyes and took off his glasses. "So, what's been going on?"

"You tell me. The last time I was here, I was a prisoner." He rubbed his neck. "Now I'm… here? Where exactly?"

"It's my old place outside of DC. We needed a good hiding spot." The tall and rangy man stood up. He eased his way into the kitchenette and grabbed the handle of the refrigerator. "Thirsty?"

"No. How'd I escape?"

"You had some help. When you were in the lair of the Time Tunnel, getting the science-fair show, I was there too, posing as a guard." Smoke cracked open the tab on a can of Coke and took his seat in the recliner. "I was one of the drivers taking you in and out. Once we got back out, I took care of those thug orderlies and brought you here. It's been two weeks since all of that happened." He drank. "It's been busy."

"Busy?" Abraham looked at the TV. "Doing what?"

"Learning." Smoke pushed back into the recliner. "Turns out that your counterpart, Ruger, is a very quick study. Sid and I have been teaching him how to use modern weapons: pistols, assault rifles, M-60 machine guns, LAW rockets."

"LAW rockets?"

"It's a personal favorite of mine. Lots of fun. And seeing how they are sending tanks into Titanuus, I think they would be useful."

"So Ruger can use those things now?"

"Oh yeah." Smoke smiled. "He wanted to know it all. That man wants to war." Smoke crossed his ankles. "We've got to know each other well, and he's told me a lot about Titanuus. I'd like to see it for myself."

"No, you don't. I'm not saying it's a bad place, but I'm not so sure it's a good place. I'll say this: we don't belong there."

"Sid hates it when I talk about it. Keep it between us."

"A man belongs with his family."

"Agreed, but I'd be lying if I didn't fantasize about taking them with me. Dragons and monsters—I've seen my share in this world, but I'd like to take on more of them. Things have been quiet around here lately, until now."

Abraham gave Smoke a perplexed look and asked, "What is it that you do? I thought you were a bounty hunter and Sid was in the FBI."

"I was a Navy SEAL too, but Sid gave up on the FBI not long after we got together. She was my handler."

He cocked an eyebrow and said, "Handler?"

"I was in prison for beating the crap out of a criminal that had a really good attorney and an inside connection with the judge. The FBI was low on manpower for some of their projects, and they didn't want to risk their agents on some of the smaller projects. Sid was assigned to a file called the Black Slate. You know, *X-Files* kind of stuff. I was given a chance to shorten my sentence by helping her." He pointed at the TV. "Man, I love this part."

Abraham gestured with his arms and said, "Well?"

"Oh, yeah, I was pretty cozy, waiting out my term, and I didn't really have any interest in helping the FBI. My past experience with big government entities strongly led me to believe that they all are shady, and I wanted no part of them. You see, I have a knack for sniffing the truth out. But, as fate would have it, the moment I saw Sid, my heart changed. That was a woman that I'd break out of jail for. In this case, I took the free ticket."

"Huh, so did the Black Slate turn out to be anything?" Abraham asked.

"Did it ever. Those things that you don't believe exist in this world... Well, let me tell you, they exist. Heck, some of them might have even come through one of your portals. There were werewolves, giants, harpies, shapeshifters, and clones. It was a deep operation invested in evil. I hate evil."

"You're serious?"

"If you don't believe me, you could ask Sid. She'll tell you. Besides, is my story any more bizarre than yours?"

"I didn't mean any disrespect, but I never would have imagined such things go on in this world." He rubbed his palms on his jeans, which he'd never seen before. He looked at his sweatshirt and read the upside-down lettering, Darkslayer Brew: The Beer for What Ales You. "Where'd you dig this shirt up?"

"Luther Vancross gave it to us."

"You didn't get him involved, did you?"

"Yeah, well, the old man is pretty persistent. He cares. Sounds like a good friend."

"He's not here, is he?"

"No." Smoke finished off his can of Coke, crushed the can, and made a hook shot into the trash can by the kitchen. "I overheard your conversation with Dr. Jack Lassiter."

"Which part?"

"All of it, but the part I was referring to was the part where you could be sent back in time to be with your family."

Abraham leaned back into the sofa and asked, "Yeah, what about it?"

With a fiery intensity lingering in his dark eyes, Smoke said, "Would you do it? Go back?"

Abraham didn't say a word. He'd been so busy fighting to survive that he hadn't had much time to give the matter deep thought. "You know, when I lost everyone, I didn't think I'd ever be able to live without them. I was lost. I'd think of them every day, and the guilt whittled down my soul. My soul was nothing but numb inside." He sighed mournfully. "It took ten years of falling flat on my face before I could lift my head up. I picked up the pieces and started walking again." His eyes started to water, and he dried them on his shirt cuff. "I'd do almost anything to hold them one last time. But I'm not traveling back in time. Even if it's possible. Life moves forward, not backward. Once you start going the wrong way, you die."

Smoke nodded. "I wouldn't do it either. And neither would Ruger, for that matter."

"You talked about this?"

"Yeah, we've gotten to be pretty big buds. I mean, he's a bit rigid, but so was Sid when we met. I've worn him down some. I've got him watching TV, didn't I?"

"The last thing Titanuus needs is more crazy ideas pouring into that world. I fear it's ruined already. I'm not so sure that what we are doing will make a difference."

"Heh heh, it sounds like that portal opened Pandora's Box."

"Based off what I've seen, that world is better off without us, but our invasion is pushing it toward an accelerated ending." He turned his gaze toward Smoke. "We recovered two more gems for King Hector. Now he has four out of the six. But I fear it's making him mad with power."

"How so?"

"He's getting irrational. Oh, and now he knows that Ruger is the father of his daughter, Clarice." He sat right up. "Oh man, I hope Ruger gets the heads-up about that. He's about to be reunited with his family. Well, assuming that they get through the barbarian horde that is raiding the castle." He glanced at the TV. It was showing the scene in the movie where Conan painted himself up in black-and-white war paint. "How do I know that I'm not dreaming?"

"Hey, I saw the Time Tunnel with my own eyes. Trust me when I say it's real. I had my doubts until I saw that thing come on. I saw that horned halfling and those huge tattooed barbarians. Ruger told me about them. The Gond. They all looked real to me. Made my hair stand up on my arms."

"Yeah, I know what you mean. I've got to find a way to shut down those portals."

"We're working on it."

Abraham took a long look around the living room. "Say, where's Mandi and Sid? Nothing happened to them, did it?"

Smoke frowned.

CHAPTER 44

ABRAHAM'S HEART BEAT BEHIND HIS ears. "What's wrong? Did something happen to Mandi? Sid?"

"What?" Smoke tore his eyes away from the TV and shook his head. "No. I hate this part when Valeria gets shot. I mean, Thulsa Doom shot her with a snake. Who does that?"

He threw a pillow at Smoke. "I ought to knock you out."

Smoke put the pillow behind his head and said, "I might be big, but I'm not easy to hit. Ruger found that out when he had an episode."

"Episode? What do you mean?"

"Let's just say that I think that this world makes him jumpy sometimes. I slipped behind him, and he, or you, nearly coldcocked me. I have a feeling that, were it his body, he would have got me. He's a warrior, isn't he? What's he look like in Titanuus?"

"Funny that you should ask." Abraham plucked a car magazine from the table, with an old blue four-door Volvo on the cover. He made a funny look and leafed through the pages. "I've only got a good look at myself a few times. Or Ruger. I'm sort of a mix of young Sean Connery and Hugh Jackman on steroids. He's strong. I'm talking animal strong. Moves like the wind and fights like the devil."

"Humph," Smoke said. He stretched his arms out over his head and yawned. "Sounds like me."

Headlights shone through the windows of the remodeled gas station. The crunch of rubber wheels on gravel caught Abraham's ear. The approaching car engine had a throaty rumble to it.

Smoke nodded. "You were asking about the girls. They are here. I can tell by the noise of the engine. It's a SRT8 Jeep Cherokee. It's got a nice groan and rides really smooth on the road. We'll be taking that back." He leaned forward and rested his elbows between his knees with his arms folded. "Say, why don't you play along and have a little fun with them."

"You mean, play Ruger."

Smoke shrugged his eyebrows. "Why not? Mandi's been kinda down, and she'll be thrilled to see you." He turned the volume up on the TV.

The car doors slammed shut.

Abraham leaned back and faced the TV.

"No, you have to sit with your back straight, like Ruger," Smoke said. "I've never seen the man slouch. He's big on posture."

Abraham sat up and put his hands on his knees.

"That's better," Smoke said with a smirk. "And don't say anything. He doesn't talk much. I'll handle it."

The front door opened. It was made of glass with a steel frame. Sid had a brown grocery bag in one hand and a box of Cokes in the other. Bags of cheese popcorn and boxes of Nutty Butty bars were sticking out of the top of the bag. She wore a pink tank top and low-rise jeans that showed off her navel. Her hair was pulled back in a silky black ponytail.

Mandi entered the room and closed the door behind her. She had four large pizza boxes in her hands.

"Hello, lordlings," Sid said in a sarcastic voice. "We have completed your snack run." She dropped the food on the kitchen counter. "How else may we serve you today?"

Abraham watched out the corner of his eye. Turning his head slightly, he could see the women with their backs to them. Mandi set the pizza boxes on the table. She wore a tight gray top and a pair of low-rise jeans that flowed over her curvy hips and flat belly. Her wavy black hair hung down her back. The intoxicating smell of perfume wafted through the air. As the women turned around, he did also. His body temperature started to rise. *What is with that sexy getup? Where did they go to buy groceries, the Lion's Den?*

"I see he hasn't changed the channel." Mandi walked over, her high heels clicking on the floor. She sat down beside Abraham and glanced between the TV and him. "It's really not that good."

Abraham fought the urge to grab Mandi and kiss her.

Sid walked over and sat down on the right side of the sofa, closer to Smoke. She had a slice of pizza in her hand. "Don't even say, 'Where is mine?' You can get it yourself. It's bad enough we had to run into town to buy your snacks, looking like a pair of hookers." She started unlacing the straps to her high-heeled shoes. "And you thought this idea wouldn't arouse suspicion. Do you know how may catcalls we got?"

"Two," Smoke guessed.

"Huh, I wish it was two. More like twenty," she glanced at the TV. "Geez, Ruger, won't you watch something else? Smoke, show him *The Punisher* or something. *Rambo*, maybe."

"If he wants to watch something else, he'll ask, won't you, Ruger?"

Abraham kept his stare fixed on the TV and nodded.

Mandi took off her high heels and rubbed her ankles. "I wish you loved rubbing feet as much as you like watching *Conan*. Did you ever think we might want to watch something else? I'd like to watch women's Wimbledon."

"I didn't know that you were a tennis player," Smoke said.

"Well, I was—a good one." She shrugged her chest. "A bit too bouncy, but when I played, the stands were full." She leaned back on the sofa's plush arm.

Abraham bent over and lifted her legs up into his lap. Mandi's painted eyes grew as big as saucers. He started rubbing her feet.

Sid gaped.

Smoke grinned.

He winked at Mandi.

She sat up and threw her arms around him and said, "Abraham, it's you? Isn't it?"

CHAPTER 45

"IT'S ME," HE SAID WITH a warm smile.

Mandi dug her fingernails into his back and said, "You sneaky snake! Why didn't you tell me?"

"We wanted to surprise you. Well, Smoke did."

"Of course he did," Sid said. "My man just loves surprises. But they don't always work out." She stood up and said, "I guess it's time to celebrate. I guess I'll serve the pizza."

Smoke slammed the recliner shut, jumped out of the chair, and said, "I'll take care of it. Anything for my queen."

The group dug into the pizza. Smoke and Abraham had their own separate boxes on their laps. The women ate from them.

Mandi held Abraham's hand with one hand and ate with the other. "It's okay," he said, "I'm not going anywhere."

"I want to hold on to you as long as I can. I never know when you're coming back or going again. I just want this to stop." Mandi wiped her free hand on a napkin. "Abraham, tell me you won't leave again."

"I wish I could." He swallowed the last bite of the Hawaiian-style pizza. "Ruger isn't that bad, is he?"

She wiped some pizza sauce off the corner of his mouth. "No, but he's not you. He's more—"

"Intense." Sid patted her flat stomach. "I'm stuffed."

"You only had two pieces," Smoke said.

"Yes, and that's twice as much as I normally eat. The celebration is over. We need to get back at it." Sid moved over to the computer desk in the corner of the room by the TV. She sat down in a black office chair. The screens on the two large monitors came on. "I'll see if Phat Sam and Guppy found anything."

"Who?" Abraham asked.

"Family, co-workers, special people like us." Sid typed on the computer and clicked the mouse. "Uh-huh. That's what we thought."

"What is it?" Smoke asked.

"Guppy confirmed what we believed. Drakeland Corporation is another branch of the old Drake Company. They use the shadow company's name as the Corporation. It's the same old government conspiracies. Powerful men and women hungry for more power. And to think that we thought we got them the last time."

"You've dealt with this before?" Abraham asked.

"People like this, yeah," Smoke said. He slapped two pieces of pizza together and bit into half of it. Speaking with his mouth full, he added, "These evil empires like to team up. More than likely, one of these old corps got wind of the Drake and propped them up. It's old money and old business that we've dealt with—hundreds if not thousands of years old."

"I don't care about the details. I just want to destroy that Time Tunnel and stop all of this from happening." Abraham tossed the pizza box on the table. "I don't have time to sit around and do research either. We know where the tunnel is, and we have to destroy it."

Sid swiveled around in her chair and said, "They know that you'll be coming back. Not to mention that they are already looking all over for you. Trust me when I say we have been putting a plan together, and Ruger has been helping."

Abraham crossed his arms. "Is that so? How? How can he help?"

"Well, for starters, he has a lot of novel ideas on how to kill people." Smoke let out a sinister chuckle. "One at a time, two at a time. Blow them up. Bomb them. Use tanks, swords, and guns. He thought he could do it on his own but wasn't so sure that your body could hold up."

Abraham gave himself a once-over. He'd continued to slim down, but he was a long way from being Ruger. "Hey, he could have done it with me. I used to be a superstar athlete. But if he wasn't going after it head-on, how is he, me, or we going to attack it?" He clutched his head. "Ah, this is maddening!" He kicked the table. "Don't you two play games with me. Spit it out!"

Mandi wrapped his arm up. "Abraham, they are on our side. Believe me, you can trust them, the same as I trust you." She pulled him toward the couch. "You need to hear them out. Be patient. We've covered a lot of ground on this."

He sank into the sofa, pinching his temples with one hand. He broke out in a cold sweat.

"Abraham, you are trembling." Mandi started rubbing his back. "It's okay. It's going to be okay."

"Don't you get it?" he asked in a throaty voice. "It's not okay. It hasn't been okay since my family died. It's not going to be okay either." He flung his hands in the air. "I don't even know if any of this is real. I don't know if you are real." He jabbed his long fingers at Sid and Smoke. "Or if they are real! You aren't the one bouncing back and forth between one reality and another. Are you!"

"Please don't yell," Mandi said in a soothing voice. "I love you. I'm here for you. This might all seem insane, and it does to me, and it scares me, but trust your heart. You know that some crazy stuff is going on. You're in the middle of it for a reason. But you can't do it on your own. Just like your Henchmen help you on the other side, we are here to help you on this side."

"Hear, hear," Smoke said.

Abraham gave the rangy man a hard-eyed look. "What did you say?" he asked with a cracking voice.

Smoke tilted his head to one side and said, "Hear, hear. Why? Is that a secret word or something in the other realm?"

Abraham let out a wild scream and pounced on Smoke.

CHAPTER 46

ABRAHAM LANDED FLAT ON TOP of Smoke. The recliner tipped over backward. The men rolled over the floor, over the top of one another.

"Stop it!" Mandi yelled. "Stop it, Abraham!"

Her words did not register with Abraham. All his frustrations had come to the surface. All the doubt and anger swelled up inside and came out. He locked his arms around Smoke's waist and slung the man into the wall.

Smoke rolled up onto his feet and hunkered down with his fingers clutching outward. "Come on, big fella."

"John, don't goad him!" Sid ordered.

Abraham lowered his shoulder and attacked like a charging bull.

Smoke braced himself for impact.

Abraham slammed him into the limestone block wall. A clock hanging on the wall fell to the ground, and its casing cracked. He kept shoving Smoke back into the wall.

Smoke's corded arms flexed. He coiled his arms around Abraham's waist and slung him aside.

Abraham stumbled backward. He lost his footing and crashed into the coffee table. Two of the legs of the table snapped.

Mandi hopped up onto the edge of the sofa. "Stop it, you two idiots! Stop it!"

In a moment, Abraham rolled onto his feet and rushed Smoke again. The fire in his blood was racing. He was mad—mad at everything, mad at the mad, mad world he'd been thrust into. He tipped his shoulder, stopped, and threw a hard punch at Smoke's face.

Smoke blocked the strong punch with his deft hands. The punch still grazed his face.

Abraham started whaling away on Smoke. He brought his hands down like hammers. The hard blows knocked through Smoke's defenses. He connected with chin and nose. He slapped his head into Smoke's mouth.

"Have you gone mad?" Mandi yelled. "Abraham, stop this! Stop this now! Listen to me!"

Her words were drowned out by the tide of anger rushing behind his ears. He kept hitting harder and harder.

Smoke snaked his head away from the heavy punches. He caught Abraham around the waist and held him chest to chest. "Go ahead! Let it out!" Smoke said fiercely in Abraham's ear. "Let it out!"

Abraham beat Smoke's back like a drum. He whaled on the man like a gorilla beating his chest. "I've had enough! I've had enough! How do I know this is real?" He hit again and again. "How do I know that you aren't one of them?" He kept at it. "How do I know? How do I know?"

"You have to have faith," Smoke said. "It's all you got. You're a good man. Don't let the enemy take that from you!"

Abraham's long arms turned to lead. The strength in his limbs failed. His last punches had no weight behind them. He sagged into Smoke's shoulder and sobbed. "I'm sorry." He let out another wet sob.

"Don't be." Smoke led Abraham to the couch and sat him down beside Mandi. He put a strong hand on Abraham's shoulder and said, "You've been at war. It happens to the best of them. Let it out. Have a good cry."

He let out a shuddering breath, straightened his back, and said, "Henchmen don't cry."

Smoke wiped the blood from the corner of his mouth and added, "Maybe not, but they sure can hit." He gave Abraham a firm slap on the back. "How about an ice-cold Coke."

Abraham nodded. He looked between Mandi and Sid and said, "I'm sorry. I bet you think I'm nuts. And why wouldn't you? I think I'm nuts."

Laying a gentle hand on his back, Mandi said, "I always liked the crazy ones."

He choked out a laugh.

Smoke handed him a Coke.

Sid got out of her chair and said, "John, let's give the two of them some privacy. Plus, I need to get out of these clothes." She held up a palm. "Don't say it."

"Say what?" He picked up a pizza and followed her back to their bedroom and closed the door.

Abraham lifted his eyes to Mandi's. "Look at me, sitting here and sobbing like a baby."

"Now isn't the time to doubt yourself. We are getting close to the end. I can feel it. I don't know why, but I do." She reached across Abraham's legs, grabbed the remote, and turned off the TV. "That's better. I think you need some Yacht Rock radio." She dusted the hair out of his eyes. "You need to mellow."

"Huh. Easier said than done. You look great, by the way."

"Thanks." She held his hand. "You sure are full of surprises."

"What do you mean?"

"When you attacked Smoke? I didn't see that coming." She put his head over her chest. "Feel it. My heart's still racing."

He felt the rapid beat of her heart under his fingers. Her perfumed scent wafted under his nose. "I didn't mean to scare you."

"Oh, it didn't scare me. I liked seeing you come alive like that. You gave Smoke a fit. That surprised me. But he handled it well." She kissed his cheek. "It's going to be okay, Abraham. I believe in you. You keep believing in yourself. I know in my heart you are doing the right thing. You should know it too."

"How do I know that my heart is right? Maybe I've been wrong about everything. Like that zillon said."

"You mean the alien woman? Ottum?"

He nodded.

"Yeah, Smoke told us about her. Now, that gave me goose bumps. But let me tell you, Sid and Smoke have let me in on the stuff they've seen. I believe it's real. Stuff like that hides in the dark and wears many disguises." She kissed his hand. "Do you want to know how I know that you are a good guy?"

He shrugged. "I guess."

"You never hit on me, and I get hit on all of the time. That's what got my attention. And you looked like a big ol' teddy bear." She gave him a warm smile. "There was something gentle about you and something broken too. I don't know, but I just knew that you were, well, my kind of guy. My mom, you know, Martha, always told me to find a sweet man. I never listened. My relationships were one drama fest after another."

"And this isn't drama?"

"Well, this is different. You are sweet, Abe, and this is crazy, but I just know that you are a special man. It's not all of this excitement that turns me on like a dreamy-eyed schoolgirl lusting after the latest hottie in *Tiger Beat* magazine. There is something deeper, a spark that I felt. Didn't you feel it too?"

"I suppose, but I'd never admitted it. Because, you know, I felt guilty." He frowned. "I always feel like I let them down."

She wiped her eyes and sniffed. "I'm ashamed to say this, but I did my homework on you. Everything about that accident says that it wasn't your fault. You need to believe it too."

"I try," he said, "but no matter how hard it is, I can't. I think that might be why I like Titanuus. There, I don't have to think about it."

CHAPTER 47

"YOU BELONG IN THIS WORLD," Mandi said. "You know, I think that maybe that's why you go back and forth. You can't decide between the two. Have you ever thought about that?"

Abraham shrugged. "Maybe. So, what are you saying—that if I concentrate long enough, I can go back to Titanuus?"

"Perhaps. But I don't want you to do that. I want to keep you here as long as I can." She crawled into his lap, straddling him. Cupping his face in her hands, she said, "I want to stare into those soft brown eyes. It's hard seeing you with Ruger in there. His stare is hard as iron—not mean, but penetrating. It freaks me out. Like Martha said, I need a sweet man. A teddy bear. One that I can trust." She started kissing him.

He kissed back. Her soft lips ignited his blood. While he was kissing her, he thought of Sticks. He broke off the kiss.

"Uh..."

Panting with her eyes closed, she said, "What? Don't worry about them. They won't bother us."

"No, it's not that. It's the other women, in Titanuus. I'm close with them."

Mandi slid off his lap. She tied her hair into a ponytail and said, "Look, let's keep a rule, what happens in Titanuus stays in Titanuus. I don't want to know. Ruger's rambled on a good deal about Queen Clarann. I can't bear to hear any more."

"Well, it's not Clarann. It's—"

She put her hand over his lips and said, "I don't want to know. Believe me, I have a very jealous bone. But we aren't married—or exclusive, exactly. Look, the reason I married Barry was because some other woman made me jealous. I didn't want her to have him. I didn't want her to win. So I took him and regretted it ever since. So for you to do what you need to do, you'll have to decide without my intervention."

"You're a little too cool about that. I mean, it's not like I'm out to fool around. It happens, but it hasn't happened in a while."

Mandi plugged her ears with her fingers. "Nah nah nah. I am not listening. Please quit talking about it. Nah nah nah."

He lifted up his hands in a sign of surrender. "Okay, not a word." He took a long drink of Coke then glanced over his shoulder at the bedroom door. "Do you really think they can help? There is an army out to get us."

"They have a plan. They went over it with Ruger too. He was on board with it."

He tilted his head and asked, "So everyone knows but me?"

"We've been waiting for you to arrive." She bit her bottom lip. "Man, I was hoping to have a little one-on-one time before we got into this. There's another bedroom, you know. The plan would make very good pillow talk."

"I can't believe I'm saying this, but I really need to know what is going on." He ran his stare over her body. "And I think it's best that I don't... you know, until all of this is over."

"Okay, suit yourself." She lifted her arms up, chest out, and stretched. She twisted side to side. "But if you change your mind..."

With a dry throat, he said, "You don't take no for an answer, do you?"

"What do you think?"

"And you said that you didn't want to be a distraction."

"Okay, fine." She eased back into the sofa cushions and curled her legs underneath her body. "I might not be able to explain it as well, but I'll let them explain the details. So if you have questions, they'll have to wait. Got it?"

He nodded. "Okay."

Mandi propped her head on a pillow. "We've been hoping that you would return. At least, that is what we've been waiting for and why we are hiding. Everyone agrees that we need to all meet at the Time Tunnel at the same time."

Abraham lifted a finger.

"No." She pushed the finger down. "Hear me out. From our side, we need to be there when you come from the other side. No, wait—that doesn't sound good." She stroked her ponytail. "When you are in Titanuus, well, you or Ruger, you need to work your way to the place where the tunnel is. Ruger believes the Time Tunnel will have to be destroyed from both sides. Does that make sense?"

"Yeah, it makes sense, but there is one big problem."

"What is that?"

"I still don't know where the Time Tunnel is."

"Yes, you do. You've been there."

"I'm not talking about the one in this world. I'm talking about the location in Titanuus. I don't know where it is."

"Oh," she said. "Well, that's a problem. We thought you would have known that already."

"Well, I don't." He crushed his Coke can and tossed it toward the waste bin. He missed. "And now, it looks like it's up to Ruger to find out."

CHAPTER 48
TITANUUS

"THE CAPTAIN IS BACK! THE captain is back!" Horace bellowed. He'd helped Ruger, who had fallen out of his saddle a moment earlier, to his feet.

What now? Sticks thought. She rode back to see what all the commotion was about.

Ruger shook his head, a grim smile forming on his face. He bumped forearms with his original crew, Horace, Vern, Bearclaw, Prospero, and Apollo. Shades sneaked up on Ruger's back, picked him up, and spun him around.

"Ha, I see you are as slippery as ever, Shades," Ruger said.

Sticks managed an uncharacteristic frown. It wasn't that she didn't like the real Ruger, but she missed Abraham. He was gone again. Ruger was different. He walked differently and talked differently. His voice was polished and carried authority. It wasn't that Abraham was bad, but he was a different sort of leader, gutsy and all heart. She didn't know what to make of Ruger yet, but the original Henchmen liked him.

Ruger gazed at the tank rolling up behind the company. He pulled out Black Bane. "The enemy is in our midst!"

"No," Horace said. "We conquered the metal dragon. It rides with us. Skitts, a Red Tunic, is in the belly."

Ruger flipped Black Bane over his hand with a twist of the wrist and stuffed it back in the sheath. "I see. Well done, then."

He eyed Horace and his closest men. They were all painted in white and bare chested. Not a stitch of armor was on them.

"You no longer don the King's Armor? Your appearance is hardly standard or uniform."

Vern stepped forward with a crooked sneer on his face. "Abraham did this. It was his idea to use this disguise to fool the Gond."

"The Gond?"

"The barbarians have laid siege to the House of Steel, Captain," Horace said. "Disguised as them, we hoped to catch them off guard—cut through their forces and attack. We have hornet blasters. Like them."

Ruger glanced at his own painted body. Jagged black striping and white were painted all over. He showed a mouthful of white teeth. "I like it. Now, tell me about the Gond." He slowly spun around with his fists on his hips. "The House of Steel is close, isn't it?"

"Aye," Horace said.

"Abraham came up with a foolish idea to disguise ourselves as Gond, win their favor, and attack," Vern said scornfully.

Ruger stepped over to Vern, looked down at him, and said, "I gather that you take issue with Abraham. Why is that? He is your captain."

Vern swallowed. "No, you are my—"

Ruger swatted Vern across the face with a loud smack. "You follow that captain. Do you understand that?"

Vern shrank underneath Ruger's steely gaze. "Yes, Captain."

"Listen to me, all of you!" Ruger lifted his voice. "There is no time to doubt me or the other. I am the captain. Abraham is the captain! I can see that he has done well to lead you this far. Now, the time has come to finish this quest. Our king, our kingdom, our way of life is in great peril! You cannot doubt. Doubt is death. Do you understand me?"

"Aye, Captain!" the gathering group said.

Ruger marched down the line of men, around the tank, and back to the group. He grabbed Vern by the neck. "I like this plan. The Gond are fierce fighters, but they can be stupid. I would have done something very similar. What would you have done, Vern?"

"I would not have shed my armor. And what happens if they recognize our Brands?" Vern said. "We need a better idea is all."

"So that is it? That is your plan?" Ruger laughed. "Vern, it does not sound like you are a better creator than Abraham. However, I can see immediately where his plan is flawed. The barbarians might be dumb, but it will take more cunning to fool them." He climbed back into the saddle of his horse. "Let us ride while I contemplate. Come, Horace, Bearclaw. Advise me."

Sticks fell to the back of the company with Solomon, out of earshot of Ruger.

With his long, hairy arms swinging by his sides, Solomon said, "A tight-knit group. It looks like you're now on the outside, looking in."

"We're probably better off," she said dryly.

"I think you should insert yourself. Ruger needs to understand your value." The crease between his eyes crinkled. "I would."

"Maybe you should insert yourself."

"No, that's not my style. I'm more of a follower than a leader."

The tank rolled up beside them. Smiling, Shades ran up to the slow-moving tank and climbed on. He saluted Sticks and Solomon and dropped back inside the hatch with Skitts.

"Ruger really does lift them up and out of their boots," Solomon said. "I like him. He's different, very military, but I can respect that. I think he's a man of his word."

"Yeah," she mumbled.

"You are a hard one to figure out, do you know that?" Solomon said. "I've known a lot of women, but you don't wear your heart on your sleeve, do you?"

Sticks gave him a look and said, "Life is what it is. I learned long ago that there isn't much I can do to change it. I do prefer to stay with one personality over another. Is it so bad that I'd like to have continuity?"

"In this crazy world? Huh, I don't think it is possible. Of course, my world was crazy too." He reached over and patted her on the back. "I think you need to assert yourself. Horace will back your play."

Sticks tugged the reins, turning the horse's head aside. Without a word, she drifted farther back from the group, unable to shake the gnawing inside her stomach. She wiped the corner of her eye and looked up into the heavens. *Come back, Abraham. I miss you.*

CHAPTER 49

"Good evening," Ruger said to Sticks.

She was sitting alone, away from the camp the Henchmen had set up. She was sharpening a dagger on a stone. The day had been long as they pushed over the rolling hills of Kingsland, trying to gain as much ground as they could. She nodded at him.

"May I sit?"

She shrugged.

Ruger planted himself beside her and leaned back on his hands and looked into the sky. "It's a beautiful thing, seeing my stars again. In the other world, they are very different." He cleared his throat. "Horace tells me that you have been second in command of the Henchmen, alongside him." He raised an eyebrow at her. "Yet you avoid your station."

"It seemed to me that moment changed when you arrived. You and the other men are better acquainted."

"True, and I'm happy to see them. But I need to get to know the rest of you as well. I imagine it has been very odd dealing with the same man who has shared many different personalities."

She switched one dagger out for another from her bandolier. She ran the blade's edge across the stone. "It is what it is. I do as I'm told."

He nodded. "The other one, the one before Abraham, his real name was Eugene. You spent most all of your time with him, eh?"

"Intimately and unfortunately."

"I am aware of his exploitation of the Henchmen. He dishonored this body, my body, and used the Henchmen like fish bait." He balled up his fists, and his knuckles cracked. "I will kill that man."

"Isn't he in the other world?"

"Yes, but I'll be going back. I don't know when, but like the sands of an hourglass, the time for this is running out."

She scraped her knife over the stone while stiffening at the same time. Ruger was right. He could sense it. She could sense it. Their mission was coming to an end.

Ruger unslung a backpack from his shoulder. It was Abraham's. He unzipped the backpack and pulled an item out. It was a small card with a picture on it. It was a decent-looking man, clean shaven, cheeky, wearing a strange cap with a bill. He held a smooth club over his shoulder. "That's Abraham. Had you seen that before?"

She slid her knife into her leather bandolier, set down the stone, and took the card. She squinted. "He looks a lot different."

"Oh, that was a long time ago. He looks much worse now. Bearded and shaggy, and in very poor condition. It's been very challenging to overcome the disadvantages of that body." He dusted the hair from his eyes. "A broken body of a broken man." He lifted a finger. "But he has heart."

She flipped the card around and asked, "Why are you showing me this?"

"I thought you would want a good look at the man that you are in love with."

"I'm not in love." She flicked the card at Ruger. "Not with him, anyway."

"No, but you are in love with the him in me. It's a twisted scenario. I know something about that. I'm in love with the bride of my king." He leaned his head down and sighed. "The only thing harder than war is love. War I understand, but love I don't."

"I guess Horace filled you in. I think the king is pretty mad at you." She looked him in the eye. "He's probably going to kill you."

Ruger chuckled. "Yes, and yet I ride to save him." He rubbed shoulders with Sticks. "I saw her first, you know. He snatched her away from me, though I do not blame him. I cannot wait for the moment when I cast my gaze upon my own daughter. All of these years, and I never knew."

She drew her knees up to her chest and said, "I wouldn't have told you either."

"Yes, I don't blame Clarann. Though I would have liked to have had a hand in raising my daughter. I hear that she is a fine sword."

"Feisty like a raccoon too."

He tossed his head back and laughed. "That she gets from her mother. Anyhow, Sticks…" He picked up the card and put in inside the backpack. "Why don't you hold on to this for Abraham." He stood up. "And don't be a stranger. I need your counsel the same as before. Rest well."

She watched Ruger amble back toward the main camp's fire. She cradled Abraham's backpack to her chest. Ruger seemed to be everything the others thought him to be, an honest knight and compassionate leader. No wonder his men followed him with such fierce loyalty.

Sticks unzipped the backpack and fished out the card again. She took a long and hard look at the image. She traced the face with her finger. *Who are you?*

The image of the man wasn't anything like the man she'd become accustomed to. She wondered what it would be like in Abraham's world. *Would I be out of place? I can't make something like that work. Why would I want to? What's wrong with me?* She tucked the card into one of her pockets. *I need to forget about this. I need to let go.* She rubbed the brand on her chest. *Once this is over, if I live, I no longer want to be a Henchmen. I want to be my own.*

Sticks lay down on her bedroll and closed her eyes. She fell fast asleep. She'd never dreamed before, but she did that night. She saw Abraham fighting Ruger, each with a sword in hand. They were the same but different. Steel flashed. Thunder rolled. Ruger's sword pierced Abraham's heart in two.

"Wake up! Wake, Sticks! Wake!"

She sat straight up, gasping for breath.

Shades was in her face. The new dawn had come. "Time to move." He helped her to her feet and swatted her behind. "Game on, girlie. Game on."

Sticks rolled up her bedroll, fingers trembling. She couldn't shake away the image of Abraham dying.

CHAPTER 50

A SMOKING BALL OF FLAME SAILED out of a small catapult and over the perimeter wall of the House of Steel. The Gond barbarians let out a chorus of wild cheers. Not one of the bare-chested painted warriors stood under six feet in height. Dozens of them towered over seven feet tall. Their bodies were packed with hard muscle. They carried crude weapons, swords, battle axes, and machine guns. They loaded another decapitated head into another catapult. They lit the skull on fire and let it fly.

"How many do you count?" Tark asked. The athletic black warrior was lying flat in tall grasses. His smoky eyes moved over the sea of savage men dancing and screaming outside the castle.

Dominga was hunkered down on one knee with a spyglass over one eye. "It would help if they didn't move all the time. But I'm counting over five hundred. You?"

"About the same," Tark said, his head slowly turning from side to side. "I don't like Ruger's plan. I don't like it at all. Those men are bloodthirsty. So many of them, too."

"They aren't men." Sticks low crawled over to Dominga and took the spyglass to view the camp below.

Many bonfires were spread out along the castle walls, burning thirty feet away. They'd been made from wood and the flesh of men. A Gond warrior dragged a dead man by his head of hair and tossed him on one huge fire. The road leading up to the castle had been dressed on both sides with severed heads spiked on poles.

She swallowed. "They are Gond."

Dusk was nearing. The shining sun was setting behind them, which made for perfect cover from anyone looking their way.

The trio watched the Gond fire the assault rifles at the castle guards that popped up on the high wall. A guard fell over the twenty-five-foot-high wall, clutching his neck. Two Gond rushed the wall and dragged the kicking man away. One held the soldier down while the other Gond cut his head off and held it high for all to see.

The House of Steel wasn't without its defenses. Crossbows were fired out of arrow slits, but the ballista towers were no longer manned. They'd all been shot to pieces.

The distinct popping of weapon fire came and went in spurts. The moment a castle soldier showed his face, a burst of gunfire followed.

Dominga rubbed her arms. "Those brutes are giving me chill bumps. They are heartless." She looked at her assault rifle and ran her fingers over the stock. She forced a smile. "But I like the idea of being able to kill them from one hundred yards away. It doesn't seem possible." She stared down the gun barrel's sight and closed and eye. She made a gunfire sound and said, "At least they are big targets."

"I know," Sticks said. She held out her rifle. "Do you both remember how to reload and fire this thing? I can show you again."

"No. We got it." Tark bumped forearms with Dominga. Sweat glistened on his forehead. "Personally, I can't wait to shoot one of those Gond. Look at them. They kill without discrimination. They are evil beasts."

"Just wait for the signal," she said.

"What is the signal?" Dominga asked.

"You'll know it when you see it." Sticks crawled down the bank.

They were positioned just over one hundred yards away from the castle. The surrounding plains were grassy, with a few small trees scattered about. The castle sat on the highest point of the gentle slope that led to the steep sea cliffs behind it. The castle's towers had a perfect view of anyone that approached its walls. When the Henchmen came, with a tank in tow, the Gond and the castle would know it.

Sticks crawled over the next rise, and with the sun in her eyes, she ran low to where the grasslands dipped and the castle fell out of sight. She jogged over a mile and didn't stop until she caught back up with the Henchmen, who were waiting by the tank. She reported to Ruger.

"What did you find?" he asked sternly.

"Roughly five hundred Gond lay siege to the castle and many citizens. Half of them are armed with rifles. They mass near the front gates, mocking the king by catapulting burning heads of the dead over the Wall."

Ruger stroked his chin. "I see. And Tark and Dominga are in a secure position?"

"They are planted right where you said."

He nodded. "Henchmen, gather."

The company quickly formed a semicircle around Ruger, who stood with his back to the treads of the tank. "The Gond are waiting on this hunk of metal." He slapped his hand on the tank. "They wait for the tank to come and blast the House of Steel's gates to a thousand pieces, but we'll have a surprise for them… won't we?"

"Aye!" Horace stated.

Solomon and Sticks exchanged a quick look.

The plan had changed. Not all the Henchmen were disguised as Gond. The war paint had been washed off. Ruger wore his breastplate. Vern, Cudgel, Apollo, and Prospero wore their tunics over chainmail. They looked like soldiers, nothing less and nothing more. Horace, Bearclaw, and Cudgel remained painted up and bare-chested. All of them were big men. Bearclaw was the most Gond looking of them all.

Skitts and Iris were inside the tank.

Shades roped up Ruger, Vern, Apollo, and Prospero. He tied knots around their wrists and put ropes around their necks. None of the men appeared to be armed. Shades tugged on the rope. "One jerk here, and they'll pull free. Elder's Fortune to you, Captain." He climbed up into the tank and vanished inside the hatch.

Ruger waved Sticks and Solomon over. "I want you to get word to Prince Lewis. Let him know my plan. If we engage, I expect his full support. I hope he brought some."

"I'd rather stay close," Sticks said.

He put his hand on her shoulder and said, "Ride now, and I hope that it isn't over before you return." He looked at Solomon. "There is a large black case on the back of the tank. I need you to look into that."

Solomon gave him a curious look, shrugged, and said, "Okay."

With a frown, Sticks rode away.

CHAPTER 51

Sticks caught up with Prince Lewis over a league away. Lewis and Pratt were marching a force just over two hundred men over the grasslands. They were all knights in full suits of armor, riding on horseback. The banners of the House of Steel flapped in the wind.

"Five hundred Gond, you say?" Prince Lewis said. His face was ashen and his shoulders slumping. He held one hand over his side and the other on the reins of his horse. A stiff breeze rustled his hair. "And Ruger rides into the jaws of death. So like him." He glanced at his second in command. "What do you think, Pratt? Do you care to taste the sting of the lead hornets?"

"Those cowardly barbarians fear a straight-up fight." Pratt shook his head. "If it is true what you say, that one man can kill many from a great distance, then I say we need a fuller army."

Lewis scratched an eyelid and said, "True." He eyeballed the rifle slung over Sticks's shoulder. "Why, she could take you out, Pratt, at close range."

Pratt blanched.

"I'd never assault the crown," Sticks said as she continued to ride alongside the prince. She didn't know what else to say. She'd already given the prince all the information she had at her disposal. She'd shared Ruger's plan too, which was, for lack of a better word, insane. "Prince Lewis, might I ask what you are thinking? I should return quickly."

Prince Lewis leaned his head her way and said, "It's a big decision. And I'd be lying if I didn't admit that I didn't want to face those rifles again." He tapped his chest. Underneath his cape, he wore a full breastplate made from the King's Steel. A helmet of the King's Guardians hung from the saddle. "The things I have to do to become king."

They kept riding, eyes ahead, without saying a word.

Pratt finally broke the silence and said, "I like this part of the country. I prefer the seaside for retirement, but I must admit, after this trek, the fields of wildflowers are growing on me."

"Is that all you think about? Retirement?"

"I'll be old someday," Pratt replied. "My bones groan. My father told me when your joints start feeling as stiff as wood, the old time is coming."

"You aren't going to have an old time. You'll be the Guardian Commander, protecting me and my family. Assuming I get the chance to have one." Lewis waved his hand at a pair of men riding not far behind him. "Derek. Gravely. Come."

Two rugged men rode up into the group. They were Guardians in full armor. Derek had a full smile on his face. Gravely was stone-faced and ashen.

"My finest scouts," Lewis said to Sticks. "They will ride with you and report back to me."

Derek gave Sticks a flirty nod. Gravely didn't even look her direction.

Prince Lewis sucked his teeth. "If you chance upon Ruger, tell him that we'll get there when we get there. Oh, and one more thing. Don't get ambushed."

"Thanks for the advice." Sticks whipped the reins of her horse and galloped off with Derek and Gravely right on her tail. She didn't know what to make of Lewis's response. He didn't seem eager at all to engage in full battle with the Gond. She didn't blame him either. The Henchmen were in way over their heads.

What in the Elders is Ruger going to do? If the Gond sniff us out, they'll slaughter them.

She spurred her horse onward, faster and faster. They rode nonstop before slowing to a trot.

"Why did we slow down?" Gravely asked in a dry voice.

Sticks felt spiders crawling up her back. The prairie breeze died down. Ahead were long fields of tall grasses. She'd ridden through it once already, but something seemed different. She slowed her horse to a walk.

Derek exchanged a look with Gravely. "Say, pretty, what's got you all twitchy? Didn't you just pass through here?"

"Yeah." She unshouldered the rifle and flipped the safety mechanism from Safe to Fire. "That doesn't mean something might not have crawled in there since I passed. I have a feeling. Keep your eyes open."

She led the trio into the high grass. The stretch of field was hundreds of yards long. She followed the flattened path in the waist-high grasses she'd plowed through over an hour earlier.

A spotted deer burst out of the grass.

Sticks and the men jumped in their saddles.

Derek chuckled. "Now my heart is moved by the sight of a comely woman. Heh heh heh. If there is something in this grass that's not a bug or varmint, I think we'd be better suited to speed along."

Sticks led her horse in a zigzag pattern, keeping the rifle barrel pointed ahead and downward. She noticed small trees sticking up only a few feet out of the high grass. She didn't remember seeing them before. She pointed her weapon at the trees.

Derek and Gravely acknowledged her signal. They pulled their swords free, split away from each other, and moved toward the little trees. Both men stopped short of the trees. Leaning over their saddle horns, they looked at the trees and shrugged.

Sticks took a close look at a tree sticking up out of the grasses. She could have sworn it had just been planted there, but nothing about it was remarkable.

"Perhaps you overlooked them when you rode straight through," Derek said. "Who's going to notice a little tree?" He glanced about. "I see many."

Gravely led his horse forward.

Sticks did the same, but she could have sworn the trees hadn't been there before.

They cleared the high grasses, and the tightness in her chest eased. She put the rifle on Safe and slung it over her shoulder. The terrain was clear ahead. She walked her horse forward and lifted the reins to snap them, then her instincts caught fire. She twisted her head around.

Gond sprinted out of the edge of the grasses and launched javelins into the trio's horses.

Sticks flew out of the bucking horse's saddle and landed hard on her back.

CHAPTER 52

With the wind knocked out of her, Sticks pulled a dagger free of her bandolier the moment a Gond leapt on top of her. She punched a hole in the painted man's belly and ripped him open. Warm blood ran over his fingers. The barbarian whaled on her with mighty fists in his death throes. She twisted the blade inside the man.

The Gond died on top of her.

Sucking for breath, Sticks pushed out from underneath the heavy warrior.

Another Gond rushed her from the thickets. He carried a crude war axe cocked over his shoulder and came on with a fierce swing.

Sticks leapt to one side, ducking underneath the swing. She poked a hole behind the Gond's ribs.

The savage warrior whirled around and let out a bloodcurdling cry. The wild-eyed warrior closed in with an over-headed chop.

Sticks sprang away. Striking like a snake, she slashed him across the wrist.

The Gond let out a throaty chuckle and clamped his big fingers around her neck. He lifted her off the ground and shook her like a rag.

She pulled another dagger free and stabbed the wild man in the throat.

His knees buckled, and he released her. She stumbled away and fell flat on the ground. He bled out in the field.

Coughing and clutching her throat, Sticks spun around to the clamor of battle. Derek was fighting sword against axe with a Gond. The barbarian stood a half a foot taller than Derek and swung his battle axe with might. A powerful blow smote Derek full in the chest and sent the Guardian scout spinning to the ground.

Sticks pulled the rifle to her shoulder and aimed at the Gond. She pulled the trigger. The weapon didn't fire. "Titanuus's Crotch." She flipped the safety to Fire.

The Gond's axe came down. Blood spurted up.

She fired.

The bullet blew out one side of the Gond's head. The axe fell free of his fingers. He fell over dead.

Sticks rushed over to Derek. His smiling face had been split open by the axe. She ground her teeth and shook her head. She put the rifle on her shoulder and searched the fields.

Gravely lay on the ground, twitching.

A Gond wandered the field with a sword jutting from his side. He turned his heavy gaze on Sticks. He pulled the sword free of his wound in a blood-dripping grip and charged.

Sticks blasted a hole in his heart.

The last Gond fell.

She kept her aim on the tall grasses and walked toward Gravely. She counted eight dead Gond on the ground. Derek and Gravely had chopped up two apiece but couldn't overcome the third. She knelt by Gravely. He spat up blood. A deep cut had opened his neck. His eyes fluttered. His cold gaze froze on the clouds above.

Sticks cursed. Two of the horses lay dead on the ground. Her horse had galloped away. She would have to complete the journey on foot. She shouldered her weapon and ran east toward the House of Steel.

She moved at a brisk jog, stopping to rest only a few times. She reloaded her magazine clips along the way and kept her rifle ready. The Gond had set up two ambushes that she knew of. She'd just survived one of them. For all she knew, the Gond were privy to Ruger's plan.

Maybe they don't know. Those barbarians might not have joined the rest. Either way...

An hour into the run, her legs were aching, and her lungs burned. She wasn't used to carrying much of a load, but the rifle tightened the muscles through her shoulder blades. She moved on at three-quarters speed, making her stride as long as she could.

Night had fallen. The thick clouds made the sky pitch-black.

Finally, Sticks caught up to a muddy spot in the back roads where the tank and the Henchmen had passed. She gathered her wind and raced to the spot where she'd left Dominga and Tark. The pair lay deep in the grasses and pointed their weapons at her. Panting, she lifted a hand and said in a low voice. "It's me."

"Well, *Me*, the next time you sneak up on our backside, you might want to signal sooner," Tark said. "I about took your head off with this rifle."

Sticks lay down in the grass between the pair. She sucked for breath. "Oh, I think if you shot me, I'd feel a lot better. I don't think I've ever run that far before."

"What happened to your horse?" Dominga asked. From the prone position, she eyed the activity at the castle with a spyglass.

Sticks briefly shared the story of the battle.

"There are more Gond behind us?" Tark said.

"I didn't come across any more. It might have been a patrol, or they were on their way to join the rest. I don't know," Sticks said. She took the spyglass from Dominga. She could see the tank sitting fifty yards away from the castle's main gate. "It's quiet down there. What is happening?"

"They rolled up with the tank a few hours ago," Tark said with an impatient sigh. "Ruger and the others have been lying on their bellies ever since. Do you see them?"

Sticks saw a row of men lying in front of the tank. It was Ruger, Vern, Apollo, and Prospero. All of them lay with their faces down in the dirt. She scanned the area and found Bearclaw and Horace talking with a huge barbarian that appeared to be the leader. He towered a full head taller than Bearclaw, who was taller than Horace. The barbarian had a mighty frame covered in tattoos and piercings. They appeared to be arguing. "That is a big man."

Tark nodded. "You can say that again. And I don't think it's going well either. They've been arguing back and forth the entire time. The Gond keeps pointing at the tank and motioning at our men that are kissing dirt."

"What do you think he wants?" she asked.

Speaking innocently, Dominga said, "I think he wants that iron chariot to run over them."

CHAPTER 53

Ruger Slade lay in the dirt with his belly on the ground. The Gond would spit on him and his men when they walked by. Regardless, he kept his head down, his eyes and ears open. He was glad to be back on Titanuus. *But for how long?* He moved his head slowly to one side and faced Vern. No barbarians were within earshot.

He said, "Glad to see things haven't changed."

"Yeah." Vern twisted his thick lips into a smile. "Just like back in the day. Glad it's you. So are we going to lie here all night?"

"Patience."

So far, Bearclaw and Horace had managed to fool the Gond leader. The wild warriors were craftier than they were smart. Ruger could hear bits and pieces of the conversation carrying under the clamor of the siege going on at the Wall. Bearclaw was making a case that more armies and tanks were coming and that the Gond needed to wait. The Gond leader, a grizzly of a man named Glaag, had taken command of the tribes. He was calling the shots. The other leaders that had opposed him were dead. That was the story Ruger had caught.

Glaag led Bearclaw and Horace over to the tank. The roaring bonfires cast dark shadows on all their faces. The barbarian rapped his knuckles on the metal and pointed at the machine and at the Henchmen lying on the ground. "Iron chariot run them over." He spoke in a bearish voice. "I want to see their heads pop from their shoulders. I want their bodies to squish. I want King Hector to hear the bones in their bodies pop."

"I want my tribe to see it too!" Bearclaw argued. "They be here at the dawn. More armies come with the Shield of Steel down. I say that we should wait."

Glaag thumped his muscular tattooed chest with his fist. "Don't try me. I am in command. Roll the iron chariot now!" He had an assault rifle slung over his shoulder and carried a single-bladed war axe in one hand. He put the flat of his big blade in front of Bearclaw's face. "Do you want to challenge me?"

Bearclaw lifted his eyes to meet Glaag's iron gaze with his own. "Yes."

Horace pulled Bearclaw away by the collar. "We are here to conquer the House of Steel, not one another! You can play your games later!"

The wild-eyed Glaag thrust his axe into the air. "The challenge has been made! I accept!" He pointed his axe at Bearclaw. "Do you change your mind and cower?"

Bearclaw brought his twin-bladed battle axe around to his front, slapped his chest, and said, "No!"

"What is Bearclaw doing?" Vern said under his breath.

"Buying time. You aren't in a rush to get trampled by that tank, are you?"

"No," Vern replied.

Ruger twisted his head around for a better look at Glaag. He and Bearclaw squared off in front of the tank. The Gond gathered in a huge circle, yelling and chortling at a fever pitch. They'd forgotten about their prisoners for the moment and chanted for their leader.

"Glaag! Glaag! Glaag! Glaag! Glaag!"

Horace dared a look at Ruger. Ruger pointed his lips at him, telling him to wait for his signal. Horace nodded subtly. The plan was still on. How he was going to execute the plan was another thing. He had to wait for the moment and hope it came.

"Be ready," he whispered to his men.

Glaag waved a big arm over to one of his men. "Bring the shields."

A Gond with a long braided ponytail handed a small round shield to Glaag. Glaag beat his axe against the shield's steel. He tossed it to Bearclaw. Brimming with confidence, Glaag said, "To make the match last longer." He took the other shield offered to him, tossed his head back and yelled, "Haaa-hoooom!"

Bearclaw's eyes narrowed. He lowered his gaze to the top rim of the shield and spun his war axe by the handle.

Glaag charged. He brought down his battle axe on Bearclaw's shield with bone-jarring impact.

Bearclaw's knees buckled underneath him. He shuffled backward and struck out with his axe. The blade's edge clipped Glaag's shield.

The Gond leader moved smoothly and easily for such a large man. He fended off Bearclaw's attacks with well-timed ease.

To the hungry howling of the tribes, the titanic, wild-haired, tattooed warriors danced back and forth. They exchanged a flurry of axe blows to the shields with quick and resounding effects.

Ruger tensed. Glaag's powerful and precise strokes beat on Bearclaw like a hammer. The metal and the wood on Bearclaw's shield started to chip away. His friend groaned underneath the barbarian's superior strength and weight.

"By the Elders, that is a barbarian of barbarians," Vern said with a gasp.

A Gond guard rushed over to Vern and kicked him in the ribs.

Vern let out a groan.

Bearclaw snaked in a few strikes at Glaag's belly. The barbarian backpedaled and knocked the jabs away.

Glaag let out a wild, howling scream and yelled, "I will drink your blood, brother!" He unleashed a windmill chop that blasted through Bearclaw's shield.

Bearclaw dropped to a knee.

The clustering Gond horde let out earsplitting screams.

The well-knit Bearclaw, large in stature for a normal man, could not match Glaag's greater length and superior strength.

The weight of Glaag's axe, powered by muscle as hard as iron, bore down on Bearclaw's shield.

Bearclaw lifted his shield.

Glaag knocked it down. He twisted the direction of his axe. With a hard swipe, Bearclaw's shield was ripped out of his grip.

Bearclaw chopped at Glaag's knees.

The barbarian knocked Bearclaw's axe aside with his shield. He tossed his shield away and spun his axe in the air. "Come! Die!" he said with throaty words.

Gasping for breath, Bearclaw came to his feet. Sweat dripped from his hair into his eyes. His broad shoulders sagged. He gripped his war axe with two hands and rushed Glaag.

Axe heads met and locked with a sharp *clank* of steel.

They wrestled back and forth chest to chest, with the bigger man leaning on the other.

In one fierce motion, blades locked together, Glaag ripped Bearclaw's axe out of his grip. The barbarian flattened Bearclaw with a hard boot to his chest.

Standing right in front of the tank, Bearclaw fell on his backside. He clutched his chest. His head hung down.

To the shrill howling of the blood-hungry throng, Glaag lifted his mighty axe high in the air with both hands and let out a triumphant bellow.

CHAPTER 54

THE MOMENT HAD COME.

Glaag stood in front of the tank, preparing to deliver the death blow to a broken Bearclaw.

Ruger sat straight up and, over the clamor of the crowd, shouted, "Shades, fire now!"

The tank gun squared up right behind Glaag's broad back erupted with a deafening *kaboom!*

Glaag's body sailed head over heels past a ducking Bearclaw and slammed into the barbarian crowd.

The silenced barbarians had hunkered down. Their eyes were big, and fingers plugged their ears.

Inside the tank, behind the gun slits, the Henchmen opened fire with their machine guns. Bullets ripped into the shell-shocked Gond. Tattooed and painted bodies were ripped to pieces.

Ruger was on the move. He, Vern, Apollo, and Prospero had slipped out of their knots. They hustled straight to cover behind the tank.

There, Horace waited. Their weapons were strapped up in burlap bags on the tank's sides, and he fished their swords out for them. "It's fighting time."

Ruger ripped Black Bane out of the scabbard, not stopping to chat. He sought out the closest barbarian and attacked. He tore the first Gond attacker's head from his shoulders then disemboweled two more. Black Bane became a living weapon in his hands. He split skulls to the chin and severed limbs with single strikes.

The tank started to move slowly. Inside the metal cabin, Skitts and Iris were firing the machine guns, mowing down the barbarians. It kept the savage men's fever-pitched advances at bay. The strategy wrought confusion.

Ruger, Vern, and Horace defended from the front of the tank.

Apollo and Prospero fought at the rear of the tank with swords in each hand.

Horace punched his spear into one bare-chested attacker after another.

Vern gutted the exposed abdomens of his opponents.

Ruger hacked off more limbs.

Without Glaag to lead them, the Gond were in complete confusion, but hundreds of them stood against only a few Henchmen.

Shades shouted from inside the tank. "Fire in the hole!"

Ruger, Vern, and Horace split away from the tank gun.

The long gun barrel exploded.

Many of the Gond dove to the ground. Others died in pieces.

"Keep that fire coming!" Ruger lunged and stabbed his sword through a Gond's chest. He yanked it out and poked through another man. "Get away from the gate!"

"What?" Shades yelled from inside.

"Away from the gate! Away from the gate!" Ruger shouted back.

The tank stopped and started rolling the opposite direction, westward. The big gun fired again. The blast blew away a host of Gond.

The barbarians fought on with swords and axes. They rushed the Henchmen in a disorganized throng, fearless of the skilled carnage the Henchmen wrought on their bodies.

Three Gond charged Ruger at once. He parried a sword and caught the axe hand of another, while the third painted reaver tried to split him in half with an axe as he cocked back to swing. A war axe brained Ruger's free attacker.

It was Bearclaw. The bearish man was back on his feet and smiling.

Ruger ended the men he was engaged with in a single stroke. "Outstanding execution, brother!"

"Did you ever doubt me?" Bearclaw replied as he brained one more Gond.

"Of course not, I knew that you could take him." Ruger sliced an attacker's sword arm off. "You wield the best axe in Titanuus!"

"Perhaps. That Gond was good. I've never seen such a large man move so well!" Bearclaw chopped a man down by the legs. "I'd rather have had a fair crack at him."

"Methinks you were losing!" Vern cut a barbarian in the neck and stabbed a hole with a dagger in another. "That big fella bowed you over like a spoon."

Bearclaw let out a fierce harrumph and killed another man.

The tank gun fired again.

The Gond that weren't blown to bits scattered. A loud howling like a whistle started, and the Gond broke away from the tank.

"What's happening?" Vern asked as he slung blood from his sword.

"They are regrouping." Ruger could see the Gond grabbing their assault rifles. Someone had finally taken charge. "And rearming themselves. Stay close to the tank." He banged his sword on the side. "Shades, stop." He pointed at the ground. "Everyone grab a dead body and get under the tank."

CHAPTER 55

THROUGH THE SPYGLASS, STICKS WATCHED Bearclaw and the Gond leader battle. Beside her, Tark and Dominga were squinting, each having taken a knee.

"What's happening?" Dominga asked over and again.

Sticks gave a dry description of the events as they unfolded.

Tark's head slid side to side on his shoulders. "I don't like this plan. I don't understand it. Wait for a signal? What signal?"

The tank rocked backward on its treads. The Gond leader disappeared from the scene. A loud *boooom* carried across the field.

"That's the signal." Sticks dropped the spyglass and shouldered her weapon. She flipped off the safety and started firing into the cluster of shocked savages gathering themselves one hundred yards away.

Inside the tank's slits, muzzle fire flashed. The barbarians were being ripped to pieces and dropped like flies. Ruger, Horace, and Vern fought the hordes at the front, and Vern and Apollo fought at the back. Sticks fired into the men attacking the front

"Fire at the ones in the back of the tank!" she ordered.

Tark and Dominga supplied deadly cover fire on the tank's backside. The Gond dropped in threes and fours.

"Am I killing them?" Dominga said with growing elation. "This is so easy. They fall like raindrops!"

Tark had a big grin on his face and said, "Now this is a crossbow!" He fired bullet after bullet until the clip emptied. He loaded another and charged the rifle's chamber.

"Don't talk. Keep your breath. Make every bullet count," Sticks demanded. She squeezed off round after round until her weapon emptied. She reloaded another magazine, took aim, and fired.

Bullets whizzed overhead. Bright muzzle flashes erupted, pointed in the trio's direction.

"Looks like we are going to have some visitors."

A large group of Gond barbarians broke away from the main army and ran toward them. The element of surprise was gone. Sticks started firing at the score of men running at them. The long-limbed raiders were closing the one-hundred-plus-yard gap quickly.

She whacked Dominga on the shoulder, pointed, and said, "Aim for them! Aim for them!"

"What about Ruger?" Dominga said.

"We can't help them if we are dead." Sticks picked off one Gond after the other. Some of the Gond took a knee and fired their guns. Others charged on, full speed, with edged weapons bared and mouths wide open, screaming as if their heads were on fire.

Many of the big men fell to the firepower. Some of them got up again and kept running. None of them turned back.

Sticks shot at one black silhouette after another. A bullet whizzed by her head, causing a sudden stir of her hair. "Aim at the men with weapons in hand. I'll take on the ones with rifles!" She aimed at the muzzle flashes. In the darkness, the attackers that fired dropped.

"Sticks, I think I have a problem!" Tark said. "This is my last magazine." He kept firing. A steady *pop-pop-pop* sounded out over the plains. "What do we do?"

She emptied her clip. The magazine pouch on her gun belt was empty. They'd taken down at least a score of the berserk warriors. Another score were coming. She pulled her short swords free, and all she could think to say was, "Fight."

CHAPTER 56

Underneath the tank, dead bodies were being turned into piles of goo. Ruger, Vern, Bearclaw, Apollo, and Prospero had crammed themselves underneath the tank the best they could. Bullets ripped into the dead Gond, which were stacked up like bags of sand.

Ruger returned fire with a rifle Shades had given him through the escape hatch on the tank's underside.

Bullets blasted from the machine guns inside the tank.

The Gond fired back at the tank from all directions. Bullets clattered off the steel bulk, followed by the sound of bullets that ricocheted in the air.

Shades shouted down through the escape hatch and said, "Captain, we have room for more inside. Climb up!"

Horace lay flat on his back and peered at the portal. "If you want the hole plugged, then I'll say that's what I'm good for. One of the slighter men can go."

"Get in there, Vern!" Ruger ordered. "And pass another rifle down!"

Shades dropped a rifle into the hole.

Ruger passed the rifle to Apollo. "Start shooting."

Bearclaw let out a pained grunt. A bullet hit him in the shoulder.

Prospero belted out a howl right after him.

Ruger laid down a line of suppressing fire. His last jaunt with Smoke and Sid had served him well. They'd taught him a lot about modern weapons, which gave him an edge over the raving Gond attacking him.

"We are going to get ripped to pieces lying down here like pigs stuck in a mudhole," Horace said. "If it's no different to you, Captain, I'd rather die on my feet."

"No one goes anywhere until I say so," Ruger said. He cracked off round after round. Barbarians fell on their faces with gaping holes in their backs. "We'll hold out as long as we can." He pounded the ceiling above him. "Shades, use that cannon!"

The tank gun fired.

Something nearby exploded.

Body parts fell down like rain.

Again the tank gun fired.

The loud *boom* sent the tank rocking back.

Ruger could sense the barbarians gathering their forces. They were putting a plan together. Some Gond fired weapons. Others streaked over the grounds and jumped up onto the tank. A full-fledged wild-man assault had begun. That wasn't all. They started lobbing burning logs and bodies at both ends of the tank. Their efforts were covering the ground with smoke.

The men underneath the tank started to cough.

Ruger's eyes watered.

They were being smoked out.

CHAPTER 57

STICKS, TARK, AND DOMINGA CROUCHED down in the grasses. They were only seconds away from locking into mortal combat with men over twice the size of the women. The Gond even made the strapping Tark appear smallish in build.

"Go for the guts," Sticks said.

She could take care of herself in a fight, but hand-to-hand combat wasn't her strength. She would have to fight smart, but the barbarians would overwhelm her in only a short matter of time—seconds, possibly.

A presence fell over her shoulder. Someone with a deep but friendly voice said, "Stay down."

Dominga looked over her shoulder and gasped then dropped onto her belly.

A distinct *whirring* sound started up. The superfast *rat-a-tat* of a machine gun followed. Suddenly, the charging Gond started dropping like flies. Their bodies were chewed up and ripped in half.

Sticks dared a look over her shoulder.

Solomon stood tall, taller than ever before. He carried a huge machine gun in his mighty paws and wore a red bandana around his head. The round gun barrel spun like a pinwheel and glowed like fire. The troglin had a long bandolier of ammo strapped over one shoulder. A fierce grin was on his face.

"How's this for some hippie power! Come get some!"

"Sweet Elders!" Tark said with an elated and horrified look. "What is that thing?"

Solomon kept firing. "It's called a Vulcan." He led the march toward the castle. Everything Gond that moved toward him died.

Sticks had never seen the likes of it before. Men were torn to pieces. Their bodies were shredded like wheat.

She pointed at the tank, which was surrounded by smoke and fire. "We have to free them! They are trapped in there!"

"I'm going! I'm going!" Solomon said. The Vulcan machine gun took out the Gond in twos and threes. Their bodies started to pile up by the dozens. "So this is war. I think I like it!"

The barrels of the Vulcan machine gun stopped spinning.

The large trigger housing started to click.

"Uh-oh," Solomon said.

"Uh-oh, what?" Sticks replied.

"No more bullets," he said

"No more bullets?" she asked.

Over a hundred Gond lay dead on the battlefield thanks to the power of the Vulcan machine gun. The problem was that there were still hundreds left. The scattered horde began to cluster again. They pointed down the gentle slope at the Henchmen below the rise. They raised their weapons and rifles and charged.

"Do the Henchmen ever retreat?" Solomon said.

"Death before failure," Dominga quietly said.

"I was afraid that you were going to say that." Solomon picked the Vulcan back up. "I guess I can use it as a club. Just remember, I'm not a man of violence—not at close quarters, anyway."

Sticks swallowed the lump in her throat. She'd been through her share of bloody skirmishes, but not many without Ruger by her side. They were going to lose, just as they did with Eugene Drisk, who'd inhabited Ruger before. This time, they were going to lose big.

She spun her swords and said, "I just want everyone to know that it's been fun."

"You can say that again," Tark said. "I just hope that they leave enough of us to be buried."

Bullets started whizzing by their bodies.

Solomon flinched as he took a bullet in a shoulder. With a snarl, he said, "I'm not standing around for this. Charge!"

Before he took a step, loud war horns from inside the House of Steel blasted. The great brass horns made a *poom-pooow*.

The front gate of the House of Steel quickly rose. Guardians on white horses rode out by the dozen. They wore full suits of armor plated in gold. White manes of hair flapped like banners behind their lion-faced helmets. They lowered lances and spears and thundered into the swarming barbarian hordes.

"The Golden Riders!" Tark exclaimed.

The Gond charging Sticks set their eyes on her group and kept coming.

Another series of loud horns carried over from the west. Suddenly, the sound of more galloping horses caught their ears.

Sticks turned around. Prince Lewis and Pratt were leading the King's Guardians and dozens of other riders right at them. Armored in full plate, they rode with their swords raised. In a heartbeat, Sticks wondered what side Prince Lewis was on when he looked upon her with narrowed eyes. She set her feet.

The regiment of Guardians rode right past the group and galloped roughshod over the barbarians.

Solomon let out a sigh of relief as he watched the last of the riders pass by. He stretched out his arms and said, "Thank you, Lord Almighty!"

Tark lifted his sword high and said, "Ha ha! Let's go!" He and Dominga ran stride for stride toward the heated battle.

Solomon tilted his head down toward her and asked, "Are you going?"

"It's not really my style." She rested her short swords on her shoulders. "We'll make sure that no one slips through."

"I like the way you think." He patted her head with a big paw.

Together they watched the carnage unfold.

The Gond became an unglued, undisciplined mass of disorganized bodies. They fought like wild demons and jerked the knights out of their saddles. They ripped helmets off and pounded them into submission.

"I used to abhor violence. I'm kind of used to it now. I guess the overt exposure has desensitized me to such things," he said.

Two Golden Riders gored a Gond with lances as they charged from different directions.

The barbarians countered the ground pounding they took by firing their assault rifles. Bullets bounced away from the armor made from the King's Steel. Other men died beneath the hail of gunfire.

Tight groups of horse riders trampled the enemy.

Not one Gond fled from the field of slaughter. They died on their feet, bloody from head to toe and swinging. An hour later, every last Gond was severely wounded or dead. Their bodies littered the bloodstained battlefield. The wounded were finally slain.

"Show's over." Solomon walked toward the castle.

"No, I get the feeling the show has only just begun."

CHAPTER 58
BACK HOME

STILL HERE. STILL HERE.

Abraham rode in the back seat of Sid's Jeep Grand Cherokee, staring out a window. Mandi sat in the back seat with him, leaning her head against her window with her eyes closed. Sid drove. Smoke was in the passenger seat, humming to a soft-rock song playing on the radio.

He counted the mile markers and watched the hills and leafless trees pass by. Only the pine trees scattered through the woodland showed any green at all. He knew these roads. He knew them well. They were on the hilly climbs and twisting interstate curves of the West Virginia Turnpike.

The car slowed. They were in a car line backing up at the tolls.

Smoke leaned forward in his seat, lifted his sunglasses, and stared hard at the toll signs. "Four dollars. The toll is four dollars."

"Yeah, and we have three more to go unless you want to take the back roads," Abraham suggested as he tapped his knuckle on the glass. "But that will take twice as long."

"No thanks," Smoke said. "I heard that Hank Williams died on those roads."

"Are you saying that you don't trust my driving?" Sid asked.

"No, I'm saying the road might be in poor condition." Smoke dropped his glasses back down and pushed back into his seat. "You might hit a lethal pothole or something."

"You got that right," Abraham mumbled. "It's bad enough that they have trouble taking care of this toll road."

Smoke started to sing out loud the lyrics to the song "Into the Night."

Abraham continued, "You know, there is only so much yacht rock a man can take. I mean, it's nice and soothing for a while, but every couple of hours, you're either getting slammed by Barry Manilow or Benny Mardones again."

Smoke chuckled.

"I wouldn't mind some country," Mandi said, her eyes still closed. "As long as we are in West 'by God' Virginia, I think some mountain music would be fitting."

"No," Sid said flatly.

"She's not a country music fan even though she does look like a giant Shania Twain," Smoke said.

Sid punched him in the leg. "I do not, and I told you to stop saying that."

"I'm sorry. You're right," Smoke replied coolly. "You are much prettier than she is."

"*And* I'm not a giant either."

"Well…" Smoke muttered.

Sid punched him again. "Don't push it, buddy."

"You know that I'm just teasing."

"Oh, I know, but that doesn't mean that I like it."

Abraham's deep thoughts drowned out Smoke and Sid's playful banter. He had more important matters on his mind. He'd just had a mental breakdown a couple of days before. Now, he was getting into the middle of God knew what. He couldn't stop thinking about his friends in Titanuus either.

I was riding on a horse, and boom, here I am. The question is, where are they now? Is Ruger taking care of the Henchmen? Do they even need me?

He didn't have any doubt in his mind that Ruger was better equipped to handle these high-risk and dangerous situations. But Abraham hadn't done half bad on his own.

If I only had his body in this world, I'd be better off. The kind of stuff Ruger is made of is incredible. But I used to be a top athlete. I could run and hit with the best long before I mastered pitching.

Abraham glanced at Mandi. Curled up in the seat, she snored softly. He couldn't let her get hurt. She'd somehow gotten dragged into this, which was the last thing he wanted. Every time he left and came back, she was deeper into the adventure. He couldn't let that happen again, but she clung to him.

What she sees in me, I'll never know.

He dug his fingers into his palm. He couldn't know when he might switch back over to Titanuus. When he'd left, they were heading back to the House of Steel, under siege by the Gond. He only hoped Ruger was back in his body to help them. His own plan had been pretty thin.

I wish I knew what was going on. I wish I knew for certain that I wasn't crazy.

He scratched the scruff on his neck and yawned and closed his eyes. Part of him wanted to stay home. Part of him wanted to go back to Titanuus.

Perhaps all I need to do is make a choice. Home or Titanuus?

Abraham rested. He didn't sleep, and he only opened his eyes when they slowed to pay at the toll booths.

Sid didn't stop the black SUV otherwise. The ride was smooth, the cabin quiet. It seemed as though everyone had a lot on their minds.

Finally, the Jeep dropped off the exit ramp near Bluefield, West Virginia. The blacktop on the main highway was bumpy, but the Jeep absorbed the bumps well. They followed the old highway a few more miles and turned right at an old brown sign that read Country Roads Microbrewery.

They pulled into the gravel parking lot of the small beer distributor that Abraham worked for. The time was after seven in the evening. Several beer trucks were parked on the lot. Otherwise, the place was abandoned, save for one man that came out of the main two-story building. It was Luther Vancross. He wore a vest over a flannel shirt and a pair of jeans. He was at least seventy years old and mostly bald, with a neatly trimmed goatee.

Abraham got out of the car. He and Luther shook hands.

"It's good to see you again." Luther looked him up and down. "You look well. Better."

Abraham shrugged his eyebrows. "I don't know about that. So, are you really wanting to do this?"

Luther smiled. "I'm old. Why not?"

CHAPTER 59
TITANUUS

"Make sure that they are all dead," Horace said. He jabbed his spear into the heart of a Gond whose leg was cut off and who had a few bullets in him.

The Gond were the heartiest of fighters. They might be mortally wounded or crippled, but they would still try to kill. One of the king's soldiers had found that out the hard way when a barbarian shoved a hidden knife in his back.

Horace walked over to a huge barbarian that lay twitching on the ground. "Ho ho ho, look at this one. Isn't he the Gond leader?"

Bearclaw and Vern walked over to the spot where the man lay on the ground in spasms.

Bearclaw grunted. "That's him. I should know. I fought him."

The Gond leader, Glaag, clutched his big bloody hands open and closed like clamps. His remaining eye bulged inside its socket. His chest was caved in, and ribs were sticking out of the wound.

Vern made a sour face and said, "Ew. How is the man still living?"

"He's a Gond. They don't know when dying is good for them." Horace stuck the tip of his spear in Glaag's face.

Glaag knocked the spear aside with a shaking hand. His body shook like a leaf. He breathed bubbles of snot out of his nose.

Iris scurried over to the Gond. Her eyes were as big as saucers. "How can this be? Wasn't this barbarian shot with that cannon thing? The fact that he breathes defies reason. I'm the one that pulled the trigger."

"A shame. He'd have made a fine Henchmen," Horace said.

"Agreed. He could swing an axe like no man I've ever seen." Bearclaw looked at Horace. "Should I do the deed?"

"You fought him. If you want to show mercy, show mercy. If you want to let him live—and suffer—so be it." Horace spat. "This Gond deserves no better."

Bearclaw rubbed his chin. "I can't help but be curious. Iris, is there any chance that he'll survive?"

She looked at Bearclaw as though he was crazy and said, "Elders no. He'll be dead by the dawn. His innards are scattered all over. I'm still scratching my head as to why he's not in pieces. It's as if the shell bounced off of him or he bounced off of it."

Bearclaw took a knee in front of the Gond. He stared into the man's bulging eye. "Do you want mercy, Gond? Eh? Blink twice if you do."

Glaag stared right back at Bearclaw with a defiant and unblinking eye.

Bearclaw nodded. "So be it. You can die on your own then." He stood up and shrugged. "What now?"

Horace looked at the House of Steel. Ruger, Prince Lewis, and a host of Guardians and Golden Riders had returned behind the closed gate. He clenched his jaws and said, "I suppose that we wait."

CHAPTER 60

Inside the House of Steel, Ruger stood on the king's terrace. His gaze hung on the shining waters of the Bay of Elders. Warships patrolled the choppy waters over a mile away from land. The boats, docks, and beaches were a hive of activity. Supplies were loaded onto ships by men and women that appeared as tiny as ants.

Ruger breathed the salty air in deep. It smelled like home. He could taste it though he knew it was temporary.

Prince Lewis and Pratt were the only other men on the terrace. They were both sitting at the table on the raised patio by the doors leading back inside the castle. They were drinking wine and eating from plates of food that had been brought forth.

With a leg of turkey in one hand, Lewis walked over to Ruger and offered it to him. "You must be hungry. That was an impressive feat you pulled off against the Gond. Care to share your strategy?"

"Simple. Cut off the head of the snake, and the body goes crazy." Ruger wasn't hungry, but he took the turkey leg anyway, not wanting to insult the prince. "Thank you." He picked off a hunk of meat with his blood-stained hands and ate. "It's good."

"You always did have a knack for getting things done quickly. Cut off the head of the snake. Hmm. I like it." Lewis drank from his goblet and set the cup down on the terrace wall. Looking down at the boats below, he said, "I hate sailing. I'd rather do anything else." His handsome face soured. "It leaves me queasy. And my footing is uncertain. Is that how you feel, Ruger? Or is it Abraham?"

"No, it's Ruger, and I'm not sure that I understand the question."

Lewis tilted his head from side to side and said, "Moving from one body to another. Never knowing what world you are going to wake up in. Isn't that like loose sand underneath your feet?"

"I suppose it is." He took a big bite of turkey leg and chewed.

Lewis leaned against the wall, rubbed his eyes, and yawned. "Riding all night isn't as easy as it used to be. Especially when bullets ripped your backside out." He fixed his stare on Ruger. "Tell me, isn't what you are going through… maddening? Frankly, I think I would go mad."

Ruger lifted his shoulders. He wasn't sure what Lewis was angling at, but he answered honestly. "I focused on one thing."

"And what's that? Wait, don't answer." Lewis snapped his fingers and pointed at Ruger. "Getting home."

"That's part of it. But I always focus on what I have always focused on. Serving the king."

Lewis raised an eyebrow. "How can you serve a king when you exist on another world?"

"By doing whatever I can to get back."

Lewis quickly shook his head and said, "I envy you, Ruger. Perhaps I always have. I'm the king's own flesh and blood, but you've been a better son to him than me. But my perspective has changed."

"How so?" Ruger asked.

"When I discovered that you had a flaw, I delighted in it. Now that the king knows that you are the father of Clarice and that Clarann is your mistress, I don't feel as… hmm, how shall I put this?" The prince grinned. "*Unfavored* anymore."

"I didn't know," Ruger said. "I never did."

"True." Lewis took up his goblet and drank. "But we both know that won't matter to my father. Will it? And speaking of change, well, the king has changed too. I'd be worried about that." He threw the goblet over the wall. "Very worried."

Ruger picked more meat off the bone and flicked it to the sea birds hovering nearby on the wind. The ones that missed the meal dove after it. He picked the bone clean and flicked it over the wall.

Lewis and Pratt remained seated at the table, talking quietly from time to time. At least two hours had passed with no sign of the king.

That gave Ruger time to think. He needed to figure out the next step. First off, he needed to locate the lair of the Time Tunnel on Titanuus. He knew it was in the Spine, but the Spine was very dark and unexplored territory. His best chance would be to track the enemy's armies back to the location. He couldn't do that if he was in Titanuus. He had no idea what King Hector would task him to do either. The king might kill him.

Ruger wiped the grease off his fingers on his blood-soaked leggings.

This is no way to stand in the presence of the king.

The curtains parted behind the patio table. A beautiful woman stepped through, dressed in the armor of the Guardian Maidens. Prince Lewis and Pratt stood.

"Leah!" Lewis said with a broad white smile on his face. "Forgive me for not wrapping you up in my arms, love, but as you can see"—he fanned out his battle-marred cape—"I'm all bloody."

"It suits you well, Prince." Leah gave Lewis a peck on the cheek. She shifted her attention to Pratt. "Good to see that you are alive and breathing."

"Another day. Another battle to come," Pratt replied grimly.

Leah's golden-brown braid hung down her back. She was as fit as she was pretty. She turned her attention toward Ruger and said to Lewis in a quieter voice, "The king comes."

Lewis opened his hands and said, "That's what I've been waiting for." He patted her on the lower back. "But not as much as you, of course."

"Of course," she said. "Is that… him?"

"Yes," Lewis replied. "Ruger in the flesh. For now, anyway. There is no telling when the next possession might take over."

Leah marched toward Ruger and stopped right in front of him. "It's been a long time. We haven't spoken since before your fall from grace. Do you remember me?"

"Of course. I remember everyone that I trained," Ruger replied. He noticed the lioness insignia on the strap of her breastplate. "You've come a very long way. The commander of the Guardian Maidens. Perhaps I did something right."

"Don't be modest, Ruger," Lewis said with his thumbs hitched in his belt. "You trained all of us, and look, we are still alive."

Leah patted Ruger on a shoulder and said, "I just wanted to say that it's good to see you again. I hope to fight by your side one day."

"I wouldn't hope too much. It might happen sooner than you think."

"Well, that is what you trained us for."

Lewis cleared his throat. "Ahem."

Leodor and Melris walked out onto the patio. The older and wizened-looking Leodor wore the customary robes of the viceroy. He maintained the same froward, tired-eyed, and chinless expression.

Melris the Elderling wore the same purple robes and carried the cast-iron Rod of Devastation cradled in his arms. His hood was down, and he maintained his short tawny hair and youthful face. The irises of his eyes were light purple.

The newcomers made a beeline for Ruger.

Leah stepped away.

"Who is with us today?" Leodor asked brightly.

"Ruger," he replied.

Leodor tilted his head side to side and gave him further study. His eyes landed on the hilt of Ruger's sword. "I need to retain your weapons. All of them."

Ruger unbuckled his sword and dagger belt. He tried to hand them to Leodor.

"Elders, no. I'm not touching those things." Leodor lifted a fragile hand and snapped his fingers with a loud pop. "Pratt. Make yourself useful."

Pratt hustled over, his armor jangling. He took the sword belt from Ruger and moved away.

"That's better," Leodor said as he hid his hand back inside his sleeves. "I'm going to need you to cross your hands behind your back."

Ruger gave Leodor a doubting look but complied. He caught a hint of surprise on Lewis's and Leah's faces.

"Please understand that King Hector can't take any chances these days," Leodor continued. "As you have seen, there are many persons of interest trying to kill him."

Unable to contain the edge in his voice, Ruger replied, "I wear the King's Brand, for Elder's sake. I'd never lift my hand against the king."

"Times change. And we can't take any chances that you aren't you." Leodor nodded at Melris. "Secure him."

Melris's hands glowed like purple sunshine. A coil of ropelike energy bands formed inside the palm of one hand. He stepped behind Ruger and bound his hands.

The mystic coils constricted and burned hot without searing the flesh.

"Do not strain against your bindings," Melris said softly. "The more you struggle, the more they will hurt." He moved back beside Leodor.

Leodor nodded at Ruger and said, "Now, get on your knees and bow for the coming king."

CHAPTER 61

RUGER TOOK A KNEE AND bowed his head. He heard the rustling of armor and clothing as the others on the terrace also took a knee. The hairs on his forearms stood on end. He wanted to look up but dared not. The sound of soft footsteps approached, and the hem of robes dusted over the terrace's tiles. Two polished boots made from black leather appeared underneath Ruger's nose.

The king's robes were black and trimmed in gold.

In a voice with the strength of a lion behind it, King Hector said, "Rise, my subjects, including you, Ruger."

Ruger slowly rose. His gaze ran over the black sword belt tightly wrapped around King Hector's waist. It held no sword, only a dagger in a sheath with tiny gems encrusted in the hilt. It was the Dagger of Death, the only weapon Ruger had ever seen King Hector carry, and that was rare.

He met eyes with the king for the first time in a long time. King Hector's eyes were as hard and bright as diamonds. The bow in his back had straightened, and he stood almost as tall as Ruger. The graying hair had been filled with brown, and his once-sagging angular jawline had hardened. On the king's head was the Crown of Stones. Four stones—red, orange, green, and blue—twinkled in the dawn's early light.

Ruger nodded and said softly, "Your Majesty."

King Hector crossed his arms but cupped his elbows in his hands. He looked Ruger up and down. "You always were a glutton for punishment, Ruger. Look at you, bathed in blood and still standing strong as a mighty oak. Normally, this would be the part where I would say that it is good to see you. I would celebrate our victory over the barbarian horde. But greater evil is afoot. For there is no wound so deep as when one friend betrays another."

Ruger had no doubt what the king was talking about—Ruger and Clarann's affair and their daughter, Clarice. For over fifteen years, the king had been fooled. When he found out, it must have been humiliating.

Ruger avoided the king's heated stare. Something disturbing lurked in the king's eyes. It made Ruger's spine tingle. This was the king, but it wasn't the king he knew. He couldn't help but feel that it was someone else. "I never knew."

"I wish that I could take your word for it." King Hector spoke into Ruger's ear. "But you know me. Ignorance is not an excuse." He stepped back. "If I would have killed you months ago, this never would have been an issue. Yet I found it so strange the Clarann desperately came to your aid. It all makes sense now."

King Hector's hand fell to his dagger. He slid the blade quietly out of the sheath. He touched Ruger on the cheek with the flat of the blade. "One prick from the tooth of this dagger will kill any living thing instantly. Instantly! I've used it before to end my troubles. Given the circumstances, I foresee myself using it again."

"You are the king. Do as you will."

King Hector spun the blade in front of Ruger's eyes and said, "I won't waste it on you, Ruger. That would be too simple. It's crude by my standards. Now, I have much more sophisticated weapons at my disposal." He sheathed the blade.

Ruger looked the king in the eyes. The irises in the king's eyes shifted from brown to an emerald green. He had the appearance of a man possessed, a man consumed by unfathomable magic. Ruger's jaw tightened. He tried to look away but could not.

"Now, you will sample my power. Now, you will share the truth," King Hector said.

By an unseen force that was not his own, Ruger's body rose up on tiptoe. His back suddenly arched, and his body became rigid. Slowly, in midair, he began to spin. He spun around once and stopped again in front of King Hector. Their eyes locked. The intensity in the king's emerald eyes bore straight into Ruger's soul. Ruger let out an agonizing scream.

King Hector probed Ruger's thoughts. He rummaged through the warrior's memories. He saw everything he wanted to see about Ruger and the queen and more. He saw torture, blood, war, monsters, and devastation, but most importantly of all, he saw full glimpses of the other world.

Ruger fell from the air and landed hard on his knees. He trembled like a leaf and broke out in a cold sweat. His strength was drained. He fell over and slumped against a wall. His entire life had been exposed.

The emerald gleam in the king's irises faded. His broad shoulders slumped, and he staggered back a step.

Leodor and Melris, who were standing behind the king, grabbed hold of his elbows and steadied him.

King Hector jerked away from both of them. "Unhand me!" He looked at Ruger and pointed a finger at his chest. "You spoke truly that you did not have knowledge of my daughter. And I must say I am disappointed. Your guilt would have made this easy. I could have turned you to dust. Instead!" He retracted his finger. "I see all you have done. So much you have suffered. All for the sake of the Crown. Where most men break, you never gave in. Your service is without question. Yet I stand here, still wounded." King Hector let out a heavy sigh. "Ruger, you will live. In what capacity, I do not know."

Ruger caught his breath. He forced himself back to his knees. He felt as if his soul had been ripped out and stuffed back inside of him again. *Is this what Clarann went through? Where is she?* He wanted to ask but dared not.

The king turned his back to Ruger and addressed the others. "I have seen this other world. I find it fascinating." His fingertips sparkled with mystic power, which flared up. "These invaders attempt to conquer us. Perhaps it is we that should conquer them!"

CHAPTER 62

King Hector addressed his constituents with grand ideas of new world conquest. Prince Lewis, Pratt, and Leah hung on every word. Leodor and Melris stood by the king, quietly nodding in agreement.

He's going mad, Ruger thought. *It must be from the stones. This is not the King Hector that I know.* He remained in place, kneeling quietly, not wanting to draw any attention to himself. He needed a greater understanding of what Hector had in mind. He needed to find a way to talk the king out of his quest—either that or knock the Crown of Stones off his head.

As King Hector rambled on about the visions he'd seen in Ruger's mind of a new world, Leodor interrupted when the lathered-up king caught his breath. "Your Majesty, are we abandoning the quest for the other two stones?"

King Hector turned on Leodor, his eyes filled with anger. He glanced at Ruger and calmed. "I have more than enough power with four stones. Besides, I thought that you and Melris agreed further pursuit of the stones is futile."

"It is only futile because I do not sense the presence of the other stones. It is possible that they are lost or destroyed. Their whereabouts are unknown," the soft-spoken Melris said.

Ruger could no longer maintain his silence. "How are you going to close the portal, then?"

King Hector glared at him and said, "Haven't you been listening? I am not going to close the portal. I am going to use it to invade the other world."

"Your Majesty, please listen. I have been there. That world is vastly bigger than this one. Ten times, a hundred times, perhaps a thousand times. You don't want to try this," Ruger pleaded.

"It only takes one man to change the world," King Hector retorted. "Perhaps this world needs a more suitable ruler." He adjusted his crown. "One filled with wisdom and omnipotent power."

"We don't know that our powers work in that world the same as ours. There is no evidence of it," Ruger said. "My king, you must trust in what I say."

"Despite your brave deeds, Ruger, I no longer trust you. You or Clarann. Perhaps in the other world, I will find a more suitable queen."

Ruger's chin dipped to his chest. *He's gone mad. This I am certain.*

"Your Majesty," Leodor said, "perhaps the time has come for you to meet with the Elders. As Melris suggested."

King Hector's fingers needled his palms. "Ah yes, the Elders. I think that it is high time that I meet with my equals." He looked at Melris. "Can you arrange this?"

"Certainly," Melris said. "After all, it was the Elders that sent me to aid you. It will take some time, but if I depart immediately, I can arrange a rendezvous in the next few mornings."

"Take your leave, then," the king said.

Melris bowed, walked over to the wall, and jumped off the ledge.

Leah gasped as the Elderling fell out of sight.

Melris rose up from behind the wall and sailed away to the north, over the handle of the sword of the House of Steel, and vanished behind the blankets of clouds.

"Whoa," Leah said with her mouth hanging open.

King Hector put an arm around her waist and said, "Oh, that is nothing. Wait until you see what I can do. Son," he said to Prince Lewis, "get yourself cleaned up. I want to meet with the leaders in the War Room."

Prince Lewis nodded. "And what about Ruger? What do we do with him?"

King Hector gave Ruger a long, unforgiving look and said, "Take him to the dungeon. I'll deal with him later."

Lewis looked at Pratt and said, "You heard the king. Take him to the dungeon and lock him up in a cold, damp, and smelly cell with the rats, where he belongs."

"My pleasure," Pratt said. In a few big strides, he crossed the patio and yanked Ruger to his feet. He shoved him ahead, using the outside exit of the patio.

Ruger caught a slight smile of victory in Lewis's face. Leodor stared at Ruger with a darker intent. Something was truly off with him.

Black Bane remained propped up against the wall.

Pratt added two more guards and took Ruger to the bottom of the castle. He locked him inside a cell in the very back.

"Listen to me, Pratt. You know that the king is not right. What he is planning is madness. He will get everyone in all of Titanuus killed." Ruger pressed his face to the bars. "You saw those tanks. Those weapons. They will have thousands of them. We have to find a way to close the portal. It's the only way!"

Pratt looked down at him and said, "Though I might agree, that does not change the fact that I serve the king. Where he says march, I march. What happened to you, Ruger, you who never questioned the king, the one who held the standard and the one that never failed? You have become a disgrace. I think the king should put a noose around your neck and hang you for all to see." He chuckled. "But I have a warm feeling that the king's thoughts are headed in that direction." He started to walk away, turned his head over his shoulder, and added, "Enjoy your stay."

Ruger backed up against the wall, sat down on a bed of rotting hay, put his head between his legs, and sighed.

CHAPTER 63

BACK HOME

"You know, if I switch with Ruger when all of this goes down, we might have an issue," Abraham said.

Smoke had stitched a small tracking device—like a tiny fuse—underneath the skin of his forearm. "At least we can keep track of you this way. You and Ruger, that is." He bit off the string. "Perfect. They'll never suspect a thing."

Abraham was inside Luther's office. It was the same place where he'd interviewed not so long before for a job as a trucker. Luther was looking out his window at the truck lot, his hands behind his back.

"Luther, I really hate to see you getting involved in this," Abraham said. "There might be another way."

"Don't think anything about it. I'm only making a phone call," Luther said in a reassuring voice. "How dangerous can that be? Besides, it's been a long time since I've done anything meaningful. I want to help."

"To a lot of people, making beer is pretty meaningful," Abraham said while he rubbed his stitched-up forearm.

"True, but you know that's not the kind of meaningful that I mean. Anybody can tap a keg and serve beer." Luther turned around and sat behind his desk. Abraham and Smoke sat in the chairs across from him. "Should I make the call now?" Luther smiled nervously. "I have to admit my fingers are itching like the first time I unhooked a bra."

"Just hold on," Abraham said.

"You know, I knew this was big trouble when those three men showed up," Luther said as he leaned back in his leather office chair. "Colonel Drew Dexter, Eugene Drisk, and Dr. Jack Lassiter. I won't forget them. They were the pushy kind. I never like a pushy kind, unless you're selling me something. I can respect that. But they were threatening me without saying it."

"A pretty good sign that they are the bad guys." Smoke grabbed a can of Coke off the corner of Luther's desk and drank.

Luther made a sour face and said, "I'm surprised that a fit fella like yourself drinks that. That crap will kill you."

"Every man has his poison," Smoke said.

Mandi and Sid entered the office and closed the door behind them. Like Smoke, they were wearing bulletproof sweetheart suits that looked like skintight scuba suits. The two women were drinking bottles of original green Gatorade.

"We are all packed," Sid said.

Abraham gave Mandi a sheepish look. She sat down on the arm of his chair and rubbed his back. "You really need to get that worried look off of your face. We are all going to be fine."

"Somehow, I get the feeling that is the suit talking," he said. "Mandi, you can't be a part of this. It's too dangerous." He glanced at the others. "None of you need to do this. Ruger and I will have to figure it out on our own."

"There won't be any turning back now," Smoke said as he grabbed Sid's hand. "That's not our style. Besides, I really want a peek at Titanuus."

Sid tugged the back of Smoke's hair. "You need to avoid any more thoughts of your crazy vacation ideas. As for Mandi, don't worry about her. She's going to be in a very safe place."

"I'd feel better if she wasn't wearing the suit and was on a plane to Texas," Abraham said.

"Sorry, honey, but I don't do long-distance relationships." Mandi took a long drink. "Man, this stuff really makes a difference."

"We added some more electrolytes to the formula." Sid looked at the phone. "I guess it's time to make the call."

An awkward moment of silence passed.

Luther jumped in his seat and leaned forward. "Oh, I guess that's my cue." He picked up Drew Dexter's business card and dialed. He cupped his hand over the phone receiver. "No one picked up. I'm getting a recorded message."

"So leave him one, short and sweet," Sid said calmly.

Luther's forehead beaded with sweat. "Uh, hello, this is Luther Vancross. You stopped by my place a few days ago. Um, I have some information. He's here. Acting kinda crazy. Oops, got to go." He hung up quickly and smiled. "How'd I do?"

"Fabulous." Smoke stood up. "Now, that's our cue to go."

Abraham shook hands with Smoke and Sid. "Good luck."

The husband-and-wife team nodded, shook hands with Luther, and left.

"Uh, Luther, can Mandi and I have a moment?"

"Sure, sure." Luther hustled from behind his desk and out the office door.

Abraham sat down and pulled Mandi into his lap. He touched foreheads with her. "I really wish I understood why you were doing this for me. But I guess I'll never understand." He looked into her eyes. "I'm honored, Mandi. I don't know how I can—"

Mandi put two fingers on his lips and said, "Don't think so much, just do."

He kissed her fingers, moved them aside, and kissed her fully on the lips. He reeled her body in closer as her fingers grabbed a handful of his hair. Her heart beat against his. Their lips locked in a more passionate kiss.

Someone knocked on the office door's frame. "What is this, a Big Red commercial? I've been standing out here ten minutes already."

They broke off the kiss.

Outside, someone was honking a car horn.

Mandi crawled out of his lap with her chest heaving. "Boy, this suit really does something for the libido. No wonder Sid has such a happy marriage." She caressed his face and kissed his cheek. "It's going to work out. Have faith. Believe in yourself. I do." Mandi gave Luther a hug and left.

From the office window, Abraham and Luther together watched the black Jeep Cherokee drive away.

"Now what?" Luther said.

"We wait."

"Hmm… How about some coffee?"

CHAPTER 64

LUTHER SAT IN HIS CHAIR, leaning back and staring out the window. He sipped his coffee. "You know, I was working on moving into a new line of business. I was going to make coffee—something super dark that would keep you up all night."

"Don't they have enough coffees in the world to choose from?"

Abraham was looking at Luther's desktop computer. They had the security cameras on. It was Sunday morning, and the office was closed.

"Eh." Luther shrugged. "It's all about the branding. You know, I should be in church right now. They're going to miss me. I'll tell you, miss one Sunday, and they are all over you the next like a pack of wolves with dentures. I like that. Don't really have anything else. It's good to know someone cares."

"Yeah, I suppose it is." Abraham toggled from one camera view to another. Three hours had passed since Luther made the call, and they weren't very far away from Facility 117. "For so long, I figured everyone in the world hated me."

"Our nation has become an incubator for hair-trigger emotions. Is it like that on Titanuus?"

"No, and it won't be if we can prevent it. Huh."

Luther leaned forward in his chair and turned toward the monitor. He put his glasses on.

Abraham pointed at the screen. "You have a black SUV pulling up to the entrance gate. Another one behind it." Soldiers with machine guns spilled out of the vehicles and dashed into the woods. "They're here."

Luther shivered. "I hated the *Poltergeist* movie. My late wife took me to see it. I never liked scary."

"That wasn't a very scary movie."

"Says you!"

Outside, the distinct sound of a helicopter could be heard above: *wuppa-wuppa-wuppa-wuppa-wuppa-wuppa…*

"I'm starting to think that letting myself get captured wasn't such a good idea." He glanced out of the window. The chopper was landing on the distillery's grounds. "I need to make a run for it."

A man was sitting in the back of the helicopter, pointing a grenade launcher at the window. It was Colonel Drew Dexter—there was no mistaking the moustache. Drew saw Abraham standing in the window and fired.

"Get down, Luther!" Abraham yelled. He dove over the desk and knocked Luther to the ground.

The glass window shattered. The grenade round exploded with white gas.

"Smoke grenade," Abraham said.

Luther broke out in a fit of coughing. "Go!" he spat. "Go!" He coughed more. "Oh my, this is awful. Worse than I remember."

Abraham couldn't see a thing. He fumbled his way through the office doorway and headed down the stairs. He coughed and hacked. His lungs burned like fire, and tears streamed down his face. He couldn't avoid the smoke.

More grenades rocketed into the lower floors of the building and exploded. More white smoke flared up, but it was worse.

Tear gas!

Abraham's eyes watered up. His breathing choked. Holding his breath, he stumbled blindly through the mist, knocking over whatever he bumped into. Unable to see a thing, he swam through the smoke. A man popped up in front of his eyes. He grabbed the man by the mask and ripped it off.

The soldier sucked in a painful breath of air and clutched at Abraham's clothing.

Abraham shoved the man aside. He barreled straight forward and smacked into a wall. His fingers felt along the edges. All he wanted to do was escape.

A pair of men came out of nowhere and tackled him. He wrestled over the floor with one of them. The second soldier cracked him in the skull with the butt of his weapon. Abraham saw stars and collapsed. The soldiers in gas masks hooked him underneath the arms and dragged him out of the building.

Abraham couldn't have been happier. He coughed and hacked while sucking in the fresh morning air. Tears streamed down his face as he spat the foul-tasting mist out of his mouth. Someone cuffed his legs together. His hands were locked behind his back and strapped.

"That was easy," Colonel Drew Dexter said.

Abraham was stood up face-to-face with Drew. He got a good look through his watery eyes.

Colonel Dexter tilted his head to one side and said, "Who are we dealing with today? Hmm?"

A soldier brought Luther out of the building in a fireman's carry. He set the old man on the ground while he hacked his lungs out.

"Make sure the building is clear. There might be three more persons of interest," Colonel Dexter said. "Go! Go!"

Abraham didn't say a word. He wanted Drew to think he was Ruger. He set his watery eyes on Luther. He felt sorry for the old man writhing on the ground and coughing his guts out, but he glared at the old man anyway.

"Not speaking, huh?" Colonel Dexter asked with a twitch of his moustache. "Don't worry, we'll find a way to make you talk. The same as we always do."

Abraham glared at Colonel Dexter. He fought against the men that held him and snorted. One of the soldiers cracked him in the back of the knee with the butt of his rifle.

"Easy—no need to bust him up too bad. We need him." Colonel Dexter pulled out his phone and made a call. "It's me, Jack. We have them. What do you want me to do with the old man, Luther?" He looked down at Luther. "Uh-huh. Uh-huh. You're the boss." He put away his phone and pulled out his pistol.

Abraham tensed.

CHAPTER 65

"Only a coward would kill a defenseless old man. Do you kill women and children too?" Abraham asked in as stern a voice as he could muster.

Colonel Dexter spun the automatic pistol on his finger and studied Abraham's face. "The way I see it, this is war, and war has casualties." He gave Abraham a harder look. "I didn't have any plans to kill him. I was more curious to see how you would react to it. Seems like the two of you are friendly. Makes me think that it might be you in there, Abraham, and not Ruger." He stuffed his weapon back in his holster.

Abraham—still pretending to be Ruger—said, "I'm not that soft-bellied goat. But I live with honor. I don't slaughter the weak for sport. It disgusts me. Take these shackles off, and I'll be more than happy to show you which man I am. I challenge you Gin-gin!"

"What is Gin-gin?"

"A duel. Have you ever fought with a blade, or do you always cower behind your tiny crossbows?"

Colonel Dexter chuckled. "All right, load this head case onto the chopper. Gin-gin. Huh." He pointed at Luther, who was still gagging and spitting. "Take the old man too. Dr. Drisk wants him."

Handling Abraham and Luther roughly, the soldiers secured them in the seats of the large chopper.

Colonel Dexter loaded in and shut the door.

The chopper lifted off, and into the sky they went.

Four seats were in the back of the chopper. Abraham was in the backseat with Colonel Dexter seated beside him. His growing disdain for the man was as bad as the foul taste of tear gas in his mouth. He spat on the floor.

"Don't do that," the colonel said.

Abraham spat again.

Colonel Dexter didn't say another word for the rest of the trip.

Abraham stared out the window. Just over an hour into the trip, he noticed streaks of purplish lightning coursing through the sky. A tempest was forming over the mountains. The hairs on the nape of his neck stood on end.

What in the world?

It was the same sort of lightning he had seen the moment before his plane was struck by it and he crashed.

"What the hell are they doing?" Colonel Dexter asked as he peered through Abraham's window. "Those idiots shouldn't be tinkering with the tunnel when they know we are airborne. Get this chopper lower. Get it on the ground ASAP! Somebody's going to get an ass chewing!"

Abraham kept his eyes fixed on the flashing sky. He wanted to ask Colonel Dexter how long this had been going on, but in his heart, he knew the answer. His blood started to rise as everything came together. The plane crash hadn't been his fault. Men like Eugene Drisk, Jack Lassiter, and Drew Dexter caused it with their experiments. They were the ones that killed Jenny, Jake, and his best friend, Buddy Parker. And all this time, he'd blamed himself. With his temperature rising, he clenched a fist and looked Colonel Dexter dead in the eye.

Colonel Dexter shrank under his gaze, said, "What?" and looked away.

They landed in the parking lot of Facility 117.

Abraham and Luther were hurried into the building. They were separated at the elevators. Otis and Haymaker appeared, hard scowls on their faces. They took Abraham to a padded cell, put him in a full-body straitjacket, and lay him on a rolling table. He wriggled against their efforts, just for show.

Otis grabbed Abraham's face in his big black hand and squeezed it. "Welcome back, Looney Tunes." He nodded at Haymaker.

Haymaker held a stun rod and smacked it into his hand. He had a twisted smile on his face.

"Dr. Jack has special orders for you. Very special," Otis continued. He removed Abraham's boots and socks. He eyeballed Otis. "Hit him."

Haymaker jabbed the stun rod against the bottom of Abraham's foot.

Abraham arched his back inside his bonds. He convulsed on the table and let out a loud scream. Every nerve inside his body caught fire. He shivered head to toe.

"Look at that. Shaking like a leaf. You aren't so tough, are you, Ruger?" Otis asked. He glanced up in the corner of the cell where a security camera hung. He grinned. "Or is it Abraham? So tell us—what are the king's plans?"

Abraham clammed up. He needed to play it tough like Ruger.

Haymaker hit him with the stun rod again.

He jumped on the table. He started to see bright spots and stars. *No! Don't go back, Abraham. Don't go back. Hang in there. We are getting close. Play along.*

Haymaker hit him with the stun rod time and again.

Otis peppered him with heated questions.

"What is your name?"

"Tell us the king's plans!"

"Do you want to see your family again?"

"Where is the sword?"

Abraham kept his mouth shut. It was what he thought Ruger would do if they tried to break him. He had to sell it. Maybe he would have broken before, but not now. The tide had turned inside him. His lingering doubt had been crushed. He focused on the purple storm in the sky, and the lust for vengeance fueled his body.

They killed my family. Now it's payback time.

The torment went on for over an hour. Abraham hung tough. His sweat-drenched hair dripped onto the table.

Otis and Haymaker dabbed their shiny foreheads with cloths. Haymaker was about to hit him with the stun rod again when the padded cell door opened.

Dr. Jack Lassiter and the zillon woman, Ottum, entered. Dr. Jack nodded at the orderlies and said, "I'll take it from here, gentlemen."

The brutish orderlies departed, and the door closed behind them.

"You are tough," Dr. Jack said as he leaned over Abraham's face. "But no one beats the needle."

Ottum stuck Abraham in the neck with a needle longer than his finger and depressed the plunger.

Nooo!

CHAPTER 66
TITANUUS

CHAINS RATTLED AND SCRAPED OVER the ground. The air smelled damp and musty. The floor was cold. Something nibbled on his fingers.

Abraham woke up. He knocked a large rat away from his fingers. The creature skipped over the floor and scurried away. He sat up and wiped sticky straw away from his face. His head was splitting. He rubbed his temples. From the hallway flickered a dim source of light that he could see through the steel bars.

He crawled to the bars and peered outside. He was in a dungeon, as medieval as it could get. The floors were coated in a film of slime and mold. The place smelled like mold. Water ran down the limestone walls. He touched the breastplate armor on his chest.

"Great, it looks like I'm back in Titanuus."

A chill went through him as he rubbed his head. He had a sinking feeling that Dr. Jack Lassiter had figured out how to send him back and forth. Perhaps the zillon, Ottum, had helped him.

Where am I?

The last time he'd been in Titanuus, he was preparing the Henchmen to fight the Gond at the House of Steel. Perhaps they had lost and he was a Gond prisoner. He had no way of knowing where he was without seeing someone. He called out loudly. "Hello!"

His voice cracked. He thirsted, and his throat was as dry as a bone. He searched the dungeon cell. A wooden bucket was tilted over, and he saw no sign of water or food.

How long have I been in here?

"Hello!" He grabbed the bucket and banged it against the cell bars. "Hello! Hello! Hello! Somebody, please!"

His words echoed hollowly down the hallway. No response came his way. The dungeons were deadly quiet, abandoned to the lingering gloom and stench of death.

Abraham rifled through his recent memories. He'd gained more knowledge since his last trip back home. The lightning that had struck his plane was man-made. The time had come to forgive himself. The time had come to make the monsters that had done that pay.

How many other innocent deaths have the monsters of the Corporation caused?

He shook his head.

I'm getting closer, but I need to get out of here.

He jerked on the bars. He kicked them.

Ruger's body was strong, unnaturally so. He grabbed the inch-thick corroding steel bars in two hands and pulled. The metal peeled back a fraction of an inch. He put more muscle into it. His back muscles knotted up. He let out a loud groan.

Somewhere in the dungeon, a door squeaked on the hinges.

Heavy footsteps came Abraham's way. He let go of the bars, sucking for breath. His belly growled, and he felt weak. His knees buckled underneath him, and he slid down the bars.

"Are you making racket again?" someone with a gruff voice asked. The heavy-set man behind the voice appeared down the hall. He waddled more than he walked and carried a short sword on his belt. "Still trying to bend those bars, eh? Goodness sake, no man can bend them. Those are the King's Steel. You of all people should know that, Ruger."

Abraham studied the pudgy man's face. He was built like Horace but fatter. His forearms were chubby, cheeks flabby, and chins saggy.

He narrowed his eyes on the man and asked, "Do we know each other?"

"Boy, you really are daffy, aren't you, Ruger? Of course. I rode with you over a decade ago. We talked about this, remember? A myrmidon cut the back of my knees out. Haven't been very able ever since. No spring in me boots. Can't climb that saddle either." The jailer made a chipper face. "But I'm here and thankful. Make the most of the worst circumstances, like you always said." He searched Abraham's face. "You really don't remember, do you?"

"Uh, what is your name again?"

"Carlton. Boy, you really have taken too many lumps on the noggin. I never thought I'd see the day when you'd deteriorate. But it happens to the best of us. Look at me. Fat as a cow, and I don't even drink. Well, not at work. Usually."

"What about the standard, Carlton?"

"Ain't no standards down here. None. Just me and the rats. The king tends to kill more that cross him than let them live. Now, you keep it quiet. I'm trying to sleep."

"Carlton, what about the Gond?"

"What Gond? The ones you slaughtered on the other side of the Wall? Why, they are all dead. Fertilizer, as I understand it." Carlton swiped his hand over his greasy black combover. "I miss all of the action. I only hear what I hear if they tell me." He leaned his shoulder on a bar and looked away from Abraham. "They treat me like I never wore that armor before, but I tell them I did. The laugh because I can't fit in it."

"How long's it been since we fought off the Gond?"

Carlton turned his head and said, "By the Elders, being incarcerated really takes a toll, doesn't it? That was three days ago." He counted on his fingers. "Three days since you've been here. You've mostly been quiet. Model prisoner." A distant look came over him. "Sometimes I feel like a prisoner."

Abraham got the sinking feeling that Carlton might be crazy, but he didn't notice a key ring on the man's belt either. He carried only a short sword, and his hand stayed on the pommel.

Carlton moved away from the cell bars. He eyed Abraham suspiciously. "I know what you are thinking. You want to escape. Well, that's impossible. You have to get by me, and ten more Guardians are waiting on guard if you get by me. Plus, you can't get out of the cell without the key because I don't keep the key on me." He tapped his finger to his head. "You see, I am smart. Very smart."

"Carlton, what about King Hector? Where is he? I need to speak to him."

"No, I won't tell you that either because I don't know, and I wouldn't if I did. It's just like you said—ignorance is bliss. Well, I'm chock-full of ignorant."

CHAPTER 67

INSIDE THE STRONGHOLD ON THE first floor, Solomon watched Horace pace around the farm table. He'd kept to himself, listening to what the others had to say while worrying about Abraham.

It's not the same without him, Solomon thought.

Horace punched a hand into his meaty fist, saying, "Need to know! 'Need to know,' the Prince of Cowards says! We have a right to know where Ruger is!"

"Don't let your mind bubble." Iris was sitting on one of the benches at the farm table, knitting a blanket with needles. The rest of the Henchmen were present except for Shades and Sticks. "You know that Ruger, or Abraham, whichever, for I can't keep up, can take care of himself."

Horace pointed at the wall behind the fireplace and said, "An army marches to the Spine, and we are not with it. That is preposterous! Ruger should be leading it. The world ends. All we do is sit here and watch."

"We need to break Abraham out of the House of Steel," Tark suggested. He was sitting at the table, beside Cudgel, sawing up his food with a knife.

"No, that's just what they want," Vern said after he finished a sip of wine. "That's why the prince provokes us. He wants to hang all of us. He always did."

"So, what do we do?" Cudgel asked, wide eyed. "We can't continue to sit here."

Solomon sat in the corner of the room nearest the grand fireplace. He'd been listening to the bickering for days, but he didn't have any answers either. He was as lost as the rest of the Henchmen. "We need to wait for Shades and Sticks."

"What if they are dead?" Vern asked.

"Don't say that," Dominga fired back, nudging him with an elbow.

"Why?" Vern shrugged. "For all we know, Ruger is dead too. I hope not, but why wouldn't they kill him? Especially if the king has gone crazy."

"He's not dead," Horace growled. "Shame on you for saying so."

"I'm being realistic," Vern said.

Prospero, who was digging a spoon into a bowl of stew, let out a loud belch.

"I share his sentiments," Cudgel said. "Vern, your outlook is deplorable."

"Deplorable, huh? Well, nothing wrong with being deplorable if I'm still living and breathing. We have to face the facts: the world is changing, and none of you even know what side we are on."

"We side with the king!" Horace grabbed a log and flung it into the fireplace. "We cannot doubt it, or we are lost!"

CHAPTER 68
RASCHEL/LEAH THE ASSASSIN

"I HATE THIS PLACE," PRINCE LEWIS said.

He, Leodor, and Leah were in the crypts underneath the largest of the Sects cathedrals in the city of Burgess. It was the same crypt where Leodor had arranged a meeting with Arcayis the Underlord before. He swiped his hand through a cobweb. "Please get on with it quick. I prefer the company of the living and not the dead."

Leah moseyed through the temple's underbelly with a seductive gait. She bent over and lifted a very tall candlestand. "I like gruesome places. I walk by a sarcophagus and wonder how a person died. After all, death is my business."

Lewis opened his arms to the woman, who crossed the room and filled his arms with her body. He kissed her deeply. "It's so very comforting to have you by my side again, Raschel. It was a shame to put an end to Leah. I was very fond of her. But I'm much fonder of the crown."

Giggling delightedly, Raschel opened her hand and showed off the ring on her finger. "Yes, the Ring of Tarsus makes my evil deeds so much easier to execute. Literally. You should have seen your former love when I drained the life from her bones and took it for my own. Talk about gruesome."

"If the two of you are quite finished bragging about your exploits, I could use your hands over here," Leodor said. The older mystic tugged on a great cloth hanging over a very tall mirror. "It's snagged."

Lewis and Raschel yanked the cloth away and dropped it on the backside of the huge mirror. Lewis snarled at the twisted figures wrought in iron around the rim. "I hate this twisted thing too."

"I don't know," Raschel said as she tapped her fingernails on her chin. "I think it would look very nice in my new chambers inside the castle."

"Yes, when you are queen, you should need a mirror that will match your ego." Lewis put his arm around her waist, lowered his hand to her rear, and said, "And when will I get to see my ravishing Raschel again? This body is fine, but yours is much more… sensual."

"When it is all over… and that should be soon."

Leodor finished setting up all the candlestands. Each one had a small skull on its top. He said a mystic word, and a green flame came to life in the shape of a tiny burning imp that danced. It jumped from candle to candle until all the stands were aflame.

"Everyone stay within the triangle," Leodor said.

Lewis and Raschel stepped inside the frame.

Leodor drew invisible symbols in the air and chanted at a feverish pace.

The trio's reflection in the dark mirror warped and twisted. The dull colors swirled like a vortex and slowed, then a new image formed and became clear. Standing inside a cavern was a very tall hooded wraith in dark ghostly robes. A man with receding blond hair, maroon shirt, and black vest stood with a pistol on his hip. They were accompanied by a bare-chested horned halfling who bulged with muscle and smoked a cigar.

Leodor cleared his throat and made quick introductions. "I am Viceroy Leodor, once banished, now reinstated mystic of the Sect. This is Prince Lewis of Kingsland and our colleague, Raschel, from the Brotherhood of Ravens." He bowed. "We are humbly at your service. Especially you, Great Fleece, Master of Shadows and the Sect."

"Let's not forget who the true master is here," the halfling said as he ran a finger inside his collar. He huffed out a smoke ring. "I'm Big Apple, and this is Lord Hawk, leader of the Shell." He hopped up onto a wooden crate. "Tell me all that is happening. I don't need any more slipups like the last time."

"Us being branded was an unforeseen circumstance, but now that King Hector has liberated us from the Brand, well"—Leodor shrugged his scrawny shoulders—"we are back in business. The moment this happened, we did not hesitate to contact you either."

"And you were wise to do so," Big Apple said. "So, where is King Hector now?"

Leodor chuckled. "He and Melris the Elderling are seeking counsel with the Elders. At the same time, King Hector rallies his armies. He plans to march on the Spine to roust you out once he learns of your location."

Big Apple and Lord Hawk chuckled and grinned at one another. "Feel free to let them know exactly where we are. At the tip-top peaks at the bottom of the Spine. Let him try to march an army all of the way through South Tiotan, where we are strongest."

"He'll send ships," Prince Lewis stated.

"Let him. We'll be ready and waiting for him," Big Apple huffed out rings of smoke. "And how is King Hector these days?"

"Everything is going according to plan. The crown's stones are too powerful for him to manage. They are making him mad with power. The Crown of Stones's gems are only meant for individual use or to function as a whole. Otherwise, they create a great deal of imbalance to the wielder's mind. That is why King Hector removed the Brand from us. He was overconfident in his power. Unknowingly, he exposed himself. Still, there is the matter of the other stones. I would not be surprised if he doesn't petition the Elders to help seek them out."

"Oh, don't worry about that. The king can search all that he wants, but he will never find them." Big Apple grinned impishly. "The white diamond and yellow fire gems do exist, but they are not in this world. They are secure in the other world, called Earth, and he will never find them. Heh heh heh."

Leodor gave an approving nod. "It's no wonder that we have not been able to locate them."

"No, we have been working on this conquest a long time. I've thought of everything," Big Apple said. "I can't believe that King Hector is so delusional that he wants to invade my home. This couldn't have worked out more perfectly. The old fool rushes to his death. But feel free to kill him at your earliest opportunity." He looked at the assassin, Raschel. "I'm sure you'll have a dozen opportunities between now and then."

"Dozens, actually," she said. "I'm only waiting on the perfect moment to strike."

Prince Lewis pushed forward. "And the Crown of Stones—what is to become of it?"

"That is not something that you need to concern yourself with," Lord Hawk said. He had his thumbs hitched in his gun belt. "We'll take care of the crown. After all, there will be a new king ruling all of Titanuus."

Prince Lewis puffed up and said, "But I get Kingsland and the House of Steel. That is the arrangement, correct?"

"You will have your little castle and the southern tip of the lands," Big Apple said. "Things will happen so fast it will hardly matter. A new era comes to Titanuus. It will be amazing."

"And what about these otherworlders that are invading? What are their plans?"

Big Apple shrugged. "We'll guide them as we please. The important matter is securing the functionality of the Time Tunnel and the other portals."

"I thought the King's Steel that I sent you was more than enough to get it working," Prince Lewis said.

"Oh, it's an ample supply, but the more we have, the longer we can keep the tunnel open, the more we can make. The process is almost perfected," Big Apple said.

"Almost?" Prince Lewis stated. "I'd assume it was finished."

"The tunnel is, but there is still one part that the men of my world have not mastered. But I think they have almost figured it out. That's why we still need Abraham Jenkins and Ruger Slade alive. They hold the key," Big Apple said. The image in the mirror warped. He glared up at Fleece. "Can't you keep it open longer?"

The towering figure clad in dark wavy robes slowly shook his head.

"This will be the last time we have to speak," Big Apple said. "Let us lure King Hector into a false sense of security. Lead him right to us in the peaks. We'll leave a trail to our location. Once you make it to the lair, we will see you there. Oh, and bring the sword too. Our new alliance would like a trophy."

"What about the Elders?" Leodor asked. "Is it not possible that they will help?"

"Those monsters? I hardly think so. They are very selfish, but one never knows. If they get involved, we will be ready," Big Apple said.

"And Ruger Slade? What do we do with him?"

"After we kill the king, we'll deal with him later. Let him rot in his cell for now."

"And the Henchmen?" Prince Lewis asked.

"Pfft," Big Apple laughed. "They are useless without their leader."

The images in the mirror faded.

The bright candles went out.

As the trio of villains covered the mirror, Prince Lewis smirked and said, "I just can't wait to be king."

CHAPTER 69

STICKS REMAINED HUDDLED AGAINST A corner wall inside the crypt. She watched Lewis, Leodor, and Leah depart. She'd seen and heard the entire conversation. After the group was several minutes gone, she slid from her hiding spot into the darkness of the crypt, which was also used for storage.

"That was an earful, wasn't it?" someone else said out in the darkness.

Sticks made out the faint outline of Shades. He'd hidden himself on the other side of the chambers. The two of them had been keeping tabs on Lewis and Leodor since they'd left the castle.

"It answers a lot of questions, doesn't it?" she said.

"The sad thing is that I thought Prince Lewis might have turned a corner. I guess once a bad seed, always a bad seed." Shades bumped into Sticks on his way out.

"Watch your hands," she said.

"Pardon me. It is dark, you know."

"And I know you know your way around the dark better than anybody but me," she said.

"True." He made his way toward the stairs. "At least we know that Ruger is alive and in the castle. That's good to know even though it will be near impossible to get him out of there."

They walked up the crypt stairs shoulder to shoulder. "I don't think a mad king will heed our warnings either," she said. "Talk about a rock and a hard spot. No one is going to believe us."

A heavy stone door sealed the entrance to the crypt. Shades put his shoulder into it and started to push it open. "Cripes, this thing is heavy. I could use some assistance."

Sticks leaned on the door. "We can get Abraham out of the House of Steel, can't we?"

"I think it would be far easier to reach out to the king."

"But he won't listen. He doesn't trust Abraham or the Henchmen anymore," she said as she shoved the door.

"True, but if we can get that crown off of his head, he might begin to see clearer."

"I thought the king was a good man. Now, he's ruined."

"He's probably still a good man. The power is corrupting him. It happens to everyone these days." Shades grunted as he pushed the door open. "Except for humble men like me." With the door wide open, he stepped aside. "After you."

They were in the back end of the great temple, in the rooms behind the altars.

Sticks moved out of the crypt stairwell. "Back to the Stronghold?"

Shades started to push the door shut. "Oh, crap on this door. Let someone else shut it." He turned, and suddenly his eyes widened.

Sticks pulled a dagger free and spun around. Raschel ran a knife deep into her gut. Sticks sliced the woman across the cheek, but her strength quickly fled her.

Shades pulled out a short sword just in time to have his sword hand cut off by Prince Lewis, who was lurking behind the curtains. Shades gaped as his missing hand and sword dropped to the floor. Blood spurted from the wound. Prince Lewis sank his sword deep in the man's chest.

Sticks sagged to her knees, clutching her belly. Her jaw hung open. She looked up at the woman in Leah's body.

Raschel smirked as she wiped the blood on her blade on the shoulder of Sticks's cloak. "The wound is fatal. You'll be dead in a few minutes. Any last words that you would like to share? I like to keep a record. It provides for excellent reading with a bottle of wine."

Sticks didn't respond. She tried to stand but could not. With tremendous effort, she knee walked over to Shades. His eyes were wide, and his hands clutched the wound in his chest. He spat blood out of his mouth.

Leodor stepped out from behind the curtain. "Did you really think that interlopers like you could sneak into a house of the Sect and not be noticed? Tsk tsk. Our eyes are everywhere. Even the likes of you could not avoid them."

"And to think you were once one of us," Sticks struggled to say. "You'll get yours."

"I like that quote," Raschel added. "I might even write it down in your own blood."

"Leodor, what are we doing? Watching them bleed to death?" Lewis asked. He wiped his sword blade off on one of the curtains. "We have more pressing matters to attend to."

"Of course. Put them in the crypt. It's a fit place for them to die. The servants of the Sect can dispose of the bodies later, after the rats have nibbled down to the bones. They are excellent when it comes to cleaning up."

Lewis sheathed his sword, grabbed Shades by the collar, dragged him to the top of the stairs, and rolled him down the steps. "A very light little fellow. He must have bones like a bird."

Sticks tried to pull a knife out of her bandolier with her numb fingers. The burning fire in her gut kept her doubled over. The strength in her limbs failed completely. Helpless, she let Prince Lewis grab her by the braids and haul her to the top of the steps.

"Hmph, I think you are heavier than Shades was." Lewis gave her a quaint smile. "It was a pleasure working with you for a time. I'll always cherish the memories."

Sticks offered the prince one last burning look and said, "We saved you."

"And I'll always be grateful. 'Tis a shame that I won't be doing the same for you." With a shove of his boot, he rolled Sticks down the steps, where she landed right on top of Shades's body. Prince Lewis waved his gloved fingers. "Ta ta."

Sticks watched in burning misery. The wicked trio stood at the top of the stairs, gloating. With a shove that made closing the stone door look easy, Lewis sealed them inside the crypt to die in darkness and their own blood.

CHAPTER 70

Water dripped from the dungeon's cell beams onto the stone floor. Abraham sat with his head sunk between his legs, listening to the steady, maddening drip of water splashing on the floor. He didn't know which was worse, being locked up in the cell or wrapped up like a pig in a blanket in a padded room.

Switch. Switch. Switch.

A big part of him wanted to go back home the longer he sat in the murk. His trips to Titanuus had at one time been very appealing, but now, its treachery had gotten old. The time for normalcy had come.

Maybe Ruger can put an end to all of this.

He let out a wet cough. Typically, when he was in Ruger's body, he felt a wellspring of endless vitality. Now, he felt drained. He'd never been the same since the wraith—the Underlord, Fleece—drained him. Perhaps all the back and forth between bodies had worn him down. Maybe Ruger's body had begun to take on Abraham's body from back home.

He leaned his head back and bumped it against the slime-slick wall.

Ah man, this isn't good.

A rat crawled into his cell. Its long whiskers twitched as it stared at Abraham with beady red eyes.

"Don't even think about it. I'm not dead yet." He flicked his fingers at the rat, but it remained frozen in its spot. "Getting bolder, eh? Maybe you can see that I'm dead already." He sniffed. "Maybe I am and I don't know it. This better be real."

If he'd had some idea of what was going on, it wouldn't have been so bad. He'd left his friends at home in the lurch. Luther was in danger, and thanks to Abraham, he'd been dragged into everything. Mandi, Sid, Smoke—all of them had endangered themselves too. And there were the Henchmen.

What in Titanuus had happened to them? What if King Hector had disbanded them? He wouldn't have killed them, would he?

The large rat with little white feet scuttled out of the cell and vanished in the hallway.

The grinding of rusting door hinges echoed through the dungeon.

Abraham heard Carlton's heavy footsteps. The former Guardian-turned-jailer rambled on like a deranged man during his visits. He remained steadfast about his duties, as he was still sharp enough to not reveal anything to Abraham. Whenever he pressed for information, Carlton would button his lip and storm away.

"Are you thirsty, Ruger? Hmm," the hefty Carlton said as he appeared in front of the cell. "Fresh water from the king's own spring." He rattled a wooden ladle inside the bucket, sloshing the water out as he did so. "You can have water but no food. Those are my orders. Do you want a drink, my old friend?"

"Of course I do. I'm dying of thirst, and I'd be grateful."

"Hum-hee! You would do the same for me—I know that. I'm not here to make you suffer. No, no. I only make sure that you don't escape. Now, you stay back. Any sudden moves, and I'll spill it." Carlton stuck a key in the keyhole and stared at Ruger with a bulging eye. "No no no!" He yanked the key out. "I see what you are thinking. You will try to overpower me and escape. I won't have that!"

"I'm not moving," Abraham said calmly.

He had no idea how Carlton had been assigned as his jailer. The man appeared inept. But he didn't come across as someone worthy of living in the House of Steel. Perhaps Ruger had arranged it long before. "I am very thirsty. I swear on my honor that I won't move."

"Ha! Henchmen have no honor! You said so long ago to me." Carlton slammed the bucket down on the ground. Precious water splashed up over the rim. "You can drink through the bars. Good day, Ruger! I'll be back tomorrow." He waddled away, and somewhere far down the hall, the door slammed shut.

Eyeing the bucket, Abraham crawled across the cell.

Probably sewer water.

He stretched his fingers through the bars far enough and squeezed his thick forearm muscles through. With two fingers, he grabbed the bucket and pulled it over to the bars. To his surprise, the water inside the wooden pail was clear as rain. Parched, he grabbed the ladle and drank. He licked his cracked, dry lips.

"Ah…"

Through the bars, he sucked in ladleful after ladleful until he couldn't scrape any more out of the bucket. He picked up the bucket, tilted it up, and drained the last swallow.

He let out a throaty "Ah!"

He'd never enjoyed water so much before. Something about it was exquisite. The throbbing in his body eased. Hot blood raced through his system. He eyed the inside of the upside-down bucket. Only a drop came out. The bucket was drained.

Abraham clutched his fingers in and out. A spring of hot energy coursed through his limbs.

Blazing saddles! What is going on? I feel like I could run through a wall!

Something was afoot. Someone somewhere was helping him. Perhaps Iris had spiked the water with her magic. He couldn't think of anything else at the time.

He grabbed hold of the bars and heaved against them. The muscles popped in his mighty forearms. Blue veins rose like corded snakes. He put his feet against the wall of steel bars and pulled hard against it. The corroded metal started to bend.

King's Steel, my big ol' butt!

He tossed his head back and threw his back into it. "Hurk!"

The entire wall of bars ripped out of its frame and fell on top of him with a loud *bang*. For a long moment, he was trapped underneath the wall. He fought the urge to giggle. He'd meant to bend the metal, not rip the entire wall down. He crawled out from underneath the bars and said, "Conan, eat your heart out."

He didn't make it two steps down the hall before crossing a woman wearing a dark-red cloak barring his path. She brandished a razor-sharp sword.

CHAPTER 71

THE WOMAN CLOAKED IN RED dropped her hood. It was Princess Clarice.

"What are you doing here?" Abraham asked.

"Rescuing you, uh…"

"Abraham," he said.

She stepped around him and looked at the fallen wall of steel bars. Bewildered, she asked, "What did you do that for?"

"To get out."

She picked up the bucket and turned it upside down. A key was attached to a claylike material on the bottom of it. "Easy peasy?"

"Ah. I thought the water—"

The jailer's dungeon door opened.

"Let's go!" Clarice whispered. She grabbed his hand and led him to another dungeon passage. At the end of the passage, a stone wall was partially split open.

Abraham pulled free of her grip. "You go. I'll catch up. I have to deal with him."

"But…"

He took off back to his cell. He stepped inside, lifted the wall of bars up, and fit them back into the frame. Metal scraped loudly against the stone fitting.

"Har! What is that racket?" Carlton jogged on heavy feet to Abraham's cell. By the time he made it to the cell, he was lathered in sweat and puffing for breath. With his hands on his knees, he eyeballed Abraham. "What did you do?"

"Me?" Abraham asked innocently as he leaned into the dungeon bars, holding them nonchalantly in place. "Sorry, I dropped the bucket. It made such a clatter. Did you hear that?"

"The deaf in Burgess could have heard it." Carlton eyed his surroundings. "What are you doing? You have a sneaky look about you." He eyed the bars and the lock. Rubbing his flabby chin, he said, "Something stinks down here."

"It's been a time since I last bathed," he said even though Carlton smelled so bad it could knock over someone with unprepared nostrils. "Sorry."

Carlton pulled his short sword. "Step back."

"Why?"

"Do it!"

Slowly, Abraham stepped two steps back, thinking he could have handled the situation better.

But he needed to fool Carlton. Otherwise, the guard wouldn't hesitate to alert the soldiers of his escape. He didn't want to kill the man either. *Why didn't I just knock him out?*

"Step back further, to the back wall!" Carlton said. The moment Abraham moved back, Carlton grabbed the bars with one hand and tugged on them.

The bars teetered.

"Huh?" Carlton said.

The cell's bars tipped all the way over and crashed down on Carlton, pinning him underneath.

Carlton let out a loud scream.

Abraham jumped over the fallen cell bars and said, "Sorry, Carlton, but I have to go! But try to keep it down, will you?"

"I'll get you! Guards! Guards!"

Abraham didn't wait around to see if the guards showed up. He dashed down the dungeon hall and into the secret passage.

Clarice met him on the other side of the wall. She closed the passage door and dropped a locking bar behind it. "Well, that was a stupid idea," she said. "Come on."

Moving quickly, he followed her through the darkness with her hand fitted in his. The narrow passage wound through the castle's interior in an endless maze.

"Where are we going?" he asked.

"Shhh, the walls can be thin in spots." Clarice hustled onward. "We've known about these networks since we were children. I think most have forgotten about them. We go outside. Horses wait for our escape. There is a ship ready at the port."

He pulled her to a stop and said, "No. We go to the Stronghold. That is the first place they will look. We have to warn the Henchmen."

"But it will be certain death," she said.

"That's why they have to know. Besides, we are Henchmen. We take care of our own."

They made it outside into the pouring rain and stood underneath the northernmost wall of the castle by the sea cliff. It was night, and the waves crashed hard against the rocky shores below.

"Where are the horses?" he said.

"I'll show you," she replied.

Loud brass horns and moaning whistles erupted from inside the castle walls. The clamor of soldiers running along the castle walls began to grow.

Abraham could hear the grinding of the front gate opening. Horses and riders by the score rode out of the castle with hooves sounding like thunder.

"Blazing saddles! They are heading to the Stronghold. I know it." He let out a regretful sigh. "We'll never beat them there. God help them. God help me."

CHAPTER 72

"ABRAHAM, WE MUST GO. THERE is not anything we can do for them now," Clarice said as she dragged him through the darkness. "They are Henchmen. They can handle themselves. Maybe they won't be there. They are savvy, are they not?"

"Yes, but I won't abandon them," he said as he ran over the rain-slick grasses. "I'll help fight."

"But you don't have Black Bane." Clarann stopped running as soon as the castle was out of sight. She caught her breath. "The horses are ahead." She pointed. "See?"

Four horses were there. Two of them had riders. One of the riders was the amazon of a woman, Swan. He could only guess that the other was Queen Clarann. They all met up.

"Ruger?" Clarice asked.

"No." He climbed into the saddle. "Listen, ladies, it would be best if you went back. They are looking for me, not you."

"Where you sail, we sail," Clarann said.

"Sorry, dear, but we aren't sailing. I'm thankful, but I am going to the Stronghold. I have to beat the king's Riders there."

"You won't beat the Golden Riders," Swan said. "They have the fastest horses in the kingdom. They ride like the wind."

With the rain in his face he said, "Then I guess I will have to do the same thing." He felt like a new man and looked at Clarice and said, "What was in the bucket of water?"

"The Guardian Maidens aren't without their own mystical resources. That was ahber root. It restores vitality. Feeling yourself?"

"Sort of." He nodded at the women and tipped his head. "Ladies, I have to go. You need to lie low until it's o—"

"Golden Riders!" Swan said. "We've been spotted."

A half score of the men in full suits of golden armor rode like bats from hell through the rain. They were less than one hundred yards away and closing fast.

"It looks like we are all going the same way now." Clarann snapped her reins. "Eeyah!" Her horse bolted away.

The small group rode like thunder.

Abraham looked over his shoulder. The Golden Riders would ride them down in minutes. He dug his heels into his horse. "Yah! Yah!"

The foursome rode into the brush where a large tree had fallen. Clarann's horse leapt it first, landed hard on the other side, and tossed her from the saddle.

Thunder popped with a loud boom. Lightning streaked across the sky.

Clarann's horse kept running.

Abraham, Clarice, and Swan gathered around the queen. Clarann was holding her ankle. A hard grimace was on her face.

He jumped off his horse and said, "Tell me it's not broken."

Clarann frowned as she nodded and said, "Ride! Ride on!"

"It's too late now." Standing behind the fallen tree, he faced the oncoming riders. He stretched out his hand. "Swan, tell me you brought an extra sword."

"No," Swan replied, "because I only need one." She lifted her sword high, and her horse reared up with a lightning bolt streaking the sky behind her. "Yah!" Her horse jumped the log, and she thundered toward the Golden Riders.

"She's crazy!" Clarice pulled out her rapier and got a wild-eyed look. "I'm crazy too."

"Clarice, don't you dare! Abraham, stop her!" the queen said.

He took a swipe at the reins of Clarice's horse and narrowly missed.

Over the log went the queen's daughter.

The Golden Riders lowered their lances.

Empty-handed, Abraham watched in horror. *They are gonna die!*

A giant black shadow passed over him and the queen.

Gazing up with eyes bigger than saucers, Clarann said, "What in Titanuus's Crotch is that?"

Abraham pumped his fist and said, "Holy sheetrock! It's Simon the Fenix!"

The Fenix dropped in front of the Golden Riders, wings spread wide like a black cloud of death. The fearless knights thundering out of the House of Steel didn't slow their charge. With lances lowered, they spurred their mighty beasts onward at breathtaking speed.

Simon—the Elder Spawn—opened his great mouth. With his eight large eyes narrowing on the charge, he unleashed a stream of misty breath. The white cloud of geyserlike mist covered the charging knights from head to toe.

One of the Golden Riders evaded the stream. His lance busted off of Simon's shoulder with a loud snap.

The horses snorted and bucked as they slowed their pace. They wriggled their mighty necks as if shaking away a swarm of stinging insects. Covered in the milky grime sprayed by Simon, the horses' efforts slowed. The knights climbed out of their saddles at an agonizing pace. Many of them fell from their horses and no longer moved.

Abraham picked up Queen Clarann, climbed over the log, and moved to a spot where he could get a better view.

The horses that didn't fall lay in the grass, frozen stiff. The same could be said for the Golden Riders. Many were stuck in their saddles as if frozen in time. Others were on the ground, snoring loudly and asleep.

He caught up with Clarice and Swan. Both women walked through the field of sleeping men and beasts. Their jaws were hanging open.

"Should I kill them?" Swan asked. Her nostrils were flared, and her chest heaved behind her breastplate. "I wanted to kill something."

"Count your blessings, and let them be. They aren't our enemy." Abraham looked at the queen. "I need to set you down."

Clarann nodded and gave him a quick kiss on the cheek. "I'll be fine."

Clarice steadied her mother.

Abraham approached the great beast, which had nestled on the ground. "My, you just keep on growing like a weed, don't you?"

Simon snorted. He was an ugly creature that looked more like a gargantuan hammerhead bat than anything else—an eight-eyed bat, that is. He was covered in brown fur that appeared coarse.

Abraham touched the Elder Spawn. The thick coat of fur was soft. He petted Simon's flat head, which was almost as big as an entire horse. "Your timing couldn't have been better." He looked at the Golden Riders, not one of which moved a muscle. "Thanks for not killing them. Let's see how this shakes out because you might have to snack on them later." He climbed onto Simon's back.

"Wait! What are you doing?" Clarann asked.

"I'm going to the Stronghold to warn the Henchmen. With Simon, I can easily beat the king's forces there."

With Clarice holding her side, Clarann hobbled over. "We have nowhere to go. We are coming too."

"I'm not getting on that thing," Swan said with a disgusted face. "I'll keep an eye on the Golden Riders. You can all go."

"Are you sure?" Clarice asked her friend.

With a raised eyebrow pointed at Simon, Swan said, "Oh, I'm sure—unless you're going to order me to do so."

"No, I wouldn't do that." Clarice hugged Swan and moved over to the Elder Spawn's monstrous side. "There should be a saddle and stirrup."

"Sorry, ladies," Abraham said as he reached over Simon's side. "Grab some fur."

Abraham, Clarann, and Clarice positioned themselves uncomfortably behind Simon's head. Clarann wrapped her arms around Abraham, and Clarice wrapped her arms around her mother.

Taking in the bizarre situation, Abraham said, "This is crazy. This is crazy!"

"What's crazy?" Clarann asked.

"Nothing. Just hang on. The Stronghold is over a league away. Let's just hope we can beat them there." He firmly patted Simon on the back of the head. "Simon, we're ready for liftoff!"

Simon's monstrous bat wings spread out. He leapt into the sky, let out a ferocious screech, and bolted toward the Stronghold.

CHAPTER 73

SIMON LANDED IN THE STRONGHOLD'S muddy courtyard in a matter of minutes. Sopping wet from head to toe, Abraham, Clarann, and Clarice barreled through the front door, taking everyone by surprise.

Clarann and Clarice sat by the fireplace, underneath wool blankets, shivering like leaves. The flight on Simon's back had proven to be a gut-wrenching journey as they flew high and fast through the icy sheets of rain.

Abraham embraced his men with forearm bumps and the women with wet hugs. Everyone in the household was gathered, including the triplets and the servant hags, Elga and Eileen. He stood at the head of the farm table with a foot propped up on his chair. "We have to get out of here, all of us. King Hector's soldiers are looking for me, and they'll be here within the hour."

"Where are we going to go, Captain?" Horace asked. "There is no place in Kingsland for a Henchman to hide. If we flee now, we can never come back."

"We only need to lie low for now." He lifted his voice and scanned every face in the room. "Listen, all of you. Everyone must go. They'll stop at nothing to find me. They'll torture you to find out. I'd think most of you would be thrown back into Baracha." He wiped his face on a towel that Dominga handed him. "There is no choice but to split up and run."

Vern slammed his fist on the table. "We are Henchmen! Sworn to serve the king. We can't go against him whether he is a mad king or not. Perhaps we should turn you in. That would be best for all of us."

"I'm going to break your neck!" Horace said as he stormed around the table toward Vern.

It took Bearclaw and Cudgel to bar his path.

"Easy!" Bearclaw warned. "We aren't against each other."

Abraham had already explained his meeting with the king. He cast a hard look at Vern, who was still seated, and said, "Is that what you want? Is that what most of you want? If it is, I can turn myself in."

No one said a word.

Vern broke the silence. "It's always going to be your word against the king's. Siding with you is a threat to my longevity. If you were Ruger, well"—he shrank in his chain-mail armor—"I'd be more apt to believe you."

"I believe you, Abraham," Cudgel said loudly. "You've never led us wrong. Ever."

"Maybe it would be best if you got on your ugly dragon and flew out of here." Vern got up. "I'm not going to stand around here and wait to fight soldiers from my kingdom either."

"I'm going to kill him!" Horace blurted out.

Bearclaw pushed Horace back and said, "He speaks from the heart. There is nothing wrong with him having doubt. But we all need to remember that this is still the body of Ruger Slade. And if he were here, I think he'd say the same thing."

"The only truth that I can give you is my word," Abraham said. His backpack was on the table, and he hung it over his shoulder. "Perhaps it might be best if I did go. We can meet somewhere else." He scanned the table and found Sticks's seat empty. He'd been so busy that he hadn't even noticed. "Where's Sticks? Where's Shades?"

"They were following Prince Lewis, but they haven't come back," Iris said. "It's been days, and no sign of either of them."

The muscles between Abraham's shoulder blades tightened.

Outside, a horse let out a shrieking whinny.

"They can't be here already!" Abraham jumped onto the table and ran for the door. Solomon beat him to the door and rushed outside right before him.

Simon had a horse frozen in its hooves. One rider leaned over the body of another that was slumped over the saddle.

Even through the heavy rain, Abraham could see they were smaller people and not heavily armed knights. He immediately recognized the shape of one figure and called out, "Sticks!"

She fell out of the saddle and into the mud.

Abraham raced to pick Sticks up. She was pale as a ghost, with clammy skin. She clutched at her bleeding gut. He scooped her up and rushed her inside and set her on the table. "Iris! Iris! Do something!"

Solomon walked inside and set Shades down on the table, head to head with Sticks. "His hand's missing," the troglin said. "He's not breathing."

Shades had a crude bandage wrapped around his bloody stump. He was out cold. Sticks, on the other hand, was barely breathing, and her eyes fluttered open and closed.

Holding Sticks's hand, Abraham said, "Talk to me. Talk to me, Sticks! Who did this to you? Prince Lewis?"

Sticks managed to say a soft "Yes."

Iris leaned right over Sticks and asked, "Did you use the salve I gave you?"

With a nod, Sticks said, "On Shades. He was worse than me. Did I save him?"

"Doesn't look like it," Vern said.

Everyone glared at Vern.

"What? Look at him. Death happens. We're all lucky we made it this far."

Iris tore Sticks's shirt open. "Oh my, that's bad. Why didn't you use the salve on yourself? Don't answer." She held her middle and index finger together. They glowed with a red-hot rosy fire. "This might hurt a bit. Hold her still, fellas." She plunged her fingers inside Sticks's wound.

Sticks's back arched like a bridge, and her wide eyes bulged, but she did not scream.

CHAPTER 74

With a groan, Sticks sat up with Ruger and Iris's help. A cold sweat ran down from her forehead to her cheeks. She panted and said, "Thanks."

"Don't do anything crazy," Iris warned. "I sealed your guts with magic fire. It will hold, but it's gonna hurt like the Brand for a while."

Sticks leaned over and touched Shades. "Is he… dead?"

"I'm afraid so," Iris said as she laid her head on the small man's chest. "Not even a beat."

"I tried," Sticks said with a straight face.

Abraham could still see the agony lurking behind her eyes. "What happened?"

Sticks swallowed as everyone gathered around the table, from the stunning Clarann to the scraggly Eileen. "We followed Prince Lewis, Leodor, and Leah to Burgess. They went back to the Cathedral of Elders. Down in the crypt. They uncovered the mirror and lit the candlestands."

Abraham's skin crawled. He remembered the last time he'd been down in the crypt.

Sticks went on. "Images of Big Apple, Fleece, and Lord Hawk appeared. They spoke and talked about their plans."

"You heard all of it," he said.

She nodded. "Lewis and Leodor have already turned on the king. As soon as King Hector removed the Brand, they went back to their old ways."

Clarice spoke up and said, "Leah is with them. I can't believe that. She'd never betray the crown. Never."

"Leah is dead," Sticks said quietly. "The Leah you see is not the one that you know. Raschel the assassin used the Ring of Tarsus to take her form."

Clarice let out a gasp, and her eyes watered as her mother put a comforting arm around her shoulder. "I'll kill Lewis. I swear it!" she said through gritted teeth.

"What else?" Abraham asked.

Sticks cleared her throat.

"Get her a drink," Horace ordered.

"Big Apple is waiting for the king. He wants to trap him in the Spine. Their lair is located at the bottom of the Spine, west of Titanuus's Crotch." Sticks grabbed Abraham by the forearm. "Leodor has greatly deceived King Hector. He says that the stones are only meant to be used individually or as a whole. The king is going mad with power, and he will eventually destroy himself if the Sect doesn't first."

"We need the other stones," Abraham said.

She shook her head. "You will never find the stones. Big Apple took them out of this world. I believe he hid them in your world."

"He wouldn't be hiding them if they didn't matter." Abraham stroked his chin. "I need to get back home and find them." He put his thoughts aside. "What happened to Leodor, Lewis, and Raschel?"

"After they thought they'd killed us, they sealed us in the crypt, leaving us for dead. I had enough of Iris's salve to keep us alive and escape."

"So, they think that you are dead, and they don't know that we know this," he said.

"I don't see how. They won't have contact again with Big Apple either until they make it to the lair."

"You know this for certain?"

"Big Apple said so."

Abraham moved from the table and paced around it. "Finally, we have an advantage that they don't have. We have to find the king and warn him."

"He marches to the Spine. No doubt that Prince Lewis will lead him to that trap," Horace offered. "Will the king take your word over his own son's?"

Abraham glanced at Clarann. "Probably not. Does Prince Lewis still have Black Bane?"

"He does," Sticks said. "Big Apple says the other side wants it as a trophy."

"Yeah, that's the same thing they told me."

"You'd think they'd want the crown as a trophy," Shades said.

Everyone looked at the dead man on the table. Shades's eyes were still closed.

"What's everyone looking at?" he said.

The Henchmen exchanged shocked, bewildered looks.

Iris put her ear on his chest. "His pumper beats again."

"Of course it does," Shades said. "I managed to slow my heart rate down so that I wouldn't die. I've just been resting." He kissed Iris on the top of her head and sat up. He held his stump before his eyes. "This is a wee bit of a problem, though."

Sticks embraced Shades and said, "I never thought I'd say this, but thank the Elders you're alive."

Shades stroked her hair. "I'm the one that owes you." He swung his legs over the table and kicked Vern in the nuggets.

Vern doubled over. "I guess I had that coming."

"Captain, what about the Golden Riders? They'll be here soon. It's time we departed and met at the Rendezvous."

"The Rendezvous?" Abraham had never heard of the place before, but a part of him thought it sounded familiar.

"Aye, our hiding spot. It wouldn't be the first time we've been in poor light with the king and many others," Horace said.

The sound of horses galloping through the rain caught everyone's attention. All of them turned toward the door.

"Looks like our time is up," Solomon said.

"No, I have a better idea." He approached the door and smiled. "Simon can keep them at bay. For a long time."

He flung the door open, expecting the see Simon the Fenix guarding the courtyard. The rain came down in heavy drops. Simon the Fenix was gone. Only two score riders remained.

He closed the door, put his back to it, and said, "Henchmen, we have a problem."

CHAPTER 75

Vern stared out one of the portal windows and said, "I'm not fighting them again, only to be hunted down and get my neck stretched later." He eyeballed Abraham. "No offense. I believe the story, but will they? I doubt it."

Abraham quickly got over the shock of Simon being gone, realizing he shouldn't have been surprised, for the Fenix came and went as it pleased. He said to Horace, "I need a banner of negotiation."

"Aye." Horace hustled away.

"They'll kill you if you go out there," Vern said. "The Golden Riders are a death squad. They don't accept surrender."

"Maybe they'll accept some reason." Abraham looked out the portals. The Golden Riders' steel armor was trimmed in gold. They wore great helmets fashioned like the heads of lions. The rider in the very front was very big. "Is that Pratt?"

"It's got to be. There's no bigger man in the Guardians than him," Vern replied. "What are you going to do, go out there and shake his hand? He'll kill you." Vern took off his sword belt. He handed it to Abraham. "Take this. You'll need it."

Abraham put a hand out and said, "No, I'm fine."

Horace returned to the room, holding a small flag. It had a thin orange stripe in the middle of a white field. "I'll go with you."

Sticks hustled over to Abraham. She was bent over slightly. "Me too."

Together, the three of them strode out into the rain.

Abraham stopped twenty yards from the row of knights. Holding the banner, he said, "Wait here." He moved ten yards closer to Pratt and lifted the banner high. "I want to talk."

Pratt removed his helmet and handed it to the rider on his left. Glowering at Abraham, he said in a rugged voice, "Golden Riders don't negotiate with traitors, escapees, or anyone else, for that matter."

"You might not like me or Ruger Slade, but when have you known either one of us to lead you wrong?" Abraham lowered the flag. "Can you say the same about Lewis and Leodor, two men that you know tried to kill the king? King Hector took the Brand from them. They are up to their same old tricks."

"I don't care," Pratt said.

"You always were looking for a fight, Pratt," Horace said.

"No, I'm looking forward to retirement." Pratt eyeballed the Stronghold. "This might make a suitable place."

"You can have it," Abraham said, "if you hear me out. And if you value your men, as I do mine, we can part ways without any blood on our hands. Listen, and if you don't agree, I'll come in peace. All of us will."

"Let me guess, if I don't, you'll fight all of us to the death." Pratt chuckled lowly and rubbed his lantern jaw. "Hmm... I can respect that. Spit it out."

Sticks rattled off everything she'd told the Henchmen minutes before. She didn't miss a single detail but added a few.

Tall in the saddle, Pratt sat in silence.

"Come on," Abraham said. "You saw those tanks. The machine guns. That's going to take over Titanuus if we don't stop it. We are the only hope King Hector has."

Pratt flexed the metal gauntlets covering his hands. He scoffed. "I hate to miss out on an opportunity to fight, but the woman's words ring with truth. Bloody blades!" He shook his head. "What are you going to do?"

"I have to try to warn King Hector."

"Ha, you won't get within a mile of him," Pratt said.

Abraham eyed the knights, grinned, and said, "Yeah, but I have an idea."

CHAPTER 76

"May fortune favor the foolish," Abraham said.

He wore a suit of Golden Knight armor. So did the rest of the Henchmen as they rode north toward the Spine.

"Who said that, someone in your world?" Sticks asked. She rode to the right of Abraham, while Horace and Pratt were on the left.

"Captain James Tiberius Kirk," Abraham said. "*Star Trek IV, the Voyage Home*. He quoted another person. I think it was Latin, but I don't know who said it originally." Oddly enough, he found his situation similar to the *Star Trek* movie, where the whittled-down crew of the *USS Enterprise* had to time travel with two whales to save the world. "It wasn't the most popular movie in the series, but I liked it."

"Humph," Sticks said quickly.

The Henchmen, along with a handful of Golden Riders, hadn't stopped moving since Pratt agreed, surprisingly, to the idea. The big, gruff man had a better head on his shoulders than it appeared. The next tricky part was getting close enough to King Hector while hoping the king hadn't completely lost his mind to the power of the Crown of Stones.

"There isn't any hiding where they are going," Horace said.

Tark and Dominga were still riding far out in the front on scout duty.

"They march thousands of soldiers. They even took more from the Wall."

The moment when the Henchmen rode through the Shield of Steel was bleak. The great doors were gone. The enemy had taken them. The forces of Southern Tiotan, however, were nowhere in sight. The King's Army scouts stated that they'd moved back north, toward the sea. They left the path to the Spine wide open. As far as Abraham was concerned, King Hector was being led into a trap.

Making it to Giant's Vein River took over three days of hard riding. The company crossed the river and moved toward the Spine. Late on the third night, they made camp.

Sitting by the campfire, Horace said, "The King's Army moves slow compared to us. We will catch them late in the day tomorrow. But I'd say that they will be in the bottom of the Spine by them. I wouldn't want to navigate those mountains with any army. The terrain is too dangerous."

"The king thinks he is invincible," Abraham said. He chewed on a piece of dried meat and drank from his water skin. "No doubt Lewis and Leodor have caught up with him. I am sure that he has the king's pride puffed up."

"What sort of son could betray such a father?" Pratt said. He was lurking nearby, sharpening his sword with a stone. "King Hector is a good man. It is something I never understood about Lewis. He was treated well."

"Perhaps too well," Clarice said as she and her mother joined Abraham by the fire and sat down. "Lewis has always been an entitled brat. May the Elders help Kingsland if he ever gains the crown."

"And I thought he might have turned the corner the last time we saved him," Abraham said. "Listen to me everyone. If Ruger comes back, you know the drill."

"We'll fill his ears with your plans," Horace said. "We understand now."

"I need to go back. I need to tell them what is going on," he said. "If I could only control it."

"Isn't that the problem? Isn't that what the Sect wants to do?" Clarann asked.

"Yeah. Be careful what you wish for."

He warmed his hands at the fire. The rain had stopped a day before, but he was still damp all over. The armor, though light, was heavier than what he was used to as well. Even the queen and princess had armor on as well. It wasn't a good fit but was good enough to fool someone from a distance. Not all the Golden Riders were tall, only most of them.

"Everyone get some rest," Abraham said. "The crack of dawn will be here before you know it."

The present company moved away. Some of them lay on their bedrolls and others underneath a blanket. Clarann and Clarice were both yawning when they left. Pratt had set up a tent for them to sleep in.

Only Sticks and Horace remained with Abraham. "I said 'everyone.'"

"We aren't everyone," Sticks said.

"Look, I'm going to get some shut-eye too." He scooted back to a spot where his feet were several feet from the flames. He lay his head back on his bedroll and looked up into the odd pattern of stars. "Do you have names for the stars in the sky?"

With a heavy upward stare, Horace said, "They are named after the Elders." He pointed at the sky. "That's the Elder of Turtles. That's the Elder of Flowers. That's the Elder of—"

"I get it." Abraham closed his eyes. "It's not very different from back home. Our stars are named after legends and heroes from an age long ago. Geez, I can't believe I'm talking about this. Those aren't my stars, but they should be, and if they are not, then I must be at least a galaxy away from home." He sighed. "This can't be real."

Solomon plopped down beside Abraham. "Now isn't the time to start doubting. Not when we are so close to the end. It's real. You have to believe it's real. I have to believe it's real."

Abraham clicked his steel-shod boots together, yawned, and said, "There's no place like home."

"If only it was that easy," Solomon said. "But I don't think those ruby slippers would ever fit on my feet." He lifted a hairy two-foot-long foot. "That would be expensive."

"I bet. Try and get some sleep." He settled in for the night.

The campfire's embers crackled. The soft rustling of the company settling down surrounded him. The fire's warmth ran from his head to his toes. With a soft breeze passing through the night, he drifted off into a heavy slumber.

He woke from his sleep, sitting up and gasping for air. The stars in the sky were long gone. So were the Henchmen.

CHAPTER 77
BACK HOME

Dr. Jack Lassiter slapped Abraham rapidly on the cheek. He snapped his fingers in front of his face. "Who do we have with us today?" He made a throaty laugh. "It's very hard to tell who I am dealing with when I inject you."

Abraham's veins were burning like fire, but they started to cool to an icy feeling. His eyes shifted side to side. He could see Dr. Jack and the zillon woman, Ottum. They were riding in the back of an ambulance on a bumpy road. He was strapped in to the gurney.

Don't say a word. Figure out your circumstances first.

Dr. Jack kept his finger in Abraham's face and said, "Watch my finger."

Abraham glared at him.

"Hmm… look at those brooding eyes. I think this is Ruger. What do you think, Ottum?"

The zillon woman leaned over Abraham. Her voluminous, pitch-black, probing eyes searched his. "I think it's Abraham."

"Really, why so?"

"I see softness, perhaps panic."

Dr. Jack shook his head. "I saw more softness that last time we shot him. Of course, we can't say for sure if this experiment is working at all." He pinched Abraham's cheek. "Of course, you aren't going to tell us, are you? You're being stubborn, aren't you?"

Looks like me and Ruger are on the same page. They don't know who is who. That's a good thing.

The bumpy ride jostled the cabin.

Dr. Jack slipped into his seat. "Heh heh heh." He grabbed a black strap that hung from the ceiling. "It's like riding in the back of a deuce."

"What is a deuce?" Ottum asked.

"A big military transport truck. I used to be a soldier. Spent time in the jungles in Vietnam. God, I'm old."

Abraham kept his heated stare on the man. He didn't hate many people, but he hated Dr. Jack.

A soldier, huh? Maybe he'll pick up a sword so I can kill him. One slice, and off with your big ol' tater head.

The truck's brakes squealed, and it came to a stop.

Abraham's gurney bumped to the front of the cabin.

Seconds later, the back doors were opened by Otis and Haymaker. They hauled Abraham, gurney and all, out of the ambulance with their long, powerful arms.

He didn't look at either one of them. His eyes slid from side to side. He was inside the abandoned train tunnel where the Time Tunnel had been set up.

I wonder where Luther is.

A few seconds later, he got his answer. Luther was strapped in a gurney just like his. Both of them had been placed behind the five computer stations standing in front of the Time Tunnel. Luther was hooked to an IV with orange fluid. Propped up at a forty-five-degree angle, the old man was twitching his fingers underneath his wrist restraints. Abraham wanted to scream. *What have you done to him?*

The Time Tunnel was in full operation. The lights in the main center ring glowed like blue star fire. Inside the ring was the tunnel made up with the metal plates of King's Steel. More plates were there this time. The patches in the tunnel had been filled in. It ran deeper into the mountainside. A row of train cars loaded with tanks and racks of assault weapons was being pushed into the tunnel, where citizens of Titanuus waited.

Dr. Jack stood beside Abraham, watching the railcars crossing from one world to another. "Amazing progress, isn't it?" He pointed at the stacks of goldlike bars that looked like the King's Steel. "And that's what made it all happen, thanks to Prince Lewis winning back favor with King Hector. He shipped it out immediately. Now, here we are. The Time Tunnel is complete, and only one thing is missing."

Abraham kept his lips sealed as he searched the area. He saw Colonel Drew Dexter and Eugene Drisk milling about with the other scientists. They were checking computer screens and giving orders. Dozens of armed guards were there too. The tunnel was a hive of activity. He didn't see any other familiar faces—no sign of Smoke, Sid, or Mandi, which gave him some relief.

"Come on, Abraham, talk to me. I know it's you," Dr. Jack said. "I've had plenty of patients with schizophrenia. Enough to know the difference between you and Ruger." He put a cigar in his mouth. "Man, I wish they'd let me smoke in here."

Seeing Luther spasm, Abraham's heart softened, and he broke down and asked, "What are you doing with Luther? He's no part of this. Let him go."

"The moment he got involved, he became a part of all of this." Dr. Jack looked at him with his dark beady eyes. "There is no way out now. Besides, being older, he's a prime candidate to start a new life on Titanuus."

"What do you mean?"

Dr. Jack pointed at the Time Tunnel. A smaller tunnel had been built to the left of it, standing about seven feet high. It was pitch-black inside, but the small outer lights of the metal ring glowed orange. "That's a portal, one of the random ones that pops up randomly in the tunnels. We caught it, so to speak, thanks to our friend on the other side, Fleece. You see, he has mastered combining the magic of his world with the technology of our world. Heh heh heh." He rolled the cigar from one side of his mouth to the other. "That's the test gate."

Abraham flexed against his bonds. "Then test it on me!"

"No, we want to see how this goes first. And we are using your friend to let you know that we mean business." Dr. Jack flagged down Colonel Dexter. "Are we ready?"

Dressed in a black suit of camouflage clothing, Colonel Dexter said, "Absolutely."

Dr. Jack looked at Luther and said, "Then take him away."

Luther cast a nervous look in Abraham's direction and said, "I'll be all right." Otis and Haymaker unhooked the IV and pushed him toward the tunnel.

The black image inside the smaller Time Tunnel twisted with vibrant colors. An image formed, showing Fleece standing on the other side. His hands glowed with white fire inside the sleeves of his robes.

Standing behind the computer station closest to the small tunnel, Eugene Drisk pounded away at the computer keys. "The moving portal is intact. Now is the time to cross. Go now!"

Otis shoved the horrified Luther into the doorway.

Fleece grabbed the gurney on the other side and ripped him through. The image on the other side of the tunnel went black.

Eugene feverishly tapped the keys. "Where did he go?"

Abraham craned his neck. He could see Eugene's monitor clearly from his position. The screens were all black.

"We put a tracking fluid in him. It's supposed to send us his vitals from one side to the other. In theory, that is. We only have the inanimate mastered. Not the living."

"Couldn't you have tested on a rat?" Abraham yelled.

"We aren't in business with rats. We are in business with people. People with a lot of money, something the animal *and* plant kingdom can't offer."

"I don't have any vitals. I don't have anything," Eugene said. "It's as if he disappeared completely."

"No, wait." Colonel Dexter pointed at the larger tunnel.

Fleece stepped into view from the other side. He dragged the gurney behind him. Luther lay on the bed with his head rolled to the side and eyes closed. He didn't move a muscle.

Colonel Dexter walked right up to the Time Tunnel and stood across from Fleece. He looked toward Luther and asked, "Is he dead?"

The shadowy hood of Fleece nodded.

CHAPTER 78

"I'm going to kill you, Jack," Abraham said. His jaws clenched, and his fists were balled up. He'd never ever had any urge to kill a man in cold blood until he met Jack.

"Don't be so dramatic. Luther was old. Chances are that he had a heart attack." Dr. Jack pulled Abraham over to Eugene's computer station. "What happened?"

"We are checking the readout." Eugene glanced at Abraham. "A shame about your friend. He could have been a true pioneer. Like us." He rubbed an eye. "It's possible that he might still be alive. He could have soul swapped, but we'll never know." He punched the keyboard. "Bloody systems should have worked."

"Why don't you go through it? You've been through before," Abraham suggested.

"That's what we brought you for, you blundering fool," Eugene said.

"You know, you're going to die. Ruger is coming for you."

Eugene paled. "Shut up!"

"It's only a matter of time."

"The only reason that you or he is still alive is because you are the only one coming back and forth through the soul swap. But once we are able to keep the tunnel open for the living, that won't matter anymore. You'll be dust in the wind once this is over."

"Quit bickering and get this thing working," Dr. Jack said. "Otis, get Mr. Jenkins out of the gurney. He can walk, but keep him bound up and all eyes on him." He kicked the gurney's wheels. "I'm tired of rolling this thing around."

Abraham was moved upright. The orderlies left a straitjacket on him and kept their stun rods ready in hand. Abraham could run, but he had nowhere else to go. He had to see things through.

Colonel Dexter flagged Jack and Eugene over. Drew stood in front of the Time Tunnel, eyeing Fleece. Big Apple and Lord Hawk had joined the wraith.

"What is it?" Dr. Jack asked Big Apple.

The horned halfling huffed on a cigar and said, "We believe it is going to take more magic to keep the portal open and be able to get it to work as you wish."

"How do you know this?"

"Fleece is the most adept user of magic in all of Titanuus. He can sense what the issue is. He knew the moment that this man died." Big Apple pointed at Luther. "You need power on our end that is more permanent. You'll need to harness the Crown of Stones's power."

"The king's crown, you say?" Dr. Jack said. "I thought that wasn't a factor."

"So long as it is incomplete, then no man can wield it, but"—Big Apple glanced up—"if you use it to power this ring, it will strengthen the tunnel. Bring me the two that you have in your possession. Perhaps that will be enough to give it a try."

"What about King Hector?" Dr. Jack asked.

"He's marching on the lair, but he is being taken care of. I wouldn't be surprised if he was dead already. But we'll know soon enough. I have scouts in the sky." Big Apple eyed Ottum. "Zillon dragon riders will be reporting soon. And we should have your trophy, the sword Black Bane as well. Perhaps you can kill Abraham with it. Ruger too."

"We'll shoot Ruger before he makes it within one hundred yards of me," Eugene said. He eyed Dr. Jack. "This plan is worth a try. The addition of magic might be just what we need. I can rig something up for Fleece."

"Do it," Dr. Jack said. "Big Apple, keep me updated on the king's location. I don't want any surprises."

"What do you want us to do with him?" Big Apple asked of Luther.

Dr. Jack replied coolly, "I don't know—feed him to a dragon."

Even though Abraham couldn't see Fleece's face, he could see his diamond-hard eyes boring into him like a drill. A moment passed as their eyes locked. Fleece broke off the stare and looked down at Big Apple. His shiny eyes fixed on the collar. Then he dragged Luther's gurney behind himself as they moved away.

What was that? With a strange shiver up his spine, he pushed by the orderlies as he moved after Dr. Jack. "You know, you are really sick. Aren't you sworn to help people?"

"If you are talking about the Hippocratic Oath, well, yeah, you'd be right. But that was written centuries ago, you know, before universal health care." Dr. Jack grabbed a chair outside one of the trailers and sat down. He propped his feet up on the table. "Sit down, Abraham. Relax. Who knows? Maybe when all of this is over, we'll find you a cozy place to live in one of Titanuus's prisons."

Abraham sat down in a folding chair. "I didn't ask for this. Luther didn't ask for this either. This all happened because of what you did."

"There are always incidental consequences on the journey to universal greatness. Don't you realize what we have done? You, of all people, should understand. We've created a gateway to another world." Dr. Jack dabbed his forehead with a handkerchief. "You could have had it better than anybody if you only cooperated. You could have been an ambassador to both worlds."

"Just so you know, I gave King Hector your offer. So I kept my end of the bargain. You can't blame him for wanting to fight it out. That's what any one of us would do."

Jack wagged his fingers. "No, no, no, read your history. Most kings compromise."

"Oh yeah, that's right. I forgot those scenes in *Braveheart*. Thanks for reminding me, Longshanks."If he wasn't in a straight-jacked he would've wagged his finger at Jack. "And how did that end?"

"Robert the Bruce took England out," Otis said.

Jack glared at Otis and said, "Will you shut up?"

"Sorry, Dr. Jack." Otis stepped away.

"Listen to me, Abraham, this fight is over. There isn't stopping progress like this. We've either opened a gateway to another dimension or created a bridge across the universe."

"Or all of this is a part of my imagination. I'm hoping for the latter, considering my fate is sealed." He crinkled his nose. "Say, Otis, could you scratch my nose? I've got a bad itch."

"How about I break it? It won't itch after that," the orderly said.

"You really have a poor bedside manner."

Jack pulled a small case out of his pocket and opened it. It contained another syringe. "You know I can send you to Titanuus whenever I want and bring you back the same. It's only a matter of time before I master it. All I know is that the lightning strike made you special. It changed your DNA." He eyed the needle. "But I think that DNA can be replicated if all else fails with the portals. Once we control them, I think I'll be able to code the body that someone jumps into."

"Aren't you full of clever ideas, playing God and all?"

"We are talking about immortality. What is more godlike than that?"

"No one lives forever in Titanuus either, moron. In case you hadn't noticed, they have dragons over there!"

"Otis. Haymaker. Secure him." Dr. Jack plunged the needle into Abraham's neck. "Next time you see a dragon, give him a kiss for me."

CHAPTER 79
TITANUUS

Abraham woke with his face in the dirt. Someone was shaking him.

"Captain! Captain!" Horace said, rolling Abraham over onto his side. "Are you well? You appeared to faint."

"Yeah, I probably did. It's me, Abraham."

The sun was shining overhead.

"Oh." Horace lay on his belly.

They were on a bluff, looking down upon a valley below the base of the bottom of the Spine. The King's Army had gathered down there, numbering in the thousands. They were making a steady march toward the winding hills of the Spine. Foot soldiers led the way, followed by heavy cavalry and support troops.

"So we caught up with them?" Abraham asked. "Have we made contact with the king?"

"No, this just happened. You, or Ruger, hadn't made up your mind on how to approach it." Horace took a knee and stood up with a grunt. "What do you think?"

"I think we'd better act quick." He eyed the sky. "Keep a lookout for zillon dragon riders. I know they are out there. The other side told me." He put a hand on Horace's shoulder. "And keep an eye on me too. They have me jumping back and forth like a frog on a lily pad. It's getting old." He made his way down the hill where he met up with the others.

Pratt stepped forward and asked, "What is the plan, Ruger?"

"It's Abraham—ah, heck, never mind. Does it even matter at this point? Man, I feel like the Tin Man in his suit of armor." He pinched the bridge of his nose. "Anyway, we won't stand here, watching from a distance. The King's Army will see us if they haven't already and get suspicious. The sooner we meet with him, the better."

"What are you going to do? March up to the king and tell him that his son the prince betrayed him again?" Pratt said.

"I wanted you to do that?"

"Prince Lewis will skin me alive," the Guardian said.

"We all need to get as close as we can. It's the only way to keep King Hector from getting slaughtered." He glanced at the distant hills. "The Sect will be waiting with an army of guns and big tanks. We have to stop the king. Now, they want the crown to keep the tunnel open. We can't let them have it."

"Why don't we destroy it?" Horace said.

"If there is no other way. This is the only way. It's going to have to be done one way or the other. Who's with me?"

"Death before failure," Horace said.

All the Henchmen nodded. Even Pratt.

Solomon brought Abraham's horse over. "This is big, isn't it?"

"Why do you say that?"

"I can feel the hair standing up on my neck. I've been lost here for decades, and I've never felt a feeling like this. If it happens, it happens." He offered his huge hand to Abraham. "I just want to say thanks for trying."

Abraham shook his hand and said, "Do you still want to go home?"

"I'm not sure. You?"

"Honestly, I think I'm ready to go back now that I know my past wasn't my fault. It was theirs. There's no telling how many lives they ruined. I just know that I have to stop it."

"I support you." Solomon looked at all the people dressed in the full armor of the Golden Riders. "Man, I wish I could have fit into a suit of that cool armor."

"Well, stay out of sight."

"Don't worry about me. Once we hit the Spine, they'll never find me. Besides, I have an idea."

Abraham raised a brow. "You do? What is it?"

"I'll surprise you."

Led by Pratt and Abraham, the Henchmen, with full helmets on, rode onward and joined up with the King's Army. The soldiers they passed saluted the Golden Riders as they trotted their horses by them. Many of the king's men let out encouraging cheers as they headed deeper into the front ranks.

Pratt cleared his throat and said to Abraham, "I'm not the sort of man that is good with crafty words. Never in my life would I wish to accuse the king's son of treason. I cannot lie either. What should I say?"

"Tell him that you have a message about Ruger, just for him."

"I'll never get by Prince Lewis if he is there. He'll demand to hear the words himself, and he is my commander." Pratt shifted in his saddle. "I'd rather fight a dozen Gond than do this."

"Tell them the truth. Tell them that Ruger escaped the prison and that you felt he should hear it directly from you. That's not a lie, now is it?"

"Well… no, I suppose." Pratt turned his head aside and pointed. "Ah, there is the king's banner." Pratt kept looking around as though he was nervous. He continued to shift in his saddle.

"Play it cool, Pratt. You have to do this for king and country."

"What does *play it cool* mean?"

"Being more like Shades."

"Ah, I think I can understand."

Abraham caught the first glimpse of King Hector. Surrounded by a host of the King's Guardians, he wore a black suit of armor trimmed in gold plate, with a white fur cloak over his shoulders. The Crown of Stones shined dully in the sunlight. Melris, Prince Lewis, Leodor, and Leah were all riding close to his side. His heart jumped.

Prince Lewis was the first to turn around at the sound of the Henchmen's approach. He wore his black cape and had Black Bane strapped between his shoulders. He cut through the Guardians with Leah in tow. "Pratt, what are you doing here?"

With his helmet still on, Pratt bowed and said, "I bear a message."

"Take your helmet off, fool! I can't understand a word you are saying."

Pratt removed his helmet, hooked it underneath his arm, and said, "I wanted you to know that Ruger Slade has escaped from the House of Steel. Our forces are searching for him now."

"Did you search for him at the Stronghold?" Lewis said with growing irritation in his voice. His gloves tightened on his reins. "Well?"

"Er… uh," Pratt blanched. "It was the first place we looked, to no avail." He scratched his thick sideburns. "They were gone. Er… escaped and hiding."

Abraham watched as new sweat trickled down the side of Pratt's cheek. *He's cracking like an egg. Too late to abort now.*

Lewis scanned the ranks of the Henchmen disguised as Golden Riders. His stare moved from one person to another. With a froward expression, he said, "Take off your helmets. All of you." He slid his sword from his sheath, but Black Bane remained fastened to his back. "Now!"

CHAPTER 80

Slowly, Abraham took his helmet off as the other Henchmen followed suit. With a smile, he said to the shock-faced Lewis, "Surprise." He flung his helmet at Lewis and shouted, "King Hector! You are in danger!"

Lewis knocked the helmet aside with his hand. "I am no such thing!"

King Hector stopped his forces and turned around.

Pratt called out in a booming voice, "It is true, Your Majesty! Your son betrays you!"

"Traitor!" Lewis stabbed the unsuspecting Pratt through the heart with his sword. "Die, you lying dog, die!"

Pratt fell out of the saddle with his eyes frozen wide open. He hit the ground with a loud thud.

"Kill the traitors! Kill the traitors!" Lewis screamed.

"Henchmen! Protect the king!" Abraham spurred his horse forward. He rammed Raschel and knocked her from the saddle. He galloped by the Guardians that were still drawing their weapons and headed toward the wide-eyed king. "King Hector, you must listen! You are in danger!"

The ground exploded underneath Abraham's horse's feet, courtesy of a purple bolt of power hurled by Melris.

Abraham flew out of his saddle and hit the ground like a bag of bricks. He popped up to one knee and found himself surrounded by a ring of spears pointed right at him. The King's Guardians had him dead to rights. He lifted his hands over his head. "King Hector, you must listen! Lewis and Leodor betray you again. I have proof!"

"You have nothing!" Lewis said with rage. "Guardians, kill him!"

"Hold!" King Hector said in a voice that froze everyone in their tracks. His eyes burned with inner fire. The stones in his crown twinkled with mystical life. He moved his horse closer to Abraham and glowered down on him. "This time, you try to assassinate me. How deep will your betrayal go?"

"You must believe me, King Hector. I have been on your side always. You march into a trap. The Sect is waiting."

"Don't listen to him, Father! He is an otherworlder, like them, a possessed man that has only brought you trouble." Lewis slid out of his saddle with his sword in hand. "Let me kill this dog myself."

"I'll handle it this time," the king said. He opened his hand and slowly closed his fingers in a crushing manner.

Abraham choked. His full suit of armor constricted as the king's distant fingers crushed him like a can. His face reddened, and his eyes bulged in their sockets.

"Hector! Stop this madness!" Queen Clarann cried out.

The fiery stare in King's Hector's eyes cooled.

Abraham fell to the ground, gasping. His armor's breastplate had a deep bend in the middle.

All the Henchmen were disarmed, dismounted, and brought to their knees. They were set down in a row beside Abraham, including the queen, who kneeled in front of Hector.

"My king, you must listen to them. They do not lie," she said.

"Of course they lie," Leodor said quickly. "All of them are otherworlders that serve the Sect. We have proven this. The only solace you will find is in their execution. It is the only way to defeat the enemy."

With Clarice by her side, Clarann said, "Search your heart, Hector. I know that you are far too wise to fall for the poison that spills from Leodor's lips. Trust me once more!"

King Hector flicked a hand. The subtle motion flattened the mother and daughter on the ground. "I've heard enough talk from you. Bind them all up. Hands behind their backs. Guardians, ready your swords. I'll end these interruptions once and for all."

"You heard your king. Bind them up," Lewis said with a victorious smirk.

The Henchmen's hands were bound behind their backs, and they were set on their knees, including Clarann and Clarice.

The King's Guardians stood behind them with their swords ready to strike.

King Hector stood on the ground, with Melris, Lewis, Leodor, and Raschel disguised as Leah by his side. They talked quietly among themselves.

A few Henchmen down, Vern leaned forward and said, "Great plan, Abraham."

The Guardian behind him cracked him in the back of the head with his pommel and said, "Silence."

Farther down the row, Tark said, "It's been an honor to serve with you, Abraham. All of you!" A Guardian blindsided him with a mailed fist.

The king turned and faced the Henchmen with a glowering stare ripe with madness. "You are interlopers, invaders, traitors, otherworlders, and betrayers." He glanced at Queen Clarann. "As the king, I am the judge, and I am the jury. The sentence for your actions is death. In my mercy, I will allow one of you to speak a final plea for all. Make it short."

Abraham exchanged a look with Clarann, whose lip was split and shoulders slumped. "Maybe you should."

"No," she said softly. "I can feel his anger. He won't listen to me. My words will only wound him. It must be you. Speak as Abraham."

Down the row to his right, he noticed Sticks leaning forward and staring at him. Her face was expressionless as ever. She winked at him and gave a stiff nod as if to say goodbye. He nodded back to her, to Horace, to all of them. "God help us." He lifted his eyes to the king. "May I stand?"

With his nose in the air, King Hector flipped up his fingers.

Abraham cleared his throat. "I am not Ruger Slade, I am Abraham Jenkins, from another world. Since I have been put into your service, I have faithfully served your will. First, I ask for mercy for my friends. They will fight for Kingsland always. Second," he looked at Lewis and Leodor, "I beg that if you will not believe my words, then use the emerald of truth to test my accusations that Lewis, Leodor, and Leah are all traitors that once again serve the Sect. It happened right after you took the Brand from them."

Lewis stepped forward, gestured at Abraham, and said, "Father, this is preposterous. We've been through all of this. He is a snake, a liar, a curse from another world. I move that you let me strike his head from his shoulders immediately!"

"Have my actions ever shown me to be untrue?" Abraham pleaded.

King Hector lifted his hand. "Silence. You have had your say. My mind remains unchanged. Execute them."

CHAPTER 81

ABRAHAM'S HEART THUMPED INSIDE HIS chest. If ever there was a time to jump back home, that time had come. The king was going to execute him, and the queen couldn't bail him out this time either. She was going to be executed too.

He glared at the smug expressions on Lewis and Leodor. "Boy, the seed of evil must run deep in you."

"That will be enough out of you," King Hector said as he lifted his arm in the air. "Guardians, lift your swords and prepare to strike."

Clarann's shoulders trembled beside his.

"I'm sorry," he whispered to her.

"It's not your fault," she said. "It's mine. I should have always been truthful."

The King's Guardians' swords scraped out of their scabbards. The blades caught the sunlight as they were lifted over the Henchmen's heads.

Abraham swallowed. He hadn't even gotten a chance to explain all that the king was facing. He hadn't warned him about the stones, and he'd never see Mandi again either. He kept his head up.

"It's over," Lewis scoffed.

Abraham started to say, "It ain't over until it's over," but he knew it was. The king had him dead to rights.

An earsplitting shriek that shook bones sounded off in the sky above.

Everyone's heads turned upward.

Simon the Fenix made a slow spiral in the air a couple of hundred feet above.

"It's a sign from the Elders," Melris the Elderling said to the king. "Remember what they said: 'The Spawn of the Elders will heed the call of the one that saves the land.'"

King Hector blinked as though a part of him that had long been dormant had awakened. His arm slowly dropped, and he said, "Guardians, sheathe your weapons."

"Father, what are you doing?" Lewis demanded.

The king's eyes burned like green wildfires, and he said, "I will have the truth!" He spread his fingers out.

Lewis and Leodor were lifted a foot off the ground as their bodies arched backward.

"Who do you serve?"

"Father, nooo!" Lewis cried out. He shook and convulsed as if his soul was being wrenched from his body.

"Your wicked heart is exposed!" King Hector said. "I have seen the truth! The truth has set me—"

Raschel sneaked up behind the king, snatched the Dagger of Death from his scabbard, and stabbed him in the belly.

King Hector threw his arms wide, staggered, and fell down.

"Nooo!" the queen and princess screamed. They ran to the king's aid. Melris knelt beside them.

Prince Lewis landed on his feet and quickly regained his composure. Seeing his dead father on the ground, he climbed onto his horse and said, "I am the king now! Follow my orders! Kill the Henchmen!" He pointed at Raschel. "Bring me that assassin! But kill the Henchmen!"

Loud explosions echoed through the valley, coming from the mountains in the Spine: *Boooom! Booooom! Boooooom!*

Groups of the king's soldiers were blasted off their feet.

The tank gunfire kept coming. The deadly shells came down.

Prince Lewis's face drew up with shock. A split second later, he was ripped from the saddle by a tank shell.

"The king is down!" the Guardian behind Abraham cried out. "The prince is down as well!"

"Who is in charge now?" asked the Guardian behind Horace amidst the explosions.

"I am," Leodor called out. "As the king's viceroy—"

"The queen is in charge now!" Horace belted out. "Every Guardian should know that!"

"No, I am!" Leodor said.

Princess Clarice stood up and kicked him in the gut. "Shut up, you old fool!"

Out of the corner of his eye, Abraham caught Raschel sneaking up behind Queen Clarann, her dagger poised to strike. He came to his feet and dashed toward the assassin. "Move! Clarann, move!"

Clarann turned just in time to see the assassin's dagger coming down.

Sticks dove into Raschel and grabbed her wrist in both hands. The pair wrestled over the ground.

Abraham tried to free his hands. He twisted his strong hands free from the knots.

Raschel flipped on top of Sticks and punched the dagger down.

Abraham caught the woman's quick hands just in time to save Sticks from being gored. He wrenched the dagger free.

Sticks took the Dagger of Death out of his hands and jabbed it into Raschel's chest. "Remember me!"

Raschel let out an abrupt croak. Her body spasmed. Her face turned from that of Leah to the face of the dusky beauty Raschel, and she died.

"Thanks," Sticks said as she tucked the dagger into her belt. "Time to get out of this armor." She started stripping it off.

The tank fire continued to erupt all around them.

"Captain, what do we do? We need a leader, or we are doomed." Horace said.

Queen Clarann clung to King Hector. She rocked him in her arms with tears streaming down her face. "He was a sweet man. Honest. This foul crown corrupted him."

"Your Highness, you must make a decision," Abraham said. "Your soldiers are being slaughtered."

"Certainly." With plenty of witnesses among the Guardians and the Henchmen, Queen Clarann said, "I declare Ruger Slade is the full-fledged Guardian Commander." She eyed him. "End this madness. Save Titanuus."

He nodded at her, turned his back, and said to the Guardians, "Cut the Henchmen loose. Get on your horses." He slapped his hand on Horace's back. "Get them organized. We have to get away from those tanks."

From the high peaks of the Spine's jagged hills, a small wave of ten zillon dragon riders flew over the army. They soared over one hundred feet in the air and dropped small objects from their saddles.

"What are they doing?" Sticks asked.

The objects plummeted to the ground and exploded among the troops.

"Holy sheetrock! They're dropping hand grenades!" Abraham said. "Crap, I need to get up there." He waved his hands, searching for Simon, but he saw no sign of the Fenix. He caught the dragon riders' eyes and stopped waving. "Oops, that was a bad idea. Incoming! Incoming!" He dove to the ground and covered his head.

Boom! Boom! Boom! Boom!

The ground exploded. Bodies went flying. Soldiers started dying. Abandoned horses bolted.

The King's Army was being bombarded.

CHAPTER 82

Abraham climbed to his feet and saw Tark and Cudgel waving him over. He ran to them. They were huddled over what was left of Prince Lewis. His body was missing between his head and legs, a sad demise for Prince Lewis. The master swordsman had shown promise, but his heart deceived him.

Tark picked up the battered scabbard of Black Bane. The sword and casing were still intact. "You'll need this, Captain."

Abraham buckled on the sword belt. "Thanks." He checked the skies and saw no sign of the Fenix, but the dragon riders were turning for another pass. "Listen to Horace and get his army out of the tank guns' range. Get the archers shooting at those dragons." He hurried back to the queen.

Queen Clarann wiped the tears from her face. "I can't help but think it is all my fault. He didn't deserve this."

"No, he didn't. He was firm, but he was fair. I'd do anything to bring him back if I could." He glanced at Melris. "Can't you do something?"

"I've done all I can to preserve his body from decay. There is little more that I can do. The dagger's tooth is fatal." Melris surveyed the scrambling army. More tanks and troops were advancing from the Spine. "It seems the Sect had no plans to work with the likes of Lewis and Leodor very long. They come for the Crown of Stones now."

The crown was still grafted to King Hector's head.

"Well, make sure that they don't get it. You are on our side, aren't you?" he asked Melris.

"Yes, I was sent to aid the king—or the queen—by the Elders."

"Don't they want to play a part in all of this? It's their world being invaded, you know. They could lend a hand."

"They did lend a hand: me," Melris replied. "The Elders spoke with King Hector and decided to not get directly involved. That would only bring war between the Elders. They would rather see how matters unfold."

"So much for tradition." Abraham didn't know what else to do. He put his fingers inside his mouth and whistled. "Come on, Simon!" Another bombardment of grenades exploded all around. "I need you! Those fish-eyed fiends are going to blow this army to pieces."

A dark blot with wings appeared in the sky. It was Simon. He dove to the ground and landed, startling the King's Army.

"It's about time." Abraham hustled over to the huge Fenix, which was the size of at least three zillon dragons. He grabbed a handful of hair and climbed up. He sat in an odd nook in the Fenix's back that was perfect for his legs. He spoke down into Simon's earhole. "See those tiny dragons? Go get 'em!"

With the pounding beating of his wings, Simon launched himself into the air. Abraham watched the field of battle dwindle away below him. A bright twinkle beside the queen caught his eye. His heart skipped. A portal opened between Clarann, Clarice and Melris. Fleece stepped halfway out of the portal, snatched the king's body in his long ghostly arms, and pulled him into the portal. The portal closed. The king and crown were gone, leaving Melris with his jaw hanging.

The queen and the princess screamed.

Abraham cried out in disbelief, "Bloody biscuits!"

CHAPTER 83

WITH AN ACHING HEART, ABRAHAM took to the sky on Simon's back. He watched the King's Army retreat from the tank's heavy fire. Soon they would be out of range, but the new army of the Sect was still coming. More tanks and foot soldiers of Tiotan and Gond were marching out from the Spine. With the heavy modern weaponry on the ground and in the air, the king dead, the the crown in the enemy's possession, there would be no stopping the enemy. He had to act quickly.

Below, Clarann and Clarice, walked with the retreating army, arm-in-arm, with their heads hung low.

He turned Simon toward the wave of dragon riders bombarding the army. "Simon, get after them. Let's put those lizards to sleep! Permanently!"

Simon bent in the sky, and his bat wings pounded the air. He made a beeline for the flying pack and closed in from behind.

With the wind tearing through his hair, Abraham pulled his sword free of his scabbard. "Black Bane, can you hear me?"

"Of course I can hear you. I am not deaf. Old, possibly. I'm not really sure. How can I help you?"

"I have about ten dragon riders that I could use some help taking out," he said.

"Hmm… that's a lot. Don't you have any other options?"

"Well, I have a Fenix," he said with irritation growing in his voice. He shook the sword. "We are closing in. Do something!"

The zillon dragon riders looked back over their shoulders. Their alien faces filled with shock. They narrowed their eyes and barked orders to one another, and the flock split up.

"Crap!" Abraham said.

Simon snaked through the air after one of the dragons, sticking to its tail end like glue, and quickly caught up.

The zillon on the dragon's back twisted around and threw a hand grenade at Abraham.

Simon bent away from the grenade, opened his jaws, and bit down on the back end of the dragon, taking its tail and legs clean off. The zillon and dragon fell from the sky and blew up when they hit the ground below.

"One down. Only…" Abraham searched the skies, "nine to go."

Three dragon riders dropped in behind him. Each of them was carrying an assault rifle and fired.

Simon barrel rolled through the sky.

Abraham hung on for dear life with his fingers clutching the Fenix's pelt. He twisted his head over his shoulders. The dragon riders raced after the Fenix. Bullets blasted from their barrels.

He had an idea. "Get lower, Simon! Get lower!"

The Fenix dropped and turned back toward the King's Army.

Abraham flew them right over the ranks of hundreds of archers below.

The archers let loose a volley of hundreds of arrows. The feathered shafts ripped through dragons' wings and bodies and impaled the zillon riders. All but one of them plunged to a violent crash on the ground. The king's foot soldiers slaughtered them.

Abraham led the chase after the last two dragon riders. The riders turned in their saddles and fired at him. "Black Bane, now would be a really good time for you to lend a hand!"

"If only I did have a hand. Now, that would be useful. How about this?"

A ball of blue light dropped out of the sky. It crackled with energy like lightning. Keeping pace between the two dragon riders, its sparkling tendrils lashed out. The strands of energy tore through the zillons and dragons. They shook, smoked, and started to burn, their wings and limbs on fire. They dropped out of their saddles and crashed to the hard ground below.

"Yes! Good job, Black Bane!"

"Certainly. Is there anything else?"

The ball of blue energy flew alongside them. Abraham noticed the tanks on the ground still firing and said, "Can you take those tanks out?"

"What's a tank?"

Five tanks were below that Abraham could see. "Those metal chariots on the ground!"

"Oh."

The ball of energy careened downward and smacked right into a tank. It exploded with a loud *boom*. The energy ball disappeared.

"Did I kill it?"

"Yes! But there are more of them."

"I'll see what I can do. After my nap."

"What?" Abraham shook his sword. "Wait. We are in the middle of a war!"

The presence inside Black Bane checked out.

He tugged on Simon's fur and said, "I guess we need to do this on our own. Simon, let's take those tanks out."

Simon landed by the nearest tank, which was nestled at the bottom hills of the Spine. Huge by comparison, the Fenix bit down on the barrel, bent the metal like a spoon, and ripped the gun turret clean off the tank.

The eyes of the three men inside the tank were big as saucers. They climbed out and attacked with short swords in hand.

Abraham hewed them down with three quick thrusts of Black Bane. He searched the area for the other tanks, looked at the monstrous Fenix, and said, "Let's finish them!"

Simon the Fenix took off on his own. He jumped on the top of one tank; sank his clawed feet into the metal; beat his wings, lifting it off the ground; flew toward another tank; and flung the one tank into the others.

The tanks bashed together, turned side over side, and rolled down from their perches in the hills.

Three tanks were down, with two more to go. Abraham raced across the base of the hills, where a tank gun turned toward Simon's backside.

He shouted out a warning: "Look out!"

The tank fired, and the shell hit Simon square in the middle of his back. His wings spread out and quavered. He fell flat on his ugly face and spasmed.

"Nooo!" Abraham raised his sword high. He closed the gap between himself and the tank. With a mighty swing, he chopped clear through the tank barrel, which dropped to the ground.

A soldier popped up from the top hatch of the tank, firing an assault rifle.

Abraham dove underneath the tank and crawled to the other side. He sneaked up on the man, who was craning his neck side to side. The soldier turned Abraham's direction too late. He split open the soldier's skull, grabbed his rifle, and fired into the hole. The tank gunner died.

Simon climbed back to his feet and shook his neck like a wet dog. All eight of his eyes narrowed on the last tank. The tank gun fired at him, and the shell exploded on his chest. He stumbled backward, let out an angry, earsplitting shriek, and stormed the tank. Glowering at the vehicle, Simon expanded his chest. A blast of red-hot fire erupted out of his mouth and curled the metal barrel of the tank gun.

Abraham pumped his sword in the air. "Now that's a Fenix!"

A shadow passed over head.

He glanced up and saw another dragon rider in the sky. This time, a zillon wasn't in the saddle—it was the burly horned halfling, Big Apple. The pair of adversaries locked eyes.

Big Apple grinned devilishly and tossed two hand grenades down at Abraham.

Abraham dove for cover toward the rocks. The world exploded around him.

CHAPTER 84

A rustle of armor caught Abraham's ear. His head pounded, and his body ached. He felt as though he had tiny burns all over. He opened his eyelids. The pie-faced Iris had a pair a tweezers. She was picking shards of rock and metal out of his leg.

"Well, look who decided to join us," the mystic said happily. "Glad to see that you had a good nap."

Abraham touched the bandage on his hand. The sky was dark and filled with stars.

"How long have I been out?"

"Only since this afternoon," she said.

He didn't know whether to be surprised or relieved that he was still in Titanuus. Normally in such tragic events, he was boosted from one world to the other. They were in a typical camp, with fires burning nearby, soldiers and Henchmen huddled in groups everywhere.

He noticed Solomon sitting beside him. "How's it going?"

Solomon flipped his big paw at him and said, "Better now that you have awakened, I think. When I plucked you out of a pile of rocks, I thought you were a goner. The King's Armor saved you. I wish I had a suit that could fit me." He shrugged. "Sort of."

Sticks huddled nearby, rocking on her toes. Shades and Horace were with her, sharing a log for a seat.

"So, what is going on?"

"Bad news, Captain." Horace scratched his meaty neck with a finger. "Armies from Tiotan have us boxed in from the south. They outnumber us too. The only way out one way or the other is to fight."

"What about the lair in the Spine?" he asked.

"I can navigate those hills better than any," Solomon said. "I took Dominga and Cudgel with me. We found the lair. It's a huge cave entrance, forty feet high at least and half as wide. A wide channel like a highway leads straight to it. It's guarded by tanks on the road, Gond and soldiers positioned down the length of the road. It's the only way in or out." He shook his head. "It looks impossible to march an army through there. Plus, more tanks and weapons are coming out."

"Yeah well, the Henchmen never needed an army before, did they?" he said.

The group nodded.

He rubbed his face. Dr. Jack, Eugene Drisk, Colonel Dexter, and Big Apple had everything they wanted. The only hope Abraham had was that their theory for completing the Time Tunnel wouldn't work. If that was the case, he'd be stranded. He winced as Twila pulled a strip of shrapnel out of the meat of his calf. *I don't suppose it matters what world I live in. Evil is evil. I have to stop it in one world or the other.*

"I'm ready," Sticks said. Her gaze landed on his. "Just say the word. It all has to end sometime."

"Well, that's the last of the shrapnel," Iris said as she began stitching up his leg. "I'll put some salve on it, and you should be good to go kill something."

"Great. I can't wait." He craned his neck. "So, is the Fenix gone?"

"Yup," Solomon said.

"What about my sword?" He felt the scabbard underneath his hand. "Oh, there it is. This ought to do it. A magic sword, the King's Steel, the deadliest fighters in the world… Who can stop us?"

A military helicopter flew overhead.

Wuppa-wuppa-wuppa-wuppa-wuppa!

"No, no, no, no!"

The Henchmen and armies stared up into the sky.

"What sort of dragon is that?" Horace said.

Abraham forced himself to his feet. He kept it simple. "It's called a chopper."

Solomon stood behind Abraham's shoulders and said, "This is bad. Really bad. Isn't it?"

"It's certainly not better." He buckled on his sword. "Henchmen, gather around."

The Henchmen formed a circle around him, including Clarann and Clarice. The hard-eyed group hadn't softened a bit since he'd first met them. They looked as invincible as ever in their armor.

"This is it. Last call. The final hour. A do-or-die mission. I don't care if any of you back out. You can even though I know you won't." He pointed toward the Spine. "The end is near, and it's in there. We're going to find it!"

"Hear! Hear!" Horace said.

"We are going to beat it!" He slung his son's backpack over his shoulder.

More Henchmen joined in. "Hear! Hear!"

"Because the King's Army has never been defeated, and it won't be defeated today!"

The Henchmen let out battle-hungry grunts.

He lifted his sword high. Everyone joined him, pointing their weapons high into the sky. United, Abraham and the Henchmen shouted, "Death before failure!"

CHAPTER 85

SOLOMON LED THE TREK INTO the jagged hills of the Spine. The Henchmen, including Clarann and Melris, moved through the night like a snake slithering up a rut. All of them were in full armor but no helmets as they made the rugged climb.

Down on the battlefield, the King's Army attacked at first light. Led by the King's Guardians, under the queen's orders, the soldiers stormed the channel leading into the Spine. They had no choice but to engage as the chopper flying overhead, with dragon riders in tow, whittled away at the army with machine-gun fire and bombardments of grenades.

Abraham could hear the explosions and clamor of battle as the brave soldiers marched forward to their doom. They would be slaughtered if some sort of help didn't arrive soon. He searched the skies. *Simon, where are you?*

He tried summoning the Fenix with whistles and calls but to no avail. Possibly the Elder Spawn had moved on. Still, he kept trying by concentrating. He didn't want to make more noise after they crossed a gap and started down the other side of the mountain. The journey took hours, and the longer it took, the more soldiers died.

Solomon flagged him down.

He slipped up to the front ranks, where he met with Tark and Dominga. She carried a spyglass and handed it to Abraham. They were on a ledge that overlooked a chasm five hundred feet down. The channel deep in the middle made for a perfect roadway.

He put the spyglass to his eye. "Blazing saddles."

The channel road dead-ended at the entrance to the tunnel leading inside the lair. Tanks were positioned down the road thirty feet apart as far as he could see. Gond savages and Tiotan soldiers in suits of chain-mail armor were positioned along the road and hidden in the rocky shelving above them. Hundreds were there in all, but thousands would be needed to penetrate their strategic positioning.

"It doesn't look good, does it?" Solomon said.

"We can kill them," Horace said.

"If we can sneak in behind them, we can fight our way in. That's the only way I can think of," Abraham said. He turned his ear toward the sky. "Everyone get down."

The Henchmen pressed against the rocks as the chopper flew overhead. It hovered for a long time then moved back down over the channel.

"Do you think they saw us?" Clarann asked.

"Doesn't seem like it. Listen up, everyone. We need to make our way closer. Follow me."

Abraham led the way down the slippery slope. The company wouldn't be entirely defenseless. In addition to their weapons, they'd managed to pack away some grenades and assault rifles from the fallen dragon riders. The company made it within two hundred feet of the tunnel entrance.

The morning mist and shadowed canyon shielded them from the sun. Now, they were within earshot.

"Horace, get a message down to Melris and Iris," he said.

The Elderling and the mystic were at the far end of the company.

"Tell them we are going to need some cover."

"What sort of cover, Captain?" Horace asked.

"Fog. Smoke. They should know—something subtle."

A minute later, fog spilled over the rocky ledges where the Henchmen waited. It came from Iris's and Melris's fingers. It wasn't enough to fill the huge chasm, but it would do for better cover.

Abraham nodded his head at Sticks, Shades, Dominga, and Tark, who weren't wearing the heavy armor. "Lead the way, but if it gets too hot down there, fall back behind us."

"Aye," Tark said.

"You're the boss, Captain," Shades added.

Silently, the group crept down the mountainside.

The chopper came flying up the channel with six dragon riders in tow. They made a beeline on Abraham's position. The fog created by the mystics was blown out of the channel. The chopper hovered right in front of the Henchmen. The alerted Gond and soldiers popped up from their hiding spots and climbed the mountain by the score, with blood in their eyes.

"Everyone get down!" Abraham ordered.

The chopper's machine guns opened fire.

CHAPTER 86

With chunks of rock being busted up all around him, Abraham shouted, "Good lord, where is my Fenix when I need him?"

Overhead, dragon riders dropped bombardments of grenades. The Henchmen scrambled over the rocks. Bullets ricocheted off metal armor. Men cried out and cursed.

On his elbows, Abraham crawled behind the lip of the rocky ledges and hunkered down in a crack. The chopper hovered only fifty feet away from them. Its machine-gun bullets pounded the mountainside.

"Take cover! Take cover!" he shouted.

Dust and debris blossomed all over. The more the bullets and grenades chewed up the rocks, the more smoke arose.

Having had little wartime experience, he finally remembered that the Henchmen had their own guns and shouted, "Return fire! Return fire!"

Nearby, the sound of machine guns rattled away. A zillon rider fell from his dragon and fell to a jagged death below.

Melris moved out to the end of the ledge with his purple robes billowing in the wind. He held out the Rod of Devastation. A bolt of scintillating purple energy blasted from the top of the rod and tore into the chopper's body. The chopper veered hard left and spun in circles before crashing and exploding below.

The Henchmen let out a triumphant chorus of cheers.

A grenade fell from the sky landed and beside Melris. The explosion blew his legs out from underneath his robes. He lay dashed against the rocks and bleeding.

"Melris!" Iris called out and rushed to his aid.

Horace walled off the mystic and the Elderling. He screamed at the dragon riders in the sky. "Fight like men, you cowards!"

With the chopper out of the way, Abraham moved out of his cover and scanned the surrounding scene. The armies in the trenches moved like a swarm of ants. Hundreds of enemy soldiers were in the rocks, climbing quickly up the steep banks. They fired their assault rifles and howled for blood.

Tark and Skitts lay on the ledge, firing downward at the swarming foot troops.

The tank guns turned and pointed toward the Henchmen.

"Devil's donuts! We're going to get blown to bits! Everybody move! Everybody move!" Abraham led them away from the gunfire.

"Come on, Iris!" Horace said. "There is nothing you can do for Melris now. Let the Elders take care of him."

Above, the dragon riders made another pass. They closed in quickly with grenades poised to drop from their bony white hands.

Like a black bolt of lightning shot from the sky, Simon the Fenix slammed into the dragon riders. His great jaws clamped down on zillon and dragon. The other dragon riders veered away and scattered.

Down below, Sticks, Tark, and Dominga shot three more dragon riders out of the air. Simon chased away the others.

A tank gun fired. The rocks two dozen feet behind Abraham's head exploded. Rocks started to slide down the mountain.

"Keep moving! Keep moving!" Abraham yelled.

"I'm tired of running. I want to start fighting!" Horace said.

With a glance at the barbarians and soldiers scrabbling up the slopes, Abraham said, "You'll get your chance."

They were outnumbered at least thirty to one, which didn't include the tanks and the other scores of soldiers guarding the tunnel entrance that had yet to move. A bullet whizzed by his face and ricocheted off the rocks behind him.

"Keep moving!" he shouted. "They can't keep shooting at us once we are engaged."

The Gond raced up to the higher ledges in a flanking move. They moved like squirrels over the rocks and positioned themselves in the rocks above the Henchmen, rapidly sealing them in, shutting off their escape from all directions. The Henchmen were trapped.

"Well isn't this a dung heap of fun!" Abraham led them to a small plateau on the mountainside that gave them a good view of the activity below and above.

Sticks, Shades, Tark, and Dominga scrambled up to the spot. They had nowhere else to go. They shot at the enemies aboveground and below. The savages and soldiers fell, only to have three more overtake their positions for each one fallen.

Abraham gripped Black Bane in hand and said, "Well, Horace, you wanted a fight. Now, you're going to get it."

Horace spat juice on the ground and said, "We can kill them."

Simon soared overhead in a black streak. A dragon and rider were crushed in his mouth. Behind him, two more choppers gave chase with machine guns firing.

"Devil's donuts! They have more of those things!" Abraham's heart sank as he watched Simon's tail end take a barrage of bullets.

The Fenix tucked his tail and curled away before disappearing over the ridges. He'd hoped the Elder Spawn would have taken out the tanks and ground troops.

"Run, Simon, run," he muttered.

Bearclaw spun his double-bladed axe. Eyeing the enemy, he said, "It will be a great fight."

Prospero and Apollo drew their pairs of swords.

Vern filled his hands with sword and dagger.

Cudgel readied his two-handed mace.

The advancing enemy stopped. The gunfire ceased. A silence fell over the chasm.

Abraham scanned the faces of their enemies. High and low, the soldiers had halted, poised to attack. He sought out why and quickly discovered the reason. Two of the tanks on the road below had their tank guns pointed right at them. His jaw dropped. The tank guns fired.

The shells rocketed into the small cliff beneath the Henchmen. The shelf gave way as the company was tossed from their feet and dropped into the rocky carnage below.

CHAPTER 87

Abraham gasped for air. His wide eyes beheld the Time Tunnel. Otis and Haymaker were on either side of him. He'd been strapped to the gurney again. Ottum stood beside him with a needle in her hand.

She tossed the needle into a waste bin. "How do you feel?" she asked.

"Like punching you in the face." He was upright and positioned behind the five computer stands. Dr. Jack, Eugene Drisk, and Colonel Dexter stood behind the center station with triumphant smiles on their faces. "And them."

"This isn't something that you need get upset about. It is a glorious day. The tunnel is working, and I can go back home."

"What do you mean, it's working?"

"See for yourself." She turned him away from the computer and directly toward the Time Tunnel.

He could see Big Apple, Fleece, and Lord Hawk talking amongst themselves on the other side. Lord Hawk pointed at the fiery gemstones from the Crown of Stones mounted in the ring. They were placed in order at the one, three, five, seven, nine, and eleven o'clock positions. A chronic hum came from the Time Tunnel, almost as loud as the diesel generators.

"It works?"

"No one has passed through it yet, but in theory, according to your experts, yes," she said. She petted his face. "It's a shame that you picked the wrong side to be on. But don't feel bad. Ruger did too."

Dr. Jack and Colonel Dexter broke out in laughter. Eugene Drisk had a gleeful look on his face.

Jack turned and looked at Abraham. "Bring him over. He needs to see this."

The orderlies wheeled him over to the central computer station.

"This is Abraham, isn't it?" Jack asked.

Brushing Abraham's hair out of his eyes, Ottum said, "Yes, it's him."

"Yeah, it's me, jerk. I'm surprised you didn't know that."

"I've been busy." Jack pointed at the screens. "Look at what we have here." He chuckled.

The images were moving on the screens. The images showed aerial views of the canyon leading up to the tunnel on some screens, while Abraham could see soldiers standing on the rocky ledges on the other monitors. They were the same ones attacking the Henchmen. The second screen showed what appeared to be a chopper chasing after the Fenix. Ripped-off flesh and blood dripped from Simon's body. The third screen showed a dusty scene of the Henchmen, including Ruger Slade, half buried in rubble. Abraham's stomach turned into knots.

"Those are drones," Jack said. "I don't know why we didn't think of it earlier."

"I thought of it," the older Eugene Drisk said. He pushed his glasses up the bridge of his nose. I thought of everything. And thanks to the retrieval of the Crown of Stones, not only will we be able to move back and forth in our own bodies, but we can use the smaller door to soul swap as well. Two men enter at the same time and swap. Just as easy as *Freaky Friday*."

"Why would you want to do that?" Abraham asked with an incredulous look.

Eugene tossed his head back. "Ha! You of all people should know why after being in Ruger Slade's body. Oh, how I can't wait to take it back." He studied the monitor. "I hope the last round of fire didn't damage him too bad."

Jack flipped his hands out and said, "There you have it. A new world awaits. And we have it all under control."

"We who?"

Jack pointed at Big Apple's trio. "The Sect, the Shell, the Corporation, or Drakeland. Does it really matter at this point? We won. We are the conquerors of a bold new world."

Abraham laughed. "Be careful what you wish for. Titanuus is full of surprises."

"I think we've seen them all," Jack said.

"So what do you need me for?"

"Funny you should ask. Quite possibly, we don't, but you make for an excellent test subject," Jack said. "You know, with your special connection to Ruger. After all, you are the one that led us to all of this. If it wasn't for you, we never would have realized the potential to swap our essence from one body to the other." He looked at Colonel Dexter. "We need to fetch Ruger. Bring him here."

"My pleasure," the deep-voiced Colonel Dexter said. He gave Abraham a cocky look. "It's going to be fun catching up with Mandi."

"Look at this!" Eugene pointed at the screen. Simon huddled in the rocks with his wings shielding his back. The chopper's gunfire was tearing him to pieces. "And to think that flying rodent had me worried. It looks like their doom is sealed." He motioned toward the Time Tunnel. "Come on, everything is in order. Titanuus awaits."

With nothing but the Time Tunnel ring between them, the two groups on either side faced off. Ottum stepped forward and stood right beside the tracks leading inside. "I would like to go first." She lifted her narrow shoulders. "I really don't have anything to lose."

"Be my guest," Dr. Jack said.

"Red rover, red rover, let the zillon babe come on over," Big Apple said as he blew a smoke ring from his side to the other side." He clapped his stubby hands. "Come on, now."

Ottum hopped from one side to the other. She swooned, started to fall, bounced up, and showed a big smile.

Jack clapped his hands. "Hot dog! We've got it mastered."

Abraham dipped his chin to his chest. *This can't be happening. What happened to Smoke and Sid? Are they captured? Somebody has to stop these madmen! I have to do something!* Behind Fleece, Luther and King Hector were lying on separate gurneys. The crown looked as though it had been ripped off King Hector's head. A sick feeling formed in the pit of Abraham's stomach. *Somebody needs to pay for this!*

"Dr. Jack!" a scientist said from behind the central computer station. She pointed at the monitors. "You should come and see this."

A wellspring of hope built up inside Abraham as Jack hustled over to the station.

Jack's eyebrows lifted. He put a cigar in his mouth and lit it. "Well, will you look at that? It appears Ruger Slade has surrendered."

CHAPTER 88

WHAT?

Abraham couldn't believe his ears. Ruger wouldn't ever surrender. Nor would the Henchmen. *This can't be right.*

"Come and take a look, Abraham," Jack said.

Otis and Haymaker wheeled him over to the station. Sure enough, the dust had settled, and Ruger had his hands and weapons raised over his head. Soldiers were climbing up the rocky trails with swords in hand to greet them.

Jack slapped him on the shoulder. "Tough loss. My gain." He lifted his voice. "Say, Eugene, looks like your new body is coming. He surrendered."

Eugene had stepped to the other side of the Time Tunnel's frame. The smile on his face vanished. He hurried back to the other side. "It's a trap. Ruger Slade never surrenders." He studied the screens and grunted in his throat. "He still holds the sword! Take it from him!"

As soon as the nearest soldier stepped into striking range, Ruger's blade flashed and took the man's head from his shoulders.

Eugene pounded the keyboard. "I told you! I told you!"

"Relax," Colonel Dexter said. They can't take out five hundred soldiers with assault rifles, and don't forget about the tanks. He fixed his eyes on the monitors. "They don't stand a chan—" He stiffened. "What the hell are those things?"

Abraham watched as the ridges in the Spine's canyon erupted with new life. Terramen, the race of men that looked and walked like snapping turtles, sprouted up all over. Their shells were naturally camouflaged with rock and brush. Their stout arms and legs were thick with scales. Their jaws snapped off hands at the wrists and feet at the ankles. With powerful claws, they tore through chain mail, skin, and chest bone.

"What are those things?" Jack demanded.

Abraham shrugged. "Ninja turtles?"

In a moment, the script of the battlefield flipped. The cameras in the sky caught it all.

Barath, the twelve-foot-tall leader of the terramen, stood down on the road and turned over tanks like they were boxes.

Eugene jabbed his fingers into the screen. "What is that thing? Kill it, Drew! Kill it!"

"Let me get my choppers on it," Colonel Dexter said. He touched his earpiece. "Eagle One! Eagle Two! Is that giant bat dead?" He nodded. "I need you to break away. We have a, uh, well, the thing looks like Bowser. Fly down there and turn it into turtle soup!"

Big Apple crept over to the bunch, jumped on an office chair, and asked, "What seems to be the problem, gentlemen?"

Dr. Jack gave Big Apple a surprised look and said, "It seems we overlooked something. Do you know how to stop those… turtles?"

"Kill them," Big Apple responded.

"That's what I'd do," Lord Hawk added.

The group broke out into a heated argument.

On the screen, the runes in Black Bane's blade glowed red hot. Ruger Slade chopped through soldiers and Gond like a hot knife through butter. Abraham never imagined a sword blade could move so fast. Each stroke took life and limb, heads from shoulders. The Henchmen were rolling. Abraham grinned. *Come on, guys! Come on!*

"Look at this massacre! The Henchmen are going to be here in minutes!" Eugene yelled. "Send more reinforcements! Send more now!"

Colonel Dexter threw up his arms and stormed toward the Time Tunnel. He pointed to the armed guards in the gray tunnel. "Go! Go! Go! Don't let anything or anyone make it into the tunnel!"

The soldiers ran into the tunnel and joined the ranks of the Tiotan army at the end of the funnel.

Abraham caught a glimpse of Fleece hovering between Luther's and King Hector's gurneys.

The Underlord had his bony fingers stretched over both of their faces. He held their faces a moment and pulled his fingers away. He stood tall, tattered ghostly robes drifting around his body. His diamond-hard eyes locked on Abraham then slid toward Big Apple, and he ran his finger across his neck.

Huh?

Big Apple yelled at Colonel Dexter. "How hard is it to kill a man with a bullet? Just shoot him!"

Colonel Dexter poked Big Apple in the chest. "Listen to me, you little billy goat! You don't talk to me like that. I'll stuff you in a suitcase and ship you out of here!"

Big Apple rammed his horns into Colonel Dexter's groin, doubling the man over. "Watch your tongue, fool! In this body, I can tear any man up!"

"We don't have time for this! We have to stop Ruger and stop him now!" Eugene flagged down Ottum. "Put another shot in Abraham's neck! He's not the kind of killer that Ruger is!"

Ottum ran over to the gurney. Otis handed her a shot. She stuck the needle in Abraham's neck and depressed the plunger.

Abraham's head snapped back. His blood churned. Star streaks raced through his eyes. He stood in the heat of battle. Black Bane crashed against another blade. The smelting fires in the sword's engravings cooled. His legs wobbled beneath him. *Crap! I need time to adjust!* His body didn't respond to his thoughts. He and Ruger weren't one.

A Gond jumped from a ledge above him and planted himself on Abraham's back. They tumbled down the hill, rolling without stopping until they hit bottom.

He cracked his head on a rock. Blood ran into his eyes. Black Bane slipped from his fingers. The bearded, burly, wild-eyed Gond grabbed a handful of his hair and punched him in the head over and over.

Ruger found his essence transported back into Abraham's body. His nostrils flared the moment he saw Eugene Drisk.

Eugene, Jack, and Lord Hawk let out a chorus of cheers. They threw up their hands and slapped them together.

"Perfect! Perfect! Ruger is done for!" Eugene shouted.

"You're going to die, Drisk," Ruger stated.

Eugene's and Jack's heads snapped around. Big Apple and Lord Hawk faced Ruger.

"Well, look who's back—Ruger Slade," Eugene said in a gloating manner. "Guess what, Ruger, now that I have you trapped in Abraham's body, I have no need for you anymore. I want the body on the other side." He looked Abraham's figure up and down. "Not this trash heap. So I can kill you and swap with your body next."

"You always were a coward," he said.

"Like any of that matters now. I'm going to be filthy rich for all eternity." Eugene typed on the keyboard as he watched the screen. "Look at that. Look at that. The choppers are taking it to the giant turtle man. I like it! The game is almost over. Someone kill him, will ya? I don't want to ever sense his presence again."

Lord Hawk pulled his revolver. He spun the gun around on his finger. "I'll do it." He pointed at Ruger's head and cocked back the hammer. "Sweet dreams."

"Don't shoot him here. I don't want blood all over my equipment. Stop being such a savage," Eugene quipped. "Take him over to the wall and blast his brains out."

A blaring alarm sounded. Flashing red emergency lights lit up the tunnel.

"What is going on?" Jack said.

"I don't know!" Eugene hammered at the keyboard and shouted at the female scientist beside him, "Fix it!"

She gave him a blank stare.

He shoved her out of the chair. "What idiot set the alarm off, huh?" He pecked away at a few keys. The alarms and red light went off. "When I find out who did that, I'm going to kill them! This was intentional. It was a hack!"

Someone let out a *woo-hoo* whistle. Everyone turned toward the source.

Smoke stepped out from behind a railcar. He held a pistol in one hand and small box in the other. "Listen up, everyone. In my hand is a detonator. And while you slappy happy bunch of idiots have been high-fiving each other, me and my partner, well, my wife, have been planting remote bombs all around."

Eugene's, Drew's, and Jack's wary eyes searched all over.

Smoke pointed his gun at the orderlies. "Listen up, big fellas. Let my friend loose before I put a hole in you."

Otis retuned Smoke's stare with a glower of his own.

Smoke shot the man in the shoulder. "Don't make me ask again."

The orderlies started to free Ruger from his restraints.

"No, no, no, no, don't you dare let him loose!" Eugene pleaded. "Lord Hawk, kill him! Kill him now!"

Lord Hawk smiled at Smoke. He still had the cocked gun pointed right at Ruger's head. Smoke had his weapon pointed at Otis.

"No one is that quick," Hawk said. "But you are welcome to try."

Smoke winked.

Blam!

Everyone jumped as Lord Hawk fell to the ground with a bullet in his head.

Smoke hadn't moved.

Sidney stepped out of the shadows with vapors coming out of her gun barrel. She put her gun on Haymaker's neck. "Finish untying my friend."

Haymaker undid the straps holding Ruger in place.

Ruger jumped away from the gurney and hit Eugene in the face so hard that his neck snapped backward and he hit the desk. The old man was out cold.

"All right, all right, let's all talk here," Jack said as he wiggled his fingers in the air. "What do you want, huh? Just take it. There is too much here to give up."

Colonel Dexter eyeballed the area and said, "There's no bomb in here. I don't see one."

"Oh yes, there is." Smoke held up his phone. "They are hidden."

"He's bluffing," Colonel Dexter said. "He wouldn't kill himself anyway. Or his deceptively pretty lady."

Soldiers were racing back from the front end of the Time Tunnel. They took a knee and aimed their guns at Smoke and Sid.

"John," Sid said. "Show them!"

Smoke pressed a button on his phone. Computer station one, farthest left of the tunnel, exploded. "I have a lot more where that came from. Care to try me?"

"I do," Big Apple grinned. "Fleece!"

Smoke, Sid, and Ruger were yanked up off their feet. They sailed a foot above ground and were violently slammed together. Their weapons were ripped from their fingers by an unseen force. Limbs tangled, they stuck together like glue.

Puffing on his cigar, Big Apple strode over to them, blew smoke in their faces, and said, "Nice try, fools!"

A spear burst through the chest of the Gond attacking Abraham. Horace flung the savage warrior aside.

"The fighting isn't over yet, Captain!" Horace punched his spear through two Tiotan soldiers at once and ripped the shaft free. "Grab some steel, and dance like you taught me!"

Abraham rolled to his side and plucked Black Bane from the ground. The handle ignited in his hand. With energy surging through him, he pounced back to his feet. "Abraham's back. It's time to attack!" He set his burning gaze on the tunnel down below. He'd had enough of the enemy. It was time to end them all. "It's time to burn some couches. Let's gooo!"

The Henchmen stormed down the mountain, creating a river of blood on their way down.

The bare-chested Gond were split open like ripe melons by the heavily armed fighters swinging steel with lethal precision.

Vern sliced open a Gond belly clean through the spine.

Bearclaw chopped skulls into bloody bits and pieces.

Cudgel busted a man's knees and cracked his face open.

Apollo and Prospero whittled down the enemy with ease.

Nothing could stop the seasoned fighters cloaked in the King's Steel.

Solomon hurled a Gond head over heels. He beat his chest and yelled, "Hairy hippie power!"

Two helicopters dropped down into the channel. One of them started spitting out bullets at the terramen leader, Barath. With bullets ricocheting off his face, Barath picked up a dead Gond and threw it at the chopper. The body flipped over in the air and fell short of the chopper by one hundred feet. The bullets began to chew Barath up. He tucked his body into his shell.

The second chopper aimed its guns at the Henchmen. The machine guns tore through Gond, terramen, and Tiotan soldiers, making a pathway to them. Apollo and Prospero were caught in the fire. Bullets ripped into their bodies and knocked them down.

"Take cover! Take cover!" Abraham shouted, moving in front of Sticks as she fired her rifle at the chopper. "Get down! You don't have any armor on!"

"No," she said, pulling the trigger over and over.

Chopper bullets spat their way up the road, making a beeline for Abraham. Like a statue, he stood in front of Sticks, facing the heavy fire. "Fine. Keep shooting then. Lord protect us!"

Warriors locked in battle fell before his eyes. Calls of the dying went out.

Simon the Fenix streaked across the sky and slammed into the nearest choppers. The chopper's blades broke off against his hide. The chopper spiraled to the ground and crashed into a ball of flame.

Abraham let out a shout. "That's what I call an entrance!"

The second chopper rose out of the channel and fired bullets into Simon.

Shredded wings beating fiercely, Simon curled away from the stream of bullets and rammed the chopper in the side headfirst. The chopper was knocked out of the sky and hit the mountainside in a fiery boom.

The gore-coated Henchmen let out a new elated battle cry: "Death and devastation!"

The great Fenix worked his way down the channel. A geyser of flame blasted from his mouth into the tanks and sea of bodies below. The road began to burn as far as the eye could see. He left nothing but charred bodies, roasting metal, black smoke, and flames in his wake.

The Gond scrambled back into the hills with the terramen giving chase. The soldiers of Tiotan scattered as the King's Army made its way up the channel.

Abraham couldn't believe his eyes. The enemies fled like water being shed from a dog. They'd won.

He grabbed Sticks by the arm and aimed her toward the tunnel. "Let's go."

A small force of soldiers guarded the entrance. Standing behind shields, they fired assault rifles.

The terramen gathered into a stampeding cluster. Barath was back on his feet and led the charge. The fierce terramen fighters hit the enemy soldiers like a wrecking ball hitting a wall.

Abraham swung Black Bane into the swarming enemy with wroth force. Sword blades shattered against his might. Bullets ricocheted from his spinning steel. The sword's engraving burned like hot coals. He waded deeper into the tunnel, leaving a path of the dead behind him. He didn't fight like Abraham Jenkins any longer. He fought like a man possessed. He fought like Ruger Slade.

"Death before failure!" Horace bellowed out. He gored a man and slung him aside. "I told you we could kill them!"

With blood in their eyes and with wild howling, the Henchmen stormed the Time Tunnel.

One hundred feet away, at the front end of the Time Tunnel, the Underlord Fleece stood waiting.

Mandi sat inside the cabin of the ambulance parked near the front end of the tunnel. She'd watched everything that happened up to the point when Abraham's, Smoke's, and Sid's bodies were ripped from the ground and slammed together.

"Oh boy," she said as she nibbled on the tips of her nails. That was something that she never did. Now, she sat in the stuffy ambulance cabin, sweating like a whore in church. "Oh boy."

Smoke and Sid had ordered her to stay in the ambulance. She was supposed to have it ready when the time came to run. Slipping inside had been tough, but all of them were disguised as soldiers, wearing blue-and-black camo with black ball caps.

She took a sip of Gatorade and decided to drain the entire sixty-four-ounce jug. With her heart pounding in her chest, she got out of the ambulance. Pistol in hand, she said to herself, "Here goes nothing."

Inside the Time Tunnel, she saw the ghostly, tattered robes of the wraith whipping about his body. Her skin crawled. Spiders made of ice scurried down her spine.

"I hate ghosts. I hate ghost stories." She swallowed an emerald-green supervitamin. A moment later, her blood ignited. Her slumped shoulders pulled back, and her eyes narrowed. She looked at her gun. "I can do this. I can do anything."

Mandi snaked down the tunnel wall, using the cover of shadows and railcars. She moved as quietly as a cat with the noise of the generators drowning her footsteps out. She bolted from the wall and the railing and huddled behind a Jeep's back bumper. The computer stations were only twenty feet away. The ghostly wraith was no more than fifty feet away. She lined up the wraith in her gunsights.

"Say goodnight, you dirty dishrag." The pistol was loaded with blue-tipped bullets that were supposed to rip through anything. She squeezed the trigger and unloaded a burst that tore right through the wraith. The wraith, Fleece, didn't budge.

Big Apple pointed his finger at her and with gnashing teeth said, "Get her!"

Mandi cracked off two shots at the horned halfling.

The halfling dove behind the computer station.

Colonel Drew Dexter took cover behind the computer station and returned fire. He said, "You don't want to do this, Mandi! It's over. You're too pretty. I'd hate to see you die."

"Shut up!" She blasted over a succession of bullets at Drew. "You dirty liar." Bullets zinged over her head.

"I'm not playing games, Mandi!" Drew said. "Give up, or they will kill you."

She hunkered down behind the Jeep's wheel well, flattened out, caught a glimpse of Drew's feet, and fired.

"Ow!" Drew jumped behind the computer station. "She shot me in the foot!"

"The next bullet's going to take off more than your—hey!" The gun was ripped from her hand by an unseen force. The gun hurtled over to Big Apple, who snatched it out of the air. Mandi's entire body floated up into the air and flew into the cluster of her friends. Her head cracked against Sid's.

"Ow!"

"I told you to stay in the ambulance," Sid said.

"It looked to me like you needed some help. What was I supposed to do? I had the superpill," Mandi said.

"Supervitamin," Smoke corrected.

They were all jammed together in a human ball.

"It was for an emergency."

"This isn't an emergency?" she said with incredulity as the ball of bodies slowly spun around.

"Nope," Smoke said. "But I can see how by your standards you'd think so."

"Abraham, is that you?" she asked Ruger.

"No, young lady. It's me, Ruger." He winked at her. "I'm impressed with your bravery."

"Yes, so am I." Drew limped over to the group, pointing his gun at all of them.

Big Apple did the same. Eugene Drisk had managed to get back on his feet.

"I would have let you live if you hadn't shot me in the foot. I'm going to have to go on disability." Drew grimaced. "But I'm going to kill you last."

Eugene slammed his fists on the computer desk. "No! No! Impossible!"

Dr. Jack, who had been gloating, gaped at the screens. "This can't be right. This can't be right!"

"What is it?" Colonel Dexter asked. He limped over to the screens. "No, no, no, no! Where did my choppers go!"

"That bat thing destroyed them!" Eugene pounded the desk. "Now the Henchmen are routing our army! Oh my, they are in the tunnel. The Henchmen are coming! The Henchmen are coming!"

Dr. Jack glared at Big Apple and said, "Sic your wraith on them and stop them!"

"Don't talk to me like that. And don't worry," Big Apple said. "They aren't a match for the Underlord." He ran his finger underneath the black collar he wore. "As long as I have this, I control everything."

Ruger chuckled. "You spawn of a billy goat. You can't stop them. They are going to kill you. You're less than one hundred feet from death's door. And I'm going to enjoy watching you die. All of you."

"I've had enough of this chatter." Dr. Jack grabbed a nearby rifle and pointed it at the group. "I'm going to kill all of you." He took aim. "Then I'm going to kill all of the Henchmen."

The blaring alarms sounded again. The red emergency lights came on, and strobe lights flashed.

"What is going on now?" Eugene screamed. "Why is there a countdown on my screen? Detonation in five minutes?" He gave Jack a blank look. "Who did this?"

Smoke spoke up and said, "I did. Remember, I told you about those detonators. All of them are armed now. It's a safety mechanism that can't be turned off. In five minutes, this tunnel will go boom."

"He's bluffing!" Dr. Jack said.

"No, he's not." Sid pointed out the detonators. They were mounted on the Time Tunnel ring, the generators, and the power lines. "You can try to disarm them, but chances are you won't get half of them all done in time."

"Fleece!" Big Apple shouted. "Finish the Henchmen. We'll take care of them."

The bodies of Ruger, Smoke, Sid, and Mandi were separated and hovered over the ground. They lay still, paralyzed, slowly rotating in the air.

Big Apple tore the phone from Smoke's grip. A countdown was on it. "What's the passcode?"

"Eight. Six. Seven. Five. Three. Oh. Nine," Smoke said.

"That's it! I've had it with all of you." Big Apple tossed the phone to Eugene and started shooting.

A great gust of wind started up inside the tunnel. Abraham could see Fleece at the opposite end of the tunnel. The Underlord's arms made slow, arcane patterns in the air. Dead soldiers and their equipment went rolling down the tunnel, past Abraham's feet.

The Henchmen gathered in a knot behind Abraham. Like the tip of a spear, with the wind tearing at their faces, they trucked on.

"Forward, men! Forward!" Horace shouted with the wind tearing at his beard. For every step the group took forward, they slid half a step backward.

Abraham could see the light at the end of the tunnel. He could see his own body, Smoke, and Sid, spinning like rotisserie chickens on the other side. Then he saw another woman's hair dangling down. "Mandi!"

The Henchmen marched on against the tunnel tempest with the wind tearing at their cheeks. The farther they marched the stronger the winds became.

"Black Bane, can't you do something about this?" he shouted.

"Why would I do that? I'm quite fond of the breeze."

Big Apple started shooting into Abraham's friends.

"Nooo!" Abraham yelled. They were only twenty-five feet away from the haunting wraith. He set his eyes on the demon and said, "Iris! Now!"

The Henchmen hunkered down. Horace had his great arms locked around one of Iris's legs. Bearclaw had a hold of the other.

In her hand, Iris held Melris's Rod of Devastation, which glowed with the fire of a hundred burning purple stars. "Taste my purple power!"

A bolt of power rocketed out of the tip of the rod. The blast smote Fleece square in the chest and sent him flying backward out of the tunnel.

Mandi, Smoke, Sid, and Ruger fell to the ground. Ruger, in Abraham's body, popped up to his knees just as Fleece gathered himself.

On impulse, Abraham threw Black Bane at Ruger just as Big Apple pointed his gun barrel at Ruger's head. Ruger snatched the blade out of the air, and in a single lightning-quick stroke, he sliced off Big Apple's head.

Before the horned halfling's head hit the ground, Fleece glided back into the tunnel. At the same time, he pulled the collar from Big Apple's neck into his hand as if using a magnet. The wind had died, but he blocked Abraham and the Henchmen's passage. With the collar in one hand, he wagged his bony finger with the other. Fleece said in a deep, ghostly, but soothing voice, "No, no, no." The collar disintegrated in his hand. His dark robes shifted to light gray and white. Muscles and skin gathered over his bones in a miraculous transformation. "Ah. I am free now. The Sect thanks you, Abraham. Now I must go and restore order." He opened a portal of swirling mist and disappeared in a puff of misty smoke.

Abraham watched in fascination as Ruger Slade, using his own out-of-shape body, finished off the enemy. Ruger blocked a bullet fired by Drew Dexter and sliced him in half. Dr. Jack turned to run, but not before Ruger gored him in the back. He finally faced off with Eugene Drisk, who, on hands and knees, pleaded for his life. Ruger split the man in half.

"Come on, hurry up!" Sid said as she beckoned him to the other side of the Time Tunnel.

That was when Abraham heard the emergency alarms going off. With the bright flashing strobe lights in his eyes, he shielded his gaze and said, "What's the hurry? We won."

"I'm destroying the Time Tunnel," Smoke said. "You have less than two minutes left."

"But you guys were shot." He looked at Mandi.

She had a grimace on her face and held her hand over her ribs. "We have the sweetheart suits on. It hurts, but we'll live. Now are you coming home or not?"

Abraham looked back over his shoulder. There stood the Henchmen, battered, bruised, and bloodied from head to toe. They looked like cans that had been spat out of a meat grinder. Horace had a bullet hole through one cheek. Bearclaw showed two teeth busted out. Dominga was holding a flap of skin in place on her arm. Those strangers had given him everything they'd had.

"Uh"—he lifted a finger—"hold on." Abraham made his way around the group, shaking hands with everyone as he did so. He started with Horace.

"Horace, I couldn't ask for a more faithful friend. You can deliver beer with me anytime."

"Bearclaw, what can I say? If I didn't know you, you'd scare the hell out of me."

"Vern, you're a dick. But in an honest kind of way."

"Thank you, Captain," Vern said.

He hugged Iris. "You've been nothing but faithful and amazing.

"Dominga, wow." He kissed her on the cheek. "Just wow."

"Apollo and Prospero…" He shook their hands. "Every time I see a homeless person, I'll think of the two of you. And Nick Nolte."

He gave Tark and Cudgel brief hugs. "You both remind me of one of my closest teammates, Buddy Parker. I'll always keep you close to my heart."

"Skitts, you might not have the Brand, but you're a Henchmen."

The young brown-haired man nodded.

Abraham stood before Shades and gave the little fella an approving look. "What can I say? It was nice knowing you."

Shades sniffed. "Nice knowing you too, Captain."

He hugged Clarann and Clarice at the same time. "I pray that it all works out." He kissed Clarice on the cheek. "You deserve to know your father. Clarann, thanks for having faith in me in the beginning."

Clarann gave him a soft kiss. "Thanks for saving me. I would have been dead without you."

Sticks was the last one to thank. He laid his hands on her shoulders and studied her creaseless and expressionless face. "I want you to know that you meant the most to me out of everyone here."

"Don't get weepy on me. I know."

"I don't suppose you'd show me a smile, would you?"

"Nope."

He chuckled. "Thanks, Sticks. I'm truly going to miss you."

He gave her a kiss. She tightened her lips then suddenly kissed him back. They shared a long, passionate kiss. He broke it off and swallowed.

"That's the best good-bye I've ever had." He squeezed her hand and bumped into Iris.

Iris's smile was as big as a rainbow, and she said, "I bet I can top that." She puckered up, pulled Abraham down, and kissed him.

Abraham caught his breath, gave Iris a pat on the rear end, and headed over to Solomon. "What's it going to be? You coming home or staying here?"

Solomon stroked the hairs on his chin, looked at his friends, and said, "I've kinda gotten used to these guys. I think I'm going to stick around and see what happens."

Abraham reached up and squeezed Solomon's shoulder. "Thanks for believing me."

"Thanks for delivering."

Abraham moved toward the other side of the Time Tunnel, where he saw himself, Mandi, Smoke, and Sid waiting.

"Will you hurry up?" Mandi demanded.

"I'm coming." Before he crossed the threshold, he smiled and waved good-bye.

Then he met Ruger on the Time Tunnel's threshold. Ruger held out Black Bane. He grabbed the sword handle, and both men locked eyes. His soul slid from one body to the other. He found himself face-to-face with the one true Ruger Slade.

"I think I'm going to miss being you."

"I know. I missed me too," Ruger Slade said.

"Aren't you going to miss being me?"

Taking the sword with him, Ruger walked backward toward Titanuus, saluted with the blade, and said, "Well done, Abraham Jenkins. Well done."

The Henchmen gathered King Hector's body.

Smoke grabbed Luther and put the man over his shoulder. He stood in Titanuus for a moment and said, "Now I can say I've been here."

"Come on, John, we only have thirty seconds," Sid said.

The company ran to the ambulance and loaded in. Abraham got into the front seat with Mandi. As the ambulance made the turn in the tunnel, he waved one last time with the emergency lights flashing in his eyes. The Henchmen were gone.

The ambulance roared at full speed out of the tunnel. It hit the dirt road doing ninety. With purple lightning in the sky, the mountainside exploded. Everything went white after that.

CHAPTER 89

BEEP. BEEP. BEEP. BEEP. BEEP.

Abraham's nose twitched. That all-too-familiar hospital smell lingered in his nose. His eyes were closed. The sheets were stiff.

I don't want to look.

The last thing he remembered was riding out of the tunnel inside an ambulance. Mandi drove. Everyone else—Smoke, Sid, and a catatonic Luther—was in the back. A blinding flash of light was followed by an earth-shattering *kaboom.*

Time to face the music.

Taking a deep breath, he opened his eyes. He was right. There he lay in a hospital bed with an IV hooked to him. The curtain, with light sea patterns, was drawn. He blinked several times. His throat tightened.

Aside from the steady beeping of a vital-statistics monitor, he didn't hear anything else. He lifted his arms and saw no handcuffs, flexicuffs, or shackles of any shape or form. His limbs were free. With a grunt, he sat up and swung his legs over the side. His toes touched the cold floor. He rubbed his forehead with his fingers.

Let's see what is behind curtain number one, Monty.

With his pulse pounding behind his ears, he slowly pushed the curtain back. He was inside a single hospital room. A wooden door with a partial glass pane window was closed. A nurse walked by, stopped, and looked in. She was short and full-figured, with a blond ponytail and wearing black Hello Kitty scrubs.

Nurse Nancy. No!

Nurse Nancy opened the door and said, "Well, look who is finally awake." She checked the monitors, grabbed a clipboard, and jotted down some notes.

He studied her with wary eyes. She'd been close to Dr. Jack Lassiter, or so he thought.

Looking at the clipboard, she smirked.

"What?" he said.

She looked at him and replied. "What?"

"Uh… what time is it?"

"Morning time." She hooked the clipboard on the end of the bed. "And I'm finishing up a twelve-hour shift. So I hope you don't mind that I'm not very chatty. I'll let your friends or family know that you are awake. You seem to be in good shape, so the doctor will swing by and sign off your release."

"Doctor who?" he asked because he couldn't stop thinking about Jack Lassiter.

"No, not Doctor Who, the time-travel guy. Doctor Uy will come by. He's in a real good mood since he returned from his fishing trip. Don't worry, he won't release you if you ain't right." She looked him up and down. "You look fine to me. You've even slimmed down. Stay put, and I'll see to it that they bring you something to eat." She closed the door behind herself.

Abraham waited on pins and needles for another half hour. He lay in bed, uncertain what to think. His gaze was fixed on the door. He wasn't sure he wanted to know what was on the other side of it. *Did everything I remember happen, or was it all just a dream?* He held his sheets with his fingers clutching in and out.

Mandi knocked on the door and quickly came inside. She had on a black polo shirt and blue jeans. Her bouncing brown hair hung down to her shoulders, and she carried a vase of flowers. "Hi!" she said cheerfully as she crept into the room and closed the door behind her.

"Mandi," he said with a shaky voice, "tell me what is going on. Did we just blow up a Time Tunnel or not?"

She set the vase of flowers on the table, unslung her purse, and set it on the chair. She sat down beside Abraham and took him by the hand. "No, we didn't blow up the Time Tunnel."

His shoulders sagged. "Oh."

"Smoke and Sid did."

He perked up. "What? It's all real." He grabbed her shoulders. "Don't mess with me, Mandi. Tell me it's over."

"Oh, it's over. I saved this for you." She pulled a newspaper out of her oversized purse. "Read."

He read the headline out loud: "Freak earthquake causes massive mountain slide." He skimmed the article. It didn't mention any names or report any injuries. It was vague and only stated that the National Guard was cleaning up. He looked at Mandi and asked, "So it's over?"

Mandi smiled brightly and nodded. "It's over."

He hugged her. She hugged back and kissed his face. Deep inside, he knew it was over. But he still wondered if all of it was even true. Giving her a black look, he said, "How do we even know that it happened?"

"Oh, we know." She opened his robe and gently ran her fingers over his chest. "And you'll have this."

He looked down to see a brand-new scar shaped like a crown on his chest. His jaw dropped. "How?"

Mandi shrugged. "I don't know, and I don't care. I'm just glad to have you back."

"Where are Smoke and Sid?"

"They are cleaning up things at Facility 117. Apparently, they have a lot of experience with this sort of thing. They told me to tell you hello and they hope to see you at the wedding."

"What wedding?"

"Our wedding," she said playfully. "You didn't think I'd go through all of that without marrying you?"

"Huh-huh," he was stunned, but he didn't mind her saying it. He felt peace. "Uh, what about Luther? Is he… gone?"

"No, he's alive and well back at the brewery—just, well, different." She patted him on a thigh. "Oh, wait, you don't want to forget this before we get out of here." Mandi moved to the clothing cabinet, opened the door, and reached up top. She tossed Jake's backpack onto the bed. "Just like you, it's been to Titanuus and back."

His eyes watered, not with tears of sadness but tears of joy. The guilt he'd felt for losing his family was gone. He realized it wasn't his fault, once and for all. He kissed the backpack. "I miss you guys."

Mandi wiped a tear away with a tissue. "You know they miss you too."

"Hmm… it feels heavier." He unzipped the backpack. The first thing he pulled out was the Rubik's cube. All the sides were solved. Immediately, he thought of the Crown of Stones and King Hector. He hoped King Hector made it. The second thing he pulled out was a leather pouch bigger than his fist. It had a lot of heft to it.

"What's that?"

"I don't know." He opened it to find the leather pouch was filled to the brim with gold and silver shards. He poured the coins into his hand. "Holy sheetrock."

Torched by Simon the Fenix, the armies of Tiotan fled shortly after the Time Tunnel collapsed. On foot, Ruger Slade and the Henchmen started the journey back home. King Hector was alive and well, except he wasn't King Hector at all. He had the essence of someone else. And he was talking to Ruger and the queen.

"So I'm the King of Kingsland?" King Hector asked. He wore the Crown of Stones on his head, but the stones were missing. All of them had been buried in hundreds of tons of rubble behind him. "I've never been a king before."

Queen Clarann had her arm hooked in Hector's. "You'll make a fine king, Luther Vancross. I can see it in your eyes. Hector would approve."

With a cheerful tone, Hector said, "I can't wait to see my castle. Do I have a queen? A harem?"

"I'm your queen," Clarann said as she looked at Ruger. "But we need to talk about that. We have a delicate situation. You see…" She explained everything about her and Ruger's past.

Luther was very understanding. "We'll work it out." He stretched out a hand to Ruger. "So you're Ruger Slade. I've heard a lot about you."

Dominga and Tark returned from the front lines of the King's Army.

Dominga reported to Ruger, saying, "There's no sign of Leodor. One of the King's Guardians said that he jumped through a swirl in the sky."

Ruger nodded. "We'll find the snake on our next mission. Home first, before the House of Steel crumbles."

Shades strolled alongside Ruger, the thumb of his remaining hand hitched inside his belt, and said, "It's good to have you back once and for all, Captain."

"Hear, hear," Horace, Bearclaw, and Vern agreed.

"But we still have a problem," Shades added.

"What's that?" Ruger asked.

"Sticks is gone. And I didn't even see her leave," Shades said with a grim voice.

With one hand on his sword handle and the other hand on Shades's shoulder, Ruger said with a smile in his voice, "She isn't the only one that is gone. The presence within Black Bane is gone too. But I have a strong feeling that everything is going to be all right."

Abraham sat at the counter at Woody's Grill, eating a basketful of cheese fries loaded down with jalapeños. A tall chocolate milkshake he was sucking on was half empty. Mandi's stepfather, Herb, sat beside him, watching the TV. The old man was covered in age spots, his hair had thinned down to almost nothing, and he wore a Members Only jacket.

"Man, the Pirates really suck this year," Herb said. "I bet they wish that they had Jenkins the Jet back." He punched Abraham in the shoulder. "Man, could you throw a fastball."

Mandi's mother, Martha, came through the double doors leading into the kitchen. The older version of Mandi always had a warm smile on her face. She wore a maroon homemade apron that read in white letters, "Peace. Love. Joy." She wiped her hands off on a dish towel and asked, "Can I get you another milkshake, Abraham?"

"No ma'am. Mandi's probably gonna kill me for having this one," he said.

"You mean two," Herb said with a chuckle.

"Shhh…" Abraham said with a grin.

Herb spun around in his chair, eyed the front doors of the store, checked his watch, and said, "They're late. Aren't they late? I hate waiting. I haven't seen Luther in decades, and here I am waiting." He stuck his bottom lip out. "He probably won't come. Probably got abducted by aliens or something." He spun around on his stool and eyed the TV.

Abraham finished his fries and wiped off his fingers. Being back home was good, but a part of him felt as if he'd slip back into Titanuus at any moment. Now, however, he was content. He was more than happy to move on with Mandi.

"Oh, there they are." Martha took off her apron, revealing a black Woody's Grill T-shirt underneath. "My, I should have gotten fixed up. I look horrible."

"You never look horrible," Herb said.

"Oh, what do you know? You can't see a thing." Martha hurried to the door and opened it. Mandi was the first one through.

Luther Vancross came in next. His white hair was almost shaved down to the skin, and he sported a white moustache. In his flannel shirt and jeans, he looked strong and healthy. Even with the age spots, he didn't look a day over seventy. The woman accompanying Luther made Abraham jump off his stool.

"Sticks!"

Sticks still wore her brown hair tied back, showing her pretty, creaseless tomboy face. She'd donned a pair of jeans and a flannel shirt that was tied off over her belly button.

Abraham gave her a fragile hug. "Uh, I don't know what to say. Are you the only one?"

"Sort of," she said.

He looked at Mandi. "Why didn't you tell me?"

"I wasn't sure how I felt about your girlfriend from the other side. But we talked," Mandi said.

Sticks slapped him on the shoulder and said, "I like you, but…" she looked him up and down, "I like you better with Ruger's body. I guess I'm shallow."

Wringing her hands, Martha whispered to her daughter, "Who is Ruger, and where is the other side?"

"I'll explain later." Mandi hooked her mom by the arm and said, "Let's give them a moment."

"So why did you come?" Abraham asked Sticks. He noticed a knife strapped to the side of her leg, the Dagger of Death.

Sticks moseyed over to the stool beside him and sat down. She took in everything from the diner to the general store. "I thought it was time for a change."

"I see." He turned his attention to Luther. "And how are you doing?"

"The longer I stay, the better," Luther said.

Herb got right in Luther's face. His bulging eyes were squinting. "You look like Luther, but you don't sound like Luther. Who are you?"

"I assure you that I am Luther, Herb, but the years have changed me." Luther motioned to the diner booths. "Abraham, can we sit down?" He rubbed Herb's shoulder. "I'll be right back, and we'll catch up where we left off."

Abraham joined Luther and Sticks in the booth. He sat across from both of them with one knee bouncing up and down.

Luther scanned the diner as if he'd never been anywhere else before. He carried himself with a different air, much stronger than before. He asked, "Don't you know who I am, Abraham?"

"King Hector?"

"No." Luther's eyes fell on Martha. "It's good to see that this world is ripe with ample women."

Abraham's knee hit the table, making the salt and pepper shakers jump. "Black Bane!"

"Yes," Luther said with a glimmer in his eyes. "But that isn't my real name."

Abraham leaned forward. He noticed a Mona Lisa smile on Sticks's face. "So what is your name?"

Luther spread out his fingers. Tiny tendrils of blue lightning danced from fingertip to fingertip. "I am Boon."

Abraham had never heard the name before. He leaned back in the booth and asked, "So where are you from, Boon?"

"Bish."

THE HENCHMEN CHRONICLES:
BONUS BACKSTORY

Several years earlier… when Ruger Slade was still Ruger Slade

CHAPTER 1

"IT'S GOOD TO SEE YOU, Pratt," Ruger said. He'd been summoned to the House of Steel, where one of his top knights greeted him at the gateway leading to the upper terrace that overlooked the Bay of Elders. "Are you keeping at your daily routine?"

Pratt swung the black gate open and stepped aside. He wore a suit of plate-mail armor, which made the man look colossal to ordinary men. He was well-groomed and a fine specimen of a warrior. "I haven't failed to miss a day of your grueling routine yet, Captain." He patted his stomach. "See, I'm flatter in the midriff. I can trot to the top of the spires now, in full armor."

"I had no doubt that you had it in you." Ruger gave Pratt a pat on the back. He was a man of extraordinary physique himself, but Pratt had noticeable inches and girth on him. "You are a big target. You have to be quicker. The enemy will always aim at the easiest target. The biggest one."

"Then that would be you when I'm not along," Pratt joked.

"That's why I like to bring you, Pratt. You make a fine moving shield."

The pair shared a chuckle.

"King Hector and Leodor are waiting." Pratt locked his heels together and said, "I'm ready for the field as soon as you request me, Captain. The castle detail… well, it's very boring."

Ruger returned his salute and said, "It's easier breathing. Make the most of it."

He marched toward the terrace. The day was overcast. Seabirds glided through the sky. Many of the birds nested in the gigantic pommel of the sword buried in the crown of the House of Steel. He stopped and gazed at it.

Every time Ruger saw the great sword of the legendary celestial being, Antagonus, he envisioned two great swordsmen battling in the heavens. He took the pommel of his sword, Black Bane, his grip tightening. *If only I could have seen it.*

He marched out onto the terrace. King Hector was tossing bread crumbs up over the terrace wall, feeding the seabirds. The king wore a rich set of forest-green robes trimmed in gold. A small crown of six horns rested atop his head. A single emerald was set in the horn in the front.

Viceroy Leodor stood beside the king. The hair of the oldest man in the group stirred in the wind. His little chin sagged, and his hands were hidden inside the oversized sleeves of his deep-brown robes. He noticed Ruger's approach and whispered in the king's ear.

King Hector dusted off his hands and turned toward his guest.

Ruger took a knee and bowed.

"Captain Ruger Slade," King Hector said in a rich voice full of charm. "Is there something that I can do for you?"

Ruger lifted his eyes and said, "My king, I was told that I was summoned."

King Hector chuckled. "Ruger, you were summoned. I was only jesting with you. Please, my champion servant, rise and properly greet your king."

Ruger stood at attention.

King Hector walked up to him, put his hands on his shoulders, and said, "Ruger, you are more than my servant and finest knight. I consider you a friend. Will you please relax?"

"A Guardian is always vigilant and mindful in the presence of the crown."

"Then I will take it off." King Hector handed the crown to Leodor and said, "Take that inside. It's making my champion uncomfortable."

Leodor's face tightened. He gently bowed and said, "Certainly, Your Majesty." He short-stepped up to the terrace's raised patio and vanished through the curtains leading inside the castle.

King Hector led them to the table on the terrace. A tall carafe filled with wine sat there, along with plates of fruit, meats, and cheeses. "Will you have a drink with me, Ruger?"

"Certainly, Your Majesty." He poured two golden goblets half full. He handed one to the king and said, "To the king."

King Hector smiled, raised his goblet, and said, "To Kingsland."

They drank together.

"Please sit," the king said as he sat at the head of the table. "Every time I see you, I feel a degree of envy."

Ruger gave him a confused look.

"What I wouldn't do to ride the way of the warrior again. I'm not so old, I'm still fit, and I miss the saddle between my legs. I hated to give up that life." He pointed at Ruger. "I hope you are still cherishing these moments."

"I was born to serve the crown of Kingsland. Every day I strap on my steel, I find satisfaction in the purpose that I serve. It is the highest honor."

"Here's to that," the king said and took another drink. "The standard is the standard."

"Hear, hear," Ruger replied.

King Hector tapped a finger on the side of his goblet and said, "Well, let's get down to business. As much as I'd like to think that we were meeting for social causes, I fear, once again, that is not the case. I need your services, Ruger. There is trouble afoot in Kingsland. I need you to deal with it."

Ruger leaned forward. "What is it, Your Majesty?"

The king reached for a scroll sitting on the table. It was bound by a short string of leather. He rolled the scroll over to Ruger. "Read it."

CHAPTER 2

Ruger unrolled the scroll and read. His eyes slid side to side and worked their way down the parchment. His cheek muscles flexed. His fingers pinched the scroll tighter. Barely able to control himself, he said, "This is an outrage. Roderick did this?"

The king's warm smile was gone, replaced with a much more serious look. He nodded. "The crown of Kingsland will always have enemies, but never did I anticipate one to move boldly in my very fields."

Ruger glanced at the scroll again. "Over fifty Kingsland soldiers were killed. An outpost burned to the ground. This is treason. Murder." He set the scroll down and balled up a fist. "Please, Your Majesty, let me deal with this scourge."

"That is why you are here, Captain Slade," the king said.

Leodor appeared through the curtains. The viceroy took a seat beside the king. With a froward expression, Leodor said, "I take it he knows."

"Aye, he does," King Hector replied.

Leodor nodded. "I see."

King Hector said, "Viceroy, go ahead and explain."

"Certainly, Your Majesty." Leodor pulled his hands out, locked his fingers, and rested them on the table. "The history of Roderick the Regal is well-known. He's openly challenged King Hector's right to wear the crown. He's always claimed that he was the heir to Kingsland. But over the past decades, he's been very quiet about it until now. Now, it appears, he is fully equipped to challenge the crown again. He has his own castle, his own knights, and a sizeable force that can wreak havoc."

"I will lead a thousand Guardians to his castle in Pompley and lay siege. I'll put an end to his madness," Ruger said.

King Hector lifted a hand and said, "That is what I brought you here for, Ruger. But we aren't going to pin our ears back and bull rush his gates. Roderick is no fool. He wants to make a spectacle of our situation. He wants the people of Kingsland to side with him. He'll divide in order to conquer."

"What are you proposing?" he asked.

Leodor cleared his throat and said, "The king wants to handle this matter quietly. If we send an army north to Pompley, the people will become restless. When they become restless, they start thinking for themselves, and they will begin choosing sides."

King Hector twisted the golden wedding ring on his finger. "I don't want to drag my people into this. I'm sworn to protect them, but Roderick wants to use them against me. As we speak, he feeds their minds with his poison. He preaches that I neglect their wants and needs. All he really wants is the House of Steel. My cousin is nothing but a greedy thief."

Ruger looked the king dead in the eye and asked, "Do you want me to kill him?"

He could see intent in Hector's eyes. The king was a fair man, but he ruled with an iron hand. Those who broke the law suffered the consequences.

Before King Hector could reply, Leodor said, "The matter is to be taken care of discreetly. If Roderick is eliminated, it will quell the rebellion."

"They will only blame King Hector for it," he said.

"That is why we want the matter to be handled discreetly," Leodor added.

Ruger narrowed his eyes on Leodor. The viceroy and he never saw eye to eye. He felt the king put too much trust in the Sect member. "If you want the matter handled discreetly, Leodor, why don't you use the Sect and send a shade to deal with him."

"Those are fables," Leodor said smugly.

King Hector chuckled. "Ruger, I have more faith in your steel than the shades of the Elders."

"So do I," Ruger said as he stood up. "The viceroy is welcome to come along if the king wishes."

Leodor's tired eyes grew big. "My services are best utilized here. But I will provide you with any means that I have. For the king and the crown."

Ruger opened his mouth to speak.

King Hector cut him off. "Let's remember that all of us serve the crown." The king stood and gazed between the two men. "Wizards and warriors. They never can get along. Leodor, you are dismissed."

Leodor bowed and departed.

King Hector hooked his arm in Ruger's, led him down the patio steps, and said, "I don't know anyone who cares for Leodor. It's disappointing. I find his knowledge invaluable."

"I meant no disrespect to you, King Hector."

"No need to apologize. Leodor's smugness is very tiresome. I know. But everyone that serves my court serves a purpose."

"I have faith in your wisdom, my king," he said.

"Tell me." The king looked him in the eye. "Is there any better way than this?"

"Your way is my way. I will find the snake and crush his head."

King Hector offered a smile. "The truth is, I trust you more than Leodor and his arcane powers." He looked at the sword on Ruger's hip. "Steel speaks to me. Besides, you and Black Bane are legendary."

"What if Roderick suspects that I am coming?"

"It's best that he doesn't, but if he does, then let his limbs quake."

Ruger offered a smile. "He won't have any limbs left once I find him."

"Elder speed, Ruger," the king said. He headed back to the terrace wall overlooking the sea and started feeding the seabirds again.

Ruger made his way back to the terrace gate and met up with Pratt, who had an eager look on his face.

"Captain, you have to take me. It's been too long since I've ridden into battle." He clenched a mailed fist. "I need a fight."

"Keep the king safe. That is the only fight you need to worry about. Do your duty… with honor."

Pratt stood rigid as a post and saluted. "Aye, Captain. Aye."

Ruger saluted Pratt then walked through the gate and down the steps, heading for the Guardians' garrison.

CHAPTER 3

The Guardian garrison resided within the House of Steel's great walls, but it was a separate entity unto itself. It was the place where the knights trained and slept, stocked with full accommodations of the finest families. The barracks slept two men to a room, complete with dressing quarters that contained modest furnishings. A common room, food galley, and the king's servants were at their disposal.

The training ground was the busiest place that time of morning. The Guardians, stationed there on a three-month rotation, were hard at it like gladiators in the battle courtyards. Men in pairs squared off with one another, fighting hard with wooden weapons.

The proving grounds were filled with the clamor of encouraging shouts, chants, and heated practice battles.

Some groups of men were lined up, practicing sword techniques from their instructors. Others were lifting heavy objects such as bags of sand and wagon wheels.

Ruger stood in the shade underneath the archways that held up the terraces above him. He trained his men hard, day and night, always running drills they would never be prepared for. It was his way. It was the Guardians' way to be prepared for anything.

One man stood out among the rest. He was in a tug-of-war with a pair of horses while other men cheered him on.

"Do it, Horace. Do it! Tug those nags out of the gate!" a wee man was shouting at Horace's face. He wasn't dressed like the other men. He didn't wear armor, didn't carry a weapon, and didn't have the strapping build of the rest of the knights. "Come on, man. I have ten shards of silver on this! Don't let me down!"

Horace puffed out of his great jaws. His round red face beaded with sweat. He was burly as a bear, built like a grizzly, and bare chested. His mighty muscles heaved underneath a firm layer of fat. "Be silent, Shades!"

The two old horses, with deep bows in their backs, whinnied and nickered. Their hooves stamped the hard ground. They snorted.

The small man, Shades, grabbed the taut rope and shook it. "I bet I could walk on this. Stand still, Horace."

"Quit being a fool!" Horace said.

A group of Guardians were gathered around the contest. Bearclaw, Vern, Apollo, and Prospero were all present. They wore plate-mail armor that glinted in the daylight. All of them were clean-shaven, and their hair was well-kept.

"I'll take that wager," Bearclaw said in his rugged voice. "Five silvers says you can't stand on the rope twenty seconds."

"I say he does," the young, bright-eyed, and blond-haired Vern said cheerfully. "My five against yours." He tossed his coins on the ground.

Prospero and Apollo threw their own coins on the ground. "We wager against the squirrel of a man," Apollo said.

"Quit your fooling!" Horace said.

"Be still, Horace." Shades climbed on the rope. He spread his arms wide and balanced himself as delicately as a trapeze artist. "Someone count."

"I'll count." Bearclaw chuckled. He started counting slowly. "One… two… three… four…"

The rope wobbled.

Shades suddenly squatted. "Pull harder, Horace. The rope is too slack. It makes it hard to stand."

Horace let out a yell. "Arrrrggh!" He pulled hard.

The rope tightened. The horses' hooves dragged.

"Zoofan," Vern commented with eyes big as saucers.

"Nine… ten… eleven," Bearclaw continued.

Ruger stole his way across the grounds. With the men's attention turned away from him, he pulled a dagger and cut the tug rope.

Shades dropped to the ground.

Horace stumbled backward, fell down, and rolled head over heels.

"What in Titanuus?" Vern exclaimed. He whirled around and saw Ruger. "Captain!" He stood up straight and saluted.

"Captain on the grounds! Captain on the grounds!" Apollo shouted as he came to attention.

Every Guardian on the grounds stopped what they were doing and stood at attention. Not one of them moved a hair.

Horace finally climbed back to his feet and stood at attention. He panted heavily and dripped with sweat.

Ruger kneeled over the pile of coins and scooped them up. "Gambling, are we? I think all of you are well aware of how I feel about gambling." His strong voice carried easily through the training grounds. He bounced the coins in his hands. "When one errs, we all err." He looked at Bearclaw. "The standard is the standard still, isn't it?"

"Yes, Captain."

He shouted, "Does everyone agree with Bearclaw?"

The entire unit of men spoke as one. "Yes, Captain!"

"Good, then you will be glad to accept these men's punishment unilaterally. I want every man in full-plate armor. We begin the run to Burgess and back now!"

The trek to Burgess was a league-long, back-breaking run loaded down with full armor. The run downhill into the city wasn't difficult, but the climb back up was pure hell.

Ruger Slade led the way, running in his own full suit of armor at a brisk pace. No man could keep up with him, except for Shades. The smallish man wore only a suit of leather because the Guardians had no full set of armor small enough to fit him.

By the time they returned to the garrison gate, every man was heaving for breath or hacking their guts out. One hundred men in all staggered inside the gate. Ruger, barely winded, greeted them all with a hearty slap on the back.

He pulled Horace, Bearclaw, Vern, Apollo, Prospero, and Shades aside as he did so. "Gather in the war room. We have an urgent mission." Inside the war room, Ruger locked them inside to secure their privacy.

Horace was glowering at all the men in the room. He had been the last man to finish the race, by many minutes. "I should bust a hole in all of you." He poked a meaty finger at Shades. "Especially you. You started the betting, and you aren't even a Guardian. You're a squire."

"He's a squirrel," Vern said.

"He's my squirrel," Ruger said. "Does anyone take issue with that?" He studied every face in the room.

No man batted an eyelash.

"Good. Now listen."

CHAPTER 4

Ruger and his five best Guardians—Horace, Bearclaw, Vern, Apollo, and Prospero—plus Shades were riding horses toward Pompley. They wore common riding cloaks and shirts of chain-mail armor underneath dyed-leather tunics. Ruger had no doubt that Roderick the Regal would be expecting the Guardians. He had chosen to be discreet.

"Captain," Horace said. The beefy warrior rode alongside Ruger.

Bearclaw and Vern were forming a column behind them as Apollo and Prospero brought up the rear. Shades was nowhere in sight but was scouting ahead.

"Do you think it is wise to ride separately from the rest of the cavalry? How will we communicate with them?"

"I only want them to spook Roderick," he replied. Ruger had ordered two hundred heavy cavalry to make the march to Pompley, which would be more than enough to get the duke's attention.

"We'll make it to Pompley a day ahead of them. That will give us time to get a feel for what is happening. Roderick shouldn't be looking for a smaller force. Hopefully, the cavalry will serve as a distraction while the Duke of Pompley's back is turned."

Horace clawed at his beard and grunted. "So, this is a mission to kill."

"Duke Roderick is a traitor. He attacked the crown. He killed our brethren soldiers. He must go down."

"How many men does Roderick have guarding his keep?" Vern asked.

"He boasts a thousand loyal soldiers or more. But it could be significantly less. Once we arrive in Pompley, we will find out exactly how many he has," Ruger said.

"The more the better," Vern proudly said. "I aim to kill more than you this time, Captain."

"I'll try to save you some," Ruger quipped. "I hope this can be resolved with little blood spilled."

"They are traitors," the broad-faced Bearclaw said. A double-bladed battle-axe hung between his shoulders. "All of them should die. I will show no mercy."

"We will follow the laws of Kingsland. It is King Hector's command that any soldier or knight that willingly surrenders will be spared and face a just punishment." Ruger eyed the sky. Birds of prey circled over the distant hills. He wiped the drizzling rain from his face. "All of us have that understanding, don't we?"

"Aye, Captain," all of them grumbled, except for Prospero, who always said little to nothing.

"I've never fought against my own countrymen before," Vern said. He was the youngest in the group. He brushed his flaxen hair over his eyes. "Not soldiers, that is."

"They aren't your countrymen when they turn against their king," Horace said. "When they come to kill you, well, you won't see them as countrymen anymore. Not when it's them or you. It's a shame that this Roderick would turn against his cousin. I feel that Hector is a good king."

"There is darkness in all men's hearts. Sometimes it controls them and feeds a hunger that cannot be satisfied." Ruger turned back in his saddle and said, "Don't ever let that hunger control you. We are Guardians. We control it."

Shades rode into view, bouncing in the saddle of his trotting horse. The hood of his cloak half covered his face. He stopped fifty yards away and waited on the group. "We might have trouble ahead."

"How so?" Ruger asked.

"There is a large group of men guarding the bridge that leads to Pompley," Shades said.

"Soldiers?"

"I can't say. I was distant, but I didn't notice any insignias or waving banners of Pompley. It was a cluster of armed men. I counted a score of them."

Ruger rubbed his chin and said, "Lead us."

The Guardians remained behind the last rise on the hill before the road led down to the bridge. They dismounted, crept up the hill, flattened out on the top, and spied the bridge below.

Sure enough, just as Shades had said, twenty well-armed men were gathered at the bridge, at the entrance and the exit. The bridge spanned a thirty-foot-wide river too deep for horses to cross. The road they were on was one of the less-traveled roads leading to Pompley.

"Strange." Ruger could see by the way that group moved that they were not soldiers. The men paced, leaned over the bridge, spat, muttered, and jested. They carried swords, hatchets, spears, and other assorted weapons. "They aren't in soldiers' uniforms—that is for certain. Perhaps they are highwaymen."

"Brigands?" Horace asked. "That is a quite a patch of them."

"It appears they are looking for someone," Ruger said. "I think we'll be safe if we are not the ones that they are looking for." He reached over and slapped Shades on the shoulder. "I'll let you do the talking."

"Yes, if anyone can speak their language, Shades can," Bearclaw quipped.

"And you should be thankful for that. If we let you do the talking, no doubt they would be calling for our heads," Shades fired back.

The Guardians mounted up, crested the hill, and slowly walked the horses down to the bridge. Ruger and Shades led the way. The moment the men at the bridge caught sight of them, they pulled their weapons free and gathered at the foot of the bridge.

Shades boldly moved out in front of Ruger and greeted the man that stood at the front of the gang. "Hail and well met, fellow citizens. Quite an ugly day, isn't it?"

The man in front was tall and lean. His brown hair was parted in the middle and hung down past his chin. His eyes were narrow, and many small white scars marked his chest. He was rugged looking, the same as the rest of the bunch behind him. A longsword hung on his back. "Do I look like the sort of fellow that cares about the weather?"

"Er… no," Shades politely replied. "You look like the sort of fellow that doesn't care about anything."

"Is that a jest?" the brigand leader said in a gruff manner. He nodded his head forward.

His men spread out to surround the Guardians.

CHAPTER 5

Shades's head followed the men moving to enclose the Guardians. He turned his attention back to their spokesman and said, "Far be it from me to try and make light on a dreary day." He glanced at the others again. "Is there something in particular that you are looking for?"

The brigand grabbed Shades's horse by the bridle, eyed the beast carefully, and said, "That's a fine horse." He peered farther back at the other horses. "All of them look fine." He moved away from Shades toward Ruger.

"Excuse me," Shades said. "We are trying to make haste. Is there any reason that you are blocking our passage?"

"There's always a reason," the leader said. "Be silent, little man. I'm busy." He eyeballed Ruger's horse and circled it. He checked the saddle and appeared to be looking for a brand underneath.

Ruger's horse nickered.

"She gets nervous around strangers," Ruger said.

The leader fixed his eyes on Ruger. He gave him a heavy look and turned his attention to Ruger's sword. "That is a big sword that you carry."

"Yes, big enough to split your face with," Ruger replied.

The brigand stepped away from the horse. His stare hardened on Ruger.

"Only jesting," Ruger assured the brigand. "I become nervous when confronted by too many people. I'm a lot like my horse in many ways."

"I don't take you for the nervous type." The leader eyed the group. "None of you. What is your business?"

Shades pulled on his reins and turned his horse toward the leader. "We are traveling to Southern Tiotan. We always do this time of year. My retainers escort me up, to purchase wares from my store, and we bring wagonloads back down."

The leader stuck his chin out, chewing something, then spat on the ground. "You won't be crossing this bridge. Go around."

"And waste a day's ride? Sir, I cannot afford to lose a day. That will prove costly."

The brigands clutched at their weapons. Blood-hungry tongues licked their lips. They crowded the horses and held their weapons ready.

The leader said, "I'm going to need all of you to get off your horses. They are mine now."

Shades and Ruger exchanged a look.

"Uh," Shades said, "certainly we can come up with a more reasonable solution. I can pay you money. We need our horses."

"You fool. Why would you say that?" Horace asked. "Can't you see that these men are robbing us?"

"The fat one speaks truth," the leader said. He backed away and let more of his men surround the horses.

One brigand held each horse's bridle while other men pointed weapons at the Guardians from either side of the beast.

"Toss down your weapons and get off of your horses," the leader said.

"Sire, certainly we can come to a reasonable compromise. I'd hate to see anyone get hurt," Shades suggested.

"Who said anything about anyone getting hurt?" the leader asked. "But you're pushing for it. You." He looked at Ruger. "Take off that sword belt and hand it over."

Ruger unbuckled his sword belt, his blood churning. He handed the sword to another brigand standing by his side. The brigand grabbed the weapon by the sheath. The moment the brigand locked his fingers on the scabbard, Ruger yanked his sword free.

Black Bane flashed downward.

Slice!

The blade cleaved the brigand's skull down to the neck.

The leader ripped his sword free and shouted, "Kill them! Kill them all!"

Horace spun his horse around. The rear of the horse knocked one of the three brigands over. He jabbed his spear into the brigand holding the bridle, goring the man through the neck. He swung his leg out of the saddle and hopped to the ground before his horse bolted away. He squared off with a brigand carrying a hand axe and grinned. "You better throw it. It's the only chance you'll get."

The brigand cocked his arm back and hurled the hand axe at Horace.

Horace plucked the axe out of the air and threw it back.

The axe's blade split the brigand right between the eyes.

Horace rumbled with laughter. "And you thought I was going to kill you with my spear."

Bearclaw stood up on his horse saddle and leapt on the brigand to his right. Both men crashed hard into the muddy road.

The brigand flailed his sword at the much bigger Guardian. His short sword bit into the links in the chain armor. Bearclaw slipped a dagger into the man's heart and rolled up to one knee. He brandished his battle-axe in both hands.

Two brigands flanked him. They came at him with short swords and knives.

The wild-eyed warrior spun between the brigands' charging attacks. His axe whistled through the air. He hacked into the side of one man, and blood exploded out of the man's side. Like an angry woodsman, he chopped down the other, slower brigand like a tree with sap for blood.

Vern whisked his dagger out and slashed the man holding his horse bridle across the wrist.

The man let out a curse.

He dove out of the saddle as two more brigands came at him. He hit the ground, rolled up to a knee, and pulled his longsword free. He started in the high-guard position and chopped off the arm of the first man at the elbow. Then he parried a strike from a hand axe, reversed his swing, and sliced the man's belly open. The third attacker ran.

The older Prospero and Apollo each wore a pair of longswords crossed over their backs. Before the brigands could strike, both Guardians had fists full of steel. The jumped from their horses, and soon their blades whistled through the air.

The brigands fell underneath the furious assault of whirling steel. They were no match for the skilled knights. It quickly showed. Hand, arms, and legs were lost to the superior steel. Some brigands that didn't die, ran, while others limped.

Prospero and Apollo chased them all down the riverbank and killed them.

With two fists full of daggers, Shades made quick work of his three attackers. He ducked an overhanded sword chop and stabbed.

Glitch!

He gored a brigand in the kidneys. Moving with catlike agility, he twisted away from two larger men chopping at him with short swords. They missed him by a foot and found themselves gawking as he stood between them and stabbed both clean through the ribs.

Both men crumbled to the ground, gurgling in their own blood.

Shades spun his daggers, wiped the blades on the clothing of the dying, and said, "That was easy."

Slice!

Ruger cut a brigand's head clean from the shoulders. He zeroed in on the last one near his horse. The man blindly rushed him with fear-filled eyes. Ruger ended it quickly with a one-step jab to the heart. He ripped Black Bane free.

The hairs rose on his neck. He ducked.

A sword sliced over the top of his head. He dove away and rolled up to one knee.

The Guardians quickly surrounded the brigand leader by forming a circle around him. As one, they advanced on the wary-eyed brigand.

"Hold!" Ruger ordered. He moved into the circle of men. He faced the brigand leader. "Before you die, tell me who you serve."

"I'll tell you nothing." The brigand ran his gaze over Ruger's sword. "But tell me this. That sword you carry… I've never seen the likes. It is Black Bane, and you are Ruger Slade."

The Guardians exchanged a few glances among themselves.

"I am," Ruger said as he flipped his sword with a spin of the wrist. "And it is."

The lanky brigand nodded with his chin jutted out. There was a natural grace in the way he moved. His longsword, unlike the other brigands', was of the finest craft. "Then you are the man I was hoping for. I am Kazan Rue, sword master of Tiotan. It is my mission to kill you."

"And why is that?" Ruger asked.

"For sport."

Ruger knew better. He could see the cleverness lurking in the man's eyes. "Now isn't the time to be coy, Kazan Rue. You are about die."

"You overestimate yourself, Slade." Kazan Rue spun his sword around his body in a unique twisting fashion. "No man that has fought me has lived to tell about it. I've heard about you, your sword. When I received the invitation, I came to see you myself."

Vern stepped forward and said, "Let me fight this windbag, Captain! I'll skin his lips off."

"Yes, let the young knight be the first to die," Kazan Rue said with smug confidence. He thumbed the edge of his blade. "As for lips, little knight, it looks like you suckled on your mother too long."

Vern jumped out of his boots.

"Hold your place," Ruger said firmly.

Vern shook in place. Bearclaw towed his younger comrade back by the elbow.

"Widen the circle," Ruger ordered and started circling Kazan Rue. "For a master swordsman, you missed my neck by a length a moment ago. I believe you overestimate yourself."

"Nay. I wanted the duel to be fair. These men you slaughtered, they are hirelings from Pompley's hovels. They showed me what I wanted to see. I know what I am up against." Kazan Rue stuck his sword in the ground, spat in his hands, and rubbed them together.

"So, Duke Roderick wants *me* dead?"

"I didn't say that. The way I see it, there are many that want you dead." Kazan Rue picked up his sword. "Mainly me, at the moment."

"It would be your gain to share the truth of the matter." Ruger got into his sword-fighting stance.

"Plow guard. I like it," Kazan Rue said. "Most old knights start in that very stance. I hate knights." He spat on the ground and readied himself with his sword raised in the high-guard position. "I'm ready."

Ruger didn't want to mince words with the man. It wasn't his way. But something about the man gnawed at his stomach. The man had clearly sought him out, but why? "I'm ready. Shades, give the word."

Shades took a step into the ring of men and said, "Duel!"

Kazan poked his sword like a striking snake straight at Ruger's neck.

Ruger slid his head to the side, lunged forward, and stabbed.

Kazan's ginger feet backed away from Black Bane's lethal strike. He danced backward, grinning. Suddenly, his expression fell. He looked down at the blood spreading through his clothing. His legs swayed. "So fast." He fell flat on his back. His sword slipped out of his fingers.

Ruger looked down on his dying opponent. "Kazan Rue, you thought you knew what you were up against. You were wrong." He took a knee, bent down, and said, "Tell me, and die with honor. I bested you. Who sent you?"

Kazar Rue spat blood.

Shades lifted the man's head up. "He chokes on his words."

As the life fled from Kazan Rue's eyes, the sword master said, "I-I'll never tell." He managed a smile, his jaw locked up, and he died.

Ruger shook his head. "Fetch the horses. This warrior might have taken the truth of his purpose to the grave, but he will have left a trail."

"Why would he be coming after you, Captain?" Horace asked.

"That's what we are going to Pompley to find out."

CHAPTER 6

Pompley was the second-largest city in Kingsland but by no large margin. Hundreds of thousands of people thrived within its borders. Much like the capital city, Burgess, which rested below the House of Steel, it had everything a citizen could want, aside from the beachfronts and the sea.

It was early evening when Ruger and his men stabled their horses at an inn and settled themselves inside. They sat near a fireplace and ate heartily. Plates of roasted beast, baskets of bread, and flagons of wine and ale covered more than half the table. All the Guardians were present except for Shades, who was scouting.

Horace chewed on a turkey leg and washed it down with ale. He belched loudly. "Excuse me."

"If you didn't swallow your food whole, you wouldn't toss it back up," Vern said. "We are knights. Show some table manners. Use a knife and fork."

Ruger nudged his young Guardian and said, "We aren't Guardians here. It'll be fine to loosen our tunics." He peeled off strips of roast from his plate and went at them with his hands. He didn't bother to dab the juice from his face either until he wiped it on his forearm.

Vern mimicked his mentor. He took a long swig of wine from a flagon then suddenly gulped it down. He slammed the flagon on the table, wiped his chin across his arm, and said, "I could get used to this."

With his back toward the wall, Ruger quietly sat while the rest of his men devoured their meal. The tavern dwellers paid the group of large men no mind as they ate and drank heartily this time of night. He could overhear murmurings about the rivalry between Roderick and Hector. There was boasting among many that took pride in their fair city and the duke. King Hector wasn't as beloved by the people of Pompley as he was by the people of Burgess. The rivalry between the two quickly became clear.

One man in the inn spoke boldly. He leaned against the bar, dressed in fine linen clothing. His voice carried like the wind. "King Hector will bow down and kiss Roderick's boot one day." He chuckled, drank his ale, and smiled. "And that isn't all that he's going to kiss either!"

The small group surrounding the blowhard erupted in laughter.

The Guardians tensed. Horace started to rise from his seat as all Ruger's men set hard stares on the man.

"Horace, ignore," Ruger quietly ordered.

"But, Captain," Horace pleaded.

"Don't call me Captain." Ruger scooted closer to the table. "I don't care what you hear. Pretend you didn't hear it. We have more important business than dealing with the gusty winds of that fellow. Maintain your discipline."

The Guardians grumbled except for Prospero, who never stopped eating.

Horace drummed a meaty finger on the table. "I don't like that man. He'd never think such words in Burgess."

"He'd never utter them in the presence of Guardians either," Bearclaw added.

A waitress refilled the men's tankards of ale. The comely young woman smiled at Vern and said, "I'll fetch more wine for you, masters." She had one tooth missing.

As she walked away, Bearclaw ribbed Vern with his elbow. "Someone has an admirer. Perhaps a future wife to breed many strapping swordsmen."

"Stop it," Vern said as his cheeks reddened. "I'd never forsake my honor without a proper arrangement."

"We are on a mission," Apollo said discreetly. "What happens in Pompley stays in Pompley. We won't tell the entire garrison. Just a few."

The Guardians rumbled with laughter.

Ruger peeled away from the table. The blowhard was still spouting off about King Hector with one insult after the other.

"They say King Hector is a wee man," the blowhard said. "And I'm not talking about his stature."

"He always sleeps with his harem… of goats."

"I once saw him… and could have sworn that it was a woman."

"And have you seen his queen? Why, she's as pretty as a newborn baby, a newborn baby kraken. I've seen her. She has tentacles!"

Ruger slung his tankard across the room, and the clay tankard smashed the blowhard in the face.

The tavern fell silent as the drunken throng turned toward the Guardians' table.

Ruger's men started to rise, but he motioned them to stay put as he rose himself.

The blowhard wiped his face off with a rag. A cut on his face was bleeding, and his clothing was soaked. The red-faced man's hand went to his rapier.

"It's one thing to insult the king—he's a man," Ruger said, "but it's quite another thing to attack a woman. No man should lower himself to that."

There were grumbles of agreement.

Another drunken patron said, "Yes, we should not insult a lady. Especially when that lady is also the king's sister!"

The people howled with laughter.

Ruger's men stood. Their chairs scooted behind them.

He eyed his men and said, "Guardians, take them."

Horace punched out the man talking that stood the nearest to him. A full-on fistfight broke out. A sea of bodies swarmed the strangers. Over forty men and women jumped into a frenzied fray.

Vern had a woman on his back, beating his head with a tray.

Bearclaw hip tossed one man over his shoulder.

No blades whisked out. It was fists, feet, and biting.

Three men rammed Ruger back into the back wall, which shook. A painting fell on his head. He twisted his hands free and hit a man so hard his jaw broke. Two hard punches to the other two men's ribs dropped them straight to the floor.

Horace slung a man into Bearclaw's arms. Bearclaw slammed the man on the ground.

A flagon shattered on Horace's head. He turned and hit the man so hard that teeth came out.

Apollo grabbed two men by the hair of the head and smacked their skulls together.

Prospero's dinner plate was knocked on the floor. He grabbed an arm of the man who did it and jerked it out of its socket.

Chairs were thrown. Tables were knocked over.

Two men dragged Vern across the bar.

Women screamed.

Elders cackled.

Merchants and their guards were slammed through the tables.

In a minute, the Guardians had their bold attackers fleeing out the door. Within two minutes, they stood alone among the fallen and the wreckage they'd wrought. All of them were still standing.

Horace spit. "For the king."

"Aye," Ruger agreed. "For the queen."

The tavern's keeper peeked up from behind the bar. He was an older man, lanky and wizened. He pointed a shaking finger at Ruger. His voice cracking, he said, "Get out! Get out, all of you strangers! Get out!"

The waitress that was missing a tooth handed Vern a damp rag. His eye was swollen.

"Thank you," he said. "Sorry about the mess."

She gave him a goofy smile and said, "Don't worry. I'll clean it up." She threw her arms around him and kissed him.

Ruger and his men picked their way through the clutter of knocked-out men and busted furnishings. They exited the tavern's swinging doors and went outside into the night.

At least fifty well-armed soldiers, some on horseback and some on foot, were waiting outside. Ten crossbows were aimed at the company's chests. The soldiers were Guardians who were wearing the insignia of Kingsland—a lion's head with white wings—upside-down.

Ruger lifted his hands and said, "I demand to speak to Roderick."

CHAPTER 7

The Guardians were marched to Roderick's castle, where Ruger was separated from his men, who were taken to the dungeon. The castle didn't compare to the House of Steel. It was made of huge slabs of gray stone instead of the exquisite marble that decorated King Hector's halls.

Their heavy guard consisted of Kingsland soldiers, some of whom were Guardians themselves. Their captain was a man named Jasper, a striking blond with an aloof look about him. He led the march through the grand halls.

"Jasper, I am the captain of all King Hector's armies. What you are doing is treason."

"Mind your tongue, Ruger Slade," Jasper said with a sneer in his voice. "Times are changing. It would be in your best interests to join with us and not follow your wayward king."

"You don't sound like yourself, man. What has happened to you?"

"Be silent, or I will silence you," Jasper said.

Two oversized oaken doors leading into Roderick's throne room were hacked apart and opened. A massive fireplace was filled with a bonfire of burning wood. Ancient tapestries of landscapes of Titanuus decorated the walls. Torches hung in brackets. A huge wrought-iron chandelier filled with white candles hung above them.

Roderick the Regal sat on a bronze throne resting on a raised platform. He had a shaggy head full of black hair and a grizzly white beard. His eyes were menacing, and he was strongly built. He wore a full suit of black-dyed leather armor.

A woman stood on either side of the throne. Much like Leodor, they appeared to be Roderick's personal advisors. They wore off-white robes trimmed with brown and laced with golden leaves. They were mature and beautiful, with flowing white hair, and carried the spooky nature of the Sect about them. They touched the duke, fawning silently over him. They were mystics.

The soldiers escorting Ruger inside took a knee and bowed.

Jasper pushed Ruger forward and said, "Bow to your new king!"

"I'll die first." Ruger stood tall with his hands shackled in front of him. He was unarmed, and his sword was in Jasper's hand.

Jasper pulled his dagger and said, "Then you will die."

"That won't be necessary, Jasper," Roderick said in a strong voice. He kept his eyes fixed on Ruger. "Put your blade away. I wouldn't expect anything less from the captain of the King's Guardians."

The women stroked Roderick's hair.

He waved them away. "Enough of that."

The mystic women hissed at him, revealing filed teeth. They fell in by his side and went silent.

Ruger glimpsed at one of the women. She was more witch than mystic, with pitch-black eyes that sent a chill to his marrow.

"So, my cousin sent you to assassinate me, did he?" Roderick said.

"You murdered the king's soldiers at the Newfair Outpost. Their blood is on your hands. But I would be curious about your reasoning." Ruger looked at the soldiers in the room. "You are no match for the King's Army. He'll ride you down and destroy your town if need be. I am here to ask you to surrender before more blood of our kinsmen is shed."

Roderick made a rusty laugh. "Do you think that I would have gone to great lengths only to give up so easily?"

"You share the same royal blood as King Hector. Surrender now and receive his mercy."

"That is the problem!" Roderick slammed his fists on the arms of his chairs. His eyes glazed over with madness. "I am a full-blood. King Hector is only half. The House of Steel should be mine!" He pounded his first on the throne. "Mine! Mine! Mine!"

The viceroys hissed and clawed at the air, chanting strange words in an odd tongue.

Ruger heard Jasper swallow. His own hair stood up on his arms. Something was off with Roderick. He'd met the duke in passing at a few ceremonial functions. Even though the man had a clear grudge against Hector, he'd always seemed composed.

The mystics' voices shifted into the common tongue. Like sirens from the sea, they said, "The tide shifts. The Elders return."

Roderick caught his breath. "They are right. They have shown me, Ruger. Times are changing in Kingsland. In the north, King Hector's enemies have now spread from Hancha to the Old Kingdom. It's only a matter of time before Kingsland falls." He held out his balled-up fist. "Kingsland needs a king that rules with might, one that won't compromise so easily with his enemies. Woe to them that would dare test my borders. I would put an end to them." He stood up. "For I am the one and true king!" He beat his chest. "I am an Elder! I am the king!"

You are mad.

CHAPTER 8

RODERICK DROPPED BACK ONTO HIS throne, his eyes blazing. "Ruger Slade, I am a fair ruler. I believe in giving second chances. Swear your allegiance to me, and you and your men will be spared. I will even let you lead Kingsland's new army."

Jasper's jaw dropped. He quickly clamped it back shut.

Ruger wanted answers. "If you wanted me to lead your forces, then why did you hire Kazan Rue to try and kill me?"

Roderick raised an eyebrow. "This is not something that I am aware of. Who is Kazan Rue?"

"You don't know who he is? But you knew that I was coming?"

"Don't be a fool, Ruger. The same as King Hector, I have my spies too. I knew that you would be coming before you left." He reached out and grabbed the hands of his mystics. "My personal viceroys offer me many advantages. They see the future. They see change. They see me at the forefront of it."

"It sounds to me that you have placed your faith in the mysterious workings of the Sect." Ruger looked Roderick dead-on. "You know the old saying, 'None know their true intentions, not even their own.'"

"I am well assured that the Elders support me and my ambitions. They have revealed to me a changing world, a world beyond a simple warrior's feeble comprehension." Roderick leaned forward. "What will it be, Ruger Slade? Will you serve me, or will you die serving a false king?"

"King Hector has my life and my sword."

"I thought as much." Roderick showed modest disappointment. "Take him to the dungeon with the others and have them prepared to be sacrificed to the Elders. As for the five hundred riders that King Hector sent, I assume you speak for them as well. Jasper, send out fifteen hundred of my finest riders and slaughter them all."

The mystics clapped and danced with glee.

Ruger was hauled away to the deep.

Ruger was hauled away to the dungeon and tossed into a cell with his Guardians, but only after he'd been beaten severely.

"Captain!" Horace said as he came to his leader's aid. He propped Ruger up against the wall. "I take it the negotiations didn't go well."

One of Ruger's eyes was swollen shut, and he held his sore ribs. "What gave it away?" he asked. Aside from Shades, who wasn't present, all the Guardians were stripped down to their trousers, including Ruger. "Roderick is mad."

"Yes, we know that he is angry with King Hector. And we can tell by looking at you," Horace replied.

"No, that isn't what he meant." Vern had his arms folded over his chest. "He means the stones in Roderick's skull are bouncing. Right, Captain?"

"Yes." He leaned his head against the wall and closed his eyes. His head throbbed. "He has two mystics with him. They look more like frights. They thought we would be a fine sacrifice to the Elders."

"A sacrifice? You mean we'll be slaughtered on an altar like a fatted calf?" Bearclaw asked.

"It could be anything. Roderick sends his army to battle the Guardians in the field. Fifteen hundred of them, he said. Even the Guardians can't stand against such a force. Not on his terrain. We need to get word to them."

"I'll get us out, Captain. I was only waiting on your arrival." Horace grabbed the steel bars that trapped them inside the cell and tried to pull them apart. "Hurk!"

Two guards holding spears hustled down the hall and thrust the spears at Horace.

Bearclaw jerked his friend back just in time before he took a spear to the gut.

"Back, you!" one guard said.

They were well-armed men in full chain-mail armor and metal skullcaps. They had swords and daggers on their belts. Both of them stood in front of the bars.

"Touch the bars again, big belly, or any of you, and we'll gore you."

"Give me that spear, and I'll show you how to gore somebody!" Horace blurted out.

The guard holding the spear stuck his chin out and grinned ear to ear. "Come and take a crack at it. All you have to do is squeeze through the bars, heifer."

Horace stormed forward.

"Let it go," Ruger ordered.

Horace stopped in his tracks, moved back to the wall, and sat down on the cot. The rotting wood broke underneath him.

The guards and the Guardians laughed for a moment, then the dungeon fell silent again. Only the tiny claws of scurrying rats scraping over the rock floor could be heard.

Vern eased toward the front of the large cell and asked the guards, "They say we will be sacrificed. What sort of sacrifice are they talking about?"

The guards looked at one another and almost laughed.

The one with the spear and many freckles and strawberry hair said, "You'll be taken to the cave. There is only one way in and one way out. They say an Elder lives in there." He hammed it up. "A slavering flesh-hungry abomination that eats entire people alive." He clacked his teeth together and licked his lips. "The Elder delights on flesh and bones and howls with satisfaction. I've heard it myself. Turned my red hair white the first time I heard it." He eyed Horace. "I bet it turns the fat one skinny."

Horace gave the guard a hard-eyed look and said, "You do know that we are Guardians and not urchins given swords, like you. When we escape, I'm going to kill you."

Both guards swallowed, looked away, and moved back to their spots.

Just as everything fell dead quiet again, the walls of the castle moaned like a living thing.

The Guardians looked all around.

The guards became wide-eyed. The redhead gathered his courage after the moaning ended, looked at the prisoners, and said with a wicked voice, "You thought I was jesting, did you?"

CHAPTER 9

An hour or so passed in the dungeon. The Guardians sat glumly in the dingy dimness. Horace's and Prospero's bellies rumbled. The slimy hole reeked of rot.

Ruger's nose twitched. He opened his eyes. The guards were leaning against the wall, fighting to keep their eyes open. He smelled smoke. He elbowed Vern, who was sitting beside him.

Vern's eyelids fluttered open. He wiped his mouth and sniffed. He showed Ruger a curious expression.

The rest of the small company shifted in their seats. All of them were leaning against the dungeon wall, and their backs straightened.

"Wait for it," Ruger silently mouthed to his men.

The red-haired guard started coughing. He looked down at the floor and saw smoke rolling over his feet. He fanned his nose. "What in Titanuus is going on?"

"Something burns," said the other guard. He was bowlegged and teetered when he walked. He sniffed loudly and started coughing.

"Fire! Fire! Fire!" a voice cried out from down the hallway.

The redheaded guard handed his spear over to his companion. "Keep an eye on the prisoners. I'll go see what is happening."

The smoke thickened in the hallway. The Guardians jumped to their feet and ran for the bars. "You have to let us out of here," Ruger demanded. "We'll be burned alive."

The guard poked a spear at Ruger. "You get back." He started coughing, and his eyes watered. "It's not my problem. You're going to die anyway."

Thud!

"What was that?" The guard jumped around and pointed his spear down the hall. "Elgin! Elgin!" he called out. "What is happening? Where is the fire?"

A man glided through the thickening smoke.

"You're not Elgin!" the guard said with a nervous voice. "Stay ba-ack!"

A dagger spun through the air and pierced the guard's neck. The young bowlegged guard collapsed in a pool of his blood.

On the other side of the cell bars, the light-haired Shades grinned. "Are you happy to see me?"

All the Guardians were coughing.

"What took you so long?" Horace asked.

Using a ring of keys, Shades unlocked the door. "It's not always easy to find flammable materials. I have to find oils, tinder, suitable wood. It's very damp out there."

Horace was the first one to push through the cell door. "Don't talk to me like I'm a Gond. Any fool can light a fire using a torch."

The Guardians hurried out of the cell and followed Shades down the hall.

"I don't think you understand the timing and planning that is involved with my scheme." Shades jumped over a dead guard. It was the red-headed man, his throat cut.

At the end of the hall, four more guards lay dead on the floor. They were half inside and outside the doorway. A stool sitting beside the wooden frame and door was burning. Everything they passed that could burn, was burning.

The company equipped themselves with the fallen men's weapons and spears. They plowed though the smoke and up the stairwell, which was filling with smoke.

"Give me a report, Shades," Ruger said as he tried not to cough.

"Roderick's riders rode out over an hour ago. A small host of fifty men remained, but they are preoccupied with the numerous fires I set. The servants were running a chain of buckets from a pond nearby. The fire spread quickly." He made a winning smile. "It's some of our better work."

"What about Roderick? My sword, Black Bane? Did Jasper take it?"

"Roderick is under guard in his throne room. Your gear is stowed away safely." He looked at Horace. "Except your spear. I had to use it for kindling."

"What?" Horace grunted.

"Only jesting." Shades put his ear to the door then pushed it open and said, "Follow me."

A lot of shouting and hollering was coming from the castle's main floor. The company advanced, naked from the waist up with steel swords in hand. Servants scuttled back and forth. The kitchen and galley were full of smoke and flames. Buckets of water were being tossed on the fire.

Shades led them quickly through the corridors. A closed doorway sat across from a living room filled with burning couches. He tipped his head and said, "Let's go!"

On the other side of the door was a den. Its mahogany furniture had been spared from the fires. The Guardians' weapons lay on a leather sofa.

"You'll have to do without your armor." Shades shrugged. "Too heavy for me."

Ruger didn't see Black Bane. The length of steel he was carrying was less than adequate.

"Take my sword, Captain," Vern offered. "It's the King's Steel. You deserve it."

"No, I'll be fine."

The Guardians buckled on their sword belts. Prospero and Apollo each carried their two blades crossed over their backs.

Apollo tossed Ruger one of his. "I'm well enough with one. Make sure that I get that one back. There is nothing better to fight with than the King's Steel."

Ruger flipped the sword with a quick twist of the wrist. The weapon was much lighter than the other even though it wasn't Black Bane. "It will more than do. Listen to me, men. I'm going after Roderick. Shades, you stay with me. The rest of you find riding horses. Get out in front of that army, warn the Guardians, and when you face Jasper, tell him that Roderick is dead. Tell him I said to come and see for himself. Tell him I have his duke's head, and I'll have his if he doesn't surrender."

CHAPTER 10

Ruger and Shades stole through the castle toward the throne room. They ducked underneath a set of steps as a trio of soldiers raced toward the distressed voices.

The smoke in the castle thickened. Panic-stricken screams grew louder. The fires were spreading.

Ruger looked at Shades and said, "Were you trying to burn the entire castle down?"

"Let's just say that I'm a man of lofty ambitions and flaming passions."

"I can see that." He took the lead through the smoke and down the corridor that led to Roderick's throne room. Eight soldiers were guarding the double doors that led inside. The guards pulled their swords the moment they saw Ruger approach.

A stout soldier wearing chain mail underneath a red tunic with a fighting-cock emblem of a ranking sergeant embroidered on it stepped forward, longsword in hand. "Halt! Who goes there?"

Bare chested, Ruger moved forward. The muscles in his mighty frame rippled with every step. He held his sword out and said, "I am Captain Ruger Slade, and I will have a word with your duke."

The sergeant swallowed. In a shaky voice, he said, "I won't allow that. My men won't allow that."

"I will warn you one last time, Sergeant. The duke has betrayed his king and his countrymen. All who stand with him will suffer the inevitable consequence. Death. As captain of the King's Guardians, I can spare you the king's wrath, but you must stand down."

The sergeant shook his head. "No, we've made our bond with the duke. He is our leader."

Ruger nodded. "Then prepare to face the king's wrath."

"Trio formation," the sergeant ordered.

Carrying swords, two soldiers moved to flank their sergeant.

Ruger sprang forward like a leaping panther and gored the sergeant in the chest with his sword. The man's jaw opened wide as his eyes filled with shock. Ruger pulled his blade free and ducked just as a sword whistled over his head and hit the dying sergeant full in the chest.

From a knee, he thrust his sword into his attacker's belly. Then he twisted around and chopped a leg off the third attacker.

Five soldiers guarding the door came at Ruger all as one in a frenzied attack.

Ruger put his unrivaled sword skill to work. His arms pumped with power and might. His strikes were lethal. His blade crashed through their blades. Metal snapped against metal. Chain mail, flesh, and bone were mutilated by his butchery.

Chop! Slice! Stab! Hack!

A soldier's head leapt from his shoulders.

Hands were cut off at the wrist in an instant.

Bowels spilled on the stony floor.

Skulls were split like ripe melons.

Five soldiers had once stood. Five soldiers died in their own blood.

Ruger's blood-splattered frame didn't have a scratch on it.

Shades gently applauded. "You make it look so easy." He tiptoed across the gory floor to the throne room's doors and pulled on the large iron handles. "You might find this hard to believe, but it's locked. Shall I fetch a battering ram?"

"You're the fence. Can't you figure something else out?"

Shades patted his hands over his body and said, "I don't have a key for this."

Blood dripped from the edge of Ruger's sword. He pounded on the door. "Roderick! I know you are in there, and I'm coming for you!" He glanced at Shades. "Stand back." He hacked at the door with his sword.

"You won't ever get through that without a hatchet," Shades said. "I'll fetch one." He turned and almost ran into Bearclaw.

"Is someone looking for an axe?" Bearclaw said with his double-bladed axe in hand.

"Why aren't you with the others?" Ruger demanded.

"There weren't enough horses." Bearclaw cocked his axe back over his shoulders. "Stand back, Captain."

Ruger watched Bearclaw butcher the door with thunderous chops. Hunks of the door splintered and flew away. Within a minute, Bearclaw carved out a hole that revealed the locking bar on the other side of the door.

"I have it!" Bearclaw roared. He hacked into the beam in a series of heavy chops. The last chop busted through the beam.

Ruger kicked the doors wide open.

They hurried inside.

The throne room was empty.

Ruger spun around. "Shades, are you certain that he was in here?"

Shades shrugged. "It was merely a guess. But a well-thought-out one. He was in here." Shades made his way to the edge of the room and ran his hands over the walls. "There must be another exit."

"There is," a woman said.

Ruger looked up. One of the mystics was standing on the throne room's ceiling as casually as if she were standing on the floor. Not a strand of her hair or robes hung out of place.

"That's something you don't see every day," Shades said.

At a flick of her fingers, the throne room's doors slammed shut. The mystic spat something out of her mouth, onto the doors. A gooey webbing quickly spread over the doors, sealing the men inside.

"I don't suppose she's going to tell us where Roderick is?" Shades asked Ruger.

Ruger kept his eyes fixed on the mystic. The hairs on his arms stood on end. He watched her walking over the beams that made up the ceiling. "You're on the losing side of this battle, witch. You'd be wise to surrender now."

"Oh, is that so?" She rolled her hands one over the other, creating a ball of gooey yarn. "I believe it is you that has failed to accept your fate. Today is the day that your life changes forever."

"We need something to shoot that thing. It's not natural," Bearclaw said. He cocked his axe back and slung it at the woman.

She bounded away like a jumping spider and huddled in the rafters.

The axe fell back down to the floor with a clatter.

"Shades, find a way out of here. We'll take care of her," Ruger said.

"Oh, take care of me, will you?" She cackled with evil delight as her body convulsed. Six spidery legs burst through her robes. She became part woman, part spider in an instant, a wall-walking abomination. "We shall *see* about that, won't we?" She muttered words that no natural-born man could utter.

The air turned chill.

The throne room went pitch-black.

CHAPTER 11

The blackness that fell over the room reeked of dark magic. Ruger lost all sense of awareness for a moment. "Don't try to see. Close your eyes. Trust your other senses."

"Aye, Captain," Bearclaw said.

"Where are you, Shades?" he asked.

"On the move," the rogue replied.

"It won't make any difference, mortal fools. You are in the grave. You just don't know it yet," the mystic said in a gloating voice full of triumph. "It is a glorious thing. For I can see, and you can't."

The voice gave Ruger a feel for the room. He took his own advice and listened for the slightest scuffle. He could hear Bearclaw breathing about fifteen feet to the right. Shades's soft footsteps dusted over the floor.

"Garg!" Bearclaw cried out. "Something has me! Ulp!" He made muffled murmurings as if he'd been gagged with something. His wild swings whistled through the air.

"Compose yourself!" Ruger ordered.

Bearclaw's efforts fell silent.

"One fool has fallen. Soon there will be two," she said.

"Crickets!" Shades called out. "She webbed me! She's right behind me, Ruger! Right behind me!"

On cat's feet, Ruger crept toward the sound of Shades's voice.

The witchy woman cackled. "You can't kill what you cannot see. Your brawn and weapons are useless against the likes of me." Her voiced carried throughout the room as though it was an echo chamber. "Don't fear. I won't kill you. I only prepare you for the Elder's feast. He likes his meals to be warm."

"I have no idea where she strikes from," Shades said.

"Be silent," Ruger replied. He moved through the darkness, trusting his senses and getting a feel for things. Unlike most men, he had a gift, a special instinct that had served him well in countless battles.

He slowly cut his sword back and forth, probing the darkness. He stubbed his toe on what he thought was the throne's platform. "Guh! I could see better in a dung heap."

In that moment, he felt a lurking presence behind him. He thrust his sword straight behind himself. Steel pierced flesh and bone. *Glitch!*

The dark witch let out a bloodcurdling scream.

Light banished the darkness with torchlight and candles.

Ruger stood and looked at the mystic impaled on the end of his sword. Her mouth gawped like a fish out of water.

"I only pretended to fall. You truly fell for it." He pushed her off his sword with his boot.

Bearclaw was alive but covered in webbing.

Ruger cleared his mouth and nose.

Bearclaw gasped. "Thanks, Captain. Now get me out of these abominable strands."

"Captain, I think I've found the exit." Shades's legs were pinned down to the ground. He was on the raised stone platform that supported the throne. He pointed at a small lever below the throne's legs. He stretched out his fingers but couldn't reach it. "Some days, I regret my slight build."

Ruger squatted down and pulled the lever. Stone scraped over stone. The throne and its platform slid backward, revealing steps leading downward.

The castle walls moaned again as if a great living thing had been unloosed.

"Free us, Captain," Bearclaw asked.

Ruger went to the wall and grabbed two torches. He handed one to Shades. "Free yourselves. You know where I am going." With a sword in one hand and a torch in the other, he descended the steps.

The stairwell led deep down into a tunnel carved out of rock. A series of elbow turns connected thirty-yard stretches. The deeper it went, the damper it became before it finally opened up into a cavern.

Ruger stopped.

Torches had been lit in brackets mounted on the cavern's walls. Two huge urns taller than men were churning with flames. They were on either side of a cave mouth standing over twenty feet high.

The monstrous moaning started again. It was coming out of the cave. The ground trembled.

The other mystic appeared inside the mouth of the cave. Her wispy white hair moved about as if stirred by a gentle breeze. She beckoned Ruger with a crooked finger and said, "Come. Roderick awaits you."

Her siren-like words carried power.

Ruger's feet moved on their own toward the eerie call of her voice.

She didn't move. She waited, watching his every step, like a cat waiting to devour a blind mouse.

Spellbound, he moved with limbs that were no longer his own, straight into the gaping maw of death that awaited him. Dark tendrils tugged at his iron will.

"That's it. That's a good man," she said with open arms. "Release your sword. Release your torch. Embrace the fate that awaits you."

Ruger's arms dropped and hung at his sides. He dragged his sword's tip across the ground. The torch fell out of his hand.

"That's close enough," the mystic said. "You can stop now."

Ruger kept going.

She shrieked with rage as her hands filled with white fire. "You can stop now!"

Ruger struck, taking her head from her shoulders. The head fell, bounced, and rolled, still screaming.

"I said stop! I said stop!" The strength of her voice faded. "Mighty Elder, take him!"

The cavern shook from a mighty bellow that came from within the cave.

"*Maaa-haaa-roooooooom!*"

A beast scurried out of the darkness. Bigger than a horse, it came with the body of a scorpion and the broad, disfigured face of a man. Its jaws slavered and dripped with venom that sizzled on the ground. The ringed scorpion tail behind its back struck.

Ruger dove out of the way.

CHAPTER 12

Ruger struck, parrying the monster's tail. The monster ran over him and pinned him underneath its body. Its jagged feet pierced Ruger's flesh. He kicked his way out from underneath it and dashed away.

The monster came at him again with large pincers snapping at its sides.

With a fierce downward chop, Ruger sliced the left pincer off. The right one clutched around his sides, drawing blood from his flesh. He cried out.

Ruger hacked at the appendage with wroth force. Hunks of the hard shell chipped off. Ooze spat out of the monster's wound.

The abominable Elder let out a bellowing howl. Its stinger reared up over its head and struck.

In a split second, Ruger twisted his shoulder away. The stinger slammed into the rock wall and stuck. Ruger's corded arms brought his sword up and down with fury. He hacked through the pincer, hobbled away, and peeled the pincer from his body.

He clutched the bloody wound on his side. It burned like fire.

The creature yanked its stinger out of the rock and came at him again.

Ruger limped away with his sword swinging.

The horrid eyes of the Elder monster burned with evil. A deep intelligence lurked behind them. It was a monster hungry for prey. A black tongue rolled inside its mouth. In a resonant, garbled voice, it said, "No mortal can slay me. I'm more than shell and bones." The stinger struck.

He jumped aside and hit it with the flat of his sword. He staggered away.

"You are weary. You are dying. I want to feast on your warmth," the creature said. It shifted around on its quick feet, keeping Ruger right in front of him. The stinger lashed out and recoiled.

Ruger's well-timed swing twisted him off balance.

The stinger lashed out and broadsided Ruger like a fist.

The sword slipped free of his fingers. He dove underneath the monster's legs just as the stinger came down on him again.

The creature scurried side to side, thinking to pin him down underneath itself. Its long tail poked at the ground.

In a valiant effort, Ruger scurried out from underneath the monster and climbed onto its back. The tail curled up behind its back. As if it had eyes of its own, the tail moved with Ruger, tracking his every move.

"Sacrifice yourself to me." The Elder stood still as a stone. "There is no greater honor than feeding me."

Blood dripped from Ruger's side. He kept his gaze fastened on the stinger. "You are right. I'm bleeding to death." He opened his arms, exposing his chest. He dropped onto his knees and knelt upon the monster's broad back. "But I won't be taken alive. You'll have to kill me."

"You are wise. Your death will be quick."

Venom dripped from the monster's stinger. It struck in the wink of an eye.

Ruger caught the tail inches from his face, used its momentum, and pushed it down into the monster's body. The stinger went deep.

The Elder cried out, "Nooo! You tricked me!" It bucked on its many legs and tossed Ruger from its body.

He landed hard and rolled back to a knee. He held his burning side and winced.

The Elder lay on its back, legs up, stiff as a piece of petrified wood.

Roderick slunk out from behind one of the burning urns. He carried Black Bane with two hands and crept forward. "You are gravely wounded, Ruger. Too wounded to fight, but that was quite a show of your prowess."

Blood seeped between Ruger's fingertips. He fought hard to catch his breath. His sword was on the far side of the cavern. He had nothing to defend himself with and knew full well that Roderick was a skilled swordsman, one of the best. "It's not too late to surrender," he said.

"I've made the same offer to you. 'Tis a shame that you won't be around to see your cherished King Hector fall." Roderick stood only a few feet away. He held Black Bane down low in the plow-guard position. "The scheme has long been set in motion. Titanuus is going to undergo change. Unbeknownst to Hector, he has many traitors among him."

"Who?"

"I'll never tell." Roderick prepared to strike. "Farewell, Ruger. You were more worthy than I ever imagined."

Bzzzt.

Roderick dropped the sword and jumped back. "The sword is bewitched!"

Ruger dove for the sword and snatched it up.

Roderick sprinted into the cave. With a heavy limp, Ruger trotted into the pitch-black cave, which ran as deep as a mining tunnel. Ruger could hear Roderick running and panting. Light of some sort shone from the opposite end. It clearly illuminated Roderick's silhouetted form.

The duke's fast footfalls slowed. The light became a sun ring and came right at him. He turned back toward Ruger and said, "There is nothing you can do now. The mystics have blessed me with immortality. Now comes my chariot to eternity!"

Ruger gritted his teeth and pushed himself into a full sprint. He caught up with Roderick and knocked him down to his knees. He held his sword up. "It's Sheol for you!"

"No, Ruger, no!" Roderick turned his face toward the oncoming sun ring. "I'll tell you everything! Everything!"

"You had your chance." Ruger brought his sword down and chopped off Roderick's head. He glanced up in time to see the oncoming sun ring hit him. A brilliant flash of light lit up the bones underneath his skin. Ruger's essence corkscrewed out of his body and was hurled into the unknown.

"Captain. Captain."

Ruger Slade opened his eyes. He set his eyes on Bearclaw's and Shades's faces, but his mind was not his own. He blinked. His brow furrowed. His body tingled all over.

"Ruger, are you well?" the man with sandy hair and a slighter build asked. He looked nothing like the man beside him, who had coarse black hair and a face of a hardened criminal. "We've patched you up. Can you stand? Ruger, can you hear me?"

Ruger swallowed. He looked at the man talking, gave him a puzzled look, and asked, "Who is Ruger? I'm Eugene Drisk."

FROM THE AUTHOR

Thanks for reading *The Henchmen Chronicles*! I have to tell you that this was one of the toughest projects that I've ever had to tackle. There were a lot of moving parts with this series, but I wanted to challenge myself and you with something new.

I attempted this portal fantasy because it thought it would be fun to include the modern vernacular that we are so connected to. I felt I had an original idea with the body-switching/soul-swapping angle too. (*Special note: The map of Titanuus is the same shape as my home state, West "by God" Virginia.)

I hoped to take you to a new world, where you could experience new backgrounds and races too. All in all, it's been a ton of fun, but this series was work! I'm glad it's done, but more importantly, I hope you enjoyed it. Let me know.

As I've mentioned, I have a lot of book series, and I'm slowly tying them all together. If Smoke and Sid piqued your interest and you like urban fantasy, give the *Supernatural Bounty Hunter Files* a try. It's a complete ten-book series. Collector's Set Link.

At the end, I reveal who the presence is inside the sword, Black Bane. This is the wizard Boon from my favorite series, *The Darkslayer*—pure hard-hitting action-packed sword and sorcery. You can check it out at The Darkslayer Omnibus Link.

I have written everything you could ask for in fantasy. Scroll on down and see more of what I have to offer.

Please leave a review. They are a huge help to me! Here is a link.

*I'd love it if you would subscribe to my mailing list: www.craighalloran.com.

*Follow me on BookBub at https://www.bookbub.com/authors/craig-halloran.

*On Facebook, you can find me at The Darkslayer Report or Craig Halloran.

*Twitter, twitter, twitter. I am there, too: www.twitter.com/CraigHalloran.

*And of course, you can always email me at craig@thedarkslayer.com.

OTHER BOOKS AND AUTHOR INFO

Craig Halloran resides with his family outside his hometown of Charleston, West Virginia. When he isn't entertaining mankind, he is seeking adventure, working out, or watching sports. To learn more about him, go to www.thedarkslayer.com.

CHECK OUT ALL OF MY GREAT STORIES ...

Free Books

The Darkslayer: Brutal Beginnings

Nath Dragon—The Quest for the Thunderstone

The Henchmen Chronicles

The King's Henchmen

The King's Assassin

The King's Prisoner

The King's Conjurer

The King's Spies

The Odyssey of Nath Dragon Series (New Series) (Prequel to Chronicles of Dragon)

Exiled

Enslaved

Deadly

Hunted

Strife

The Chronicles of Dragon Series 1 (10 Books)

The Hero, the Sword, and the Dragons (Book 1)

Dragon Bones and Tombstones (Book 2)

Terror at the Temple (Book 3)

Clutch of the Cleric (Book 4)

Hunt for the Hero (Book 5)

Siege at the Settlements (Book 6)

Strife in the Sky (Book 7)

Fight and the Fury (Book 8)

War in the Winds (Book 9)

Finale (Book 10)

Box set 1–5

Box set 6–10

Collector's Edition 1–10

Tail of the Dragon, The Chronicles of Dragon, Series 2 (10 books)

Tail of the Dragon #1

Claws of the Dragon #2

Battle of the Dragon #3

Eyes of the Dragon #4

Flight of the Dragon #5

Trial of the Dragon #6

Judgement of the Dragon #7

Wrath of the Dragon #8

Power of the Dragon #9

Hour of the Dragon #10

Box set 1–5

Box set 6–10

Collector's Edition 1–10

The Darkslayer, Series 1 (6 books)

Wrath of the Royals (Book 1)

Blades in the Night (Book 2)

Underling Revenge (Book 3)

Danger and the Druid (Book 4)

Outrage in the Outlands (Book 5)

Chaos at the Castle (Book 6)

Box set 1–3

Box set 4–6

Omnibus 1–6

The Darkslayer: Bish and Bone, Series 2 (10 books)

Bish and Bone (Book 1)

Black Blood (Book 2)

Red Death (Book 3)

Lethal Liaisons (Book 4)

Torment and Terror (Book 5)

Brigands and Badlands (Book 6)

War in the Wasteland (Book 7)

Slaughter in the Streets (Book 8)

Hunt of the Beast (Book 9)

The Battle for Bone (Book 10)

Box set 1–5

Box set 6–10

Bish and Bone Omnibus (Books 1–10)

CLASH OF HEROES: Nath Dragon meets The Darkslayer miniseries

Book 1

Book 2

Book 3

The Gamma Earth Cycle

Escape from the Dominion

Flight from the Dominion

Prison of the Dominion

The Supernatural Bounty Hunter Files (10 books)

Smoke Rising: Book 1

I Smell Smoke: Book 2

Where There's Smoke: Book 3

Smoke on the Water: Book 4

Smoke and Mirrors: Book 5

Up in Smoke: Book 6

Smoke Signals: Book 7

Holy Smoke: Book 8

Smoke Happens: Book 9

Smoke Out: Book 10

Box set 1–5

Box set 6–10

Collector's Edition 1–10

Zombie Impact Series

Zombie Day Care: Book 1

Zombie Rehab: Book 2

Zombie Warfare: Book 3

Box set: Books 1–3

OTHER WORKS & NOVELLAS

The Scarab's Curse—Sword & Sorcery Novella

The Scarab's Power

The Scarab's Command

The Scarab's Trick

The Scarab's War

Made in the USA
Middletown, DE
19 October 2021